I0763242

The Three Musketeers Omnibus, Volume One

(six books in two volumes)

By

Alexandre Dumas

Cover Photograph: ap.

ISBN: 978-1-78139-352-9

Contents

THE THREE MUSKETEERS

TWENTY YEARS AFTER

THE THREE MUSKETEERS

Author's Preface

In which it is proved that, notwithstanding their names' ending in OS and IS, the heroes of the story which we are about to have the honor to relate to our readers have nothing mythological about them.

A short time ago, while making researches in the Royal Library for my History of Louis XIV, I stumbled by chance upon the Memoirs of M. d'Artagnan, printed--as were most of the works of that period, in which authors could not tell the truth without the risk of a residence, more or less long, in the Bastille--at Amsterdam, by Pierre Rouge. The title attracted me; I took them home with me, with the permission of the guardian, and devoured them.

It is not my intention here to enter into an analysis of this curious work; and I shall satisfy myself with referring such of my readers as appreciate the pictures of the period to its pages. They will therein find portraits penciled by the hand of a master; and although these squibs may be, for the most part, traced upon the doors of barracks and the walls of cabarets, they will not find the likenesses of Louis XIII, Anne of Austria, Richelieu, Mazarin, and the courtiers of the period, less faithful than in the history of M. Anquetil.

But, it is well known, what strikes the capricious mind of the poet is not always what affects the mass of readers. Now, while admiring, as others doubtless will admire, the details we have to relate, our main preoccupation concerned a matter to which no one before ourselves had given a thought.

D'Artagnan relates that on his first visit to M. de Treville, captain of the king's Musketeers, he met in the antechamber three young men, serving in the illustrious corps into which he was soliciting the honor of being received, bearing the names of Athos, Porthos, and Aramis.

We must confess these three strange names struck us; and it immediately occurred to us that they were but pseudonyms, under which d'Artagnan had disguised names perhaps illustrious, or else that the bearers of these borrowed names had themselves chosen them on the day in which, from caprice, discontent, or want of fortune, they had donned the simple Musketeer's uniform.

From the moment we had no rest till we could find some trace in contemporary works of these extraordinary names which had so strongly awakened our curiosity.

The catalogue alone of the books we read with this object would fill a whole chapter, which, although it might be very instructive, would certainly afford our readers but little amusement. It will suffice, then, to tell them that at the moment at which, discouraged by so many fruitless investigations, we were about to abandon our search, we at length found, guided by the counsels of our illustrious friend Paulin Paris, a manuscript in folio, endorsed 4772 or 4773, we do not recollect which, having for title, "Memoirs of the Comte de la Fere, Touching Some Events Which Passed in France Toward the End of the Reign of King Louis XIII and the Commencement of the Reign of King Louis XIV."

It may be easily imagined how great was our joy when, in turning over this manuscript, our last hope, we found at the twentieth page the name of Athos, at the twenty-seventh the name of Porthos, and at the thirty-first the name of Aramis.

The discovery of a completely unknown manuscript at a period in which historical science is carried to such a high degree appeared almost miraculous. We hastened, therefore, to obtain permission to print it, with the view of presenting ourselves someday with the pack of others at the doors of the Academie des Inscriptions et Belles Lettres, if we should not succeed--a very probable thing, by the by--in gaining admission to the Academie Francaise with our own proper pack. This permission, we feel bound to say, was graciously granted; which compels us here to give a public contradiction to the slanderers who pretend that we live under a government but moderately indulgent to men of letters.

Now, this is the first part of this precious manuscript which we offer to our readers, restoring it to the title which belongs to it, and entering into an engagement that if (of which we have no doubt) this first part should obtain the success it merits, we will publish the second immediately.

In the meanwhile, as the godfather is a second father, we beg the reader to lay to our account, and not to that of the Comte de la Fere, the pleasure or the ENNUI he may experience.

This being understood, let us proceed with our history.

1 The Three Presents Of D'Artagnan The Elder

On the first Monday of the month of April, 1625, the market town of Meung, in which the author of ROMANCE OF THE ROSE was born, appeared to be in as perfect a state of revolution as if the Huguenots had just made a second La Rochelle of it. Many citizens, seeing the women flying toward the High Street, leaving their children crying at the open doors, hastened to don the cuirass, and supporting their somewhat uncertain courage with a musket or a partisan, directed their steps toward the hostelry of the Jolly Miller, before which was gathered, increasing every minute, a compact group, vociferous and full of curiosity.

In those times panics were common, and few days passed without some city or other registering in its archives an event of this kind. There were nobles, who made war against each other; there was the king, who made war against the cardinal; there was Spain, which made war against the king. Then, in addition to these concealed or public, secret or open wars, there were robbers, mendicants, Huguenots, wolves, and scoundrels, who made war upon everybody. The citizens always took up arms readily against thieves, wolves or scoundrels, often against nobles or Huguenots, sometimes against the king, but never against cardinal or Spain. It resulted, then, from this habit that on the said first Monday of April, 1625, the citizens, on hearing the clamor, and seeing neither the red-and-yellow standard nor the livery of the Duc de Richelieu, rushed toward the hostel of the Jolly Miller. When arrived there, the cause of the hubbub was apparent to all.

A young man--we can sketch his portrait at a dash. Imagine to yourself a Don Quixote of eighteen; a Don Quixote without his corselet, without his coat of mail, without his cuisses; a Don Quixote clothed in a woolen doublet, the blue color of which had faded into a nameless shade between lees of wine and a heavenly azure; face long and brown; high cheek bones, a sign of sagacity; the maxillary muscles enormously developed, an infallible sign by which a Gascon may always be detected, even without his cap--and our young man wore a cap set off with a sort of feather; the eye open and intelligent; the nose hooked, but finely chiseled. Too big for a youth, too small for a grown man, an experienced eye might have taken him for a farmer's son upon a journey had it not been for the long sword which, dangling from a leather baldric, hit against the calves of its owner as he walked, and against the rough side of his steed when he was on horseback.

For our young man had a steed which was the observed of all observers. It was a Bearn pony, from twelve to fourteen years old, yellow in his hide, without a hair in his tail, but not without windgalls on his legs, which, though going with his head lower than his knees, rendering a martingale quite unnecessary, contrived nevertheless to perform his eight leagues a day. Unfortunately, the qualities of this horse were so well concealed under his strange-colored hide and his unaccountable gait, that at a time when everybody was a connoisseur in horseflesh, the appearance of the aforesaid pony at Meung--which place he had entered about a quarter of an hour before, by the gate of Beaugency--produced an unfavorable feeling, which extended to his rider.

And this feeling had been more painfully perceived by young d'Artagnan--for so was the Don Quixote of this second Rosinante named--from his not being able to conceal from himself the ridiculous appearance that such a steed gave him, good horseman as he was. He had sighed deeply, therefore, when accepting the gift of the pony from M. d'Artagnan the elder. He was not ignorant that such a beast was worth at least twenty livres; and the words which had accompanied the present were above all price.

"My son," said the old Gascon gentleman, in that pure Bearn PATOIS of which Henry IV could never rid himself, "this horse was born in the house of your father about thirteen years ago, and has remained in it ever since, which ought to make you love it. Never sell it; allow it to die tranquilly and honorably of old age, and if you make a campaign with it, take as much care of it as you would of an old servant. At court, provided you have ever the honor to go there," continued M. d'Artagnan the elder, "--an honor to which, remember, your ancient nobility gives you the right--sustain worthily your name of gentleman, which has been worthily borne by your ancestors for five hundred years, both for your own sake and the sake of those who belong to you. By the latter I mean your relatives and friends. Endure nothing from any-one except Monsieur the Cardinal and the king. It is by his courage, please observe, by his courage alone, that a gentleman can make his way nowadays. Who-ever hesitates for a second perhaps allows the bait to escape which during that exact second fortune held out to him. You are young. You ought to be brave for two reasons: the first is that you are a Gascon, and the second is that you are my son. Never fear quarrels, but seek adventures. I have taught you how to handle a sword; you have thews of iron, a wrist of steel. Fight on all occasions. Fight the more for duels being forbidden, since consequently there is twice as much courage in fighting. I have nothing to give you, my son, but fifteen crowns, my horse, and the counsels you have just heard. Your mother will add to them a recipe for a certain balsam, which she had from a Bohemian and which has the miraculous virtue of curing all wounds that do not reach the heart. Take advantage of all, and live happily and long. I have but one word to add, and that is to propose an example to you--not mine, for I myself have never appeared at court, and have only taken part in religious wars as a volunteer; I speak of Monsieur de Treville, who was formerly my neighbor, and who had the honor to be, as a child, the play-fellow of our king, Louis XIII, whom God preserve! Sometimes their play degenerated into battles, and in these battles the king was not always the stronger. The blows which he received increased greatly his esteem and friendship for Monsieur de Treville. Afterward, Monsieur de Treville fought with others: in his first journey to Paris, five times; from the death of the late king till the young one came of age, without reckoning wars and sieges, seven times; and from that date up to the present day, a hundred times, perhaps! So that in spite of edicts, ordinances, and decrees, there he is, captain of the Musketeers; that is to say, chief of a legion of Caesars, whom the king holds in great esteem and whom the cardinal dreads--he who dreads nothing, as it is said. Still further, Monsieur de Treville gains ten thousand crowns a year; he is therefore a great noble. He began as you begin. Go to him with this letter, and make him your model in order that you may do as he has done."

Upon which M. d'Artagnan the elder girded his own sword round his son, kissed him tenderly on both cheeks, and gave him his benediction.

On leaving the paternal chamber, the young man found his mother, who was waiting for him with the famous recipe of which the counsels we have just repeated would necessitate frequent employment. The adieux were on this side longer and more tender than they had been on the other--not that M. d'Artagnan did not love his son, who was his only offspring, but M. d'Artagnan was a man, and he would have considered it unworthy of a man to give way to his feelings; whereas Mme. d'Artagnan was a woman, and still more, a mother. She wept abundantly; and--let us speak it to the praise of M. d'Artagnan the younger--notwithstanding the efforts he made to remain firm, as a future Musketeer ought, nature prevailed, and he shed many tears, of which he succeeded with great difficulty in concealing the half.

The same day the young man set forward on his journey, furnished with the three paternal gifts, which consisted, as we have said, of fifteen crowns, the horse, and the letter for M. de Treville--the counsels being thrown into the bargain.

With such a VADE MECUM d'Artagnan was morally and physically an exact copy of the hero of Cervantes, to whom we so happily compared him when our duty of an historian placed us under the necessity of sketching his portrait. Don Quixote took windmills for giants, and sheep for armies; d'Artagnan took every smile for an insult, and every look as a provocation--whence it resulted that from Tarbes to Meung his fist was constantly doubled, or his hand on the hilt of his sword; and yet the fist did not descend upon any jaw, nor did the sword issue from its scabbard. It was not that the sight of the wretched pony did not excite numerous smiles on the countenances of passers-by; but as against the side of this pony rattled a sword of respectable length, and as over this sword gleamed an eye rather ferocious than haughty, these passers-by repressed their hilarity, or if hilarity prevailed over prudence, they endeavored to laugh only on one side, like the masks of the ancients. D'Artagnan, then, remained majestic and intact in his susceptibility, till he came to this unlucky city of Meung.

But there, as he was alighting from his horse at the gate of the Jolly Miller, without anyone--host, waiter, or hostler--coming to hold his stirrup or take his horse, d'Artagnan spied, though an open window on the ground floor, a gentleman, well-made and of good carriage, although of rather a stern countenance, talking with two persons who appeared to listen to him with respect. d'Artagnan fancied quite naturally, according to his custom, that he must be the object of their conversation, and listened. This time d'Artagnan was only in part mistaken; he himself was not in question, but his horse was. The gentleman appeared to be enumerating all his qualities to his auditors; and, as I have said, the auditors seeming to have great deference for the narrator, they every moment burst into fits of laughter. Now, as a half-smile was sufficient to awaken the irascibility of the young man, the effect produced upon him by this vociferous mirth may be easily imagined.

Nevertheless, d'Artagnan was desirous of examining the appearance of this impertinent personage who ridiculed him. He fixed his haughty eye upon the stranger, and perceived a man of from forty to forty-five years of age, with black and piercing eyes, pale complexion, a strongly marked nose, and a black and well-shaped mustache. He was dressed in a doublet and hose of a violet color, with aiguillettes of the same color, without any other ornaments than the customary slashes, through which the shirt appeared. This doublet and hose, though new, were creased, like traveling clothes for a long time packed in a portmanteau. d'Artagnan made all these remarks with the rapidity of a most minute observer, and doubtless from an instinctive feeling that this stranger was destined to have a great influence over his future life.

Now, as at the moment in which d'Artagnan fixed his eyes upon the gentleman in the violet doublet, the gentleman made one of his most knowing and profound remarks respecting the Bearnese pony, his two auditors laughed even louder than before, and he himself, though contrary to his custom, allowed a pale smile (if I may allowed to use such an expression) to stray over his countenance. This time there could be no doubt; d'Artagnan was really insulted. Full, then, of this conviction, he pulled his cap down over his eyes, and endeavoring to copy some of the court airs he had picked up in Gascony among young traveling nobles, he advanced with one hand on the hilt of his sword and the other resting on his hip. Unfortunately, as he advanced, his anger increased at every step; and instead of the proper and lofty speech he had prepared as a prelude to his challenge, he found nothing at the tip of his tongue but a gross personality, which he accompanied with a furious gesgesture.

"I say, sir, you sir, who are hiding yourself behind that shutter--yes, you, sir, tell me what you are laughing at, and we will laugh together!"

The gentleman raised his eyes slowly from the nag to his cavalier, as if he required some time to ascertain whether it could be to him that such strange reproaches were addressed; then, when he could not possibly entertain any doubt of the matter, his eyebrows slightly bent, and with an accent of irony and insolence impossible to be described, he replied to d'Artagnan, "I was not speaking to you, sir."

"But I am speaking to you!" replied the young man, additionally exasperated with this mixture of insolence and good manners, of politeness and scorn.

The stranger looked at him again with a slight smile, and retiring from the window, came out of the hostelry with a slow step, and placed himself before the horse, within two paces of d'Artagnan. His quiet manner and the ironical expression of his countenance redoubled the mirth of the persons with whom he had been talking, and who still remained at the window.

D'Artagnan, seeing him approach, drew his sword a foot out of the scabbard.

"This horse is decidedly, or rather has been in his youth, a buttercup," resumed the stranger, continuing the remarks he had begun, and addressing himself to his auditors at the window, without paying the least attention to the exasperation of d'Artagnan, who, however placed himself between him and them. "It is a color very well known in botany, but till the present time very rare among horses."

"There are people who laugh at the horse that would not dare to laugh at the master," cried the young emulator of the furious Treville.

"I do not often laugh, sir," replied the stranger, "as you may perceive by the expression of my countenance; but nevertheless I retain the privilege of laughing when I please."

"And I," cried d'Artagnan, "will allow no man to laugh when it displeases me!"

"Indeed, sir," continued the stranger, more calm than ever; "well, that is perfectly right!" and turning on his heel, was about to re-enter the hostelry by the front gate, beneath which d'Artagnan on arriving had observed a saddled horse.

But, d'Artagnan was not of a character to allow a man to escape him thus who had the insolence to ridicule him. He drew his sword entirely from the scabbard, and followed him, crying, "Turn, turn, Master Joker, lest I strike you behind!"

"Strike me!" said the other, turning on his heels, and surveying the young man with as much astonishment as contempt. "Why, my good fellow, you must be mad!" Then, in a suppressed tone, as if speaking to himself, "This is annoying," continued he. "What a godsend this would be for his Majesty, who is seeking everywhere for brave fellows to recruit for his Musketeers!"

He had scarcely finished, when d'Artagnan made such a furious lunge at him that if he had not sprung nimbly backward, it is probable he would have jested for the last time. The stranger, then perceiving that the matter went beyond raillery, drew his sword, saluted his adversary, and seriously placed himself on guard. But at the same moment, his two auditors, accompanied by the host, fell upon d'Artagnan with sticks, shovels and tongs. This caused so rapid and complete a diversion from the attack that d'Artagnan's adversary, while the latter turned round to face this shower of blows, sheathed his sword with the same precision, and instead of an actor, which he had nearly been, became a spectator of the fight--a part in which he acquitted himself with his usual impassiveness, muttering, nevertheless, "A plague upon these Gascons! Replace him on his orange horse, and let him begone!"

"Not before I have killed you, poltroon!" cried d'Artagnan, making the best face possible, and never retreating one step before his three assailants, who continued to shower blows upon him.

"Another gasconade!" murmured the gentleman. "By my honor, these Gascons are incorrigible! Keep up the dance, then, since he will have it so. When he is tired, he will perhaps tell us that he has had enough of it."

But the stranger knew not the headstrong personage he had to do with; d'Artagnan was not the man ever to cry for quarter. The fight was therefore prolonged for some seconds; but at length d'Artagnan dropped his sword, which was broken in two pieces by the blow of a stick. Another blow full upon his forehead at the same moment brought him to the ground, covered with blood and almost fainting.

It was at this moment that people came flocking to the scene of action from all sides. The host, fearful of consequences, with the help of his servants carried the wounded man into the kitchen, where some trifling attentions were bestowed upon him.

As to the gentleman, he resumed his place at the window, and surveyed the crowd with a certain impatience, evidently annoyed by their remaining undispersed.

"Well, how is it with this madman?" exclaimed he, turning round as the noise of the door announced the entrance of the host, who came in to inquire if he was unhurt.

"Your excellency is safe and sound?" asked the host.

"Oh, yes! Perfectly safe and sound, my good host; and I wish to know what has become of our young man."

"He is better," said the host, "he fainted quite away."

"Indeed!" said the gentleman.

"But before he fainted, he collected all his strength to challenge you, and to defy you while challenging you."

"Why, this fellow must be the devil in person!" cried the stranger.

"Oh, no, your Excellency, he is not the devil," replied the host, with a grin of contempt; "for during his fainting we rummaged his valise and found nothing but a clean shirt and eleven crowns--which however, did not prevent his saying, as he was fainting, that if such a thing had happened in Paris, you should have cause to repent of it at a later period."

"Then," said the stranger coolly, "he must be some prince in disguise."

"I have told you this, good sir," resumed the host, "in order that you may be on your guard."

"Did he name no one in his passion?"

"Yes; he struck his pocket and said, 'We shall see what Monsieur de Treville will think of this insult offered to his protege.'"

"Monsieur de Treville?" said the stranger, becoming attentive, "he put his hand upon his pocket while pronouncing the name of Monsieur de Treville? Now, my dear host, while your young man was insensible, you did not fail, I am quite sure, to ascertain what that pocket contained. What was there in it?"

"A letter addressed to Monsieur de Treville, captain of the Musketeers."

"Indeed!"

"Exactly as I have the honor to tell your Excellency."

The host, who was not endowed with great perspicacity, did not observe the expression which his words had given to the physiognomy of the stranger. The latter rose from the front of the window, upon the sill of which he had leaned with his elbow, and knitted his brow like a man disquieted.

"The devil!" murmured he, between his teeth. "Can Treville have set this Gascon upon me? He is very young; but a sword thrust is a sword thrust, whatever be the age of him who gives it, and a youth is less to be suspected than an older man," and the stranger fell into a reverie which lasted some minutes. "A weak obstacle is sometimes sufficient to overthrow a great design.

"Host," said he, "could you not contrive to get rid of this frantic boy for me? In conscience, I cannot kill him; and yet," added he, with a coldly menacing expression, "he annoys me. Where is he?"

"In my wife's chamber, on the first flight, where they are dressing his wounds."

"His things and his bag are with him? Has he taken off his doublet?"

"On the contrary, everything is in the kitchen. But if he annoys you, this young fool--"

"To be sure he does. He causes a disturbance in your hostelry, which respectable people cannot put up with. Go; make out my bill and notify my servant."

"What, monsieur, will you leave us so soon?"

"You know that very well, as I gave my order to saddle my horse. Have they not obeyed me?"

"It is done; as your Excellency may have observed, your horse is in the great gateway, ready saddled for your departure."

"That is well; do as I have directed you, then."

"What the devil!" said the host to himself. "Can he be afraid of this boy?" But an imperious glance from the stranger stopped him short; he bowed humbly and retired.

"It is not necessary for Milady[1] to be seen by this fellow," continued the stranger. "She will soon pass; she is already late. I had better get on horseback, and go and meet her. I should like, however, to know what this letter addressed to Treville contains."

And the stranger, muttering to himself, directed his steps toward the kitchen.

In the meantime, the host, who entertained no doubt that it was the presence of the young man that drove the stranger from his hostelry, re-ascended to his wife's chamber, and found d'Artagnan just recovering his senses. Giving him to understand that the police would deal with him pretty severely for having sought a quarrel with a great lord--for the opinion of the host the stranger could be nothing less than a great lord--he insisted that notwithstanding his weakness d'Artagnan should get up and depart as quickly as possible. D'Artagnan, half stupefied, without his doublet, and with his head bound up in a linen cloth, arose then, and urged by the host, began to descend the stairs; but on arriving at the kitchen, the first thing he saw was his antagonist talking calmly at the step of a heavy carriage, drawn by two large Norman horses.

His interlocutor, whose head appeared through the carriage window, was a woman of from twenty to two-and-twenty years. We have already observed with what rapidity d'Artagnan seized the expression of a countenance. He perceived then, at a glance, that this woman was young and beautiful; and her style of beauty struck him more forcibly from its being totally different from that of the southern countries in which d'Artagnan had hitherto resided. She was pale and fair, with long curls falling in profusion over her shoulders, had large, blue, languishing eyes, rosy lips, and hands of alabaster. She was talking with great animation with the stranger.

"His Eminence, then, orders me--" said the lady.

"To return instantly to England, and to inform him as soon as the duke leaves London."

"And as to my other instructions?" asked the fair traveler.

"They are contained in this box, which you will not open until you are on the other side of the Channel."

"Very well; and you--what will you do?"

"I--I return to Paris."

"What, without chastising this insolent boy?" asked the lady.

The stranger was about to reply; but at the moment he opened his mouth, d'Artagnan, who had heard all, precipitated himself over the threshold of the door.

"This insolent boy chastises others," cried he; "and I hope that this time he whom he ought to chastise will not escape him as before."

"Will not escape him?" replied the stranger, knitting his brow.

"No; before a woman you would dare not fly, I presume?"

"Remember," said Milady, seeing the stranger lay his hand on his sword, "the least delay may ruin everything."

"You are right," cried the gentleman; "begone then, on your part, and I will depart as quickly on mine." And bowing to the lady, sprang into his sad-

[1] We are well aware that this term, milady, is only properly used when followed by a family name. But we find it thus in the manuscript, and we do not choose to take upon ourselves to alter it.

dle, while her coachman applied his whip vigorously to his horses. The two interlocutors thus separated, taking opposite directions, at full gallop.

"Pay him, booby!" cried the stranger to his servant, without checking the speed of his horse; and the man, after throwing two or three silver pieces at the foot of mine host, galloped after his master.

"Base coward! false gentleman!" cried d'Artagnan, springing forward, in his turn, after the servant. But his wound had rendered him too weak to support such an exertion. Scarcely had he gone ten steps when his ears began to tingle, a faintness seized him, a cloud of blood passed over his eyes, and he fell in the middle of the street, crying still, "Coward! coward! coward!"

"He is a coward, indeed," grumbled the host, drawing near to d'Artagnan, and endeavoring by this little flattery to make up matters with the young man, as the heron of the fable did with the snail he had despised the evening before.

"Yes, a base coward," murmured d'Artagnan; "but she--she was very beautiful."

"What she?" demanded the host.

"Milady," faltered d'Artagnan, and fainted a second time.

"Ah, it's all one," said the host; "I have lost two customers, but this one remains, of whom I am pretty certain for some days to come. There will be eleven crowns gained."

It is to be remembered that eleven crowns was just the sum that remained in d'Artagnan's purse.

The host had reckoned upon eleven days of confinement at a crown a day, but he had reckoned without his guest. On the following morning at five o'clock d'Artagnan arose, and descending to the kitchen without help, asked, among other ingredients the list of which has not come down to us, for some oil, some wine, and some rosemary, and with his mother's recipe in his hand composed a balsam, with which he anointed his numerous wounds, replacing his bandages himself, and positively refusing the assistance of any doctor, d'Artagnan walked about that same evening, and was almost cured by the morrow.

But when the time came to pay for his rosemary, this oil, and the wine, the only expense the master had incurred, as he had preserved a strict abstinence--while on the contrary, the yellow horse, by the account of the hostler at least, had eaten three times as much as a horse of his size could reasonably supposed to have done--d'Artagnan found nothing in his pocket but his little old velvet purse with the eleven crowns it contained; for as to the letter addressed to M. de Treville, it had disappeared.

The young man commenced his search for the letter with the greatest patience, turning out his pockets of all kinds over and over again, rummaging and rerummaging in his valise, and opening and reopening his purse; but when he found that he had come to the conviction that the letter was not to be found, he flew, for the third time, into such a rage as was near costing him a fresh consumption of wine, oil, and rosemary--for upon seeing this hot-headed youth become exasperated and threaten to destroy everything in the establishment if his letter were not found, the host seized a spit, his wife a broom handle, and the servants the same sticks they had used the day before.

"My letter of recommendation!" cried d'Artagnan, "my letter of recommendation! or, the holy blood, I will spit you all like ortolans!"

Unfortunately, there was one circumstance which created a powerful obstacle to the accomplishment of this threat; which was, as we have related, that his sword had been in his first conflict broken in two, and which he had entirely forgotten. Hence, it resulted when d'Artagnan proceeded to draw his sword in earnest, he found himself purely and simply armed with a stump of a sword about eight or ten inches in length, which the host had carefully placed in the scabbard. As to the rest of the blade, the master had slyly put that on one side to make himself a larding pin.

But this deception would probably not have stopped our fiery young man if the host had not reflected that the reclamation which his guest made was perfectly just.

"But, after all," said he, lowering the point of his spit, "where is this letter?"

"Yes, where is this letter?" cried d'Artagnan. "In the first place, I warn you that that letter is for Monsieur de Treville, and it must be found, he will know how to find it."

His threat completed the intimidation of the host. After the king and the cardinal, M. de Treville was the man whose name was perhaps most frequently repeated by the military, and even by citizens. There was, to be sure, Father Joseph, but his name was never pronounced but with a subdued voice, such was the terror inspired by his Gray Eminence, as the cardinal's familiar was called.

Throwing down his spit, and ordering his wife to do the same with her broom handle, and the servants with their sticks, he set the first example of commencing an earnest search for the lost letter.

"Does the letter contain anything valuable?" demanded the host, after a few minutes of useless investigation.

"Zounds! I think it does indeed!" cried the Gascon, who reckoned upon this letter for making his way at court. "It contained my fortune!"

"Bills upon Spain?" asked the disturbed host.

"Bills upon his Majesty's private treasury," answered d'Artagnan, who, reckoning upon entering into the king's service in consequence of this recommendation, believed he could make this somewhat hazardous reply without telling of a falsehood.

"The devil!" cried the host, at his wit's end.

"But it's of no importance," continued d'Artagnan, with natural assurance; "it's of no importance. The money is nothing; that letter was everything. I would rather have lost a thousand pistoles than have lost it." He would not have risked more if he had said twenty thousand; but a certain juvenile modesty restrained him.

A ray of light all at once broke upon the mind of the host as he was giving himself to the devil upon finding nothing.

"That letter is not lost!" cried he.

"What!" cried d'Artagnan.

"No, it has been stolen from you."

"Stolen? By whom?"

"By the gentleman who was here yesterday. He came down into the kitchen, where your doublet was. He remained there some time alone. I would lay a wager he has stolen it."

"Do you think so?" answered d'Artagnan, but little convinced, as he knew better than anyone else how entirely personal the value of this letter was, and was nothing in it likely to tempt cupidity. The fact was that none of his servants, none of the travelers present, could have gained anything by being possessed of this paper.

"Do you say," resumed d'Artagnan, "that you suspect that impertinent gentleman?"

"I tell you I am sure of it," continued the host. "When I informed him that your lordship was the protege of Monsieur de Treville, and that you even had a letter for that illustrious gentleman, he appeared to be very much disturbed, and asked me where that letter was, and immediately came down into the kitchen, where he knew your doublet was."

"Then that's my thief," replied d'Artagnan. "I will complain to Monsieur de Treville, and Monsieur de Treville will complain to the king." He then drew two crowns majestically from his purse and gave them to the host, who accompanied him, cap in hand, to the gate, and remounted his yellow horse, which bore him without any further accident to the gate of St. Antoine at Paris, where his owner sold him for three crowns, which was a very good price, considering that d'Artagnan had ridden him hard during the last stage. Thus the dealer to whom d'Artagnan sold him for the nine livres did not conceal from the young man that he only gave that enormous sum for him on the account of the originality of his color.

Thus d'Artagnan entered Paris on foot, carrying his little packet under his arm, and walked about till he found an apartment to be let on terms suited to the scantiness of his means. This chamber was a sort of garret, situated in the Rue des Fossoyeurs, near the Luxembourg.

As soon as the earnest money was paid, d'Artagnan took possession of his lodging, and passed the remainder of the day in sewing onto his doublet and hose some ornamental braiding which his mother had taken off an almost-new doublet of the elder M. d'Artagnan, and which she had given her son secretly. Next he went to the Quai de Feraille to have a new blade put to his sword, and then returned toward the Louvre, inquiring of the first Musketeer he met for the situation of the hotel of M. de Treville, which proved to be in the Rue du Vieux-Colombier; that is to say, in the immediate vicinity of the chamber hired by d'Artagnan--a circumstance which appeared to furnish a happy augury for the success of his journey.

After this, satisfied with the way in which he had conducted himself at Meung, without remorse for the past, confident in the present, and full of hope for the future, he retired to bed and slept the sleep of the brave.

This sleep, provincial as it was, brought him to nine o'clock in the morning; at which hour he rose, in order to repair to the residence of M. de Treville, the third personage in the kingdom, in the paternal estimation.

2 The Antechamber Of M. De Treville

M de Troisville, as his family was still called in Gascony, or M. de Treville, as he has ended by styling himself in Paris, had really commenced life as d'Artagnan now did; that is to say, without a sou in his pocket, but with a fund of audacity, shrewdness, and intelligence which makes the poorest Gascon gentleman often derive more in his hope from the paternal inheritance than the richest Perigordian or Berrichan gentleman derives in reality from his. His insolent bravery, his still more insolent success at a time when blows poured down like hail, had borne him to the top of that difficult ladder called Court Favor, which he had climbed four steps at a time.

He was the friend of the king, who honored highly, as everyone knows, the memory of his father, Henry IV. The father of M. de Treville had served him so faithfully in his wars against the league that in default of money--a thing to which the Bearnais was accustomed all his life, and who constantly paid his debts with that of which he never stood in need of borrowing, that is to say, with ready wit--in default of money, we repeat, he authorized him, after the reduction of Paris, to assume for his arms a golden lion passant upon gules, with the motto FIDELIS ET FORTIS. This was a great matter in the way of honor, but very little in the way of wealth; so that when the illustrious companion of the great Henry died, the only inheritance he was able to leave his son was his sword and his motto. Thanks to this double gift and the spotless name that accompanied it, M. de Treville was admitted into the household of the young prince where he made such good use of his sword, and was so faithful to his motto, that Louis XIII, one of the good blades of his kingdom, was accustomed to say that if he had a friend who was about to fight, he would advise him to choose as a second, himself first, and Treville next--or even, perhaps, before himself.

Thus Louis XIII had a real liking for Treville--a royal liking, a self-interested liking, it is true, but still a liking. At that unhappy period it was an important consideration to be surrounded by such men as Treville. Many might take for their device the epithet STRONG, which formed the second part of his motto, but very few gentlemen could lay claim to the FAITHFUL, which constituted the first. Treville was one of these latter. His was one of those rare organizations, endowed with an obedient intelligence like that of the dog; with a blind valor, a quick eye, and a prompt hand; to whom sight appeared only to be given to see if the king were dissatisfied with anyone, and the hand to strike this displeasing personage, whether a Besme, a Maurevers, a Poltiot de Mere, or a Vitry. In short, up to this period nothing had been wanting to Treville but opportunity; but he was ever on the watch for it, and he faithfully promised himself that he would not fail to seize it by its three hairs whenever it came within reach of his hand. At last Louis XIII made Treville the captain of his Musketeers, who were to Louis XIII in devotedness, or rather in fanaticism, what his Ordinaries had been to Henry III, and his Scotch Guard to Louis XI.

On his part, the cardinal was not behind the king in this respect. When he saw the formidable and chosen body with which Louis XIII had surrounded himself, this second, or rather this first king of France, became desirous that he, too, should have his guard. He had his Musketeers therefore, as Louis XIII had his, and these two powerful rivals vied with each other in procuring, not only from all the provinces of France, but even from all foreign states, the most celebrated swordsmen. It was not uncommon for Richelieu and Louis XIII to dispute over their evening game of chess upon the merits of their servants. Each boasted the bearing and the courage of his own people. While exclaiming loudly against duels and brawls, they excited them secretly to quarrel, deriving an immoderate satisfaction or genuine regret from the success or defeat of their own combatants. We learn this from the memoirs of a man who was concerned in some few of these defeats and in many of these victories.

Treville had grasped the weak side of his master; and it was to this address that he owed the long and constant favor of a king who has not left the reputation behind him of being very faithful in his friendships. He paraded his Musketeers before the Cardinal Armand Duplessis with an insolent air which made the gray moustache of his Eminence curl with ire. Treville understood admirably the war method of that period, in which he who could not live at the expense of the enemy must live at the expense of his compatriots. His soldiers formed a legion of devil-may-care fellows, perfectly undisciplined toward all but himself.

Loose, half-drunk, imposing, the king's Musketeers, or rather M. de Treville's, spread themselves about in the cabarets, in the public walks, and the public sports, shouting, twisting their mustaches, clanking their swords, and taking great pleasure in annoying the Guards of the cardinal whenever they could fall in with them; then drawing in the open streets, as if it were the best of all possible sports; sometimes killed, but sure in that case to be both wept and avenged; often killing others, but then certain of not rotting in prison, M. de Treville being there to claim them. Thus M. de Treville was praised to the highest note by these men, who adored him, and who, ruffians as they were, trembled before him like scholars before their master, obedient to his least word, and ready to sacrifice themselves to wash out the smallest insult.

M de Treville employed this powerful weapon for the king, in the first place, and the friends of the king--and then for himself and his own friends. For the rest, in the memoirs of this period, which has left so many memoirs, one does not find this worthy gentleman blamed even by his enemies; and he had many such among men of the pen as well as among men of the sword. In no instance, let us say, was this worthy gentleman accused of deriving personal advantage from the cooperation of his minions. Endowed with a rare genius for intrigue which rendered him the equal of the ablest intriguers, he remained an honest man. Still further, in spite of sword thrusts which weaken, and painful exercises which fatigue, he had become one of the most gallant frequenters of revels, one of the most insinuating lady's men, one of the softest whisperers of interesting nothings of his day; the BONNES FORTUNES of de Treville were talked of as those of M. de Bassompierre had been talked of twenty years before, and that was not saying a little. The captain of the Musketeers was therefore admired, feared, and loved; and this constitutes the zenith of human fortune.

Louis XIV absorbed all the smaller stars of his court in his own vast radiance; but his father, a sun PLURIBUS IMPAR, left his personal splendor to each of his favorites, his individual value to each of his courtiers. In addition to the leeves of the king and the cardinal, there might be reckoned in Paris at that time more than two hundred smaller but still noteworthy leeves. Among these two hundred leeves, that of Treville was one of the most sought.

The court of his hotel, situated in the Rue du Vieux-Colombier, resembled a camp from by six o'clock in the morning in summer and eight o'clock in winter. From fifty to sixty Musketeers, who appeared to replace one another in order always to present an imposing number, paraded constantly, armed to the teeth and ready for anything. On one of those immense staircases, upon whose space modern civilization would build a whole house, ascended and descended the office seekers of Paris, who ran after any sort of favor--gentlemen from the provinces anxious to be enrolled, and servants in all sorts of liveries, bringing and carrying messages between their masters and M. de Treville. In the antechamber, upon long circular benches, reposed the elect; that is to say, those who were called. In this apartment a continued buzzing prevailed from morning till night, while M. de Treville, in his office contiguous to this antechamber, received visits, listened to complaints, gave his orders, and like the king in his balcony at the Louvre, had only to place himself at the window to review both his men and arms.

The day on which d'Artagnan presented himself the assemblage was imposing, particularly for a provincial just arriving from his province. It is true that this provincial was a Gascon; and that, particularly at this period, the compatriots of d'Artagnan had the reputation of not being easily intimidated. When he had once passed the massive door covered with long square-headed nails, he fell into the midst of a troop of swordsmen, who crossed one another in their passage, calling out, quarreling, and playing tricks one with another. In order to make one's way amid these turbulent and conflicting waves, it was necessary to be an officer, a great noble, or a pretty woman.

It was, then, into the midst of this tumult and disorder that our young man advanced with a beating heat, ranging his long rapier up his lanky leg, and keeping one hand on the edge of his cap, with that half-smile of the embarrassed a provincial who wishes to put on a good face. When he had passed one group he began to breathe more freely; but he could not help observing that they turned round to look at him, and for the first time in his life d'Artagnan, who had till that day entertained a very good opinion of himself, felt ridiculous.

Arrived at the staircase, it was still worse. There were four Musketeers on the bottom steps, amusing themselves with the following exercise, while ten or twelve of their comrades waited upon the landing place to take their turn in the sport.

One of them, stationed upon the top stair, naked sword in hand, prevented, or at least endeavored to prevent, the three others from ascending.

These three others fenced against him with their agile swords.

D'Artagnan at first took these weapons for foils, and believed them to be buttoned; but he soon perceived by certain scratches that every weapon was pointed and sharpened, and that at each of these scratches not only the spectators, but even the actors themselves, laughed like so many madmen.

He who at the moment occupied the upper step kept his adversaries marvelously in check. A circle was formed around them. The conditions required that at every hit the man touched should quit the game, yielding his turn for the benefit of the adversary who had hit him. In five minutes three were slightly wounded, one on the hand, another on the ear, by the defender of the stair, who himself remained intact--a piece of skill which was worth to him, according to the rules agreed upon, three turns of favor.

However difficult it might be, or rather as he pretended it was, to astonish our young traveler, this pastime really astonished him. He had seen in his province--that land in which heads become so easily heated--a few of the preliminaries of duels; but the daring of these four fencers appeared to him the strongest he had ever heard of even in Gascony. He believed himself transported into that famous country of giants into which Gulliver afterward went and was so frightened; and yet he had not gained the goal, for there were still the landing place and the antechamber.

On the landing they were no longer fighting, but amused themselves with stories about women, and in the antechamber, with stories about the court. On the landing d'Artagnan blushed; in the antechamber he trembled. His warm and fickle imagination, which in Gascony had rendered formidable to young chambermaids, and even sometimes their mistresses, had never dreamed, even in moments of delirium, of half the amorous wonders or a quarter of the feats of gallantry which were here set forth in connection with names the best known and with details the least concealed. But if his morals were shocked on the landing, his respect for the cardinal was scandalized in the antechamber. There, to his great astonishment, d'Artagnan heard the policy which made all Europe tremble criticized aloud and openly, as well as the private life of the cardinal, which so many great nobles had been punished for trying to pry into. That great man who was so revered by d'Artagnan the elder served as an object of ridicule to the Musketeers of Treville, who cracked their jokes upon his bandy legs and his crooked back. Some sang ballads about Mme. d'Aguillon, his mistress, and Mme. Cambalet, his niece; while others formed parties and plans to annoy the pages and guards of the cardinal duke--all things which appeared to d'Artagnan monstrous impossibilities.

Nevertheless, when the name of the king was now and then uttered unthinkingly amid all these cardinal jests, a sort of gag seemed to close for a moment on all these jeering mouths. They looked hesitatingly around them, and appeared to doubt the thickness of the partition between them and the office of M. de Treville; but a fresh allusion soon brought back the conversation to his Eminence, and then the laughter recovered its loudness and the light was not withheld from any of his actions.

"Certes, these fellows will all either be imprisoned or hanged," thought the terrified d'Artagnan, "and I, no doubt, with them; for from the moment I have either listened to or heard them, I shall be held as an accomplice. What would my good father say, who so strongly pointed out to me the respect due to the cardinal, if he knew I was in the society of such pagans?"

We have no need, therefore, to say that d'Artagnan dared not join in the conversation, only he looked with all his eyes and listened with all his ears, stretching his five senses so as to lose nothing; and despite his confidence on the paternal admonitions, he felt himself carried by his tastes and led by his instincts to praise rather than to blame the unheard-of things which were taking place.

Although he was a perfect stranger in the court of M. de Treville's courtiers, and this his first appearance in that place, he was at length noticed, and somebody came and asked him what he wanted. At this demand d'Artagnan gave his name very modestly, emphasized the title of compatriot, and begged the servant who had put the question to him to request a moment's audience of M. de Treville--a request which the other, with an air of protection, promised to transmit in due season.

D'Artagnan, a little recovered from his first surprise, had now leisure to study costumes and physiognomy.

The center of the most animated group was a Musketeer of great height and haughty countenance, dressed in a costume so peculiar as to attract general attention. He did not wear the uniform cloak--which was not obligatory at that epoch of less liberty but more independence--but a cerulean-blue doublet, a little faded and worn, and over this a magnificent baldric, worked in gold, which shone like water ripples in the sun. A long cloak of crimson velvet fell in graceful folds from his shoulders, disclosing in front the splendid baldric, from which was suspended a gigantic rapier. This Musketeer had just come off guard, complained of having a cold, and coughed from time to time affectedly. It was for this reason, as he said to those around him, that he had put on his cloak; and while he spoke with a lofty air and twisted his mustache disdainfully, all admired his embroidered baldric, and d'Artagnan more than anyone.

"What would you have?" said the Musketeer. "This fashion is coming in. It is a folly, I admit, but still it is the fashion. Besides, one must lay out one's inheritance somehow."

"Ah, Porthos!" cried one of his companions, "don't try to make us believe you obtained that baldric by paternal generosity. It was given to you by that veiled lady I met you with the other Sunday, near the gate St. Honor."

"No, upon honor and by the faith of a gentleman, I bought it with the contents of my own purse," answered he whom they designated by the name Porthos.

"Yes; about in the same manner," said another Musketeer, "that I bought this new purse with what my mistress put into the old one."

"It's true, though," said Porthos; "and the proof is that I paid twelve pistoles for it."

The wonder was increased, though the doubt continued to exist.

"Is it not true, Aramis?" said Porthos, turning toward another Musketeer.

This other Musketeer formed a perfect contrast to his interrogator, who had just designated him by the name of Aramis. He was a stout man, of about two- or three-and-twenty, with an open, ingenuous countenance, a black, mild eye, and cheeks rosy and downy as an autumn peach. His delicate mustache marked a perfectly straight line upon his upper lip; he appeared to dread to lower his hands lest their veins should swell, and he pinched the tips of his ears from time to time to preserve their delicate pink transparency. Habitually he spoke little and slowly, bowed frequently, laughed without noise, showing his teeth, which were fine and of which, as the rest of his person, he appeared to take great care. He answered the appeal of his friend by an affirmative nod of the head.

This affirmation appeared to dispel all doubts with regard to the baldric. They continued to admire it, but said no more about it; and with a rapid change of thought, the conversation passed suddenly to another subject.

"What do you think of the story Chalais's esquire relates?" asked another Musketeer, without addressing anyone in particular, but on the contrary speaking to everybody.

"And what does he say?" asked Porthos, in a self-sufficient tone.

"He relates that he met at Brussels Rochefort, the AME DAMNEE of the cardinal disguised as a Capuchin, and that this cursed Rochefort, thanks to his disguise, had tricked Monsieur de Laigues, like a ninny as he is."

"A ninny, indeed!" said Porthos; "but is the matter certain?"

"I had it from Aramis," replied the Musketeer.

"Indeed?"

"Why, you knew it, Porthos," said Aramis. "I told you of it yesterday. Let us say no more about it."

"Say no more about it? That's YOUR opinion!" replied Porthos.

"Say no more about it! PESTE! You come to your conclusions quickly. What! The cardinal sets a spy upon a gentleman, has his letters stolen from him by means of a traitor, a brigand, a rascal-has, with the help of this spy and thanks to this correspondence, Chalais's throat cut, under the stupid pretext that he wanted to kill the king and marry Monsieur to the queen! Nobody knew a word of this enigma. You unraveled it yesterday to the great satisfaction of all; and while we are still gaping with wonder at the news, you come and tell us today, 'Let us say no more about it.'"

"Well, then, let us talk about it, since you desire it," replied Aramis, patiently.

"This Rochefort," cried Porthos, "if I were the esquire of poor Chalais, should pass a minute or two very uncomfortably with me."

"And you--you would pass rather a sad quarter-hour with the Red Duke," replied Aramis.

"Oh, the Red Duke! Bravo! Bravo! The Red Duke!" cried Porthos, clapping his hands and nodding his head. "The Red Duke is capital. I'll circulate that saying, be assured, my dear fellow. Who says this Aramis is not a wit? What a misfortune it is you did not follow your first vocation; what a delicious abbe you would have made!"

"Oh, it's only a temporary postponement," replied Aramis; "I shall be one someday. You very well know, Porthos, that I continue to study theology for that purpose."

"He will be one, as he says," cried Porthos; "he will be one, sooner or later."

"Sooner." said Aramis.

"He only waits for one thing to determine him to resume his cassock, which hangs behind his uniform," said another Musketeer.

"What is he waiting for?" asked another.

"Only till the queen has given an heir to the crown of France."

"No jesting upon that subject, gentlemen," said Porthos; "thank God the queen is still of an age to give one!"

"They say that Monsieur de Buckingham is in France," replied Aramis, with a significant smile which gave to this sentence, apparently so simple, a tolerably scandalous meaning.

"Aramis, my good friend, this time you are wrong," interrupted Porthos. "Your wit is always leading you beyond bounds; if Monsieur de Treville heard you, you would repent of speaking thus."

"Are you going to give me a lesson, Porthos?" cried Aramis, from whose usually mild eye a flash passed like lightning.

"My dear fellow, be a Musketeer or an abbe. Be one or the other, but not both," replied Porthos. "You know what Athos told you the other day; you eat at everybody's mess. Ah, don't be angry, I beg of you, that would be useless; you know what is agreed upon between you, Athos and me. You go to Madame d'Aguillon's, and you pay your court to her; you go to Madame de Bois-Tracy's, the cousin of Madame de Chevreuse, and you pass for being far advanced in the good graces of that lady. Oh, good Lord! Don't trouble yourself to reveal your good luck; no one asks for your secret-all the world knows your discretion. But since you possess that virtue, why the devil don't you make use of it with respect to her Majesty? Let whoever likes talk of the king and the cardinal, and how he likes; but the queen is sacred, and if anyone speaks of her, let it be respectfully."

"Porthos, you are as vain as Narcissus; I plainly tell you so," replied Aramis. "You know I hate moralizing, except when it is done by Athos. As to you, good sir, you wear too magnificent a baldric to be strong on that head. I will be an abbe if it suits me. In the meanwhile I am a Musketeer; in that quality I say what I please, and at this moment it pleases me to say that you weary me."

"Aramis!"

"Porthos!"

"Gentlemen! Gentlemen!" cried the surrounding group.

"Monsieur de Treville awaits Monsieur d'Artagnan," cried a servant, throwing open the door of the cabinet.

At this announcement, during which the door remained open, everyone became mute, and amid the general silence the young man crossed part of the length of the antechamber, and entered the apartment of the captain of the Musketeers, congratulating himself with all his heart at having so narrowly escaped the end of this strange quarrel.

3 The Audience

M de Treville was at the moment in rather ill-humor, nevertheless he saluted the young man politely, who bowed to the very ground; and he smiled on receiving d'Artagnan's response, the Bearnese accent of which recalled to him at the same time his youth and his country--a double remembrance which makes a man smile at all ages; but stepping toward the antechamber and making a sign to d'Artagnan with his hand, as if to ask his permission to finish with others before he began with him, he called three times, with a louder voice at each time, so that he ran through the intervening tones between the imperative accent and the angry accent.

"Athos! Porthos! Aramis!"

The two Musketeers with whom we have already made acquaintance, and who answered to the last of these three names, immediately quitted the group of which they had formed a part, and advanced toward the cabinet, the door of which closed after them as soon as they had entered. Their appearance, although it was not quite at ease, excited by its carelessness, at once full of dignity and submission, the admiration of d'Artagnan, who beheld in these two men demi-gods, and in their leader an Olympian Jupiter, armed with all his thunders.

When the two Musketeers had entered; when the door was closed behind them; when the buzzing murmur of the antechamber, to which the summons which had been made had doubtless furnished fresh food, had recommenced; when M. de Treville had three or four times paced in silence, and with a frowning brow, the whole length of his cabinet, passing each time before Porthos and Aramis, who were as upright and silent as if on parade--he stopped all at once full in front of them, and covering them from head to foot with an angry look, "Do you know what the king said to me," cried he, "and that no longer ago than yesterday evening--do you know, gentlemen?"

"No," replied the two Musketeers, after a moment's silence, "no, sir, we do not."

"But I hope that you will do us the honor to tell us," added Aramis, in his politest tone and with his most graceful bow.

"He told me that he should henceforth recruit his Musketeers from among the Guards of Monsieur the Cardinal."

"The Guards of the cardinal! And why so?" asked Porthos, warmly.

"Because he plainly perceives that his piquette[1] stands in need of being enlivened by a mixture of good wine."

The two Musketeers reddened to the whites of their eyes. d'Artagnan did not know where he was, and wished himself a hundred feet underground.

"Yes, yes," continued M. de Treville, growing warmer as he spoke, "and his majesty was right; for, upon my honor, it is true that the Musketeers make but a miserable figure at court. The cardinal related yesterday while playing with the king, with an air of condolence very displeasing to me, that the day before yesterday those DAMNED MUSKETEERS, those DAREDEVILS--he dwelt upon those words with an ironical tone still more displeasing to me--those BRAGGARTS, added he, glancing at me with his tiger-cat's eye, had made a riot in the Rue Ferou in a cabaret, and that a party of his Guards (I thought he was going to laugh in my face) had been forced to arrest the rioters! MORBLEU! You must know something about it. Arrest Musketeers! You were among them--you were! Don't deny it; you were recognized, and the cardinal named you. But it's all my fault; yes, it's all my fault, because it is myself who

---

[1] A watered liquor, made from the second pressing of the grape.

selects my men. You, Aramis, why the devil did you ask me for a uniform when you would have been so much better in a cassock? And you, Porthos, do you only wear such a fine golden baldric to suspend a sword of straw from it? And Athos--I don't see Athos. Where is he?"

"Ill--"

"Very ill, say you? And of what malady?"

"It is feared that it may be the smallpox, sir," replied Porthos, desirous of taking his turn in the conversation; "and what is serious is that it will certainly spoil his face."

"The smallpox! That's a great story to tell me, Porthos! Sick of the smallpox at his age! No, no; but wounded without doubt, killed, perhaps. Ah, if I knew! S'blood! Messieurs Musketeers, I will not have this haunting of bad places, this quarreling in the streets, this swordplay at the crossways; and above all, I will not have occasion given for the cardinal's Guards, who are brave, quiet, skillful men who never put themselves in a position to be arrested, and who, besides, never allow themselves to be arrested, to laugh at you! I am sure of it--they would prefer dying on the spot to being arrested or taking back a step. To save yourselves, to scamper away, to flee--that is good for the king's Musketeers!"

Porthos and Aramis trembled with rage. They could willingly have strangled M. de Treville, if, at the bottom of all this, they had not felt it was the great love he bore them which made him speak thus. They stamped upon the carpet with their feet; they bit their lips till the blood came, and grasped the hilts of their swords with all their might. All without had heard, as we have said, Athos, Porthos, and Aramis called, and had guessed, from M. de Treville's tone of voice, that he was very angry about something. Ten curious heads were glued to the tapestry and became pale with fury; for their ears, closely applied to the door, did not lose a syllable of what he said, while their mouths repeated as he went on, the insulting expressions of the captain to all the people in the antechamber. In an instant, from the door of the cabinet to the street gate, the whole hotel was boiling.

"Ah! The king's Musketeers are arrested by the Guards of the cardinal, are they?" continued M. de Treville, as furious at heart as his soldiers, but emphasizing his words and plunging them, one by one, so to say, like so many blows of a stiletto, into the bosoms of his auditors. "What! Six of his Eminence's Guards arrest six of his Majesty's Musketeers! MORBLEU! My part is taken! I will go straight to the louvre; I will give in my resignation as captain of the king's Musketeers to take a lieutenancy in the cardinal's Guards, and if he refuses me, MORBLEU! I will turn abbe."

At these words, the murmur without became an explosion; nothing was to be heard but oaths and blasphemies. The MORBLEUS, the SANG DIEUS, the MORTS TOUTS LES DIABLES, crossed one another in the air. D'Artagnan looked for some tapestry behind which he might hide himself, and felt an immense inclination to crawl under the table.

"Well, my Captain," said Porthos, quite beside himself, "the truth is that we were six against six. But we were not captured by fair means; and before we had time to draw our swords, two of our party were dead, and Athos, grievously wounded, was very little better. For you know Athos. Well, Captain, he endeavored twice to get up, and fell again twice. And we did not surrender--no! They dragged us away by force. On the way we escaped. As for Athos, they believed him to be dead, and left him very quiet on the field of battle, not thinking it worth the trouble to carry him away. That's the whole story. What the devil, Captain, one cannot win all one's battles! The great Pompey lost that of Pharsalia; and Francis the First, who was, as I have heard say, as good as other folks, nevertheless lost the Battle of Pavia."

"And I have the honor of assuring you that I killed one of them with his own sword," said Aramis; "for mine was broken at the first parry. Killed him, or poniarded him, sir, as is most agreeable to you."

"I did not know that," replied M. de Treville, in a somewhat softened tone. "The cardinal exaggerated, as I perceive."

"But pray, sir," continued Aramis, who, seeing his captain become appeased, ventured to risk a prayer, "do not say that Athos is wounded. He would be in despair if that should come to the ears of the king; and as the wound is very serious, seeing that after crossing the shoulder it penetrates into the chest, it is to be feared--"

At this instant the tapestry was raised and a noble and handsome head, but frightfully pale, appeared under the fringe.

"Athos!" cried the two Musketeers.

"Athos!" repeated M. de Treville himself.

"You have sent for me, sir," said Athos to M. de Treville, in a feeble yet perfectly calm voice, "you have sent for me, as my comrades inform me, and I have hastened to receive your orders. I am here; what do you want with me?"

And at these words, the Musketeer, in irreproachable costume, belted as usual, with a tolerably firm step, entered the cabinet. M. de Treville, moved to the bottom of his heart by this proof of courage, sprang toward him.

"I was about to say to these gentlemen," added he, "that I forbid my Musketeers to expose their lives needlessly; for brave men are very dear to the king, and the king knows that his Musketeers are the bravest on the earth. Your hand, Athos!"

And without waiting for the answer of the newcomer to this proof of affection, M. de Treville seized his right hand and pressed it with all his might, without perceiving that Athos, whatever might be his self-command, allowed a slight murmur of pain to escape him, and if possible, grew paler than he was before.

The door had remained open, so strong was the excitement produced by the arrival of Athos, whose wound, though kept as a secret, was known to all. A burst of satisfaction hailed the last words of the captain; and two or three heads, carried away by the enthusiasm of the moment, appeared through the openings of the tapestry. M. de Treville was about to reprehend this breach of the rules of etiquette, when he felt the hand of Athos, who had rallied all his energies to contend against pain, at length overcome by it, fell upon the floor as if he were dead.

"A surgeon!" cried M. de Treville, "mine! The king's! The best! A surgeon! Or, s'blood, my brave Athos will die!"

At the cries of M. de Treville, the whole assemblage rushed into the cabinet, he not thinking to shut the door against anyone, and all crowded round the wounded man. But all this eager attention might have been useless if the doctor so loudly called for had not chanced to be in the hotel. He pushed through the crowd, approached Athos, still insensible, and as all this noise and commotion inconvenienced him greatly, he required, as the first and most urgent thing, that the Musketeer should be carried into an adjoining chamber. Immediately M. de Treville opened and pointed the way to Porthos and Aramis, who bore their comrade in their arms. Behind this group walked the surgeon; and behind the surgeon the door closed.

The cabinet of M. de Treville, generally held so sacred, became in an instant the annex of the antechamber. Everyone spoke, harangued, and vociferated, swearing, cursing, and consigning the cardinal and his Guards to all the devils.

An instant after, Porthos and Aramis re-entered, the surgeon and M. de Treville alone remaining with the wounded.

At length, M. de Treville himself returned. The injured man had recovered his senses. The surgeon declared that the situation of the Musketeer had nothing in it to render his friends uneasy, his weakness having been purely and simply caused by loss of blood.

Then M. de Treville made a sign with his hand, and all retired except d'Artagnan, who did not forget that he had an audience, and with the tenacity of a Gascon remained in his place.

When all had gone out and the door was closed, M. de Treville, on turning round, found himself alone with the young man. The event which had occurred had in some degree broken the thread of his ideas. He inquired what was the will of his persevering visitor. d'Artagnan then repeated his name, and in an instant recovering all his remembrances of the present and the past, M. de Treville grasped the situation.

"Pardon me," said he, smiling, "pardon me my dear compatriot, but I had wholly forgotten you. But what help is there for it! A captain is nothing but a father of a family, charged with even a greater responsibility than the father of an ordinary family. Soldiers are big children; but as I maintain that the orders of the king, and more particularly the orders of the cardinal, should be executed--"

D'Artagnan could not restrain a smile. By this smile M. de Treville judged that he had not to deal with a fool, and changing the conversation, came straight to the point.

"I respected your father very much," said he. "What can I do for the son? Tell me quickly; my time is not my own."

"Monsieur," said d'Artagnan, "on quitting Tarbes and coming hither, it was my intention to request of you, in remembrance of the friendship which you have not forgotten, the uniform of a Musketeer; but after all that I have seen during the last two hours, I comprehend that such a favor is enormous, and tremble lest I should not merit it."

"It is indeed a favor, young man," replied M. de Treville, "but it may not be so far beyond your hopes as you believe, or rather as you appear to believe. But his majesty's decision is always necessary; and I inform you with regret that no one becomes a Musketeer without the preliminary ordeal of several campaigns, certain brilliant actions, or a service of two years in some other regiment less favored than ours."

D'Artagnan bowed without replying, feeling his desire to don the Musketeer's uniform vastly increased by the great difficulties which preceded the attainment of it.

"But," continued M. de Treville, fixing upon his compatriot a look so piercing that it might be said he wished to read the thoughts of his heart, "on account of my old companion, your father, as I have said, I will do something for you, young man. Our recruits from Bearn are not generally very rich, and I have no reason to think matters have much changed in this respect since I left the province. I dare say you have not brought too large a stock of money with you?"

D'Artagnan drew himself up with a proud air which plainly said, "I ask alms of no man."

"Oh, that's very well, young man," continued M. de Treville, "that's all very well. I know these airs; I myself came to Paris with four crowns in my purse, and would have fought with anyone who dared to tell me I was not in a condition to purchase the Louvre."

D'Artagnan's bearing became still more imposing. Thanks to the sale of his horse, he commenced his career with four more crowns than M. de Treville possessed at the commencement of his.

"You ought, I say, then, to husband the means you have, however large the sum may be; but you ought also to endeavor to perfect yourself in the exercises becoming a gentleman. I will write a letter today to the Director of the Royal Academy, and tomorrow he will admit you without any expense to yourself. Do not refuse this little service. Our best-born and richest gentlemen sometimes solicit it without being able to obtain it. You will learn horsemanship, swordsmanship in all its branches, and dancing. You will make some desirable acquaintances; and from time to time you can call upon me, just to tell me how you are getting on, and to say whether I can be of further service to you."

D'Artagnan, stranger as he was to all the manners of a court, could not but perceive a little coldness in this reception.

"Alas, sir," said he, "I cannot but perceive how sadly I miss the letter of introduction which my father gave me to present to you."

"I certainly am surprised," replied M. de Treville, "that you should undertake so long a journey without that necessary passport, the sole resource of us poor Bearnese."

"I had one, sir, and, thank God, such as I could wish," cried d'Artagnan; "but it was perfidiously stolen from me."

He then related the adventure of Meung, described the unknown gentleman with the greatest minuteness, and all with a warmth and truthfulness that delighted M. de Treville.

"This is all very strange," said M. de Treville, after meditating a minute; "you mentioned my name, then, aloud?"

"Yes, sir, I certainly committed that imprudence; but why should I have done otherwise? A name like yours must be as a buckler to me on my way. Judge if I should not put myself under its protection."

Flattery was at that period very current, and M. de Treville loved incense as well as a king, or even a cardinal. He could not refrain from a smile of visible satisfaction; but this smile soon disappeared, and returning to the adventure of Meung, "Tell me," continued he, "had not this gentlemen a slight scar on his cheek?"

"Yes, such a one as would be made by the grazing of a ball."

"Was he not a fine-looking man?"

"Yes."

"Of lofty stature."

"Yes."

"Of complexion and brown hair?"

"Yes, yes, that is he; how is it, sir, that you are acquainted with this man? If I ever find him again--and I will find him, I swear, were it in hell!"

"He was waiting for a woman," continued Treville.

"He departed immediately after having conversed for a minute with her whom he awaited."

"You know not the subject of their conversation?"

"He gave her a box, told her not to open it except in London."

"Was this woman English?"

"He called her Milady."

"It is he; it must be he!" murmured Treville. "I believed him still at Brussels."

"Oh, sir, if you know who this man is," cried d'Artagnan, "tell me who he is, and whence he is. I will then release you from all your promises--even that of procuring my admission into the Musketeers; for before everything, I wish to avenge myself."

"Beware, young man!" cried Treville. "If you see him coming on one side of the street, pass by on the other. Do not cast yourself against such a rock; he would break you like glass."

"That will not prevent me," replied d'Artagnan, "if ever I find him."

"In the meantime," said Treville, "seek him not--if I have a right to advise you."

All at once the captain stopped, as if struck by a sudden suspicion. This great hatred which the young traveler manifested so loudly for this man, who--a rather improbable thing--had stolen his father's letter from him--was there not some perfidy concealed under this hatred? Might not this young man be sent by his Eminence? Might he not have come for the purpose of laying a snare for him? This pretended d'Artagnan--was he not an emissary of the cardinal, whom the cardinal sought to introduce into Treville's house, to place near him, to win his confidence, and afterward to ruin him as had been done in a thousand other instances? He fixed his eyes upon d'Artagnan even more earnestly than before. He was moderately reassured however, by the aspect of that countenance, full of astute intelligence and affected humility. "I know he is a Gascon," reflected he, "but he may be one for the cardinal as well as for me. Let us try him."

"My friend," said he, slowly, "I wish, as the son of an ancient friend--for I consider this story of the lost letter perfectly true--I wish, I say, in order to repair the coldness you may have remarked in my reception of you, to discover to you the secrets of our policy. The king and the cardinal are the best of friends; their apparent bickerings are only feints to deceive fools. I am not willing that a compatriot, a handsome cavalier, a brave youth, quite fit to make his way, should become the dupe of all these artifices and fall into the snare after the example of so many others who have been ruined by it. Be assured that I am devoted to both these all-powerful masters, and that my earnest endeavors have no other aim than the service of the king, and also the cardinal--one of the most illustrious geniuses that France has ever produced.

"Now, young man, regulate your conduct accordingly; and if you entertain, whether from your family, your relations, or even from your instincts, any of these enmities which we see constantly breaking out against the cardinal, bid me adieu and let us separate. I will aid you in many ways, but without attaching you to my person. I hope that my frankness at least will make you my friend; for you are the only young man to whom I have hitherto spoken as I have done to you."

Treville said to himself: "If the cardinal has set this young fox upon me, he will certainly not have failed--he, who knows how bitterly I execrate him--to tell his spy that the best means of making his court to me is to rail at him. Therefore, in spite of all my protestations, if it be as I suspect, my cunning gossip will assure me that he holds his Eminence in horror."

It, however, proved otherwise. D'Artagnan answered, with the greatest simplicity: "I came to Paris with exactly such intentions. My father advised me to stoop to nobody but the king, the cardinal, and yourself--whom he considered the first three personages in France."

D'Artagnan added M. de Treville to the others, as may be perceived; but he thought this addition would do no harm.

"I have the greatest veneration for the cardinal," continued he, "and the most profound respect for his actions. So much the better for me, sir, if you speak to me, as you say, with frankness--for then you will do me the honor to esteem the resemblance of our opinions; but if you have entertained any doubt, as naturally you may, I feel that I am ruining myself by speaking the truth. But I still trust you will not esteem me the less for it, and that is my object beyond all others."

M de Treville was surprised to the greatest degree. So much penetration, so much frankness, created admiration, but did not entirely remove his suspicions. The more this young man was superior to others, the more he was to be dreaded if he meant to deceive him; "You are an honest youth; but at the present moment I can only do for you that which I just now offered. My hotel will be always open to you. Hereafter, being able to ask for me at all hours, and consequently to take advantage of all opportunities, you will probably obtain that which you desire."

"That is to say," replied d'Artagnan, "that you will wait until I have proved myself worthy of it. Well, be assured," added he, with the familiarity of a Gascon, "you shall not wait long." And he bowed in order to retire, and as if he considered the future in his own hands.

"But wait a minute," said M. de Treville, stopping him. "I promised you a letter for the director of the Academy. Are you too proud to accept it, young gentleman?"

"No, sir," said d'Artagnan; "and I will guard it so carefully that I will be sworn it shall arrive at its address, and woe be to him who shall attempt to take it from me!"

M de Treville smiled at this flourish; and leaving his young man compatriot in the embrasure of the window, where they had talked together, he seated himself at a table in order to write the promised letter of recommendation. While he was doing this, d'Artagnan, having no better employment, amused himself with beating a march upon the window and with looking at the Musketeers, who went away, one after another, following them with his eyes until they disappeared.

M de Treville, after having written the letter, sealed it, and rising, approached the young man in order to give it to him. But at the very moment when d'Artagnan stretched out his hand to receive it, M. de Treville was highly astonished to see his protege make a sudden spring, become crimson with passion, and rush from the cabinet crying, "S'blood, he shall not escape me this time!"

"And who?" asked M. de Treville.

"He, my thief!" replied d'Artagnan. "Ah, the traitor!" and he disappeared.

"The devil take the madman!" murmured M. de Treville, "unless," added he, "this is a cunning mode of escaping, seeing that he had failed in his purpose!"

4 The Shoulder Of Athos, The Baldric Of Porthos And The Handkerchief Of Aramis

D'Artagnan, in a state of fury, crossed the antechamber at three bounds, and was darting toward the stairs, which he reckoned upon descending four at a time, when, in his heedless course, he ran head foremost against a Musketeer who was coming out of one of M. de Treville's private rooms, and striking his shoulder violently, made him utter a cry, or rather a howl.

"Excuse me," said d'Artagnan, endeavoring to resume his course, "excuse me, but I am in a hurry."

Scarcely had he descended the first stair, when a hand of iron seized him by the belt and stopped him.

"You are in a hurry?" said the Musketeer, as pale as a sheet. "Under that pretense you run against me! You say. 'Excuse me,' and you believe that is sufficient? Not at all my young man. Do you fancy because you have heard Monsieur de Treville speak to us a little cavalierly today that other people are to treat us as he speaks to us? Undeceive yourself, comrade, you are not Monsieur de Treville."

"My faith!" replied d'Artagnan, recognizing Athos, who, after the dressing performed by the doctor, was returning to his own apartment. "I did not do it intentionally, and not doing it intentionally, I said 'Excuse me.' It appears to me that this is quite enough. I repeat to you, however, and this time on my word of honor--I think perhaps too often--that I am in haste, great haste. Leave your hold, then, I beg of you, and let me go where my business calls me."

"Monsieur," said Athos, letting him go, "you are not polite; it is easy to perceive that you come from a distance."

D'Artagnan had already strode down three or four stairs, but at Athos's last remark he stopped short.

"MORBLEU, monsieur!" said he, "however far I may come, it is not you who can give me a lesson in good manners, I warn you."

"Perhaps," said Athos.

"Ah! If I were not in such haste, and if I were not running after someone," said d'Artagnan.

"Monsieur Man-in-a-hurry, you can find me without running--ME, you understand?"

"And where, I pray you?"

"Near the Carmes-Deschaux."

"At what hour?"

"About noon."

"About noon? That will do; I will be there."

"Endeavor not to make me wait; for at quarter past twelve I will cut off your ears as you run."

"Good!" cried d'Artagnan, "I will be there ten minutes before twelve." And he set off running as if the devil possessed him, hoping that he might yet find the stranger, whose slow pace could not have carried him far.

But at the street gate, Porthos was talking with the soldier on guard. Between the two talkers there was just enough room for a man to pass. D'Artagnan thought it would suffice for him, and he sprang forward like a dart between them. But d'Artagnan had reckoned without the wind. As he was about to pass, the wind blew out Porthos's long cloak, and d'Artagnan rushed straight into the middle of it. Without doubt, Porthos had reasons for not abandoning this part of his vestments, for instead of quitting his hold on the flap in his hand, he pulled it toward him, so that d'Artagnan rolled himself up in the velvet by a movement of rotation explained by the persistency of Porthos.

D'Artagnan, hearing the Musketeer swear, wished to escape from the cloak, which blinded him, and sought to find his way from under the folds of it. He was particularly anxious to avoid marring the freshness of the magnificent baldric we are acquainted with; but on timidly opening his eyes, he found himself with his nose fixed between the two shoulders of Porthos--that is to say, exactly upon the baldric.

Alas, like most things in this world which have nothing in their favor but appearances, the baldric was glittering with gold in the front, but was nothing but simple buff behind. Vainglorious as he was, Porthos could not afford to have a baldric wholly of gold, but had at least half. One could comprehend the necessity of the cold and the urgency of the cloak.

"Bless me!" cried Porthos, making strong efforts to disembarrass himself of d'Artagnan, who was wriggling about his back; "you must be mad to run against people in this manner."

"Excuse me," said d'Artagnan, reappearing under the shoulder of the giant, "but I am in such haste--I was running after someone and--"

"And do you always forget your eyes when you run?" asked Porthos.

"No," replied d'Artagnan, piqued, "and thanks to my eyes, I can see what other people cannot see."

Whether Porthos understood him or did not understand him, giving way to his anger, "Monsieur," said he, "you stand a chance of getting chastised if you rub Musketeers in this fashion."

"Chastised, Monsieur!" said d'Artagnan, "the expression is strong."

"It is one that becomes a man accustomed to look his enemies in the face."

"Ah, PARDIEU! I know full well that you don't turn your back to yours."

And the young man, delighted with his joke, went away laughing loudly.

Porthos foamed with rage, and made a movement to rush after d'Artagnan.

"Presently, presently," cried the latter, "when you haven't your cloak on."

"At one o'clock, then, behind the Luxembourg."

"Very well, at one o'clock, then," replied d'Artagnan, turning the angle of the street.

But neither in the street he had passed through, nor in the one which his eager glance pervaded, could he see anyone; however slowly the stranger had walked, he was gone on his way, or perhaps had entered some house. D'Artagnan inquired of everyone he met with, went down to the ferry, came up again by the Rue de Seine, and the Red Cross; but nothing, absolutely nothing! This chase was, however, advantageous to him in one sense, for in proportion as the perspiration broke from his forehead, his heart began to cool.

He began to reflect upon the events that had passed; they were numerous and inauspicious. It was scarcely eleven o'clock in the morning, and yet this morning had already brought him into disgrace with M. de Treville, who could not fail to think the manner in which d'Artagnan had left him a little cavalier.

Besides this, he had drawn upon himself two good duels with two men, each capable of killing three d'Artagnans--with two Musketeers, in short, with two of those beings whom he esteemed so greatly that he placed them in his mind and heart above all other men.

The outlook was sad. Sure of being killed by Athos, it may easily be understood that the young man was not very uneasy about Porthos. As hope, however, is the last thing extinguished in the heart of man, he finished by hoping that he might survive, even though with terrible wounds, in both these duels; and in case of surviving, he made the following reprehensions upon his own conduct:

"What a madcap I was, and what a stupid fellow I am! That brave and unfortunate Athos was wounded on that very shoulder against which I must run head foremost, like a ram. The only thing that astonishes me is that he did not strike me dead at once. He had good cause to do so; the pain I gave him must have been atrocious. As to Porthos--oh, as to Porthos, faith, that's a droll affair!"

And in spite of himself, the young man began to laugh aloud, looking round carefully, however, to see that his solitary laugh, without a cause in the eyes of passers-by, offended no one.

"As to Porthos, that is certainly droll; but I am not the less a giddy fool. Are people to be run against without warning? No! And have I any right to go and peep under their cloaks to see what is not there? He would have pardoned me, he would certainly have pardoned me, if I had not said anything to him about that cursed baldric--in ambiguous words, it is true, but rather drolly ambiguous. Ah, cursed Gascon that I am, I get from one hobble into another. Friend d'Artagnan," continued he, speaking to himself with all the amenity that he thought due himself, "if you escape, of which there is not much chance, I would advise you to practice perfect politeness for the future. You must henceforth be admired and quoted as a model of it. To be obliging and polite does not necessarily make a man a coward. Look at Aramis, now; Aramis is mildness and grace personified. Well, did anybody ever dream of calling Aramis a coward? No, certainly not, and from this moment I will endeavor to model myself after him. Ah! That's strange! Here he is!"

D'Artagnan, walking and soliloquizing, had arrived within a few steps of the hotel d'Arguillon and in front of that hotel perceived Aramis, chatting gaily with three gentlemen; but as he had not forgotten that it was in presence of this young man that M. de Treville had been so angry in the morning, and as a witness of the rebuke the Musketeers had received was not likely to be at all agreeable, he pretended not to see him. D'Artagnan, on the contrary, quite full of his plans of conciliation and courtesy, approached the young men with a profound bow, accompanied by a most gracious smile. All four, besides, immediately broke off their conversation.

D'Artagnan was not so dull as not to perceive that he was one too many; but he was not sufficiently broken into the fashions of the gay world to know how to extricate himself gallantly from a false position, like that of a man who begins to mingle with people he is scarcely acquainted with and in a conversation that does not concern him. He was seeking in his mind, then, for the least awkward means of retreat, when he remarked that Aramis had let his handkerchief fall, and by mistake, no doubt, had placed his foot upon it. This appeared to be a favorable opportunity to repair his intrusion. He stooped, and with the most gracious air he could assume, drew the handkerchief from under the foot of the Musketeer in spite of the efforts the latter made to detain it, and holding it out to him, said, "I believe, monsieur, that this is a handkerchief you would be sorry to lose?"

The handkerchief was indeed richly embroidered, and had a coronet and arms at one of its corners. Aramis blushed excessively, and snatched rather than took the handkerchief from the hand of the Gascon.

"Ah, ah!" cried one of the Guards, "will you persist in saying, most discreet Aramis, that you are not on good terms with Madame de Bois-Tracy, when that gracious lady has the kindness to lend you one of her handkerchiefs?"

Aramis darted at d'Artagnan one of those looks which inform a man that he has acquired a mortal enemy. Then, resuming his mild air, "You are deceived, gentlemen," said he, "this handkerchief is not mine, and I cannot fancy why Monsieur has taken it into his head to offer it to me rather than to one of you; and as a proof of what I say, here is mine in my pocket."

So saying, he pulled out his own handkerchief, likewise a very elegant handkerchief, and of fine cambric--though cambric was dear at the period--but a handkerchief without embroidery and without arms, only ornamented with a single cipher, that of its proprietor.

This time d'Artagnan was not hasty. He perceived his mistake; but the friends of Aramis were not at all convinced by his denial, and one of them addressed the young Musketeer with affected seriousness. "If it were as you pretend it is," said he, "I should be forced, my dear Aramis, to reclaim it myself; for, as you very well know, Bois-Tracy is an intimate friend of mine, and I cannot allow the property of his wife to be sported as a trophy."

"You make the demand badly," replied Aramis; "and while acknowledging the justice of your reclamation, I refuse it on account of the form."

"The fact is," hazarded d'Artagnan, timidly, "I did not see the handkerchief fall from the pocket of Monsieur Aramis. He had his foot upon it, that is all; and I thought from having his foot upon it the handkerchief was his."

"And you were deceived, my dear sir," replied Aramis, coldly, very little sensible to the reparation. Then turning toward that one of the guards who had declared himself the friend of Bois-Tracy, "Besides," continued he, "I have reflected, my dear intimate of Bois-Tracy, that I am not less tenderly his friend than you can possibly be; so that decidedly this handkerchief is as likely to have fallen from your pocket as mine."

"No, upon my honor!" cried his Majesty's Guardsman.

"You are about to swear upon your honor and I upon my word, and then it will be pretty evident that one of us will have lied. Now, here, Montaran, we will do better than that--let each take a half."

"Of the handkerchief?"

"Yes."

"Perfectly just," cried the other two Guardsmen, "the judgment of King Solomon! Aramis, you certainly are full of wisdom!"

The young men burst into a laugh, and as may be supposed, the affair had no other sequel. In a moment or two the conversation ceased, and the three Guardsmen and the Musketeer, after having cordially shaken hands, separated, the Guardsmen going one way and Aramis another.

"Now is my time to make peace with this gallant man," said d'Artagnan to himself, having stood on one side during the whole of the latter part of the conversation; and with this good feeling drawing near to Aramis, who was departing without paying any attention to him, "Monsieur," said he, "you will excuse me, I hope."

"Ah, monsieur," interrupted Aramis, "permit me to observe to you that you have not acted in this affair as a gallant man ought."

"What, monsieur!" cried d'Artagnan, "and do you suppose--"

"I suppose, monsieur that you are not a fool, and that you knew very well, although coming from Gascony, that people do not tread upon handkerchiefs without a reason. What the devil! Paris is not paved with cambric!"

"Monsieur, you act wrongly in endeavoring to mortify me," said d'Artagnan, in whom the natural quarrelsome spirit began to speak more loudly than his pacific resolutions. "I am from Gascony, it is true; and since you know it, there is no occasion to tell you that Gascons are not very patient, so that when they have begged to be excused once, were it even for a folly, they are convinced that they have done already at least as much again as they ought to have done."

"Monsieur, what I say to you about the matter," said Aramis, "is not for the sake of seeking a quarrel. Thank God, I am not a bravo! And being a Musketeer but for a time, I only fight when I am forced to do so, and always with great repugnance; but this time the affair is serious, for here is a lady compromised by you."

"By US, you mean!" cried d'Artagnan.

"Why did you so maladroitly restore me the handkerchief?"

"Why did you so awkwardly let it fall?"

"I have said, monsieur, and I repeat, that the handkerchief did not fall from my pocket."

"And thereby you have lied twice, monsieur, for I saw it fall."

"Ah, you take it with that tone, do you, Master Gascon? Well, I will teach you how to behave yourself."

"And I will send you back to your Mass book, Master Abbe. Draw, if you please, and instantly--"

"Not so, if you please, my good friend--not here, at least. Do you not perceive that we are opposite the Hotel d'Arguillon, which is full of the cardinal's creatures? How do I know that this is not his Eminence who has honored you with the commission to procure my head? Now, I entertain a ridiculous partiality for my head, it seems to suit my shoulders so correctly. I wish to kill you, be at rest as to that, but to kill you quietly in a snug, remote place, where you will not be able to boast of your death to anybody."

"I agree, monsieur; but do not be too confident. Take your handkerchief; whether it belongs to you or another, you may perhaps stand in need of it."

"Monsieur is a Gascon?" asked Aramis.

"Yes. Monsieur does not postpone an interview through prudence?"

"Prudence, monsieur, is a virtue sufficiently useless to Musketeers, I know, but indispensable to churchmen; and as I am only a Musketeer provisionally, I hold it good to be prudent. At two o'clock I shall have the honor of expecting you at the hotel of Monsieur de Treville. There I will indicate to you the best place and time."

The two young men bowed and separated, Aramis ascending the street which led to the Luxembourg, while d'Artagnan, perceiving the appointed hour was approaching, took the road to the Carmes-Deschaux, saying to himself, "Decidedly I can't draw back; but at least, if I am killed, I shall be killed by a Musketeer."

5 The King's Musketeers And The Cardinal's Guards

D'Artagnan was acquainted with nobody in Paris. He went therefore to his appointment with Athos without a second, determined to be satisfied with those his adversary should choose. Besides, his intention was formed to make the brave Musketeer all suitable apologies, but without meanness or weakness, fearing that might result from this duel which generally results from an affair of this kind, when a young and vigorous man fights with an adversary who is wounded and weakened--if conquered, he doubles the triumph of his antagonist; if a conqueror, he is accused of foul play and want of courage.

Now, we must have badly painted the character of our adventure seeker, or our readers must have already perceived that d'Artagnan was not an ordinary man; therefore, while repeating to himself that his death was inevitable, he did not make up his mind to die quietly, as one less courageous and less restrained might have done in his place. He reflected upon the different characters of men he had to fight with, and began to view his situation more clearly. He hoped, by means of loyal excuses, to make a friend of Athos, whose lordly air and austere bearing pleased him much. He flattered himself he should be able to frighten Porthos with the adventure of the baldric, which he might, if not killed upon the spot, relate to everybody a recital which, well managed, would cover Porthos with ridicule. As to the astute Aramis, he did not entertain much dread of him; and supposing he should be able to get so far, he determined to dispatch him in good style or at least, by hitting him in the face, as Caesar recommended his soldiers do to those of Pompey, to damage forever the beauty of which he was so proud.

In addition to this, d'Artagnan possessed that invincible stock of resolution which the counsels of his father had implanted in his heart: "Endure nothing from anyone but the king, the cardinal, and Monsieur de Treville." He flew, then, rather than walked, toward the convent of the Carmes Dechausses, or rather Deschaux, as it was called at that period, a sort of building without a window, surrounded by barren fields--an accessory to the Preaux-Clercs, and which was generally employed as the place for the duels of men who had no time to lose.

When d'Artagnan arrived in sight of the bare spot of ground which extended along the foot of the monastery, Athos had been waiting about five minutes, and twelve o'clock was striking. He was, then, as punctual as the Samaritan woman, and the most rigorous casuist with regard to duels could have nothing to say.

Athos, who still suffered grievously from his wound, though it had been dressed anew by M. de Treville's surgeon, was seated on a post and waiting for his adversary with hat in hand, his feather even touching the ground.

"Monsieur," said Athos, "I have engaged two of my friends as seconds; but these two friends are not yet come, at which I am astonished, as it is not at all their custom."

"I have no seconds on my part, monsieur," said d'Artagnan; "for having only arrived yesterday in Paris, I as yet know no one but Monsieur de Treville, to whom I was recommended by my father, who has the honor to be, in some degree, one of his friends."

Athos reflected for an instant. "You know no one but Monsieur de Treville?" he asked.

"Yes, monsieur, I know only him."

"Well, but then," continued Athos, speaking half to himself, "if I kill you, I shall have the air of a boy-slayer."

"Not too much so," replied d'Artagnan, with a bow that was not deficient in dignity, "since you do me the honor to draw a sword with me while suffering from a wound which is very inconvenient."

"Very inconvenient, upon my word; and you hurt me devilishly, I can tell you. But I will take the left hand--it is my custom in such circumstances. Do not fancy that I do you a favor; I use either hand easily. And it will be even a disadvantage to you; a left-handed man is very troublesome to people who are not prepared for it. I regret I did not inform you sooner of this circumstance."

"You have truly, monsieur," said d'Artagnan, bowing again, "a courtesy, for which, I assure you, I am very grateful."

"You confuse me," replied Athos, with his gentlemanly air; "let us talk of something else, if you please. Ah, s'blood, how you have hurt me! My shoulder quite burns."

"If you would permit me--" said d'Artagnan, with timidity.

"What, monsieur?"

"I have a miraculous balsam for wounds--a balsam given to me by my mother and of which I have made a trial upon myself."

"Well?"

"Well, I am sure that in less than three days this balsam would cure you; and at the end of three days, when you would be cured--well, sir, it would still do me a great honor to be your man."

D'Artagnan spoke these words with a simplicity that did honor to his courtesy, without throwing the least doubt upon his courage.

"PARDIEU, monsieur!" said Athos, "that's a proposition that pleases me; not that I can accept it, but a league off it savors of the gentleman. Thus spoke and acted the gallant knights of the time of Charlemagne, in whom every cavalier ought to seek his model. Unfortunately, we do not live in the times of the great emperor, we live in the times of the cardinal; and three days hence, however well the secret might be guarded, it would be known, I say, that we were to fight, and our combat would be prevented. I think these fellows will never come."

"If you are in haste, monsieur," said d'Artagnan, with the same simplicity with which a moment before he had proposed to him to put off the duel for three days, "and if it be your will to dispatch me at once, do not inconvenience yourself, I pray you."

"There is another word which pleases me," cried Athos, with a gracious nod to d'Artagnan. "That did not come from a man without a heart. Monsieur, I love men of your kidney; and I foresee plainly that if we don't kill each other, I shall hereafter have much pleasure in your conversation. We will wait for these gentlemen, so please you; I have plenty of time, and it will be more correct. Ah, here is one of them, I believe."

In fact, at the end of the Rue Vaugirard the gigantic Porthos appeared.

"What!" cried d'Artagnan, "is your first witness Monsieur Porthos?"

"Yes, that disturbs you?"

"By no means."

"And here is the second."

D'Artagnan turned in the direction pointed to by Athos, and perceived Aramis.

"What!" cried he, in an accent of greater astonishment than before, "your second witness is Monsieur Aramis?"

"Doubtless! Are you not aware that we are never seen one without the others, and that we are called among the Musketeers and the Guards, at court and in the city, Athos, Porthos, and Aramis, or the Three Inseparables? And yet, as you come from Dax or Pau--"

"From Tarbes," said d'Artagnan.

"It is probable you are ignorant of this little fact," said Athos.

"My faith!" replied d'Artagnan, "you are well named, gentlemen; and my adventure, if it should make any noise, will prove at least that your union is not founded upon contrasts."

In the meantime, Porthos had come up, waved his hand to Athos, and then turning toward d'Artagnan, stood quite astonished.

Let us say in passing that he had changed his baldric and relinquished his cloak.

"Ah, ah!" said he, "what does this mean?"

"This is the gentleman I am going to fight with," said Athos, pointing to d'Artagnan with his hand and saluting him with the same gesture.

"Why, it is with him I am also going to fight," said Porthos.

"But not before one o'clock," replied d'Artagnan.

"And I also am to fight with this gentleman," said Aramis, coming in his turn onto the place.

"But not until two o'clock," said d'Artagnan, with the same calmness.

"But what are you going to fight about, Athos?" asked Aramis.

"Faith! I don't very well know. He hurt my shoulder. And you, Porthos?"

"Faith! I am going to fight--because I am going to fight," answered Porthos, reddening.

Athos, whose keen eye lost nothing, perceived a faintly sly smile pass over the lips of the young Gascon as he replied, "We had a short discussion upon dress."

"And you, Aramis?" asked Athos.

"Oh, ours is a theological quarrel," replied Aramis, making a sign to d'Artagnan to keep secret the cause of their duel.

Athos indeed saw a second smile on the lips of d'Artagnan.

"Indeed?" said Athos.

"Yes; a passage of St. Augustine, upon which we could not agree," said the Gascon.

"Decidedly, this is a clever fellow," murmured Athos.

"And now you are assembled, gentlemen," said d'Artagnan, "permit me to offer you my apologies."

At this word APOLOGIES, a cloud passed over the brow of Athos, a haughty smile curled the lip of Porthos, and a negative sign was the reply of Aramis.

"You do not understand me, gentlemen," said d'Artagnan, throwing up his head, the sharp and bold lines of which were at the moment gilded by a bright ray of the sun. "I asked to be excused in case I should not be able to discharge my debt to all three; for Monsieur Athos has the right to kill me first, which must much diminish the face-value of your bill, Monsieur Porthos, and render yours almost null, Monsieur Aramis. And now, gentlemen, I repeat, excuse me, but on that account only, and--on guard!"

At these words, with the most gallant air possible, d'Artagnan drew his sword.

The blood had mounted to the head of d'Artagnan, and at that moment he would have drawn his sword against all the Musketeers in the kingdom as willingly as he now did against Athos, Porthos, and Aramis.

It was a quarter past midday. The sun was in its zenith, and the spot chosen for the scene of the duel was exposed to its full ardor.

"It is very hot," said Athos, drawing his sword in its turn, "and yet I cannot take off my doublet; for I just now felt my wound begin to bleed again, and I should not like to annoy Monsieur with the sight of blood which he has not drawn from me himself."

"That is true, Monsieur," replied d'Artagnan, "and whether drawn by myself or another, I assure you I shall always view with regret the blood of so brave a gentleman. I will therefore fight in my doublet, like yourself."

"Come, come, enough of such compliments!" cried Porthos. "Remember, we are waiting for our turns."

"Speak for yourself when you are inclined to utter such incongruities," interrupted Aramis. "For my part, I think what they say is very well said, and quite worthy of two gentlemen."

"When you please, monsieur," said Athos, putting himself on guard.

"I waited your orders," said d'Artagnan, crossing swords.

But scarcely had the two rapiers clashed, when a company of the Guards of his Eminence, commanded by M. de Jussac, turned the corner of the convent.

"The cardinal's Guards!" cried Aramis and Porthos at the same time. "Sheathe your swords, gentlemen, sheathe your swords!"

But it was too late. The two combatants had been seen in a position which left no doubt of their intentions.

"Halloo!" cried Jussac, advancing toward them and making a sign to his men to do so likewise, "halloo, Musketeers? Fighting here, are you? And the edicts? What is become of them?"

"You are very generous, gentlemen of the Guards," said Athos, full of rancor, for Jussac was one of the aggressors of the preceding day. "If we were to see you fighting, I can assure you that we would make no effort to prevent you. Leave us alone, then, and you will enjoy a little amusement without cost to yourselves."

"Gentlemen," said Jussac, "it is with great regret that I pronounce the thing impossible. Duty before everything. Sheathe, then, if you please, and follow us."

"Monsieur," said Aramis, parodying Jussac, "it would afford us great pleasure to obey your polite invitation if it depended upon ourselves; but unfortunately the thing is impossible--Monsieur de Treville has forbidden it. Pass on your way, then; it is the best thing to do."

This raillery exasperated Jussac. "We will charge upon you, then," said he, "if you disobey."

"There are five of them," said Athos, half aloud, "and we are but three; we shall be beaten again, and must die on the spot, for, on my part, I declare I will never appear again before the captain as a conquered man."

Athos, Porthos, and Aramis instantly drew near one another, while Jussac drew up his soldiers.

This short interval was sufficient to determine d'Artagnan on the part he was to take. It was one of those events which decide the life of a man; it was a choice between the king and the cardinal--the choice made, it must be persisted in. To fight, that was to disobey the law, that was to risk his head, that was to make at one blow an enemy of a minister more powerful than the king himself. All this young man perceived, and yet, to his praise we speak it, he did not hesitate a second. Turning towards Athos and his friends, "Gentlemen," said he, "allow me to correct your words, if you please. You said you were but three, but it appears to me we are four."

"But you are not one of us," said Porthos.

"That's true," replied d'Artagnan; "I have not the uniform, but I have the spirit. My heart is that of a Musketeer; I feel it, monsieur, and that impels me on."

"Withdraw, young man," cried Jussac, who doubtless, by his gestures and the expression of his countenance, had guessed d'Artagnan's design. "You may retire; we consent to that. Save your skin; begone quickly."

D'Artagnan did not budge.

"Decidedly, you are a brave fellow," said Athos, pressing the young man's hand.

"Come, come, choose your part," replied Jussac.

"Well," said Porthos to Aramis, "we must do something."

"Monsieur is full of generosity," said Athos.

But all three reflected upon the youth of d'Artagnan, and dreaded his inexperience.

"We should only be three, one of whom is wounded, with the addition of a boy," resumed Athos; "and yet it will not be the less said we were four men."

"Yes, but to yield!" said Porthos.

"That IS difficult," replied Athos.

D'Artagnan comprehended their irresolution.

"Try me, gentlemen," said he, "and I swear to you by my honor that I will not go hence if we are conquered."

"What is your name, my brave fellow?" said Athos.

"d'Artagnan, monsieur."

"Well, then, Athos, Porthos, Aramis, and d'Artagnan, forward!" cried Athos.

"Come, gentlemen, have you decided?" cried Jussac for the third time.

"It is done, gentlemen," said Athos.

"And what is your choice?" asked Jussac.

"We are about to have the honor of charging you," replied Aramis, lifting his hat with one hand and drawing his sword with the other.

"Ah! You resist, do you?" cried Jussac.

"S'blood; does that astonish you?"

And the nine combatants rushed upon each other with a fury which however did not exclude a certain degree of method.

Athos fixed upon a certain Cahusac, a favorite of the cardinal's. Porthos had Bicarat, and Aramis found himself opposed to two adversaries. As to d'Artagnan, he sprang toward Jussac himself.

The heart of the young Gascon beat as if it would burst through his side--not from fear, God be thanked, he had not the shade of it, but with emulation; he fought like a furious tiger, turning ten times round his adversary, and changing his ground and his guard twenty times. Jussac was, as was then said, a fine blade, and had had much practice; nevertheless it required all his skill to defend himself against an adversary who, active and energetic, departed every instant from received rules, attacking him on all sides at once, and yet parrying like a man who had the greatest respect for his own epidermis.

This contest at length exhausted Jussac's patience. Furious at being held in check by one whom he had considered a boy, he became warm and began to make mistakes. D'Artagnan, who though wanting in practice had a sound theory, redoubled his agility. Jussac, anxious to put an end to this, springing forward, aimed a terrible thrust at his adversary, but the latter parried it; and while Jussac was recovering himself, glided like a serpent beneath his blade, and passed his sword through his body. Jussac fell like a dead mass.

D'Artagnan then cast an anxious and rapid glance over the field of battle.

Aramis had killed one of his adversaries, but the other pressed him warmly. Nevertheless, Aramis was in a good situation, and able to defend himself.

Bicarat and Porthos had just made counterhits. Porthos had received a thrust through his arm, and Bicarat one through his thigh. But neither of these two wounds was serious, and they only fought more earnestly.

Athos, wounded anew by Cahusac, became evidently paler, but did not give way a foot. He only changed his sword hand, and fought with his left hand.

According to the laws of dueling at that period, d'Artagnan was at liberty to assist whom he pleased. While he was endeavoring to find out which of his companions stood in greatest need, he caught a glance from Athos. The glance was of sublime eloquence. Athos would have died rather than appeal for help; but he could look, and with that look ask assistance. D'Artagnan interpreted it; with a terrible bound he sprang to the side of Cahusac, crying, "To me, Monsieur Guardsman; I will slay you!"

Cahusac turned. It was time; for Athos, whose great courage alone supported him, sank upon his knee.

"S'blood!" cried he to d'Artagnan, "do not kill him, young man, I beg of you. I have an old affair to settle with him when I am cured and sound again. Disarm him only--make sure of his sword. That's it! Very well done!"

The exclamation was drawn from Athos by seeing the sword of Cahusac fly twenty paces from him. D'Artagnan and Cahusac sprang forward at the same instant, the one to recover, the other to obtain, the sword; but d'Artagnan, being the more active, reached it first and placed his foot upon it.

Cahusac immediately ran to the Guardsman whom Aramis had killed, seized his rapier, and returned toward d'Artagnan; but on his way he met Athos, who during his relief which d'Artagnan had procured him had recovered his breath, and who, for fear that d'Artagnan would kill his enemy, wished to resume the fight.

D'Artagnan perceived that it would be disobliging Athos not to leave him alone; and in a few minutes Cahusac fell, with a sword thrust through his throat.

At the same instant Aramis placed his sword point on the breast of his fallen enemy, and forced him to ask for mercy.

There only then remained Porthos and Bicarat. Porthos made a thousand flourishes, asking Bicarat what o'clock it could be, and offering him his compliments upon his brother's having just obtained a company in the regiment of Navarre; but, jest as he might, he gained nothing. Bicarat was one of those iron men who never fell dead.

Nevertheless, it was necessary to finish. The watch might come up and take all the combatants, wounded or not, royalists or cardinalists. Athos, Aramis, and d'Artagnan surrounded Bicarat, and required him to surrender. Though alone against all and with a wound in his thigh, Bicarat wished to hold out; but Jussac, who had risen upon his elbow, cried out to him to yield. Bicarat was a Gascon, as d'Artagnan was; he turned a deaf ear, and contented himself with laughing, and between two parries finding time to point to a spot of earth with his sword, "Here," cried he, parodying a verse of the Bible, "here will Bicarat die; for I only am left, and they seek my life."

"But there are four against you; leave off, I command you."

"Ah, if you command me, that's another thing," said Bicarat. "As you are my commander, it is my duty to obey." And springing backward, he broke his sword across his knee to avoid the necessity of surrendering it, threw the pieces over the convent wall, and crossed him arms, whistling a cardinalist air.

Bravery is always respected, even in an enemy. The Musketeers saluted Bicarat with their swords, and returned them to their sheaths. D'Artagnan did the same. Then, assisted by Bicarat, the only one left standing, he bore Jussac, Cahusac, and one of Aramis's adversaries who was only wounded, under the porch of the convent. The fourth, as we have said, was dead. They then rang the bell, and carrying away four swords out of five, they took their road, intoxicated with joy, toward the hotel of M. de Treville.

They walked arm in arm, occupying the whole width of the street and taking in every Musketeer they met, so that in the end it became a triumphal march. The heart of d'Artagnan swam in delirium; he marched between Athos and Porthos, pressing them tenderly.

"If I am not yet a Musketeer," said he to his new friends, as he passed through the gateway of M. de Treville's hotel, "at least I have entered upon my apprenticeship, haven't I?"

6 His Majesty King Louis Xiii

This affair made a great noise. M. de Treville scolded his Musketeers in public, and congratulated them in private; but as no time was to be lost in gaining the king, M. de Treville hastened to report himself at the Louvre. It was already too late. The king was closeted with the cardinal, and M. de Treville was informed that the king was busy and could not receive him at that moment. In the evening M. de Treville attended the king's gaming table. The king was winning; and as he was very avaricious, he was in an excellent humor. Perceiving M. de Treville at a distance--

"Come here, Monsieur Captain," said he, "come here, that I may growl at you. Do you know that his Eminence has been making fresh complaints against your Musketeers, and that with so much emotion, that this evening his Eminence is indisposed? Ah, these Musketeers of yours are very devils--fellows to be hanged."

"No, sire," replied Treville, who saw at the first glance how things would go, "on the contrary, they are good creatures, as meek as lambs, and have but one desire, I'll be their warranty. And that is that their swords may never leave their scabbards but in your majesty's service. But what are they to do? The Guards of Monsieur the Cardinal are forever seeking quarrels with them, and for the honor of the corps even, the poor young men are obliged to defend themselves."

"Listen to Monsieur de Treville," said the king; "listen to him! Would not one say he was speaking of a religious community? In truth, my dear Captain, I have a great mind to take away your commission and give it to Mademoiselle de Chemerault, to whom I promised an abbey. But don't fancy that I am going to take you on your bare word. I am called Louis the Just, Monsieur de Treville, and by and by, by and by we will see."

"Ah, sire; it is because I confide in that justice that I shall wait patiently and quietly the good pleasure of your Majesty."

"Wait, then, monsieur, wait," said the king; "I will not detain you long."

In fact, fortune changed; and as the king began to lose what he had won, he was not sorry to find an excuse for playing Charlemagne--if we may use a gaming phrase of whose origin we confess our ignorance. The king therefore arose a minute after, and putting the money which lay before him into his pocket, the major part of which arose from his winnings, "La Vieuville," said he, "take my place; I must speak to Monsieur de Treville on an affair of importance. Ah, I had eighty louis before me; put down the same sum, so that they who have lost may have nothing to complain of. Justice before everything."

Then turning toward M. de Treville and walking with him toward the embrasure of a window, "Well, monsieur," continued he, "you say it is his Eminence's Guards who have sought a quarrel with your Musketeers?"

"Yes, sire, as they always do."

"And how did the thing happen? Let us see, for you know, my dear Captain, a judge must hear both sides."

"Good Lord! In the most simple and natural manner possible. Three of my best soldiers, whom your Majesty knows by name, and whose devotedness you have more than once appreciated, and who have, I dare affirm to the king, his service much at heart--three of my best soldiers, I say, Athos, Porthos, and Aramis, had made a party of pleasure with a young fellow from Gascony, whom I had introduced to them the same morning. The party was to take place at St. Germain, I believe, and they had appointed to meet at the Carmes-Deschaux, when they were disturbed by de Jussac, Cahusac, Bicarat, and two other Guardsmen, who certainly did not go there in such a numerous company without some ill intention against the edicts."

"Ah, ah! You incline me to think so," said the king. "There is no doubt they went thither to fight themselves."

"I do not accuse them, sire; but I leave your Majesty to judge what five armed men could possibly be going to do in such a deserted place as the neighborhood of the Convent des Carmes."

"Yes, you are right, Treville, you are right!"

"Then, upon seeing my Musketeers they changed their minds, and forgot their private hatred for partisan hatred; for your Majesty cannot be ignorant that the Musketeers, who belong to the king and nobody but the king, are the natural enemies of the Guardsmen, who belong to the cardinal."

"Yes, Treville, yes," said the king, in a melancholy tone; "and it is very sad, believe me, to see thus two parties in France, two heads to royalty. But all this will come to an end, Treville, will come to an end. You say, then, that the Guardsmen sought a quarrel with the Musketeers?"

"I say that it is probable that things have fallen out so, but I will not swear to it, sire. You know how difficult it is to discover the truth; and unless a man be endowed with that admirable instinct which causes Louis XIII to be named the Just--"

"You are right, Treville; but they were not alone, your Musketeers. They had a youth with them?"

"Yes, sire, and one wounded man; so that three of the king's Musketeers--one of whom was wounded--and a youth not only maintained their ground against five of the most terrible of the cardinal's Guardsmen, but absolutely brought four of them to earth."

"Why, this is a victory!" cried the king, all radiant, "a complete victory!"

"Yes, sire; as complete as that of the Bridge of Ce."

"Four men, one of them wounded, and a youth, say you?"

"One hardly a young man; but who, however, behaved himself so admirably on this occasion that I will take the liberty of recommending him to your Majesty."

"How does he call himself?"

"d'Artagnan, sire; he is the son of one of my oldest friends--the son of a man who served under the king your father, of glorious memory, in the civil war."

"And you say this young man behaved himself well? Tell me how, Treville--you know how I delight in accounts of war and fighting."

And Louis XIII twisted his mustache proudly, placing his hand upon his hip.

"Sire," resumed Treville, "as I told you, Monsieur d'Artagnan is little more than a boy; and as he has not the honor of being a Musketeer, he was dressed as a citizen. The Guards of the cardinal, perceiving his youth and that he did not belong to the corps, invited him to retire before they attacked."

"So you may plainly see, Treville," interrupted the king, "it was they who attacked?"

"That is true, sire; there can be no more doubt on that head. They called upon him then to retire; but he answered that he was a Musketeer at heart, entirely devoted to your Majesty, and that therefore he would remain with Messieurs the Musketeers."

"Brave young man!" murmured the king.

"Well, he did remain with them; and your Majesty has in him so firm a champion that it was he who gave Jussac the terrible sword thrust which has made the cardinal so angry."

"He who wounded Jussac!" cried the king, "he, a boy! Treville, that's impossible!"

"It is as I have the honor to relate it to your Majesty."

"Jussac, one of the first swordsmen in the kingdom?"

"Well, sire, for once he found his master."

"I will see this young man, Treville--I will see him; and if anything can be done--well, we will make it our business."

"When will your Majesty deign to receive him?"

"Tomorrow, at midday, Treville."

"Shall I bring him alone?"

"No, bring me all four together. I wish to thank them all at once. Devoted men are so rare, Treville, by the back staircase. It is useless to let the cardinal know."

"Yes, sire."

"You understand, Treville--an edict is still an edict, it is forbidden to fight, after all."

"But this encounter, sire, is quite out of the ordinary conditions of a duel. It is a brawl; and the proof is that there were five of the cardinal's Guardsmen against my three Musketeers and Monsieur d'Artagnan."

"That is true," said the king; "but never mind, Treville, come still by the back staircase."

Treville smiled; but as it was indeed something to have prevailed upon this child to rebel against his master, he saluted the king respectfully, and with this agreement, took leave of him.

That evening the three Musketeers were informed of the honor accorded them. As they had long been acquainted with the king, they were not much excited; but d'Artagnan, with his Gascon imagination, saw in it his future fortune, and passed the night in golden dreams. By eight o'clock in the morning he was at the apartment of Athos.

D'Artagnan found the Musketeer dressed and ready to go out. As the hour to wait upon the king was not till twelve, he had made a party with Porthos and Aramis to play a game at tennis in a tennis court situated near the stables of the Luxembourg. Athos invited d'Artagnan to follow them; and although ignorant of the game, which he had never played, he accepted, not knowing what to do with his time from nine o'clock in the morning, as it then scarcely was, till twelve.

The two Musketeers were already there, and were playing together. Athos, who was very expert in all bodily exercises, passed with d'Artagnan to the opposite side and challenged them; but at the first effort he made, although he played with his left hand, he found that his wound was yet too recent to allow of such exertion. D'Artagnan remained, therefore, alone; and as he declared he was too ignorant of the game to play it regularly they only continued giving balls to one another without counting. But one of these balls, launched by Porthos' herculean hand, passed so close to d'Artagnan's face that he thought that if, instead of passing near, it had hit him, his audience would have been probably lost, as it would have been impossible for him to present himself before the king. Now, as upon this audience, in his Gascon imagination, depended his future life, he saluted Aramis and Porthos politely, declaring that he would not resume the game until he should be prepared to play with them on more equal terms, and went and took his place near the cord and in the gallery.

Unfortunately for d'Artagnan, among the spectators was one of his Eminence's Guardsmen, who, still irritated by the defeat of his companions, which had happened only the day before, had promised himself to seize the first opportunity of avenging it. He believed this opportunity was now come and addressed his neighbor: "It is not astonishing that that young man should be afraid of a ball, for he is doubtless a Musketeer apprentice."

D'Artagnan turned round as if a serpent had stung him, and fixed his eyes intensely upon the Guardsman who had just made this insolent speech.

"PARDIEU," resumed the latter, twisting his mustache, "look at me as long as you like, my little gentleman! I have said what I have said."

"And as since that which you have said is too clear to require any explanation," replied d'Artagnan, in a low voice, "I beg you to follow me."

"And when?" asked the Guardsman, with the same jeering air.

"At once, if you please."

"And you know who I am, without doubt?"

"I? I am completely ignorant; nor does it much disquiet me."

"You're in the wrong there; for if you knew my name, perhaps you would not be so pressing."

"What is your name?"

"Bernajoux, at your service."

"Well, then, Monsieur Bernajoux," said d'Artagnan, tranquilly, "I will wait for you at the door."

"Go, monsieur, I will follow you."

"Do not hurry yourself, monsieur, lest it be observed that we go out together. You must be aware that for our undertaking, company would be in the way."

"That's true," said the Guardsman, astonished that his name had not produced more effect upon the young man.

Indeed, the name of Bernajoux was known to all the world, d'Artagnan alone excepted, perhaps; for it was one of those which figured most frequently in the daily brawls which all the edicts of the cardinal could not repress.

Porthos and Aramis were so engaged with their game, and Athos was watching them with so much attention, that they did not even perceive their young companion go out, who, as he had told the Guardsman of his Eminence, stopped outside the door. An instant after, the Guardsman descended in his turn. As d'Artagnan had no time to lose, on account of the audience of the king, which was fixed for midday, he cast his eyes around, and seeing that the street was empty, said to his adversary, "My faith! It is fortunate for you, although your name is Bernajoux, to have only to deal with an apprentice Musketeer. Never mind; be content, I will do my best. On guard!"

"But," said he whom d'Artagnan thus provoked, "it appears to me that this place is badly chosen, and that we should be better behind the Abbey St. Germain or in the Pre-aux-Clercs."

"What you say is full of sense," replied d'Artagnan; "but unfortunately I have very little time to spare, having an appointment at twelve precisely. On guard, then, monsieur, on guard!"

Bernajoux was not a man to have such a compliment paid to him twice. In an instant his sword glittered in his hand, and he sprang upon his adversary, whom, thanks to his great youthfulness, he hoped to intimidate.

But d'Artagnan had on the preceding day served his apprenticeship. Fresh sharpened by his victory, full of hopes of future favor, he was resolved not to recoil a step. So the two swords were crossed close to the hilts, and as d'Artagnan stood firm, it was his adversary who made the retreating step; but d'Artagnan seized the moment at which, in this movement, the sword of Bernajoux deviated from the line. He freed his weapon, made a lunge, and touched his adversary on the shoulder. d'Artagnan immediately made a step backward and raised his sword; but Bernajoux cried out that it was nothing, and rushing blindly upon him, absolutely spitted himself upon d'Artagnan's sword. As, however, he did not fall, as he did not declare himself conquered, but only broke away toward the hotel of M. de la Tremouille, in whose service he had a relative, d'Artagnan was ignorant of the seriousness of the last wound his adversary had received, and pressing him warmly, without doubt would soon have completed his work with a third blow, when the noise which arose from the street being heard in the tennis court, two of the friends of the Guardsman, who had seen him go out after exchanging some words with d'Artagnan, rushed, sword in hand, from the court, and fell upon the conqueror. But Athos, Porthos, and Aramis quickly appeared in their turn, and the moment the two Guardsmen attacked their young companion, drove them back. Bernajoux now fell, and as the Guardsmen were only two against four, they began to cry, "To the rescue! The Hotel de la Tremouille!" At these cries, all who were in the hotel rushed out and fell upon the four companions, who on their side cried aloud, "To the rescue, Musketeers!"

This cry was generally heeded; for the Musketeers were known to be enemies of the cardinal, and were beloved on account of the hatred they bore to his Eminence. Thus the soldiers of other companies than those which belonged to the Red Duke, as Aramis had called him, often took part with the king's Musketeers in these quarrels. Of three Guardsmen of the company of M. Dessessart who were passing, two came to the assistance of the four companions, while the other ran toward the hotel of M. de Treville, crying, "To the rescue, Musketeers! To the rescue!" As usual, this hotel was full of soldiers of this company, who hastened to the succor of their comrades. The MELEE became general, but strength was on the side of the Musketeers. The cardinal's Guards and M. de la Tremouille's people retreated into the hotel, the doors of which they closed just in time to prevent their enemies from entering with them. As to the wounded man, he had been taken in at once, and, as we have said, in a very bad state.

Excitement was at its height among the Musketeers and their allies, and they even began to deliberate whether they should not set fire to the hotel to punish the insolence of M. de la Tremouille's domestics in daring to make a SORTIE upon the king's Musketeers. The proposition had been made, and received with enthusiasm, when fortunately eleven o'clock struck. D'Artagnan and his companions remembered their audience, and as they would very much have regretted that such an opportunity should be lost, they succeeded in calming their friends, who contented themselves with hurling some paving stones against the gates; but the gates were too strong. They soon tired of the sport. Besides, those who must be considered the leaders of the enterprise had quit the group and were making their way toward the hotel of M. de Treville, who was waiting for them, already informed of this fresh disturbance.

"Quick to the Louvre," said he, "to the Louvre without losing an instant, and let us endeavor to see the king before he is prejudiced by the cardinal. We will describe the thing to him as a consequence of the affair of yesterday, and the two will pass off together."

M de Treville, accompanied by the four young fellows, directed his course toward the Louvre; but to the great astonishment of the captain of the Musketeers, he was informed that the king had gone stag hunting in the forest of St. Germain. M. de Treville required this intelligence to be repeated to him twice, and each time his companions saw his brow become darker.

"Had his Majesty," asked he, "any intention of holding this hunting party yesterday?"

"No, your Excellency," replied the valet de chambre, "the Master of the Hounds came this morning to inform him that he had marked down a stag. At first the king answered that he would not go; but he could not resist his love of sport, and set out after dinner."

"And the king has seen the cardinal?" asked M. de Treville.

"In all probability he has," replied the valet, "for I saw the horses harnessed to his Eminence's carriage this morning, and when I asked where he was going, they told me, 'To St. Germain.'"

"He is beforehand with us," said M. de Treville. "Gentlemen, I will see the king this evening; but as to you, I do not advise you to risk doing so."

This advice was too reasonable, and moreover came from a man who knew the king too well, to allow the four young men to dispute it. M. de Treville recommended everyone to return home and wait for news.

On entering his hotel, M. de Treville thought it best to be first in making the complaint. He sent one of his servants to M. de la Tremouille with a letter in which he begged of him to eject the cardinal's Guardsmen from his house, and to reprimand his people for their audacity in making SORTIE against the king's Musketeers. But M. de la Tremouille--already prejudiced by his esquire, whose relative, as we already know, Bernajoux was--replied that it was neither for M. de Treville nor the Musketeers to complain, but, on the contrary, for him, whose people the Musketeers had assaulted and whose hotel they had endeavored to burn. Now, as the debate between these two nobles might last a long time, each becoming, naturally, more firm in his own opinion, M. de Treville thought of an expedient which might terminate it quietly. This was to go himself to M. de la Tremouille.

He repaired, therefore, immediately to his hotel, and caused himself to be announced.

The two nobles saluted each other politely, for if no friendship existed between them, there was at least esteem. Both were men of courage and honor; and as M. de la Tremouille--a Protestant, and seeing the king seldom--was of no party, he did not, in general, carry any bias into his social relations. This time, however, his address, although polite, was cooler than usual.

"Monsieur," said M. de Treville, "we fancy that we have each cause to complain of the other, and I am come to endeavor to clear up this affair."

"I have no objection," replied M. de la Tremouille, "but I warn you that I am well informed, and all the fault is with your Musketeers."

"You are too just and reasonable a man, monsieur!" said Treville, "not to accept the proposal I am about to make to you."

"Make it, monsieur, I listen."

"How is Monsieur Bernajoux, your esquire's relative?"

"Why, monsieur, very ill indeed! In addition to the sword thrust in his arm, which is not dangerous, he has received another right through his lungs, of which the doctor says bad things."

"But has the wounded man retained his senses?"

"Perfectly."

"Does he talk?"

"With difficulty, but he can speak."

"Well, monsieur, let us go to him. Let us adjure him, in the name of the God before whom he must perhaps appear, to speak the truth. I will take him for judge in his own cause, monsieur, and will believe what he will say."

M de la Tremouille reflected for an instant; then as it was difficult to suggest a more reasonable proposal, he agreed to it.

Both descended to the chamber in which the wounded man lay. The latter, on seeing these two noble lords who came to visit him, endeavored to raise himself up in his bed; but he was too weak, and exhausted by the effort, he fell back again almost senseless.

M de la Tremouille approached him, and made him inhale some salts, which recalled him to life. Then M. de Treville, unwilling that it should be thought that he had influenced the wounded man, requested M. de la Tremouille to interrogate him himself.

That happened which M. de Treville had foreseen. Placed between life and death, as Bernajoux was, he had no idea for a moment of concealing the truth; and he described to the two nobles the affair exactly as it had passed.

This was all that M. de Treville wanted. He wished Bernajoux a speedy convalescence, took leave of M. de la Tremouille, returned to his hotel, and immediately sent word to the four friends that he awaited their company at dinner.

M de Treville entertained good company, wholly anticardinalist, though. It may easily be understood, therefore, that the conversation during the whole of dinner turned upon the two checks that his Eminence's Guardsmen had received. Now, as d'Artagnan had been the hero of these two fights, it was upon him that all the felicitations fell, which Athos, Porthos, and Aramis abandoned to him, not only as good comrades, but as men who had so often had their turn that could very well afford him his.

Toward six o'clock M. de Treville announced that it was time to go to the Louvre; but as the hour of audience granted by his Majesty was past, instead of claiming the ENTREE by the back stairs, he placed himself with the four young men in the antechamber. The king had not yet returned from hunting. Our young men had been waiting about half an hour, amid a crowd of courtiers, when all the doors were thrown open, and his Majesty was announced.

At his announcement d'Artagnan felt himself tremble to the very marrow of his bones. The coming instant would in all probability decide the rest of his life. His eyes therefore were fixed in a sort of agony upon the door through which the king must enter.

Louis XIII appeared, walking fast. He was in hunting costume covered with dust, wearing large boots, and holding a whip in his hand. At the first glance, d'Artagnan judged that the mind of the king was stormy.

This disposition, visible as it was in his Majesty, did not prevent the courtiers from ranging themselves along his pathway. In royal antechambers it is worth more to be viewed with an angry eye than not to be seen at all. The three Musketeers therefore did not hesitate to make a step forward. D'Artagnan on the contrary remained concealed behind them; but although the king knew Athos, Porthos, and Aramis personally, he passed before them without speaking or looking--indeed, as if he had never seen them before. As for M. de Treville, when the eyes of the king fell upon him, he sustained the look with so much firmness that it was the king who dropped his eyes; after which his Majesty, grumbling, entered his apartment.

"Matters go but badly," said Athos, smiling; "and we shall not be made Chevaliers of the Order this time."

"Wait here ten minutes," said M. de Treville; "and if at the expiration of ten minutes you do not see me come out, return to my hotel, for it will be useless for you to wait for me longer."

The four young men waited ten minutes, a quarter of an hour, twenty minutes; and seeing that M. de Treville did not return, went away very uneasy as to what was going to happen.

M de Treville entered the king's cabinet boldly, and found his Majesty in a very ill humor, seated on an armchair, beating his boot with the handle of his whip. This, however, did not prevent his asking, with the greatest coolness, after his Majesty's health.

"Bad, monsieur, bad!" replied the king; "I am bored."

This was, in fact, the worst complaint of Louis XIII, who would sometimes take one of his courtiers to a window and say, "Monsieur So-and-so, let us weary ourselves together."

"How! Your Majesty is bored? Have you not enjoyed the pleasures of the chase today?"

"A fine pleasure, indeed, monsieur! Upon my soul, everything degenerates; and I don't know whether it is the game which leaves no scent, or the dogs that have no noses. We started a stag of ten branches. We chased him for six hours, and when he was near being taken--when St.-Simon was already putting his horn to his mouth to sound the mort--crack, all the pack takes the wrong scent and sets off after a two-year-older. I shall be obliged to give up hunting, as I have given up hawking. Ah, I am an unfortunate king, Monsieur de Treville! I had but one gerfalcon, and he died day before yesterday."

"Indeed, sire, I wholly comprehend your disappointment. The misfortune is great; but I think you have still a good number of falcons, sparrow hawks, and tiercets."

"And not a man to instruct them. Falconers are declining. I know no one but myself who is acquainted with the noble art of venery. After me it will all be over, and people will hunt with gins, snares, and traps. If I had but the time to train pupils! But there is the cardinal always at hand, who does not leave me a moment's repose; who talks to me about Spain, who talks to me about Austria, who talks to me about England! Ah! A PROPOS of the cardinal, Monsieur de Treville, I am vexed with you!"

This was the chance at which M. de Treville waited for the king. He knew the king of old, and he knew that all these complaints were but a preface--a sort of excitation to encourage himself--and that he had now come to his point at last.

"And in what have I been so unfortunate as to displease your Majesty?" asked M. de Treville, feigning the most profound astonishment.

"Is it thus you perform your charge, monsieur?" continued the king, without directly replying to de Treville's question. "Is it for this I name you captain of my Musketeers, that they should assassinate a man, disturb a whole quarter, and endeavor to set fire to Paris, without your saying a word? But yet," continued the king, "undoubtedly my haste accuses you wrongfully; without doubt the rioters are in prison, and you come to tell me justice is done."

"Sire," replied M. de Treville, calmly, "on the contrary, I come to demand it of you."

"And against whom?" cried the king.

"Against calumniators," said M. de Treville.

"Ah! This is something new," replied the king. "Will you tell me that your three damned Musketeers, Athos, Porthos, and Aramis, and your youngster from Bearn, have not fallen, like so many furies, upon poor Bernajoux, and have not maltreated him in such a fashion that probably by this time he is dead? Will you tell me that they did not lay siege to the hotel of the Duc de la Tremouille, and that they did not endeavor to burn it?--which would not, perhaps, have been a great misfortune in time of war, seeing that it is nothing but a nest of Huguenots, but which is, in time of peace, a frightful example. Tell me, now, can you deny all this?"

"And who told you this fine story, sire?" asked Treville, quietly.

"Who has told me this fine story, monsieur? Who should it be but he who watches while I sleep, who labors while I amuse myself, who conducts everything at home and abroad--in France as in Europe?"

"Your Majesty probably refers to God," said M. de Treville; "for I know no one except God who can be so far above your Majesty."

"No, monsieur; I speak of the prop of the state, of my only servant, of my only friend--of the cardinal."

"His Eminence is not his holiness, sire."

"What do you mean by that, monsieur?"

"That it is only the Pope who is infallible, and that this infallibility does not extend to cardinals."

"You mean to say that he deceives me; you mean to say that he betrays me? You accuse him, then? Come, speak; avow freely that you accuse him!"

"No, sire, but I say that he deceives himself. I say that he is ill-informed. I say that he has hastily accused your Majesty's Musketeers, toward whom he is unjust, and that he has not obtained his information from good sources."

"The accusation comes from Monsieur de la Tremouille, from the duke himself. What do you say to that?"

"I might answer, sire, that he is too deeply interested in the question to be a very impartial witness; but so far from that, sire, I know the duke to be a royal gentleman, and I refer the matter to him--but upon one condition, sire."

"What?"

"It is that your Majesty will make him come here, will interrogate him yourself, TETE-A-TETE, without witnesses, and that I shall see your Majesty as soon as you have seen the duke."

"What, then! You will bind yourself," cried the king, "by what Monsieur de la Tremouille shall say?"

"Yes, sire."

"You will accept his judgment?"

"Undoubtedly."

"Any you will submit to the reparation he may require?"

"Certainly."

"La Chesnaye," said the king. "La Chesnaye!"

Louis XIII's confidential valet, who never left the door, entered in reply to the call.

"La Chesnaye," said the king, "let someone go instantly and find Monsieur de la Tremouille; I wish to speak with him this evening."

"Your Majesty gives me your word that you will not see anyone between Monsieur de la Tremouille and myself?"

"Nobody, by the faith of a gentleman."

"Tomorrow, then, sire?"

"Tomorrow, monsieur."

"At what o'clock, please your Majesty?"

"At any hour you will."

"But in coming too early I should be afraid of awakening your Majesty."

"Awaken me! Do you think I ever sleep, then? I sleep no longer, monsieur. I sometimes dream, that's all. Come, then, as early as you like--at seven o'clock; but beware, if you and your Musketeers are guilty."

"If my Musketeers are guilty, sire, the guilty shall be placed in your Majesty's hands, who will dispose of them at your good pleasure. Does your Majesty require anything further? Speak, I am ready to obey."

"No, monsieur, no; I am not called Louis the Just without reason. Tomorrow, then, monsieur--tomorrow."

"Till then, God preserve your Majesty!"

However ill the king might sleep, M. de Treville slept still worse. He had ordered his three Musketeers and their companion to be with him at half past six in the morning. He took them with him, without encouraging them or promising them anything, and without concealing from them that their luck, and even his own, depended upon the cast of the dice.

Arrived at the foot of the back stairs, he desired them to wait. If the king was still irritated against them, they would depart without being seen; if the king consented to see them, they would only have to be called.

On arriving at the king's private antechamber, M. de Treville found La Chesnaye, who informed him that they had not been able to find M. de la Tremouille on the preceding evening at his hotel, that he returned too late to present himself at the Louvre, that he had only that moment arrived and that he was at that very hour with the king.

This circumstance pleased M. de Treville much, as he thus became certain that no foreign suggestion could insinuate itself between M. de la Tremouille's testimony and himself.

In fact, ten minutes had scarcely passed away when the door of the king's closet opened, and M. de Treville saw M. de la Tremouille come out. The duke came straight up to him, and said: "Monsieur de Treville, his Majesty has just sent for me in order to inquire respecting the circumstances which took place yesterday at my hotel. I have told him the truth; that is to say, that the fault lay with my people, and that I was ready to offer you my excuses. Since I have the good fortune to meet you, I beg you to receive them, and to hold me always as one of your friends."

"Monsieur the Duke," said M. de Treville, "I was so confident of your loyalty that I required no other defender before his Majesty than yourself. I find that I have not been mistaken, and I thank you that there is still one man in France of whom may be said, without disappointment, what I have said of you."

"That's well said," cried the king, who had heard all these compliments through the open door; "only tell him, Treville, since he wishes to be considered your friend, that I also wish to be one of his, but he neglects me; that it is nearly three years since I have seen him, and that I never do see him unless I send for him. Tell him all this for me, for these are things which a king cannot say for himself."

"Thanks, sire, thanks," said the duke; "but your Majesty may be assured that it is not those--I do not speak of Monsieur de Treville--whom your Majesty sees at all hours of the day that are most devoted to you."

"Ah! You have heard what I said? So much the better, Duke, so much the better," said the king, advancing toward the door. "Ah! It is you, Treville. Where are your Musketeers? I told you the day before yesterday to bring them with you; why have you not done so?"

"They are below, sire, and with your permission La Chesnaye will bid them come up."

"Yes, yes, let them come up immediately. It is nearly eight o'clock, and at nine I expect a visit. Go, Monsieur Duke, and return often. Come in, Treville."

The Duke saluted and retired. At the moment he opened the door, the three Musketeers and d'Artagnan, conducted by La Chesnaye, appeared at the top of the staircase.

"Come in, my braves," said the king, "come in; I am going to scold you."

The Musketeers advanced, bowing, d'Artagnan following closely behind them.

"What the devil!" continued the king. "Seven of his Eminence's Guards placed HORS DE COMBAT by you four in two days! That's too many, gentlemen, too many! If you go on so, his Eminence will be forced to renew his company in three weeks, and I to put the edicts in force in all their rigor. One now and then I don't say much about; but seven in two days, I repeat, it is too many, it is far too many!"

"Therefore, sire, your Majesty sees that they are come, quite contrite and repentant, to offer you their excuses."

"Quite contrite and repentant! Hem!" said the king. "I place no confidence in their hypocritical faces. In particular, there is one yonder of a Gascon look. Come hither, monsieur."

D'Artagnan, who understood that it was to him this compliment was addressed, approached, assuming a most deprecating air.

"Why you told me he was a young man? This is a boy, Treville, a mere boy! Do you mean to say that it was he who bestowed that severe thrust at Jussac?"

"And those two equally fine thrusts at Bernajoux."

"Truly!"

"Without reckoning," said Athos, "that if he had not rescued me from the hands of Cahusac, I should not now have the honor of making my very humble reverence to your Majesty."

"Why he is a very devil, this Bearnais! VENTRE-SAINT-GRIS, Monsieur de Treville, as the king my father would have said. But at this sort of work, many doublets must be slashed and many swords broken. Now, Gascons are always poor, are they not?"

"Sire, I can assert that they have hitherto discovered no gold mines in their mountains; though the Lord owes them this miracle in recompense for the manner in which they supported the pretensions of the king your father."

"Which is to say that the Gascons made a king of me, myself, seeing that I am my father's son, is it not, Treville? Well, happily, I don't say nay to it. La Chesnaye, go and see if by rummaging all my pockets you can find forty pistoles; and if you can find them, bring them to me. And now let us see, young man, with your hand upon your conscience, how did all this come to pass?"

D'Artagnan related the adventure of the preceding day in all its details; how, not having been able to sleep for the joy he felt in the expectation of seeing his Majesty, he had gone to his three friends three hours before the hour of audience; how they had gone together to the tennis court, and how, upon the fear he had manifested lest he receive a ball in the face, he had been jeered at by Bernajoux who had nearly paid for his jeer with his life and M. de la Tremouille, who had nothing to do with the matter, with the loss of his hotel.

"This is all very well," murmured the king, "yes, this is just the account the duke gave me of the affair. Poor cardinal! Seven men in two days, and those of his very best! But that's quite enough, gentlemen; please to understand, that's enough. You have taken your revenge for the Rue Ferou, and even exceeded it; you ought to be satisfied."

"If your Majesty is so," said Treville, "we are."

"Oh, yes; I am," added the king, taking a handful of gold from La Chesnaye, and putting it into the hand of d'Artagnan. "Here," said he, "is a proof of my satisfaction."

At this epoch, the ideas of pride which are in fashion in our days did not prevail. A gentleman received, from hand to hand, money from the king, and was not the least in the world humiliated. D'Artagnan put his forty pistoles into his pocket without any scruple--on the contrary, thanking his Majesty greatly.

"There," said the king, looking at a clock, "there, now, as it is half past eight, you may retire; for as I told you, I expect someone at nine. Thanks for your devotedness, gentlemen. I may continue to rely upon it, may I not?"

"Oh, sire!" cried the four companions, with one voice, "we would allow ourselves to be cut to pieces in your Majesty's service."

"Well, well, but keep whole; that will be better, and you will be more useful to me. Treville," added the king, in a low voice, as the others were retiring, "as you have no room in the Musketeers, and as we have besides decided that a novitiate is necessary before entering that corps, place this young man in the company of the Guards of Monsieur Dessessart, your brother-in-law. Ah, PARDIEU, Treville! I enjoy beforehand the face the cardinal will make. He will be furious; but I don't care. I am doing what is right."

The king waved his hand to Treville, who left him and rejoined the Musketeers, whom he found sharing the forty pistoles with d'Artagnan.

The cardinal, as his Majesty had said, was really furious, so furious that during eight days he absented himself from the king's gaming table. This did not prevent the king from being as complacent to him as possible whenever he met him, or from asking in the kindest tone, "Well, Monsieur Cardinal, how fares it with that poor Jussac and that poor Bernajoux of yours?"

7 THE INTERIOR OF "THE MUSKETEERS"

When d'Artagnan was out of the Louvre, and consulted his friends upon the use he had best make of his share of the forty pistoles, Athos advised him to order a good repast at the Pomme-de-Pin, Porthos to engage a lackey, and Aramis to provide himself with a suitable mistress.

The repast was carried into effect that very day, and the lackey waited at table. The repast had been ordered by Athos, and the lackey furnished by Porthos. He was a Picard, whom the glorious Musketeer had picked up on the Bridge Tournelle, making rings and plashing in the water.

Porthos pretended that this occupation was proof of a reflective and contemplative organization, and he had brought him away without any other recommendation. The noble carriage of this gentleman, for whom he believed himself to be engaged, had won Planchet--that was the name of the Picard. He felt a slight disappointment, however, when he saw that this place was already taken by a compeer named Mousqueton, and when Porthos signified to him that the state of his household, though great, would not support two servants, and that he must enter into the service of d'Artagnan. Nevertheless, when he waited at the dinner given by his master, and saw him take out a handful of gold to pay for it, he believed his fortune made, and returned thanks to heaven for having thrown him into the service of such a Croesus. He preserved this opinion even after the feast, with the remnants of which he repaired his own long abstinence; but when in the evening he made his master's bed, the chimeras of Planchet faded away. The bed was the only one in the apartment, which consisted of an antechamber and a bedroom. Planchet slept in the antechamber upon a coverlet taken from the bed of d'Artagnan, and which d'Artagnan from that time made shift to do without.

Athos, on his part, had a valet whom he had trained in his service in a thoroughly peculiar fashion, and who was named Grimaud. He was very taciturn, this worthy signor. Be it understood we are speaking of Athos. During the five or six years that he had lived in the strictest intimacy with his companions, Porthos and Aramis, they could remember having often seen him smile, but had never heard him laugh. His words were brief and expressive, conveying all that was meant, and no more; no embellishments, no embroidery, no arabesques. His conversation a matter of fact, without a single romance.

Although Athos was scarcely thirty years old, and was of great personal beauty and intelligence of mind, no one knew whether he had ever had a mistress. He never spoke of women. He certainly did not prevent others from speaking of them before him, although it was easy to perceive that this kind of conversation, in which he only mingled by bitter words and misanthropic remarks, was very disagreeable to him. His reserve, his roughness, and his silence made almost an old man of him. He had, then, in order not to disturb his habits, accustomed Grimaud to obey him upon a simple gesture or upon a simple movement of his lips. He never spoke to him, except under the most extraordinary occasions.

Sometimes, Grimaud, who feared his master as he did fire, while entertaining a strong attachment to his person and a great veneration for his talents, believed he perfectly understood what he wanted, flew to execute the order received, and did precisely the contrary. Athos then shrugged his shoulders, and, without putting himself in a passion, thrashed Grimaud. On these days he spoke a little.

Porthos, as we have seen, had a character exactly opposite to that of Athos. He not only talked much, but he talked loudly, little caring, we must render him that justice, whether anybody listened to him or not. He talked for the pleasure of talking and for the pleasure of hearing himself talk. He spoke upon all subjects except the sciences, alleging in this respect the inveterate hatred he had borne to scholars from his childhood. He had not so noble an air as Athos, and the commencement of their intimacy often rendered him unjust toward that gentleman, whom he endeavored to eclipse by his splendid dress. But with his simple Musketeer's uniform and nothing but the manner in which he threw back his head and advanced his foot, Athos instantly took the place which was his due and consigned the ostentatious Porthos to the second rank. Porthos consoled himself by filling the antechamber of M. de Treville and the guardroom of the Louvre with the accounts of his love scrapes, after having passed from professional ladies to military ladies, from the lawyer's dame to the baroness, there was question of nothing less with Porthos than a foreign princess, who was enormously fond of him.

An old proverb says, "Like master, like man." Let us pass, then, from the valet of Athos to the valet of Porthos, from Grimaud to Mousqueton.

Mousqueton was a Norman, whose pacific name of Boniface his master had changed into the infinitely more sonorous name of Mousqueton. He had entered the service of Porthos upon condition that he should only be clothed and lodged, though in a handsome manner; but he claimed two hours a day to himself, consecrated to an employment which would provide for his other wants. Porthos agreed to the bargain; the thing suited him wonderfully well. He had doublets cut out of his old clothes and cast-off cloaks for Mousqueton, and thanks to a very intelligent tailor, who made his clothes look as good as new by turning them, and whose wife was suspected of wishing to make Porthos descend from his aristocratic habits, Mousqueton made a very good figure when attending on his master.

As for Aramis, of whom we believe we have sufficiently explained the character--a character which, like that of his lackey was called Bazin. Thanks to the hopes which his master entertained of someday entering into orders, he was always clothed in black, as became the servant of a churchman. He was a Berrichon, thirty-five or forty years old, mild, peaceable, sleek, employing the leisure his master left him in the perusal of pious works, providing rigorously for two a dinner of few dishes, but excellent. For the rest, he was dumb, blind, and deaf, and of unimpeachable fidelity.

And now that we are acquainted, superficially at least, with the masters and the valets, let us pass on to the dwellings occupied by each of them.

Athos dwelt in the Rue Ferou, within two steps of the Luxembourg. His apartment consisted of two small chambers, very nicely fitted up, in a furnished house, the hostess of which, still young and still really handsome, cast tender glances uselessly at him. Some fragments of past splendor appeared here and there upon the walls of this modest lodging; a sword, for example, richly embossed, which belonged by its make to the times of Francis I, the hilt of which alone, encrusted with precious stones, might be worth two hundred pistoles, and which, nevertheless, in his moments of greatest distress Athos had never pledged or offered for sale. It had long been an object of ambition for Porthos. Porthos would have given ten years of his life to possess this sword.

One day, when he had an appointment with a duchess, he endeavored even to borrow it of Athos. Athos, without saying anything, emptied his pockets, got together all his jewels, purses, aiguillettes, and gold chains, and offered them all to Porthos; but as to the sword, he said it was sealed to its place and should never quit it until its master should himself quit his lodgings. In addition to the sword, there was a portrait representing a nobleman of the time of Henry III, dressed with the greatest elegance, and who wore the Order of the Holy Ghost; and this portrait had certain resemblances of lines with Athos, certain family likenesses which indicated that this great noble, a knight of the Order of the King, was his ancestor.

Besides these, a casket of magnificent goldwork, with the same arms as the sword and the portrait, formed a middle ornament to the mantelpiece, and assorted badly with the rest of the furniture. Athos always carried the key of this coffer about him; but he one day opened it before Porthos, and Porthos was convinced that this coffer contained nothing but letters and papers--love letters and family papers, no doubt.

Porthos lived in an apartment, large in size and of very sumptuous appearance, in the Rue du Vieux-Colombier. Every time he passed with a friend before his windows, at one of which Mousqueton was sure to be placed in full livery, Porthos raised his head and his hand, and said, "That is my abode!" But he was never to be found at home; he never invited anybody to go up with him, and no one could form an idea of what his sumptuous apartment contained in the shape of real riches.

As to Aramis, he dwelt in a little lodging composed of a boudoir, an eating room, and a bedroom, which room, situated, as the others were, on the ground floor, looked out upon a little fresh green garden, shady and impenetrable to the eyes of his neighbors.

With regard to d'Artagnan, we know how he was lodged, and we have already made acquaintance with his lackey, Master Planchet.

D'Artagnan, who was by nature very curious--as people generally are who possess the genius of intrigue--did all he could to make out who Athos, Porthos, and Aramis really were (for under these pseudonyms each of these young men concealed his family name)--Athos in particular, who, a league away, savored of nobility. He addressed himself then to Porthos to gain information respecting Athos and Aramis, and to Aramis in order to learn something of Porthos.

Unfortunately Porthos knew nothing of the life of his silent companion but what revealed itself. It was said Athos had met with great crosses in love, and that a frightful treachery had forever poisoned the life of this gallant man. What could this treachery be? All the world was ignorant of it.

As to Porthos, except his real name (as was the case with those of his two comrades), his life was very easily known. Vain and indiscreet, it was as easy to see through him as through a crystal. The only thing to mislead the investigator would have been belief in all the good things he said of himself.

With respect to Aramis, though having the air of having nothing secret about him, he was a young fellow made up of mysteries, answering little to questions put to him about others, and having learned from him the report which prevailed concerning the success of the Musketeer with a princess, wished to gain a little insight into the amorous adventures of his interlocutor. "And you, my dear companion," said he, "you speak of the baronesses, countesses, and princesses of others?"

"PARDIEU! I spoke of them because Porthos talked of them himself, because he had paraded all these fine things before me. But be assured, my dear Monsieur d'Artagnan, that if I had obtained them from any other source, or if they had been confided to me, there exists no confessor more discreet than myself."

"Oh, I don't doubt that," replied d'Artagnan; "but it seems to me that you are tolerably familiar with coats of arms--a certain embroidered handkerchief, for instance, to which I owe the honor of your acquaintance?"

This time Aramis was not angry, but assumed the most modest air and replied in a friendly tone, "My dear friend, do not forget that I wish to belong to the Church, and that I avoid all mundane opportunities. The handkerchief you saw had not been given to me, but it had been forgotten and left at my house by one of my friends. I was obliged to pick it up in order not to compromise him and the lady he loves. As for myself, I neither have, nor desire to have, a mistress, following in that respect the very judicious example of Athos, who has none any more than I have."

"But what the devil! You are not a priest, you are a Musketeer!"

"A Musketeer for a time, my friend, as the cardinal says, a Musketeer against my will, but a churchman at heart, believe me. Athos and Porthos dragged me into this to occupy me. I had, at the moment of being ordained, a little difficulty with--But that would not interest you, and I am taking up your valuable time."

"Not at all; it interests me very much," cried d'Artagnan; "and at this moment I have absolutely nothing to do."

"Yes, but I have my breviary to repeat," answered Aramis; "then some verses to compose, which Madame d'Aiguillon begged of me. Then I must go to the Rue St. Honore in order to purchase some rouge for Madame de Chevreuse. So you see, my dear friend, that if you are not in a hurry, I am very much in a hurry."

Aramis held out his hand in a cordial manner to his young companion, and took leave of him.

Notwithstanding all the pains he took, d'Artagnan was unable to learn any more concerning his three new-made friends. He formed, therefore, the resolution of believing for the present all that was said of their past, hoping for more certain and extended revelations in the future. In the meanwhile, he looked upon Athos as an Achilles, Porthos as an Ajax, and Aramis as a Joseph.

As to the rest, the life of the four young friends was joyous enough. Athos played, and that as a rule unfortunately. Nevertheless, he never borrowed a sou of his companions, although his purse was ever at their service; and when he had played upon honor, he always awakened his creditor by six o'clock the next morning to pay the debt of the preceding evening.

Porthos had his fits. On the days when he won he was insolent and ostentatious; if he lost, he disappeared completely for several days, after which he reappeared with a pale face and thinner person, but with money in his purse.

As to Aramis, he never played. He was the worst Musketeer and the most unconvivial companion imaginable. He had always something or other to do. Sometimes in the midst of dinner, when everyone, under the attraction of wine and in the warmth of conversation, believed they had two or three hours longer to enjoy themselves at table, Aramis looked at his watch, arose with a bland smile, and took leave of the company, to go, as he said, to consult a casuist with whom he had an appointment. At other times he would return home to write a treatise, and requested his friends not to disturb him.

At this Athos would smile, with his charming, melancholy smile, which so became his noble countenance, and Porthos would drink, swearing that Aramis would never be anything but a village CURE.

Planchet, d'Artagnan's valet, supported his good fortune nobly. He received thirty sous per day, and for a month he returned to his lodgings gay as a chaffinch, and affable toward his master. When the wind of adversity began to blow upon the housekeeping of the Rue des Fossoyeurs--that is to say, when the forty pistoles of King Louis XIII were consumed or nearly so--he commenced complaints which Athos thought nauseous, Porthos indecent, and Aramis ridiculous. Athos counseled d'Artagnan to dismiss the fellow; Porthos was of opinion that he should give him a good thrashing first; and Aramis contended that a master should never attend to anything but the civilities paid to him.

"This is all very easy for you to say," replied d'Artagnan, "for you, Athos, who live like a dumb man with Grimaud, who forbid him to speak, and consequently never exchange ill words with him; for you, Porthos, who carry matters in such a magnificent style, and are a god to your valet, Mousqueton; and for you, Aramis, who, always abstracted by your theological studies, inspire your servant, Bazin, a mild, religious man, with a profound respect; but for me, who am without any settled means and without resources--for me, who am neither a Musketeer nor even a Guardsman, what I am to do to inspire either the affection, the terror, or the respect in Planchet?"

"This is serious," answered the three friends; "it is a family affair. It is with valets as with wives, they must be placed at once upon the footing in which you wish them to remain. Reflect upon it."

D'Artagnan did reflect, and resolved to thrash Planchet provisionally; which he did with the conscientiousness that d'Artagnan carried into everything. After having well beaten him, he forbade him to leave his service without his permission. "For," added he, "the future cannot fail to mend; I inevitably look for better times. Your fortune is therefore made if you remain with me, and I am too good a master to allow you to miss such a chance by granting you the dismissal you require."

This manner of acting roused much respect for d'Artagnan's policy among the Musketeers. Planchet was equally seized with admiration, and said no more about going away.

The life of the four young men had become fraternal. D'Artagnan, who had no settled habits of his own, as he came from his province into the midst of his world quite new to him, fell easily into the habits of his friends.

They rose about eight o'clock in the winter, about six in summer, and went to take the countersign and see how things went on at M. de Treville's. D'Artagnan, although he was not a Musketeer, performed the duty of one with remarkable punctuality.

He went on guard because he always kept company with whoever of his friends was on duty. He was well known at the Hotel of the Musketeers, where everyone considered him a good comrade. M. de Treville, who had appreciated him at the first glance and who bore him a real affection, never ceased recommending him to the king.

On their side, the three Musketeers were much attached to their young comrade. The friendship which united these four men, and the need they felt of seeing another three or four times a day, whether for dueling, business, or pleasure, caused them to be continually running after one another like shadows; and the Inseparables were constantly to be met with seeking one another, from the Luxembourg to the Place St. Sulpice, or from the Rue du Vieux-Colombier to the Luxembourg.

In the meanwhile the promises of M. de Treville went on prosperously. One fine morning the king commanded M. de Chevalier Dessessart to admit d'Artagnan as a cadet in his company of Guards. D'Artagnan, with a sigh, donned his uniform, which he would have exchanged for that of a Musketeer at the expense of ten years of his existence. But M. de Treville promised this favor after a novitiate of two years--a novitiate which might besides be abridged if an opportunity should present itself for d'Artagnan to render the king any signal service, or to distinguish himself by some brilliant action. Upon this promise d'Artagnan withdrew, and the next day he began service.

Then it became the turn of Athos, Porthos, and Aramis to mount guard with d'Artagnan when he was on duty. The company of M. le Chevalier Dessessart thus received four instead of one when it admitted d'Artagnan.

8 Concerning A Court Intrigue

In the meantime, the forty pistoles of King Louis XIII, like all other things of this world, after having had a beginning had an end, and after this end our four companions began to be somewhat embarrassed. At first, Athos supported the association for a time with his own means.

Porthos succeeded him; and thanks to one of those disappearances to which he was accustomed, he was able to provide for the wants of all for a fortnight. At last it became Aramis's turn, who performed it with a good grace and who succeeded--as he said, by selling some theological books--in procuring a few pistoles.

Then, as they had been accustomed to do, they had recourse to M. de Treville, who made some advances on their pay; but these advances could not go far with three Musketeers who were already much in arrears and a Guardsman who as yet had no pay at all.

At length when they found they were likely to be really in want, they got together, as a last effort, eight or ten pistoles, with which Porthos went to the gaming table. Unfortunately he was in a bad vein; he lost all, together with twenty-five pistoles for which he had given his word.

Then the inconvenience became distress. The hungry friends, followed by their lackeys, were seen haunting the quays and Guard rooms, picking up among their friends abroad all the dinners they could meet with; for according to the advice of Aramis, it was prudent to sow repasts right and left in prosperity, in order to reap a few in time of need.

Athos was invited four times, and each time took his friends and their lackeys with him. Porthos had six occasions, and contrived in the same manner that his friends should partake of them; Aramis had eight of them. He was a man, as must have been already perceived, who made but little noise, and yet was much sought after.

As to d'Artagnan, who as yet knew nobody in the capital, he only found one chocolate breakfast at the house of a priest of his own province, and one dinner at the house of a cornet of the Guards. He took his army to the priest's, where they devoured as much provision as would have lasted him for two months, and to the cornet's, who performed wonders; but as Planchet said, "People do not eat at once for all time, even when they eat a good deal."

D'Artagnan thus felt himself humiliated in having only procured one meal and a half for his companions--as the breakfast at the priest's could only be counted as half a repast--in return for the feasts which Athos, Porthos, and Aramis had procured him. He fancied himself a burden to the society, forgetting in his perfectly juvenile good faith that he had fed this society for a month; and he set his mind actively to work. He reflected that this coalition of four young, brave, enterprising, and active men ought to have some other object than swaggering walks, fencing lessons, and practical jokes, more or less witty.

In fact, four men such as they were--four men devoted to one another, from their purses to their lives; four men always supporting one another, never yielding, executing singly or together the resolutions formed in common; four arms threatening the four cardinal points, or turning toward a single point--must inevitably, either subterraneously, in open day, by mining, in the trench, by cunning, or by force, open themselves a way toward the object they wished to attain, however well it might be defended, or however distant it may seem. The only thing that astonished d'Artagnan was that his friends had never thought of this.

He was thinking by himself, and even seriously racking his brain to find a direction for this single force four times multiplied, with which he did not doubt, as with the lever for which Archimedes sought, they should succeed in moving the world, when someone tapped gently at his door. D'Artagnan awakened Planchet and ordered him to open it.

From this phrase, "d'Artagnan awakened Planchet," the reader must not suppose it was night, or that day was hardly come. No, it had just struck four. Planchet, two hours before, had asked his master for some dinner, and he had answered him with the proverb, "He who sleeps, dines." And Planchet dined by sleeping.

A man was introduced of simple mien, who had the appearance of a tradesman. Planchet, by way of dessert, would have liked to hear the conversation; but the citizen declared to d'Artagnan that what he had to say being important and confidential, he desired to be left alone with him.

D'Artagnan dismissed Planchet, and requested his visitor to be seated. There was a moment of silence, during which the two men looked at each other, as if to make a preliminary acquaintance, after which d'Artagnan bowed, as a sign that he listened.

"I have heard Monsieur d'Artagnan spoken of as a very brave young man," said the citizen; "and this reputation which he justly enjoys had decided me to confide a secret to him."

"Speak, monsieur, speak," said d'Artagnan, who instinctively scented something advantageous.

The citizen made a fresh pause and continued, "I have a wife who is seamstress to the queen, monsieur, and who is not deficient in either virtue or beauty. I was induced to marry her about three years ago, although she had but very little dowry, because Monsieur Laporte, the queen's cloak bearer, is her godfather, and befriends her."

"Well, monsieur?" asked d'Artagnan.

"Well!" resumed the citizen, "well, monsieur, my wife was abducted yesterday morning, as she was coming out of her workroom."

"And by whom was your wife abducted?"

"I know nothing surely, monsieur, but I suspect someone."

"And who is the person whom you suspect?"

"A man who has pursued her a long time."

"The devil!"

"But allow me to tell you, monsieur," continued the citizen, "that I am convinced that there is less love than politics in all this."

"Less love than politics," replied d'Artagnan, with a reflective air; "and what do you suspect?"

"I do not know whether I ought to tell you what I suspect."

"Monsieur, I beg you to observe that I ask you absolutely nothing. It is you who have come to me. It is you who have told me that you had a secret to confide in me. Act, then, as you think proper; there is still time to withdraw."

"No, monsieur, no; you appear to be an honest young man, and I will have confidence in you. I believe, then, that it is not on account of any intrigues of her own that my wife has been arrested, but because of those of a lady much greater than herself."

"Ah, ah! Can it be on account of the amours of Madame de Bois-Tracy?" said d'Artagnan, wishing to have the air, in the eyes of the citizen, of being posted as to court affairs.

"Higher, monsieur, higher."

"Of Madame d'Aiguillon?"

"Still higher."

"Of Madame de Chevreuse?"

"Of the--" d'Artagnan checked himself.

"Yes, monsieur," replied the terrified citizen, in a tone so low that he was scarcely audible.

"And with whom?"

"With whom can it be, if not the Duke of--"

"The Duke of--"

"Yes, monsieur," replied the citizen, giving a still fainter intonation to his voice.

"But how do you know all this?"

"How do I know it?"

"Yes, how do you know it? No half-confidence, or--you understand!"

"I know it from my wife, monsieur--from my wife herself."

"Who learns it from whom?"

"From Monsieur Laporte. Did I not tell you that she was the goddaughter of Monsieur Laporte, the confidential man of the queen? Well, Monsieur Laporte placed her near her Majesty in order that our poor queen might at least have someone in whom she could place confidence, abandoned as she is by the king, watched as she is by the cardinal, betrayed as she is by everybody."

"Ah, ah! It begins to develop itself," said d'Artagnan.

"Now, my wife came home four days ago, monsieur. One of her conditions was that she should come and see me twice a week; for, as I had the honor to tell you, my wife loves me dearly--my wife, then, came and confided to me that the queen at that very moment entertained great fears."

"Truly!"

"Yes. The cardinal, as it appears, pursues he and persecutes her more than ever. He cannot pardon her the history of the Saraband. You know the history of the Saraband?"

"PARDIEU! Know it!" replied d'Artagnan, who knew nothing about it, but who wished to appear to know everything that was going on.

"So that now it is no longer hatred, but vengeance."

"Indeed!"

"And the queen believes--"

"Well, what does the queen believe?"

"She believes that someone has written to the Duke of Buckingham in her name."

"In the queen's name?"

"Yes, to make him come to Paris; and when once come to Paris, to draw him into some snare."

"The devil! But your wife, monsieur, what has she to do with all this?"

"Her devotion to the queen is known; and they wish either to remove her from her mistress, or to intimidate her, in order to obtain her Majesty's secrets, or to seduce her and make use of her as a spy."

"That is likely," said d'Artagnan; "but the man who has abducted her--do you know him?"

"I have told you that I believe I know him."

"His name?"

"I do not know that; what I do know is that he is a creature of the cardinal, his evil genius."

"But you have seen him?"

"Yes, my wife pointed him out to me one day."

"Has he anything remarkable about him by which one may recognize him?"

"Oh, certainly; he is a noble of very lofty carriage, black hair, swarthy complexion, piercing eye, white teeth, and has a scar on his temple."

"A scar on his temple!" cried d'Artagnan; "and with that, white teeth, a piercing eye, dark complexion, black hair, and haughty carriage--why, that's my man of Meung."

"He is your man, do you say?"

"Yes, yes; but that has nothing to do with it. No, I am wrong. On the contrary, that simplifies the matter greatly. If your man is mine, with one blow I shall obtain two revenges, that's all; but where to find this man?"

"I know not."

"Have you no information as to his abiding place?"

"None. One day, as I was conveying my wife back to the Louvre, he was coming out as she was going in, and she showed him to me."

"The devil! The devil!" murmured d'Artagnan; "all this is vague enough. From whom have you learned of the abduction of your wife?"

"From Monsieur Laporte."

"Did he give you any details?"

"He knew none himself."

"And you have learned nothing from any other quarter?"

"Yes, I have received--"

"What?"

"I fear I am committing a great imprudence."

"You always come back to that; but I must make you see this time that it is too late to retreat."

"I do not retreat, MORDIEU!" cried the citizen, swearing in order to rouse his courage. "Besides, by the faith of Bonacieux--"

"You call yourself Bonacieux?" interrupted d'Artagnan.

"Yes, that is my name."

"You said, then, by the word of Bonacieux. Pardon me for interrupting you, but it appears to me that that name is familiar to me."

"Possibly, monsieur. I am your landlord."

"Ah, ah!" said d'Artagnan, half rising and bowing; "you are my landlord?"

"Yes, monsieur, yes. And as it is three months since you have been here, and though, distracted as you must be in your important occupations, you have forgotten to pay me my rent--as, I say, I have not tormented you a single instant, I thought you would appreciate my delicacy."

"How can it be otherwise, my dear Bonacieux?" replied d'Artagnan; "trust me, I am fully grateful for such unparalleled conduct, and if, as I told you, I can be of any service to you--"

"I believe you, monsieur, I believe you; and as I was about to say, by the word of Bonacieux, I have confidence in you."

"Finish, then, what you were about to say."

The citizen took a paper from his pocket, and presented it to d'Artagnan.

"A letter?" said the young man.

"Which I received this morning."

D'Artagnan opened it, and as the day was beginning to decline, he approached the window to read it. The citizen followed him.

"'Do not seek your wife,'" read d'Artagnan; "'she will be restored to you when there is no longer occasion for her. If you make a single step to find her you are lost.'

"That's pretty positive," continued d'Artagnan; "but after all, it is but a menace."

"Yes; but that menace terrifies me. I am not a fighting man at all, monsieur, and I am afraid of the Bastille."

"Hum!" said d'Artagnan. "I have no greater regard for the Bastille than you. If it were nothing but a sword thrust, why then--"

"I have counted upon you on this occasion, monsieur."

"Yes?"

"Seeing you constantly surrounded by Musketeers of a very superb appearance, and knowing that these Musketeers belong to Monsieur de Treville, and were consequently enemies of the cardinal, I thought that you and your friends, while rendering justice to your poor queen, would be pleased to play his Eminence an ill turn."

"Without doubt."

"And then I have thought that considering three months' lodging, about which I have said nothing--"

"Yes, yes; you have already given me that reason, and I find it excellent."

"Reckoning still further, that as long as you do me the honor to remain in my house I shall never speak to you about rent--"

"Very kind!"

"And adding to this, if there be need of it, meaning to offer you fifty pistoles, if, against all probability, you should be short at the present moment."

"Admirable! You are rich then, my dear Monsieur Bonacieux?"

"I am comfortably off, monsieur, that's all; I have scraped together some such thing as an income of two or three thousand crown in the haberdashery business, but more particularly in venturing some funds in the last voyage of the celebrated navigator Jean Moquet; so that you understand, monsieur--But--" cried the citizen.

"What!" demanded d'Artagnan.

"Whom do I see yonder?"

"Where?"

"In the street, facing your window, in the embrasure of that door--a man wrapped in a cloak."

"It is he!" cried d'Artagnan and the citizen at the same time, each having recognized his man.

"Ah, this time," cried d'Artagnan, springing to his sword, "this time he will not escape me!"

Drawing his sword from its scabbard, he rushed out of the apartment. On the staircase he met Athos and Porthos, who were coming to see him. They separated, and d'Artagnan rushed between them like a dart.

"Pah! Where are you going?" cried the two Musketeers in a breath.

"The man of Meung!" replied d'Artagnan, and disappeared.

D'Artagnan had more than once related to his friends his adventure with the stranger, as well as the apparition of the beautiful foreigner, to whom this man had confided some important missive.

The opinion of Athos was that d'Artagnan had lost his letter in the skirmish. A gentleman, in his opinion--and according to d'Artagnan's portrait of him, the stranger must be a gentleman--would be incapable of the baseness of stealing a letter.

Porthos saw nothing in all this but a love meeting, given by a lady to a cavalier, or by a cavalier to a lady, which had been disturbed by the presence of d'Artagnan and his yellow horse.

Aramis said that as these sorts of affairs were mysterious, it was better not to fathom them.

They understood, then, from the few words which escaped from d'Artagnan, what affair was in hand, and as they thought that overtaking his man, or losing sight of him, d'Artagnan would return to his rooms, they kept on their way.

When they entered d'Artagnan's chamber, it was empty; the landlord, dreading the consequences of the encounter which was doubtless about to take place between the young man and the stranger, had, consistent with the character he had given himself, judged it prudent to decamp.

9 D'Artagnan Shows Himself

As Athos and Porthos had foreseen, at the expiration of a half hour, d'Artagnan returned. He had again missed his man, who had disappeared as if by enchantment. D'Artagnan had run, sword in hand, through all the neighboring streets, but had found nobody resembling the man he sought for. Then he came back to the point where, perhaps, he ought to have begun, and that was to knock at the door against which the stranger had leaned; but this proved useless--for though he knocked ten or twelve times in succession, no one answered, and some of the neighbors, who put their noses out of their windows or were brought to their doors by the noise, had assured him that that house, all the openings of which were tightly closed, had not been inhabited for six months.

While d'Artagnan was running through the streets and knocking at doors, Aramis had joined his companions; so that on returning home d'Artagnan found the reunion complete.

"Well!" cried the three Musketeers all together, on seeing d'Artagnan enter with his brow covered with perspiration and his countenance upset with anger.

"Well!" cried he, throwing his sword upon the bed, "this man must be the devil in person; he has disappeared like a phantom, like a shade, like a specter."

"Do you believe in apparitions?" asked Athos of Porthos.

"I never believe in anything I have not seen, and as I never have seen apparitions, I don't believe in them."

"The Bible," said Aramis, "make our belief in them a law; the ghost of Samuel appeared to Saul, and it is an article of faith that I should be very sorry to see any doubt thrown upon, Porthos."

"At all events, man or devil, body or shadow, illusion or reality, this man is born for my damnation; for his flight has caused us to miss a glorious affair, gentlemen--an affair by which there were a hundred pistoles, and perhaps more, to be gained."

"How is that?" cried Porthos and Aramis in a breath.

As to Athos, faithful to his system of reticence, he contented himself with interrogating d'Artagnan by a look.

"Planchet," said d'Artagnan to his domestic, who just then insinuated his head through the half-open door in order to catch some fragments of the conversation, "go down to my landlord, Monsieur Bonacieux, and ask him to send me half a dozen bottles of Beaugency wine; I prefer that."

"Ah, ah! You have credit with your landlord, then?" asked Porthos.

"Yes," replied d'Artagnan, "from this very day; and mind, if the wine is bad, we will send him to find better."

"We must use, and not abuse," said Aramis, sententiously.

"I always said that d'Artagnan had the longest head of the four," said Athos, who, having uttered his opinion, to which d'Artagnan replied with a bow, immediately resumed his accustomed silence.

"But come, what is this about?" asked Porthos.

"Yes," said Aramis, "impart it to us, my dear friend, unless the honor of any lady be hazarded by this confidence; in that case you would do better to keep it to yourself."

"Be satisfied," replied d'Artagnan; "the honor of no one will have cause to complain of what I have to tell."

He then related to his friends, word for word, all that had passed between him and his host, and how the man who had abducted the wife of his worthy landlord was the same with whom he had had the difference at the hostelry of the Jolly Miller.

"Your affair is not bad," said Athos, after having tasted like a connoisseur and indicated by a nod of his head that he thought the wine good; "and one may draw fifty or sixty pistoles from this good man.

Then there only remains to ascertain whether these fifty or sixty pistoles are worth the risk of four heads."

"But observe," cried d'Artagnan, "that there is a woman in the affair--a woman carried off, a woman who is doubtless threatened, tortured perhaps, and all because she is faithful to her mistress."

"Beware, d'Artagnan, beware," said Aramis. "You grow a little too warm, in my opinion, about the fate of Madame Bonacieux. Woman was created for our destruction, and it is from her we inherit all our miseries."

At this speech of Aramis, the brow of Athos became clouded and he bit his lips.

"It is not Madame Bonacieux about whom I am anxious," cried d'Artagnan, "but the queen, whom the king abandons, whom the cardinal persecutes, and who sees the heads of all her friends fall, one after the other."

"Why does she love what we hate most in the world, the Spaniards and the English?"

"Spain is her country," replied d'Artagnan; "and it is very natural that she should love the Spanish, who are the children of the same soil as herself. As to the second reproach, I have heard it said that she does not love the English, but an Englishman."

"Well, and by my faith," said Athos, "it must be acknowledged that this Englishman is worthy of being loved. I never saw a man with a nobler air than his."

"Without reckoning that he dresses as nobody else can," said Porthos. "I was at the Louvre on the day when he scattered his pearls; and, PARDIEU, I picked up two that I sold for ten pistoles each. Do you know him, Aramis?"

"As well as you do, gentlemen; for I was among those who seized him in the garden at Amiens, into which Monsieur Putange, the queen's equerry, introduced me. I was at school at the time, and the adventure appeared to me to be cruel for the king."

"Which would not prevent me," said d'Artagnan, "if I knew where the Duke of Buckingham was, from taking him by the hand and conducting him to the queen, were it only to enrage the cardinal, and if we could find means to play him a sharp turn, I vow that I would voluntarily risk my head in doing it."

"And did the mercer[1]," rejoined Athos, "tell you, d'Artagnan, that the queen thought that Buckingham had been brought over by a forged letter?"

"She is afraid so."

"Wait a minute, then," said Aramis.

"What for?" demanded Porthos.

"Go on, while I endeavor to recall circumstances."

"And now I am convinced," said d'Artagnan, "that this abduction of the queen's woman is connected with the events of which we are speaking, and perhaps with the presence of Buckingham in Paris."

"The Gascon is full of ideas," said Porthos, with admiration.

"I like to hear him talk," said Athos; "his dialect amuses me."

"Gentlemen," cried Aramis, "listen to this."

"Listen to Aramis," said his three friends.

"Yesterday I was at the house of a doctor of theology, whom I sometimes consult about my studies."

Athos smiled.

"He resides in a quiet quarter," continued Aramis; "his tastes and his profession require it. Now, at the moment when I left his house--"

Here Aramis paused.

"Well," cried his auditors; "at the moment you left his house?"

Aramis appeared to make a strong inward effort, like a man who, in the full relation of a falsehood, finds himself stopped by some unforeseen obstacle; but the eyes of his three companions were fixed upon him, their ears were wide open, and there were no means of retreat.

"This doctor has a niece," continued Aramis.

"Ah, he has a niece!" interrupted Porthos.

"A very respectable lady," said Aramis.

The three friends burst into laughter.

"Ah, if you laugh, if you doubt me," replied Aramis, "you shall know nothing."

"We believe like Mohammedans, and are as mute as tombstones," said Athos.

"I will continue, then," resumed Aramis. "This niece comes sometimes to see her uncle; and by chance was there yesterday at the same time that I was, and it was my duty to offer to conduct her to her carriage."

"Ah! She has a carriage, then, this niece of the doctor?" interrupted Porthos, one of whose faults was a great looseness of tongue. "A nice acquaintance, my friend!"

"Porthos," replied Aramis, "I have had the occasion to observe to you more than once that you are very indiscreet; and that is injurious to you among the women."

"Gentlemen, gentlemen," cried d'Artagnan, who began to get a glimpse of the result of the adventure,

[1] Haberdasher

"the thing is serious. Let us try not to jest, if we can. Go on Aramis, go on."

"All at once, a tall, dark gentleman--just like yours, d'Artagnan."

"The same, perhaps," said he.

"Possibly," continued Aramis, "came toward me, accompanied by five or six men who followed about ten paces behind him; and in the politest tone, 'Monsieur Duke,' said he to me, 'and you madame,' continued he, addressing the lady on my arm--"

"The doctor's niece?"

"Hold your tongue, Porthos," said Athos; "you are insupportable."

"'--will you enter this carriage, and that without offering the least resistance, without making the least noise?'"

"He took you for Buckingham!" cried d'Artagnan.

"I believe so," replied Aramis.

"But the lady?" asked Porthos.

"He took her for the queen!" said d'Artagnan.

"Just so," replied Aramis.

"The Gascon is the devil!" cried Athos; "nothing escapes him."

"The fact is," said Porthos, "Aramis is of the same height, and something of the shape of the duke; but it nevertheless appears to me that the dress of a Musketeer--"

"I wore an enormous cloak," said Aramis.

"In the month of July? The devil!" said Porthos. "Is the doctor afraid that you may be recognized?"

"I can comprehend that the spy may have been deceived by the person; but the face--"

"I had a large hat," said Aramis.

"Oh, good lord," cried Porthos, "what precautions for the study of theology!"

"Gentlemen, gentlemen," said d'Artagnan, "do not let us lose our time in jesting. Let us separate, and let us seek the mercer's wife--that is the key of the intrigue."

"A woman of such inferior condition! Can you believe so?" said Porthos, protruding his lips with contempt.

"She is goddaughter to Laporte, the confidential valet of the queen. Have I not told you so, gentlemen? Besides, it has perhaps been her Majesty's calculation to seek on this occasion for support so lowly. High heads expose themselves from afar, and the cardinal is longsighted."

"Well," said Porthos, "in the first place make a bargain with the mercer, and a good bargain."

"That's useless," said d'Artagnan; "for I believe if he does not pay us, we shall be well enough paid by another party."

At this moment a sudden noise of footsteps was heard upon the stairs; the door was thrown violently open, and the unfortunate mercer rushed into the chamber in which the council was held.

"Save me, gentlemen, for the love of heaven, save me!" cried he. "There are four men come to arrest me. Save me! Save me!"

Porthos and Aramis arose.

"A moment," cried d'Artagnan, making them a sign to replace in the scabbard their half-drawn swords. "It is not courage that is needed; it is prudence."

"And yet," cried Porthos, "we will not leave--"

"You will leave d'Artagnan to act as he thinks proper," said Athos. "He has, I repeat, the longest head of the four, and for my part I declare that I will obey him. Do as you think best, d'Artagnan."

At this moment the four Guards appeared at the door of the antechamber, but seeing four Musketeers standing, and their swords by their sides, they hesitated about going farther.

"Come in, gentlemen, come in," called d'Artagnan; "you are here in my apartment, and we are all faithful servants of the king and cardinal."

"Then, gentlemen, you will not oppose our executing the orders we have received?" asked one who appeared to be the leader of the party.

"On the contrary, gentlemen, we would assist you if it were necessary."

"What does he say?" grumbled Porthos.

"You are a simpleton," said Athos. "Silence!"

"But you promised me--" whispered the poor mercer.

"We can only save you by being free ourselves," replied d'Artagnan, in a rapid, low tone; "and if we appear inclined to defend you, they will arrest us with you."

"It seems, nevertheless--"

"Come, gentlemen, come!" said d'Artagnan, aloud; "I have no motive for defending Monsieur. I saw him today for the first time, and he can tell you on what occasion; he came to demand the rent of my lodging. Is that not true, Monsieur Bonacieux? Answer!"

"That is the very truth," cried the mercer; "but Monsieur does not tell you--"

"Silence, with respect to me, silence, with respect to my friends; silence about the queen, above all, or you will ruin everybody without saving yourself!

Come, come, gentlemen, remove the fellow." And d'Artagnan pushed the half-stupefied mercer among the Guards, saying to him, "You are a shabby old fellow, my dear. You come to demand money of me--of a Musketeer! To prison with him! Gentlemen, once more, take him to prison, and keep him under key as long as possible; that will give me time to pay him."

The officers were full of thanks, and took away their prey. As they were going down d'Artagnan laid his hand on the shoulder of their leader.

"May I not drink to your health, and you to mine?" said d'Artagnan, filling two glasses with the Beaugency wine which he had obtained from the liberality of M. Bonacieux.

"That will do me great honor," said the leader of the posse, "and I accept thankfully."

"Then to yours, monsieur--what is your name?"

"Boisrenard."

"Monsieur Boisrenard."

"To yours, my gentlemen! What is your name, in your turn, if you please?"

"d'Artagnan."

"To yours, monsieur."

"And above all others," cried d'Artagnan, as if carried away by his enthusiasm, "to that of the king and the cardinal."

The leader of the posse would perhaps have doubted the sincerity of d'Artagnan if the wine had been bad; but the wine was good, and he was convinced.

"What diabolical villainy you have performed here," said Porthos, when the officer had rejoined his companions and the four friends found themselves alone. "Shame, shame, for four Musketeers to allow an unfortunate fellow who cried for help to be arrested in their midst! And a gentleman to hobnob with a bailiff!"

"Porthos," said Aramis, "Athos has already told you that you are a simpleton, and I am quite of his opinion. D'Artagnan, you are a great man; and when you occupy Monsieur de Treville's place, I will come and ask your influence to secure me an abbey."

"Well, I am in a maze," said Porthos; "do YOU approve of what d'Artagnan has done?"

"PARBLEU! Indeed I do," said Athos; "I not only approve of what he has done, but I congratulate him upon it."

"And now, gentlemen," said d'Artagnan, without stopping to explain his conduct to Porthos, "All for one, one for all--that is our motto, is it not?"

"And yet--" said Porthos.

"Hold out your hand and swear!" cried Athos and Aramis at once.

Overcome by example, grumbling to himself, nevertheless, Porthos stretched out his hand, and the four friends repeated with one voice the formula dictated by d'Artagnan:

"All for one, one for all."

"That's well! Now let us everyone retire to his own home," said d'Artagnan, as if he had done nothing but command all his life; "and attention! For from this moment we are at feud with the cardinal."

10 A Mousetrap In The Seventeenth Century

The invention of the mousetrap does not date from our days; as soon as societies, in forming, had invented any kind of police, that police invented mousetraps.

As perhaps our readers are not familiar with the slang of the Rue de Jerusalem, and as it is fifteen years since we applied this word for the first time to this thing, allow us to explain to them what is a mousetrap.

When in a house, of whatever kind it may be, an individual suspected of any crime is arrested, the arrest is held secret. Four or five men are placed in ambuscade in the first room. The door is opened to all who knock. It is closed after them, and they are arrested; so that at the end of two or three days they have in their power almost all the HABITUES of the establishment. And that is a mousetrap.

The apartment of M. Bonacieux, then, became a mousetrap; and whoever appeared there was taken and interrogated by the cardinal's people. It must be observed that as a separate passage led to the first floor, in which d'Artagnan lodged, those who called on him were exempted from this detention.

Besides, nobody came thither but the three Musketeers; they had all been engaged in earnest search and inquiries, but had discovered nothing. Athos had even gone so far as to question M. de Treville--a thing which, considering the habitual reticence of the worthy Musketeer, had very much astonished his captain. But M. de Treville knew nothing, except that the last time he had seen the cardinal, the king, and the queen, the cardinal looked very thoughtful, the king uneasy, and the redness of the queen's eyes donated that she had been sleepless or tearful. But this last circumstance was not striking, as the queen since her marriage had slept badly and wept much.

M de Treville requested Athos, whatever might happen, to be observant of his duty to the king, but particularly to the queen, begging him to convey his desires to his comrades.

As to d'Artagnan, he did not budge from his apartment. He converted his chamber into an observatory. From his windows he saw all the visitors who were caught. Then, having removed a plank from his floor, and nothing remaining but a simple ceiling between him and the room beneath, in which the interrogatories were made, he heard all that passed between the inquisitors and the accused.

The interrogatories, preceded by a minute search operated upon the persons arrested, were almost always framed thus: "Has Madame Bonacieux sent anything to you for her husband, or any other person? Has Monsieur Bonacieux sent anything to you for his wife, or for any other person? Has either of them confided anything to you by word of mouth?"

"If they knew anything, they would not question people in this manner," said d'Artagnan to himself. "Now, what is it they want to know? Why, they want to know if the Duke of Buckingham is in Paris, and if he has had, or is likely to have, an interview with the queen."

D'Artagnan held onto this idea, which, from what he had heard, was not wanting in probability.

In the meantime, the mousetrap continued in operation, and likewise d'Artagnan's vigilance.

On the evening of the day after the arrest of poor Bonacieux, as Athos had just left d'Artagnan to report at M. de Treville's, as nine o'clock had just struck, and as Planchet, who had not yet made the bed, was beginning his task, a knocking was heard at the street door. The door was instantly opened and shut; someone was taken in the mousetrap.

D'Artagnan flew to his hole, laid himself down on the floor at full length, and listened.

Cries were soon heard, and then moans, which someone appeared to be endeavoring to stifle. There were no questions.

"The devil!" said d'Artagnan to himself. "It seems like a woman! They search her; she resists; they use force--the scoundrels!"

In spite of his prudence, d'Artagnan restrained himself with great difficulty from taking a part in the scene that was going on below.

"But I tell you that I am the mistress of the house, gentlemen! I tell you I am Madame Bonacieux; I tell you I belong to the queen!" cried the unfortunate woman.

"Madame Bonacieux!" murmured d'Artagnan. "Can I be so lucky as to find what everybody is seeking for?"

The voice became more and more indistinct; a tumultuous movement shook the partition. The victim resisted as much as a woman could resist four men.

"Pardon, gentlemen--par--" murmured the voice, which could now only be heard in inarticulate sounds.

"They are binding her; they are going to drag her away," cried d'Artagnan to himself, springing up from the floor. "My sword! Good, it is by my side! Planchet!"

"Monsieur."

"Run and seek Athos, Porthos and Aramis. One of the three will certainly be at home, perhaps all three. Tell them to take arms, to come here, and to run! Ah, I remember, Athos is at Monsieur de Treville's."

"But where are you going, monsieur, where are you going?"

"I am going down by the window, in order to be there the sooner," cried d'Artagnan. "You put back the boards, sweep the floor, go out at the door, and run as I told you."

"Oh, monsieur! Monsieur! You will kill yourself," cried Planchet.

"Hold your tongue, stupid fellow," said d'Artagnan; and laying hold of the casement, he let himself gently down from the first story, which fortunately was not very elevated, without doing himself the slightest injury.

He then went straight to the door and knocked, murmuring, "I will go myself and be caught in the mousetrap, but woe be to the cats that shall pounce upon such a mouse!"

The knocker had scarcely sounded under the hand of the young man before the tumult ceased, steps approached, the door was opened, and d'Artagnan, sword in hand, rushed into the rooms of M. Bonacieux, the door of which doubtless acted upon by a spring, closed after him.

Then those who dwelt in Bonacieux's unfortunate house, together with the nearest neighbors, heard loud cries, stamping of feet, clashing of swords, and breaking of furniture. A moment after, those who, surprised by this tumult, had gone to their windows to learn the cause of it, saw the door open, and four men, clothed in black, not COME out of it, but FLY, like so many frightened crows, leaving on the ground and on the corners of the furniture, feathers from their wings; that is to say, patches of their clothes and fragments of their cloaks.

D'Artagnan was conqueror--without much effort, it must be confessed, for only one of the officers was armed, and even he defended himself for form's sake. It is true that the three others had endeavored to knock the young man down with chairs, stools, and crockery; but two or three scratches made by the Gascon's blade terrified them. Ten minutes sufficed for their defeat, and d'Artagnan remained master of the field of battle.

The neighbors who had opened their windows, with the coolness peculiar to the inhabitants of Paris in these times of perpetual riots and disturbances, closed them again as soon as they saw the four men in black flee--their instinct telling them that for the time all was over. Besides, it began to grow late, and then, as today, people went to bed early in the quarter of the Luxembourg.

On being left alone with Mme. Bonacieux, d'Artagnan turned toward her; the poor woman reclined where she had been left, half-fainting upon an armchair. D'Artagnan examined her with a rapid glance.

She was a charming woman of twenty-five or twenty-six years, with dark hair, blue eyes, and a nose slightly turned up, admirable teeth, and a complexion marbled with rose and opal. There, however, ended the signs which might have confounded her with a lady of rank. The hands were white, but without delicacy; the feet did not bespeak the woman of quality. Happily, d'Artagnan was not yet acquainted with such niceties.

While d'Artagnan was examining Mme. Bonacieux, and was, as we have said, close to her, he saw on the ground a fine cambric handkerchief, which he picked up, as was his habit, and at the corner of which he recognized the same cipher he had seen on the handkerchief which had nearly caused him and Aramis to cut each other's throat.

From that time, d'Artagnan had been cautious with respect to handkerchiefs with arms on them, and he therefore placed in the pocket of Mme. Bonacieux the one he had just picked up.

At that moment Mme. Bonacieux recovered her senses. She opened her eyes, looked around her with terror, saw that the apartment was empty and that she was alone with her liberator. She extended her hands to him with a smile. Mme. Bonacieux had the sweetest smile in the world.

"Ah, monsieur!" said she, "you have saved me; permit me to thank you."

"Madame," said d'Artagnan, "I have only done what every gentleman would have done in my place; you owe me no thanks."

"Oh, yes, monsieur, oh, yes; and I hope to prove to you that you have not served an ingrate. But what could these men, whom I at first took for robbers, want with me, and why is Monsieur Bonacieux not here?"

"Madame, those men were more dangerous than any robbers could have been, for they are the agents of the cardinal; and as to your husband, Monsieur Bonacieux, he is not here because he was yesterday evening conducted to the Bastille."

"My husband in the Bastille!" cried Mme. Bonacieux. "Oh, my God! What has he done? Poor dear man, he is innocence itself!"

And something like a faint smile lighted the still-terrified features of the young woman.

"What has he done, madame?" said d'Artagnan. "I believe that his only crime is to have at the same time the good fortune and the misfortune to be your husband."

"But, monsieur, you know then--"

"I know that you have been abducted, madame."

"And by whom? Do you know him? Oh, if you know him, tell me!"

"By a man of from forty to forty-five years, with black hair, a dark complexion, and a scar on his left temple."

"That is he, that is he; but his name?"

"Ah, his name? I do not know that."

"And did my husband know I had been carried off?"

"He was informed of it by a letter, written to him by the abductor himself."

"And does he suspect," said Mme. Bonacieux, with some embarrassment, "the cause of this event?"

"He attributed it, I believe, to a political cause."

"I doubted from the first; and now I think entirely as he does. Then my dear Monsieur Bonacieux has not suspected me a single instant?"

"So far from it, madame, he was too proud of your prudence, and above all, of your love."

A second smile, almost imperceptible, stole over the rosy lips of the pretty young woman.

"But," continued d'Artagnan, "how did you escape?"

"I took advantage of a moment when they left me alone; and as I had known since morning the reason of my abduction, with the help of the sheets I let myself down from the window. Then, as I believed my husband would be at home, I hastened hither."

"To place yourself under his protection?"

"Oh, no, poor dear man! I knew very well that he was incapable of defending me; but as he could serve us in other ways, I wished to inform him."

"Of what?"

"Oh, that is not my secret; I must not, therefore, tell you."

"Besides," said d'Artagnan, "pardon me, madame, if, guardsman as I am, I remind you of prudence--besides, I believe we are not here in a very proper place for imparting confidences. The men I have put to flight will return reinforced; if they find us here, we are lost. I have sent for three of my friends, but who knows whether they were at home?"

"Yes, yes! You are right," cried the affrighted Mme. Bonacieux; "let us fly! Let us save ourselves."

At these words she passed her arm under that of d'Artagnan, and urged him forward eagerly.

"But whither shall we fly--whither escape?"

"Let us first withdraw from this house; afterward we shall see."

The young woman and the young man, without taking the trouble to shut the door after them, descended the Rue des Fossoyeurs rapidly, turned into the Rue des Fosses-Monsieur-le-Prince, and did not stop till they came to the Place St. Sulpice.

"And now what are we to do, and where do you wish me to conduct you?" asked d'Artagnan.

"I am at quite a loss how to answer you, I admit," said Mme. Bonacieux. "My intention was to inform Monsieur Laporte, through my husband, in order that Monsieur Laporte might tell us precisely what had taken place at the Louvre in the last three days, and whether there is any danger in presenting myself there."

"But I," said d'Artagnan, "can go and inform Monsieur Laporte."

"No doubt you could, only there is one misfortune, and that is that Monsieur Bonacieux is known at the Louvre, and would be allowed to pass; whereas you are not known there, and the gate would be closed against you."

"Ah, bah!" said d'Artagnan; "you have at some wicket of the Louvre a CONCIERGE who is devoted to you, and who, thanks to a password, would--"

Mme. Bonacieux looked earnestly at the young man.

"And if I give you this password," said she, "would you forget it as soon as you used it?"

"By my honor, by the faith of a gentleman!" said d'Artagnan, with an accent so truthful that no one could mistake it.

"Then I believe you. You appear to be a brave young man; besides, your fortune may perhaps be the result of your devotedness."

"I will do, without a promise and voluntarily, all that I can do to serve the king and be agreeable to the queen. Dispose of me, then, as a friend."

"But I--where shall I go meanwhile?"

"Is there nobody from whose house Monsieur Laporte can come and fetch you?"

"No, I can trust nobody."

"Stop," said d'Artagnan; "we are near Athos's door. Yes, here it is."

"Who is this Athos?"

"One of my friends."

"But if he should be at home and see me?"

"He is not at home, and I will carry away the key, after having placed you in his apartment."

"But if he should return?"

"Oh, he won't return; and if he should, he will be told that I have brought a woman with me, and that woman is in his apartment."

"But that will compromise me sadly, you know."

"Of what consequence? Nobody knows you. Besides, we are in a situation to overlook ceremony."

"Come, then, let us go to your friend's house. Where does he live?"

"Rue Ferou, two steps from here."

"Let us go!"

Both resumed their way. As d'Artagnan had foreseen, Athos was not within. He took the key, which was customarily given him as one of the family, ascended the stairs, and introduced Mme. Bonacieux into the little apartment of which we have given a description.

"You are at home," said he. "Remain here, fasten the door inside, and open it to nobody unless you hear three taps like this;" and he tapped thrice--two taps close together and pretty hard, the other after an interval, and lighter.

"That is well," said Mme. Bonacieux. "Now, in my turn, let me give you my instructions."

"I am all attention."

"Present yourself at the wicket of the Louvre, on the side of the Rue de l'Echelle, and ask for Germain."

"Well, and then?"

"He will ask you what you want, and you will answer by these two words, 'Tours' and 'Bruxelles.' He will at once put himself at your orders."

"And what shall I command him?"

"To go and fetch Monsieur Laporte, the queen's VALET DE CHAMBRE."

"And when he shall have informed him, and Monsieur Laporte is come?"

"You will send him to me."

"That is well; but where and how shall I see you again?"

"Do you wish to see me again?"

"Certainly."

"Well, let that care be mine, and be at ease."

"I depend upon your word."

"You may."

D'Artagnan bowed to Mme. Bonacieux, darting at her the most loving glance that he could possibly concentrate upon her charming little person; and while he descended the stairs, he heard the door closed and double-locked. In two bounds he was at the Louvre; as he entered the wicket of L'Echelle, ten o'clock struck. All the events we have described had taken place within a half hour.

Everything fell out as Mme. Bonacieux prophesied. On hearing the password, Germain bowed. In a few minutes, Laporte was at the lodge; in two words d'Artagnan informed him where Mme. Bonacieux was. Laporte assured himself, by having it twice repeated, of the accurate address, and set off at a run. Hardly, however, had he taken ten steps before he returned.

"Young man," said he to d'Artagnan, "a suggestion."

"What?"

"You may get into trouble by what has taken place."

"You believe so?"

"Yes. Have you any friend whose clock is too slow?"

"Well?"

"Go and call upon him, in order that he may give evidence of your having been with him at half past nine. In a court of justice that is called an alibi."

D'Artagnan found his advice prudent. He took to his heels, and was soon at M. de Treville's; but instead of going into the saloon with the rest of the crowd, he asked to be introduced to M. de Treville's office. As d'Artagnan so constantly frequented the hotel, no difficulty was made in complying with his request, and a servant went to inform M. de Treville that his young compatriot, having something important to communicate, solicited a private audience. Five minutes after, M. de Treville was asking d'Artagnan what he could do to serve him, and what caused his visit at so late an hour.

"Pardon me, monsieur," said d'Artagnan, who had profited by the moment he had been left alone to put back M. de Treville's clock three-quarters of an hour, "but I thought, as it was yet only twenty-five minutes past nine, it was not too late to wait upon you."

"Twenty-five minutes past nine!" cried M. de Treville, looking at the clock; "why, that's impossible!"

"Look, rather, monsieur," said d'Artagnan, "the clock shows it."

"That's true," said M. de Treville; "I believed it later. But what can I do for you?"

Then d'Artagnan told M. de Treville a long history about the queen. He expressed to him the fears he entertained with respect to her Majesty; he related to him what he had heard of the projects of the cardinal with regard to Buckingham, and all with a tranquillity and candor of which M. de Treville was the more the dupe, from having himself, as we have said, observed something fresh between the cardinal, the king, and the queen.

As ten o'clock was striking, d'Artagnan left M. de Treville, who thanked him for his information, recommended him to have the service of the king and queen always at heart, and returned to the saloon; but at the foot of the stairs, d'Artagnan remembered he had forgotten his cane. He consequently sprang up again, re-entered the office, with a turn of his finger set the clock right again, that it might not be perceived the next day that it had been put wrong, and certain from that time that he had a witness to prove his alibi, he ran downstairs and soon found himself in the street.

11 In Which The Plot Thickens

His visit to M. de Treville being paid, the pensive d'Artagnan took the longest way homeward.

On what was d'Artagnan thinking, that he strayed thus from his path, gazing at the stars of heaven, and sometimes sighing, sometimes smiling?

He was thinking of Mme. Bonacieux. For an apprentice Musketeer the young woman was almost an ideal of love. Pretty, mysterious, initiated in almost all the secrets of the court, which reflected such a charming gravity over her pleasing features, it might be surmised that she was not wholly unmoved; and this is an irresistible charm to novices in love. Moreover, d'Artagnan had delivered her from the hands of the demons who wished to search and ill treat her; and this important service had established between them one of those sentiments of gratitude which so easily assume a more tender character.

D'Artagnan already fancied himself, so rapid is the flight of our dreams upon the wings of imagination, accosted by a messenger from the young woman, who brought him some billet appointing a meeting, a gold chain, or a diamond. We have observed that young cavaliers received presents from their king without shame. Let us add that in these times of lax morality they had no more delicacy with respect to the mistresses; and that the latter almost always left them valuable and durable remembrances, as if they essayed to conquer the fragility of their sentiments by the solidity of their gifts.

Without a blush, men made their way in the world by the means of women blushing. Such as were only beautiful gave their beauty, whence, without doubt, comes the proverb, "The most beautiful girl in the world can only give what she has." Such as were rich gave in addition a part of their money; and a vast number of heroes of that gallant period may be cited who would neither have won their spurs in the first place, nor their battles afterward, without the purse, more or less furnished, which their mistress fastened to the saddle bow.

D'Artagnan owned nothing. Provincial diffidence, that slight varnish, the ephemeral flower, that down of the peach, had evaporated to the winds through the little orthodox counsels which the three Musketeers gave their friend. D'Artagnan, following the strange custom of the times, considered himself at Paris as on a campaign, neither more nor less than if he had been in Flanders--Spain yonder, woman here. In each there was an enemy to contend with, and contributions to be levied.

But, we must say, at the present moment d'Artagnan was ruled by a feeling much more noble and disinterested. The mercer had said that he was rich; the young man might easily guess that with so weak a man as M. Bonacieux; and interest was almost foreign to this commencement of love, which had been the consequence of it. We say ALMOST, for the idea that a young, handsome, kind, and witty woman is at the same time rich takes nothing from the beginning of love, but on the contrary strengthens it.

There are in affluence a crowd of aristocratic cares and caprices which are highly becoming to beauty. A fine and white stocking, a silken robe, a lace kerchief, a pretty slipper on the foot, a tasty ribbon on the head do not make an ugly woman pretty, but they make a pretty woman beautiful, without reckoning the hands, which gain by all this; the hands, among women particularly, to be beautiful must be idle.

Then d'Artagnan, as the reader, from whom we have not concealed the state of his fortune, very well knows--d'Artagnan was not a millionaire; he hoped to become one someday, but the time which in his own mind he fixed upon for this happy change was still far distant. In the meanwhile, how disheartening to see the woman one loves long for those thousands of nothings which constitute a woman's happiness, and be unable to give her those thousands of nothings. At least, when the woman is rich and the lover is not, that which he cannot offer she offers to herself; and although it is generally with her husband's money that she procures herself this indulgence, the gratitude for it seldom reverts to him.

Then d'Artagnan, disposed to become the most tender of lovers, was at the same time a very devoted friend, In the midst of his amorous projects for the mercer's wife, he did not forget his friends. The pretty Mme. Bonacieux was just the woman to walk with in the Plain St. Denis or in the fair of St. Germain, in company with Athos, Porthos, and Aramis, to whom d'Artagnan had often remarked this. Then one could enjoy charming little dinners, where one touches on one side the hand of a friend, and on the other the foot of a mistress. Besides, on pressing occasions, in extreme difficulties, d'Artagnan would become the preserver of his friends.

And M. Bonacieux? whom d'Artagnan had pushed into the hands of the officers, denying him aloud although he had promised in a whisper to save him. We are compelled to admit to our readers that d'Artagnan thought nothing about him in any way; or that if he did think of him, it was only to say to himself that he was very well where he was, wherever it might be. Love is the most selfish of all the passions.

Let our readers reassure themselves. IF d'Artagnan forgets his host, or appears to forget him, under the pretense of not knowing where he has been carried, we will not forget him, and we know where he is. But for the moment, let us do as did the amorous Gascon; we will see after the worthy mercer later.

D'Artagnan, reflecting on his future amours, addressing himself to the beautiful night, and smiling at the stars, ascended the Rue Cherish-Midi, or Chase-Midi, as it was then called. As he found himself in the quarter in which Aramis lived, he took it into his head to pay his friend a visit in order to explain the motives which had led him to send Planchet with a request that he would come instantly to the mousetrap. Now, if Aramis had been at home when Planchet came to his abode, he had doubtless hastened to the Rue des Fossoyeurs, and finding nobody there but his other two companions perhaps, they would not be able to conceive what all this meant. This mystery required an explanation; at least, so d'Artagnan declared to himself.

He likewise thought this was an opportunity for talking about pretty little Mme. Bonacieux, of whom his head, if not his heart, was already full. We must never look for discretion in first love. First love is accompanied by such excessive joy that unless the joy be allowed to overflow, it will stifle you.

Paris for two hours past had been dark, and seemed a desert. Eleven o'clock sounded from all the clocks of the Faubourg St. Germain. It was delightful weather. D'Artagnan was passing along a lane on the spot where the Rue d'Assas is now situated, breathing the balmy emanations which were borne upon the wind from the Rue de Vaugirard, and which arose from the gardens refreshed by the dews of evening and the breeze of night. From a distance resounded, deadened, however, by good shutters, the songs of the tipplers, enjoying themselves in the cabarets scattered along the plain. Arrived at the end of the lane, d'Artagnan turned to the left. The house in which Aramis dwelt was situated between the Rue Cassette and the Rue Servandoni.

D'Artagnan had just passed the Rue Cassette, and already perceived the door of his friend's house, shaded by a mass of sycamores and clematis which formed a vast arch opposite the front of it, when he perceived something like a shadow issuing from the Rue Servandoni. This something was enveloped in a cloak, and d'Artagnan at first believed it was a man; but by the smallness of the form, the hesitation of the walk, and the indecision of the step, he soon discovered that it was a woman. Further, this woman, as if not certain of the house she was seeking, lifted up her eyes to look around her, stopped, went backward, and then returned again. D'Artagnan was perplexed.

"Shall I go and offer her my services?" thought he. "By her step she must be young; perhaps she is pretty. Oh, yes! But a woman who wanders in the streets at this hour only ventures out to meet her lover. If I should disturb a rendezvous, that would not be the best means of commencing an acquaintance."

Meantime the young woman continued to advance, counting the houses and windows. This was neither long nor difficult. There were but three hotels in this part of the street; and only two windows looking toward the road, one of which was in a pavilion parallel to that which Aramis occupied, the other belonging to Aramis himself.

"PARIDIEU!" said d'Artagnan to himself, to whose mind the niece of the theologian reverted, "PARDIEU, it would be droll if this belated dove should be in search of our friend's house. But on my soul, it looks so. Ah, my dear Aramis, this time I shall find you out." And d'Artagnan, making himself as small as he could, concealed himself in the darkest side of the street near a stone bench placed at the back of a niche.

The young woman continued to advance; and in addition to the lightness of her step, which had betrayed her, she emitted a little cough which denoted a sweet voice. D'Artagnan believed this cough to be a signal.

Nevertheless, whether the cough had been answered by a similar signal which had fixed the irresolution of the nocturnal seeker, or whether without this aid she saw that she had arrived at the end of her journey, she resolutely drew near to Aramis's shutter, and tapped, at three equal intervals, with her bent finger.

"This is all very fine, dear Aramis," murmured d'Artagnan. "Ah, Monsieur Hypocrite, I understand how you study theology."

The three blows were scarcely struck, when the inside blind was opened and a light appeared through the panes of the outside shutter.

"Ah, ah!" said the listener, "not through doors, but through windows! Ah, this visit was expected. We shall see the windows open, and the lady enter by escalade. Very pretty!"

But to the great astonishment of d'Artagnan, the shutter remained closed. Still more, the light which had shone for an instant disappeared, and all was again in obscurity.

D'Artagnan thought this could not last long, and continued to look with all his eyes and listen with all his ears.

He was right; at the end of some seconds two sharp taps were heard inside. The young woman in the street replied by a single tap, and the shutter was opened a little way.

It may be judged whether d'Artagnan looked or listened with avidity. Unfortunately the light had been removed into another chamber; but the eyes of the young man were accustomed to the night. Besides, the eyes of the Gascons have, as it is asserted, like those of cats, the faculty of seeing in the dark.

D'Artagnan then saw that the young woman took from her pocket a white object, which she unfolded quickly, and which took the form of a handkerchief. She made her interlocutor observe the corner of this unfolded object.

This immediately recalled to d'Artagnan's mind the handkerchief which he had found at the feet of Mme. Bonacieux, which had reminded him of that which he had dragged from under the feet of Aramis.

"What the devil could that handkerchief signify?"

Placed where he was, d'Artagnan could not perceive the face of Aramis. We say Aramis, because the young man entertained no doubt that it was his friend who held this dialogue from the interior with the lady of the exterior. Curiosity prevailed over prudence; and profiting by the preoccupation into which the sight of the handkerchief appeared to have plunged the two personages now on the scene, he stole from his hiding place, and quick as lightning, but stepping with utmost caution, he ran and placed himself close to the angle of the wall, from which his eye could pierce the interior of Aramis's room.

Upon gaining this advantage d'Artagnan was near uttering a cry of surprise; it was not Aramis who was conversing with the nocturnal visitor, it was a woman! D'Artagnan, however, could only see enough to recognize the form of her vestments, not enough to distinguish her features.

At the same instant the woman inside drew a second handkerchief from her pocket, and exchanged it for that which had just been shown to her. Then some words were spoken by the two women. At length the shutter closed. The woman who was outside the window turned round, and passed within four steps of d'Artagnan, pulling down the hood of her mantle; but the precaution was too late, d'Artagnan had already recognized Mme. Bonacieux.

Mme. Bonacieux! The suspicion that it was she had crossed the mind of d'Artagnan when she drew the handkerchief from her pocket; but what probability was there that Mme. Bonacieux, who had sent for M. Laporte in order to be reconducted to the Louvre, should be running about the streets of Paris at half past eleven at night, at the risk of being abducted a second time?

This must be, then, an affair of importance; and what is the most important affair to a woman of twenty-five! Love.

But was it on her own account, or on account of another, that she exposed herself to such hazards? This was a question the young man asked himself, whom the demon of jealousy already gnawed, being in heart neither more nor less than an accepted lover.

There was a very simple means of satisfying himself whither Mme. Bonacieux was going; that was to follow her. This method was so simple that d'Artagnan employed it quite naturally and instinctively.

But at the sight of the young man, who detached himself from the wall like a statue walking from its niche, and at the noise of the steps which she heard resound behind her, Mme. Bonacieux uttered a little cry and fled.

D'Artagnan ran after her. It was not difficult for him to overtake a woman embarrassed with her cloak. He came up with her before she had traversed a third of the street. The unfortunate woman was exhausted, not by fatigue, but by terror, and when d'Artagnan placed his hand upon her shoulder, she sank upon one knee, crying in a choking voice, "Kill me, if you please, you shall know nothing!"

D'Artagnan raised her by passing his arm round her waist; but as he felt by her weight she was on the point of fainting, he made haste to reassure her by protestations of devotedness. These protestations were nothing for Mme. Bonacieux, for such protestations may be made with the worst intentions in the world; but the voice was all. Mme. Bonacieux thought she recognized the sound of that voice; she reopened her eyes, cast a quick glance upon the man who had terrified her so, and at once perceiving it was d'Artagnan, she uttered a cry of joy, "Oh, it is you, it is you! Thank God, thank God!"

"Yes, it is I," said d'Artagnan, "it is I, whom God has sent to watch over you."

"Was it with that intention you followed me?" asked the young woman, with a coquettish smile, whose somewhat bantering character resumed its influence, and with whom all fear had disappeared from the moment in which she recognized a friend in one she had taken for an enemy.

"No," said d'Artagnan; "no, I confess it. It was chance that threw me in your way; I saw a woman knocking at the window of one of my friends."

"One of your friends?" interrupted Mme. Bonacieux.

"Without doubt; Aramis is one of my best friends."

"Aramis! Who is he?"

"Come, come, you won't tell me you don't know Aramis?"

"This is the first time I ever heard his name pronounced."

"It is the first time, then, that you ever went to that house?"

"Undoubtedly."

"And you did not know that it was inhabited by a young man?"

"No."

"By a Musketeer?"

"No, indeed!"

"It was not he, then, you came to seek?"

"Not the least in the world. Besides, you must have seen that the person to whom I spoke was a woman."

"That is true; but this woman is a friend of Aramis--"

"I know nothing of that."

"--since she lodges with him."

"That does not concern me."

"But who is she?"

"Oh, that is not my secret."

"My dear Madame Bonacieux, you are charming; but at the same time you are one of the most mysterious women."

"Do I lose by that?"

"No; you are, on the contrary, adorable."

"Give me your arm, then."

"Most willingly. And now?"

"Now escort me."

"Where?"

"Where I am going."

"But where are you going?"

"You will see, because you will leave me at the door."

"Shall I wait for you?"

"That will be useless."

"You will return alone, then?"

"Perhaps yes, perhaps no."

"But will the person who shall accompany you afterward be a man or a woman?"

"I don't know yet."

"But I will know it!"

"How so?"

"I will wait until you come out."

"In that case, adieu."

"Why so?"

"I do not want you."

"But you have claimed--"

"The aid of a gentleman, not the watchfulness of a spy."

"The word is rather hard."

"How are they called who follow others in spite of them?"

"They are indiscreet."

"The word is too mild."

"Well, madame, I perceive I must do as you wish."

"Why did you deprive yourself of the merit of doing so at once?"

"Is there no merit in repentance?"

"And do you really repent?"

"I know nothing about it myself. But what I know is that I promise to do all you wish if you allow me to accompany you where you are going."

"And you will leave me then?"

"Yes."

"Without waiting for my coming out again?"

"Yes."

"Word of honor?"

"By the faith of a gentleman. Take my arm, and let us go."

D'Artagnan offered his arm to Mme. Bonacieux, who willingly took it, half laughing, half trembling, and both gained the top of Rue de la Harpe. Arriving there, the young woman seemed to hesitate, as she had before done in the Rue Vaugirard. She seemed, however, by certain signs, to recognize a door, and approaching that door, "And now, monsieur," said she, "it is here I have business; a thousand thanks for your honorable company, which has saved me from all the dangers to which, alone I was exposed. But the moment is come to keep your word; I have reached my destination."

"And you will have nothing to fear on your return?"

"I shall have nothing to fear but robbers."

"And that is nothing?"

"What could they take from me? I have not a penny about me."

"You forget that beautiful handkerchief with the coat of arms."

"Which?"

"That which I found at your feet, and replaced in your pocket."

"Hold your tongue, imprudent man! Do you wish to destroy me?"

"You see very plainly that there is still danger for you, since a single word makes you tremble; and you confess that if that word were heard you would be ruined. Come, come, madame!" cried d'Artagnan, seizing her hands, and surveying her with an ardent glance, "come, be more generous. Confide in me. Have you not read in my eyes that there is nothing but devotion and sympathy in my heart?"

"Yes," replied Mme. Bonacieux; "therefore, ask my own secrets, and I will reveal them to you; but those of others--that is quite another thing."

"Very well," said d'Artagnan, "I shall discover them; as these secrets may have an influence over your life, these secrets must become mine."

"Beware of what you do!" cried the young woman, in a manner so serious as to make d'Artagnan start in spite of himself. "Oh, meddle in nothing which concerns me. Do not seek to assist me in that which I am accomplishing. This I ask of you in the name of the interest with which I inspire you, in the name of the service you have rendered me and which I never shall forget while I have life. Rather, place faith in what I tell you. Have no more concern about me; I exist no longer for you, any more than if you had never seen me."

"Must Aramis do as much as I, madame?" said d'Artagnan, deeply piqued.

"This is the second or third time, monsieur, that you have repeated that name, and yet I have told you that I do not know him."

"You do not know the man at whose shutter you have just knocked? Indeed, madame, you believe me too credulous!"

"Confess that it is for the sake of making me talk that you invent this story and create this personage."

"I invent nothing, madame; I create nothing. I only speak that exact truth."

"And you say that one of your friends lives in that house?"

"I say so, and I repeat it for the third time; that house is one inhabited by my friend, and that friend is Aramis."

"All this will be cleared up at a later period," murmured the young woman; "no, monsieur, be silent."

"If you could see my heart," said d'Artagnan, "you would there read so much curiosity that you would pity me and so much love that you would instantly satisfy my curiosity. We have nothing to fear from those who love us."

"You speak very suddenly of love, monsieur," said the young woman, shaking her head.

"That is because love has come suddenly upon me, and for the first time; and because I am only twenty."

The young woman looked at him furtively.

"Listen; I am already upon the scent," resumed d'Artagnan. "About three months ago I was near having a duel with Aramis concerning a handkerchief resembling the one you showed to the woman in his house--for a handkerchief marked in the same manner, I am sure."

"Monsieur," said the young woman, "you weary me very much, I assure you, with your questions."

"But you, madame, prudent as you are, think, if you were to be arrested with that handkerchief, and that handkerchief were to be seized, would you not be compromised?"

"In what way? The initials are only mine--C. B., Constance Bonacieux."

"Or Camille de Bois-Tracy."

"Silence, monsieur! Once again, silence! Ah, since the dangers I incur on my own account cannot stop you, think of those you may yourself run!"

"Me?"

"Yes; there is peril of imprisonment, risk of life in knowing me."

"Then I will not leave you."

"Monsieur!" said the young woman, supplicating him and clasping her hands together, "monsieur, in the name of heaven, by the honor of a soldier, by the courtesy of a gentleman, depart! There, there midnight sounds! That is the hour when I am expected."

"Madame," said the young man, bowing; "I can refuse nothing asked of me thus. Be content; I will depart."

"But you will not follow me; you will not watch me?"

"I will return home instantly."

"Ah, I was quite sure you were a good and brave young man," said Mme. Bonacieux, holding out her hand to him, and placing the other upon the knocker of a little door almost hidden in the wall.

D'Artagnan seized the hand held out to him, and kissed it ardently.

"Ah! I wish I had never seen you!" cried d'Artagnan, with that ingenuous roughness which women often prefer to the affectations of politeness, because it betrays the depths of the thought and proves that feeling prevails over reason.

"Well!" resumed Mme. Bonacieux, in a voice almost caressing, and pressing the hand of d'Artagnan, who had not relinquished hers, "well: I will not say as much as you do; what is lost for today may not be lost forever. Who knows, when I shall be at liberty, that I may not satisfy your curiosity?"

"And will you make the same promise to my love?" cried d'Artagnan, beside himself with joy.

"Oh, as to that, I do not engage myself. That depends upon the sentiments with which you may inspire me."

"Then today, madame--"

"Oh, today, I am no further than gratitude."

"Ah! You are too charming," said d'Artagnan, sorrowfully; "and you abuse my love."

"No, I use your generosity, that's all. But be of good cheer; with certain people, everything comes round."

"Oh, you render me the happiest of men! Do not forget this evening--do not forget that promise."

"Be satisfied. In the proper time and place I will remember everything. Now then, go, go, in the name of heaven! I was expected at sharp midnight, and I am late."

"By five minutes."

"Yes; but in certain circumstances five minutes are five ages."

"When one loves."

"Well! And who told you I had no affair with a lover?"

"It is a man, then, who expects you?" cried d'Artagnan. "A man!"

"The discussion is going to begin again!" said Mme. Bonacieux, with a half-smile which was not exempt from a tinge of impatience.

"No, no; I go, I depart! I believe in you, and I would have all the merit of my devotion, even if that devotion were stupidity. Adieu, madame, adieu!"

And as if he only felt strength to detach himself by a violent effort from the hand he held, he sprang away, running, while Mme. Bonacieux knocked, as at the shutter, three light and regular taps. When he had gained the angle of the street, he turned. The door had been opened, and shut again; the mercer's pretty wife had disappeared.

D'Artagnan pursued his way. He had given his word not to watch Mme. Bonacieux, and if his life had depended upon the spot to which she was going or upon the person who should accompany her, d'Artagnan would have returned home, since he had so promised. Five minutes later he was in the Rue des Fossoyeurs.

"Poor Athos!" said he; "he will never guess what all this means. He will have fallen asleep waiting for me, or else he will have returned home, where he will have learned that a woman had been there. A woman with Athos! After all," continued d'Artagnan, "there was certainly one with Aramis. All this is very strange; and I am curious to know how it will end."

"Badly, monsieur, badly!" replied a voice which the young man recognized as that of Planchet; for, soliloquizing aloud, as very preoccupied people do, he had entered the alley, at the end of which were the stairs which led to his chamber.

"How badly? What do you mean by that, you idiot?" asked d'Artagnan. "What has happened?"

"All sorts of misfortunes."

"What?"

"In the first place, Monsieur Athos is arrested."

"Arrested! Athos arrested! What for?"

"He was found in your lodging; they took him for you."

"And by whom was he arrested?"

"By Guards brought by the men in black whom you put to flight."

"Why did he not tell them his name? Why did he not tell them he knew nothing about this affair?"

"He took care not to do so, monsieur; on the contrary, he came up to me and said, 'It is your master that needs his liberty at this moment and not I, since he knows everything and I know nothing. They will believe he is arrested, and that will give him time; in three days I will tell them who I am, and they cannot fail to let me go.'"

"Bravo, Athos! Noble heart!" murmured d'Artagnan. "I know him well there! And what did the officers do?"

"Four conveyed him away, I don't know where--to the Bastille or Fort l'Eveque. Two remained with the men in black, who rummaged every place and took all the papers. The last two mounted guard at the door during this examination; then, when all was over, they went away, leaving the house empty and exposed."

"And Porthos and Aramis?"

"I could not find them; they did not come."

"But they may come any moment, for you left word that I awaited them?"

"Yes, monsieur."

"Well, don't budge, then; if they come, tell them what has happened. Let them wait for me at the Pomme-de-Pin. Here it would be dangerous; the house may be watched. I will run to Monsieur de Treville to tell them all this, and will meet them there."

"Very well, monsieur," said Planchet.

"But you will remain; you are not afraid?" said d'Artagnan, coming back to recommend courage to his lackey.

"Be easy, monsieur," said Planchet; "you do not know me yet. I am brave when I set about it. It is all in beginning. Besides, I am a Picard."

"Then it is understood," said d'Artagnan; "you would rather be killed than desert your post?"

"Yes, monsieur; and there is nothing I would not do to prove to Monsieur that I am attached to him."

"Good!" said d'Artagnan to himself. "It appears that the method I have adopted with this boy is decidedly the best. I shall use it again upon occasion."

And with all the swiftness of his legs, already a little fatigued however, with the perambulations of the day, d'Artagnan directed his course toward M. de Treville's.

M de Treville was not at his hotel. His company was on guard at the Louvre; he was at the Louvre with his company.

It was necessary to reach M. de Treville; it was important that he should be informed of what was passing. D'Artagnan resolved to try and enter the Louvre. His costume of Guardsman in the company of M. Dessessart ought to be his passport.

He therefore went down the Rue des Petits Augustins, and came up to the quay, in order to take the New Bridge. He had at first an idea of crossing by the ferry; but on gaining the riverside, he had mechanically put his hand into his pocket, and perceived that he had not wherewithal to pay his passage.

As he gained the top of the Rue Guenegaud, he saw two persons coming out of the Rue Dauphine whose appearance very much struck him. Of the two persons who composed this group, one was a man and the other a woman. The woman had the outline of Mme. Bonacieux; the man resembled Aramis so much as to be mistaken for him.

Besides, the woman wore that black mantle which d'Artagnan could still see outlined on the shutter of the Rue de Vaugirard and on the door of the Rue de la Harpe; still further, the man wore the uniform of a Musketeer.

The woman's hood was pulled down, and the man held a handkerchief to his face. Both, as this double precaution indicated, had an interest in not being recognized.

They took the bridge. That was d'Artagnan's road, as he was going to the Louvre. D'Artagnan followed them.

He had not gone twenty steps before he became convinced that the woman was really Mme. Bonacieux and that the man was Aramis.

He felt at that instant all the suspicions of jealousy agitating his heart. He felt himself doubly betrayed, by his friend and by her whom he already loved like a mistress. Mme. Bonacieux had declared to him, by all the gods, that she did not know Aramis; and a quarter of an hour after having made this assertion, he found her hanging on the arm of Aramis.

D'Artagnan did not reflect that he had only known the mercer's pretty wife for three hours; that she owed him nothing but a little gratitude for having delivered her from the men in black, who wished to carry her off, and that she had promised him nothing. He considered himself an outraged, betrayed, and ridiculed lover. Blood and anger mounted to his face; he was resolved to unravel the mystery.

The young man and young woman perceived they were watched, and redoubled their speed. D'Artagnan determined upon his course. He passed them, then returned so as to meet them exactly before the Samaritaine. Which was illuminated by a lamp which threw its light over all that part of the bridge.

D'Artagnan stopped before them, and they stopped before him.

"What do you want, monsieur?" demanded the Musketeer, recoiling a step, and with a foreign accent, which proved to d'Artagnan that he was deceived in one of his conjectures.

"It is not Aramis!" cried he.

"No, monsieur, it is not Aramis; and by your exclamation I perceive you have mistaken me for another, and pardon you."

"You pardon me?" cried d'Artagnan.

"Yes," replied the stranger. "Allow me, then, to pass on, since it is not with me you have anything to do."

"You are right, monsieur, it is not with you that I have anything to do; it is with Madame."

"With Madame! You do not know her," replied the stranger.

"You are deceived, monsieur; I know her very well."

"Ah," said Mme. Bonacieux; in a tone of reproach, "ah, monsieur, I had your promise as a soldier and your word as a gentleman. I hoped to be able to rely upon that."

"And I, madame!" said d'Artagnan, embarrassed; "you promised me--"

"Take my arm, madame," said the stranger, "and let us continue our way."

D'Artagnan, however, stupefied, cast down, annihilated by all that happened, stood, with crossed arms, before the Musketeer and Mme. Bonacieux.

The Musketeer advanced two steps, and pushed d'Artagnan aside with his hand. D'Artagnan made a spring backward and drew his sword. At the same time, and with the rapidity of lightning, the stranger drew his.

"In the name of heaven, my Lord!" cried Mme. Bonacieux, throwing herself between the combatants and seizing the swords with her hands.

"My Lord!" cried d'Artagnan, enlightened by a sudden idea, "my Lord! Pardon me, monsieur, but you are not--"

"My Lord the Duke of Buckingham," said Mme. Bonacieux, in an undertone; "and now you may ruin us all."

"My Lord, Madame, I ask a hundred pardons! But I love her, my Lord, and was jealous. You know what it is to love, my Lord. Pardon me, and then tell me how I can risk my life to serve your Grace?"

"You are a brave young man," said Buckingham, holding out his hand to d'Artagnan, who pressed it respectfully. "You offer me your services; with the same frankness I accept them. Follow us at a distance of twenty paces, as far as the Louvre, and if anyone watches us, slay him!"

D'Artagnan placed his naked sword under his arm, allowed the duke and Mme. Bonacieux to take twenty steps ahead, and then followed them, ready to execute the instructions of the noble and elegant minister of Charles I.

Fortunately, he had no opportunity to give the duke this proof of his devotion, and the young woman and the handsome Musketeer entered the Louvre by the wicket of the Echelle without any interference.

As for d'Artagnan, he immediately repaired to the cabaret of the Pomme-de-Pin, where he found Porthos and Aramis awaiting him. Without giving them any explanation of the alarm and inconvenience he had caused them, he told them that he had terminated the affair alone in which he had for a moment believed he should need their assistance.

Meanwhile, carried away as we are by our narrative, we must leave our three friends to themselves, and follow the Duke of Buckingham and his guide through the labyrinths of the Louvre.

12 George Villiers, Duke Of Buckingham

Mme. Bonacieux and the duke entered the Louvre without difficulty. Mme. Bonacieux was known to belong to the queen; the duke wore the uniform of the Musketeers of M. de Treville, who, as we have said, were that evening on guard. Besides, Germain was in the interests of the queen; and if anything should happen, Mme. Bonacieux would be accused of having introduced her lover into the Louvre, that was all. She took the risk upon herself. Her reputation would be lost, it is true; but of what value in the world was the reputation of the little wife of a mercer?

Once within the interior of the court, the duke and the young woman followed the wall for the space of about twenty-five steps. This space passed, Mme. Bonacieux pushed a little servants' door, open by day but generally closed at night. The door yielded. Both entered, and found themselves in darkness; but Mme. Bonacieux was acquainted with all the turnings and windings of this part of the Louvre, appropriated for the people of the household. She closed the door after her, took the duke by the hand, and after a few experimental steps, grasped a balustrade, put her foot upon the bottom step, and began to ascend the staircase. The duke counted two stories. She then turned to the right, followed the course of a long corridor, descended a flight, went a few steps farther, introduced a key into a lock, opened a door, and pushed the duke into an apartment lighted only by a lamp, saying, "Remain here, my Lord Duke; someone will come." She then went out by the same door, which she locked, so that the duke found himself literally a prisoner.

Nevertheless, isolated as he was, we must say that the Duke of Buckingham did not experience an instant of fear. One of the salient points of his character was the search for adventures and a love of romance. Brave, rash, and enterprising, this was not the first time he had risked his life in such attempts. He had learned that the pretended message from Anne of Austria, upon the faith of which he had come to Paris, was a snare; but instead of regaining England, he had, abusing the position in which he had been placed, declared to the queen that he would not depart without seeing her. The queen had at first positively refused; but at length became afraid that the duke, if exasperated, would commit some folly. She had already decided upon seeing him and urging his immediate departure, when, on the very evening of coming to this decision, Mme. Bonacieux, who was charged with going to fetch the duke and conducting him to the Louvre, was abducted. For two days no one knew what had become of her, and everything remained in suspense; but once free, and placed in communication with Laporte, matters resumed their course, and she accomplished the perilous enterprise which, but for her arrest, would have been executed three days earlier.

Buckingham, left alone, walked toward a mirror. His Musketeer's uniform became him marvelously.

At thirty-five, which was then his age, he passed, with just title, for the handsomest gentleman and the most elegant cavalier of France or England.

The favorite of two kings, immensely rich, all-powerful in a kingdom which he disordered at his fancy and calmed again at his caprice, George Villiers, Duke of Buckingham, had lived one of those fabulous existences which survive, in the course of centuries, to astonish posterity.

Sure of himself, convinced of his own power, certain that the laws which rule other men could not reach him, he went straight to the object he aimed at, even were this object were so elevated and so dazzling that it would have been madness for any other even to have contemplated it. It was thus he had succeeded in approaching several times the beautiful and proud Anne of Austria, and in making himself loved by dazzling her.

George Villiers placed himself before the glass, as we have said, restored the undulations to his beautiful hair, which the weight of his hat had disordered, twisted his mustache, and, his heart swelling with joy, happy and proud at being near the moment he had so long sighed for, he smiled upon himself with pride and hope.

At this moment a door concealed in the tapestry opened, and a woman appeared. Buckingham saw this apparition in the glass; he uttered a cry. It was the queen!

Anne of Austria was then twenty-six or twenty-seven years of age; that is to say, she was in the full splendor of her beauty.

Her carriage was that of a queen or a goddess; her eyes, which cast the brilliancy of emeralds, were perfectly beautiful, and yet were at the same time full of sweetness and majesty.

Her mouth was small and rosy; and although her underlip, like that of all princes of the House of Austria, protruded slightly beyond the other, it was eminently lovely in its smile, but as profoundly disdainful in its contempt.

Her skin was admired for its velvety softness; her hands and arms were of surpassing beauty, all the poets of the time singing them as incomparable.

Lastly, her hair, which, from being light in her youth, had become chestnut, and which she wore curled very plainly, and with much powder, admirably set off her face, in which the most rigid critic could only have desired a little less rouge, and the most fastidious sculptor a little more fineness in the nose.

Buckingham remained for a moment dazzled. Never had Anne of Austria appeared to him so beautiful, amid balls, fetes, or carousals, as she appeared to him at this moment, dressed in a simple robe of white satin, and accompanied by Donna Estafania--the only one of her Spanish women who had not been driven from her by the jealousy of the king or by the persecutions of Richelieu.

Anne of Austria took two steps forward. Buckingham threw himself at her feet, and before the queen could prevent him, kissed the hem of her robe.

"Duke, you already know that it is not I who caused you to be written to."

"Yes, yes, madame! Yes, your Majesty!" cried the duke. "I know that I must have been mad, senseless, to believe that snow would become animated or marble warm; but what then! They who love believe easily in love. Besides, I have lost nothing by this journey because I see you."

"Yes," replied Anne, "but you know why and how I see you; because, insensible to all my sufferings, you persist in remaining in a city where, by remaining, you run the risk of your life, and make me run the risk of my honor. I see you to tell you that everything separates us--the depths of the sea, the enmity of kingdoms, the sanctity of vows. It is sacrilege to struggle against so many things, my Lord. In short, I see you to tell you that we must never see each other again."

"Speak on, madame, speak on, Queen," said Buckingham; "the sweetness of your voice covers the harshness of your words. You talk of sacrilege! Why, the sacrilege is the separation of two hearts formed by God for each other."

"My Lord," cried the queen, "you forget that I have never said that I love you."

"But you have never told me that you did not love me; and truly, to speak such words to me would be, on the part of your Majesty, too great an ingratitude. For tell me, where can you find a love like mine--a love which neither time, nor absence, nor despair can extinguish, a love which contents itself with a lost ribbon, a stray look, or a chance word? It is now three years, madame, since I saw you for the first time, and during those three years I have loved you thus. Shall I tell you each ornament of your toilet? Mark! I see you now. You were seated upon cushions in the Spanish fashion; you wore a robe of green satin embroidered with gold and silver, hanging sleeves knotted upon your beautiful arms--those lovely arms--with large diamonds. You wore a close ruff, a small cap upon your head of the same color as your robe, and in that cap a heron's feather. Hold! Hold! I shut my eyes, and I can see you as you then were; I open them again, and I see what you are now--a hundred time more beautiful!"

"What folly," murmured Anne of Austria, who had not the courage to find fault with the duke for having so well preserved her portrait in his heart, "what folly to feed a useless passion with such remembrances!"

"And upon what then must I live? I have nothing but memory. It is my happiness, my treasure, my hope. Every time I see you is a fresh diamond which I enclose in the casket of my heart. This is the fourth which you have let fall and I have picked up; for in three years, madame, I have only seen you four times--the first, which I have described to you; the second, at the mansion of Madame de Chevreuse; the third, in the gardens of Amiens."

"Duke," said the queen, blushing, "never speak of that evening."

"Oh, let us speak of it; on the contrary, let us speak of it! That is the most happy and brilliant evening of my life! You remember what a beautiful night it was? How soft and perfumed was the air; how lovely the blue heavens and star-enameled sky! Ah, then, madame, I was able for one instant to be alone with you. Then you were about to tell me all--the isolation of your life, the griefs of your heart. You leaned upon my arm--upon this, madame! I felt, in bending my head toward you, your beautiful hair touch my cheek; and every time that it touched me I trembled from head to foot. Oh, Queen! Queen! You do not know what felicity from heaven, what joys from paradise, are comprised in a moment like that. Take my wealth, my fortune, my glory, all the days I have to live, for such an instant, for a night like that. For that night, madame, that night you loved me, I will swear it."

"My Lord, yes; it is possible that the influence of the place, the charm of the beautiful evening, the fascination of your look--the thousand circumstances, in short, which sometimes unite to destroy a woman--were grouped around me on that fatal evening; but, my Lord, you saw the queen come to the aid of the woman who faltered. At the first word you dared to utter, at the first freedom to which I had to reply, I called for help."

"Yes, yes, that is true. And any other love but mine would have sunk beneath this ordeal; but my love came out from it more ardent and more eternal. You believed that you would fly from me by returning to Paris; you believed that I would not dare to quit the treasure over which my master had charged me to watch. What to me were all the treasures in the world, or all the kings of the earth! Eight days after, I was back again, madame. That time you had nothing to say to me; I had risked my life and favor to see you but for a second. I did not even touch your hand, and you pardoned me on seeing me so submissive and so repentant."

"Yes, but calumny seized upon all those follies in which I took no part, as you well know, my Lord. The king, excited by the cardinal, made a terrible clamor. Madame de Vernet was driven from me, Putange was exiled, Madame de Chevreuse fell into disgrace, and when you wished to come back as ambassador to France, the king himself--remember, my lord--the king himself opposed to it."

"Yes, and France is about to pay for her king's refusal with a war. I am not allowed to see you, madame, but you shall every day hear of me. What object, think you, have this expedition to Re and this league with the Protestants of La Rochelle which I am projecting? The pleasure of seeing you. I have no hope of penetrating, sword in hand, to Paris, I know that well. But this war may bring round a peace; this peace will require a negotiator; that negotiator will be me. They will not dare to refuse me then; and I will return to Paris, and will see you again, and will be happy for an instant. Thousands of men, it is true, will have to pay for my happiness with their lives; but what is that to me, provided I see you again! All this is perhaps folly--perhaps insanity; but tell me what woman has a lover more truly in love; what queen a servant more ardent?"

"My Lord, my Lord, you invoke in your defense things which accuse you more strongly. All these proofs of love which you would give me are almost crimes."

"Because you do not love me, madame! If you loved me, you would view all this otherwise. If you loved me, oh, if you loved me, that would be too great happiness, and I should run mad. Ah, Madame de Chevreuse was less cruel than you. Holland loved her, and she responded to his love."

"Madame de Chevreuse was not queen," murmured Anne of Austria, overcome, in spite of herself, by the expression of so profound a passion.

"You would love me, then, if you were not queen! Madame, say that you would love me then! I can believe that it is the dignity of your rank alone which makes you cruel to me; I can believe that you had been Madame de Chevreuse, poor Buckingham might have hoped. Thanks for those sweet words! Oh, my beautiful sovereign, a hundred times, thanks!"

"Oh, my Lord! You have ill understood, wrongly interpreted; I did not mean to say--"

"Silence, silence!" cried the duke. "If I am happy in an error, do not have the cruelty to lift me from it. You have told me yourself, madame, that I have been drawn into a snare; I, perhaps, may leave my life in it--for, although it may be strange, I have for some time had a presentiment that I should shortly die." And the duke smiled, with a smile at once sad and charming.

"Oh, my God!" cried Anne of Austria, with an accent of terror which proved how much greater an interest she took in the duke than she ventured to tell.

"I do not tell you this, madame, to terrify you; no, it is even ridiculous for me to name it to you, and, believe me, I take no heed of such dreams. But the words you have just spoken, the hope you have almost given me, will have richly paid all--were it my life."

"Oh, but I," said Anne, "I also, duke, have had presentiments; I also have had dreams. I dreamed that I saw you lying bleeding, wounded."

"In the left side, was it not, and with a knife?" interrupted Buckingham.

"Yes, it was so, my Lord, it was so--in the left side, and with a knife. Who can possibly have told you I had had that dream? I have imparted it to no one but my God, and that in my prayers."

"I ask for no more. You love me, madame; it is enough."

"I love you, I?"

"Yes, yes. Would God send the same dreams to you as to me if you did not love me? Should we have the same presentiments if our existences did not touch at the heart? You love me, my beautiful queen, and you will weep for me?"

"Oh, my God, my God!" cried Anne of Austria, "this is more than I can bear. In the name of heaven, Duke, leave me, go! I do not know whether I love you or love you not; but what I know is that I will not be perjured. Take pity on me, then, and go! Oh, if you are struck in France, if you die in France, if I could imagine that your love for me was the cause of your death, I could not console myself; I should run mad. Depart then, depart, I implore you!"

"Oh, how beautiful you are thus! Oh, how I love you!" said Buckingham.

"Go, go, I implore you, and return hereafter! Come back as ambassador, come back as minister, come back surrounded with guards who will defend you, with servants who will watch over you, and then I shall no longer fear for your days, and I shall be happy in seeing you."

"Oh, is this true what you say?"

"Yes."

"Oh, then, some pledge of your indulgence, some object which came from you, and may remind me that I have not been dreaming; something you have worn, and that I may wear in my turn--a ring, a necklace, a chain."

"Will you depart--will you depart, if I give you that you demand?"

"Yes."

"This very instant?"

"Yes."

"You will leave France, you will return to England?"

"I will, I swear to you."

"Wait, then, wait."

Anne of Austria re-entered her apartment, and came out again almost immediately, holding a rosewood casket in her hand, with her cipher encrusted with gold.

"Here, my Lord, here," said she, "keep this in memory of me."

Buckingham took the casket, and fell a second time on his knees.

"You have promised me to go," said the queen.

"And I keep my word. Your hand, madame, your hand, and I depart!"

Anne of Austria stretched forth her hand, closing her eyes, and leaning with the other upon Estafania, for she felt that her strength was about to fail her.

Buckingham pressed his lips passionately to that beautiful hand, and then rising, said, "Within six months, if I am not dead, I shall have seen you again, madame--even if I have to overturn the world." And faithful to the promise he had made, he rushed out of the apartment.

In the corridor he met Mme. Bonacieux, who waited for him, and who, with the same precautions and the same good luck, conducted him out of the Louvre.

13 Monsieur Bonacieux

There was in all this, as may have been observed, one personage concerned, of whom, notwithstanding his precarious position, we have appeared to take but very little notice. This personage was M. Bonacieux, the respectable martyr of the political and amorous intrigues which entangled themselves so nicely together at this gallant and chivalric period.

Fortunately, the reader may remember, or may not remember--fortunately we have promised not to lose sight of him.

The officers who arrested him conducted him straight to the Bastille, where he passed trembling before a party of soldiers who were loading their muskets. Thence, introduced into a half-subterranean gallery, he became, on the part of those who had brought him, the object of the grossest insults and the harshest treatment. The officers perceived that they had not to deal with a gentleman, and they treated him like a very peasant.

At the end of half an hour or thereabouts, a clerk came to put an end to his tortures, but not to his anxiety, by giving the order to conduct M. Bonacieux to the Chamber of Examination. Ordinarily, prisoners were interrogated in their cells; but they did not do so with M. Bonacieux.

Two guards attended the mercer who made him traverse a court and enter a corridor in which were three sentinels, opened a door and pushed him unceremoniously into a low room, where the only furniture was a table, a chair, and a commissary. The commissary was seated in the chair, and was writing at the table.

The two guards led the prisoner toward the table, and upon a sign from the commissary drew back so far as to be unable to hear anything.

The commissary, who had till this time held his head down over his papers, looked up to see what sort of person he had to do with. This commissary was a man of very repulsive mien, with a pointed nose, with yellow and salient cheek bones, with eyes small but keen and penetrating, and an expression of countenance resembling at once the polecat and the fox. His head, supported by a long and flexible neck, issued from his large black robe, balancing itself with a motion very much like that of the tortoise thrusting his head out of his shell. He began by asking M. Bonacieux his name, age, condition, and abode.

The accused replied that his name was Jacques Michel Bonacieux, that he was fifty-one years old, a retired mercer, and lived Rue des Fossoyeurs, No. 14.

The commissary then, instead of continuing to interrogate him, made him a long speech upon the danger there is for an obscure citizen to meddle with public matters. He complicated this exordium by an exposition in which he painted the power and the deeds of the cardinal, that incomparable minister, that conqueror of past ministers, that example for ministers to come--deeds and power which none could thwart with impunity.

After this second part of his discourse, fixing his hawk's eye upon poor Bonacieux, he bade him reflect upon the gravity of his situation.

The reflections of the mercer were already made; he cursed the instant when M. Laporte formed the idea of marrying him to his goddaughter, and particularly the moment when that goddaughter had been received as Lady of the Linen to her Majesty.

At bottom the character of M. Bonacieux was one of profound selfishness mixed with sordid avarice, the whole seasoned with extreme cowardice. The love with which his young wife had inspired him was a secondary sentiment, and was not strong enough to contend with the primitive feelings we have just enumerated. Bonacieux indeed reflected on what had just been said to him.

"But, Monsieur Commissary," said he, calmly, "believe that I know and appreciate, more than anybody, the merit of the incomparable eminence by whom we have the honor to be governed."

"Indeed?" asked the commissary, with an air of doubt. "If that is really so, how came you in the Bastille?"

"How I came there, or rather why I am there," replied Bonacieux, "that is entirely impossible for me to tell you, because I don't know myself; but to a certainty it is not for having, knowingly at least, disobliged Monsieur the Cardinal."

"You must, nevertheless, have committed a crime, since you are here and are accused of high treason."

"Of high treason!" cried Bonacieux, terrified; "of high treason! How is it possible for a poor mercer, who detests Huguenots and who abhors Spaniards, to be accused of high treason? Consider, monsieur, the thing is absolutely impossible."

"Monsieur Bonacieux," said the commissary, looking at the accused as if his little eyes had the faculty of reading to the very depths of hearts, "you have a wife?"

"Yes, monsieur," replied the mercer, in a tremble, feeling that it was at this point affairs were likely to become perplexing; "that is to say, I HAD one."

"What, you 'had one'? What have you done with her, then, if you have her no longer?"

"They have abducted her, monsieur."

"They have abducted her? Ah!"

Bonacieux inferred from this "Ah" that the affair grew more and more intricate.

"They have abducted her," added the commissary; "and do you know the man who has committed this deed?"

"I think I know him."

"Who is he?"

"Remember that I affirm nothing, Monsieur the Commissary, and that I only suspect."

"Whom do you suspect? Come, answer freely."

M Bonacieux was in the greatest perplexity possible. Had he better deny everything or tell everything? By denying all, it might be suspected that he must know too much to avow; by confessing all he might prove his good will. He decided, then, to tell all.

"I suspect," said he, "a tall, dark man, of lofty carriage, who has the air of a great lord. He has followed us several times, as I think, when I have waited for my wife at the wicket of the Louvre to escort her home."

The commissary now appeared to experience a little uneasiness.

"And his name?" said he.

"Oh, as to his name, I know nothing about it; but if I were ever to meet him, I should recognize him in an instant, I will answer for it, were he among a thousand persons."

The face of the commissary grew still darker.

"You should recognize him among a thousand, say you?" continued he.

"That is to say," cried Bonacieux, who saw he had taken a false step, "that is to say--"

"You have answered that you should recognize him," said the commissary. "That is all very well, and enough for today; before we proceed further, someone must be informed that you know the ravisher of your wife."

"But I have not told you that I know him!" cried Bonacieux, in despair. "I told you, on the contrary--"

"Take away the prisoner," said the commissary to the two guards.

"Where must we place him?" demanded the chief.

"In a dungeon."

"Which?"

"Good Lord! In the first one handy, provided it is safe," said the commissary, with an indifference which penetrated poor Bonacieux with horror.

"Alas, alas!" said he to himself, "misfortune is over my head; my wife must have committed some frightful crime. They believe me her accomplice, and will punish me with her. She must have spoken; she must have confessed everything--a woman is so weak! A dungeon! The first he comes to! That's it! A night is soon passed; and tomorrow to the wheel, to the gallows! Oh, my God, my God, have pity on me!"

Without listening the least in the world to the lamentations of M. Bonacieux--lamentations to which, besides, they must have been pretty well accustomed--the two guards took the prisoner each by an arm, and led him away, while the commissary wrote a letter in haste and dispatched it by an officer in waiting.

Bonacieux could not close his eyes; not because his dungeon was so very disagreeable, but because his uneasiness was so great. He sat all night on his stool, starting at the least noise; and when the first rays of the sun penetrated into his chamber, the dawn itself appeared to him to have taken funereal tints.

All at once he heard his bolts drawn, and made a terrified bound. He believed they were come to conduct him to the scaffold; so that when he saw merely and simply, instead of the executioner he expected, only his commissary of the preceding evening, attended by his clerk, he was ready to embrace them both.

"Your affair has become more complicated since yesterday evening, my good man, and I advise you to tell the whole truth; for your repentance alone can remove the anger of the cardinal."

"Why, I am ready to tell everything," cried Bonacieux, "at least, all that I know. Interrogate me, I entreat you!"

"Where is your wife, in the first place?"

"Why, did not I tell you she had been stolen from me?"

"Yes, but yesterday at five o'clock in the afternoon, thanks to you, she escaped."

"My wife escaped!" cried Bonacieux. "Oh, unfortunate creature! Monsieur, if she has escaped, it is not my fault, I swear."

"What business had you, then, to go into the chamber of Monsieur d'Artagnan, your neighbor, with whom you had a long conference during the day?"

"Ah, yes, Monsieur Commissary; yes, that is true, and I confess that I was in the wrong. I did go to Monsieur d'Artagnan's."

"What was the aim of that visit?"

"To beg him to assist me in finding my wife. I believed I had a right to endeavor to find her. I was deceived, as it appears, and I ask your pardon."

"And what did Monsieur d'Artagnan reply?"

"Monsieur d'Artagnan promised me his assistance; but I soon found out that he was betraying me."

"You impose upon justice. Monsieur d'Artagnan made a compact with you; and in virtue of that compact put to flight the police who had arrested your wife, and has placed her beyond reach."

"Fortunately, Monsieur d'Artagnan is in our hands, and you shall be confronted with him."

"By my faith, I ask no better," cried Bonacieux; "I shall not be sorry to see the face of an acquaintance."

"Bring in the Monsieur d'Artagnan," said the commissary to the guards. The two guards led in Athos.

"Monsieur d'Artagnan," said the commissary, addressing Athos, "declare all that passed yesterday between you and Monsieur."

"But," cried Bonacieux, "this is not Monsieur d'Artagnan whom you show me."

"What! Not Monsieur d'Artagnan?" exclaimed the commissary.

"Not the least in the world," replied Bonacieux.

"What is this gentleman's name?" asked the commissary.

"I cannot tell you; I don't know him."

"How! You don't know him?"

"No."

"Did you never see him?"

"Yes, I have seen him, but I don't know what he calls himself."

"Your name?" replied the commissary.

"Athos," replied the Musketeer.

"But that is not a man's name; that is the name of a mountain," cried the poor questioner, who began to lose his head.

"That is my name," said Athos, quietly.

"But you said that your name was d'Artagnan."

"Who, I?"

"Yes, you."

"Somebody said to me, 'You are Monsieur d'Artagnan?' I answered, 'You think so?' My guards exclaimed that they were sure of it. I did not wish to contradict them; besides, I might be deceived."

"Monsieur, you insult the majesty of justice."

"Not at all," said Athos, calmly.

"You are Monsieur d'Artagnan."

"You see, monsieur, that you say it again."

"But I tell you, Monsieur Commissary," cried Bonacieux, in his turn, "there is not the least doubt about the matter. Monsieur d'Artagnan is my tenant, although he does not pay me my rent--and even better on that account ought I to know him. Monsieur d'Artagnan is a young man, scarcely nineteen or twenty, and this gentleman must be thirty at least. Monsieur d'Artagnan is in Monsieur Dessessart's Guards, and this gentleman is in the company of Monsieur de Treville's Musketeers. Look at his uniform, Monsieur Commissary, look at his uniform!"

"That's true," murmured the commissary; "PARDIEU, that's true."

At this moment the door was opened quickly, and a messenger, introduced by one of the gatekeepers of the Bastille, gave a letter to the commissary.

"Oh, unhappy woman!" cried the commissary.

"How? What do you say? Of whom do you speak? It is not of my wife, I hope!"

"On the contrary, it is of her. Yours is a pretty business."

"But," said the agitated mercer, "do me the pleasure, monsieur, to tell me how my own proper affair can become worse by anything my wife does while I am in prison?"

"Because that which she does is part of a plan concerted between you--of an infernal plan."

"I swear to you, Monsieur Commissary, that you are in the profoundest error, that I know nothing in the world about what my wife had to do, that I am entirely a stranger to what she has done; and that if she has committed any follies, I renounce her, I abjure her, I curse her!"

"Bah!" said Athos to the commissary, "if you have no more need of me, send me somewhere. Your Monsieur Bonacieux is very tiresome."

The commissary designated by the same gesture Athos and Bonacieux, "Let them be guarded more closely than ever."

"And yet," said Athos, with his habitual calmness, "if it be Monsieur d'Artagnan who is concerned in this matter, I do not perceive how I can take his place."

"Do as I bade you," cried the commissary, "and preserve absolute secrecy. You understand!"

Athos shrugged his shoulders, and followed his guards silently, while M. Bonacieux uttered lamentations enough to break the heart of a tiger.

They locked the mercer in the same dungeon where he had passed the night, and left him to himself during the day. Bonacieux wept all day, like a true mercer, not being at all a military man, as he himself informed us. In the evening, about nine o'clock, at the moment he had made up his mind to go to bed, he heard steps in his corridor. These steps drew near to his dungeon, the door was thrown open, and the guards appeared.

"Follow me," said an officer, who came up behind the guards.

"Follow you!" cried Bonacieux, "follow you at this hour! Where, my God?"

"Where we have orders to lead you."

"But that is not an answer."

"It is, nevertheless, the only one we can give."

"Ah, my God, my God!" murmured the poor mercer, "now, indeed, I am lost!" And he followed the guards who came for him, mechanically and without resistance.

He passed along the same corridor as before, crossed one court, then a second side of a building; at length, at the gate of the entrance court he found a carriage surrounded by four guards on horseback. They made him enter this carriage, the officer placed himself by his side, the door was locked, and they were left in a rolling prison. The carriage was put in motion as slowly as a funeral car. Through the closely fastened windows the prisoner could perceive the houses and the pavement, that was all; but, true Parisian as he was, Bonacieux could recognize every street by the milestones, the signs, and the lamps. At the moment of arriving at St. Paul--the spot where such as were condemned at the Bastille were executed--he was near fainting and crossed himself twice. He thought the carriage was about to stop there. The carriage, however, passed on.

Farther on, a still greater terror seized him on passing by the cemetery of St. Jean, where state criminals were buried. One thing, however, reassured him; he remembered that before they were buried their heads were generally cut off, and he felt that his head was still on his shoulders. But when he saw the carriage take the way to La Greve, when he perceived the pointed roof of the Hotel de Ville, and the carriage passed under the arcade, he believed it was over with him. He wished to confess to the officer, and upon his refusal, uttered such pitiable cries that the officer told him that if he continued to deafen him thus, he should put a gag in his mouth.

This measure somewhat reassured Bonacieux. If they meant to execute him at La Greve, it could scarcely be worth while to gag him, as they had nearly reached the place of execution. Indeed, the carriage crossed the fatal spot without stopping. There remained, then, no other place to fear but the Traitor's Cross; the carriage was taking the direct road to it.

This time there was no longer any doubt; it was at the Traitor's Cross that lesser criminals were executed. Bonacieux had flattered himself in believing himself worthy of St. Paul or of the Place de Greve; it was at the Traitor's Cross that his journey and his destiny were about to end! He could not yet see that dreadful cross, but he felt somehow as if it were coming to meet him. When he was within twenty paces of it, he heard a noise of people and the carriage stopped. This was more than poor Bonacieux could endure, depressed as he was by the successive emotions which he had experienced; he uttered a feeble groan which night have been taken for the last sigh of a dying man, and fainted.

14 The Man Of Meung

The crowd was caused, not by the expectation of a man to be hanged, but by the contemplation of a man who was hanged.

The carriage, which had been stopped for a minute, resumed its way, passed through the crowd, threaded the Rue St. Honore, turned into the Rue des Bons Enfants, and stopped before a low door.

The door opened; two guards received Bonacieux in their arms from the officer who supported him. They carried him through an alley, up a flight of stairs, and deposited him in an antechamber.

All these movements had been effected mechanically, as far as he was concerned. He had walked as one walks in a dream; he had a glimpse of objects as through a fog. His ears had perceived sounds without comprehending them; he might have been executed at that moment without his making a single gesture in his own defense or uttering a cry to implore mercy.

He remained on the bench, with his back leaning against the wall and his hands hanging down, exactly on the spot where the guards placed him.

On looking around him, however, as he could perceive no threatening object, as nothing indicated that he ran any real danger, as the bench was comfortably covered with a well-stuffed cushion, as the wall was ornamented with a beautiful Cordova leather, and as large red damask curtains, fastened back by gold clasps, floated before the window, he perceived by degrees that his fear was exaggerated, and he began to turn his head to the right and the left, upward and downward.

At this movement, which nobody opposed, he resumed a little courage, and ventured to draw up one leg and then the other. At length, with the help of his two hands he lifted himself from the bench, and found himself on his feet.

At this moment an officer with a pleasant face opened a door, continued to exchange some words with a person in the next chamber and then came up to the prisoner. "Is your name Bonacieux?" said he.

"Yes, Monsieur Officer," stammered the mercer, more dead than alive, "at your service."

"Come in," said the officer.

And he moved out of the way to let the mercer pass. The latter obeyed without reply, and entered the chamber, where he appeared to be expected.

It was a large cabinet, close and stifling, with the walls furnished with arms offensive and defensive, and in which there was already a fire, although it was scarcely the end of the month of September. A square table, covered with books and papers, upon which was unrolled an immense plan of the city of La Rochelle, occupied the center of the room.

Standing before the chimney was a man of middle height, of a haughty, proud mien; with piercing eyes, a large brow, and a thin face, which was made still longer by a ROYAL (or IMPERIAL, as it is now called), surmounted by a pair of mustaches. Although this man was scarcely thirty-six or thirty-seven years of age, hair, mustaches, and royal, all began to be gray. This man, except a sword, had all the appearance of a soldier; and his buff boots still slightly covered with dust, indicated that he had been on horseback in the course of the day.

This man was Armand Jean Duplessis, Cardinal de Richelieu; not such as he is now represented--broken down like an old man, suffering like a martyr, his body bent, his voice failing, buried in a large armchair as in an anticipated tomb; no longer living but by the strength of his genius, and no longer maintaining the struggle with Europe but by the eternal application of his thoughts--but such as he really was at this period; that is to say, an active and gallant cavalier, already weak of body, but sustained by that moral power which made of him one of the most extraordinary men that ever lived, preparing, after having supported the Duc de Nevers in his duchy of Mantua, after having taken Nimes, Castres, and Uzes, to drive the English from the Isle of Re and lay siege to La Rochelle.

At first sight, nothing denoted the cardinal; and it was impossible for those who did not know his face to guess in whose presence they were.

The poor mercer remained standing at the door, while the eyes of the personage we have just described were fixed upon him, and appeared to wish to penetrate even into the depths of the past.

"Is this that Bonacieux?" asked he, after a moment of silence.

"Yes, monseigneur," replied the officer.

"That's well. Give me those papers, and leave us."

The officer took from the table the papers pointed out, gave them to him who asked for them, bowed to the ground, and retired.

Bonacieux recognized in these papers his interrogatories of the Bastille. From time to time the man by the chimney raised his eyes from the writings, and plunged them like poniards into the heart of the poor mercer.

At the end of ten minutes of reading and ten seconds of examination, the cardinal was satisfied.

"That head has never conspired," murmured he, "but it matters not; we will see."

"You are accused of high treason," said the cardinal, slowly.

"So I have been told already, monseigneur," cried Bonacieux, giving his interrogator the title he had heard the officer give him, "but I swear to you that I know nothing about it."

The cardinal repressed a smile.

"You have conspired with your wife, with Madame de Chevreuse, and with my Lord Duke of Buckingham."

"Indeed, monseigneur," responded the mercer, "I have heard her pronounce all those names."

"And on what occasion?"

"She said that the Cardinal de Richelieu had drawn the Duke of Buckingham to Paris to ruin him and to ruin the queen."

"She said that?" cried the cardinal, with violence.

"Yes, monseigneur, but I told her she was wrong to talk about such things; and that his Eminence was incapable--"

"Hold your tongue! You are stupid," replied the cardinal.

"That's exactly what my wife said, monseigneur."

"Do you know who carried off your wife?"

"No, monseigneur."

"You have suspicions, nevertheless?"

"Yes, monseigneur; but these suspicions appeared to be disagreeable to Monsieur the Commissary, and I no longer have them."

"Your wife has escaped. Did you know that?"

"No, monseigneur. I learned it since I have been in prison, and that from the conversation of Monsieur the Commissary--an amiable man."

The cardinal repressed another smile.

"Then you are ignorant of what has become of your wife since her flight."

"Absolutely, monseigneur; but she has most likely returned to the Louvre."

"At one o'clock this morning she had not returned."

"My God! What can have become of her, then?"

"We shall know, be assured. Nothing is concealed from the cardinal; the cardinal knows everything."

"In that case, monseigneur, do you believe the cardinal will be so kind as to tell me what has become of my wife?"

"Perhaps he may; but you must, in the first place, reveal to the cardinal all you know of your wife's relations with Madame de Chevreuse."

"But, monseigneur, I know nothing about them; I have never seen her."

"When you went to fetch your wife from the Louvre, did you always return directly home?"

"Scarcely ever; she had business to transact with linen drapers, to whose houses I conducted her."

"And how many were there of these linen drapers?"

"Two, monseigneur."

"And where did they live?"

"One in Rue de Vaugirard, the other Rue de la Harpe."

"Did you go into these houses with her?"

"Never, monseigneur; I waited at the door."

"And what excuse did she give you for entering all alone?"

"She gave me none; she told me to wait, and I waited."

"You are a very complacent husband, my dear Monsieur Bonacieux," said the cardinal.

"He calls me his dear Monsieur," said the mercer to himself. "PESTE! Matters are going all right."

"Should you know those doors again?"

"Yes."

"Do you know the numbers?"

"Yes."

"What are they?"

"No. 25 in the Rue de Vaugirard; 75 in the Rue de la Harpe."

"That's well," said the cardinal.

At these words he took up a silver bell, and rang it; the officer entered.

"Go," said he, in a subdued voice, "and find Rochefort. Tell him to come to me immediately, if he has returned."

"The count is here," said the officer, "and requests to speak with your Eminence instantly."

"Let him come in, then!" said the cardinal, quickly.

The officer sprang out of the apartment with that alacrity which all the servants of the cardinal displayed in obeying him.

"To your Eminence!" murmured Bonacieux, rolling his eyes round in astonishment.

Five seconds has scarcely elapsed after the disappearance of the officer, when the door opened, and a new personage entered.

"It is he!" cried Bonacieux.

"He! What he?" asked the cardinal.

"The man who abducted my wife."

The cardinal rang a second time. The officer reappeared.

"Place this man in the care of his guards again, and let him wait till I send for him."

"No, monseigneur, no, it is not he!" cried Bonacieux; "no, I was deceived. This is quite another man, and does not resemble him at all. Monsieur is, I am sure, an honest man."

"Take away that fool!" said the cardinal.

The officer took Bonacieux by the arm, and led him into the antechamber, where he found his two guards.

The newly introduced personage followed Bonacieux impatiently with his eyes till he had gone out; and the moment the door closed, "They have seen each other;" said he, approaching the cardinal eagerly.

"Who?" asked his Eminence.

"He and she."

"The queen and the duke?" cried Richelieu.

"Yes."

"Where?"

"At the Louvre."

"Are you sure of it?"

"Perfectly sure."

"Who told you of it?"

"Madame de Lannoy, who is devoted to your Eminence, as you know."

"Why did she not let me know sooner?"

"Whether by chance or mistrust, the queen made Madame de Surgis sleep in her chamber, and detained her all day."

"Well, we are beaten! Now let us try to take our revenge."

"I will assist you with all my heart, monseigneur; be assured of that."

"How did it come about?"

"At half past twelve the queen was with her women--"

"Where?"

"In her bedchamber--"

"Go on."

"When someone came and brought her a handkerchief from her laundress."

"And then?"

"The queen immediately exhibited strong emotion; and despite the rouge with which her face was covered evidently turned pale--"

"And then, and then?"

"She then arose, and with altered voice, 'Ladies,' said she, 'wait for me ten minutes, I shall soon return.' She then opened the door of her alcove, and went out."

"Why did not Madame de Lannoy come and inform you instantly?"

"Nothing was certain; besides, her Majesty had said, 'Ladies, wait for me,' and she did not dare to disobey the queen."

"How long did the queen remain out of the chamber?"

"Three-quarters of an hour."

"None of her women accompanied her?"

"Only Donna Estafania."

"Did she afterward return?"

"Yes; but only to take a little rosewood casket, with her cipher upon it, and went out again immediately."

"And when she finally returned, did she bring that casket with her?"

"No."

"Does Madame de Lannoy know what was in that casket?"

"Yes; the diamond studs which his Majesty gave the queen."

"And she came back without this casket?"

"Yes."

"Madame de Lannoy, then, is of opinion that she gave them to Buckingham?"

"She is sure of it."

"How can she be so?"

"In the course of the day Madame de Lannoy, in her quality of tire-woman of the queen, looked for this casket, appeared uneasy at not finding it, and at length asked information of the queen."

"And then the queen?"

"The queen became exceedingly red, and replied that having in the evening broken one of those studs, she had sent it to her goldsmith to be repaired."

"He must be called upon, and so ascertain if the thing be true or not."

"I have just been with him."

"And the goldsmith?"

"The goldsmith has heard nothing of it."

"Well, well! Rochefort, all is not lost; and perhaps--perhaps everything is for the best."

"The fact is that I do not doubt your Eminence's genius--"

"Will repair the blunders of his agent--is that it?"

"That is exactly what I was going to say, if your Eminence had let me finish my sentence."

"Meanwhile, do you know where the Duchesse de Chevreuse and the Duke of Buckingham are now concealed?"

"No, monseigneur; my people could tell me nothing on that head."

"But I know."

"You, monseigneur?"

"Yes; or at least I guess. They were, one in the Rue de Vaugirard, No. 25; the other in the Rue de la Harpe, No. 75."

"Does your Eminence command that they both be instantly arrested?"

"It will be too late; they will be gone."

"But still, we can make sure that they are so."

"Take ten men of my Guardsmen, and search the two houses thoroughly."

"Instantly, monseigneur." And Rochefort went hastily out of the apartment.

The cardinal being left alone, reflected for an instant and then rang the bell a third time. The same officer appeared.

"Bring the prisoner in again," said the cardinal.

M Bonacieux was introduced afresh, and upon a sign from the cardinal, the officer retired.

"You have deceived me!" said the cardinal, sternly.

"I," cried Bonacieux, "I deceive your Eminence!"

"Your wife, in going to Rue de Vaugirard and Rue de la Harpe, did not go to find linen drapers."

"Then why did she go, just God?"

"She went to meet the Duchesse de Chevreuse and the Duke of Buckingham."

"Yes," cried Bonacieux, recalling all his remembrances of the circumstances, "yes, that's it. Your Eminence is right. I told my wife several times that it was surprising that linen drapers should live in such houses as those, in houses that had no signs; but she always laughed at me. Ah, monseigneur!" continued Bonacieux, throwing himself at his Eminence's feet, "ah, how truly you are the cardinal, the great cardinal, the man of genius whom all the world reveres!"

The cardinal, however contemptible might be the triumph gained over so vulgar a being as Bonacieux, did not the less enjoy it for an instant; then, almost immediately, as if a fresh thought has occurred, a smile played upon his lips, and he said, offering his hand to the mercer, "Rise, my friend, you are a worthy man."

"The cardinal has touched me with his hand! I have touched the hand of the great man!" cried Bonacieux. "The great man has called me his friend!"

"Yes, my friend, yes," said the cardinal, with that paternal tone which he sometimes knew how to assume, but which deceived none who knew him; "and as you have been unjustly suspected, well, you must be indemnified. Here, take this purse of a hundred pistoles, and pardon me."

"I pardon you, monseigneur!" said Bonacieux, hesitating to take the purse, fearing, doubtless, that this pretended gift was but a pleasantry. "But you are able to have me arrested, you are able to have me tortured, you are able to have me hanged; you are the master, and I could not have the least word to say. Pardon you, monseigneur! You cannot mean that!"

"Ah, my dear Monsieur Bonacieux, you are generous in this matter. I see it and I thank you for it. Thus, then, you will take this bag, and you will go away without being too malcontent."

"I go away enchanted."

"Farewell, then, or rather, AU REVOIR!"

And the cardinal made him a sign with his hand, to which Bonacieux replied by bowing to the ground. He then went out backward, and when he was in the antechamber the cardinal heard him, in his enthusiasm, crying aloud, "Long life to the Monseigneur! Long life to his Eminence! Long life to the great cardinal!" The cardinal listened with a smile to this vociferous manifestation of the feelings of M. Bonacieux; and then, when Bonacieux's cries were no longer audible, "Good!" said he, "that man would henceforward lay down his life for me." And the cardinal began to examine with the greatest attention the map of La Rochelle, which, as we have said, lay open on the desk, tracing with a pencil the line in which the famous dyke was to pass which, eighteen months later, shut up the port of the besieged city. As he was in the deepest of his strategic meditations, the door opened, and Rochefort returned.

"Well?" said the cardinal, eagerly, rising with a promptitude which proved the degree of importance he attached to the commission with which he had charged the count.

"Well," said the latter, "a young woman of about twenty-six or twenty-eight years of age, and a man of from thirty-five to forty, have indeed lodged at the two houses pointed out by your Eminence; but the woman left last night, and the man this morning."

"It was they!" cried the cardinal, looking at the clock; "and now it is too late to have them pursued. The duchess is at Tours, and the duke at Boulogne. It is in London they must be found."

"What are your Eminence's orders?"

"Not a word of what has passed. Let the queen remain in perfect security; let her be ignorant that we know her secret. Let her believe that we are in search of some conspiracy or other. Send me the keeper of the seals, Seguier."

"And that man, what has your Eminence done with him?"

"What man?" asked the cardinal.

"That Bonacieux."

"I have done with him all that could be done. I have made him a spy upon his wife."

The Comte de Rochefort bowed like a man who acknowledges the superiority of the master as great, and retired.

Left alone, the cardinal seated himself again and wrote a letter, which he secured with his special seal. Then he rang. The officer entered for the fourth time.

"Tell Vitray to come to me," said he, "and tell him to get ready for a journey."

An instant after, the man he asked for was before him, booted and spurred.

"Vitray," said he, "you will go with all speed to London. You must not stop an instant on the way. You will deliver this letter to Milady. Here is an order for two hundred pistoles; call upon my treasurer and get the money. You shall have as much again if you are back within six days, and have executed your commission well."

The messenger, without replying a single word, bowed, took the letter, with the order for the two hundred pistoles, and retired.

Here is what the letter contained:

MILADY, Be at the first ball at which the Duke of Buckingham shall be present. He will wear on his doublet twelve diamond studs; get as near to him as you can, and cut off two.

As soon as these studs shall be in your possession, inform me.

15 Men Of The Robe And Men Of The Sword

On the day after these events had taken place, Athos not having reappeared, M. de Treville was informed by d'Artagnan and Porthos of the circumstance. As to Aramis, he had asked for leave of absence for five days, and was gone, it was said, to Rouen on family business.

M de Treville was the father of his soldiers. The lowest or the least known of them, as soon as he assumed the uniform of the company, was as sure of his aid and support as if he had been his own brother.

He repaired, then, instantly to the office of the LIEUTENANT-CRIMINEL. The officer who commanded the post of the Red Cross was sent for, and by successive inquiries they learned that Athos was then lodged in the Fort l'Eveque.

Athos had passed through all the examinations we have seen Bonacieux undergo.

We were present at the scene in which the two captives were confronted with each other. Athos, who had till that time said nothing for fear that d'Artagnan, interrupted in his turn, should not have the time necessary, from this moment declared that his name was Athos, and not d'Artagnan. He added that he did not know either M. or Mme. Bonacieux; that he had never spoken to the one or the other; that he had come, at about ten o'clock in the evening, to pay a visit to his friend M. d'Artagnan, but that till that hour he had been at M. de Treville's, where he had dined. "Twenty witnesses," added he, "could attest the fact"; and he named several distinguished gentlemen, and among them was M. le Duc de la Tremouille.

The second commissary was as much bewildered as the first had been by the simple and firm declaration of the Musketeer, upon whom he was anxious to take the revenge which men of the robe like at all times to gain over men of the sword; but the name of M. de Treville, and that of M. de la Tremouille, commanded a little reflection.

Athos was then sent to the cardinal; but unfortunately the cardinal was at the Louvre with the king.

It was precisely at this moment that M. de Treville, on leaving the residence of the LIEUTENANT-CRIMINEL and the governor of the Fort l'Eveque without being able to find Athos, arrived at the palace.

As captain of the Musketeers, M. de Treville had the right of entry at all times.

It is well known how violent the king's prejudices were against the queen, and how carefully these prejudices were kept up by the cardinal, who in affairs of intrigue mistrusted women infinitely more than men. One of the grand causes of this prejudice was the friendship of Anne of Austria for Mme. de Chevreuse. These two women gave him more uneasiness than the war with Spain, the quarrel with England, or the embarrassment of the finances. In his eyes and to his conviction, Mme. de Chevreuse not only served the queen in her political intrigues, but, what tormented him still more, in her amorous intrigues.

At the first word the cardinal spoke of Mme. de Chevreuse--who, though exiled to Tours and believed to be in that city, had come to Paris, remained there five days, and outwitted the police--the king flew into a furious passion. Capricious and unfaithful, the king wished to be called Louis the Just and Louis the Chaste. Posterity will find a difficulty in understanding this character, which history explains only by facts and never by reason.

But when the cardinal added that not only Mme. de Chevreuse had been in Paris, but still further, that the queen had renewed with her one of those mysterious correspondences which at that time was named a CABAL; when he affirmed that he, the cardinal, was about to unravel the most closely twisted thread of this intrigue; that at the moment of arresting in the very act, with all the proofs about her, the queen's emissary to the exiled duchess, a Musketeer had dared to interrupt the course of justice violently, by falling sword in hand upon the honest men of the law, charged with investigating impartially the whole affair in order to place it before the eyes of the king--Louis XIII could not contain himself, and he made a step toward the queen's apartment with that pale and mute indignation which, when in broke out, led this prince to the commission of the most pitiless cruelty. And yet, in all this, the cardinal had not yet said a word about the Duke of Buckingham.

At this instant M. de Treville entered, cool, polite, and in irreproachable costume.

Informed of what had passed by the presence of the cardinal and the alteration in the king's countenance, M. de Treville felt himself something like Samson before the Philistines.

Louis XIII had already placed his hand on the knob of the door; at the noise of M. de Treville's entrance he turned round. "You arrive in good time, monsieur," said the king, who, when his passions were raised to a certain point, could not dissemble; "I have learned some fine things concerning your Musketeers."

"And I," said Treville, coldly, "I have some pretty things to tell your Majesty concerning these gownsmen."

"What?" said the king, with hauteur.

"I have the honor to inform your Majesty," continued M. de Treville, in the same tone, "that a party of PROCUREURS, commissaries, and men of the police--very estimable people, but very inveterate, as it appears, against the uniform--have taken upon themselves to arrest in a house, to lead away through the open street, and throw into the Fort l'Eveque, all upon an order which they have refused to show me, one of my, or rather your Musketeers, sire, of irreproachable conduct, of an almost illustrious reputation, and whom your Majesty knows favorably, Monsieur Athos."

"Athos," said the king, mechanically; "yes, certainly I know that name."

"Let your Majesty remember," said Treville, "that Monsieur Athos is the Musketeer who, in the annoying duel which you are acquainted with, had the misfortune to wound Monsieur de Cahusac so seriously. A PROPOS, monseigneur," continued Treville. Addressing the cardinal, "Monsieur de Cahusac is quite recovered, is he not?"

"Thank you," said the cardinal, biting his lips with anger.

"Athos, then, went to pay a visit to one of his friends absent at the time," continued Treville, "to a young Bearnais, a cadet in his Majesty's Guards, the company of Monsieur Dessessart, but scarcely had he arrived at his friend's and taken up a book, while waiting his return, when a mixed crowd of bailiffs and soldiers came and laid siege to the house, broke open several doors--"

The cardinal made the king a sign, which signified, "That was on account of the affair about which I spoke to you."

"We all know that," interrupted the king; "for all that was done for our service."

"Then," said Treville, "it was also for your Majesty's service that one of my Musketeers, who was innocent, has been seized, that he has been placed between two guards like a malefactor, and that this gallant man, who has ten times shed his blood in your Majesty's service and is ready to shed it again, has been paraded through the midst of an insolent populace?"

"Bah!" said the king, who began to be shaken, "was it so managed?"

"Monsieur de Treville," said the cardinal, with the greatest phlegm, "does not tell your Majesty that this innocent Musketeer, this gallant man, had only an hour before attacked, sword in hand, four commissaries of inquiry, who were delegated by myself to examine into an affair of the highest importance."

"I defy your Eminence to prove it," cried Treville, with his Gascon freedom and military frankness; "for one hour before, Monsieur Athos, who, I will confide it to your Majesty, is really a man of the highest quality, did me the honor after having dined with me to be conversing in the saloon of my hotel, with the Duc de la Tremouille and the Comte de Chalus, who happened to be there."

The king looked at the cardinal.

"A written examination attests it," said the cardinal, replying aloud to the mute interrogation of his Majesty; "and the ill-treated people have drawn up the following, which I have the honor to present to your Majesty."

"And is the written report of the gownsmen to be placed in comparison with the word of honor of a swordsman?" replied Treville haughtily.

"Come, come, Treville, hold your tongue," said the king.

"If his Eminence entertains any suspicion against one of my Musketeers," said Treville, "the justice of Monsieur the Cardinal is so well known that I demand an inquiry."

"In the house in which the judicial inquiry was made," continued the impassive cardinal, "there lodges, I believe, a young Bearnais, a friend of the Musketeer."

"Your Eminence means Monsieur d'Artagnan."

"I mean a young man whom you patronize, Monsieur de Treville."

"Yes, your Eminence, it is the same."

"Do you not suspect this young man of having given bad counsel?"

"To Athos, to a man double his age?" interrupted Treville. "No, monseigneur. Besides, d'Artagnan passed the evening with me."

"Well," said the cardinal, "everybody seems to have passed the evening with you."

"Does your Eminence doubt my word?" said Treville, with a brow flushed with anger.

"No, God forbid," said the cardinal; "only, at what hour was he with you?"

"Oh, as to that I can speak positively, your Eminence; for as he came in I remarked that it was but half past nine by the clock, although I had believed it to be later."

"At what hour did he leave your hotel?"

"At half past ten--an hour after the event."

"Well," replied the cardinal, who could not for an instant suspect the loyalty of Treville, and who felt that the victory was escaping him, "well, but Athos WAS taken in the house in the Rue des Fossoyeurs."

"Is one friend forbidden to visit another, or a Musketeer of my company to fraternize with a Guard of Dessessart's company?"

"Yes, when the house where he fraternizes is suspected."

"That house is suspected, Treville," said the king; "perhaps you did not know it?"

"Indeed, sire, I did not. The house may be suspected; but I deny that it is so in the part of it inhabited my Monsieur d'Artagnan, for I can affirm, sire, if I can believe what he says, that there does not exist a more devoted servant of your Majesty, or a more profound admirer of Monsieur the Cardinal."

"Was it not this d'Artagnan who wounded Jussac one day, in that unfortunate encounter which took place near the Convent of the Carmes-Dechausses?" asked the king, looking at the cardinal, who colored with vexation.

"And the next day, Bernajoux. Yes, sire, yes, it is the same; and your Majesty has a good memory."

"Come, how shall we decide?" said the king.

"That concerns your Majesty more than me," said the cardinal. "I should affirm the culpability."

"And I deny it," said Treville. "But his Majesty has judges, and these judges will decide."

"That is best," said the king. "Send the case before the judges; it is their business to judge, and they shall judge."

"Only," replied Treville, "it is a sad thing that in the unfortunate times in which we live, the purest life, the most incontestable virtue, cannot exempt a man from infamy and persecution. The army, I will answer for it, will be but little pleased at being exposed to rigorous treatment on account of police affairs."

The expression was imprudent; but M. de Treville launched it with knowledge of his cause. He was desirous of an explosion, because in that case the mine throws forth fire, and fire enlightens.

"Police affairs!" cried the king, taking up Treville's words, "police affairs! And what do you know about them, Monsieur? Meddle with your Musketeers, and do not annoy me in this way. It appears, according to your account, that if by mischance a Musketeer is arrested, France is in danger. What a noise about a Musketeer! I would arrest ten of them, VENTREBLEU, a hundred, even, all the company, and I would not allow a whisper."

"From the moment they are suspected by your Majesty," said Treville, "the Musketeers are guilty; therefore, you see me prepared to surrender my sword--for after having accused my soldiers, there can be no doubt that Monsieur the Cardinal will end by accusing me. It is best to constitute myself at once a prisoner with Athos, who is already arrested, and with d'Artagnan, who most probably will be."

"Gascon-headed man, will you have done?" said the king.

"Sire," replied Treville, without lowering his voice in the least, "either order my Musketeer to be restored to me, or let him be tried."

"He shall be tried," said the cardinal.

"Well, so much the better; for in that case I shall demand of his Majesty permission to plead for him."

The king feared an outbreak.

"If his Eminence," said he, "did not have personal motives--"

The cardinal saw what the king was about to say and interrupted him:

"Pardon me," said he; "but the instant your Majesty considers me a prejudiced judge, I withdraw."

"Come," said the king, "will you swear, by my father, that Athos was at your residence during the event and that he took no part in it?"

"By your glorious father, and by yourself, whom I love and venerate above all the world, I swear it."

"Be so kind as to reflect, sire," said the cardinal. "If we release the prisoner thus, we shall never know the truth."

"Athos may always be found," replied Treville, "ready to answer, when it shall please the gownsmen to interrogate him. He will not desert, Monsieur the Cardinal, be assured of that; I will answer for him."

"No, he will not desert," said the king; "he can always be found, as Treville says. Besides," added he, lowering his voice and looking with a suppliant air at the cardinal, "let us give them apparent security; that is policy."

This policy of Louis XIII made Richelieu smile.

"Order it as you please, sire; you possess the right of pardon."

"The right of pardoning only applies to the guilty," said Treville, who was determined to have the last word, "and my Musketeer is innocent. It is not mercy, then, that you are about to accord, sire, it is justice."

"And he is in the Fort l'Eveque?" said the king.

"Yes, sire, in solitary confinement, in a dungeon, like the lowest criminal."

"The devil!" murmured the king; "what must be done?"

"Sign an order for his release, and all will be said," replied the cardinal. "I believe with your Majesty that Monsieur de Treville's guarantee is more than sufficient."

Treville bowed very respectfully, with a joy that was not unmixed with fear; he would have preferred an obstinate resistance on the part of the cardinal to this sudden yielding.

The king signed the order for release, and Treville carried it away without delay. As he was about to leave the presence, the cardinal gave him a friendly smile, and said, "A perfect harmony reigns, sire, between the leaders and the soldiers of your Musketeers, which must be profitable for the service and honorable to all."

"He will play me some dog's trick or other, and that immediately," said Treville. "One has never the last word with such a man. But let us be quick--the king may change his mind in an hour; and at all events it is more difficult to replace a man in the Fort l'Eveque or the Bastille who has got out, than to keep a prisoner there who is in."

M de Treville made his entrance triumphantly into the Fort l'Eveque, whence he delivered the Musketeer, whose peaceful indifference had not for a moment abandoned him.

The first time he saw d'Artagnan, "You have come off well," said he to him; "there is your Jussac thrust paid for. There still remains that of Bernajoux, but you must not be too confident."

As to the rest, M. de Treville had good reason to mistrust the cardinal and to think that all was not over, for scarcely had the captain of the Musketeers closed the door after him, than his Eminence said to the king, "Now that we are at length by ourselves, we will, if your Majesty pleases, converse seriously. Sire, Buckingham has been in Paris five days, and only left this morning."

16 In Which M. Seguier, Keeper Of The Seals, Looks More Than Once For The Bell

It is impossible to form an idea of the impression these few words made upon Louis XIII. He grew pale and red alternately; and the cardinal saw at once that he had recovered by a single blow all the ground he had lost.

"Buckingham in Paris!" cried he, "and why does he come?"

"To conspire, no doubt, with your enemies, the Huguenots and the Spaniards."

"No, PARDIEU, no! To conspire against my honor with Madame de Chevreuse, Madame de Longueville, and the Condes."

"Oh, sire, what an idea! The queen is too virtuous; and besides, loves your Majesty too well."

"Woman is weak, Monsieur Cardinal," said the king; "and as to loving me much, I have my own opinion as to that love."

"I not the less maintain," said the cardinal, "that the Duke of Buckingham came to Paris for a project wholly political."

"And I am sure that he came for quite another purpose, Monsieur Cardinal; but if the queen be guilty, let her tremble!"

"Indeed," said the cardinal, "whatever repugnance I may have to directing my mind to such a treason, your Majesty compels me to think of it. Madame de Lannoy, whom, according to your Majesty's command, I have frequently interrogated, told me this morning that the night before last her Majesty sat up very late, that this morning she wept much, and that she was writing all day."

"That's it!" cried the king; "to him, no doubt. Cardinal, I must have the queen's papers."

"But how to take them, sire? It seems to me that it is neither your Majesty nor myself who can charge himself with such a mission."

"How did they act with regard to the Marechale d'Ancre?" cried the king, in the highest state of choler; "first her closets were thoroughly searched, and then she herself."

"The Marechale d'Ancre was no more than the Marechale d'Ancre. A Florentine adventurer, sire, and that was all; while the august spouse of your Majesty is Anne of Austria, Queen of France--that is to say, one of the greatest princesses in the world."

"She is not the less guilty, Monsieur Duke! The more she has forgotten the high position in which she was placed, the more degrading is her fall. Besides, I long ago determined to put an end to all these petty intrigues of policy and love. She has near her a certain Laporte."

"Who, I believe, is the mainspring of all this, I confess," said the cardinal.

"You think then, as I do, that she deceives me?" said the king.

"I believe, and I repeat it to your Majesty, that the queen conspires against the power of the king, but I have not said against his honor."

"And I--I tell you against both. I tell you the queen does not love me; I tell you she loves another; I tell you she loves that infamous Buckingham! Why did you not have him arrested while in Paris?"

"Arrest the Duke! Arrest the prime minister of King Charles I! Think of it, sire! What a scandal! And if the suspicions of your Majesty, which I still continue to doubt, should prove to have any foundation, what a terrible disclosure, what a fearful scandal!"

"But as he exposed himself like a vagabond or a thief, he should have been--"

Louis XIII stopped, terrified at what he was about to say, while Richelieu, stretching out his neck, waited uselessly for the word which had died on the lips of the king.

"He should have been--?"

"Nothing," said the king, "nothing. But all the time he was in Paris, you, of course, did not lose sight of him?"

"No, sire."

"Where did he lodge?"

"Rue de la Harpe. No. 75."

"Where is that?"

"By the side of the Luxembourg."

"And you are certain that the queen and he did not see each other?"

"I believe the queen to have too high a sense of her duty, sire."

"But they have corresponded; it is to him that the queen has been writing all the day. Monsieur Duke, I must have those letters!"

"Sire, notwithstanding--"

"Monsieur Duke, at whatever price it may be, I will have them."

"I would, however, beg your Majesty to observe--"

"Do you, then, also join in betraying me, Monsieur Cardinal, by thus always opposing my will? Are you also in accord with Spain and England, with Madame de Chevreuse and the queen?"

"Sire," replied the cardinal, sighing, "I believed myself secure from such a suspicion."

"Monsieur Cardinal, you have heard me; I will have those letters."

"There is but one way."

"What is that?"

"That would be to charge Monsieur de Seguier, the keeper of the seals, with this mission. The matter enters completely into the duties of the post."

"Let him be sent for instantly."

"He is most likely at my hotel. I requested him to call, and when I came to the Louvre I left orders if he came, to desire him to wait."

"Let him be sent for instantly."

"Your Majesty's orders shall be executed; but--"

"But what?"

"But the queen will perhaps refuse to obey."

"My orders?"

"Yes, if she is ignorant that these orders come from the king."

"Well, that she may have no doubt on that head, I will go and inform her myself."

"Your Majesty will not forget that I have done everything in my power to prevent a rupture."

"Yes, Duke, yes, I know you are very indulgent toward the queen, too indulgent, perhaps; we shall have occasion, I warn you, at some future period to speak of that."

"Whenever it shall please your Majesty; but I shall be always happy and proud, sire, to sacrifice myself to the harmony which I desire to see reign between you and the Queen of France."

"Very well, Cardinal, very well; but, meantime, send for Monsieur the Keeper of the Seals. I will go to the queen."

And Louis XIII, opening the door of communication, passed into the corridor which led from his apartments to those of Anne of Austria.

The queen was in the midst of her women--Mme. de Guitaut, Mme. de Sable, Mme. de Montbazon, and Mme. de Guemene. In a corner was the Spanish companion, Donna Estafania, who had followed her from Madrid. Mme. Guemene was reading aloud, and everybody was listening to her with attention with the exception of the queen, who had, on the contrary, desired this reading in order that she might be able, while feigning to listen, to pursue the thread of her own thoughts.

These thoughts, gilded as they were by a last reflection of love, were not the less sad. Anne of Austria, deprived of the confidence of her husband, pursued by the hatred of the cardinal, who could not pardon her for having repulsed a more tender feeling, having before her eyes the example of the queen-mother whom that hatred had tormented all her life--though Marie de Medicis, if the memoirs of the time are to be believed, had begun by according to the cardinal that sentiment which Anne of Austria always refused him--Anne of Austria had seen her most devoted servants fall around her, her most intimate confidants, her dearest favorites. Like those unfortunate persons endowed with a fatal gift, she brought misfortune upon everything she touched. Her friendship was a fatal sign which called down persecution. Mme. de Chevreuse and Mme. de Bernet were exiled, and Laporte did not conceal from his mistress that he expected to be arrested every instant.

It was at the moment when she was plunged in the deepest and darkest of these reflections that the door of the chamber opened, and the king entered.

The reader hushed herself instantly. All the ladies rose, and there was a profound silence. As to the king, he made no demonstration of politeness, only stopping before the queen. "Madame," said he, "you are about to receive a visit from the chancellor, who will communicate certain matters to you with which I have charged him."

The unfortunate queen, who was constantly threatened with divorce, exile, and trial even, turned pale under her rouge, and could not refrain from saying, "But why this visit, sire? What can the chancellor have to say to me that your Majesty could not say yourself?"

The king turned upon his heel without reply, and almost at the same instant the captain of the Guards, M. de Guitant, announced the visit of the chancellor.

When the chancellor appeared, the king had already gone out by another door.

The chancellor entered, half smiling, half blushing. As we shall probably meet with him again in the course of our history, it may be well for our readers to be made at once acquainted with him.

This chancellor was a pleasant man. He was Des Roches le Masle, canon of Notre Dame, who had formerly been valet of a bishop, who introduced him to his Eminence as a perfectly devout man. The cardinal trusted him, and therein found his advantage.

There are many stories related of him, and among them this. After a wild youth, he had retired into a convent, there to expiate, at least for some time, the follies of adolescence. On entering this holy place, the poor penitent was unable to shut the door so close as to prevent the passions he fled from entering with him. He was incessantly attacked by them, and the superior, to whom he had confided this misfortune, wishing as much as in him lay to free him from them, had advised him, in order to conjure away the tempting demon, to have recourse to the bell rope, and ring with all his might. At the denunciating sound, the monks would be rendered aware that temptation was besieging a brother, and all the community would go to prayers.

This advice appeared good to the future chancellor. He conjured the evil spirit with abundance of prayers offered up by the monks. But the devil does not suffer himself to be easily dispossessed from a place in which he has fixed his garrison. In proportion as they redoubled the exorcisms he redoubled the temptations; so that day and night the bell was ringing full swing, announcing the extreme desire for mortification which the penitent experienced.

The monks had no longer an instant of repose. By day they did nothing but ascend and descend the steps which led to the chapel; at night, in addition to complines and matins, they were further obliged to leap twenty times out of their beds and prostrate themselves on the floor of their cells.

It is not known whether it was the devil who gave way, or the monks who grew tired; but within three months the penitent reappeared in the world with the reputation of being the most terrible POSSESSED that ever existed.

On leaving the convent he entered into the magistracy, became president on the place of his uncle, embraced the cardinal's party, which did not prove want of sagacity, became chancellor, served his Eminence with zeal in his hatred against the queen-mother and his vengeance against Anne of Austria, stimulated the judges in the affair of Calais, encouraged the attempts of M. de Laffemas, chief gamekeeper of France; then, at length, invested with the entire confidence of the cardinal--a confidence which he had so well earned--he received the singular commission for the execution of which he presented himself in the queen's apartments.

The queen was still standing when he entered; but scarcely had she perceived him then she reseated herself in her armchair, and made a sign to her women to resume their cushions and stools, and with an air of supreme hauteur, said, "What do you desire, monsieur, and with what object do you present yourself here?"

"To make, madame, in the name of the king, and without prejudice to the respect which I have the honor to owe to your Majesty a close examination into all your papers."

"How, monsieur, an investigation of my papers--mine! Truly, this is an indignity!"

"Be kind enough to pardon me, madame; but in this circumstance I am but the instrument which the king employs. Has not his Majesty just left you, and has he not himself asked you to prepare for this visit?"

"Search, then, monsieur! I am a criminal, as it appears. Estafania, give up the keys of my drawers and my desks."

For form's sake the chancellor paid a visit to the pieces of furniture named; but he well knew that it was not in a piece of furniture that the queen would place the important letter she had written that day.

When the chancellor had opened and shut twenty times the drawers of the secretaries, it became necessary, whatever hesitation he might experience--it became necessary, I say, to come to the conclusion of the affair; that is to say, to search the queen herself. The chancellor advanced, therefore, toward Anne of Austria, and said with a very perplexed and embarrassed air, "And now it remains for me to make the principal examination."

"What is that?" asked the queen, who did not understand, or rather was not willing to understand.

"His majesty is certain that a letter has been written by you during the day; he knows that it has not yet been sent to its address. This letter is not in your table nor in your secretary; and yet this letter must be somewhere."

"Would you dare to lift your hand to your queen?" said Anne of Austria, drawing herself up to her full height, and fixing her eyes upon the chancellor with an expression almost threatening.

"I am a faithful subject of the king, madame, and all that his Majesty commands I shall do."

"Well, it is true!" said Anne of Austria; "and the spies of the cardinal have served him faithfully. I have written a letter today; that letter is not yet gone. The letter is here." And the queen laid her beautiful hand on her bosom.

"Then give me that letter, madame," said the chancellor.

"I will give it to none but the king monsieur," said Anne.

"If the king had desired that the letter should be given to him, madame, he would have demanded it of you himself. But I repeat to you, I am charged with reclaiming it; and if you do not give it up--"

"Well?"

"He has, then, charged me to take it from you."

"How! What do you say?"

"That my orders go far, madame; and that I am authorized to seek for the suspected paper, even on the person of your Majesty."

"What horror!" cried the queen.

"Be kind enough, then, madame, to act more compliantly."

"The conduct is infamously violent! Do you know that, monsieur?"

"The king commands it, madame; excuse me."

"I will not suffer it! No, no, I would rather die!" cried the queen, in whom the imperious blood of Spain and Austria began to rise.

The chancellor made a profound reverence. Then, with the intention quite patent of not drawing back a foot from the accomplishment of the commission with which he was charged, and as the attendant of an executioner might have done in the chamber of torture, he approached Anne of Austria, for whose eyes at the same instant sprang tears of rage.

The queen was, as we have said, of great beauty. The commission might well be called delicate; and the king had reached, in his jealousy of Buckingham, the point of not being jealous of anyone else.

Without doubt the chancellor, Seguier looked about at that moment for the rope of the famous bell; but not finding it he summoned his resolution, and stretched forth his hands toward the place where the queen had acknowledged the paper was to be found.

Anne of Austria took one step backward, became so pale that it might be said she was dying, and leaning with her left hand upon a table behind her to keep herself from falling, she with her right hand drew the paper from her bosom and held it out to the keeper of the seals.

"There, monsieur, there is that letter!" cried the queen, with a broken and trembling voice; "take it, and deliver me from your odious presence."

The chancellor, who, on his part, trembled with an emotion easily to be conceived, took the letter, bowed to the ground, and retired. The door was scarcely closed upon him, when the queen sank, half fainting, into the arms of her women.

The chancellor carried the letter to the king without having read a single word of it. The king took it with a trembling hand, looked for the address, which was wanting, became very pale, opened it slowly, then seeing by the first words that it was addressed to the King of Spain, he read it rapidly.

It was nothing but a plan of attack against the cardinal. The queen pressed her brother and the Emperor of Austria to appear to be wounded, as they really were, by the policy of Richelieu--the eternal object of which was the abasement of the house of Austria--to declare war against France, and as a condition of peace, to insist upon the dismissal of the cardinal; but as to love, there was not a single word about it in all the letter.

The king, quite delighted, inquired if the cardinal was still at the Louvre; he was told that his Eminence awaited the orders of his Majesty in the business cabinet.

The king went straight to him.

"There, Duke," said he, "you were right and I was wrong. The whole intrigue is political, and there is not the least question of love in this letter; but, on the other hand, there is abundant question of you."

The cardinal took the letter, and read it with the greatest attention; then, when he had arrived at the end of it, he read it a second time. "Well, your Majesty," said he, "you see how far my enemies go; they menace you with two wars if you do not dismiss me. In your place, in truth, sire, I should yield to such powerful instance; and on my part, it would be a real happiness to withdraw from public affairs."

"What say you, Duke?"

"I say, sire, that my health is sinking under these excessive struggles and these never-ending labors. I say that according to all probability I shall not be able to undergo the fatigues of the siege of La Rochelle, and that it would be far better that you should appoint there either Monsieur de Conde, Monsieur de Bassopierre, or some valiant gentleman whose business is war, and not me, who am a churchman, and who am constantly turned aside for my real vocation to look after matters for which I have no aptitude. You would be the happier for it at home, sire, and I do not doubt you would be the greater for it abroad."

"Monsieur Duke," said the king, "I understand you. Be satisfied, all who are named in that letter shall be punished as they deserve, even the queen herself."

"What do you say, sire? God forbid that the queen should suffer the least inconvenience or uneasiness on my account! She has always believed me, sire, to be her enemy; although your Majesty can bear witness that I have always taken her part warmly, even against you. Oh, if she betrayed your Majesty on the side of your honor, it would be quite another thing, and I should be the first to say, 'No grace, sire--no grace for the guilty!' Happily, there is nothing of the kind, and your Majesty has just acquired a new proof of it."

"That is true, Monsieur Cardinal," said the king, "and you were right, as you always are; but the queen, not the less, deserves all my anger."

"It is you, sire, who have now incurred hers. And even if she were to be seriously offended, I could well understand it; your Majesty has treated her with a severity--"

"It is thus I will always treat my enemies and yours, Duke, however high they may be placed, and whatever peril I may incur in acting severely toward them."

"The queen is my enemy, but is not yours, sire; on the contrary, she is a devoted, submissive, and irreproachable wife. Allow me, then, sire, to intercede for her with your Majesty."

"Let her humble herself, then, and come to me first."

"On the contrary, sire, set the example. You have committed the first wrong, since it was you who suspected the queen."

"What! I make the first advances?" said the king. "Never!"

"Sire, I entreat you to do so."

"Besides, in what manner can I make advances first?"

"By doing a thing which you know will be agreeable to her."

"What is that?"

"Give a ball; you know how much the queen loves dancing. I will answer for it, her resentment will not hold out against such an attention."

"Monsieur Cardinal, you know that I do not like worldly pleasures."

"The queen will only be the more grateful to you, as she knows your antipathy for that amusement; besides, it will be an opportunity for her to wear those beautiful diamonds which you gave her recently on her birthday and with which she has since had no occasion to adorn herself."

"We shall see, Monsieur Cardinal, we shall see," said the king, who, in his joy at finding the queen guilty of a crime which he cared little about, and innocent of a fault of which he had great dread, was ready to make up all differences with her, "we shall see, but upon my honor, you are too indulgent toward her."

"Sire," said the cardinal, "leave severity to your ministers. Clemency is a royal virtue; employ it, and you will find that you derive advantage therein."

Thereupon the cardinal, hearing the clock strike eleven, bowed low, asking permission of the king to retire, and supplicating him to come to a good understanding with the queen.

Anne of Austria, who, in consequence of the seizure of her letter, expected reproaches, was much astonished the next day to see the king make some attempts at reconciliation with her. Her first movement was repellent. Her womanly pride and her queenly dignity had both been so cruelly offended that she could not come round at the first advance; but, overpersuaded by the advice of her women, she at last had the appearance of beginning to forget. The king took advantage of this favorable moment to tell her that her had the intention of shortly giving a fete.

A fete was so rare a thing for poor Anne of Austria that at this announcement, as the cardinal had predicted, the last trace of her resentment disappeared, if not from her heart at least from her countenance. She asked upon what day this fete would take place, but the king replied that he must consult the cardinal upon that head.

Indeed, every day the king asked the cardinal when this fete should take place; and every day the cardinal, under some pretext, deferred fixing it. Ten days passed away thus.

On the eighth day after the scene we have described, the cardinal received a letter with the

London stamp which only contained these lines: "I have them; but I am unable to leave London for want of money. Send me five hundred pistoles, and four or five days after I have received them I shall be in Paris."

On the same day the cardinal received this letter the king put his customary question to him.

Richelieu counted on his fingers, and said to himself, "She will arrive, she says, four or five days after having received the money. It will require four or five days for the transmission of the money, four or five days for her to return; that makes ten days. Now, allowing for contrary winds, accidents, and a woman's weakness, there are twelve days."

"Well, Monsieur Duke," said the king, "have you made your calculations?"

"Yes, sire. Today is the twentieth of September. The aldermen of the city give a fete on the third of October. That will fall in wonderfully well; you will not appear to have gone out of your way to please the queen."

Then the cardinal added, "A PROPOS, sire, do not forget to tell her Majesty the evening before the fete that you should like to see how her diamond studs become her."

17 Bonacieux At Home

It was the second time the cardinal had mentioned these diamond studs to the king. Louis XIII was struck with this insistence, and began to fancy that this recommendation concealed some mystery.

More than once the king had been humiliated by the cardinal, whose police, without having yet attained the perfection of the modern police, were excellent, being better informed than himself, even upon what was going on in his own household. He hoped, then, in a conversation with Anne of Austria, to obtain some information from that conversation, and afterward to come upon his Eminence with some secret which the cardinal either knew or did not know, but which, in either case, would raise him infinitely in the eyes of his minister.

He went then to the queen, and according to custom accosted her with fresh menaces against those who surrounded her. Anne of Austria lowered her head, allowed the torrent to flow on without replying, hoping that it would cease of itself; but this was not what Louis XIII meant. Louis XIII wanted a discussion from which some light or other might break, convinced as he was that the cardinal had some afterthought and was preparing for him one of those terrible surprises which his Eminence was so skillful in getting up. He arrived at this end by his persistence in accusation.

"But," cried Anne of Austria, tired of these vague attacks, "but, sire, you do not tell me all that you have in your heart. What have I done, then? Let me know what crime I have committed. It is impossible that your Majesty can make all this ado about a letter written to my brother."

The king, attacked in a manner so direct, did not know what to answer; and he thought that this was the moment for expressing the desire which he was not going to have made until the evening before the fete.

"Madame," said he, with dignity, "there will shortly be a ball at the Hotel de Ville. I wish, in order to honor our worthy aldermen, you should appear in ceremonial costume, and above all, ornamented with the diamond studs which I gave you on your birthday. That is my answer."

The answer was terrible. Anne of Austria believed that Louis XIII knew all, and that the cardinal had persuaded him to employ this long dissimulation of seven or eight days, which, likewise, was characteristic. She became excessively pale, leaned her beautiful hand upon a CONSOLE, which hand appeared then like one of wax, and looking at the king with terror in her eyes, she was unable to reply by a single syllable.

"You hear, madame," said the king, who enjoyed the embarrassment to its full extent, but without guessing the cause. "You hear, madame?"

"Yes, sire, I hear," stammered the queen.

"You will appear at this ball?"

"Yes."

"With those studs?"

"Yes."

The queen's paleness, if possible, increased; the king perceived it, and enjoyed it with that cold cruelty which was one of the worst sides of his character.

"Then that is agreed," said the king, "and that is all I had to say to you."

"But on what day will this ball take place?" asked Anne of Austria.

Louis XIII felt instinctively that he ought not to reply to this question, the queen having put it in an almost dying voice.

"Oh, very shortly, madame," said he; "but I do not precisely recollect the date of the day. I will ask the cardinal."

"It was the cardinal, then, who informed you of this fete?"

"Yes, madame," replied the astonished king; "but why do you ask that?"

"It was he who told you to invite me to appear with these studs?"

"That is to say, madame--"

"It was he, sire, it was he!"

"Well, and what does it signify whether it was he or I? Is there any crime in this request?"

"No, sire."

"Then you will appear?"

"Yes, sire."

"That is well," said the king, retiring, "that is well; I count upon it."

The queen made a curtsy, less from etiquette than because her knees were sinking under her. The king went away enchanted.

"I am lost," murmured the queen, "lost!--for the cardinal knows all, and it is he who urges on the king, who as yet knows nothing but will soon know everything. I am lost! My God, my God, my God!"

She knelt upon a cushion and prayed, with her head buried between her palpitating arms.

In fact, her position was terrible. Buckingham had returned to London; Mme. Chevreuse was at Tours. More closely watched than ever, the queen felt certain, without knowing how to tell which, that one of her women had betrayed her. Laporte could not leave the Louvre; she had not a soul in the world in whom she could confide. Thus, while contemplating the misfortune which threatened her and the abandonment in which she was left, she broke out into sobs and tears.

"Can I be of service to your Majesty?" said all at once a voice full of sweetness and pity.

The queen turned sharply round, for there could be no deception in the expression of that voice; it was a friend who spoke thus.

In fact, at one of the doors which opened into the queen's apartment appeared the pretty Mme. Bonacieux. She had been engaged in arranging the dresses and linen in a closet when the king entered; she could not get out and had heard all.

The queen uttered a piercing cry at finding herself surprised--for in her trouble she did not at first recognize the young woman who had been given to her by Laporte.

"Oh, fear nothing, madame!" said the young woman, clasping her hands and weeping herself at the queen's sorrows; "I am your Majesty's, body and soul, and however far I may be from you, however inferior may be my position, I believe I have discovered a means of extricating your Majesty from your trouble."

"You, oh, heaven, you!" cried the queen; "but look me in the face. I am betrayed on all sides. Can I trust in you?"

"Oh, madame!" cried the young woman, falling on her knees; "upon my soul, I am ready to die for your Majesty!"

This expression sprang from the very bottom of the heart, and, like the first, there was no mistaking it.

"Yes," continued Mme. Bonacieux, "yes, there are traitors here; but by the holy name of the Virgin, I swear that no one is more devoted to your Majesty than I am. Those studs which the king speaks of, you gave them to the Duke of Buckingham, did you not? Those studs were enclosed in a little rosewood box which he held under his arm? Am I deceived? Is it not so, madame?"

"Oh, my God, my God!" murmured the queen, whose teeth chattered with fright.

"Well, those studs," continued Mme. Bonacieux, "we must have them back again."

"Yes, without doubt, it is necessary," cried the queen; "but how am I to act? How can it be effected?"

"Someone must be sent to the duke."

"But who, who? In whom can I trust?"

"Place confidence in me, madame; do me that honor, my queen, and I will find a messenger."

"But I must write."

"Oh, yes; that is indispensable. Two words from the hand of your Majesty and your private seal."

"But these two words would bring about my condemnation, divorce, exile!"

"Yes, if they fell into infamous hands. But I will answer for these two words being delivered to their address."

"Oh, my God! I must then place my life, my honor, my reputation, in your hands?"

"Yes, yes, madame, you must; and I will save them all."

"But how? Tell me at least the means."

"My husband had been at liberty these two or three days. I have not yet had time to see him again. He is a worthy, honest man who entertains neither love nor hatred for anybody. He will do anything I wish. He will set out upon receiving an order from me, without knowing what he carries, and he will carry your Majesty's letter, without even knowing it is from your Majesty, to the address which is on it."

The queen took the two hands of the young woman with a burst of emotion, gazed at her as if to read her very heart, and seeing nothing but sincerity in her beautiful eyes, embraced her tenderly.

"Do that," cried she, "and you will have saved my life, you will have saved my honor!"

"Do not exaggerate the service I have the happiness to render your Majesty. I have nothing to save for your Majesty; you are only the victim of perfidious plots."

"That is true, that is true, my child," said the queen, "you are right."

"Give me then, that letter, madame; time presses."

The queen ran to a little table, on which were ink, paper, and pens. She wrote two lines, sealed the letter with her private seal, and gave it to Mme. Bonacieux.

"And now," said the queen, "we are forgetting one very necessary thing."

"What is that, madame?"

"Money."

Mme. Bonacieux blushed.

"Yes, that is true," said she, "and I will confess to your Majesty that my husband--"

"Your husband has none. Is that what you would say?"

"He has some, but he is very avaricious; that is his fault. Nevertheless, let not your Majesty be uneasy, we will find means."

"And I have none, either," said the queen. Those who have read the MEMOIRS of Mme. de Motteville will not be astonished at this reply. "But wait a minute."

Anne of Austria ran to her jewel case.

"Here," said she, "here is a ring of great value, as I have been assured. It came from my brother, the King of Spain. It is mine, and I am at liberty to dispose of it. Take this ring; raise money with it, and let your husband set out."

"In an hour you shall be obeyed."

"You see the address," said the queen, speaking so low that Mme. Bonacieux could hardly hear what she said, "To my Lord Duke of Buckingham, London."

"The letter shall be given to himself."

"Generous girl!" cried Anne of Austria.

Mme. Bonacieux kissed the hands of the queen, concealed the paper in the bosom of her dress, and disappeared with the lightness of a bird.

Ten minutes afterward she was at home. As she told the queen, she had not seen her husband since his liberation; she was ignorant of the change that had taken place in him with respect to the cardinal--a change which had since been strengthened by two or three visits from the Comte de Rochefort, who had become the best friend of Bonacieux, and had persuaded him, without much trouble, was putting his house in order, the furniture of which he had found mostly broken and his closets nearly empty--justice not being one of the three things which King Solomon names as leaving no traces of their passage. As to the servant, she had run away at the moment of her master's arrest. Terror had had such an effect upon the poor girl that she had never ceased walking from Paris till she reached Burgundy, her native place.

The worthy mercer had, immediately upon reentering his house, informed his wife of his happy return, and his wife had replied by congratulating him, and telling him that the first moment she could steal from her duties should be devoted to paying him a visit.

This first moment had been delayed five days, which, under any other circumstances, might have appeared rather long to M. Bonacieux; but he had, in the visit he had made to the cardinal and in the visits Rochefort had made him, ample subjects for reflection, and as everybody knows, nothing makes time pass more quickly than reflection.

This was the more so because Bonacieux's reflections were all rose-colored. Rochefort called him his friend, his dear Bonacieux, and never ceased telling him that the cardinal had a great respect for him. The mercer fancied himself already on the high road to honors and fortune.

On her side Mme. Bonacieux had also reflected; but, it must be admitted, upon something widely different from ambition. In spite of herself her thoughts constantly reverted to that handsome young man who was so brave and appeared to be so much in love. Married at eighteen to M. Bonacieux, having always lived among her husband's friends--people little capable of inspiring any sentiment whatever in a young woman whose heart was above her position--Mme. Bonacieux had remained insensible to vulgar seductions; but at this period the title of gentleman had great influence with the citizen class, and d'Artagnan was a gentleman. Besides, he wore the uniform of the Guards, which next to that of the Musketeers was most admired by the ladies. He was, we repeat, handsome, young, and bold; he spoke of love like a man who did love and was anxious to be loved in return. There was certainly enough in all this to turn a head only twenty-three years old, and Mme. Bonacieux had just attained that happy period of life.

The couple, then, although they had not seen each other for eight days, and during that time serious events had taken place in which both were concerned, accosted each other with a degree of preoccupation. Nevertheless, Bonacieux manifested real joy, and advanced toward his wife with open arms. Madame Bonacieux presented her cheek to him.

"Let us talk a little," said she.

"How!" said Bonacieux, astonished.

"Yes, I have something of the highest importance to tell you."

"True," said he, "and I have some questions sufficiently serious to put to you. Describe to me your abduction, I pray you."

"Oh, that's of no consequence just now," said Mme. Bonacieux.

"And what does it concern, then--my captivity?"

"I heard of it the day it happened; but as you were not guilty of any crime, as you were not guilty of any intrigue, as you, in short, knew nothing that could compromise yourself or anybody else, I attached no more importance to that event than it merited."

"You speak very much at your ease, madame," said Bonacieux, hurt at the little interest his wife showed in him. "Do you know that I was plunged during a day and night in a dungeon of the Bastille?"

"Oh, a day and night soon pass away. Let us return to the object that brings me here."

"What, that which brings you home to me? Is it not the desire of seeing a husband again from whom you have been separated for a week?" asked the mercer, piqued to the quick.

"Yes, that first, and other things afterward."

"Speak."

"It is a thing of the highest interest, and upon which our future fortune perhaps depends."

"The complexion of our fortune has changed very much since I saw you, Madam Bonacieux, and I should not be astonished if in the course of a few months it were to excite the envy of many folks."

"Yes, particularly if you follow the instructions I am about to give you."

"Me?"

"Yes, you. There is good and holy action to be performed, monsieur, and much money to be gained at the same time."

Mme. Bonacieux knew that in talking of money to her husband, she took him on his weak side. But a man, were he even a mercer, when he had talked for ten minutes with Cardinal Richelieu, is no longer the same man.

"Much money to be gained?" said Bonacieux, protruding his lip.

"Yes, much."

"About how much?"

"A thousand pistoles, perhaps."

"What you demand of me is serious, then?"

"It is indeed."

"What must be done?"

"You must go away immediately. I will give you a paper which you must not part with on any account, and which you will deliver into the proper hands."

"And whither am I to go?"

"To London."

"I go to London? Go to! You jest! I have no business in London."

"But others wish that you should go there."

"But who are those others? I warn you that I will never again work in the dark, and that I will know not only to what I expose myself, but for whom I expose myself."

"An illustrious person sends you; an illustrious person awaits you. The recompense will exceed your expectations; that is all I promise you."

"More intrigues! Nothing but intrigues! Thank you, madame, I am aware of them now; Monsieur Cardinal has enlightened me on that head."

"The cardinal?" cried Mme. Bonacieux. "Have you seen the cardinal?"

"He sent for me," answered the mercer, proudly.

"And you responded to his bidding, you imprudent man?"

"Well, I can't say I had much choice of going or not going, for I was taken to him between two guards. It is true also, that as I did not then know his Eminence, if I had been able to dispense with the visit, I should have been enchanted."

"He ill-treated you, then; he threatened you?"

"He gave me his hand, and called me his friend. His friend! Do you hear that, madame? I am the friend of the great cardinal!"

"Of the great cardinal!"

"Perhaps you would contest his right to that title, madame?"

"I would contest nothing; but I tell you that the favor of a minister is ephemeral, and that a man must be mad to attach himself to a minister. There are powers above his which do not depend upon a man or the issue of an event; it is to these powers we should rally."

"I am sorry for it, madame, but I acknowledge not her power but that of the great man whom I have the honor to serve."

"You serve the cardinal?"

"Yes, madame; and as his servant, I will not allow you to be concerned in plots against the safety of the state, or to serve the intrigues of a woman who is not

French and who has a Spanish heart. Fortunately we have the great cardinal; his vigilant eye watches over and penetrates to the bottom of the heart."

Bonacieux was repeating, word for word, a sentence which he had heard from the Comte de Rochefort; but the poor wife, who had reckoned on her husband, and who, in that hope, had answered for him to the queen, did not tremble the less, both at the danger into which she had nearly cast herself and at the helpless state to which she was reduced. Nevertheless, knowing the weakness of her husband, and more particularly his cupidity, she did not despair of bringing him round to her purpose.

"Ah, you are a cardinalist, then, monsieur, are you?" cried she; "and you serve the party of those who maltreat your wife and insult your queen?"

"Private interests are as nothing before the interests of all. I am for those who save the state," said Bonacieux, emphatically.

"And what do you know about the state you talk of?" said Mme. Bonacieux, shrugging her shoulders. "Be satisfied with being a plain, straightforward citizen, and turn to that side which offers the most advantages."

"Eh, eh!" said Bonacieux, slapping a plump, round bag, which returned a sound a money; "what do you think of this, Madame Preacher?"

"Whence comes that money?"

"You do not guess?"

"From the cardinal?"

"From him, and from my friend the Comte de Rochefort."

"The Comte de Rochefort! Why it was he who carried me off!"

"That may be, madame!"

"And you receive silver from that man?"

"Have you not said that that abduction was entirely political?"

"Yes; but that abduction had for its object the betrayal of my mistress, to draw from me by torture confessions that might compromise the honor, and perhaps the life, of my august mistress."

"Madame," replied Bonacieux, "your august mistress is a perfidious Spaniard, and what the cardinal does is well done."

"Monsieur," said the young woman, "I know you to be cowardly, avaricious, and foolish, but I never till now believed you infamous!"

"Madame," said Bonacieux, who had never seen his wife in a passion, and who recoiled before this conjugal anger, "madame, what do you say?"

"I say you are a miserable creature!" continued Mme. Bonacieux, who saw she was regaining some little influence over her husband. "You meddle with politics, do you--and still more, with cardinalist politics? Why, you sell yourself, body and soul, to the demon, the devil, for money!"

"No, to the cardinal."

"It's the same thing," cried the young woman. "Who calls Richelieu calls Satan."

"Hold your tongue, hold your tongue, madame! You may be overheard."

"Yes, you are right; I should be ashamed for anyone to know your baseness."

"But what do you require of me, then? Let us see."

"I have told you. You must depart instantly, monsieur. You must accomplish loyally the commission with which I deign to charge you, and on that condition I pardon everything, I forget everything; and what is more," and she held out her hand to him, "I restore my love."

Bonacieux was cowardly and avaricious, but he loved his wife. He was softened. A man of fifty cannot long bear malice with a wife of twenty-three. Mme. Bonacieux saw that he hesitated.

"Come! Have you decided?" said she.

"But, my dear love, reflect a little upon what you require of me. London is far from Paris, very far, and perhaps the commission with which you charge me is not without dangers?"

"What matters it, if you avoid them?"

"Hold, Madame Bonacieux," said the mercer, "hold! I positively refuse; intrigues terrify me. I have seen the Bastille. My! Whew! That's a frightful place, that Bastille! Only to think of it makes my flesh crawl. They threatened me with torture. Do you know what torture is? Wooden points that they stick in between your legs till your bones stick out! No, positively I will not go. And, MORBLEU, why do you not go yourself? For in truth, I think I have hitherto been deceived in you. I really believe you are a man, and a violent one, too."

"And you, you are a woman--a miserable woman, stupid and brutal. You are afraid, are you? Well, if you do not go this very instant, I will have you arrested by the queen's orders, and I will have you placed in the Bastille which you dread so much."

Bonacieux fell into a profound reflection. He weighed the two angers in his brain--that of the cardinal and that of the queen; that of the cardinal predominated enormously.

"Have me arrested on the part of the queen," said he, "and I--I will appeal to his Eminence."

At once Mme. Bonacieux saw that she had gone too far, and she was terrified at having communicated so much. She for a moment contemplated with fright that stupid countenance, impressed with the invincible resolution of a fool that is overcome by fear.

"Well, be it so!" said she. "Perhaps, when all is considered, you are right. In the long run, a man knows more about politics than a woman, particularly such as, like you, Monsieur Bonacieux, have conversed with the cardinal. And yet it is very hard," added she, "that a man upon whose affection I thought I might depend, treats me thus unkindly and will not comply with any of my fancies."

"That is because your fancies go too far," replied the triumphant Bonacieux, "and I mistrust them."

"Well, I will give it up, then," said the young woman, sighing. "It is well as it is; say no more about it."

"At least you should tell me what I should have to do in London," replied Bonacieux, who remembered a little too late that Rochefort had desired him to endeavor to obtain his wife's secrets.

"It is of no use for you to know anything about it," said the young woman, whom an instinctive mistrust now impelled to draw back. "It was about one of those purchases that interest women--a purchase by which much might have been gained."

But the more the young woman excused herself, the more important Bonacieux thought the secret which she declined to confide to him. He resolved then to hasten immediately to the residence of the Comte de Rochefort, and tell him that the queen was seeking for a messenger to send to London.

"Pardon me for quitting you, my dear Madame Bonacieux," said he; "but, not knowing you would come to see me, I had made an engagement with a friend. I shall soon return; and if you will wait only a few minutes for me, as soon as I have concluded my business with that friend, as it is growing late, I will come back and reconduct you to the Louvre."

"Thank you, monsieur, you are not brave enough to be of any use to me whatever," replied Mme. Bonacieux. "I shall return very safely to the Louvre all alone."

"As you please, Madame Bonacieux," said the ex-mercer. "Shall I see you again soon?"

"Next week I hope my duties will afford me a little liberty, and I will take advantage of it to come and put things in order here, as they must necessarily be much deranged."

"Very well; I shall expect you. You are not angry with me?"

"Not the least in the world."

"Till then, then?"

"Till then."

Bonacieux kissed his wife's hand, and set off at a quick pace.

"Well," said Mme. Bonacieux, when her husband had shut the street door and she found herself alone; "that imbecile lacked but one thing to become a cardinalist. And I, who have answered for him to the queen--I, who have promised my poor mistress--ah, my God, my God! She will take me for one of those wretches with whom the palace swarms and who are placed about her as spies! Ah, Monsieur Bonacieux, I never did love you much, but now it is worse than ever. I hate you, and on my word you shall pay for this!"

At the moment she spoke these words a rap on the ceiling made her raise her head, and a voice which reached her through the ceiling cried, "Dear Madame Bonacieux, open for me the little door on the alley, and I will come down to you."

18 Lover And Husband

"Ah, Madame," said d'Artagnan, entering by the door which the young woman opened for him, "allow me to tell you that you have a bad sort of a husband."

"You have, then, overheard our conversation?" asked Mme. Bonacieux, eagerly, and looking at d'Artagnan with disquiet.

"The whole."

"But how, my God?"

"By a mode of proceeding known to myself, and by which I likewise overheard the more animated conversation which he had with the cardinal's police."

"And what did you understand by what we said?"

"A thousand things. In the first place, that, unfortunately, your husband is a simpleton and a fool; in the next place, you are in trouble, of which I am very glad, as it gives me a opportunity of placing myself at your service, and God knows I am ready to throw myself into the fire for you; finally, that the queen wants a brave, intelligent, devoted man to make a journey to London for her. I have at least two of the three qualities you stand in need of, and here I am."

Mme. Bonacieux made no reply; but her heart beat with joy and secret hope shone in her eyes.

"And what guarantee will you give me," asked she, "if I consent to confide this message to you?"

"My love for you. Speak! Command! What is to be done?"

"My God, my God!" murmured the young woman, "ought I to confide such a secret to you, monsieur? You are almost a boy."

"I see that you require someone to answer for me?"

"I admit that would reassure me greatly."

"Do you know Athos?"

"No."

"Porthos?"

"No."

"Aramis?"

"No. Who are these gentleman?"

"Three of the king's Musketeers. Do you know Monsieur de Treville, their captain?"

"Oh, yes, him! I know him; not personally, but from having heard the queen speak of him more than once as a brave and loyal gentleman."

"You do not fear lest he should betray you to the cardinal?"

"Oh, no, certainly not!"

"Well, reveal your secret to him, and ask him whether, however important, however valuable, however terrible it may be, you may not confide it to me."

"But this secret is not mine, and I cannot reveal it in this manner."

"You were about to confide it to Monsieur Bonacieux," said d'Artagnan, with chagrin.

"As one confides a letter to the hollow of a tree, to the wing of a pigeon, to the collar of a dog."

"And yet, me--you see plainly that I love you."

"You say so."

"I am an honorable man."

"You say so."

"I am a gallant fellow."

"I believe it."

"I am brave."

"Oh, I am sure of that!"

"Then, put me to the proof."

Mme. Bonacieux looked at the young man, restrained for a minute by a last hesitation; but there was such an ardor in his eyes, such persuasion in his voice, that she felt herself constrained to confide in him. Besides, she found herself in circumstances where everything must be risked for the sake of everything. The queen might be as much injured by too much reticence as by too much confidence; and--let us admit it--the involuntary sentiment which she felt for her young protector decided her to speak.

"Listen," said she; "I yield to your protestations, I yield to your assurances. But I swear to you, before God who hears us, that if you betray me, and my enemies pardon me, I will kill myself, while accusing you of my death."

"And I--I swear to you before God, madame," said d'Artagnan, "that if I am taken while accomplishing the orders you give me, I will die sooner than do anything that may compromise anyone."

Then the young woman confided in him the terrible secret of which chance had already communicated to him a part in front of the Samaritaine. This was their mutual declaration of love.

D'Artagnan was radiant with joy and pride. This secret which he possessed, this woman whom he loved! Confidence and love made him a giant.

"I go," said he; "I go at once."

"How, you will go!" said Mme. Bonacieux; "and your regiment, your captain?"

"By my soul, you had made me forget all that, dear Constance! Yes, you are right; a furlough is needful."

"Still another obstacle," murmured Mme. Bonacieux, sorrowfully.

"As to that," cried d'Artagnan, after a moment of reflection, "I shall surmount it, be assured."

"How so?"

"I will go this very evening to Treville, whom I will request to ask this favor for me of his brother-in-law, Monsieur Dessessart."

"But another thing."

"What?" asked d'Artagnan, seeing that Mme. Bonacieux hesitated to continue.

"You have, perhaps, no money?"

"PERHAPS is too much," said d'Artagnan, smiling.

"Then," replied Mme. Bonacieux, opening a cupboard and taking from it the very bag which a half hour before her husband had caressed so affectionately, "take this bag."

"The cardinal's?" cried d'Artagnan, breaking into a loud laugh, he having heard, as may be remembered, thanks to the broken boards, every syllable of the conversation between the mercer and his wife.

"The cardinal's," replied Mme. Bonacieux. "You see it makes a very respectable appearance."

"PARDIEU," cried d'Artagnan, "it will be a double amusing affair to save the queen with the cardinal's money!"

"You are an amiable and charming young man," said Mme. Bonacieux. "Be assured you will not find her Majesty ungrateful."

"Oh, I am already grandly recompensed!" cried d'Artagnan. "I love you; you permit me to tell you that I do--that is already more happiness than I dared to hope."

"Silence!" said Mme. Bonacieux, starting.

"What!"

"Someone is talking in the street."

"It is the voice of--"

"Of my husband! Yes, I recognize it!"

D'Artagnan ran to the door and pushed the bolt.

"He shall not come in before I am gone," said he; "and when I am gone, you can open to him."

"But I ought to be gone, too. And the disappearance of his money; how am I to justify it if I am here?"

"You are right; we must go out."

"Go out? How? He will see us if we go out."

"Then you must come up into my room."

"Ah," said Mme. Bonacieux, "you speak that in a tone that frightens me!"

Mme. Bonacieux pronounced these words with tears in her eyes. d'Artagnan saw those tears, and much disturbed, softened, he threw himself at her feet.

"With me you will be as safe as in a temple; I give you my word of a gentleman."

"Let us go," said she, "I place full confidence in you, my friend!"

D'Artagnan drew back the bolt with precaution, and both, light as shadows, glided through the interior door into the passage, ascended the stairs as quietly as possible, and entered d'Artagnan's chambers.

Once there, for greater security, the young man barricaded the door. They both approached the window, and through a slit in the shutter they saw Bonacieux talking with a man in a cloak.

At sight of this man, d'Artagnan started, and half drawing his sword, sprang toward the door.

It was the man of Meung.

"What are you going to do?" cried Mme. Bonacieux; "you will ruin us all!"

"But I have sworn to kill that man!" said d'Artagnan.

"Your life is devoted from this moment, and does not belong to you. In the name of the queen I forbid you to throw yourself into any peril which is foreign to that of your journey."

"And do you command nothing in your own name?"

"In my name," said Mme. Bonacieux, with great emotion, "in my name I beg you! But listen; they appear to be speaking of me."

D'Artagnan drew near the window, and lent his ear.

M Bonacieux had opened his door, and seeing the apartment, had returned to the man in the cloak, whom he had left alone for an instant.

"She is gone," said he; "she must have returned to the Louvre."

"You are sure," replied the stranger, "that she did not suspect the intentions with which you went out?"

"No," replied Bonacieux, with a self-sufficient air, "she is too superficial a woman."

"Is the young Guardsman at home?"

"I do not think he is; as you see, his shutter is closed, and you can see no light shine through the chinks of the shutters."

"All the same, it is well to be certain."

"How so?"

"By knocking at his door. Go."

"I will ask his servant."

Bonacieux re-entered the house, passed through the same door that had afforded a passage for the two fugitives, went up to d'Artagnan's door, and knocked.

No one answered. Porthos, in order to make a greater display, had that evening borrowed Planchet. As to d'Artagnan, he took care not to give the least sign of existence.

The moment the hand of Bonacieux sounded on the door, the two young people felt their hearts bound within them.

"There is nobody within," said Bonacieux.

"Never mind. Let us return to your apartment. We shall be safer there than in the doorway."

"Ah, my God!" whispered Mme. Bonacieux, "we shall hear no more."

"On the contrary," said d'Artagnan, "we shall hear better."

D'Artagnan raised the three or four boards which made his chamber another ear of Dionysius, spread a carpet on the floor, went upon his knees, and made a sign to Mme. Bonacieux to stoop as he did toward the opening.

"You are sure there is nobody there?" said the stranger.

"I will answer for it," said Bonacieux.

"And you think that your wife--"

"Has returned to the Louvre."

"Without speaking to anyone but yourself?"

"I am sure of it."

"That is an important point, do you understand?"

"Then the news I brought you is of value?"

"The greatest, my dear Bonacieux; I don't conceal this from you."

"Then the cardinal will be pleased with me?"

"I have no doubt of it."

"The great cardinal!"

"Are you sure, in her conversation with you, that your wife mentioned no names?"

"I think not."

"She did not name Madame de Chevreuse, the Duke of Buckingham, or Madame de Vernet?"

"No; she only told me she wished to send me to London to serve the interests of an illustrious personage."

"The traitor!" murmured Mme. Bonacieux.

"Silence!" said d'Artagnan, taking her hand, which, without thinking of it, she abandoned to him.

"Never mind," continued the man in the cloak; "you were a fool not to have pretended to accept the mission. You would then be in present possession of the letter. The state, which is now threatened, would be safe, and you--"

"And I?"

"Well you--the cardinal would have given you letters of nobility."

"Did he tell you so?"

"Yes, I know that he meant to afford you that agreeable surprise."

"Be satisfied," replied Bonacieux; "my wife adores me, and there is yet time."

"The ninny!" murmured Mme. Bonacieux.

"Silence!" said d'Artagnan, pressing her hand more closely.

"How is there still time?" asked the man in the cloak.

"I go to the Louvre; I ask for Mme. Bonacieux; I say that I have reflected; I renew the affair; I obtain the letter, and I run directly to the cardinal."

"Well, go quickly! I will return soon to learn the result of your trip."

The stranger went out.

"Infamous!" said Mme. Bonacieux, addressing this epithet to her husband.

"Silence!" said d'Artagnan, pressing her hand still more warmly.

A terrible howling interrupted these reflections of d'Artagnan and Mme. Bonacieux. It was her husband, who had discovered the disappearance of the moneybag, and was crying "Thieves!"

"Oh, my God!" cried Mme. Bonacieux, "he will rouse the whole quarter."

Bonacieux called a long time; but as such cries, on account of their frequency, brought nobody in the Rue des Fossoyeurs, and as lately the mercer's house had a bad name, finding that nobody came, he went out continuing to call, his voice being heard fainter and fainter as he went in the direction of the Rue du Bac.

"Now he is gone, it is your turn to get out," said Mme. Bonacieux. "Courage, my friend, but above all, prudence, and think what you owe to the queen."

"To her and to you!" cried d'Artagnan. "Be satisfied, beautiful Constance. I shall become worthy of her gratitude; but shall I likewise return worthy of your love?"

The young woman only replied by the beautiful glow which mounted to her cheeks. A few seconds afterward d'Artagnan also went out enveloped in a large cloak, which ill-concealed the sheath of a long sword.

Mme. Bonacieux followed him with her eyes, with that long, fond look with which he had turned the angle of the street, she fell on her knees, and clasping her hands, "Oh, my God," cried she, "protect the queen, protect me!"

19 Plan Of Campaign

D'Artagnan went straight to M. de Treville's. He had reflected that in a few minutes the cardinal would be warned by this cursed stranger, who appeared to be his agent, and he judged, with reason, he had not a moment to lose.

The heart of the young man overflowed with joy. An opportunity presented itself to him in which there would be at the same time glory to be acquired, and money to be gained; and as a far higher encouragement, it brought him into close intimacy with a woman he adored. This chance did, then, for him at once more than he would have dared to ask of Providence.

M de Treville was in his saloon with his habitual court of gentlemen. D'Artagnan, who was known as a familiar of the house, went straight to his office, and sent word that he wished to see him on something of importance.

D'Artagnan had been there scarcely five minutes when M. de Treville entered. At the first glance, and by the joy which was painted on his countenance, the worthy captain plainly perceived that something new was on foot.

All the way along d'Artagnan had been consulting with himself whether he should place confidence in M. de Treville, or whether he should only ask him to give him CARTE BLANCHE for some secret affair. But M. de Treville had always been so thoroughly his friend, had always been so devoted to the king and queen, and hated the cardinal so cordially, that the young man resolved to tell him everything.

"Did you ask for me, my good friend?" said M. de Treville.

"Yes, monsieur," said d'Artagnan, lowering his voice, "and you will pardon me, I hope, for having disturbed you when you know the importance of my business."

"Speak, then, I am all attention."

"It concerns nothing less," said d'Artagnan, "than the honor, perhaps the life of the queen."

"What did you say?" asked M. de Treville, glancing round to see if they were surely alone, and then fixing his questioning look upon d'Artagnan.

"I say, monsieur, that chance has rendered me master of a secret--"

"Which you will guard, I hope, young man, as your life."

"But which I must impart to you, monsieur, for you alone can assist me in the mission I have just received from her Majesty."

"Is this secret your own?"

"No, monsieur; it is her Majesty's."

"Are you authorized by her Majesty to communicate it to me?"

"No, monsieur, for, on the contrary, I am desired to preserve the profoundest mystery."

"Why, then, are you about to betray it to me?"

"Because, as I said, without you I can do nothing; and I am afraid you will refuse me the favor I come to ask if you do not know to what end I ask it."

"Keep your secret, young man, and tell me what you wish."

"I wish you to obtain for me, from Monsieur Dessessart, leave of absence for fifteen days."

"When?"

"This very night."

"You leave Paris?"

"I am going on a mission."

"May you tell me whither?"

"To London."

"Has anyone an interest in preventing your arrival there?"

"The cardinal, I believe, would give the world to prevent my success."

"And you are going alone?"

"I am going alone."

"In that case you will not get beyond Bondy. I tell you so, by the faith of de Treville."

"How so?"

"You will be assassinated."

"And I shall die in the performance of my duty."

"But your mission will not be accomplished."

"That is true," replied d'Artagnan.

"Believe me," continued Treville, "in enterprises of this kind, in order that one may arrive, four must set out."

"Ah, you are right, monsieur," said d'Artagnan; "but you know Athos, Porthos, and Aramis, and you know if I can dispose of them."

"Without confiding to them the secret which I am not willing to know?"

"We are sworn, once for all, to implicit confidence and devotedness against all proof. Besides, you can tell them that you have full confidence in me, and they will not be more incredulous than you."

"I can send to each of them leave of absence for fifteen days, that is all--to Athos, whose wound still makes him suffer, to go to the waters of Forges; to Porthos and Aramis to accompany their friend, whom they are not willing to abandon in such a painful condition. Sending their leave of absence will be proof enough that I authorize their journey."

"Thanks, monsieur. You are a hundred times too good."

"Begone, then, find them instantly, and let all be done tonight! Ha! But first write your request to Dessessart. Perhaps you had a spy at your heels; and your visit, if it should ever be known to the cardinal, will thus seem legitimate."

D'Artagnan drew up his request, and M. de Treville, on receiving it, assured him that by two o'clock in the morning the four leaves of absence should be at the respective domiciles of the travelers.

"Have the goodness to send mine to Athos's residence. I should dread some disagreeable encounter if I were to go home."

"Be easy. Adieu, and a prosperous voyage. A PROPOS," said M. de Treville, calling him back.

D'Artagnan returned.

"Have you any money?"

D'Artagnan tapped the bag he had in his pocket.

"Enough?" asked M. de Treville.

"Three hundred pistoles."

"Oh, plenty! That would carry you to the end of the world. Begone, then!"

D'Artagnan saluted M. de Treville, who held out his hand to him; d'Artagnan pressed it with a respect mixed with gratitude. Since his first arrival at Paris, he had had constant occasion to honor this excellent man, whom he had always found worthy, loyal, and great.

His first visit was to Aramis, at whose residence he had not been since the famous evening on which he had followed Mme. Bonacieux. Still further, he had seldom seen the young Musketeer; but every time he had seen him, he had remarked a deep sadness imprinted on his countenance.

This evening, especially, Aramis was melancholy and thoughtful. d'Artagnan asked some questions about this prolonged melancholy. Aramis pleaded as his excuse a commentary upon the eighteenth chapter of St. Augustine, which he was forced to write in Latin for the following week, and which preoccupied him a good deal.

After the two friends had been chatting a few moments, a servant from M. de Treville entered, bringing a sealed packet.

"What is that?" asked Aramis.

"The leave of absence Monsieur has asked for," replied the lackey.

"For me! I have asked for no leave of absence."

"Hold your tongue and take it!" said d'Artagnan. "And you, my friend, there is a demipistole for your trouble; you will tell Monsieur de Treville that Monsieur Aramis is very much obliged to him. Go."

The lackey bowed to the ground and departed.

"What does all this mean?" asked Aramis.

"Pack up all you want for a journey of a fortnight, and follow me."

"But I cannot leave Paris just now without knowing--"

Aramis stopped.

"What is become of her? I suppose you mean--" continued d'Artagnan.

"Become of whom?" replied Aramis.

"The woman who was here--the woman with the embroidered handkerchief."

"Who told you there was a woman here?" replied Aramis, becoming as pale as death.

"I saw her."

"And you know who she is?"

"I believe I can guess, at least."

"Listen!" said Aramis. "Since you appear to know so many things, can you tell me what is become of that woman?"

"I presume that she has returned to Tours."

"To Tours? Yes, that may be. You evidently know her. But why did she return to Tours without telling me anything?"

"Because she was in fear of being arrested."

"Why has she not written to me, then?"

"Because she was afraid of compromising you."

"d'Artagnan, you restore me to life!" cried Aramis. "I fancied myself despised, betrayed. I was so delighted to see her again! I could not have believed she would risk her liberty for me, and yet for what other cause could she have returned to Paris?"

"For the cause which today takes us to England."

"And what is this cause?" demanded Aramis.

"Oh, you'll know it someday, Aramis; but at present I must imitate the discretion of 'the doctor's niece.'"

Aramis smiled, as he remembered the tale he had told his friends on a certain evening. "Well, then, since she has left Paris, and you are sure of it, d'Artagnan, nothing prevents me, and I am ready to follow you. You say we are going--"

"To see Athos now, and if you will come thither, I beg you to make haste, for we have lost much time already. A PROPOS, inform Bazin."

"Will Bazin go with us?" asked Aramis.

"Perhaps so. At all events, it is best that he should follow us to Athos's."

Aramis called Bazin, and, after having ordered him to join them at Athos's residence, said "Let us go then," at the same time taking his cloak, sword, and three pistols, opening uselessly two or three drawers to see if he could not find stray coin. When well assured this search was superfluous, he followed d'Artagnan, wondering to himself how this young Guardsman should know so well who the lady was to whom he had given hospitality, and that he should know better than himself what had become of her.

Only as they went out Aramis placed his hand upon the arm of d'Artagnan, and looking at him earnestly, "You have not spoken of this lady?" said he.

"To nobody in the world."

"Not even to Athos or Porthos?"

"I have not breathed a syllable to them."

"Good enough!"

Tranquil on this important point, Aramis continued his way with d'Artagnan, and both soon arrived at Athos's dwelling. They found him holding his leave of absence in one hand, and M. de Treville's note in the other.

"Can you explain to me what signify this leave of absence and this letter, which I have just received?" said the astonished Athos.

My dear Athos,

I wish, as your health absolutely requires it, that you should rest for a fortnight. Go, then, and take the waters of Forges, or any that may be more agreeable to you, and recuperate yourself as quickly as possible.

Yours affectionate,

de Treville

"Well, this leave of absence and that letter mean that you must follow me, Athos."

"To the waters of Forges?"

"There or elsewhere."

"In the king's service?"

"Either the king's or the queen's. Are we not their Majesties' servants?"

At that moment Porthos entered. "PARDIEU!" said he, "here is a strange thing! Since when, I wonder, in the Musketeers, did they grant men leave of absence without their asking for it?"

"Since," said d'Artagnan, "they have friends who ask it for them."

"Ah, ah!" said Porthos, "it appears there's something fresh here."

"Yes, we are going--" said Aramis.

"To what country?" demanded Porthos.

"My faith! I don't know much about it," said Athos. "Ask d'Artagnan."

"To London, gentlemen," said d'Artagnan.

"To London!" cried Porthos; "and what the devil are we going to do in London?"

"That is what I am not at liberty to tell you, gentlemen; you must trust to me."

"But in order to go to London," added Porthos, "money is needed, and I have none."

"Nor I," said Aramis.

"Nor I," said Athos.

"I have," replied d'Artagnan, pulling out his treasure from his pocket, and placing it on the table. "There are in this bag three hundred pistoles. Let each take seventy-five; that is enough to take us to London and back. Besides, make yourselves easy; we shall not all arrive at London."

"Why so?"

"Because, in all probability, some one of us will be left on the road."

"Is this, then, a campaign upon which we are now entering?"

"One of a most dangerous kind, I give you notice."

"Ah! But if we do risk being killed," said Porthos, "at least I should like to know what for."

"You would be all the wiser," said Athos.

"And yet," said Aramis, "I am somewhat of Porthos's opinion."

"Is the king accustomed to give you such reasons? No. He says to you jauntily, 'Gentlemen, there is fighting going on in Gascony or in Flanders; go and fight,' and you go there. Why? You need give yourselves no more uneasiness about this."

"d'Artagnan is right," said Athos; "here are our three leaves of absence which came from Monsieur de Treville, and here are three hundred pistoles which came from I don't know where. So let us go and get killed where we are told to go. Is life worth the trouble of so many questions? D'Artagnan, I am ready to follow you."

"And I also," said Porthos.

"And I also," said Aramis. "And, indeed, I am not sorry to quit Paris; I had need of distraction."

"Well, you will have distractions enough, gentlemen, be assured," said d'Artagnan.

"And, now, when are we to go?" asked Athos.

"Immediately," replied d'Artagnan; "we have not a minute to lose."

"Hello, Grimaud! Planchet! Mousqueton! Bazin!" cried the four young men, calling their lackeys, "clean my boots, and fetch the horses from the hotel."

Each Musketeer was accustomed to leave at the general hotel, as at a barrack, his own horse and that of his lackey. Planchet, Grimaud, Mousqueton, and Bazin set off at full speed.

"Now let us lay down the plan of campaign," said Porthos. "Where do we go first?"

"To Calais," said d'Artagnan; "that is the most direct line to London."

"Well," said Porthos, "this is my advice--"

"Speak!"

"Four men traveling together would be suspected. D'Artagnan will give each of us his instructions. I will go by the way of Boulogne to clear the way; Athos will set out two hours after, by that of Amiens; Aramis will follow us by that of Noyon; as to d'Artagnan, he will go by what route he thinks is best, in Planchet's clothes, while Planchet will follow us like d'Artagnan, in the uniform of the Guards."

"Gentlemen," said Athos, "my opinion is that it is not proper to allow lackeys to have anything to do in such an affair. A secret may, by chance, be betrayed by gentlemen; but it is almost always sold by lackeys."

"Porthos's plan appears to me to be impracticable," said d'Artagnan, "inasmuch as I am myself ignorant of what instructions I can give you. I am the bearer of a letter, that is all. I have not, and I cannot make three copies of that letter, because it is sealed. We must, then, as it appears to me, travel in company. This letter is here, in this pocket," and he pointed to the pocket which contained the letter. "If I should be killed, one of you must take it, and continue the route; if he be killed, it will be another's turn, and so on--provided a single one arrives, that is all that is required."

"Bravo, d'Artagnan, your opinion is mine," cried Athos, "Besides, we must be consistent; I am going to take the waters, you will accompany me. Instead of taking the waters of Forges, I go and take sea waters; I am free to do so. If anyone wishes to stop us, I will show Monsieur de Treville's letter, and you will show your leaves of absence. If we are attacked, we will defend ourselves; if we are tried, we will stoutly maintain that we were only anxious to dip ourselves a certain number of times in the sea. They would have an easy bargain of four isolated men; whereas four men together make a troop. We will arm our four lackeys with pistols and musketoons; if they send an army out against us, we will give battle, and the survivor, as d'Artagnan says, will carry the letter."

"Well said," cried Aramis; "you don't often speak, Athos, but when you do speak, it is like St. John of the Golden Mouth. I agree to Athos's plan. And you, Porthos?"

"I agree to it, too," said Porthos, "if d'Artagnan approves of it. D'Artagnan, being the bearer of the letter, is naturally the head of the enterprise; let him decide, and we will execute."

"Well," said d'Artagnan, "I decide that we should adopt Athos's plan, and that we set off in half an hour."

"Agreed!" shouted the three Musketeers in chorus.

Each one, stretching out his hand to the bag, took his seventy-five pistoles, and made his preparations to set out at the time appointed.

20 The Journey

At two o'clock in the morning, our four adventurers left Paris by the Barriere St. Denis. As long as it was dark they remained silent; in spite of themselves they submitted to the influence of the obscurity, and apprehended ambushes on every side.

With the first rays of day their tongues were loosened; with the sun gaiety revived. It was like the eve of a battle; the heart beat, the eyes laughed, and they felt that the life they were perhaps going to lose, was, after all, a good thing.

Besides, the appearance of the caravan was formidable. The black horses of the Musketeers, their martial carriage, with the regimental step of these noble companions of the soldier, would have betrayed the most strict incognito. The lackeys followed, armed to the teeth.

All went well till they arrived at Chantilly, which they reached about eight o'clock in the morning. They needed breakfast, and alighted at the door of an AUBERGE, recommended by a sign representing St. Martin giving half his cloak to a poor man. They ordered the lackeys not to unsaddle the horses, and to hold themselves in readiness to set off again immediately.

They entered the common hall, and placed themselves at table. A gentleman, who had just arrived by the route of Dammartin, was seated at the same table, and was breakfasting. He opened the conversation about rain and fine weather; the travelers replied. He drank to their good health, and the travelers returned his politeness.

But at the moment Mousqueton came to announce that the horses were ready, and they were arising from table, the stranger proposed to Porthos to drink the health of the cardinal. Porthos replied that he asked no better if the stranger, in his turn, would drink the health of the king. The stranger cried that he acknowledged no other king but his Eminence. Porthos called him drunk, and the stranger drew his sword.

"You have committed a piece of folly," said Athos, "but it can't be helped; there is no drawing back. Kill the fellow, and rejoin us as soon as you can."

All three remounted their horses, and set out at a good pace, while Porthos was promising his adversary to perforate him with all the thrusts known in the fencing schools.

"There goes one!" cried Athos, at the end of five hundred paces.

"But why did that man attack Porthos rather than any other one of us?" asked Aramis.

"Because, as Porthos was talking louder than the rest of us, he took him for the chief," said d'Artagnan.

"I always said that this cadet from Gascony was a well of wisdom," murmured Athos; and the travelers continued their route.

At Beauvais they stopped two hours, as well to breathe their horses a little as to wait for Porthos. At the end of two hours, as Porthos did not come, not any news of him, they resumed their journey.

At a league from Beauvais, where the road was confined between two high banks, they fell in with eight or ten men who, taking advantage of the road being unpaved in this spot, appeared to be employed in digging holes and filling up the ruts with mud.

Aramis, not liking to soil his boots with this artificial mortar, apostrophized them rather sharply. Athos wished to restrain him, but it was too late. The laborers began to jeer the travelers and by their insolence disturbed the equanimity even of the cool Athos, who urged on his horse against one of them.

Then each of these men retreated as far as the ditch, from which each took a concealed musket; the result was that our seven travelers were outnumbered in weapons. Aramis received a ball which passed through his shoulder, and Mousqueton another ball which lodged in the fleshy part which prolongs the lower portion of the loins. Therefore Mousqueton alone fell from his horse, not because he was severely wounded, but not being able to see the wound, he judged it to be more serious than it really was.

"It was an ambuscade!" shouted d'Artagnan. "Don't waste a charge! Forward!"

Aramis, wounded as he was, seized the mane of his horse, which carried him on with the others. Mousqueton's horse rejoined them, and galloped by the side of his companions.

"That will serve us for a relay," said Athos.

"I would rather have had a hat," said d'Artagnan. "Mine was carried away by a ball. By my faith, it is very fortunate that the letter was not in it."

"They'll kill poor Porthos when he comes up," said Aramis.

"If Porthos were on his legs, he would have rejoined us by this time," said Athos. "My opinion is that on the ground the drunken man was not intoxicated."

They continued at their best speed for two hours, although the horses were so fatigued that it was to be feared they would soon refuse service.

The travelers had chosen crossroads in the hope that they might meet with less interruption; but at Crevecoeur, Aramis declared he could proceed no farther. In fact, it required all the courage which he concealed beneath his elegant form and polished manners to bear him so far. He grew more pale every minute, and they were obliged to support him on his horse. They lifted him off at the door of a cabaret, left Bazin with him, who, besides, in a skirmish was more embarrassing than useful, and set forward again in the hope of sleeping at Amiens.

"MORBLEU," said Athos, as soon as they were again in motion, "reduced to two masters and Grimaud and Planchet! MORBLEU! I won't be their dupe, I will answer for it. I will neither open my mouth nor draw my sword between this and Calais. I swear by--"

"Don't waste time in swearing," said d'Artagnan; "let us gallop, if our horses will consent."

And the travelers buried their rowels in their horses' flanks, who thus vigorously stimulated recovered their energies. They arrived at Amiens at midnight, and alighted at the AUBERGE of the Golden Lily.

The host had the appearance of as honest a man as any on earth. He received the travelers with his candlestick in one hand and his cotton nightcap in the other. He wished to lodge the two travelers each in a charming chamber; but unfortunately these charming chambers were at the opposite extremities of the hotel. d'Artagnan and Athos refused them. The host replied that he had no other worthy of their Excellencies; but the travelers declared they would sleep in the common chamber, each on a mattress which might be thrown upon the ground. The host insisted; but the travelers were firm, and he was obliged to do as they wished.

They had just prepared their beds and barricaded their door within, when someone knocked at the yard shutter; they demanded who was there, and recognizing the voices of their lackeys, opened the shutter. It was indeed Planchet and Grimaud.

"Grimaud can take care of the horses," said Planchet. "If you are willing, gentlemen, I will sleep across your doorway, and you will then be certain that nobody can reach you."

"And on what will you sleep?" said d'Artagnan.

"Here is my bed," replied Planchet, producing a bundle of straw.

"Come, then," said d'Artagnan, "you are right. Mine host's face does not please me at all; it is too gracious."

"Nor me either," said Athos.

Planchet mounted by the window and installed himself across the doorway, while Grimaud went and shut himself up in the stable, undertaking that by five o'clock in the morning he and the four horses should be ready.

The night was quiet enough. Toward two o'clock in the morning somebody endeavored to open the door; but as Planchet awoke in an instant and cried, "Who goes there?" somebody replied that he was mistaken, and went away.

At four o'clock in the morning they heard a terrible riot in the stables. Grimaud had tried to waken the stable boys, and the stable boys had beaten him. When they opened the window, they saw the poor lad lying senseless, with his head split by a blow with a pitchfork.

Planchet went down into the yard, and wished to saddle the horses; but the horses were all used up. Mousqueton's horse which had traveled for five or six hours without a rider the day before, might have been able to pursue the journey; but by an inconceivable error the veterinary surgeon, who had been sent for, as it appeared, to bleed one of the host's horses, had bled Mousqueton's.

This began to be annoying. All these successive accidents were perhaps the result of chance; but they might be the fruits of a plot. Athos and d'Artagnan went out, while Planchet was sent to inquire if there were not three horses for sale in the neighborhood. At the door stood two horses, fresh, strong, and fully equipped. These would just have suited them. He asked where their masters were, and was informed that they had passed the night in the inn, and were then settling their bill with the host.

Athos went down to pay the reckoning, while d'Artagnan and Planchet stood at the street door. The host was in a lower and back room, to which Athos was requested to go.

Athos entered without the least mistrust, and took out two pistoles to pay the bill. The host was alone, seated before his desk, one of the drawers of which was partly open. He took the money which Athos offered to him, and after turning and turning it over and over in his hands, suddenly cried out that it was bad, and that he would have him and his companions arrested as forgers.

"You blackguard!" cried Athos, going toward him, "I'll cut your ears off!"

At the same instant, four men, armed to the teeth, entered by side doors, and rushed upon Athos.

"I am taken!" shouted Athos, with all the power of his lungs. "Go on, d'Artagnan! Spur, spur!" and he fired two pistols.

D'Artagnan and Planchet did not require twice bidding; they unfastened the two horses that were waiting at the door, leaped upon them, buried their spurs in their sides, and set off at full gallop.

"Do you know what has become of Athos?" asked d'Artagnan of Planchet, as they galloped on.

"Ah, monsieur," said Planchet, "I saw one fall at each of his two shots, and he appeared to me, through the glass door, to be fighting with his sword with the others."

"Brave Athos!" murmured d'Artagnan, "and to think that we are compelled to leave him; maybe the same fate awaits us two paces hence. Forward, Planchet, forward! You are a brave fellow."

"As I told you, monsieur," replied Planchet, "Picards are found out by being used. Besides, I am here in my own country, and that excites me."

And both, with free use of the spur, arrived at St. Omer without drawing bit. At St. Omer they breathed their horses with the bridles passed under their arms for fear of accident, and ate a morsel from their hands on the stones of the street, after they departed again.

At a hundred paces from the gates of Calais, d'Artagnan's horse gave out, and could not by any means be made to get up again, the blood flowing from his eyes and his nose. There still remained Planchet's horse; but he stopped short, and could not be made to move a step.

Fortunately, as we have said, they were within a hundred paces of the city; they left their two nags upon the high road, and ran toward the quay. Planchet called his master's attention to a gentleman who had just arrived with his lackey, and only preceded them by about fifty paces. They made all speed to come up to this gentleman, who appeared to be in great haste. His boots were covered with dust, and he inquired if he could not instantly cross over to England.

"Nothing would be more easy," said the captain of a vessel ready to set sail, "but this morning came an order to let no one leave without express permission from the cardinal."

"I have that permission," said the gentleman, drawing the paper from his pocket; "here it is."

"Have it examined by the governor of the port," said the shipmaster, "and give me the preference."

"Where shall I find the governor?"

"At his country house."

"And that is situated?"

"At a quarter of a league from the city. Look, you may see it from here--at the foot of that little hill, that slated roof."

"Very well," said the gentleman. And, with his lackey, he took the road to the governor's country house.

D'Artagnan and Planchet followed the gentleman at a distance of five hundred paces. Once outside the city, d'Artagnan overtook the gentleman as he was entering a little wood.

"Monsieur, you appear to be in great haste?"

"No one can be more so, monsieur."

"I am sorry for that," said d'Artagnan; "for as I am in great haste likewise, I wish to beg you to render me a service."

"What?"

"To let me sail first."

"That's impossible," said the gentleman; "I have traveled sixty leagues in forty hours, and by tomorrow at midday I must be in London."

"I have performed that same distance in forty hours, and by ten o'clock in the morning I must be in London."

"Very sorry, monsieur; but I was here first, and will not sail second."

"I am sorry, too, monsieur; but I arrived second, and must sail first."

"The king's service!" said the gentleman.

"My own service!" said d'Artagnan.

"But this is a needless quarrel you seek with me, as it seems to me."

"PARBLEU! What do you desire it to be?"

"What do you want?"

"Would you like to know?"

"Certainly."

"Well, then, I wish that order of which you are bearer, seeing that I have not one of my own and must have one."

"You jest, I presume."

"I never jest."

"Let me pass!"

"You shall not pass."

"My brave young man, I will blow out your brains. HOLA, Lubin, my pistols!"

"Planchet," called out d'Artagnan, "take care of the lackey; I will manage the master."

Planchet, emboldened by the first exploit, sprang upon Lubin; and being strong and vigorous, he soon got him on the broad of his back, and placed his knee upon his breast.

"Go on with your affair, monsieur," cried Planchet; "I have finished mine."

Seeing this, the gentleman drew his sword, and sprang upon d'Artagnan; but he had too strong an adversary. In three seconds d'Artagnan had wounded him three times, exclaiming at each thrust, "One for Athos, one for Porthos; and one for Aramis!"

At the third hit the gentleman fell like a log. D'Artagnan believed him to be dead, or at least insensible, and went toward him for the purpose of taking the order; but the moment he extended his hand to search for it, the wounded man, who had not dropped his sword, plunged the point into d'Artagnan's breast, crying, "One for you!"

"And one for me--the best for last!" cried d'Artagnan, furious, nailing him to the earth with a fourth thrust through his body.

This time the gentleman closed his eyes and fainted. D'Artagnan searched his pockets, and took from one of them the order for the passage. It was in the name of Comte de Wardes.

Then, casting a glance on the handsome young man, who was scarcely twenty-five years of age, and whom he was leaving in his gore, deprived of sense and perhaps dead, he gave a sigh for that unaccountable destiny which leads men to destroy each other for the interests of people who are strangers to them and who often do not even know that they exist. But he was soon aroused from these reflections by Lubin, who uttered loud cries and screamed for help with all his might.

Planchet grasped him by the throat, and pressed as hard as he could. "Monsieur," said he, "as long as I hold him in this manner, he can't cry, I'll be bound; but as soon as I let go he will howl again. I know him for a Norman, and Normans are obstinate."

In fact, tightly held as he was, Lubin endeavored still to cry out.

"Stay!" said d'Artagnan; and taking out his handkerchief, he gagged him.

"Now," said Planchet, "let us bind him to a tree."

This being properly done, they drew the Comte de Wardes close to his servant; and as night was approaching, and as the wounded man and the bound man were at some little distance within the wood, it was evident they were likely to remain there till the next day.

"And now," said d'Artagnan, "to the Governor's."

"But you are wounded, it seems," said Planchet.

"Oh, that's nothing! Let us attend to what is more pressing first, and then we will attend to my wound; besides, it does not seem very dangerous."

And they both set forward as fast as they could toward the country house of the worthy functionary.

The Comte de Wardes was announced, and d'Artagnan was introduced.

"You have an order signed by the cardinal?" said the governor.

"Yes, monsieur," replied d'Artagnan; "here it is."

"Ah, ah! It is quite regular and explicit," said the governor.

"Most likely," said d'Artagnan; "I am one of his most faithful servants."

"It appears that his Eminence is anxious to prevent someone from crossing to England?"

"Yes; a certain d'Artagnan, a Bearnese gentleman who left Paris in company with three of his friends, with the intention of going to London."

"Do you know him personally?" asked the governor.

"Whom?"

"This d'Artagnan."

"Perfectly well."

"Describe him to me, then."

"Nothing more easy."

And d'Artagnan gave, feature for feature, a description of the Comte de Wardes.

"Is he accompanied?"

"Yes; by a lackey named Lubin."

"We will keep a sharp lookout for them; and if we lay hands on them his Eminence may be assured they will be reconducted to Paris under a good escort."

"And by doing so, Monsieur the Governor," said d'Artagnan, "you will deserve well of the cardinal."

"Shall you see him on your return, Monsieur Count?"

"Without a doubt."

"Tell him, I beg you, that I am his humble servant."

"I will not fail."

Delighted with this assurance the governor countersigned the passport and delivered it to d'Artagnan. D'Artagnan lost no time in useless compliments. He thanked the governor, bowed, and departed. Once outside, he and Planchet set off as fast as they could; and by making a long detour avoided the wood and reentered the city by another gate.

The vessel was quite ready to sail, and the captain was waiting on the wharf. "Well?" said he, on perceiving d'Artagnan.

"Here is my pass countersigned," said the latter.

"And that other gentleman?

"He will not go today," said d'Artagnan; "but here, I'll pay you for us two."

"In that case let us go," said the shipmaster.

"Let us go," repeated d'Artagnan.

He leaped with Planchet into the boat, and five minutes after they were on board. It was time; for they had scarcely sailed half a league, when d'Artagnan saw a flash and heard a detonation. It was the cannon which announced the closing of the port.

He had now leisure to look to his wound. Fortunately, as d'Artagnan had thought, it was not dangerous. The point of the sword had touched a rib, and glanced along the bone. Still further, his shirt had stuck to the wound, and he had lost only a few drops of blood.

D'Artagnan was worn out with fatigue. A mattress was laid upon the deck for him. He threw himself upon it, and fell asleep.

On the morrow, at break of day, they were still three or four leagues from the coast of England. The breeze had been so light all night, they had made but little progress. At ten o'clock the vessel cast anchor in the harbor of Dover, and at half past ten d'Artagnan placed his foot on English land, crying, "Here I am at last!"

But that was not all; they must get to London. In England the post was well served. D'Artagnan and Planchet took each a post horse, and a postillion rode before them. In a few hours they were in the capital.

D'Artagnan did not know London; he did not know a word of English; but he wrote the name of Buckingham on a piece of paper, and everyone pointed out to him the way to the duke's hotel.

The duke was at Windsor hunting with the king. D'Artagnan inquired for the confidential valet of the duke, who, having accompanied him in all his voyages, spoke French perfectly well; he told him that he came from Paris on an affair of life and death, and that he must speak with his master instantly.

The confidence with which d'Artagnan spoke convinced Patrick, which was the name of this minister of the minister. He ordered two horses to be saddled, and himself went as guide to the young Guardsman. As for Planchet, he had been lifted from his horse as stiff as a rush; the poor lad's strength was almost exhausted. d'Artagnan seemed iron.

On their arrival at the castle they learned that Buckingham and the king were hawking in the marshes two or three leagues away. In twenty minutes they were on the spot named. Patrick soon caught the sound of his master's voice calling his falcon.

"Whom must I announce to my Lord Duke?" asked Patrick.

"The young man who one evening sought a quarrel with him on the Pont Neuf, opposite the Samaritaine."

"A singular introduction!"

"You will find that it is as good as another."

Patrick galloped off, reached the duke, and announced to him in the terms directed that a messenger awaited him.

Buckingham at once remembered the circumstance, and suspecting that something was going on in France of which it was necessary he should be informed, he only took the time to inquire where the messenger was, and recognizing from afar the uniform of the Guards, he put his horse into a gallop, and rode straight up to d'Artagnan. Patrick discreetly kept in the background.

"No misfortune has happened to the queen?" cried Buckingham, the instant he came up, throwing all his fear and love into the question.

"I believe not; nevertheless I believe she runs some great peril from which your Grace alone can extricate her."

"I!" cried Buckingham. "What is it? I should be too happy to be of any service to her. Speak, speak!"

"Take this letter," said d'Artagnan.

"This letter! From whom comes this letter?"

"From her Majesty, as I think."

"From her Majesty!" said Buckingham, becoming so pale that d'Artagnan feared he would faint as he broke the seal.

"What is this rent?" said he, showing d'Artagnan a place where it had been pierced through.

"Ah," said d'Artagnan, "I did not see that; it was the sword of the Comte de Wardes which made that hole, when he gave me a good thrust in the breast."

"You are wounded?" asked Buckingham, as he opened the letter.

"Oh, nothing but a scratch," said d'Artagnan.

"Just heaven, what have I read?" cried the duke. "Patrick, remain here, or rather join the king, wherever he may be, and tell his Majesty that I humbly beg him to excuse me, but an affair of the greatest importance recalls me to London. Come, monsieur, come!" and both set off towards the capital at full gallop.

21 The Countess De Winter

As they rode along, the duke endeavored to draw from d'Artagnan, not all that had happened, but what d'Artagnan himself knew. By adding all that he heard from the mouth of the young man to his own remembrances, he was enabled to form a pretty exact idea of a position of the seriousness of which, for the rest, the queen's letter, short but explicit, gave him the clue. But that which astonished him most was that the cardinal, so deeply interested in preventing this young man from setting his foot in England, had not succeeded in arresting him on the road. It was then, upon the manifestation of this astonishment, that d'Artagnan related to him the precaution taken, and how, thanks to the devotion of his three friends, whom he had left scattered and bleeding on the road, he had succeeded in coming off with a single sword thrust, which had pierced the queen's letter and for which he had repaid M. de Wardes with such terrible coin. While he was listening to this recital, delivered with the greatest simplicity, the duke looked from time to time at the young man with astonishment, as if he could not comprehend how so much prudence, courage, and devotedness could be allied with a countenance which indicated not more than twenty years.

The horses went like the wind, and in a few minutes they were at the gates of London. D'Artagnan imagined that on arriving in town the duke would slacken his pace, but it was not so. He kept on his way at the same rate, heedless about upsetting those whom he met on the road. In fact, in crossing the city two or three accidents of this kind happened; but Buckingham did not even turn his head to see what became of those he had knocked down. d'Artagnan followed him amid cries which strongly resembled curses.

On entering the court of his hotel, Buckingham sprang from his horse, and without thinking what became of the animal, threw the bridle on his neck, and sprang toward the vestibule. D'Artagnan did the same, with a little more concern, however, for the noble creatures, whose merits he fully appreciated; but he had the satisfaction of seeing three or four grooms run from the kitchens and the stables, and busy themselves with the steeds.

The duke walked so fast that d'Artagnan had some trouble in keeping up with him. He passed through several apartments, of an elegance of which even the greatest nobles of France had not even an idea, and arrived at length in a bedchamber which was at once a miracle of taste and of richness. In the alcove of this chamber was a door concealed in the tapestry which the duke opened with a little gold key which he wore suspended from his neck by a chain of the same metal. With discretion d'Artagnan remained behind; but at the moment when Buckingham crossed the threshold, he turned round, and seeing the hesitation of the young man, "Come in!" cried he, "and if you have the good fortune to be admitted to her Majesty's presence, tell her what you have seen."

Encouraged by this invitation, d'Artagnan followed the duke, who closed the door after them. The two found themselves in a small chapel covered with a tapestry of Persian silk worked with gold, and brilliantly lighted with a vast number of candles. Over a species of altar, and beneath a canopy of blue velvet, surmounted by white and red plumes, was a full-length portrait of Anne of Austria, so perfect in its resemblance that d'Artagnan uttered a cry of surprise on beholding it. One might believe the queen was about to speak. On the altar, and beneath the portrait, was the casket containing the diamond studs.

The duke approached the altar, knelt as a priest might have done before a crucifix, and opened the casket. "There," said he, drawing from the casket a large bow of blue ribbon all sparkling with diamonds, "there are the precious studs which I have taken an oath should be buried with me. The queen gave them to me, the queen requires them again. Her will be done, like that of God, in all things."

Then, he began to kiss, one after the other, those dear studs with which he was about to part. All at once he uttered a terrible cry.

"What is the matter?" exclaimed d'Artagnan, anxiously; "what has happened to you, my Lord?"

"All is lost!" cried Buckingham, becoming as pale as a corpse; "two of the studs are wanting, there are only ten."

"Can you have lost them, my Lord, or do you think they have been stolen?"

"They have been stolen," replied the duke, "and it is the cardinal who has dealt this blow. Hold; see! The ribbons which held them have been cut with scissors."

"If my Lord suspects they have been stolen, perhaps the person who stole them still has them in his hands."

"Wait, wait!" said the duke. "The only time I have worn these studs was at a ball given by the king eight days ago at Windsor. The Comtesse de Winter, with whom I had quarreled, became reconciled to me at that ball. That reconciliation was nothing but the vengeance of a jealous woman. I have never seen her from that day. The woman is an agent of the cardinal."

"He has agents, then, throughout the world?" cried d'Artagnan.

"Oh, yes," said Buckingham, grating his teeth with rage. "Yes, he is a terrible antagonist. But when is this ball to take place?"

"Monday next."

"Monday next! Still five days before us. That's more time than we want. Patrick!" cried the duke, opening the door of the chapel, "Patrick!" His confidential valet appeared.

"My jeweler and my secretary."

The valet went out with a mute promptitude which showed him accustomed to obey blindly and without reply.

But although the jeweler had been mentioned first, it was the secretary who first made his appearance. This was simply because he lived in the hotel. He found Buckingham seated at a table in his bedchamber, writing orders with his own hand.

"Mr. Jackson," said he, "go instantly to the Lord Chancellor, and tell him that I charge him with the execution of these orders. I wish them to be promulgated immediately."

"But, my Lord, if the Lord Chancellor interrogates me upon the motives which may have led your Grace to adopt such an extraordinary measure, what shall I reply?"

"That such is my pleasure, and that I answer for my will to no man."

"Will that be the answer," replied the secretary, smiling, "which he must transmit to his Majesty if, by chance, his Majesty should have the curiosity to know why no vessel is to leave any of the ports of Great Britain?"

"You are right, Mr. Jackson," replied Buckingham. "He will say, in that case, to the king that I am determined on war, and that this measure is my first act of hostility against France."

The secretary bowed and retired.

"We are safe on that side," said Buckingham, turning toward d'Artagnan. "If the studs are not yet gone to Paris, they will not arrive till after you."

"How so?"

"I have just placed an embargo on all vessels at present in his Majesty's ports, and without particular permission, not one dare lift an anchor."

D'Artagnan looked with stupefaction at a man who thus employed the unlimited power with which he was clothed by the confidence of a king in the prosecution of his intrigues. Buckingham saw by the expression of the young man's face what was passing in his mind, and he smiled.

"Yes," said he, "yes, Anne of Austria is my true queen. Upon a word from her, I would betray my country, I would betray my king, I would betray my God. She asked me not to send the Protestants of La Rochelle the assistance I promised them; I have not done so. I broke my word, it is true; but what signifies that? I obeyed my love; and have I not been richly paid for that obedience? It was to that obedience I owe her portrait."

D'Artagnan was amazed to note by what fragile and unknown threads the destinies of nations and the lives of men are suspended. He was lost in these reflections when the goldsmith entered. He was an Irishman--one of the most skillful of his craft, and who himself confessed that he gained a hundred thousand livres a year by the Duke of Buckingham.

"Mr. O'Reilly," said the duke, leading him into the chapel, "look at these diamond studs, and tell me what they are worth apiece."

The goldsmith cast a glance at the elegant manner in which they were set, calculated, one with another, what the diamonds were worth, and without hesitation said, "Fifteen hundred pistoles each, my Lord."

"How many days would it require to make two studs exactly like them? You see there are two wanting."

"Eight days, my Lord."

"I will give you three thousand pistoles apiece if I can have them by the day after tomorrow."

"My Lord, they shall be yours."

"You are a jewel of a man, Mr. O'Reilly; but that is not all. These studs cannot be trusted to anybody; it must be done in the palace."

"Impossible, my Lord! There is no one but myself can so execute them that one cannot tell the new from the old."

"Therefore, my dear Mr. O'Reilly, you are my prisoner. And if you wish ever to leave my palace, you cannot; so make the best of it. Name to me such of your workmen as you need, and point out the tools they must bring."

The goldsmith knew the duke. He knew all objection would be useless, and instantly determined how to act.

"May I be permitted to inform my wife?" said he.

"Oh, you may even see her if you like, my dear Mr. O'Reilly. Your captivity shall be mild, be assured; and as every inconvenience deserves its indemnification, here is, in addition to the price of the studs, an order for a thousand pistoles, to make you forget the annoyance I cause you."

D'Artagnan could not get over the surprise created in him by this minister, who thus open-handed, sported with men and millions.

As to the goldsmith, he wrote to his wife, sending her the order for the thousand pistoles, and charging her to send him, in exchange, his most skillful apprentice, an assortment of diamonds, of which he gave the names and the weight, and the necessary tools.

Buckingham conducted the goldsmith to the chamber destined for him, and which, at the end of half an hour, was transformed into a workshop. Then he placed a sentinel at each door, with an order to admit nobody upon any pretense but his VALET DE CHAMBRE, Patrick. We need not add that the goldsmith, O'Reilly, and his assistant, were prohibited from going out under any pretext. This point, settled, the duke turned to d'Artagnan. "Now, my young friend," said he, "England is all our own. What do you wish for? What do you desire?"

"A bed, my Lord," replied d'Artagnan. "At present, I confess, that is the thing I stand most in need of."

Buckingham gave d'Artagnan a chamber adjoining his own. He wished to have the young man at hand--not that he at all mistrusted him, but for the sake of having someone to whom he could constantly talk of the queen.

In one hour after, the ordinance was published in London that no vessel bound for France should leave port, not even the packet boat with letters. In the eyes of everybody this was a declaration of war between the two kingdoms.

On the day after the morrow, by eleven o'clock, the two diamond studs were finished, and they were so completely imitated, so perfectly alike, that Buckingham could not tell the new ones from the old ones, and experts in such matters would have been deceived as he was. He immediately called d'Artagnan. "Here," said he to him, "are the diamond studs that you came to bring; and be my witness that I have done all that human power could do."

"Be satisfied, my Lord, I will tell all that I have seen. But does your Grace mean to give me the studs without the casket?"

"The casket would encumber you. Besides, the casket is the more precious from being all that is left to me. You will say that I keep it."

"I will perform your commission, word for word, my Lord."

"And now," resumed Buckingham, looking earnestly at the young man, "how shall I ever acquit myself of the debt I owe you?"

D'Artagnan blushed up to the whites of his eyes. He saw that the duke was searching for a means of making him accept something and the idea that the blood of his friends and himself was about to be paid for with English gold was strangely repugnant to him.

"Let us understand each other, my Lord," replied d'Artagnan, "and let us make things clear beforehand in order that there may be no mistake. I am in the service of the King and Queen of France, and form part of the company of Monsieur Dessessart, who, as well as his brother-in-law, Monsieur de Treville, is particularly attached to their Majesties. What I have done, then, has been for the queen, and not at all for your Grace. And still further, it is very probable I should not have done anything of this, if it had not been to make myself agreeable to someone who is my lady, as the queen is yours."

"Yes," said the duke, smiling, "and I even believe that I know that other person; it is--"

"My Lord, I have not named her!" interrupted the young man, warmly.

"That is true," said the duke; "and it is to this person I am bound to discharge my debt of gratitude."

"You have said, my Lord; for truly, at this moment when there is question of war, I confess to you that I see nothing in your Grace but an Englishman, and consequently an enemy whom I should have much greater pleasure in meeting on the field of battle than in the park at Windsor or the corridors of the Louvre--all which, however, will not prevent me from executing to the very point my commission or from laying down my life, if there be need of it, to accomplish it; but I repeat it to your Grace, without your having personally on that account more to thank me for in this second interview than for what I did for you in the first."

"We say, 'Proud as a Scotsman,'" murmured the Duke of Buckingham.

"And we say, 'Proud as a Gascon,'" replied d'Artagnan. "The Gascons are the Scots of France."

D'Artagnan bowed to the duke, and was retiring.

"Well, are you going away in that manner? Where, and how?"

"That's true!"

"Fore Gad, these Frenchmen have no consideration!"

"I had forgotten that England was an island, and that you were the king of it."

"Go to the riverside, ask for the brig SUND, and give this letter to the captain; he will convey you to a little port, where certainly you are not expected, and which is ordinarily only frequented by fishermen."

"The name of that port?"

"St. Valery; but listen. When you have arrived there you will go to a mean tavern, without a name and without a sign--a mere fisherman's hut. You cannot be mistaken; there is but one."

"Afterward?"

"You will ask for the host, and will repeat to him the word 'Forward!'"

"Which means?"

"In French, EN AVANT. It is the password. He will give you a horse all saddled, and will point out to you the road you ought to take. You will find, in the same way, four relays on your route. If you will give at each of these relays your address in Paris, the four horses will follow you thither. You already know two of them, and you appeared to appreciate them like a judge. They were those we rode on; and you may rely upon me for the others not being inferior to them. These horses are equipped for the field. However proud you may be, you will not refuse to accept one of them, and to request your three companions to accept the others--that is, in order to make war against us. Besides, the end justified the means, as you Frenchmen say, does it not?"

"Yes, my Lord, I accept them," said d'Artagnan; "and if it please God, we will make a good use of your presents."

"Well, now, your hand, young man. Perhaps we shall soon meet on the field of battle; but in the meantime we shall part good friends, I hope."

"Yes, my Lord; but with the hope of soon becoming enemies."

"Be satisfied; I promise you that."

"I depend upon your word, my Lord."

D'Artagnan bowed to the duke, and made his way as quickly as possible to the riverside. Opposite the Tower of London he found the vessel that had been named to him, delivered his letter to the captain, who after having it examined by the governor of the port made immediate preparations to sail.

Fifty vessels were waiting to set out. Passing alongside one of them, d'Artagnan fancied he perceived on board it the woman of Meung--the same whom the unknown gentleman had called Milady, and whom d'Artagnan had thought so handsome; but thanks to the current of the stream and a fair wind, his vessel passed so quickly that he had little more than a glimpse of her.

The next day about nine o'clock in the morning, he landed at St. Valery. D'Artagnan went instantly in search of the inn, and easily discovered it by the riotous noise which resounded from it. War between England and France was talked of as near and certain, and the jolly sailors were having a carousal.

D'Artagnan made his way through the crowd, advanced toward the host, and pronounced the word "Forward!" The host instantly made him a sign to follow, went out with him by a door which opened into a yard, led him to the stable, where a saddled horse awaited him, and asked him if he stood in need of anything else.

"I want to know the route I am to follow," said d'Artagnan.

"Go from hence to Blangy, and from Blangy to Neufchatel. At Neufchatel, go to the tavern of the Golden Harrow, give the password to the landlord, and you will find, as you have here, a horse ready saddled."

"Have I anything to pay?" demanded d'Artagnan.

"Everything is paid," replied the host, "and liberally. Begone, and may God guide you!"

"Amen!" cried the young man, and set off at full gallop.

Four hours later he was in Neufchatel. He strictly followed the instructions he had received. At Neufchatel, as at St. Valery, he found a horse quite ready and awaiting him. He was about to remove the pistols from the saddle he had quit to the one he was about to fill, but he found the holsters furnished with similar pistols.

"Your address at Paris?"

"Hotel of the Guards, company of Dessessart."

"Enough," replied the questioner.

"Which route must I take?" demanded d'Artagnan, in his turn.

"That of Rouen; but you will leave the city on your right. You must stop at the little village of Eccuis, in which there is but one tavern--the Shield of France. Don't condemn it from appearances; you will find a horse in the stables quite as good as this."

"The same password?"

"Exactly."

"Adieu, master!"

"A good journey, gentlemen! Do you want anything?"

D'Artagnan shook his head, and set off at full speed. At Eccuis, the same scene was repeated. He found as provident a host and a fresh horse. He left his address as he had done before, and set off again at the same pace for Pontoise. At Pontoise he changed his horse for the last time, and at nine o'clock galloped into the yard of Treville's hotel. He had made nearly sixty leagues in little more than twelve hours.

M de Treville received him as if he had seen him that same morning; only, when pressing his hand a little more warmly than usual, he informed him that the company of Dessessart was on duty at the Louvre, and that he might repair at once to his post.

22 The Ballet Of La Merlaison

On the morrow, nothing was talked of in Paris but the ball which the aldermen of the city were to give to the king and queen, and in which their Majesties were to dance the famous La Merlaison--the favorite ballet of the king.

Eight days had been occupied in preparations at the Hotel de Ville for this important evening. The city carpenters had erected scaffolds upon which the invited ladies were to be placed; the city grocer had ornamented the chambers with two hundred FLAMBEAUX of white wax, a piece of luxury unheard of at that period; and twenty violins were ordered, and the price for them fixed at double the usual rate, upon condition, said the report, that they should be played all night.

At ten o'clock in the morning the Sieur de la Coste, ensign in the king's Guards, followed by two officers and several archers of that body, came to the city registrar, named Clement, and demanded of him all the keys of the rooms and offices of the hotel. These keys were given up to him instantly. Each of them had ticket attached to it, by which it might be recognized; and from that moment the Sieur de la Coste was charged with the care of all the doors and all the avenues.

At eleven o'clock came in his turn Duhallier, captain of the Guards, bringing with him fifty archers, who were distributed immediately through the Hotel de Ville, at the doors assigned them.

At three o'clock came two companies of the Guards, one French, the other Swiss. The company of French guards was composed of half of M. Duhallier's men and half of M. Dessessart's men.

At six in the evening the guests began to come. As fast as they entered, they were placed in the grand saloon, on the platforms prepared for them.

At nine o'clock Madame la Premiere Presidente arrived. As next to the queen, she was the most considerable personage of the fete, she was received by the city officials, and placed in a box opposite to that which the queen was to occupy.

At ten o'clock, the king's collation, consisting of preserves and other delicacies, was prepared in the little room on the side of the church of St. Jean, in front of the silver buffet of the city, which was guarded by four archers.

At midnight great cries and loud acclamations were heard. It was the king, who was passing through the streets which led from the Louvre to the Hotel de Ville, and which were all illuminated with colored lanterns.

Immediately the aldermen, clothed in their cloth robes and preceded by six sergeants, each holding a FLAMBEAU in his hand, went to attend upon the king, whom they met on the steps, where the provost of the merchants made him the speech of welcome--a compliment to which his Majesty replied with an apology for coming so late, laying the blame upon the cardinal, who had detained him till eleven o'clock, talking of affairs of state.

His Majesty, in full dress, was accompanied by his royal Highness, M. le Comte de Soissons, by the Grand Prior, by the Duc de Longueville, by the Duc d'Euboeuf, by the Comte d'Harcourt, by the Comte de la Roche-Guyon, by M. de Liancourt, by M. de Baradas, by the Comte de Cramail, and by the Chevalier de Souveray. Everybody noticed that the king looked dull and preoccupied.

A private room had been prepared for the king and another for Monsieur. In each of these closets were placed masquerade dresses. The same had been done for the queen and Madame the President. The nobles and ladies of their Majesties' suites were to dress, two by two, in chambers prepared for the purpose. Before entering his closet the king desired to be informed the moment the cardinal arrived.

Half an hour after the entrance of the king, fresh acclamations were heard; these announced the arrival of the queen. The aldermen did as they had done before, and preceded by their sergeants, advanced to receive their illustrious guest. The queen entered the great hall; and it was remarked that, like the king, she looked dull and even weary.

At the moment she entered, the curtain of a small gallery which to that time had been closed, was drawn, and the pale face of the cardinal appeared, he being dressed as a Spanish cavalier. His eyes were fixed upon those of the queen, and a smile of terrible joy passed over his lips; the queen did not wear her diamond studs.

The queen remained for a short time to receive the compliments of the city dignitaries and to reply to the salutations of the ladies. All at once the king appeared with the cardinal at one of the doors of the hall. The cardinal was speaking to him in a low voice, and the king was very pale.

The king made his way through the crowd without a mask, and the ribbons of his doublet scarcely tied. He went straight to the queen, and in an altered voice said, "Why, madame, have you not thought proper to wear your diamond studs, when you know it would give me so much gratification?"

The queen cast a glance around her, and saw the cardinal behind, with a diabolical smile on his countenance.

"Sire," replied the queen, with a faltering voice, "because, in the midst of such a crowd as this, I feared some accident might happen to them."

"And you were wrong, madame. If I made you that present it was that you might adorn yourself therewith. I tell you that you were wrong."

The voice of the king was tremulous with anger. Everybody looked and listened with astonishment, comprehending nothing of what passed.

"Sire," said the queen, "I can send for them to the Louvre, where they are, and thus your Majesty's wishes will be complied with."

"Do so, madame, do so, and that at once; for within an hour the ballet will commence."

The queen bent in token of submission, and followed the ladies who were to conduct her to her room. On his part the king returned to his apartment.

There was a moment of trouble and confusion in the assembly. Everybody had remarked that something had passed between the king and queen; but both of them had spoken so low that everybody, out of respect, withdrew several steps, so that nobody had heard anything. The violins began to sound with all their might, but nobody listened to them.

The king came out first from his room. He was in a most elegant hunting costume; and Monsieur and the other nobles were dressed like him. This was the costume that best became the king. So dressed, he really appeared the first gentleman of his kingdom.

The cardinal drew near to the king, and placed in his hand a small casket. The king opened it, and found in it two diamond studs.

"What does this mean?" demanded he of the cardinal.

"Nothing," replied the latter; "only, if the queen has the studs, which I very much doubt, count them, sire, and if you only find ten, ask her Majesty who can have stolen from her the two studs that are here."

The king looked at the cardinal as if to interrogate him; but he had not time to address any question to him--a cry of admiration burst from every mouth. If the king appeared to be the first gentleman of his kingdom, the queen was without doubt the most beautiful woman in France.

It is true that the habit of a huntress became her admirably. She wore a beaver hat with blue feathers, a surtout of gray-pearl velvet, fastened with diamond clasps, and a petticoat of blue satin, embroidered with silver. On her left shoulder sparkled the diamond studs, on a bow of the same color as the plumes and the petticoat.

The king trembled with joy and the cardinal with vexation; although, distant as they were from the queen, they could not count the studs. The queen had them. The only question was, had she ten or twelve?

At that moment the violins sounded the signal for the ballet. The king advanced toward Madame the President, with whom he was to dance, and his Highness Monsieur with the queen. They took their places, and the ballet began.

The king danced facing the queen, and every time he passed by her, he devoured with his eyes those studs of which he could not ascertain the number. A cold sweat covered the brow of the cardinal.

The ballet lasted an hour, and had sixteen ENTREES. The ballet ended amid the applause of the whole assemblage, and everyone reconducted his lady to her place; but the king took advantage of the privilege he had of leaving his lady, to advance eagerly toward the queen.

"I thank you, madame," said he, "for the deference you have shown to my wishes, but I think you want two of the studs, and I bring them back to you."

With these words he held out to the queen the two studs the cardinal had given him.

"How, sire?" cried the young queen, affecting surprise, "you are giving me, then, two more: I shall have fourteen."

In fact the king counted them, and the twelve studs were all on her Majesty's shoulder.

The king called the cardinal.

"What does this mean, Monsieur Cardinal?" asked the king in a severe tone.

"This means, sire," replied the cardinal, "that I was desirous of presenting her Majesty with these two studs, and that not daring to offer them myself, I adopted this means of inducing her to accept them."

"And I am the more grateful to your Eminence," replied Anne of Austria, with a smile that proved she was not the dupe of this ingenious gallantry, "from being certain that these two studs alone have cost you as much as all the others cost his Majesty."

Then saluting the king and the cardinal, the queen resumed her way to the chamber in which she had dressed, and where she was to take off her costume.

The attention which we have been obliged to give, during the commencement of the chapter, to the illustrious personages we have introduced into it, has diverted us for an instant from him to whom Anne of Austria owed the extraordinary triumph she had obtained over the cardinal; and who, confounded, unknown, lost in the crowd gathered at one of the doors, looked on at this scene, comprehensible only to four persons--the king, the queen, his Eminence, and himself.

The queen had just regained her chamber, and d'Artagnan was about to retire, when he felt his shoulder lightly touched. He turned and saw a young woman, who made him a sign to follow her. The face of this young woman was covered with a black velvet mask; but notwithstanding this precaution, which was in fact taken rather against others than against him, he at once recognized his usual guide, the light and intelligent Mme. Bonacieux.

On the evening before, they had scarcely seen each other for a moment at the apartment of the Swiss guard, Germain, whither d'Artagnan had sent for her. The haste which the young woman was in to convey to the queen the excellent news of the happy return of her messenger prevented the two lovers from exchanging more than a few words. D'Artagnan therefore followed Mme. Bonacieux moved by a double sentiment--love and curiosity. All the way, and in proportion as the corridors became more deserted, d'Artagnan wished to stop the young woman, seize her and gaze upon her, were it only for a minute; but quick as a bird she glided between his hands, and when he wished to speak to her, her finger placed upon her mouth, with a little imperative gesture full of grace, reminded him that he was under the command of a power which he must blindly obey, and which forbade him even to make the slightest complaint. At length, after winding about for a minute or two, Mme. Bonacieux opened the door of a closet, which was entirely dark, and led d'Artagnan into it. There she made a fresh sign of silence, and opened a second door concealed by tapestry. The opening of this door disclosed a brilliant light, and she disappeared.

D'Artagnan remained for a moment motionless, asking himself where he could be; but soon a ray of light which penetrated through the chamber, together with the warm and perfumed air which reached him from the same aperture, the conversation of two of three ladies in language at once respectful and refined, and the word "Majesty" several times repeated, indicated clearly that he was in a closet attached to the queen's apartment. The young man waited in comparative darkness and listened.

The queen appeared cheerful and happy, which seemed to astonish the persons who surrounded her and who were accustomed to see her almost always sad and full of care. The queen attributed this joyous feeling to the beauty of the fete, to the pleasure she had experienced in the ballet; and as it is not permissible to contradict a queen, whether she smile or weep, everybody expatiated on the gallantry of the aldermen of the city of Paris.

Although d'Artagnan did not at all know the queen, he soon distinguished her voice from the others, at first by a slightly foreign accent, and next by that tone of domination naturally impressed upon all royal words. He heard her approach and withdraw from the partially open door; and twice or three times he even saw the shadow of a person intercept the light.

At length a hand and an arm, surpassingly beautiful in their form and whiteness, glided through the tapestry. D'Artagnan at once comprehended that this was his recompense. He cast himself on his knees, seized the hand, and touched it respectfully with his lips. Then the hand was withdrawn, leaving in his an object which he perceived to be a ring. The door immediately closed, and d'Artagnan found himself again in complete obscurity.

D'Artagnan placed the ring on his finger, and again waited; it was evident that all was not yet over. After the reward of his devotion, that of his love was to come. Besides, although the ballet was danced, the evening had scarcely begun. Supper was to be served at three, and the clock of St. Jean had struck three quarters past two.

The sound of voices diminished by degrees in the adjoining chamber. The company was then heard departing; then the door of the closet in which d'Artagnan was, was opened, and Mme. Bonacieux entered.

"You at last?" cried d'Artagnan.

"Silence!" said the young woman, placing her hand upon his lips; "silence, and go the same way you came!"

"But where and when shall I see you again?" cried d'Artagnan.

"A note which you will find at home will tell you. Begone, begone!"

At these words she opened the door of the corridor, and pushed d'Artagnan out of the room. D'Artagnan obeyed like a child, without the least resistance or objection, which proved that he was really in love.

23 The Rendezvous

D'Artagnan ran home immediately, and although it was three o'clock in the morning and he had some of the worst quarters of Paris to traverse, he met with no misadventure. Everyone knows that drunkards and lovers have a protecting deity.

He found the door of his passage open, sprang up the stairs and knocked softly in a manner agreed upon between him and his lackey. Planchet[1], whom he had sent home two hours before from the Hotel de Ville, telling him to sit up for him, opened the door for him.

"Has anyone brought a letter for me?" asked d'Artagnan, eagerly.

"No one has BROUGHT a letter, monsieur," replied Planchet; "but one has come of itself."

"What do you mean, blockhead?"

"I mean to say that when I came in, although I had the key of your apartment in my pocket, and that key had never quit me, I found a letter on the green table cover in your bedroom."

"And where is that letter?"

"I left it where I found it, monsieur. It is not natural for letters to enter people's houses in this manner. If the window had been open or even ajar, I should think nothing of it; but, no--all was hermetically sealed. Beware, monsieur; there is certainly some magic underneath."

Meanwhile, the young man had darted in to his chamber, and opened the letter. It was from Mme. Bonacieux, and was expressed in these terms:

"There are many thanks to be offered to you, and to be transmitted to you. Be this evening about ten o'clock at St. Cloud, in front of the pavilion which stands at the corner of the house of M. d'Estrees.--C.B."

While reading this letter, d'Artagnan felt his heart dilated and compressed by that delicious spasm which tortures and caresses the hearts of lovers.

It was the first billet he had received; it was the first rendezvous that had been granted him. His heart, swelled by the intoxication of joy, felt ready to dissolve away at the very gate of that terrestrial paradise called Love!

"Well, monsieur," said Planchet, who had observed his master grow red and pale successively, "did I not guess truly? Is it not some bad affair?"

"You are mistaken, Planchet," replied d'Artagnan; "and as a proof, there is a crown to drink my health."

"I am much obliged to Monsieur for the crown he had given me, and I promise him to follow his instructions exactly; but it is not the less true that letters which come in this way into shut-up houses--"

"Fall from heaven, my friend, fall from heaven."

"Then Monsieur is satisfied?" asked Planchet.

"My dear Planchet, I am the happiest of men!"

"And I may profit by Monsieur's happiness, and go to bed?"

"Yes, go."

"May the blessings of heaven fall upon Monsieur! But it is not the less true that that letter--"

And Planchet retired, shaking his head with an air of doubt, which the liberality of d'Artagnan had not entirely effaced.

Left alone, d'Artagnan read and reread his billet. Then he kissed and rekissed twenty times the lines traced by the hand of his beautiful mistress. At length he went to bed, fell asleep, and had golden dreams.

At seven o'clock in the morning he arose and called Planchet, who at the second summons opened the door, his countenance not yet quite freed from the anxiety of the preceding night.

"Planchet," said d'Artagnan, "I am going out for all day, perhaps. You are, therefore, your own master

[1] The reader may ask, "How came Planchet here?" when he was left "stiff as a rush" in London. In the intervening time Buckingham perhaps sent him to Paris, as he did the horses.

till seven o'clock in the evening; but at seven o'clock you must hold yourself in readiness with two horses."

"There!" said Planchet. "We are going again, it appears, to have our hides pierced in all sorts of ways."

"You will take your musketoon and your pistols."

"There, now! Didn't I say so?" cried Planchet. "I was sure of it--the cursed letter!"

"Don't be afraid, you idiot; there is nothing in hand but a party of pleasure."

"Ah, like the charming journey the other day, when it rained bullets and produced a crop of steel traps!"

"Well, if you are really afraid, Monsieur Planchet," resumed d'Artagnan, "I will go without you. I prefer traveling alone to having a companion who entertains the least fear."

"Monsieur does me wrong," said Planchet; "I thought he had seen me at work."

"Yes, but I thought perhaps you had worn out all your courage the first time."

"Monsieur shall see that upon occasion I have some left; only I beg Monsieur not to be too prodigal of it if he wishes it to last long."

"Do you believe you have still a certain amount of it to expend this evening?"

"I hope so, monsieur."

"Well, then, I count on you."

"At the appointed hour I shall be ready; only I believed that Monsieur had but one horse in the Guard stables."

"Perhaps there is but one at this moment; but by this evening there will be four."

"It appears that our journey was a remounting journey, then?"

"Exactly so," said d'Artagnan; and nodding to Planchet, he went out.

M Bonacieux was at his door. D'Artagnan's intention was to go out without speaking to the worthy mercer; but the latter made so polite and friendly a salutation that his tenant felt obliged, not only to stop, but to enter into conversation with him.

Besides, how is it possible to avoid a little condescension toward a husband whose pretty wife has appointed a meeting with you that same evening at St. Cloud, opposite D'Estrees's pavilion? D'Artagnan approached him with the most amiable air he could assume.

The conversation naturally fell upon the incarceration of the poor man. M. Bonacieux, who was ignorant that d'Artagnan had overheard his conversation with the stranger of Meung, related to his young tenant the persecutions of that monster, M. de Laffemas, whom he never ceased to designate, during his account, by the title of the "cardinal's executioner," and expatiated at great length upon the Bastille, the bolts, the wickets, the dungeons, the gratings, the instruments of torture.

D'Artagnan listened to him with exemplary complaisance, and when he had finished said, "And Madame Bonacieux, do you know who carried her off?--For I do not forget that I owe to that unpleasant circumstance the good fortune of having made your acquaintance."

"Ah!" said Bonacieux, "they took good care not to tell me that; and my wife, on her part, has sworn to me by all that's sacred that she does not know. But you," continued M. Bonacieux, in a tine of perfect good fellowship, "what has become of you all these days? I have not seen you nor your friends, and I don't think you could gather all that dust that I saw Planchet brush off your boots yesterday from the pavement of Paris."

"You are right, my dear Monsieur Bonacieux, my friends and I have been on a little journey."

"Far from here?"

"Oh, Lord, no! About forty leagues only. We went to take Monsieur Athos to the waters of Forges, where my friends still remain."

"And you have returned, have you not?" replied M. Bonacieux, giving to his countenance a most sly air. "A handsome young fellow like you does not obtain long leaves of absence from his mistress; and we were impatiently waited for at Paris, were we not?"

"My faith!" said the young man, laughing, "I confess it, and so much more the readily, my dear Bonacieux, as I see there is no concealing anything from you. Yes, I was expected, and very impatiently, I acknowledge."

A slight shade passed over the brow of Bonacieux, but so slight that d'Artagnan did not perceive it.

"And we are going to be recompensed for our diligence?" continued the mercer, with a trifling alteration in his voice--so trifling, indeed, that d'Artagnan did not perceive it any more than he had the momentary shade which, an instant before, had darkened the countenance of the worthy man.

"Ah, may you be a true prophet!" said d'Artagnan, laughing.

"No; what I say," replied Bonacieux, "is only that I may know whether I am delaying you."

"Why that question, my dear host?" asked d'Artagnan. "Do you intend to sit up for me?"

"No; but since my arrest and the robbery that was committed in my house, I am alarmed every time I hear a door open, particularly in the night. What the deuce can you expect? I am no swordsman."

"Well, don't be alarmed if I return at one, two or three o'clock in the morning; indeed, do not be alarmed if I do not come at all."

This time Bonacieux became so pale that d'Artagnan could not help perceiving it, and asked him what was the matter.

"Nothing," replied Bonacieux, "nothing. Since my misfortunes I have been subject to faintnesses, which seize me all at once, and I have just felt a cold shiver. Pay no attention to it; you have nothing to occupy yourself with but being happy."

"Then I have full occupation, for I am so."

"Not yet; wait a little! This evening, you said."

"Well, this evening will come, thank God! And perhaps you look for it with as much impatience as I do; perhaps this evening Madame Bonacieux will visit the conjugal domicile."

"Madame Bonacieux is not at liberty this evening," replied the husband, seriously; "she is detained at the Louvre this evening by her duties."

"So much the worse for you, my dear host, so much the worse! When I am happy, I wish all the world to be so; but it appears that is not possible."

The young man departed, laughing at the joke, which he thought he alone could comprehend.

"Amuse yourself well!" replied Bonacieux, in a sepulchral tone.

But d'Artagnan was too far off to hear him; and if he had heard him in the disposition of mind he then enjoyed, he certainly would not have remarked it.

He took his way toward the hotel of M. de Treville; his visit of the day before, it is to be remembered, had been very short and very little explicative.

He found Treville in a joyful mood. He had thought the king and queen charming at the ball. It is true the cardinal had been particularly ill-tempered. He had retired at one o'clock under the pretense of being indisposed. As to their Majesties, they did not return to the Louvre till six o'clock in the morning.

"Now," said Treville, lowering his voice, and looking into every corner of the apartment to see if they were alone, "now let us talk about yourself, my young friend; for it is evident that your happy return has something to do with the joy of the king, the triumph of the queen, and the humiliation of his Eminence. You must look out for yourself."

"What have I to fear," replied d'Artagnan, "as long as I shall have the luck to enjoy the favor of their Majesties?"

"Everything, believe me. The cardinal is not the man to forget a mystification until he has settled account with the mystifier; and the mystifier appears to me to have the air of being a certain young Gascon of my acquaintance."

"Do you believe that the cardinal is as well posted as yourself, and knows that I have been to London?"

"The devil! You have been to London! Was it from London you brought that beautiful diamond that glitters on your finger? Beware, my dear d'Artagnan! A present from an enemy is not a good thing. Are there not some Latin verses upon that subject? Stop!"

"Yes, doubtless," replied d'Artagnan, who had never been able to cram the first rudiments of that language into his head, and who had by his ignorance driven his master to despair, "yes, doubtless there is one."

"There certainly is one," said M. de Treville, who had a tincture of literature, "and Monsieur de Benserade was quoting it to me the other day. Stop a minute--ah, this is it: 'Timeo Danaos et dona ferentes,' which means, 'Beware of the enemy who makes you presents."

"This diamond does not come from an enemy, monsieur," replied d'Artagnan, "it comes from the queen."

"From the queen! Oh, oh!" said M. de Treville. "Why, it is indeed a true royal jewel, which is worth a thousand pistoles if it is worth a denier. By whom did the queen send you this jewel?"

"She gave it to me herself."

"Where?"

"In the room adjoining the chamber in which she changed her toilet."

"How?"

"Giving me her hand to kiss."

"You have kissed the queen's hand?" said M. de Treville, looking earnestly at d'Artagnan.

"Her Majesty did me the honor to grant me that favor."

"And that in the presence of witnesses! Imprudent, thrice imprudent!"

"No, monsieur, be satisfied; nobody saw her," replied d'Artagnan, and he related to M. de Treville how the affair came to pass.

"Oh, the women, the women!" cried the old soldier. "I know them by their romantic imagination. Everything that savors of mystery charms them. So you have seen the arm, that was all. You would meet the queen, and she would not know who you are?"

"No; but thanks to this diamond," replied the young man.

"Listen," said M. de Treville; "shall I give you counsel, good counsel, the counsel of a friend?"

"You will do me honor, monsieur," said d'Artagnan.

"Well, then, off to the nearest goldsmith's, and sell that diamond for the highest price you can get from him. However much of a Jew he may be, he will give you at least eight hundred pistoles. Pistoles have no name, young man, and that ring has a terrible one, which may betray him who wears it."

"Sell this ring, a ring which comes from my sovereign? Never!" said d'Artagnan.

"Then, at least turn the gem inside, you silly fellow; for everybody must be aware that a cadet from Gascony does not find such stones in his mother's jewel case."

"You think, then, I have something to dread?" asked d'Artagnan.

"I mean to say, young man, that he who sleeps over a mine the match of which is already lighted, may consider himself in safety in comparison with you."

"The devil!" said d'Artagnan, whom the positive tone of M. de Treville began to disquiet, "the devil! What must I do?"

"Above all things be always on your guard. The cardinal has a tenacious memory and a long arm; you may depend upon it, he will repay you by some ill turn."

"But of what sort?"

"Eh! How can I tell? Has he not all the tricks of a demon at his command? The least that can be expected is that you will be arrested."

"What! Will they dare to arrest a man in his Majesty's service?"

"PARDIEU! They did not scruple much in the case of Athos. At all events, young man, rely upon one who has been thirty years at court. Do not lull yourself in security, or you will be lost; but, on the contrary--and it is I who say it--see enemies in all directions. If anyone seeks a quarrel with you, shun it, were it with a child of ten years old. If you are attacked by day or by night, fight, but retreat, without shame; if you cross a bridge, feel every plank of it with your foot, lest one should give way beneath you; if you pass before a house which is being built, look up, for fear a stone should fall upon your head; if you stay out late, be always followed by your lackey, and let your lackey be armed--if, by the by, you can be sure of your lackey. Mistrust everybody, your friend, your brother, your mistress--your mistress above all."

D'Artagnan blushed.

"My mistress above all," repeated he, mechanically; "and why her rather than another?"

"Because a mistress is one of the cardinal's favorite means; he has not one that is more expeditious. A woman will sell you for ten pistoles, witness Delilah. You are acquainted with the Scriptures?"

D'Artagnan thought of the appointment Mme. Bonacieux had made with him for that very evening; but we are bound to say, to the credit of our hero, that the bad opinion entertained by M. de Treville of women in general, did not inspire him with the least suspicion of his pretty hostess.

"But, A PROPOS," resumed M. de Treville, "what has become of your three companions?"

"I was about to ask you if you had heard any news of them?"

"None, monsieur."

"Well, I left them on my road--Porthos at Chantilly, with a duel on his hands; Aramis at Crevecoeur, with a ball in his shoulder; and Athos at Amiens, detained by an accusation of coining."

"See there, now!" said M. de Treville; "and how the devil did you escape?"

"By a miracle, monsieur, I must acknowledge, with a sword thrust in my breast, and by nailing the Comte de Wardes on the byroad to Calais, like a butterfly on a tapestry."

"There again! De Wardes, one of the cardinal's men, a cousin of Rochefort! Stop, my friend, I have an idea."

"Speak, monsieur."

"In your place, I would do one thing."

"What?"

"While his Eminence was seeking for me in Paris, I would take, without sound of drum or trumpet, the road to Picardy, and would go and make some inquiries concerning my three companions. What the devil! They merit richly that piece of attention on your part."

"The advice is good, monsieur, and tomorrow I will set out."

"Tomorrow! Any why not this evening?"

"This evening, monsieur, I am detained in Paris by indispensable business."

"Ah, young man, young man, some flirtation or other. Take care, I repeat to you, take care. It is woman who has ruined us, still ruins us, and will ruin us, as long as the world stands. Take my advice and set out this evening."

"Impossible, monsieur."

"You have given your word, then?"

"Yes, monsieur."

"Ah, that's quite another thing; but promise me, if you should not be killed tonight, that you will go tomorrow."

"I promise it."

"Do you need money?"

"I have still fifty pistoles. That, I think, is as much as I shall want."

"But your companions?"

"I don't think they can be in need of any. We left Paris, each with seventy-five pistoles in his pocket."

"Shall I see you again before your departure?"

"I think not, monsieur, unless something new should happen."

"Well, a pleasant journey."

"Thanks, monsieur."

D'Artagnan left M. de Treville, touched more than ever by his paternal solicitude for his Musketeers.

He called successively at the abodes of Athos, Porthos, and Aramis. Neither of them had returned. Their lackeys likewise were absent, and nothing had been heard of either the one or the other. He would have inquired after them of their mistresses, but he was neither acquainted with Porthos's nor Aramis's, and as to Athos, he had none.

As he passed the Hotel des Gardes, he took a glance in to the stables. Three of the four horses had already arrived. Planchet, all astonishment, was busy grooming them, and had already finished two.

"Ah, monsieur," said Planchet, on perceiving d'Artagnan, "how glad I am to see you."

"Why so, Planchet?" asked the young man.

"Do you place confidence in our landlord--Monsieur Bonacieux?"

"I? Not the least in the world."

"Oh, you do quite right, monsieur."

"But why this question?"

"Because, while you were talking with him, I watched you without listening to you; and, monsieur, his countenance changed color two or three times!"

"Bah!"

"Preoccupied as Monsieur was with the letter he had received, he did not observe that; but I, whom the strange fashion in which that letter came into the house had placed on my guard--I did not lose a movement of his features."

"And you found it?"

"Traitorous, monsieur."

"Indeed!"

"Still more; as soon as Monsieur had left and disappeared round the corner of the street, Monsieur Bonacieux took his hat, shut his door, and set off at a quick pace in an opposite direction."

"It seems you are right, Planchet; all this appears to be a little mysterious; and be assured that we will not pay him our rent until the matter shall be categorically explained to us."

"Monsieur jests, but Monsieur will see."

"What would you have, Planchet? What must come is written."

"Monsieur does not then renounce his excursion for this evening?"

"Quite the contrary, Planchet; the more ill will I have toward Monsieur Bonacieux, the more punctual I shall be in keeping the appointment made by that letter which makes you so uneasy."

"Then that is Monsieur's determination?"

"Undeniably, my friend. At nine o'clock, then, be ready here at the hotel, I will come and take you."

Planchet seeing there was no longer any hope of making his master renounce his project, heaved a profound sigh and set to work to groom the third horse.

As to d'Artagnan, being at bottom a prudent youth, instead of returning home, went and dined with the Gascon priest, who, at the time of the distress of the four friends, had given them a breakfast of chocolate.

24 The Pavilion

At nine o'clock d'Artagnan was at the Hotel des Gardes; he found Planchet all ready. The fourth horse had arrived.

Planchet was armed with his musketoon and a pistol. D'Artagnan had his sword and placed two pistols in his belt; then both mounted and departed quietly. It was quite dark, and no one saw them go out. Planchet took place behind his master, and kept at a distance of ten paces from him.

D'Artagnan crossed the quays, went out by the gate of La Conference and followed the road, much more beautiful then than it is now, which leads to St. Cloud.

As long as he was in the city, Planchet kept at the respectful distance he had imposed upon himself; but as soon as the road began to be more lonely and dark, he drew softly nearer, so that when they entered the Bois de Boulogne he found himself riding quite naturally side by side with his master. In fact, we must not dissemble that the oscillation of the tall trees and the reflection of the moon in the dark underwood gave him serious uneasiness. D'Artagnan could not help perceiving that something more than usual was passing in the mind of his lackey and said, "Well, Monsieur Planchet, what is the matter with us now?"

"Don't you think, monsieur, that woods are like churches?"

"How so, Planchet?"

"Because we dare not speak aloud in one or the other."

"But why did you not dare to speak aloud, Planchet--because you are afraid?"

"Afraid of being heard? Yes, monsieur."

"Afraid of being heard! Why, there is nothing improper in our conversation, my dear Planchet, and no one could find fault with it."

"Ah, monsieur!" replied Planchet, recurring to his besetting idea, "that Monsieur Bonacieux has something vicious in his eyebrows, and something very unpleasant in the play of his lips."

"What the devil makes you think of Bonacieux?"

"Monsieur, we think of what we can, and not of what we will."

"Because you are a coward, Planchet."

"Monsieur, we must not confound prudence with cowardice; prudence is a virtue."

"And you are very virtuous, are you not, Planchet?"

"Monsieur, is not that the barrel of a musket which glitters yonder? Had we not better lower our heads?"

"In truth," murmured d'Artagnan, to whom M. de Treville's recommendation recurred, "this animal will end by making me afraid." And he put his horse into a trot.

Planchet followed the movements of his master as if he had been his shadow, and was soon trotting by his side.

"Are we going to continue this pace all night?" asked Planchet.

"No; you are at your journey's end."

"How, monsieur! And you?"

"I am going a few steps farther."

"And Monsieur leaves me here alone?"

"You are afraid, Planchet?"

"No; I only beg leave to observe to Monsieur that the night will be very cold, that chills bring on rheumatism, and that a lackey who has the rheumatism makes but a poor servant, particularly to a master as active as Monsieur."

"Well, if you are cold, Planchet, you can go into one of those cabarets that you see yonder, and be in waiting for me at the door by six o'clock in the morning."

"Monsieur, I have eaten and drunk respectfully the crown you gave me this morning, so that I have not a sou left in case I should be cold."

"Here's half a pistole. Tomorrow morning."

D'Artagnan sprang from his horse, threw the bridle to Planchet, and departed at a quick pace, folding his cloak around him.

"Good Lord, how cold I am!" cried Planchet, as soon as he had lost sight of his master; and in such haste was he to warm himself that he went straight to a house set out with all the attributes of a suburban tavern, and knocked at the door.

In the meantime d'Artagnan, who had plunged into a bypath, continued his route and reached St. Cloud; but instead of following the main street he turned behind the chateau, reached a sort of retired lane, and found himself soon in front of the pavilion named. It was situated in a very private spot. A high wall, at the angle of which was the pavilion, ran along one side of this lane, and on the other was a little garden connected with a poor cottage which was protected by a hedge from passers-by.

He gained the place appointed, and as no signal had been given him by which to announce his presence, he waited.

Not the least noise was to be heard; it might be imagined that he was a hundred miles from the capital. D'Artagnan leaned against the hedge, after having cast a glance behind it. Beyond that hedge, that garden, and that cottage, a dark mist enveloped with its folds that immensity where Paris slept--a vast void from which glittered a few luminous points, the funeral stars of that hell!

But for d'Artagnan all aspects were clothed happily, all ideas wore a smile, all shades were diaphanous. The appointed hour was about to strike. In fact, at the end of a few minutes the belfry of St. Cloud let fall slowly ten strokes from its sonorous jaws. There was something melancholy in this brazen voice pouring out its lamentations in the middle of the night; but each of those strokes, which made up the expected hour, vibrated harmoniously to the heart of the young man.

His eyes were fixed upon the little pavilion situated at the angle of the wall, of which all the windows were closed with shutters, except one on the first story. Through this window shone a mild light which silvered the foliage of two or three linden trees which formed a group outside the park. There could be no doubt that behind this little window, which threw forth such friendly beams, the pretty Mme. Bonacieux expected him.

Wrapped in this sweet idea, d'Artagnan waited half an hour without the least impatience, his eyes fixed upon that charming little abode of which he could perceive a part of the ceiling with its gilded moldings, attesting the elegance of the rest of the apartment.

The belfry of St. Cloud sounded half past ten.

This time, without knowing why, d'Artagnan felt a cold shiver run through his veins. Perhaps the cold began to affect him, and he took a perfectly physical sensation for a moral impression.

Then the idea seized him that he had read incorrectly, and that the appointment was for eleven o'clock. He drew near to the window, and placing himself so that a ray of light should fall upon the letter as he held it, he drew it from his pocket and read it again; but he had not been mistaken, the appointment was for ten o'clock. He went and resumed his post, beginning to be rather uneasy at this silence and this solitude.

Eleven o'clock sounded.

D'Artagnan began now really to fear that something had happened to Mme. Bonacieux. He clapped his hands three times--the ordinary signal of lovers; but nobody replied to him, not even an echo.

He then thought, with a touch of vexation, that perhaps the young woman had fallen asleep while waiting for him. He approached the wall, and tried to climb it; but the wall had been recently pointed, and d'Artagnan could get no hold.

At that moment he thought of the trees, upon whose leaves the light still shone; and as one of them drooped over the road, he thought that from its branches he might get a glimpse of the interior of the pavilion.

The tree was easy to climb. Besides, d'Artagnan was but twenty years old, and consequently had not yet forgotten his schoolboy habits. In an instant he was among the branches, and his keen eyes plunged through the transparent panes into the interior of the pavilion.

It was a strange thing, and one which made d'Artagnan tremble from the sole of his foot to the roots of his hair, to find that this soft light, this calm lamp, enlightened a scene of fearful disorder. One of the windows was broken, the door of the chamber had been beaten in and hung, split in two, on its hinges. A table, which had been covered with an elegant supper, was overturned. The decanters broken in pieces, and the fruits crushed, strewed the floor. Everything in the apartment gave evidence of a violent and desperate struggle. D'Artagnan even fancied he could recognize amid this strange disorder, fragments of garments, and some bloody spots staining the cloth and the curtains. He hastened to descend into the street, with a frightful beating at his heart; he wished to see if he could find other traces of violence.

The little soft light shone on in the calmness of the night. d'Artagnan then perceived a thing that he had not before remarked--for nothing had led him to the examination--that the ground, trampled here and hoofmarked there, presented confused traces of men and horses. Besides, the wheels of a carriage, which appeared to have come from Paris, had made a deep impression in the soft earth, which did not extend beyond the pavilion, but turned again toward Paris.

At length d'Artagnan, in pursuing his researches, found near the wall a woman's torn glove. This glove, wherever it had not touched the muddy ground, was of irreproachable odor. It was one of those perfumed gloves that lovers like to snatch from a pretty hand.

As d'Artagnan pursued his investigations, a more abundant and more icy sweat rolled in large drops from his forehead; his heart was oppressed by a horrible anguish; his respiration was broken and short. And yet he said, to reassure himself, that this pavilion perhaps had nothing in common with Mme. Bonacieux; that the young woman had made an appointment with him before the pavilion, and not in the pavilion; that she might have been detained in Paris by her duties, or perhaps by the jealousy of her husband.

But all these reasons were combated, destroyed, overthrown, by that feeling of intimate pain which, on certain occasions, takes possession of our being, and cries to us so as to be understood unmistakably that some great misfortune is hanging over us.

Then d'Artagnan became almost wild. He ran along the high road, took the path he had before taken, and reaching the ferry, interrogated the boatman.

About seven o'clock in the evening, the boatman had taken over a young woman, wrapped in a black mantle, who appeared to be very anxious not to be recognized; but entirely on account of her precautions, the boatman had paid more attention to her and discovered that she was young and pretty.

There were then, as now, a crowd of young and pretty women who came to St. Cloud, and who had reasons for not being seen, and yet d'Artagnan did not for an instant doubt that it was Mme. Bonacieux whom the boatman had noticed.

D'Artagnan took advantage of the lamp which burned in the cabin of the ferryman to read the billet of Mme. Bonacieux once again, and satisfy himself that he had not been mistaken, that the appointment was at St. Cloud and not elsewhere, before the D'Estrees's pavilion and not in another street. Everything conspired to prove to d'Artagnan that his presentiments had not deceived him, and that a great misfortune had happened.

He again ran back to the chateau. It appeared to him that something might have happened at the pavilion in his absence, and that fresh information awaited him. The lane was still deserted, and the same calm soft light shone through the window.

D'Artagnan then thought of that cottage, silent and obscure, which had no doubt seen all, and could tell its tale. The gate of the enclosure was shut; but he leaped over the hedge, and in spite of the barking of a chained-up dog, went up to the cabin.

No one answered to his first knocking. A silence of death reigned in the cabin as in the pavilion; but as the cabin was his last resource, he knocked again.

It soon appeared to him that he heard a slight noise within--a timid noise which seemed to tremble lest it should be heard.

Then d'Artagnan ceased knocking, and prayed with an accent so full of anxiety and promises, terror and cajolery, that his voice was of a nature to reassure the most fearful. At length an old, worm-eaten shutter was opened, or rather pushed ajar, but closed again as soon as the light from a miserable lamp which burned in the corner had shone upon the baldric, sword belt, and pistol pommels of d'Artagnan. Nevertheless, rapid as the movement had been, d'Artagnan had had time to get a glimpse of the head of an old man.

"In the name of heaven!" cried he, "listen to me; I have been waiting for someone who has not come. I am dying with anxiety. Has anything particular happened in the neighborhood? Speak!"

The window was again opened slowly, and the same face appeared, only it was now still more pale than before.

D'Artagnan related his story simply, with the omission of names. He told how he had a rendezvous with a young woman before that pavilion, and how, not seeing her come, he had climbed the linden tree, and by the light of the lamp had seen the disorder of the chamber.

The old man listened attentively, making a sign only that it was all so; and then, when d'Artagnan had ended, he shook his head with an air that announced nothing good.

"What do you mean?" cried d'Artagnan. "In the name of heaven, explain yourself!"

"Oh! Monsieur," said the old man, "ask me nothing; for if I dared tell you what I have seen, certainly no good would befall me."

"You have, then, seen something?" replied d'Artagnan. "In that case, in the name of heaven," continued he, throwing him a pistole, "tell me what you have seen, and I will pledge you the word of a gentleman that not one of your words shall escape from my heart."

The old man read so much truth and so much grief in the face of the young man that he made him a sign to listen, and repeated in a low voice: "It was scarcely nine o'clock when I heard a noise in the street, and was wondering what it could be, when on coming to my door, I found that somebody was endeavoring to open it. As I am very poor and am not afraid of being robbed, I went and opened the gate and saw three men at a few paces from it. In the shadow was a carriage with two horses, and some saddlehorses. These horses evidently belonged to the three men, who were dressed as cavaliers. 'Ah, my worthy gentlemen,' cried I, 'what do you want?' 'You must have a ladder?' said he who appeared to be the leader of the party. 'Yes, monsieur, the one with which I gather my fruit.' 'Lend it to us, and go into your house again; there is a crown for the annoyance we have caused you. Only remember this--if you speak a word of what you may see or what you may hear (for you will look and you will listen, I am quite sure, however we may threaten you), you are lost.' At these words he threw me a crown, which I picked up, and he took the ladder. After shutting the gate behind them, I pretended to return to the house, but I immediately went out a back door, and stealing along in the shade of the hedge, I gained yonder clump of elder, from which I could hear and see everything. The three men brought the carriage up quietly, and took out of it a little man, stout, short, elderly, and commonly dressed in clothes of a dark color, who ascended the ladder very carefully, looked suspiciously in at the window of the pavilion, came down as quietly as he had gone up, and whispered, 'It is she!' Immediately, he who had spoken to me approached the door of the pavilion, opened it with a key he had in his hand, closed the door and disappeared, while at the same time the other two men ascended the ladder. The little old man remained at the coach door; the coachman took care of his horses, the lackey held the saddlehorses. All at once great cries resounded in the pavilion, and a woman came to the window, and opened it, as if to throw herself out of it; but as soon as she perceived the other two men, she fell back and they went into the chamber. Then I saw no more; but I heard the noise of breaking furniture. The woman screamed, and cried for help; but her cries were soon stifled. Two of the men appeared, bearing the woman in their arms, and carried her to the carriage, into which the little old man got after her. The leader closed the window, came out an instant after by the door, and satisfied himself that the woman was in the carriage. His two companions were already on horseback. He sprang into his saddle; the lackey took his place by the coachman; the carriage went off at a quick pace, escorted by the three horsemen, and all was over. From that moment I have neither seen nor heard anything."

D'Artagnan, entirely overcome by this terrible story, remained motionless and mute, while all the demons of anger and jealousy were howling in his heart.

"But, my good gentleman," resumed the old man, upon whom this mute despair certainly produced a greater effect than cries and tears would have done, "do not take on so; they did not kill her, and that's a comfort."

"Can you guess," said d'Artagnan, "who was the man who headed this infernal expedition?"

"I don't know him."

"But as you spoke to him you must have seen him."

"Oh, it's a description you want?"

"Exactly so."

"A tall, dark man, with black mustaches, dark eyes, and the air of a gentleman."

"That's the man!" cried d'Artagnan, "again he, forever he! He is my demon, apparently. And the other?"

"Which?"

"The short one."

"Oh, he was not a gentleman, I'll answer for it; besides, he did not wear a sword, and the others treated him with small consideration."

"Some lackey," murmured d'Artagnan. "Poor woman, poor woman, what have they done with you?"

"You have promised to be secret, my good monsieur?" said the old man.

"And I renew my promise. Be easy, I am a gentleman. A gentleman has but his word, and I have given you mine."

With a heavy heart, d'Artagnan again bent his way toward the ferry. Sometimes he hoped it could not be Mme. Bonacieux, and that he should find her next day at the Louvre; sometimes he feared she had had an intrigue with another, who, in a jealous fit, had surprised her and carried her off. His mind was torn by doubt, grief, and despair.

"Oh, if I had my three friends here," cried he, "I should have, at least, some hopes of finding her; but who knows what has become of them?"

It was past midnight; the next thing was to find Planchet. d'Artagnan went successively into all the cabarets in which there was a light, but could not find Planchet in any of them.

At the sixth he began to reflect that the search was rather dubious. D'Artagnan had appointed six o'clock in the morning for his lackey, and wherever he might be, he was right.

Besides, it came into the young man's mind that by remaining in the environs of the spot on which this sad event had passed, he would, perhaps, have some light thrown upon the mysterious affair. At the sixth cabaret, then, as we said, d'Artagnan stopped, asked for a bottle of wine of the best quality, and placing himself in the darkest corner of the room, determined thus to wait till daylight; but this time again his hopes were disappointed, and although he listened with all his ears, he heard nothing, amid the oaths, coarse jokes, and abuse which passed between the laborers, servants, and carters who comprised the honorable society of which he formed a part, which could put him upon the least track of her who had been stolen from him. He was compelled, then, after having swallowed the contents of his bottle, to pass the time as well as to evade suspicion, to fall into the easiest position in his corner and to sleep, whether well or ill. D'Artagnan, be it remembered, was only twenty years old, and at that age sleep has its imprescriptible rights which it imperiously insists upon, even with the saddest hearts.

Toward six o'clock d'Artagnan awoke with that uncomfortable feeling which generally accompanies the break of day after a bad night. He was not long in making his toilet. He examined himself to see if advantage had been taken of his sleep, and having found his diamond ring on his finger, his purse in his pocket, and his pistols in his belt, he rose, paid for his bottle, and went out to try if he could have any better luck in his search after his lackey than he had had the night before. The first thing he perceived through the damp gray mist was honest Planchet, who, with the two horses in hand, awaited him at the door of a little blind cabaret, before which d'Artagnan had passed without even a suspicion of its existence.

25 Porthos

Instead of returning directly home, d'Artagnan alighted at the door of M. de Treville, and ran quickly up the stairs. This time he had decided to relate all that had passed. M. de Treville would doubtless give him good advice as to the whole affair. Besides, as M. de Treville saw the queen almost daily, he might be able to draw from her Majesty some intelligence of the poor young woman, whom they were doubtless making pay very dearly for her devotedness to her mistress.

M de Treville listened to the young man's account with a seriousness which proved that he saw something else in this adventure besides a love affair. When d'Artagnan had finished, he said, "Hum! All this savors of his Eminence, a league off."

"But what is to be done?" said d'Artagnan.

"Nothing, absolutely nothing, at present, but quitting Paris, as I told you, as soon as possible. I will see the queen; I will relate to her the details of the disappearance of this poor woman, of which she is no doubt ignorant. These details will guide her on her part, and on your return, I shall perhaps have some good news to tell you. Rely on me."

D'Artagnan knew that, although a Gascon, M. de Treville was not in the habit of making promises, and that when by chance he did promise, he more than kept his word. He bowed to him, then, full of gratitude for the past and for the future; and the worthy captain, who on his side felt a lively interest in this young man, so brave and so resolute, pressed his hand kindly, wishing him a pleasant journey.

Determined to put the advice of M. de Treville in practice instantly, d'Artagnan directed his course toward the Rue des Fossoyeurs, in order to superintend the packing of his valise. On approaching the house, he perceived M. Bonacieux in morning costume, standing at his threshold. All that the prudent Planchet had said to him the preceding evening about the sinister character of the old man recurred to the mind of d'Artagnan, who looked at him with more attention than he had done before. In fact, in addition to that yellow, sickly paleness which indicates the insinuation of the bile in the blood, and which might, besides, be accidental, d'Artagnan remarked something perfidiously significant in the play of the wrinkled features of his countenance. A rogue does not laugh in the same way that an honest man does; a hypocrite does not shed the tears of a man of good faith. All falsehood is a mask; and however well made the mask may be, with a little attention we may always succeed in distinguishing it from the true face.

It appeared, then, to d'Artagnan that M. Bonacieux wore a mask, and likewise that that mask was most disagreeable to look upon. In consequence of this feeling of repugnance, he was about to pass without speaking to him, but, as he had done the day before, M. Bonacieux accosted him.

"Well, young man," said he, "we appear to pass rather gay nights! Seven o'clock in the morning! PESTE! You seem to reverse ordinary customs, and come home at the hour when other people are going out."

"No one can reproach you for anything of the kind, Monsieur Bonacieux," said the young man; "you are a model for regular people. It is true that when a man possesses a young and pretty wife, he has no need to seek happiness elsewhere. Happiness comes to meet him, does it not, Monsieur Bonacieux?"

Bonacieux became as pale as death, and grinned a ghastly smile.

"Ah, ah!" said Bonacieux, "you are a jocular companion! But where the devil were you gladding last night, my young master? It does not appear to be very clean in the crossroads."

D'Artagnan glanced down at his boots, all covered with mud; but that same glance fell upon the shoes and stockings of the mercer, and it might have been said they had been dipped in the same mud heap. Both were stained with splashes of mud of the same appearance.

Then a sudden idea crossed the mind of d'Artagnan. That little stout man, short and elderly, that sort of lackey, dressed in dark clothes, treated without ceremony by the men wearing swords who composed the escort, was Bonacieux himself. The husband had presided at the abduction of his wife.

A terrible inclination seized d'Artagnan to grasp the mercer by the throat and strangle him; but, as we have said, he was a very prudent youth, and he restrained himself. However, the revolution which appeared upon his countenance was so visible that Bonacieux was terrified at it, and he endeavored to draw back a step or two; but as he was standing before the half of the door which was shut, the obstacle compelled him to keep his place.

"Ah, but you are joking, my worthy man!" said d'Artagnan. "It appears to me that if my boots need a sponge, your stockings and shoes stand in equal need of a brush. May you not have been philandering a little also, Monsieur Bonacieux? Oh, the devil! That's unpardonable in a man of your age, and who besides, has such a pretty wife as yours."

"Oh, Lord! no," said Bonacieux, "but yesterday I went to St. Mande to make some inquiries after a servant, as I cannot possibly do without one; and the roads were so bad that I brought back all this mud, which I have not yet had time to remove."

The place named by Bonacieux as that which had been the object of his journey was a fresh proof in support of the suspicions d'Artagnan had conceived. Bonacieux had named Mande because Mande was in an exactly opposite direction from St. Cloud. This probability afforded him his first consolation. If Bonacieux knew where his wife was, one might, by extreme means, force the mercer to open his teeth and let his secret escape. The question, then, was how to change this probability into a certainty.

"Pardon, my dear Monsieur Bonacieux, if I don't stand upon ceremony," said d'Artagnan, "but nothing makes one so thirsty as want of sleep. I am parched with thirst. Allow me to take a glass of water in your apartment; you know that is never refused among neighbors."

Without waiting for the permission of his host, d'Artagnan went quickly into the house, and cast a rapid glance at the bed. It had not been used. Bonacieux had not been abed. He had only been back an hour or two; he had accompanied his wife to the place of her confinement, or else at least to the first relay.

"Thanks, Monsieur Bonacieux," said d'Artagnan, emptying his glass, "that is all I wanted of you. I will now go up into my apartment. I will make Planchet brush my boots; and when he has done, I will, if you like, send him to you to brush your shoes."

He left the mercer quite astonished at his singular farewell, and asking himself if he had not been a little inconsiderate.

At the top of the stairs he found Planchet in a great fright.

"Ah, monsieur!" cried Planchet, as soon as he perceived his master, "here is more trouble. I thought you would never come in."

"What's the matter now, Planchet?" demanded d'Artagnan.

"Oh! I give you a hundred, I give you a thousand times to guess, monsieur, the visit I received in your absence."

"When?"

"About half an hour ago, while you were at Monsieur de Treville's."

"Who has been here? Come, speak."

"Monsieur de Cavois."

"Monsieur de Cavois?"

"In person."

"The captain of the cardinal's Guards?"

"Himself."

"Did he come to arrest me?"

"I have no doubt that he did, monsieur, for all his wheedling manner."

"Was he so sweet, then?"

"Indeed, he was all honey, monsieur."

"Indeed!"

"He came, he said, on the part of his Eminence, who wished you well, and to beg you to follow him to the Palais-Royal[1]."

"What did you answer him?"

"That the thing was impossible, seeing that you were not at home, as he could see."

"Well, what did he say then?"

"That you must not fail to call upon him in the course of the day; and then he added in a low voice, 'Tell your master that his Eminence is very well disposed toward him, and that his fortune perhaps depends upon this interview.'"

"The snare is rather MALADROIT for the cardinal," replied the young man, smiling.

"Oh, I saw the snare, and I answered you would be quite in despair on your return.

"'Where has he gone?' asked Monsieur de Cavois.

"'To Troyes, in Champagne,' I answered.

[1] It was called the Palais-Cardinal before Richelieu gave it to the King.

"'And when did he set out?'

"'Yesterday evening.'"

"Planchet, my friend," interrupted d'Artagnan, "you are really a precious fellow."

"You will understand, monsieur, I thought there would be still time, if you wish, to see Monsieur de Cavois to contradict me by saying you were not yet gone. The falsehood would then lie at my door, and as I am not a gentleman, I may be allowed to lie."

"Be of good heart, Planchet, you shall preserve your reputation as a veracious man. In a quarter of an hour we set off."

"That's the advice I was about to give Monsieur; and where are we going, may I ask, without being too curious?"

"PARDIEU! In the opposite direction to that which you said I was gone. Besides, are you not as anxious to learn news of Grimaud, Mousqueton, and Bazin as I am to know what has become of Athos, Porthos, and Aramis?"

"Yes, monsieur," said Planchet, "and I will go as soon as you please. Indeed, I think provincial air will suit us much better just now than the air of Paris. So then--"

"So then, pack up our luggage, Planchet, and let us be off. On my part, I will go out with my hands in my pockets, that nothing may be suspected. You may join me at the Hotel des Gardes. By the way, Planchet, I think you are right with respect to our host, and that he is decidedly a frightfully low wretch."

"Ah, monsieur, you may take my word when I tell you anything. I am a physiognomist, I assure you."

D'Artagnan went out first, as had been agreed upon. Then, in order that he might have nothing to reproach himself with, he directed his steps, for the last time, toward the residences of his three friends. No news had been received of them; only a letter, all perfumed and of an elegant writing in small characters, had come for Aramis. D'Artagnan took charge of it. Ten minutes afterward Planchet joined him at the stables of the Hotel des Gardes. D'Artagnan, in order that there might be no time lost, had saddled his horse himself.

"That's well," said he to Planchet, when the latter added the portmanteau to the equipment. "Now saddle the other three horses."

"Do you think, then, monsieur, that we shall travel faster with two horses apiece?" said Planchet, with his shrewd air.

"No, Monsieur Jester," replied d'Artagnan; "but with our four horses we may bring back our three friends, if we should have the good fortune to find them living."

"Which is a great chance," replied Planchet, "but we must not despair of the mercy of God."

"Amen!" said d'Artagnan, getting into his saddle.

As they went from the Hotel des Gardes, they separated, leaving the street at opposite ends, one having to quit Paris by the Barriere de la Villette and the other by the Barriere Montmartre, to meet again beyond St. Denis--a strategic maneuver which, having been executed with equal punctuality, was crowned with the most fortunate results. D'Artagnan and Planchet entered Pierrefitte together.

Planchet was more courageous, it must be admitted, by day than by night. His natural prudence, however, never forsook him for a single instant. He had forgotten not one of the incidents of the first journey, and he looked upon everybody he met on the road as an enemy. It followed that his hat was forever in his hand, which procured him some severe reprimands from d'Artagnan, who feared that his excess of politeness would lead people to think he was the lackey of a man of no consequence.

Nevertheless, whether the passengers were really touched by the urbanity of Planchet or whether this time nobody was posted on the young man's road, our two travelers arrived at Chantilly without any accident, and alighted at the tavern of Great St. Martin, the same at which they had stopped on their first journey.

The host, on seeing a young man followed by a lackey with two extra horses, advanced respectfully to the door. Now, as they had already traveled eleven leagues, d'Artagnan thought it time to stop, whether Porthos were or were not in the inn. Perhaps it would not be prudent to ask at once what had become of the Musketeer. The result of these reflections was that d'Artagnan, without asking information of any kind, alighted, commended the horses to the care of his lackey, entered a small room destined to receive those who wished to be alone, and desired the host to bring him a bottle of his best wine and as good a breakfast as possible--a desire which further corroborated the high opinion the innkeeper had formed of the traveler at first sight.

D'Artagnan was therefore served with miraculous celerity. The regiment of the Guards was recruited among the first gentlemen of the kingdom; and d'Artagnan, followed by a lackey, and traveling with four magnificent horses, despite the simplicity of his uniform, could not fail to make a sensation. The host desired himself to serve him; which d'Artagnan perceiving, ordered two glasses to be brought, and commenced the following conversation.

"My faith, my good host," said d'Artagnan, filling the two glasses, "I asked for a bottle of your best wine, and if you have deceived me, you will be punished in what you have sinned; for seeing that I hate drinking my myself, you shall drink with me. Take your glass, then, and let us drink. But what shall we drink to, so as to avoid wounding any susceptibility? Let us drink to the prosperity of your establishment."

"Your Lordship does me much honor," said the host, "and I thank you sincerely for your kind wish."

"But don't mistake," said d'Artagnan, "there is more selfishness in my toast than perhaps you may think--for it is only in prosperous establishments that one is well received. In hotels that do not flourish, everything is in confusion, and the traveler is a victim to the embarrassments of his host. Now, I travel a great deal, particularly on this road, and I wish to see all innkeepers making a fortune."

"It seems to me," said the host, "that this is not the first time I have had the honor of seeing Monsieur."

"Bah, I have passed perhaps ten times through Chantilly, and out of the ten times I have stopped three or four times at your house at least. Why I was here only ten or twelve days ago. I was conducting some friends, Musketeers, one of whom, by the by, had a dispute with a stranger--a man who sought a quarrel with him, for I don't know what."

"Exactly so," said the host; "I remember it perfectly. It is not Monsieur Porthos that your Lordship means?"

"Yes, that is my companion's name. My God, my dear host, tell me if anything has happened to him?"

"Your Lordship must have observed that he could not continue his journey."

"Why, to be sure, he promised to rejoin us, and we have seen nothing of him."

"He has done us the honor to remain here."

"What, he had done you the honor to remain here?"

"Yes, monsieur, in this house; and we are even a little uneasy--"

"On what account?"

"Of certain expenses he has contracted."

"Well, but whatever expenses he may have incurred, I am sure he is in a condition to pay them."

"Ah, monsieur, you infuse genuine balm into my blood. We have made considerable advances; and this very morning the surgeon declared that if Monsieur Porthos did not pay him, he should look to me, as it was I who had sent for him."

"Porthos is wounded, then?"

"I cannot tell you, monsieur."

"What! You cannot tell me? Surely you ought to be able to tell me better than any other person."

"Yes; but in our situation we must not say all we know--particularly as we have been warned that our ears should answer for our tongues."

"Well, can I see Porthos?"

"Certainly, monsieur. Take the stairs on your right; go up the first flight and knock at Number One. Only warn him that it is you."

"Why should I do that?"

"Because, monsieur, some mischief might happen to you."

"Of what kind, in the name of wonder?"

"Monsieur Porthos may imagine you belong to the house, and in a fit of passion might run his sword through you or blow out your brains."

"What have you done to him, then?"

"We have asked him for money."

"The devil! Ah, I can understand that. It is a demand that Porthos takes very ill when he is not in funds; but I know he must be so at present."

"We thought so, too, monsieur. As our house is carried on very regularly, and we make out our bills every week, at the end of eight days we presented our account; but it appeared we had chosen an unlucky moment, for at the first word on the subject, he sent us to all the devils. It is true he had been playing the day before."

"Playing the day before! And with whom?"

"Lord, who can say, monsieur? With some gentleman who was traveling this way, to whom he proposed a game of LANSQUENET."

"That's it, then, and the foolish fellow lost all he had?"

"Even to his horse, monsieur; for when the gentleman was about to set out, we perceived that his lackey was saddling Monsieur Porthos's horse, as well as his master's. When we observed this to him, he told us all to trouble ourselves about our own business, as this horse belonged to him. We also informed Monsieur Porthos of what was going on; but he told us we were scoundrels to doubt a gentleman's word, and that as he had said the horse was his, it must be so."

"That's Porthos all over," murmured d'Artagnan.

"Then," continued the host, "I replied that as from the moment we seemed not likely to come to a good understanding with respect to payment, I hoped that he would have at least the kindness to grant the favor of his custom to my brother host of the Golden Eagle; but Monsieur Porthos replied that, my house being the best, he should remain where he was. This reply was too flattering to allow me to insist on his departure. I confined myself then to begging him to give up his chamber, which is the handsomest in the hotel, and to be satisfied with a pretty little room on the third floor; but to this Monsieur Porthos replied that as he every moment expected his mistress, who was one of the greatest ladies in the court, I might easily comprehend that the chamber he did me the honor to occupy in my house was itself very mean for the visit of such a personage. Nevertheless, while acknowledging the truth of what he said, I thought proper to insist; but without even giving himself the trouble to enter into any discussion with me, he took one of his pistols, laid it on his table, day and night, and said that at the first word that should be spoken to him about removing, either within the house or out of it, he would blow out the brains of the person who should be so imprudent as to meddle with a matter which only concerned himself. Since that time, monsieur, nobody entered his chamber but his servant."

"What! Mousqueton is here, then?"

"Oh, yes, monsieur. Five days after your departure, he came back, and in a very bad condition, too. It appears that he had met with disagreeableness, likewise, on his journey. Unfortunately, he is more nimble than his master; so that for the sake of his master, he puts us all under his feet, and as he thinks we might refuse what he asked for, he takes all he wants without asking at all."

"The fact is," said d'Artagnan, "I have always observed a great degree of intelligence and devotedness in Mousqueton."

"That is possible, monsieur; but suppose I should happen to be brought in contact, even four times a year, with such intelligence and devotedness--why, I should be a ruined man!"

"No, for Porthos will pay you."

"Hum!" said the host, in a doubtful tone.

"The favorite of a great lady will not be allowed to be inconvenienced for such a paltry sum as he owes you."

"If I durst say what I believe on that head--"

"What you believe?"

"I ought rather to say, what I know."

"What you know?"

"And even what I am sure of."

"And of what are you so sure?"

"I would say that I know this great lady."

"You?"

"Yes; I."

"And how do you know her?"

"Oh, monsieur, if I could believe I might trust in your discretion."

"Speak! By the word of a gentleman, you shall have no cause to repent of your confidence."

"Well, monsieur, you understand that uneasiness makes us do many things."

"What have you done?"

"Oh, nothing which was not right in the character of a creditor."

"Well?"

"Monsieur Porthos gave us a note for his duchess, ordering us to put it in the post. This was before his servant came. As he could not leave his chamber, it was necessary to charge us with this commission."

"And then?"

"Instead of putting the letter in the post, which is never safe, I took advantage of the journey of one of my lads to Paris, and ordered him to convey the letter to this duchess himself. This was fulfilling the intentions of Monsieur Porthos, who had desired us to be so careful of this letter, was it not?"

"Nearly so."

"Well, monsieur, do you know who this great lady is?"

"No; I have heard Porthos speak of her, that's all."

"Do you know who this pretended duchess is?

"I repeat to you, I don't know her."

"Why, she is the old wife of a procurator[1] of the Chatelet, monsieur, named Madame Coquenard, who, although she is at least fifty, still gives herself jealous airs. It struck me as very odd that a princess should live in the Rue aux Ours."

"But how do you know all this?"

"Because she flew into a great passion on receiving the letter, saying that Monsieur Porthos was a weathercock, and that she was sure it was for some woman he had received this wound."

"Has he been wounded, then?"

"Oh, good Lord! What have I said?"

"You said that Porthos had received a sword cut."

"Yes, but he has forbidden me so strictly to say so."

"And why so."

"Zounds, monsieur! Because he had boasted that he would perforate the stranger with whom you left him in dispute; whereas the stranger, on the contrary, in spite of all his rodomontades quickly threw him on his back. As Monsieur Porthos is a very boastful man, he insists that nobody shall know he has re-

[1] Attorney

ceived this wound except the duchess, whom he endeavored to interest by an account of his adventure."

"It is a wound that confines him to his bed?"

"Ah, and a master stroke, too, I assure you. Your friend's soul must stick tight to his body."

"Were you there, then?"

"Monsieur, I followed them from curiosity, so that I saw the combat without the combatants seeing me."

"And what took place?"

"Oh! The affair was not long, I assure you. They placed themselves on guard; the stranger made a feint and a lunge, and that so rapidly that when Monsieur Porthos came to the PARADE, he had already three inches of steel in his breast. He immediately fell backward. The stranger placed the point of his sword at his throat; and Monsieur Porthos, finding himself at the mercy of his adversary, acknowledged himself conquered. Upon which the stranger asked his name, and learning that it was Porthos, and not d'Artagnan, he assisted him to rise, brought him back to the hotel, mounted his horse, and disappeared."

"So it was with Monsieur d'Artagnan this stranger meant to quarrel?"

"It appears so."

"And do you know what has become of him?"

"No, I never saw him until that moment, and have not seen him since."

"Very well; I know all that I wish to know. Porthos's chamber is, you say, on the first story, Number One?"

"Yes, monsieur, the handsomest in the inn--a chamber that I could have let ten times over."

"Bah! Be satisfied," said d'Artagnan, laughing, "Porthos will pay you with the money of the Duchess Coquenard."

"Oh, monsieur, procurator's wife or duchess, if she will but loosen her pursestrings, it will be all the same; but she positively answered that she was tired of the exigencies and infidelities of Monsieur Porthos, and that she would not send him a denier."

"And did you convey this answer to your guest?"

"We took good care not to do that; he would have found in what fashion we had executed his commission."

"So that he still expects his money?"

"Oh, Lord, yes, monsieur! Yesterday he wrote again; but it was his servant who this time put the letter in the post."

"Do you say the procurator's wife is old and ugly?"

"Fifty at least, monsieur, and not at all handsome, according to Pathaud's account."

"In that case, you may be quite at ease; she will soon be softened. Besides, Porthos cannot owe you much."

"How, not much! Twenty good pistoles, already, without reckoning the doctor. He denies himself nothing; it may easily be seen he has been accustomed to live well."

"Never mind; if his mistress abandons him, he will find friends, I will answer for it. So, my dear host, be not uneasy, and continue to take all the care of him that his situation requires."

"Monsieur has promised me not to open his mouth about the procurator's wife, and not to say a word of the wound?"

"That's agreed; you have my word."

"Oh, he would kill me!"

"Don't be afraid; he is not so much of a devil as he appears."

Saying these words, d'Artagnan went upstairs, leaving his host a little better satisfied with respect to two things in which he appeared to be very much interested--his debt and his life.

At the top of the stairs, upon the most conspicuous door of the corridor, was traced in black ink a gigantic number "1." d'Artagnan knocked, and upon the bidding to come in which came from inside, he entered the chamber.

Porthos was in bed, and was playing a game at LANSQUENET with Mousqueton, to keep his hand in; while a spit loaded with partridges was turning before the fire, and on each side of a large chimney-piece, over two chafing dishes, were boiling two stewpans, from which exhaled a double odor of rabbit and fish stews, rejoicing to the smell. In addition to this he perceived that the top of a wardrobe and the marble of a commode were covered with empty bottles.

At the sight of his friend, Porthos uttered a loud cry of joy; and Mousqueton, rising respectfully, yielded his place to him, and went to give an eye to the two stewpans, of which he appeared to have the particular inspection.

"Ah, PARDIEU! Is that you?" said Porthos to d'Artagnan. "You are right welcome. Excuse my not coming to meet you; but," added he, looking at d'Artagnan with a certain degree of uneasiness, "you know what has happened to me?"

"No."

"Has the host told you nothing, then?"

"I asked after you, and came up as soon as I could."

Porthos seemed to breathe more freely.

"And what has happened to you, my dear Porthos?" continued d'Artagnan.

"Why, on making a thrust at my adversary, whom I had already hit three times, and whom I meant to finish with the fourth, I put my foot on a stone, slipped, and strained my knee."

"Truly?"

"Honor! Luckily for the rascal, for I should have left him dead on the spot, I assure you."

"And what has became of him?"

"Oh, I don't know; he had enough, and set off without waiting for the rest. But you, my dear d'Artagnan, what has happened to you?"

"So that this strain of the knee," continued d'Artagnan, "my dear Porthos, keeps you in bed?"

"My God, that's all. I shall be about again in a few days."

"Why did you not have yourself conveyed to Paris? You must be cruelly bored here."

"That was my intention; but, my dear friend, I have one thing to confess to you."

"What's that?"

"It is that as I was cruelly bored, as you say, and as I had the seventy-five pistoles in my pocket which you had distributed to me, in order to amuse myself I invited a gentleman who was traveling this way to walk up, and proposed a cast of dice. He accepted my challenge, and, my faith, my seventy-five pistoles passed from my pocket to his, without reckoning my horse, which he won into the bargain. But you, my dear d'Artagnan?"

"What can you expect, my dear Porthos; a man is not privileged in all ways," said d'Artagnan. "You know the proverb 'Unlucky at play, lucky in love.' You are too fortunate in your love for play not to take its revenge. What consequence can the reverses of fortune be to you? Have you not, happy rogue that you are--have you not your duchess, who cannot fail to come to your aid?"

"Well, you see, my dear d'Artagnan, with what ill luck I play," replied Porthos, with the most careless air in the world. "I wrote to her to send me fifty louis or so, of which I stood absolutely in need on account of my accident."

"Well?"

"Well, she must be at her country seat, for she has not answered me."

"Truly?"

"No; so I yesterday addressed another epistle to her, still more pressing than the first. But you are here, my dear fellow, let us speak of you. I confess I began to be very uneasy on your account."

"But your host behaves very well toward you, as it appears, my dear Porthos," said d'Artagnan, directing the sick man's attention to the full stewpans and the empty bottles.

"So, so," replied Porthos. "Only three or four days ago the impertinent jackanapes gave me his bill, and I was forced to turn both him and his bill out of the door; so that I am here something in the fashion of a conqueror, holding my position, as it were, my conquest. So you see, being in constant fear of being forced from that position, I am armed to the teeth."

"And yet," said d'Artagnan, laughing, "it appears to me that from time to time you must make SORTIES." And he again pointed to the bottles and the stewpans.

"Not I, unfortunately!" said Porthos. "This miserable strain confines me to my bed; but Mousqueton forages, and brings in provisions. Friend Mousqueton, you see that we have a reinforcement, and we must have an increase of supplies."

"Mousqueton," said d'Artagnan, "you must render me a service."

"What, monsieur?"

"You must give your recipe to Planchet. I may be besieged in my turn, and I shall not be sorry for him to be able to let me enjoy the same advantages with which you gratify your master."

"Lord, monsieur! There is nothing more easy," said Mousqueton, with a modest air. "One only needs to be sharp, that's all. I was brought up in the country, and my father in his leisure time was something of a poacher."

"And what did he do the rest of his time?"

"Monsieur, he carried on a trade which I have always thought satisfactory."

"Which?"

"As it was a time of war between the Catholics and the Huguenots, and as he saw the Catholics exterminate the Huguenots and the Huguenots exterminate the Catholics--all in the name of religion--he adopted a mixed belief which permitted him to be sometimes Catholic, sometimes a Huguenot. Now, he was accustomed to walk with his fowling piece on his shoulder, behind the hedges which border the roads, and when he saw a Catholic coming alone, the Protestant religion immediately prevailed in his mind. He lowered his gun in the direction of the traveler; then, when he was within ten paces of him, he commenced a conversation which almost always ended by the traveler's abandoning his purse to save his life. It goes without saying that when he saw a Huguenot coming, he felt himself filled with such ardent Catholic zeal that he could not understand how, a quarter of an hour before, he had been able to have any doubts upon the superiority of our holy religion. For my part, monsieur, I am Catholic--my father, faithful to his principles, having made my elder brother a Huguenot."

"And what was the end of this worthy man?" asked d'Artagnan.

"Oh, of the most unfortunate kind, monsieur. One day he was surprised in a lonely road between a Huguenot and a Catholic, with both of whom he had before had business, and who both knew him again; so they united against him and hanged him on a tree. Then they came and boasted of their fine exploit in the cabaret of the next village, where my brother and I were drinking."

"And what did you do?" said d'Artagnan.

"We let them tell their story out," replied Mousqueton. "Then, as in leaving the cabaret they took different directions, my brother went and hid himself on the road of the Catholic, and I on that of the Huguenot. Two hours after, all was over; we had done the business of both, admiring the foresight of our poor father, who had taken the precaution to bring each of us up in a different religion."

"Well, I must allow, as you say, your father was a very intelligent fellow. And you say in his leisure moments the worthy man was a poacher?"

"Yes, monsieur, and it was he who taught me to lay a snare and ground a line. The consequence is that when I saw our laborers, which did not at all suit two such delicate stomachs as ours, I had recourse to a little of my old trade. While walking near the wood of Monsieur le Prince, I laid a few snare in the runs; and while reclining on the banks of his Highness's pieces of water, I slipped a few lines into his fish ponds. So that now, thanks be to God, we do not want, as Monsieur can testify, for partridges, rabbits, carp or eels--all light, wholesome food, suitable for the sick."

"But the wine," said d'Artagnan, "who furnishes the wine? Your host?"

"That is to say, yes and no."

"How yes and no?"

"He furnishes it, it is true, but he does not know that he has that honor."

"Explain yourself, Mousqueton; your conversation is full of instructive things."

"That is it, monsieur. It has so chanced that I met with a Spaniard in my peregrinations who had seen many countries, and among them the New World."

"What connection can the New World have with the bottles which are on the commode and the wardrobe?"

"Patience, monsieur, everything will come in its turn."

"This Spaniard had in his service a lackey who had accompanied him in his voyage to Mexico. This lackey was my compatriot; and we became the more intimate from there being many resemblances of character between us. We loved sporting of all kinds better than anything; so that he related to me how in the plains of the Pampas the natives hunt the tiger and the wild bull with simple running nooses which they throw to a distance of twenty or thirty paces the end of a cord with such nicety; but in face of the proof I was obliged to acknowledge the truth of the recital. My friend placed a bottle at the distance of thirty paces, and at each cast he caught the neck of the bottle in his running noose. I practiced this exercise, and as nature has endowed me with some faculties, at this day I can throw the lasso with any man in the world. Well, do you understand, monsieur? Our host has a well-furnished cellar the key of which never leaves him; only this cellar has a ventilating hole. Now through this ventilating hole I throw my lasso, and as I now know in which part of the cellar is the best wine, that's my point for sport. You see, monsieur, what the New World has to do with the bottles which are on the commode and the wardrobe. Now, will you taste our wine, and without prejudice say what you think of it?"

"Thank you, my friend, thank you; unfortunately, I have just breakfasted."

"Well," said Porthos, "arrange the table, Mousqueton, and while we breakfast, d'Artagnan will relate to us what has happened to him during the ten days since he left us."

"Willingly," said d'Artagnan.

While Porthos and Mousqueton were breakfasting, with the appetites of convalescents and with that brotherly cordiality which unites men in misfortune, d'Artagnan related how Aramis, being wounded, was obliged to stop at Crevecoeur, how he had left Athos fighting at Amiens with four men who accused him of being a coiner, and how he, d'Artagnan, had been forced to run the Comtes de Wardes through the body in order to reach England.

But there the confidence of d'Artagnan stopped. He only added that on his return from Great Britain he had brought back four magnificent horses--one for himself, and one for each of his companions; then he informed Porthos that the one intended for him was already installed in the stable of the tavern.

At this moment Planchet entered, to inform his master that the horses were sufficiently refreshed and that it would be possible to sleep at Clermont.

As d'Artagnan was tolerably reassured with regard to Porthos, and as he was anxious to obtain news of his two other friends, he held out his hand to the wounded man, and told him he was about to resume his route in order to continue his researches. For the rest, as he reckoned upon returning by the same route in seven or eight days, if Porthos were still at the Great St. Martin, he would call for him on his way.

Porthos replied that in all probability his sprain would not permit him to depart yet awhile. Besides, it was necessary he should stay at Chantilly to wait for the answer from his duchess.

D'Artagnan wished that answer might be prompt and favorable; and having again recommended Porthos to the care of Mousqueton, and paid his bill to the host, he resumed his route with Planchet, already relieved of one of his led horses.

26 Aramis And His Thesis

D'Artagnan had said nothing to Porthos of his wound or of his procurator's wife. Our Bearnais was a prudent lad, however young he might be. Consequently he had appeared to believe all that the vainglorious Musketeer had told him, convinced that no friendship will hold out against a surprised secret. Besides, we feel always a sort of mental superiority over those whose lives we know better than they suppose. In his projects of intrigue for the future, and determined as he was to make his three friends the instruments of his fortune, d'Artagnan was not sorry at getting into his grasp beforehand the invisible strings by which he reckoned upon moving them.

And yet, as he journeyed along, a profound sadness weighed upon his heart. He thought of that young and pretty Mme. Bonacieux who was to have paid him the price of his devotedness; but let us hasten to say that this sadness possessed the young man less from the regret of the happiness he had missed, than from the fear he entertained that some serious misfortune had befallen the poor woman. For himself, he had no doubt she was a victim of the cardinal's vengeance; and, and as was well known, the vengeance of his Eminence was terrible. How he had found grace in the eyes of the minister, he did not know; but without doubt M. de Cavois would have revealed this to him if the captain of the Guards had found him at home.

Nothing makes time pass more quickly or more shortens a journey than a thought which absorbs in itself all the faculties of the organization of him who thinks. External existence then resembles a sleep of which this thought is the dream. By its influence, time has no longer measure, space has no longer distance. We depart from one place, and arrive at another, that is all. Of the interval passed, nothing remains in the memory but a vague mist in which a thousand confused images of trees, mountains, and landscapes are lost. It was as a prey to this hallucination that d'Artagnan traveled, at whatever pace his horse pleased, the six or eight leagues that separated Chantilly from Crevecoeur, without his being able to remember on his arrival in the village any of the things he had passed or met with on the road.

There only his memory returned to him. He shook his head, perceived the cabaret at which he had left Aramis, and putting his horse to the trot, he shortly pulled up at the door.

This time it was not a host but a hostess who received him. d'Artagnan was a physiognomist. His eye took in at a glance the plump, cheerful countenance of the mistress of the place, and he at once perceived there was no occasion for dissembling with her, or of fearing anything from one blessed with such a joyous physiognomy.

"My good dame," asked d'Artagnan, "can you tell me what has become of one of my friends, whom we were obliged to leave here about a dozen days ago?"

"A handsome young man, three- or four-and-twenty years old, mild, amiable, and well made?"

"That is he--wounded in the shoulder."

"Just so. Well, monsieur, he is still here."

"Ah, PARDIEU! My dear dame," said d'Artagnan, springing from his horse, and throwing the bridle to Planchet, "you restore me to life; where is this dear Aramis? Let me embrace him, I am in a hurry to see him again."

"Pardon, monsieur, but I doubt whether he can see you at this moment."

"Why so? Has he a lady with him?"

"Jesus! What do you mean by that? Poor lad! No, monsieur, he has not a lady with him."

"With whom is he, then?"

"With the curate of Montdidier and the superior of the Jesuits of Amiens."

"Good heavens!" cried d'Artagnan, "is the poor fellow worse, then?"

"No, monsieur, quite the contrary; but after his illness grace touched him, and he determined to take orders."

"That's it!" said d'Artagnan, "I had forgotten that he was only a Musketeer for a time."

"Monsieur still insists upon seeing him?"

"More than ever."

"Well, monsieur has only to take the right-hand staircase in the courtyard, and knock at Number Five on the second floor."

D'Artagnan walked quickly in the direction indicated, and found one of those exterior staircases that are still to be seen in the yards of our old-fashioned taverns. But there was no getting at the place of sojourn of the future abbe; the defiles of the chamber of Aramis were as well guarded as the gardens of Armida. Bazin was stationed in the corridor, and barred his passage with the more intrepidity that, after many years of trial, Bazin found himself near a result of which he had ever been ambitious.

In fact, the dream of poor Bazin had always been to serve a churchman; and he awaited with impatience the moment, always in the future, when Aramis would throw aside the uniform and assume the cassock. The daily-renewed promise of the young man that the moment would not long be delayed, had alone kept him in the service of a Musketeer--a service in which, he said, his soul was in constant jeopardy.

Bazin was then at the height of joy. In all probability, this time his master would not retract. The union of physical pain with moral uneasiness had produced the effect so long desired. Aramis, suffering at once in body and mind, had at length fixed his eyes and his thoughts upon religion, and he had considered as a warning from heaven the double accident which had happened to him; that is to say, the sudden disappearance of his mistress and the wound in his shoulder.

It may be easily understood that in the present disposition of his master nothing could be more disagreeable to Bazin than the arrival of d'Artagnan, which might cast his master back again into that vortex of mundane affairs which had so long carried him away. He resolved, then, to defend the door bravely; and as, betrayed by the mistress of the inn, he could not say that Aramis was absent, he endeavored to prove to the newcomer that it would be the height of indiscretion to disturb his master in his pious conference, which had commenced with the morning and would not, as Bazin said, terminate before night.

But d'Artagnan took very little heed of the eloquent discourse of M. Bazin; and as he had no desire to support a polemic discussion with his friend's valet, he simply moved him out of the way with one hand, and with the other turned the handle of the door of Number Five. The door opened, and d'Artagnan went into the chamber.

Aramis, in a black gown, his head enveloped in a sort of round flat cap, not much unlike a CALOTTE, was seated before an oblong table, covered with rolls of paper and enormous volumes in folio. At his right hand was placed the superior of the Jesuits, and on his left the curate of Montdidier. The curtains were half drawn, and only admitted the mysterious light calculated for beatific reveries. All the mundane objects that generally strike the eye on entering the room of a young man, particularly when that young man is a Musketeer, had disappeared as if by enchantment; and for fear, no doubt, that the sight of them might bring his master back to ideas of this world, Bazin had laid his hands upon sword, pistols, plumed hat, and embroideries and laces of all kinds and sorts. In their stead d'Artagnan thought he perceived in an obscure corner a discipline cord suspended from a nail in the wall.

At the noise made by d'Artagnan in entering, Aramis lifted up his head, and beheld his friend; but to the great astonishment of the young man, the sight of him did not produce much effect upon the Musketeer, so completely was his mind detached from the things of this world.

"Good day, dear d'Artagnan," said Aramis; "believe me, I am glad to see you."

"So am I delighted to see you," said d'Artagnan, "although I am not yet sure that it is Aramis I am speaking to."

"To himself, my friend, to himself! But what makes you doubt it?"

"I was afraid I had made a mistake in the chamber, and that I had found my way into the apartment of some churchman. Then another error seized me on seeing you in company with these gentlemen--I was afraid you were dangerously ill."

The two men in black, who guessed d'Artagnan's meaning, darted at him a glance which might have been thought threatening; but d'Artagnan took no heed of it.

"I disturb you, perhaps, my dear Aramis," continued d'Artagnan, "for by what I see, I am led to believe that you are confessing to these gentlemen."

Aramis colored imperceptibly. "You disturb me? Oh, quite the contrary, dear friend, I swear; and as a proof of what I say, permit me to declare I am rejoiced to see you safe and sound."

"Ah, he'll come round," thought d'Artagnan; "that's not bad!"

"This gentleman, who is my friend, has just escaped from a serious danger," continued Aramis, with unction, pointing to d'Artagnan with his hand, and addressing the two ecclesiastics.

"Praise God, monsieur," replied they, bowing together.

"I have not failed to do so, your Reverences," replied the young man, returning their salutation.

"You arrive in good time, dear d'Artagnan," said Aramis, "and by taking part in our discussion may assist us with your intelligence. Monsieur the Principal of Amiens, Monsieur the Curate of Montdidier, and I are arguing certain theological questions in which we have been much interested; I shall be delighted to have your opinion."

"The opinion of a swordsman can have very little weight," replied d'Artagnan, who began to be uneasy at the turn things were taking, "and you had better be satisfied, believe me, with the knowledge of these gentlemen."

The two men in black bowed in their turn.

"On the contrary," replied Aramis, "your opinion will be very valuable. The question is this: Monsieur the Principal thinks that my thesis ought to be dogmatic and didactic."

"Your thesis! Are you then making a thesis?"

"Without doubt," replied the Jesuit. "In the examination which precedes ordination, a thesis is always a requisite."

"Ordination!" cried d'Artagnan, who could not believe what the hostess and Bazin had successively told him; and he gazed, half stupefied, upon the three persons before him.

"Now," continued Aramis, taking the same graceful position in his easy chair that he would have assumed in bed, and complacently examining his hand, which was as white and plump as that of a woman, and which he held in the air to cause the blood to descend, "now, as you have heard, d'Artagnan, Monsieur the Principal is desirous that my thesis should be dogmatic, while I, for my part, would rather it should be ideal. This is the reason why Monsieur the Principal has proposed to me the following subject, which has not yet been treated upon, and in which I perceive there is matter for magnificent elaboration-'UTRAQUE MANUS IN BENEDICENDO CLERICIS INFERIORIBUS NECESSARIA EST.'"

D'Artagnan, whose erudition we are well acquainted with, evinced no more interest on hearing this quotation than he had at that of M. de Treville in allusion to the gifts he pretended that d'Artagnan had received from the Duke of Buckingham.

"Which means," resumed Aramis, that he might perfectly understand, "'The two hands are indispensable for priests of the inferior orders, when they bestow the benediction.'"

"An admirable subject!" cried the Jesuit.

"Admirable and dogmatic!" repeated the curate, who, about as strong as d'Artagnan with respect to Latin, carefully watched the Jesuit in order to keep step with him, and repeated his words like an echo.

As to d'Artagnan, he remained perfectly insensible to the enthusiasm of the two men in black.

"Yes, admirable! PRORSUS ADMIRABILE!" continued Aramis; "but which requires a profound study of both the Scriptures and the Fathers. Now, I have confessed to these learned ecclesiastics, and that in all humility, that the duties of mounting guard and the service of the king have caused me to neglect study a little. I should find myself, therefore, more at my ease, FACILUS NATANS, in a subject of my own choice, which would be to these hard theological questions what morals are to metaphysics in philosophy."

D'Artagnan began to be tired, and so did the curate.

"See what an exordium!" cried the Jesuit.

"Exordium," repeated the curate, for the sake of saying something. "QUEMADMODUM INTER COELORUM IMMNSITATEM."

Aramis cast a glance upon d'Artagnan to see what effect all this produced, and found his friend gaping enough to split his jaws.

"Let us speak French, my father," said he to the Jesuit; "Monsieur d'Artagnan will enjoy our conversation better."

"Yes," replied d'Artagnan; "I am fatigued with reading, and all this Latin confuses me."

"Certainly," replied the Jesuit, a little put out, while the curate, greatly delighted, turned upon d'Artagnan a look full of gratitude. "Well, let us see what is to be derived from this gloss. Moses, the servant of God-he was but a servant, please to understand-Moses blessed with the hands; he held out both his arms while the Hebrews beat their enemies, and then he blessed them with his two hands. Besides, what does the Gospel say? IMPONITE MANUS, and not MANUM-place the HANDS, not the HAND."

"Place the HANDS," repeated the curate, with a gesture.

"St. Peter, on the contrary, of whom the Popes are the successors," continued the Jesuit; "PORRIGE DIGITOS-present the fingers. Are you there, now?"

"CERTES," replied Aramis, in a pleased tone, "but the thing is subtle."

"The FINGERS," resumed the Jesuit, "St. Peter blessed with the FINGERS. The Pope, therefore blesses with the fingers. And with how many fingers does he bless? With THREE fingers, to be sure-one for the Father, one for the Son, and one for the Holy Ghost."

All crossed themselves. D'Artagnan thought it was proper to follow this example.

"The Pope is the successor of St. Peter, and represents the three divine powers; the rest-ORDINES INFERIORES-of the ecclesiastical hierarchy bless in the name of the holy archangels and angels. The most humble clerks such as our deacons and sacristans, bless with holy water sprinklers, which resemble an infinite number of blessing fingers. There is the subject simplified. ARGUMENTUM OMNI DENUDATUM ORNAMENTO. I could make of that subject two volumes the size of this," continued the Jesuit; and in his enthusiasm he struck a St. Chrysostom in folio, which made the table bend beneath its weight.

D'Artagnan trembled.

"CERTES," said Aramis, "I do justice to the beauties of this thesis; but at the same time I perceive it would be overwhelming for me. I had chosen this text-tell me, dear d'Artagnan, if it is not to your taste-'NON INUTILE EST DESIDERIUM IN OBLATIONE'; that is, 'A little regret is not unsuitable in an offering to the Lord.'"

"Stop there!" cried the Jesuit, "for that thesis touches closely upon heresy. There is a proposition almost like it in the AUGUSTINUS of the heresiarch Jansenius, whose book will sooner or later be burned by the hands of the executioner. Take care, my young friend. You are inclining toward false doctrines, my young friend; you will be lost."

"You will be lost," said the curate, shaking his head sorrowfully.

"You approach that famous point of free will which is a mortal rock. You face the insinuations of the Pelagians and the semi-Pelagians."

"But, my Reverend-" replied Aramis, a little amazed by the shower of arguments that poured upon his head.

"How will you prove," continued the Jesuit, without allowing him time to speak, "that we ought to regret the world when we offer ourselves to God? Listen to this dilemma: God is God, and the world is the devil. To regret the world is to regret the devil; that is my conclusion."

"And that is mine also," said the curate.

"But, for heaven's sake-" resumed Aramis.

"DESIDERAS DIABOLUM, unhappy man!" cried the Jesuit.

"He regrets the devil! Ah, my young friend," added the curate, groaning, "do not regret the devil, I implore you!"

D'Artagnan felt himself bewildered. It seemed to him as though he were in a madhouse, and was becoming as mad as those he saw. He was, however, forced to hold his tongue from not comprehending half the language they employed.

"But listen to me, then," resumed Aramis with politeness mingled with a little impatience. "I do not say I regret; no, I will never pronounce that sentence, which would not be orthodox."

The Jesuit raised his hands toward heaven, and the curate did the same.

"No; but pray grant me that it is acting with an ill grace to offer to the Lord only that with which we are perfectly disgusted! Don't you think so, d'Artagnan?"

"I think so, indeed," cried he.

The Jesuit and the curate quite started from their chairs.

"This is the point of departure; it is a syllogism. The world is not wanting in attractions. I quit the world; then I make a sacrifice. Now, the Scripture says positively, 'Make a sacrifice unto the Lord.'"

"That is true," said his antagonists.

"And then," said Aramis, pinching his ear to make it red, as he rubbed his hands to make them white, "and then I made a certain RONDEAU upon it last year, which I showed to Monsieur Voiture, and that great man paid me a thousand compliments."

"A RONDEAU!" said the Jesuit, disdainfully.

"A RONDEAU!" said the curate, mechanically.

"Repeat it! Repeat it!" cried d'Artagnan; "it will make a little change."

"Not so, for it is religious," replied Aramis; "it is theology in verse."

"The devil!" said d'Artagnan.

"Here it is," said Aramis, with a little look of diffidence, which, however, was not exempt from a shade of hypocrisy:

"Vous qui pleurez un passe plein de charmes, Et qui trainez des jours infortunes, Tous vos malheurs se verront termines, Quand a Dieu seul vous offrirez vos larmes, Vous qui pleurez!"

"You who weep for pleasures fled, While dragging on a life of care, All your woes will melt in air, If to God your tears are shed, You who weep!"

d'Artagnan and the curate appeared pleased. The Jesuit persisted in his opinion. "Beware of a profane taste in your theological style. What says Augustine on this subject: 'SEVERUS SIT CLERICORUM VERBO.'"

"Yes, let the sermon be clear," said the curate.

"Now," hastily interrupted the Jesuit, on seeing that his acolyte was going astray, "now your thesis would please the ladies; it would have the success of one of Monsieur Patru's pleadings."

"Please God!" cried Aramis, transported.

"There it is," cried the Jesuit; "the world still speaks within you in a loud voice, ALTISIMM VOCE. You follow the world, my young friend, and I tremble lest grace prove not efficacious."

"Be satisfied, my reverend father, I can answer for myself."

"Mundane presumption!"

"I know myself, Father; my resolution is irrevocable."

"Then you persist in continuing that thesis?"

"I feel myself called upon to treat that, and no other. I will see about the continuation of it, and tomorrow I hope you will be satisfied with the corrections I shall have made in consequence of your advice."

"Work slowly," said the curate; "we leave you in an excellent tone of mind."

"Yes, the ground is all sown," said the Jesuit, "and we have not to fear that one portion of the seed may have fallen upon stone, another upon the highway, or that the birds of heaven have eaten the rest, AVES COELI COMEDERUNT ILLAM."

"Plague stifle you and your Latin!" said d'Artagnan, who began to feel all his patience exhausted.

"Farewell, my son," said the curate, "till tomorrow."

"Till tomorrow, rash youth," said the Jesuit. "You promise to become one of the lights of the Church. Heaven grant that this light prove not a devouring fire!"

D'Artagnan, who for an hour past had been gnawing his nails with impatience, was beginning to attack the quick.

The two men in black rose, bowed to Aramis and d'Artagnan, and advanced toward the door. Bazin, who had been standing listening to all this controversy with a pious jubilation, sprang toward them, took the breviary of the curate and the missal of the Jesuit, and walked respectfully before them to clear their way.

Aramis conducted them to the foot of the stairs, and then immediately came up again to d'Artagnan, whose senses were still in a state of confusion.

When left alone, the two friends at first kept an embarrassed silence. It however became necessary for one of them to break it first, and as d'Artagnan appeared determined to leave that honor to his companion, Aramis said, "you see that I am returned to my fundamental ideas."

"Yes, efficacious grace has touched you, as that gentleman said just now."

"Oh, these plans of retreat have been formed for a long time. You have often heard me speak of them, have you not, my friend?"

"Yes; but I confess I always thought you jested."

"With such things! Oh, d'Artagnan!"

"The devil! Why, people jest with death."

"And people are wrong, d'Artagnan; for death is the door which leads to perdition or to salvation."

"Granted; but if you please, let us not theologize, Aramis. You must have had enough for today. As for me, I have almost forgotten the little Latin I have ever known. Then I confess to you that I have eaten nothing since ten o'clock this morning, and I am devilish hungry."

"We will dine directly, my friend; only you must please to remember that this is Friday. Now, on such a day I can neither eat flesh nor see it eaten. If you can be satisfied with my dinner-it consists of cooked tetragones and fruits."

"What do you mean by tetragones?" asked d'Artagnan, uneasily.

"I mean spinach," replied Aramis; "but on your account I will add some eggs, and that is a serious infraction of the rule-for eggs are meat, since they engender chickens."

"This feast is not very succulent; but never mind, I will put up with it for the sake of remaining with you."

"I am grateful to you for the sacrifice," said Aramis; "but if your body be not greatly benefited by it, be assured your soul will."

"And so, Aramis, you are decidedly going into the Church? What will our two friends say? What will Monsieur de Treville say? They will treat you as a deserter, I warn you."

"I do not enter the Church; I re-enter it. I deserted the Church for the world, for you know that I forced myself when I became a Musketeer."

"I? I know nothing about it."

"You don't know I quit the seminary?"

"Not at all."

"This is my story, then. Besides, the Scriptures say, 'Confess yourselves to one another,' and I confess to you, d'Artagnan."

"And I give you absolution beforehand. You see I am a good sort of a man."

"Do not jest about holy things, my friend."

"Go on, then, I listen."

"I had been at the seminary from nine years old; in three days I should have been twenty. I was about to become an abbe, and all was arranged. One evening I went, according to custom, to a house which I frequented with much pleasure: when one is young, what can be expected?--one is weak. An officer who saw me, with a jealous eye, reading the LIVES OF THE SAINTS to the mistress of the house, entered suddenly and without being announced. That evening I had translated an episode of Judith, and had just communicated my verses to the lady, who gave me all sorts of compliments, and leaning on my shoulder, was reading them a second time with me. Her pose, which I must admit was rather free, wounded this officer. He said nothing; but when I went out he followed, and quickly came up with me. 'Monsieur the Abbe,' said he, 'do you like blows with a cane?' 'I cannot say, monsieur,' answered I; 'no one has ever dared to give me any.' 'Well, listen to me, then, Monsieur the Abbe! If you venture again into the house in which I have met you this evening, I will dare it myself.' I really think I must have been frightened. I became very pale; I felt my legs fail me; I sought for a reply, but could find none-I was silent. The officer waited for his reply, and seeing it so long coming, he burst into a laugh, turned upon his heel, and reentered the house. I returned to the seminary.

"I am a gentleman born, and my blood is warm, as you may have remarked, my dear d'Artagnan. The insult was terrible, and although unknown to the rest of the world, I felt it live and fester at the bottom of my heart. I informed my superiors that I did not feel myself sufficiently prepared for ordination, and at my request the ceremony was postponed for a year. I sought out the best fencing master in Paris, I made an agreement with him to take a lesson every day, and every day for a year I took that lesson. Then, on the anniversary of the day on which I had been insulted, I hung my cassock on a peg, assumed the costume of a cavalier, and went to a ball given by a lady friend of mine and to which I knew my man was invited. It was in the Rue des France-Bourgeois, close to La Force. As I expected, my officer was there. I went up to him as he was singing a love ditty and looking tenderly at a lady, and interrupted him exactly in the middle of the second couplet. 'Monsieur,' said I, 'does it still displease you that I should frequent a certain house of La Rue Payenne? And would you still cane me if I took it into my head to disobey you? The officer looked at me with astonishment, and then said, 'What is your business with me, monsieur? I do not know you.' 'I am,' said I, 'the little abbe who reads LIVES OF THE SAINTS, and translates Judith into verse.' 'Ah, ah! I recollect now,' said the officer, in a jeering tone; 'well, what do you want with me?' 'I want you to spare time to take a walk with me.' 'Tomorrow morning, if you like, with the greatest pleasure.' 'No, not tomorrow morning, if you please, but immediately.' 'If you absolutely insist.' 'I do insist upon it.' 'Come, then. Ladies,' said the officer, 'do not disturb yourselves; allow me time just to kill this gentleman, and I will return and finish the last couplet.'

"We went out. I took him to the Rue Payenne, to exactly the same spot where, a year before, at the very same hour, he had paid me the compliment I have related to you. It was a superb moonlight night. We immediately drew, and at the first pass I laid him stark dead."

"The devil!" cried d'Artagnan.

"Now," continued Aramis, "as the ladies did not see the singer come back, and as he was found in the Rue Payenne with a great sword wound through his body, it was supposed that I had accommodated him thus; and the matter created some scandal which obliged me to renounce the cassock for a time. Athos, whose acquaintance I made about that period, and Porthos, who had in addition to my lessons taught me some effective tricks of fence, prevailed upon me to solicit the uniform of a Musketeer. The king entertained great regard for my father, who had fallen at the siege of Arras, and the uniform was granted. You may understand that the moment has come for me to re-enter the bosom of the Church."

"And why today, rather than yesterday or tomorrow? What has happened to you today, to raise all these melancholy ideas?"

"This wound, my dear d'Artagnan, has been a warning to me from heaven."

"This wound? Bah, it is now nearly healed, and I am sure it is not that which gives you the most pain."

"What, then?" said Aramis, blushing.

"You have one at heart, Aramis, one deeper and more painful--a wound made by a woman."

The eye of Aramis kindled in spite of himself.

"Ah," said he, dissembling his emotion under a feigned carelessness, "do not talk of such things, and suffer love pains? VANITAS VANITATUM! According to your idea, then, my brain is turned. And for whom-for some GRISETTE, some chambermaid with whom I have trifled in some garrison? Fie!"

"Pardon, my dear Aramis, but I thought you carried your eyes higher."

"Higher? And who am I, to nourish such ambition? A poor Musketeer, a beggar, an unknown-who hates slavery, and finds himself ill-placed in the world."

"Aramis, Aramis!" cried d'Artagnan, looking at his friend with an air of doubt.

"Dust I am, and to dust I return. Life is full of humiliations and sorrows," continued he, becoming still more melancholy; "all the ties which attach him to life break in the hand of man, particularly the golden ties. Oh, my dear d'Artagnan," resumed Aramis, giving to his voice a slight tone of bitterness, "trust me! Conceal your wounds when you have any; silence is the last joy of the unhappy. Beware of giving anyone the clue to your griefs; the curious suck our tears as flies suck the blood of a wounded hart."

"Alas, my dear Aramis," said d'Artagnan, in his turn heaving a profound sigh, "that is my story you are relating!"

"How?"

"Yes; a woman whom I love, whom I adore, has just been torn from me by force. I do not know where she is or whither they have conducted her. She is perhaps a prisoner; she is perhaps dead!"

"Yes, but you have at least this consolation, that you can say to yourself she has not quit you voluntarily, that if you learn no news of her, it is because all communication with you is interdicted; while I--"

"Well?"

"Nothing," replied Aramis, "nothing."

"So you renounce the world, then, forever; that is a settled thing--a resolution registered!"

"Forever! You are my friend today; tomorrow you will be no more to me than a shadow, or rather, even, you will no longer exist. As for the world, it is a sepulcher and nothing else."

"The devil! All this is very sad which you tell me."

"What will you? My vocation commands me; it carries me away."

D'Artagnan smiled, but made no answer.

Aramis continued, "And yet, while I do belong to the earth, I wish to speak of you--of our friends."

"And on my part," said d'Artagnan, "I wished to speak of you, but I find you so completely detached from everything! To love you cry, 'Fie! Friends are shadows! The world is a sepulcher!'"

"Alas, you will find it so yourself," said Aramis, with a sigh.

"Well, then, let us say no more about it," said d'Artagnan; "and let us burn this letter, which, no doubt, announces to you some fresh infidelity of your GRISETTE or your chambermaid."

"What letter?" cried Aramis, eagerly.

"A letter which was sent to your abode in your absence, and which was given to me for you."

"But from whom is that letter?"

"Oh, from some heartbroken waiting woman, some desponding GRISETTE; from Madame de Chevreuse's chambermaid, perhaps, who was obliged to return to Tours with her mistress, and who, in order to appear smart and attractive, stole some perfumed paper, and sealed her letter with a duchess's coronet."

"What do you say?"

"Hold! I must have lost it," said the young man maliciously, pretending to search for it. "But fortunately the world is a sepulcher; the men, and consequently the women, are but shadows, and love is a sentiment to which you cry, 'Fie! Fie!'"

"d'Artagnan, d'Artagnan," cried Aramis, "you are killing me!"

"Well, here it is at last!" said d'Artagnan, as he drew the letter from his pocket.

Aramis made a bound, seized the letter, read it, or rather devoured it, his countenance radiant.

"This same waiting maid seems to have an agreeable style," said the messenger, carelessly.

"Thanks, d'Artagnan, thanks!" cried Aramis, almost in a state of delirium. "She was forced to return to Tours; she is not faithless; she still loves me! Come, my friend, come, let me embrace you. Happiness almost stifles me!"

The two friends began to dance around the venerable St. Chrysostom, kicking about famously the sheets of the thesis, which had fallen on the floor.

At that moment Bazin entered with the spinach and the omelet.

"Be off, you wretch!" cried Aramis, throwing his skullcap in his face. "Return whence you came; take back those horrible vegetables, and that poor kickshaw! Order a larded hare, a fat capon, mutton leg dressed with garlic, and four bottles of old Burgundy."

Bazin, who looked at his master, without comprehending the cause of this change, in a melancholy manner, allowed the omelet to slip into the spinach, and the spinach onto the floor.

"Now this is the moment to consecrate your existence to the King of kings," said d'Artagnan, "if you persist in offering him a civility. NON INUTILE DESIDERIUM OBLATIONE."

"Go to the devil with your Latin. Let us drink, my dear d'Artagnan, MORBLEU! Let us drink while the wine is fresh! Let us drink heartily, and while we do so, tell me a little of what is going on in the world yonder."

27 The Wife Of Athos

"We have now to search for Athos," said d'Artagnan to the vivacious Aramis, when he had informed him of all that had passed since their departure from the capital, and an excellent dinner had made one of them forget his thesis and the other his fatigue.

"Do you think, then, that any harm can have happened to him?" asked Aramis. "Athos is so cool, so brave, and handles his sword so skillfully."

"No doubt. Nobody has a higher opinion of the courage and skill of Athos than I have; but I like better to hear my sword clang against lances than against staves. I fear lest Athos should have been beaten down by serving men. Those fellows strike hard, and don't leave off in a hurry. This is why I wish to set out again as soon as possible."

"I will try to accompany you," said Aramis, "though I scarcely feel in a condition to mount on horseback. Yesterday I undertook to employ that cord which you see hanging against the wall, but pain prevented my continuing the pious exercise."

"That's the first time I ever heard of anybody trying to cure gunshot wounds with cat-o'-nine-tails; but you were ill, and illness renders the head weak, therefore you may be excused."

"When do you mean to set out?"

"Tomorrow at daybreak. Sleep as soundly as you can tonight, and tomorrow, if you can, we will take our departure together."

"Till tomorrow, then," said Aramis; "for iron-nerved as you are, you must need repose."

The next morning, when d'Artagnan entered Aramis's chamber, he found him at the window.

"What are you looking at?" asked d'Artagnan.

"My faith! I am admiring three magnificent horses which the stable boys are leading about. It would be a pleasure worthy of a prince to travel upon such horses."

"Well, my dear Aramis, you may enjoy that pleasure, for one of those three horses is yours."

"Ah, bah! Which?"

"Whichever of the three you like, I have no preference."

"And the rich caparison, is that mine, too?"

"Without doubt."

"You laugh, d'Artagnan."

"No, I have left off laughing, now that you speak French."

"What, those rich holsters, that velvet housing, that saddle studded with silver-are they all for me?"

"For you and nobody else, as the horse which paws the ground is mine, and the other horse, which is caracoling, belongs to Athos."

"PESTE! They are three superb animals!"

"I am glad they please you."

"Why, it must have been the king who made you such a present."

"Certainly it was not the cardinal; but don't trouble yourself whence they come, think only that one of the three is your property."

"I choose that which the red-headed boy is leading."

"It is yours!"

"Good heaven! That is enough to drive away all my pains; I could mount him with thirty balls in my body. On my soul, handsome stirrups! HOLA, Bazin, come here this minute."

Bazin appeared on the threshold, dull and spiritless.

"That last order is useless," interrupted d'Artagnan; "there are loaded pistols in your holsters."

Bazin sighed.

"Come, Monsieur Bazin, make yourself easy," said d'Artagnan; "people of all conditions gain the kingdom of heaven."

"Monsieur was already such a good theologian," said Bazin, almost weeping; "he might have become a bishop, and perhaps a cardinal."

"Well, but my poor Bazin, reflect a little. Of what use is it to be a churchman, pray? You do not avoid going to war by that means; you see, the cardinal is about to make the next campaign, helm on head and partisan in hand. And Monsieur de Nogaret de la Valette, what do you say of him? He is a cardinal likewise. Ask his lackey how often he has had to prepare lint of him."

"Alas!" sighed Bazin. "I know it, monsieur; everything is turned topsy-turvy in the world nowadays."

While this dialogue was going on, the two young men and the poor lackey descended.

"Hold my stirrup, Bazin," cried Aramis; and Aramis sprang into the saddle with his usual grace and agility, but after a few vaults and curvets of the noble animal his rider felt his pains come on so insupportably that he turned pale and became unsteady in his seat. D'Artagnan, who, foreseeing such an event, had kept his eye on him, sprang toward him, caught him in his arms, and assisted him to his chamber.

"That's all right, my dear Aramis, take care of yourself," said he; "I will go alone in search of Athos."

"You are a man of brass," replied Aramis.

"No, I have good luck, that is all. But how do you mean to pass your time till I come back? No more theses, no more glosses upon the fingers or upon benedictions, hey?"

Aramis smiled. "I will make verses," said he.

"Yes, I dare say; verses perfumed with the odor of the billet from the attendant of Madame de Chevreuse. Teach Bazin prosody; that will console him. As to the horse, ride him a little every day, and that will accustom you to his maneuvers."

"Oh, make yourself easy on that head," replied Aramis. "You will find me ready to follow you."

They took leave of each other, and in ten minutes, after having commended his friend to the cares of the hostess and Bazin, d'Artagnan was trotting along in the direction of Amiens.

How was he going to find Athos? Should he find him at all? The position in which he had left him was critical. He probably had succumbed. This idea, while darkening his brow, drew several sighs from him, and caused him to formulate to himself a few vows of vengeance. Of all his friends, Athos was the eldest, and the least resembling him in appearance, in his tastes and sympathies.

Yet he entertained a marked preference for this gentleman. The noble and distinguished air of Athos, those flashes of greatness which from time to time broke out from the shade in which he voluntarily kept himself, that unalterable equality of temper which made him the most pleasant companion in the world, that forced and cynical gaiety, that bravery which might have been termed blind if it had not been the result of the rarest coolness--such qualities attracted more than the esteem, more than the friendship of d'Artagnan; they attracted his admiration.

Indeed, when placed beside M. de Treville, the elegant and noble courtier, Athos in his most cheerful days might advantageously sustain a comparison. He was of middle height; but his person was so admirably shaped and so well proportioned that more than once in his struggles with Porthos he had overcome the giant whose physical strength was proverbial among the Musketeers. His head, with piercing eyes, a straight nose, a chin cut like that of Brutus, had altogether an indefinable character of grandeur and grace. His hands, of which he took little care, were the despair of Aramis, who cultivated his with almond paste and perfumed oil. The sound of his voice was at once penetrating and melodious; and then, that which was inconceivable in Athos, who was always retiring, was that delicate knowledge of the world and of the usages of the most brilliant society--those manners of a high degree which appeared, as if unconsciously to himself, in his least actions.

If a repast were on foot, Athos presided over it better than any other, placing every guest exactly in the rank which his ancestors had earned for him or that he had made for himself. If a question in heraldry were started, Athos knew all the noble families of the kingdom, their genealogy, their alliances, their coats of arms, and the origin of them. Etiquette had no minutiae unknown to him. He knew what were the rights of the great land owners. He was profoundly versed in hunting and falconry, and had one day when conversing on this great art astonished even Louis XIII himself, who took a pride in being considered a past master therein.

Like all the great nobles of that period, Athos rode and fenced to perfection. But still further, his education had been so little neglected, even with respect to scholastic studies, so rare at this time among gentlemen, that he smiled at the scraps of Latin which Aramis sported and which Porthos pretended to understand. Two or three times, even, to the great astonishment of his friends, he had, when Aramis allowed some rudimental error to escape him, replaced a verb in its right tense and a noun in its case. Besides, his probity was irreproachable, in an age in which soldiers compromised so easily with their religion and their consciences, lovers with the rigorous delicacy of our era, and the poor with God's Seventh

Commandment. This Athos, then, was a very extraordinary man.

And yet this nature so distinguished, this creature so beautiful, this essence so fine, was seen to turn insensibly toward material life, as old men turn toward physical and moral imbecility. Athos, in his hours of gloom--and these hours were frequent--was extinguished as to the whole of the luminous portion of him, and his brilliant side disappeared as into profound darkness.

Then the demigod vanished; he remained scarcely a man. His head hanging down, his eye dull, his speech slow and painful, Athos would look for hours together at his bottle, his glass, or at Grimaud, who, accustomed to obey him by signs, read in the faint glance of his master his least desire, and satisfied it immediately. If the four friends were assembled at one of these moments, a word, thrown forth occasionally with a violent effort, was the share Athos furnished to the conversation. In exchange for his silence Athos drank enough for four, and without appearing to be otherwise affected by wine than by a more marked constriction of the brow and by a deeper sadness.

D'Artagnan, whose inquiring disposition we are acquainted with, had not--whatever interest he had in satisfying his curiosity on this subject--been able to assign any cause for these fits of for the periods of their recurrence. Athos never received any letters; Athos never had concerns which all his friends did not know.

It could not be said that it was wine which produced this sadness; for in truth he only drank to combat this sadness, which wine however, as we have said, rendered still darker. This excess of bilious humor could not be attributed to play; for unlike Porthos, who accompanied the variations of chance with songs or oaths, Athos when he won remained as unmoved as when he lost. He had been known, in the circle of the Musketeers, to win in one night three thousand pistoles; to lose them even to the gold-embroidered belt for gala days, win all this again with the addition of a hundred louis, without his beautiful eyebrow being heightened or lowered half a line, without his hands losing their pearly hue, without his conversation, which was cheerful that evening, ceasing to be calm and agreeable.

Neither was it, as with our neighbors, the English, an atmospheric influence which darkened his countenance; for the sadness generally became more intense toward the fine season of the year. June and July were the terrible months with Athos.

For the present he had no anxiety. He shrugged his shoulders when people spoke of the future. His secret, then, was in the past, as had often been vaguely said to d'Artagnan.

This mysterious shade, spread over his whole person, rendered still more interesting the man whose eyes or mouth, even in the most complete intoxication, had never revealed anything, however skillfully questions had been put to him.

"Well," thought d'Artagnan, "poor Athos is perhaps at this moment dead, and dead by my fault--for it was I who dragged him into this affair, of which he did not know the origin, of which he is ignorant of the result, and from which he can derive no advantage."

"Without reckoning, monsieur," added Planchet to his master's audibly expressed reflections, "that we perhaps owe our lives to him. Do you remember how he cried, 'On, d'Artagnan, on, I am taken'? And when he had discharged his two pistols, what a terrible noise he made with his sword! One might have said that twenty men, or rather twenty mad devils, were fighting."

These words redoubled the eagerness of d'Artagnan, who urged his horse, though he stood in need of no incitement, and they proceeded at a rapid pace. About eleven o'clock in the morning they perceived Ameins, and at half past eleven they were at the door of the cursed inn.

D'Artagnan had often meditated against the perfidious host one of those hearty vengeances which offer consolation while they are hoped for. He entered the hostelry with his hat pulled over his eyes, his left hand on the pommel of the sword, and cracking his whip with his right hand.

"Do you remember me?" said he to the host, who advanced to greet him.

"I have not that honor, monseigneur," replied the latter, his eyes dazzled by the brilliant style in which d'Artagnan traveled.

"What, you don't know me?"

"No, monseigneur."

"Well, two words will refresh your memory. What have you done with that gentleman against whom you had the audacity, about twelve days ago, to make an accusation of passing false money?"

The host became as pale as death; for d'Artagnan had assumed a threatening attitude, and Planchet modeled himself after his master.

"Ah, monseigneur, do not mention it!" cried the host, in the most pitiable voice imaginable. "Ah, monseigneur, how dearly have I paid for that fault, unhappy wretch as I am!"

"That gentleman, I say, what has become of him?"

"Deign to listen to me, monseigneur, and be merciful! Sit down, in mercy!"

D'Artagnan, mute with anger and anxiety, took a seat in the threatening attitude of a judge. Planchet glared fiercely over the back of his armchair.

"Here is the story, monseigneur," resumed the trembling host; "for I now recollect you. It was you who rode off at the moment I had that unfortunate difference with the gentleman you speak of."

"Yes, it was I; so you may plainly perceive that you have no mercy to expect if you do not tell me the whole truth."

"Condescend to listen to me, and you shall know all."

"I listen."

"I had been warned by the authorities that a celebrated coiner of bad money would arrive at my inn, with several of his companions, all disguised as Guards or Musketeers. Monseigneur, I was furnished with a description of your horses, your lackeys, your countenances--nothing was omitted."

"Go on, go on!" said d'Artagnan, who quickly understood whence such an exact description had come.

"I took then, in conformity with the orders of the authorities, who sent me a reinforcement of six men, such measures as I thought necessary to get possession of the persons of the pretended coiners."

"Again!" said d'Artagnan, whose ears chafed terribly under the repetition of this word COINERs.

"Pardon me, monseigneur, for saying such things, but they form my excuse. The authorities had terrified me, and you know that an innkeeper must keep on good terms with the authorities."

"But once again, that gentleman--where is he? What has become of him? Is he dead? Is he living?"

"Patience, monseigneur, we are coming to it. There happened then that which you know, and of which your precipitate departure," added the host, with an acuteness that did not escape d'Artagnan, "appeared to authorize the issue. That gentleman, your friend, defended himself desperately. His lackey, who, by an unforeseen piece of ill luck, had quarreled with the officers, disguised as stable lads--"

"Miserable scoundrel!" cried d'Artagnan, "you were all in the plot, then! And I really don't know what prevents me from exterminating you all."

"Alas, monseigneur, we were not in the plot, as you will soon see. Monsieur your friend (pardon for not calling him by the honorable name which no doubt he bears, but we do not know that name), Monsieur your friend, having disabled two men with his pistols, retreated fighting with his sword, with which he disabled one of my men, and stunned me with a blow of the flat side of it."

"You villain, will you finish?" cried d'Artagnan, "Athos--what has become of Athos?"

"While fighting and retreating, as I have told Monseigneur, he found the door of the cellar stairs behind him, and as the door was open, he took out the key, and barricaded himself inside. As we were sure of finding him there, we left him alone."

"Yes," said d'Artagnan, "you did not really wish to kill; you only wished to imprison him."

"Good God! To imprison him, monseigneur? Why, he imprisoned himself, I swear to you he did. In the first place he had made rough work of it; one man was killed on the spot, and two others were severely wounded. The dead man and the two wounded were carried off by their comrades, and I have heard nothing of either of them since. As for myself, as soon as I recovered my senses I went to Monsieur the Governor, to whom I related all that had passed, and asked, what I should do with my prisoner. Monsieur the Governor was all astonishment. He told me he knew nothing about the matter, that the orders I had received did not come from him, and that if I had the audacity to mention his name as being concerned in this disturbance he would have me hanged. It appears that I had made a mistake, monsieur, that I had arrested the wrong person, and that he whom I ought to have arrested had escaped."

"But Athos!" cried d'Artagnan, whose impatience was increased by the disregard of the authorities, "Athos, where is he?"

"As I was anxious to repair the wrongs I had done the prisoner," resumed the innkeeper, "I took my way straight to the cellar in order to set him at liberty. Ah, monsieur, he was no longer a man, he was a devil! To my offer of liberty, he replied that it was nothing but a snare, and that before he came out he intended to impose his own conditions. I told him very humbly--for I could not conceal from myself the scrape I had got into by laying hands on one of his Majesty's Musketeers--I told him I was quite ready to submit to his conditions.

"'In the first place,' said he, 'I wish my lackey placed with me, fully armed.' We hastened to obey this order; for you will please to understand, monsieur, we were disposed to do everything your friend could desire. Monsieur Grimaud (he told us his name, although he does not talk much)--Monsieur Grimaud, then, went down to the cellar, wounded as he was; then his master, having admitted him, barricaded the door afresh, and ordered us to remain quietly in our own bar."

"But where is Athos now?" cried d'Artagnan. "Where is Athos?"

"In the cellar, monsieur."

"What, you scoundrel! Have you kept him in the cellar all this time?"

"Merciful heaven! No, monsieur! We keep him in the cellar! You do not know what he is about in the cellar. Ah! If you could but persuade him to come out, monsieur, I should owe you the gratitude of my whole life; I should adore you as my patron saint!"

"Then he is there? I shall find him there?"

"Without doubt you will, monsieur; he persists in remaining there. We every day pass through the air hole some bread at the end of a fork, and some meat when he asks for it; but alas! It is not of bread and meat of which he makes the greatest consumption. I once endeavored to go down with two of my servants; but he flew into terrible rage. I heard the noise he made in loading his pistols, and his servant in loading his musketoon. Then, when we asked them what were their intentions, the master replied that he had forty charges to fire, and that he and his lackey would fire to the last one before he would allow a single soul of us to set foot in the cellar. Upon this I went and complained to the governor, who replied that I only had what I deserved, and that it would teach me to insult honorable gentlemen who took up their abode in my house."

"So that since that time--" replied d'Artagnan, totally unable to refrain from laughing at the pitiable face of the host.

"So from that time, monsieur," continued the latter, "we have led the most miserable life imaginable; for you must know, monsieur, that all our provisions are in the cellar. There is our wine in bottles, and our wine in casks; the beer, the oil, and the spices, the bacon, and sausages. And as we are prevented from going down there, we are forced to refuse food and drink to the travelers who come to the house; so that our hostelry is daily going to ruin. If your friend remains another week in my cellar I shall be a ruined man."

"And not more than justice, either, you ass! Could you not perceive by our appearance that we were people of quality, and not coiners--say?"

"Yes, monsieur, you are right," said the host. "But, hark, hark! There he is!"

"Somebody has disturbed him, without doubt," said d'Artagnan.

"But he must be disturbed," cried the host; "Here are two English gentlemen just arrived."

"Well?"

"Well, the English like good wine, as you may know, monsieur; these have asked for the best. My wife has perhaps requested permission of Monsieur Athos to go into the cellar to satisfy these gentlemen; and he, as usual, has refused. Ah, good heaven! There is the hullabaloo louder than ever!"

D'Artagnan, in fact, heard a great noise on the side next the cellar. He rose, and preceded by the host wringing his hands, and followed by Planchet with his musketoon ready for use, he approached the scene of action.

The two gentlemen were exasperated; they had had a long ride, and were dying with hunger and thirst.

"But this is tyranny!" cried one of them, in very good French, though with a foreign accent, "that this madman will not allow these good people access to their own wine! Nonsense, let us break open the door, and if he is too far gone in his madness, well, we will kill him!"

"Softly, gentlemen!" said d'Artagnan, drawing his pistols from his belt, "you will kill nobody, if you please!"

"Good, good!" cried the calm voice of Athos, from the other side of the door, "let them just come in, these devourers of little children, and we shall see!"

Brave as they appeared to be, the two English gentlemen looked at each other hesitatingly. One might have thought there was in that cellar one of those famished ogres--the gigantic heroes of popular legends, into whose cavern nobody could force their way with impunity.

There was a moment of silence; but at length the two Englishmen felt ashamed to draw back, and the angrier one descended the five or six steps which led to the cellar, and gave a kick against the door enough to split a wall.

"Planchet," said d'Artagnan, cocking his pistols, "I will take charge of the one at the top; you look to the one below. Ah, gentlemen, you want battle; and you shall have it."

"Good God!" cried the hollow voice of Athos, "I can hear d'Artagnan, I think."

"Yes," cried d'Artagnan, raising his voice in turn, "I am here, my friend."

"Ah, good, then," replied Athos, "we will teach them, these door breakers!"

The gentlemen had drawn their swords, but they found themselves taken between two fires. They still hesitated an instant; but, as before, pride prevailed, and a second kick split the door from bottom to top.

"Stand on one side, d'Artagnan, stand on one side," cried Athos. "I am going to fire!"

"Gentlemen," exclaimed d'Artagnan, whom reflection never abandoned, "gentlemen, think of what you are about. Patience, Athos! You are running your heads into a very silly affair; you will be riddled. My lackey and I will have three shots at you, and you will get as many from the cellar. You will then have our swords, with which, I can assure you, my friend and I can play tolerably well. Let me conduct your business and my own. You shall soon have something to drink; I give you my word."

"If there is any left," grumbled the jeering voice of Athos.

The host felt a cold sweat creep down his back.

"How! 'If there is any left!'" murmured he.

"What the devil! There must be plenty left," replied d'Artagnan. "Be satisfied of that; these two cannot have drunk all the cellar. Gentlemen, return your swords to their scabbards."

"Well, provided you replace your pistols in your belt."

"Willingly."

And d'Artagnan set the example. Then, turning toward Planchet, he made him a sign to uncock his musketoon.

The Englishmen, convinced of these peaceful proceedings, sheathed their swords grumblingly. The history of Athos's imprisonment was then related to them; and as they were really gentlemen, they pronounced the host in the wrong.

"Now, gentlemen," said d'Artagnan, "go up to your room again; and in ten minutes, I will answer for it, you shall have all you desire."

The Englishmen bowed and went upstairs.

"Now I am alone, my dear Athos," said d'Artagnan; "open the door, I beg of you."

"Instantly," said Athos.

Then was heard a great noise of fagots being removed and of the groaning of posts; these were the counterscarps and bastions of Athos, which the besieged himself demolished.

An instant after, the broken door was removed, and the pale face of Athos appeared, who with a rapid glance took a survey of the surroundings.

D'Artagnan threw himself on his neck and embraced him tenderly. He then tried to draw him from his moist abode, but to his surprise he perceived that Athos staggered.

"You are wounded," said he.

"I! Not at all. I am dead drunk, that's all, and never did a man more strongly set about getting so. By the Lord, my good host! I must at least have drunk for my part a hundred and fifty bottles."

"Mercy!" cried the host, "if the lackey has drunk only half as much as the master, I am a ruined man."

"Grimaud is a well-bred lackey. He would never think of faring in the same manner as his master; he only drank from the cask. Hark! I don't think he put the faucet in again. Do you hear it? It is running now."

D'Artagnan burst into a laugh which changed the shiver of the host into a burning fever.

In the meantime, Grimaud appeared in his turn behind his master, with the musketoon on his shoulder, and his head shaking. Like one of those drunken satyrs in the pictures of Rubens. He was moistened before and behind with a greasy liquid which the host recognized as his best olive oil.

The four crossed the public room and proceeded to take possession of the best apartment in the house, which d'Artagnan occupied with authority.

In the meantime the host and his wife hurried down with lamps into the cellar, which had so long been interdicted to them and where a frightful spectacle awaited them.

Beyond the fortifications through which Athos had made a breach in order to get out, and which were composed of fagots, planks, and empty casks, heaped up according to all the rules of the strategic art, they found, swimming in puddles of oil and wine, the bones and fragments of all the hams they had eaten; while a heap of broken bottles filled the whole left-hand corner of the cellar, and a tun, the cock of which was left running, was yielding, by this means, the last drop of its blood. "The image of devastation and death," as the ancient poet says, "reigned as over a field of battle."

Of fifty large sausages, suspended from the joists, scarcely ten remained.

Then the lamentations of the host and hostess pierced the vault of the cellar. D'Artagnan himself was moved by them. Athos did not even turn his head.

To grief succeeded rage. The host armed himself with a spit, and rushed into the chamber occupied by the two friends.

"Some wine!" said Athos, on perceiving the host.

"Some wine!" cried the stupefied host, "some wine? Why you have drunk more than a hundred pistoles' worth! I am a ruined man, lost, destroyed!"

"Bah," said Athos, "we were always dry."

"If you had been contented with drinking, well and good; but you have broken all the bottles."

"You pushed me upon a heap which rolled down. That was your fault."

"All my oil is lost!"

"Oil is a sovereign balm for wounds; and my poor Grimaud here was obliged to dress those you had inflicted on him."

"All my sausages are gnawed!"

"There is an enormous quantity of rats in that cellar."

"You shall pay me for all this," cried the exasperated host.

"Triple ass!" said Athos, rising; but he sank down again immediately. He had tried his strength to the utmost. d'Artagnan came to his relief with his whip in his hand.

The host drew back and burst into tears.

"This will teach you," said d'Artagnan, "to treat the guests God sends you in a more courteous fashion."

"God? Say the devil!"

"My dear friend," said d'Artagnan, "if you annoy us in this manner we will all four go and shut ourselves up in your cellar, and we will see if the mischief is as great as you say."

"Oh, gentlemen," said the host, "I have been wrong. I confess it, but pardon to every sin! You are gentlemen, and I am a poor innkeeper. You will have pity on me."

"Ah, if you speak in that way," said Athos, "you will break my heart, and the tears will flow from my eyes as the wine flowed from the cask. We are not such devils as we appear to be. Come hither, and let us talk."

The host approached with hesitation.

"Come hither, I say, and don't be afraid," continued Athos. "At the very moment when I was about to pay you, I had placed my purse on the table."

"Yes, monsieur."

"That purse contained sixty pistoles; where is it?"

"Deposited with the justice; they said it was bad money."

"Very well; get me my purse back and keep the sixty pistoles."

"But Monseigneur knows very well that justice never lets go that which it once lays hold of. If it were bad money, there might be some hopes; but unfortunately, those were all good pieces."

"Manage the matter as well as you can, my good man; it does not concern me, the more so as I have not a livre left."

"Come," said d'Artagnan, "let us inquire further. Athos's horse, where is that?"

"In the stable."

"How much is it worth?"

"Fifty pistoles at most."

"It's worth eighty. Take it, and there ends the matter."

"What," cried Athos, "are you selling my horse--my Bajazet? And pray upon what shall I make my campaign; upon Grimaud?"

"I have brought you another," said d'Artagnan.

"Another?"

"And a magnificent one!" cried the host.

"Well, since there is another finer and younger, why, you may take the old one; and let us drink."

"What?" asked the host, quite cheerful again.

"Some of that at the bottom, near the laths. There are twenty-five bottles of it left; all the rest were broken by my fall. Bring six of them."

"Why, this man is a cask!" said the host, aside. "If he only remains here a fortnight, and pays for what he drinks, I shall soon re-establish my business."

"And don't forget," said d'Artagnan, "to bring up four bottles of the same sort for the two English gentlemen."

"And now," said Athos, "while they bring the wine, tell me, d'Artagnan, what has become of the others, come!"

D'Artagnan related how he had found Porthos in bed with a strained knee, and Aramis at a table between two theologians. As he finished, the host entered with the wine ordered and a ham which, fortunately for him, had been left out of the cellar.

"That's well!" said Athos, filling his glass and that of his friend; "here's to Porthos and Aramis! But you, d'Artagnan, what is the matter with you, and what has happened to you personally? You have a sad air."

"Alas," said d'Artagnan, "it is because I am the most unfortunate."

"Tell me."

"Presently," said d'Artagnan.

"Presently! And why presently? Because you think I am drunk? d'Artagnan, remember this! My ideas are never so clear as when I have had plenty of wine. Speak, then, I am all ears."

D'Artagnan related his adventure with Mme. Bonacieux. Athos listened to him without a frown; and when he had finished, said, "Trifles, only trifles!" That was his favorite word.

"You always say TRIFLES, my dear Athos!" said d'Artagnan, "and that come very ill from you, who have never loved."

The drink-deadened eye of Athos flashed out, but only for a moment; it became as dull and vacant as before.

"That's true," said he, quietly, "for my part I have never loved."

"Acknowledge, then, you stony heart," said d'Artagnan, "that you are wrong to be so hard upon us tender hearts."

"Tender hearts! Pierced hearts!" said Athos.

"What do you say?"

"I say that love is a lottery in which he who wins, wins death! You are very fortunate to have lost, believe me, my dear d'Artagnan. And if I have any counsel to give, it is, always lose!"

"She seemed to love me so!"

"She SEEMED, did she?"

"Oh, she DID love me!"

"You child, why, there is not a man who has not believed, as you do, that his mistress loved him, and there lives not a man who has not been deceived by his mistress."

"Except you, Athos, who never had one."

"That's true," said Athos, after a moment's silence, "that's true! I never had one! Let us drink!"

"But then, philosopher that you are," said d'Artagnan, "instruct me, support me. I stand in need of being taught and consoled."

"Consoled for what?"

"For my misfortune."

"Your misfortune is laughable," said Athos, shrugging his shoulders; "I should like to know what you would say if I were to relate to you a real tale of love!"

"Which has happened to you?"

"Or one of my friends, what matters?"

"Tell it, Athos, tell it."

"Better if I drink."

"Drink and relate, then."

"Not a bad idea!" said Athos, emptying and refilling his glass. "The two things agree marvelously well."

"I am all attention," said d'Artagnan.

Athos collected himself, and in proportion as he did so, d'Artagnan saw that he became pale. He was at that period of intoxication in which vulgar drinkers fall on the floor and go to sleep. He kept himself upright and dreamed, without sleeping. This somnambulism of drunkenness had something frightful in it.

"You particularly wish it?" asked he.

"I pray for it," said d'Artagnan.

"Be it then as you desire. One of my friends--one of my friends, please to observe, not myself," said Athos, interrupting himself with a melancholy smile, "one of the counts of my province--that is to say, of Berry--noble as a Dandolo or a Montmorency, at twenty-five years of age fell in love with a girl of sixteen, beautiful as fancy can paint. Through the ingenuousness of her age beamed an ardent mind, not of the woman, but of the poet. She did not please; she intoxicated. She lived in a small town with her brother, who was a curate. Both had recently come into the country. They came nobody knew whence; but when seeing her so lovely and her brother so pious, nobody thought of asking whence they came. They were said, however, to be of good extraction. My friend, who was seigneur of the country, might have seduced her, or taken her by force, at his will--for he was master. Who would have come to the assistance of two strangers, two unknown persons? Unfortunately he was an honorable man; he married her. The fool! The ass! The idiot!"

"How so, if he love her?" asked d'Artagnan.

"Wait," said Athos. "He took her to his chateau, and made her the first lady in the province; and in justice it must be allowed that she supported her rank becomingly."

"Well?" asked d'Artagnan.

"Well, one day when she was hunting with her husband," continued Athos, in a low voice, and speaking very quickly, "she fell from her horse and fainted. The count flew to her to help, and as she appeared to be oppressed by her clothes, he ripped them open with his ponaird, and in so doing laid bare her shoulder. d'Artagnan," said Athos, with a maniacal burst of laughter, "guess what she had on her shoulder."

"How can I tell?" said d'Artagnan.

"A FLEUR-DE-LIS," said Athos. "She was branded."

Athos emptied at a single draught the glass he held in his hand.

"Horror!" cried d'Artagnan. "What do you tell me?"

"Truth, my friend. The angel was a demon; the poor young girl had stolen the sacred vessels from a church."

"And what did the count do?"

"The count was of the highest nobility. He had on his estates the rights of high and low tribunals. He tore the dress of the countess to pieces; he tied her hands behind her, and hanged her on a tree."

"Heavens, Athos, a murder?" cried d'Artagnan.

"No less," said Athos, as pale as a corpse. "But methinks I need wine!" and he seized by the neck the last bottle that was left, put it to his mouth, and emptied it at a single draught, as he would have emptied an ordinary glass.

Then he let his head sink upon his two hands, while d'Artagnan stood before him, stupefied.

"That has cured me of beautiful, poetical, and loving women," said Athos, after a considerable pause, raising his head, and forgetting to continue the fiction of the count. "God grant you as much! Let us drink."

"Then she is dead?" stammered d'Artagnan.

"PARBLEU!" said Athos. "But hold out your glass. Some ham, my boy, or we can't drink."

"And her brother?" added d'Artagnan, timidly.

"Her brother?" replied Athos.

"Yes, the priest."

"Oh, I inquired after him for the purpose of hanging him likewise; but he was beforehand with me, he had quit the curacy the night before."

"Was it ever known who this miserable fellow was?"

"He was doubtless the first lover and accomplice of the fair lady. A worthy man, who had pretended to be a curate for the purpose of getting his mistress married, and securing her a position. He has been hanged and quartered, I hope."

"My God, my God!" cried d'Artagnan, quite stunned by the relation of this horrible adventure.

"Taste some of this ham, d'Artagnan; it is exquisite," said Athos, cutting a slice, which he placed on the young man's plate.

"What a pity it is there were only four like this in the cellar. I could have drunk fifty bottles more."

D'Artagnan could no longer endure this conversation, which had made him bewildered. Allowing his head to sink upon his two hands, he pretended to sleep.

"These young fellows can none of them drink," said Athos, looking at him with pity, "and yet this is one of the best!"

28 The Return

D'Artagnan was astounded by the terrible confidence of Athos; yet many things appeared very obscure to him in this half revelation. In the first place it had been made by a man quite drunk to one who was half drunk; and yet, in spite of the incertainty which the vapor of three or four bottles of Burgundy carries with it to the brain, d'Artagnan, when awaking on the following morning, had all the words of Athos as present to his memory as if they then fell from his mouth--they had been so impressed upon his mind. All this doubt only gave rise to a more lively desire of arriving at a certainty, and he went into his friend's chamber with a fixed determination of renewing the conversation of the preceding evening; but he found Athos quite himself again--that is to say, the most shrewd and impenetrable of men. Besides which, the Musketeer, after having exchanged a hearty shake of the hand with him, broached the matter first.

"I was pretty drunk yesterday, d'Artagnan," said he, "I can tell that by my tongue, which was swollen and hot this morning, and by my pulse, which was very tremulous. I wager that I uttered a thousand extravagances."

While saying this he looked at his friend with an earnestness that embarrassed him.

"No," replied d'Artagnan, "if I recollect well what you said, it was nothing out of the common way."

"Ah, you surprise me. I thought I had told you a most lamentable story." And he looked at the young man as if he would read the bottom of his heart.

"My faith," said d'Artagnan, "it appears that I was more drunk than you, since I remember nothing of the kind."

Athos did not trust this reply, and he resumed; "you cannot have failed to remark, my dear friend, that everyone has his particular kind of drunkenness, sad or gay. My drunkenness is always sad, and when I am thoroughly drunk my mania is to relate all the lugubrious stories which my foolish nurse inculcated into my brain. That is my failing--a capital failing, I admit; but with that exception, I am a good drinker."

Athos spoke this in so natural a manner that d'Artagnan was shaken in his conviction.

"It is that, then," replied the young man, anxious to find out the truth, "it is that, then, I remember as we remember a dream. We were speaking of hanging."

"Ah, you see how it is," said Athos, becoming still paler, but yet attempting to laugh; "I was sure it was so--the hanging of people is my nightmare."

"Yes, yes," replied d'Artagnan. "I remember now; yes, it was about--stop a minute--yes, it was about a woman."

"That's it," replied Athos, becoming almost livid; "that is my grand story of the fair lady, and when I relate that, I must be very drunk."

"Yes, that was it," said d'Artagnan, "the story of a tall, fair lady, with blue eyes."

"Yes, who was hanged."

"By her husband, who was a nobleman of your acquaintance," continued d'Artagnan, looking intently at Athos.

"Well, you see how a man may compromise himself when he does not know what he says," replied Athos, shrugging his shoulders as if he thought himself an object of pity. "I certainly never will get drunk again, d'Artagnan; it is too bad a habit."

D'Artagnan remained silent; and then changing the conversation all at once, Athos said:

"By the by, I thank you for the horse you have brought me."

"Is it to your mind?" asked d'Artagnan.

"Yes; but it is not a horse for hard work."

"You are mistaken; I rode him nearly ten leagues in less than an hour and a half, and he appeared no more distressed than if he had only made the tour of the Place St. Sulpice."

"Ah, you begin to awaken my regret."

"Regret?"

"Yes; I have parted with him."

"How?"

"Why, here is the simple fact. This morning I awoke at six o'clock. You were still fast asleep, and I did not know what to do with myself; I was still stupid from our yesterday's debauch. As I came into the public room, I saw one of our Englishman bargaining with a dealer for a horse, his own having died yesterday from bleeding. I drew near, and found he was bidding a hundred pistoles for a chestnut nag. 'PARDIEU,' said I, 'my good gentleman, I have a horse to sell, too.' 'Ay, and a very fine one! I saw him yesterday; your friend's lackey was leading him.' 'Do you think he is worth a hundred pistoles?' 'Yes! Will you sell him to me for that sum?' 'No; but I will play for him.' 'What?' 'At dice.' No sooner said than done, and I lost the horse. Ah, ah! But please to observe I won back the equipage," cried Athos.

D'Artagnan looked much disconcerted.

"This vexes you?" said Athos.

"Well, I must confess it does," replied d'Artagnan. "That horse was to have identified us in the day of battle. It was a pledge, a remembrance. Athos, you have done wrong."

"But, my dear friend, put yourself in my place," replied the Musketeer. "I was hipped to death; and still further, upon my honor, I don't like English horses. If it is only to be recognized, why the saddle will suffice for that; it is quite remarkable enough. As to the horse, we can easily find some excuse for its disappearance. Why the devil! A horse is mortal; suppose mine had had the glanders or the farcy?"

D'Artagnan did not smile.

"It vexes me greatly," continued Athos, "that you attach so much importance to these animals, for I am not yet at the end of my story."

"What else have you done."

"After having lost my own horse, nine against ten--see how near--I formed an idea of staking yours."

"Yes; but you stopped at the idea, I hope?"

"No; for I put it in execution that very minute."

"And the consequence?" said d'Artagnan, in great anxiety.

"I threw, and I lost."

"What, my horse?"

"Your horse, seven against eight; a point short--you know the proverb."

"Athos, you are not in your right senses, I swear."

"My dear lad, that was yesterday, when I was telling you silly stories, it was proper to tell me that, and not this morning. I lost him then, with all his appointments and furniture."

"Really, this is frightful."

"Stop a minute; you don't know all yet. I should make an excellent gambler if I were not too hot-headed; but I was hot-headed, just as if I had been drinking. Well, I was not hot-headed then--"

"Well, but what else could you play for? You had nothing left?"

"Oh, yes, my friend; there was still that diamond left which sparkles on your finger, and which I had observed yesterday."

"This diamond!" said d'Artagnan, placing his hand eagerly on his ring.

"And as I am a connoisseur in such things, having had a few of my own once, I estimated it at a thousand pistoles."

"I hope," said d'Artagnan, half dead with fright, "you made no mention of my diamond?"

"On the contrary, my dear friend, this diamond became our only resource; with it I might regain our horses and their harnesses, and even money to pay our expenses on the road."

"Athos, you make me tremble!" cried d'Artagnan.

"I mentioned your diamond then to my adversary, who had likewise remarked it. What the devil, my dear, do you think you can wear a star from heaven on your finger, and nobody observe it? Impossible!"

"Go on, go on, my dear fellow!" said d'Artagnan; "for upon my honor, you will kill me with your indifference."

"We divided, then, this diamond into ten parts of a hundred pistoles each."

"You are laughing at me, and want to try me!" said d'Artagnan, whom anger began to take by the hair, as Minerva takes Achilles, in the ILLIAD.

"No, I do not jest, MORDIEU! I should like to have seen you in my place! I had been fifteen days without seeing a human face, and had been left to brutalize myself in the company of bottles."

"That was no reason for staking my diamond!" replied d'Artagnan, closing his hand with a nervous spasm.

"Hear the end. Ten parts of a hundred pistoles each, in ten throws, without revenge; in thirteen throws I had lost all--in thirteen throws. The number thirteen was always fatal to me; it was on the thirteenth of July that--"

"VENTREBLEU!" cried d'Artagnan, rising from the table, the story of the present day making him forget that of the preceding one.

"Patience!" said Athos; "I had a plan. The Englishman was an original; I had seen him conversing that morning with Grimaud, and Grimaud had told me that he had made him proposals to enter into his service. I staked Grimaud, the silent Grimaud, divided into ten portions."

"Well, what next?" said d'Artagnan, laughing in spite of himself.

"Grimaud himself, understand; and with the ten parts of Grimaud, which are not worth a ducatoon, I regained the diamond. Tell me, now, if persistence is not a virtue?"

"My faith! But this is droll," cried d'Artagnan, consoled, and holding his sides with laughter.

"You may guess, finding the luck turned, that I again staked the diamond."

"The devil!" said d'Artagnan, becoming angry again.

"I won back your harness, then your horse, then my harness, then my horse, and then I lost again. In brief, I regained your harness and then mine. That's where we are. That was a superb throw, so I left off there."

D'Artagnan breathed as if the whole hostelry had been removed from his breast.

"Then the diamond is safe?" said he, timidly.

"Intact, my dear friend; besides the harness of your Bucephalus and mine."

"But what is the use of harnesses without horses?"

"I have an idea about them."

"Athos, you make me shudder."

"Listen to me. You have not played for a long time, d'Artagnan."

"And I have no inclination to play."

"Swear to nothing. You have not played for a long time, I said; you ought, then, to have a good hand."

"Well, what then?"

"Well; the Englishman and his companion are still here. I remarked that he regretted the horse furniture very much. You appear to think much of your horse. In your place I would stake the furniture against the horse."

"But he will not wish for only one harness."

"Stake both, PARDIEU! I am not selfish, as you are."

"You would do so?" said d'Artagnan, undecided, so strongly did the confidence of Athos begin to prevail, in spite of himself.

"On my honor, in one single throw."

"But having lost the horses, I am particularly anxious to preserve the harnesses."

"Stake your diamond, then."

"This? That's another matter. Never, never!"

"The devil!" said Athos. "I would propose to you to stake Planchet, but as that has already been done, the Englishman would not, perhaps, be willing."

"Decidedly, my dear Athos," said d'Artagnan, "I should like better not to risk anything."

"That's a pity," said Athos, coolly. "The Englishman is overflowing with pistoles. Good Lord, try one throw! One throw is soon made!"

"And if I lose?"

"You will win."

"But if I lose?"

"Well, you will surrender the harnesses."

"Have with you for one throw!" said d'Artagnan.

Athos went in quest of the Englishman, whom he found in the stable, examining the harnesses with a greedy eye. The opportunity was good. He proposed the conditions--the two harnesses, either against one horse or a hundred pistoles. The Englishman calculated fast; the two harnesses were worth three hundred pistoles. He consented.

D'Artagnan threw the dice with a trembling hand, and turned up the number three; his paleness terrified Athos, who, however, consented himself with saying, "That's a sad throw, comrade; you will have the horses fully equipped, monsieur."

The Englishman, quite triumphant, did not even give himself the trouble to shake the dice. He threw them on the table without looking at them, so sure was he of victory; d'Artagnan turned aside to conceal his ill humor.

"Hold, hold, hold!" said Athos, wit his quiet tone; "that throw of the dice is extraordinary. I have not seen such a one four times in my life. Two aces!"

The Englishman looked, and was seized with astonishment. d'Artagnan looked, and was seized with pleasure.

"Yes," continued Athos, "four times only; once at the house of Monsieur Crequy; another time at my own house in the country, in my chateau at--when I had a chateau; a third time at Monsieur de Treville's where it surprised us all; and the fourth time at a cabaret, where it fell to my lot, and where I lost a hundred louis and a supper on it."

"Then Monsieur takes his horse back again," said the Englishman.

"Certainly," said d'Artagnan.

"Then there is no revenge?"

"Our conditions said, 'No revenge,' you will please to recollect."

"That is true; the horse shall be restored to your lackey, monsieur."

"A moment," said Athos; "with your permission, monsieur, I wish to speak a word with my friend."

"Say on."

Athos drew d'Artagnan aside.

"Well, Tempter, what more do you want with me?" said d'Artagnan. "You want me to throw again, do you not?"

"No, I would wish you to reflect."

"On what?"

"You mean to take your horse?"

"Without doubt."

"You are wrong, then. I would take the hundred pistoles. You know you have staked the harnesses against the horse or a hundred pistoles, at your choice."

"Yes."

"Well, then, I repeat, you are wrong. What is the use of one horse for us two? I could not ride behind. We should look like the two sons of Anmon, who had lost their brother. You cannot think of humiliating me by prancing along by my side on that magnificent charger. For my part, I should not hesitate a moment; I should take the hundred pistoles. We want money for our return to Paris."

"I am much attached to that horse, Athos."

"And there again you are wrong. A horse slips and injures a joint; a horse stumbles and breaks his knees to the bone; a horse eats out of a manger in which a glandered horse has eaten. There is a horse, while on the contrary, the hundred pistoles feed their master."

"But how shall we get back?"

"Upon our lackey's horses, PARDIEU. Anybody may see by our bearing that we are people of condition."

"Pretty figures we shall cut on ponies while Aramis and Porthos caracole on their steeds."

"Aramis! Porthos!" cried Athos, and laughed aloud.

"What is it?" asked d'Artagnan, who did not at all comprehend the hilarity of his friend.

"Nothing, nothing! Go on!"

"Your advice, then?"

"To take the hundred pistoles, d'Artagnan. With the hundred pistoles we can live well to the end of the month. We have undergone a great deal of fatigue, remember, and a little rest will do no harm."

"I rest? Oh, no, Athos. Once in Paris, I shall prosecute my search for that unfortunate woman!"

"Well, you may be assured that your horse will not be half so serviceable to you for that purpose as good golden louis. Take the hundred pistoles, my friend; take the hundred pistoles!"

D'Artagnan only required one reason to be satisfied. This last reason appeared convincing. Besides, he feared that by resisting longer he should appear selfish in the eyes of Athos. He acquiesced, therefore, and chose the hundred pistoles, which the Englishman paid down on the spot.

They then determined to depart. Peace with the landlord, in addition to Athos's old horse, cost six pistoles. D'Artagnan and Athos took the nags of Planchet and Grimaud, and the two lackeys started on foot, carrying the saddles on their heads.

However ill our two friends were mounted, they were soon far in advance of their servants, and arrived at Creveccoeur. From a distance they perceived Aramis, seated in a melancholy manner at his window, looking out, like Sister Anne, at the dust in the horizon.

"HOLA, Aramis! What the devil are you doing there?" cried the two friends.

"Ah, is that you, d'Artagnan, and you, Athos?" said the young man. "I was reflecting upon the rapidity with which the blessings of this world leave us. My English horse, which has just disappeared amid a cloud of dust, has furnished me with a living image of the fragility of the things of the earth. Life itself may be resolved into three words: ERAT, EST, FUIT."

"Which means--" said d'Artagnan, who began to suspect the truth.

"Which means that I have just been duped-sixty louis for a horse which by the manner of his gait can do at least five leagues an hour."

D'Artagnan and Athos laughed aloud.

"My dear d'Artagnan," said Aramis, "don't be too angry with me, I beg. Necessity has no law; besides, I am the person punished, as that rascally horsedealer has robbed me of fifty louis, at least. Ah, you fellows are good managers! You ride on our lackey's horses, and have your own gallant steeds led along carefully by hand, at short stages."

At the same instant a market cart, which some minutes before had appeared upon the Amiens road, pulled up at the inn, and Planchet and Grimaud came out of it with the saddles on their heads. The cart was returning empty to Paris, and the two lackeys had agreed, for their transport, to slake the wagoner's thirst along the route.

"What is this?" said Aramis, on seeing them arrive. "Nothing but saddles?"

"Now do you understand?" said Athos.

"My friends, that's exactly like me! I retained my harness by instinct. HOLA, Bazin! Bring my new saddle and carry it along with those of these gentlemen."

"And what have you done with your ecclesiastics?" asked d'Artagnan.

"My dear fellow, I invited them to a dinner the next day," replied Aramis. "They have some capital wine here--please to observe that in passing. I did my best to make them drunk. Then the curate forbade me to quit my uniform, and the Jesuit entreated me to get him made a Musketeer."

"Without a thesis?" cried d'Artagnan, "without a thesis? I demand the suppression of the thesis."

"Since then," continued Aramis, "I have lived very agreeably. I have begun a poem in verses of one syllable. That is rather difficult, but the merit in all things consists in the difficulty. The matter is gallant. I will read you the first canto. It has four hundred lines, and lasts a minute."

"My faith, my dear Aramis," said d'Artagnan, who detested verses almost as much as he did Latin, "add to the merit of the difficulty that of the brevity, and you are sure that your poem will at least have two merits."

"You will see," continued Aramis, "that it breathes irreproachable passion. And so, my friends, we return to Paris? Bravo! I am ready. We are going to rejoin that good fellow, Porthos. So much the better. You can't think how I have missed him, the great simpleton. To see him so self-satisfied reconciles me with myself. He would not sell his horse; not for a kingdom! I think I can see him now, mounted upon his superb animal and seated in his handsome saddle. I am sure he will look like the Great Mogul!"

They made a halt for an hour to refresh their horses. Aramis discharged his bill, placed Bazin in the cart with his comrades, and they set forward to join Porthos.

They found him up, less pale than when d'Artagnan left him after his first visit, and seated at a table on which, though he was alone, was spread enough for four persons. This dinner consisted of meats nicely dressed, choice wines, and superb fruit.

"Ah, PARDIEU!" said he, rising, "you come in the nick of time, gentlemen. I was just beginning the soup, and you will dine with me."

"Oh, oh!" said d'Artagnan, "Mousqueton has not caught these bottles with his lasso. Besides, here is a piquant FRICANDEAU and a fillet of beef."

"I am recruiting myself," said Porthos, "I am recruiting myself. Nothing weakens a man more than these devilish strains. Did you ever suffer from a strain, Athos?"

"Never! Though I remember, in our affair of the Rue Ferou, I received a sword wound which at the end of fifteen or eighteen days produced the same effect."

"But this dinner was not intended for you alone, Porthos?" said Aramis.

"No," said Porthos, "I expected some gentlemen of the neighborhood, who have just sent me word they could not come. You will take their places and I shall not lose by the exchange. HOLA, Mousqueton, seats, and order double the bottles!"

"Do you know what we are eating here?" said Athos, at the end of ten minutes.

"PARDIEU!" replied d'Artagnan, "for my part, I am eating veal garnished with shrimps and vegetables."

"And I some lamb chops," said Porthos.

"And I a plain chicken," said Aramis.

"You are all mistaken, gentlemen," answered Athos, gravely; "you are eating horse."

"Eating what?" said d'Artagnan.

"Horse!" said Aramis, with a grimace of disgust.

Porthos alone made no reply.

"Yes, horse. Are we not eating a horse, Porthos? And perhaps his saddle, therewith."

"No, gentlemen, I have kept the harness," said Porthos.

"My faith," said Aramis, "we are all alike. One would think we had tipped the wink."

"What could I do?" said Porthos. "This horse made my visitors ashamed of theirs, and I don't like to humiliate people."

"Then your duchess is still at the waters?" asked d'Artagnan.

"Still," replied Porthos. "And, my faith, the governor of the province--one of the gentlemen I expected today--seemed to have such a wish for him, that I gave him to him."

"Gave him?" cried d'Artagnan.

"My God, yes, GAVE, that is the word," said Porthos; "for the animal was worth at least a hundred and fifty louis, and the stingy fellow would only give me eighty."

"Without the saddle?" said Aramis.

"Yes, without the saddle."

"You will observe, gentlemen," said Athos, "that Porthos has made the best bargain of any of us."

And then commenced a roar of laughter in which they all joined, to the astonishment of poor Porthos; but when he was informed of the cause of their hilarity, he shared it vociferously according to his custom.

"There is one comfort, we are all in cash," said d'Artagnan.

"Well, for my part," said Athos, "I found Aramis's Spanish wine so good that I sent on a hamper of sixty bottles of it in the wagon with the lackeys. That has weakened my purse."

"And I," said Aramis, "imagined that I had given almost my last sou to the church of Montdidier and the Jesuits of Amiens, with whom I had made engagements which I ought to have kept. I have ordered Masses for myself, and for you, gentlemen, which will be said, gentlemen, for which I have not the least doubt you will be marvelously benefited."

"And I," said Porthos, "do you think my strain cost me nothing?--without reckoning Mousqueton's wound, for which I had to have the surgeon twice a day, and who charged me double on account of that foolish Mousqueton having allowed himself a ball in a part which people generally only show to an apothecary; so I advised him to try never to get wounded there any more."

"Ay, ay!" said Athos, exchanging a smile with d'Artagnan and Aramis, "it is very clear you acted nobly with regard to the poor lad; that is like a good master."

"In short," said Porthos, "when all my expenses are paid, I shall have, at most, thirty crowns left."

"And I about ten pistoles," said Aramis.

"Well, then it appears that we are the Croesuses of the society. How much have you left of your hundred pistoles, d'Artagnan?"

"Of my hundred pistoles? Why, in the first place I gave you fifty."

"You think so?"

"PARDIEU!" "Ah, that is true. I recollect."

"Then I paid the host six."

"What a brute of a host! Why did you give him six pistoles?"

"You told me to give them to him."

"It is true; I am too good-natured. In brief, how much remains?"

"Twenty-five pistoles," said d'Artagnan.

"And I," said Athos, taking some small change from his pocket, "I--"

"You? Nothing!"

"My faith! So little that it is not worth reckoning with the general stock."

"Now, then, let us calculate how much we posses in all."

"Porthos?"

"Thirty crowns."

"Aramis?"

"Ten pistoles."

"And you, d'Artagnan?"

"Twenty-five."

"That makes in all?" said Athos.

"Four hundred and seventy-five livres," said d'Artagnan, who reckoned like Archimedes.

"On our arrival in Paris, we shall still have four hundred, besides the harnesses," said Porthos.

"But our troop horses?" said Aramis.

"Well, of the four horses of our lackeys we will make two for the masters, for which we will draw lots. With the four hundred livres we will make the half of one for one of the unmounted, and then we will give the turnings out of our pockets to d'Artagnan, who has a steady hand, and will go and play in the first gaming house we come to. There!"

"Let us dine, then," said Porthos; "it is getting cold."

The friends, at ease with regard to the future, did honor to the repast, the remains of which were abandoned to Mousqueton, Bazin, Planchet, and Grimaud.

On arriving in Paris, d'Artagnan found a letter from M. de Treville, which informed him that, at his request, the king had promised that he should enter the company of the Musketeers.

As this was the height of d'Artagnan's worldly ambition--apart, be it well understood, from his desire of finding Mme. Bonacieux--he ran, full of joy, to seek his comrades, whom he had left only half an hour before, but whom he found very sad and deeply preoccupied. They were assembled in council at the residence of Athos, which always indicated an event of some gravity. M. de Treville had intimated to them his Majesty's fixed intention to open the campaign on the first of May, and they must immediately prepare their outfits.

The four philosophers looked at one another in a state of bewilderment. M. de Treville never jested in matters relating to discipline.

"And what do you reckon your outfit will cost?" said d'Artagnan.

"Oh, we can scarcely say. We have made our calculations with Spartan economy, and we each require fifteen hundred livres."

"Four times fifteen makes sixty--six thousand livres," said Athos.

"It seems to me," said d'Artagnan, "with a thousand livres each--I do not speak as a Spartan, but as a procurator--"

This word PROCURATOR roused Porthos. "Stop," said he, "I have an idea."

"Well, that's something, for I have not the shadow of one," said Athos coolly; "but as to d'Artagnan, gentlemen, the idea of belonging to OURS has driven him out of his senses. A thousand livres! For my part, I declare I want two thousand."

"Four times two makes eight," then said Aramis; "it is eight thousand that we want to complete our outfits, toward which, it is true, we have already the saddles."

"Besides," said Athos, waiting till d'Artagnan, who went to thank Monsieur de Treville, had shut the door, "besides, there is that beautiful ring which beams from the finger of our friend. What the devil! D'Artagnan is too good a comrade to leave his brothers in embarrassment while he wears the ransom of a king on his finger."

29 Hunting For The Equipments

The most preoccupied of the four friends was certainly d'Artagnan, although he, in his quality of Guardsman, would be much more easily equipped than Messieurs the Musketeers, who were all of high rank; but our Gascon cadet was, as may have been observed, of a provident and almost avaricious character, and with that (explain the contradiction) so vain as almost to rival Porthos. To this preoccupation of his vanity, d'Artagnan at this moment joined an uneasiness much less selfish. Notwithstanding all his inquiries respecting Mme. Bonacieux, he could obtain no intelligence of her. M. de Treville had spoken of her to the queen. The queen was ignorant where the mercer's young wife was, but had promised to have her sought for; but this promise was very vague and did not at all reassure d'Artagnan.

Athos did not leave his chamber; he made up his mind not to take a single step to equip himself.

"We have still fifteen days before us," said he to his friends, "well, if at the end of a fortnight I have found nothing, or rather if nothing has come to find me, as I, too good a Catholic to kill myself with a pistol bullet, I will seek a good quarrel with four of his Eminence's Guards or with eight Englishmen, and I will fight until one of them has killed me, which, considering the number, cannot fail to happen. It will then be said of me that I died for the king; so that I shall have performed my duty without the expense of an outfit."

Porthos continued to walk about with his hands behind him, tossing his head and repeating, "I shall follow up on my idea."

Aramis, anxious and negligently dressed, said nothing.

It may be seen by these disastrous details that desolation reigned in the community.

The lackeys on their part, like the coursers of Hippolytus, shared the sadness of their masters. Mousqueton collected a store of crusts; Bazin, who had always been inclined to devotion, never quit the churches; Planchet watched the flight of flies; and Grimaud, whom the general distress could not induce to break the silence imposed by his master, heaved sighs enough to soften the stones.

The three friends--for, as we have said, Athos had sworn not to stir a foot to equip himself--went out early in the morning, and returned late at night. They wandered about the streets, looking at the pavement as if to see whether the passengers had not left a purse behind them. They might have been supposed to be following tracks, so observant were they wherever they went. When they met they looked desolately at one another, as much as to say, "Have you found anything?"

However, as Porthos had first found an idea, and had thought of it earnestly afterward, he was the first to act. He was a man of execution, this worthy Porthos. D'Artagnan perceived him one day walking toward the church of St. Leu, and followed him instinctively. He entered, after having twisted his mustache and elongated his imperial, which always announced on his part the most triumphant resolutions. As d'Artagnan took some precautions to conceal himself, Porthos believed he had not been seen. d'Artagnan entered behind him. Porthos went and leaned against the side of a pillar. D'Artagnan, still unperceived, supported himself against the other side.

There happened to be a sermon, which made the church very full of people. Porthos took advantage of this circumstance to ogle the women. Thanks to the cares of Mousqueton, the exterior was far from announcing the distress of the interior. His hat was a little napless, his feather was a little faded, his gold lace was a little tarnished, his laces were a trifle frayed; but in the obscurity of the church these things were not seen, and Porthos was still the handsome Porthos.

D'Artagnan observed, on the bench nearest to the pillar against which Porthos leaned, a sort of ripe beauty, rather yellow and rather dry, but erect and haughty under her black hood. The eyes of Porthos were furtively cast upon this lady, and then roved about at large over the nave.

On her side the lady, who from time to time blushed, darted with the rapidity of lightning a glance toward the inconstant Porthos; and then immediately the eyes of Porthos wandered anxiously. It was plain that this mode of proceeding piqued the lady in the black hood, for she bit her lips till they bled, scratched the end of her nose, and could not sit still in her seat.

Porthos, seeing this, retwisted his mustache, elongated his imperial a second time, and began to make signals to a beautiful lady who was near the choir, and who not only was a beautiful lady, but still further, no doubt, a great lady--for she had behind her a Negro boy who had brought the cushion on which she knelt, and a female servant who held the emblazoned bag in which was placed the book from which she read the Mass.

The lady with the black hood followed through all their wanderings the looks of Porthos, and perceived that they rested upon the lady with the velvet cushion, the little Negro, and the maid-servant.

During this time Porthos played close. It was almost imperceptible motions of his eyes, fingers placed upon the lips, little assassinating smiles, which really did assassinate the disdained beauty.

Then she cried, "Ahem!" under cover of the MEA CULPA, striking her breast so vigorously that everybody, even the lady with the red cushion, turned round toward her. Porthos paid no attention. Nevertheless, he understood it all, but was deaf.

The lady with the red cushion produced a great effect--for she was very handsome--upon the lady with the black hood, who saw in her a rival really to be dreaded; a great effect upon Porthos, who thought her much prettier than the lady with the black hood; a great effect upon d'Artagnan, who recognized in her the lady of Meung, of Calais, and of Dover, whom his persecutor, the man with the scar, had saluted by the name of Milady.

D'Artagnan, without losing sight of the lady of the red cushion, continued to watch the proceedings of Porthos, which amused him greatly. He guessed that the lady of the black hood was the procurator's wife of the Rue aux Ours, which was the more probable from the church of St. Leu being not far from that locality.

He guessed, likewise, by induction, that Porthos was taking his revenge for the defeat of Chantilly, when the procurator's wife had proved so refractory with respect to her purse.

Amid all this, d'Artagnan remarked also that not one countenance responded to the gallantries of Porthos. There were only chimeras and illusions; but for real love, for true jealousy, is there any reality except illusions and chimeras?

The sermon over, the procurator's wife advanced toward the holy font. Porthos went before her, and instead of a finger, dipped his whole hand in. The procurator's wife smiled, thinking that it was for her Porthos had put himself to this trouble; but she was cruelly and promptly undeceived. When she was only about three steps from him, he turned his head round, fixing his eyes steadfastly upon the lady with the red cushion, who had risen and was approaching, followed by her black boy and her woman.

When the lady of the red cushion came close to Porthos, Porthos drew his dripping hand from the font. The fair worshipper touched the great hand of Porthos with her delicate fingers, smiled, made the sign of the cross, and left the church.

This was too much for the procurator's wife; she doubted not there was an intrigue between this lady and Porthos. If she had been a great lady she would have fainted; but as she was only a procurator's wife, she contented herself saying to the Musketeer with concentrated fury, "Eh, Monsieur Porthos, you don't offer me any holy water?"

Porthos, at the sound of that voice, started like a man awakened from a sleep of a hundred years.

"Ma-madame!" cried he; "is that you? How is your husband, our dear Monsieur Coquenard? Is he still as stingy as ever? Where can my eyes have been not to have seen you during the two hours of the sermon?"

"I was within two paces of you, monsieur," replied the procurator's wife; "but you did not perceive me because you had no eyes but for the pretty lady to whom you just now gave the holy water."

Porthos pretended to be confused. "Ah," said he, "you have remarked--"

"I must have been blind not to have seen."

"Yes," said Porthos, "that is a duchess of my acquaintance whom I have great trouble to meet on account of the jealousy of her husband, and who sent me word that she should come today to this poor church, buried in this vile quarter, solely for the sake of seeing me."

"Monsieur Porthos," said the procurator's wife, "will you have the kindness to offer me your arm for five minutes? I have something to say to you."

"Certainly, madame," said Porthos, winking to himself, as a gambler does who laughs at the dupe he is about to pluck.

At that moment d'Artagnan passed in pursuit of Milady; he cast a passing glance at Porthos, and beheld this triumphant look.

"Eh, eh!" said he, reasoning to himself according to the strangely easy morality of that gallant period, "there is one who will be equipped in good time!"

Porthos, yielding to the pressure of the arm of the procurator's wife, as a bark yields to the rudder, arrived at the cloister St. Magloire--a little-frequented passage, enclosed with a turnstile at each end. In the daytime nobody was seen there but mendicants devouring their crusts, and children at play.

"Ah, Monsieur Porthos," cried the procurator's wife, when she was assured that no one who was a stranger to the population of the locality could either see or hear her, "ah, Monsieur Porthos, you are a great conqueror, as it appears!"

"I, madame?" said Porthos, drawing himself up proudly; "how so?"

"The signs just now, and the holy water! But that must be a princess, at least--that lady with her Negro boy and her maid!"

"My God! Madame, you are deceived," said Porthos; "she is simply a duchess."

"And that running footman who waited at the door, and that carriage with a coachman in grand livery who sat waiting on his seat?"

Porthos had seen neither the footman nor the carriage, but with the eye of a jealous woman, Mme. Coquenard had seen everything.

Porthos regretted that he had not at once made the lady of the red cushion a princess.

"Ah, you are quite the pet of the ladies, Monsieur Porthos!" resumed the procurator's wife, with a sigh.

"Well," responded Porthos, "you may imagine, with the physique with which nature has endowed me, I am not in want of good luck."

"Good Lord, how quickly men forget!" cried the procurator's wife, raising her eyes toward heaven.

"Less quickly than the women, it seems to me," replied Porthos; "for I, madame, I may say I was your victim, when wounded, dying, I was abandoned by the surgeons. I, the offspring of a noble family, who placed reliance upon your friendship--I was near dying of my wounds at first, and of hunger afterward, in a beggarly inn at Chantilly, without you ever deigning once to reply to the burning letters I addressed to you."

"But, Monsieur Porthos," murmured the procurator's wife, who began to feel that, to judge by the conduct of the great ladies of the time, she was wrong.

"I, who had sacrificed for you the Baronne de--"

"I know it well."

"The Comtesse de--"

"Monsieur Porthos, be generous!"

"You are right, madame, and I will not finish."

"But it was my husband who would not hear of lending."

"Madame Coquenard," said Porthos, "remember the first letter you wrote me, and which I preserve engraved in my memory."

The procurator's wife uttered a groan.

"Besides," said she, "the sum you required me to borrow was rather large."

"Madame Coquenard, I gave you the preference. I had but to write to the Duchesse--but I won't repeat her name, for I am incapable of compromising a woman; but this I know, that I had but to write to her and she would have sent me fifteen hundred."

The procurator's wife shed a tear.

"Monsieur Porthos," said she, "I can assure you that you have severely punished me; and if in the time to come you should find yourself in a similar situation, you have but to apply to me."

"Fie, madame, fie!" said Porthos, as if disgusted. "Let us not talk about money, if you please; it is humiliating."

"Then you no longer love me!" said the procurator's wife, slowly and sadly.

Porthos maintained a majestic silence.

"And that is the only reply you make? Alas, I understand."

"Think of the offense you have committed toward me, madame! It remains HERE!" said Porthos, placing his hand on his heart, and pressing it strongly.

"I will repair it, indeed I will, my dear Porthos."

"Besides, what did I ask of you?" resumed Porthos, with a movement of the shoulders full of good fellowship. "A loan, nothing more! After all, I am not an unreasonable man. I know you are not rich, Madame Coquenard, and that your husband is obliged to bleed his poor clients to squeeze a few paltry crowns from them. Oh! If you were a duchess, a marchioness, or a countess, it would be quite a different thing; it would be unpardonable."

The procurator's wife was piqued.

"Please to know, Monsieur Porthos," said she, "that my strongbox, the strongbox of a procurator's wife though it may be, is better filled than those of your affected minxes."

"The doubles the offense," said Porthos, disengaging his arm from that of the procurator's wife; "for if you are rich, Madame Coquenard, then there is no excuse for your refusal."

"When I said rich," replied the procurator's wife, who saw that she had gone too far, "you must not take the word literally. I am not precisely rich, though I am pretty well off."

"Hold, madame," said Porthos, "let us say no more upon the subject, I beg of you. You have misunderstood me, all sympathy is extinct between us."

"Ingrate that you are!"

"Ah! I advise you to complain!" said Porthos.

"Begone, then, to your beautiful duchess; I will detain you no longer."

"And she is not to be despised, in my opinion."

"Now, Monsieur Porthos, once more, and this is the last! Do you love me still?"

"Ah, madame," said Porthos, in the most melancholy tone he could assume, "when we are about to enter upon a campaign--a campaign, in which my presentiments tell me I shall be killed--"

"Oh, don't talk of such things!" cried the procurator's wife, bursting into tears.

"Something whispers me so," continued Porthos, becoming more and more melancholy.

"Rather say that you have a new love."

"Not so; I speak frankly to you. No object affects me; and I even feel here, at the bottom of my heart, something which speaks for you. But in fifteen days, as you know, or as you do not know, this fatal campaign is to open. I shall be fearfully preoccupied with my outfit. Then I must make a journey to see my family, in the lower part of Brittany, to obtain the sum necessary for my departure."

Porthos observed a last struggle between love and avarice.

"And as," continued he, "the duchess whom you saw at the church has estates near to those of my family, we mean to make the journey together. Journeys, you know, appear much shorter when we travel two in company."

"Have you no friends in Paris, then, Monsieur Porthos?" said the procurator's wife.

"I thought I had," said Porthos, resuming his melancholy air; "but I have been taught my mistake."

"You have some!" cried the procurator's wife, in a transport that surprised even herself. "Come to our house tomorrow. You are the son of my aunt, consequently my cousin; you come from Noyon, in Picardy; you have several lawsuits and no attorney. Can you recollect all that?"

"Perfectly, madame."

"Come at dinnertime."

"Very well."

"And be upon your guard before my husband, who is rather shrewd, notwithstanding his seventy-six years."

"Seventy-six years! PESTE! That's a fine age!" replied Porthos.

"A great age, you mean, Monsieur Porthos. Yes, the poor man may be expected to leave me a widow, any hour," continued she, throwing a significant glance at Porthos. "Fortunately, by our marriage contract, the survivor takes everything."

"All?"

"Yes, all."

"You are a woman of precaution, I see, my dear Madame Coquenard," said Porthos, squeezing the hand of the procurator's wife tenderly.

"We are then reconciled, dear Monsieur Porthos?" said she, simpering.

"For life," replied Porthos, in the same manner.

"Till we meet again, then, dear traitor!"

"Till we meet again, my forgetful charmer!"

"Tomorrow, my angel!"

"Tomorrow, flame of my life!"

30 D'Artagnan And The Englishman

D'Artagnan followed Milady without being perceived by her. He saw her get into her carriage, and heard her order the coachman to drive to St. Germain.

It was useless to try to keep pace on foot with a carriage drawn by two powerful horses. D'Artagnan therefore returned to the Rue Ferou.

In the Rue de Seine he met Planchet, who had stopped before the house of a pastry cook, and was contemplating with ecstasy a cake of the most appetizing appearance.

He ordered him to go and saddle two horses in M. de Treville's stables--one for himself, d'Artagnan, and one for Planchet--and bring them to Athens's place. Once for all, Treville had placed his stable at d'Artagnan's service.

Planchet proceeded toward the Rue du Colombier, and d'Artagnan toward the Rue Ferou. Athos was at home, emptying sadly a bottle of the famous Spanish wine he had brought back with him from his journey into Picardy. He made a sign for Grimaud to bring a glass for d'Artagnan, and Grimaud obeyed as usual.

D'Artagnan related to Athos all that had passed at the church between Porthos and the procurator's wife, and how their comrade was probably by that time in a fair way to be equipped.

"As for me," replied Athos to this recital, "I am quite at my ease; it will not be women that will defray the expense of my outfit."

"Handsome, well-bred, noble lord as you are, my dear Athos, neither princesses nor queens would be secure from your amorous solicitations."

"How young this d'Artagnan is!" said Athos, shrugging his shoulders; and he made a sign to Grimaud to bring another bottle.

At that moment Planchet put his head modestly in at the half-open door, and told his master that the horses were ready.

"What horses?" asked Athos.

"Two horses that Monsieur de Treville lends me at my pleasure, and with which I am now going to take a ride to St. Germain."

"Well, and what are you going to do at St. Germain?" then demanded Athos.

Then d'Artagnan described the meeting which he had at the church, and how he had found that lady who, with the seigneur in the black cloak and with the scar near his temple, filled his mind constantly.

"That is to say, you are in love with this lady as you were with Madame Bonacieux," said Athos, shrugging his shoulders contemptuously, as if he pitied human weakness.

"I? not at all!" said d'Artagnan. "I am only curious to unravel the mystery to which she is attached. I do not know why, but I imagine that this woman, wholly unknown to me as she is, and wholly unknown to her as I am, has an influence over my life."

"Well, perhaps you are right," said Athos. "I do not know a woman that is worth the trouble of being sought for when she is once lost. Madame Bonacieux is lost; so much the worse for her if she is found."

"No, Athos, no, you are mistaken," said d'Artagnan; "I love my poor Constance more than ever, and if I knew the place in which she is, were it at the end of the world, I would go to free her from the hands of her enemies; but I am ignorant. All my researches have been useless. What is to be said? I must divert my attention!"

"Amuse yourself with Milady, my dear d'Artagnan; I wish you may with all my heart, if that will amuse you."

"Hear me, Athos," said d'Artagnan. "Instead of shutting yourself up here as if you were under arrest, get on horseback and come and take a ride with me to St. Germain."

"My dear fellow," said Athos, "I ride horses when I have any; when I have none, I go afoot."

"Well," said d'Artagnan, smiling at the misanthropy of Athos, which from any other person would have offended him, "I ride what I can get; I am not so proud as you. So AU REVOIR, dear Athos."

"AU REVOIR," said the Musketeer, making a sign to Grimaud to uncork the bottle he had just brought.

D'Artagnan and Planchet mounted, and took the road to St. Germain.

All along the road, what Athos had said respecting Mme. Bonacieux recurred to the mind of the young man. Although d'Artagnan was not of a very sentimental character, the mercer's pretty wife had made a real impression upon his heart. As he said, he was ready to go to the end of the world to seek her; but the world, being round, has many ends, so that he did not know which way to turn. Meantime, he was going to try to find out Milady. Milady had spoken to the man in the black cloak; therefore she knew him. Now, in the opinion of d'Artagnan, it was certainly the man in the black cloak who had carried off Mme. Bonacieux the second time, as he had carried her off the first. d'Artagnan then only half-lied, which is lying but little, when he said that by going in search of Milady he at the same time went in search of Constance.

Thinking of all this, and from time to time giving a touch of the spur to his horse, d'Artagnan completed his short journey, and arrived at St. Germain. He had just passed by the pavilion in which ten years later Louis XIV was born. He rode up a very quiet street, looking to the right and the left to see if he could catch any vestige of his beautiful Englishwoman, when from the ground floor of a pretty house, which, according to the fashion of the time, had no window toward the street, he saw a face peep out with which he thought he was acquainted. This person walked along the terrace, which was ornamented with flowers. Planchet recognized him first.

"Eh, monsieur!" said he, addressing d'Artagnan, "don't you remember that face which is blinking yonder?"

"No," said d'Artagnan, "and yet I am certain it is not the first time I have seen that visage."

"PARBLEU, I believe it is not," said Planchet. "Why, it is poor Lubin, the lackey of the Comte de Wardes--he whom you took such good care of a month ago at Calais, on the road to the governor's country house!"

"So it is!" said d'Artagnan; "I know him now. Do you think he would recollect you?"

"My faith, monsieur, he was in such trouble that I doubt if he can have retained a very clear recollection of me."

"Well, go and talk with the boy," said d'Artagnan, "and make out if you can from his conversation whether his master is dead."

Planchet dismounted and went straight up to Lubin, who did not at all remember him, and the two lackeys began to chat with the best understanding possible; while d'Artagnan turned the two horses into a lane, went round the house, and came back to watch the conference from behind a hedge of filberts.

At the end of an instant's observation he heard the noise of a vehicle, and saw Milady's carriage stop opposite to him. He could not be mistaken; Milady was in it. D'Artagnan leaned upon the neck of his horse, in order that he might see without being seen.

Milady put her charming blond head out at the window, and gave her orders to her maid.

The latter--a pretty girl of about twenty or twenty-two years, active and lively, the true SOUBRETTE of a great lady--jumped from the step upon which, according to the custom of the time, she was seated, and took her way toward the terrace upon which d'Artagnan had perceived Lubin.

D'Artagnan followed the soubrette with his eyes, and saw her go toward the terrace; but it happened that someone in the house called Lubin, so that Planchet remained alone, looking in all directions for the road where d'Artagnan had disappeared.

The maid approached Planchet, whom she took for Lubin, and holding out a little billet to him said, "For your master."

"For my master?" replied Planchet, astonished.

"Yes, and important. Take it quickly."

Thereupon she ran toward the carriage, which had turned round toward the way it came, jumped upon the step, and the carriage drove off.

Planchet turned and returned the billet. Then, accustomed to passive obedience, he jumped down from the terrace, ran toward the lane, and at the end of twenty paces met d'Artagnan, who, having seen all, was coming to him.

"For you, monsieur," said Planchet, presenting the billet to the young man.

"For me?" said d'Artagnan; "are you sure of that?"

"PARDIEU, monsieur, I can't be more sure. The SOUBRETTE said, 'For your master.' I have no other master but you; so--a pretty little lass, my faith, is that SOUBRETTE!"

D'Artagnan opened the letter, and read these words:

"A person who takes more interest in you than she is willing to confess wishes to know on what day it will suit you to walk in the forest? Tomorrow, at the Hotel Field of the Cloth of Gold, a lackey in black and red will wait for your reply."

"Oh!" said d'Artagnan, "this is rather warm; it appears that Milady and I are anxious about the health of the same person. Well, Planchet, how is the good Monsieur de Wardes? He is not dead, then?"

"No, monsieur, he is as well as a man can be with four sword wounds in his body; for you, without question, inflicted four upon the dear gentleman, and he is still very weak, having lost almost all his blood. As I said, monsieur, Lubin did not know me, and told me our adventure from one end to the other."

"Well done, Planchet! you are the king of lackeys. Now jump onto your horse, and let us overtake the carriage."

This did not take long. At the end of five minutes they perceived the carriage drawn up by the roadside; a cavalier, richly dressed, was close to the door.

The conversation between Milady and the cavalier was so animated that d'Artagnan stopped on the other side of the carriage without anyone but the pretty SOUBRETTE perceiving his presence.

The conversation took place in English--a language which d'Artagnan could not understand; but by the accent the young man plainly saw that the beautiful Englishwoman was in a great rage. She terminated it by an action which left no doubt as to the nature of this conversation; this was a blow with her fan, applied with such force that the little feminine weapon flew into a thousand pieces.

The cavalier laughed aloud, which appeared to exasperate Milady still more.

D'Artagnan thought this was the moment to interfere. He approached the other door, and taking off his hat respectfully, said, "Madame, will you permit me to offer you my services? It appears to me that this cavalier has made you very angry. Speak one word, madame, and I take upon myself to punish him for his want of courtesy."

At the first word Milady turned, looking at the young man with astonishment; and when he had finished, she said in very good French, "Monsieur, I should with great confidence place myself under your protection if the person with whom I quarrel were not my brother."

"Ah, excuse me, then," said d'Artagnan. "You must be aware that I was ignorant of that, madame."

"What is that stupid fellow troubling himself about?" cried the cavalier whom Milady had designated as her brother, stooping down to the height of the coach window. "Why does not he go about his business?"

"Stupid fellow yourself!" said d'Artagnan, stooping in his turn on the neck of his horse, and answering on his side through the carriage window. "I do not go on because it pleases me to stop here."

The cavalier addressed some words in English to his sister.

"I speak to you in French," said d'Artagnan; "be kind enough, then, to reply to me in the same language. You are Madame's brother, I learn--be it so; but fortunately you are not mine."

It might be thought that Milady, timid as women are in general, would have interposed in this commencement of mutual provocations in order to prevent the quarrel from going too far; but on the contrary, she threw herself back in her carriage, and called out coolly to the coachman, "Go on--home!"

The pretty SOUBRETTE cast an anxious glance at d'Artagnan, whose good looks seemed to have made an impression on her.

The carriage went on, and left the two men facing each other; no material obstacle separated them.

The cavalier made a movement as if to follow the carriage; but d'Artagnan, whose anger, already excited, was much increased by recognizing in him the Englishman of Amiens who had won his horse and had been very near winning his diamond of Athos, caught at his bridle and stopped him.

"Well, monsieur," said he, "you appear to be more stupid than I am, for you forget there is a little quarrel to arrange between us two."

"Ah," said the Englishman, "is it you, my master? It seems you must always be playing some game or other."

"Yes; and that reminds me that I have a revenge to take. We will see, my dear monsieur, if you can handle a sword as skillfully as you can a dice box."

"You see plainly that I have no sword," said the Englishman. "Do you wish to play the braggart with an unarmed man?"

"I hope you have a sword at home; but at all events, I have two, and if you like, I will throw with you for one of them."

"Needless," said the Englishman; "I am well furnished with such playthings."

"Very well, my worthy gentleman," replied d'Artagnan, "pick out the longest, and come and show it to me this evening."

"Where, if you please?"

"Behind the Luxembourg; that's a charming spot for such amusements as the one I propose to you."

"That will do; I will be there."

"Your hour?"

"Six o'clock."

"A PROPOS, you have probably one or two friends?"

"I have three, who would be honored by joining in the sport with me."

"Three? Marvelous! That falls out oddly! Three is just my number!"

"Now, then, who are you?" asked the Englishman.

"I am Monsieur d'Artagnan, a Gascon gentleman, serving in the king's Musketeers. And you?"

"I am Lord de Winter, Baron Sheffield."

"Well, then, I am your servant, Monsieur Baron," said d'Artagnan, "though you have names rather difficult to recollect." And touching his horse with the spur, he cantered back to Paris. As he was accustomed to do in all cases of any consequence, d'Artagnan went straight to the residence of Athos.

He found Athos reclining upon a large sofa, where he was waiting, as he said, for his outfit to come and find him. He related to Athos all that had passed, except the letter to M. de Wardes.

Athos was delighted to find he was going to fight an Englishman. We might say that was his dream.

They immediately sent their lackeys for Porthos and Aramis, and on their arrival made them acquainted with the situation.

Porthos drew his sword from the scabbard, and made passes at the wall, springing back from time to time, and making contortions like a dancer.

Aramis, who was constantly at work at his poem, shut himself up in Athos's closet, and begged not to be disturbed before the moment of drawing swords.

Athos, by signs, desired Grimaud to bring another bottle of wine.

D'Artagnan employed himself in arranging a little plan, of which we shall hereafter see the execution, and which promised him some agreeable adventure, as might be seen by the smiles which from time to time passed over his countenance, whose thoughtfulness they animated.

31 English And French

The hour having come, they went with their four lackeys to a spot behind the Luxembourg given up to the feeding of goats. Athos threw a piece of money to the goatkeeper to withdraw. The lackeys were ordered to act as sentinels.

A silent party soon drew near to the same enclosure, entered, and joined the Musketeers. Then, according to foreign custom, the presentations took place.

The Englishmen were all men of rank; consequently the odd names of their adversaries were for them not only a matter of surprise, but of annoyance.

"But after all," said Lord de Winter, when the three friends had been named, "we do not know who you are. We cannot fight with such names; they are names of shepherds."

"Therefore your lordship may suppose they are only assumed names," said Athos.

"Which only gives us a greater desire to know the real ones," replied the Englishman.

"You played very willingly with us without knowing our names," said Athos, "by the same token that you won our horses."

"That is true, but we then only risked our pistoles; this time we risk our blood. One plays with anybody; but one fights only with equals."

"And that is but just," said Athos, and he took aside the one of the four Englishmen with whom he was to fight, and communicated his name in a low voice.

Porthos and Aramis did the same.

"Does that satisfy you?" said Athos to his adversary. "Do you find me of sufficient rank to do me the honor of crossing swords with me?"

"Yes, monsieur," said the Englishman, bowing.

"Well! now shall I tell you something?" added Athos, coolly.

"What?" replied the Englishman.

"Why, that is that you would have acted much more wisely if you had not required me to make myself known."

"Why so?"

"Because I am believed to be dead, and have reasons for wishing nobody to know I am living; so that I shall be obliged to kill you to prevent my secret from roaming over the fields."

The Englishman looked at Athos, believing that he jested, but Athos did not jest the least in the world.

"Gentlemen," said Athos, addressing at the same time his companions and their adversaries, "are we ready?"

"Yes!" answered the Englishmen and the Frenchmen, as with one voice.

"On guard, then!" cried Athos.

Immediately eight swords glittered in the rays of the setting sun, and the combat began with an animosity very natural between men twice enemies.

Athos fenced with as much calmness and method as if he had been practicing in a fencing school.

Porthos, abated, no doubt, of his too-great confidence by his adventure of Chantilly, played with skill and prudence. Aramis, who had the third canto of his poem to finish, behaved like a man in haste.

Athos killed his adversary first. He hit him but once, but as he had foretold, that hit was a mortal one; the sword pierced his heart.

Second, Porthos stretched his upon the grass with a wound through his thigh, As the Englishman, without making any further resistance, then surrendered his sword, Porthos took him up in his arms and bore him to his carriage.

Aramis pushed his so vigorously that after going back fifty paces, the man ended by fairly taking to his heels, and disappeared amid the hooting of the lackeys.

As to d'Artagnan, he fought purely and simply on the defensive; and when he saw his adversary pretty well fatigued, with a vigorous side thrust sent his sword flying. The baron, finding himself disarmed, took two or three steps back, but in this movement his foot slipped and he fell backward.

D'Artagnan was over him at a bound, and said to the Englishman, pointing his sword to his throat, "I could kill you, my Lord, you are completely in my hands; but I spare your life for the sake of your sister."

D'Artagnan was at the height of joy; he had realized the plan he had imagined beforehand, whose picturing had produced the smiles we noted upon his face.

The Englishman, delighted at having to do with a gentleman of such a kind disposition, pressed d'Artagnan in his arms, and paid a thousand compliments to the three Musketeers, and as Porthos's adversary was already installed in the carriage, and as Aramis's had taken to his heels, they had nothing to think about but the dead.

As Porthos and Aramis were undressing him, in the hope of finding his wound not mortal, a large purse dropped from his clothes. D'Artagnan picked it up and offered it to Lord de Winter.

"What the devil would you have me do with that?" said the Englishman.

"You can restore it to his family," said d'Artagnan.

"His family will care much about such a trifle as that! His family will inherit fifteen thousand louis a year from him. Keep the purse for your lackeys."

D'Artagnan put the purse into his pocket.

"And now, my young friend, for you will permit me, I hope, to give you that name," said Lord de Winter, "on this very evening, if agreeable to you, I will present you to my sister, Milady Clarik, for I am desirous that she should take you into her good graces; and as she is not in bad odor at court, she may perhaps on some future day speak a word that will not prove useless to you."

D'Artagnan blushed with pleasure, and bowed a sign of assent.

At this time Athos came up to d'Artagnan.

"What do you mean to do with that purse?" whispered he.

"Why, I meant to pass it over to you, my dear Athos."

"Me! why to me?"

"Why, you killed him! They are the spoils of victory."

"I, the heir of an enemy!" said Athos; "for whom, then, do you take me?"

"It is the custom in war," said d'Artagnan, "why should it not be the custom in a duel?"

"Even on the field of battle, I have never done that."

Porthos shrugged his shoulders; Aramis by a movement of his lips endorsed Athos.

"Then," said d'Artagnan, "let us give the money to the lackeys, as Lord de Winter desired us to do."

"Yes," said Athos; "let us give the money to the lackeys--not to our lackeys, but to the lackeys of the Englishmen."

Athos took the purse, and threw it into the hand of the coachman. "For you and your comrades."

This greatness of spirit in a man who was quite destitute struck even Porthos; and this French generosity, repeated by Lord de Winter and his friend, was highly applauded, except by MM Grimaud, Bazin, Mousqueton and Planchet.

Lord de Winter, on quitting d'Artagnan, gave him his sister's address. She lived in the Place Royale--then the fashionable quarter--at Number 6, and he undertook to call and take d'Artagnan with him in order to introduce him. d'Artagnan appointed eight o'clock at Athos's residence.

This introduction to Milady Clarik occupied the head of our Gascon greatly. He remembered in what a strange manner this woman had hitherto been mixed up in his destiny. According to his conviction, she was some creature of the cardinal, and yet he felt himself invincibly drawn toward her by one of those sentiments for which we cannot account. His only fear was that Milady would recognize in him the man of Meung and of Dover. Then she knew that he was one of the friends of M. de Treville, and consequently, that he belonged body and soul to the king; which would make him lose a part of his advantage, since when known to Milady as he knew her, he played only an equal game with her. As to the commencement of an intrigue between her and M. de Wardes, our presumptuous hero gave but little heed to that, although the marquis was young, handsome, rich, and high in the cardinal's favor. It is not for nothing we are but twenty years old, above all if we were born at Tarbes.

D'Artagnan began by making his most splendid toilet, then returned to Athos's, and according to custom, related everything to him. Athos listened to his projects, then shook his head, and recommended prudence to him with a shade of bitterness.

"What!" said he, "you have just lost one woman, whom you call good, charming, perfect; and here you are, running headlong after another."

D'Artagnan felt the truth of this reproach.

"I loved Madame Bonacieux with my heart, while I only love Milady with my head," said he. "In getting introduced to her, my principal object is to ascertain what part she plays at court."

"The part she plays, PARDIEU! It is not difficult to divine that, after all you have told me. She is some emissary of the cardinal; a woman who will draw you into a snare in which you will leave your head."

"The devil! my dear Athos, you view things on the dark side, methinks."

"My dear fellow, I mistrust women. Can it be otherwise? I bought my experience dearly--particularly fair women. Milady is fair, you say?"

"She has the most beautiful light hair imaginable!"

"Ah, my poor d'Artagnan!" said Athos.

"Listen to me! I want to be enlightened on a subject; then, when I shall have learned what I desire to know, I will withdraw."

"Be enlightened!" said Athos, phlegmatically.

Lord de Winter arrived at the appointed time; but Athos, being warned of his coming, went into the other chamber. He therefore found d'Artagnan alone, and as it was nearly eight o'clock he took the young man with him.

An elegant carriage waited below, and as it was drawn by two excellent horses, they were soon at the Place Royale.

Milady Clarik received d'Artagnan ceremoniously. Her hotel was remarkably sumptuous, and while the most part of the English had quit, or were about to quit, France on account of the war, Milady had just been laying out much money upon her residence; which proved that the general measure which drove the English from France did not affect her.

"You see," said Lord de Winter, presenting d'Artagnan to his sister, "a young gentleman who has held my life in his hands, and who has not abused his advantage, although we have been twice enemies, although it was I who insulted him, and although I am an Englishman. Thank him, then, madame, if you have any affection for me."

Milady frowned slightly; a scarcely visible cloud passed over her brow, and so peculiar a smile appeared upon her lips that the young man, who saw and observed this triple shade, almost shuddered at it.

The brother did not perceive this; he had turned round to play with Milady's favorite monkey, which had pulled him by the doublet.

"You are welcome, monsieur," said Milady, in a voice whose singular sweetness contrasted with the symptoms of ill-humor which d'Artagnan had just remarked; "you have today acquired eternal rights to my gratitude."

The Englishman then turned round and described the combat without omitting a single detail. Milady listened with the greatest attention, and yet it was easily to be perceived, whatever effort she made to conceal her impressions, that this recital was not agreeable to her. The blood rose to her head, and her little foot worked with impatience beneath her robe.

Lord de Winter perceived nothing of this. When he had finished, he went to a table upon which was a salver with Spanish wine and glasses. He filled two glasses, and by a sign invited d'Artagnan to drink.

D'Artagnan knew it was considered disobliging by an Englishman to refuse to pledge him. He therefore drew near to the table and took the second glass. He did not, however, lose sight of Milady, and in a mirror he perceived the change that came over her face. Now that she believed herself to be no longer observed, a sentiment resembling ferocity animated her countenance. She bit her handkerchief with her beautiful teeth.

That pretty little SOUBRETTE whom d'Artagnan had already observed then came in. She spoke some words to Lord de Winter in English, who thereupon requested d'Artagnan's permission to retire, excusing himself on account of the urgency of the business that had called him away, and charging his sister to obtain his pardon.

D'Artagnan exchanged a shake of the hand with Lord de Winter, and then returned to Milady. Her countenance, with surprising mobility, had recovered its gracious expression; but some little red spots on her handkerchief indicated that she had bitten her lips till the blood came. Those lips were magnificent; they might be said to be of coral.

The conversation took a cheerful turn. Milady appeared to have entirely recovered. She told d'Artagnan that Lord de Winter was her brother-in-law, and not her brother. She had married a younger brother of the family, who had left her a widow with one child. This child was the only heir to Lord de Winter, if Lord de Winter did not marry. All this showed d'Artagnan that there was a veil which concealed something; but he could not yet see under this veil.

In addition to this, after a half hour's conversation d'Artagnan was convinced that Milady was his compatriot; she spoke French with an elegance and a purity that left no doubt on that head.

D'Artagnan was profuse in gallant speeches and protestations of devotion. To all the simple things which escaped our Gascon, Milady replied with a smile of kindness. The hour came for him to retire. D'Artagnan took leave of Milady, and left the saloon the happiest of men.

On the staircase he met the pretty SOUBRETTE, who brushed gently against him as she passed, and then, blushing to the eyes, asked his pardon for having touched him in a voice so sweet that the pardon was granted instantly.

D'Artagnan came again on the morrow, and was still better received than on the evening before. Lord de Winter was not at home; and it was Milady who this time did all the honors of the evening. She appeared to take a great interest in him, asked him whence he came, who were his friends, and whether he had not sometimes thought of attaching himself to the cardinal.

D'Artagnan, who, as we have said, was exceedingly prudent for a young man of twenty, then remembered his suspicions regarding Milady. He launched into a eulogy of his Eminence, and said that he should not have failed to enter into the Guards of the cardinal instead of the king's Guards if he had happened to know M. de Cavois instead of M. de Treville.

Milady changed the conversation without any appearance of affectation, and asked d'Artagnan in the most careless manner possible if he had ever been in England.

D'Artagnan replied that he had been sent thither by M. de Treville to treat for a supply of horses, and that he had brought back four as specimens.

Milady in the course of the conversation twice or thrice bit her lips; she had to deal with a Gascon who played close.

At the same hour as on the preceding evening, d'Artagnan retired. In the corridor he again met the pretty Kitty; that was the name of the SOUBRETTE. She looked at him with an expression of kindness which it was impossible to mistake; but d'Artagnan was so preoccupied by the mistress that he noticed absolutely nothing but her.

D'Artagnan came again on the morrow and the day after that, and each day Milady gave him a more gracious reception.

Every evening, either in the antechamber, the corridor, or on the stairs, he met the pretty SOUBRETTE. But, as we have said, d'Artagnan paid no attention to this persistence of poor Kitty.

32 A Procurator's Dinner

However brilliant had been the part played by Porthos in the duel, it had not made him forget the dinner of the procurator's wife.

On the morrow he received the last touches of Mousqueton's brush for an hour, and took his way toward the Rue aux Ours with the steps of a man who was doubly in favor with fortune.

His heart beat, but not like d'Artagnan's with a young and impatient love. No; a more material interest stirred his blood. He was about at last to pass that mysterious threshold, to climb those unknown stairs by which, one by one, the old crowns of M. Coquenard had ascended. He was about to see in reality a certain coffer of which he had twenty times beheld the image in his dreams--a coffer long and deep, locked, bolted, fastened in the wall; a coffer of which he had so often heard, and which the hands--a little wrinkled, it is true, but still not without elegance--of the procurator's wife were about to open to his admiring looks.

And then he--a wanderer on the earth, a man without fortune, a man without family, a soldier accustomed to inns, cabarets, taverns, and restaurants, a lover of wine forced to depend upon chance treats--was about to partake of family meals, to enjoy the pleasures of a comfortable establishment, and to give himself up to those little attentions which "the harder one is, the more they please," as old soldiers say.

To come in the capacity of a cousin, and seat himself every day at a good table; to smooth the yellow, wrinkled brow of the old procurator; to pluck the clerks a little by teaching them BASSETTE, PASSE-DIX, and LANSQUENET, in their utmost nicety, and winning from them, by way of fee for the lesson he would give them in an hour, their savings of a month--all this was enormously delightful to Porthos.

The Musketeer could not forget the evil reports which then prevailed, and which indeed have survived them, of the procurators of the period--meanness, stinginess, fasts; but as, after all, excepting some few acts of economy which Porthos had always found very unseasonable, the procurator's wife had been tolerably liberal--that is, be it understood, for a procurator's wife--he hoped to see a household of a highly comfortable kind.

And yet, at the very door the Musketeer began to entertain some doubts. The approach was not such as to prepossess people--an ill-smelling, dark passage, a staircase half-lighted by bars through which stole a glimmer from a neighboring yard; on the first floor a low door studded with enormous nails, like the principal gate of the Grand Chatelet.

Porthos knocked with his hand. A tall, pale clerk, his face shaded by a forest of virgin hair, opened the door, and bowed with the air of a man forced at once to respect in another lofty stature, which indicated strength, the military dress, which indicated rank, and a ruddy countenance, which indicated familiarity with good living.

A shorter clerk came behind the first, a taller clerk behind the second, a stripling of a dozen years rising behind the third. In all, three clerks and a half, which, for the time, argued a very extensive clientage.

Although the Musketeer was not expected before one o'clock, the procurator's wife had been on the watch ever since midday, reckoning that the heart, or perhaps the stomach, of her lover would bring him before his time.

Mme. Coquenard therefore entered the office from the house at the same moment her guest entered from the stairs, and the appearance of the worthy lady relieved him from an awkward embarrassment. The clerks surveyed him with great curiosity, and he, not knowing well what to say to this ascending and descending scale, remained tongue-tied.

"It is my cousin!" cried the procurator's wife. "Come in, come in, Monsieur Porthos!"

The name of Porthos produced its effect upon the clerks, who began to laugh; but Porthos turned sharply round, and every countenance quickly recovered its gravity.

They reached the office of the procurator after having passed through the antechamber in which the clerks were, and the study in which they ought to have been. This last apartment was a sort of dark room, littered with papers. On quitting the study they left the kitchen on the right, and entered the reception room.

All these rooms, which communicated with one another, did not inspire Porthos favorably. Words might be heard at a distance through all these open doors. Then, while passing, he had cast a rapid, investigating glance into the kitchen; and he was obliged to confess to himself, to the shame of the procurator's wife and his own regret, that he did not see that fire, that animation, that bustle, which when a good repast is on foot prevails generally in that sanctuary of good living.

The procurator had without doubt been warned of his visit, as he expressed no surprise at the sight of Porthos, who advanced toward him with a sufficiently easy air, and saluted him courteously.

"We are cousins, it appears, Monsieur Porthos?" said the procurator, rising, yet supporting his weight upon the arms of his cane chair.

The old man, wrapped in a large black doublet, in which the whole of his slender body was concealed, was brisk and dry. His little gray eyes shone like carbuncles, and appeared, with his grinning mouth, to be the only part of his face in which life survived. Unfortunately the legs began to refuse their service to this bony machine. During the last five or six months that this weakness had been felt, the worthy procurator had nearly become the slave of his wife.

The cousin was received with resignation, that was all. M. Coquenard, firm upon his legs, would have declined all relationship with M. Porthos.

"Yes, monsieur, we are cousins," said Porthos, without being disconcerted, as he had never reckoned upon being received enthusiastically by the husband.

"By the female side, I believe?" said the procurator, maliciously.

Porthos did not feel the ridicule of this, and took it for a piece of simplicity, at which he laughed in his large mustache. Mme. Coquenard, who knew that a simple-minded procurator was a very rare variety in the species, smiled a little, and colored a great deal.

M Coquenard had, since the arrival of Porthos, frequently cast his eyes with great uneasiness upon a large chest placed in front of his oak desk. Porthos comprehended that this chest, although it did not correspond in shape with that which he had seen in his dreams, must be the blessed coffer, and he congratulated himself that the reality was several feet higher than the dream.

M Coquenard did not carry his genealogical investigations any further; but withdrawing his anxious look from the chest and fixing it upon Porthos, he contented himself with saying, "Monsieur our cousin will do us the favor of dining with us once before his departure for the campaign, will he not, Madame Coquenard?"

This time Porthos received the blow right in his stomach, and felt it. It appeared likewise that Mme. Coquenard was not less affected by it on her part, for she added, "My cousin will not return if he finds that we do not treat him kindly; but otherwise he has so little time to pass in Paris, and consequently to spare to us, that we must entreat him to give us every instant he can call his own previous to his departure."

"Oh, my legs, my poor legs! where are you?" murmured Coquenard, and he tried to smile.

This succor, which came to Porthos at the moment in which he was attacked in his gastronomic hopes, inspired much gratitude in the Musketeer toward the procurator's wife.

The hour of dinner soon arrived. They passed into the eating room--a large dark room situated opposite the kitchen.

The clerks, who, as it appeared, had smelled unusual perfumes in the house, were of military punctuality, and held their stools in hand quite ready to sit down. Their jaws moved preliminarily with fearful threatenings.

"Indeed!" thought Porthos, casting a glance at the three hungry clerks--for the errand boy, as might be expected, was not admitted to the honors of the magisterial table, "in my cousin's place, I would not keep such gourmands! They look like shipwrecked sailors who have not eaten for six weeks."

M Coquenard entered, pushed along upon his armchair with casters by Mme. Coquenard, whom Porthos assisted in rolling her husband up to the table. He had scarcely entered when he began to agitate his nose and his jaws after the example of his clerks.

"Oh, oh!" said he; "here is a soup which is rather inviting."

"What the devil can they smell so extraordinary in this soup?" said Porthos, at the sight of a pale liquid, abundant but entirely free from meat, on the surface of which a few crusts swam about as rare as the islands of an archipelago.

Mme. Coquenard smiled, and upon a sign from her everyone eagerly took his seat.

M Coquenard was served first, then Porthos. Afterward Mme. Coquenard filled her own plate, and distributed the crusts without soup to the impatient clerks. At this moment the door of the dining room unclosed with a creak, and Porthos perceived through the half-open flap the little clerk who, not being allowed to take part in the feast, ate his dry bread in the passage with the double odor of the dining room and kitchen.

After the soup the maid brought a boiled fowl--a piece of magnificence which caused the eyes of the diners to dilate in such a manner that they seemed ready to burst.

"One may see that you love your family, Madame Coquenard," said the procurator, with a smile that was almost tragic. "You are certainly treating your cousin very handsomely!"

The poor fowl was thin, and covered with one of those thick, bristly skins through which the teeth cannot penetrate with all their efforts. The fowl must have been sought for a long time on the perch, to which it had retired to die of old age.

"The devil!" thought Porthos, "this is poor work. I respect old age, but I don't much like it boiled or roasted."

And he looked round to see if anybody partook of his opinion; but on the contrary, he saw nothing but eager eyes which were devouring, in anticipation, that sublime fowl which was the object of his contempt.

Mme. Coquenard drew the dish toward her, skillfully detached the two great black feet, which she placed upon her husband's plate, cut off the neck, which with the head she put on one side for herself, raised the wing for Porthos, and then returned the bird otherwise intact to the servant who had brought it in, who disappeared with it before the Musketeer had time to examine the variations which disappointment produces upon faces, according to the characters and temperaments of those who experience it.

In the place of the fowl a dish of haricot beans made its appearance--an enormous dish in which some bones of mutton that at first sight one might have believed to have some meat on them pretended to show themselves.

But the clerks were not the dupes of this deceit, and their lugubrious looks settled down into resigned countenances.

Mme. Coquenard distributed this dish to the young men with the moderation of a good housewife.

The time for wine came. M. Coquenard poured from a very small stone bottle the third of a glass for each of the young men, served himself in about the same proportion, and passed the bottle to Porthos and Mme. Coquenard.

The young men filled up their third of a glass with water; then, when they had drunk half the glass, they filled it up again, and continued to do so. This brought them, by the end of the repast, to swallowing a drink which from the color of the ruby had passed to that of a pale topaz.

Porthos ate his wing of the fowl timidly, and shuddered when he felt the knee of the procurator's wife under the table, as it came in search of his. He also drank half a glass of this sparingly served wine, and found it to be nothing but that horrible Montreuil--the terror of all expert palates.

M Coquenard saw him swallowing this wine undiluted, and sighed deeply.

"Will you eat any of these beans, Cousin Porthos?" said Mme. Coquenard, in that tone which says, "Take my advice, don't touch them."

"Devil take me if I taste one of them!" murmured Porthos to himself, and then said aloud, "Thank you, my cousin, I am no longer hungry."

There was silence. Porthos could hardly keep his countenance.

The procurator repeated several times, "Ah, Madame Coquenard! Accept my compliments; your dinner has been a real feast. Lord, how I have eaten!"

M Coquenard had eaten his soup, the black feet of the fowl, and the only mutton bone on which there was the least appearance of meat.

Porthos fancied they were mystifying him, and began to curl his mustache and knit his eyebrows; but the knee of Mme. Coquenard gently advised him to be patient.

This silence and this interruption in serving, which were unintelligible to Porthos, had, on the contrary, a terrible meaning for the clerks. Upon a look from the procurator, accompanied by a smile from Mme. Coquenard, they arose slowly from the table, folded their napkins more slowly still, bowed, and retired.

"Go, young men! go and promote digestion by working," said the procurator, gravely.

The clerks gone, Mme. Coquenard rose and took from a buffet a piece of cheese, some preserved quinces, and a cake which she had herself made of almonds and honey.

M Coquenard knit his eyebrows because there were too many good things. Porthos bit his lips because he saw not the wherewithal to dine. He looked to see if the dish of beans was still there; the dish of beans had disappeared.

"A positive feast!" cried M. Coquenard, turning about in his chair, "a real feast, EPULCE EPULORUM. Lucullus dines with Lucullus."

Porthos looked at the bottle, which was near him, and hoped that with wine, bread, and cheese, he might make a dinner; but wine was wanting, the bottle was empty. M. and Mme. Coquenard did not seem to observe it.

"This is fine!" said Porthos to himself; "I am prettily caught!"

He passed his tongue over a spoonful of preserves, and stuck his teeth into the sticky pastry of Mme. Coquenard.

"Now," said he, "the sacrifice is consummated! Ah! if I had not the hope of peeping with Madame Coquenard into her husband's chest!"

M Coquenard, after the luxuries of such a repast, which he called an excess, felt the want of a siesta. Porthos began to hope that the thing would take place at the present sitting, and in that same locality; but the procurator would listen to nothing, he would be taken to his room, and was not satisfied till he was close to his chest, upon the edge of which, for still greater precaution, he placed his feet.

The procurator's wife took Porthos into an adjoining room, and they began to lay the basis of a reconciliation.

"You can come and dine three times a week," said Mme. Coquenard.

"Thanks, madame!" said Porthos, "but I don't like to abuse your kindness; besides, I must think of my outfit!"

"That's true," said the procurator's wife, groaning, "that unfortunate outfit!"

"Alas, yes," said Porthos, "it is so."

"But of what, then, does the equipment of your company consist, Monsieur Porthos?"

"Oh, of many things!" said Porthos. "The Musketeers are, as you know, picked soldiers, and they require many things useless to the Guardsmen or the Swiss."

"But yet, detail them to me."

"Why, they may amount to--", said Porthos, who preferred discussing the total to taking them one by one.

The procurator's wife waited tremblingly.

"To how much?" said she. "I hope it does not exceed--" She stopped; speech failed her.

"Oh, no," said Porthos, "it does not exceed two thousand five hundred livres! I even think that with economy I could manage it with two thousand livres."

"Good God!" cried she, "two thousand livres! Why, that is a fortune!"

Porthos made a most significant grimace; Mme. Coquenard understood it.

"I wished to know the detail," said she, "because, having many relatives in business, I was almost sure of obtaining things at a hundred per cent less than you would pay yourself."

"Ah, ah!" said Porthos, "that is what you meant to say!"

"Yes, dear Monsieur Porthos. Thus, for instance, don't you in the first place want a horse?"

"Yes, a horse."

"Well, then! I can just suit you."

"Ah!" said Porthos, brightening, "that's well as regards my horse; but I must have the appointments complete, as they include objects which a Musketeer alone can purchase, and which will not amount, besides, to more than three hundred livres."

"Three hundred livres? Then put down three hundred livres," said the procurator's wife, with a sigh.

Porthos smiled. It may be remembered that he had the saddle which came from Buckingham. These three hundred livres he reckoned upon putting snugly into his pocket.

"Then," continued he, "there is a horse for my lackey, and my valise. As to my arms, it is useless to trouble you about them; I have them."

"A horse for your lackey?" resumed the procurator's wife, hesitatingly; "but that is doing things in lordly style, my friend."

"Ah, madame!" said Porthos, haughtily; "do you take me for a beggar?"

"No; I only thought that a pretty mule makes sometimes as good an appearance as a horse, and it seemed to me that by getting a pretty mule for Mousqueton--"

"Well, agreed for a pretty mule," said Porthos; "you are right, I have seen very great Spanish nobles whose whole suite were mounted on mules. But then you understand, Madame Coquenard, a mule with feathers and bells."

"Be satisfied," said the procurator's wife.

"There remains the valise," added Porthos.

"Oh, don't let that disturb you," cried Mme. Coquenard. "My husband has five or six valises; you shall choose the best. There is one in particular which he prefers in his journeys, large enough to hold all the world."

"Your valise is then empty?" asked Porthos, with simplicity.

"Certainly it is empty," replied the procurator's wife, in real innocence.

"Ah, but the valise I want," cried Porthos, "is a well-filled one, my dear."

Madame uttered fresh sighs. Moliere had not written his scene in "L'Avare" then. Mme. Coquenard was in the dilemma of Harpagan.

Finally, the rest of the equipment was successively debated in the same manner; and the result of the sitting was that the procurator's wife should give eight hundred livres in money, and should furnish the horse and the mule which should have the honor of carrying Porthos and Mousqueton to glory.

These conditions being agreed to, Porthos took leave of Mme. Coquenard. The latter wished to detain him by darting certain tender glances; but Porthos urged the commands of duty, and the procurator's wife was obliged to give place to the king.

The Musketeer returned home hungry and in bad humor.

33 Soubrette And Mistress

Meantime, as we have said, despite the cries of his conscience and the wise counsels of Athos, d'Artagnan became hourly more in love with Milady. Thus he never failed to pay his diurnal court to her; and the self-satisfied Gascon was convinced that sooner or later she could not fail to respond.

One day, when he arrived with his head in the air, and as light at heart as a man who awaits a shower of gold, he found the SOUBRETTE under the gateway of the hotel; but this time the pretty Kitty was not contented with touching him as he passed, she took him gently by the hand.

"Good!" thought d'Artagnan, "She is charged with some message for me from her mistress; she is about to appoint some rendezvous of which she had not courage to speak." And he looked down at the pretty girl with the most triumphant air imaginable.

"I wish to say three words to you, Monsieur Chevalier," stammered the SOUBRETTE.

"Speak, my child, speak," said d'Artagnan; "I listen."

"Here? Impossible! That which I have to say is too long, and above all, too secret."

"Well, what is to be done?"

"If Monsieur Chevalier would follow me?" said Kitty, timidly.

"Where you please, my dear child."

"Come, then."

And Kitty, who had not let go the hand of d'Artagnan, led him up a little dark, winding staircase, and after ascending about fifteen steps, opened a door.

"Come in here, Monsieur Chevalier," said she; "here we shall be alone, and can talk."

"And whose room is this, my dear child?"

"It is mine, Monsieur Chevalier; it communicates with my mistress's by that door. But you need not fear. She will not hear what we say; she never goes to bed before midnight."

D'Artagnan cast a glance around him. The little apartment was charming for its taste and neatness; but in spite of himself, his eyes were directed to that door which Kitty said led to Milady's chamber.

Kitty guessed what was passing in the mind of the young man, and heaved a deep sigh.

"You love my mistress, then, very dearly, Monsieur Chevalier?" said she.

"Oh, more than I can say, Kitty! I am mad for her!"

Kitty breathed a second sigh.

"Alas, monsieur," said she, "that is too bad."

"What the devil do you see so bad in it?" said d'Artagnan.

"Because, monsieur," replied Kitty, "my mistress loves you not at all."

"HEIN!" said d'Artagnan, "can she have charged you to tell me so?"

"Oh, no, monsieur; but out of the regard I have for you, I have taken the resolution to tell you so."

"Much obliged, my dear Kitty; but for the intention only--for the information, you must agree, is not likely to be at all agreeable."

"That is to say, you don't believe what I have told you; is it not so?"

"We have always some difficulty in believing such things, my pretty dear, were it only from self-love."

"Then you don't believe me?"

"I confess that unless you deign to give me some proof of what you advance--"

"What do you think of this?"

Kitty drew a little note from her bosom.

"For me?" said d'Artagnan, seizing the letter.

"No; for another."

"For another?"

"Yes."

"His name; his name!" cried d'Artagnan.

"Read the address."

"Monsieur El Comte de Wardes."

The remembrance of the scene at St. Germain presented itself to the mind of the presumptuous Gascon. As quick as thought, he tore open the letter, in spite of the cry which Kitty uttered on seeing what he was going to do, or rather, what he was doing.

"Oh, good Lord, Monsieur Chevalier," said she, "what are you doing?"

"I?" said d'Artagnan; "nothing," and he read,

"You have not answered my first note. Are you indisposed, or have you forgotten the glances you favored me with at the ball of Mme. de Guise? You have an opportunity now, Count; do not allow it to escape."

d'Artagnan became very pale; he was wounded in his SELF-love: he thought that it was in his LOVE.

"Poor dear Monsieur d'Artagnan," said Kitty, in a voice full of compassion, and pressing anew the young man's hand.

"You pity me, little one?" said d'Artagnan.

"Oh, yes, and with all my heart; for I know what it is to be in love."

"You know what it is to be in love?" said d'Artagnan, looking at her for the first time with much attention.

"Alas, yes."

"Well, then, instead of pitying me, you would do much better to assist me in avenging myself on your mistress."

"And what sort of revenge would you take?"

"I would triumph over her, and supplant my rival."

"I will never help you in that, Monsieur Chevalier," said Kitty, warmly.

"And why not?" demanded d'Artagnan.

"For two reasons."

"What ones?"

"The first is that my mistress will never love you."

"How do you know that?"

"You have cut her to the heart."

"I? In what can I have offended her--I who ever since I have known her have lived at her feet like a slave? Speak, I beg you!"

"I will never confess that but to the man--who should read to the bottom of my soul!"

D'Artagnan looked at Kitty for the second time. The young girl had freshness and beauty which many duchesses would have purchased with their coronets.

"Kitty," said he, "I will read to the bottom of your soul when-ever you like; don't let that disturb you." And he gave her a kiss at which the poor girl became as red as a cherry.

"Oh, no," said Kitty, "it is not me you love! It is my mistress you love; you told me so just now."

"And does that hinder you from letting me know the second reason?"

"The second reason, Monsieur the Chevalier," replied Kitty, emboldened by the kiss in the first place, and still further by the expression of the eyes of the young man, "is that in love, everyone for herself!"

Then only d'Artagnan remembered the languishing glances of Kitty, her constantly meeting him in the antechamber, the corridor, or on the stairs, those touches of the hand every time she met him, and her deep sighs; but absorbed by his desire to please the great lady, he had disdained the soubrette. He whose game is the eagle takes no heed of the sparrow.

But this time our Gascon saw at a glance all the advantage to be derived from the love which Kitty had just confessed so innocently, or so boldly: the interception of letters addressed to the Comte de Wardes, news on the spot, entrance at all hours into Kitty's chamber, which was contiguous to her mistress's. The perfidious deceiver was, as may plainly be perceived, already sacrificing, in intention, the poor girl in order to obtain Milady, willy-nilly.

"Well," said he to the young girl, "are you willing, my dear Kitty, that I should give you a proof of that love which you doubt?"

"What love?" asked the young girl.

"Of that which I am ready to feel toward you."

"And what is that proof?"

"Are you willing that I should this evening pass with you the time I generally spend with your mistress?"

"Oh, yes," said Kitty, clapping her hands, "very willing."

"Well, then, come here, my dear," said d'Artagnan, establishing himself in an easy chair; "come, and let me tell you that you are the prettiest SOUBRETTE I ever saw!"

And he did tell her so much, and so well, that the poor girl, who asked nothing better than to believe him, did believe him. Nevertheless, to d'Artagnan's great astonishment, the pretty Kitty defended herself resolutely.

Time passes quickly when it is passed in attacks and defenses. Midnight sounded, and almost at the same time the bell was rung in Milady's chamber.

"Good God," cried Kitty, "there is my mistress calling me! Go; go directly!"

D'Artagnan rose, took his hat, as if it had been his intention to obey, then, opening quickly the door of a large closet instead of that leading to the staircase, he buried himself amid the robes and dressing gowns of Milady.

"What are you doing?" cried Kitty.

D'Artagnan, who had secured the key, shut himself up in the closet without reply.

"Well," cried Milady, in a sharp voice. "Are you asleep, that you don't answer when I ring?"

And d'Artagnan heard the door of communication opened violently.

"Here am I, Milady, here am I!" cried Kitty, springing forward to meet her mistress.

Both went into the bedroom, and as the door of communication remained open, d'Artagnan could hear Milady for some time scolding her maid. She was at length appeased, and the conversation turned upon him while Kitty was assisting her mistress.

"Well," said Milady, "I have not seen our Gascon this evening."

"What, Milady! has he not come?" said Kitty. "Can he be inconstant before being happy?"

"Oh, no; he must have been prevented by Monsieur de Treville or Monsieur Dessessart. I understand my game, Kitty; I have this one safe."

"What will you do with him, madame?"

"What will I do with him? Be easy, Kitty, there is something between that man and me that he is quite ignorant of: he nearly made me lose my credit with his Eminence. Oh, I will be revenged!"

"I believed that Madame loved him."

"I love him? I detest him! An idiot, who held the life of Lord de Winter in his hands and did not kill him, by which I missed three hundred thousand livres' income."

"That's true," said Kitty; "your son was the only heir of his uncle, and until his majority you would have had the enjoyment of his fortune."

D'Artagnan shuddered to the marrow at hearing this suave creature reproach him, with that sharp voice which she took such pains to conceal in conversation, for not having killed a man whom he had seen load her with kindnesses.

"For all this," continued Milady, "I should long ago have revenged myself on him if, and I don't know why, the cardinal had not requested me to conciliate him."

"Oh, yes; but Madame has not conciliated that little woman he was so fond of."

"What, the mercer's wife of the Rue des Fossoyeurs? Has he not already forgotten she ever existed? Fine vengeance that, on my faith!"

A cold sweat broke from d'Artagnan's brow. Why, this woman was a monster! He resumed his listening, but unfortunately the toilet was finished.

"That will do," said Milady; "go into your own room, and tomorrow endeavor again to get me an answer to the letter I gave you."

"For Monsieur de Wardes?" said Kitty.

"To be sure; for Monsieur de Wardes."

"Now, there is one," said Kitty, "who appears to me quite a different sort of a man from that poor Monsieur d'Artagnan."

"Go to bed, mademoiselle," said Milady; "I don't like comments."

D'Artagnan heard the door close; then the noise of two bolts by which Milady fastened herself in. On her side, but as softly as possible, Kitty turned the key of the lock, and then d'Artagnan opened the closet door.

"Oh, good Lord!" said Kitty, in a low voice, "what is the matter with you? How pale you are!"

"The abominable creature," murmured d'Artagnan.

"Silence, silence, begone!" said Kitty. "There is nothing but a wainscot between my chamber and Milady's; every word that is uttered in one can be heard in the other."

"That's exactly the reason I won't go," said d'Artagnan.

"What!" said Kitty, blushing.

"Or, at least, I will go--later."

He drew Kitty to him. She had the less motive to resist, resistance would make so much noise. Therefore Kitty surrendered.

It was a movement of vengeance upon Milady. D'Artagnan believed it right to say that vengeance is the pleasure of the gods. With a little more heart, he might have been contented with this new conquest; but the principal features of his character were ambition and pride. It must, however, be confessed in his justification that the first use he made of his influence over Kitty was to try and find out what had become of Mme. Bonacieux; but the poor girl swore upon the crucifix to d'Artagnan that she was entirely ignorant on that head, her mistress never admitting her into half her secrets--only she believed she could say she was not dead.

As to the cause which was near making Milady lose her credit with the cardinal, Kitty knew nothing about it; but this time d'Artagnan was better informed than she was. As he had seen Milady on board a vessel at the moment he was leaving England, he suspected that it was, almost without a doubt, on account of the diamond studs.

But what was clearest in all this was that the true hatred, the profound hatred, the inveterate hatred of Milady, was increased by his not having killed her brother-in-law.

D'Artagnan came the next day to Milady's, and finding her in a very ill-humor, had no doubt that it was lack of an answer from M. de Wardes that provoked her thus. Kitty came in, but Milady was very cross with her. The poor girl ventured a glance at d'Artagnan which said, "See how I suffer on your account!"

Toward the end of the evening, however, the beautiful lioness became milder; she smilingly listened to the soft speeches of d'Artagnan, and even gave him her hand to kiss.

D'Artagnan departed, scarcely knowing what to think, but as he was a youth who did not easily lose his head, while continuing to pay his court to Milady, he had framed a little plan in his mind.

He found Kitty at the gate, and, as on the preceding evening, went up to her chamber. Kitty had been accused of negligence and severely scolded. Milady could not at all comprehend the silence of the Comte de Wardes, and she ordered Kitty to come at nine o'clock in the morning to take a third letter.

D'Artagnan made Kitty promise to bring him that letter on the following morning. The poor girl promised all her lover desired; she was mad.

Things passed as on the night before. D'Artagnan concealed himself in his closet; Milady called, undressed, sent away Kitty, and shut the door. As the night before, d'Artagnan did not return home till five o'clock in the morning.

At eleven o'clock Kitty came to him. She held in her hand a fresh billet from Milady. This time the poor girl did not even argue with d'Artagnan; she gave it to him at once. She belonged body and soul to her handsome soldier.

D'Artagnan opened the letter and read as follows:

This is the third time I have written to you to tell you that I love you. Beware that I do not write to you a fourth time to tell you that I detest you.

If you repent of the manner in which you have acted toward me, the young girl who brings you this will tell you how a man of spirit may obtain his pardon.

d'Artagnan colored and grew pale several times in reading this billet.

"Oh, you love her still," said Kitty, who had not taken her eyes off the young man's countenance for an instant.

"No, Kitty, you are mistaken. I do not love her, but I will avenge myself for her contempt."

"Oh, yes, I know what sort of vengeance! You told me that!"

"What matters it to you, Kitty? You know it is you alone whom I love."

"How can I know that?"

"By the scorn I will throw upon her."

D'Artagnan took a pen and wrote:

Madame, Until the present moment I could not believe that it was to me your first two letters were addressed, so unworthy did I feel myself of such an honor; besides, I was so seriously indisposed that I could not in any case have replied to them.

But now I am forced to believe in the excess of your kindness, since not only your letter but your servant assures me that I have the good fortune to be beloved by you.

She has no occasion to teach me the way in which a man of spirit may obtain his pardon. I will come and ask mine at eleven o'clock this evening.

To delay it a single day would be in my eyes now to commit a fresh offense.

From him whom you have rendered the happiest of men, Comte de Wardes

This note was in the first place a forgery; it was likewise an indelicacy. It was even, according to our present manners, something like an infamous action; but at that period people did not manage affairs as they do today. Besides, d'Artagnan from her own admission knew Milady culpable of treachery in matters more important, and could entertain no respect for her. And yet, notwithstanding this want of respect, he felt an uncontrollable passion for this woman boiling in his veins--passion drunk with contempt; but passion or thirst, as the reader pleases.

D'Artagnan's plan was very simple. By Kitty's chamber he could gain that of her mistress. He would take advantage of the first moment of surprise, shame, and terror, to triumph over her. He might fail, but something must be left to chance. In eight days the campaign would open, and he would be compelled to leave Paris; d'Artagnan had no time for a prolonged love siege.

"There," said the young man, handing Kitty the letter sealed; "give that to Milady. It is the count's reply."

Poor Kitty became as pale as death; she suspected what the letter contained.

"Listen, my dear girl," said d'Artagnan; "you cannot but perceive that all this must end, some way or other. Milady may discover that you gave the first billet to my lackey instead of to the count's; that it is I who have opened the others which ought to have been opened by de Wardes. Milady will then turn you out of doors, and you know she is not the woman to limit her vengeance."

"Alas!" said Kitty, "for whom have I exposed myself to all that?"

"For me, I well know, my sweet girl," said d'Artagnan. "But I am grateful, I swear to you."

"But what does this note contain?"

"Milady will tell you."

"Ah, you do not love me!" cried Kitty, "and I am very wretched."

To this reproach there is always one response which deludes women. D'Artagnan replied in such a manner that Kitty remained in her great delusion. Although she cried freely before deciding to transmit the letter to her mistress, she did at last so decide, which was all d'Artagnan wished. Finally he promised that he would leave her mistress's presence at an early hour that evening, and that when he left the mistress he would ascend with the maid. This promise completed poor Kitty's consolation.

34 IN WHICH THE EQUIPMENT OF ARAMIS AND PORTHOS IS TREATED OF

Since the four friends had been each in search of his equipments, there had been no fixed meeting between them. They dined apart from one another, wherever they might happen to be, or rather where they could. Duty likewise on its part took a portion of that precious time which was gliding away so rapidly--only they had agreed to meet once a week, about one o'clock, at the residence of Athos, seeing that he, in agreement with the vow he had formed, did not pass over the threshold of his door.

This day of reunion was the same day as that on which Kitty came to find d'Artagnan. Soon as Kitty left him, d'Artagnan directed his steps toward the Rue Ferou.

He found Athos and Aramis philosophizing. Aramis had some slight inclination to resume the cassock. Athos, according to his system, neither encouraged nor dissuaded him. Athos believed that everyone should be left to his own free will. He never gave advice but when it was asked, and even then he required to be asked twice.

"People, in general," he said, "only ask advice not to follow it; or if they do follow it, it is for the sake of having someone to blame for having given it."

Porthos arrived a minute after d'Artagnan. The four friends were reunited.

The four countenances expressed four different feelings: that of Porthos, tranquillity; that of d'Artagnan, hope; that of Aramis, uneasiness; that of Athos, carelessness.

At the end of a moment's conversation, in which Porthos hinted that a lady of elevated rank had condescended to relieve him from his embarrassment, Mousqueton entered. He came to request his master to return to his lodgings, where his presence was urgent, as he piteously said.

"Is it my equipment?"

"Yes and no," replied Mousqueton.

"Well, but can't you speak?"

"Come, monsieur."

Porthos rose, saluted his friends, and followed Mousqueton. An instant after, Bazin made his appearance at the door.

"What do you want with me, my friend?" said Aramis, with that mildness of language which was observable in him every time that his ideas were directed toward the Church.

"A man wishes to see Monsieur at home," replied Bazin.

"A man! What man?"

"A mendicant."

"Give him alms, Bazin, and bid him pray for a poor sinner."

"This mendicant insists upon speaking to you, and pretends that you will be very glad to see him."

"Has he sent no particular message for me?"

"Yes. If Monsieur Aramis hesitates to come," he said, "tell him I am from Tours."

"From Tours!" cried Aramis. "A thousand pardons, gentlemen; but no doubt this man brings me the news I expected." And rising also, he went off at a quick pace. There remained Athos and d'Artagnan.

"I believe these fellows have managed their business. What do you think, d'Artagnan?" said Athos.

"I know that Porthos was in a fair way," replied d'Artagnan; "and as to Aramis to tell you the truth, I have never been seriously uneasy on his account. But you, my dear Athos--you, who so generously distributed the Englishman's pistoles, which were our legitimate property--what do you mean to do?"

"I am satisfied with having killed that fellow, my boy, seeing that it is blessed bread to kill an Englishman; but if I had pocketed his pistoles, they would have weighed me down like a remorse.

"Go to, my dear Athos; you have truly inconceivable ideas."

"Let it pass. What do you think of Monsieur de Treville telling me, when he did me the honor to call upon me yesterday, that you associated with the suspected English, whom the cardinal protects?"

"That is to say, I visit an Englishwoman--the one I named."

"Oh, ay! the fair woman on whose account I gave you advice, which naturally you took care not to adopt."

"I gave you my reasons."

"Yes; you look there for your outfit, I think you said."

"Not at all. I have acquired certain knowledge that that woman was concerned in the abduction of Madame Bonacieux."

"Yes, I understand now: to find one woman, you court another. It is the longest road, but certainly the most amusing."

D'Artagnan was on the point of telling Athos all; but one consideration restrained him. Athos was a gentleman, punctilious in points of honor; and there were in the plan which our lover had devised for Milady, he was sure, certain things that would not obtain the assent of this Puritan. He was therefore silent; and as Athos was the least inquisitive of any man on earth, d'Artagnan's confidence stopped there. We will therefore leave the two friends, who had nothing important to say to each other, and follow Aramis.

Upon being informed that the person who wanted to speak to him came from Tours, we have seen with what rapidity the young man followed, or rather went before, Bazin; he ran without stopping from the Rue Ferou to the Rue de Vaugirard. On entering he found a man of short stature and intelligent eyes, but covered with rags.

"You have asked for me?" said the Musketeer.

"I wish to speak with Monsieur Aramis. Is that your name, monsieur?"

"My very own. You have brought me something?"

"Yes, if you show me a certain embroidered handkerchief."

"Here it is," said Aramis, taking a small key from his breast and opening a little ebony box inlaid with mother of pearl, "here it is. Look."

"That is right," replied the mendicant; "dismiss your lackey."

In fact, Bazin, curious to know what the mendicant could want with his master, kept pace with him as well as he could, and arrived almost at the same time he did; but his quickness was not of much use to him. At the hint from the mendicant his master made him a sign to retire, and he was obliged to obey.

Bazin gone, the mendicant cast a rapid glance around him in order to be sure that nobody could either see or hear him, and opening his ragged vest, badly held together by a leather strap, he began to rip the upper part of his doublet, from which he drew a letter.

Aramis uttered a cry of joy at the sight of the seal, kissed the superscription with an almost religious respect, and opened the epistle, which contained what follows:

"My Friend, it is the will of fate that we should be still for some time separated; but the delightful days of youth are not lost beyond return. Perform your duty in camp; I will do mine elsewhere. Accept that which the bearer brings you; make the campaign like a handsome true gentleman, and think of me, who kisses tenderly your black eyes.

"Adieu; or rather, AU REVOIR."

The mendicant continued to rip his garments; and drew from amid his rags a hundred and fifty Spanish double pistoles, which he laid down on the table; then he opened the door, bowed, and went out before the young man, stupefied by his letter, had ventured to address a word to him.

Aramis then reperused the letter, and perceived a postscript:

PS. You may behave politely to the bearer, who is a count and a grandee of Spain!

"Golden dreams!" cried Aramis. "Oh, beautiful life! Yes, we are young; yes, we shall yet have happy days! My love, my blood, my life! all, all, all, are thine, my adored mistress!"

And he kissed the letter with passion, without even vouchsafing a look at the gold which sparkled on the table.

Bazin scratched at the door, and as Aramis had no longer any reason to exclude him, he bade him come in.

Bazin was stupefied at the sight of the gold, and forgot that he came to announce d'Artagnan, who, curious to know who the mendicant could be, came to Aramis on leaving Athos.

Now, as d'Artagnan used no ceremony with Aramis, seeing that Bazin forgot to announce him, he announced himself.

"The devil! my dear Aramis," said d'Artagnan, "if these are the prunes that are sent to you from Tours, I beg you will make my compliments to the gardener who gathers them."

"You are mistaken, friend d'Artagnan," said Aramis, always on his guard; "this is from my publisher, who has just sent me the price of that poem in one-syllable verse which I began yonder."

"Ah, indeed," said d'Artagnan. "Well, your publisher is very generous, my dear Aramis, that's all I can say."

"How, monsieur?" cried Bazin, "a poem sell so dear as that! It is incredible! Oh, monsieur, you can write as much as you like; you may become equal to Monsieur de Voiture and Monsieur de Benserade. I like that. A poet is as good as an abbe. Ah! Monsieur Aramis, become a poet, I beg of you."

"Bazin, my friend," said Aramis, "I believe you meddle with my conversation."

Bazin perceived he was wrong; he bowed and went out.

"Ah!" said d'Artagnan with a smile, "you sell your productions at their weight in gold. You are very fortunate, my friend; but take care or you will lose that letter which is peeping from your doublet, and which also comes, no doubt, from your publisher."

Aramis blushed to the eyes, crammed in the letter, and re-buttoned his doublet.

"My dear d'Artagnan," said he, "if you please, we will join our friends; as I am rich, we will today begin to dine together again, expecting that you will be rich in your turn."

"My faith!" said d'Artagnan, with great pleasure. "It is long since we have had a good dinner; and I, for my part, have a somewhat hazardous expedition for this evening, and shall not be sorry, I confess, to fortify myself with a few glasses of good old Burgundy."

"Agreed, as to the old Burgundy; I have no objection to that," said Aramis, from whom the letter and the gold had removed, as by magic, his ideas of conversion.

And having put three or four double pistoles into his pocket to answer the needs of the moment, he placed the others in the ebony box, inlaid with mother of pearl, in which was the famous handkerchief which served him as a talisman.

The two friends repaired to Athos's, and he, faithful to his vow of not going out, took upon him to order dinner to be brought to them. As he was perfectly acquainted with the details of gastronomy, d'Artagnan and Aramis made no objection to abandoning this important care to him.

They went to find Porthos, and at the corner of the Rue Bac met Mousqueton, who, with a most pitiable air, was driving before him a mule and a horse.

D'Artagnan uttered a cry of surprise, which was not quite free from joy.

"Ah, my yellow horse," cried he. "Aramis, look at that horse!"

"Oh, the frightful brute!" said Aramis.

"Ah, my dear," replied d'Artagnan, "upon that very horse I came to Paris."

"What, does Monsieur know this horse?" said Mousqueton.

"It is of an original color," said Aramis; "I never saw one with such a hide in my life."

"I can well believe it," replied d'Artagnan, "and that was why I got three crowns for him. It must have been for his hide, for, CERTES, the carcass is not worth eighteen livres. But how did this horse come into your bands, Mousqueton?"

"Pray," said the lackey, "say nothing about it, monsieur; it is a frightful trick of the husband of our duchess!"

"How is that, Mousqueton?"

"Why, we are looked upon with a rather favorable eye by a lady of quality, the Duchesse de--but, your pardon; my master has commanded me to be discreet. She had forced us to accept a little souvenir, a magnificent Spanish GENET and an Andalusian mule, which were beautiful to look upon. The husband heard of the affair; on their way he confiscated the two magnificent beasts which were being sent to us, and substituted these horrible animals."

"Which you are taking back to him?" said d'Artagnan.

"Exactly!" replied Mousqueton. "You may well believe that we will not accept such steeds as these in exchange for those which had been promised to us."

"No, PARDIEU; though I should like to have seen Porthos on my yellow horse. That would give me an idea of how I looked when I arrived in Paris. But don't let us hinder you, Mousqueton; go and perform your master's orders. Is he at home?"

"Yes, monsieur," said Mousqueton, "but in a very ill humor. Get up!"

He continued his way toward the Quai des Grands Augustins, while the two friends went to ring at the bell of the unfortunate Porthos. He, having seen them crossing the yard, took care not to answer, and they rang in vain.

Meanwhile Mousqueton continued on his way, and crossing the Pont Neuf, still driving the two sorry animals before him, he reached the Rue aux Ours.

Arrived there, he fastened, according to the orders of his master, both horse and mule to the knocker of the procurator's door; then, without taking any thought for their future, he returned to Porthos, and told him that his commission was completed.

In a short time the two unfortunate beasts, who had not eaten anything since the morning, made such a noise in raising and letting fall the knocker that the procurator ordered his errand boy to go and inquire in the neighborhood to whom this horse and mule belonged.

Mme. Coquenard recognized her present, and could not at first comprehend this restitution; but the visit of Porthos soon enlightened her. The anger which fired the eyes of the Musketeer, in spite of his efforts to suppress it, terrified his sensitive inamorata. In fact, Mousqueton had not concealed from his master that he had met d'Artagnan and Aramis, and that d'Artagnan in the yellow horse had recognized the Bearnese pony upon which he had come to Paris, and which he had sold for three crowns.

Porthos went away after having appointed a meeting with the procurator's wife in the cloister of St. Magloire. The procurator, seeing he was going, invited him to dinner--an invitation which the Musketeer refused with a majestic air.

Mme. Coquenard repaired trembling to the cloister of St. Magloire, for she guessed the reproaches that awaited her there; but she was fascinated by the lofty airs of Porthos.

All that which a man wounded in his self-love could let fall in the shape of imprecations and reproaches upon the head of a woman Porthos let fall upon the bowed head of the procurator's wife.

"Alas," said she, "I did all for the best! One of our clients is a horsedealer; he owes money to the office, and is backward in his pay. I took the mule and the horse for what he owed us; he assured me that they were two noble steeds."

"Well, madame," said Porthos, "if he owed you more than five crowns, your horsedealer is a thief."

"There is no harm in trying to buy things cheap, Monsieur Porthos," said the procurator's wife, seeking to excuse herself.

"No, madame; but they who so assiduously try to buy things cheap ought to permit others to seek more generous friends." And Porthos, turning on his heel, made a step to retire.

"Monsieur Porthos! Monsieur Porthos!" cried the procurator's wife. "I have been wrong; I see it. I ought not to have driven a bargain when it was to equip a cavalier like you."

Porthos, without reply, retreated a second step. The procurator's wife fancied she saw him in a brilliant cloud, all surrounded by duchesses and marchionesses, who cast bags of money at his feet.

"Stop, in the name of heaven, Monsieur Porthos!" cried she. "Stop, and let us talk."

"Talking with you brings me misfortune," said Porthos.

"But, tell me, what do you ask?"

"Nothing; for that amounts to the same thing as if I asked you for something."

The procurator's wife hung upon the arm of Porthos, and in the violence of her grief she cried out, "Monsieur Porthos, I am ignorant of all such matters! How should I know what a horse is? How should I know what horse furniture is?"

"You should have left it to me, then, madame, who know what they are; but you wished to be frugal, and consequently to lend at usury."

"It was wrong, Monsieur Porthos; but I will repair that wrong, upon my word of honor."

"How so?" asked the Musketeer.

"Listen. This evening M. Coquenard is going to the house of the Due de Chaulnes, who has sent for him. It is for a consultation, which will last three hours at least. Come! We shall be alone, and can make up our accounts."

"In good time. Now you talk, my dear."

"You pardon me?"

"We shall see," said Porthos, majestically; and the two separated saying, "Till this evening."

"The devil!" thought Porthos, as he walked away, "it appears I am getting nearer to Monsieur Coquenard's strongbox at last."

35 A Gascon A Match For Cupid

The evening so impatiently waited for by Porthos and by d'Artagnan at last arrived.

As was his custom, d'Artagnan presented himself at Milady's at about nine o'clock. He found her in a charming humor. Never had he been so well received. Our Gascon knew, by the first glance of his eye, that his billet had been delivered, and that this billet had had its effect.

Kitty entered to bring some sherbet. Her mistress put on a charming face, and smiled on her graciously; but alas! the poor girl was so sad that she did not even notice Milady's condescension.

D'Artagnan looked at the two women, one after the other, and was forced to acknowledge that in his opinion Dame Nature had made a mistake in their formation. To the great lady she had given a heart vile and venal; to the SOUBRETTE she had given the heart of a duchess.

At ten o'clock Milady began to appear restless. D'Artagnan knew what she wanted. She looked at the clock, rose, reseated herself, smiled at d'Artagnan with an air which said, "You are very amiable, no doubt, but you would be charming if you would only depart."

D'Artagnan rose and took his hat; Milady gave him her hand to kiss. The young man felt her press his hand, and comprehended that this was a sentiment, not of coquetry, but of gratitude because of his departure.

"She loves him devilishly," he murmured. Then he went out.

This time Kitty was nowhere waiting for him; neither in the antechamber, nor in the corridor, nor beneath the great door. It was necessary that d'Artagnan should find alone the staircase and the little chamber. She heard him enter, but she did not raise her head. The young man went to her and took her hands; then she sobbed aloud.

As d'Artagnan had presumed, on receiving his letter, Milady in a delirium of joy had told her servant everything; and by way of recompense for the manner in which she had this time executed the commission, she had given Kitty a purse.

Returning to her own room, Kitty had thrown the purse into a corner, where it lay open, disgorging three or four gold pieces on the carpet. The poor girl, under the caresses of d'Artagnan, lifted her head. D'Artagnan himself was frightened by the change in her countenance. She joined her hands with a suppliant air, but without venturing to speak a word. As little sensitive as was the heart of d'Artagnan, he was touched by this mute sorrow; but he held too tenaciously to his projects, above all to this one, to change the program which he had laid out in advance. He did not therefore allow her any hope that he would flinch; only he represented his action as one of simple vengeance.

For the rest this vengeance was very easy; for Milady, doubtless to conceal her blushes from her lover, had ordered Kitty to extinguish all the lights in the apartment, and even in the little chamber itself. Before daybreak M. de Wardes must take his departure, still in obscurity.

Presently they heard Milady retire to her room. D'Artagnan slipped into the wardrobe. Hardly was he concealed when the little bell sounded. Kitty went to her mistress, and did not leave the door open; but the partition was so thin that one could hear nearly all that passed between the two women.

Milady seemed overcome with joy, and made Kitty repeat the smallest details of the pretended interview of the soubrette with de Wardes when he received the letter; how he had responded; what was the expression of his face; if he seemed very amorous. And to all these questions poor Kitty, forced to put on a pleasant face, responded in a stifled voice whose dolorous accent her mistress did not however remark, solely because happiness is egotistical.

Finally, as the hour for her interview with the count approached, Milady had everything about her darkened, and ordered Kitty to return to her own chamber, and introduce de Wardes whenever he presented himself.

Kitty's detention was not long. Hardly had d'Artagnan seen, through a crevice in his closet, that the whole apartment was in obscurity, than he slipped out of his concealment, at the very moment when Kitty reclosed the door of communication.

"What is that noise?" demanded Milady.

"It is I," said d'Artagnan in a subdued voice, "I, the Comte de Wardes."

"Oh, my God, my God!" murmured Kitty, "he has not even waited for the hour he himself named!"

"Well," said Milady, in a trembling voice, "why do you not enter? Count, Count," added she, "you know that I wait for you."

At this appeal d'Artagnan drew Kitty quietly away, and slipped into the chamber.

If rage or sorrow ever torture the heart, it is when a lover receives under a name which is not his own protestations of love addressed to his happy rival. D'Artagnan was in a dolorous situation which he had not foreseen. Jealousy gnawed his heart; and he suffered almost as much as poor Kitty, who at that very moment was crying in the next chamber.

"Yes, Count," said Milady, in her softest voice, and pressing his hand in her own, "I am happy in the love which your looks and your words have expressed to me every time we have met. I also--I love you. Oh, tomorrow, tomorrow, I must have some pledge from you which will prove that you think of me; and that you may not forget me, take this!" and she slipped a ring from her finger onto d'Artagnan's. d'Artagnan remembered having seen this ring on the finger of Milady; it was a magnificent sapphire, encircled with brilliants.

The first movement of d'Artagnan was to return it, but Milady added, "No, no! Keep that ring for love of me. Besides, in accepting it," she added, in a voice full of emotion, "you render me a much greater service than you imagine."

"This woman is full of mysteries," murmured d'Artagnan to himself. At that instant he felt himself ready to reveal all. He even opened his mouth to tell Milady who he was, and with what a revengeful purpose he had come; but she added, "Poor angel, whom that monster of a Gascon barely failed to kill."

The monster was himself.

"Oh," continued Milady, "do your wounds still make you suffer?"

"Yes, much," said d'Artagnan, who did not well know how to answer.

"Be tranquil," murmured Milady; "I will avenge you--and cruelly!"

"PESTE!" said d'Artagnan to himself, "the moment for confidences has not yet come."

It took some time for d'Artagnan to resume this little dialogue; but then all the ideas of vengeance which he had brought with him had completely vanished. This woman exercised over him an unaccountable power; he hated and adored her at the same time. He would not have believed that two sentiments so opposite could dwell in the same heart, and by their union constitute a passion so strange, and as it were, diabolical.

Presently it sounded one o'clock. It was necessary to separate. D'Artagnan at the moment of quitting Milady felt only the liveliest regret at the parting; and as they addressed each other in a reciprocally passionate adieu, another interview was arranged for the following week.

Poor Kitty hoped to speak a few words to d'Artagnan when he passed through her chamber; but Milady herself reconducted him through the darkness, and only quit him at the staircase.

The next morning d'Artagnan ran to find Athos. He was engaged in an adventure so singular that he wished for counsel. He therefore told him all.

"Your Milady," said he, "appears to be an infamous creature, but not the less you have done wrong to deceive her. In one fashion or another you have a terrible enemy on your hands."

While thus speaking Athos regarded with attention the sapphire set with diamonds which had taken, on d'Artagnan's finger, the place of the queen's ring, carefully kept in a casket.

"You notice my ring?" said the Gascon, proud to display so rich a gift in the eyes of his friends.

"Yes," said Athos, "it reminds me of a family jewel."

"It is beautiful, is it not?" said d'Artagnan.

"Yes," said Athos, "magnificent. I did not think two sapphires of such a fine water existed. Have you traded it for your diamond?"

"No. It is a gift from my beautiful Englishwoman, or rather Frenchwoman--for I am convinced she was born in France, though I have not questioned her."

"That ring comes from Milady?" cried Athos, with a voice in which it was easy to detect strong emotion.

"Her very self; she gave it me last night. Here it is," replied d'Artagnan, taking it from his finger.

Athos examined it and became very pale. He tried it on his left hand; it fit his finger as if made for it.

A shade of anger and vengeance passed across the usually calm brow of this gentleman.

"It is impossible it can be she," said he. "How could this ring come into the hands of Milady Clarik? And yet it is difficult to suppose such a resemblance should exist between two jewels."

"Do you know this ring?" said d'Artagnan.

"I thought I did," replied Athos; "but no doubt I was mistaken." And he returned d'Artagnan the ring without, however, ceasing to look at it.

"Pray, d'Artagnan," said Athos, after a minute, "either take off that ring or turn the mounting inside; it recalls such cruel recollections that I shall have no head to converse with you. Don't ask me for counsel; don't tell me you are perplexed what to do. But stop! let me look at that sapphire again; the one I mentioned to you had one of its faces scratched by accident."

D'Artagnan took off the ring, giving it again to Athos.

Athos started. "Look," said he, "is it not strange?" and he pointed out to d'Artagnan the scratch he had remembered.

"But from whom did this ring come to you, Athos?"

"From my mother, who inherited it from her mother. As I told you, it is an old family jewel."

"And you--sold it?" asked d'Artagnan, hesitatingly.

"No," replied Athos, with a singular smile. "I gave it away in a night of love, as it has been given to you."

D'Artagnan became pensive in his turn; it appeared as if there were abysses in Milady's soul whose depths were dark and unknown. He took back the ring, but put it in his pocket and not on his finger.

"d'Artagnan," said Athos, taking his hand, "you know I love you; if I had a son I could not love him better. Take my advice, renounce this woman. I do not know her, but a sort of intuition tells me she is a lost creature, and that there is something fatal about her."

"You are right," said d'Artagnan; "I will have done with her. I own that this woman terrifies me."

"Shall you have the courage?" said Athos.

"I shall," replied d'Artagnan, "and instantly."

"In truth, my young friend, you will act rightly," said the gentleman, pressing the Gascon's hand with an affection almost paternal; "and God grant that this woman, who has scarcely entered into your life, may not leave a terrible trace in it!" And Athos bowed to d'Artagnan like a man who wishes it understood that he would not be sorry to be left alone with his thoughts.

On reaching home d'Artagnan found Kitty waiting for him. A month of fever could not have changed her more than this one night of sleeplessness and sorrow.

She was sent by her mistress to the false de Wardes. Her mistress was mad with love, intoxicated with joy. She wished to know when her lover would meet her a second night; and poor Kitty, pale and trembling, awaited d'Artagnan's reply. The counsels of his friend, joined to the cries of his own heart, made him determine, now his pride was saved and his vengeance satisfied, not to see Milady again. As a reply, he wrote the following letter:

Do not depend upon me, madame, for the next meeting. Since my convalescence I have so many affairs of this kind on my hands that I am forced to regulate them a little. When your turn comes, I shall have the honor to inform you of it. I kiss your hands.

Comte de Wardes

Not a word about the sapphire. Was the Gascon determined to keep it as a weapon against Milady, or else, let us be frank, did he not reserve the sapphire as a last resource for his outfit? It would be wrong to judge the actions of one period from the point of view of another. That which would now be considered as disgraceful to a gentleman was at that time quite a simple and natural affair, and the younger sons of the best families were frequently supported by their mistresses. D'Artagnan gave the open letter to Kitty, who at first was unable to comprehend it, but who became almost wild with joy on reading it a second time. She could scarcely believe in her happiness; and d'Artagnan was forced to renew with the living voice the assurances which he had written. And whatever might be--considering the violent character of Milady--the danger which the poor girl incurred in giving this billet to her mistress, she ran back to the Place Royale as fast as her legs could carry her.

The heart of the best woman is pitiless toward the sorrows of a rival.

Milady opened the letter with eagerness equal to Kitty's in bringing it; but at the first words she read she became livid. She crushed the paper in her hand, and turning with flashing eyes upon Kitty, she cried, "What is this letter?"

"The answer to Madame's," replied Kitty, all in a tremble.

"Impossible!" cried Milady. "It is impossible a gentleman could have written such a letter to a woman." Then all at once, starting, she cried, "My God! can he have--" and she stopped. She ground her teeth; she was of the color of ashes. She tried to go toward the window for air, but she could only stretch forth her arms; her legs failed her, and she sank into an armchair. Kitty, fearing she was ill, hastened toward her and was beginning to open her dress; but Milady started up, pushing her away. "What do you want with me?" said she, "and why do you place your hand on me?"

"I thought that Madame was ill, and I wished to bring her help," responded the maid, frightened at the terrible expression which had come over her mistress's face.

"I faint? I? I? Do you take me for half a woman? When I am insulted I do not faint; I avenge myself!"

And she made a sign for Kitty to leave the room.

36 Dream Of Vengeance

That evening Milady gave orders that when M. d'Artagnan came as usual, he should be immediately admitted; but he did not come.

The next day Kitty went to see the young man again, and related to him all that had passed on the preceding evening. d'Artagnan smiled; this jealous anger of Milady was his revenge.

That evening Milady was still more impatient than on the preceding evening. She renewed the order relative to the Gascon; but as before she expected him in vain.

The next morning, when Kitty presented herself at d'Artagnan's, she was no longer joyous and alert as on the two preceding days; but on the contrary sad as death.

D'Artagnan asked the poor girl what was the matter with her; but she, as her only reply, drew a letter from her pocket and gave it to him.

This letter was in Milady's handwriting; only this time it was addressed to M. d'Artagnan, and not to M. de Wardes.

He opened it and read as follows:

Dear M. d'Artagnan, It is wrong thus to neglect your friends, particularly at the moment you are about to leave them for so long a time. My brother-in-law and myself expected you yesterday and the day before, but in vain. Will it be the same this evening?

Your very grateful, Milady Clarik

"That's all very simple," said d'Artagnan; "I expected this letter. My credit rises by the fall of that of the Comte de Wardes."

"And will you go?" asked Kitty.

"Listen to me, my dear girl," said the Gascon, who sought for an excuse in his own eyes for breaking the promise he had made Athos; "you must understand it would be impolitic not to accept such a positive invitation. Milady, not seeing me come again, would not be able to understand what could cause the interruption of my visits, and might suspect something; who could say how far the vengeance of such a woman would go?"

"Oh, my God!" said Kitty, "you know how to represent things in such a way that you are always in the right. You are going now to pay your court to her again, and if this time you succeed in pleasing her in your own name and with your own face, it will be much worse than before."

Instinct made poor Kitty guess a part of what was to happen. d'Artagnan reassured her as well as he could, and promised to remain insensible to the seductions of Milady.

He desired Kitty to tell her mistress that he could not be more grateful for her kindnesses than he was, and that he would be obedient to her orders. He did not dare to write for fear of not being able--to such experienced eyes as those of Milady--to disguise his writing sufficiently.

As nine o'clock sounded, d'Artagnan was at the Place Royale. It was evident that the servants who waited in the antechamber were warned, for as soon as d'Artagnan appeared, before even he had asked if Milady were visible, one of them ran to announce him.

"Show him in," said Milady, in a quick tone, but so piercing that d'Artagnan heard her in the antechamber.

He was introduced.

"I am at home to nobody," said Milady; "observe, to nobody." The servant went out.

D'Artagnan cast an inquiring glance at Milady. She was pale, and looked fatigued, either from tears or want of sleep. The number of lights had been intentionally diminished, but the young woman could not conceal the traces of the fever which had devoured her for two days.

D'Artagnan approached her with his usual gallantry. She then made an extraordinary effort to receive him, but never did a more distressed countenance give the lie to a more amiable smile.

To the questions which d'Artagnan put concerning her health, she replied, "Bad, very bad."

"Then," replied he, "my visit is ill-timed; you, no doubt, stand in need of repose, and I will withdraw."

"No, no!" said Milady. "On the contrary, stay, Monsieur d'Artagnan; your agreeable company will divert me."

"Oh, oh!" thought d'Artagnan. "She has never been so kind before. On guard!"

Milady assumed the most agreeable air possible, and conversed with more than her usual brilliancy. At the same time the fever, which for an instant abandoned her, returned to give luster to her eyes, color to her cheeks, and vermillion to her lips. D'Artagnan was again in the presence of the Circe who had before surrounded him with her enchantments. His love, which he believed to be extinct but which was only asleep, awoke again in his heart. Milady smiled, and d'Artagnan felt that he could damn himself for that smile. There was a moment at which he felt something like remorse.

By degrees, Milady became more communicative. She asked d'Artagnan if he had a mistress.

"Alas!" said d'Artagnan, with the most sentimental air he could assume, "can you be cruel enough to put such a question to me--to me, who, from the moment I saw you, have only breathed and sighed through you and for you?"

Milady smiled with a strange smile.

"Then you love me?" said she.

"Have I any need to tell you so? Have you not perceived it?"

"It may be; but you know the more hearts are worth the capture, the more difficult they are to be won."

"Oh, difficulties do not affright me," said d'Artagnan. "I shrink before nothing but impossibilities."

"Nothing is impossible," replied Milady, "to true love."

"Nothing, madame?"

"Nothing," replied Milady.

"The devil!" thought d'Artagnan. "The note is changed. Is she going to fall in love with me, by chance, this fair inconstant; and will she be disposed to give me myself another sapphire like that which she gave me for de Wardes?"

D'Artagnan rapidly drew his seat nearer to Milady's.

"Well, now," she said, "let us see what you would do to prove this love of which you speak."

"All that could be required of me. Order; I am ready."

"For everything?"

"For everything," cried d'Artagnan, who knew beforehand that he had not much to risk in engaging himself thus.

"Well, now let us talk a little seriously," said Milady, in her turn drawing her armchair nearer to d'Artagnan's chair.

"I am all attention, madame," said he.

Milady remained thoughtful and undecided for a moment; then, as if appearing to have formed a resolution, she said, "I have an enemy."

"You, madame!" said d'Artagnan, affecting surprise; "is that possible, my God?--good and beautiful as you are!"

"A mortal enemy."

"Indeed!"

"An enemy who has insulted me so cruelly that between him and me it is war to the death. May I reckon on you as an auxiliary?"

D'Artagnan at once perceived the ground which the vindictive creature wished to reach.

"You may, madame," said he, with emphasis. "My arm and my life belong to you, like my love."

"Then," said Milady, "since you are as generous as you are loving--"

She stopped.

"Well?" demanded d'Artagnan.

"Well," replied Milady, after a moment of silence, "from the present time, cease to talk of impossibilities."

"Do not overwhelm me with happiness," cried d'Artagnan, throwing himself on his knees, and covering with kisses the hands abandoned to him.

"Avenge me of that infamous de Wardes," said Milady, between her teeth, "and I shall soon know how to get rid of you--you double idiot, you animated sword blade!"

"Fall voluntarily into my arms, hypocritical and dangerous woman," said d'Artagnan, likewise to himself, "after having abused me with such effrontery, and afterward I will laugh at you with him whom you wish me to kill."

D'Artagnan lifted up his head.

"I am ready," said he.

"You have understood me, then, dear Monsieur d'Artagnan," said Milady.

"I could interpret one of your looks."

"Then you would employ for me your arm which has already acquired so much renown?"

"Instantly!"

"But on my part," said Milady, "how should I repay such a service? I know these lovers. They are men who do nothing for nothing."

"You know the only reply that I desire," said d'Artagnan, "the only one worthy of you and of me!"

And he drew nearer to her.

She scarcely resisted.

"Interested man!" cried she, smiling.

"Ah," cried d'Artagnan, really carried away by the passion this woman had the power to kindle in his heart, "ah, that is because my happiness appears so impossible to me; and I have such fear that it should fly away from me like a dream that I pant to make a reality of it."

"Well, merit this pretended happiness, then!"

"I am at your orders," said d'Artagnan.

"Quite certain?" said Milady, with a last doubt.

"Only name to me the base man that has brought tears into your beautiful eyes!"

"Who told you that I had been weeping?" said she.

"It appeared to me--"

"Such women as I never weep," said Milady.

"So much the better! Come, tell me his name!"

"Remember that his name is all my secret."

"Yet I must know his name."

"Yes, you must; see what confidence I have in you!"

"You overwhelm me with joy. What is his name?"

"You know him."

"Indeed."

"Yes."

"It is surely not one of my friends?" replied d'Artagnan, affecting hesitation in order to make her believe him ignorant.

"If it were one of your friends you would hesitate, then?" cried Milady; and a threatening glance darted from her eyes.

"Not if it were my own brother!" cried d'Artagnan, as if carried away by his enthusiasm.

Our Gascon promised this without risk, for he knew all that was meant.

"I love your devotedness," said Milady.

"Alas, do you love nothing else in me?" asked d'Artagnan.

"I love you also, YOU!" said she, taking his hand.

The warm pressure made d'Artagnan tremble, as if by the touch that fever which consumed Milady attacked himself.

"You love me, you!" cried he. "Oh, if that were so, I should lose my reason!"

And he folded her in his arms. She made no effort to remove her lips from his kisses; only she did not respond to them. Her lips were cold; it appeared to d'Artagnan that he had embraced a statue.

He was not the less intoxicated with joy, electrified by love. He almost believed in the tenderness of Milady; he almost believed in the crime of de Wardes. If de Wardes had at that moment been under his hand, he would have killed him.

Milady seized the occasion.

"His name is--" said she, in her turn.

"De Wardes; I know it," cried d'Artagnan.

"And how do you know it?" asked Milady, seizing both his hands, and endeavoring to read with her eyes to the bottom of his heart.

D'Artagnan felt he had allowed himself to be carried away, and that he had committed an error.

"Tell me, tell me, tell me, I say," repeated Milady, "how do you know it?"

"How do I know it?" said d'Artagnan.

"Yes."

"I know it because yesterday Monsieur de Wardes, in a saloon where I was, showed a ring which he said he had received from you."

"Wretch!" cried Milady.

The epithet, as may be easily understood, resounded to the very bottom of d'Artagnan's heart.

"Well?" continued she.

"Well, I will avenge you of this wretch," replied d'Artagnan, giving himself the airs of Don Japhet of Armenia.

"Thanks, my brave friend!" cried Milady; "and when shall I be avenged?"

"Tomorrow--immediately--when you please!"

Milady was about to cry out, "Immediately," but she reflected that such precipitation would not be very gracious toward d'Artagnan.

Besides, she had a thousand precautions to take, a thousand counsels to give to her defender, in order that he might avoid explanations with the count before witnesses. All this was answered by an expression of d'Artagnan's. "Tomorrow," said he, "you will be avenged, or I shall be dead."

"No," said she, "you will avenge me; but you will not be dead. He is a coward."

"With women, perhaps; but not with men. I know something of him."

"But it seems you had not much reason to complain of your fortune in your contest with him."

"Fortune is a courtesan; favorable yesterday, she may turn her back tomorrow."

"Which means that you now hesitate?"

"No, I do not hesitate; God forbid! But would it be just to allow me to go to a possible death without having given me at least something more than hope?"

Milady answered by a glance which said, "Is that all?--speak, then." And then accompanying the glance with explanatory words, "That is but too just," said she, tenderly.

"Oh, you are an angel!" exclaimed the young man.

"Then all is agreed?" said she.

"Except that which I ask of you, dear love."

"But when I assure you that you may rely on my tenderness?"

"I cannot wait till tomorrow."

"Silence! I hear my brother. It will be useless for him to find you here."

She rang the bell and Kitty appeared.

"Go out this way," said she, opening a small private door, "and come back at eleven o'clock; we will then terminate this conversation. Kitty will conduct you to my chamber."

The poor girl almost fainted at hearing these words.

"Well, mademoiselle, what are you thinking about, standing there like a statue? Do as I bid you: show the chevalier out; and this evening at eleven o'clock--you have heard what I said."

"It appears that these appointments are all made for eleven o'clock," thought d'Artagnan; "that's a settled custom."

Milady held out her hand to him, which he kissed tenderly.

"But," said he, as he retired as quickly as possible from the reproaches of Kitty, "I must not play the fool. This woman is certainly a great liar. I must take care."

37 Milady's Secret

D'Artagnan left the hotel instead of going up at once to Kitty's chamber, as she endeavored to persuade him to do--and that for two reasons: the first, because by this means he should escape reproaches, recriminations, and prayers; the second, because he was not sorry to have an opportunity of reading his own thoughts and endeavoring, if possible, to fathom those of this woman.

What was most clear in the matter was that d'Artagnan loved Milady like a madman, and that she did not love him at all. In an instant d'Artagnan perceived that the best way in which he could act would be to go home and write Milady a long letter, in which he would confess to her that he and de Wardes were, up to the present moment absolutely the same, and that consequently he could not undertake, without committing suicide, to kill the Comte de Wardes. But he also was spurred on by a ferocious desire of vengeance. He wished to subdue this woman in his own name; and as this vengeance appeared to him to have a certain sweetness in it, he could not make up his mind to renounce it.

He walked six or seven times round the Place Royale, turning at every ten steps to look at the light in Milady's apartment, which was to be seen through the blinds. It was evident that this time the young woman was not in such haste to retire to her apartment as she had been the first.

At length the light disappeared. With this light was extinguished the last irresolution in the heart of d'Artagnan. He recalled to his mind the details of the first night, and with a beating heart and a brain on fire he re-entered the hotel and flew toward Kitty's chamber.

The poor girl, pale as death and trembling in all her limbs, wished to delay her lover; but Milady, with her ear on the watch, had heard the noise d'Artagnan had made, and opening the door, said, "Come in."

All this was of such incredible immodesty, of such monstrous effrontery, that d'Artagnan could scarcely believe what he saw or what he heard. He imagined himself to be drawn into one of those fantastic intrigues one meets in dreams. He, however, darted not the less quickly toward Milady, yielding to that magnetic attraction which the loadstone exercises over iron.

As the door closed after them Kitty rushed toward it. Jealousy, fury, offended pride, all the passions in short that dispute the heart of an outraged woman in love, urged her to make a revelation; but she reflected that she would be totally lost if she confessed having assisted in such a machination, and above all, that d'Artagnan would also be lost to her forever. This last thought of love counseled her to make this last sacrifice.

D'Artagnan, on his part, had gained the summit of all his wishes. It was no longer a rival who was beloved; it was himself who was apparently beloved. A secret voice whispered to him, at the bottom of his heart, that he was but an instrument of vengeance, that he was only caressed till he had given death; but pride, but self-love, but madness silenced this voice and stifled its murmurs. And then our Gascon, with that large quantity of conceit which we know he possessed, compared himself with de Wardes, and asked himself why, after all, he should not be beloved for himself?

He was absorbed entirely by the sensations of the moment. Milady was no longer for him that woman of fatal intentions who had for a moment terrified him; she was an ardent, passionate mistress, abandoning herself to love which she also seemed to feel. Two hours thus glided away. When the transports of the two lovers were calmer, Milady, who had not the same motives for forgetfulness that d'Artagnan had, was the first to return to reality, and asked the young man if the means which were on the morrow to bring on the encounter between him and de Wardes were already arranged in his mind.

But d'Artagnan, whose ideas had taken quite another course, forgot himself like a fool, and answered gallantly that it was too late to think about duels and sword thrusts.

This coldness toward the only interests that occupied her mind terrified Milady, whose questions became more pressing.

Then d'Artagnan, who had never seriously thought of this impossible duel, endeavored to turn the conversation; but he could not succeed. Milady kept him within the limits she had traced beforehand with her irresistible spirit and her iron will.

D'Artagnan fancied himself very cunning when advising Milady to renounce, by pardoning de Wardes, the furious projects she had formed.

But at the first word the young woman started, and exclaimed in a sharp, bantering tone, which sounded strangely in the darkness, "Are you afraid, dear Monsieur d'Artagnan?"

"You cannot think so, dear love!" replied d'Artagnan; "but now, suppose this poor Comte de Wardes were less guilty than you think him?"

"At all events," said Milady, seriously, "he has deceived me, and from the moment he deceived me, he merited death."

"He shall die, then, since you condemn him!" said d'Artagnan, in so firm a tone that it appeared to Milady an undoubted proof of devotion. This reassured her.

We cannot say how long the night seemed to Milady, but d'Artagnan believed it to be hardly two hours before the daylight peeped through the window blinds, and invaded the chamber with its paleness. Seeing d'Artagnan about to leave her, Milady recalled his promise to avenge her on the Comte de Wardes.

"I am quite ready," said d'Artagnan; "but in the first place I should like to be certain of one thing."

"And what is that?" asked Milady.

"That is, whether you really love me?"

"I have given you proof of that, it seems to me."

"And I am yours, body and soul!"

"Thanks, my brave lover; but as you are satisfied of my love, you must, in your turn, satisfy me of yours. Is it not so?"

"Certainly; but if you love me as much as you say," replied d'Artagnan, "do you not entertain a little fear on my account?"

"What have I to fear?"

"Why, that I may be dangerously wounded--killed even."

"Impossible!" cried Milady, "you are such a valiant man, and such an expert swordsman."

"You would not, then, prefer a method," resumed d'Artagnan, "which would equally avenge you while rendering the combat useless?"

Milady looked at her lover in silence. The pale light of the first rays of day gave to her clear eyes a strangely frightful expression.

"Really," said she, "I believe you now begin to hesitate."

"No, I do not hesitate; but I really pity this poor Comte de Wardes, since you have ceased to love him. I think that a man must be so severely punished by the loss of your love that he stands in need of no other chastisement."

"Who told you that I loved him?" asked Milady, sharply.

"At least, I am now at liberty to believe, without too much fatuity, that you love another," said the young man, in a caressing tone, "and I repeat that I am really interested for the count."

"You?" asked Milady.

"Yes, I."

"And why YOU?"

"Because I alone know--"

"What?"

"That he is far from being, or rather having been, so guilty toward you as he appears."

"Indeed!" said Milady, in an anxious tone; "explain yourself, for I really cannot tell what you mean."

And she looked at d'Artagnan, who embraced her tenderly, with eyes which seemed to burn themselves away.

"Yes; I am a man of honor," said d'Artagnan, determined to come to an end, "and since your love is mine, and I am satisfied I possess it--for I do possess it, do I not?"

"Entirely; go on."

"Well, I feel as if transformed--a confession weighs on my mind."

"A confession!"

"If I had the least doubt of your love I would not make it, but you love me, my beautiful mistress, do you not?"

"Without doubt."

"Then if through excess of love I have rendered myself culpable toward you, you will pardon me?"

"Perhaps."

D'Artagnan tried with his sweetest smile to touch his lips to Milady's, but she evaded him.

"This confession," said she, growing paler, "what is this confession?"

"You gave de Wardes a meeting on Thursday last in this very room, did you not?"

"No, no! It is not true," said Milady, in a tone of voice so firm, and with a countenance so unchanged, that if d'Artagnan had not been in such perfect possession of the fact, he would have doubted.

"Do not lie, my angel," said d'Artagnan, smiling; "that would be useless."

"What do you mean? Speak! you kill me."

"Be satisfied; you are not guilty toward me, and I have already pardoned you."

"What next? what next?"

"De Wardes cannot boast of anything."

"How is that? You told me yourself that that ring--"

"That ring I have! The Comte de Wardes of Thursday and the d'Artagnan of today are the same person."

The imprudent young man expected a surprise, mixed with shame--a slight storm which would resolve itself into tears; but he was strangely deceived, and his error was not of long duration.

Pale and trembling, Milady repulsed d'Artagnan's attempted embrace by a violent blow on the chest, as she sprang out of bed.

It was almost broad daylight.

D'Artagnan detained her by her night dress of fine India linen, to implore her pardon; but she, with a strong movement, tried to escape. Then the cambric was torn from her beautiful shoulders; and on one of those lovely shoulders, round and white, d'Artagnan recognized, with inexpressible astonishment, the FLEUR-DE-LIS--that indelible mark which the hand of the infamous executioner had imprinted.

"Great God!" cried d'Artagnan, loosing his hold of her dress, and remaining mute, motionless, and frozen.

But Milady felt herself denounced even by his terror. He had doubtless seen all. The young man now knew her secret, her terrible secret--the secret she concealed even from her maid with such care, the secret of which all the world was ignorant, except himself.

She turned upon him, no longer like a furious woman, but like a wounded panther.

"Ah, wretch!" cried she, "you have basely betrayed me, and still more, you have my secret! You shall die."

And she flew to a little inlaid casket which stood upon the dressing table, opened it with a feverish and trembling hand, drew from it a small poniard, with a golden haft and a sharp thin blade, and then threw herself with a bound upon d'Artagnan.

Although the young man was brave, as we know, he was terrified at that wild countenance, those terribly dilated pupils, those pale cheeks, and those bleeding lips. He recoiled to the other side of the room as he would have done from a serpent which was crawling toward him, and his sword coming in contact with his nervous hand, he drew it almost unconsciously from the scabbard. But without taking any heed of the sword, Milady endeavored to get near enough to him to stab him, and did not stop till she felt the sharp point at her throat.

She then tried to seize the sword with her hands; but d'Artagnan kept it free from her grasp, and presenting the point, sometimes at her eyes, sometimes at her breast, compelled her to glide behind the bedstead, while he aimed at making his retreat by the door which led to Kitty's apartment.

Milady during this time continued to strike at him with horrible fury, screaming in a formidable way.

As all this, however, bore some resemblance to a duel, d'Artagnan began to recover himself little by little.

"Well, beautiful lady, very well," said he; "but, PARDIEU, if you don't calm yourself, I will design a second FLEUR-DE-LIS upon one of those pretty cheeks!"

"Scoundrel, infamous scoundrel!" howled Milady.

But d'Artagnan, still keeping on the defensive, drew near to Kitty's door. At the noise they made, she in overturning the furniture in her efforts to get at him, he in screening himself behind the furniture to keep out of her reach, Kitty opened the door. D'Artagnan, who had unceasingly maneuvered to gain this point, was not at more than three paces from it. With one spring he flew from the chamber of Milady into that of the maid, and quick as lightning, he slammed to the door, and placed all his weight against it, while Kitty pushed the bolts.

Then Milady attempted to tear down the doorcase, with a strength apparently above that of a woman; but finding she could not accomplish this, she in her fury stabbed at the door with her poniard, the point of which repeatedly glittered through the wood. Every blow was accompanied with terrible imprecations.

"Quick, Kitty, quick!" said d'Artagnan, in a low voice, as soon as the bolts were fast, "let me get out of the hotel; for if we leave her time to turn round, she will have me killed by the servants."

"But you can't go out so," said Kitty; "you are naked."

"That's true," said d'Artagnan, then first thinking of the costume he found himself in, "that's true. But dress me as well as you are able, only make haste; think, my dear girl, it's life and death!"

Kitty was but too well aware of that. In a turn of the hand she muffled him up in a flowered robe, a large hood, and a cloak. She gave him some slippers, in which he placed his naked feet, and then conducted him down the stairs. It was time. Milady had already rung her bell, and roused the whole hotel. The porter was drawing the cord at the moment Milady cried from her window, "Don't open!"

The young man fled while she was still threatening him with an impotent gesture. The moment she lost sight of him, Milady tumbled fainting into her chamber.

38 How, Without Incommding Himself, Athos Procures His Equipment

D'Artagnan was so completely bewildered that without taking any heed of what might become of Kitty he ran at full speed across half Paris, and did not stop till he came to Athos's door. The confusion of his mind, the terror which spurred him on, the cries of some of the patrol who started in pursuit of him, and the hooting of the people who, notwithstanding the early hour, were going to their work, only made him precipitate his course.

He crossed the court, ran up the two flights to Athos's apartment, and knocked at the door enough to break it down.

Grimaud came, rubbing his half-open eyes, to answer this noisy summons, and d'Artagnan sprang with such violence into the room as nearly to overturn the astonished lackey.

In spite of his habitual silence, the poor lad this time found his speech.

"Holloa, there!" cried he; "what do you want, you strumpet? What's your business here, you hussy?"

D'Artagnan threw off his hood, and disengaged his hands from the folds of the cloak. At sight of the mustaches and the naked sword, the poor devil perceived he had to deal with a man. He then concluded it must be an assassin.

"Help! murder! help!" cried he.

"Hold your tongue, you stupid fellow!" said the young man; "I am d'Artagnan; don't you know me? Where is your master?"

"You, Monsieur d'Artagnan!" cried Grimaud, "impossible."

"Grimaud," said Athos, coming out of his apartment in a dressing gown, "Grimaud, I thought I heard you permitting yourself to speak?"

"Ah, monsieur, it is--"

"Silence!"

Grimaud contented himself with pointing d'Artagnan out to his master with his finger.

Athos recognized his comrade, and phlegmatic as he was, he burst into a laugh which was quite excused by the strange masquerade before his eyes--petticoats falling over his shoes, sleeves tucked up, and mustaches stiff with agitation.

"Don't laugh, my friend!" cried d'Artagnan; "for heaven's sake, don't laugh, for upon my soul, it's no laughing matter!"

And he pronounced these words with such a solemn air and with such a real appearance of terror, that Athos eagerly seized his hand, crying, "Are you wounded, my friend? How pale you are!"

"No, but I have just met with a terrible adventure! Are you alone, Athos?"

"PARBLEU! whom do you expect to find with me at this hour?"

"Well, well!" and d'Artagnan rushed into Athos's chamber.

"Come, speak!" said the latter, closing the door and bolting it, that they might not be disturbed. "Is the king dead? Have you killed the cardinal? You are quite upset! Come, come, tell me; I am dying with curiosity and uneasiness!"

"Athos," said d'Artagnan, getting rid of his female garments, and appearing in his shirt, "prepare yourself to hear an incredible, an unheard-of story."

"Well, but put on this dressing gown first," said the Musketeer to his friend.

D'Artagnan donned the robe as quickly as he could, mistaking one sleeve for the other, so greatly was he still agitated.

"Well?" said Athos.

"Well," replied d'Artagnan, bending his mouth to Athos's ear, and lowering his voice, "Milady is marked with a FLEUR-DE-LIS upon her shoulder!"

"Ah!" cried the Musketeer, as if he had received a ball in his heart.

"Let us see," said d'Artagnan. "Are you SURE that the OTHER is dead?"

"THE OTHER?" said Athos, in so stifled a voice that d'Artagnan scarcely heard him.

"Yes, she of whom you told me one day at Amiens."

Athos uttered a groan, and let his head sink on his hands.

"This is a woman of twenty-six or twenty-eight years."

"Fair," said Athos, "is she not?"

"Very."

"Blue and clear eyes, of a strange brilliancy, with black eyelids and eyebrows?"

"Yes."

"Tall, well-made? She has lost a tooth, next to the eyetooth on the left?"

"Yes."

"The FLEUR-DE-LIS is small, rosy in color, and looks as if efforts had been made to efface it by the application of poultices?"

"Yes."

"But you say she is English?"

"She is called Milady, but she may be French. Lord de Winter is only her brother-in-law."

"I will see her, d'Artagnan!"

"Beware, Athos, beware. You tried to kill her; she is a woman to return you the like, and not to fail."

"She will not dare to say anything; that would be to denounce herself."

"She is capable of anything or everything. Did you ever see her furious?"

"No," said Athos.

"A tigress, a panther! Ah, my dear Athos, I am greatly afraid I have drawn a terrible vengeance on both of us!"

D'Artagnan then related all--the mad passion of Milady and her menaces of death.

"You are right; and upon my soul, I would give my life for a hair," said Athos. "Fortunately, the day after tomorrow we leave Paris. We are going according to all probability to La Rochelle, and once gone--"

"She will follow you to the end of the world, Athos, if she recognizes you. Let her, then, exhaust her vengeance on me alone!"

"My dear friend, of what consequence is it if she kills me?" said Athos. "Do you, perchance, think I set any great store by life?"

"There is something horribly mysterious under all this, Athos; this woman is one of the cardinal's spies, I am sure of that."

"In that case, take care! If the cardinal does not hold you in high admiration for the affair of London, he entertains a great hatred for you; but as, considering everything, he cannot accuse you openly, and as hatred must be satisfied, particularly when it's a cardinal's hatred, take care of yourself. If you go out, do not go out alone; when you eat, use every precaution. Mistrust everything, in short, even your own shadow."

"Fortunately," said d'Artagnan, "all this will be only necessary till after tomorrow evening, for when once with the army, we shall have, I hope, only men to dread."

"In the meantime," said Athos, "I renounce my plan of seclusion, and wherever you go, I will go with you. You must return to the Rue des Fossoyeurs; I will accompany you."

"But however near it may be," replied d'Artagnan, "I cannot go thither in this guise."

"That's true," said Athos, and he rang the bell.

Grimaud entered.

Athos made him a sign to go to d'Artagnan's residence, and bring back some clothes. Grimaud replied by another sign that he understood perfectly, and set off.

"All this will not advance your outfit," said Athos; "for if I am not mistaken, you have left the best of your apparel with Milady, and she will certainly not have the politeness to return it to you. Fortunately, you have the sapphire."

"The jewel is yours, my dear Athos! Did you not tell me it was a family jewel?"

"Yes, my grandfather gave two thousand crowns for it, as he once told me. It formed part of the nuptial present he made his wife, and it is magnificent. My mother gave it to me, and I, fool as I was, instead of keeping the ring as a holy relic, gave it to this wretch."

"Then, my friend, take back this ring, to which I see you attach much value."

"I take back the ring, after it has passed through the hands of that infamous creature? Never; that ring is defiled, d'Artagnan."

"Sell it, then."

"Sell a jewel which came from my mother! I vow I should consider it a profanation."

"Pledge it, then; you can borrow at least a thousand crowns on it. With that sum you can extricate yourself from your present difficulties; and when you are full of money again, you can redeem it, and take it back cleansed from its ancient stains, as it will have passed through the hands of usurers."

Athos smiled.

"You are a capital companion, d'Artagnan," said be; "your never-failing cheerfulness raises poor souls in affliction. Well, let us pledge the ring, but upon one condition."

"What?"

"That there shall be five hundred crowns for you, and five hundred crowns for me."

"Don't dream it, Athos. I don't need the quarter of such a sum--I who am still only in the Guards--and by selling my saddles, I shall procure it. What do I want? A horse for Planchet, that's all. Besides, you forget that I have a ring likewise."

"To which you attach more value, it seems, than I do to mine; at least, I have thought so."

"Yes, for in any extreme circumstance it might not only extricate us from some great embarrassment, but even a great danger. It is not only a valuable diamond, but it is an enchanted talisman."

"I don't at all understand you, but I believe all you say to be true. Let us return to my ring, or rather to yours. You shall take half the sum that will be advanced upon it, or I will throw it into the Seine; and I doubt, as was the case with Polycrates, whether any fish will be sufficiently complaisant to bring it back to us."

"Well, I will take it, then," said d'Artagnan.

At this moment Grimaud returned, accompanied by Planchet; the latter, anxious about his master and curious to know what had happened to him, had taken advantage of the opportunity and brought the garments himself.

d'Artagnan dressed himself, and Athos did the same. When the two were ready to go out, the latter made Grimaud the sign of a man taking aim, and the lackey immediately took down his musketoon, and prepared to follow his master.

They arrived without accident at the Rue des Fossoyeurs. Bonacieux was standing at the door, and looked at d'Artagnan hatefully.

"Make haste, dear lodger," said he; "there is a very pretty girl waiting for you upstairs; and you know women don't like to be kept waiting."

"That's Kitty!" said d'Artagnan to himself, and darted into the passage.

Sure enough! Upon the landing leading to the chamber, and crouching against the door, he found the poor girl, all in a tremble. As soon as she perceived him, she cried, "You have promised your protection; you have promised to save me from her anger. Remember, it is you who have ruined me!"

"Yes, yes, to be sure, Kitty," said d'Artagnan; "be at ease, my girl. But what happened after my departure?"

"How can I tell!" said Kitty. "The lackeys were brought by the cries she made. She was mad with passion. There exist no imprecations she did not pour out against you. Then I thought she would remember it was through my chamber you had penetrated hers, and that then she would suppose I was your accomplice; so I took what little money I had and the best of my things, and I got away.

"Poor dear girl! But what can I do with you? I am going away the day after tomorrow."

"Do what you please, Monsieur Chevalier. Help me out of Paris; help me out of France!"

"I cannot take you, however, to the siege of La Rochelle," aid d'Artagnan.

"No; but you can place me in one of the provinces with some lady of your acquaintance--in your own country, for instance."

"My dear little love! In my country the ladies do without chambermaids. But stop! I can manage your business for you. Planchet, go and find Aramis. Request him to come here directly. We have something very important to say to him."

"I understand," said Athos; "but why not Porthos? I should have thought that his duchess--"

"Oh, Porthos's duchess is dressed by her husband's clerks," said d'Artagnan, laughing. "Besides, Kitty would not like to live in the Rue aux Ours. Isn't it so, Kitty?"

"I do not care where I live," said Kitty, "provided I am well concealed, and nobody knows where I am."

"Meanwhile, Kitty, when we are about to separate, and you are no longer jealous of me--"

"Monsieur Chevalier, far off or near," said Kitty, "I shall always love you."

"Where the devil will constancy niche itself next?" murmured Athos.

"And I, also," said d'Artagnan, "I also. I shall always love you; be sure of that. But now answer me. I attach great importance to the question I am about to put to you. Did you never hear talk of a young woman who was carried off one night?"

"There, now! Oh, Monsieur Chevalier, do you love that woman still?"

"No, no; it is one of my friends who loves her--Monsieur Athos, this gentleman here."

"I?" cried Athos, with an accent like that of a man who perceives he is about to tread upon an adder.

"You, to be sure!" said d'Artagnan, pressing Athos's hand. "You know the interest we both take in this poor little Madame Bonacieux. Besides, Kitty will tell nothing; will you, Kitty? You understand, my dear girl," continued d'Artagnan, "she is the wife of that frightful baboon you saw at the door as you came in."

"Oh, my God! You remind me of my fright! If he should have known me again!"

"How? know you again? Did you ever see that man before?"

"He came twice to Milady's."

"That's it. About what time?"

"Why, about fifteen or eighteen days ago."

"Exactly so."

"And yesterday evening he came again."

"Yesterday evening?"

"Yes, just before you came."

"My dear Athos, we are enveloped in a network of spies. And do you believe he knew you again, Kitty?"

"I pulled down my hood as soon as I saw him, but perhaps it was too late."

"Go down, Athos--he mistrusts you less than me--and see if he be still at his door."

Athos went down and returned immediately.

"He has gone," said he, "and the house door is shut."

"He has gone to make his report, and to say that all the pigeons are at this moment in the dovecot."

"Well, then, let us all fly," said Athos, "and leave nobody here but Planchet to bring us news."

"A minute. Aramis, whom we have sent for!"

"That's true," said Athos; "we must wait for Aramis."

At that moment Aramis entered.

The matter was all explained to him, and the friends gave him to understand that among all his high connections he must find a place for Kitty.

Aramis reflected for a minute, and then said, coloring, "Will it be really rendering you a service, d'Artagnan?"

"I shall be grateful to you all my life."

"Very well. Madame de Bois-Tracy asked me, for one of her friends who resides in the provinces, I believe, for a trustworthy maid. If you can, my dear d'Artagnan, answer for Mademoiselle-"

"Oh, monsieur, be assured that I shall be entirely devoted to the person who will give me the means of quitting Paris."

"Then," said Aramis, "this falls out very well."

He placed himself at the table and wrote a little note which he sealed with a ring, and gave the billet to Kitty.

"And now, my dear girl," said d'Artagnan, "you know that it is not good for any of us to be here. Therefore let us separate. We shall meet again in better days."

"And whenever we find each other, in whatever place it may be," said Kitty, "you will find me loving you as I love you today."

"Dicers' oaths!" said Athos, while d'Artagnan went to conduct Kitty downstairs.

An instant afterward the three young men separated, agreeing to meet again at four o'clock with Athos, and leaving Planchet to guard the house.

Aramis returned home, and Athos and d'Artagnan busied themselves about pledging the sapphire.

As the Gascon had foreseen, they easily obtained three hundred pistoles on the ring. Still further, the Jew told them that if they would sell it to him, as it would make a magnificent pendant for earrings, he would give five hundred pistoles for it.

Athos and d'Artagnan, with the activity of two soldiers and the knowledge of two connoisseurs, hardly required three hours to purchase the entire equipment of the Musketeer. Besides, Athos was very easy, and a noble to his fingers' ends. When a thing suited him he paid the price demanded, without thinking to ask for any abatement. D'Artagnan would have remonstrated at this; but Athos put his hand upon his shoulder, with a smile, and d'Artagnan understood that it was all very well for such a little Gascon gentleman as himself to drive a bargain, but not for a man who had the bearing of a prince. The Musketeer met with a superb Andalusian horse, black as jet, nostrils of fire, legs clean and elegant, rising six years. He examined him, and found him sound and without blemish. They asked a thousand livres for him.

He might perhaps have been bought for less; but while d'Artagnan was discussing the price with the dealer, Athos was counting out the money on the table.

Grimaud had a stout, short Picard cob, which cost three hundred livres.

But when the saddle and arms for Grimaud were purchased, Athos had not a sou left of his hundred and fifty pistoles. d'Artagnan offered his friend a part of his share which he should return when convenient.

But Athos only replied to this proposal by shrugging his shoulders.

"How much did the Jew say he would give for the sapphire if he purchased it?" said Athos.

"Five hundred pistoles."

"That is to say, two hundred more--a hundred pistoles for you and a hundred pistoles for me. Well, now, that would be a real fortune to us, my friend; let us go back to the Jew's again."

"What! will you--"

"This ring would certainly only recall very bitter remembrances; then we shall never be masters of three hundred pistoles to redeem it, so that we really should lose two hundred pistoles by the bargain. Go and tell him the ring is his, d'Artagnan, and bring back the two hundred pistoles with you."

"Reflect, Athos!"

"Ready money is needful for the present time, and we must learn how to make sacrifices. Go, d'Artagnan, go; Grimaud will accompany you with his musketoon."

A half hour afterward, d'Artagnan returned with the two thousand livres, and without having met with any accident.

It was thus Athos found at home resources which he did not expect.

39 A Vision

At four o'clock the four friends were all assembled with Athos. Their anxiety about their outfits had all disappeared, and each countenance only preserved the expression of its own secret disquiet--for behind all present happiness is concealed a fear for the future.

Suddenly Planchet entered, bringing two letters for d'Artagnan.

The one was a little billet, genteelly folded, with a pretty seal in green wax on which was impressed a dove bearing a green branch.

The other was a large square epistle, resplendent with the terrible arms of his Eminence the cardinal duke.

At the sight of the little letter the heart of d'Artagnan bounded, for he believed he recognized the handwriting, and although he had seen that writing but once, the memory of it remained at the bottom of his heart.

He therefore seized the little epistle, and opened it eagerly.

"Be," said the letter, "on Thursday next, at from six to seven o'clock in the evening, on the road to Chaillot, and look carefully into the carriages that pass; but if you have any consideration for your own life or that of those who love you, do not speak a single word, do not make a movement which may lead anyone to believe you have recognized her who exposes herself to everything for the sake of seeing you but for an instant."

No signature.

"That's a snare," said Athos; "don't go, d'Artagnan."

"And yet," replied d'Artagnan, "I think I recognize the writing."

"It may be counterfeit," said Athos. "Between six and seven o'clock the road of Chaillot is quite deserted; you might as well go and ride in the forest of Bondy."

"But suppose we all go," said d'Artagnan; "what the devil! They won't devour us all four, four lackeys, horses, arms, and all!"

"And besides, it will be a chance for displaying our new equipments," said Porthos.

"But if it is a woman who writes," said Aramis, "and that woman desires not to be seen, remember, you compromise her, d'Artagnan; which is not the part of a gentleman."

"We will remain in the background," said Porthos, "and he will advance alone."

"Yes; but a pistol shot is easily fired from a carriage which goes at a gallop."

"Bah!" said d'Artagnan, "they will miss me; if they fire we will ride after the carriage, and exterminate those who may be in it. They must be enemies."

"He is right," said Porthos; "battle. Besides, we must try our own arms."

"Bah, let us enjoy that pleasure," said Aramis, with his mild and careless manner.

"As you please," said Athos.

"Gentlemen," said d'Artagnan, "it is half past four, and we have scarcely time to be on the road of Chaillot by six."

"Besides, if we go out too late, nobody will see us," said Porthos, "and that will be a pity. Let us get ready, gentlemen."

"But this second letter," said Athos, "you forget that; it appears to me, however, that the seal denotes that it deserves to be opened. For my part, I declare, d'Artagnan, I think it of much more consequence than the little piece of waste paper you have so cunningly slipped into your bosom."

D'Artagnan blushed.

"Well," said he, "let us see, gentlemen, what are his Eminence's commands," and d'Artagnan unsealed the letter and read,

"M. d'Artagnan, of the king's Guards, company Dessessart, is expected at the Palais-Cardinal this evening, at eight o'clock.

"La Houdiniere, CAPTAIN OF THE GUARDS"

"The devil!" said Athos; "here's a rendezvous much more serious than the other."

"I will go to the second after attending the first," said d'Artagnan. "One is for seven o'clock, and the other for eight; there will be time for both."

"Hum! I would not go at all," said Aramis. "A gallant knight cannot decline a rendezvous with a lady; but a prudent gentleman may excuse himself from not waiting on his Eminence, particularly when he has reason to believe he is not invited to make his compliments."

"I am of Aramis's opinion," said Porthos.

"Gentlemen," replied d'Artagnan, "I have already received by Monsieur de Cavois a similar invitation from his Eminence. I neglected it, and on the morrow a serious misfortune happened to me--Constance disappeared. Whatever may ensue, I will go."

"If you are determined," said Athos, "do so."

"But the Bastille?" said Aramis.

"Bah! you will get me out if they put me there," said d'Artagnan.

"To be sure we will," replied Aramis and Porthos, with admirable promptness and decision, as if that were the simplest thing in the world, "to be sure we will get you out; but meantime, as we are to set off the day after tomorrow, you would do much better not to risk this Bastille."

"Let us do better than that," said Athos; "do not let us leave him during the whole evening. Let each of us wait at a gate of the palace with three Musketeers behind him; if we see a close carriage, at all suspicious in appearance, come out, let us fall upon it. It is a long time since we have had a skirmish with the Guards of Monsieur the Cardinal; Monsieur de Treville must think us dead."

"To a certainty, Athos," said Aramis, "you were meant to be a general of the army! What do you think of the plan, gentlemen?"

"Admirable!" replied the young men in chorus.

"Well," said Porthos, "I will run to the hotel, and engage our comrades to hold themselves in readiness by eight o'clock; the rendezvous, the Place du Palais-Cardinal. Meantime, you see that the lackeys saddle the horses."

"I have no horse," said d'Artagnan; "but that is of no consequence, I can take one of Monsieur de Treville's."

"That is not worth while," said Aramis, "you can have one of mine."

"One of yours! how many have you, then?" asked d'Artagnan.

"Three," replied Aramis, smiling.

"Certes," cried Athos, "you are the best-mounted poet of France or Navarre."

"Well, my dear Aramis, you don't want three horses? I cannot comprehend what induced you to buy three!"

"Therefore I only purchased two," said Aramis.

"The third, then, fell from the clouds, I suppose?"

"No, the third was brought to me this very morning by a groom out of livery, who would not tell me in whose service he was, and who said he had received orders from his master."

"Or his mistress," interrupted d'Artagnan.

"That makes no difference," said Aramis, coloring; "and who affirmed, as I said, that he had received orders from his master or mistress to place the horse in my stable, without informing me whence it came."

"It is only to poets that such things happen," said Athos, gravely.

"Well, in that case, we can manage famously," said d'Artagnan; "which of the two horses will you ride--that which you bought or the one that was given to you?"

"That which was given to me, assuredly. You cannot for a moment imagine, d'Artagnan, that I would commit such an offense toward--"

"The unknown giver," interrupted d'Artagnan.

"Or the mysterious benefactress," said Athos.

"The one you bought will then become useless to you?"

"Nearly so."

"And you selected it yourself?"

"With the greatest care. The safety of the horseman, you know, depends almost always upon the goodness of his horse."

"Well, transfer it to me at the price it cost you?"

"I was going to make you the offer, my dear d'Artagnan, giving you all the time necessary for repaying me such a trifle."

"How much did it cost you?"

"Eight hundred livres."

"Here are forty double pistoles, my dear friend," said d'Artagnan, taking the sum from his pocket; "I know that is the coin in which you were paid for your poems."

"You are rich, then?" said Aramis.

"Rich? Richest, my dear fellow!"

And d'Artagnan chinked the remainder of his pistoles in his pocket.

"Send your saddle, then, to the hotel of the Musketeers, and your horse can be brought back with ours."

"Very well; but it is already five o'clock, so make haste."

A quarter of an hour afterward Porthos appeared at the end of the Rue Ferou on a very handsome genet. Mousqueton followed him upon an Auvergne horse, small but very handsome. Porthos was resplendent with joy and pride.

At the same time, Aramis made his appearance at the other end of the street upon a superb English charger. Bazin followed him upon a roan, holding by the halter a vigorous Mecklenburg horse; this was d'Artagnan's mount.

The two Musketeers met at the gate. Athos and d'Artagnan watched their approach from the window.

"The devil!" cried Aramis, "you have a magnificent horse there, Porthos."

"Yes," replied Porthos, "it is the one that ought to have been sent to me at first. A bad joke of the husband's substituted the other; but the husband has been punished since, and I have obtained full satisfaction."

Planchet and Grimaud appeared in their turn, leading their masters' steeds. D'Artagnan and Athos put themselves into saddle with their companions, and all four set forward; Athos upon a horse he owed to a woman, Aramis on a horse he owed to his mistress, Porthos on a horse he owed to his procurator's wife, and d'Artagnan on a horse he owed to his good fortune--the best mistress possible.

The lackeys followed.

As Porthos had foreseen, the cavalcade produced a good effect; and if Mme. Coquenard had met Porthos and seen what a superb appearance he made upon his handsome Spanish genet, she would not have regretted the bleeding she had inflicted upon the strongbox of her husband.

Near the Louvre the four friends met with M. de Treville, who was returning from St. Germain; he stopped them to offer his compliments upon their appointments, which in an instant drew round them a hundred gapers.

D'Artagnan profited by the circumstance to speak to M. de Treville of the letter with the great red seal and the cardinal's arms. It is well understood that he did not breathe a word about the other.

M de Treville approved of the resolution he had adopted, and assured him that if on the morrow he did not appear, he himself would undertake to find him, let him be where he might.

At this moment the clock of La Samaritaine struck six; the four friends pleaded an engagement, and took leave of M. de Treville.

A short gallop brought them to the road of Chaillot; the day began to decline, carriages were passing and repassing. d'Artagnan, keeping at some distance from his friends, darted a scrutinizing glance into every carriage that appeared, but saw no face with which he was acquainted.

At length, after waiting a quarter of an hour and just as twilight was beginning to thicken, a carriage appeared, coming at a quick pace on the road of Sevres. A presentiment instantly told d'Artagnan that this carriage contained the person who had appointed the rendezvous; the young man was himself astonished to find his heart beat so violently. Almost instantly a female head was put out at the window, with two fingers placed upon her mouth, either to enjoin silence or to send him a kiss. D'Artagnan uttered a slight cry of joy; this woman, or rather this apparition--for the carriage passed with the rapidity of a vision--was Mme. Bonacieux.

By an involuntary movement and in spite of the injunction given, d'Artagnan put his horse into a gallop, and in a few strides overtook the carriage; but the window was hermetically closed, the vision had disappeared.

D'Artagnan then remembered the injunction: "If you value your own life or that of those who love you, remain motionless, and as if you had seen nothing."

He stopped, therefore, trembling not for himself but for the poor woman who had evidently exposed herself to great danger by appointing this rendezvous.

The carriage pursued its way, still going at a great pace, till it dashed into Paris, and disappeared.

D'Artagnan remained fixed to the spot, astounded and not knowing what to think. If it was Mme. Bonacieux and if she was returning to Paris, why this fugitive rendezvous, why this simple exchange of a glance, why this lost kiss? If, on the other side, it was not she--which was still quite possible--for the little light that remained rendered a mistake easy--might it not be the commencement of some plot against him through the allurement of this woman, for whom his love was known?

His three companions joined him. All had plainly seen a woman's head appear at the window, but none of them, except Athos, knew Mme. Bonacieux. The opinion of Athos was that it was indeed she; but less preoccupied by that pretty face than d'Artagnan, he had fancied he saw a second head, a man's head, inside the carriage.

"If that be the case," said d'Artagnan, "they are doubtless transporting her from one prison to another. But what can they intend to do with the poor creature, and how shall I ever meet her again?"

"Friend," said Athos, gravely, "remember that it is the dead alone with whom we are not likely to meet again on this earth. You know something of that, as well as I do, I think. Now, if your mistress is not dead, if it is she we have just seen, you will meet with her again some day or other. And perhaps, my God!" added he, with that misanthropic tone which was peculiar to him, "perhaps sooner than you wish."

Half past seven had sounded. The carriage had been twenty minutes behind the time appointed. D'Artagnan's friends reminded him that he had a visit to pay, but at the same time bade him observe that there was yet time to retract.

But d'Artagnan was at the same time impetuous and curious. He had made up his mind that he would go to the Palais-Cardinal, and that he would learn what his Eminence had to say to him. Nothing could turn him from his purpose.

They reached the Rue St. Honore, and in the Place du Palais-Cardinal they found the twelve invited Musketeers, walking about in expectation of their comrades. There only they explained to them the matter in hand.

D'Artagnan was well known among the honorable corps of the king's Musketeers, in which it was known he would one day take his place; he was considered beforehand as a comrade. It resulted from these antecedents that everyone entered heartily into the purpose for which they met; besides, it would not be unlikely that they would have an opportunity of playing either the cardinal or his people an ill turn, and for such expeditions these worthy gentlemen were always ready.

Athos divided them into three groups, assumed the command of one, gave the second to Aramis, and the third to Porthos; and then each group went and took their watch near an entrance.

D'Artagnan, on his part, entered boldly at the principal gate.

Although he felt himself ably supported, the young man was not without a little uneasiness as he ascended the great staircase, step by step. His conduct toward Milady bore a strong resemblance to treachery, and he was very suspicious of the political relations which existed between that woman and the cardinal. Still further, de Wardes, whom he had treated so ill, was one of the tools of his Eminence; and d'Artagnan knew that while his Eminence was terrible to his enemies, he was strongly attached to his friends.

"If de Wardes has related all our affair to the cardinal, which is not to be doubted, and if he has recognized me, as is probable, I may consider myself almost as a condemned man," said d'Artagnan, shaking his head. "But why has he waited till now? That's all plain enough. Milady has laid her complaints against me with that hypocritical grief which renders her so interesting, and this last offense has made the cup overflow."

"Fortunately," added he, "my good friends are down yonder, and they will not allow me to be carried away without a struggle. Nevertheless, Monsieur de Treville's company of Musketeers alone cannot maintain a war against the cardinal, who disposes of the forces of all France, and before whom the queen is without power and the king without will. d'Artagnan, my friend, you are brave, you are prudent, you have excellent qualities; but the women will ruin you!"

He came to this melancholy conclusion as he entered the antechamber. He placed his letter in the hands of the usher on duty, who led him into the waiting room and passed on into the interior of the palace.

In this waiting room were five or six of the cardinals Guards, who recognized d'Artagnan, and knowing that it was he who had wounded Jussac, they looked upon him with a smile of singular meaning.

This smile appeared to d'Artagnan to be of bad augury. Only, as our Gascon was not easily intimidated--or rather, thanks to a great pride natural to the men of his country, he did not allow one easily to see what was passing in his mind when that which was passing at all resembled fear--he placed himself haughtily in front of Messieurs the Guards, and waited with his hand on his hip, in an attitude by no means deficient in majesty.

The usher returned and made a sign to d'Artagnan to follow him. It appeared to the young man that the Guards, on seeing him depart, chuckled among themselves.

He traversed a corridor, crossed a grand saloon, entered a library, and found himself in the presence of a man seated at a desk and writing.

The usher introduced him, and retired without speaking a word. D'Artagnan remained standing and examined this man.

D'Artagnan at first believed that he had to do with some judge examining his papers; but he perceived that the man at the desk wrote, or rather corrected, lines of unequal length, scanning the words on his fingers. He saw then that he was with a poet. At the end of an instant the poet closed his manuscript, upon the cover of which was written "Mirame, a Tragedy in Five Acts," and raised his head.

D'Artagnan recognized the cardinal.

40 A Terrible Vision

The cardinal leaned his elbow on his manuscript, his cheek upon his hand, and looked intently at the young man for a moment. No one had a more searching eye than the Cardinal de Richelieu, and d'Artagnan felt this glance run through his veins like a fever.

He however kept a good countenance, holding his hat in his hand and awaiting the good pleasure of his Eminence, without too much assurance, but also without too much humility.

"Monsieur," said the cardinal, "are you a d'Artagnan from Bearn?"

"Yes, monseigneur," replied the young man.

"There are several branches of the d'Artagnans at Tarbes and in its environs," said the cardinal; "to which do you belong?"

"I am the son of him who served in the Religious Wars under the great King Henry, the father of his gracious Majesty."

"That is well. It is you who set out seven or eight months ago from your country to seek your fortune in the capital?"

"Yes, monseigneur."

"You came through Meung, where something befell you. I don't very well know what, but still something."

"Monseigneur," said d'Artagnan, "this was what happened to me--"

"Never mind, never mind!" resumed the cardinal, with a smile which indicated that he knew the story as well as he who wished to relate it. "You were recommended to Monsieur de Treville, were you not?"

"Yes, monseigneur; but in that unfortunate affair at Meung--"

"The letter was lost," replied his Eminence; "yes, I know that. But Monsieur de Treville is a skilled physiognomist, who knows men at first sight; and he placed you in the company of his brother-in-law, Monsieur Dessessart, leaving you to hope that one day or other you should enter the Musketeers."

"Monseigneur is correctly informed," said d'Artagnan.

"Since that time many things have happened to you. You were walking one day behind the Chartreux, when it would have been better if you had been elsewhere. Then you took with your friends a journey to the waters of Forges; they stopped on the road, but you continued yours. That is all very simple: you had business in England."

"Monseigneur," said d'Artagnan, quite confused, "I went--"

"Hunting at Windsor, or elsewhere--that concerns nobody. I know, because it is my office to know everything. On your return you were received by an august personage, and I perceive with pleasure that you preserve the souvenir she gave you."

D'Artagnan placed his hand upon the queen's diamond, which he wore, and quickly turned the stone inward; but it was too late.

"The day after that, you received a visit from Cavois," resumed the cardinal. "He went to desire you to come to the palace. You have not returned that visit, and you were wrong."

"Monseigneur, I feared I had incurred disgrace with your Eminence."

"How could that be, monsieur? Could you incur my displeasure by having followed the orders of your superiors with more intelligence and courage than another would have done? It is the people who do not obey that I punish, and not those who, like you, obey--but too well. As a proof, remember the date of the day on which I had you bidden to come to me, and seek in your memory for what happened to you that very night."

That was the very evening when the abduction of Mme. Bonacieux took place. D'Artagnan trembled; and he likewise recollected that during the past half hour the poor woman had passed close to him, without doubt carried away by the same power that had caused her disappearance.

"In short," continued the cardinal, "as I have heard nothing of you for some time past, I wished to know what you were doing. Besides, you owe me some thanks. You must yourself have remarked how much you have been considered in all the circumstances."

D'Artagnan bowed with respect.

"That," continued the cardinal, "arose not only from a feeling of natural equity, but likewise from a plan I have marked out with respect to you."

D'Artagnan became more and more astonished.

"I wished to explain this plan to you on the day you received my first invitation; but you did not come. Fortunately, nothing is lost by this delay, and you are now about to hear it. Sit down there, before me, d'Artagnan; you are gentleman enough not to listen standing." And the cardinal pointed with his finger to a chair for the young man, who was so astonished at what was passing that he awaited a second sign from his interlocutor before he obeyed.

"You are brave, Monsieur d'Artagnan," continued his Eminence; "you are prudent, which is still better. I like men of head and heart. Don't be afraid," said he, smiling. "By men of heart I mean men of courage. But young as you are, and scarcely entering into the world, you have powerful enemies; if you do not take great heed, they will destroy you."

"Alas, monseigneur!" replied the young man, "very easily, no doubt, for they are strong and well supported, while I am alone."

"Yes, that's true; but alone as you are, you have done much already, and will do still more, I don't doubt. Yet you have need, I believe, to be guided in the adventurous career you have undertaken; for, if I mistake not, you came to Paris with the ambitious idea of making your fortune."

"I am at the age of extravagant hopes, monseigneur," said d'Artagnan.

"There are no extravagant hopes but for fools, monsieur, and you are a man of understanding. Now, what would you say to an ensign's commission in my Guards, and a company after the campaign?"

"Ah, monseigneur."

"You accept it, do you not?"

"Monseigneur," replied d'Artagnan, with an embarrassed air.

"How? You refuse?" cried the cardinal, with astonishment.

"I am in his Majesty's Guards, monseigneur, and I have no reason to be dissatisfied."

"But it appears to me that my Guards--mine--are also his Majesty's Guards; and whoever serves in a French corps serves the king."

"Monseigneur, your Eminence has ill understood my words."

"You want a pretext, do you not? I comprehend. Well, you have this excuse: advancement, the opening campaign, the opportunity which I offer you--so much for the world. As regards yourself, the need of protection; for it is fit you should know, Monsieur d'Artagnan, that I have received heavy and serious complaints against you. You do not consecrate your days and nights wholly to the king's service."

D'Artagnan colored.

"In fact," said the cardinal, placing his hand upon a bundle of papers, "I have here a whole pile which concerns you. I know you to be a man of resolution; and your services, well directed, instead of leading you to ill, might be very advantageous to you. Come; reflect, and decide."

"Your goodness confounds me, monseigneur," replied d'Artagnan, "and I am conscious of a greatness of soul in your Eminence that makes me mean as an earthworm; but since Monseigneur permits me to speak freely--"

D'Artagnan paused.

"Yes; speak."

"Then, I will presume to say that all my friends are in the king's Musketeers and Guards, and that by an inconceivable fatality my enemies are in the service of your Eminence; I should, therefore, be ill received here and ill regarded there if I accepted what Monseigneur offers me."

"Do you happen to entertain the haughty idea that I have not yet made you an offer equal to your value?" asked the cardinal, with a smile of disdain.

"Monseigneur, your Eminence is a hundred times too kind to me; and on the contrary, I think I have not proved myself worthy of your goodness. The siege of La Rochelle is about to be resumed, monseigneur. I shall serve under the eye of your Eminence, and if I have the good fortune to conduct myself at the siege in such a manner as merits your attention, then I shall at least leave behind me some brilliant action to justify the protection with which you honor me. Everything is best in its time, monseigneur. Hereafter, perhaps, I shall have the right of giving myself; at present I shall appear to sell myself."

"That is to say, you refuse to serve me, monsieur," said the cardinal, with a tone of vexation, through which, however, might be seen a sort of esteem; "remain free, then, and guard your hatreds and your sympathies."

"Monseigneur--"

"Well, well," said the cardinal, "I don't wish you any ill; but you must be aware that it is quite trouble enough to defend and recompense our friends. We owe nothing to our enemies; and let me give you a piece of advice; take care of yourself, Monsieur d'Artagnan, for from the moment I withdraw my hand from behind you, I would not give an obolus for your life."

"I will try to do so, monseigneur," replied the Gascon, with a noble confidence.

"Remember at a later period and at a certain moment, if any mischance should happen to you," said Richelieu, significantly, "that it was I who came to seek you, and that I did all in my power to prevent this misfortune befalling you."

"I shall entertain, whatever may happen," said d'Artagnan, placing his hand upon his breast and bowing, "an eternal gratitude toward your Eminence for that which you now do for me."

"Well, let it be, then, as you have said, Monsieur d'Artagnan; we shall see each other again after the campaign. I will have my eye upon you, for I shall be there," replied the cardinal, pointing with his finger to a magnificent suit of armor he was to wear, "and on our return, well--we will settle our account!"

"Young man," said Richelieu, "if I shall be able to say to you at another time what I have said to you today, I promise you to do so."

This last expression of Richelieu's conveyed a terrible doubt; it alarmed d'Artagnan more than a menace would have done, for it was a warning. The cardinal, then, was seeking to preserve him from some misfortune which threatened him. He opened his mouth to reply, but with a haughty gesture the cardinal dismissed him.

D'Artagnan went out, but at the door his heart almost failed him, and he felt inclined to return. Then the noble and severe countenance of Athos crossed his mind; if he made the compact with the cardinal which he required, Athos would no more give him his hand--Athos would renounce him.

It was this fear that restrained him, so powerful is the influence of a truly great character on all that surrounds it.

D'Artagnan descended by the staircase at which he had entered, and found Athos and the four Musketeers waiting his appearance, and beginning to grow uneasy. With a word, d'Artagnan reassured them; and Planchet ran to inform the other sentinels that it was useless to keep guard longer, as his master had come out safe from the Palais-Cardinal.

Returned home with Athos, Aramis and Porthos inquired eagerly the cause of the strange interview; but d'Artagnan confined himself to telling them that M. de Richelieu had sent for him to propose to him to enter into his guards with the rank of ensign, and that he had refused.

"And you were right," cried Aramis and Porthos, with one voice.

Athos fell into a profound reverie and answered nothing. But when they were alone he said, "You have done that which you ought to have done, d'Artagnan; but perhaps you have been wrong."

D'Artagnan sighed deeply, for this voice responded to a secret voice of his soul, which told him that great misfortunes awaited him.

The whole of the next day was spent in preparations for departure. D'Artagnan went to take leave of M. de Treville. At that time it was believed that the separation of the Musketeers and the Guards would be but momentary, the king holding his Parliament that very day and proposing to set out the day after. M. de Treville contented himself with asking d'Artagnan if he could do anything for him, but d'Artagnan answered that he was supplied with all he wanted.

That night brought together all those comrades of the Guards of M. Dessessart and the company of Musketeers of M. de Treville who had been accustomed to associate together. They were parting to meet again when it pleased God, and if it pleased God. That night, then, was somewhat riotous, as may be imagined. In such cases extreme preoccupation is only to be combated by extreme carelessness.

At the first sound of the morning trumpet the friends separated; the Musketeers hastening to the hotel of M. de Treville, the Guards to that of M. Dessessart. Each of the captains then led his company to the Louvre, where the king held his review.

The king was dull and appeared ill, which detracted a little from his usual lofty bearing. In fact, the evening before, a fever had seized him in the midst of the Parliament, while he was holding his Bed of Justice. He had, not the less, decided upon setting out that same evening; and in spite of the remonstrances that had been offered to him, he persisted in having the review, hoping by setting it at defiance to conquer the disease which began to lay hold upon him.

The review over, the Guards set forward alone on their march, the Musketeers waiting for the king, which allowed Porthos time to go and take a turn in his superb equipment in the Rue aux Ours.

The procurator's wife saw him pass in his new uniform and on his fine horse. She loved Porthos too dearly to allow him to part thus; she made him a sign to dismount and come to her. Porthos was magnificent; his spurs jingled, his cuirass glittered, his sword knocked proudly against his ample limbs. This time the clerks evinced no inclination to laugh, such a real ear clipper did Porthos appear.

The Musketeer was introduced to M. Coquenard, whose little gray eyes sparkled with anger at seeing his cousin all blazing new. Nevertheless, one thing afforded him inward consolation; it was expected by everybody that the campaign would be a severe one. He whispered a hope to himself that this beloved relative might be killed in the field.

Porthos paid his compliments to M. Coquenard and bade him farewell. M. Coquenard wished him all sorts of prosperities. As to Mme. Coquenard, she could not restrain her tears; but no evil impressions were taken from her grief as she was known to be very much attached to her relatives, about whom she was constantly having serious disputes with her husband.

But the real adieux were made in Mme. Coquenard's chamber; they were heartrending.

As long as the procurator's wife could follow him with her eyes, she waved her handkerchief to him, leaning so far out of the window as to lead people to believe she wished to precipitate herself. Porthos received all these attentions like a man accustomed to such demonstrations, only on turning the corner of the street he lifted his hat gracefully, and waved it to her as a sign of adieu.

On his part Aramis wrote a long letter. To whom? Nobody knew. Kitty, who was to set out that evening for Tours, was waiting in the next chamber.

Athos sipped the last bottle of his Spanish wine.

In the meantime d'Artagnan was defiling with his company. Arriving at the Faubourg St. Antoine, he turned round to look gaily at the Bastille; but as it was the Bastille alone he looked at, he did not observe Milady, who, mounted upon a light chestnut horse, designated him with her finger to two ill-looking men who came close up to the ranks to take notice of him. To a look of interrogation which they made, Milady replied by a sign that it was he. Then, certain that there could be no mistake in the execution of her orders, she started her horse and disappeared.

The two men followed the company, and on leaving the Faubourg St. Antoine, mounted two horses properly equipped, which a servant without livery had waiting for them.

41 The Seige Of La Rochelle

The Siege of La Rochelle was one of the great political events of the reign of Louis XIII, and one of the great military enterprises of the cardinal. It is, then, interesting and even necessary that we should say a few words about it, particularly as many details of this siege are connected in too important a manner with the story we have undertaken to relate to allow us to pass it over in silence.

The political plans of the cardinal when he undertook this siege were extensive. Let us unfold them first, and then pass on to the private plans which perhaps had not less influence upon his Eminence than the others.

Of the important cities given up by Henry IV to the Huguenots as places of safety, there only remained La Rochelle. It became necessary, therefore, to destroy this last bulwark of Calvinism--a dangerous leaven with which the ferments of civil revolt and foreign war were constantly mingling.

Spaniards, Englishmen, and Italian malcontents, adventurers of all nations, and soldiers of fortune of every sect, flocked at the first summons under the standard of the Protestants, and organized themselves like a vast association, whose branches diverged freely over all parts of Europe.

La Rochelle, which had derived a new importance from the ruin of the other Calvinist cities, was, then, the focus of dissensions and ambition. Moreover, its port was the last in the kingdom of France open to the English, and by closing it against England, our eternal enemy, the cardinal completed the work of Joan of Arc and the Duc de Guise.

Thus Bassompierre, who was at once Protestant and Catholic--Protestant by conviction and Catholic as commander of the order of the Holy Ghost; Bassompierre, who was a German by birth and a Frenchman at heart--in short, Bassompierre, who had a distinguished command at the siege of La Rochelle, said, in charging at the head of several other Protestant nobles like himself, "You will see, gentlemen, that we shall be fools enough to take La Rochelle."

And Bassompierre was right. The cannonade of the Isle of Re presaged to him the dragonnades of the Cevennes; the taking of La Rochelle was the preface to the revocation of the Edict of Nantes.

We have hinted that by the side of these views of the leveling and simplifying minister, which belong to history, the chronicler is forced to recognize the lesser motives of the amorous man and jealous rival.

Richelieu, as everyone knows, had loved the queen. Was this love a simple political affair, or was it naturally one of those profound passions which Anne of Austria inspired in those who approached her? That we are not able to say; but at all events, we have seen, by the anterior developments of this story, that Buckingham had the advantage over him, and in two or three circumstances, particularly that of the diamond studs, had, thanks to the devotedness of the three Musketeers and the courage and conduct of d'Artagnan, cruelly mystified him.

It was, then, Richelieu's object, not only to get rid of an enemy of France, but to avenge himself on a rival; but this vengeance must be grand and striking and worthy in every way of a man who held in his hand, as his weapon for combat, the forces of a kingdom.

Richelieu knew that in combating England he combated Buckingham; that in triumphing over England he triumphed over Buckingham--in short, that in humiliating England in the eyes of Europe he humiliated Buckingham in the eyes of the queen.

On his side Buckingham, in pretending to maintain the honor of England, was moved by interests exactly like those of the cardinal. Buckingham also was pursuing a private vengeance. Buckingham could not under any pretense be admitted into France as an ambassador; he wished to enter it as a conqueror.

It resulted from this that the real stake in this game, which two most powerful kingdoms played for the good pleasure of two amorous men, was simply a kind look from Anne of Austria.

The first advantage had been gained by Buckingham. Arriving unexpectedly in sight of the Isle of Re with ninety vessels and nearly twenty thousand men, he had surprised the Comte de Toiras, who commanded for the king in the Isle, and he had, after a bloody conflict, effected his landing.

Allow us to observe in passing that in this fight perished the Baron de Chantal; that the Baron de Chantal left a little orphan girl eighteen months old, and that this little girl was afterward Mme. de Sevigne.

The Comte de Toiras retired into the citadel St. Martin with his garrison, and threw a hundred men into a little fort called the fort of La Pree.

This event had hastened the resolutions of the cardinal; and till the king and he could take the command of the siege of La Rochelle, which was determined, he had sent Monsieur to direct the first operations, and had ordered all the troops he could dispose of to march toward the theater of war. It was of this detachment, sent as a vanguard, that our friend d'Artagnan formed a part.

The king, as we have said, was to follow as soon as his Bed of Justice had been held; but on rising from his Bed of Justice on the twenty-eighth of June, he felt himself attacked by fever. He was, notwithstanding, anxious to set out; but his illness becoming more serious, he was forced to stop at Villeroy.

Now, whenever the king halted, the Musketeers halted. It followed that d'Artagnan, who was as yet purely and simply in the Guards, found himself, for the time at least, separated from his good friends--Athos, Porthos, and Aramis. This separation, which was no more than an unpleasant circumstance, would have certainly become a cause of serious uneasiness if he had been able to guess by what unknown dangers he was surrounded.

He, however, arrived without accident in the camp established before La Rochelle, of the tenth of the month of September of the year 1627.

Everything was in the same state. The Duke of Buckingham and his English, masters of the Isle of Re, continued to besiege, but without success, the citadel St. Martin and the fort of La Pree; and hostilities with La Rochelle had commenced, two or three days before, about a fort which the Duc d'Angouleme had caused to be constructed near the city.

The Guards, under the command of M. Dessessart, took up their quarters at the Minimes; but, as we know, d'Artagnan, possessed with ambition to enter the Musketeers, had formed but few friendships among his comrades, and he felt himself isolated and given up to his own reflections.

His reflections were not very cheerful. From the time of his arrival in Paris, he had been mixed up with public affairs; but his own private affairs had made no great progress, either in love or fortune. As to love, the only woman he could have loved was Mme. Bonacieux; and Mme. Bonacieux had disappeared, without his being able to discover what had become of her. As to fortune, he had made--he, humble as he was--an enemy of the cardinal; that is to say, of a man before whom trembled the greatest men of the kingdom, beginning with the king.

That man had the power to crush him, and yet he had not done so. For a mind so perspicuous as that of d'Artagnan, this indulgence was a light by which he caught a glimpse of a better future.

Then he had made himself another enemy, less to be feared, he thought; but nevertheless, he instinctively felt, not to be despised. This enemy was Milady.

In exchange for all this, he had acquired the protection and good will of the queen; but the favor of the queen was at the present time an additional cause of persecution, and her protection, as it was known, protected badly--as witness Chalais and Mme. Bonacieux.

What he had clearly gained in all this was the diamond, worth five or six thousand livres, which he wore on his finger; and even this diamond--supposing that d'Artagnan, in his projects of ambition, wished to keep it, to make it someday a pledge for the gratitude of the queen--had not in the meanwhile, since he could not part with it, more value than the gravel he trod under his feet.

We say the gravel he trod under his feet, for d'Artagnan made these reflections while walking solitarily along a pretty little road which led from the camp to the village of Angoutin. Now, these reflections had led him further than he intended, and the day was beginning to decline when, by the last ray of the setting sun, he thought he saw the barrel of a musket glitter from behind a hedge.

D'Artagnan had a quick eye and a prompt understanding. He comprehended that the musket had not come there of itself, and that he who bore it had not concealed himself behind a hedge with any friendly intentions. He determined, therefore, to direct his course as clear from it as he could when, on the opposite side of the road, from behind a rock, he perceived the extremity of another musket.

This was evidently an ambuscade.

The young man cast a glance at the first musket and saw, with a certain degree of inquietude, that it was leveled in his direction; but as soon as he perceived that the orifice of the barrel was motionless, he threw himself upon the ground. At the same instant the gun was fired, and he heard the whistling of a ball pass over his head.

No time was to be lost. D'Artagnan sprang up with a bound, and at the same instant the ball from the other musket tore up the gravel on the very spot on the road where he had thrown himself with his face to the ground.

D'Artagnan was not one of those foolhardy men who seek a ridiculous death in order that it may be said of them that they did not retreat a single step. Besides, courage was out of the question here; d'Artagnan had fallen into an ambush.

"If there is a third shot," said he to himself, "I am a lost man."

He immediately, therefore, took to his heels and ran toward the camp, with the swiftness of the young men of his country, so renowned for their agility; but whatever might be his speed, the first who fired, having had time to reload, fired a second shot, and this time so well aimed that it struck his hat, and carried it ten paces from him.

As he, however, had no other hat, he picked up this as he ran, and arrived at his quarters very pale and quite out of breath. He sat down without saying a word to anybody, and began to reflect.

This event might have three causes:

The first and the most natural was that it might be an ambuscade of the Rochellais, who might not be sorry to kill one of his Majesty's Guards, because it would be an enemy the less, and this enemy might have a well-furnished purse in his pocket.

D'Artagnan took his hat, examined the hole made by the ball, and shook his head. The ball was not a musket ball--it was an arquebus ball. The accuracy of the aim had first given him the idea that a special weapon had been employed. This could not, then, be a military ambuscade, as the ball was not of the regular caliber.

This might be a kind remembrance of Monsieur the Cardinal. It may be observed that at the very moment when, thanks to the ray of the sun, he perceived the gun barrel, he was thinking with astonishment on the forbearance of his Eminence with respect to him.

But d'Artagnan again shook his head. For people toward whom he had but to put forth his hand, his Eminence had rarely recourse to such means.

It might be a vengeance of Milady; that was most probable.

He tried in vain to remember the faces or dress of the assassins; he had escaped so rapidly that he had not had leisure to notice anything.

"Ah, my poor friends!" murmured d'Artagnan; "where are you? And that you should fail me!"

D'Artagnan passed a very bad night. Three or four times he started up, imagining that a man was approaching his bed for the purpose of stabbing him. Nevertheless, day dawned without darkness having brought any accident.

But d'Artagnan well suspected that that which was deferred was not relinquished.

D'Artagnan remained all day in his quarters, assigning as a reason to himself that the weather was bad.

At nine o'clock the next morning, the drums beat to arms. The Duc d'Orleans visited the posts. The guards were under arms, and d'Artagnan took his place in the midst of his comrades.

Monsieur passed along the front of the line; then all the superior officers approached him to pay their compliments, M. Dessessart, captain of the Guards, as well as the others.

At the expiration of a minute or two, it appeared to d'Artagnan that M. Dessessart made him a sign to approach. He waited for a fresh gesture on the part of his superior, for fear he might be mistaken; but this gesture being repeated, he left the ranks, and advanced to receive orders.

"Monsieur is about to ask for some men of good will for a dangerous mission, but one which will do honor to those who shall accomplish it; and I made you a sign in order that you might hold yourself in readiness."

"Thanks, my captain!" replied d'Artagnan, who wished for nothing better than an opportunity to distinguish himself under the eye of the lieutenant general.

In fact the Rochellais had made a sortie during the night, and had retaken a bastion of which the royal army had gained possession two days before. The matter was to ascertain, by reconnoitering, how the enemy guarded this bastion.

At the end of a few minutes Monsieur raised his voice, and said, "I want for this mission three or four volunteers, led by a man who can be depended upon."

"As to the man to be depended upon, I have him under my hand, monsieur," said M. Dessessart, pointing to d'Artagnan; "and as to the four or five volunteers, Monsieur has but to make his intentions known, and the men will not be wanting."

"Four men of good will who will risk being killed with me!" said d'Artagnan, raising his sword.

Two of his comrades of the Guards immediately sprang forward, and two other soldiers having joined them, the number was deemed sufficient. D'Artagnan declined all others, being unwilling to take the first chance from those who had the priority.

It was not known whether, after the taking of the bastion, the Rochellais had evacuated it or left a garrison in it; the object then was to examine the place near enough to verify the reports.

D'Artagnan set out with his four companions, and followed the trench; the two Guards marched abreast with him, and the two soldiers followed behind.

They arrived thus, screened by the lining of the trench, till they came within a hundred paces of the bastion. There, on turning round, d'Artagnan perceived that the two soldiers had disappeared.

He thought that, beginning to be afraid, they had stayed behind, and he continued to advance.

At the turning of the counterscarp they found themselves within about sixty paces of the bastion. They saw no one, and the bastion seemed abandoned.

The three composing our forlorn hope were deliberating whether they should proceed any further, when all at once a circle of smoke enveloped the giant of stone, and a dozen balls came whistling around d'Artagnan and his companions.

They knew all they wished to know; the bastion was guarded. A longer stay in this dangerous spot would have been useless imprudence. D'Artagnan and his two companions turned their backs, and commenced a retreat which resembled a flight.

On arriving at the angle of the trench which was to serve them as a rampart, one of the Guardsmen fell. A ball had passed through his breast. The other, who was safe and sound, continued his way toward the camp.

D'Artagnan was not willing to abandon his companion thus, and stooped to raise him and assist him in regaining the lines; but at this moment two shots were fired. One ball struck the head of the already-wounded guard, and the other flattened itself against a rock, after having passed within two inches of d'Artagnan.

The young man turned quickly round, for this attack could not have come from the bastion, which was hidden by the angle of the trench. The idea of the two soldiers who had abandoned him occurred to his mind, and with them he remembered the assassins of two evenings before. He resolved this time to know with whom he had to deal, and fell upon the body of his comrade as if he were dead.

He quickly saw two heads appear above an abandoned work within thirty paces of him; they were the heads of the two soldiers. D'Artagnan had not been deceived; these two men had only followed for the purpose of assassinating him, hoping that the young man's death would be placed to the account of the enemy.

As he might be only wounded and might denounce their crime, they came up to him with the purpose of making sure. Fortunately, deceived by d'Artagnan's trick, they neglected to reload their guns.

When they were within ten paces of him, d'Artagnan, who in falling had taken care not to let go his sword, sprang up close to them.

The assassins comprehended that if they fled toward the camp without having killed their man, they should be accused by him; therefore their first idea was to join the enemy. One of them took his gun by the barrel, and used it as he would a club. He aimed a terrible blow at d'Artagnan, who avoided it by springing to one side; but by this movement he left a passage free to the bandit, who darted off toward the bastion. As the Rochellais who guarded the bastion were ignorant of the intentions of the man they saw coming toward them, they fired upon him, and he fell, struck by a ball which broke his shoulder.

Meantime d'Artagnan had thrown himself upon the other soldier, attacking him with his sword. The conflict was not long; the wretch had nothing to defend himself with but his discharged arquebus. The sword of the Guardsman slipped along the barrel of the now-useless weapon, and passed through the thigh of the assassin, who fell.

D'Artagnan immediately placed the point of his sword at his throat.

"Oh, do not kill me!" cried the bandit. "Pardon, pardon, my officer, and I will tell you all."

"Is your secret of enough importance to me to spare your life for it?" asked the young man, withholding his arm.

"Yes; if you think existence worth anything to a man of twenty, as you are, and who may hope for everything, being handsome and brave, as you are."

"Wretch," cried d'Artagnan, "speak quickly! Who employed you to assassinate me?"

"A woman whom I don't know, but who is called Milady."

"But if you don't know this woman, how do you know her name?"

"My comrade knows her, and called her so. It was with him she agreed, and not with me; he even has in his pocket a letter from that person, who attaches great importance to you, as I have heard him say."

"But how did you become concerned in this villainous affair?"

"He proposed to me to undertake it with him, and I agreed."

"And how much did she give you for this fine enterprise?"

"A hundred louis."

"Well, come!" said the young man, laughing, "she thinks I am worth something. A hundred louis? Well, that was a temptation for two wretches like you. I understand why you accepted it, and I grant you my pardon; but upon one condition."

"What is that?" said the soldier, uneasy at perceiving that all was not over.

"That you will go and fetch me the letter your comrade has in his pocket."

"But," cried the bandit, "that is only another way of killing me. How can I go and fetch that letter under the fire of the bastion?"

"You must nevertheless make up your mind to go and get it, or I swear you shall die by my hand."

"Pardon, monsieur; pity! In the name of that young lady you love, and whom you perhaps believe dead but who is not!" cried the bandit, throwing himself upon his knees and leaning upon his hand--for he began to lose his strength with his blood.

"And how do you know there is a young woman whom I love, and that I believed that woman dead?" asked d'Artagnan.

"By that letter which my comrade has in his pocket."

"You see, then," said d'Artagnan, "that I must have that letter. So no more delay, no more hesitation; or else whatever may be my repugnance to soiling my sword a second time with the blood of a wretch like you, I swear by my faith as an honest man--" and at these words d'Artagnan made so fierce a gesture that the wounded man sprang up.

"Stop, stop!" cried he, regaining strength by force of terror. "I will go--I will go!"

D'Artagnan took the soldier's arquebus, made him go on before him, and urged him toward his companion by pricking him behind with his sword.

It was a frightful thing to see this wretch, leaving a long track of blood on the ground he passed over, pale with approaching death, trying to drag himself along without being seen to the body of his accomplice, which lay twenty paces from him.

Terror was so strongly painted on his face, covered with a cold sweat, that d'Artagnan took pity on him, and casting upon him a look of contempt, "Stop," said he, "I will show you the difference between a man of courage and such a coward as you. Stay where you are; I will go myself."

And with a light step, an eye on the watch, observing the movements of the enemy and taking advantage of the accidents of the ground, d'Artagnan succeeded in reaching the second soldier.

There were two means of gaining his object--to search him on the spot, or to carry him away, making a buckler of his body, and search him in the trench.

D'Artagnan preferred the second means, and lifted the assassin onto his shoulders at the moment the enemy fired.

A slight shock, the dull noise of three balls which penetrated the flesh, a last cry, a convulsion of agony, proved to d'Artagnan that the would-be assassin had saved his life.

D'Artagnan regained the trench, and threw the corpse beside the wounded man, who was as pale as death.

Then he began to search. A leather pocketbook, a purse, in which was evidently a part of the sum which the bandit had received, with a dice box and dice, completed the possessions of the dead man.

He left the box and dice where they fell, threw the purse to the wounded man, and eagerly opened the pocketbook.

Among some unimportant papers he found the following letter, that which he had sought at the risk of his life:

"Since you have lost sight of that woman and she is now in safety in the convent, which you should never have allowed her to reach, try, at least, not to miss the man. If you do, you know that my hand stretches far, and that you shall pay very dearly for the hundred louis you have from me."

No signature. Nevertheless it was plain the letter came from Milady. He consequently kept it as a piece of evidence, and being in safety behind the angle of the trench, he began to interrogate the wounded man. He confessed that he had undertaken with his comrade--the same who was killed--to carry off a young woman who was to leave Paris by the Barriere de La Villette; but having stopped to drink at a cabaret, they had missed the carriage by ten minutes.

"But what were you to do with that woman?" asked d'Artagnan, with anguish.

"We were to have conveyed her to a hotel in the Place Royale," said the wounded man.

"Yes, yes!" murmured d'Artagnan; "that's the place--Milady's own residence!"

Then the young man tremblingly comprehended what a terrible thirst for vengeance urged this woman on to destroy him, as well as all who loved him, and how well she must be acquainted with the affairs of the court, since she had discovered all. There could be no doubt she owed this information to the cardinal.

But amid all this he perceived, with a feeling of real joy, that the queen must have discovered the prison in which poor Mme. Bonacieux was explaining her devotion, and that she had freed her from that prison; and the letter he had received from the young woman, and her passage along the road of Chaillot like an apparition, were now explained.

Then also, as Athos had predicted, it became possible to find Mme. Bonacieux, and a convent was not impregnable.

This idea completely restored clemency to his heart. He turned toward the wounded man, who had watched with intense anxiety all the various expressions of his countenance, and holding out his arm to him, said, "Come, I will not abandon you thus. Lean upon me, and let us return to the camp."

"Yes," said the man, who could scarcely believe in such magnanimity, "but is it not to have me hanged?"

"You have my word," said he; "for the second time I give you your life."

The wounded man sank upon his knees, to again kiss the feet of his preserver; but d'Artagnan, who had no longer a motive for staying so near the enemy, abridged the testimonials of his gratitude.

The Guardsman who had returned at the first discharge announced the death of his four companions. They were therefore much astonished and delighted in the regiment when they saw the young man come back safe and sound.

D'Artagnan explained the sword wound of his companion by a sortie which he improvised. He described the death of the other soldier, and the perils they had encountered. This recital was for him the occasion of veritable triumph. The whole army talked of this expedition for a day, and Monsieur paid him his compliments upon it. Besides this, as every great action bears its recompense with it, the brave exploit of d'Artagnan resulted in the restoration of the tranquility he had lost. In fact, d'Artagnan believed that he might be tranquil, as one of his two enemies was killed and the other devoted to his interests.

This tranquillity proved one thing--that d'Artagnan did not yet know Milady.

42 The Anjou Wine

After the most disheartening news of the king's health, a report of his convalescence began to prevail in the camp; and as he was very anxious to be in person at the siege, it was said that as soon as he could mount a horse he would set forward.

Meantime, Monsieur, who knew that from one day to the other he might expect to be removed from his command by the Duc d'Angouleme, by Bassompierre, or by Schomberg, who were all eager for his post, did but little, lost his days in wavering, and did not dare to attempt any great enterprise to drive the English from the Isle of Re, where they still besieged the citadel St. Martin and the fort of La Pree, as on their side the French were besieging La Rochelle.

D'Artagnan, as we have said, had become more tranquil, as always happens after a past danger, particularly when the danger seems to have vanished. He only felt one uneasiness, and that was at not hearing any tidings from his friends.

But one morning at the commencement of the month of November everything was explained to him by this letter, dated from Villeroy:

M d'Artagnan,

MM Athos, Porthos, and Aramis, after having had an entertainment at my house and enjoying themselves very much, created such a disturbance that the provost of the castle, a rigid man, has ordered them to be confined for some days; but I accomplish the order they have given me by forwarding to you a dozen bottles of my Anjou wine, with which they are much pleased. They are desirous that you should drink to their health in their favorite wine. I have done this, and am, monsieur, with great respect,

Your very humble and obedient servant,

Godeau, Purveyor of the Musketeers

"That's all well!" cried d'Artagnan. "They think of me in their pleasures, as I thought of them in my troubles. Well, I will certainly drink to their health with all my heart, but I will not drink alone."

And d'Artagnan went among those Guardsmen with whom he had formed greater intimacy than with the others, to invite them to enjoy with him this present of delicious Anjou wine which had been sent him from Villeroy.

One of the two Guardsmen was engaged that evening, and another the next, so the meeting was fixed for the day after that.

D'Artagnan, on his return, sent the twelve bottles of wine to the refreshment room of the Guards, with strict orders that great care should be taken of it; and then, on the day appointed, as the dinner was fixed for midday d'Artagnan sent Planchet at nine in the morning to assist in preparing everything for the entertainment.

Planchet, very proud of being raised to the dignity of landlord, thought he would make all ready, like an intelligent man; and with this view called in the assistance of the lackey of one of his master's guests, named Fourreau, and the false soldier who had tried to kill d'Artagnan and who, belonging to no corps, had entered into the service of d'Artagnan, or rather of Planchet, after d'Artagnan had saved his life.

The hour of the banquet being come, the two guards arrived, took their places, and the dishes were arranged on the table. Planchet waited, towel on arm; Fourreau uncorked the bottles; and Brisemont, which was the name of the convalescent, poured the wine, which was a little shaken by its journey, carefully into decanters. Of this wine, the first bottle being a little thick at the bottom, Brisemont poured the lees into a glass, and d'Artagnan desired him to drink it, for the poor devil had not yet recovered his strength.

The guests having eaten the soup, were about to lift the first glass of wine to their lips, when all at once the cannon sounded from Fort Louis and Fort Neuf. The Guardsmen, imagining this to be caused by some unexpected attack, either of the besieged or the English, sprang to their swords. D'Artagnan, not less forward than they, did likewise, and all ran out, in order to repair to their posts.

But scarcely were they out of the room before they were made aware of the cause of this noise. Cries of "Live the king! Live the cardinal!" resounded on every side, and the drums were beaten in all directions.

In short, the king, impatient, as has been said, had come by forced marches, and had that moment arrived with all his household and a reinforcement of ten thousand troops. His Musketeers proceeded and followed him. D'Artagnan, placed in line with his company, saluted with an expressive gesture his three friends, whose eyes soon discovered him, and M. de Treville, who detected him at once.

The ceremony of reception over, the four friends were soon in one another's arms.

"Pardieu!" cried d'Artagnan, "you could not have arrived in better time; the dinner cannot have had time to get cold! Can it, gentlemen?" added the young man, turning to the two Guards, whom he introduced to his friends.

"Ah, ah!" said Porthos, "it appears we are feasting!"

"I hope," said Aramis, "there are no women at your dinner."

"Is there any drinkable wine in your tavern?" asked Athos.

"Well, pardieu! there is yours, my dear friend," replied d'Artagnan.

"Our wine!" said Athos, astonished.

"Yes, that you sent me."

"We sent you wine?"

"You know very well--the wine from the hills of Anjou."

"Yes, I know what brand you are talking about."

"The wine you prefer."

"Well, in the absence of champagne and chambertin, you must content yourselves with that."

"And so, connoisseurs in wine as we are, we have sent you some Anjou wine?" said Porthos.

"Not exactly, it is the wine that was sent by your order."

"On our account?" said the three Musketeers.

"Did you send this wine, Aramis?" said Athos.

"No; and you, Porthos?"

"No; and you, Athos?"

"No!"

"If it was not you, it was your purveyor," said d'Artagnan.

"Our purveyor!"

"Yes, your purveyor, Godeau--the purveyor of the Musketeers."

"My faith! never mind where it comes from," said Porthos, "let us taste it, and if it is good, let us drink it."

"No," said Athos; "don't let us drink wine which comes from an unknown source."

"You are right, Athos," said d'Artagnan. "Did none of you charge your purveyor, Godeau, to send me some wine?"

"No! And yet you say he has sent you some as from us?"

"Here is his letter," said d'Artagnan, and he presented the note to his comrades.

"This is not his writing!" said Athos. "I am acquainted with it; before we left Villeroy I settled the accounts of the regiment."

"A false letter altogether," said Porthos, "we have not been disciplined."

"d'Artagnan," said Aramis, in a reproachful tone, "how could you believe that we had made a disturbance?"

D'Artagnan grew pale, and a convulsive trembling shook all his limbs.

"Thou alarmest me!" said Athos, who never used thee and thou but upon very particular occasions, "what has happened?"

"Look you, my friends!" cried d'Artagnan, "a horrible suspicion crosses my mind! Can this be another vengeance of that woman?"

It was now Athos who turned pale.

D'Artagnan rushed toward the refreshment room, the three Musketeers and the two Guards following him.

The first object that met the eyes of d'Artagnan on entering the room was Brisemont, stretched upon the ground and rolling in horrible convulsions.

Planchet and Fourreau, as pale as death, were trying to give him succor; but it was plain that all assistance was useless--all the features of the dying man were distorted with agony.

"Ah!" cried he, on perceiving d'Artagnan, "ah! this is frightful! You pretend to pardon me, and you poison me!"

"I!" cried d'Artagnan. "I, wretch? What do you say?"

"I say that it was you who gave me the wine; I say that it was you who desired me to drink it. I say you wished to avenge yourself on me, and I say that it is horrible!"

"Do not think so, Brisemont," said d'Artagnan; "do not think so. I swear to you, I protest--"

"Oh, but God is above! God will punish you! My God, grant that he may one day suffer what I suffer!"

"Upon the Gospel," said d'Artagnan, throwing himself down by the dying man, "I swear to you that the wine was poisoned and that I was going to drink of it as you did."

"I do not believe you," cried the soldier, and he expired amid horrible tortures.

"Frightful! frightful!" murmured Athos, while Porthos broke the bottles and Aramis gave orders, a little too late, that a confessor should be sent for.

"Oh, my friends," said d'Artagnan, "you come once more to save my life, not only mine but that of these gentlemen. Gentlemen," continued he, addressing the Guardsmen, "I request you will be silent with regard to this adventure. Great personages may have had a hand in what you have seen, and if talked about, the evil would only recoil upon us."

"Ah, monsieur!" stammered Planchet, more dead than alive, "ah, monsieur, what an escape I have had!"

"How, sirrah! you were going to drink my wine?"

"To the health of the king, monsieur; I was going to drink a small glass of it if Fourreau had not told me I was called."

"Alas!" said Fourreau, whose teeth chattered with terror, "I wanted to get him out of the way that I might drink myself."

"Gentlemen," said d'Artagnan, addressing the Guardsmen, "you may easily comprehend that such a feast can only be very dull after what has taken place; so accept my excuses, and put off the party till another day, I beg of you."

The two Guardsmen courteously accepted d'Artagnan's excuses, and perceiving that the four friends desired to be alone, retired.

When the young Guardsman and the three Musketeers were without witnesses, they looked at one another with an air which plainly expressed that each of them perceived the gravity of their situation.

"In the first place," said Athos, "let us leave this chamber; the dead are not agreeable company, particularly when they have died a violent death."

"Planchet," said d'Artagnan, "I commit the corpse of this poor devil to your care. Let him be interred in holy ground. He committed a crime, it is true; but he repented of it."

And the four friends quit the room, leaving to Planchet and Fourreau the duty of paying mortuary honors to Brisemont.

The host gave them another chamber, and served them with fresh eggs and some water, which Athos went himself to draw at the fountain. In a few words, Porthos and Aramis were posted as to the situation.

"Well," said d'Artagnan to Athos, "you see, my dear friend, that this is war to the death."

Athos shook his head.

"Yes, yes," replied he, "I perceive that plainly; but do you really believe it is she?"

"I am sure of it."

"Nevertheless, I confess I still doubt."

"But the fleur-de-lis on her shoulder?"

"She is some Englishwoman who has committed a crime in France, and has been branded in consequence."

"Athos, she is your wife, I tell you," repeated d'Artagnan; "only reflect how much the two descriptions resemble each other."

"Yes; but I should think the other must be dead, I hanged her so effectually."

It was d'Artagnan who now shook his head in his turn.

"But in either case, what is to be done?" said the young man.

"The fact is, one cannot remain thus, with a sword hanging eternally over his head," said Athos. "We must extricate ourselves from this position."

"But how?"

"Listen! You must try to see her, and have an explanation with her. Say to her: 'Peace or war! My word as a gentleman never to say anything of you, never to do anything against you; on your side, a solemn oath to remain neutral with respect to me. If not, I will apply to the chancellor, I will apply to the king, I will apply to the hangman, I will move the courts against you, I will denounce you as branded, I will bring you to trial; and if you are acquitted, well, by the faith of a gentleman, I will kill you at the corner of some wall, as I would a mad dog.'"

"I like the means well enough," said d'Artagnan, "but where and how to meet with her?"

"Time, dear friend, time brings round opportunity; opportunity is the martingale of man. The more we have ventured the more we gain, when we know how to wait."

"Yes; but to wait surrounded by assassins and poisoners."

"Bah!" said Athos. "God has preserved us hitherto, God will preserve us still."

"Yes, we. Besides, we are men; and everything considered, it is our lot to risk our lives; but she," asked he, in an undertone.

"What she?" asked Athos.

"Constance."

"Madame Bonacieux! Ah, that's true!" said Athos. "My poor friend, I had forgotten you were in love."

"Well, but," said Aramis, "have you not learned by the letter you found on the wretched corpse that she is in a convent? One may be very comfortable in a convent; and as soon as the siege of La Rochelle is terminated, I promise you on my part--"

"Good," cried Athos, "good! Yes, my dear Aramis, we all know that your views have a religious tendency."

"I am only temporarily a Musketeer," said Aramis, humbly.

"It is some time since we heard from his mistress," said Athos, in a low voice. "But take no notice; we know all about that."

"Well," said Porthos, "it appears to me that the means are very simple."

"What?" asked d'Artagnan.

"You say she is in a convent?" replied Porthos.

"Yes."

"Very well. As soon as the siege is over, we'll carry her off from that convent."

"But we must first learn what convent she is in."

"That's true," said Porthos.

"But I think I have it," said Athos. "Don't you say, dear d'Artagnan, that it is the queen who has made choice of the convent for her?"

"I believe so, at least."

"In that case Porthos will assist us."

"And how so, if you please?"

"Why, by your marchioness, your duchess, your princess. She must have a long arm."

"Hush!" said Porthos, placing a finger on his lips. "I believe her to be a cardinalist; she must know nothing of the matter."

"Then," said Aramis, "I take upon myself to obtain intelligence of her."

"You, Aramis?" cried the three friends. "You! And how?"

"By the queen's almoner, to whom I am very intimately allied," said Aramis, coloring.

And on this assurance, the four friends, who had finished their modest repast, separated, with the promise of meeting again that evening. D'Artagnan returned to less important affairs, and the three Musketeers repaired to the king's quarters, where they had to prepare their lodging.

43 The Sign Of The Red Dovecot

Meanwhile the king, who, with more reason than the cardinal, showed his hatred for Buckingham, although scarcely arrived was in such a haste to meet the enemy that he commanded every disposition to be made to drive the English from the Isle of Re, and afterward to press the siege of La Rochelle; but notwithstanding his earnest wish, he was delayed by the dissensions which broke out between MM Bassompierre and Schomberg, against the Duc d'Angouleme.

MM Bassompierre and Schomberg were marshals of France, and claimed their right of commanding the army under the orders of the king; but the cardinal, who feared that Bassompierre, a Huguenot at heart, might press but feebly the English and Rochellais, his brothers in religion, supported the Duc d'Angouleme, whom the king, at his instigation, had named lieutenant general. The result was that to prevent MM Bassompierre and Schomberg from deserting the army, a separate command had to be given to each. Bassompierre took up his quarters on the north of the city, between Leu and Dompierre; the Duc d'Angouleme on the east, from Dompierre to Perigny; and M. de Schomberg on the south, from Perigny to Angoutin.

The quarters of Monsieur were at Dompierre; the quarters of the king were sometimes at Estree, sometimes at Jarrie; the cardinal's quarters were upon the downs, at the bridge of La Pierre, in a simple house without any entrenchment. So that Monsieur watched Bassompierre; the king, the Duc d'Angouleme; and the cardinal, M. de Schomberg.

As soon as this organization was established, they set about driving the English from the Isle.

The juncture was favorable. The English, who require, above everything, good living in order to be good soldiers, only eating salt meat and bad biscuit, had many invalids in their camp. Still further, the sea, very rough at this period of the year all along the sea coast, destroyed every day some little vessel; and the shore, from the point of l'Aiguillon to the trenches, was at every tide literally covered with the wrecks of pinnacles, roberges, and feluccas. The result was that even if the king's troops remained quietly in their camp, it was evident that some day or other, Buckingham, who only continued in the Isle from obstinacy, would be obliged to raise the siege.

But as M. de Toiras gave information that everything was preparing in the enemy's camp for a fresh assault, the king judged that it would be best to put an end to the affair, and gave the necessary orders for a decisive action.

As it is not our intention to give a journal of the siege, but on the contrary only to describe such of the events of it as are connected with the story we are relating, we will content ourselves with saying in two words that the expedition succeeded, to the great astonishment of the king and the great glory of the cardinal. The English, repulsed foot by foot, beaten in all encounters, and defeated in the passage of the Isle of Loie, were obliged to re-embark, leaving on the field of battle two thousand men, among whom were five colonels, three lieutenant colonels, two hundred and fifty captains, twenty gentlemen of rank, four pieces of cannon, and sixty flags, which were taken to Paris by Claude de St. Simon, and suspended with great pomp in the arches of Notre Dame.

Te Deums were chanted in camp, and afterward throughout France.

The cardinal was left free to carry on the siege, without having, at least at the present, anything to fear on the part of the English.

But it must be acknowledged, this response was but momentary. An envoy of the Duke of Buckingham, named Montague, was taken, and proof was obtained of a league between the German Empire, Spain, England, and Lorraine. This league was directed against France.

Still further, in Buckingham's lodging, which he had been forced to abandon more precipitately than he expected, papers were found which confirmed this alliance and which, as the cardinal asserts in his memoirs, strongly compromised Mme. de Chevreuse and consequently the queen.

It was upon the cardinal that all the responsibility fell, for one is not a despotic minister without responsibility. All, therefore, of the vast resources of his genius were at work night and day, engaged in listening to the least report heard in any of the great kingdoms of Europe.

The cardinal was acquainted with the activity, and more particularly the hatred, of Buckingham. If the league which threatened France triumphed, all his influence would be lost. Spanish policy and Austrian policy would have their representatives in the cabinet of the Louvre, where they had as yet but partisans; and he, Richelieu--the French minister, the national minister--would be ruined. The king, even while obeying him like a child, hated him as a child hates his master, and would abandon him to the personal vengeance of Monsieur and the queen. He would then be lost, and France, perhaps, with him. All this must be prepared against.

Courtiers, becoming every instant more numerous, succeeded one another, day and night, in the little house of the bridge of La Pierre, in which the cardinal had established his residence.

There were monks who wore the frock with such an ill grace that it was easy to perceive they belonged to the church militant; women a little inconvenienced by their costume as pages and whose large trousers could not entirely conceal their rounded forms; and peasants with blackened hands but with fine limbs, savoring of the man of quality a league off.

There were also less agreeable visits--for two or three times reports were spread that the cardinal had nearly been assassinated.

It is true that the enemies of the cardinal said that it was he himself who set these bungling assassins to work, in order to have, if wanted, the right of using reprisals; but we must not believe everything ministers say, nor everything their enemies say.

These attempts did not prevent the cardinal, to whom his most inveterate detractors have never denied personal bravery, from making nocturnal excursions, sometimes to communicate to the Duc d'Angouleme important orders, sometimes to confer with the king, and sometimes to have an interview with a messenger whom he did not wish to see at home.

On their part the Musketeers, who had not much to do with the siege, were not under very strict orders and led a joyous life. The was the more easy for our three companions in particular; for being friends of M. de Treville, they obtained from him special permission to be absent after the closing of the camp.

Now, one evening when d'Artagnan, who was in the trenches, was not able to accompany them, Athos, Porthos, and Aramis, mounted on their battle steeds, enveloped in their war cloaks, with their hands upon their pistol butts, were returning from a drinking place called the Red Dovecot, which Athos had discovered two days before upon the route to Jarrie, following the road which led to the camp and quite on their guard, as we have stated, for fear of an ambuscade, when, about a quarter of a league from the village of Boisnau, they fancied they heard the sound of horses approaching them. They immediately all three halted, closed in, and waited, occupying the middle of the road. In an instant, and as the moon broke from behind a cloud, they saw at a turning of the road two horsemen who, on perceiving them, stopped in their turn, appearing to deliberate whether they should continue their route or go back. The hesitation created some suspicion in the three friends, and Athos, advancing a few paces in front of the others, cried in a firm voice, "Who goes there?"

"Who goes there, yourselves?" replied one of the horsemen.

"That is not an answer," replied Athos. "Who goes there? Answer, or we charge."

"Beware of what you are about, gentlemen!" said a clear voice which seemed accustomed to command.

"It is some superior officer making his night rounds," said Athos. "What do you wish, gentlemen?"

"Who are you?" said the same voice, in the same commanding tone. "Answer in your turn, or you may repent of your disobedience."

"King's Musketeers," said Athos, more and more convinced that he who interrogated them had the right to do so.

"What company?"

"Company of Treville."

"Advance, and give an account of what you are doing here at this hour."

The three companions advanced rather humbly--for all were now convinced that they had to do with someone more powerful than themselves--leaving Athos the post of speaker.

One of the two riders, he who had spoken second, was ten paces in front of his companion. Athos made a sign to Porthos and Aramis also to remain in the rear, and advanced alone.

"Your pardon, my officer," said Athos; "but we were ignorant with whom we had to do, and you may see that we were good guard."

"Your name?" said the officer, who covered a part of his face with his cloak.

"But yourself, monsieur," said Athos, who began to be annoyed by this inquisition, "give me, I beg you, the proof that you have the right to question me."

"Your name?" repeated the cavalier a second time, letting his cloak fall, and leaving his face uncovered.

"Monsieur the Cardinal!" cried the stupefied Musketeer.

"Your name?" cried his Eminence, for the third time.

"Athos," said the Musketeer.

The cardinal made a sign to his attendant, who drew near. "These three Musketeers shall follow us," said he, in an undertone. "I am not willing it should be known I have left the camp; and if they follow us we shall be certain they will tell nobody."

"We are gentlemen, monseigneur," said Athos; "require our parole, and give yourself no uneasiness. Thank God, we can keep a secret."

The cardinal fixed his piercing eyes on this courageous speaker.

"You have a quick ear, Monsieur Athos," said the cardinal; "but now listen to this. It is not from mistrust that I request you to follow me, but for my security. Your companions are no doubt Messieurs Porthos and Aramis."

"Yes, your Eminence," said Athos, while the two Musketeers who had remained behind advanced hat in hand.

"I know you, gentlemen," said the cardinal, "I know you. I know you are not quite my friends, and I am sorry you are not so; but I know you are brave and loyal gentlemen, and that confidence may be placed in you. Monsieur Athos, do me, then, the honor to accompany me; you and your two friends, and then I shall have an escort to excite envy in his Majesty, if we should meet him."

The three Musketeers bowed to the necks of their horses.

"Well, upon my honor," said Athos, "your Eminence is right in taking us with you; we have seen several ill-looking faces on the road, and we have even had a quarrel at the Red Dovecot with four of those faces."

"A quarrel, and what for, gentlemen?" said the cardinal; "you know I don't like quarrelers."

"And that is the reason why I have the honor to inform your Eminence of what has happened; for you might learn it from others, and upon a false account believe us to be in fault."

"What have been the results of your quarrel?" said the cardinal, knitting his brow.

"My friend, Aramis, here, has received a slight sword wound in the arm, but not enough to prevent him, as your Eminence may see, from mounting to the assault tomorrow, if your Eminence orders an escalade."

"But you are not the men to allow sword wounds to be inflicted upon you thus," said the cardinal. "Come, be frank, gentlemen, you have settled accounts with somebody! Confess; you know I have the right of giving absolution."

"I, monseigneur?" said Athos. "I did not even draw my sword, but I took him who offended me round the body, and threw him out of the window. It appears that in falling," continued Athos, with some hesitation, "he broke his thigh."

"Ah, ah!" said the cardinal; "and you, Monsieur Porthos?"

"I, monseigneur, knowing that dueling is prohibited--I seized a bench, and gave one of those brigands such a blow that I believe his shoulder is broken."

"Very well," said the cardinal; "and you, Monsieur Aramis?"

"Monseigneur, being of a very mild disposition, and being, likewise, of which Monseigneur perhaps is not aware, about to enter into orders, I endeavored to appease my comrades, when one of these wretches gave me a wound with a sword, treacherously, across my left arm. Then I admit my patience failed me; I drew my sword in my turn, and as he came back to the charge, I fancied I felt that in throwing himself upon me, he let it pass through his body. I only know for a certainty that he fell; and it seemed to me that he was borne away with his two companions."

"The devil, gentlemen!" said the cardinal, "three men placed hors de combat in a cabaret squabble! You don't do your work by halves. And pray what was this quarrel about?"

"These fellows were drunk," said Athos, "and knowing there was a lady who had arrived at the cabaret this evening, they wanted to force her door."

"Force her door!" said the cardinal, "and for what purpose?"

"To do her violence, without doubt," said Athos. "I have had the honor of informing your Eminence that these men were drunk."

"And was this lady young and handsome?" asked the cardinal, with a certain degree of anxiety.

"We did not see her, monseigneur," said Athos.

"You did not see her? Ah, very well," replied the cardinal, quickly. "You did well to defend the honor of a woman; and as I am going to the Red Dovecot myself, I shall know if you have told me the truth."

"Monseigneur," said Athos, haughtily, "we are gentlemen, and to save our heads we would not be guilty of a falsehood."

"Therefore I do not doubt what you say, Monsieur Athos, I do not doubt it for a single instant; but," added he, "to change the conversation, was this lady alone?"

"The lady had a cavalier shut up with her," said Athos, "but as notwithstanding the noise, this cavalier did not show himself, it is to be presumed that he is a coward."

"'Judge not rashly', says the Gospel," replied the cardinal.

Athos bowed.

"And now, gentlemen, that's well," continued the cardinal. "I know what I wish to know; follow me."

The three Musketeers passed behind his Eminence, who again enveloped his face in his cloak, and put his horse in motion, keeping from eight to ten paces in advance of his four companions.

They soon arrived at the silent, solitary inn. No doubt the host knew what illustrious visitor was expected, and had consequently sent intruders out of the way.

Ten paces from the door the cardinal made a sign to his esquire and the three Musketeers to halt. A saddled horse was fastened to the window shutter. The cardinal knocked three times, and in a peculiar manner.

A man, enveloped in a cloak, came out immediately, and exchanged some rapid words with the cardinal; after which he mounted his horse, and set off in the direction of Surgeres, which was likewise the way to Paris.

"Advance, gentlemen," said the cardinal.

"You have told me the truth, my gentlemen," said he, addressing the Musketeers, "and it will not be my fault if our encounter this evening be not advantageous to you. In the meantime, follow me."

The cardinal alighted; the three Musketeers did likewise. The cardinal threw the bridle of his horse to his esquire; the three Musketeers fastened the horses to the shutters.

The host stood at the door. For him, the cardinal was only an officer coming to visit a lady.

"Have you any chamber on the ground floor where these gentlemen can wait near a good fire?" said the cardinal.

The host opened the door of a large room, in which an old stove had just been replaced by a large and excellent chimney.

"I have this," said he.

"That will do," replied the cardinal. "Enter, gentlemen, and be kind enough to wait for me; I shall not be more than half an hour."

And while the three Musketeers entered the ground floor room, the cardinal, without asking further information, ascended the staircase like a man who has no need of having his road pointed out to him.

44 The Utility Of Stovepipes

It was evident that without suspecting it, and actuated solely by their chivalrous and adventurous character, our three friends had just rendered a service to someone the cardinal honored with his special protection.

Now, who was that someone? That was the question the three Musketeers put to one another. Then, seeing that none of their replies could throw any light on the subject, Porthos called the host and asked for dice.

Porthos and Aramis placed themselves at the table and began to play. Athos walked about in a contemplative mood.

While thinking and walking, Athos passed and repassed before the pipe of the stove, broken in halves, the other extremity passing into the chamber above; and every time he passed and repassed he heard a murmur of words, which at length fixed his attention. Athos went close to it, and distinguished some words that appeared to merit so great an interest that he made a sign to his friends to be silent, remaining himself bent with his ear directed to the opening of the lower orifice.

"Listen, Milady," said the cardinal, "the affair is important. Sit down, and let us talk it over."

"Milady!" murmured Athos.

"I listen to your Eminence with greatest attention," replied a female voice which made the Musketeer start.

"A small vessel with an English crew, whose captain is on my side, awaits you at the mouth of Charente, at fort of the Point. He will set sail tomorrow morning."

"I must go thither tonight?"

"Instantly! That is to say, when you have received my instructions. Two men, whom you will find at the door on going out, will serve you as escort. You will allow me to leave first; then, after half an hour, you can go away in your turn."

"Yes, monseigneur. Now let us return to the mission with which you wish to charge me; and as I desire to continue to merit the confidence of your Eminence, deign to unfold it to me in terms clear and precise, that I may not commit an error."

There was an instant of profound silence between the two interlocutors. It was evident that the cardinal was weighing beforehand the terms in which he was about to speak, and that Milady was collecting all her intellectual faculties to comprehend the things he was about to say, and to engrave them in her memory when they should be spoken.

Athos took advantage of this moment to tell his two companions to fasten the door inside, and to make them a sign to come and listen with him.

The two Musketeers, who loved their ease, brought a chair for each of themselves and one for Athos. All three then sat down with their heads together and their ears on the alert.

"You will go to London," continued the cardinal. "Arrived in London, you will seek Buckingham."

"I must beg your Eminence to observe," said Milady, "that since the affair of the diamond studs, about which the duke always suspected me, his Grace distrusts me."

"Well, this time," said the cardinal, "it is not necessary to steal his confidence, but to present yourself frankly and loyally as a negotiator."

"Frankly and loyally," repeated Milady, with an unspeakable expression of duplicity.

"Yes, frankly and loyally," replied the cardinal, in the same tone. "All this negotiation must be carried on openly."

"I will follow your Eminence's instructions to the letter. I only wait till you give them."

"You will go to Buckingham in my behalf, and you will tell him I am acquainted with all the preparations he has made; but that they give me no uneasiness, since at the first step he takes I will ruin the queen."

"Will he believe that your Eminence is in a position to accomplish the threat thus made?"

"Yes; for I have the proofs."

"I must be able to present these proofs for his appreciation."

"Without doubt. And you will tell him I will publish the report of Bois-Robert and the Marquis de Beautru, upon the interview which the duke had at the residence of Madame the Constable with the queen on the evening Madame the Constable gave a masquerade. You will tell him, in order that he may not doubt, that he came there in the costume of the Great Mogul, which the Chevalier de Guise was to have worn, and that he purchased this exchange for the sum of three thousand pistoles."

"Well, monseigneur?"

"All the details of his coming into and going out of the palace--on the night when he introduced himself in the character of an Italian fortune teller--you will tell him, that he may not doubt the correctness of my information; that he had under his cloak a large white robe dotted with black tears, death's heads, and crossbones--for in case of a surprise, he was to pass for the phantom of the White Lady who, as all the world knows, appears at the Louvre every time any great event is impending."

"Is that all, monseigneur?"

"Tell him also that I am acquainted with all the details of the adventure at Amiens; that I will have a little romance made of it, wittily turned, with a plan of the garden and portraits of the principal actors in that nocturnal romance."

"I will tell him that."

"Tell him further that I hold Montague in my power; that Montague is in the Bastille; that no letters were found upon him, it is true, but that torture may make him tell much of what he knows, and even what he does not know."

"Exactly."

"Then add that his Grace has, in the precipitation with which he quit the Isle of Re, forgotten and left behind him in his lodging a certain letter from Madame de Chevreuse which singularly compromises the queen, inasmuch as it proves not only that her Majesty can love the enemies of the king but that she can conspire with the enemies of France. You recollect perfectly all I have told you, do you not?"

"Your Eminence will judge: the ball of Madame the Constable; the night at the Louvre; the evening at Amiens; the arrest of Montague; the letter of Madame de Chevreuse."

"That's it," said the cardinal, "that's it. You have an excellent memory, Milady."

"But," resumed she to whom the cardinal addressed this flattering compliment, "if, in spite of all these reasons, the duke does not give way and continues to menace France?"

"The duke is in love to madness, or rather to folly," replied Richelieu, with great bitterness. "Like the ancient paladins, he has only undertaken this war to obtain a look from his lady love. If he becomes certain that this war will cost the honor, and perhaps the liberty, of the lady of his thoughts, as he says, I will answer for it he will look twice."

"And yet," said Milady, with a persistence that proved she wished to see clearly to the end of the mission with which she was about to be charged, "if he persists?"

"If he persists?" said the cardinal. "That is not probable."

"It is possible," said Milady.

"If he persists--" His Eminence made a pause, and resumed: "If he persists--well, then I shall hope for one of those events which change the destinies of states."

"If your Eminence would quote to me some one of these events in history," said Milady, "perhaps I should partake of your confidence as to the future."

"Well, here, for example," said Richelieu: "when, in 1610, for a cause similar to that which moves the duke, King Henry IV, of glorious memory, was about, at the same time, to invade Flanders and Italy, in order to attack Austria on both sides. Well, did there not happen an event which saved Austria? Why should not the king of France have the same chance as the emperor?"

"Your Eminence means, I presume, the knife stab in the Rue de la Feronnerie?"

"Precisely," said the cardinal.

"Does not your Eminence fear that the punishment inflicted upon Ravaillac may deter anyone who might entertain the idea of imitating him?"

"There will be, in all times and in all countries, particularly if religious divisions exist in those countries, fanatics who ask nothing better than to become martyrs. Ay, and observe--it just occurs to me that the Puritans are furious against Buckingham, and their preachers designate him as the Antichrist."

"Well?" said Milady.

"Well," continued the cardinal, in an indifferent tone, "the only thing to be sought for at this moment is some woman, handsome, young, and clever, who has cause of quarrel with the duke. The duke has had many affairs of gallantry; and if he has fostered his amours by promises of eternal constancy, he must likewise have sown the seeds of hatred by his eternal infidelities."

"No doubt," said Milady, coolly, "such a woman may be found."

"Well, such a woman, who would place the knife of Jacques Clement or of Ravaillac in the hands of a fanatic, would save France."

"Yes; but she would then be the accomplice of an assassination."

"Were the accomplices of Ravaillac or of Jacques Clement ever known?"

"No; for perhaps they were too high-placed for anyone to dare look for them where they were. The Palace of Justice would not be burned down for everybody, monseigneur."

"You think, then, that the fire at the Palace of Justice was not caused by chance?" asked Richelieu, in the tone with which he would have put a question of no importance.

"I, monseigneur?" replied Milady. "I think nothing; I quote a fact, that is all. Only I say that if I were named Madame de Montpensier, or the Queen Marie de Medicis, I should use less precautions than I take, being simply called Milady Clarik."

"That is just," said Richelieu. "What do you require, then?"

"I require an order which would ratify beforehand all that I should think proper to do for the greatest good of France."

"But in the first place, this woman I have described must be found who is desirous of avenging herself upon the duke."

"She is found," said Milady.

"Then the miserable fanatic must be found who will serve as an instrument of God's justice."

"He will be found."

"Well," said the cardinal, "then it will be time to claim the order which you just now required."

"Your Eminence is right," replied Milady; "and I have been wrong in seeing in the mission with which you honor me anything but that which it really is--that is, to announce to his Grace, on the part of your Eminence, that you are acquainted with the different disguises by means of which he succeeded in approaching the queen during the fete given by Madame the Constable; that you have proofs of the interview granted at the Louvre by the queen to a certain Italian astrologer who was no other than the Duke of Buckingham; that you have ordered a little romance of a satirical nature to be written upon the adventures of Amiens, with a plan of the gardens in which those adventures took place, and portraits of the actors who figured in them; that Montague is in the Bastille, and that the torture may make him say things he remembers, and even things he has forgotten; that you possess a certain letter from Madame de Chevreuse, found in his Grace's lodging, which singularly compromises not only her who wrote it, but her in whose name it was written. Then, if he persists, notwithstanding all this--as that is, as I have said, the limit of my mission--I shall have nothing to do but to pray God to work a miracle for the salvation of France. That is it, is it not, monseigneur, and I shall have nothing else to do?"

"That is it," replied the cardinal, dryly.

"And now," said Milady, without appearing to remark the change of the duke's tone toward her--"now that I have received the instructions of your Eminence as concerns your enemies, Monseigneur will permit me to say a few words to him of mine?"

"Have you enemies, then?" asked Richelieu.

"Yes, monseigneur, enemies against whom you owe me all your support, for I made them by serving your Eminence."

"Who are they?" replied the duke.

"In the first place, there is a little intrigante named Bonacieux."

"She is in the prison of Nantes."

"That is to say, she was there," replied Milady; "but the queen has obtained an order from the king by means of which she has been conveyed to a convent."

"To a convent?" said the duke.

"Yes, to a convent."

"And to which?"

"I don't know; the secret has been well kept."

"But I will know!"

"And your Eminence will tell me in what convent that woman is?"

"I can see nothing inconvenient in that," said the cardinal.

"Well, now I have an enemy much more to be dreaded by me than this little Madame Bonacieux."

"Who is that?"

"Her lover."

"What is his name?"

"Oh, your Eminence knows him well," cried Milady, carried away by her anger. "He is the evil genius of both of us. It is he who in an encounter with your Eminence's Guards decided the victory in favor of the king's Musketeers; it is he who gave three desperate wounds to de Wardes, your emissary, and who caused the affair of the diamond studs to fail; it is he who, knowing it was I who had Madame Bonacieux carried off, has sworn my death."

"Ah, ah!" said the cardinal, "I know of whom you speak."

"I mean that miserable d'Artagnan."

"He is a bold fellow," said the cardinal.

"And it is exactly because he is a bold fellow that he is the more to be feared."

"I must have," said the duke, "a proof of his connection with Buckingham."

"A proof?" cried Milady; "I will have ten."

"Well, then, it becomes the simplest thing in the world; get me that proof, and I will send him to the Bastille."

"So far good, monseigneur; but afterwards?"

"When once in the Bastille, there is no afterward!" said the cardinal, in a low voice. "Ah, pardieu!" continued he, "if it were as easy for me to get rid of my enemy as it is easy to get rid of yours, and if it were against such people you require impunity--"

"Monseigneur," replied Milady, "a fair exchange. Life for life, man for man; give me one, I will give you the other."

"I don't know what you mean, nor do I even desire to know what you mean," replied the cardinal; "but I wish to please you, and see nothing out of the way in giving you what you demand with respect to so infamous a creature--the more so as you tell me this d'Artagnan is a libertine, a duelist, and a traitor."

"An infamous scoundrel, monseigneur, a scoundrel!"

"Give me paper, a quill, and some ink, then," said the cardinal.

"Here they are, monseigneur."

There was a moment of silence, which proved that the cardinal was employed in seeking the terms in which he should write the note, or else in writing it. Athos, who had not lost a word of the conversation, took his two companions by the hand, and led them to the other end of the room.

"Well," said Porthos, "what do you want, and why do you not let us listen to the end of the conversation?"

"Hush!" said Athos, speaking in a low voice. "We have heard all it was necessary we should hear; besides, I don't prevent you from listening, but I must be gone."

"You must be gone!" said Porthos; "and if the cardinal asks for you, what answer can we make?"

"You will not wait till he asks; you will speak first, and tell him that I am gone on the lookout, because certain expressions of our host have given me reason to think the road is not safe. I will say two words about it to the cardinal's esquire likewise. The rest concerns myself; don't be uneasy about that."

"Be prudent, Athos," said Aramis.

"Be easy on that head," replied Athos; "you know I am cool enough."

Porthos and Aramis resumed their places by the stovepipe.

As to Athos, he went out without any mystery, took his horse, which was tied with those of his friends to the fastenings of the shutters, in four words convinced the attendant of the necessity of a vanguard for their return, carefully examined the priming of his pistols, drew his sword, and took, like a forlorn hope, the road to the camp.

45 A Conjugal Scene

As Athos had foreseen, it was not long before the cardinal came down. He opened the door of the room in which the Musketeers were, and found Porthos playing an earnest game of dice with Aramis. He cast a rapid glance around the room, and perceived that one of his men was missing.

"What has become of Monseigneur Athos?" asked he.

"Monseigneur," replied Porthos, "he has gone as a scout, on account of some words of our host, which made him believe the road was not safe."

"And you, what have you done, Monsieur Porthos?"

"I have won five pistoles of Aramis."

"Well; now will you return with me?"

"We are at your Eminence's orders."

"To horse, then, gentlemen; for it is getting late."

The attendant was at the door, holding the cardinal's horse by the bridle. At a short distance a group of two men and three horses appeared in the shade. These were the two men who were to conduct Milady to the fort of the Point, and superintend her embarkation.

The attendant confirmed to the cardinal what the two Musketeers had already said with respect to Athos. The cardinal made an approving gesture, and retraced his route with the same precautions he had used incoming.

Let us leave him to follow the road to the camp protected by his esquire and the two Musketeers, and return to Athos.

For a hundred paces he maintained the speed at which he started; but when out of sight he turned his horse to the right, made a circuit, and came back within twenty paces of a high hedge to watch the passage of the little troop. Having recognized the laced hats of his companions and the golden fringe of the cardinal's cloak, he waited till the horsemen had turned the angle of the road, and having lost sight of them, he returned at a gallop to the inn, which was opened to him without hesitation.

The host recognized him.

"My officer," said Athos, "has forgotten to give a piece of very important information to the lady, and has sent me back to repair his forgetfulness."

"Go up," said the host; "she is still in her chamber."

Athos availed himself of the permission, ascended the stairs with his lightest step, gained the landing, and through the open door perceived Milady putting on her hat.

He entered the chamber and closed the door behind him. At the noise he made in pushing the bolt, Milady turned round.

Athos was standing before the door, enveloped in his cloak, with his hat pulled down over his eyes. On seeing this figure, mute and immovable as a statue, Milady was frightened.

"Who are you, and what do you want?" cried she.

"Humph," murmured Athos, "it is certainly she!"

And letting fall his cloak and raising his hat, he advanced toward Milady.

"Do you know me, madame?" said he.

Milady made one step forward, and then drew back as if she had seen a serpent.

"So far, well," said Athos, "I perceive you know me."

"The Comte de la Fere!" murmured Milady, becoming exceedingly pale, and drawing back till the wall prevented her from going any farther.

"Yes, Milady," replied Athos; "the Comte de la Fere in person, who comes expressly from the other world to have the pleasure of paying you a visit. Sit down, madame, and let us talk, as the cardinal said."

Milady, under the influence of inexpressible terror, sat down without uttering a word.

"You certainly are a demon sent upon the earth!" said Athos. "Your power is great, I know; but you also know that with the help of God men have often conquered the most terrible demons. You have once before thrown yourself in my path. I thought I had crushed you, madame; but either I was deceived or hell has resuscitated you!"

Milady at these words, which recalled frightful remembrances, hung down her head with a suppressed groan.

"Yes, hell has resuscitated you," continued Athos. "Hell has made you rich, hell has given you another name, hell has almost made you another face; but it has neither effaced the stains from your soul nor the brand from your body."

Milady arose as if moved by a powerful spring, and her eyes flashed lightning. Athos remained sitting.

"You believed me to be dead, did you not, as I believed you to be? And the name of Athos as well concealed the Comte de la Fere, as the name Milady Clarik concealed Anne de Breuil. Was it not so you were called when your honored brother married us? Our position is truly a strange one," continued Athos, laughing. "We have only lived up to the present time because we believed each other dead, and because a remembrance is less oppressive than a living creature, though a remembrance is sometimes devouring."

"But," said Milady, in a hollow, faint voice, "what brings you back to me, and what do you want with me?"

"I wish to tell you that though remaining invisible to your eyes, I have not lost sight of you."

"You know what I have done?"

"I can relate to you, day by day, your actions from your entrance to the service of the cardinal to this evening."

A smile of incredulity passed over the pale lips of Milady.

"Listen! It was you who cut off the two diamond studs from the shoulder of the Duke of Buckingham; it was you had the Madame Bonacieux carried off; it was you who, in love with de Wardes and thinking to pass the night with him, opened the door to Monsieur d'Artagnan; it was you who, believing that de Wardes had deceived you, wished to have him killed by his rival; it was you who, when this rival had discovered your infamous secret, wished to have him killed in his turn by two assassins, whom you sent in pursuit of him; it was you who, finding the balls had missed their mark, sent poisoned wine with a forged letter, to make your victim believe that the wine came from his friends. In short, it was you who have but now in this chamber, seated in this chair I now fill, made an engagement with Cardinal Richelieu to cause the Duke of Buckingham to be assassinated, in exchange for the promise he has made you to allow you to assassinate d'Artagnan."

Milady was livid.

"You must be Satan!" cried she.

"Perhaps," said Athos; "But at all events listen well to this. Assassinate the Duke of Buckingham, or cause him to be assassinated--I care very little about that! I don't know him. Besides, he is an Englishman. But do not touch with the tip of your finger a single hair of d'Artagnan, who is a faithful friend whom I love and defend, or I swear to you by the head of my father the crime which you shall have endeavored to commit, or shall have committed, shall be the last."

"Monsieur d'Artagnan has cruelly insulted me," said Milady, in a hollow tone; "Monsieur d'Artagnan shall die!"

"Indeed! Is it possible to insult you, madame?" said Athos, laughing; "he has insulted you, and he shall die!"

"He shall die!" replied Milady; "she first, and he afterward."

Athos was seized with a kind of vertigo. The sight of this creature, who had nothing of the woman about her, recalled awful remembrances. He thought how one day, in a less dangerous situation than the one in which he was now placed, he had already endeavored to sacrifice her to his honor. His desire for blood returned, burning his brain and pervading his frame like a raging fever; he arose in his turn, reached his hand to his belt, drew forth a pistol, and cocked it.

Milady, pale as a corpse, endeavored to cry out; but her swollen tongue could utter no more than a hoarse sound which had nothing human in it and resembled the rattle of a wild beast. Motionless against the dark tapestry, with her hair in disorder, she appeared like a horrid image of terror.

Athos slowly raised his pistol, stretched out his arm so that the weapon almost touched Milady's forehead, and then, in a voice the more terrible from having the supreme calmness of a fixed resolution, "Madame," said he, "you will this instant deliver to me the paper the cardinal signed; or upon my soul, I will blow your brains out."

With another man, Milady might have preserved some doubt; but she knew Athos. Nevertheless, she remained motionless.

"You have one second to decide," said he.

Milady saw by the contraction of his countenance that the trigger was about to be pulled; she reached her hand quickly to her bosom, drew out a paper, and held it toward Athos.

"Take it," said she, "and be accursed!"

Athos took the paper, returned the pistol to his belt, approached the lamp to be assured that it was the paper, unfolded it, and read:

Dec. 3, 1627

It is by my order and for the good of the state that the bearer of this has done what he has done.

Richelieu

"And now," said Athos, resuming his cloak and putting on his hat, "now that I have drawn your teeth, viper, bite if you can."

And he left the chamber without once looking behind him.

At the door he found the two men and the spare horse which they held.

"Gentlemen," said he, "Monseigneur's order is, you know, to conduct that woman, without losing time, to the fort of the Point, and never to leave her till she is on board."

As these words agreed wholly with the order they had received, they bowed their heads in sign of assent.

With regard to Athos, he leaped lightly into the saddle and set out at full gallop; only instead of following the road, he went across the fields, urging his horse to the utmost and stopping occasionally to listen.

In one of those halts he heard the steps of several horses on the road. He had no doubt it was the cardinal and his escort. He immediately made a new point in advance, rubbed his horse down with some heath and leaves of trees, and placed himself across the road, about two hundred paces from the camp.

"Who goes there?" cried he, as soon as he perceived the horsemen.

"That is our brave Musketeer, I think," said the cardinal.

"Yes, monseigneur," said Porthos, "it is he."

"Monsieur Athos," said Richelieu, "receive my thanks for the good guard you have kept. Gentlemen, we are arrived; take the gate on the left. The watchword is, 'King and Re.'"

Saying these words, the cardinal saluted the three friends with an inclination of his head, and took the right hand, followed by his attendant--for that night he himself slept in the camp.

"Well!" said Porthos and Aramis together, as soon as the cardinal was out of hearing, "well, he signed the paper she required!"

"I know it," said Athos, coolly, "since here it is."

And the three friends did not exchange another word till they reached their quarters, except to give the watchword to the sentinels. Only they sent Mousqueton to tell Planchet that his master was requested, the instant that he left the trenches, to come to the quarters of the Musketeers.

Milady, as Athos had foreseen, on finding the two men that awaited her, made no difficulty in following them. She had had for an instant an inclination to be reconducted to the cardinal, and relate everything to him; but a revelation on her part would bring about a revelation on the part of Athos. She might say that Athos had hanged her; but then Athos would tell that she was branded. She thought it was best to preserve silence, to discreetly set off to accomplish her difficult mission with her usual skill; and then, all things being accomplished to the satisfaction of the cardinal, to come to him and claim her vengeance.

In consequence, after having traveled all night, at seven o'clock she was at the fort of the Point; at eight o'clock she had embarked; and at nine, the vessel, which with letters of marque from the cardinal was supposed to be sailing for Bayonne, raised anchor, and steered its course toward England.

46 The Bastion Saint-Gervais

On arriving at the lodgings of his three friends, d'Artagnan found them assembled in the same chamber. Athos was meditating; Porthos was twisting his mustache; Aramis was saying his prayers in a charming little Book of Hours, bound in blue velvet.

"Pardieu, gentlemen," said he. "I hope what you have to tell me is worth the trouble, or else, I warn you, I will not pardon you for making me come here instead of getting a little rest after a night spent in taking and dismantling a bastion. Ah, why were you not there, gentlemen? It was warm work."

"We were in a place where it was not very cold," replied Porthos, giving his mustache a twist which was peculiar to him.

"Hush!" said Athos.

"Oh, oh!" said d'Artagnan, comprehending the slight frown of the Musketeer. "It appears there is something fresh aboard."

"Aramis," said Athos, "you went to breakfast the day before yesterday at the inn of the Parpaillot, I believe?"

"Yes."

"How did you fare?"

"For my part, I ate but little. The day before yesterday was a fish day, and they had nothing but meat."

"What," said Athos, "no fish at a seaport?"

"They say," said Aramis, resuming his pious reading, "that the dyke which the cardinal is making drives them all out into the open sea."

"But that is not quite what I mean to ask you, Aramis," replied Athos. "I want to know if you were left alone, and nobody interrupted you."

"Why, I think there were not many intruders. Yes, Athos, I know what you mean: we shall do very well at the Parpaillot."

"Let us go to the Parpaillot, then, for here the walls are like sheets of paper."

D'Artagnan, who was accustomed to his friend's manner of acting, and who perceived immediately, by a word, a gesture, or a sign from him, that the circumstances were serious, took Athos's arm, and went out without saying anything. Porthos followed, chatting with Aramis.

On their way they met Grimaud. Athos made him a sign to come with them. Grimaud, according to custom, obeyed in silence; the poor lad had nearly come to the pass of forgetting how to speak.

They arrived at the drinking room of the Parpaillot. It was seven o'clock in the morning, and daylight began to appear. The three friends ordered breakfast, and went into a room in which the host said they would not be disturbed.

Unfortunately, the hour was badly chosen for a private conference. The morning drum had just been beaten; everyone shook off the drowsiness of night, and to dispel the humid morning air, came to take a drop at the inn. Dragoons, Swiss, Guardsmen, Musketeers, light-horsemen, succeeded one another with a rapidity which might answer the purpose of the host very well, but agreed badly with the views of the four friends. Thus they applied very curtly to the salutations, healths, and jokes of their companions.

"I see how it will be," said Athos: "we shall get into some pretty quarrel or other, and we have no need of one just now. D'Artagnan, tell us what sort of a night you have had, and we will describe ours afterward."

"Ah, yes," said a light-horseman, with a glass of brandy in his hand, which he sipped slowly. "I hear you gentlemen of the Guards have been in the trenches tonight, and that you did not get much the best of the Rochellais."

D'Artagnan looked at Athos to know if he ought to reply to this intruder who thus mixed unasked in their conversation.

"Well," said Athos, "don't you hear Monsieur de Busigny, who does you the honor to ask you a question? Relate what has passed during the night, since these gentlemen desire to know it."

"Have you not taken a bastion?" said a Swiss, who was drinking rum out of a beer glass.

"Yes, monsieur," said d'Artagnan, bowing, "we have had that honor. We even have, as you may have heard, introduced a barrel of powder under one of the angles, which in blowing up made a very pretty breach. Without reckoning that as the bastion was not built yesterday all the rest of the building was badly shaken."

"And what bastion is it?" asked a dragoon, with his saber run through a goose which he was taking to be cooked.

"The bastion St. Gervais," replied d'Artagnan, "from behind which the Rochellais annoyed our workmen."

"Was that affair hot?"

"Yes, moderately so. We lost five men, and the Rochellais eight or ten."

"Balzempleu!" said the Swiss, who, notwithstanding the admirable collection of oaths possessed by the German language, had acquired a habit of swearing in French.

"But it is probable," said the light-horseman, "that they will send pioneers this morning to repair the bastion."

"Yes, that's probable," said d'Artagnan.

"Gentlemen," said Athos, "a wager!"

"Ah, wooi, a vager!" cried the Swiss.

"What is it?" said the light-horseman.

"Stop a bit," said the dragoon, placing his saber like a spit upon the two large iron dogs which held the firebrands in the chimney, "stop a bit, I am in it. You cursed host! a dripping pan immediately, that I may not lose a drop of the fat of this estimable bird."

"You was right," said the Swiss; "goose grease is kood with basdry."

"There!" said the dragoon. "Now for the wager! We listen, Monsieur Athos."

"Yes, the wager!" said the light-horseman.

"Well, Monsieur de Busigny, I will bet you," said Athos, "that my three companions, Messieurs Porthos, Aramis, and d'Artagnan, and myself, will go and breakfast in the bastion St. Gervais, and we will remain there an hour, by the watch, whatever the enemy may do to dislodge us."

Porthos and Aramis looked at each other; they began to comprehend.

"But," said d'Artagnan, in the ear of Athos, "you are going to get us all killed without mercy."

"We are much more likely to be killed," said Athos, "if we do not go."

"My faith, gentlemen," said Porthos, turning round upon his chair and twisting his mustache, "that's a fair bet, I hope."

"I take it," said M. de Busigny; "so let us fix the stake."

"You are four gentlemen," said Athos, "and we are four; an unlimited dinner for eight. Will that do?"

"Capitally," replied M. de Busigny.

"Perfectly," said the dragoon.

"That shoots me," said the Swiss.

The fourth auditor, who during all this conversation had played a mute part, made a sign of the head in proof that he acquiesced in the proposition.

"The breakfast for these gentlemen is ready," said the host.

"Well, bring it," said Athos.

The host obeyed. Athos called Grimaud, pointed to a large basket which lay in a corner, and made a sign to him to wrap the viands up in the napkins.

Grimaud understood that it was to be a breakfast on the grass, took the basket, packed up the viands, added the bottles, and then took the basket on his arm.

"But where are you going to eat my breakfast?" asked the host.

"What matter, if you are paid for it?" said Athos, and he threw two pistoles majestically on the table.

"Shall I give you the change, my officer?" said the host.

"No, only add two bottles of champagne, and the difference will be for the napkins."

The host had not quite so good a bargain as he at first hoped for, but he made amends by slipping in two bottles of Anjou wine instead of two bottles of champagne.

"Monsieur de Busigny," said Athos, "will you be so kind as to set your watch with mine, or permit me to regulate mine by yours?"

"Which you please, monsieur!" said the light-horseman, drawing from his fob a very handsome watch, studded with diamonds; "half past seven."

"Thirty-five minutes after seven," said Athos, "by which you perceive I am five minutes faster than you."

And bowing to all the astonished persons present, the young men took the road to the bastion St. Gervais, followed by Grimaud, who carried the basket, ignorant of where he was going but in the passive obedience which Athos had taught him not even thinking of asking.

As long as they were within the circle of the camp, the four friends did not exchange one word;

besides, they were followed by the curious, who, hearing of the wager, were anxious to know how they would come out of it. But when once they passed the line of circumvallation and found themselves in the open plain, d'Artagnan, who was completely ignorant of what was going forward, thought it was time to demand an explanation.

"And now, my dear Athos," said he, "do me the kindness to tell me where we are going?"

"Why, you see plainly enough we are going to the bastion."

"But what are we going to do there?"

"You know well that we go to breakfast there."

"But why did we not breakfast at the Parpaillot?"

"Because we have very important matters to communicate to one another, and it was impossible to talk five minutes in that inn without being annoyed by all those importunate fellows, who keep coming in, saluting you, and addressing you. Here at least," said Athos, pointing to the bastion, "they will not come and disturb us."

"It appears to me," said d'Artagnan, with that prudence which allied itself in him so naturally with excessive bravery, "that we could have found some retired place on the downs or the seashore."

"Where we should have been seen all four conferring together, so that at the end of a quarter of an hour the cardinal would have been informed by his spies that we were holding a council."

"Yes," said Aramis, "Athos is right: ANIMADVERTUNTUR IN DESERTIS."

"A desert would not have been amiss," said Porthos; "but it behooved us to find it."

"There is no desert where a bird cannot pass over one's head, where a fish cannot leap out of the water, where a rabbit cannot come out of its burrow, and I believe that bird, fish, and rabbit each becomes a spy of the cardinal. Better, then, pursue our enterprise; from which, besides, we cannot retreat without shame. We have made a wager--a wager which could not have been foreseen, and of which I defy anyone to divine the true cause. We are going, in order to win it, to remain an hour in the bastion. Either we shall be attacked, or not. If we are not, we shall have all the time to talk, and nobody will hear us--for I guarantee the walls of the bastion have no ears; if we are, we will talk of our affairs just the same. Moreover, in defending ourselves, we shall cover ourselves with glory. You see that everything is to our advantage."

"Yes," said d'Artagnan; "but we shall indubitably attract a ball."

"Well, my dear," replied Athos, "you know well that the balls most to be dreaded are not from the enemy."

"But for such an expedition we surely ought to have brought our muskets."

"You are stupid, friend Porthos. Why should we load ourselves with a useless burden?"

"I don't find a good musket, twelve cartridges, and a powder flask very useless in the face of an enemy."

"Well," replied Athos, "have you not heard what d'Artagnan said?"

"What did he say?" demanded Porthos.

"d'Artagnan said that in the attack of last night eight or ten Frenchmen were killed, and as many Rochellais."

"What then?"

"The bodies were not plundered, were they? It appears the conquerors had something else to do."

"Well?"

"Well, we shall find their muskets, their cartridges, and their flasks; and instead of four musketoons and twelve balls, we shall have fifteen guns and a hundred charges to fire."

"Oh, Athos!" said Aramis, "truly you are a great man."

Porthos nodded in sign of agreement. D'Artagnan alone did not seem convinced.

Grimaud no doubt shared the misgivings of the young man, for seeing that they continued to advance toward the bastion--something he had till then doubted--he pulled his master by the skirt of his coat.

"Where are we going?" asked he, by a gesture.

Athos pointed to the bastion.

"But," said Grimaud, in the same silent dialect, "we shall leave our skins there."

Athos raised his eyes and his finger toward heaven.

Grimaud put his basket on the ground and sat down with a shake of the head.

Athos took a pistol from his belt, looked to see if it was properly primed, cocked it, and placed the muzzle close to Grimaud's ear.

Grimaud was on his legs again as if by a spring. Athos then made him a sign to take up his basket and to walk on first. Grimaud obeyed. All that Grimaud gained by this momentary pantomime was to pass from the rear guard to the vanguard.

Arrived at the bastion, the four friends turned round.

More than three hundred soldiers of all kinds were assembled at the gate of the camp; and in a separate group might be distinguished M. de Busigny, the dragoon, the Swiss, and the fourth bettor.

Athos took off his hat, placed it on the end of his sword, and waved it in the air.

All the spectators returned him his salute, accompanying this courtesy with a loud hurrah which was audible to the four; after which all four disappeared in the bastion, whither Grimaud had preceded them.

47 The Council Of The Musketeers

As Athos had foreseen, the bastion was only occupied by a dozen corpses, French and Rochellais.

"Gentlemen," said Athos, who had assumed the command of the expedition, "while Grimaud spreads the table, let us begin by collecting the guns and cartridges together. We can talk while performing that necessary task. These gentlemen," added he, pointing to the bodies, "cannot hear us."

"But we could throw them into the ditch," said Porthos, "after having assured ourselves they have nothing in their pockets."

"Yes," said Athos, "that's Grimaud's business."

"Well, then," cried d'Artagnan, "pray let Grimaud search them and throw them over the walls."

"Heaven forfend!" said Athos; "they may serve us."

"These bodies serve us?" said Porthos. "You are mad, dear friend."

"Judge not rashly, say the gospel and the cardinal," replied Athos. "How many guns, gentlemen?"

"Twelve," replied Aramis.

"How many shots?"

"A hundred."

"That's quite as many as we shall want. Let us load the guns."

The four Musketeers went to work; and as they were loading the last musket Grimaud announced that the breakfast was ready.

Athos replied, always by gestures, that that was well, and indicated to Grimaud, by pointing to a turret that resembled a pepper caster, that he was to stand as sentinel. Only, to alleviate the tediousness of the duty, Athos allowed him to take a loaf, two cutlets, and a bottle of wine.

"And now to table," said Athos.

The four friends seated themselves on the ground with their legs crossed like Turks, or even tailors.

"And now," said d'Artagnan, "as there is no longer any fear of being overheard, I hope you are going to let me into your secret."

"I hope at the same time to procure you amusement and glory, gentlemen," said Athos. "I have induced you to take a charming promenade; here is a delicious breakfast; and yonder are five hundred persons, as you may see through the loopholes, taking us for heroes or madmen--two classes of imbeciles greatly resembling each other."

"But the secret!" said d'Artagnan.

"The secret is," said Athos, "that I saw Milady last night."

D'Artagnan was lifting a glass to his lips; but at the name of Milady, his hand trembled so, that he was obliged to put the glass on the ground again for fear of spilling the contents."

"You saw your wi--"

"Hush!" interrupted Athos. "You forget, my dear, you forget that these gentlemen are not initiated into my family affairs like yourself. I have seen Milady."

"Where?" demanded d'Artagnan.

"Within two leagues of this place, at the inn of the Red Dovecot."

"In that case I am lost," said d'Artagnan.

"Not so bad yet," replied Athos; "for by this time she must have quit the shores of France."

D'Artagnan breathed again.

"But after all," asked Porthos, "who is Milady?"

"A charming woman!" said Athos, sipping a glass of sparkling wine. "Villainous host!" cried he, "he has given us Anjou wine instead of champagne, and fancies we know no better! Yes," continued he, "a charming woman, who entertained kind views toward our friend d'Artagnan, who, on his part, has given her some offense for which she tried to revenge herself a month ago by having him killed by two musket shots, a week ago by trying to poison him, and yesterday by demanding his head of the cardinal."

"What! by demanding my head of the cardinal?" cried d'Artagnan, pale with terror.

"Yes, that is true as the Gospel," said Porthos; "I heard her with my own ears."

"I also," said Aramis.

"Then," said d'Artagnan, letting his arm fall with discouragement, "it is useless to struggle longer. I may as well blow my brains out, and all will be over."

"That's the last folly to be committed," said Athos, "seeing it is the only one for which there is no remedy."

"But I can never escape," said d'Artagnan, "with such enemies. First, my stranger of Meung; then de Wardes, to whom I have given three sword wounds; next Milady, whose secret I have discovered; finally, the cardinal, whose vengeance I have balked."

"Well," said Athos, "that only makes four; and we are four--one for one. Pardieu! if we may believe the signs Grimaud is making, we are about to have to do with a very different number of people. What is it, Grimaud? Considering the gravity of the occasion, I permit you to speak, my friend; but be laconic, I beg. What do you see?"

"A troop."

"Of how many persons?"

"Twenty men."

"What sort of men?"

"Sixteen pioneers, four soldiers."

"How far distant?"

"Five hundred paces."

"Good! We have just time to finish this fowl and to drink one glass of wine to your health, d'Artagnan."

"To your health!" repeated Porthos and Aramis.

"Well, then, to my health! although I am very much afraid that your good wishes will not be of great service to me."

"Bah!" said Athos, "God is great, as say the followers of Mohammed, and the future is in his hands."

Then, swallowing the contents of his glass, which he put down close to him, Athos arose carelessly, took the musket next to him, and drew near to one of the loopholes.

Porthos, Aramis and d'Artagnan followed his example. As to Grimaud, he received orders to place himself behind the four friends in order to reload their weapons.

"Pardieu!" said Athos, "it was hardly worth while to distribute ourselves for twenty fellows armed with pickaxes, mattocks, and shovels. Grimaud had only to make them a sign to go away, and I am convinced they would have left us in peace."

"I doubt that," replied d'Artagnan, "for they are advancing very resolutely. Besides, in addition to the pioneers, there are four soldiers and a brigadier, armed with muskets."

"That's because they don't see us," said Athos.

"My faith," said Aramis, "I must confess I feel a great repugnance to fire on these poor devils of civilians."

"He is a bad priest," said Porthos, "who has pity for heretics."

"In truth," said Athos, "Aramis is right. I will warn them."

"What the devil are you going to do?" cried d'Artagnan, "you will be shot."

But Athos heeded not his advice. Mounting on the breach, with his musket in one hand and his hat in the other, he said, bowing courteously and addressing the soldiers and the pioneers, who, astonished at this apparition, stopped fifty paces from the bastion: "Gentlemen, a few friends and myself are about to breakfast in this bastion. Now, you know nothing is more disagreeable than being disturbed when one is at breakfast. We request you, then, if you really have business here, to wait till we have finished or repast, or to come again a short time hence, unless; unless, which would be far better, you form the salutary resolution to quit the side of the rebels, and come and drink with us to the health of the King of France."

"Take care, Athos!" cried d'Artagnan; "don't you see they are aiming?"

"Yes, yes," said Athos; "but they are only civilians--very bad marksmen, who will be sure not to hit me."

In fact, at the same instant four shots were fired, and the balls were flattened against the wall around Athos, but not one touched him.

Four shots replied to them almost instantaneously, but much better aimed than those of the aggressors; three soldiers fell dead, and one of the pioneers was wounded.

"Grimaud," said Athos, still on the breach, "another musket!"

Grimaud immediately obeyed. On their part, the three friends had reloaded their arms; a second discharge followed the first. The brigadier and two pioneers fell dead; the rest of the troop took to flight.

"Now, gentlemen, a sortie!" cried Athos.

And the four friends rushed out of the fort, gained the field of battle, picked up the four muskets of the privates and the half-pike of the brigadier, and convinced that the fugitives would not stop till they reached the city, turned again toward the bastion, bearing with them the trophies of their victory.

"Reload the muskets, Grimaud," said Athos, "and we, gentlemen, will go on with our breakfast, and resume our conversation. Where were we?"

"I recollect you were saying," said d'Artagnan, "that after having demanded my head of the cardinal, Milady had quit the shores of France. Whither goes she?" added he, strongly interested in the route Milady followed.

"She goes into England," said Athos.

"With what view?"

"With the view of assassinating, or causing to be assassinated, the Duke of Buckingham."

D'Artagnan uttered an exclamation of surprise and indignation.

"But this is infamous!" cried he.

"As to that," said Athos, "I beg you to believe that I care very little about it. Now you have done, Grimaud, take our brigadier's half-pike, tie a napkin to it, and plant it on top of our bastion, that these rebels of Rochellais may see that they have to deal with brave and loyal soldiers of the king."

Grimaud obeyed without replying. An instant afterward, the white flag was floating over the heads of the four friends. A thunder of applause saluted its appearance; half the camp was at the barrier.

"How?" replied d'Artagnan, "you care little if she kills Buckingham or causes him to be killed? But the duke is our friend."

"The duke is English; the duke fights against us. Let her do what she likes with the duke; I care no more about him than an empty bottle." And Athos threw fifteen paces from him an empty bottle from which he had poured the last drop into his glass.

"A moment," said d'Artagnan. "I will not abandon Buckingham thus. He gave us some very fine horses."

"And moreover, very handsome saddles," said Porthos, who at the moment wore on his cloak the lace of his own.

"Besides," said Aramis, "God desires the conversion and not the death of a sinner."

"Amen!" said Athos, "and we will return to that subject later, if such be your pleasure; but what for the moment engaged my attention most earnestly, and I am sure you will understand me, d'Artagnan, was the getting from this woman a kind of carte blanche which she had extorted from the cardinal, and by means of which she could with impunity get rid of you and perhaps of us."

"But this creature must be a demon!" said Porthos, holding out his plate to Aramis, who was cutting up a fowl.

"And this carte blanche," said d'Artagnan, "this carte blanche, does it remain in her hands?"

"No, it passed into mine; I will not say without trouble, for if I did I should tell a lie."

"My dear Athos, I shall no longer count the number of times I am indebted to you for my life."

"Then it was to go to her that you left us?" said Aramis.

"Exactly."

"And you have that letter of the cardinal?" said d'Artagnan.

"Here it is," said Athos; and he took the invaluable paper from the pocket of his uniform. D'Artagnan unfolded it with one hand, whose trembling he did not even attempt to conceal, to read:

Dec. 3, 1627

It is by my order and for the good of the state that the bearer of this has done what he has done.

"Richelieu"

"In fact," said Aramis, "it is an absolution according to rule."

"That paper must be torn to pieces," said d'Artagnan, who fancied he read in it his sentence of death.

"On the contrary," said Athos, "it must be preserved carefully. I would not give up this paper if covered with as many gold pieces."

"And what will she do now?" asked the young man.

"Why," replied Athos, carelessly, "she is probably going to write to the cardinal that a damned Musketeer, named Athos, has taken her safe-conduct from her by force; she will advise him in the same letter to get rid of his two friends, Aramis and Porthos, at the same time. The cardinal will remember that these are the same men who have often crossed his path; and then some fine morning he will arrest d'Artagnan, and for fear he should feel lonely, he will send us to keep him company in the Bastille."

"Go to! It appears to me you make dull jokes, my dear," said Porthos.

"I do not jest," said Athos.

"Do you know," said Porthos, "that to twist that damned Milady's neck would be a smaller sin than to twist those of these poor devils of Huguenots, who have committed no other crime than singing in French the psalms we sing in Latin?"

"What says the abbe?" asked Athos, quietly.

"I say I am entirely of Porthos's opinion," replied Aramis.

"And I, too," said d'Artagnan.

"Fortunately, she is far off," said Porthos, "for I confess she would worry me if she were here."

"She worries me in England as well as in France," said Athos.

"She worries me everywhere," said d'Artagnan.

"But when you held her in your power, why did you not drown her, strangle her, hang her?" said Porthos. "It is only the dead who do not return."

"You think so, Porthos?" replied the Musketeer, with a sad smile which d'Artagnan alone understood.

"I have an idea," said d'Artagnan.

"What is it?" said the Musketeers.

"To arms!" cried Grimaud.

The young men sprang up, and seized their muskets.

This time a small troop advanced, consisting of from twenty to twenty-five men; but they were not pioneers, they were soldiers of the garrison.

"Shall we return to the camp?" said Porthos. "I don't think the sides are equal."

"Impossible, for three reasons," replied Athos. "The first, that we have not finished breakfast; the second, that we still have some very important things to say; and the third, that it yet wants ten minutes before the lapse of the hour."

"Well, then," said Aramis, "we must form a plan of battle."

"That's very simple," replied Athos. "As soon as the enemy are within musket shot, we must fire upon them. If they continue to advance, we must fire again. We must fire as long as we have loaded guns. If those who remain of the troop persist in coming to the assault, we will allow the besiegers to get as far as the ditch, and then we will push down upon their heads that strip of wall which keeps its perpendicular by a miracle."

"Bravo!" cried Porthos. "Decidedly, Athos, you were born to be a general, and the cardinal, who fancies himself a great soldier, is nothing beside you."

"Gentlemen," said Athos, "no divided attention, I beg; let each one pick out his man."

"I cover mine," said d'Artagnan.

"And I mine," said Porthos.

"And I mine," said Aramis.

"Fire, then," said Athos.

The four muskets made but one report, but four men fell.

The drum immediately beat, and the little troop advanced at charging pace.

Then the shots were repeated without regularity, but always aimed with the same accuracy. Nevertheless, as if they had been aware of the numerical weakness of the friends, the Rochellais continued to advance in quick time.

With every three shots at least two men fell; but the march of those who remained was not slackened.

Arrived at the foot of the bastion, there were still more than a dozen of the enemy. A last discharge welcomed them, but did not stop them; they jumped into the ditch, and prepared to scale the breach.

"Now, my friends," said Athos, "finish them at a blow. To the wall; to the wall!"

And the four friends, seconded by Grimaud, pushed with the barrels of their muskets an enormous sheet of the wall, which bent as if pushed by the wind, and detaching itself from its base, fell with a horrible crash into the ditch. Then a fearful crash was heard; a cloud of dust mounted toward the sky--and all was over!

"Can we have destroyed them all, from the first to the last?" said Athos.

"My faith, it appears so!" said d'Artagnan.

"No," cried Porthos; "there go three or four, limping away."

In fact, three or four of these unfortunate men, covered with dirt and blood, fled along the hollow way, and at length regained the city. These were all who were left of the little troop.

Athos looked at his watch.

"Gentlemen," said he, "we have been here an hour, and our wager is won; but we will be fair players. Besides, d'Artagnan has not told us his idea yet."

And the Musketeer, with his usual coolness, reseated himself before the remains of the breakfast.

"My idea?" said d'Artagnan.

"Yes; you said you had an idea," said Athos.

"Oh, I remember," said d'Artagnan. "Well, I will go to England a second time; I will go and find Buckingham."

"You shall not do that, d'Artagnan," said Athos, coolly.

"And why not? Have I not been there once?"

"Yes; but at that period we were not at war. At that period Buckingham was an ally, and not an enemy. What you would now do amounts to treason."

D'Artagnan perceived the force of this reasoning, and was silent.

"But," said Porthos, "I think I have an idea, in my turn."

"Silence for Monsieur Porthos's idea!" said Aramis.

"I will ask leave of absence of Monsieur de Treville, on some pretext or other which you must invent; I am not very clever at pretexts. Milady does not know me; I will get access to her without her suspecting me, and when I catch my beauty, I will strangle her."

"Well," replied Athos, "I am not far from approving the idea of Monsieur Porthos."

"For shame!" said Aramis. "Kill a woman? No, listen to me; I have the true idea."

"Let us see your idea, Aramis," said Athos, who felt much deference for the young Musketeer.

"We must inform the queen."

"Ah, my faith, yes!" said Porthos and d'Artagnan, at the same time; "we are coming nearer to it now."

"Inform the queen!" said Athos; "and how? Have we relations with the court? Could we send anyone to Paris without its being known in the camp? From here to Paris it is a hundred and forty leagues; before our letter was at Angers we should be in a dungeon."

"As to remitting a letter with safety to her Majesty," said Aramis, coloring, "I will take that upon myself. I know a clever person at Tours--"

Aramis stopped on seeing Athos smile.

"Well, do you not adopt this means, Athos?" said d'Artagnan.

"I do not reject it altogether," said Athos; "but I wish to remind Aramis that he cannot quit the camp, and that nobody but one of ourselves is trustworthy; that two hours after the messenger has set out, all the Capuchins, all the police, all the black caps of the cardinal, will know your letter by heart, and you and your clever person will be arrested."

"Without reckoning," objected Porthos, "that the queen would save Monsieur de Buckingham, but would take no heed of us."

"Gentlemen," said d'Artagnan, "what Porthos says is full of sense."

"Ah, ah! but what's going on in the city yonder?" said Athos.

"They are beating the general alarm."

The four friends listened, and the sound of the drum plainly reached them.

"You see, they are going to send a whole regiment against us," said Athos.

"You don't think of holding out against a whole regiment, do you?" said Porthos.

"Why not?" said Musketeer. "I feel myself quite in a humor for it; and I would hold out before an army if we had taken the precaution to bring a dozen more bottles of wine."

"Upon my word, the drum draws near," said d'Artagnan.

"Let it come," said Athos. "It is a quarter of an hour's journey from here to the city, consequently a quarter of an hour's journey from the city to hither. That is more than time enough for us to devise a plan. If we go from this place we shall never find another so suitable. Ah, stop! I have it, gentlemen; the right idea has just occurred to me."

"Tell us."

"Allow me to give Grimaud some indispensable orders."

Athos made a sign for his lackey to approach.

"Grimaud," said Athos, pointing to the bodies which lay under the wall of the bastion, "take those gentlemen, set them up against the wall, put their hats upon their heads, and their guns in their hands."

"Oh, the great man!" cried d'Artagnan. "I comprehend now."

"You comprehend?" said Porthos.

"And do you comprehend, Grimaud?" said Aramis.

Grimaud made a sign in the affirmative.

"That's all that is necessary," said Athos; "now for my idea."

"I should like, however, to comprehend," said Porthos.

"That is useless."

"Yes, yes! Athos's idea!" cried Aramis and d'Artagnan, at the same time.

"This Milady, this woman, this creature, this demon, has a brother-in-law, as I think you told me, d'Artagnan?"

"Yes, I know him very well; and I also believe that he has not a very warm affection for his sister-in-law."

"There is no harm in that. If he detested her, it would be all the better," replied Athos.

"In that case we are as well off as we wish."

"And yet," said Porthos, "I would like to know what Grimaud is about."

"Silence, Porthos!" said Aramis.

"What is her brother-in-law's name?"

"Lord de Winter."

"Where is he now?"

"He returned to London at the first sound of war."

"Well, there's just the man we want," said Athos. "It is he whom we must warn. We will have him informed that his sister-in-law is on the point of having someone assassinated, and beg him not to lose sight of her. There is in London, I hope, some establishment like that of the Magdalens, or of the Repentant Daughters. He must place his sister in one of these, and we shall be in peace."

"Yes," said d'Artagnan, "till she comes out."

"Ah, my faith!" said Athos, "you require too much, d'Artagnan. I have given you all I have, and I beg leave to tell you that this is the bottom of my sack."

"But I think it would be still better," said Aramis, "to inform the queen and Lord de Winter at the same time."

"Yes; but who is to carry the letter to Tours, and who to London?"

"I answer for Bazin," said Aramis.

"And I for Planchet," said d'Artagnan.

"Ay," said Porthos, "if we cannot leave the camp, our lackeys may."

"To be sure they may; and this very day we will write the letters," said Aramis. "Give the lackeys money, and they will start."

"We will give them money?" replied Athos. "Have you any money?"

The four friends looked at one another, and a cloud came over the brows which but lately had been so cheerful.

"Look out!" cried d'Artagnan, "I see black points and red points moving yonder. Why did you talk of a regiment, Athos? It is a veritable army!"

"My faith, yes," said Athos; "there they are. See the sneaks come, without drum or trumpet. Ah, ah! have you finished, Grimaud?"

Grimaud made a sign in the affirmative, and pointed to a dozen bodies which he had set up in the most picturesque attitudes. Some carried arms, others seemed to be taking aim, and the remainder appeared merely to be sword in hand.

"Bravo!" said Athos; "that does honor to your imagination."

"All very well," said Porthos, "but I should like to understand."

"Let us decamp first, and you will understand afterward."

"A moment, gentlemen, a moment; give Grimaud time to clear away the breakfast."

"Ah, ah!" said Aramis, "the black points and the red points are visibly enlarging. I am of d'Artagnan's opinion; we have no time to lose in regaining our camp."

"My faith," said Athos, "I have nothing to say against a retreat. We bet upon one hour, and we have stayed an hour and a half. Nothing can be said; let us be off, gentlemen, let us be off!"

Grimaud was already ahead, with the basket and the dessert. The four friends followed, ten paces behind him.

"What the devil shall we do now, gentlemen?" cried Athos.

"Have you forgotten anything?" said Aramis.

"The white flag, morbleu! We must not leave a flag in the hands of the enemy, even if that flag be but a napkin."

And Athos ran back to the bastion, mounted the platform, and bore off the flag; but as the Rochellais had arrived within musket range, they opened a terrible fire upon this man, who appeared to expose himself for pleasure's sake.

But Athos might be said to bear a charmed life. The balls passed and whistled all around him; not one struck him.

Athos waved his flag, turning his back on the guards of the city, and saluting those of the camp. On both sides loud cries arose--on the one side cries of anger, on the other cries of enthusiasm.

A second discharge followed the first, and three balls, by passing through it, made the napkin really a flag. Cries were heard from the camp, "Come down! come down!"

Athos came down; his friends, who anxiously awaited him, saw him returned with joy.

"Come along, Athos, come along!" cried d'Artagnan; "now we have found everything except money, it would be stupid to be killed."

But Athos continued to march majestically, whatever remarks his companions made; and they, finding their remarks useless, regulated their pace by his.

Grimaud and his basket were far in advance, out of the range of the balls.

At the end of an instant they heard a furious fusillade.

"What's that?" asked Porthos, "what are they firing at now? I hear no balls whistle, and I see nobody!"

"They are firing at the corpses," replied Athos.

"But the dead cannot return their fire."

"Certainly not! They will then fancy it is an ambuscade, they will deliberate; and by the time they have found out the pleasantry, we shall be out of the range of their balls. That renders it useless to get a pleurisy by too much haste."

"Oh, I comprehend now," said the astonished Porthos.

"That's lucky," said Athos, shrugging his shoulders.

On their part, the French, on seeing the four friends return at such a step, uttered cries of enthusiasm.

At length a fresh discharge was heard, and this time the balls came rattling among the stones around the four friends, and whistling sharply in their ears. The Rochellais had at last taken possession of the bastion.

"These Rochellais are bungling fellows," said Athos; "how many have we killed of them--a dozen?"

"Or fifteen."

"How many did we crush under the wall?"

"Eight or ten."

"And in exchange for all that not even a scratch! Ah, but what is the matter with your hand, d'Artagnan? It bleeds, seemingly."

"Oh, it's nothing," said d'Artagnan.

"A spent ball?"

"Not even that."

"What is it, then?"

We have said that Athos loved d'Artagnan like a child, and this somber and inflexible personage felt the anxiety of a parent for the young man.

"Only grazed a little," replied d'Artagnan; "my fingers were caught between two stones--that of the wall and that of my ring--and the skin was broken."

"That comes of wearing diamonds, my master," said Athos, disdainfully.

"Ah, to be sure," cried Porthos, "there is a diamond. Why the devil, then, do we plague ourselves about money, when there is a diamond?"

"Stop a bit!" said Aramis.

"Well thought of, Porthos; this time you have an idea."

"Undoubtedly," said Porthos, drawing himself up at Athos's compliment; "as there is a diamond, let us sell it."

"But," said d'Artagnan, "it is the queen's diamond."

"The stronger reason why it should be sold," replied Athos. The queen saving Monsieur de Buckingham, her lover; nothing more just. The queen saving us, her friends; nothing more moral. Let us sell the diamond. What says Monsieur the Abbe? I don't ask Porthos; his opinion has been given."

"Why, I think," said Aramis, blushing as usual, "that his ring not coming from a mistress, and consequently not being a love token, d'Artagnan may sell it."

"My dear Aramis, you speak like theology personified. Your advice, then, is--"

"To sell the diamond," replied Aramis.

"Well, then," said d'Artagnan, gaily, "let us sell the diamond, and say no more about it."

The fusillade continued; but the four friends were out of reach, and the Rochellais only fired to appease their consciences.

"My faith, it was time that idea came into Porthos's head. Here we are at the camp; therefore, gentlemen, not a word more of this affair. We are observed; they are coming to meet us. We shall be carried in triumph."

In fact, as we have said, the whole camp was in motion. More than two thousand persons had assisted, as at a spectacle, in this fortunate but wild undertaking of the four friends--an undertaking of which they were far from suspecting the real motive. Nothing was heard but cries of "Live the Musketeers! Live the Guards!" M. de Busigny was the first to come and shake Athos by the hand, and acknowledge that the wager was lost. The dragoon and the Swiss followed him, and all their comrades followed the dragoon and the Swiss. There was nothing but felicitations, pressures of the hand, and embraces; there was no end to the inextinguishable laughter at the Rochellais. The tumult at length became so great that the cardinal fancied there must be some riot, and sent La Houdiniere, his captain of the Guards, to inquire what was going on.

The affair was described to the messenger with all the effervescence of enthusiasm.

"Well?" asked the cardinal, on seeing La Houdiniere return.

"Well, monseigneur," replied the latter, "three Musketeers and a Guardsman laid a wager with Monsieur de Busigny that they would go and breakfast in the bastion St. Gervais; and while breakfasting they held it for two hours against the enemy, and have killed I don't know how many Rochellais."

"Did you inquire the names of those three Musketeers?"

"Yes, monseigneur."

"What are their names?"

"Messieurs Athos, Porthos, and Aramis."

"Still my three brave fellows!" murmured the cardinal. "And the Guardsman?"

"d'Artagnan."

"Still my young scapegrace. Positively, these four men must be on my side."

The same evening the cardinal spoke to M. de Treville of the exploit of the morning, which was the talk of the whole camp. M. de Treville, who had received the account of the adventure from the mouths of the heroes of it, related it in all its details to his Eminence, not forgetting the episode of the napkin.

"That's well, Monsieur de Treville," said the cardinal; "pray let that napkin be sent to me. I will have three fleur-de-lis embroidered on it in gold, and will give it to your company as a standard."

"Monseigneur," said M. de Treville, "that will be unjust to the Guardsmen. Monsieur d'Artagnan is not with me; he serves under Monsieur Dessessart."

"Well, then, take him," said the cardinal; "when four men are so much attached to one another, it is only fair that they should serve in the same company."

That same evening M. de Treville announced this good news to the three Musketeers and d'Artagnan, inviting all four to breakfast with him next morning.

D'Artagnan was beside himself with joy. We know that the dream of his life had been to become a Musketeer. The three friends were likewise greatly delighted.

"My faith," said d'Artagnan to Athos, "you had a triumphant idea! As you said, we have acquired glory, and were enabled to carry on a conversation of the highest importance."

"Which we can resume now without anybody suspecting us, for, with the help of God, we shall henceforth pass for cardinalists."

That evening d'Artagnan went to present his respects to M. Dessessart, and inform him of his promotion.

M Dessessart, who esteemed d'Artagnan, made him offers of help, as this change would entail expenses for equipment.

D'Artagnan refused; but thinking the opportunity a good one, he begged him to have the diamond he put into his hand valued, as he wished to turn it into money.

The next day, M. Dessessart's valet came to d'Artagnan's lodging, and gave him a bag containing seven thousand livres.

This was the price of the queen's diamond.

48 A Family Affair

Athos had invented the phrase, family affair. A family affair was not subject to the investigation of the cardinal; a family affair concerned nobody. People might employ themselves in a family affair before all the world. Therefore Athos had invented the phrase, family affair.

Aramis had discovered the idea, the lackeys.

Porthos had discovered the means, the diamond.

D'Artagnan alone had discovered nothing--he, ordinarily the most inventive of the four; but it must be also said that the very name of Milady paralyzed him.

Ah! no, we were mistaken; he had discovered a purchaser for his diamond.

The breakfast at M. de Treville's was as gay and cheerful as possible. D'Artagnan already wore his uniform--for being nearly of the same size as Aramis, and as Aramis was so liberally paid by the publisher who purchased his poem as to allow him to buy everything double, he sold his friend a complete outfit.

D'Artagnan would have been at the height of his wishes if he had not constantly seen Milady like a dark cloud hovering in the horizon.

After breakfast, it was agreed that they should meet again in the evening at Athos's lodging, and there finish their plans.

D'Artagnan passed the day in exhibiting his Musketeer's uniform in every street of the camp.

In the evening, at the appointed hour, the four friends met. There only remained three things to decide--what they should write to Milady's brother; what they should write to the clever person at Tours; and which should be the lackeys to carry the letters.

Everyone offered his own. Athos talked of the discretion of Grimaud, who never spoke a word but when his master unlocked his mouth. Porthos boasted of the strength of Mousqueton, who was big enough to thrash four men of ordinary size. Aramis, confiding in the address of Bazin, made a pompous eulogium on his candidate. Finally, d'Artagnan had entire faith in the bravery of Planchet, and reminded them of the manner in which he had conducted himself in the ticklish affair of Boulogne.

These four virtues disputed the prize for a length of time, and gave birth to magnificent speeches which we do not repeat here for fear they should be deemed too long.

"Unfortunately," said Athos, "he whom we send must possess in himself alone the four qualities united."

"But where is such a lackey to be found?"

"Not to be found!" cried Athos. "I know it well, so take Grimaud."

"Take Mousqueton."

"Take Bazin."

"Take Planchet. Planchet is brave and shrewd; they are two qualities out of the four."

"Gentlemen," said Aramis, "the principal question is not to know which of our four lackeys is the most discreet, the most strong, the most clever, or the most brave; the principal thing is to know which loves money the best."

"What Aramis says is very sensible," replied Athos; "we must speculate upon the faults of people, and not upon their virtues. Monsieur Abbe, you are a great moralist."

"Doubtless," said Aramis, "for we not only require to be well served in order to succeed, but moreover, not to fail; for in case of failure, heads are in question, not for our lackeys--"

"Speak lower, Aramis," said Athos.

"That's wise--not for the lackeys," resumed Aramis, "but for the master--for the masters, we may say. Are our lackeys sufficiently devoted to us to risk their lives for us? No."

"My faith," said d'Artagnan. "I would almost answer for Planchet."

"Well, my dear friend, add to his natural devotedness a good sum of money, and then, instead of answering for him once, answer for him twice."

"Why, good God! you will be deceived just the same," said Athos, who was an optimist when things were concerned, and a pessimist when men were in question. "They will promise everything for the sake of the money, and on the road fear will prevent them from acting. Once taken, they will be pressed; when pressed, they will confess everything. What the devil! we are not children. To reach England"--Athos lowered his voice--"all France, covered with spies and creatures of the cardinal, must be crossed. A passport for embarkation must be obtained; and the party must be acquainted with English in order to ask the way to London. Really, I think the thing very difficult."

"Not at all," cried d'Artagnan, who was anxious the matter should be accomplished; "on the contrary, I think it very easy. It would be, no doubt, parbleu, if we write to Lord de Winter about affairs of vast importance, of the horrors of the cardinal--"

"Speak lower!" said Athos.

"--of intrigues and secrets of state," continued d'Artagnan, complying with the recommendation. "There can be no doubt we would all be broken on the wheel; but for God's sake, do not forget, as you yourself said, Athos, that we only write to him concerning a family affair; that we only write to him to entreat that as soon as Milady arrives in London he will put it out of her power to injure us. I will write to him, then, nearly in these terms."

"Let us see," said Athos, assuming in advance a critical look.

"Monsieur and dear friend--"

"Ah, yes! Dear friend to an Englishman," interrupted Athos; "well commenced! Bravo, d'Artagnan! Only with that word you would be quartered instead of being broken on the wheel."

"Well, perhaps. I will say, then, Monsieur, quite short."

"You may even say, My Lord," replied Athos, who stickled for propriety.

"My Lord, do you remember the little goat pasture of the Luxembourg?"

"Good, the Luxembourg! One might believe this is an allusion to the queen-mother! That's ingenious," said Athos.

"Well, then, we will put simply, My Lord, do you remember a certain little enclosure where your life was spared?"

"My dear d'Artagnan, you will never make anything but a very bad secretary. Where your life was spared! For shame! that's unworthy. A man of spirit is not to be reminded of such services. A benefit reproached is an offense committed."

"The devil!" said d'Artagnan, "you are insupportable. If the letter must be written under your censure, my faith, I renounce the task."

"And you will do right. Handle the musket and the sword, my dear fellow. You will come off splendidly at those two exercises; but pass the pen over to Monsieur Abbe. That's his province."

"Ay, ay!" said Porthos; "pass the pen to Aramis, who writes theses in Latin."

"Well, so be it," said d'Artagnan. "Draw up this note for us, Aramis; but by our Holy Father the Pope, cut it short, for I shall prune you in my turn, I warn you."

"I ask no better," said Aramis, with that ingenious air of confidence which every poet has in himself; "but let me be properly acquainted with the subject. I have heard here and there that this sister-in-law was a hussy. I have obtained proof of it by listening to her conversation with the cardinal."

"Lower! SACRE BLEU!" said Athos.

"But," continued Aramis, "the details escape me."

"And me also," said Porthos.

D'Artagnan and Athos looked at each other for some time in silence. At length Athos, after serious reflection and becoming more pale than usual, made a sign of assent to d'Artagnan, who by it understood he was at liberty to speak.

"Well, this is what you have to say," said d'Artagnan: "My Lord, your sister-in-law is an infamous woman, who wished to have you killed that she might inherit your wealth; but she could not marry your brother, being already married in France, and having been--" d'Artagnan stopped, as if seeking for the word, and looked at Athos.

"Repudiated by her husband," said Athos.

"Because she had been branded," continued d'Artagnan.

"Bah!" cried Porthos. "Impossible! What do you say--that she wanted to have her brother-in-law killed?"

"Yes."

"She was married?" asked Aramis.

"Yes."

"And her husband found out that she had a fleur-de-lis on her shoulder?" cried Porthos.

"Yes."

These three yeses had been pronounced by Athos, each with a sadder intonation.

"And who has seen this fleur-de-lis?" inquired Aramis.

"d'Artagnan and I. Or rather, to observe the chronological order, I and d'Artagnan," replied Athos.

"And does the husband of this frightful creature still live?" said Aramis.

"He still lives."

"Are you quite sure of it?"

"I am he."

There was a moment of cold silence, during which everyone was affected according to his nature.

"This time," said Athos, first breaking the silence, "d'Artagnan has given us an excellent program, and the letter must be written at once."

"The devil! You are right, Athos," said Aramis; "and it is a rather difficult matter. The chancellor himself would be puzzled how to write such a letter, and yet the chancellor draws up an official report very readily. Never mind! Be silent, I will write."

Aramis accordingly took the quill, reflected for a few moments, wrote eight or ten lines in a charming little female hand, and then with a voice soft and slow, as if each word had been scrupulously weighed, he read the following:

"My Lord, The person who writes these few lines had the honor of crossing swords with you in the little enclosure of the Rue d'Enfer. As you have several times since declared yourself the friend of that person, he thinks it his duty to respond to that friendship by sending you important information. Twice you have nearly been the victim of a near relative, whom you believe to be your heir because you are ignorant that before she contracted a marriage in England she was already married in France. But the third time, which is the present, you may succumb. Your relative left La Rochelle for England during the night. Watch her arrival, for she has great and terrible projects. If you require to know positively what she is capable of, read her past history on her left shoulder."

"Well, now that will do wonderfully well," said Athos. "My dear Aramis, you have the pen of a secretary of state. Lord de Winter will now be upon his guard if the letter should reach him; and even if it should fall into the hands of the cardinal, we shall not be compromised. But as the lackey who goes may make us believe he has been to London and may stop at Chatellerault, let us give him only half the sum promised him, with the letter, with an agreement that he shall have the other half in exchange for the reply. Have you the diamond?" continued Athos.

"I have what is still better. I have the price;" and d'Artagnan threw the bag upon the table. At the sound of the gold Aramis raised his eyes and Porthos started. As to Athos, he remained unmoved.

"How much in that little bag?"

"Seven thousand livres, in louis of twelve francs."

"Seven thousand livres!" cried Porthos. "That poor little diamond was worth seven thousand livres?"

"It appears so," said Athos, "since here they are. I don't suppose that our friend d'Artagnan has added any of his own to the amount."

"But, gentlemen, in all this," said d'Artagnan, "we do not think of the queen. Let us take some heed of the welfare of her dear Buckingham. That is the least we owe her."

"That's true," said Athos; "but that concerns Aramis."

"Well," replied the latter, blushing, "what must I say?"

"Oh, that's simple enough!" replied Athos. "Write a second letter for that clever personage who lives at Tours."

Aramis resumed his pen, reflected a little, and wrote the following lines, which he immediately submitted to the approbation of his friends.

"My dear cousin."

"Ah, ah!" said Athos. "This clever person is your relative, then?"

"Cousin-german."

"Go on, to your cousin, then!"

Aramis continued:

"My dear Cousin, His Eminence, the cardinal, whom God preserve for the happiness of France and the confusion of the enemies of the kingdom, is on the point of putting an end to the hectic rebellion of La Rochelle. It is probable that the succor of the English fleet will never even arrive in sight of the place. I will even venture to say that I am certain M. de Buckingham will be prevented from setting out by some great event. His Eminence is the most illustrious politician of times past, of times present, and probably of times to come. He would extinguish the sun if the sun incommoded him. Give these happy tidings to your sister, my dear cousin. I have dreamed that the unlucky Englishman was dead. I cannot recollect whether it was by steel or by poison; only of this I am sure, I have dreamed he was dead, and you know my dreams never deceive me. Be assured, then, of seeing me soon return."

"Capital!" cried Athos; "you are the king of poets, my dear Aramis. You speak like the Apocalypse, and you are as true as the Gospel. There is nothing now to do but to put the address to this letter."

"That is easily done," said Aramis.

He folded the letter fancifully, and took up his pen and wrote:

"To Mlle. Michon, seamstress, Tours."

The three friends looked at one another and laughed; they were caught.

"Now," said Aramis, "you will please to understand, gentlemen, that Bazin alone can carry this letter to Tours. My cousin knows nobody but Bazin, and places confidence in nobody but him; any other person would fail. Besides, Bazin is ambitious and learned; Bazin has read history, gentlemen, he knows that Sixtus the Fifth became Pope after having kept pigs. Well, as he means to enter the Church at the same time as myself, he does not despair of becoming Pope in his turn, or at least a cardinal. You can understand that a man who has such views will never allow himself to be taken, or if taken, will undergo martyrdom rather than speak."

"Very well," said d'Artagnan, "I consent to Bazin with all my heart, but grant me Planchet. Milady had him one day turned out of doors, with sundry blows of a good stick to accelerate his motions. Now, Planchet has an excellent memory; and I will be bound that sooner than relinquish any possible means of vengeance, he will allow himself to be beaten to death. If your arrangements at Tours are your arrangements, Aramis, those of London are mine. I request, then, that Planchet may be chosen, more particularly as he has already been to London with me, and knows how to speak correctly: London, sir, if you please, and my master, Lord d'Artagnan. With that you may be satisfied he can make his way, both going and returning."

"In that case," said Athos, "Planchet must receive seven hundred livres for going, and seven hundred livres for coming back; and Bazin, three hundred livres for going, and three hundred livres for returning--that will reduce the sum to five thousand livres. We will each take a thousand livres to be employed as seems good, and we will leave a fund of a thousand livres under the guardianship of Monsieur Abbe here, for extraordinary occasions or common wants. Will that do?"

"My dear Athos," said Aramis, "you speak like Nestor, who was, as everyone knows, the wisest among the Greeks."

"Well, then," said Athos, "it is agreed. Planchet and Bazin shall go. Everything considered, I am not sorry to retain Grimaud; he is accustomed to my ways, and I am particular. Yesterday's affair must have shaken him a little; his voyage would upset him quite."

Planchet was sent for, and instructions were given him. The matter had been named to him by d'Artagnan, who in the first place pointed out the money to him, then the glory, and then the danger.

"I will carry the letter in the lining of my coat," said Planchet; "and if I am taken I will swallow it."

"Well, but then you will not be able to fulfill your commission," said d'Artagnan.

"You will give me a copy this evening, which I shall know by heart tomorrow."

D'Artagnan looked at his friends, as if to say, "Well, what did I tell you?"

"Now," continued he, addressing Planchet, "you have eight days to get an interview with Lord de Winter; you have eight days to return--in all sixteen days. If, on the sixteenth day after your departure, at eight o'clock in the evening you are not here, no money--even if it be but five minutes past eight."

"Then, monsieur," said Planchet, "you must buy me a watch."

"Take this," said Athos, with his usual careless generosity, giving him his own, "and be a good lad. Remember, if you talk, if you babble, if you get drunk, you risk your master's head, who has so much confidence in your fidelity, and who answers for you. But remember, also, that if by your fault any evil happens to d'Artagnan, I will find you, wherever you may be, for the purpose of ripping up your belly."

"Oh, monsieur!" said Planchet, humiliated by the suspicion, and moreover, terrified at the calm air of the Musketeer.

"And I," said Porthos, rolling his large eyes, "remember, I will skin you alive."

"Ah, monsieur!"

"And I," said Aramis, with his soft, melodius voice, "remember that I will roast you at a slow fire, like a savage."

"Ah, monsieur!"

Planchet began to weep. We will not venture to say whether it was from terror created by the threats or from tenderness at seeing four friends so closely united.

D'Artagnan took his hand. "See, Planchet," said he, "these gentlemen only say this out of affection for me, but at bottom they all like you."

"Ah, monsieur," said Planchet, "I will succeed or I will consent to be cut in quarters; and if they do cut me in quarters, be assured that not a morsel of me will speak."

It was decided that Planchet should set out the next day, at eight o'clock in the morning, in order, as he had said, that he might during the night learn the letter by heart. He gained just twelve hours by this engagement; he was to be back on the sixteenth day, by eight o'clock in the evening.

In the morning, as he was mounting his horse, d'Artagnan, who felt at the bottom of his heart a partiality for the duke, took Planchet aside.

"Listen," said he to him. "When you have given the letter to Lord de Winter and he has read it, you will further say to him: Watch over his Grace Lord Buckingham, for they wish to assassinate him. But this, Planchet, is so serious and important that I have not informed my friends that I would entrust this secret to you; and for a captain's commission I would not write it."

"Be satisfied, monsieur," said Planchet, "you shall see if confidence can be placed in me."

Mounted on an excellent horse, which he was to leave at the end of twenty leagues in order to take the post, Planchet set off at a gallop, his spirits a little depressed by the triple promise made him by the Musketeers, but otherwise as light-hearted as possible.

Bazin set out the next day for Tours, and was allowed eight days for performing his commission.

The four friends, during the period of these two absences, had, as may well be supposed, the eye on the watch, the nose to the wind, and the ear on the hark. Their days were passed in endeavoring to catch all that was said, in observing the proceeding of the cardinal, and in looking out for all the couriers who arrived. More than once an involuntary trembling seized them when called upon for some unexpected service. They had, besides, to look constantly to their own proper safety; Milady was a phantom which, when it had once appeared to people, did not allow them to sleep very quietly.

On the morning of the eighth day, Bazin, fresh as ever, and smiling, according to custom, entered the cabaret of the Parpaillot as the four friends were sitting down to breakfast, saying, as had been agreed upon: "Monsieur Aramis, the answer from your cousin."

The four friends exchanged a joyful glance; half of the work was done. It is true, however, that it was the shorter and easier part.

Aramis, blushing in spite of himself, took the letter, which was in a large, coarse hand and not particular for its orthography.

"Good God!" cried he, laughing, "I quite despair of my poor Michon; she will never write like Monsieur de Voiture."

"What does you mean by boor Michon?" said the Swiss, who was chatting with the four friends when the letter came.

"Oh, pardieu, less than nothing," said Aramis; "a charming little seamstress, whom I love dearly and from whose hand I requested a few lines as a sort of keepsake."

"The duvil!" said the Swiss, "if she is as great a lady as her writing is large, you are a lucky fellow, gomrade!"

Aramis read the letter, and passed it to Athos.

"See what she writes to me, Athos," said he.

Athos cast a glance over the epistle, and to disperse all the suspicions that might have been created, read aloud:

"My cousin, My sister and I are skillful in interpreting dreams, and even entertain great fear of them; but of yours it may be said, I hope, every dream is an illusion. Adieu! Take care of yourself, and act so that we may from time to time hear you spoken of.

"Marie Michon"

"And what dream does she mean?" asked the dragoon, who had approached during the reading.

"Yez; what's the dream?" said the Swiss.

"Well, pardieu!" said Aramis, "it was only this: I had a dream, and I related it to her."

"Yez, yez," said the Swiss; "it's simple enough to dell a dream, but I neffer dream."

"You are very fortunate," said Athos, rising; "I wish I could say as much!"

"Neffer," replied the Swiss, enchanted that a man like Athos could envy him anything. "Neffer, neffer!"

D'Artagnan, seeing Athos rise, did likewise, took his arm, and went out.

Porthos and Aramis remained behind to encounter the jokes of the dragoon and the Swiss.

As to Bazin, he went and lay down on a truss of straw; and as he had more imagination than the Swiss, he dreamed that Aramis, having become pope, adorned his head with a cardinal's hat.

But, as we have said, Bazin had not, by his fortunate return, removed more than a part of the uneasiness which weighed upon the four friends. The days of expectation are long, and d'Artagnan, in particular, would have wagered that the days were forty-four hours. He forgot the necessary slowness of navigation; he exaggerated to himself the power of

Milady. He credited this woman, who appeared to him the equal of a demon, with agents as supernatural as herself; at the least noise, he imagined himself about to be arrested, and that Planchet was being brought back to be confronted with himself and his friends. Still further, his confidence in the worthy Picard, at one time so great, diminished day by day. This anxiety became so great that it even extended to Aramis and Porthos. Athos alone remained unmoved, as if no danger hovered over him, and as if he breathed his customary atmosphere.

On the sixteenth day, in particular, these signs were so strong in d'Artagnan and his two friends that they could not remain quiet in one place, and wandered about like ghosts on the road by which Planchet was expected.

"Really," said Athos to them, "you are not men but children, to let a woman terrify you so! And what does it amount to, after all? To be imprisoned. Well, but we should be taken out of prison; Madame Bonacieux was released. To be decapitated? Why, every day in the trenches we go cheerfully to expose ourselves to worse than that--for a bullet may break a leg, and I am convinced a surgeon would give us more pain in cutting off a thigh than an executioner in cutting off a head. Wait quietly, then; in two hours, in four, in six hours at latest, Planchet will be here. He promised to be here, and I have very great faith in Planchet, who appears to me to be a very good lad."

"But if he does not come?" said d'Artagnan.

"Well, if he does not come, it will be because he has been delayed, that's all. He may have fallen from his horse, he may have cut a caper from the deck; he may have traveled so fast against the wind as to have brought on a violent catarrh. Eh, gentlemen, let us reckon upon accidents! Life is a chaplet of little miseries which the philosopher counts with a smile. Be philosophers, as I am, gentlemen; sit down at the table and let us drink. Nothing makes the future look so bright as surveying it through a glass of chambertin."

"That's all very well," replied d'Artagnan; "but I am tired of fearing when I open a fresh bottle that the wine may come from the cellar of Milady."

"You are very fastidious," said Athos; "such a beautiful woman!"

"A woman of mark!" said Porthos, with his loud laugh.

Athos started, passed his hand over his brow to remove the drops of perspiration that burst forth, and rose in his turn with a nervous movement he could not repress.

The day, however, passed away; and the evening came on slowly, but finally it came. The bars were filled with drinkers. Athos, who had pocketed his share of the diamond, seldom quit the Parpaillot. He had found in M. de Busigny, who, by the by, had given them a magnificent dinner, a partner worthy of his company. They were playing together, as usual, when seven o'clock sounded; the patrol was heard passing to double the posts. At half past seven the retreat was sounded.

"We are lost," said d'Artagnan, in the ear of Athos.

"You mean to say we have lost," said Athos, quietly, drawing four pistoles from his pocket and throwing them upon the table. "Come, gentlemen," said he, "they are beating the tattoo. Let us to bed!"

And Athos went out of the Parpaillot, followed by d'Artagnan. Aramis came behind, giving his arm to Porthos. Aramis mumbled verses to himself, and Porthos from time to time pulled a hair or two from his mustache, in sign of despair.

But all at once a shadow appeared in the darkness the outline of which was familiar to d'Artagnan, and a well-known voice said, "Monsieur, I have brought your cloak; it is chilly this evening."

"Planchet!" cried d'Artagnan, beside himself with joy.

"Planchet!" repeated Aramis and Porthos.

"Well, yes, Planchet, to be sure," said Athos, "what is there so astonishing in that? He promised to be back by eight o'clock, and eight is striking. Bravo, Planchet, you are a lad of your word, and if ever you leave your master, I will promise you a place in my service."

"Oh, no, never," said Planchet, "I will never leave Monsieur d'Artagnan."

At the same time d'Artagnan felt that Planchet slipped a note into his hand.

D'Artagnan felt a strong inclination to embrace Planchet as he had embraced him on his departure; but he feared lest this mark of affection, bestowed upon his lackey in the open street, might appear extraordinary to passers-by, and he restrained himself.

"I have the note," said he to Athos and to his friends.

"That's well," said Athos, "let us go home and read it."

The note burned the hand of d'Artagnan. He wished to hasten their steps; but Athos took his arm and passed it under his own, and the young man was forced to regulate his pace by that of his friend.

At length they reached the tent, lit a lamp, and while Planchet stood at the entrance that the four friends might not be surprised, d'Artagnan, with a trembling hand, broke the seal and opened the so anxiously expected letter.

It contained half a line, in a hand perfectly British, and with a conciseness as perfectly Spartan:

Thank you; be easy.

d'Artagnan translated this for the others.

Athos took the letter from the hands of d'Artagnan, approached the lamp, set fire to the paper, and did not let go till it was reduced to a cinder.

Then, calling Planchet, he said, "Now, my lad, you may claim your seven hundred livres, but you did not run much risk with such a note as that."

"I am not to blame for having tried every means to compress it," said Planchet.

"Well!" cried d'Artagnan, "tell us all about it."

"Dame, that's a long job, monsieur."

"You are right, Planchet," said Athos; "besides, the tattoo has been sounded, and we should be observed if we kept a light burning much longer than the others."

"So be it," said d'Artagnan. "Go to bed, Planchet, and sleep soundly."

"My faith, monsieur! that will be the first time I have done so for sixteen days."

"And me, too!" said d'Artagnan.

"And me, too!" said Porthos.

"And me, too!" said Aramis.

"Well, if you will have the truth, and me, too!" said Athos.

49 Fatality

Meantime Milady, drunk with passion, roaring on the deck like a lioness that has been embarked, had been tempted to throw herself into the sea that she might regain the coast, for she could not get rid of the thought that she had been insulted by d'Artagnan, threatened by Athos, and that she had quit France without being revenged on them. This idea soon became so insupportable to her that at the risk of whatever terrible consequences might result to herself from it, she implored the captain to put her on shore; but the captain, eager to escape from his false position--placed between French and English cruisers, like the bat between the mice and the birds--was in great haste to regain England, and positively refused to obey what he took for a woman's caprice, promising his passenger, who had been particularly recommended to him by the cardinal, to land her, if the sea and the French permitted him, at one of the ports of Brittany, either at Lorient or Brest. But the wind was contrary, the sea bad; they tacked and kept offshore. Nine days after leaving the Charente, pale with fatigue and vexation, Milady saw only the blue coasts of Finisterre appear.

She calculated that to cross this corner of France and return to the cardinal it would take her at least three days. Add another day for landing, and that would make four. Add these four to the nine others, that would be thirteen days lost--thirteen days, during which so many important events might pass in London. She reflected likewise that the cardinal would be furious at her return, and consequently would be more disposed to listen to the complaints brought against her than to the accusations she brought against others.

She allowed the vessel to pass Lorient and Brest without repeating her request to the captain, who, on his part, took care not to remind her of it. Milady therefore continued her voyage, and on the very day that Planchet embarked at Portsmouth for France, the messenger of his Eminence entered the port in triumph.

All the city was agitated by an extraordinary movement. Four large vessels, recently built, had just been launched. At the end of the jetty, his clothes richly laced with gold, glittering, as was customary with him, with diamonds and precious stones, his hat ornamented with a white feather which drooped upon his shoulder, Buckingham was seen surrounded by a staff almost as brilliant as himself.

It was one of those rare and beautiful days in winter when England remembers that there is a sun. The star of day, pale but nevertheless still splendid, was setting in the horizon, glorifying at once the heavens and the sea with bands of fire, and casting upon the towers and the old houses of the city a last ray of gold which made the windows sparkle like the reflection of a conflagration. Breathing that sea breeze, so much more invigorating and balsamic as the land is approached, contemplating all the power of those preparations she was commissioned to destroy, all the power of that army which she was to combat alone--she, a woman with a few bags of gold--Milady compared herself mentally to Judith, the terrible Jewess, when she penetrated the camp of the Assyrians and beheld the enormous mass of chariots, horses, men, and arms, which a gesture of her hand was to dissipate like a cloud of smoke.

They entered the roadstead; but as they drew near in order to cast anchor, a little cutter, looking like a coastguard formidably armed, approached the merchant vessel and dropped into the sea a boat which directed its course to the ladder. This boat contained an officer, a mate, and eight rowers. The officer alone went on board, where he was received with all the deference inspired by the uniform.

The officer conversed a few instants with the captain, gave him several papers, of which he was the bearer, to read, and upon the order of the merchant captain the whole crew of the vessel, both passengers and sailors, were called upon deck.

When this species of summons was made the officer inquired aloud the point of the brig's departure, its route, its landings; and to all these questions the captain replied without difficulty and without hesitation. Then the officer began to pass in review all the people, one after the other, and stopping when he came to Milady, surveyed her very closely, but without addressing a single word to her.

He then returned to the captain, said a few words to him, and as if from that moment the vessel was under his command, he ordered a maneuver which the crew executed immediately. Then the vessel resumed its course, still escorted by the little cutter, which sailed side by side with it, menacing it with the mouths of its six cannon. The boat followed in the wake of the ship, a speck near the enormous mass.

During the examination of Milady by the officer, as may well be imagined, Milady on her part was not less scrutinizing in her glances. But however great was the power of this woman with eyes of flame in reading the hearts of those whose secrets she wished to divine, she met this time with a countenance of such impassivity that no discovery followed her investigation. The officer who had stopped in front of her and studied her with so much care might have been twenty-five or twenty-six years of age. He was of pale complexion, with clear blue eyes, rather deeply set; his mouth, fine and well cut, remained motionless in its correct lines; his chin, strongly marked, denoted that strength of will which in the ordinary Britannic type denotes mostly nothing but obstinacy; a brow a little receding, as is proper for poets, enthusiasts, and soldiers, was scarcely shaded by short thin hair which, like the beard which covered the lower part of his face, was of a beautiful deep chestnut color.

When they entered the port, it was already night. The fog increased the darkness, and formed round the sternlights and lanterns of the jetty a circle like that which surrounds the moon when the weather threatens to become rainy. The air they breathed was heavy, damp, and cold.

Milady, that woman so courageous and firm, shivered in spite of herself.

The officer desired to have Milady's packages pointed out to him, and ordered them to be placed in the boat. When this operation was complete, he invited her to descend by offering her his hand.

Milady looked at this man, and hesitated. "Who are you, sir," asked she, "who has the kindness to trouble yourself so particularly on my account?"

"You may perceive, madame, by my uniform, that I am an officer in the English navy," replied the young man.

"But is it the custom for the officers in the English navy to place themselves at the service of their female compatriots when they land in a port of Great Britain, and carry their gallantry so far as to conduct them ashore?"

"Yes, madame, it is the custom, not from gallantry but prudence, that in time of war foreigners should be conducted to particular hotels, in order that they may remain under the eye of the government until full information can be obtained about them."

These words were pronounced with the most exact politeness and the most perfect calmness. Nevertheless, they had not the power of convincing Milady.

"But I am not a foreigner, sir," said she, with an accent as pure as ever was heard between Portsmouth and Manchester; "my name is Lady Clarik, and this measure--"

"This measure is general, madame; and you will seek in vain to evade it."

"I will follow you, then, sir."

Accepting the hand of the officer, she began the descent of the ladder, at the foot of which the boat waited. The officer followed her. A large cloak was spread at the stern; the officer requested her to sit down upon this cloak, and placed himself beside her.

"Row!" said he to the sailors.

The eight oars fell at once into the sea, making but a single sound, giving but a single stroke, and the boat seemed to fly over the surface of the water.

In five minutes they gained the land.

The officer leaped to the pier, and offered his hand to Milady. A carriage was in waiting.

"Is this carriage for us?" asked Milady.

"Yes, madame," replied the officer.

"The hotel, then, is far away?"

"At the other end of the town."

"Very well," said Milady; and she resolutely entered the carriage.

The officer saw that the baggage was fastened carefully behind the carriage; and this operation ended, he took his place beside Milady, and shut the door.

Immediately, without any order being given or his place of destination indicated, the coachman set off at a rapid pace, and plunged into the streets of the city.

So strange a reception naturally gave Milady ample matter for reflection; so seeing that the young officer did not seem at all disposed for conversation, she reclined in her corner of the carriage, and one after the other passed in review all the surmises which presented themselves to her mind.

At the end of a quarter of an hour, however, surprised at the length of the journey, she leaned forward toward the door to see whither she was being conducted. Houses were no longer to be seen; trees appeared in the darkness like great black phantoms chasing one another. Milady shuddered.

"But we are no longer in the city, sir," said she.

The young officer preserved silence.

"I beg you to understand, sir, I will go no farther unless you tell me whither you are taking me."

This threat brought no reply.

"Oh, this is too much," cried Milady. "Help! help!"

No voice replied to hers; the carriage continued to roll on with rapidity; the officer seemed a statue.

Milady looked at the officer with one of those terrible expressions peculiar to her countenance, and which so rarely failed of their effect; anger made her eyes flash in the darkness.

The young man remained immovable.

Milady tried to open the door in order to throw herself out.

"Take care, madame," said the young man, coolly, "you will kill yourself in jumping."

Milady reseated herself, foaming. The officer leaned forward, looked at her in his turn, and appeared surprised to see that face, just before so beautiful, distorted with passion and almost hideous. The artful creature at once comprehended that she was injuring herself by allowing him thus to read her soul; she collected her features, and in a complaining voice said: "In the name of heaven, sir, tell me if it is to you, if it is to your government, if it is to an enemy I am to attribute the violence that is done me?"

"No violence will be offered to you, madame, and what happens to you is the result of a very simple measure which we are obliged to adopt with all who land in England."

"Then you don't know me, sir?"

"It is the first time I have had the honor of seeing you."

"And on your honor, you have no cause of hatred against me?"

"None, I swear to you."

There was so much serenity, coolness, mildness even, in the voice of the young man, that Milady felt reassured.

At length after a journey of nearly an hour, the carriage stopped before an iron gate, which closed an avenue leading to a castle severe in form, massive, and isolated. Then, as the wheels rolled over a fine gravel, Milady could hear a vast roaring, which she at once recognized as the noise of the sea dashing against some steep cliff.

The carriage passed under two arched gateways, and at length stopped in a court large, dark, and square. Almost immediately the door of the carriage was opened, the young man sprang lightly out and presented his hand to Milady, who leaned upon it, and in her turn alighted with tolerable calmness.

"Still, then, I am a prisoner," said Milady, looking around her, and bringing back her eyes with a most gracious smile to the young officer; "but I feel assured it will not be for long," added she. "My own conscience and your politeness, sir, are the guarantees of that."

However flattering this compliment, the officer made no reply; but drawing from his belt a little silver whistle, such as boatswains use in ships of war, he whistled three times, with three different modulations. Immediately several men appeared, who unharnessed the smoking horses, and put the carriage into a coach house.

Then the officer, with the same calm politeness, invited his prisoner to enter the house. She, with a still-smiling countenance, took his arm, and passed with him under a low arched door, which by a vaulted passage, lighted only at the farther end, led to a stone staircase around an angle of stone. They then came to a massive door, which after the introduction into the lock of a key which the young man carried with him, turned heavily upon its hinges, and disclosed the chamber destined for Milady.

With a single glance the prisoner took in the apartment in its minutest details. It was a chamber whose furniture was at once appropriate for a prisoner or a free man; and yet bars at the windows and outside bolts at the door decided the question in favor of the prison.

In an instant all the strength of mind of this creature, though drawn from the most vigorous sources, abandoned her; she sank into a large easy chair, with her arms crossed, her head lowered, and expecting every instant to see a judge enter to interrogate her.

But no one entered except two or three marines, who brought her trunks and packages, deposited them in a corner, and retired without speaking.

The officer superintended all these details with the same calmness Milady had constantly seen in him, never pronouncing a word himself, and making himself obeyed by a gesture of his hand or a sound of his whistle.

It might have been said that between this man and his inferiors spoken language did not exist, or had become useless.

At length Milady could hold out no longer; she broke the silence. "In the name of heaven, sir," cried she, "what means all that is passing? Put an end to my doubts; I have courage enough for any danger I can foresee, for every misfortune which I understand. Where am I, and why am I here? If I am free, why these bars and these doors? If I am a prisoner, what crime have I committed?"

"You are here in the apartment destined for you, madame. I received orders to go and take charge of you on the sea, and to conduct you to this castle. This order I believe I have accomplished with all the exactness of a soldier, but also with the courtesy of a gentleman. There terminates, at least to the present moment, the duty I had to fulfill toward you; the rest concerns another person."

"And who is that other person?" asked Milady, warmly. "Can you not tell me his name?"

At the moment a great jingling of spurs was heard on the stairs. Some voices passed and faded away, and the sound of a single footstep approached the door.

"That person is here, madame," said the officer, leaving the entrance open, and drawing himself up in an attitude of respect.

At the same time the door opened; a man appeared on the threshold. He was without a hat, carried a sword, and flourished a handkerchief in his hand.

Milady thought she recognized this shadow in the gloom; she supported herself with one hand upon the arm of the chair, and advanced her head as if to meet a certainty.

The stranger advanced slowly, and as he advanced, after entering into the circle of light projected by the lamp, Milady involuntarily drew back.

Then when she had no longer any doubt, she cried, in a state of stupor, "What, my brother, is it you?"

"Yes, fair lady!" replied Lord de Winter, making a bow, half courteous, half ironical; "it is I, myself."

"But this castle, then?"

"Is mine."

"This chamber?"

"Is yours."

"I am, then, your prisoner?"

"Nearly so."

"But this is a frightful abuse of power!"

"No high-sounding words! Let us sit down and chat quietly, as brother and sister ought to do."

Then, turning toward the door, and seeing that the young officer was waiting for his last orders, he said. "All is well, I thank you; now leave us alone, Mr. Felton."

50 Chat Between Brother And Sister

During the time which Lord de Winter took to shut the door, close a shutter, and draw a chair near to his sister-in-law's fauteuil, Milady, anxiously thoughtful, plunged her glance into the depths of possibility, and discovered all the plan, of which she could not even obtain a glance as long as she was ignorant into whose hands she had fallen. She knew her brother-in-law to be a worthy gentleman, a bold hunter, an intrepid player, enterprising with women, but by no means remarkable for his skill in intrigues. How had he discovered her arrival, and caused her to be seized? Why did he detain her?

Athos had dropped some words which proved that the conversation she had with the cardinal had fallen into outside ears; but she could not suppose that he had dug a countermine so promptly and so boldly. She rather feared that her preceding operations in England might have been discovered. Buckingham might have guessed that it was she who had cut off the two studs, and avenge himself for that little treachery; but Buckingham was incapable of going to any excess against a woman, particularly if that woman was supposed to have acted from a feeling of jealousy.

This supposition appeared to her most reasonable. It seemed to her that they wanted to revenge the past, and not to anticipate the future. At all events, she congratulated herself upon having fallen into the hands of her brother-in-law, with whom she reckoned she could deal very easily, rather than into the hands of an acknowledged and intelligent enemy.

"Yes, let us chat, brother," said she, with a kind of cheerfulness, decided as she was to draw from the conversation, in spite of all the dissimulation Lord de Winter could bring, the revelations of which she stood in need to regulate her future conduct.

"You have, then, decided to come to England again," said Lord de Winter, "in spite of the resolutions you so often expressed in Paris never to set your feet on British ground?"

Milady replied to this question by another question. "To begin with, tell me," said she, "how have you watched me so closely as to be aware beforehand not only of my arrival, but even of the day, the hour, and the port at which I should arrive?"

Lord de Winter adopted the same tactics as Milady, thinking that as his sister-in-law employed them they must be the best.

"But tell me, my dear sister," replied he, "what makes you come to England?"

"I come to see you," replied Milady, without knowing how much she aggravated by this reply the suspicions to which d'Artagnan's letter had given birth in the mind of her brother-in-law, and only desiring to gain the good will of her auditor by a falsehood.

"Ah, to see me?" said de Winter, cunningly.

"To be sure, to see you. What is there astonishing in that?"

"And you had no other object in coming to England but to see me?"

"No."

"So it was for me alone you have taken the trouble to cross the Channel?"

"For you alone."

"The deuce! What tenderness, my sister!"

"But am I not your nearest relative?" demanded Milady, with a tone of the most touching ingenuousness.

"And my only heir, are you not?" said Lord de Winter in his turn, fixing his eyes on those of Milady.

Whatever command she had over herself, Milady could not help starting; and as in pronouncing the last words Lord de Winter placed his hand upon the arm of his sister, this start did not escape him.

In fact, the blow was direct and severe. The first idea that occurred to Milady's mind was that she had been betrayed by Kitty, and that she had recounted to the baron the selfish aversion toward himself of which she had imprudently allowed some marks to escape before her servant. She also recollected the furious and imprudent attack she had made upon d'Artagnan when he spared the life of her brother.

"I do not understand, my Lord," said she, in order to gain time and make her adversary speak out. "What do you mean to say? Is there any secret meaning concealed beneath your words?"

"Oh, my God, no!" said Lord de Winter, with apparent good nature. "You wish to see me, and you come to England. I learn this desire, or rather I suspect that you feel it; and in order to spare you all the annoyances of a nocturnal arrival in a port and all the fatigues of landing, I send one of my officers to meet you, I place a carriage at his orders, and he brings you hither to this castle, of which I am governor, whither I come every day, and where, in order to satisfy our mutual desire of seeing each other, I have prepared you a chamber. What is there more astonishing in all that I have said to you than in what you have told me?"

"No; what I think astonishing is that you should expect my coming."

"And yet that is the most simple thing in the world, my dear sister. Have you not observed that the captain of your little vessel, on entering the roadstead, sent forward, in order to obtain permission to enter the port, a little boat bearing his logbook and the register of his voyagers? I am commandant of the port. They brought me that book. I recognized your name in it. My heart told me what your mouth has just confirmed--that is to say, with what view you have exposed yourself to the dangers of a sea so perilous, or at least so troublesome at this moment--and I sent my cutter to meet you. You know the rest."

Milady knew that Lord de Winter lied, and she was the more alarmed.

"My brother," continued she, "was not that my Lord Buckingham whom I saw on the jetty this evening as we arrived?"

"Himself. Ah, I can understand how the sight of him struck you," replied Lord de Winter. "You came from a country where he must be very much talked of, and I know that his armaments against France greatly engage the attention of your friend the cardinal."

"My friend the cardinal!" cried Milady, seeing that on this point as on the other Lord de Winter seemed well instructed.

"Is he not your friend?" replied the baron, negligently. "Ah, pardon! I thought so; but we will return to my Lord Duke presently. Let us not depart from the sentimental turn our conversation had taken. You came, you say, to see me?"

"Yes."

"Well, I reply that you shall be served to the height of your wishes, and that we shall see each other every day."

"Am I, then, to remain here eternally?" demanded Milady, with a certain terror.

"Do you find yourself badly lodged, sister? Demand anything you want, and I will hasten to have you furnished with it."

"But I have neither my women nor my servants."

"You shall have all, madame. Tell me on what footing your household was established by your first husband, and although I am only your brother-in-law, I will arrange one similar."

"My first husband!" cried Milady, looking at Lord de Winter with eyes almost starting from their sockets.

"Yes, your French husband. I don't speak of my brother. If you have forgotten, as he is still living, I can write to him and he will send me information on the subject."

A cold sweat burst from the brow of Milady.

"You jest!" said she, in a hollow voice.

"Do I look so?" asked the baron, rising and going a step backward.

"Or rather you insult me," continued she, pressing with her stiffened hands the two arms of her easy chair, and raising herself upon her wrists.

"I insult you!" said Lord de Winter, with contempt. "In truth, madame, do you think that can be possible?"

"Indeed, sir," said Milady, "you must be either drunk or mad. Leave the room, and send me a woman."

"Women are very indiscreet, my sister. Cannot I serve you as a waiting maid? By that means all our secrets will remain in the family."

"Insolent!" cried Milady; and as if acted upon by a spring, she bounded toward the baron, who awaited her attack with his arms crossed, but nevertheless with one hand on the hilt of his sword.

"Come!" said he. "I know you are accustomed to assassinate people; but I warn you I shall defend myself, even against you."

"You are right," said Milady. "You have all the appearance of being cowardly enough to lift your hand against a woman."

"Perhaps so; and I have an excuse, for mine would not be the first hand of a man that has been placed upon you, I imagine."

And the baron pointed, with a slow and accusing gesture, to the left shoulder of Milady, which he almost touched with his finger.

Milady uttered a deep, inward shriek, and retreated to a corner of the room like a panther which crouches for a spring.

"Oh, growl as much as you please," cried Lord de Winter, "but don't try to bite, for I warn you that it would be to your disadvantage. There are here no procurators who regulate successions beforehand. There is no knight-errant to come and seek a quarrel with me on account of the fair lady I detain a prisoner; but I have judges quite ready who will quickly dispose of a woman so shameless as to glide, a bigamist, into the bed of Lord de Winter, my brother. And these judges, I warn you, will soon send you to an executioner who will make both your shoulders alike."

The eyes of Milady darted such flashes that although he was a man and armed before an unarmed woman, he felt the chill of fear glide through his whole frame. However, he continued all the same, but with increasing warmth: "Yes, I can very well understand that after having inherited the fortune of my brother it would be very agreeable to you to be my heir likewise; but know beforehand, if you kill me or cause me to be killed, my precautions are taken. Not a penny of what I possess will pass into your hands. Were you not already rich enough--you who possess nearly a million? And could you not stop your fatal career, if you did not do evil for the infinite and supreme joy of doing it? Oh, be assured, if the memory of my brother were not sacred to me, you should rot in a state dungeon or satisfy the curiosity of sailors at Tyburn. I will be silent, but you must endure your captivity quietly. In fifteen or twenty days I shall set out for La Rochelle with the army; but on the eve of my departure a vessel which I shall see depart will take you hence and convey you to our colonies in the south. And be assured that you shall be accompanied by one who will blow your brains out at the first attempt you make to return to England or the Continent."

Milady listened with an attention that dilated her inflamed eyes.

"Yes, at present," continued Lord de Winter, "you will remain in this castle. The walls are thick, the doors strong, and the bars solid; besides, your window opens immediately over the sea. The men of my crew, who are devoted to me for life and death, mount guard around this apartment, and watch all the passages that lead to the courtyard. Even if you gained the yard, there would still be three iron gates for you to pass. The order is positive. A step, a gesture, a word, on your part, denoting an effort to escape, and you are to be fired upon. If they kill you, English justice will be under an obligation to me for having saved it trouble. Ah! I see your features regain their calmness, your countenance recovers its assurance. You are saying to yourself: 'Fifteen days, twenty days? Bah! I have an inventive mind; before that is expired some idea will occur to me. I have an infernal spirit. I shall meet with a victim. Before fifteen days are gone by I shall be away from here.' Ah, try it!"

Milady, finding her thoughts betrayed, dug her nails into her flesh to subdue every emotion that might give to her face any expression except agony.

Lord de Winter continued: "The officer who commands here in my absence you have already seen, and therefore know him. He knows how, as you must have observed, to obey an order--for you did not, I am sure, come from Portsmouth hither without endeavoring to make him speak. What do you say of him? Could a statue of marble have been more impassive and more mute? You have already tried the power of your seductions upon many men, and unfortunately you have always succeeded; but I give you leave to try them upon this one. PARDIEU! if you succeed with him, I pronounce you the demon himself."

He went toward the door and opened it hastily.

"Call Mr. Felton," said he. "Wait a minute longer, and I will introduce him to you."

There followed between these two personages a strange silence, during which the sound of a slow and regular step was heard approaching. Shortly a human form appeared in the shade of the corridor, and the young lieutenant, with whom we are already acquainted, stopped at the threshold to receive the orders of the baron.

"Come in, my dear John," said Lord de Winter, "come in, and shut the door."

The young officer entered.

"Now," said the baron, "look at this woman. She is young; she is beautiful; she possesses all earthly seductions. Well, she is a monster, who, at twenty-five years of age, has been guilty of as many crimes as you could read of in a year in the archives of our tribunals. Her voice prejudices her hearers in her favor; her beauty serves as a bait to her victims; her body even pays what she promises--I must do her that justice. She will try to seduce you, perhaps she will try to kill you. I have extricated you from misery, Felton; I have caused you to be named lieutenant; I once saved your life, you know on what occasion. I am for you not only a protector, but a friend; not only a benefactor, but a father. This woman has come back again into England for the purpose of conspiring against my life. I hold this serpent in my hands. Well, I call you, and say to you: Friend Felton, John, my child, guard me, and more particularly guard yourself, against this woman. Swear, by your hopes of salvation, to keep her safely for the chastisement she has merited. John Felton, I trust your word! John Felton, I put faith in your loyalty!"

"My Lord," said the young officer, summoning to his mild countenance all the hatred he could find in his heart, "my Lord, I swear all shall be done as you desire."

Milady received this look like a resigned victim; it was impossible to imagine a more submissive or a more mild expression than that which prevailed on her beautiful countenance. Lord de Winter himself could scarcely recognize the tigress who, a minute before, prepared apparently for a fight.

"She is not to leave this chamber, understand, John," continued the baron. "She is to correspond with nobody; she is to speak to no one but you--if you will do her the honor to address a word to her."

"That is sufficient, my Lord! I have sworn."

"And now, madame, try to make your peace with God, for you are judged by men!"

Milady let her head sink, as if crushed by this sentence. Lord de Winter went out, making a sign to Felton, who followed him, shutting the door after him.

One instant after, the heavy step of a marine who served as sentinel was heard in the corridor--his ax in his girdle and his musket on his shoulder.

Milady remained for some minutes in the same position, for she thought they might perhaps be examining her through the keyhole; she then slowly raised her head, which had resumed its formidable expression of menace and defiance, ran to the door to listen, looked out of her window, and returning to bury herself again in her large armchair, she reflected.

51 Officer

Meanwhile, the cardinal looked anxiously for news from England; but no news arrived that was not annoying and threatening.

Although La Rochelle was invested, however certain success might appear--thanks to the precautions taken, and above all to the dyke, which prevented the entrance of any vessel into the besieged city--the blockade might last a long time yet. This was a great affront to the king's army, and a great inconvenience to the cardinal, who had no longer, it is true, to embroil Louis XIII with Anne of Austria--for that affair was over--but he had to adjust matters for M. de Bassompierre, who was embroiled with the Duc d'Angouleme.

As to Monsieur, who had begun the siege, he left to the cardinal the task of finishing it.

The city, notwithstanding the incredible perseverance of its mayor, had attempted a sort of mutiny for a surrender; the mayor had hanged the mutineers. This execution quieted the ill-disposed, who resolved to allow themselves to die of hunger--this death always appearing to them more slow and less sure than strangulation.

On their side, from time to time, the besiegers took the messengers which the Rochellais sent to Buckingham, or the spies which Buckingham sent to the Rochellais. In one case or the other, the trial was soon over. The cardinal pronounced the single word, "Hanged!" The king was invited to come and see the hanging. He came languidly, placing himself in a good situation to see all the details. This amused him sometimes a little, and made him endure the siege with patience; but it did not prevent his getting very tired, or from talking at every moment of returning to Paris--so that if the messengers and the spies had failed, his Eminence, notwithstanding all his inventiveness, would have found himself much embarrassed.

Nevertheless, time passed on, and the Rochellais did not surrender. The last spy that was taken was the bearer of a letter. This letter told Buckingham that the city was at an extremity; but instead of adding, "If your succor does not arrive within fifteen days, we will surrender," it added, quite simply, "If your succor comes not within fifteen days, we shall all be dead with hunger when it comes."

The Rochellais, then, had no hope but in Buckingham. Buckingham was their Messiah. It was evident that if they one day learned positively that they must not count on Buckingham, their courage would fail with their hope.

The cardinal looked, then, with great impatience for the news from England which would announce to him that Buckingham would not come.

The question of carrying the city by assault, though often debated in the council of the king, had been always rejected. In the first place, La Rochelle appeared impregnable. Then the cardinal, whatever he said, very well knew that the horror of bloodshed in this encounter, in which Frenchman would combat against Frenchman, was a retrograde movement of sixty years impressed upon his policy; and the cardinal was at that period what we now call a man of progress. In fact, the sack of La Rochelle, and the assassination of three of four thousand Huguenots who allowed themselves to be killed, would resemble too closely, in 1628, the massacre of St. Bartholomew in 1572; and then, above all this, this extreme measure, which was not at all repugnant to the king, good Catholic as he was, always fell before this argument of the besieging generals--La Rochelle is impregnable except to famine.

The cardinal could not drive from his mind the fear he entertained of his terrible emissary--for he comprehended the strange qualities of this woman, sometimes a serpent, sometimes a lion. Had she betrayed him? Was she dead? He knew her well enough in all cases to know that, whether acting for or against him, as a friend or an enemy, she would not remain motionless without great impediments;

but whence did these impediments arise? That was what he could not know.

And yet he reckoned, and with reason, on Milady. He had divined in the past of this woman terrible things which his red mantle alone could cover; and he felt, from one cause or another, that this woman was his own, as she could look to no other but himself for a support superior to the danger which threatened her.

He resolved, then, to carry on the war alone, and to look for no success foreign to himself, but as we look for a fortunate chance. He continued to press the raising of the famous dyke which was to starve La Rochelle. Meanwhile, he cast his eyes over that unfortunate city, which contained so much deep misery and so many heroic virtues, and recalling the saying of Louis XI, his political predecessor, as he himself was the predecessor of Robespierre, he repeated this maxim of Tristan's gossip: "Divide in order to reign."

Henry IV, when besieging Paris, had loaves and provisions thrown over the walls. The cardinal had little notes thrown over in which he represented to the Rochellais how unjust, selfish, and barbarous was the conduct of their leaders. These leaders had corn in abundance, and would not let them partake of it; they adopted as a maxim--for they, too, had maxims--that it was of very little consequence that women, children, and old men should die, so long as the men who were to defend the walls remained strong and healthy. Up to that time, whether from devotedness or from want of power to act against it, this maxim, without being generally adopted, nevertheless passed from theory into practice; but the notes did it injury. The notes reminded the men that the children, women, and old men whom they allowed to die were their sons, their wives, and their fathers, and that it would be more just for everyone to be reduced to the common misery, in order that equal conditions should give birth to unanimous resolutions.

These notes had all the effect that he who wrote them could expect, in that they induced a great number of the inhabitants to open private negotiations with the royal army.

But at the moment when the cardinal saw his means already bearing fruit, and applauded himself for having put it in action, an inhabitant of La Rochelle who had contrived to pass the royal lines--God knows how, such was the watchfulness of Bassompierre, Schomberg, and the Duc d'Angouleme, themselves watched over by the cardinal--an inhabitant of La Rochelle, we say, entered the city, coming from Portsmouth, and saying that he had seen a magnificent fleet ready to sail within eight days. Still further, Buckingham announced to the mayor that at length the great league was about to declare itself against France, and that the kingdom would be at once invaded by the English, Imperial, and Spanish armies. This letter was read publicly in all parts of the city. Copies were put up at the corners of the streets; and even they who had begun to open negotiations interrupted them, being resolved to await the succor so pompously announced.

This unexpected circumstance brought back Richelieu's former anxiety, and forced him in spite of himself once more to turn his eyes to the other side of the sea.

During this time, exempt from the anxiety of its only and true chief, the royal army led a joyous life, neither provisions nor money being wanting in the camp. All the corps rivaled one another in audacity and gaiety. To take spies and hang them, to make hazardous expeditions upon the dyke or the sea, to imagine wild plans, and to execute them coolly--such were the pastimes which made the army find these days short which were not only so long to the Rochellais, a prey to famine and anxiety, but even to the cardinal, who blockaded them so closely.

Sometimes when the cardinal, always on horseback, like the lowest GENDARME of the army, cast a pensive glance over those works, so slowly keeping pace with his wishes, which the engineers, brought from all the corners of France, were executing under his orders, if he met a Musketeer of the company of Treville, he drew near and looked at him in a peculiar manner, and not recognizing in him one of our four companions, he turned his penetrating look and profound thoughts in another direction.

One day when oppressed with a mortal weariness of mind, without hope in the negotiations with the city, without news from England, the cardinal went out, without any other aim than to be out of doors, and accompanied only by Cahusac and La Houdiniere, strolled along the beach. Mingling the immensity of his dreams with the immensity of the ocean, he came, his horse going at a foot's pace, to a hill from the top of which he perceived behind a hedge, reclining on the sand and catching in its passage one of those rays of the sun so rare at this period of the year, seven men surrounded by empty bottles. Four of these men were our Musketeers, preparing to listen to a letter one of them had just received. This letter was so important that it made them forsake their cards and their dice on the drumhead.

The other three were occupied in opening an enormous flagon of Collicure wine; these were the lackeys of these gentlemen.

The cardinal was, as we have said, in very low spirits; and nothing when he was in that state of mind increased his depression so much as gaiety in others. Besides, he had another strange fancy, which was always to believe that the causes of his sadness created the gaiety of others. Making a sign to La Houdiniere and Cahusac to stop, he alighted from his horse, and went toward these suspected merry companions, hoping, by means of the sand which deadened the sound of his steps and of the hedge which concealed his approach, to catch some words of this conversation which appeared so interesting. At ten paces from the hedge he recognized the talkative Gascon; and as he had already perceived that these men were Musketeers, he did not doubt that the three others were those called the Inseparables; that is to say, Athos, Porthos, and Aramis.

It may be supposed that his desire to hear the conversation was augmented by this discovery. His eyes took a strange expression, and with the step of a tiger-cat he advanced toward the hedge; but he had not been able to catch more than a few vague syllables without any positive sense, when a sonorous and short cry made him start, and attracted the attention of the Musketeers.

"Officer!" cried Grimaud.

"You are speaking, you scoundrel!" said Athos, rising upon his elbow, and transfixing Grimaud with his flaming look.

Grimaud therefore added nothing to his speech, but contented himself with pointing his index finger in the direction of the hedge, announcing by this gesture the cardinal and his escort.

With a single bound the Musketeers were on their feet, and saluted with respect.

The cardinal seemed furious.

"It appears that Messieurs the Musketeers keep guard," said he. "Are the English expected by land, or do the Musketeers consider themselves superior officers?"

"Monseigneur," replied Athos, for amid the general fright he alone had preserved the noble calmness and coolness that never forsook him, "Monseigneur, the Musketeers, when they are not on duty, or when their duty is over, drink and play at dice, and they are certainly superior officers to their lackeys."

"Lackeys?" grumbled the cardinal. "Lackeys who have the order to warn their masters when anyone passes are not lackeys, they are sentinels."

"Your Eminence may perceive that if we had not taken this precaution, we should have been exposed to allowing you to pass without presenting you our respects or offering you our thanks for the favor you have done us in uniting us. D'Artagnan," continued Athos, "you, who but lately were so anxious for such an opportunity for expressing your gratitude to Monseigneur, here it is; avail yourself of it."

These words were pronounced with that imperturbable phlegm which distinguished Athos in the hour of danger, and with that excessive politeness which made of him at certain moments a king more majestic than kings by birth.

D'Artagnan came forward and stammered out a few words of gratitude which soon expired under the gloomy looks of the cardinal.

"It does not signify, gentlemen," continued the cardinal, without appearing to be in the least swerved from his first intention by the diversion which Athos had started, "it does not signify, gentlemen. I do not like to have simple soldiers, because they have the advantage of serving in a privileged corps, thus to play the great lords; discipline is the same for them as for everybody else."

Athos allowed the cardinal to finish his sentence completely, and bowed in sign of assent. Then he resumed in his turn: "Discipline, Monseigneur, has, I hope, in no way been forgotten by us. We are not on duty, and we believed that not being on duty we were at liberty to dispose of our time as we pleased. If we are so fortunate as to have some particular duty to perform for your Eminence, we are ready to obey you. Your Eminence may perceive," continued Athos, knitting his brow, for this sort of investigation began to annoy him, "that we have not come out without our arms."

And he showed the cardinal, with his finger, the four muskets piled near the drum, on which were the cards and dice.

"Your Eminence may believe," added d'Artagnan, "that we would have come to meet you, if we could have supposed it was Monseigneur coming toward us with so few attendants."

The cardinal bit his mustache, and even his lips a little.

"Do you know what you look like, all together, as you are armed and guarded by your lackeys?" said the cardinal. "You look like four conspirators."

"Oh, as to that, Monseigneur, it is true," said Athos; "we do conspire, as your Eminence might have seen the other morning. Only we conspire against the Rochellais."

"Ah, you gentlemen of policy!" replied the cardinal, knitting his brow in his turn, "the secret of many unknown things might perhaps be found in your brains, if we could read them as you read that letter which you concealed as soon as you saw me coming."

The color mounted to the face of Athos, and he made a step toward his Eminence.

"One might think you really suspected us, monseigneur, and we were undergoing a real interrogatory. If it be so, we trust your Eminence will deign to explain yourself, and we should then at least be acquainted with our real position."

"And if it were an interrogatory!" replied the cardinal. "Others besides you have undergone such, Monsieur Athos, and have replied thereto."

"Thus I have told your Eminence that you had but to question us, and we are ready to reply."

"What was that letter you were about to read, Monsieur Aramis, and which you so promptly concealed?"

"A woman's letter, monseigneur."

"Ah, yes, I see," said the cardinal; "we must be discreet with this sort of letters; but nevertheless, we may show them to a confessor, and you know I have taken orders."

"Monseigneur," said Athos, with a calmness the more terrible because he risked his head in making this reply, "the letter is a woman's letter, but it is neither signed Marion de Lorme, nor Madame d'Aiguillon."

The cardinal became as pale as death; lightning darted from his eyes. He turned round as if to give an order to Cahusac and Houdiniere. Athos saw the movement; he made a step toward the muskets, upon which the other three friends had fixed their eyes, like men ill-disposed to allow themselves to be taken. The cardinalists were three; the Musketeers, lackeys included, were seven. He judged that the match would be so much the less equal, if Athos and his companions were really plotting; and by one of those rapid turns which he always had at command, all his anger faded away into a smile.

"Well, well!" said he, "you are brave young men, proud in daylight, faithful in darkness. We can find no fault with you for watching over yourselves, when you watch so carefully over others. Gentlemen, I have not forgotten the night in which you served me as an escort to the Red Dovecot. If there were any danger to be apprehended on the road I am going, I would request you to accompany me; but as there is none, remain where you are, finish your bottles, your game, and your letter. Adieu, gentlemen!"

And remounting his horse, which Cahusac led to him, he saluted them with his hand, and rode away.

The four young men, standing and motionless, followed him with their eyes without speaking a single word until he had disappeared. Then they looked at one another.

The countenances of all gave evidence of terror, for notwithstanding the friendly adieu of his Eminence, they plainly perceived that the cardinal went away with rage in his heart.

Athos alone smiled, with a self-possessed, disdainful smile.

When the cardinal was out of hearing and sight, "That Grimaud kept bad watch!" cried Porthos, who had a great inclination to vent his ill-humor on somebody.

Grimaud was about to reply to excuse himself. Athos lifted his finger, and Grimaud was silent.

"Would you have given up the letter, Aramis?" said d'Artagnan.

"I," said Aramis, in his most flutelike tone, "I had made up my mind. If he had insisted upon the letter being given up to him, I would have presented the letter to him with one hand, and with the other I would have run my sword through his body."

"I expected as much," said Athos; "and that was why I threw myself between you and him. Indeed, this man is very much to blame for talking thus to other men; one would say he had never had to do with any but women and children."

"My dear Athos, I admire you, but nevertheless we were in the wrong, after all."

"How, in the wrong?" said Athos. "Whose, then, is the air we breathe? Whose is the ocean upon which we look? Whose is the sand upon which we were reclining? Whose is that letter of your mistress? Do these belong to the cardinal? Upon my honor, this man fancies the world belongs to him. There you stood, stammering, stupefied, annihilated. One might have supposed the Bastille appeared before you, and that the gigantic Medusa had converted you into stone. Is being in love conspiring? You are in love with a woman whom the cardinal has caused to be shut up, and you wish to get her out of the hands of the cardinal. That's a match you are playing with his Eminence; this letter is your game. Why should you expose your game to your adversary? That is never done. Let him find it out if he can! We can find out his!"

"Well, that's all very sensible, Athos," said d'Artagnan.

"In that case, let there be no more question of what's past, and let Aramis resume the letter from his cousin where the cardinal interrupted him."

Aramis drew the letter from his pocket; the three friends surrounded him, and the three lackeys grouped themselves again near the wine jar.

"You had only read a line or two," said d'Artagnan; "read the letter again from the commencement."

"Willingly," said Aramis.

"My dear Cousin, I think I shall make up my mind to set out for Bethune, where my sister has placed our little servant in the convent of the Carmelites; this poor child is quite resigned, as she knows she cannot live elsewhere without the salvation of her soul being in danger. Nevertheless, if the affairs of our family are arranged, as we hope they will be, I believe she will run the risk of being damned, and will return to those she regrets, particularly as she knows they are always thinking of her. Meanwhile, she is not very wretched; what she most desires is a letter from her intended. I know that such viands pass with difficulty through convent gratings; but after all, as I have given you proofs, my dear cousin, I am not unskilled in such affairs, and I will take charge of the commission. My sister thanks you for your good and eternal remembrance. She has experienced much anxiety; but she is now at length a little reassured, having sent her secretary away in order that nothing may happen unexpectedly.

"Adieu, my dear cousin. Tell us news of yourself as often as you can; that is to say, as often as you can with safety. I embrace you.

"Marie Michon."

"Oh, what do I not owe you, Aramis?" said d'Artagnan. "Dear Constance! I have at length, then, intelligence of you. She lives; she is in safety in a convent; she is at Bethune! Where is Bethune, Athos?"

"Why, upon the frontiers of Artois and of Flanders. The siege once over, we shall be able to make a tour in that direction."

"And that will not be long, it is to be hoped," said Porthos; "for they have this morning hanged a spy who confessed that the Rochellais were reduced to the leather of their shoes. Supposing that after having eaten the leather they eat the soles, I cannot see much that is left unless they eat one another."

"Poor fools!" said Athos, emptying a glass of excellent Bordeaux wine which, without having at that period the reputation it now enjoys, merited it no less, "poor fools! As if the Catholic religion was not the most advantageous and the most agreeable of all religions! All the same," resumed he, after having clicked his tongue against his palate, "they are brave fellows! But what the devil are you about, Aramis?" continued Athos. "Why, you are squeezing that letter into your pocket!"

"Yes," said d'Artagnan, "Athos is right, it must be burned. And yet if we burn it, who knows whether Monsieur Cardinal has not a secret to interrogate ashes?"

"He must have one," said Athos.

"What will you do with the letter, then?" asked Porthos.

"Come here, Grimaud," said Athos. Grimaud rose and obeyed. "As a punishment for having spoken without permission, my friend, you will please to eat this piece of paper; then to recompense you for the service you will have rendered us, you shall afterward drink this glass of wine. First, here is the letter. Eat heartily."

Grimaud smiled; and with his eyes fixed upon the glass which Athos held in his hand, he ground the paper well between his teeth and then swallowed it.

"Bravo, Monsieur Grimaud!" said Athos; "and now take this. That's well. We dispense with your saying grace."

Grimaud silently swallowed the glass of Bordeaux wine; but his eyes, raised toward heaven during this delicious occupation, spoke a language which, though mute, was not the less expressive.

"And now," said Athos, "unless Monsieur Cardinal should form the ingenious idea of ripping up Grimaud, I think we may be pretty much at our ease respecting the letter."

Meantime, his Eminence continued his melancholy ride, murmuring between his mustaches, "These four men must positively be mine."

52 Captivity: The First Day

Let us return to Milady, whom a glance thrown upon the coast of France has made us lose sight of for an instant.

We shall find her still in the despairing attitude in which we left her, plunged in an abyss of dismal reflection--a dark hell at the gate of which she has almost left hope behind, because for the first time she doubts, for the first time she fears.

On two occasions her fortune has failed her, on two occasions she has found herself discovered and betrayed; and on these two occasions it was to one fatal genius, sent doubtlessly by the Lord to combat her, that she has succumbed. D'Artagnan has conquered her--her, that invincible power of evil.

He has deceived her in her love, humbled her in her pride, thwarted her in her ambition; and now he ruins her fortune, deprives her of liberty, and even threatens her life. Still more, he has lifted the corner of her mask--that shield with which she covered herself and which rendered her so strong.

D'Artagnan has turned aside from Buckingham, whom she hates as she hates everyone she has loved, the tempest with which Richelieu threatened him in the person of the queen. D'Artagnan had passed himself upon her as de Wardes, for whom she had conceived one of those tigerlike fancies common to women of her character. D'Artagnan knows that terrible secret which she has sworn no one shall know without dying. In short, at the moment in which she has just obtained from Richelieu a carte blanche by the means of which she is about to take vengeance on her enemy, this precious paper is torn from her hands, and it is d'Artagnan who holds her prisoner and is about to send her to some filthy Botany Bay, some infamous Tyburn of the Indian Ocean.

All this she owes to d'Artagnan, without doubt. From whom can come so many disgraces heaped upon her head, if not from him? He alone could have transmitted to Lord de Winter all these frightful secrets which he has discovered, one after another, by a train of fatalities. He knows her brother-in-law. He must have written to him.

What hatred she distills! Motionless, with her burning and fixed glances, in her solitary apartment, how well the outbursts of passion which at times escape from the depths of her chest with her respiration, accompany the sound of the surf which rises, growls, roars, and breaks itself like an eternal and powerless despair against the rocks on which is built this dark and lofty castle! How many magnificent projects of vengeance she conceives by the light of the flashes which her tempestuous passion casts over her mind against Mme. Bonacieux, against Buckingham, but above all against d'Artagnan--projects lost in the distance of the future.

Yes; but in order to avenge herself she must be free. And to be free, a prisoner has to pierce a wall, detach bars, cut through a floor--all undertakings which a patient and strong man may accomplish, but before which the feverish irritations of a woman must give way. Besides, to do all this, time is necessary--months, years; and she has ten or twelve days, as Lord de Winter, her fraternal and terrible jailer, has told her.

And yet, if she were a man she would attempt all this, and perhaps might succeed; why, then, did heaven make the mistake of placing that manlike soul in that frail and delicate body?

The first moments of her captivity were terrible; a few convulsions of rage which she could not suppress paid her debt of feminine weakness to nature. But by degrees she overcame the outbursts of her mad passion; and nervous tremblings which agitated her frame disappeared, and she remained folded within herself like a fatigued serpent in repose.

"Go to, go to! I must have been mad to allow myself to be carried away so," says she, gazing into the glass, which reflects back to her eyes the burning glance by which she appears to interrogate herself. "No violence; violence is the proof of weakness. In the first place, I have never succeeded by that means.

Perhaps if I employed my strength against women I might perchance find them weaker than myself, and consequently conquer them; but it is with men that I struggle, and I am but a woman to them. Let me fight like a woman, then; my strength is in my weakness."

Then, as if to render an account to herself of the changes she could place upon her countenance, so mobile and so expressive, she made it take all expressions from that of passionate anger, which convulsed her features, to that of the most sweet, most affectionate, and most seducing smile. Then her hair assumed successively, under her skillful hands, all the undulations she thought might assist the charms of her face. At length she murmured, satisfied with herself, "Come, nothing is lost; I am still beautiful."

It was then nearly eight o'clock in the evening. Milady perceived a bed; she calculated that the repose of a few hours would not only refresh her head and her ideas, but still further, her complexion. A better idea, however, came into her mind before going to bed. She had heard something said about supper. She had already been an hour in this apartment; they could not long delay bringing her a repast. The prisoner did not wish to lose time; and she resolved to make that very evening some attempts to ascertain the nature of the ground she had to work upon, by studying the characters of the men to whose guardianship she was committed.

A light appeared under the door; this light announced the reappearance of her jailers. Milady, who had arisen, threw herself quickly into the armchair, her head thrown back, her beautiful hair unbound and disheveled, her bosom half bare beneath her crumpled lace, one hand on her heart, and the other hanging down.

The bolts were drawn; the door groaned upon its hinges. Steps sounded in the chamber, and drew near.

"Place that table there," said a voice which the prisoner recognized as that of Felton.

The order was executed.

"You will bring lights, and relieve the sentinel," continued Felton.

And this double order which the young lieutenant gave to the same individuals proved to Milady that her servants were the same men as her guards; that is to say, soldiers.

Felton's orders were, for the rest, executed with a silent rapidity that gave a good idea of the way in which he maintained discipline.

At length Felton, who had not yet looked at Milady, turned toward her.

"Ah, ah!" said he, "she is asleep; that's well. When she wakes she can sup." And he made some steps toward the door.

"But, my lieutenant," said a soldier, less stoical than his chief, and who had approached Milady, "this woman is not asleep."

"What, not asleep!" said Felton; "what is she doing, then?"

"She has fainted. Her face is very pale, and I have listened in vain; I do not hear her breathe."

"You are right," said Felton, after having looked at Milady from the spot on which he stood without moving a step toward her. "Go and tell Lord de Winter that his prisoner has fainted--for this event not having been foreseen, I don't know what to do."

The soldier went out to obey the orders of his officer. Felton sat down upon an armchair which happened to be near the door, and waited without speaking a word, without making a gesture. Milady possessed that great art, so much studied by women, of looking through her long eyelashes without appearing to open the lids. She perceived Felton, who sat with his back toward her. She continued to look at him for nearly ten minutes, and in these ten minutes the immovable guardian never turned round once.

She then thought that Lord de Winter would come, and by his presence give fresh strength to her jailer. Her first trial was lost; she acted like a woman who reckons up her resources. As a result she raised her head, opened her eyes, and sighed deeply.

At this sigh Felton turned round.

"Ah, you are awake, madame," he said; "then I have nothing more to do here. If you want anything you can ring."

"Oh, my God, my God! how I have suffered!" said Milady, in that harmonious voice which, like that of the ancient enchantresses, charmed all whom she wished to destroy.

And she assumed, upon sitting up in the armchair, a still more graceful and abandoned position than when she reclined.

Felton arose.

"You will be served, thus, madame, three times a day," said he. "In the morning at nine o'clock, in the day at one o'clock, and in the evening at eight. If that does not suit you, you can point out what other hours you prefer, and in this respect your wishes will be complied with."

"But am I to remain always alone in this vast and dismal chamber?" asked Milady.

"A woman of the neighbourhood has been sent for, who will be tomorrow at the castle, and will return as often as you desire her presence."

"I thank you, sir," replied the prisoner, humbly.

Felton made a slight bow, and directed his steps toward the door. At the moment he was about to go out, Lord de Winter appeared in the corridor, followed by the soldier who had been sent to inform him of the swoon of Milady. He held a vial of salts in his hand.

"Well, what is it--what is going on here?" said he, in a jeering voice, on seeing the prisoner sitting up and Felton about to go out. "Is this corpse come to life already? Felton, my lad, did you not perceive that you were taken for a novice, and that the first act was being performed of a comedy of which we shall doubtless have the pleasure of following out all the developments?"

"I thought so, my lord," said Felton; "but as the prisoner is a woman, after all, I wish to pay her the attention that every man of gentle birth owes to a woman, if not on her account, at least on my own."

Milady shuddered through her whole system. These words of Felton's passed like ice through her veins.

"So," replied de Winter, laughing, "that beautiful hair so skillfully disheveled, that white skin, and that languishing look, have not yet seduced you, you heart of stone?"

"No, my Lord," replied the impassive young man; "your Lordship may be assured that it requires more than the tricks and coquetry of a woman to corrupt me."

"In that case, my brave lieutenant, let us leave Milady to find out something else, and go to supper; but be easy! She has a fruitful imagination, and the second act of the comedy will not delay its steps after the first."

And at these words Lord de Winter passed his arm through that of Felton, and led him out, laughing.

"Oh, I will be a match for you!" murmured Milady, between her teeth; "be assured of that, you poor spoiled monk, you poor converted soldier, who has cut his uniform out of a monk's frock!"

"By the way," resumed de Winter, stopping at the threshold of the door, "you must not, Milady, let this check take away your appetite. Taste that fowl and those fish. On my honor, they are not poisoned. I have a very good cook, and he is not to be my heir; I have full and perfect confidence in him. Do as I do. Adieu, dear sister, till your next swoon!"

This was all that Milady could endure. Her hands clutched her armchair; she ground her teeth inwardly; her eyes followed the motion of the door as it closed behind Lord de Winter and Felton, and the moment she was alone a fresh fit of despair seized her. She cast her eyes upon the table, saw the glittering of a knife, rushed toward it and clutched it; but her disappointment was cruel. The blade was round, and of flexible silver.

A burst of laughter resounded from the other side of the ill-closed door, and the door reopened.

"Ha, ha!" cried Lord de Winter; "ha, ha! Don't you see, my brave Felton; don't you see what I told you? That knife was for you, my lad; she would have killed you. Observe, this is one of her peculiarities, to get rid thus, after one fashion or another, of all the people who bother her. If I had listened to you, the knife would have been pointed and of steel. Then no more of Felton; she would have cut your throat, and after that everybody else's. See, John, see how well she knows how to handle a knife."

In fact, Milady still held the harmless weapon in her clenched hand; but these last words, this supreme insult, relaxed her hands, her strength, and even her will. The knife fell to the ground.

"You were right, my Lord," said Felton, with a tone of profound disgust which sounded to the very bottom of the heart of Milady, "you were right, my Lord, and I was wrong."

And both again left the room.

But this time Milady lent a more attentive ear than the first, and she heard their steps die away in the distance of the corridor.

"I am lost," murmured she; "I am lost! I am in the power of men upon whom I can have no more influence than upon statues of bronze or granite; they know me by heart, and are steeled against all my weapons. It is, however, impossible that this should end as they have decreed!"

In fact, as this last reflection indicated--this instinctive return to hope--sentiments of weakness or fear did not dwell long in her ardent spirit. Milady sat down to table, ate from several dishes, drank a little Spanish wine, and felt all her resolution return.

Before she went to bed she had pondered, analyzed, turned on all sides, examined on all points, the words, the steps, the gestures, the signs, and even the silence of her interlocutors; and of this profound, skillful, and anxious study the result was that Felton, everything considered, appeared the more vulnerable of her two persecutors.

One expression above all recurred to the mind of the prisoner: "If I had listened to you," Lord de Winter had said to Felton.

Felton, then, had spoken in her favor, since Lord de Winter had not been willing to listen to him.

"Weak or strong," repeated Milady, "that man has, then, a spark of pity in his soul; of that spark I will make a flame that shall devour him. As to the other, he knows me, he fears me, and knows what he has to expect of me if ever I escape from his hands. It is useless, then, to attempt anything with him. But Felton--that's another thing. He is a young, ingenuous, pure man who seems virtuous; him there are means of destroying."

And Milady went to bed and fell asleep with a smile upon her lips. Anyone who had seen her sleeping might have said she was a young girl dreaming of the crown of flowers she was to wear on her brow at the next festival.

53 Captivity: The Second Day

Milady dreamed that she at length had d'Artagnan in her power, that she was present at his execution; and it was the sight of his odious blood, flowing beneath the ax of the headsman, which spread that charming smile upon her lips.

She slept as a prisoner sleeps, rocked by his first hope.

In the morning, when they entered her chamber she was still in bed. Felton remained in the corridor. He brought with him the woman of whom he had spoken the evening before, and who had just arrived; this woman entered, and approaching Milady's bed, offered her services.

Milady was habitually pale; her complexion might therefore deceive a person who saw her for the first time.

"I am in a fever," said she; "I have not slept a single instant during all this long night. I suffer horribly. Are you likely to be more humane to me than others were yesterday? All I ask is permission to remain abed."

"Would you like to have a physician called?" said the woman.

Felton listened to this dialogue without speaking a word.

Milady reflected that the more people she had around her the more she would have to work upon, and Lord de Winter would redouble his watch. Besides, the physician might declare the ailment feigned; and Milady, after having lost the first trick, was not willing to lose the second.

"Go and fetch a physician?" said she. "What could be the good of that? These gentlemen declared yesterday that my illness was a comedy; it would be just the same today, no doubt--for since yesterday evening they have had plenty of time to send for a doctor."

"Then," said Felton, who became impatient, "say yourself, madame, what treatment you wish followed."

"Eh, how can I tell? My God! I know that I suffer, that's all. Give me anything you like, it is of little consequence."

"Go and fetch Lord de Winter," said Felton, tired of these eternal complaints.

"Oh, no, no!" cried Milady; "no, sir, do not call him, I conjure you. I am well, I want nothing; do not call him."

She gave so much vehemence, such magnetic eloquence to this exclamation, that Felton in spite of himself advanced some steps into the room.

"He has come!" thought Milady.

"Meanwhile, madame, if you really suffer," said Felton, "a physician shall be sent for; and if you deceive us--well, it will be the worse for you. But at least we shall not have to reproach ourselves with anything."

Milady made no reply, but turning her beautiful head round upon her pillow, she burst into tears, and uttered heartbreaking sobs.

Felton surveyed her for an instant with his usual impassiveness; then, seeing that the crisis threatened to be prolonged, he went out. The woman followed him, and Lord de Winter did not appear.

"I fancy I begin to see my way," murmured Milady, with a savage joy, burying herself under the clothes to conceal from anybody who might be watching her this burst of inward satisfaction.

Two hours passed away.

"Now it is time that the malady should be over," said she; "let me rise, and obtain some success this very day. I have but ten days, and this evening two of them will be gone."

In the morning, when they entered Milady's chamber they had brought her breakfast. Now, she thought, they could not long delay coming to clear the table, and that Felton would then reappear.

Milady was not deceived. Felton reappeared, and without observing whether Milady had or had not touched her repast, made a sign that the table should be carried out of the room, it having been brought in ready spread.

Felton remained behind; he held a book in his hand.

Milady, reclining in an armchair near the chimney, beautiful, pale, and resigned, looked like a holy virgin awaiting martyrdom.

Felton approached her, and said, "Lord de Winter, who is a Catholic, like yourself, madame, thinking that the deprivation of the rites and ceremonies of your church might be painful to you, has consented that you should read every day the ordinary of your Mass; and here is a book which contains the ritual."

At the manner in which Felton laid the book upon the little table near which Milady was sitting, at the tone in which he pronounced the two words, YOUR MASS, at the disdainful smile with which he accompanied them, Milady raised her head, and looked more attentively at the officer.

By that plain arrangement of the hair, by that costume of extreme simplicity, by the brow polished like marble and as hard and impenetrable, she recognized one of those gloomy Puritans she had so often met, not only in the court of King James, but in that of the King of France, where, in spite of the remembrance of the St. Bartholomew, they sometimes came to seek refuge.

She then had one of those sudden inspirations which only people of genius receive in great crises, in supreme moments which are to decide their fortunes or their lives.

Those two words, YOUR MASS, and a simple glance cast upon Felton, revealed to her all the importance of the reply she was about to make; but with that rapidity of intelligence which was peculiar to her, this reply, ready arranged, presented itself to her lips:

"I?" said she, with an accent of disdain in unison with that which she had remarked in the voice of the young officer, "I, sir? MY MASS? Lord de Winter, the corrupted Catholic, knows very well that I am not of his religion, and this is a snare he wishes to lay for me!"

"And of what religion are you, then, madame?" asked Felton, with an astonishment which in spite of the empire he held over himself he could not entirely conceal.

"I will tell it," cried Milady, with a feigned exultation, "on the day when I shall have suffered sufficiently for my faith."

The look of Felton revealed to Milady the full extent of the space she had opened for herself by this single word.

The young officer, however, remained mute and motionless; his look alone had spoken.

"I am in the hands of my enemies," continued she, with that tone of enthusiasm which she knew was familiar to the Puritans. "Well, let my God save me, or let me perish for my God! That is the reply I beg you to make to Lord de Winter. And as to this book," added she, pointing to the manual with her finger but without touching it, as if she must be contaminated by it, "you may carry it back and make use of it yourself, for doubtless you are doubly the accomplice of Lord de Winter--the accomplice in his persecutions, the accomplice in his heresies."

Felton made no reply, took the book with the same appearance of repugnance which he had before manifested, and retired pensively.

Lord de Winter came toward five o'clock in the evening. Milady had had time, during the whole day, to trace her plan of conduct. She received him like a woman who had already recovered all her advantages.

"It appears," said the baron, seating himself in the armchair opposite that occupied by Milady, and stretching out his legs carelessly upon the hearth, "it appears we have made a little apostasy!"

"What do you mean, sir!"

"I mean to say that since we last met you have changed your religion. You have not by chance married a Protestant for a third husband, have you?"

"Explain yourself, my Lord," replied the prisoner, with majesty; "for though I hear your words, I declare I do not understand them."

"Then you have no religion at all; I like that best," replied Lord de Winter, laughing.

"Certainly that is most in accord with your own principles," replied Milady, frigidly.

"Oh, I confess it is all the same to me."

"Oh, you need not avow this religious indifference, my Lord; your debaucheries and crimes would vouch for it."

"What, you talk of debaucheries, Madame Messalina, Lady Macbeth! Either I misunderstand you or you are very shameless!"

"You only speak thus because you are overheard," coolly replied Milady; "and you wish to interest your jailers and your hangmen against me."

"My jailers and my hangmen! Heyday, madame! you are taking a poetical tone, and the comedy of yesterday turns to a tragedy this evening. As to the rest, in eight days you will be where you ought to be, and my task will be completed."

"Infamous task! impious task!" cried Milady, with the exultation of a victim who provokes his judge.

"My word," said de Winter, rising, "I think the hussy is going mad! Come, come, calm yourself, Madame Puritan, or I'll remove you to a dungeon. It's my Spanish wine that has got into your head, is it not? But never mind; that sort of intoxication is not dangerous, and will have no bad effects."

And Lord de Winter retired swearing, which at that period was a very knightly habit.

Felton was indeed behind the door, and had not lost one word of this scene. Milady had guessed aright.

"Yes, go, go!" said she to her brother; "the effects ARE drawing near, on the contrary; but you, weak fool, will not see them until it is too late to shun them."

Silence was re-established. Two hours passed away. Milady's supper was brought in, and she was found deeply engaged in saying her prayers aloud--prayers which she had learned of an old servant of her second husband, a most austere Puritan. She appeared to be in ecstasy, and did not pay the least attention to what was going on around her. Felton made a sign that she should not be disturbed; and when all was arranged, he went out quietly with the soldiers.

Milady knew she might be watched, so she continued her prayers to the end; and it appeared to her that the soldier who was on duty at her door did not march with the same step, and seemed to listen. For the moment she wished nothing better. She arose, came to the table, ate but little, and drank only water.

An hour after, her table was cleared; but Milady remarked that this time Felton did not accompany the soldiers. He feared, then, to see her too often.

She turned toward the wall to smile--for there was in this smile such an expression of triumph that this smile alone would have betrayed her.

She allowed, therefore, half an hour to pass away; and as at that moment all was silence in the old castle, as nothing was heard but the eternal murmur of the waves--that immense breaking of the ocean--with her pure, harmonious, and powerful voice, she began the first couplet of the psalm then in great favor with the Puritans:

"Thou leavest thy servants, Lord, To see if they be strong; But soon thou dost afford Thy hand to lead them on."

These verses were not excellent--very far from it; but as it is well known, the Puritans did not pique themselves upon their poetry.

While singing, Milady listened. The soldier on guard at her door stopped, as if he had been changed into stone. Milady was then able to judge of the effect she had produced.

Then she continued her singing with inexpressible fervor and feeling. It appeared to her that the sounds spread to a distance beneath the vaulted roofs, and carried with them a magic charm to soften the hearts of her jailers. It however likewise appeared that the soldier on duty--a zealous Catholic, no doubt--shook off the charm, for through the door he called: "Hold your tongue, madame! Your song is as dismal as a 'De profundis'; and if besides the pleasure of being in garrison here, we must hear such things as these, no mortal can hold out."

"Silence!" then exclaimed another stern voice which Milady recognized as that of Felton. "What are you meddling with, stupid? Did anybody order you to prevent that woman from singing? No. You were told to guard her--to fire at her if she attempted to fly. Guard her! If she flies, kill her; but don't exceed your orders."

An expression of unspeakable joy lightened the countenance of Milady; but this expression was fleeting as the reflection of lightning. Without appearing to have heard the dialogue, of which she had not lost a word, she began again, giving to her voice all the charm, all the power, all the seduction the demon had bestowed upon it:

"For all my tears, my cares, My exile, and my chains, I have my youth, my prayers, And God, who counts my pains."

Her voice, of immense power and sublime expression, gave to the rude, unpolished poetry of these psalms a magic and an effect which the most exalted Puritans rarely found in the songs of their brethren, and which they were forced to ornament with all the resources of their imagination. Felton believed he heard the singing of the angel who consoled the three Hebrews in the furnace.

Milady continued:

"One day our doors will ope, With God come our desire; And if betrays that hope, To death we can aspire."

This verse, into which the terrible enchantress threw her whole soul, completed the trouble which had seized the heart of the young officer. He opened the door quickly; and Milady saw him appear, pale as usual, but with his eye inflamed and almost wild.

"Why do you sing thus, and with such a voice?" said he.

"Your pardon, sir," said Milady, with mildness. "I forgot that my songs are out of place in this castle. I have perhaps offended you in your creed; but it was without wishing to do so, I swear. Pardon me, then, a fault which is perhaps great, but which certainly was involuntary."

Milady was so beautiful at this moment, the religious ecstasy in which she appeared to be plunged gave such an expression to her countenance, that Felton was so dazzled that he fancied he beheld the angel whom he had only just before heard.

"Yes, yes," said he; "you disturb, you agitate the people who live in the castle."

The poor, senseless young man was not aware of the incoherence of his words, while Milady was reading with her lynx's eyes the very depths of his heart.

"I will be silent, then," said Milady, casting down her eyes with all the sweetness she could give to her voice, with all the resignation she could impress upon her manner.

"No, no, madame," said Felton, "only do not sing so loud, particularly at night."

And at these words Felton, feeling that he could not long maintain his severity toward his prisoner, rushed out of the room.

"You have done right, Lieutenant," said the soldier. "Such songs disturb the mind; and yet we become accustomed to them, her voice is so beautiful."

54 Captivity: The Third Day

Felton had fallen; but there was still another step to be taken. He must be retained, or rather he must be left quite alone; and Milady but obscurely perceived the means which could lead to this result.

Still more must be done. He must be made to speak, in order that he might be spoken to--for Milady very well knew that her greatest seduction was in her voice, which so skillfully ran over the whole gamut of tones from human speech to language celestial.

Yet in spite of all this seduction Milady might fail--for Felton was forewarned, and that against the least chance. From that moment she watched all his actions, all his words, from the simplest glance of his eyes to his gestures--even to a breath that could be interpreted as a sigh. In short, she studied everything, as a skillful comedian does to whom a new part has been assigned in a line to which he is not accustomed.

Face to face with Lord de Winter her plan of conduct was more easy. She had laid that down the preceding evening. To remain silent and dignified in his presence; from time to time to irritate him by affected disdain, by a contemptuous word; to provoke him to threats and violence which would produce a contrast with her own resignation--such was her plan. Felton would see all; perhaps he would say nothing, but he would see.

In the morning, Felton came as usual; but Milady allowed him to preside over all the preparations for breakfast without addressing a word to him. At the moment when he was about to retire, she was cheered with a ray of hope, for she thought he was about to speak; but his lips moved without any sound leaving his mouth, and making a powerful effort to control himself, he sent back to his heart the words that were about to escape from his lips, and went out. Toward midday, Lord de Winter entered.

It was a tolerably fine winter's day, and a ray of that pale English sun which lights but does not warm came through the bars of her prison.

Milady was looking out at the window, and pretended not to hear the door as it opened.

"Ah, ah!" said Lord de Winter, "after having played comedy, after having played tragedy, we are now playing melancholy?"

The prisoner made no reply.

"Yes, yes," continued Lord de Winter, "I understand. You would like very well to be at liberty on that beach! You would like very well to be in a good ship dancing upon the waves of that emerald-green sea; you would like very well, either on land or on the ocean, to lay for me one of those nice little ambuscades you are so skillful in planning. Patience, patience! In four days' time the shore will be beneath your feet, the sea will be open to you--more open than will perhaps be agreeable to you, for in four days England will be relieved of you."

Milady folded her hands, and raising her fine eyes toward heaven, "Lord, Lord," said she, with an angelic meekness of gesture and tone, "pardon this man, as I myself pardon him."

"Yes, pray, accursed woman!" cried the baron; "your prayer is so much the more generous from your being, I swear to you, in the power of a man who will never pardon you!" and he went out.

At the moment he went out a piercing glance darted through the opening of the nearly closed door, and she perceived Felton, who drew quickly to one side to prevent being seen by her.

Then she threw herself upon her knees, and began to pray.

"My God, my God!" said she, "thou knowest in what holy cause I suffer; give me, then, strength to suffer."

The door opened gently; the beautiful supplicant pretended not to hear the noise, and in a voice broken by tears, she continued:

"God of vengeance! God of goodness! wilt thou allow the frightful projects of this man to be accomplished?"

Then only she pretended to hear the sound of Felton's steps, and rising quick as thought, she blushed, as if ashamed of being surprised on her knees.

"I do not like to disturb those who pray, madame," said Felton, seriously; "do not disturb yourself on my account, I beseech you."

"How do you know I was praying, sir?" said Milady, in a voice broken by sobs. "You were deceived, sir; I was not praying."

"Do you think, then, madame," replied Felton, in the same serious voice, but with a milder tone, "do you think I assume the right of preventing a creature from prostrating herself before her Creator? God forbid! Besides, repentance becomes the guilty; whatever crimes they may have committed, for me the guilty are sacred at the feet of God!"

"Guilty? I?" said Milady, with a smile which might have disarmed the angel of the last judgment. "Guilty? Oh, my God, thou knowest whether I am guilty! Say I am condemned, sir, if you please; but you know that God, who loves martyrs, sometimes permits the innocent to be condemned."

"Were you condemned, were you innocent, were you a martyr," replied Felton, "the greater would be the necessity for prayer; and I myself would aid you with my prayers."

"Oh, you are a just man!" cried Milady, throwing herself at his feet. "I can hold out no longer, for I fear I shall be wanting in strength at the moment when I shall be forced to undergo the struggle, and confess my faith. Listen, then, to the supplication of a despairing woman. You are abused, sir; but that is not the question. I only ask you one favor; and if you grant it me, I will bless you in this world and in the next."

"Speak to the master, madame," said Felton; "happily I am neither charged with the power of pardoning nor punishing. It is upon one higher placed than I am that God has laid this responsibility."

"To you--no, to you alone! Listen to me, rather than add to my destruction, rather than add to my ignominy!"

"If you have merited this shame, madame, if you have incurred this ignominy, you must submit to it as an offering to God."

"What do you say? Oh, you do not understand me! When I speak of ignominy, you think I speak of some chastisement, of imprisonment or death. Would to heaven! Of what consequence to me is imprisonment or death?"

"It is I who no longer understand you, madame," said Felton.

"Or, rather, who pretend not to understand me, sir!" replied the prisoner, with a smile of incredulity.

"No, madame, on the honor of a soldier, on the faith of a Christian."

"What, you are ignorant of Lord de Winter's designs upon me?"

"I am."

"Impossible; you are his confidant!"

"I never lie, madame."

"Oh, he conceals them too little for you not to divine them."

"I seek to divine nothing, madame; I wait till I am confided in, and apart from that which Lord de Winter has said to me before you, he has confided nothing to me."

"Why, then," cried Milady, with an incredible tone of truthfulness, "you are not his accomplice; you do not know that he destines me to a disgrace which all the punishments of the world cannot equal in horror?"

"You are deceived, madame," said Felton, blushing; "Lord de Winter is not capable of such a crime."

"Good," said Milady to herself; "without thinking what it is, he calls it a crime!" Then aloud, "The friend of THAT WRETCH is capable of everything."

"Whom do you call 'that wretch'?" asked Felton.

"Are there, then, in England two men to whom such an epithet can be applied?"

"You mean George Villiers?" asked Felton, whose looks became excited.

"Whom Pagans and unbelieving Gentiles call Duke of Buckingham," replied Milady. "I could not have thought that there was an Englishman in all England who would have required so long an explanation to make him understand of whom I was speaking."

"The hand of the Lord is stretched over him," said Felton; "he will not escape the chastisement he deserves."

Felton only expressed, with regard to the duke, the feeling of execration which all the English had declared toward him whom the Catholics themselves called the extortioner, the pillager, the debauchee, and whom the Puritans styled simply Satan.

"Oh, my God, my God!" cried Milady; "when I supplicate thee to pour upon this man the chastisement which is his due, thou knowest it is not my own vengeance I pursue, but the deliverance of a whole nation that I implore!"

"Do you know him, then?" asked Felton.

"At length he interrogates me!" said Milady to herself, at the height of joy at having obtained so quickly such a great result. "Oh, know him? Yes, yes! to my misfortune, to my eternal misfortune!" and Milady twisted her arms as if in a paroxysm of grief.

Felton no doubt felt within himself that his strength was abandoning him, and he made several steps toward the door; but the prisoner, whose eye never left him, sprang in pursuit of him and stopped him.

"Sir," cried she, "be kind, be clement, listen to my prayer! That knife, which the fatal prudence of the baron deprived me of, because he knows the use I would make of it! Oh, hear me to the end! that knife, give it to me for a minute only, for mercy's, for pity's sake! I will embrace your knees! You shall shut the door that you may be certain I contemplate no injury to you! My God! to you--the only just, good, and compassionate being I have met with! To you--my preserver, perhaps! One minute that knife, one minute, a single minute, and I will restore it to you through the grating of the door. Only one minute, Mr. Felton, and you will have saved my honor!"

"To kill yourself?" cried Felton, with terror, forgetting to withdraw his hands from the hands of the prisoner, "to kill yourself?"

"I have told, sir," murmured Milady, lowering her voice, and allowing herself to sink overpowered to the ground; "I have told my secret! He knows all! My God, I am lost!"

Felton remained standing, motionless and undecided.

"He still doubts," thought Milady; "I have not been earnest enough."

Someone was heard in the corridor; Milady recognized the step of Lord de Winter.

Felton recognized it also, and made a step toward the door.

Milady sprang toward him. "Oh, not a word," said she in a concentrated voice, "not a word of all that I have said to you to this man, or I am lost, and it would be you--you--"

Then as the steps drew near, she became silent for fear of being heard, applying, with a gesture of infinite terror, her beautiful hand to Felton's mouth.

Felton gently repulsed Milady, and she sank into a chair.

Lord de Winter passed before the door without stopping, and they heard the noise of his footsteps soon die away.

Felton, as pale as death, remained some instants with his ear bent and listening; then, when the sound was quite extinct, he breathed like a man awaking from a dream, and rushed out of the apartment.

"Ah!" said Milady, listening in her turn to the noise of Felton's steps, which withdrew in a direction opposite to those of Lord de Winter; "at length you are mine!"

Then her brow darkened. "If he tells the baron," said she, "I am lost--for the baron, who knows very well that I shall not kill myself, will place me before him with a knife in my hand, and he will discover that all this despair is but acted."

She placed herself before the glass, and regarded herself attentively; never had she appeared more beautiful.

"Oh, yes," said she, smiling, "but we won't tell him!"

In the evening Lord de Winter accompanied the supper.

"Sir," said Milady, "is your presence an indispensable accessory of my captivity? Could you not spare me the increase of torture which your visits cause me?"

"How, dear sister!" said Lord de Winter. "Did not you sentimentally inform me with that pretty mouth of yours, so cruel to me today, that you came to England solely for the pleasure of seeing me at your ease, an enjoyment of which you told me you so sensibly felt the deprivation that you had risked everything for it--seasickness, tempest, captivity? Well, here I am; be satisfied. Besides, this time, my visit has a motive."

Milady trembled; she thought Felton had told all. Perhaps never in her life had this woman, who had experienced so many opposite and powerful emotions, felt her heart beat so violently.

She was seated. Lord de Winter took a chair, drew it toward her, and sat down close beside her. Then taking a paper out of his pocket, he unfolded it slowly.

"Here," said he, "I want to show you the kind of passport which I have drawn up, and which will serve you henceforward as the rule of order in the life I consent to leave you."

Then turning his eyes from Milady to the paper, he read: "'Order to conduct--' The name is blank," interrupted Lord de Winter. "If you have any preference you can point it out to me; and if it be not within a thousand leagues of London, attention will be paid to your wishes. I will begin again, then:

"'Order to conduct to--the person named Charlotte Backson, branded by the justice of the kingdom of France, but liberated after chastisement. She is to dwell in this place without ever going more than three leagues from it. In case of any attempt to escape, the penalty of death is to be applied. She will receive five shillings per day for lodging and food'".

"That order does not concern me," replied Milady, coldly, "since it bears another name than mine."

"A name? Have you a name, then?"

"I bear that of your brother."

"Ay, but you are mistaken. My brother is only your second husband; and your first is still living. Tell me his name, and I will put it in the place of the name of Charlotte Backson. No? You will not? You are silent? Well, then you must be registered as Charlotte Backson."

Milady remained silent; only this time it was no longer from affectation, but from terror. She believed the order ready for execution. She thought that Lord de Winter had hastened her departure; she thought she was condemned to set off that very evening. Everything in her mind was lost for an instant; when all at once she perceived that no signature was attached to the order. The joy she felt at this discovery was so great she could not conceal it.

"Yes, yes," said Lord de Winter, who perceived what was passing in her mind; "yes, you look for the signature, and you say to yourself: 'All is not lost, for that order is not signed. It is only shown to me to terrify me, that's all.' You are mistaken. Tomorrow this order will be sent to the Duke of Buckingham. The day after tomorrow it will return signed by his hand and marked with his seal; and four-and-twenty hours afterward I will answer for its being carried into execution. Adieu, madame. That is all I had to say to you."

"And I reply to you, sir, that this abuse of power, this exile under a fictitious name, are infamous!"

"Would you like better to be hanged in your true name, Milady? You know that the English laws are inexorable on the abuse of marriage. Speak freely. Although my name, or rather that of my brother, would be mixed up with the affair, I will risk the scandal of a public trial to make myself certain of getting rid of you."

Milady made no reply, but became as pale as a corpse.

"Oh, I see you prefer peregrination. That's well madame; and there is an old proverb that says, 'Traveling trains youth.' My faith! you are not wrong after all, and life is sweet. That's the reason why I take such care you shall not deprive me of mine. There only remains, then, the question of the five shillings to be settled. You think me rather parsimonious, don't you? That's because I don't care to leave you the means of corrupting your jailers. Besides, you will always have your charms left to seduce them with. Employ them, if your check with regard to Felton has not disgusted you with attempts of that kind."

"Felton has not told him," said Milady to herself. "Nothing is lost, then."

"And now, madame, till I see you again! Tomorrow I will come and announce to you the departure of my messenger."

Lord de Winter rose, saluted her ironically, and went out.

Milady breathed again. She had still four days before her. Four days would quite suffice to complete the seduction of Felton.

A terrible idea, however, rushed into her mind. She thought that Lord de Winter would perhaps send Felton himself to get the order signed by the Duke of Buckingham. In that case Felton would escape her--for in order to secure success, the magic of a continuous seduction was necessary. Nevertheless, as we have said, one circumstance reassured her. Felton had not spoken.

As she would not appear to be agitated by the threats of Lord de Winter, she placed herself at the table and ate.

Then, as she had done the evening before, she fell on her knees and repeated her prayers aloud. As on the evening before, the soldier stopped his march to listen to her.

Soon after she heard lighter steps than those of the sentinel, which came from the end of the corridor and stopped before her door.

"It is he," said she. And she began the same religious chant which had so strongly excited Felton the evening before.

But although her voice--sweet, full, and sonorous--vibrated as harmoniously and as affectingly as ever, the door remained shut. It appeared however to Milady that in one of the furtive glances she darted from time to time at the grating of the door she thought she saw the ardent eyes of the young man through the narrow opening. But whether this was reality or vision, he had this time sufficient self-command not to enter.

However, a few instants after she had finished her religious song, Milady thought she heard a profound sigh. Then the same steps she had heard approach slowly withdrew, as if with regret.

55 Captivity: The Fourth Day

The next day, when Felton entered Milady's apartment he found her standing, mounted upon a chair, holding in her hands a cord made by means of torn cambric handkerchiefs, twisted into a kind of rope one with another, and tied at the ends. At the noise Felton made in entering, Milady leaped lightly to the ground, and tried to conceal behind her the improvised cord she held in her hand.

The young man was more pale than usual, and his eyes, reddened by want of sleep, denoted that he had passed a feverish night. Nevertheless, his brow was armed with a severity more austere than ever.

He advanced slowly toward Milady, who had seated herself, and taking an end of the murderous rope which by neglect, or perhaps by design, she allowed to be seen, "What is this, madame?" he asked coldly.

"That? Nothing," said Milady, smiling with that painful expression which she knew so well how to give to her smile. "Ennui is the mortal enemy of prisoners; I had ennui, and I amused myself with twisting that rope."

Felton turned his eyes toward the part of the wall of the apartment before which he had found Milady standing in the armchair in which she was now seated, and over her head he perceived a gilt-headed screw, fixed in the wall for the purpose of hanging up clothes or weapons.

He started, and the prisoner saw that start--for though her eyes were cast down, nothing escaped her.

"What were you doing on that armchair?" asked he.

"Of what consequence?" replied Milady.

"But," replied Felton, "I wish to know."

"Do not question me," said the prisoner; "you know that we who are true Christians are forbidden to lie."

"Well, then," said Felton, "I will tell you what you were doing, or rather what you meant to do; you were going to complete the fatal project you cherish in your mind. Remember, madame, if our God forbids falsehood, he much more severely condemns suicide."

"When God sees one of his creatures persecuted unjustly, placed between suicide and dishonor, believe me, sir," replied Milady, in a tone of deep conviction, "God pardons suicide, for then suicide becomes martyrdom."

"You say either too much or too little; speak, madame. In the name of heaven, explain yourself."

"That I may relate my misfortunes for you to treat them as fables; that I may tell you my projects for you to go and betray them to my persecutor? No, sir. Besides, of what importance to you is the life or death of a condemned wretch? You are only responsible for my body, is it not so? And provided you produce a carcass that may be recognized as mine, they will require no more of you; nay, perhaps you will even have a double reward."

"I, madame, I?" cried Felton. "You suppose that I would ever accept the price of your life? Oh, you cannot believe what you say!"

"Let me act as I please, Felton, let me act as I please," said Milady, elated. "Every soldier must be ambitious, must he not? You are a lieutenant? Well, you will follow me to the grave with the rank of captain."

"What have I, then, done to you," said Felton, much agitated, "that you should load me with such a responsibility before God and before men? In a few days you will be away from this place; your life, madame, will then no longer be under my care, and," added he, with a sigh, "then you can do what you will with it."

"So," cried Milady, as if she could not resist giving utterance to a holy indignation, "you, a pious man, you who are called a just man, you ask but one thing--and that is that you may not be inculpated, annoyed, by my death!"

"It is my duty to watch over your life, madame, and I will watch."

"But do you understand the mission you are fulfilling? Cruel enough, if I am guilty; but what name can you give it, what name will the Lord give it, if I am innocent?"

"I am a soldier, madame, and fulfill the orders I have received."

"Do you believe, then, that at the day of the Last Judgment God will separate blind executioners from iniquitous judges? You are not willing that I should kill my body, and you make yourself the agent of him who would kill my soul."

"But I repeat it again to you," replied Felton, in great emotion, "no danger threatens you; I will answer for Lord de Winter as for myself."

"Dunce," cried Milady, "dunce! who dares to answer for another man, when the wisest, when those most after God's own heart, hesitate to answer for themselves, and who ranges himself on the side of the strongest and the most fortunate, to crush the weakest and the most unfortunate."

"Impossible, madame, impossible," murmured Felton, who felt to the bottom of his heart the justness of this argument. "A prisoner, you will not recover your liberty through me; living, you will not lose your life through me."

"Yes," cried Milady, "but I shall lose that which is much dearer to me than life, I shall lose my honor, Felton; and it is you, you whom I make responsible, before God and before men, for my shame and my infamy."

This time Felton, immovable as he was, or appeared to be, could not resist the secret influence which had already taken possession of him. To see this woman, so beautiful, fair as the brightest vision, to see her by turns overcome with grief and threatening; to resist at once the ascendancy of grief and beauty--it was too much for a visionary; it was too much for a brain weakened by the ardent dreams of an ecstatic faith; it was too much for a heart furrowed by the love of heaven that burns, by the hatred of men that devours.

Milady saw the trouble. She felt by intuition the flame of the opposing passions which burned with the blood in the veins of the young fanatic. As a skillful general, seeing the enemy ready to surrender, marches toward him with a cry of victory, she rose, beautiful as an antique priestess, inspired like a Christian virgin, her arms extended, her throat uncovered, her hair disheveled, holding with one hand her robe modestly drawn over her breast, her look illumined by that fire which had already created such disorder in the veins of the young Puritan, and went toward him, crying out with a vehement air, and in her melodious voice, to which on this occasion she communicated a terrible energy:

"Let this victim to Baal be sent, To the lions the martyr be thrown! Thy God shall teach thee to repent! From th' abyss he'll give ear to my moan."

Felton stood before this strange apparition like one petrified.

"Who art thou? Who art thou?" cried he, clasping his hands. "Art thou a messenger from God; art thou a minister from hell; art thou an angel or a demon; callest thou thyself Eloa or Astarte?"

"Do you not know me, Felton? I am neither an angel nor a demon; I am a daughter of earth, I am a sister of thy faith, that is all."

"Yes, yes!" said Felton, "I doubted, but now I believe."

"You believe, and still you are an accomplice of that child of Belial who is called Lord de Winter! You believe, and yet you leave me in the hands of mine enemies, of the enemy of England, of the enemy of God! You believe, and yet you deliver me up to him who fills and defiles the world with his heresies and debaucheries--to that infamous Sardanapalus whom the blind call the Duke of Buckingham, and whom believers name Antichrist!"

"I deliver you up to Buckingham? I? what mean you by that?"

"They have eyes," cried Milady, "but they see not; ears have they, but they hear not."

"Yes, yes!" said Felton, passing his hands over his brow, covered with sweat, as if to remove his last doubt. "Yes, I recognize the voice which speaks to me in my dreams; yes, I recognize the features of the angel who appears to me every night, crying to my soul, which cannot sleep: 'Strike, save England, save thyself--for thou wilt die without having appeased God!' Speak, speak!" cried Felton, "I can understand you now."

A flash of terrible joy, but rapid as thought, gleamed from the eyes of Milady.

However fugitive this homicide flash, Felton saw it, and started as if its light had revealed the abysses of this woman's heart. He recalled, all at once, the warnings of Lord de Winter, the seductions of Milady, her first attempts after her arrival. He drew back a step, and hung down his head, without, however, ceasing to look at her, as if, fascinated by this strange creature, he could not detach his eyes from her eyes.

Milady was not a woman to misunderstand the meaning of this hesitation. Under her apparent emotions her icy coolness never abandoned her. Before

Felton replied, and before she should be forced to resume this conversation, so difficult to be sustained in the same exalted tone, she let her hands fall; and as if the weakness of the woman overpowered the enthusiasm of the inspired fanatic, she said: "But no, it is not for me to be the Judith to deliver Bethulia from this Holofernes. The sword of the eternal is too heavy for my arm. Allow me, then, to avoid dishonor by death; let me take refuge in martyrdom. I do not ask you for liberty, as a guilty one would, nor for vengeance, as would a pagan. Let me die; that is all. I supplicate you, I implore you on my knees--let me die, and my last sigh shall be a blessing for my preserver."

Hearing that voice, so sweet and suppliant, seeing that look, so timid and downcast, Felton reproached himself. By degrees the enchantress had clothed herself with that magic adornment which she assumed and threw aside at will; that is to say, beauty, meekness, and tears--and above all, the irresistible attraction of mystical voluptuousness, the most devouring of all voluptuousness.

"Alas!" said Felton, "I can do but one thing, which is to pity you if you prove to me you are a victim! But Lord de Winter makes cruel accusations against you. You are a Christian; you are my sister in religion. I feel myself drawn toward you--I, who have never loved anyone but my benefactor--I who have met with nothing but traitors and impious men. But you, madame, so beautiful in reality, you, so pure in appearance, must have committed great iniquities for Lord de Winter to pursue you thus."

"They have eyes," repeated Milady, with an accent of indescribable grief, "but they see not; ears have they, but they hear not."

"But," cried the young officer, "speak, then, speak!"

"Confide my shame to you," cried Milady, with the blush of modesty upon her countenance, "for often the crime of one becomes the shame of another--confide my shame to you, a man, and I a woman? Oh," continued she, placing her hand modestly over her beautiful eyes, "never! never!--I could not!"

"To me, to a brother?" said Felton.

Milady looked at him for some time with an expression which the young man took for doubt, but which, however, was nothing but observation, or rather the wish to fascinate.

Felton, in his turn a suppliant, clasped his hands.

"Well, then," said Milady, "I confide in my brother; I will dare to--"

At this moment the steps of Lord de Winter were heard; but this time the terrible brother-in-law of Milady did not content himself, as on the preceding day, with passing before the door and going away again. He paused, exchanged two words with the sentinel; then the door opened, and he appeared.

During the exchange of these two words Felton drew back quickly, and when Lord de Winter entered, he was several paces from the prisoner.

The baron entered slowly, sending a scrutinizing glance from Milady to the young officer.

"You have been here a very long time, John," said he. "Has this woman been relating her crimes to you? In that case I can comprehend the length of the conversation."

Felton started; and Milady felt she was lost if she did not come to the assistance of the disconcerted Puritan.

"Ah, you fear your prisoner should escape!" said she. "Well, ask your worthy jailer what favor I this instant solicited of him."

"You demanded a favor?" said the baron, suspiciously.

"Yes, my Lord," replied the young man, confused.

"And what favor, pray?" asked Lord de Winter.

"A knife, which she would return to me through the grating of the door a minute after she had received it," replied Felton.

"There is someone, then, concealed here whose throat this amiable lady is desirous of cutting," said de Winter, in an ironical, contemptuous tone.

"There is myself," replied Milady.

"I have given you the choice between America and Tyburn," replied Lord de Winter. "Choose Tyburn, madame. Believe me, the cord is more certain than the knife."

Felton grew pale, and made a step forward, remembering that at the moment he entered Milady had a rope in her hand.

"You are right," said she, "I have often thought of it." Then she added in a low voice, "And I will think of it again."

Felton felt a shudder run to the marrow of his bones; probably Lord de Winter perceived this emotion.

"Mistrust yourself, John," said he. "I have placed reliance upon you, my friend. Beware! I have warned you! But be of good courage, my lad; in three days we shall be delivered from this creature, and where I shall send her she can harm nobody."

"You hear him!" cried Milady, with vehemence, so that the baron might believe she was addressing heaven, and that Felton might understand she was addressing him.

Felton lowered his head and reflected.

The baron took the young officer by the arm, and turned his head over his shoulder, so as not to lose sight of Milady till he was gone out.

"Well," said the prisoner, when the door was shut, "I am not so far advanced as I believed. De Winter has changed his usual stupidity into a strange prudence. It is the desire of vengeance, and how desire molds a man! As to Felton, he hesitates. Ah, he is not a man like that cursed d'Artagnan. A Puritan only adores virgins, and he adores them by clasping his hands. A Musketeer loves women, and he loves them by clasping his arms round them."

Milady waited, then, with much impatience, for she feared the day would pass away without her seeing Felton again. At last, in an hour after the scene we have just described, she heard someone speaking in a low voice at the door. Presently the door opened, and she perceived Felton.

The young man advanced rapidly into the chamber, leaving the door open behind him, and making a sign to Milady to be silent; his face was much agitated.

"What do you want with me?" said she.

"Listen," replied Felton, in a low voice. "I have just sent away the sentinel that I might remain here without anybody knowing it, in order to speak to you without being overheard. The baron has just related a frightful story to me."

Milady assumed her smile of a resigned victim, and shook her head.

"Either you are a demon," continued Felton, "or the baron--my benefactor, my father--is a monster. I have known you four days; I have loved him four years. I therefore may hesitate between you. Be not alarmed at what I say; I want to be convinced. Tonight, after twelve, I will come and see you, and you shall convince me."

"No, Felton, no, my brother," said she; "the sacrifice is too great, and I feel what it must cost you. No, I am lost; do not be lost with me. My death will be much more eloquent than my life, and the silence of the corpse will convince you much better than the words of the prisoner."

"Be silent, madame," cried Felton, "and do not speak to me thus; I came to entreat you to promise me upon your honor, to swear to me by what you hold most sacred, that you will make no attempt upon your life."

"I will not promise," said Milady, "for no one has more respect for a promise or an oath than I have; and if I make a promise I must keep it."

"Well," said Felton, "only promise till you have seen me again. If, when you have seen me again, you still persist--well, then you shall be free, and I myself will give you the weapon you desire."

"Well," said Milady, "for you I will wait."

"Swear."

"I swear it, by our God. Are you satisfied?"

"Well," said Felton, "till tonight."

And he darted out of the room, shut the door, and waited in the corridor, the soldier's half-pike in his hand, and as if he had mounted guard in his place.

The soldier returned, and Felton gave him back his weapon.

Then, through the grating to which she had drawn near, Milady saw the young man make a sign with delirious fervor, and depart in an apparent transport of joy.

As for her, she returned to her place with a smile of savage contempt upon her lips, and repeated, blaspheming, that terrible name of God, by whom she had just sworn without ever having learned to know Him.

"My God," said she, "what a senseless fanatic! My God, it is I--I--and this fellow who will help me to avenge myself."

56 Captivity: The Fifth Day

Milady had however achieved a half-triumph, and success doubled her forces.

It was not difficult to conquer, as she had hitherto done, men prompt to let themselves be seduced, and whom the gallant education of a court led quickly into her net. Milady was handsome enough not to find much resistance on the part of the flesh, and she was sufficiently skillful to prevail over all the obstacles of the mind.

But this time she had to contend with an unpolished nature, concentrated and insensible by force of austerity. Religion and its observances had made Felton a man inaccessible to ordinary seductions. There fermented in that sublimated brain plans so vast, projects so tumultuous, that there remained no room for any capricious or material love--that sentiment which is fed by leisure and grows with corruption. Milady had, then, made a breach by her false virtue in the opinion of a man horribly prejudiced against her, and by her beauty in the heart of a man hitherto chaste and pure. In short, she had taken the measure of motives hitherto unknown to herself, through this experiment, made upon the most rebellious subject that nature and religion could submit to her study.

Many a time, nevertheless, during the evening she despaired of fate and of herself. She did not invoke God, we very well know, but she had faith in the genius of evil--that immense sovereignty which reigns in all the details of human life, and by which, as in the Arabian fable, a single pomegranate seed is sufficient to reconstruct a ruined world.

Milady, being well prepared for the reception of Felton, was able to erect her batteries for the next day. She knew she had only two days left; that when once the order was signed by Buckingham--and Buckingham would sign it the more readily from its bearing a false name, and he could not, therefore, recognize the woman in question--once this order was signed, we say, the baron would make her embark immediately, and she knew very well that women condemned to exile employ arms much less powerful in their seductions than the pretendedly virtuous woman whose beauty is lighted by the sun of the world, whose style the voice of fashion lauds, and whom a halo of aristocracy gilds with enchanting splendors. To be a woman condemned to a painful and disgraceful punishment is no impediment to beauty, but it is an obstacle to the recovery of power. Like all persons of real genius, Milady knew what suited her nature and her means. Poverty was repugnant to her; degradation took away two-thirds of her greatness. Milady was only a queen while among queens. The pleasure of satisfied pride was necessary to her domination. To command inferior beings was rather a humiliation than a pleasure for her.

She should certainly return from her exile--she did not doubt that a single instant; but how long might this exile last? For an active, ambitious nature, like that of Milady, days not spent in climbing are inauspicious days. What word, then, can be found to describe the days which they occupy in descending? To lose a year, two years, three years, is to talk of an eternity; to return after the death or disgrace of the cardinal, perhaps; to return when d'Artagnan and his friends, happy and triumphant, should have received from the queen the reward they had well acquired by the services they had rendered her--these were devouring ideas that a woman like Milady could not endure. For the rest, the storm which raged within her doubled her strength, and she would have burst the walls of her prison if her body had been able to take for a single instant the proportions of her mind.

Then that which spurred her on additionally in the midst of all this was the remembrance of the cardinal. What must the mistrustful, restless, suspicious cardinal think of her silence--the cardinal, not merely her only support, her only prop, her only protector at present, but still further, the principal instrument of her future fortune and vengeance? She knew him; she knew that at her return from a fruitless journey it would be in vain to tell him of her imprisonment, in vain to enlarge upon the sufferings she had undergone. The cardinal would reply, with the sarcastic calmness of the skeptic, strong at once by power and genius, "You should not have allowed yourself to be taken."

Then Milady collected all her energies, murmuring in the depths of her soul the name of Felton--the only beam of light that penetrated to her in the hell into which she had fallen; and like a serpent which folds and unfolds its rings to ascertain its strength, she enveloped Felton beforehand in the thousand meshes of her inventive imagination.

Time, however, passed away; the hours, one after another, seemed to awaken the clock as they passed, and every blow of the brass hammer resounded upon the heart of the prisoner. At nine o'clock, Lord de Winter made his customary visit, examined the window and the bars, sounded the floor and the walls, looked to the chimney and the doors, without, during this long and minute examination, he or Milady pronouncing a single word.

Doubtless both of them understood that the situation had become too serious to lose time in useless words and aimless wrath.

"Well," said the baron, on leaving her "you will not escape tonight!"

At ten o'clock Felton came and placed the sentinel. Milady recognized his step. She was as well acquainted with it now as a mistress is with that of the lover of her heart; and yet Milady at the same time detested and despised this weak fanatic.

That was not the appointed hour. Felton did not enter.

Two hours after, as midnight sounded, the sentinel was relieved. This time it WAS the hour, and from this moment Milady waited with impatience. The new sentinel commenced his walk in the corridor. At the expiration of ten minutes Felton came.

Milady was all attention.

"Listen," said the young man to the sentinel. "On no pretense leave the door, for you know that last night my Lord punished a soldier for having quit his post for an instant, although I, during his absence, watched in his place."

"Yes, I know it," said the soldier.

"I recommend you therefore to keep the strictest watch. For my part I am going to pay a second visit to this woman, who I fear entertains sinister intentions upon her own life, and I have received orders to watch her."

"Good!" murmured Milady; "the austere Puritan lies."

As to the soldier, he only smiled.

"Zounds, Lieutenant!" said he; "you are not unlucky in being charged with such commissions, particularly if my Lord has authorized you to look into her bed."

Felton blushed. Under any other circumstances he would have reprimanded the soldier for indulging in such pleasantry, but his conscience murmured too loud for his mouth to dare speak.

"If I call, come," said he. "If anyone comes, call me."

"I will, Lieutenant," said the soldier.

Felton entered Milady's apartment. Milady arose.

"You are here!" said she.

"I promised to come," said Felton, "and I have come."

"You promised me something else."

"What, my God!" said the young man, who in spite of his self-command felt his knees tremble and the sweat start from his brow.

"You promised to bring a knife, and to leave it with me after our interview."

"Say no more of that, madame," said Felton. "There is no situation, however terrible it may be, which can authorize a creature of God to inflict death upon himself. I have reflected, and I cannot, must not be guilty of such a sin."

"Ah, you have reflected!" said the prisoner, sitting down in her armchair, with a smile of disdain; "and I also have reflected."

"Upon what?"

"That I can have nothing to say to a man who does not keep his word."

"Oh, my God!" murmured Felton.

"You may retire," said Milady. "I will not talk."

"Here is the knife," said Felton, drawing from his pocket the weapon which he had brought, according to his promise, but which he hesitated to give to his prisoner.

"Let me see it," said Milady.

"For what purpose?"

"Upon my honor, I will instantly return it to you. You shall place it on that table, and you may remain between it and me."

Felton offered the weapon to Milady, who examined the temper of it attentively, and who tried the point on the tip of her finger.

"Well," said she, returning the knife to the young officer, "this is fine and good steel. You are a faithful friend, Felton."

Felton took back the weapon, and laid it upon the table, as he had agreed with the prisoner.

Milady followed him with her eyes, and made a gesture of satisfaction.

"Now," said she, "listen to me."

The request was needless. The young officer stood upright before her, awaiting her words as if to devour them.

"Felton," said Milady, with a solemnity full of melancholy, "imagine that your sister, the daughter of your father, speaks to you. While yet young, unfortunately handsome, I was dragged into a snare. I resisted. Ambushes and violences multiplied around me, but I resisted. The religion I serve, the God I adore, were blasphemed because I called upon that religion and that God, but still I resisted. Then outrages were heaped upon me, and as my soul was not subdued they wished to defile my body forever. Finally--"

Milady stopped, and a bitter smile passed over her lips.

"Finally," said Felton, "finally, what did they do?"

"At length, one evening my enemy resolved to paralyze the resistance he could not conquer. One evening he mixed a powerful narcotic with my water. Scarcely had I finished my repast, when I felt myself sink by degrees into a strange torpor. Although I was without mistrust, a vague fear seized me, and I tried to struggle against sleepiness. I arose. I wished to run to the window and call for help, but my legs refused their office. It appeared as if the ceiling sank upon my head and crushed me with its weight. I stretched out my arms. I tried to speak. I could only utter inarticulate sounds, and irresistible faintness came over me. I supported myself by a chair, feeling that I was about to fall, but this support was soon insufficient on account of my weak arms. I fell upon one knee, then upon both. I tried to pray, but my tongue was frozen. God doubtless neither heard nor saw me, and I sank upon the floor a prey to a slumber which resembled death.

"Of all that passed in that sleep, or the time which glided away while it lasted, I have no remembrance. The only thing I recollect is that I awoke in bed in a round chamber, the furniture of which was sumptuous, and into which light only penetrated by an opening in the ceiling. No door gave entrance to the room. It might be called a magnificent prison.

"It was a long time before I was able to make out what place I was in, or to take account of the details I describe. My mind appeared to strive in vain to shake off the heavy darkness of the sleep from which I could not rouse myself. I had vague perceptions of space traversed, of the rolling of a carriage, of a horrible dream in which my strength had become exhausted; but all this was so dark and so indistinct in my mind that these events seemed to belong to another life than mine, and yet mixed with mine in fantastic duality.

"At times the state into which I had fallen appeared so strange that I believed myself dreaming. I arose trembling. My clothes were near me on a chair; I neither remembered having undressed myself nor going to bed. Then by degrees the reality broke upon me, full of chaste terrors. I was no longer in the house where I had dwelt. As well as I could judge by the light of the sun, the day was already two-thirds gone. It was the evening before when I had fallen asleep; my sleep, then, must have lasted twenty-four hours! What had taken place during this long sleep?

"I dressed myself as quickly as possible; my slow and stiff motions all attested that the effects of the narcotic were not yet entirely dissipated. The chamber was evidently furnished for the reception of a woman; and the most finished coquette could not have formed a wish, but on casting her eyes about the apartment, she would have found that wish accomplished.

"Certainly I was not the first captive that had been shut up in this splendid prison; but you may easily comprehend, Felton, that the more superb the prison, the greater was my terror.

"Yes, it was a prison, for I tried in vain to get out of it. I sounded all the walls, in the hopes of discovering a door, but everywhere the walls returned a full and flat sound.

"I made the tour of the room at least twenty times, in search of an outlet of some kind; but there was none. I sank exhausted with fatigue and terror into an armchair.

"Meantime, night came on rapidly, and with night my terrors increased. I did not know but I had better remain where I was seated. It appeared that I was surrounded with unknown dangers into which I was about to fall at every instant. Although I had eaten nothing since the evening before, my fears prevented my feeling hunger.

"No noise from without by which I could measure the time reached me; I only supposed it must be seven or eight o'clock in the evening, for it was in the month of October and it was quite dark.

"All at once the noise of a door, turning on its hinges, made me start. A globe of fire appeared above the glazed opening of the ceiling, casting a strong light into my chamber; and I perceived with terror that a man was standing within a few paces of me.

"A table, with two covers, bearing a supper ready prepared, stood, as if by magic, in the middle of the apartment.

"That man was he who had pursued me during a whole year, who had vowed my dishonor, and who, by the first words that issued from his mouth, gave me to understand he had accomplished it the preceding night."

"Scoundrel!" murmured Felton.

"Oh, yes, scoundrel!" cried Milady, seeing the interest which the young officer, whose soul seemed to hang on her lips, took in this strange recital. "Oh, yes, scoundrel! He believed, having triumphed over me in my sleep, that all was completed. He came, hoping that I would accept my shame, as my shame was consummated; he came to offer his fortune in exchange for my love.

"All that the heart of a woman could contain of haughty contempt and disdainful words, I poured out upon this man. Doubtless he was accustomed to such reproaches, for he listened to me calm and smiling, with his arms crossed over his breast. Then, when he thought I had said all, he advanced toward me; I sprang toward the table, I seized a knife, I placed it to my breast.

"Take one step more," said I, "and in addition to my dishonor, you shall have my death to reproach yourself with."

"There was, no doubt, in my look, my voice, my whole person, that sincerity of gesture, of attitude, of accent, which carries conviction to the most perverse minds, for he paused.

"'Your death?' said he; 'oh, no, you are too charming a mistress to allow me to consent to lose you thus, after I have had the happiness to possess you only a single time. Adieu, my charmer; I will wait to pay you my next visit till you are in a better humor.'

"At these words he blew a whistle; the globe of fire which lighted the room reascended and disappeared. I found myself again in complete darkness. The same noise of a door opening and shutting was repeated the instant afterward; the flaming globe descended afresh, and I was completely alone.

"This moment was frightful; if I had any doubts as to my misfortune, these doubts had vanished in an overwhelming reality. I was in the power of a man whom I not only detested, but despised--of a man capable of anything, and who had already given me a fatal proof of what he was able to do."

"But who, then was this man?" asked Felton.

"I passed the night on a chair, starting at the least noise, for toward midnight the lamp went out, and I was again in darkness. But the night passed away without any fresh attempt on the part of my persecutor. Day came; the table had disappeared, only I had still the knife in my hand.

"This knife was my only hope.

"I was worn out with fatigue. Sleeplessness inflamed my eyes; I had not dared to sleep a single instant. The light of day reassured me; I went and threw myself on the bed, without parting with the emancipating knife, which I concealed under my pillow.

"When I awoke, a fresh meal was served.

"This time, in spite of my terrors, in spite of my agony, I began to feel a devouring hunger. It was forty-eight hours since I had taken any nourishment. I ate some bread and some fruit; then, remembering the narcotic mixed with the water I had drunk, I would not touch that which was placed on the table, but filled my glass at a marble fountain fixed in the wall over my dressing table.

"And yet, notwithstanding these precautions, I remained for some time in a terrible agitation of mind. But my fears were this time ill-founded; I passed the day without experiencing anything of the kind I dreaded.

"I took the precaution to half empty the carafe, in order that my suspicions might not be noticed.

"The evening came on, and with it darkness; but however profound was this darkness, my eyes began to accustom themselves to it. I saw, amid the shadows, the table sink through the floor; a quarter of an hour later it reappeared, bearing my supper. In an instant, thanks to the lamp, my chamber was once more lighted.

"I was determined to eat only such things as could not possibly have anything soporific introduced into them. Two eggs and some fruit composed my repast; then I drew another glass of water from my protecting fountain, and drank it.

"At the first swallow, it appeared to me not to have the same taste as in the morning. Suspicion instantly seized me. I paused, but I had already drunk half a glass.

"I threw the rest away with horror, and waited, with the dew of fear upon my brow.

"No doubt some invisible witness had seen me draw the water from that fountain, and had taken advantage of my confidence in it, the better to assure my ruin, so coolly resolved upon, so cruelly pursued.

"Half an hour had not passed when the same symptoms began to appear; but as I had only drunk half a glass of the water, I contended longer, and instead of falling entirely asleep, I sank into a state of drowsiness which left me a perception of what was passing around me, while depriving me of the strength either to defend myself or to fly.

"I dragged myself toward the bed, to seek the only defense I had left--my saving knife; but I could not reach the bolster. I sank on my knees, my hands clasped round one of the bedposts; then I felt that I was lost."

Felton became frightfully pale, and a convulsive tremor crept through his whole body.

"And what was most frightful," continued Milady, her voice altered, as if she still experienced the same agony as at that awful minute, "was that at this time I retained a consciousness of the danger that threatened me; was that my soul, if I may say so, waked in my sleeping body; was that I saw, that I heard. It is true that all was like a dream, but it was not the less frightful.

"I saw the lamp ascend, and leave me in darkness; then I heard the well-known creaking of the door although I had heard that door open but twice.

"I felt instinctively that someone approached me; it is said that the doomed wretch in the deserts of America thus feels the approach of the serpent.

"I wished to make an effort; I attempted to cry out. By an incredible effort of will I even raised myself up, but only to sink down again immediately, and to fall into the arms of my persecutor."

"Tell me who this man was!" cried the young officer.

Milady saw at a single glance all the painful feelings she inspired in Felton by dwelling on every detail of her recital; but she would not spare him a single pang. The more profoundly she wounded his heart, the more certainly he would avenge her. She continued, then, as if she had not heard his exclamation, or as if she thought the moment was not yet come to reply to it.

"Only this time it was no longer an inert body, without feeling, that the villain had to deal with. I have told you that without being able to regain the complete exercise of my faculties, I retained the sense of my danger. I struggled, then, with all my strength, and doubtless opposed, weak as I was, a long resistance, for I heard him cry out, 'These miserable Puritans! I knew very well that they tired out their executioners, but I did not believe them so strong against their lovers!'

"Alas! this desperate resistance could not last long. I felt my strength fail, and this time it was not my sleep that enabled the coward to prevail, but my swoon."

Felton listened without uttering any word or sound, except an inward expression of agony. The sweat streamed down his marble forehead, and his hand, under his coat, tore his breast.

"My first impulse, on coming to myself, was to feel under my pillow for the knife I had not been able to reach; if it had not been useful for defense, it might at least serve for expiation.

"But on taking this knife, Felton, a terrible idea occurred to me. I have sworn to tell you all, and I will tell you all. I have promised you the truth; I will tell it, were it to destroy me."

"The idea came into your mind to avenge yourself on this man, did it not?" cried Felton.

"Yes," said Milady. "The idea was not that of a Christian, I knew; but without doubt, that eternal enemy of our souls, that lion roaring constantly around us, breathed it into my mind. In short, what shall I say to you, Felton?" continued Milady, in the tone of a woman accusing herself of a crime. "This idea occurred to me, and did not leave me; it is of this homicidal thought that I now bear the punishment."

"Continue, continue!" said Felton; "I am eager to see you attain your vengeance!"

"Oh, I resolved that it should take place as soon as possible. I had no doubt he would return the following night. During the day I had nothing to fear.

"When the hour of breakfast came, therefore, I did not hesitate to eat and drink. I had determined to make believe sup, but to eat nothing. I was forced, then, to combat the fast of the evening with the nourishment of the morning.

"Only I concealed a glass of water, which remained after my breakfast, thirst having been the chief of my sufferings when I remained forty-eight hours without eating or drinking.

"The day passed away without having any other influence on me than to strengthen the resolution I had formed; only I took care that my face should not betray the thoughts of my heart, for I had no doubt I was watched. Several times, even, I felt a smile on my lips. Felton, I dare not tell you at what idea I smiled; you would hold me in horror--"

"Go on! go on!" said Felton; "you see plainly that I listen, and that I am anxious to know the end."

"Evening came; the ordinary events took place. During the darkness, as before, my supper was brought. Then the lamp was lighted, and I sat down to table. I only ate some fruit. I pretended to pour out water from the jug, but I only drank that which I had saved in my glass. The substitution was made so carefully that my spies, if I had any, could have no suspicion of it.

"After supper I exhibited the same marks of languor as on the preceding evening; but this time, as I yielded to fatigue, or as if I had become familiarized with danger, I dragged myself toward my bed, let my robe fall, and lay down.

"I found my knife where I had placed it, under my pillow, and while feigning to sleep, my hand grasped the handle of it convulsively.

"Two hours passed away without anything fresh happening. Oh, my God! who could have said so the evening before? I began to fear that he would not come.

"At length I saw the lamp rise softly, and disappear in the depths of the ceiling; my chamber was filled with darkness and obscurity, but I made a strong effort to penetrate this darkness and obscurity.

"Nearly ten minutes passed; I heard no other noise but the beating of my own heart. I implored heaven that he might come.

"At length I heard the well-known noise of the door, which opened and shut; I heard, notwithstanding the thickness of the carpet, a step which made the floor creak; I saw, notwithstanding the darkness, a shadow which approached my bed."

"Haste! haste!" said Felton; "do you not see that each of your words burns me like molten lead?"

"Then," continued Milady, "then I collected all my strength; I recalled to my mind that the moment of vengeance, or rather, of justice, had struck. I looked upon myself as another Judith; I gathered myself up, my knife in my hand, and when I saw him near me, stretching out his arms to find his victim, then, with the last cry of agony and despair, I struck him in the middle of his breast.

"The miserable villain! He had foreseen all. His breast was covered with a coat-of-mail; the knife was bent against it.

"'Ah, ah!' cried he, seizing my arm, and wresting from me the weapon that had so badly served me, 'you want to take my life, do you, my pretty Puritan? But that's more than dislike, that's ingratitude! Come, come, calm yourself, my sweet girl! I thought you had softened. I am not one of those tyrants who detain women by force. You don't love me. With my usual fatuity I doubted it; now I am convinced. To-morrow you shall be free.'

"I had but one wish; that was that he should kill me.

"'Beware!' said I, 'for my liberty is your dishonor.'

"'Explain yourself, my pretty sibyl!'

"'Yes; for as soon as I leave this place I will tell everything. I will proclaim the violence you have used toward me. I will describe my captivity. I will denounce this place of infamy. You are placed on high, my Lord, but tremble! Above you there is the king; above the king there is God!'

"However perfect master he was over himself, my persecutor allowed a movement of anger to escape him. I could not see the expression of his countenance, but I felt the arm tremble upon which my hand was placed.

"'Then you shall not leave this place,' said he.

"'Very well,' cried I, 'then the place of my punishment will be that of my tomb. I will die here, and you will see if a phantom that accuses is not more terrible than a living being that threatens!'

"'You shall have no weapon left in your power.'

"'There is a weapon which despair has placed within the reach of every creature who has the courage to use it. I will allow myself to die with hunger.'

"'Come,' said the wretch, 'is not peace much better than such a war as that? I will restore you to liberty this moment; I will proclaim you a piece of immaculate virtue; I will name you the Lucretia of England.'

"'And I will say that you are the Sextus. I will denounce you before men, as I have denounced you before God; and if it be necessary that, like Lucretia, I should sign my accusation with my blood, I will sign it.'

"'Ah!' said my enemy, in a jeering tone, 'that's quite another thing. My faith! everything considered, you are very well off here. You shall want for nothing, and if you let yourself die of hunger that will be your own fault.'

"At these words he retired. I heard the door open and shut, and I remained overwhelmed, less, I confess it, by my grief than by the mortification of not having avenged myself.

"He kept his word. All the day, all the next night passed away without my seeing him again. But I also kept my word with him, and I neither ate nor drank. I was, as I told him, resolved to die of hunger.

"I passed the day and the night in prayer, for I hoped that God would pardon me my suicide.

"The second night the door opened; I was lying on the floor, for my strength began to abandon me.

"At the noise I raised myself up on one hand.

"'Well,' said a voice which vibrated in too terrible a manner in my ear not to be recognized, 'well! Are we softened a little? Will we not pay for our liberty with a single promise of silence? Come, I am a good sort of a prince,' added he, 'and although I like not Puritans I do them justice; and it is the same with Puritanesses, when they are pretty. Come, take a little oath for me on the cross; I won't ask anything more of you.'

"'On the cross,' cried I, rising, for at that abhorred voice I had recovered all my strength, 'on the cross I swear that no promise, no menace, no force, no torture, shall close my mouth! On the cross I swear to denounce you everywhere as a murderer, as a thief of honor, as a base coward! On the cross I swear, if I ever leave this place, to call down vengeance upon you from the whole human race!'

"'Beware!' said the voice, in a threatening accent that I had never yet heard. 'I have an extraordinary means which I will not employ but in the last extremity to close your mouth, or at least to prevent anyone from believing a word you may utter.'

"I mustered all my strength to reply to him with a burst of laughter.

"He saw that it was a merciless war between us--a war to the death.

"'Listen!' said he. 'I give you the rest of tonight and all day tomorrow. Reflect: promise to be silent, and riches, consideration, even honor, shall surround you; threaten to speak, and I will condemn you to infamy.'

"'You?' cried I. 'You?'

"'To interminable, ineffaceable infamy!'

"'You?' repeated I. Oh, I declare to you, Felton, I thought him mad!

"'Yes, yes, I!' replied he.

"'Oh, leave me!' said I. 'Begone, if you do not desire to see me dash my head against that wall before your eyes!'

"'Very well, it is your own doing. Till tomorrow evening, then!'

"'Till tomorrow evening, then!' replied I, allowing myself to fall, and biting the carpet with rage."

Felton leaned for support upon a piece of furniture; and Milady saw, with the joy of a demon, that his strength would fail him perhaps before the end of her recital.

57 Means For Classical Tragedy

After a moment of silence employed by Milady in observing the young man who listened to her, Milady continued her recital.

"It was nearly three days since I had eaten or drunk anything. I suffered frightful torments. At times there passed before me clouds which pressed my brow, which veiled my eyes; this was delirium.

"When the evening came I was so weak that every time I fainted I thanked God, for I thought I was about to die.

"In the midst of one of these swoons I heard the door open. Terror recalled me to myself.

"He entered the apartment followed by a man in a mask. He was masked likewise; but I knew his step, I knew his voice, I knew him by that imposing bearing which hell has bestowed upon his person for the curse of humanity.

"'Well,' said he to me, 'have you made your mind up to take the oath I requested of you?'

"'You have said Puritans have but one word. Mine you have heard, and that is to pursue you--on earth to the tribunal of men, in heaven to the tribunal of God.'

"'You persist, then?'

"'I swear it before the God who hears me. I will take the whole world as a witness of your crime, and that until I have found an avenger.'

"'You are a prostitute,' said he, in a voice of thunder, 'and you shall undergo the punishment of prostitutes! Branded in the eyes of the world you invoke, try to prove to that world that you are neither guilty nor mad!'

"Then, addressing the man who accompanied him, 'Executioner,' said he, 'do your duty.'"

"Oh, his name, his name!" cried Felton. "His name, tell it me!"

"Then in spite of my cries, in spite of my resistance--for I began to comprehend that there was a question of something worse than death--the executioner seized me, threw me on the floor, fastened me with his bonds, and suffocated by sobs, almost without sense, invoking God, who did not listen to me, I uttered all at once a frightful cry of pain and shame. A burning fire, a red-hot iron, the iron of the executioner, was imprinted on my shoulder."

Felton uttered a groan.

"Here," said Milady, rising with the majesty of a queen, "here, Felton, behold the new martyrdom invented for a pure young girl, the victim of the brutality of a villain. Learn to know the heart of men, and henceforth make yourself less easily the instrument of their unjust vengeance."

Milady, with a rapid gesture, opened her robe, tore the cambric that covered her bosom, and red with feigned anger and simulated shame, showed the young man the ineffaceable impression which dishonored that beautiful shoulder.

"But," cried Felton, "that is a FLEUR-DE-LIS which I see there."

"And therein consisted the infamy," replied Milady. "The brand of England!--it would be necessary to prove what tribunal had imposed it on me, and I could have made a public appeal to all the tribunals of the kingdom; but the brand of France!--oh, by that, by THAT I was branded indeed!"

This was too much for Felton.

Pale, motionless, overwhelmed by this frightful revelation, dazzled by the superhuman beauty of this woman who unveiled herself before him with an immodesty which appeared to him sublime, he ended by falling on his knees before her as the early Christians did before those pure and holy martyrs whom the persecution of the emperors gave up in the circus to the sanguinary sensuality of the populace. The brand disappeared; the beauty alone remained.

"Pardon! Pardon!" cried Felton, "oh, pardon!"

Milady read in his eyes LOVE! LOVE!

"Pardon for what?" asked she.

"Pardon me for having joined with your persecutors."

Milady held out her hand to him.

"So beautiful! so young!" cried Felton, covering that hand with his kisses.

Milady let one of those looks fall upon him which make a slave of a king.

Felton was a Puritan; he abandoned the hand of this woman to kiss her feet.

He no longer loved her; he adored her.

When this crisis was past, when Milady appeared to have resumed her self-possession, which she had never lost; when Felton had seen her recover with the veil of chastity those treasures of love which were only concealed from him to make him desire them the more ardently, he said, "Ah, now! I have only one thing to ask of you; that is, the name of your true executioner. For to me there is but one; the other was an instrument, that was all."

"What, brother!" cried Milady, "must I name him again? Have you not yet divined who he is?"

"What?" cried Felton, "he--again he--always he? What--the truly guilty?"

"The truly guilty," said Milady, "is the ravager of England, the persecutor of true believers, the base ravisher of the honor of so many women--he who, to satisfy a caprice of his corrupt heart, is about to make England shed so much blood, who protects the Protestants today and will betray them tomorrow--"

"Buckingham! It is, then, Buckingham!" cried Felton, in a high state of excitement.

Milady concealed her face in her hands, as if she could not endure the shame which this name recalled to her.

"Buckingham, the executioner of this angelic creature!" cried Felton. "And thou hast not hurled thy thunder at him, my God! And thou hast left him noble, honored, powerful, for the ruin of us all!"

"God abandons him who abandons himself," said Milady.

"But he will draw upon his head the punishment reserved for the damned!" said Felton, with increasing exultation. "He wills that human vengeance should precede celestial justice."

"Men fear him and spare him."

"I," said Felton, "I do not fear him, nor will I spare him."

The soul of Milady was bathed in an infernal joy.

"But how can Lord de Winter, my protector, my father," asked Felton, "possibly be mixed up with all this?"

"Listen, Felton," resumed Milady, "for by the side of base and contemptible men there are often found great and generous natures. I had an affianced husband, a man whom I loved, and who loved me--a heart like yours, Felton, a man like you. I went to him and told him all; he knew me, that man did, and did not doubt an instant. He was a nobleman, a man equal to Buckingham in every respect. He said nothing; he only girded on his sword, wrapped himself in his cloak, and went straight to Buckingham Palace.

"Yes, yes," said Felton; "I understand how he would act. But with such men it is not the sword that should be employed; it is the poniard."

"Buckingham had left England the day before, sent as ambassador to Spain, to demand the hand of the Infanta for King Charles I, who was then only Prince of Wales. My affianced husband returned.

"'Hear me,' said he; 'this man has gone, and for the moment has consequently escaped my vengeance; but let us be united, as we were to have been, and then leave it to Lord de Winter to maintain his own honor and that of his wife.'"

"Lord de Winter!" cried Felton.

"Yes," said Milady, "Lord de Winter; and now you can understand it all, can you not? Buckingham remained nearly a year absent. A week before his return Lord de Winter died, leaving me his sole heir. Whence came the blow? God who knows all, knows without doubt; but as for me, I accuse nobody."

"Oh, what an abyss; what an abyss!" cried Felton.

"Lord de Winter died without revealing anything to his brother. The terrible secret was to be concealed till it burst, like a clap of thunder, over the head of the guilty. Your protector had seen with pain this marriage of his elder brother with a portionless girl. I was sensible that I could look for no support from a man disappointed in his hopes of an inheritance. I went to France, with a determination to remain there for the rest of my life. But all my fortune is in England. Communication being closed by the war, I was in want of everything. I was then obliged to come back again. Six days ago, I landed at Portsmouth."

"Well?" said Felton.

"Well; Buckingham heard by some means, no doubt, of my return. He spoke of me to Lord de Winter, already prejudiced against me, and told him that his sister-in-law was a prostitute, a branded woman. The noble and pure voice of my husband was no longer here to defend me. Lord de Winter believed all that was told him with so much the more ease that it was his interest to believe it. He caused me to be arrested, had me conducted hither, and placed me under your guard. You know the rest. The day after tomorrow he banishes me, he transports me; the day after tomorrow he exiles me among the infamous. Oh, the train is well laid; the plot is clever. My honor will not survive it! You see, then, Felton, I can do nothing but die. Felton, give me that knife!"

And at these words, as if all her strength was exhausted, Milady sank, weak and languishing, into the arms of the young officer, who, intoxicated with love, anger, and voluptuous sensations hitherto unknown, received her with transport, pressed her against his heart, all trembling at the breath from that charming mouth, bewildered by the contact with that palpitating bosom.

"No, no," said he. "No, you shall live honored and pure; you shall live to triumph over your enemies."

Milady put him from her slowly with her hand, while drawing him nearer with her look; but Felton, in his turn, embraced her more closely, imploring her like a divinity.

"Oh, death, death!" said she, lowering her voice and her eyelids, "oh, death, rather than shame! Felton, my brother, my friend, I conjure you!"

"No," cried Felton, "no; you shall live and you shall be avenged."

"Felton, I bring misfortune to all who surround me! Felton, abandon me! Felton, let me die!"

"Well, then, we will live and die together!" cried he, pressing his lips to those of the prisoner.

Several strokes resounded on the door; this time Milady really pushed him away from her.

"Hark," said she, "we have been overheard! Someone is coming! All is over! We are lost!"

"No," said Felton; it is only the sentinel warning me that they are about to change the guard."

"Then run to the door, and open it yourself."

Felton obeyed; this woman was now his whole thought, his whole soul.

He found himself face to face with a sergeant commanding a watch-patrol.

"Well, what is the matter?" asked the young lieutenant.

"You told me to open the door if I heard anyone cry out," said the soldier; "but you forgot to leave me the key. I heard you cry out, without understanding what you said. I tried to open the door, but it was locked inside; then I called the sergeant."

"And here I am," said the sergeant.

Felton, quite bewildered, almost mad, stood speechless.

Milady plainly perceived that it was now her turn to take part in the scene. She ran to the table, and seizing the knife which Felton had laid down, exclaimed, "And by what right will you prevent me from dying?"

"Great God!" exclaimed Felton, on seeing the knife glitter in her hand.

At that moment a burst of ironical laughter resounded through the corridor. The baron, attracted by the noise, in his chamber gown, his sword under his arm, stood in the doorway.

"Ah," said he, "here we are, at the last act of the tragedy. You see, Felton, the drama has gone through all the phases I named; but be easy, no blood will flow."

Milady perceived that all was lost unless she gave Felton an immediate and terrible proof of her courage.

"You are mistaken, my Lord, blood will flow; and may that blood fall back on those who cause it to flow!"

Felton uttered a cry, and rushed toward her. He was too late; Milady had stabbed herself.

But the knife had fortunately, we ought to say skillfully, come in contact with the steel busk, which at that period, like a cuirass, defended the chests of women. It had glided down it, tearing the robe, and had penetrated slantingly between the flesh and the ribs. Milady's robe was not the less stained with blood in a second.

Milady fell down, and seemed to be in a swoon.

Felton snatched away the knife.

"See, my Lord," said he, in a deep, gloomy tone, "here is a woman who was under my guard, and who has killed herself!"

"Be at ease, Felton," said Lord de Winter. "She is not dead; demons do not die so easily. Be tranquil, and go wait for me in my chamber."

"But, my Lord--"

"Go, sir, I command you!"

At this injunction from his superior, Felton obeyed; but in going out, he put the knife into his bosom.

As to Lord de Winter, he contented himself with calling the woman who waited on Milady, and when she was come, he recommended the prisoner, who was still fainting, to her care, and left them alone.

Meanwhile, all things considered and notwithstanding his suspicions, as the wound might be serious, he immediately sent off a mounted man to find a physician.

58 Escape

As Lord de Winter had thought, Milady's wound was not dangerous. So soon as she was left alone with the woman whom the baron had summoned to her assistance she opened her eyes.

It was, however, necessary to affect weakness and pain--not a very difficult task for so finished an actress as Milady. Thus the poor woman was completely the dupe of the prisoner, whom, notwithstanding her hints, she persisted in watching all night.

But the presence of this woman did not prevent Milady from thinking.

There was no longer a doubt that Felton was convinced; Felton was hers. If an angel appeared to that young man as an accuser of Milady, he would take him, in the mental disposition in which he now found himself, for a messenger sent by the devil.

Milady smiled at this thought, for Felton was now her only hope--her only means of safety.

But Lord de Winter might suspect him; Felton himself might now be watched!

Toward four o'clock in the morning the doctor arrived; but since the time Milady stabbed herself, however short, the wound had closed. The doctor could therefore measure neither the direction nor the depth of it; he only satisfied himself by Milady's pulse that the case was not serious.

In the morning Milady, under the pretext that she had not slept well in the night and wanted rest, sent away the woman who attended her.

She had one hope, which was that Felton would appear at the breakfast hour; but Felton did not come.

Were her fears realized? Was Felton, suspected by the baron, about to fail her at the decisive moment? She had only one day left. Lord de Winter had announced her embarkation for the twenty-third, and it was now the morning of the twenty-second.

Nevertheless she still waited patiently till the hour for dinner.

Although she had eaten nothing in the morning, the dinner was brought in at its usual time. Milady then perceived, with terror, that the uniform of the soldiers who guarded her was changed.

Then she ventured to ask what had become of Felton.

She was told that he had left the castle an hour before on horseback. She inquired if the baron was still at the castle. The soldier replied that he was, and that he had given orders to be informed if the prisoner wished to speak to him.

Milady replied that she was too weak at present, and that her only desire was to be left alone.

The soldier went out, leaving the dinner served.

Felton was sent away. The marines were removed. Felton was then mistrusted.

This was the last blow to the prisoner.

Left alone, she arose. The bed, which she had kept from prudence and that they might believe her seriously wounded, burned her like a bed of fire. She cast a glance at the door; the baron had had a plank nailed over the grating. He no doubt feared that by this opening she might still by some diabolical means corrupt her guards.

Milady smiled with joy. She was free now to give way to her transports without being observed. She traversed her chamber with the excitement of a furious maniac or of a tigress shut up in an iron cage. CERTES, if the knife had been left in her power, she would now have thought, not of killing herself, but of killing the baron.

At six o'clock Lord de Winter came in. He was armed at all points. This man, in whom Milady till that time had only seen a very simple gentleman, had become an admirable jailer. He appeared to foresee all, to divine all, to anticipate all.

A single look at Milady apprised him of all that was passing in her mind.

"Ay!" said he, "I see; but you shall not kill me today. You have no longer a weapon; and besides, I am on my guard. You had begun to pervert my poor Felton. He was yielding to your infernal influence; but I will save him. He will never see you again; all is over. Get your clothes together. Tomorrow you will go. I had fixed the embarkation for the twenty-fourth; but I have reflected that the more promptly the affair takes place the more sure it will be. Tomorrow, by twelve o'clock, I shall have the order for your exile, signed, BUCKINGHAM. If you speak a single word to anyone before going aboard ship, my sergeant will blow your brains out. He has orders to do so. If when on the ship you speak a single word to anyone before the captain permits you, the captain will have you thrown into the sea. That is agreed upon.

"AU REVOIR; then; that is all I have to say today. Tomorrow I will see you again, to take my leave." With these words the baron went out. Milady had listened to all this menacing tirade with a smile of disdain on her lips, but rage in her heart.

Supper was served. Milady felt that she stood in need of all her strength. She did not know what might take place during this night which approached so menacingly--for large masses of cloud rolled over the face of the sky, and distant lightning announced a storm.

The storm broke about ten o'clock. Milady felt a consolation in seeing nature partake of the disorder of her heart. The thunder growled in the air like the passion and anger in her thoughts. It appeared to her that the blast as it swept along disheveled her brow, as it bowed the branches of the trees and bore away their leaves. She howled as the hurricane howled; and her voice was lost in the great voice of nature, which also seemed to groan with despair.

All at once she heard a tap at her window, and by the help of a flash of lightning she saw the face of a man appear behind the bars.

She ran to the window and opened it.

"Felton!" cried she. "I am saved."

"Yes," said Felton; "but silence, silence! I must have time to file through these bars. Only take care that I am not seen through the wicket."

"Oh, it is a proof that the Lord is on our side, Felton," replied Milady. "They have closed up the grating with a board."

"That is well; God has made them senseless," said Felton.

"But what must I do?" asked Milady.

"Nothing, nothing, only shut the window. Go to bed, or at least lie down in your clothes. As soon as I have done I will knock on one of the panes of glass. But will you be able to follow me?"

"Oh, yes!"

"Your wound?"

"Gives me pain, but will not prevent my walking."

"Be ready, then, at the first signal."

Milady shut the window, extinguished the lamp, and went, as Felton had desired her, to lie down on the bed. Amid the moaning of the storm she heard the grinding of the file upon the bars, and by the light of every flash she perceived the shadow of Felton through the panes.

She passed an hour without breathing, panting, with a cold sweat upon her brow, and her heart oppressed by frightful agony at every movement she heard in the corridor.

There are hours which last a year.

At the expiration of an hour, Felton tapped again.

Milady sprang out of bed and opened the window. Two bars removed formed an opening for a man to pass through.

"Are you ready?" asked Felton.

"Yes. Must I take anything with me?"

"Money, if you have any."

"Yes; fortunately they have left me all I had."

"So much the better, for I have expended all mine in chartering a vessel."

"Here!" said Milady, placing a bag full of louis in Felton's hands.

Felton took the bag and threw it to the foot of the wall.

"Now," said he, "will you come?"

"I am ready."

Milady mounted upon a chair and passed the upper part of her body through the window. She saw the young officer suspended over the abyss by a ladder of ropes. For the first time an emotion of terror reminded her that she was a woman.

The dark space frightened her.

"I expected this," said Felton.

"It's nothing, it's nothing!" said Milady. "I will descend with my eyes shut."

"Have you confidence in me?" said Felton.

"You ask that?"

"Put your two hands together. Cross them; that's right!"

Felton tied her two wrists together with his handkerchief, and then with a cord over the handkerchief.

"What are you doing?" asked Milady, with surprise.

"Pass your arms around my neck, and fear nothing."

"But I shall make you lose your balance, and we shall both be dashed to pieces."

"Don't be afraid. I am a sailor."

Not a second was to be lost. Milady passed her two arms round Felton's neck, and let herself slip out of the window. Felton began to descend the ladder slowly, step by step. Despite the weight of two bodies, the blast of the hurricane shook them in the air.

All at once Felton stopped.

"What is the matter?" asked Milady.

"Silence," said Felton, "I hear footsteps."

"We are discovered!"

There was a silence of several seconds.

"No," said Felton, "it is nothing."

"But what, then, is the noise?"

"That of the patrol going their rounds."

"Where is their road?"

"Just under us."

"They will discover us!"

"No, if it does not lighten."

"But they will run against the bottom of the ladder."

"Fortunately it is too short by six feet."

"Here they are! My God!"

"Silence!"

Both remained suspended, motionless and breathless, within twenty paces of the ground, while the patrol passed beneath them laughing and talking. This was a terrible moment for the fugitives.

The patrol passed. The noise of their retreating footsteps and the murmur of their voices soon died away.

"Now," said Felton, "we are safe."

Milady breathed a deep sigh and fainted.

Felton continued to descend. Near the bottom of the ladder, when he found no more support for his feet, he clung with his hands; at length, arrived at the last step, he let himself hang by the strength of his wrists, and touched the ground. He stooped down, picked up the bag of money, and placed it between his teeth. Then he took Milady in his arms, and set off briskly in the direction opposite to that which the patrol had taken. He soon left the pathway of the patrol, descended across the rocks, and when arrived on the edge of the sea, whistled.

A similar signal replied to him; and five minutes after, a boat appeared, rowed by four men.

The boat approached as near as it could to the shore; but there was not depth enough of water for it to touch land. Felton walked into the sea up to his middle, being unwilling to trust his precious burden to anybody.

Fortunately the storm began to subside, but still the sea was disturbed. The little boat bounded over the waves like a nut-shell.

"To the sloop," said Felton, "and row quickly."

The four men bent to their oars, but the sea was too high to let them get much hold of it.

However, they left the castle behind; that was the principal thing. The night was extremely dark. It was almost impossible to see the shore from the boat; they would therefore be less likely to see the boat from the shore.

A black point floated on the sea. That was the sloop. While the boat was advancing with all the speed its four rowers could give it, Felton untied the cord and then the handkerchief which bound Milady's hands together. When her hands were loosed he took some sea water and sprinkled it over her face.

Milady breathed a sigh, and opened her eyes.

"Where am I?" said she.

"Saved!" replied the young officer.

"Oh, saved, saved!" cried she. "Yes, there is the sky; here is the sea! The air I breathe is the air of liberty! Ah, thanks, Felton, thanks!"

The young man pressed her to his heart.

"But what is the matter with my hands!" asked Milady; "it seems as if my wrists had been crushed in a vice."

Milady held out her arms; her wrists were bruised.

"Alas!" said Felton, looking at those beautiful hands, and shaking his head sorrowfully.

"Oh, it's nothing, nothing!" cried Milady. "I remember now."

Milady looked around her, as if in search of something.

"It is there," said Felton, touching the bag of money with his foot.

They drew near to the sloop. A sailor on watch hailed the boat; the boat replied.

"What vessel is that?" asked Milady.

"The one I have hired for you."

"Where will it take me?"

"Where you please, after you have put me on shore at Portsmouth."

"What are you going to do at Portsmouth?" asked Milady.

"Accomplish the orders of Lord de Winter," said Felton, with a gloomy smile.

"What orders?" asked Milady.

"You do not understand?" asked Felton.

"No; explain yourself, I beg."

"As he mistrusted me, he determined to guard you himself, and sent me in his place to get Buckingham to sign the order for your transportation."

"But if he mistrusted you, how could he confide such an order to you?"

"How could I know what I was the bearer of?"

"That's true! And you are going to Portsmouth?"

"I have no time to lose. Tomorrow is the twenty-third, and Buckingham sets sail tomorrow with his fleet."

"He sets sail tomorrow! Where for?"

"For La Rochelle."

"He need not sail!" cried Milady, forgetting her usual presence of mind.

"Be satisfied," replied Felton; "he will not sail."

Milady started with joy. She could read to the depths of the heart of this young man; the death of Buckingham was written there at full length.

"Felton," cried she, "you are as great as Judas Maccabeus! If you die, I will die with you; that is all I can say to you."

"Silence!" cried Felton; "we are here."

In fact, they touched the sloop.

Felton mounted the ladder first, and gave his hand to Milady, while the sailors supported her, for the sea was still much agitated.

An instant after they were on the deck.

"Captain," said Felton, "this is the person of whom I spoke to you, and whom you must convey safe and sound to France."

"For a thousand pistoles," said the captain.

"I have paid you five hundred of them."

"That's correct," said the captain.

"And here are the other five hundred," replied Milady, placing her hand upon the bag of gold.

"No," said the captain, "I make but one bargain; and I have agreed with this young man that the other five hundred shall not be due to me till we arrive at Boulogne."

"And shall we arrive there?"

"Safe and sound, as true as my name's Jack Butler."

"Well," said Milady, "if you keep your word, instead of five hundred, I will give you a thousand pistoles."

"Hurrah for you, then, my beautiful lady," cried the captain; "and may God often send me such passengers as your Ladyship!"

"Meanwhile," said Felton, "convey me to the little bay of--; you know it was agreed you should put in there."

The captain replied by ordering the necessary maneuvers, and toward seven o'clock in the morning the little vessel cast anchor in the bay that had been named.

During this passage, Felton related everything to Milady--how, instead of going to London, he had chartered the little vessel; how he had returned; how he had scaled the wall by fastening cramps in the interstices of the stones, as he ascended, to give him foothold; and how, when he had reached the bars, he fastened his ladder. Milady knew the rest.

On her side, Milady tried to encourage Felton in his project; but at the first words which issued from her mouth, she plainly saw that the young fanatic stood more in need of being moderated than urged.

It was agreed that Milady should wait for Felton till ten o'clock; if he did not return by ten o'clock she was to sail.

In that case, and supposing he was at liberty, he was to rejoin her in France, at the convent of the Carmelites at Bethune.

59 WHAT TOOK PLACE AT PORTSMOUTH AUGUST 23, 1628

Felton took leave of Milady as a brother about to go for a mere walk takes leave of his sister, kissing her hand.

His whole body appeared in its ordinary state of calmness, only an unusual fire beamed from his eyes, like the effects of a fever; his brow was more pale than it generally was; his teeth were clenched, and his speech had a short dry accent which indicated that something dark was at work within him.

As long as he remained in the boat which conveyed him to land, he kept his face toward Milady, who, standing on the deck, followed him with her eyes. Both were free from the fear of pursuit; nobody ever came into Milady's apartment before nine o'clock, and it would require three hours to go from the castle to London.

Felton jumped onshore, climbed the little ascent which led to the top of the cliff, saluted Milady a last time, and took his course toward the city.

At the end of a hundred paces, the ground began to decline, and he could only see the mast of the sloop.

He immediately ran in the direction of Portsmouth, which he saw at nearly half a league before him, standing out in the haze of the morning, with its houses and towers.

Beyond Portsmouth the sea was covered with vessels whose masts, like a forest of poplars despoiled by the winter, bent with each breath of the wind.

Felton, in his rapid walk, reviewed in his mind all the accusations against the favorite of James I and Charles I, furnished by two years of premature meditation and a long sojourn among the Puritans.

When he compared the public crimes of this minister--startling crimes, European crimes, if so we may say--with the private and unknown crimes with which Milady had charged him, Felton found that the more culpable of the two men which formed the character of Buckingham was the one of whom the public knew not the life. This was because his love, so strange, so new, and so ardent, made him view the infamous and imaginary accusations of Milady de Winter as, through a magnifying glass, one views as frightful monsters atoms in reality imperceptible by the side of an ant.

The rapidity of his walk heated his blood still more; the idea that he left behind him, exposed to a frightful vengeance, the woman he loved, or rather whom he adored as a saint, the emotion he had experienced, present fatigue--all together exalted his mind above human feeling.

He entered Portsmouth about eight o'clock in the morning. The whole population was on foot; drums were beating in the streets and in the port; the troops about to embark were marching toward the sea.

Felton arrived at the palace of the Admiralty, covered with dust, and streaming with perspiration. His countenance, usually so pale, was purple with heat and passion. The sentinel wanted to repulse him; but Felton called to the officer of the post, and drawing from his pocket the letter of which he was the bearer, he said, "A pressing message from Lord de Winter."

At the name of Lord de Winter, who was known to be one of his Grace's most intimate friends, the officer of the post gave orders to let Felton pass, who, besides, wore the uniform of a naval officer.

Felton darted into the palace.

At the moment he entered the vestibule, another man was entering likewise, dusty, out of breath, leaving at the gate a post horse, which, on reaching the palace, tumbled on his foreknees.

Felton and he addressed Patrick, the duke's confidential lackey, at the same moment. Felton named Lord de Winter; the unknown would not name anybody, and pretended that it was to the duke alone he would make himself known. Each was anxious to gain admission before the other.

Patrick, who knew Lord de Winter was in affairs of the service, and in relations of friendship with the duke, gave the preference to the one who came in his name. The other was forced to wait, and it was easily to be seen how he cursed the delay.

The valet led Felton through a large hall in which waited the deputies from La Rochelle, headed by the Prince de Soubise, and introduced him into a closet where Buckingham, just out of the bath, was finishing his toilet, upon which, as at all times, he bestowed extraordinary attention.

"Lieutenant Felton, from Lord de Winter," said Patrick.

"From Lord de Winter!" repeated Buckingham; "let him come in."

Felton entered. At that moment Buckingham was throwing upon a couch a rich toilet robe, worked with gold, in order to put on a blue velvet doublet embroidered with pearls.

"Why didn't the baron come himself?" demanded Buckingham. "I expected him this morning."

"He desired me to tell your Grace," replied Felton, "that he very much regretted not having that honor, but that he was prevented by the guard he is obliged to keep at the castle."

"Yes, I know that," said Buckingham; "he has a prisoner."

"It is of that prisoner that I wish to speak to your Grace," replied Felton.

"Well, then, speak!"

"That which I have to say of her can only be heard by yourself, my Lord!"

"Leave us, Patrick," said Buckingham; "but remain within sound of the bell. I shall call you presently."

Patrick went out.

"We are alone, sir," said Buckingham; "speak!"

"My Lord," said Felton, "the Baron de Winter wrote to you the other day to request you to sign an order of embarkation relative to a young woman named Charlotte Backson."

"Yes, sir; and I answered him, to bring or send me that order and I would sign it."

"Here it is, my Lord."

"Give it to me," said the duke.

And taking it from Felton, he cast a rapid glance over the paper, and perceiving that it was the one that had been mentioned to him, he placed it on the table, took a pen, and prepared to sign it.

"Pardon, my Lord," said Felton, stopping the duke; "but does your Grace know that the name of

Charlotte Backson is not the true name of this young woman?"

"Yes, sir, I know it," replied the duke, dipping the quill in the ink.

"Then your Grace knows her real name?" asked Felton, in a sharp tone.

"I know it"; and the duke put the quill to the paper. Felton grew pale.

"And knowing that real name, my Lord," replied Felton, "will you sign it all the same?"

"Doubtless," said Buckingham, "and rather twice than once."

"I cannot believe," continued Felton, in a voice that became more sharp and rough, "that your Grace knows that it is to Milady de Winter this relates."

"I know it perfectly, although I am astonished that you know it."

"And will your Grace sign that order without remorse?"

Buckingham looked at the young man haughtily.

"Do you know, sir, that you are asking me very strange questions, and that I am very foolish to answer them?"

"Reply to them, my Lord," said Felton; "the circumstances are more serious than you perhaps believe."

Buckingham reflected that the young man, coming from Lord de Winter, undoubtedly spoke in his name, and softened.

"Without remorse," said he. "The baron knows, as well as myself, that Milady de Winter is a very guilty woman, and it is treating her very favorably to commute her punishment to transportation." The duke put his pen to the paper.

"You will not sign that order, my Lord!" said Felton, making a step toward the duke.

"I will not sign this order! And why not?"

"Because you will look into yourself, and you will do justice to the lady."

"I should do her justice by sending her to Tyburn," said Buckingham. "This lady is infamous."

"My Lord, Milady de Winter is an angel; you know that she is, and I demand her liberty of you."

"Bah! Are you mad, to talk to me thus?" said Buckingham.

"My Lord, excuse me! I speak as I can; I restrain myself. But, my Lord, think of what you're about to do, and beware of going too far!"

"What do you say? God pardon me!" cried Buckingham, "I really think he threatens me!"

"No, my Lord, I still plead. And I say to you: one drop of water suffices to make the full vase overflow; one slight fault may draw down punishment upon the head spared, despite many crimes."

"Mr. Felton," said Buckingham, "you will withdraw, and place yourself at once under arrest."

"You will hear me to the end, my Lord. You have seduced this young girl; you have outraged, defiled her. Repair your crimes toward her; let her go free, and I will exact nothing else from you."

"You will exact!" said Buckingham, looking at Felton with astonishment, and dwelling upon each syllable of the three words as he pronounced them.

"My Lord," continued Felton, becoming more excited as he spoke, "my Lord, beware! All England is tired of your iniquities; my Lord, you have abused the royal power, which you have almost usurped; my Lord, you are held in horror by God and men. God will punish you hereafter, but I will punish you here!"

"Ah, this is too much!" cried Buckingham, making a step toward the door.

Felton barred his passage.

"I ask it humbly of you, my Lord," said he; "sign the order for the liberation of Milady de Winter. Remember that she is a woman whom you have dishonored."

"Withdraw, sir," said Buckingham, "or I will call my attendant, and have you placed in irons."

"You shall not call," said Felton, throwing himself between the duke and the bell placed on a stand encrusted with silver. "Beware, my Lord, you are in the hands of God!"

"In the hands of the devil, you mean!" cried Buckingham, raising his voice so as to attract the notice of his people, without absolutely shouting.

"Sign, my Lord; sign the liberation of Milady de Winter," said Felton, holding out a paper to the duke.

"By force? You are joking! Holloa, Patrick!"

"Sign, my Lord!"

"Never."

"Never?"

"Help!" shouted the duke; and at the same time he sprang toward his sword.

But Felton did not give him time to draw it. He held the knife with which Milady had stabbed herself, open in his bosom; at one bound he was upon the duke.

At that moment Patrick entered the room, crying, "A letter from France, my Lord."

"From France!" cried Buckingham, forgetting everything in thinking from whom that letter came.

Felton took advantage of this moment, and plunged the knife into his side up to the handle.

"Ah, traitor," cried Buckingham, "you have killed me!"

"Murder!" screamed Patrick.

Felton cast his eyes round for means of escape, and seeing the door free, he rushed into the next chamber, in which, as we have said, the deputies from La Rochelle were waiting, crossed it as quickly as possible, and rushed toward the staircase; but upon the first step he met Lord de Winter, who, seeing him pale, confused, livid, and stained with blood both on his hands and face, seized him by the throat, crying, "I knew it! I guessed it! But too late by a minute, unfortunate, unfortunate that I am!"

Felton made no resistance. Lord de Winter placed him in the hands of the guards, who led him, while awaiting further orders, to a little terrace commanding the sea; and then the baron hastened to the duke's chamber.

At the cry uttered by the duke and the scream of Patrick, the man whom Felton had met in the antechamber rushed into the chamber.

He found the duke reclining upon a sofa, with his hand pressed upon the wound.

"Laporte," said the duke, in a dying voice, "Laporte, do you come from her?"

"Yes, monseigneur," replied the faithful cloak bearer of Anne of Austria, "but too late, perhaps."

"Silence, Laporte, you may be overheard. Patrick, let no one enter. Oh, I cannot tell what she says to me! My God, I am dying!"

And the duke swooned.

Meanwhile, Lord de Winter, the deputies, the leaders of the expedition, the officers of Buckingham's household, had all made their way into the chamber. Cries of despair resounded on all sides. The news, which filled the palace with tears and groans, soon became known, and spread itself throughout the city.

The report of a cannon announced that something new and unexpected had taken place.

Lord de Winter tore his hair.

"Too late by a minute!" cried he, "too late by a minute! Oh, my God, my God! what a misfortune!"

He had been informed at seven o'clock in the morning that a rope ladder floated from one of the windows of the castle; he had hastened to Milady's chamber, had found it empty, the window open, and the bars filed, had remembered the verbal caution d'Artagnan had transmitted to him by his messenger, had trembled for the duke, and running to the stable without taking time to have a horse saddled, had jumped upon the first he found, had galloped off like the wind, had alighted below in the courtyard, had ascended the stairs precipitately, and on the top step, as we have said, had encountered Felton.

The duke, however, was not dead. He recovered a little, reopened his eyes, and hope revived in all hearts.

"Gentlemen," said he, "leave me alone with Patrick and Laporte--ah, is that you, de Winter? You sent me a strange madman this morning! See the state in which he has put me."

"Oh, my Lord!" cried the baron, "I shall never console myself."

"And you would be quite wrong, my dear de Winter," said Buckingham, holding out his hand to him. "I do not know the man who deserves being regretted during the whole life of another man; but leave us, I pray you."

The baron went out sobbing.

There only remained in the closet of the wounded duke Laporte and Patrick. A physician was sought for, but none was yet found.

"You will live, my Lord, you will live!" repeated the faithful servant of Anne of Austria, on his knees before the duke's sofa.

"What has she written to me?" said Buckingham, feebly, streaming with blood, and suppressing his agony to speak of her he loved, "what has she written to me? Read me her letter."

"Oh, my Lord!" said Laporte.

"Obey, Laporte, do you not see I have no time to lose?"

Laporte broke the seal, and placed the paper before the eyes of the duke; but Buckingham in vain tried to make out the writing.

"Read!" said he, "read! I cannot see. Read, then! For soon, perhaps, I shall not hear, and I shall die without knowing what she has written to me."

Laporte made no further objection, and read:

"My Lord, By that which, since I have known you, have suffered by you and for you, I conjure you, if you have any care for my repose, to countermand those great armaments which you are preparing against France, to put an end to a war of which it is publicly said religion is the ostensible cause, and of which, it is generally whispered, your love for me is the concealed cause. This war may not only bring great catastrophes upon England and France, but misfortune upon you, my Lord, for which I should never console myself.

"Be careful of your life, which is menaced, and which will be dear to me from the moment I am not obliged to see an enemy in you.

"Your affectionate

"ANNE" Buckingham collected all his remaining strength to listen to the reading of the letter; then, when it was ended, as if he had met with a bitter disappointment, he asked, "Have you nothing else to say to me by the living voice, Laporte?"

"The queen charged me to tell you to watch over yourself, for she had advice that your assassination would be attempted."

"And is that all--is that all?" replied Buckingham, impatiently.

"She likewise charged me to tell you that she still loved you."

"Ah," said Buckingham, "God be praised! My death, then, will not be to her as the death of a stranger!"

Laporte burst into tears.

"Patrick," said the due, "bring me the casket in which the diamond studs were kept."

Patrick brought the object desired, which Laporte recognized as having belonged to the queen.

"Now the scent bag of white satin, on which her cipher is embroidered in pearls."

Patrick again obeyed.

"Here, Laporte," said Buckingham, "these are the only tokens I ever received from her--this silver casket and these two letters. You will restore them to her Majesty; and as a last memorial"--he looked round for some valuable object--"you will add--"

He still sought; but his eyes, darkened by death, encountered only the knife which had fallen from the hand of Felton, still smoking with the blood spread over its blade.

"And you will add to them this knife," said the duke, pressing the hand of Laporte. He had just strength enough to place the scent bag at the bottom of the silver casket, and to let the knife fall into it, making a sign to Laporte that he was no longer able to speak; than, in a last convulsion, which this time he had not the power to combat, he slipped from the sofa to the floor.

Patrick uttered a loud cry.

Buckingham tried to smile a last time; but death checked his thought, which remained engraved on his brow like a last kiss of love.

At this moment the duke's surgeon arrived, quite terrified; he was already on board the admiral's ship, where they had been obliged to seek him.

He approached the duke, took his hand, held it for an instant in his own, and letting it fall, "All is useless," said he, "he is dead."

"Dead, dead!" cried Patrick.

At this cry all the crowd re-entered the apartment, and throughout the palace and town there was nothing but consternation and tumult.

As soon as Lord de Winter saw Buckingham was dead, he ran to Felton, whom the soldiers still guarded on the terrace of the palace.

"Wretch!" said he to the young man, who since the death of Buckingham had regained that coolness and self-possession which never after abandoned him, "wretch! what have you done?"

"I have avenged myself!" said he.

"Avenged yourself," said the baron. "Rather say that you have served as an instrument to that accursed woman; but I swear to you that this crime shall be her last."

"I don't know what you mean," replied Felton, quietly, "and I am ignorant of whom you are speaking, my Lord. I killed the Duke of Buckingham because he twice refused you yourself to appoint me captain; I have punished him for his injustice, that is all."

De Winter, stupefied, looked on while the soldiers bound Felton, and could not tell what to think of such insensibility.

One thing alone, however, threw a shade over the pallid brow of Felton. At every noise he heard, the simple Puritan fancied he recognized the step and voice of Milady coming to throw herself into his arms, to accuse herself, and die with him.

All at once he started. His eyes became fixed upon a point of the sea, commanded by the terrace where he was. With the eagle glance of a sailor he had recognized there, where another would have seen only a gull hovering over the waves, the sail of a sloop which was directed toward the cost of France.

He grew deadly pale, placed his hand upon his heart, which was breaking, and at once perceived all the treachery.

"One last favor, my Lord!" said he to the baron.

"What?" asked his Lordship.

"What o'clock is it?"

The baron drew out his watch. "It wants ten minutes to nine," said he.

Milady had hastened her departure by an hour and a half. As soon as she heard the cannon which announced the fatal event, she had ordered the anchor to be weighed. The vessel was making way under a blue sky, at great distance from the coast.

"God has so willed it!" said he, with the resignation of a fanatic; but without, however, being able to take his eyes from that ship, on board of which he doubtless fancied he could distinguish the white outline of her to whom he had sacrificed his life.

De Winter followed his look, observed his feelings, and guessed all.

"Be punished ALONE, for the first, miserable man!" said Lord de Winter to Felton, who was being dragged away with his eyes turned toward the sea; "but I swear to you by the memory of my brother whom I have loved so much that your accomplice is not saved."

Felton lowered his head without pronouncing a syllable.

As to Lord de Winter, he descended the stairs rapidly, and went straight to the port.

60 In France

The first fear of the King of England, Charles I, on learning of the death of the duke, was that such terrible news might discourage the Rochellais; he tried, says Richelieu in his Memoirs, to conceal it from them as long as possible, closing all the ports of his kingdom, and carefully keeping watch that no vessel should sail until the army which Buckingham was getting together had gone, taking upon himself, in default of Buckingham, to superintend the departure.

He carried the strictness of this order so far as to detain in England the ambassadors of Denmark, who had taken their leave, and the regular ambassador of Holland, who was to take back to the port of Flushing the Indian merchantmen of which Charles I had made restitution to the United Provinces.

But as he did not think of giving this order till five hours after the event--that is to say, till two o'clock in the afternoon--two vessels had already left the port, the one bearing, as we know, Milady, who, already anticipating the event, was further confirmed in that belief by seeing the black flag flying at the masthead of the admiral's ship.

As to the second vessel, we will tell hereafter whom it carried, and how it set sail.

During this time nothing new occurred in the camp at La Rochelle; only the king, who was bored, as always, but perhaps a little more so in camp than elsewhere, resolved to go incognito and spend the festival of St. Louis at St. Germain, and asked the cardinal to order him an escort of only twenty Musketeers. The cardinal, who sometimes became weary of the king, granted this leave of absence with great pleasure to his royal lieutenant, who promised to return about the fifteenth of September.

M de Treville, being informed of this by his Eminence, packed his portmanteau; and as without knowing the cause he knew the great desire and even imperative need which his friends had of returning to Paris, it goes without saying that he fixed upon them to form part of the escort.

The four young men heard the news a quarter of an hour after M. de Treville, for they were the first to whom he communicated it. It was then that d'Artagnan appreciated the favor the cardinal had conferred upon him in making him at last enter the Musketeers--for without that circumstance he would have been forced to remain in the camp while his companions left it.

It goes without saying that this impatience to return toward Paris had for a cause the danger which Mme. Bonacieux would run of meeting at the convent of Bethune with Milady, her mortal enemy. Aramis therefore had written immediately to Marie Michon, the seamstress at Tours who had such fine acquaintances, to obtain from the queen authority for Mme. Bonacieux to leave the convent, and to retire either into Lorraine or Belgium. They had not long to wait for an answer. Eight or ten days afterward Aramis received the following letter:

My Dear Cousin, Here is the authorization from my sister to withdraw our little servant from the convent of Bethune, the air of which you think is bad for her. My sister sends you this authorization with great pleasure, for she is very partial to the little girl, to whom she intends to be more serviceable hereafter.

I salute you,

To this letter was added an order, conceived in these terms:

At the Louvre, August 10, 1628 The superior of the convent of Bethune will place in the hands of the person who shall present this note to her the novice who entered the convent upon my recommendation and under my patronage.

ANNE

It may be easily imagined how the relationship between Aramis and a seamstress who called the queen her sister amused the young men; but Aramis, after having blushed two or three times up to the whites of his eyes at the gross pleasantry of Porthos, begged his friends not to revert to the subject again, declaring that if a single word more was said to him about it, he would never again implore his cousins to interfere in such affairs.

There was no further question, therefore, about Marie Michon among the four Musketeers, who besides had what they wanted: that was, the order to withdraw Mme. Bonacieux from the convent of the Carmelites of Bethune. It was true that this order would not be of great use to them while they were in camp at La Rochelle; that is to say, at the other end of France. Therefore d'Artagnan was going to ask leave of absence of M. de Treville, confiding to him candidly the importance of his departure, when the news was transmitted to him as well as to his three friends that the king was about to set out for Paris with an escort of twenty Musketeers, and that they formed part of the escort.

Their joy was great. The lackeys were sent on before with the baggage, and they set out on the morning of the sixteenth.

The cardinal accompanied his Majesty from Surgeres to Mauzes; and there the king and his minister took leave of each other with great demonstrations of friendship.

The king, however, who sought distraction, while traveling as fast as possible--for he was anxious to be in Paris by the twenty-third--stopped from time to time to fly the magpie, a pastime for which the taste had been formerly inspired in him by de Luynes, and for which he had always preserved a great predilection. Out of the twenty Musketeers sixteen, when this took place, rejoiced greatly at this relaxation; but the other four cursed it heartily. D'Artagnan, in particular, had a perpetual buzzing in his ears, which Porthos explained thus: "A very great lady has told me that this means that somebody is talking of you somewhere."

At length the escort passed through Paris on the twenty-third, in the night. The king thanked M. de Treville, and permitted him to distribute furloughs for four days, on condition that the favored parties should not appear in any public place, under penalty of the Bastille.

The first four furloughs granted, as may be imagined, were to our four friends. Still further, Athos obtained of M. de Treville six days instead of four, and introduced into these six days two more nights--for they set out on the twenty-fourth at five o'clock in the evening, and as a further kindness M. de Treville post-dated the leave to the morning of the twenty-fifth.

"Good Lord!" said d'Artagnan, who, as we have often said, never stumbled at anything. "It appears to me that we are making a great trouble of a very simple thing. In two days, and by using up two or three horses (that's nothing; I have plenty of money), I am at Bethune. I present my letter from the queen to the superior, and I bring back the dear treasure I go to seek--not into Lorraine, not into Belgium, but to Paris, where she will be much better concealed, particularly while the cardinal is at La Rochelle. Well, once returned from the country, half by the protection of her cousin, half through what we have personally done for her, we shall obtain from the queen what we desire. Remain, then, where you are, and do not exhaust yourselves with useless fatigue. Myself and Planchet are all that such a simple expedition requires."

To this Athos replied quietly: "We also have money left--for I have not yet drunk all my share of the diamond, and Porthos and Aramis have not eaten all theirs. We can therefore use up four horses as well as one. But consider, d'Artagnan," added he, in a tone so solemn that it made the young man shudder, "consider that Bethune is a city where the cardinal has given rendezvous to a woman who, wherever she goes, brings misery with her. If you had only to deal with four men, d'Artagnan, I would allow you to go alone. You have to do with that woman! We four will go; and I hope to God that with our four lackeys we may be in sufficient number."

"You terrify me, Athos!" cried d'Artagnan. "My God! what do you fear?"

"Everything!" replied Athos.

D'Artagnan examined the countenances of his companions, which, like that of Athos, wore an impression of deep anxiety; and they continued their route as fast as their horses could carry them, but without adding another word.

On the evening of the twenty-fifth, as they were entering Arras, and as d'Artagnan was dismounting at the inn of the Golden Harrow to drink a glass of wine, a horseman came out of the post yard, where he had just had a relay, started off at a gallop, and with a fresh horse took the road to Paris. At the moment he passed through the gateway into the street, the wind blew open the cloak in which he was wrapped, although it was in the month of August, and lifted his hat, which the traveler seized with his hand the moment it had left his head, pulling it eagerly over his eyes.

D'Artagnan, who had his eyes fixed upon this man, became very pale, and let his glass fall.

"What is the matter, monsieur?" said Planchet. "Oh, come, gentlemen, my master is ill!"

The three friends hastened toward d'Artagnan, who, instead of being ill, ran toward his horse. They stopped him at the door.

"Well, where the devil are you going now?" cried Athos.

"It is he!" cried d'Artagnan, pale with anger, and with the sweat on his brow, "it is he! let me overtake him!"

"He? What he?" asked Athos.

"He, that man!"

"What man?"

"That cursed man, my evil genius, whom I have always met with when threatened by some misfortune, he who accompanied that horrible woman when I met her for the first time, he whom I was seeking when I offended our Athos, he whom I saw on the very morning Madame Bonacieux was abducted. I have seen him; that is he! I recognized him when the wind blew upon his cloak."

"The devil!" said Athos, musingly.

"To saddle, gentlemen! to saddle! Let us pursue him, and we shall overtake him!"

"My dear friend," said Aramis, "remember that he goes in an opposite direction from that in which we are going, that he has a fresh horse, and ours are fatigued, so that we shall disable our own horses without even a chance of overtaking him. Let the man go, d'Artagnan; let us save the woman."

"Monsieur, monsieur!" cried a hostler, running out and looking after the stranger, "monsieur, here is a paper which dropped out of your hat! Eh, monsieur, eh!"

"Friend," said d'Artagnan, "a half-pistole for that paper!"

"My faith, monsieur, with great pleasure! Here it is!"

The hostler, enchanted with the good day's work he had done, returned to the yard. D'Artagnan unfolded the paper.

"Well?" eagerly demanded all his three friends.

"Nothing but one word!" said d'Artagnan.

"Yes," said Aramis, "but that one word is the name of some town or village."

"Armentieres," read Porthos; "Armentieres? I don't know such a place."

"And that name of a town or village is written in her hand!" cried Athos.

"Come on, come on!" said d'Artagnan; "let us keep that paper carefully, perhaps I have not thrown away my half-pistole. To horse, my friends, to horse!"

And the four friends flew at a gallop along the road to Bethune.

61 The Carmelite Convent At Bethune

Great criminals bear about them a kind of predestination which makes them surmount all obstacles, which makes them escape all dangers, up to the moment which a wearied Providence has marked as the rock of their impious fortunes.

It was thus with Milady. She escaped the cruisers of both nations, and arrived at Boulogne without accident.

When landing at Portsmouth, Milady was an Englishwoman whom the persecutions of the French drove from La Rochelle; when landing at Boulogne, after a two days' passage, she passed for a Frenchwoman whom the English persecuted at Portsmouth out of their hatred for France.

Milady had, likewise, the best of passports--her beauty, her noble appearance, and the liberality with which she distributed her pistoles. Freed from the usual formalities by the affable smile and gallant manners of an old governor of the port, who kissed her hand, she only remained long enough at Boulogne to put into the post a letter, conceived in the following terms:

"To his Eminence Monseigneur the Cardinal Richelieu, in his camp before La Rochelle.

"Monseigneur, Let your Eminence be reassured. His Grace the Duke of Buckingham WILL NOT SET OUT for France.

"MILADY DE ---- "BOULOGNE, evening of the twenty-fifth.

"P.S.--According to the desire of your Eminence, I report to the convent of the Carmelites at Bethune, where I will await your orders."

Accordingly, that same evening Milady commenced her journey. Night overtook her; she stopped, and slept at an inn. At five o'clock the next morning she again proceeded, and in three hours after entered Bethune. She inquired for the convent of the Carmelites, and went thither immediately.

The superior met her; Milady showed her the cardinal's order. The abbess assigned her a chamber, and had breakfast served.

All the past was effaced from the eyes of this woman; and her looks, fixed on the future, beheld nothing but the high fortunes reserved for her by the cardinal, whom she had so successfully served without his name being in any way mixed up with the sanguinary affair. The ever-new passions which consumed her gave to her life the appearance of those clouds which float in the heavens, reflecting sometimes azure, sometimes fire, sometimes the opaque blackness of the tempest, and which leave no traces upon the earth behind them but devastation and death.

After breakfast, the abbess came to pay her a visit. There is very little amusement in the cloister, and the good superior was eager to make the acquaintance of her new boarder.

Milady wished to please the abbess. This was a very easy matter for a woman so really superior as she was. She tried to be agreeable, and she was charming, winning the good superior by her varied conversation and by the graces of her whole personality.

The abbess, who was the daughter of a noble house, took particular delight in stories of the court, which so seldom travel to the extremities of the kingdom, and which, above all, have so much difficulty in penetrating the walls of convents, at whose threshold the noise of the world dies away.

Milady, on the contrary, was quite conversant with all aristocratic intrigues, amid which she had constantly lived for five or six years. She made it her business, therefore, to amuse the good abbess with the worldly practices of the court of France, mixed with the eccentric pursuits of the king; she made for her the scandalous chronicle of the lords and ladies of the court, whom the abbess knew perfectly by name, touched lightly on the amours of the queen and the Duke of Buckingham, talking a great deal to induce her auditor to talk a little.

But the abbess contented herself with listening and smiling without replying a word. Milady, however, saw that this sort of narrative amused her very much, and kept at it; only she now let her conversation drift toward the cardinal.

But she was greatly embarrassed. She did not know whether the abbess was a royalist or a cardinalist; she therefore confined herself to a prudent middle course. But the abbess, on her part, maintained a reserve still more prudent, contenting herself with making a profound inclination of the head every time the fair traveler pronounced the name of his Eminence.

Milady began to think she should soon grow weary of a convent life; she resolved, then, to risk something in order that she might know how to act afterward. Desirous of seeing how far the discretion of the good abbess would go, she began to tell a story, obscure at first, but very circumstantial afterward, about the cardinal, relating the amours of the minister with Mme. d'Aiguillon, Marion de Lorme, and several other gay women.

The abbess listened more attentively, grew animated by degrees, and smiled.

"Good," thought Milady; "she takes a pleasure in my conversation. If she is a cardinalist, she has no fanaticism, at least."

She then went on to describe the persecutions exercised by the cardinal upon his enemies. The abbess only crossed herself, without approving or disapproving.

This confirmed Milady in her opinion that the abbess was rather royalist than cardinalist. Milady therefore continued, coloring her narrations more and more.

"I am very ignorant of these matters," said the abbess, at length; "but however distant from the court we may be, however remote from the interests of the world we may be placed, we have very sad examples of what you have related. And one of our boarders has suffered much from the vengeance and persecution of the cardinal!"

"One of your boarders?" said Milady; "oh, my God! Poor woman! I pity her, then."

"And you have reason, for she is much to be pitied. Imprisonment, menaces, ill treatment-she has suffered everything. But after all," resumed the abbess, "Monsieur Cardinal has perhaps plausible motives for acting thus; and though she has the look of an angel, we must not always judge people by the appearance."

"Good!" said Milady to herself; "who knows! I am about, perhaps, to discover something here; I am in the vein."

She tried to give her countenance an appearance of perfect candor.

"Alas," said Milady, "I know it is so. It is said that we must not trust to the face; but in what, then, shall we place confidence, if not in the most beautiful work of the Lord? As for me, I shall be deceived all my life perhaps, but I shall always have faith in a person whose countenance inspires me with sympathy."

"You would, then, be tempted to believe," said the abbess, "that this young person is innocent?"

"The cardinal pursues not only crimes," said she: "there are certain virtues which he pursues more severely than certain offenses."

"Permit me, madame, to express my surprise," said the abbess.

"At what?" said Milady, with the utmost ingenuousness.

"At the language you use."

"What do you find so astonishing in that language?" said Milady, smiling.

"You are the friend of the cardinal, for he sends you hither, and yet--"

"And yet I speak ill of him," replied Milady, finishing the thought of the superior.

"At least you don't speak well of him."

"That is because I am not his friend," said she, sighing, "but his victim!"

"But this letter in which he recommends you to me?"

"Is an order for me to confine myself to a sort of prison, from which he will release me by one of his satellites."

"But why have you not fled?"

"Whither should I go? Do you believe there is a spot on the earth which the cardinal cannot reach if he takes the trouble to stretch forth his hand? If I were a man, that would barely be possible; but what can a woman do? This young boarder of yours, has she tried to fly?"

"No, that is true; but she--that is another thing; I believe she is detained in France by some love affair."

"Ah," said Milady, with a sigh, "if she loves she is not altogether wretched."

"Then," said the abbess, looking at Milady with increasing interest, "I behold another poor victim?"

"Alas, yes," said Milady.

The abbess looked at her for an instant with uneasiness, as if a fresh thought suggested itself to her mind.

"You are not an enemy of our holy faith?" said she, hesitatingly.

"Who--I?" cried Milady; "I a Protestant? Oh, no! I call to witness the God who hears us, that on the contrary I am a fervent Catholic!"

"Then, madame," said the abbess, smiling, "be reassured; the house in which you are shall not be a very hard prison, and we will do all in our power to make you cherish your captivity. You will find here, moreover, the young woman of whom I spoke, who is persecuted, no doubt, in consequence of some court intrigue. She is amiable and well-behaved."

"What is her name?"

"She was sent to me by someone of high rank, under the name of Kitty. I have not tried to discover her other name."

"Kitty!" cried Milady. "What? Are you sure?"

"That she is called so? Yes, madame. Do you know her?"

Milady smiled to herself at the idea which had occurred to her that this might be her old chambermaid. There was connected with the remembrance of this girl a remembrance of anger; and a desire of vengeance disordered the features of Milady, which, however, immediately recovered the calm and benevolent expression which this woman of a hundred faces had for a moment allowed them to lose.

"And when can I see this young lady, for whom I already feel so great a sympathy?" asked Milady.

"Why, this evening," said the abbess; "today even. But you have been traveling these four days, as you told me yourself. This morning you rose at five o'clock; you must stand in need of repose. Go to bed and sleep; at dinnertime we will rouse you."

Although Milady would very willingly have gone without sleep, sustained as she was by all the excitements which a new adventure awakened in her heart, ever thirsting for intrigues, she nevertheless accepted the offer of the superior. During the last fifteen days she had experienced so many and such various emotions that if her frame of iron was still capable of supporting fatigue, her mind required repose.

She therefore took leave of the abbess, and went to bed, softly rocked by the ideas of vengeance which the name of Kitty had naturally brought to her thoughts. She remembered that almost unlimited promise which the cardinal had given her if she succeeded in her enterprise. She had succeeded; d'Artagnan was then in her power!

One thing alone frightened her; that was the remembrance of her husband, the Comte de la Fere, whom she had believed dead, or at least expatriated, and whom she found again in Athos-the best friend of d'Artagnan.

But alas, if he was the friend of d'Artagnan, he must have lent him his assistance in all the proceedings by whose aid the queen had defeated the project of his Eminence; if he was the friend of d'Artagnan, he was the enemy of the cardinal; and she doubtless would succeed in involving him in the vengeance by which she hoped to destroy the young Musketeer.

All these hopes were so many sweet thoughts for Milady; so, rocked by them, she soon fell asleep.

She was awakened by a soft voice which sounded at the foot of her bed. She opened her eyes, and saw the abbess, accompanied by a young woman with light hair and delicate complexion, who fixed upon her a look full of benevolent curiosity.

The face of the young woman was entirely unknown to her. Each examined the other with great attention, while exchanging the customary compliments; both were very handsome, but of quite different styles of beauty. Milady, however, smiled in observing that she excelled the young woman by far in her high air and aristocratic bearing. It is true that the habit of a novice, which the young woman wore, was not very advantageous in a contest of this kind.

The abbess introduced them to each other. When this formality was ended, as her duties called her to chapel, she left the two young women alone.

The novice, seeing Milady in bed, was about to follow the example of the superior; but Milady stopped her.

"How, madame," said she, "I have scarcely seen you, and you already wish to deprive me of your company, upon which I had counted a little, I must confess, for the time I have to pass here?"

"No, madame," replied the novice, "only I thought I had chosen my time ill; you were asleep, you are fatigued."

"Well," said Milady, "what can those who sleep wish for--a happy awakening? This awakening you have given me; allow me, then, to enjoy it at my ease," and taking her hand, she drew her toward the armchair by the bedside.

The novice sat down.

"How unfortunate I am!" said she; "I have been here six months without the shadow of recreation. You arrive, and your presence was likely to afford me delightful company; yet I expect, in all probability, to quit the convent at any moment."

"How, you are going soon?" asked Milady.

"At least I hope so," said the novice, with an expression of joy which she made no effort to disguise.

"I think I learned you had suffered persecutions from the cardinal," continued Milady; "that would have been another motive for sympathy between us."

"What I have heard, then, from our good mother is true; you have likewise been a victim of that wicked priest."

"Hush!" said Milady; "let us not, even here, speak thus of him. All my misfortunes arise from my having said nearly what you have said before a woman whom I thought my friend, and who betrayed me. Are you also the victim of a treachery?"

"No," said the novice, "but of my devotion--of a devotion to a woman I loved, for whom I would have laid down my life, for whom I would give it still."

"And who has abandoned you--is that it?"

"I have been sufficiently unjust to believe so; but during the last two or three days I have obtained proof to the contrary, for which I thank God--for it would have cost me very dear to think she had forgotten me. But you, madame, you appear to be free," continued the novice; "and if you were inclined to fly it only rests with yourself to do so."

"Whither would you have me go, without friends, without money, in a part of France with which I am unacquainted, and where I have never been before?"

"Oh," cried the novice, "as to friends, you would have them wherever you want, you appear so good and are so beautiful!"

"That does not prevent," replied Milady, softening her smile so as to give it an angelic expression, "my being alone or being persecuted."

"Hear me," said the novice; "we must trust in heaven. There always comes a moment when the good you have done pleads your cause before God; and see, perhaps it is a happiness for you, humble and powerless as I am, that you have met with me, for if I leave this place, well-I have powerful friends, who, after having exerted themselves on my account, may also exert themselves for you."

"Oh, when I said I was alone," said Milady, hoping to make the novice talk by talking of herself, "it is not for want of friends in high places; but these friends themselves tremble before the cardinal. The queen herself does not dare to oppose the terrible minister. I have proof that her Majesty, notwithstanding her excellent heart, has more than once been obliged to abandon to the anger of his Eminence persons who had served her."

"Trust me, madame; the queen may appear to have abandoned those persons, but we must not put faith in appearances. The more they are persecuted, the more she thinks of them; and often, when they least expect it, they have proof of a kind remembrance."

"Alas!" said Milady, "I believe so; the queen is so good!"

"Oh, you know her, then, that lovely and noble queen, that you speak of her thus!" cried the novice, with enthusiasm.

"That is to say," replied Milady, driven into her entrenchment, "that I have not the honor of knowing her personally; but I know a great number of her most intimate friends. I am acquainted with Monsieur de Putange; I met Monsieur Dujart in England; I know Monsieur de Treville."

"Monsieur de Treville!" exclaimed the novice, "do you know Monsieur de Treville?"

"Yes, perfectly well--intimately even."

"The captain of the king's Musketeers?"

"The captain of the king's Musketeers."

"Why, then, only see!" cried the novice; "we shall soon be well acquainted, almost friends. If you know Monsieur de Treville, you must have visited him?"

"Often!" said Milady, who, having entered this track, and perceiving that falsehood succeeded, was determined to follow it to the end.

"With him, then, you must have seen some of his Musketeers?"

"All those he is in the habit of receiving!" replied Milady, for whom this conversation began to have a real interest.

"Name a few of those whom you know, and you will see if they are my friends."

"Well!" said Milady, embarrassed, "I know Monsieur de Louvigny, Monsieur de Courtivron, Monsieur de Ferussac."

The novice let her speak, then seeing that she paused, she said, "Don't you know a gentleman named Athos?"

Milady became as pale as the sheets in which she was lying, and mistress as she was of herself, could not help uttering a cry, seizing the hand of the novice, and devouring her with looks.

"What is the matter? Good God!" asked the poor woman, "have I said anything that has wounded you?"

"No; but the name struck me, because I also have known that gentleman, and it appeared strange to me to meet with a person who appears to know him well."

"Oh, yes, very well; not only him, but some of his friends, Messieurs Porthos and Aramis!"

"Indeed! you know them likewise? I know them," cried Milady, who began to feel a chill penetrate her heart.

"Well, if you know them, you know that they are good and free companions. Why do you not apply to them, if you stand in need of help?"

"That is to say," stammered Milady, "I am not really very intimate with any of them. I know them from having heard one of their friends, Monsieur d'Artagnan, say a great deal about them."

"You know Monsieur d'Artagnan!" cried the novice, in her turn seizing the hands of Milady and devouring her with her eyes.

Then remarking the strange expression of Milady's countenance, she said, "Pardon me, madame; you know him by what title?"

"Why," replied Milady, embarrassed, "why, by the title of friend."

"You deceive me, madame," said the novice; "you have been his mistress!"

"It is you who have been his mistress, madame!" cried Milady, in her turn.

"I?" said the novice.

"Yes, you! I know you now. You are Madame Bonacieux!"

The young woman drew back, filled with surprise and terror.

"Oh, do not deny it! Answer!" continued Milady.

"Well, yes, madame," said the novice, "Are we rivals?"

The countenance of Milady was illumined by so savage a joy that under any other circumstances Mme. Bonacieux would have fled in terror; but she was absorbed by jealousy.

"Speak, madame!" resumed Mme. Bonacieux, with an energy of which she might not have been believed capable. "Have you been, or are you, his mistress?"

"Oh, no!" cried Milady, with an accent that admitted no doubt of her truth. "Never, never!"

"I believe you," said Mme. Bonacieux; "but why, then, did you cry out so?"

"Do you not understand?" said Milady, who had already overcome her agitation and recovered all her presence of mind.

"How can I understand? I know nothing."

"Can you not understand that Monsieur d'Artagnan, being my friend, might take me into his confidence?"

"Truly?"

"Do you not perceive that I know all--your abduction from the little house at St. Germain, his despair, that of his friends, and their useless inquiries up to this moment? How could I help being astonished when, without having the least expectation of such a thing, I meet you face to face--you, of whom we have so often spoken together, you whom he loves with all his soul, you whom he had taught me to love before I had seen you! Ah, dear Constance, I have found you, then; I see you at last!"

And Milady stretched out her arms to Mme. Bonacieux, who, convinced by what she had just said, saw nothing in this woman whom an instant before she had believed her rival but a sincere and devoted friend.

"Oh, pardon me, pardon me!" cried she, sinking upon the shoulders of Milady. "Pardon me, I love him so much!"

These two women held each other for an instant in a close embrace. Certainly, if Milady's strength had been equal to her hatred, Mme. Bonacieux would never have left that embrace alive. But not being able to stifle her, she smiled upon her.

"Oh, you beautiful, good little creature!" said Milady. "How delighted I am to have found you! Let me look at you!" and while saying these words, she absolutely devoured her by her looks. "Oh, yes it is you indeed! From what he has told me, I know you now. I recognize you perfectly."

The poor young woman could not possibly suspect what frightful cruelty was behind the rampart of that pure brow, behind those brilliant eyes in which she read nothing but interest and compassion.

"Then you know what I have suffered," said Mme. Bonacieux, "since he has told you what he has suffered; but to suffer for him is happiness."

Milady replied mechanically, "Yes, that is happiness." She was thinking of something else.

"And then," continued Mme. Bonacieux, "my punishment is drawing to a close. Tomorrow, this evening, perhaps, I shall see him again; and then the past will no longer exist."

"This evening?" asked Milady, roused from her reverie by these words. "What do you mean? Do you expect news from him?"

"I expect himself."

"Himself? D'Artagnan here?"

"Himself!"

"But that's impossible! He is at the siege of La Rochelle with the cardinal. He will not return till after the taking of the city."

"Ah, you fancy so! But is there anything impossible for my d'Artagnan, the noble and loyal gentleman?"

"Oh, I cannot believe you!"

"Well, read, then!" said the unhappy young woman, in the excess of her pride and joy, presenting a letter to Milady.

"The writing of Madame de Chevreuse!" said Milady to herself. "Ah, I always thought there was some secret understanding in that quarter!" And she greedily read the following few lines:

My Dear Child, Hold yourself ready. OUR FRIEND will see you soon, and he will only see you to release you from that imprisonment in which your safety required you should be concealed. Prepare, then, for your departure, and never despair of us.

Our charming Gascon has just proved himself as brave and faithful as ever. Tell him that certain parties are grateful for the warning he has given.

"Yes, yes," said Milady; "the letter is precise. Do you know what that warning was?"

"No, I only suspect he has warned the queen against some fresh machinations of the cardinal."

"Yes, that's it, no doubt!" said Milady, returning the letter to Mme. Bonacieux, and letting her head sink pensively upon her bosom.

At that moment they heard the gallop of a horse.

"Oh!" cried Mme. Bonacieux, darting to the window, "can it be he?"

Milady remained still in bed, petrified by surprise; so many unexpected things happened to her all at once that for the first time she was at a loss.

"He, he!" murmured she; "can it be he?" And she remained in bed with her eyes fixed.

"Alas, no!" said Mme. Bonacieux; "it is a man I don't know, although he seems to be coming here. Yes, he checks his pace; he stops at the gate; he rings."

Milady sprang out of bed.

"You are sure it is not he?" said she.

"Yes, yes, very sure!"

"Perhaps you did not see well."

"Oh, if I were to see the plume of his hat, the end of his cloak, I should know HIM!"

Milady was dressing herself all the time.

"Yes, he has entered."

"It is for you or me!"

"My God, how agitated you seem!"

"Yes, I admit it. I have not your confidence; I fear the cardinal."

"Hush!" said Mme. Bonacieux; "somebody is coming."

Immediately the door opened, and the superior entered.

"Did you come from Boulogne?" demanded she of Milady.

"Yes," replied she, trying to recover her self-possession. "Who wants me?"

"A man who will not tell his name, but who comes from the cardinal."

"And who wishes to speak with me?"

"Who wishes to speak to a lady recently come from Boulogne."

"Then let him come in, if you please."

"Oh, my God, my God!" cried Mme. Bonacieux. "Can it be bad news?"

"I fear it."

"I will leave you with this stranger; but as soon as he is gone, if you will permit me, I will return."

"PERMIT you? I BESEECH you."

The superior and Mme. Bonacieux retired.

Milady remained alone, with her eyes fixed upon the door. An instant later, the jingling of spurs was heard upon the stairs, steps drew near, the door opened, and a man appeared.

Milady uttered a cry of joy; this man was the Comte de Rochefort--the demoniacal tool of his Eminence.

62 Two Varieties Of Demons

"Ah," cried Milady and Rochefort together, "it is you!"

"Yes, it is I."

"And you come?" asked Milady.

"From La Rochelle; and you?"

"From England."

"Buckingham?"

"Dead or desperately wounded, as I left without having been able to hear anything of him. A fanatic has just assassinated him."

"Ah," said Rochefort, with a smile; "this is a fortunate chance--one that will delight his Eminence! Have you informed him of it?"

"I wrote to him from Boulogne. But what brings you here?"

"His Eminence was uneasy, and sent me to find you."

"I only arrived yesterday."

"And what have you been doing since yesterday?"

"I have not lost my time."

"Oh, I don't doubt that."

"Do you know whom I have encountered here?"

"No."

"Guess."

"How can I?"

"That young woman whom the queen took out of prison."

"The mistress of that fellow d'Artagnan?"

"Yes; Madame Bonacieux, with whose retreat the cardinal was unacquainted."

"Well, well," said Rochefort, "here is a chance which may pair off with the other! Monsieur Cardinal is indeed a privileged man!"

"Imagine my astonishment," continued Milady, "when I found myself face to face with this woman!"

"Does she know you?"

"No."

"Then she looks upon you as a stranger?"

Milady smiled. "I am her best friend."

"Upon my honor," said Rochefort, "it takes you, my dear countess, to perform such miracles!"

"And it is well I can, Chevalier," said Milady, "for do you know what is going on here?"

"No."

"They will come for her tomorrow or the day after, with an order from the queen."

"Indeed! And who?"

"d'Artagnan and his friends."

"Indeed, they will go so far that we shall be obliged to send them to the Bastille."

"Why is it not done already?"

"What would you? The cardinal has a weakness for these men which I cannot comprehend."

"Indeed!"

"Yes."

"Well, then, tell him this, Rochefort. Tell him that our conversation at the inn of the Red Dovecot was overheard by these four men; tell him that after his departure one of them came up to me and took from me by violence the safe-conduct which he had given me; tell him they warned Lord de Winter of my journey to England; that this time they nearly foiled my mission as they foiled the affair of the studs; tell him that among these four men two only are to be feared--d'Artagnan and Athos; tell him that the third, Aramis, is the lover of Madame de Chevreuse--he may be left alone, we know his secret, and it may be useful; as to the fourth, Porthos, he is a fool, a simpleton, a blustering booby, not worth troubling himself about."

"But these four men must be now at the siege of La Rochelle?"

"I thought so, too; but a letter which Madame Bonacieux has received from Madame the Constable, and which she has had the imprudence to show me, leads me to believe that these four men, on the contrary, are on the road hither to take her away."

"The devil! What's to be done?"

"What did the cardinal say about me?"

"I was to take your dispatches, written or verbal, and return by post; and when he shall know what you have done, he will advise what you have to do."

"I must, then, remain here?"

"Here, or in the neighborhood."

"You cannot take me with you?"

"No, the order is imperative. Near the camp you might be recognized; and your presence, you must be aware, would compromise the cardinal."

"Then I must wait here, or in the neighborhood?"

"Only tell me beforehand where you will wait for intelligence from the cardinal; let me know always where to find you."

"Observe, it is probable that I may not be able to remain here."

"Why?"

"You forget that my enemies may arrive at any minute."

"That's true; but is this little woman, then, to escape his Eminence?"

"Bah!" said Milady, with a smile that belonged only to herself; "you forget that I am her best friend."

"Ah, that's true! I may then tell the cardinal, with respect to this little woman--"

"That he may be at ease."

"Is that all?"

"He will know what that means."

"He will guess, at least. Now, then, what had I better do?"

"Return instantly. It appears to me that the news you bear is worth the trouble of a little diligence."

"My chaise broke down coming into Lilliers."

"Capital!"

"What, CAPITAL?"

"Yes, I want your chaise."

"And how shall I travel, then?"

"On horseback."

"You talk very comfortably,--a hundred and eighty leagues!"

"What's that?"

"One can do it! Afterward?"

"Afterward? Why, in passing through Lilliers you will send me your chaise, with an order to your servant to place himself at my disposal."

"Well."

"You have, no doubt, some order from the cardinal about you?"

"I have my FULL POWER."

"Show it to the abbess, and tell her that someone will come and fetch me, either today or tomorrow, and that I am to follow the person who presents himself in your name."

"Very well."

"Don't forget to treat me harshly in speaking of me to the abbess."

"To what purpose?"

"I am a victim of the cardinal. It is necessary to inspire confidence in that poor little Madame Bonacieux."

"That's true. Now, will you make me a report of all that has happened?"

"Why, I have related the events to you. You have a good memory; repeat what I have told you. A paper may be lost."

"You are right; only let me know where to find you that I may not run needlessly about the neighborhood."

"That's correct; wait!"

"Do you want a map?"

"Oh, I know this country marvelously!"

"You? When were you here?"

"I was brought up here."

"Truly?"

"It is worth something, you see, to have been brought up somewhere."

"You will wait for me, then?"

"Let me reflect a little! Ay, that will do--at Armentieres."

"Where is that Armentieres?"

"A little town on the Lys; I shall only have to cross the river, and I shall be in a foreign country."

"Capital! but it is understood you will only cross the river in case of danger."

"That is well understood."

"And in that case, how shall I know where you are?"

"You do not want your lackey?"

"Is he a sure man?"

"To the proof."

"Give him to me. Nobody knows him. I will leave him at the place I quit, and he will conduct you to me."

"And you say you will wait for me at Armentieres?"

"At Armentieres."

"Write that name on a bit of paper, lest I should forget it. There is nothing compromising in the name of a town. Is it not so?"

"Eh, who knows? Never mind," said Milady, writing the name on half a sheet of paper; "I will compromise myself."

"Well," said Rochefort, taking the paper from Milady, folding it, and placing it in the lining of his hat, "you may be easy. I will do as children do, for fear of losing the paper--repeat the name along the route. Now, is that all?"

"I believe so."

"Let us see: Buckingham dead or grievously wounded; your conversation with the cardinal overheard by the four Musketeers; Lord de Winter warned of your arrival at Portsmouth; d'Artagnan and Athos to the Bastille; Aramis the lover of Madame de Chevreuse; Porthos an ass; Madame Bonacieux found again; to send you the chaise as soon as possible; to place my lackey at your disposal; to make you out a victim of the cardinal in order that the abbess may entertain no suspicion; Armentieres, on the banks of the Lys. Is that all, then?"

"In truth, my dear Chevalier, you are a miracle of memory. A PROPOS, add one thing--"

"What?"

"I saw some very pretty woods which almost touch the convent garden. Say that I am permitted to walk in those woods. Who knows? Perhaps I shall stand in need of a back door for retreat."

"You think of everything."

"And you forget one thing."

"What?"

"To ask me if I want money."

"That's true. How much do you want?"

"All you have in gold."

"I have five hundred pistoles, or thereabouts."

"I have as much. With a thousand pistoles one may face everything. Empty your pockets."

"There."

"Right. And you go--"

"In an hour--time to eat a morsel, during which I shall send for a post horse."

"Capital! Adieu, Chevalier."

"Adieu, Countess."

"Commend me to the cardinal."

"Commend me to Satan."

Milady and Rochefort exchanged a smile and separated. An hour afterward Rochefort set out at a grand gallop; five hours after that he passed through Arras.

Our readers already know how he was recognized by d'Artagnan, and how that recognition by inspiring fear in the four Musketeers had given fresh activity to their journey.

63 The Drop Of Water

Rochefort had scarcely departed when Mme. Bonacieux re-entered. She found Milady with a smiling countenance.

"Well," said the young woman, "what you dreaded has happened. This evening, or tomorrow, the cardinal will send someone to take you away."

"Who told you that, my dear?" asked Milady.

"I heard it from the mouth of the messenger himself."

"Come and sit down close to me," said Milady.

"Here I am."

"Wait till I assure myself that nobody hears us."

"Why all these precautions?"

"You shall know."

Milady arose, went to the door, opened it, looked in the corridor, and then returned and seated herself close to Mme. Bonacieux.

"Then," said she, "he has well played his part."

"Who has?"

"He who just now presented himself to the abbess as a messenger from the cardinal."

"It was, then, a part he was playing?"

"Yes, my child."

"That man, then, was not--"

"That man," said Milady, lowering her voice, "is my brother."

"Your brother!" cried Mme. Bonacieux.

"No one must know this secret, my dear, but yourself. If you reveal it to anyone in the world, I shall be lost, and perhaps yourself likewise."

"Oh, my God!"

"Listen. This is what has happened: My brother, who was coming to my assistance to take me away by force if it were necessary, met with the emissary of the cardinal, who was coming in search of me. He followed him. At a solitary and retired part of the road he drew his sword, and required the messenger to deliver up to him the papers of which he was the bearer. The messenger resisted; my brother killed him."

"Oh!" said Mme. Bonacieux, shuddering.

"Remember, that was the only means. Then my brother determined to substitute cunning for force. He took the papers, and presented himself here as the emissary of the cardinal, and in an hour or two a carriage will come to take me away by the orders of his Eminence."

"I understand. It is your brother who sends this carriage."

"Exactly; but that is not all. That letter you have received, and which you believe to be from Madame de Chevreuse--"

"Well?"

"It is a forgery."

"How can that be?"

"Yes, a forgery; it is a snare to prevent your making any resistance when they come to fetch you."

"But it is d'Artagnan that will come."

"Do not deceive yourself. D'Artagnan and his friends are detained at the siege of La Rochelle."

"How do you know that?"

"My brother met some emissaries of the cardinal in the uniform of Musketeers. You would have been summoned to the gate; you would have believed yourself about to meet friends; you would have been abducted, and conducted back to Paris."

"Oh, my God! My senses fail me amid such a chaos of iniquities. I feel, if this continues," said Mme. Bonacieux, raising her hands to her forehead, "I shall go mad!"

"Stop--"

"What?"

"I hear a horse's steps; it is my brother setting off again. I should like to offer him a last salute. Come!"

Milady opened the window, and made a sign to Mme. Bonacieux to join her. The young woman complied.

Rochefort passed at a gallop.

"Adieu, brother!" cried Milady.

The chevalier raised his head, saw the two young women, and without stopping, waved his hand in a friendly way to Milady.

"The good George!" said she, closing the window with an expression of countenance full of affection and melancholy. And she resumed her seat, as if plunged in reflections entirely personal.

"Dear lady," said Mme. Bonacieux, "pardon me for interrupting you; but what do you advise me to do? Good heaven! You have more experience than I have. Speak; I will listen."

"In the first place," said Milady, "it is possible I may be deceived, and that d'Artagnan and his friends may really come to your assistance."

"Oh, that would be too much!" cried Mme. Bonacieux, "so much happiness is not in store for me!"

"Then you comprehend it would be only a question of time, a sort of race, which should arrive first. If your friends are the more speedy, you are to be saved; if the satellites of the cardinal, you are lost."

"Oh, yes, yes; lost beyond redemption! What, then, to do? What to do?"

"There would be a very simple means, very natural--"

"Tell me what!"

"To wait, concealed in the neighborhood, and assure yourself who are the men who come to ask for you."

"But where can I wait?"

"Oh, there is no difficulty in that. I shall stop and conceal myself a few leagues hence until my brother can rejoin me. Well, I take you with me; we conceal ourselves, and wait together."

"But I shall not be allowed to go; I am almost a prisoner."

"As they believe that I go in consequence of an order from the cardinal, no one will believe you anxious to follow me."

"Well?"

"Well! The carriage is at the door; you bid me adieu; you mount the step to embrace me a last time; my brother's servant, who comes to fetch me, is told how to proceed; he makes a sign to the postillion, and we set off at a gallop."

"But d'Artagnan! D'Artagnan! if he comes?"

"Shall we not know it?"

"How?"

"Nothing easier. We will send my brother's servant back to Bethune, whom, as I told you, we can trust. He shall assume a disguise, and place himself in front of the convent. If the emissaries of the cardinal arrive, he will take no notice; if it is Monsieur d'Artagnan and his friends, he will bring them to us."

"He knows them, then?"

"Doubtless. Has he not seen Monsieur d'Artagnan at my house?"

"Oh, yes, yes; you are right. Thus all may go well--all may be for the best; but we do not go far from this place?"

"Seven or eight leagues at the most. We will keep on the frontiers, for instance; and at the first alarm we can leave France."

"And what can we do there?"

"Wait."

"But if they come?"

"My brother's carriage will be here first."

"If I should happen to be any distance from you when the carriage comes for you--at dinner or supper, for instance?"

"Do one thing."

"What is that?"

"Tell your good superior that in order that we may be as much together as possible, you ask her permission to share my repast."

"Will she permit it?"

"What inconvenience can it be?"

"Oh, delightful! In this way we shall not be separated for an instant."

"Well, go down to her, then, to make your request. I feel my head a little confused; I will take a turn in the garden."

"Go and where shall I find you?"

"Here, in an hour."

"Here, in an hour. Oh, you are so kind, and I am so grateful!"

"How can I avoid interesting myself for one who is so beautiful and so amiable? Are you not the beloved of one of my best friends?"

"Dear d'Artagnan! Oh, how he will thank you!"

"I hope so. Now, then, all is agreed; let us go down."

"You are going into the garden?"

"Yes."

"Go along this corridor, down a little staircase, and you are in it."

"Excellent; thank you!"

And the two women parted, exchanging charming smiles.

Milady had told the truth--her head was confused, for her ill-arranged plans clashed one another like chaos. She required to be alone that she might put her thoughts a little into order. She saw vaguely the future; but she stood in need of a little silence and quiet to give all her ideas, as yet confused, a distinct form and a regular plan.

What was most pressing was to get Mme. Bonacieux away, and convey her to a place of safety, and there, if matters required, make her a hostage. Milady began to have doubts of the issue of this terrible duel, in which her enemies showed as much perseverance as she did animosity.

Besides, she felt as we feel when a storm is coming on--that this issue was near, and could not fail to be terrible.

The principal thing for her, then, was, as we have said, to keep Mme. Bonacieux in her power. Mme. Bonacieux was the very life of d'Artagnan. This was more than his life, the life of the woman he loved; this was, in case of ill fortune, a means of temporizing and obtaining good conditions.

Now, this point was settled; Mme. Bonacieux, without any suspicion, accompanied her. Once concealed with her at Armentieres, it would be easy to make her believe that d'Artagnan had not come to Bethune. In fifteen days at most, Rochefort would be back; besides, during that fifteen days she would have time to think how she could best avenge herself on the four friends. She would not be weary, thank God! for she should enjoy the sweetest pastime such events could accord a woman of her character--perfecting a beautiful vengeance.

Revolving all this in her mind, she cast her eyes around her, and arranged the topography of the garden in her head. Milady was like a good general who contemplates at the same time victory and defeat, and who is quite prepared, according to the chances of the battle, to march forward or to beat a retreat.

At the end of an hour she heard a soft voice calling her; it was Mme. Bonacieux's. The good abbess had naturally consented to her request; and as a commencement, they were to sup together.

On reaching the courtyard, they heard the noise of a carriage which stopped at the gate.

Milady listened.

"Do you hear anything?" said she.

"Yes, the rolling of a carriage."

"It is the one my brother sends for us."

"Oh, my God!"

"Come, come! courage!"

The bell of the convent gate was sounded; Milady was not mistaken.

"Go to your chamber," said she to Mme. Bonacieux; "you have perhaps some jewels you would like to take."

"I have his letters," said she.

"Well, go and fetch them, and come to my apartment. We will snatch some supper; we shall perhaps travel part of the night, and must keep our strength up."

"Great God!" said Mme. Bonacieux, placing her hand upon her bosom, "my heart beats so I cannot walk."

"Courage, courage! remember that in a quarter of an hour you will be safe; and think that what you are about to do is for HIS sake."

"Yes, yes, everything for him. You have restored my courage by a single word; go, I will rejoin you."

Milady ran up to her apartment quickly; she there found Rochefort's lackey, and gave him his instructions.

He was to wait at the gate; if by chance the Musketeers should appear, the carriage was to set off as fast as possible, pass around the convent, and go and wait for Milady at a little village which was situated at the other side of the wood. In this case Milady would cross the garden and gain the village on foot. As we have already said, Milady was admirably acquainted with this part of France.

If the Musketeers did not appear, things were to go on as had been agreed; Mme. Bonacieux was to get into the carriage as if to bid her adieu, and she was to take away Mme. Bonacieux.

Mme. Bonacieux came in; and to remove all suspicion, if she had any, Milady repeated to the lackey, before her, the latter part of her instructions.

Milady asked some questions about the carriage. It was a chaise drawn by three horses, driven by a postillion; Rochefort's lackey would precede it, as courier.

Milady was wrong in fearing that Mme. Bonacieux would have any suspicion. The poor young woman was too pure to suppose that any female could be guilty of such perfidy; besides, the name of the Comtesse de Winter, which she had heard the abbess pronounce, was wholly unknown to her, and she was even ignorant that a woman had had so great and so fatal a share in the misfortune of her life.

"You see," said she, when the lackey had gone out, "everything is ready. The abbess suspects nothing, and believes that I am taken by order of the cardinal. This man goes to give his last orders; take the least thing, drink a finger of wine, and let us be gone."

"Yes," said Mme. Bonacieux, mechanically, "yes, let us be gone."

Milady made her a sign to sit down opposite, poured her a small glass of Spanish wine, and helped her to the wing of a chicken.

"See," said she, "if everything does not second us! Here is night coming on; by daybreak we shall have reached our retreat, and nobody can guess where we are. Come, courage! take something."

Mme. Bonacieux ate a few mouthfuls mechanically, and just touched the glass with her lips.

"Come, come!" said Milady, lifting hers to her mouth, "do as I do."

But at the moment the glass touched her lips, her hand remained suspended; she heard something on the road which sounded like the rattling of a distant gallop. Then it grew nearer, and it seemed to her, almost at the same time, that she heard the neighing of horses.

This noise acted upon her joy like the storm which awakens the sleeper in the midst of a happy dream; she grew pale and ran to the window, while Mme. Bonacieux, rising all in a tremble, supported herself upon her chair to avoid falling. Nothing was yet to be seen, only they heard the galloping draw nearer.

"Oh, my God!" said Mme. Bonacieux, "what is that noise?"

"That of either our friends or our enemies," said Milady, with her terrible coolness. "Stay where you are, I will tell you."

Mme. Bonacieux remained standing, mute, motionless, and pale as a statue.

The noise became louder; the horses could not be more than a hundred and fifty paces distant. If they were not yet to be seen, it was because the road made an elbow. The noise became so distinct that the horses might be counted by the rattle of their hoofs.

Milady gazed with all the power of her attention; it was just light enough for her to see who was coming.

All at once, at the turning of the road she saw the glitter of laced hats and the waving of feathers; she counted two, then five, then eight horsemen. One of them preceded the rest by double the length of his horse.

Milady uttered a stifled groan. In the first horseman she recognized d'Artagnan.

"Oh, my God, my God," cried Mme. Bonacieux, "what is it?"

"It is the uniform of the cardinal's Guards. Not an instant to be lost! Fly, fly!"

"Yes, yes, let us fly!" repeated Mme. Bonacieux, but without being able to make a step, glued as she was to the spot by terror.

They heard the horsemen pass under the windows.

"Come, then, come, then!" cried Milady, trying to drag the young woman along by the arm. "Thanks to the garden, we yet can flee; I have the key, but make haste! in five minutes it will be too late!"

Mme. Bonacieux tried to walk, made two steps, and sank upon her knees. Milady tried to raise and carry her, but could not do it.

At this moment they heard the rolling of the carriage, which at the approach of the Musketeers set off at a gallop. Then three or four shots were fired.

"For the last time, will you come?" cried Milady.

"Oh, my God, my God! you see my strength fails me; you see plainly I cannot walk. Flee alone!"

"Flee alone, and leave you here? No, no, never!" cried Milady.

All at once she paused, a livid flash darted from her eyes; she ran to the table, emptied into Mme. Bonacieux's glass the contents of a ring which she opened with singular quickness. It was a grain of a reddish color, which dissolved immediately.

Then, taking the glass with a firm hand, she said, "Drink. This wine will give you strength, drink!" And she put the glass to the lips of the young woman, who drank mechanically.

"This is not the way that I wished to avenge myself," said Milady, replacing the glass upon the table, with an infernal smile, "but, my faith! we do what we can!" And she rushed out of the room.

Mme. Bonacieux saw her go without being able to follow her; she was like people who dream they are pursued, and who in vain try to walk.

A few moments passed; a great noise was heard at the gate. Every instant Mme. Bonacieux expected to see Milady, but she did not return. Several times, with terror, no doubt, the cold sweat burst from her burning brow.

At length she heard the grating of the hinges of the opening gates; the noise of boots and spurs resounded on the stairs. There was a great murmur of voices which continued to draw near, amid which she seemed to hear her own name pronounced.

All at once she uttered a loud cry of joy, and darted toward the door; she had recognized the voice of d'Artagnan.

"d'Artagnan! D'Artagnan!" cried she, "is it you? This way! this way!"

"Constance? Constance?" replied the young man, "where are you? where are you? My God!"

At the same moment the door of the cell yielded to a shock, rather than opened; several men rushed into the chamber. Mme. Bonacieux had sunk into an armchair, without the power of moving.

D'Artagnan threw down a yet-smoking pistol which he held in his hand, and fell on his knees before his mistress. Athos replaced his in his belt; Porthos and Aramis, who held their drawn swords in their hands, returned them to their scabbards.

"Oh, d'Artagnan, my beloved d'Artagnan! You have come, then, at last! You have not deceived me! It is indeed thee!"

"Yes, yes, Constance. Reunited!"

"Oh, it was in vain she told me you would not come! I hoped in silence. I was not willing to fly. Oh, I have done well! How happy I am!"

At this word SHE, Athos, who had seated himself quietly, started up.

"SHE! What she?" asked d'Artagnan.

"Why, my companion. She who out of friendship for me wished to take me from my persecutors. She who, mistaking you for the cardinal's Guards, has just fled away."

"Your companion!" cried d'Artagnan, becoming more pale than the white veil of his mistress. "Of what companion are you speaking, dear Constance?"

"Of her whose carriage was at the gate; of a woman who calls herself your friend; of a woman to whom you have told everything."

"Her name, her name!" cried d'Artagnan. "My God, can you not remember her name?"

"Yes, it was pronounced in my hearing once. Stop--but--it is very strange--oh, my God, my head swims! I cannot see!"

"Help, help, my friends! her hands are icy cold," cried d'Artagnan. "She is ill! Great God, she is losing her senses!"

While Porthos was calling for help with all the power of his strong voice, Aramis ran to the table to get a glass of water; but he stopped at seeing the horrible alteration that had taken place in the countenance of Athos, who, standing before the table, his hair rising from his head, his eyes fixed in stupor, was looking at one of the glasses, and appeared a prey to the most horrible doubt.

"Oh!" said Athos, "oh, no, it is impossible! God would not permit such a crime!"

"Water, water!" cried d'Artagnan. "Water!"

"Oh, poor woman, poor woman!" murmured Athos, in a broken voice.

Mme. Bonacieux opened her eyes under the kisses of d'Artagnan.

"She revives!" cried the young man. "Oh, my God, my God, I thank thee!"

"Madame!" said Athos, "madame, in the name of heaven, whose empty glass is this?"

"Mine, monsieur," said the young woman, in a dying voice.

"But who poured the wine for you that was in this glass?"

"She."

"But who is SHE?"

"Oh, I remember!" said Mme. Bonacieux, "the Comtesse de Winter."

The four friends uttered one and the same cry, but that of Athos dominated all the rest.

At that moment the countenance of Mme. Bonacieux became livid; a fearful agony pervaded her frame, and she sank panting into the arms of Porthos and Aramis.

D'Artagnan seized the hands of Athos with an anguish difficult to be described.

"And what do you believe?' His voice was stifled by sobs.

"I believe everything," said Athos biting his lips till the blood sprang to avoid sighing.

"d'Artagnan, d'Artagnan!" cried Mme. Bonacieux, "where art thou? Do not leave me! You see I am dying!"

D'Artagnan released the hands of Athos which he still held clasped in both his own, and hastened to her. Her beautiful face was distorted with agony; her glassy eyes had no longer their sight; a convulsive shuddering shook her whole body; the sweat rolled from her brow.

"In the name of heaven, run, call! Aramis! Porthos! Call for help!"

"Useless!" said Athos, "useless! For the poison which SHE pours there is no antidote."

"Yes, yes! Help, help!" murmured Mme. Bonacieux; "help!"

Then, collecting all her strength, she took the head of the young man between her hands, looked at him for an instant as if her whole soul passed into that look, and with a sobbing cry pressed her lips to his.

"Constance, Constance!" cried d'Artagnan.

A sigh escaped from the mouth of Mme. Bonacieux, and dwelt for an instant on the lips of d'Artagnan. That sigh was the soul, so chaste and so loving, which reascended to heaven.

D'Artagnan pressed nothing but a corpse in his arms. The young man uttered a cry, and fell by the side of his mistress as pale and as icy as herself.

Porthos wept; Aramis pointed toward heaven; Athos made the sign of the cross.

At that moment a man appeared in the doorway, almost as pale as those in the chamber. He looked around him and saw Mme. Bonacieux dead, and d'Artagnan in a swoon. He appeared just at that moment of stupor which follows great catastrophes.

"I was not deceived," said he; "here is Monsieur d'Artagnan; and you are his friends, Messieurs Athos, Porthos, and Aramis."

The persons whose names were thus pronounced looked at the stranger with astonishment. It seemed to all three that they knew him.

"Gentlemen," resumed the newcomer, "you are, as I am, in search of a woman who," added he, with a terrible smile, "must have passed this way, for I see a corpse."

The three friends remained mute--for although the voice as well as the countenance reminded them of someone they had seen, they could not remember under what circumstances.

"Gentlemen," continued the stranger, "since you do not recognize a man who probably owes his life to you twice, I must name myself. I am Lord de Winter, brother-in-law of THAT WOMAN."

The three friends uttered a cry of surprise.

Athos rose, and offering him his hand, "Be welcome, my Lord," said he, "you are one of us."

"I set out five hours after her from Portsmouth," said Lord de Winter. "I arrived three hours after her at Boulogne. I missed her by twenty minutes at St. Omer. Finally, at Lilliers I lost all trace of her. I was going about at random, inquiring of everybody, when I saw you gallop past. I recognized Monsieur d'Artagnan. I called to you, but you did not answer me; I wished to follow you, but my horse was too much fatigued to go at the same pace with yours. And yet it appears, in spite of all your diligence, you have arrived too late."

"You see!" said Athos, pointing to Mme. Bonacieux dead, and to d'Artagnan, whom Porthos and Aramis were trying to recall to life.

"Are they both dead?" asked Lord de Winter, sternly.

"No," replied Athos, "fortunately Monsieur d'Artagnan has only fainted."

"Ah, indeed, so much the better!" said Lord de Winter.

At that moment d'Artagnan opened his eyes. He tore himself from the arms of Porthos and Aramis, and threw himself like a madman on the corpse of his mistress.

Athos rose, walked toward his friend with a slow and solemn step, embraced him tenderly, and as he burst into violent sobs, he said to him with his noble and persuasive voice, "Friend, be a man! Women weep for the dead; men avenge them!"

"Oh, yes!" cried d'Artagnan, "yes! If it be to avenge her, I am ready to follow you."

Athos profited by this moment of strength which the hope of vengeance restored to his unfortunate friend to make a sign to Porthos and Aramis to go and fetch the superior.

The two friends met her in the corridor, greatly troubled and much upset by such strange events; she called some of the nuns, who against all monastic custom found themselves in the presence of five men.

"Madame," said Athos, passing his arm under that of d'Artagnan, "we abandon to your pious care the body of that unfortunate woman. She was an angel on earth before being an angel in heaven. Treat her as one of your sisters. We will return someday to pray over her grave."

D'Artagnan concealed his face in the bosom of Athos, and sobbed aloud.

"Weep," said Athos, "weep, heart full of love, youth, and life! Alas, would I could weep like you!"

And he drew away his friend, as affectionate as a father, as consoling as a priest, noble as a man who has suffered much.

All five, followed by their lackeys leading their horses, took their way to the town of Bethune, whose outskirts they perceived, and stopped before the first inn they came to.

"But," said d'Artagnan, "shall we not pursue that woman?"

"Later," said Athos. "I have measures to take."

"She will escape us," replied the young man; "she will escape us, and it will be your fault, Athos."

"I will be accountable for her," said Athos.

D'Artagnan had so much confidence in the word of his friend that he lowered his head, and entered the inn without reply.

Porthos and Aramis regarded each other, not understanding this assurance of Athos.

Lord de Winter believed he spoke in this manner to soothe the grief of d'Artagnan.

"Now, gentlemen," said Athos, when he had ascertained there were five chambers free in the hotel, "let everyone retire to his own apartment. d'Artagnan needs to be alone, to weep and to sleep. I take charge of everything; be easy."

"It appears, however," said Lord de Winter, "if there are any measures to take against the countess, it concerns me; she is my sister-in-law."

"And me," said Athos, "--she is my wife!"

D'Artagnan smiled--for he understood that Athos was sure of his vengeance when he revealed such a secret. Porthos and Aramis looked at each other, and grew pale. Lord de Winter thought Athos was mad.

"Now, retire to your chambers," said Athos, "and leave me to act. You must perceive that in my quality of a husband this concerns me. Only, d'Artagnan, if you have not lost it, give me the paper which fell from that man's hat, upon which is written the name of the village of--"

"Ah," said d'Artagnan, "I comprehend! that name written in her hand."

"You see, then," said Athos, "there is a god in heaven still!"

64 The Man In The Red Cloak

The despair of Athos had given place to a concentrated grief which only rendered more lucid the brilliant mental faculties of that extraordinary man.

Possessed by one single thought--that of the promise he had made, and of the responsibility he had taken--he retired last to his chamber, begged the host to procure him a map of the province, bent over it, examined every line traced upon it, perceived that there were four different roads from Bethune to Armentieres, and summoned the lackeys.

Planchet, Grimaud, Bazin, and Mousqueton presented themselves, and received clear, positive, and serious orders from Athos.

They must set out the next morning at daybreak, and go to Armentieres--each by a different route. Planchet, the most intelligent of the four, was to follow that by which the carriage had gone upon which the four friends had fired, and which was accompanied, as may be remembered, by Rochefort's servant.

Athos set the lackeys to work first because, since these men had been in the service of himself and his friends he had discovered in each of them different and essential qualities. Then, lackeys who ask questions inspire less mistrust than masters, and meet with more sympathy among those to whom they address themselves. Besides, Milady knew the masters, and did not know the lackeys; on the contrary, the lackeys knew Milady perfectly.

All four were to meet the next day at eleven o'clock. If they had discovered Milady's retreat, three were to remain on guard; the fourth was to return to Bethune in order to inform Athos and serve as a guide to the four friends. These arrangements made, the lackeys retired.

Athos then arose from his chair, girded on his sword, enveloped himself in his cloak, and left the hotel. It was nearly ten o'clock. At ten o'clock in the evening, it is well known, the streets in provincial towns are very little frequented. Athos nevertheless was visibly anxious to find someone of whom he could ask a question. At length he met a belated passenger, went up to him, and spoke a few words to him. The man he addressed recoiled with terror, and only answered the few words of the Musketeer by pointing. Athos offered the man half a pistole to accompany him, but the man refused.

Athos then plunged into the street the man had indicated with his finger; but arriving at four crossroads, he stopped again, visibly embarrassed. Nevertheless, as the crossroads offered him a better chance than any other place of meeting somebody, he stood still. In a few minutes a night watch passed. Athos repeated to him the same question he had asked the first person he met. The night watch evinced the same terror, refused, in his turn, to accompany Athos, and only pointed with his hand to the road he was to take.

Athos walked in the direction indicated, and reached the suburb situated at the opposite extremity of the city from that by which he and his friends had entered it. There he again appeared uneasy and embarrassed, and stopped for the third time.

Fortunately, a mendicant passed, who, coming up to Athos to ask charity, Athos offered him half a crown to accompany him where he was going. The mendicant hesitated at first, but at the sight of the piece of silver which shone in the darkness he consented, and walked on before Athos.

Arrived at the angle of a street, he pointed to a small house, isolated, solitary, and dismal. Athos went toward the house, while the mendicant, who had received his reward, left as fast as his legs could carry him.

Athos went round the house before he could distinguish the door, amid the red color in which the house was painted. No light appeared through the chinks of the shutters; no noise gave reason to believe that it was inhabited. It was dark and silent as the tomb.

Three times Athos knocked without receiving an answer. At the third knock, however, steps were heard inside. The door at length was opened, and a man appeared, of high stature, pale complexion, and black hair and beard.

Athos and he exchanged some words in a low voice, then the tall man made a sign to the Musketeer that he might come in. Athos immediately profited by the permission, and the door was closed behind him.

The man whom Athos had come so far to seek, and whom he had found with so much trouble, introduced him into his laboratory, where he was engaged in fastening together with iron wire the dry bones of a skeleton. All the frame was adjusted except the head, which lay on the table.

All the rest of the furniture indicated that the dweller in this house occupied himself with the study of natural science. There were large bottles filled with serpents, ticketed according to their species; dried lizards shone like emeralds set in great squares of black wood, and bunches of wild odoriferous herbs, doubtless possessed of virtues unknown to common men, were fastened to the ceiling and hung down in the corners of the apartment. There was no family, no servant; the tall man alone inhabited this house.

Athos cast a cold and indifferent glance upon the objects we have described, and at the invitation of him whom he came to seek sat down near him.

Then he explained to him the cause of his visit, and the service he required of him. But scarcely had he expressed his request when the unknown, who remained standing before the Musketeer, drew back with signs of terror, and refused. Then Athos took from his pocket a small paper, on which two lines were written, accompanied by a signature and a seal, and presented them to him who had made too prematurely these signs of repugnance. The tall man had scarcely read these lines, seen the signature, and recognized the seal, when he bowed to denote that he had no longer any objection to make, and that he was ready to obey.

Athos required no more. He arose, bowed, went out, returned by the same way he came, re-entered the hotel, and went to his apartment.

At daybreak d'Artagnan entered the chamber, and demanded what was to be done.

"To wait," replied Athos.

Some minutes after, the superior of the convent sent to inform the Musketeers that the burial would take place at midday. As to the poisoner, they had heard no tidings of her whatever, only that she must have made her escape through the garden, on the sand of which her footsteps could be traced, and the door of which had been found shut. As to the key, it had disappeared.

At the hour appointed, Lord de Winter and the four friends repaired to the convent; the bells tolled, the chapel was open, the grating of the choir was closed. In the middle of the choir the body of the victim, clothed in her novitiate dress, was exposed. On each side of the choir and behind the gratings opening into the convent was assembled the whole community of the Carmelites, who listened to the divine service, and mingled their chant with the chant of the priests, without seeing the profane, or being seen by them.

At the door of the chapel d'Artagnan felt his courage fall anew, and returned to look for Athos; but Athos had disappeared.

Faithful to his mission of vengeance, Athos had requested to be conducted to the garden; and there upon the sand following the light steps of this woman, who left sharp tracks wherever she went, he advanced toward the gate which led into the wood, and causing it to be opened, he went out into the forest.

Then all his suspicions were confirmed; the road by which the carriage had disappeared encircled the forest. Athos followed the road for some time, his eyes fixed upon the ground; slight stains of blood, which came from the wound inflicted upon the man who accompanied the carriage as a courier, or from one of the horses, dotted the road. At the end of three-quarters of a league, within fifty paces of Festubert, a larger bloodstain appeared; the ground was trampled by horses. Between the forest and this accursed spot, a little behind the trampled ground, was the same track of small feet as in the garden; the carriage had stopped here. At this spot Milady had come out of the wood, and entered the carriage.

Satisfied with this discovery which confirmed all his suspicions, Athos returned to the hotel, and found Planchet impatiently waiting for him.

Everything was as Athos had foreseen.

Planchet had followed the road; like Athos, he had discovered the stains of blood; like Athos, he had noted the spot where the horses had halted. But he had gone farther than Athos--for at the village of Festubert, while drinking at an inn, he had learned without needing to ask a question that the evening before, at half-past eight, a wounded man who accompanied a lady traveling in a post-chaise had been obliged to stop, unable to go further. The accident was set down to the account of robbers, who had stopped the chaise in the wood. The man remained in the village; the woman had had a relay of horses, and continued her journey.

Planchet went in search of the postillion who had driven her, and found him. He had taken the lady as far as Fromelles; and from Fromelles she had set out for Armentieres. Planchet took the crossroad, and by seven o'clock in the morning he was at Armentieres.

There was but one tavern, the Post. Planchet went and presented himself as a lackey out of a place, who was in search of a situation. He had not chatted ten minutes with the people of the tavern before he learned that a woman had come there alone about eleven o'clock the night before, had engaged a chamber, had sent for the master of the hotel, and told him she desired to remain some time in the neighborhood.

Planchet had no need to learn more. He hastened to the rendezvous, found the lackeys at their posts, placed them as sentinels at all the outlets of the hotel, and came to find Athos, who had just received this information when his friends returned.

All their countenances were melancholy and gloomy, even the mild countenance of Aramis.

"What is to be done?" asked d'Artagnan.

"To wait!" replied Athos.

Each retired to his own apartment.

At eight o'clock in the evening Athos ordered the horses to be saddled, and Lord de Winter and his friends notified that they must prepare for the expedition.

In an instant all five were ready. Each examined his arms, and put them in order. Athos came down last, and found d'Artagnan already on horseback, and growing impatient.

"Patience!" cried Athos; "one of our party is still wanting."

The four horsemen looked round them with astonishment, for they sought vainly in their minds to know who this other person could be.

At this moment Planchet brought out Athos's house; the Musketeer leaped lightly into the saddle.

"Wait for me," cried he, "I will soon be back," and he set off at a gallop.

In a quarter of an hour he returned, accompanied by a tall man, masked, and wrapped in a large red cloak.

Lord de Winter and the three Musketeers looked at one another inquiringly. Neither could give the others any information, for all were ignorant who this man could be; nevertheless, they felt convinced that all was as it should be, as it was done by the order of Athos.

At nine o'clock, guided by Planchet, the little cavalcade set out, taking the route the carriage had taken.

It was a melancholy sight--that of these six men, traveling in silence, each plunged in his own thoughts, sad as despair, gloomy as chastisement.

65 Trial

It was a stormy and dark night; vast clouds covered the heavens, concealing the stars; the moon would not rise till midnight.

Occasionally, by the light of a flash of lightning which gleamed along the horizon, the road stretched itself before them, white and solitary; the flash extinct, all remained in darkness.

Every minute Athos was forced to restrain d'Artagnan, constantly in advance of the little troop, and to beg him to keep in the line, which in an instant he again departed from. He had but one thought--to go forward; and he went.

They passed in silence through the little village of Festubert, where the wounded servant was, and then skirted the wood of Richebourg. At Herlier, Planchet, who led the column, turned to the left.

Several times Lord de Winter, Porthos, or Aramis, tried to talk with the man in the red cloak; but to every interrogation which they put to him he bowed, without response. The travelers then comprehended that there must be some reason why the unknown preserved such a silence, and ceased to address themselves to him.

The storm increased, the flashes succeeded one another more rapidly, the thunder began to growl, and the wind, the precursor of a hurricane, whistled in the plumes and the hair of the horsemen.

The cavalcade trotted on more sharply.

A little before they came to Fromelles the storm burst. They spread their cloaks. There remained three leagues to travel, and they did it amid torrents of rain.

D'Artagnan took off his hat, and could not be persuaded to make use of his cloak. He found pleasure in feeling the water trickle over his burning brow and over his body, agitated by feverish shudders.

The moment the little troop passed Goskal and were approaching the Port, a man sheltered beneath a tree detached himself from the trunk with which he had been confounded in the darkness, and advanced into the middle of the road, putting his finger on his lips.

Athos recognized Grimaud.

"What's the manner?" cried Athos. "Has she left Armentieres?"

Grimaud made a sign in the affirmative. D'Artagnan ground his teeth.

"Silence, d'Artagnan!" said Athos. "I have charged myself with this affair. It is for me, then, to interrogate Grimaud."

"Where is she?" asked Athos.

Grimaud extended his hands in the direction of the Lys. "Far from here?" asked Athos.

Grimaud showed his master his forefinger bent.

"Alone?" asked Athos.

Grimaud made the sign yes.

"Gentlemen," said Athos, "she is alone within half a league of us, in the direction of the river."

"That's well," said d'Artagnan. "Lead us, Grimaud."

Grimaud took his course across the country, and acted as guide to the cavalcade.

At the end of five hundred paces, more or less, they came to a rivulet, which they forded.

By the aid of the lightning they perceived the village of Erquinheim.

"Is she there, Grimaud?" asked Athos.

Grimaud shook his head negatively.

"Silence, then!" cried Athos.

And the troop continued their route.

Another flash illuminated all around them. Grimaud extended his arm, and by the bluish splendor of the fiery serpent they distinguished a little isolated house on the banks of the river, within a hundred paces of a ferry.

One window was lighted.

"Here we are!" said Athos.

At this moment a man who had been crouching in a ditch jumped up and came towards them. It was Mousqueton. He pointed his finger to the lighted window.

"She is there," said he.

"And Bazin?" asked Athos.

"While I watched the window, he guarded the door."

"Good!" said Athos. "You are good and faithful servants."

Athos sprang from his horse, gave the bridle to Grimaud, and advanced toward the window, after having made a sign to the rest of the troop to go toward the door.

The little house was surrounded by a low, quickset hedge, two or three feet high. Athos sprang over the hedge and went up to the window, which was without shutters, but had the half-curtains closely drawn.

He mounted the skirting stone that his eyes might look over the curtain.

By the light of a lamp he saw a woman, wrapped in a dark mantle, seated upon a stool near a dying fire. Her elbows were placed upon a mean table, and she leaned her head upon her two hands, which were white as ivory.

He could not distinguish her countenance, but a sinister smile passed over the lips of Athos. He was not deceived; it was she whom he sought.

At this moment a horse neighed. Milady raised her head, saw close to the panes the pale face of Athos, and screamed.

Athos, perceiving that she knew him, pushed the window with his knee and hand. The window yielded. The squares were broken to shivers; and Athos, like the spectre of vengeance, leaped into the room.

Milady rushed to the door and opened it. More pale and menacing than Athos, d'Artagnan stood on the threshold.

Milady recoiled, uttering a cry. D'Artagnan, believing she might have means of flight and fearing she should escape, drew a pistol from his belt; but Athos raised his hand.

"Put back that weapon, d'Artagnan!" said he; "this woman must be tried, not assassinated. Wait an instant, my friend, and you shall be satisfied. Come in, gentlemen."

D'Artagnan obeyed; for Athos had the solemn voice and the powerful gesture of a judge sent by the Lord himself. Behind d'Artagnan entered Porthos, Aramis, Lord de Winter, and the man in the red cloak.

The four lackeys guarded the door and the window.

Milady had sunk into a chair, with her hands extended, as if to conjure this terrible apparition. Perceiving her brother-in-law, she uttered a terrible cry.

"What do you want?" screamed Milady.

"We want," said Athos, "Charlotte Backson, who first was called Comtesse de la Fere, and afterwards Milady de Winter, Baroness of Sheffield."

"That is I! that is I!" murmured Milady, in extreme terror; "what do you want?"

"We wish to judge you according to your crime," said Athos; "you shall be free to defend yourself. Justify yourself if you can. M. d'Artagnan, it is for you to accuse her first."

D'Artagnan advanced.

"Before God and before men," said he, "I accuse this woman of having poisoned Constance Bonacieux, who died yesterday evening."

He turned towards Porthos and Aramis.

"We bear witness to this," said the two Musketeers, with one voice.

D'Artagnan continued: "Before God and before men, I accuse this woman of having attempted to poison me, in wine which she sent me from Villeroy, with a forged letter, as if that wine came from my friends. God preserved me, but a man named Brisemont died in my place."

"We bear witness to this," said Porthos and Aramis, in the same manner as before.

"Before God and before men, I accuse this woman of having urged me to the murder of the Baron de Wardes; but as no one else can attest the truth of this accusation, I attest it myself. I have done." And d'Artagnan passed to the other side of the room with Porthos and Aramis.

"Your turn, my Lord," said Athos.

The baron came forward.

"Before God and before men," said he, "I accuse this woman of having caused the assassination of the Duke of Buckingham."

"The Duke of Buckingham assassinated!" cried all present, with one voice.

"Yes," said the baron, "assassinated. On receiving the warning letter you wrote to me, I had this woman arrested, and gave her in charge to a loyal servant. She corrupted this man; she placed the poniard in his hand; she made him kill the duke. And at this moment, perhaps, Felton is paying with his head for the crime of this fury!"

A shudder crept through the judges at the revelation of these unknown crimes.

"That is not all," resumed Lord de Winter. "My brother, who made you his heir, died in three hours of a strange disorder which left livid traces all over the body. My sister, how did your husband die?"

"Horror!" cried Porthos and Aramis.

"Assassin of Buckingham, assassin of Felton, assassin of my brother, I demand justice upon you, and I swear that if it be not granted to me, I will execute it myself."

And Lord de Winter ranged himself by the side of d'Artagnan, leaving the place free for another accuser.

Milady let her head sink between her two hands, and tried to recall her ideas, whirling in a mortal vertigo.

"My turn," said Athos, himself trembling as the lion trembles at the sight of the serpent--"my turn. I married that woman when she was a young girl; I married her in opposition to the wishes of all my family; I gave her my wealth, I gave her my name; and one day I discovered that this woman was branded--this woman was marked with a FLEUR-DE-LIS on her left shoulder."

"Oh," said Milady, raising herself, "I defy you to find any tribunal which pronounced that infamous sentence against me. I defy you to find him who executed it."

"Silence!" said a hollow voice. "It is for me to reply to that!" And the man in the red cloak came forward in his turn.

"What man is that? What man is that?" cried Milady, suffocated by terror, her hair loosening itself, and rising above her livid countenance as if alive.

All eyes were turned towards this man--for to all except Athos he was unknown.

Even Athos looked at him with as much stupefaction as the others, for he knew not how he could in any way find himself mixed up with the horrible drama then unfolded.

After approaching Milady with a slow and solemn step, so that the table alone separated them, the unknown took off his mask.

Milady for some time examined with increasing terror that pale face, framed with black hair and whiskers, the only expression of which was icy impassibility. Then she suddenly cried, "Oh, no, no!" rising and retreating to the very wall. "No, no! it is an infernal apparition! It is not he! Help, help!" screamed she, turning towards the wall, as if she would tear an opening with her hands.

"Who are you, then?" cried all the witnesses of this scene.

"Ask that woman," said the man in the red cloak, "for you may plainly see she knows me!"

"The executioner of Lille, the executioner of Lille!" cried Milady, a prey to insensate terror, and clinging with her hands to the wall to avoid falling.

Every one drew back, and the man in the red cloak remained standing alone in the middle of the room.

"Oh, grace, grace, pardon!" cried the wretch, falling on her knees.

The unknown waited for silence, and then resumed, "I told you well that she would know me. Yes, I am the executioner of Lille, and this is my history."

All eyes were fixed upon this man, whose words were listened to with anxious attention.

"That woman was once a young girl, as beautiful as she is today. She was a nun in the convent of the Benedictines of Templemar. A young priest, with a simple and trustful heart, performed the duties of the church of that convent. She undertook his seduction, and succeeded; she would have seduced a saint.

"Their vows were sacred and irrevocable. Their connection could not last long without ruining both. She prevailed upon him to leave the country; but to leave the country, to fly together, to reach another part of France, where they might live at ease because unknown, money was necessary. Neither had any. The priest stole the sacred vases, and sold them; but as they were preparing to escape together, they were both arrested.

"Eight days later she had seduced the son of the jailer, and escaped. The young priest was condemned to ten years of imprisonment, and to be branded. I was executioner of the city of Lille, as this woman has said. I was obliged to brand the guilty one; and he, gentlemen, was my brother!

"I then swore that this woman who had ruined him, who was more than his accomplice, since she had urged him to the crime, should at least share his punishment. I suspected where she was concealed. I followed her, I caught her, I bound her; and I imprinted the same disgraceful mark upon her that I had imprinted upon my poor brother.

"The day after my return to Lille, my brother in his turn succeeded in making his escape; I was accused of complicity, and was condemned to remain in his place till he should be again a prisoner. My poor brother was ignorant of this sentence. He rejoined this woman; they fled together into Berry, and there he obtained a little curacy. This woman passed for his sister.

"The Lord of the estate on which the chapel of the curacy was situated saw this pretend sister, and became enamoured of her--amorous to such a degree that he proposed to marry her. Then she quitted him she had ruined for him she was destined to ruin, and became the Comtesse de la Fere--"

All eyes were turned towards Athos, whose real name that was, and who made a sign with his head that all was true which the executioner had said.

"Then," resumed he, "mad, desperate, determined to get rid of an existence from which she had stolen everything, honor and happiness, my poor brother returned to Lille, and learning the sentence which had condemned me in his place, surrendered himself, and hanged himself that same night from the iron bar of the loophole of his prison.

"To do justice to them who had condemned me, they kept their word. As soon as the identity of my brother was proved, I was set at liberty.

"That is the crime of which I accuse her; that is the cause for which she was branded."

"Monsieur d'Artagnan," said Athos, "what is the penalty you demand against this woman?"

"The punishment of death," replied d'Artagnan.

"My Lord de Winter," continued Athos, "what is the penalty you demand against this woman?"

"The punishment of death," replied Lord de Winter.

"Messieurs Porthos and Aramis," repeated Athos, "you who are her judges, what is the sentence you pronounce upon this woman?"

"The punishment of death," replied the Musketeers, in a hollow voice.

Milady uttered a frightful shriek, and dragged herself along several paces upon her knees toward her judges.

Athos stretched out his hand toward her.

"Charlotte Backson, Comtesse de la Fere, Milady de Winter," said he, "your crimes have wearied men on earth and God in heaven. If you know a prayer, say it--for you are condemned, and you shall die."

At these words, which left no hope, Milady raised herself in all her pride, and wished to speak; but her strength failed her. She felt that a powerful and implacable hand seized her by the hair, and dragged her away as irrevocably as fatality drags humanity. She did not, therefore, even attempt the least resistance, and went out of the cottage.

Lord de Winter, d'Artagnan, Athos, Porthos, and Aramis, went out close behind her. The lackeys followed their masters, and the chamber was left solitary, with its broken window, its open door, and its smoky lamp burning sadly on the table.

66 Execution

It was near midnight; the moon, lessened by its decline, and reddened by the last traces of the storm, arose behind the little town of Armentieres, which showed against its pale light the dark outline of its houses, and the skeleton of its high belfry. In front of them the Lys rolled its waters like a river of molten tin; while on the other side was a black mass of trees, profiled on a stormy sky, invaded by large coppery clouds which created a sort of twilight amid the night. On the left was an old abandoned mill, with its motionless wings, from the ruins of which an owl threw out its shrill, periodical, and monotonous cry. On the right and on the left of the road, which the dismal procession pursued, appeared a few low, stunted trees, which looked like deformed dwarfs crouching down to watch men traveling at this sinister hour.

From time to time a broad sheet of lightning opened the horizon in its whole width, darted like a serpent over the black mass of trees, and like a terrible scimitar divided the heavens and the waters into two parts. Not a breath of wind now disturbed the heavy atmosphere. A deathlike silence oppressed all nature. The soil was humid and glittering with the rain which had recently fallen, and the refreshed herbs sent forth their perfume with additional energy.

Two lackeys dragged Milady, whom each held by one arm. The executioner walked behind them, and Lord de Winter, d'Artagnan, Porthos, and Aramis walked behind the executioner. Planchet and Bazin came last.

The two lackeys conducted Milady to the bank of the river. Her mouth was mute; but her eyes spoke with their inexpressible eloquence, supplicating by turns each of those on whom she looked.

Being a few paces in advance she whispered to the lackeys, "A thousand pistoles to each of you, if you will assist my escape; but if you deliver me up to your masters, I have near at hand avengers who will make you pay dearly for my death."

Grimaud hesitated. Mousqueton trembled in all his members.

Athos, who heard Milady's voice, came sharply up. Lord de Winter did the same.

"Change these lackeys," said he; "she has spoken to them. They are no longer sure."

Planchet and Bazin were called, and took the places of Grimaud and Mousqueton.

On the bank of the river the executioner approached Milady, and bound her hands and feet.

Then she broke the silence to cry out, "You are cowards, miserable assassins--ten men combined to murder one woman. Beware! If I am not saved I shall be avenged."

"You are not a woman," said Athos, coldly and sternly. "You do not belong to the human species; you are a demon escaped from hell, whither we send you back again."

"Ah, you virtuous men!" said Milady; "please to remember that he who shall touch a hair of my head is himself an assassin."

"The executioner may kill, without being on that account an assassin," said the man in the red cloak, rapping upon his immense sword. "This is the last judge; that is all. NACHRICHTER, as say our neighbors, the Germans."

And as he bound her while saying these words, Milady uttered two or three savage cries, which produced a strange and melancholy effect in flying away into the night, and losing themselves in the depths of the woods.

"If I am guilty, if I have committed the crimes you accuse me of," shrieked Milady, "take me before a tribunal. You are not judges! You cannot condemn me!"

"I offered you Tyburn," said Lord de Winter. "Why did you not accept it?"

"Because I am not willing to die!" cried Milady, struggling. "Because I am too young to die!"

"The woman you poisoned at Bethune was still younger than you, madame, and yet she is dead," said d'Artagnan.

"I will enter a cloister; I will become a nun," said Milady.

"You were in a cloister," said the executioner, "and you left it to ruin my brother."

Milady uttered a cry of terror and sank upon her knees. The executioner took her up in his arms and was carrying her toward the boat.

"Oh, my God!" cried she, "my God! are you going to drown me?"

These cries had something so heartrending in them that M. d'Artagnan, who had been at first the most eager in pursuit of Milady, sat down on the stump of a tree and hung his head, covering his ears with the palms of his hands; and yet, notwithstanding, he could still hear her cry and threaten.

D'Artagnan was the youngest of all these men. His heart failed him.

"Oh, I cannot behold this frightful spectacle!" said he. "I cannot consent that this woman should die thus!"

Milady heard these few words and caught at a shadow of hope.

"d'Artagnan, d'Artagnan!" cried she; "remember that I loved you!"

The young man rose and took a step toward her.

But Athos rose likewise, drew his sword, and placed himself in the way.

"If you take one step farther, d'Artagnan," said he, "we shall cross swords together."

D'Artagnan sank on his knees and prayed.

"Come," continued Athos, "executioner, do your duty."

"Willingly, monseigneur," said the executioner; "for as I am a good Catholic, I firmly believe I am acting justly in performing my functions on this woman."

"That's well."

Athos made a step toward Milady.

"I pardon you," said he, "the ill you have done me. I pardon you for my blasted future, my lost honor, my defiled love, and my salvation forever compromised by the despair into which you have cast me. Die in peace!"

Lord de Winter advanced in his turn.

"I pardon you," said he, "for the poisoning of my brother, and the assassination of his Grace, Lord Buckingham. I pardon you for the death of poor Felton; I pardon you for the attempts upon my own person. Die in peace!"

"And I," said M. d'Artagnan. "Pardon me, madame, for having by a trick unworthy of a gentleman provoked your anger; and I, in exchange, pardon you the murder of my poor love and your cruel vengeance against me. I pardon you, and I weep for you. Die in peace!"

"I am lost!" murmured Milady in English. "I must die!"

Then she arose of herself, and cast around her one of those piercing looks which seemed to dart from an eye of flame.

She saw nothing; she listened, and she heard nothing.

"Where am I to die?" said she.

"On the other bank," replied the executioner.

Then he placed her in the boat, and as he was going to set foot in it himself, Athos handed him a sum of silver.

"Here," said he, "is the price of the execution, that it may be plain we act as judges."

"That is correct," said the executioner; "and now in her turn, let this woman see that I am not fulfilling my trade, but my debt."

And he threw the money into the river.

The boat moved off toward the left-hand shore of the Lys, bearing the guilty woman and the executioner; all the others remained on the right-hand bank, where they fell on their knees.

The boat glided along the ferry rope under the shadow of a pale cloud which hung over the water at that moment.

The troop of friends saw it gain the opposite bank; the figures were defined like black shadows on the red-tinted horizon.

Milady, during the passage had contrived to untie the cord which fastened her feet. On coming near the bank, she jumped lightly on shore and took to flight. But the soil was moist; on reaching the top of the bank, she slipped and fell upon her knees.

She was struck, no doubt, with a superstitious idea; she conceived that heaven denied its aid, and she remained in the attitude in which she had fallen, her head drooping and her hands clasped.

Then they saw from the other bank the executioner raise both his arms slowly; a moonbeam fell upon the blade of the large sword. The two arms fell with a sudden force; they heard the hissing of the scimitar and the cry of the victim, then a truncated mass sank beneath the blow.

The executioner then took off his red cloak, spread it upon the ground, laid the body in it, threw in the head, tied all up by the four corners, lifted it on his back, and entered the boat again.

In the middle of the stream he stopped the boat, and suspending his burden over the water cried in a loud voice, "Let the justice of God be done!" and he let the corpse drop into the depths of the waters, which closed over it.

Three days afterward the four Musketeers were in Paris; they had not exceeded their leave of absence, and that same evening they went to pay their customary visit to M. de Treville.

"Well, gentlemen," said the brave captain, "I hope you have been well amused during your excursion."

"Prodigiously," replied Athos in the name of himself and his comrades.

67 Conclusion

On the sixth of the following month the king, in compliance with the promise he had made the cardinal to return to La Rochelle, left his capital still in amazement at the news which began to spread itself of Buckingham's assassination.

Although warned that the man she had loved so much was in great danger, the queen, when his death was announced to her, would not believe the fact, and even imprudently exclaimed, "it is false; he has just written to me!"

But the next day she was obliged to believe this fatal intelligence; Laporte, detained in England, as everyone else had been, by the orders of Charles I, arrived, and was the bearer of the duke's dying gift to the queen.

The joy of the king was lively. He did not even give himself the trouble to dissemble, and displayed it with affectation before the queen. Louis XIII, like every weak mind, was wanting in generosity.

But the king soon again became dull and indisposed; his brow was not one of those that long remain clear. He felt that in returning to camp he should re-enter slavery; nevertheless, he did return.

The cardinal was for him the fascinating serpent, and himself the bird which flies from branch to branch without power to escape.

The return to La Rochelle, therefore, was profoundly dull. Our four friends, in particular, astonished their comrades; they traveled together, side by side, with sad eyes and heads lowered. Athos alone from time to time raised his expansive brow; a flash kindled in his eyes, and a bitter smile passed over his lips, then, like his comrades, he sank again into reverie.

As soon as the escort arrived in a city, when they had conducted the king to his quarters the four friends either retired to their own or to some secluded cabaret, where they neither drank nor played; they only conversed in a low voice, looking around attentively to see that no one overheard them.

One day, when the king had halted to fly the magpie, and the four friends, according to their custom, instead of following the sport had stopped at a cabaret on the high road, a man coming from la Rochelle on horseback pulled up at the door to drink a glass of wine, and darted a searching glance into the room where the four Musketeers were sitting.

"Holloa, Monsieur d'Artagnan!" said he, "is not that you whom I see yonder?"

D'Artagnan raised his head and uttered a cry of joy. It was the man he called his phantom; it was his stranger of Meung, of the Rue des Fossoyeurs and of Arras.

D'Artagnan drew his sword, and sprang toward the door.

But this time, instead of avoiding him the stranger jumped from his horse, and advanced to meet d'Artagnan.

"Ah, monsieur!" said the young man, "I meet you, then, at last! This time you shall not escape me!"

"Neither is it my intention, monsieur, for this time I was seeking you; in the name of the king, I arrest you."

"How! what do you say?" cried d'Artagnan.

"I say that you must surrender your sword to me, monsieur, and that without resistance. This concerns your head, I warn you."

"Who are you, then?" demanded d'Artagnan, lowering the point of his sword, but without yet surrendering it.

"I am the Chevalier de Rochefort," answered the other, "the equerry of Monsieur le Cardinal Richelieu, and I have orders to conduct you to his Eminence."

"We are returning to his Eminence, monsieur the Chevalier," said Athos, advancing; "and you will please to accept the word of Monsieur d'Artagnan that he will go straight to La Rochelle."

"I must place him in the hands of guards who will take him into camp."

"We will be his guards, monsieur, upon our word as gentlemen; but likewise, upon our word as gentlemen," added Athos, knitting his brow, "Monsieur d'Artagnan shall not leave us."

The Chevalier de Rochefort cast a glance backward, and saw that Porthos and Aramis had placed themselves between him and the gate; he understood that he was completely at the mercy of these four men.

"Gentlemen," said he, "if Monsieur d'Artagnan will surrender his sword to me and join his word to yours, I shall be satisfied with your promise to convey Monsieur d'Artagnan to the quarters of Monseigneur the Cardinal."

"You have my word, monsieur, and here is my sword."

"This suits me the better," said Rochefort, "as I wish to continue my journey."

"If it is for the purpose of rejoining Milady," said Athos, coolly, "it is useless; you will not find her."

"What has become of her, then?" asked Rochefort, eagerly.

"Return to camp and you shall know."

Rochefort remained for a moment in thought; then, as they were only a day's journey from Surgeres, whither the cardinal was to come to meet the king, he resolved to follow the advice of Athos and go with them. Besides, this return offered him the advantage of watching his prisoner.

They resumed their route.

On the morrow, at three o'clock in the afternoon, they arrived at Surgeres. The cardinal there awaited Louis XIII. The minister and the king exchanged numerous caresses, felicitating each other upon the fortunate chance which had freed France from the inveterate enemy who set all Europe against her. After which, the cardinal, who had been informed that d'Artagnan was arrested and who was anxious to see him, took leave of the king, inviting him to come the next day to view the work already done upon the dyke.

On returning in the evening to his quarters at the bridge of La Pierre, the cardinal found, standing before the house he occupied, d'Artagnan, without his sword, and the three Musketeers armed.

This time, as he was well attended, he looked at them sternly, and made a sign with his eye and hand for d'Artagnan to follow him.

D'Artagnan obeyed.

"We shall wait for you, d'Artagnan," said Athos, loud enough for the cardinal to hear him.

His Eminence bent his brow, stopped for an instant, and then kept on his way without uttering a single word.

D'Artagnan entered after the cardinal, and behind d'Artagnan the door was guarded.

His Eminence entered the chamber which served him as a study, and made a sign to Rochefort to bring in the young Musketeer.

Rochefort obeyed and retired.

D'Artagnan remained alone in front of the cardinal; this was his second interview with Richelieu, and he afterward confessed that he felt well assured it would be his last.

Richelieu remained standing, leaning against the mantelpiece; a table was between him and d'Artagnan.

"Monsieur," said the cardinal, "you have been arrested by my orders."

"So they tell me, monseigneur."

"Do you know why?"

"No, monseigneur, for the only thing for which I could be arrested is still unknown to your Eminence."

Richelieu looked steadfastly at the young man.

"Holloa!" said he, "what does that mean?"

"If Monseigneur will have the goodness to tell me, in the first place, what crimes are imputed to me, I will then tell him the deeds I have really done."

"Crimes are imputed to you which had brought down far loftier heads than yours, monsieur," said the cardinal.

"What, monseigneur?" said d'Artagnan, with a calmness which astonished the cardinal himself.

"You are charged with having corresponded with the enemies of the kingdom; you are charged with having surprised state secrets; you are charged with having tried to thwart the plans of your general."

"And who charges me with this, monseigneur?" said d'Artagnan, who had no doubt the accusation came from Milady, "a woman branded by the justice of the country; a woman who has espoused one man in France and another in England; a woman who poisoned her second husband and who attempted both to poison and assassinate me!"

"What do you say, monsieur?" cried the cardinal, astonished; "and of what woman are you speaking thus?"

"Of Milady de Winter," replied d'Artagnan, "yes, of Milady de Winter, of whose crimes your Eminence is doubtless ignorant, since you have honored her with your confidence."

"Monsieur," said the cardinal, "if Milady de Winter has committed the crimes you lay to her charge, she shall be punished."

"She has been punished, monseigneur."

"And who has punished her?"

"We."

"She is in prison?"

"She is dead."

"Dead!" repeated the cardinal, who could not believe what he heard, "dead! Did you not say she was dead?"

"Three times she attempted to kill me, and I pardoned her; but she murdered the woman I loved. Then my friends and I took her, tried her, and condemned her."

D'Artagnan then related the poisoning of Mme. Bonacieux in the convent of the Carmelites at Bethune, the trial in the isolated house, and the execution on the banks of the Lys.

A shudder crept through the body of the cardinal, who did not shudder readily.

But all at once, as if undergoing the influence of an unspoken thought, the countenance of the cardinal, till then gloomy, cleared up by degrees, and recovered perfect serenity.

"So," said the cardinal, in a tone that contrasted strongly with the severity of his words, "you have constituted yourselves judges, without remembering that they who punish without license to punish are assassins?"

"Monseigneur, I swear to you that I never for an instant had the intention of defending my head against you. I willingly submit to any punishment your Eminence may please to inflict upon me. I do not hold life dear enough to be afraid of death."

"Yes, I know you are a man of a stout heart, monsieur," said the cardinal, with a voice almost affectionate; "I can therefore tell you beforehand you shall be tried, and even condemned."

"Another might reply to your Eminence that he had his pardon in his pocket. I content myself with saying: Command, monseigneur; I am ready."

"Your pardon?" said Richelieu, surprised.

"Yes, monseigneur," said d'Artagnan.

"And signed by whom--by the king?" And the cardinal pronounced these words with a singular expression of contempt.

"No, by your Eminence."

"By me? You are insane, monsieur."

"Monseigneur will doubtless recognize his own handwriting."

And d'Artagnan presented to the cardinal the precious piece of paper which Athos had forced from Milady, and which he had given to d'Artagnan to serve him as a safeguard.

His Eminence took the paper, and read in a slow voice, dwelling upon every syllable:

"Dec. 3, 1627

"It is by my order and for the good of the state that the bearer of this has done what he has done.

"RICHELIEU" The cardinal, after having read these two lines, sank into a profound reverie; but he did not return the paper to d'Artagnan.

"He is meditating by what sort of punishment he shall cause me to die," said the Gascon to himself. "Well, my faith! he shall see how a gentleman can die."

The young Musketeer was in excellent disposition to die heroically.

Richelieu still continued thinking, rolling and unrolling the paper in his hands.

At length he raised his head, fixed his eagle look upon that loyal, open, and intelligent countenance, read upon that face, furrowed with tears, all the sufferings its possessor had endured in the course of a month, and reflected for the third or fourth time how much there was in that youth of twenty-one years before him, and what resources his activity, his courage, and his shrewdness might offer to a good master. On the other side, the crimes, the power, and the infernal genius of Milady had more than once terrified him. He felt something like a secret joy at being forever relieved of this dangerous accomplice.

Richelieu slowly tore the paper which d'Artagnan had generously relinquished.

"I am lost!" said d'Artagnan to himself. And he bowed profoundly before the cardinal, like a man who says, "Lord, Thy will be done!"

The cardinal approached the table, and without sitting down, wrote a few lines upon a parchment of which two-thirds were already filled, and affixed his seal.

"That is my condemnation," thought d'Artagnan; "he will spare me the ENNUI of the Bastille, or the tediousness of a trial. That's very kind of him."

"Here, monsieur," said the cardinal to the young man. "I have taken from you one CARTE BLANCHE to give you another. The name is wanting in this commission; you can write it yourself."

D'Artagnan took the paper hesitatingly and cast his eyes over it; it was a lieutenant's commission in the Musketeers.

D'Artagnan fell at the feet of the cardinal.

"Monseigneur," said he, "my life is yours; henceforth dispose of it. But this favor which you bestow upon me I do not merit. I have three friends who are more meritorious and more worthy--"

"You are a brave youth, d'Artagnan," interrupted the cardinal, tapping him familiarly on the shoulder, charmed at having vanquished this rebellious nature. "Do with this commission what you will; only remember, though the name be blank, it is to you I give it."

"I shall never forget it," replied d'Artagnan. "Your Eminence may be certain of that."

The cardinal turned and said in a loud voice, "Rochefort!" The chevalier, who no doubt was near the door, entered immediately.

"Rochefort," said the cardinal, "you see Monsieur d'Artagnan. I receive him among the number of my friends. Greet each other, then; and be wise if you wish to preserve your heads."

Rochefort and d'Artagnan coolly greeted each other with their lips; but the cardinal was there, observing them with his vigilant eye.

They left the chamber at the same time.

"We shall meet again, shall we not, monsieur?"

"When you please," said d'Artagnan.

"An opportunity will come," replied Rochefort.

"Hey?" said the cardinal, opening the door.

The two men smiled at each other, shook hands, and saluted his Eminence.

"We were beginning to grow impatient," said Athos.

"Here I am, my friends," replied d'Artagnan; "not only free, but in favor."

"Tell us about it."

"This evening; but for the moment, let us separate."

Accordingly, that same evening d'Artagnan repaired to the quarters of Athos, whom he found in a fair way to empty a bottle of Spanish wine--an occupation which he religiously accomplished every night.

D'Artagnan related what had taken place between the cardinal and himself, and drawing the commission from his pocket, said, "Here, my dear Athos, this naturally belongs to you."

Athos smiled with one of his sweet and expressive smiles.

"Friend," said he, "for Athos this is too much; for the Comte de la Fere it is too little. Keep the commission; it is yours. Alas! you have purchased it dearly enough."

D'Artagnan left Athos's chamber and went to that of Porthos. He found him clothed in a magnificent dress covered with splendid embroidery, admiring himself before a glass.

"Ah, ah! is that you, dear friend?" exclaimed Porthos. "How do you think these garments fit me?"

"Wonderfully," said d'Artagnan; "but I come to offer you a dress which will become you still better."

"What?" asked Porthos.

"That of a lieutenant of Musketeers."

D'Artagnan related to Porthos the substance of his interview with the cardinal, and said, taking the commission from his pocket, "Here, my friend, write your name upon it and become my chief."

Porthos cast his eyes over the commission and returned it to d'Artagnan, to the great astonishment of the young man.

"Yes," said he, "yes, that would flatter me very much; but I should not have time enough to enjoy the distinction. During our expedition to Bethune the husband of my duchess died; so, my dear, the coffer of the defunct holding out its arms to me, I shall marry the widow. Look here! I was trying on my wedding suit. Keep the lieutenancy, my dear, keep it."

The young man then entered the apartment of Aramis. He found him kneeling before a PRIEDIEU with his head leaning on an open prayer book.

He described to him his interview with the cardinal, and said, for the third time drawing his commission from his pocket, "You, our friend, our intelligence, our invisible protector, accept this commission. You have merited it more than any of us by your wisdom and your counsels, always followed by such happy results."

"Alas, dear friend!" said Aramis, "our late adventures have disgusted me with military life. This time my determination is irrevocably taken. After the siege I shall enter the house of the Lazarists. Keep the commission, d'Artagnan; the profession of arms suits you. You will be a brave and adventurous captain."

D'Artagnan, his eye moist with gratitude though beaming with joy, went back to Athos, whom he found still at table contemplating the charms of his last glass of Malaga by the light of his lamp.

"Well," said he, "they likewise have refused me."

"That, dear friend, is because nobody is more worthy than yourself."

He took a quill, wrote the name of d'Artagnan in the commission, and returned it to him.

"I shall then have no more friends," said the young man. "Alas! nothing but bitter recollections."

And he let his head sink upon his hands, while two large tears rolled down his cheeks.

"You are young," replied Athos; "and your bitter recollections have time to change themselves into sweet remembrances."

Epilogue

La Rochelle, deprived of the assistance of the English fleet and of the diversion promised by Buckingham, surrendered after a siege of a year. On the twenty-eighth of October, 1628, the capitulation was signed.

The king made his entrance into Paris on the twenty-third of December of the same year. He was received in triumph, as if he came from conquering an enemy and not Frenchmen. He entered by the Faubourg St. Jacques, under verdant arches.

D'Artagnan took possession of his command. Porthos left the service, and in the course of the following year married Mme. Coquenard; the coffer so much coveted contained eight hundred thousand livres.

Mousqueton had a magnificent livery, and enjoyed the satisfaction of which he had been ambitious all his life--that of standing behind a gilded carriage.

Aramis, after a journey into Lorraine, disappeared all at once, and ceased to write to his friends; they learned at a later period through Mme. de Chevreuse, who told it to two or three of her intimates, that, yielding to his vocation, he had retired into a convent--only into which, nobody knew.

Bazin became a lay brother.

Athos remained a Musketeer under the command of d'Artagnan till the year 1633, at which period, after a journey he made to Touraine, he also quit the service, under the pretext of having inherited a small property in Roussillon.

Grimaud followed Athos.

D'Artagnan fought three times with Rochefort, and wounded him three times.

"I shall probably kill you the fourth," said he to him, holding out his hand to assist him to rise.

"It is much better both for you and for me to stop where we are," answered the wounded man. "CORBLEU--I am more your friend than you think--for after our very first encounter, I could by saying a word to the cardinal have had your throat cut!"

They this time embraced heartily, and without retaining any malice.

Planchet obtained from Rochefort the rank of sergeant in the Piedmont regiment.

M Bonacieux lived on very quietly, wholly ignorant of what had become of his wife, and caring very little about it. One day he had the imprudence to recall himself to the memory of the cardinal. The cardinal had him informed that he would provide for him so that he should never want for anything in future. In fact, M. Bonacieux, having left his house at seven o'clock in the evening to go to the Louvre, never appeared again in the Rue des Fossoyeurs; the opinion of those who seemed to be best informed was that he was fed and lodged in some royal castle, at the expense of his generous Eminence.

TWENTY YEARS AFTER

1. The Shade of Cardinal Richelieu.

In a splendid chamber of the Palais Royal, formerly styled the Palais Cardinal, a man was sitting in deep reverie, his head supported on his hands, leaning over a gilt and inlaid table which was covered with letters and papers. Behind this figure glowed a vast fireplace alive with leaping flames; great logs of oak blazed and crackled on the polished brass andirons whose flicker shone upon the superb habiliments of the lonely tenant of the room, which was illumined grandly by twin candelabra rich with wax-lights.

Any one who happened at that moment to contemplate that red simar--the gorgeous robe of office--and the rich lace, or who gazed on that pale brow, bent in anxious meditation, might, in the solitude of that apartment, combined with the silence of the ante-chambers and the measured paces of the guards upon the landing-place, have fancied that the shade of Cardinal Richelieu lingered still in his accustomed haunt.

It was, alas! the ghost of former greatness. France enfeebled, the authority of her sovereign contemned, her nobles returning to their former turbulence and insolence, her enemies within her frontiers--all proved the great Richelieu no longer in existence.

In truth, that the red simar which occupied the wonted place was his no longer, was still more strikingly obvious from the isolation which seemed, as we have observed, more appropriate to a phantom than a living creature--from the corridors deserted by courtiers, and courts crowded with guards--from that spirit of bitter ridicule, which, arising from the streets below, penetrated through the very casements of the room, which resounded with the murmurs of a whole city leagued against the minister; as well as from the distant and incessant sounds of guns firing--let off, happily, without other end or aim, except to show to the guards, the Swiss troops and the military who surrounded the Palais Royal, that the people were possessed of arms.

The shade of Richelieu was Mazarin. Now Mazarin was alone and defenceless, as he well knew.

"Foreigner!" he ejaculated, "Italian! that is their mean yet mighty byword of reproach--the watchword with which they assassinated, hanged, and made away with Concini; and if I gave them their way they would assassinate, hang, and make away with me in the same manner, although they have nothing to complain of except a tax or two now and then. Idiots! ignorant of their real enemies, they do not perceive that it is not the Italian who speaks French badly, but those who can say fine things to them in the purest Parisian accent, who are their real foes.

"Yes, yes," Mazarin continued, whilst his wonted smile, full of subtlety, lent a strange expression to his pale lips; "yes, these noises prove to me, indeed, that the destiny of favorites is precarious; but ye shall know I am no ordinary favorite. No! The Earl of Essex, 'tis true, wore a splendid ring, set with diamonds, given him by his royal mistress, whilst I--I have nothing but a simple circlet of gold, with a cipher on it and a date; but that ring has been blessed in the chapel of the Palais Royal[1], so they will never ruin me, as they long to do, and whilst they shout, 'Down with Mazarin!' I, unknown, and unperceived by them, incite them to cry out, 'Long live the Duke de Beaufort' one day; another, 'Long live the Prince de Conde;' and again, 'Long live the parliament!'" And at this word the smile on the cardinal's lips assumed an expression of hatred, of which his mild countenance seemed incapable. "The parliament! We shall soon see how to dispose," he continued, "of the parliament! Both Orleans and Montargis are ours. It will be a work of time, but those who have begun by crying out: Down with Mazarin! will finish by shout-

[1] It is said that Mazarin, who, though a cardinal, had not taken such vows as to prevent it, was secretly married to Anne of Austria.--La Porte's Memoirs.

ing out, Down with all the people I have mentioned, each in his turn.

"Richelieu, whom they hated during his lifetime and whom they now praise after his death, was even less popular than I am. Often he was driven away, oftener still had he a dread of being sent away. The queen will never banish me, and even were I obliged to yield to the populace she would yield with me; if I fly, she will fly; and then we shall see how the rebels will get on without either king or queen.

"Oh, were I not a foreigner! were I but a Frenchman! were I but of gentle birth!"

The position of the cardinal was indeed critical, and recent events had added to his difficulties. Discontent had long pervaded the lower ranks of society in France. Crushed and impoverished by taxation--imposed by Mazarin, whose avarice impelled him to grind them down to the very dust--the people, as the Advocate-General Talon described it, had nothing left to them except their souls; and as those could not be sold by auction, they began to murmur. Patience had in vain been recommended to them by reports of brilliant victories gained by France; laurels, however, were not meat and drink, and the people had for some time been in a state of discontent.

Had this been all, it might not, perhaps, have greatly signified; for when the lower classes alone complained, the court of France, separated as it was from the poor by the intervening classes of the gentry and the bourgeoisie, seldom listened to their voice; but unluckily, Mazarin had had the imprudence to attack the magistrates and had sold no less than twelve appointments in the Court of Requests, at a high price; and as the officers of that court paid very dearly for their places, and as the addition of twelve new colleagues would necessarily lower the value of each place, the old functionaries formed a union amongst themselves, and, enraged, swore on the Bible not to allow of this addition to their number, but to resist all the persecutions which might ensue; and should any one of them chance to forfeit his post by this resistance, to combine to indemnify him for his loss.

Now the following occurrences had taken place between the two contending parties.

On the seventh of January between seven and eight hundred tradesmen had assembled in Paris to discuss a new tax which was to be levied on house property. They deputed ten of their number to wait upon the Duke of Orleans, who, according to his custom, affected popularity. The duke received them and they informed him that they were resolved not to pay this tax, even if they were obliged to defend themselves against its collectors by force of arms. They were listened to with great politeness by the duke, who held out hopes of easier measures, promised to speak in their behalf to the queen, and dismissed them with the ordinary expression of royalty, "We will see what we can do."

Two days afterward these same magistrates appeared before the cardinal and their spokesman addressed Mazarin with so much fearlessness and determination that the minister was astounded and sent the deputation away with the same answer as it had received from the Duke of Orleans--that he would see what could be done; and in accordance with that intention a council of state was assembled and the superintendent of finance was summoned.

This man, named Emery, was the object of popular detestation, in the first place because he was superintendent of finance, and every superintendent of finance deserved to be hated; in the second place, because he rather deserved the odium which he had incurred.

He was the son of a banker at Lyons named Particelli, who, after becoming a bankrupt, chose to change his name to Emery; and Cardinal Richelieu having discovered in him great financial aptitude, had introduced him with a strong recommendation to Louis XIII. under his assumed name, in order that he might be appointed to the post he subsequently held.

"You surprise me!" exclaimed the monarch. "I am rejoiced to hear you speak of Monsieur d'Emery as calculated for a post which requires a man of probity. I was really afraid that you were going to force that villain Particelli upon me."

"Sire," replied Richelieu, "rest assured that Particelli, the man to whom your majesty refers, has been hanged."

"Ah; so much the better!" exclaimed the king. "It is not for nothing that I am styled Louis the Just." and he signed Emery's appointment.

This was the same Emery who became eventually superintendent of finance.

He was sent for by the ministers and he came before them pale and trembling, declaring that his son had very nearly been assassinated the day before, near the palace. The mob had insulted him on account of the ostentatious luxury of his wife, whose house was hung with red velvet edged with gold fringe. This lady was the daughter of Nicholas de Camus, who arrived in Paris with twenty francs in his pocket, became secretary of state, and accumulated wealth enough to divide nine millions of francs among his children and to keep an income of forty thousand for himself.

The fact was that Emery's son had run a great chance of being suffocated, one of the rioters having proposed to squeeze him until he gave up all the gold he had swallowed. Nothing, therefore, was settled that day, as Emery's head was not steady enough for business after such an occurrence.

On the next day Mathieu Mole, the chief president, whose courage at this crisis, says the Cardinal de Retz, was equal to that of the Duc de Beaufort and the Prince de Conde--in other words, of the two men who were considered the bravest in France--had been attacked in his turn. The people threatened to hold him responsible for the evils that hung over them. But the chief president had replied with his habitual coolness, without betraying either disturbance or surprise, that should the agitators refuse obedience to the king's wishes he would have gallows erected in the public squares and proceed at once to hang the most active among them. To which the others had responded that they would be glad to see the gallows erected; they would serve for the hanging of those detestable judges who purchased favor at court at the price of the people's misery.

Nor was this all. On the eleventh the queen in going to mass at Notre Dame, as she always did on Saturdays, was followed by more than two hundred women demanding justice. These poor creatures had no bad intentions. They wished only to be allowed to fall on their knees before their sovereign, and that they might move her to compassion; but they were prevented by the royal guard and the queen proceeded on her way, haughtily disdainful of their entreaties.

At length parliament was convoked; the authority of the king was to be maintained.

One day--it was the morning of the day my story begins--the king, Louis XIV., then ten years of age, went in state, under pretext of returning thanks for his recovery from the small-pox, to Notre Dame. He took the opportunity of calling out his guard, the Swiss troops and the musketeers, and he had planted them round the Palais Royal, on the quays, and on the Pont Neuf. After mass the young monarch drove to the Parliament House, where, upon the throne, he hastily confirmed not only such edicts as he had already passed, but issued new ones, each one, according to Cardinal de Retz, more ruinous than the others--a proceeding which drew forth a strong remonstrance from the chief president, Mole--whilst President Blancmesnil and Councillor Broussel raised their voices in indignation against fresh taxes.

The king returned amidst the silence of a vast multitude to the Palais Royal. All minds were uneasy, most were foreboding, many of the people used threatening language.

At first, indeed, they were doubtful whether the king's visit to the parliament had been in order to lighten or increase their burdens; but scarcely was it known that the taxes were to be still further increased, when cries of "Down with Mazarin!" "Long live Broussel!" "Long live Blancmesnil!" resounded through the city. For the people had learned that Broussel and Blancmesnil had made speeches in their behalf, and, although the eloquence of these deputies had been without avail, it had none the less won for them the people's good-will. All attempts to disperse the groups collected in the streets, or silence their exclamations, were in vain. Orders had just been given to the royal guards and the Swiss guards, not only to stand firm, but to send out patrols to the streets of Saint Denis and Saint Martin, where the people thronged and where they were the most vociferous, when the mayor of Paris was announced at the Palais Royal.

He was shown in directly; he came to say that if these offensive precautions were not discontinued, in two hours Paris would be under arms.

Deliberations were being held when a lieutenant in the guards, named Comminges, made his appearance, with his clothes all torn, his face streaming with blood. The queen on seeing him uttered a cry of surprise and asked him what was going on.

As the mayor had foreseen, the sight of the guards had exasperated the mob. The tocsin was sounded. Comminges had arrested one of the ringleaders and had ordered him to be hanged near the cross of Du Trahoir; but in attempting to execute this command the soldiery were attacked in the market-place with stones and halberds; the delinquent had escaped to the Rue des Lombards and rushed into a house. They broke open the doors and searched the dwelling, but in vain. Comminges, wounded by a stone which had struck him on the forehead, had left a picket in the street and returned to the Palais Royal, followed by a menacing crowd, to tell his story.

This account confirmed that of the mayor. The authorities were not in a condition to cope with serious revolt. Mazarin endeavored to circulate among the people a report that troops had only been stationed on the quays and on the Pont Neuf, on account of the ceremonial of the day, and that they would soon withdraw. In fact, about four o'clock they were all concentrated about the Palais Royal, the courts and ground floors of which were filled with musketeers and Swiss guards, and there awaited the outcome of all this disturbance.

Such was the state of affairs at the very moment we introduced our readers to the study of Cardinal Mazarin--once that of Cardinal Richelieu. We have seen in what state of mind he listened to the murmurs from below, which even reached him in his seclusion, and to the guns, the firing of which resounded through that room. All at once he raised his head; his brow slightly contracted like that of a man who has formed a resolution; he fixed his eyes upon an enormous clock that was about to strike ten, and taking up a whistle of silver gilt that stood upon the table near him, he shrilled it twice.

A door hidden in the tapestry opened noiselessly and a man in black silently advanced and stood behind the chair on which Mazarin sat.

"Bernouin," said the cardinal, not turning round, for having whistled, he knew that it was his valet-de-chambre who was behind him; "what musketeers are now within the palace?"

"The Black Musketeers, my lord."

"What company?"

"Treville's company."

"Is there any officer belonging to this company in the ante-chamber?"

"Lieutenant d'Artagnan."

"A man on whom we can depend, I hope."

"Yes, my lord."

"Give me a uniform of one of these musketeers and help me to put it on."

The valet went out as silently as he had entered and appeared in a few minutes bringing the dress demanded.

The cardinal, in deep thought and in silence, began to take off the robes of state he had assumed in order to be present at the sitting of parliament, and to attire himself in the military coat, which he wore with a certain degree of easy grace, owing to his former campaigns in Italy. When he was completely dressed he said:

"Send hither Monsieur d'Artagnan."

The valet went out of the room, this time by the centre door, but still as silently as before; one might have fancied him an apparition.

When he was left alone the cardinal looked at himself in the glass with a feeling of self-satisfaction. Still young--for he was scarcely forty-six years of age--he possessed great elegance of form and was above the middle height; his complexion was brilliant and beautiful; his glance full of expression; his nose, though large, was well proportioned; his forehead broad and majestic; his hair, of a chestnut color, was curled slightly; his beard, which was darker than his hair, was turned carefully with a curling iron, a practice that greatly improved it. After a short time the cardinal arranged his shoulder belt, then looked with great complacency at his hands, which were most elegant and of which he took the greatest care; and throwing on one side the large kid gloves tried on at first, as belonging to the uniform, he put on others of silk only. At this instant the door opened.

"Monsieur d'Artagnan," said the valet-de-chambre.

An officer, as he spoke, entered the apartment. He was a man between thirty-nine and forty years of age, of medium height but a very well proportioned figure; with an intellectual and animated physiognomy; his beard black, and his hair turning gray, as often happens when people have found life either too gay or too sad, more especially when they happen to be of swart complexion.

D'Artagnan advanced a few steps into the apartment.

How perfectly he remembered his former entrance into that very room! Seeing, however, no one there except a musketeer of his own troop, he fixed his eyes upon the supposed soldier, in whose dress, nevertheless, he recognized at the first glance the cardinal.

The lieutenant remained standing in a dignified but respectful posture, such as became a man of good birth, who had in the course of his life been frequently in the society of the highest nobles.

The cardinal looked at him with a cunning rather than serious glance, yet he examined his countenance with attention and after a momentary silence said:

"You are Monsieur d'Artagnan?"

"I am that individual," replied the officer.

Mazarin gazed once more at a countenance full of intelligence, the play of which had been, nevertheless, subdued by age and experience; and D'Artagnan received the penetrating glance like one who had formerly sustained many a searching look, very different, indeed, from those which were inquiringly directed on him at that instant.

"Sir," resumed the cardinal, "you are to come with me, or rather, I am to go with you."

"I am at your command, my lord," returned D'Artagnan.

"I wish to visit in person the outposts which surround the Palais Royal; do you suppose that there is any danger in so doing?"

"Danger, my lord!" exclaimed D'Artagnan with a look of astonishment, "what danger?"

"I am told that there is a general insurrection."

"The uniform of the king's musketeers carries a certain respect with it, and even if that were not the case I would engage with four of my men to put to flight a hundred of these clowns."

"Did you witness the injury sustained by Comminges?"

"Monsieur de Comminges is in the guards and not in the musketeers----"

"Which means, I suppose, that the musketeers are better soldiers than the guards." The cardinal smiled as he spoke.

"Every one likes his own uniform best, my lord."

"Myself excepted," and again Mazarin smiled; "for you perceive that I have left off mine and put on yours."

"Lord bless us! this is modesty indeed!" cried D'Artagnan. "Had I such a uniform as your eminence possesses, I protest I should be mightily content, and I would take an oath never to wear any other costume----"

"Yes, but for to-night's adventure I don't suppose my dress would have been a very safe one. Give me my felt hat, Bernouin."

The valet instantly brought to his master a regimental hat with a wide brim. The cardinal put it on in military style.

"Your horses are ready saddled in their stables, are they not?" he said, turning to D'Artagnan.

"Yes, my lord."

"Well, let us set out."

"How many men does your eminence wish to escort you?"

"You say that with four men you will undertake to disperse a hundred low fellows; as it may happen that we shall have to encounter two hundred, take eight----"

"As many as my lord wishes."

"I will follow you. This way--light us downstairs Bernouin."

The valet held a wax-light; the cardinal took a key from his bureau and opening the door of a secret stair descended into the court of the Palais Royal.

2. A Nightly Patrol.

In ten minutes Mazarin and his party were traversing the street "Les Bons Enfants" behind the theatre built by Richelieu expressly for the play of "Mirame," and in which Mazarin, who was an amateur of music, but not of literature, had introduced into France the first opera that was ever acted in that country.

The appearance of the town denoted the greatest agitation. Numberless groups paraded the streets and, whatever D'Artagnan might think of it, it was obvious that the citizens had for the night laid aside their usual forbearance, in order to assume a warlike aspect. From time to time noises came in the direction of the public markets. The report of firearms was heard near the Rue Saint Denis and occasionally church bells began to ring indiscriminately and at the caprice of the populace. D'Artagnan, meantime, pursued his way with the indifference of a man upon whom such acts of folly made no impression. When he approached a group in the middle of the street he urged his horse upon it without a word of warning; and the members of the group, whether rebels or not, as if they knew with what sort of a man they had to deal, at once gave place to the patrol. The cardinal envied that composure, which he attributed to the habit of meeting danger; but none the less he conceived for the officer under whose orders he had for the moment placed himself, that consideration which even prudence pays to careless courage. On approaching an outpost near the Barriere des Sergens, the sentinel cried out, "Who's there?" and D'Artagnan answered--having first asked the word of the cardinal--"Louis and Rocroy." After which he inquired if Lieutenant Comminges were not the commanding officer at the outpost. The soldier replied by pointing out to him an officer who was conversing, on foot, his hand upon the neck of a horse on which the individual to whom he was talking sat. Here was the officer D'Artagnan was seeking.

"Here is Monsieur Comminges," said D'Artagnan, returning to the cardinal. He instantly retired, from a feeling of respectful delicacy; it was, however, evident that the cardinal was recognized by both Comminges and the other officers on horseback.

"Well done, Guitant," cried the cardinal to the equestrian; "I see plainly that, notwithstanding the sixty-four years that have passed over your head, you are still the same man, active and zealous. What were you saying to this youngster?"

"My lord," replied Guitant, "I was observing that we live in troublous times and that to-day's events are very like those in the days of the Ligue, of which I heard so much in my youth. Are you aware that the mob have even suggested throwing up barricades in the Rue Saint Denis and the Rue Saint Antoine?"

"And what was Comminges saying to you in reply, my good Guitant?"

"My lord," said Comminges, "I answered that to compose a Ligue only one ingredient was wanting--in my opinion an essential one--a Duc de Guise; moreover, no generation ever does the same thing twice."

"No, but they mean to make a Fronde, as they call it," said Guitant.

"And what is a Fronde?" inquired Mazarin.

"My lord, Fronde is the name the discontented give to their party."

"And what is the origin of this name?"

"It seems that some days since Councillor Bachaumont remarked at the palace that rebels and agitators reminded him of schoolboys slinging--qui frondent--stones from the moats round Paris, young urchins who run off the moment the constable appears, only to return to their diversion the instant his back is turned. So they have picked up the word and the insurrectionists are called 'Frondeurs,' and yesterday every article sold was 'a la Fronde;' bread 'a la Fronde,' hats 'a la Fronde,' to say nothing of gloves, pocket-handkerchiefs, and fans; but listen----"

At that moment a window opened and a man began to sing:

"A tempest from the Fronde Did blow to-day: I think 'twill blow Sieur Mazarin away."

"Insolent wretch!" cried Guitant.

"My lord," said Comminges, who, irritated by his wounds, wished for revenge and longed to give back blow for blow, "shall I fire off a ball to punish that jester, and to warn him not to sing so much out of tune in the future?"

And as he spoke he put his hand on the holster of his uncle's saddle-bow.

"Certainly not! certainly not," exclaimed Mazarin. "Diavolo! my dear friend, you are going to spoil everything--everything is going on famously. I know the French as well as if I had made them myself. They sing--let them pay the piper. During the Ligue, about which Guitant was speaking just now, the people chanted nothing except the mass, so everything went to destruction. Come, Guitant, come along, and let's see if they keep watch at the Quinze-Vingts as at the Barriere des Sergens."

And waving his hand to Comminges he rejoined D'Artagnan, who instantly put himself at the head of his troop, followed by the cardinal, Guitant and the rest of the escort.

"Just so," muttered Comminges, looking after Mazarin. "True, I forgot; provided he can get money out of the people, that is all he wants."

The street of Saint Honore, when the cardinal and his party passed through it, was crowded by an assemblage who, standing in groups, discussed the edicts of that memorable day. They pitied the young king, who was unconsciously ruining his country, and threw all the odium of his proceedings on Mazarin. Addresses to the Duke of Orleans and to Conde were suggested. Blancmesnil and Broussel seemed in the highest favor.

D'Artagnan passed through the very midst of this discontented mob just as if his horse and he had been made of iron. Mazarin and Guitant conversed together in whispers. The musketeers, who had already discovered who Mazarin was, followed in profound silence. In the street of Saint Thomas-du-Louvre they stopped at the barrier distinguished by the name of Quinze-Vingts. Here Guitant spoke to one of the subalterns, asking how matters were progressing.

"Ah, captain!" said the officer, "everything is quiet hereabout--if I did not know that something is going on in yonder house!"

And he pointed to a magnificent hotel situated on the very spot whereon the Vaudeville now stands.

"In that hotel? it is the Hotel Rambouillet," cried Guitant.

"I really don't know what hotel it is; all I do know is that I observed some suspicious looking people go in there----"

"Nonsense!" exclaimed Guitant, with a burst of laughter; "those men must be poets."

"Come, Guitant, speak, if you please, respectfully of these gentlemen," said Mazarin; "don't you know that I was in my youth a poet? I wrote verses in the style of Benserade----"

"You, my lord?"

"Yes, I; shall I repeat to you some of my verses?"

"Just as you please, my lord. I do not understand Italian."

"Yes, but you understand French," and Mazarin laid his hand upon Guitant's shoulder. "My good, my brave Guitant, whatsoever command I may give you in that language--in French--whatever I may order you to do, will you not perform it?"

"Certainly. I have already answered that question in the affirmative; but that command must come from the queen herself."

"Yes! ah yes!" Mazarin bit his lips as he spoke; "I know your devotion to her majesty."

"I have been a captain in the queen's guards for twenty years," was the reply.

"En route, Monsieur d'Artagnan," said the cardinal; "all goes well in this direction."

D'Artagnan, in the meantime, had taken the head of his detachment without a word and with that ready and profound obedience which marks the character of an old soldier.

He led the way toward the hill of Saint Roche. The Rue Richelieu and the Rue Villedot were then, owing to their vicinity to the ramparts, less frequented than any others in that direction, for the town was thinly inhabited thereabout.

"Who is in command here?" asked the cardinal.

"Villequier," said Guitant.

"Diavolo! Speak to him yourself, for ever since you were deputed by me to arrest the Duc de Beaufort, this officer and I have been on bad terms. He laid claim to that honor as captain of the royal guards."

"I am aware of that, and I have told him a hundred times that he was wrong. The king could not give that order, since at that time he was hardly four years old."

"Yes, but I could give him the order--I, Guitant--and I preferred to give it to you."

Guitant, without reply, rode forward and desired the sentinel to call Monsieur de Villequier.

"Ah! so you are here!" cried the officer, in the tone of ill-humor habitual to him; "what the devil are you doing here?"

"I wish to know--can you tell me, pray--is anything fresh occurring in this part of the town?"

"What do you mean? People cry out, 'Long live the king! down with Mazarin!' That's nothing new; no, we've been used to those acclamations for some time."

"And you sing chorus," replied Guitant, laughing.

"Faith, I've half a mind to do it. In my opinion the people are right; and cheerfully would I give up five years of my pay--which I am never paid, by the way--to make the king five years older."

"Really! And pray what would come to pass, supposing the king were five years older than he is?"

"As soon as ever the king comes of age he will issue his commands himself, and 'tis far pleasanter to obey the grandson of Henry IV. than the son of Peter Mazarin. 'Sdeath! I would die willingly for the king, but supposing I happened to be killed on account of Mazarin, as your nephew came near being to-day, there could be nothing in Paradise, however well placed I might be there, that could console me for it."

"Well, well, Monsieur de Villequier," Mazarin interposed, "I shall make it my care the king hears of your loyalty. Come, gentlemen," addressing the troop, "let us return."

"Stop," exclaimed Villequier, "so Mazarin was here! so much the better. I have been waiting for a long time to tell him what I think of him. I am obliged to you Guitant, although your intention was perhaps not very favorable to me, for such an opportunity."

He turned away and went off to his post, whistling a tune then popular among the party called the "Fronde," whilst Mazarin returned, in a pensive mood, toward the Palais Royal. All that he had heard from these three different men, Comminges, Guitant and Villequier, confirmed him in his conviction that in case of serious tumults there would be no one on his side except the queen; and then Anne of Austria had so often deserted her friends that her support seemed most precarious. During the whole of this nocturnal ride, during the whole time that he was endeavoring to understand the various characters of Comminges, Guitant and Villequier, Mazarin was, in truth, studying more especially one man. This man, who had remained immovable as bronze when menaced by the mob--not a muscle of whose face was stirred, either at Mazarin's witticisms or by the jests of the multitude--seemed to the cardinal a peculiar being, who, having participated in past events similar to those now occurring, was calculated to cope with those now on the eve of taking place.

The name of D'Artagnan was not altogether new to Mazarin, who, although he did not arrive in France before the year 1634 or 1635, that is to say, about eight or nine years after the events which we have related in a preceding narrative[1], fancied he had heard it pronounced as that of one who was said to be a model of courage, address and loyalty.

Possessed by this idea, the cardinal resolved to know all about D'Artagnan immediately; of course he could not inquire from D'Artagnan himself who he was and what had been his career; he remarked, however, in the course of conversation that the lieutenant of musketeers spoke with a Gascon accent. Now the Italians and the Gascons are too much alike and know each other too well ever to trust what any one of them may say of himself; so in reaching the walls which surrounded the Palais Royal, the cardinal knocked at a little door, and after thanking D'Artagnan and requesting him to wait in the court of the Palais Royal, he made a sign to Guitant to follow him.

They both dismounted, consigned their horses to the lackey who had opened the door, and disappeared in the garden.

"My dear friend," said the cardinal, leaning, as they walked through the garden, on his friend's arm, "you told me just now that you had been twenty years in the queen's service."

"Yes, it's true. I have," returned Guitant.

"Now, my dear Guitant, I have often remarked that in addition to your courage, which is indisputable, and your fidelity, which is invincible, you possess an admirable memory."

"You have found that out, have you, my lord? Deuce take it--all the worse for me!"

"How?"

"There is no doubt but that one of the chief accomplishments of a courtier is to know when to forget."

"But you, Guitant, are not a courtier. You are a brave soldier, one of the few remaining veterans of the days of Henry IV. Alas! how few to-day exist!"

"Plague on't, my lord, have you brought me here to get my horoscope out of me?"

---

[1] "The Three Musketeers."

"No; I only brought you here to ask you," returned Mazarin, smiling, "if you have taken any particular notice of our lieutenant of musketeers?"

"Monsieur d'Artagnan? I have had no occasion to notice him particularly; he's an old acquaintance. He's a Gascon. De Treville knows him and esteems him very highly, and De Treville, as you know, is one of the queen's greatest friends. As a soldier the man ranks well; he did his whole duty and even more, at the siege of Rochelle--as at Suze and Perpignan."

"But you know, Guitant, we poor ministers often want men with other qualities besides courage; we want men of talent. Pray, was not Monsieur d'Artagnan, in the time of the cardinal, mixed up in some intrigue from which he came out, according to report, quite cleverly?"

"My lord, as to the report you allude to"--Guitant perceived that the cardinal wished to make him speak out--"I know nothing but what the public knows. I never meddle in intrigues, and if I occasionally become a confidant of the intrigues of others I am sure your eminence will approve of my keeping them secret."

Mazarin shook his head.

"Ah!" he said; "some ministers are fortunate and find out all that they wish to know."

"My lord," replied Guitant, "such ministers do not weigh men in the same balance; they get their information on war from warriors; on intrigues, from intriguers. Consult some politician of the period of which you speak, and if you pay well for it you will certainly get to know all you want."

"Eh, pardieu!" said Mazarin, with a grimace which he always made when spoken to about money. "They will be paid, if there is no way of getting out of it."

"Does my lord seriously wish me to name any one who was mixed up in the cabals of that day?"

"By Bacchus!" rejoined Mazarin, impatiently, "it's about an hour since I asked you for that very thing, wooden-head that you are."

"There is one man for whom I can answer, if he will speak out."

"That's my concern; I will make him speak."

"Ah, my lord, 'tis not easy to make people say what they don't wish to let out."

"Pooh! with patience one must succeed. Well, this man. Who is he?"

"The Comte de Rochefort."

"The Comte de Rochefort!"

"Unfortunately he has disappeared these four or five years and I don't know where he is."

"I know, Guitant," said Mazarin.

"Well, then, how is it that your eminence complained just now of want of information?"

"You think," resumed Mazarin, "that Rochefort----"

"He was Cardinal Richelieu's creature, my lord. I warn you, however, his services will cost you something. The cardinal was lavish to his underlings."

"Yes, yes, Guitant," said Mazarin; "Richelieu was a great man, a very great man, but he had that defect. Thanks, Guitant; I shall benefit by your advice this very evening."

Here they separated and bidding adieu to Guitant in the court of the Palais Royal, Mazarin approached an officer who was walking up and down within that inclosure.

It was D'Artagnan, who was waiting for him.

"Come hither," said Mazarin in his softest voice; "I have an order to give you."

D'Artagnan bent low and following the cardinal up the secret staircase, soon found himself in the study whence they had first set out.

The cardinal seated himself before his bureau and taking a sheet of paper wrote some lines upon it, whilst D'Artagnan stood imperturbable, without showing either impatience or curiosity. He was like a soldierly automaton, or rather, like a magnificent marionette.

The cardinal folded and sealed his letter.

"Monsieur d'Artagnan," he said, "you are to take this dispatch to the Bastile and bring back here the person it concerns. You must take a carriage and an escort, and guard the prisoner with the greatest care."

D'Artagnan took the letter, touched his hat with his hand, turned round upon his heel like a drill-sergeant, and a moment afterward was heard, in his dry and monotonous tone, commanding "Four men and an escort, a carriage and a horse." Five minutes afterward the wheels of the carriage and the horses' shoes were heard resounding on the pavement of the courtyard.

3. Dead Animosities.

D'Artagnan arrived at the Bastile just as it was striking half-past eight. His visit was announced to the governor, who, on hearing that he came from the cardinal, went to meet him and received him at the top of the great flight of steps outside the door. The governor of the Bastile was Monsieur du Tremblay, the brother of the famous Capuchin, Joseph, that fearful favorite of Richelieu's, who went by the name of the Gray Cardinal.

During the period that the Duc de Bassompierre passed in the Bastile--where he remained for twelve long years--when his companions, in their dreams of liberty, said to each other: "As for me, I shall go out of the prison at such a time," and another, at such and such a time, the duke used to answer, "As for me, gentlemen, I shall leave only when Monsieur du Tremblay leaves;" meaning that at the death of the cardinal Du Tremblay would certainly lose his place at the Bastile and De Bassompierre regain his at court.

His prediction was nearly fulfilled, but in a very different way from that which De Bassompierre supposed; for after the death of Richelieu everything went on, contrary to expectation, in the same way as before; and Bassompierre had little chance of leaving his prison.

Monsieur du Tremblay received D'Artagnan with extreme politeness and invited him to sit down with him to supper, of which he was himself about to partake.

"I should be delighted to do so," was the reply; "but if I am not mistaken, the words 'In haste,' are written on the envelope of the letter which I brought."

"You are right," said Du Tremblay. "Halloo, major! tell them to order Number 25 to come downstairs."

The unhappy wretch who entered the Bastile ceased, as he crossed the threshold, to be a man--he became a number.

D'Artagnan shuddered at the noise of the keys; he remained on horseback, feeling no inclination to dismount, and sat looking at the bars, at the buttressed windows and the immense walls he had hitherto only seen from the other side of the moat, but by which he had for twenty years been awe-struck.

A bell resounded.

"I must leave you," said Du Tremblay; "I am sent for to sign the release of a prisoner. I shall be happy to meet you again, sir."

"May the devil annihilate me if I return thy wish!" murmured D'Artagnan, smiling as he pronounced the imprecation; "I declare I feel quite ill after only being five minutes in the courtyard. Go to! go to! I would rather die on straw than hoard up a thousand a year by being governor of the Bastile."

He had scarcely finished this soliloquy before the prisoner arrived. On seeing him D'Artagnan could hardly suppress an exclamation of surprise. The prisoner got into the carriage without seeming to recognize the musketeer.

"Gentlemen," thus D'Artagnan addressed the four musketeers, "I am ordered to exercise the greatest possible care in guarding the prisoner, and since there are no locks to the carriage, I shall sit beside him. Monsieur de Lillebonne, lead my horse by the bridle, if you please." As he spoke he dismounted, gave the bridle of his horse to the musketeer and placing himself by the side of the prisoner said, in a voice perfectly composed, "To the Palais Royal, at full trot."

The carriage drove on and D'Artagnan, availing himself of the darkness in the archway under which they were passing, threw himself into the arms of the prisoner.

"Rochefort!" he exclaimed; "you! is it you, indeed? I am not mistaken?"

"D'Artagnan!" cried Rochefort.

"Ah! my poor friend!" resumed D'Artagnan, "not having seen you for four or five years I concluded you were dead."

"I'faith," said Rochefort, "there's no great difference, I think, between a dead man and one who has been buried alive; now I have been buried alive, or very nearly so."

"And for what crime are you imprisoned in the Bastile."

"Do you wish me to speak the truth?"

"Yes."

"Well, then, I don't know."

"Have you any suspicion of me, Rochefort?"

"No! on the honor of a gentleman; but I cannot be imprisoned for the reason alleged; it is impossible."

"What reason?" asked D'Artagnan.

"For stealing."

"For stealing! you, Rochefort! you are laughing at me."

"I understand. You mean that this demands explanation, do you not?"

"I admit it."

"Well, this is what actually took place: One evening after an orgy in Reinard's apartment at the Tuileries with the Duc d'Harcourt, Fontrailles, De Rieux and others, the Duc d'Harcourt proposed that we should go and pull cloaks on the Pont Neuf; that is, you know, a diversion which the Duc d'Orleans made quite the fashion."

"Were you crazy, Rochefort? at your age!"

"No, I was drunk. And yet, since the amusement seemed to me rather tame, I proposed to Chevalier de Rieux that we should be spectators instead of actors, and, in order to see to advantage, that we should mount the bronze horse. No sooner said than done. Thanks to the spurs, which served as stirrups, in a moment we were perched upon the croupe; we were well placed and saw everything. Four or five cloaks had already been lifted, with a dexterity without parallel, and not one of the victims had dared to say a word, when some fool of a fellow, less patient than the others, took it into his head to cry out, 'Guard!' and drew upon us a patrol of archers. Duc d'Harcourt, Fontrailles, and the others escaped; De Rieux was inclined to do likewise, but I told him they wouldn't look for us where we were. He wouldn't listen, put his foot on the spur to get down, the spur broke, he fell with a broken leg, and, instead of keeping quiet, took to crying out like a gallows-bird. I then was ready to dismount, but it was too late; I descended into the arms of the archers. They conducted me to the Chatelet, where I slept soundly, being very sure that on the next day I should go forth free. The next day came and passed, the day after, a week; I then wrote to the cardinal. The same day they came for me and took me to the Bastile. That was five years ago. Do you believe it was because I committed the sacrilege of mounting en croupe behind Henry IV.?"

"No; you are right, my dear Rochefort, it couldn't be for that; but you will probably learn the reason soon."

"Ah, indeed! I forgot to ask you--where are you taking me?"

"To the cardinal."

"What does he want with me?"

"I do not know. I did not even know that you were the person I was sent to fetch."

"Impossible--you--a favorite of the minister!"

"A favorite! no, indeed!" cried D'Artagnan. "Ah, my poor friend! I am just as poor a Gascon as when I saw you at Meung, twenty-two years ago, you know; alas!" and he concluded his speech with a deep sigh.

"Nevertheless, you come as one in authority."

"Because I happened to be in the ante-chamber when the cardinal called me, by the merest chance. I am still a lieutenant in the musketeers and have been so these twenty years."

"Then no misfortune has happened to you?"

"And what misfortune could happen to me? To quote some Latin verses I have forgotten, or rather, never knew well, 'the thunderbolt never falls on the valleys,' and I am a valley, dear Rochefort,--one of the lowliest of the low."

"Then Mazarin is still Mazarin?"

"The same as ever, my friend; it is said that he is married to the queen."

"Married?"

"If not her husband, he is unquestionably her lover."

"You surprise me. Rebuff Buckingham and consent to Mazarin!"

"Just like the women," replied D'Artagnan, coolly.

"Like women, not like queens."

"Egad! queens are the weakest of their sex, when it comes to such things as these."

"And M. de Beaufort--is he still in prison?"

"Yes. Why?"

"Oh, nothing, but that he might get me out of this, if he were favorably inclined to me."

"You are probably nearer freedom than he is, so it will be your business to get him out."

"And," said the prisoner, "what talk is there of war with Spain?"

"With Spain, no," answered D'Artagnan; "but Paris."

"What do you mean?" cried Rochefort.

"Do you hear the guns, pray? The citizens are amusing themselves in the meantime."

"And you--do you really think that anything could be done with these bourgeois?"

"Yes, they might do well if they had any leader to unite them in one body."

"How miserable not to be free!"

"Don't be downcast. Since Mazarin has sent for you, it is because he wants you. I congratulate you! Many a long year has passed since any one has wanted to employ me; so you see in what a situation I am."

"Make your complaints known; that's my advice."

"Listen, Rochefort; let us make a compact. We are friends, are we not?"

"Egad! I bear the traces of our friendship--three slits or slashes from your sword."

"Well, if you should be restored to favor, don't forget me."

"On the honor of a Rochefort; but you must do the like for me."

"There's my hand,--I promise."

"Therefore, whenever you find any opportunity of saying something in my behalf----"

"I shall say it, and you?"

"I shall do the same."

"Apropos, are we to speak of your friends also, Athos, Porthos, and Aramis? or have you forgotten them?"

"Almost."

"What has become of them?"

"I don't know; we separated, as you know. They are alive, that's all that I can say about them; from time to time I hear of them indirectly, but in what part of the world they are, devil take me if I know, No, on my honor, I have not a friend in the world but you, Rochefort."

"And the illustrious--what's the name of the lad whom I made a sergeant in Piedmont's regiment?"

"Planchet!"

"The illustrious Planchet. What has become of him?"

"I shouldn't wonder if he were at the head of the mob at this very moment. He married a woman who keeps a confectioner's shop in the Rue des Lombards, for he's a lad who was always fond of sweetmeats; he's now a citizen of Paris. You'll see that that queer fellow will be a sheriff before I shall be a captain."

"Come, dear D'Artagnan, look up a little! Courage! It is when one is lowest on the wheel of fortune that the merry-go-round wheels and rewards us. This evening your destiny begins to change."

"Amen!" exclaimed D'Artagnan, stopping the carriage.

"What are you doing?" asked Rochefort.

"We are almost there and I want no one to see me getting out of your carriage; we are supposed not to know each other."

"You are right. Adieu."

"Au revoir. Remember your promise."

In five minutes the party entered the courtyard and D'Artagnan led the prisoner up the great staircase and across the corridor and ante-chamber.

As they stopped at the door of the cardinal's study, D'Artagnan was about to be announced when Rochefort slapped him on his shoulder.

"D'Artagnan, let me confess to you what I've been thinking about during the whole of my drive, as I looked out upon the parties of citizens who perpetually crossed our path and looked at you and your four men with fiery eyes."

"Speak out," answered D'Artagnan.

"I had only to cry out 'Help!' for you and for your companions to be cut to pieces, and then I should have been free."

"Why didn't you do it?" asked the lieutenant.

"Come, come!" cried Rochefort. "Did we not swear friendship? Ah! had any one but you been there, I don't say----"

D'Artagnan bowed. "Is it possible that Rochefort has become a better man than I am?" he said to himself. And he caused himself to be announced to the minister.

"Let M. de Rochefort enter," said Mazarin, eagerly, on hearing their names pronounced; "and beg M. d'Artagnan to wait; I shall have further need of him."

These words gave great joy to D'Artagnan. As he had said, it had been a long time since any one had needed him; and that demand for his services on the part of Mazarin seemed to him an auspicious sign.

Rochefort, rendered suspicious and cautious by these words, entered the apartment, where he found Mazarin sitting at the table, dressed in his ordinary garb and as one of the prelates of the Church, his costume being similar to that of the abbes in that day, excepting that his scarf and stockings were violet.

As the door was closed Rochefort cast a glance toward Mazarin, which was answered by one, equally furtive, from the minister.

There was little change in the cardinal; still dressed with sedulous care, his hair well arranged and curled, his person perfumed, he looked, owing to his extreme taste in dress, only half his age. But Rochefort, who had passed five years in prison, had become old in the lapse of a few years; the dark locks of this estimable friend of the defunct Cardinal Richelieu were now white; the deep bronze of his complexion had been succeeded by a mortal pallor which betokened debility. As he gazed at him Mazarin shook his head slightly, as much as to say, "This is a man who does not appear to me fit for much."

After a pause, which appeared an age to Rochefort, Mazarin took from a bundle of papers a letter, and showing it to the count, he said:

"I find here a letter in which you sue for liberty, Monsieur de Rochefort. You are in prison, then?"

Rochefort trembled in every limb at this question. "But I thought," he said, "that your eminence knew that circumstance better than any one----"

"I? Oh no! There is a congestion of prisoners in the Bastile, who were cooped up in the time of Monsieur de Richelieu; I don't even know their names."

"Yes, but in regard to myself, my lord, it cannot be so, for I was removed from the Chatelet to the Bastile owing to an order from your eminence."

"You think you were."

"I am certain of it."

"Ah, stay! I fancy I remember it. Did you not once refuse to undertake a journey to Brussels for the queen?"

"Ah! ah!" exclaimed Rochefort. "There is the true reason! Idiot that I am, though I have been trying to find it out for five years, I never found it out."

"But I do not say it was the cause of your imprisonment. I merely ask you, did you not refuse to go to Brussels for the queen, whilst you had consented to go there to do some service for the late cardinal?"

"That is the very reason I refused to go back to Brussels. I was there at a fearful moment. I was sent there to intercept a correspondence between Chalais and the archduke, and even then, when I was discovered I was nearly torn to pieces. How could I, then, return to Brussels? I should injure the queen instead of serving her."

"Well, since the best motives are liable to misconstruction, the queen saw in your refusal nothing but a refusal--a distinct refusal she had also much to complain of you during the lifetime of the late cardinal; yes, her majesty the queen----"

Rochefort smiled contemptuously.

"Since I was a faithful servant, my lord, to Cardinal Richelieu during his life, it stands to reason that now, after his death, I should serve you well, in defiance of the whole world."

"With regard to myself, Monsieur de Rochefort," replied Mazarin, "I am not, like Monsieur de Richelieu, all-powerful. I am but a minister, who wants no servants, being myself nothing but a servant of the queen's. Now, the queen is of a sensitive nature. Hearing of your refusal to obey her she looked upon it as a declaration of war, and as she considers you a man of superior talent, and consequently dangerous, she desired me to make sure of you; that is the reason of your being shut up in the Bastile. But your release can be managed. You are one of those men who can comprehend certain matters and having understood them, can act with energy----"

"Such was Cardinal Richelieu's opinion, my lord."

"The cardinal," interrupted Mazarin, "was a great politician and therein shone his vast superiority over me. I am a straightforward, simple man; that's my great disadvantage. I am of a frankness of character quite French."

Rochefort bit his lips in order to prevent a smile.

"Now to the point. I want friends; I want faithful servants. When I say I want, I mean the queen wants them. I do nothing without her commands--pray understand that; not like Monsieur de Richelieu, who went on just as he pleased. So I shall never be a great man, as he was, but to compensate for that, I shall be a good man, Monsieur de Rochefort, and I hope to prove it to you."

Rochefort knew well the tones of that soft voice, in which sounded sometimes a sort of gentle lisp, like the hissing of young vipers.

"I am disposed to believe your eminence," he replied; "though I have had but little evidence of that good-nature of which your eminence speaks. Do not forget that I have been five years in the Bastile and that no medium of viewing things is so deceptive as the grating of a prison."

"Ah, Monsieur de Rochefort! have I not told you already that I had nothing to do with that? The queen--cannot you make allowances for the pettishness of a queen and a princess? But that has passed away as suddenly as it came, and is forgotten."

"I can easily suppose, sir, that her majesty has forgotten it amid the fetes and the courtiers of the

Palais Royal, but I who have passed those years in the Bastile----"

"Ah! mon Dieu! my dear Monsieur de Rochefort! do you absolutely think that the Palais Royal is the abode of gayety? No. We have had great annoyances there. As for me, I play my game squarely, fairly, and above board, as I always do. Let us come to some conclusion. Are you one of us, Monsieur de Rochefort?"

"I am very desirous of being so, my lord, but I am totally in the dark about everything. In the Bastile one talks politics only with soldiers and jailers, and you have not an idea, my lord, how little is known of what is going on by people of that sort; I am of Monsieur de Bassompierre's party. Is he still one of the seventeen peers of France?"

"He is dead, sir; a great loss. His devotion to the queen was boundless; men of loyalty are scarce."

"I think so, forsooth," said Rochefort, "and when you find any of them, you march them off to the Bastile. However, there are plenty in the world, but you don't look in the right direction for them, my lord."

"Indeed! explain to me. Ah! my dear Monsieur de Rochefort, how much you must have learned during your intimacy with the late cardinal! Ah! he was a great man."

"Will your eminence be angry if I read you a lesson?"

"I! never! you know you may say anything to me. I try to be beloved, not feared."

"Well, there is on the wall of my cell, scratched with a nail, a proverb, which says, 'Like master, like servant.'"

"Pray, what does that mean?"

"It means that Monsieur de Richelieu was able to find trusty servants, dozens and dozens of them."

"He! the point aimed at by every poniard! Richelieu, who passed his life in warding off blows which were forever aimed at him!"

"But he did ward them off," said De Rochefort, "and the reason was, that though he had bitter enemies he possessed also true friends. I have known persons," he continued--for he thought he might avail himself of the opportunity of speaking of D'Artagnan--"who by their sagacity and address have deceived the penetration of Cardinal Richelieu; who by their valor have got the better of his guards and spies; persons without money, without support, without credit, yet who have preserved to the crowned head its crown and made the cardinal crave pardon."

"But those men you speak of," said Mazarin, smiling inwardly on seeing Rochefort approach the point to which he was leading him, "those men were not devoted to the cardinal, for they contended against him."

"No; in that case they would have met with more fitting reward. They had the misfortune to be devoted to that very queen for whom just now you were seeking servants."

"But how is it that you know so much of these matters?"

"I know them because the men of whom I speak were at that time my enemies; because they fought against me; because I did them all the harm I could and they returned it to the best of their ability; because one of them, with whom I had most to do, gave me a pretty sword-thrust, now about seven years ago, the third that I received from the same hand; it closed an old account."

"Ah!" said Mazarin, with admirable suavity, "could I but find such men!"

"My lord, there has stood for six years at your very door a man such as I describe, and during those six years he has been unappreciated and unemployed by you."

"Who is it?"

"It is Monsieur d'Artagnan."

"That Gascon!" cried Mazarin, with well acted surprise.

"'That Gascon' has saved a queen and made Monsieur de Richelieu confess that in point of talent, address and political skill, to him he was only a tyro."

"Really?"

"It is as I have the honor of telling it to your excellency."

"Tell me a little about it, my dear Monsieur de Rochefort."

"That is somewhat difficult, my lord," said Rochefort, with a smile.

"Then he will tell it me himself."

"I doubt it, my lord."

"Why do you doubt it?"

"Because the secret does not belong to him; because, as I have told you, it has to do with a great queen."

"And he was alone in achieving an enterprise like that?"

"No, my lord, he had three colleagues, three brave men, men such as you were wishing for just now."

"And were these four men attached to each other, true in heart, really united?"

"As if they had been one man--as if their four hearts had pulsated in one breast."

"You pique my curiosity, dear Rochefort; pray tell me the whole story."

"That is impossible; but I will tell you a true story, my lord."

"Pray do so, I delight in stories," cried the cardinal.

"Listen, then," returned Rochefort, as he spoke endeavoring to read in that subtle countenance the cardinal's motive. "Once upon a time there lived a queen--a powerful monarch--who reigned over one of the greatest kingdoms of the universe; and a minister; and this minister wished much to injure the queen, whom once he had loved too well. (Do not try, my lord, you cannot guess who it is; all this happened long before you came into the country where this queen reigned.) There came to the court an ambassador so brave, so magnificent, so elegant, that every woman lost her heart to him; and the queen had even the indiscretion to give him certain ornaments so rare that they could never be replaced by any like them.

"As these ornaments were given by the king the minister persuaded his majesty to insist upon the queen's appearing in them as part of her jewels at a ball which was soon to take place. There is no occasion to tell you, my lord, that the minister knew for a fact that these ornaments had sailed away with the ambassador, who was far away, beyond seas. This illustrious queen had fallen low as the least of her subjects--fallen from her high estate."

"Indeed!"

"Well, my lord, four men resolved to save her. These four men were not princes, neither were they dukes, neither were they men in power; they were not even rich. They were four honest soldiers, each with a good heart, a good arm and a sword at the service of those who wanted it. They set out. The minister knew of their departure and had planted people on the road to prevent them ever reaching their destination. Three of them were overwhelmed and disabled by numerous assailants; one of them alone arrived at the port, having either killed or wounded those who wished to stop him. He crossed the sea and brought back the set of ornaments to the great queen, who was able to wear them on her shoulder on the appointed day; and this very nearly ruined the minister. What do you think of that exploit, my lord?"

"It is magnificent!" said Mazarin, thoughtfully.

"Well, I know of ten such men."

Mazarin made no reply; he reflected.

Five or six minutes elapsed.

"You have nothing more to ask of me, my lord?" said Rochefort.

"Yes. And you say that Monsieur d'Artagnan was one of those four men?"

"He led the enterprise."

"And who were the others?"

"I leave it to Monsieur d'Artagnan to name them, my lord. They were his friends and not mine. He alone would have any influence with them; I do not even know them under their true names."

"You suspect me, Monsieur de Rochefort; I want him and you and all to aid me."

"Begin with me, my lord; for after five or six years of imprisonment it is natural to feel some curiosity as to one's destination."

"You, my dear Monsieur de Rochefort, shall have the post of confidence; you shall go to Vincennes, where Monsieur de Beaufort is confined; you will guard him well for me. Well, what is the matter?"

"The matter is that you have proposed to me what is impossible," said Rochefort, shaking his head with an air of disappointment.

"What! impossible? And why is it impossible?"

"Because Monsieur de Beaufort is one of my friends, or rather, I am one of his. Have you forgotten, my lord, that it is he who answered for me to the queen?"

"Since then Monsieur de Beaufort has become an enemy of the State."

"That may be, my lord; but since I am neither king nor queen nor minister, he is not my enemy and I cannot accept your offer."

"This, then, is what you call devotion! I congratulate you. Your devotion does not commit you too far, Monsieur de Rochefort."

"And then, my lord," continued Rochefort, "you understand that to emerge from the Bastile in order to enter Vincennes is only to change one's prison."

"Say at once that you are on the side of Monsieur de Beaufort; that will be the most sincere line of conduct," said Mazarin.

"My lord, I have been so long shut up, that I am only of one party--I am for fresh air. Employ me in any other way; employ me even actively, but let it be on the high roads."

"My dear Monsieur de Rochefort," Mazarin replied in a tone of raillery, "you think yourself still a young man; your spirit is that of the phoenix, but your strength fails you. Believe me, you ought now to take a rest. Here!"

"You decide, then, nothing about me, my lord?"

"On the contrary, I have come to a decision."

Bernouin came into the room.

"Call an officer of justice," he said; "and stay close to me," he added, in a low tone.

The officer entered. Mazarin wrote a few words, which he gave to this man; then he bowed.

"Adieu, Monsieur de Rochefort," he said.

Rochefort bent low.

"I see, my lord, I am to be taken back to the Bastile."

"You are sagacious."

"I shall return thither, my lord, but it is a mistake on your part not to employ me."

"You? the friend of my greatest foes? Don't suppose that you are the only person who can serve me, Monsieur de Rochefort. I shall find many men as able as you are."

"I wish you may, my lord," replied De Rochefort.

He was then reconducted by the little staircase, instead of passing through the ante-chamber where D'Artagnan was waiting. In the courtyard the carriage and the four musketeers were ready, but he looked around in vain for his friend.

"Ah!" he muttered to himself, "this changes the situation, and if there is still a crowd of people in the streets we will try to show Mazarin that we are still, thank God, good for something else than keeping guard over a prisoner;" and he jumped into the carriage with the alacrity of a man of five-and-twenty.

4. Anne of Austria at the Age of Forty-six.

When left alone with Bernouin, Mazarin was for some minutes lost in thought. He had gained much information, but not enough. Mazarin was a cheat at the card-table. This is a detail preserved to us by Brienne. He called it using his advantages. He now determined not to begin the game with D'Artagnan till he knew completely all his adversary's cards.

"My lord, have you any commands?" asked Bernouin.

"Yes, yes," replied Mazarin. "Light me; I am going to the queen."

Bernouin took up a candlestick and led the way.

There was a secret communication between the cardinal's apartments and those of the queen; and through this corridor[1] Mazarin passed whenever he wished to visit Anne of Austria.

In the bedroom in which this passage ended, Bernouin encountered Madame de Beauvais, like himself intrusted with the secret of these subterranean love affairs; and Madame de Beauvais undertook to prepare Anne of Austria, who was in her oratory with the young king, Louis XIV., to receive the cardinal.

Anne, reclining in a large easy-chair, her head supported by her hand, her elbow resting on a table, was looking at her son, who was turning over the leaves of a large book filled with pictures. This celebrated woman fully understood the art of being dull with dignity. It was her practice to pass hours either in her oratory or in her room, without either reading or praying.

When Madame de Beauvais appeared at the door and announced the cardinal, the child, who had been absorbed in the pages of Quintus Curtius, enlivened as they were by engravings of Alexander's feats of arms, frowned and looked at his mother.

"Why," he said, "does he enter without first asking for an audience?"

Anne colored slightly.

"The prime minister," she said, "is obliged in these unsettled days to inform the queen of all that is happening from time to time, without exciting the curiosity or remarks of the court."

"But Richelieu never came in this manner," said the pertinacious boy.

"How can you remember what Monsieur de Richelieu did? You were too young to know about such things."

"I do not remember what he did, but I have inquired and I have been told all about it."

"And who told you about it?" asked Anne of Austria, with a movement of impatience.

"I know that I ought never to name the persons who answer my questions," answered the child, "for if I do I shall learn nothing further."

At this very moment Mazarin entered. The king rose immediately, took his book, closed it and went to lay it down on the table, near which he continued standing, in order that Mazarin might be obliged to stand also.

Mazarin contemplated these proceedings with a thoughtful glance. They explained what had occurred that evening.

He bowed respectfully to the king, who gave him a somewhat cavalier reception, but a look from his mother reproved him for the hatred which, from his infancy, Louis XIV. had entertained toward Mazarin, and he endeavored to receive the minister's homage with civility.

Anne of Austria sought to read in Mazarin's face the occasion of this unexpected visit, since the cardinal usually came to her apartment only after every one had retired.

The minister made a slight sign with his head, whereupon the queen said to Madame Beauvais:

"It is time for the king to go to bed; call Laporte."

---

[1] This secret passage is still to be seen in the Palais Royal.

The queen had several times already told her son that he ought to go to bed, and several times Louis had coaxingly insisted on staying where he was; but now he made no reply, but turned pale and bit his lips with anger.

In a few minutes Laporte came into the room. The child went directly to him without kissing his mother.

"Well, Louis," said Anne, "why do you not kiss me?"

"I thought you were angry with me, madame; you sent me away."

"I do not send you away, but you have had the small-pox and I am afraid that sitting up late may tire you."

"You had no fears of my being tired when you ordered me to go to the palace to-day to pass the odious decrees which have raised the people to rebellion."

"Sire!" interposed Laporte, in order to turn the subject, "to whom does your majesty wish me to give the candle?"

"To any one, Laporte," the child said; and then added in a loud voice, "to any one except Mancini."

Now Mancini was a nephew of Mazarin's and was as much hated by Louis as the cardinal himself, although placed near his person by the minister.

And the king went out of the room without either embracing his mother or even bowing to the cardinal.

"Good," said Mazarin, "I am glad to see that his majesty has been brought up with a hatred of dissimulation."

"Why do you say that?" asked the queen, almost timidly.

"Why, it seems to me that the way in which he left us needs no explanation. Besides, his majesty takes no pains to conceal how little affection he has for me. That, however, does not hinder me from being entirely devoted to his service, as I am to that of your majesty."

"I ask your pardon for him, cardinal," said the queen; "he is a child, not yet able to understand his obligations to you."

The cardinal smiled.

"But," continued the queen, "you have doubtless come for some important purpose. What is it, then?"

Mazarin sank into a chair with the deepest melancholy painted on his countenance.

"It is likely," he replied, "that we shall soon be obliged to separate, unless you love me well enough to follow me to Italy."

"Why," cried the queen; "how is that?"

"Because, as they say in the opera of 'Thisbe,' 'The whole world conspires to break our bonds.'"

"You jest, sir!" answered the queen, endeavoring to assume something of her former dignity.

"Alas! I do not, madame," rejoined Mazarin. "Mark well what I say. The whole world conspires to break our bonds. Now as you are one of the whole world, I mean to say that you also are deserting me."

"Cardinal!"

"Heavens! did I not see you the other day smile on the Duke of Orleans? or rather at what he said?"

"And what was he saying?"

"He said this, madame: 'Mazarin is a stumbling-block. Send him away and all will then be well.'"

"What do you wish me to do?"

"Oh, madame! you are the queen!"

"Queen, forsooth! when I am at the mercy of every scribbler in the Palais Royal who covers waste paper with nonsense, or of every country squire in the kingdom."

"Nevertheless, you have still the power of banishing from your presence those whom you do not like!"

"That is to say, whom you do not like," returned the queen.

"I! persons whom I do not like!"

"Yes, indeed. Who sent away Madame de Chevreuse after she had been persecuted twelve years under the last reign?"

"A woman of intrigue, who wanted to keep up against me the spirit of cabal she had raised against M. de Richelieu."

"Who dismissed Madame de Hautefort, that friend so loyal that she refused the favor of the king that she might remain in mine?"

"A prude, who told you every night, as she undressed you, that it was a sin to love a priest, just as if one were a priest because one happens to be a cardinal."

"Who ordered Monsieur de Beaufort to be arrested?"

"An incendiary the burden of whose song was his intention to assassinate me."

"You see, cardinal," replied the queen, "that your enemies are mine."

"That is not enough madame, it is necessary that your friends should be also mine."

"My friends, monsieur?" The queen shook her head. "Alas, I have them no longer!"

"How is it that you have no friends in your prosperity when you had many in adversity?"

"It is because in my prosperity I forgot those old friends, monsieur; because I have acted like Queen

Marie de Medicis, who, returning from her first exile, treated with contempt all those who had suffered for her and, being proscribed a second time, died at Cologne abandoned by every one, even by her own son."

"Well, let us see," said Mazarin; "isn't there still time to repair the evil? Search among your friends, your oldest friends."

"What do you mean, monsieur?"

"Nothing else than I say--search."

"Alas, I look around me in vain! I have no influence with any one. Monsieur is, as usual, led by his favorite; yesterday it was Choisy, to-day it is La Riviere, to-morrow it will be some one else. Monsieur le Prince is led by the coadjutor, who is led by Madame de Guemenee."

"Therefore, madame, I ask you to look, not among your friends of to-day, but among those of other times."

"Among my friends of other times?" said the queen.

"Yes, among your friends of other times; among those who aided you to contend against the Duc de Richelieu and even to conquer him."

"What is he aiming at?" murmured the queen, looking uneasily at the cardinal.

"Yes," continued his eminence; "under certain circumstances, with that strong and shrewd mind your majesty possesses, aided by your friends, you were able to repel the attacks of that adversary."

"I!" said the queen. "I suffered, that is all."

"Yes." said Mazarin, "as women suffer in avenging themselves. Come, let us come to the point. Do you know Monsieur de Rochefort?"

"One of my bitterest enemies--the faithful friend of Cardinal Richelieu."

"I know that, and we sent him to the Bastile," said Mazarin.

"Is he at liberty?" asked the queen.

"No; still there, but I only speak of him in order that I may introduce the name of another man. Do you know Monsieur d'Artagnan?" he added, looking steadfastly at the queen.

Anne of Austria received the blow with a beating heart.

"Has the Gascon been indiscreet?" she murmured to herself, then said aloud:

"D'Artagnan! stop an instant, the name seems certainly familiar. D'Artagnan! there was a musketeer who was in love with one of my women. Poor young creature! she was poisoned on my account."

"That's all you know of him?" asked Mazarin.

The queen looked at him, surprised.

"You seem, sir," she remarked, "to be making me undergo a course of cross-examination."

"Which you answer according to your fancy," replied Mazarin.

"Tell me your wishes and I will comply with them."

The queen spoke with some impatience.

"Well, madame," said Mazarin, bowing, "I desire that you give me a share in your friends, as I have shared with you the little industry and talent that Heaven has given me. The circumstances are grave and it will be necessary to act promptly."

"Still!" said the queen. "I thought that we were finally quit of Monsieur de Beaufort."

"Yes, you saw only the torrent that threatened to overturn everything and you gave no attention to the still water. There is, however, a proverb current in France relating to water which is quiet."

"Continue," said the queen.

"Well, then, madame, not a day passes in which I do not suffer affronts from your princes and your lordly servants, all of them automata who do not perceive that I wind up the spring that makes them move, nor do they see that beneath my quiet demeanor lies the still scorn of an injured, irritated man, who has sworn to himself to master them one of these days. We have arrested Monsieur de Beaufort, but he is the least dangerous among them. There is the Prince de Conde----"

"The hero of Rocroy. Do you think of him?"

"Yes, madame, often and often, but pazienza, as we say in Italy; next, after Monsieur de Conde, comes the Duke of Orleans."

"What are you saying? The first prince of the blood, the king's uncle!"

"No! not the first prince of the blood, not the king's uncle, but the base conspirator, the soul of every cabal, who pretends to lead the brave people who are weak enough to believe in the honor of a prince of the blood--not the prince nearest to the throne, not the king's uncle, I repeat, but the murderer of Chalais, of Montmorency and of Cinq-Mars, who is playing now the same game he played long ago and who thinks that he will win the game because he has a new adversary--instead of a man who threatened, a man who smiles. But he is mistaken; I shall not leave so near the queen that source of discord with which the deceased cardinal so often caused the anger of the king to rage above the boiling point."

Anne blushed and buried her face in her hands.

"What am I to do?" she said, bowed down beneath the voice of her tyrant.

"Endeavor to remember the names of those faithful servants who crossed the Channel, in spite of Monsieur de Richelieu, tracking the roads along which they passed by their blood, to bring back to your majesty certain jewels given by you to Buckingham."

Anne arose, full of majesty, and as if touched by a spring, and looking at the cardinal with the haughty dignity which in the days of her youth had made her so powerful: "You are insulting me!" she said.

"I wish," continued Mazarin, finishing, as it were, the speech this sudden movement of the queen had cut; "I wish, in fact, that you should now do for your husband what you formerly did for your lover."

"Again that accusation!" cried the queen. "I thought that calumny was stifled or extinct; you have spared me till now, but since you speak of it, once for all, I tell you----"

"Madame, I do not ask you to tell me," said Mazarin, astounded by this returning courage.

"I will tell you all," replied Anne. "Listen: there were in truth, at that epoch, four devoted hearts, four loyal spirits, four faithful swords, who saved more than my life--my honor----"

"Ah! you confess it!" exclaimed Mazarin.

"Is it only the guilty whose honor is at the sport of others, sir? and cannot women be dishonored by appearances? Yes, appearances were against me and I was about to suffer dishonor. However, I swear I was not guilty, I swear it by----"

The queen looked around her for some sacred object by which she could swear, and taking out of a cupboard hidden in the tapestry, a small coffer of rosewood set in silver, and laying it on the altar:

"I swear," she said, "by these sacred relics that Buckingham was not my lover."

"What relics are those by which you swear?" asked Mazarin, smiling. "I am incredulous."

The queen untied from around her throat a small golden key which hung there, and presented it to the cardinal.

"Open, sir," she said, "and look for yourself."

Mazarin opened the coffer; a knife, covered with rust, and two letters, one of which was stained with blood, alone met his gaze.

"What are these things?" he asked.

"What are these things?" replied Anne, with queen-like dignity, extending toward the open coffer an arm, despite the lapse of years, still beautiful. "These two letters are the only ones I ever wrote to him. This knife is the knife with which Felton stabbed him. Read the letters and see if I have lied or spoken the truth."

But Mazarin, notwithstanding this permission, instead of reading the letters, took the knife which the dying Buckingham had snatched out of the wound and sent by Laporte to the queen. The blade was red, for the blood had become rust; after a momentary examination during which the queen became as white as the cloth which covered the altar on which she was leaning, he put it back into the coffer with an involuntary shudder.

"It is well, madame, I believe your oath."

"No, no, read," exclaimed the queen, indignantly; "read, I command you, for I am resolved that everything shall be finished to-night and never will I recur to this subject again. Do you think," she said, with a ghastly smile, "that I shall be inclined to reopen this coffer to answer any future accusations?"

Mazarin, overcome by this determination, read the two letters. In one the queen asked for the ornaments back again. This letter had been conveyed by D'Artagnan and had arrived in time. The other was that which Laporte had placed in the hands of the Duke of Buckingham, warning him that he was about to be assassinated; that communication had arrived too late.

"It is well, madame," said Mazarin; "nothing can gainsay such testimony."

"Sir," replied the queen, closing the coffer and leaning her hand upon it, "if there is anything to be said, it is that I have always been ungrateful to the brave men who saved me--that I have given nothing to that gallant officer, D'Artagnan, you were speaking of just now, but my hand to kiss and this diamond."

As she spoke she extended her beautiful hand to the cardinal and showed him a superb diamond which sparkled on her finger.

"It appears," she resumed, "that he sold it---he sold it in order to save me another time--to be able to send a messenger to the duke to warn him of his danger--he sold it to Monsieur des Essarts, on whose finger I remarked it. I bought it from him, but it belongs to D'Artagnan. Give it back to him, sir, and since you have such a man in your service, make him useful."

"Thank you, madame," said Mazarin. "I will profit by the advice."

"And now," added the queen, her voice broken by her emotion, "have you any other question to ask me?"

"Nothing,"--the cardinal spoke in his most conciliatory manner--"except to beg of you to forgive my unworthy suspicions. I love you so tenderly that I cannot help being jealous, even of the past."

A smile, which was indefinable, passed over the lips of the queen.

"Since you have no further interrogations to make, leave me, I beseech you," she said. "I wish, after such a scene, to be alone."

Mazarin bent low before her.

"I will retire, madame. Do you permit me to return?"

"Yes, to-morrow."

The cardinal took the queen's hand and pressed it with an air of gallantry to his lips.

Scarcely had he left her when the queen went into her son's room, and inquired from Laporte if the king was in bed. Laporte pointed to the child, who was asleep.

Anne ascended the steps side of the bed and softly kissed the placid forehead of her son; then she retired as silently as she had come, merely saying to Laporte:

"Try, my dear Laporte, to make the king more courteous to Monsieur le Cardinal, to whom both he and I are under such important obligations."

5. The Gascon and the Italian.

Meanwhile the cardinal returned to his own room; and after asking Bernouin, who stood at the door, whether anything had occurred during his absence, and being answered in the negative, he desired that he might be left alone.

When he was alone he opened the door of the corridor and then that of the ante-chamber. There D'Artagnan was asleep upon a bench.

The cardinal went up to him and touched his shoulder. D'Artagnan started, awakened himself, and as he awoke, stood up exactly like a soldier under arms.

"Here I am," said he. "Who calls me?"

"I," said Mazarin, with his most smiling expression.

"I ask pardon of your eminence," said D'Artagnan, "but I was so fatigued----"

"Don't ask my pardon, monsieur," said Mazarin, "for you fatigued yourself in my service."

D'Artagnan admired Mazarin's gracious manner. "Ah," said he, between his teeth, "is there truth in the proverb that fortune comes while one sleeps?"

"Follow me, monsieur," said Mazarin.

"Come, come," murmured D'Artagnan, "Rochefort has kept his promise, but where in the devil is he?" And he searched the cabinet even to the smallest recesses, but there was no sign of Rochefort.

"Monsieur d'Artagnan," said the cardinal, sitting down on a fauteuil, "you have always seemed to me to be a brave and honorable man."

"Possibly," thought D'Artagnan, "but he has taken a long time to let me know his thoughts;" nevertheless, he bowed to the very ground in gratitude for Mazarin's compliment.

"Well," continued Mazarin, "the time has come to put to use your talents and your valor."

There was a sudden gleam of joy in the officer's eyes, which vanished immediately, for he knew nothing of Mazarin's purpose.

"Order, my lord," he said; "I am ready to obey your eminence."

"Monsieur d'Artagnan," continued the cardinal, "you performed sundry superb exploits in the last reign."

"Your eminence is too good to remember such trifles in my favor. It is true I fought with tolerable success."

"I don't speak of your warlike exploits, monsieur," said Mazarin; "although they gained you much reputation, they were surpassed by others."

D'Artagnan pretended astonishment.

"Well, you do not reply?" resumed Mazarin.

"I am waiting, my lord, till you tell me of what exploits you speak."

"I speak of the adventure--Eh, you know well what I mean."

"Alas, no, my lord!" replied D'Artagnan, surprised.

"You are discreet--so much the better. I speak of that adventure in behalf of the queen, of the ornaments, of the journey you made with three of your friends."

"Aha!" thought the Gascon; "is this a snare or not? Let me be on my guard."

And he assumed a look of stupidity which Mendori or Bellerose, two of the first actors of the day, might have envied.

"Bravo!" cried Mazarin; "they told me that you were the man I wanted. Come, let us see what you will do for me."

"Everything that your eminence may please to command me," was the reply.

"You will do for me what you have done for the queen?"

"Certainly," D'Artagnan said to himself, "he wishes to make me speak out. He's not more cunning than De Richelieu was! Devil take him!" Then he said aloud:

"The queen, my lord? I don't comprehend."

"You don't comprehend that I want you and your three friends to be of use to me?"

"Which of my friends, my lord?"

"Your three friends--the friends of former days."

"Of former days, my lord! In former days I had not only three friends, I had thirty; at two-and-twenty one calls every man one's friend."

"Well, sir," returned Mazarin, "prudence is a fine thing, but to-day you might regret having been too prudent."

"My lord, Pythagoras made his disciples keep silence for five years that they might learn to hold their tongues."

"But you have been silent for twenty years, sir. Speak, now the queen herself releases you from your promise."

"The queen!" said D'Artagnan, with an astonishment which this time was not pretended.

"Yes, the queen! And as a proof of what I say she commanded me to show you this diamond, which she thinks you know."

And so saying, Mazarin extended his hand to the officer, who sighed as he recognized the ring so gracefully given to him by the queen on the night of the ball at the Hotel de Ville and which she had repurchased from Monsieur des Essarts.

"'Tis true. I remember well that diamond, which belonged to the queen."

"You see, then, that I speak to you in the queen's name. Answer me without acting as if you were on the stage; your interests are concerned in your so doing."

"Faith, my lord, it is very necessary for me to make my fortune, your eminence has so long forgotten me."

"We need only a week to amend all that. Come, you are accounted for, you are here, but where are your friends?"

"I do not know, my lord. We have parted company this long time; all three have left the service."

"Where can you find them, then?"

"Wherever they are, that's my business."

"Well, now, what are your conditions, if I employ you?"

"Money, my lord, as much money as what you wish me to undertake will require. I remember too well how sometimes we were stopped for want of money, and but for that diamond, which I was obliged to sell, we should have remained on the road."

"The devil he does! Money! and a large sum!" said Mazarin. "Pray, are you aware that the king has no money in his treasury?"

"Do then as I did, my lord. Sell the crown diamonds. Trust me, don't let us try to do things cheaply. Great undertakings come poorly off with paltry means."

"Well," returned Mazarin, "we will satisfy you."

"Richelieu," thought D'Artagnan, "would have given me five hundred pistoles in advance."

"You will then be at my service?" asked Mazarin.

"Yes, if my friends agree."

"But if they refuse can I count on you?"

"I have never accomplished anything alone," said D'Artagnan, shaking his head.

"Go, then, and find them."

"What shall I say to them by way of inducement to serve your eminence?"

"You know them better than I. Adapt your promises to their respective characters."

"What shall I promise?"

"That if they serve me as well as they served the queen my gratitude shall be magnificent."

"But what are we to do?"

"Make your mind easy; when the time for action comes you shall be put in full possession of what I require from you; wait till that time arrives and find out your friends."

"My lord, perhaps they are not in Paris. It is even probable that I shall have to make a journey. I am only a lieutenant of musketeers, very poor, and journeys cost money.

"My intention," said Mazarin, "is not that you go with a great following; my plans require secrecy, and would be jeopardized by a too extravagant equipment."

"Still, my lord, I can't travel on my pay, for it is now three months behind; and I can't travel on my savings, for in my twenty-two years of service I have accumulated nothing but debts."

Mazarin remained some moments in deep thought, as if he were fighting with himself; then, going to a large cupboard closed with a triple lock, he took from it a bag of silver, and weighing it twice in his hands before he gave it to D'Artagnan:

"Take this," he said with a sigh, "'tis merely for your journey."

"If these are Spanish doubloons, or even gold crowns," thought D'Artagnan, "we shall yet be able to do business together." He saluted the cardinal and plunged the bag into the depths of an immense pocket.

"Well, then, all is settled; you are to set off," said the cardinal.

"Yes, my lord."

"Apropos, what are the names of your friends?"

"The Count de la Fere, formerly styled Athos; Monsieur du Vallon, whom we used to call Porthos; the Chevalier d'Herblay, now the Abbe d'Herblay, whom we styled Aramis----"

The cardinal smiled.

"Younger sons," he said, "who enlisted in the musketeers under feigned names in order not to lower their family names. Long swords but light purses. Was that it?"

"If, God willing, these swords should be devoted to the service of your eminence," said D'Artagnan, "I shall venture to express a wish, which is, that in its turn the purse of your eminence may become light and theirs heavy--for with these three men your eminence may rouse all Europe if you like."

"These Gascons," said the cardinal, laughing, "almost beat the Italians in effrontery."

"At all events," answered D'Artagnan, with a smile almost as crafty as the cardinal's, "they beat them when they draw their swords."

He then withdrew, and as he passed into the courtyard he stopped near a lamp and dived eagerly into the bag of money.

"Crown pieces only--silver pieces! I suspected it. Ah! Mazarin! Mazarin! thou hast no confidence in me! so much the worse for thee, for harm may come of it!"

Meanwhile the cardinal was rubbing his hands in great satisfaction.

"A hundred pistoles! a hundred pistoles! for a hundred pistoles I have discovered a secret for which Richelieu would have paid twenty thousand crowns; without reckoning the value of that diamond"--he cast a complacent look at the ring, which he had kept, instead of restoring to D'Artagnan--"which is worth, at least, ten thousand francs."

He returned to his room, and after depositing the ring in a casket filled with brilliants of every sort, for the cardinal was a connoisseur in precious stones, he called to Bernouin to undress him, regardless of the noises of gun-fire that, though it was now near midnight, continued to resound through Paris.

In the meantime D'Artagnan took his way toward the Rue Tiquetonne, where he lived at the Hotel de la Chevrette.

We will explain in a few words how D'Artagnan had been led to choose that place of residence.

6. D'Artagnan in his Fortieth Year.

Years have elapsed, many events have happened, alas! since, in our romance of "The Three Musketeers," we took leave of D'Artagnan at No. 12 Rue des Fossoyeurs. D'Artagnan had not failed in his career, but circumstances had been adverse to him. So long as he was surrounded by his friends he retained his youth and the poetry of his character. He was one of those fine, ingenuous natures which assimilate themselves easily to the dispositions of others. Athos imparted to him his greatness of soul, Porthos his enthusiasm, Aramis his elegance. Had D'Artagnan continued his intimacy with these three men he would have become a superior character. Athos was the first to leave him, in order that he might retire to a little property he had inherited near Blois; Porthos, the second, to marry an attorney's wife; and lastly, Aramis, the third, to take orders and become an abbe. From that day D'Artagnan felt lonely and powerless, without courage to pursue a career in which he could only distinguish himself on condition that each of his three companions should endow him with one of the gifts each had received from Heaven.

Notwithstanding his commission in the musketeers, D'Artagnan felt completely solitary. For a time the delightful remembrance of Madame Bonancieux left on his character a certain poetic tinge, perishable indeed; for like all other recollections in this world, these impressions were, by degrees, effaced. A garrison life is fatal even to the most aristocratic organization; and imperceptibly, D'Artagnan, always in the camp, always on horseback, always in garrison, became (I know not how in the present age one would express it) a typical trooper. His early refinement of character was not only not lost, it grew even greater than ever; but it was now applied to the little, instead of to the great things of life--to the martial condition of the soldier--comprised under the head of a good lodging, a rich table, a congenial hostess. These important advantages D'Artagnan found to his own taste in the Rue Tiquetonne at the sign of the Roe.

From the time D'Artagnan took quarters in that hotel, the mistress of the house, a pretty and fresh looking Flemish woman, twenty-five or twenty-six years old, had been singularly interested in him; and after certain love passages, much obstructed by an inconvenient husband to whom a dozen times D'Artagnan had made a pretence of passing a sword through his body, that husband had disappeared one fine morning, after furtively selling certain choice lots of wine, carrying away with him money and jewels. He was thought to be dead; his wife, especially, who cherished the pleasing idea that she was a widow, stoutly maintained that death had taken him. Therefore, after the connection had continued three years, carefully fostered by D'Artagnan, who found his bed and his mistress more agreeable every year, each doing credit to the other, the mistress conceived the extraordinary desire of becoming a wife and proposed to D'Artagnan that he should marry her.

"Ah, fie!" D'Artagnan replied. "Bigamy, my dear! Come now, you don't really wish it?"

"But he is dead; I am sure of it."

"He was a very contrary fellow and might come back on purpose to have us hanged."

"All right; if he comes back you will kill him, you are so skillful and so brave."

"Peste! my darling! another way of getting hanged."

"So you refuse my request?"

"To be sure I do--furiously!"

The pretty landlady was desolate. She would have taken D'Artagnan not only as her husband, but as her God, he was so handsome and had so fierce a mustache.

Then along toward the fourth year came the expedition of Franche-Comte. D'Artagnan was assigned to it and made his preparations to depart. There were then great griefs, tears without end and solemn promises to remain faithful--all of course on the part of the hostess. D'Artagnan was too grand to promise anything; he purposed only to do all that he could to increase the glory of his name.

As to that, we know D'Artagnan's courage; he exposed himself freely to danger and while charging at the head of his company he received a ball through the chest which laid him prostrate on the field of battle. He had been seen falling from his horse and had not been seen to rise; every one, therefore, believed him to be dead, especially those to whom his death would give promotion. One believes readily what he wishes to believe. Now in the army, from the division-generals who desire the death of the general-in-chief, to the soldiers who desire the death of the corporals, all desire some one's death.

But D'Artagnan was not a man to let himself be killed like that. After he had remained through the heat of the day unconscious on the battle-field, the cool freshness of the night brought him to himself. He gained a village, knocked at the door of the finest house and was received as the wounded are always and everywhere received in France. He was petted, tended, cured; and one fine morning, in better health than ever before, he set out for France. Once in France he turned his course toward Paris, and reaching Paris went straight to Rue Tiquetonne.

But D'Artagnan found in his chamber the personal equipment of a man, complete, except for the sword, arranged along the wall.

"He has returned," said he. "So much the worse, and so much the better!"

It need not be said that D'Artagnan was still thinking of the husband. He made inquiries and discovered that the servants were new and that the mistress had gone for a walk.

"Alone?" asked D'Artagnan.

"With monsieur."

"Monsieur has returned, then?"

"Of course," naively replied the servant.

"If I had any money," said D'Artagnan to himself, "I would go away; but I have none. I must stay and follow the advice of my hostess, while thwarting the conjugal designs of this inopportune apparition."

He had just completed this monologue--which proves that in momentous circumstances nothing is more natural than the monologue--when the servant-maid, watching at the door, suddenly cried out:

"Ah! see! here is madame returning with monsieur."

D'Artagnan looked out and at the corner of Rue Montmartre saw the hostess coming along hanging to the arm of an enormous Swiss, who tiptoed in his walk with a magnificent air which pleasantly reminded him of his old friend Porthos.

"Is that monsieur?" said D'Artagnan to himself. "Oh! oh! he has grown a good deal, it seems to me." And he sat down in the hall, choosing a conspicuous place.

The hostess, as she entered, saw D'Artagnan and uttered a little cry, whereupon D'Artagnan, judging that he had been recognized, rose, ran to her and embraced her tenderly. The Swiss, with an air of stupefaction, looked at the hostess, who turned pale.

"Ah, it is you, monsieur! What do you want of me?" she asked, in great distress.

"Is monsieur your cousin? Is monsieur your brother?" said D'Artagnan, not in the slightest degree embarrassed in the role he was playing. And without waiting for her reply he threw himself into the arms of the Helvetian, who received him with great coldness.

"Who is that man?" he asked.

The hostess replied only by gasps.

"Who is that Swiss?" asked D'Artagnan.

"Monsieur is going to marry me," replied the hostess, between two gasps.

"Your husband, then, is at last dead?"

"How does that concern you?" replied the Swiss.

"It concerns me much," said D'Artagnan, "since you cannot marry madame without my consent and since----"

"And since?" asked the Swiss.

"And since--I do not give it," said the musketeer.

The Swiss became as purple as a peony. He wore his elegant uniform, D'Artagnan was wrapped in a sort of gray cloak; the Swiss was six feet high, D'Artagnan was hardly more than five; the Swiss considered himself on his own ground and regarded D'Artagnan as an intruder.

"Will you go away from here?" demanded the Swiss, stamping violently, like a man who begins to be seriously angry.

"I? By no means!" said D'Artagnan.

"Some one must go for help," said a lad, who could not comprehend that this little man should make a stand against that other man, who was so large.

D'Artagnan, with a sudden accession of wrath, seized the lad by the ear and led him apart, with the injunction:

"Stay you where you are and don't you stir, or I will pull this ear off. As for you, illustrious descendant of William Tell, you will straightway get together your clothes which are in my room and which annoy me, and go out quickly to another lodging."

The Swiss began to laugh boisterously. "I go out?" he said. "And why?"

"Ah, very well!" said D'Artagnan; "I see that you understand French. Come then, and take a turn with me and I will explain."

The hostess, who knew D'Artagnan's skill with the sword, began to weep and tear her hair. D'Artagnan turned toward her, saying, "Then send him away, madame."

"Pooh!" said the Swiss, who had needed a little time to take in D'Artagnan's proposal, "pooh! who are you, in the first place, to ask me to take a turn with you?"

"I am lieutenant in his majesty's musketeers," said D'Artagnan, "and consequently your superior in everything; only, as the question now is not of rank, but of quarters--you know the custom--come and seek for yours; the first to return will recover his chamber."

D'Artagnan led away the Swiss in spite of lamentations on the part of the hostess, who in reality found her heart inclining toward her former lover, though she would not have been sorry to give a lesson to that haughty musketeer who had affronted her by the refusal of her hand.

It was night when the two adversaries reached the field of battle. D'Artagnan politely begged the Swiss to yield to him the disputed chamber; the Swiss refused by shaking his head, and drew his sword.

"Then you will lie here," said D'Artagnan. "It is a wretched bed, but that is not my fault, and it is you who have chosen it." With these words he drew in his turn and crossed swords with his adversary.

He had to contend against a strong wrist, but his agility was superior to all force. The Swiss received two wounds and was not aware of it, by reason of the cold; but suddenly feebleness, occasioned by loss of blood, obliged him to sit down.

"There!" said: D'Artagnan, "what did I tell you? Fortunately, you won't be laid up more than a fortnight. Remain here and I will send you your clothes by the boy. Good-by! Oh, by the way, you'd better take lodging in the Rue Montorgueil at the Chat Qui Pelote. You will be well fed there, if the hostess remains the same. Adieu."

Thereupon he returned in a lively mood to his room and sent to the Swiss the things that belonged to him. The boy found him sitting where D'Artagnan had left him, still overwhelmed by the coolness of his adversary.

The boy, the hostess, and all the house had the same regard for D'Artagnan that one would have for Hercules should he return to earth to repeat his twelve labors.

But when he was alone with the hostess he said: "Now, pretty Madeleine, you know the difference between a Swiss and a gentleman. As for you, you have acted like a barmaid. So much the worse for you, for by such conduct you have lost my esteem and my patronage. I have driven away the Swiss to humiliate you, but I shall lodge here no longer. I will not sleep where I must scorn. Ho, there, boy! Have my valise carried to the Muid d'Amour, Rue des Bourdonnais. Adieu, madame."

In saying these words D'Artagnan appeared at the same time majestic and grieved. The hostess threw herself at his feet, asked his pardon and held him back with a sweet violence. What more need be said? The spit turned, the stove roared, the pretty Madeleine wept; D'Artagnan felt himself invaded by hunger, cold and love. He pardoned, and having pardoned he remained.

And this explains how D'Artagnan had quarters in the Rue Tiquetonne, at the Hotel de la Chevrette.

D'Artagnan then returned home in thoughtful mood, finding a somewhat lively pleasure in carrying Mazarin's bag of money and thinking of that fine diamond which he had once called his own and which he had seen on the minister's finger that night.

"Should that diamond ever fall into my hands again," he reflected, "I would turn it at once into money; I would buy with the proceeds certain lands around my father's chateau, which is a pretty place, well enough, but with no land to it at all, except a garden about the size of the Cemetery des Innocents; and I should wait in all my glory till some rich heiress, attracted by my good looks, rode along to marry me. Then I should like to have three sons; I should make the first a nobleman, like Athos; the second a good soldier, like Porthos; the third an excellent abbe, like Aramis. Faith! that would be a far better life than I lead now; but Monsieur Mazarin is a mean wretch, who won't dispossess himself of his diamond in my favor."

On entering the Rue Tiquetonne he heard a tremendous noise and found a dense crowd near the house.

"Oho!" said he, "is the hotel on fire?" On approaching the hotel of the Roe he found, however, that it was in front of the next house the mob was collected. The people were shouting and running about with torches. By the light of one of these torches D'Artagnan perceived men in uniform.

He asked what was going on.

He was told that twenty citizens, headed by one man, had attacked a carriage which was escorted by a troop of the cardinal's bodyguard; but a reinforcement having come up, the assailants had been put to flight and the leader had taken refuge in the hotel next to his lodgings; the house was now being searched.

In his youth D'Artagnan had often headed the bourgeoisie against the military, but he was cured of all those hot-headed propensities; besides, he had the cardinal's hundred pistoles in his pocket, so he went into the hotel without a word. There he found Madeleine alarmed for his safety and anxious to tell him all the events of the evening, but he cut her short by ordering her to put his supper in his room and give him with it a bottle of good Burgundy.

He took his key and candle and went upstairs to his bedroom. He had been contented, for the convenience of the house, to lodge in the fourth story; and truth obliges us even to confess that his chamber was just above the gutter and below the roof. His first care on entering it was to lock up in an old bureau with a new lock his bag of money, and then as soon as supper was ready he sent away the waiter who brought it up and sat down to table.

Not to reflect on what had passed, as one might fancy. No, D'Artagnan considered that things are never well done when they are not reserved to their proper time. He was hungry; he supped, he went to bed. Neither was he one of those who think that the necessary silence of the night brings counsel with it. In the night he slept, but in the morning, refreshed and calm, he was inspired with his clearest views of everything. It was long since he had any reason for his morning's inspiration, but he always slept all night long. At daybreak he awoke and took a turn around his room.

"In '43," he said, "just before the death of the late cardinal, I received a letter from Athos. Where was I then? Let me see. Oh! at the siege of Besancon I was in the trenches. He told me--let me think--what was it? That he was living on a small estate--but where? I was just reading the name of the place when the wind blew my letter away, I suppose to the Spaniards; there's no use in thinking any more about Athos. Let me see: with regard to Porthos, I received a letter from him, too. He invited me to a hunting party on his property in the month of September, 1646. Unluckily, as I was then in Bearn, on account of my father's death, the letter followed me there. I had left Bearn when it arrived and I never received it until the month of April, 1647; and as the invitation was for September, 1646, I couldn't accept it. Let me look for this letter; it must be with my title deeds."

D'Artagnan opened an old casket which stood in a corner of the room, and which was full of parchments referring to an estate during a period of two hundred years lost to his family. He uttered an exclamation of delight, for the large handwriting of Porthos was discernible, and underneath some lines traced by his worthy spouse.

D'Artagnan eagerly searched for the heading of this letter; it was dated from the Chateau du Vallon.

Porthos had forgotten that any other address was necessary; in his pride he fancied that every one must know the Chateau du Vallon.

"Devil take the vain fellow," said D'Artagnan. "However, I had better find him out first, since he can't want money. Athos must have become an idiot by this time from drinking. Aramis must have worn himself to a shadow of his former self by constant genuflexion."

He cast his eyes again on the letter. There was a postscript:

"I write by the same courier to our worthy friend Aramis in his convent."

"In his convent! What convent? There are about two hundred in Paris and three thousand in France; and then, perhaps, on entering the convent he changed his name. Ah! if I were but learned in theology I should recollect what it was he used to dispute about with the curate of Montdidier and the superior of the Jesuits, when we were at Crevecoeur; I should know what doctrine he leans to and I should glean from that what saint he has adopted as his patron.

"Well, suppose I go back to the cardinal and ask him for a passport into all the convents one can find, even into the nunneries? It would be a curious idea, and maybe I should find my friend under the name of Achilles. But, no! I should lose myself in the cardinal's opinion. Great people only thank you for doing the impossible; what's possible, they say, they can effect themselves, and they are right. But let us wait a little and reflect. I received a letter from him, the dear fellow, in which he even asked me for some small service, which, in fact, I rendered him. Yes, yes; but now what did I do with that letter?"

D'Artagnan thought a moment and then went to the wardrobe in which hung his old clothes. He looked for his doublet of the year 1648 and as he had orderly habits, he found it hanging on its nail. He felt in the pocket and drew from it a paper; it was the letter of Aramis:

"Monsieur D'Artagnan: You know that I have had a quarrel with a certain gentleman, who has given me an appointment for this evening in the Place Royale. As I am of the church, and the affair might injure me if I should share it with any other than a sure friend like you, I write to beg that you will serve me as second.

"You will enter by the Rue Neuve Sainte Catherine; under the second lamp on the right you will find your adversary. I shall be with mine under the third.

"Wholly yours,

"Aramis."

D'Artagnan tried to recall his remembrances. He had gone to the rendezvous, had encountered there the adversary indicated, whose name he had never known, had given him a pretty sword-stroke on the arm, then had gone toward Aramis, who at the same time came to meet him, having already finished his affair. "It is over," Aramis had said. "I think I have killed the insolent fellow. But, dear friend, if you ever need me you know that I am entirely devoted to you." Thereupon Aramis had given him a clasp of the hand and had disappeared under the arcades.

So, then, he no more knew where Aramis was than where Athos and Porthos were, and the affair was becoming a matter of great perplexity, when he fancied he heard a pane of glass break in his room window. He thought directly of his bag and rushed from the inner room where he was sleeping. He was not mistaken; as he entered his bedroom a man was getting in by the window.

"Ah! you scoundrel!" cried D'Artagnan, taking the man for a thief and seizing his sword.

"Sir!" cried the man, "in the name of Heaven put your sword back into the sheath and don't kill me unheard. I'm no thief, but an honest citizen, well off in the world, with a house of my own. My name is--ah! but surely you are Monsieur d'Artagnan?"

"And thou--Planchet!" cried the lieutenant.

"At your service, sir," said Planchet, overwhelmed with joy; "if I were still capable of serving you."

"Perhaps so," replied D'Artagnan. "But why the devil dost thou run about the tops of houses at seven o'clock of the morning in the month of January?"

"Sir," said Planchet, "you must know; but, perhaps you ought not to know----"

"Tell us what," returned D'Artagnan, "but first put a napkin against the window and draw the curtains."

"Sir," said the prudent Planchet, "in the first place, are you on good terms with Monsieur de Rochefort?"

"Perfectly; one of my dearest friends."

"Ah! so much the better!"

"But what has De Rochefort to do with this manner you have of invading my room?"

"Ah, sir! I must first tell you that Monsieur de Rochefort is----"

Planchet hesitated.

"Egad, I know where he is," said D'Artagnan. "He's in the Bastile."

"That is to say, he was there," replied Planchet. "But in returning thither last night, when fortunately you did not accompany him, as his carriage was crossing the Rue de la Ferronnerie his guards insulted the people, who began to abuse them. The prisoner thought this a good opportunity for escape; he called out his name and cried for help. I was there. I heard the name of Rochefort. I remembered him well. I said in a loud voice that he was a prisoner, a friend of the Duc de Beaufort, who called for help. The people were infuriated; they stopped the horses and cut the escort to pieces, whilst I opened the doors of the carriage and Monsieur de Rochefort jumped out and soon was lost amongst the crowd. At this moment a patrol passed by. I was obliged to sound a retreat toward the Rue Tiquetonne; I was pursued and took refuge in the house next to this, where I have been concealed between two mattresses. This morning I ventured to run along the gutters and----"

"Well," interrupted D'Artagnan, "I am delighted that De Rochefort is free, but as for thee, if thou shouldst fall into the hands of the king's servants they will hang thee without mercy. Nevertheless, I promise thee thou shalt be hidden here, though I risk by concealing thee neither more nor less than my lieutenancy, if it was found out that I gave one rebel an asylum."

"Ah! sir, you know well I would risk my life for you."

"Thou mayst add that thou hast risked it, Planchet. I have not forgotten all I owe thee. Sit down there and eat in security. I see thee cast expressive glances at the remains of my supper."

"Yes, sir; for all I've had since yesterday was a slice of bread and butter, with preserves on it. Although I don't despise sweet things in proper time and place, I found the supper rather light."

"Poor fellow!" said D'Artagnan. "Well, come; set to."

"Ah, sir, you are going to save my life a second time!" cried Planchet.

And he seated himself at the table and ate as he did in the merry days of the Rue des Fossoyeurs, whilst D'Artagnan walked to and fro and thought how he could make use of Planchet under present circumstances. While he turned this over in his mind Planchet did his best to make up for lost time at table. At last he uttered a sigh of satisfaction and paused, as if he had partially appeased his hunger.

"Come," said D'Artagnan, who thought that it was now a convenient time to begin his interrogations, "dost thou know where Athos is?"

"No, sir," replied Planchet.

"The devil thou dost not! Dost know where Porthos is?"

"No--not at all."

"And Aramis?"

"Not in the least."

"The devil! the devil! the devil!"

"But, sir," said Planchet, with a look of shrewdness, "I know where Bazin is."

"Where is he?"

"At Notre Dame."

"What has he to do at Notre Dame?"

"He is beadle."

"Bazin beadle at Notre Dame! He must know where his master is!"

"Without a doubt he must."

D'Artagnan thought for a moment, then took his sword and put on his cloak to go out.

"Sir," said Planchet, in a mournful tone, "do you abandon me thus to my fate? Think, if I am found out here, the people of the house, who have not seen me enter it, will take me for a thief."

"True," said D'Artagnan. "Let's see. Canst thou speak any patois?"

"I can do something better than that, sir, I can speak Flemish."

"Where the devil didst thou learn it?"

"In Artois, where I fought for years. Listen, sir. Goeden morgen, mynheer, eth teen begeeray le weeten the ge sond heets omstand."

"Which means?"

"Good-day, sir! I am anxious to know the state of your health."

"He calls that a language! But never mind, that will do capitally."

D'Artagnan opened the door and called out to a waiter to desire Madeleine to come upstairs.

When the landlady made her appearance she expressed much astonishment at seeing Planchet.

"My dear landlady," said D'Artagnan, "I beg to introduce to you your brother, who is arrived from Flanders and whom I am going to take into my service."

"My brother?"

"Wish your sister good-morning, Master Peter."

"Wilkom, suster," said Planchet.

"Goeden day, broder," replied the astonished landlady.

"This is the case," said D'Artagnan; "this is your brother, Madeleine; you don't know him perhaps, but I know him; he has arrived from Amsterdam. You must dress him up during my absence. When I return, which will be in about an hour, you must offer him to me as a servant, and upon your recommendation, though he doesn't speak a word of French, I take him into my service. You understand?"

"That is to say, I guess your wishes, and that is all that's necessary," said Madeleine.

"You are a precious creature, my pretty hostess, and I am much obliged to you."

The next moment D'Artagnan was on his way to Notre Dame.

7. Touches upon the Strange Effects a Half-pistole may have.

D'Artagnan, as he crossed the Pont Neuf, congratulated himself on having found Planchet again, for at that time an intelligent servant was essential to him; nor was he sorry that through Planchet and the situation which he held in Rue des Lombards, a connection with the bourgeoisie might be commenced, at that critical period when that class were preparing to make war with the court party. It was like having a spy in the enemy's camp. In this frame of mind, grateful for the accidental meeting with Planchet, pleased with himself, D'Artagnan reached Notre Dame. He ran up the steps, entered the church, and addressing a verger who was sweeping the chapel, asked him if he knew Monsieur Bazin.

"Monsieur Bazin, the beadle?" said the verger. "Yes. There he is, attending mass, in the chapel of the Virgin."

D'Artagnan nearly jumped for joy; he had despaired of finding Bazin, but now, he thought, since he held one end of the thread he would be pretty sure to reach the other end.

He knelt down just opposite the chapel in order not to lose sight of his man; and as he had almost forgotten his prayers and had omitted to take a book with him, he made use of his time in gazing at Bazin.

Bazin wore his dress, it may be observed, with equal dignity and saintly propriety. It was not difficult to understand that he had gained the crown of his ambition and that the silver-mounted wand he brandished was in his eyes as honorable a distinction as the marshal's baton which Conde threw, or did not throw, into the enemy's line of battle at Fribourg. His person had undergone a change, analogous to the change in his dress; his figure had grown rotund and, as it were, canonical. The striking points of his face were effaced; he had still a nose, but his cheeks, fattened out, each took a portion of it unto themselves; his chin had joined his throat; his eyes were swelled up with the puffiness of his cheeks; his hair, cut straight in holy guise, covered his forehead as far as his eyebrows.

The officiating priest was just finishing mass whilst D'Artagnan was looking at Bazin; he pronounced the words of the holy Sacrament and retired, giving the benediction, which was received by the kneeling communicants, to the astonishment of D'Artagnan, who recognized in the priest the coadjutor[1] himself, the famous Jean Francois Gondy, who at that time, having a presentiment of the part he was to play, was beginning to court popularity by almsgiving. It was to this end that he performed from time to time some of those early masses which the common people, generally, alone attended.

D'Artagnan knelt as well as the rest, received his share of the benediction and made the sign of the cross; but when Bazin passed in his turn, with his eyes raised to Heaven and walking, in all humility, the very last, D'Artagnan pulled him by the hem of his robe.

Bazin looked down and started, as if he had seen a serpent.

"Monsieur d'Artagnan!" he cried; "Vade retro Satanas!"

"So, my dear Bazin!" said the officer, laughing, "this is the way you receive an old friend."

"Sir," replied Bazin, "the true friends of a Christian are those who aid him in working out his salvation, not those who hinder him in doing so."

"I don't understand you, Bazin; nor can I see how I can be a stumbling-block in the way of your salvation," said D'Artagnan.

"You forget, sir, that you very nearly ruined forever that of my master; and that it was owing to you that he was very nearly being damned eternally for remaining a musketeer, whilst all the time his true vocation was the church."

"My dear Bazin, you ought to perceive," said D'Artagnan, "from the place in which you find me, that I am greatly changed in everything. Age produc-

---

[1] A sacerdotal officer.

es good sense, and, as I doubt not but that your master is on the road to salvation, I want you to tell me where he is, that he may help me to mine."

"Rather say, to take him back with you into the world. Fortunately, I don't know where he is."

"How!" cried D'Artagnan; "you don't know where Aramis is?"

"Formerly," replied Bazin, "Aramis was his name of perdition. By Aramis is meant Simara, which is the name of a demon. Happily for him he has ceased to bear that name."

"And therefore," said D'Artagnan, resolved to be patient to the end, "it is not Aramis I seek, but the Abbe d'Herblay. Come, my dear Bazin, tell me where he is."

"Didn't you hear me tell you, Monsieur d'Artagnan, that I don't know where he is?"

"Yes, certainly; but to that I answer that it is impossible."

"It is, nevertheless, the truth, monsieur--the pure truth, the truth of the good God."

D'Artagnan saw clearly that he would get nothing out of this man, who was evidently telling a falsehood in his pretended ignorance of the abode of Aramis, but whose lies were bold and decided.

"Well, Bazin," said D'Artagnan, "since you do not know where your master lives, let us speak of it no more; let us part good friends. Accept this half-pistole to drink to my health."

"I do not drink"--Bazin pushed away with dignity the officer's hand--"'tis good only for the laity."

"Incorruptible!" murmured D'Artagnan; "I am unlucky;" and whilst he was lost in thought Bazin retreated toward the sacristy, and even there he could not think himself safe until he had shut and locked the door behind him.

D'Artagnan was still in deep thought when some one touched him on the shoulder. He turned and was about to utter an exclamation of surprise when the other made to him a sign of silence.

"You here, Rochefort?" he said, in a low voice.

"Hush!" returned Rochefort. "Did you know that I am at liberty?"

"I knew it from the fountain-head--from Planchet. And what brought you here?"

"I came to thank God for my happy deliverance," said Rochefort.

"And nothing more? I suppose that is not all."

"To take my orders from the coadjutor and to see if we cannot wake up Mazarin a little."

"A bad plan; you'll be shut up again in the Bastile."

"Oh, as to that, I shall take care, I assure you. The air, the fresh, free air is so good; besides," and Rochefort drew a deep breath as he spoke, "I am going into the country to make a tour."

"Stop," cried D'Artagnan; "I, too, am going."

"And if I may without impertinence ask--where are you going?"

"To seek my friends."

"What friends?"

"Those that you asked about yesterday."

"Athos, Porthos and Aramis--you are looking for them?"

"Yes."

"On honor?"

"What, then, is there surprising in that?"

"Nothing. Queer, though. And in whose behalf are you looking for them?"

"You are in no doubt on that score."

"That is true."

"Unfortunately, I have no idea where they are."

"And you have no way to get news of them? Wait a week and I myself will give you some."

"A week is too long. I must find them within three days."

"Three days are a short time and France is large."

"No matter; you know the word must; with that word great things are done."

"And when do you set out?"

"I am now on my road."

"Good luck to you."

"And to you--a good journey."

"Perhaps we shall meet on our road."

"That is not probable."

"Who knows? Chance is so capricious. Adieu, till we meet again! Apropos, should Mazarin speak to you about me, tell him that I should have requested you to acquaint him that in a short time he will see whether I am, as he says, too old for action."

And Rochefort went away with one of those diabolical smiles which used formerly to make D'Artagnan shudder, but D'Artagnan could now see it without alarm, and smiling in his turn, with an expression of melancholy which the recollections called up by that smile could, perhaps, alone give to his countenance, he said:

"Go, demon, do what thou wilt! It matters little now to me. There's no second Constance in the world."

On his return to the cathedral, D'Artagnan saw Bazin, who was conversing with the sacristan. Bazin was making, with his spare little short arms, ridiculous gestures. D'Artagnan perceived that he was enforcing prudence with respect to himself.

D'Artagnan slipped out of the cathedral and placed himself in ambuscade at the corner of the Rue des Canettes; it was impossible that Bazin should go out of the cathedral without his seeing him.

In five minutes Bazin made his appearance, looking in every direction to see if he were observed, but he saw no one. Calmed by appearances he ventured to walk on through the Rue Notre Dame. Then D'Artagnan rushed out of his hiding place and arrived in time to see Bazin turn down the Rue de la Juiverie and enter, in the Rue de la Calandre, a respectable looking house; and this D'Artagnan felt no doubt was the habitation of the worthy beadle. Afraid of making any inquiries at this house, D'Artagnan entered a small tavern at the corner of the street and asked for a cup of hypocras. This beverage required a good half-hour to prepare. And D'Artagnan had time, therefore, to watch Bazin unsuspected.

He perceived in the tavern a pert boy between twelve and fifteen years of age whom he fancied he had seen not twenty minutes before under the guise of a chorister. He questioned him, and as the boy had no interest in deceiving, D'Artagnan learned that he exercised, from six o'clock in the morning until nine, the office of chorister, and from nine o'clock till midnight that of a waiter in the tavern.

Whilst he was talking to this lad a horse was brought to the door of Bazin's house. It was saddled and bridled. Almost immediately Bazin came downstairs.

"Look!" said the boy, "there's our beadle, who is going a journey."

"And where is he going?" asked D'Artagnan.

"Forsooth, I don't know."

"Half a pistole if you can find out," said D'Artagnan.

"For me?" cried the boy, his eyes sparkling with joy, "if I can find out where Bazin is going? That is not difficult. You are not joking, are you?"

"No, on the honor of an officer; there is the half-pistole;" and he showed him the seductive coin, but did not give it him.

"I shall ask him."

"Just the very way not to know. Wait till he is set out and then, marry, come up, ask, and find out. The half-pistole is ready," and he put it back again into his pocket.

"I understand," said the child, with that jeering smile which marks especially the "gamin de Paris." "Well, we must wait."

They had not long to wait. Five minutes afterward Bazin set off on a full trot, urging on his horse by the blows of a parapluie, which he was in the habit of using instead of a riding whip.

Scarcely had he turned the corner of the Rue de la Juiverie when the boy rushed after him like a bloodhound on full scent.

Before ten minutes had elapsed the child returned.

"Well!" said D'Artagnan.

"Well!" answered the boy, "the thing is done."

"Where is he gone?"

"The half-pistole is for me?"

"Doubtless, answer me."

"I want to see it. Give it me, that I may see it is not false."

"There it is."

The child put the piece of money into his pocket.

"And now, where is he gone?" inquired D'Artagnan.

"He is gone to Noisy."

"How dost thou know?"

"Ah, faith! there was no great cunning necessary. I knew the horse he rode; it belonged to the butcher, who lets it out now and then to M. Bazin. Now I thought that the butcher would not let his horse out like that without knowing where it was going. And he answered 'that Monsieur Bazin went to Noisy.' 'Tis his custom. He goes two or three times a week."

"Dost thou know Noisy well?"

"I think so, truly; my nurse lives there."

"Is there a convent at Noisy?"

"Isn't there a great and grand one--the convent of Jesuits?"

"What is thy name?"

"Friquet."

D'Artagnan wrote the child's name in his tablets.

"Please, sir," said the boy, "do you think I can gain any more half-pistoles in any way?"

"Perhaps," replied D'Artagnan.

And having got out all he wanted, he paid for the hypocras, which he did not drink, and went quickly back to the Rue Tiquetonne.

8. D'Artagnan, Going to a Distance to discover Aramis.

On entering the hotel D'Artagnan saw a man sitting in a corner by the fire. It was Planchet, but so completely transformed, thanks to the old clothes that the departing husband had left behind, that D'Artagnan himself could hardly recognize him. Madeleine introduced him in presence of all the servants. Planchet addressed the officer with a fine Flemish phrase; the officer replied in words that belonged to no language at all, and the bargain was concluded; Madeleine's brother entered D'Artagnan's service.

The plan adopted by D'Artagnan was soon perfected. He resolved not to reach Noisy in the day, for fear of being recognized; he had therefore plenty of time before him, for Noisy is only three or four leagues from Paris, on the road to Meaux.

He began his day by breakfasting substantially--a bad beginning when one wants to employ the head, but an excellent precaution when one wants to work the body; and about two o'clock he had his two horses saddled, and followed by Planchet he quitted Paris by the Barriere de la Villete. A most active search was still prosecuted in the house near the Hotel de la Chevrette for the discovery of Planchet.

At about a league and a half from the city, D'Artagnan, finding that in his impatience he had set out too soon, stopped to give the horses breathing time. The inn was full of disreputable looking people, who seemed as if they were on the point of commencing some nightly expedition. A man, wrapped in a cloak, appeared at the door, but seeing a stranger he beckoned to his companions, and two men who were drinking in the inn went out to speak to him.

D'Artagnan, on his side, went up to the landlady, praised her wine--which was a horrible production from the country of Montreuil--and heard from her that there were only two houses of importance in the village; one of these belonged to the Archbishop of Paris, and was at that time the abode of his niece the Duchess of Longueville; the other was a convent of Jesuits and was the property--a by no means unusual circumstance--of these worthy fathers.

At four o'clock D'Artagnan recommenced his journey. He proceeded slowly and in deep reverie. Planchet also was lost in thought, but the subject of their reflections was not the same.

One word which their landlady had pronounced had given a particular turn to D'Artagnan's deliberations; this was the name of Madame de Longueville.

That name was indeed one to inspire imagination and produce thought. Madame de Longueville was one of the highest ladies in the realm; she was also one of the greatest beauties at court. She had formerly been suspected of an intimacy of too tender a nature with Coligny, who, for her sake, had been killed in a duel, in the Place Royale, by the Duc de Guise. She was now connected by bonds of a political nature with the Prince de Marsillac, the eldest son of the old Duc de Rochefoucauld, whom she was trying to inspire with an enmity toward the Duc de Conde, her brother-in-law, whom she now hated mortally.

D'Artagnan thought of all these matters. He remembered how at the Louvre he had often seen, as she passed by him in the full radiance of her dazzling charms, the beautiful Madame de Longueville. He thought of Aramis, who, without possessing any greater advantages than himself, had formerly been the lover of Madame de Chevreuse, who had been to a former court what Madame de Longueville was in that day; and he wondered how it was that there should be in the world people who succeed in every wish, some in ambition, others in love, whilst others, either from chance, or from ill-luck, or from some natural defect or impediment, remain half-way upon the road toward fulfilment of their hopes and expectations.

He was confessing to himself that he belonged to the latter unhappy class, when Planchet approached and said:

"I will lay a wager, your honor, that you and I are thinking of the same thing."

"I doubt it, Planchet," replied D'Artagnan, "but what are you thinking of?"

"I am thinking, sir, of those desperate looking men who were drinking in the inn where we rested."

"Always cautious, Planchet."

"'Tis instinct, your honor."

"Well, what does your instinct tell you now?"

"Sir, my instinct told me that those people were assembled there for some bad purpose; and I was reflecting on what my instinct had told me, in the darkest corner of the stable, when a man wrapped in a cloak and followed by two other men, came in."

"Ah ah!" said D'Artagnan, Planchet's recital agreeing with his own observations. "Well?"

"One of these two men said, 'He must certainly be at Noisy, or be coming there this evening, for I have seen his servant.'

"'Art thou sure?' said the man in the cloak.

"'Yes, my prince.'"

"My prince!" interrupted D'Artagnan.

"Yes, 'my prince;' but listen. 'If he is here'--this is what the other man said--'let's see decidedly what to do with him.'

"'What to do with him?' answered the prince.

"'Yes, he's not a man to allow himself to be taken anyhow; he'll defend himself.'

"'Well, we must try to take him alive. Have you cords to bind him with and a gag to stop his mouth?'

"'We have.'

"'Remember that he will most likely be disguised as a horseman.'

"'Yes, yes, my lord; don't be uneasy.'

"'Besides, I shall be there.'

"'You will assure us that justice----'

"'Yes, yes! I answer for all that,' the prince said.

"'Well, then, we'll do our best.' Having said that, they went out of the stable."

"Well, what matters all that to us?" said D'Artagnan. "This is one of those attempts that happen every day."

"Are you sure that we are not its objects?"

"We? Why?"

"Just remember what they said. 'I have seen his servant,' said one, and that applies very well to me."

"Well?"

"'He must certainly be at Noisy, or be coming there this evening,' said the other; and that applies very well to you."

"What else?"

"Then the prince said: 'Take notice that in all probability he will be disguised as a cavalier;' which seems to me to leave no room for doubt, since you are dressed as a cavalier and not as an officer of musketeers. Now then, what do you say to that?"

"Alas! my dear Planchet," said D'Artagnan, sighing, "we are unfortunately no longer in those times in which princes would care to assassinate me. Those were good old days; never fear--these people owe us no grudge."

"Is your honor sure?"

"I can answer for it they do not."

"Well, we won't speak of it any more, then;" and Planchet took his place in D'Artagnan's suite with that sublime confidence he had always had in his master, which even fifteen years of separation had not destroyed.

They had traveled onward about half a mile when Planchet came close up to D'Artagnan.

"Stop, sir, look yonder," he whispered; "don't you see in the darkness something pass by, like shadows? I fancy I hear horses' feet."

"Impossible!" returned D'Artagnan. "The ground is soaking wet; yet I fancy, as thou sayest, that I see something."

At this moment the neighing of a horse struck his ear, coming through darkness and space.

"There are men somewhere about, but that's of no consequence to us," said D'Artagnan; "let us ride onward."

At about half-past eight o'clock they reached the first houses in Noisy; every one was in bed and not a light was to be seen in the village. The obscurity was broken only now and then by the still darker lines of the roofs of houses. Here and there a dog barked behind a door or an affrighted cat fled precipitately from the midst of the pavement to take refuge behind a pile of faggots, from which retreat her eyes would shine like peridores. These were the only living creatures that seemed to inhabit the village.

Toward the middle of the town, commanding the principal open space, rose a dark mass, separated from the rest of the world by two lanes and overshadowed in the front by enormous lime-trees. D'Artagnan looked attentively at the building.

"This," he said to Planchet, "must be the archbishop's chateau, the abode of the fair Madame de Longueville; but the convent, where is that?"

"The convent, your honor, is at the other end of the village; I know it well."

"Well, then, Planchet, gallop up to it whilst I tighten my horse's girth, and come back and tell me if there is a light in any of the Jesuits' windows."

In about five minutes Planchet returned.

"Sir," he said, "there is one window of the convent lighted up."

"Hem! If I were a 'Frondeur,'" said D'Artagnan, "I should knock here and should be sure of a good supper. If I were a monk I should knock yonder and should have a good supper there, too; whereas, 'tis very possible that between the castle and the convent we shall sleep on hard beds, dying with hunger and thirst."

"Yes," added Planchet, "like the famous ass of Buridan. Shall I knock?"

"Hush!" replied D'Artagnan; "the light no longer burns in yonder window."

"Do you hear nothing?" whispered Planchet.

"What is that noise?"

There came a sound like a whirlwind, at the same time two troops of horsemen, each composed of ten men, sallied forth from each of the lanes which encompassed the house and surrounded D'Artagnan and Planchet.

"Heyday!" cried D'Artagnan, drawing his sword and taking refuge behind his horse; "are you not mistaken? is it really for us that you mean your attack?"

"Here he is! we have him!" cried the horsemen, rushing on D'Artagnan with naked swords.

"Don't let him escape!" said a loud voice.

"No, my lord; be assured we shall not."

D'Artagnan thought it was now time for him to join in the conversation.

"Halloo, gentlemen!" he called out in his Gascon accent, "what do you want? what do you demand?"

"That thou shalt soon know," shouted a chorus of horsemen.

"Stop, stop!" cried he whom they had addressed as "my lord;" "'tis not his voice."

"Ah! just so, gentlemen! pray, do people get into a passion at random at Noisy? Take care, for I warn you that the first man that comes within the length of my sword--and my sword is long--I rip him up."

The chieftain of the party drew near.

"What are you doing here?" he asked in a lofty tone, as that of one accustomed to command.

"And you--what are you doing here?" replied D'Artagnan.

"Be civil, or I shall beat you; for although one may not choose to proclaim oneself, one insists on respect suitable to one's rank."

"You don't choose to discover yourself, because you are the leader of an ambuscade," returned D'Artagnan; "but with regard to myself, who am traveling quietly with my own servant, I have not the same reasons as you have to conceal my name."

"Enough! enough! what is your name?"

"I shall tell you my name in order that you may know where to find me, my lord, or my prince, as it may suit you best to be called," said our Gascon, who did not choose to seem to yield to a threat. "Do you know Monsieur d'Artagnan?"

"Lieutenant in the king's musketeers?" said the voice; "you are Monsieur d'Artagnan?"

"I am."

"Then you came here to defend him?"

"Him? whom?"

"The man we are seeking."

"It seems," said D'Artagnan, "that whilst I thought I was coming to Noisy I have entered, without suspecting it, into the kingdom of mysteries."

"Come," replied the same lofty tone, "answer! Are you waiting for him underneath these windows? Did you come to Noisy to defend him?"

"I am waiting for no one," replied D'Artagnan, who was beginning to be angry. "I propose to defend no one but myself, and I shall defend myself vigorously, I give you warning."

"Very well," said the voice; "go away from here and leave the place to us."

"Go away from here!" said D'Artagnan, whose purposes were in conflict with that order, "that is not so easy, since I am on the point of falling, and my horse, too, through fatigue; unless, indeed, you are disposed to offer me a supper and a bed in the neighborhood."

"Rascal!"

"Eh! monsieur!" said D'Artagnan, "I beg you will have a care what you say; for if you utter another word like that, be you marquis, duke, prince or king, I will thrust it down your throat! do you hear?"

"Well, well," rejoined the leader, "there's no doubt 'tis a Gascon who is speaking, and therefore not the man we are looking for. Our blow has failed for to-night; let us withdraw. We shall meet again, Master d'Artagnan," continued the leader, raising his voice.

"Yes, but never with the same advantages," said D'Artagnan, in a tone of raillery; "for when you meet me again you will perhaps be alone and there will be daylight."

"Very good, very good," said the voice. "En route, gentlemen."

And the troop, grumbling angrily, disappeared in the darkness and took the road to Paris. D'Artagnan and Planchet remained for some moments still on the defensive; then, as the noise of the horsemen became more and more distant, they sheathed their swords.

"Thou seest, simpleton," said D'Artagnan to his servant, "that they wished no harm to us."

"But to whom, then?"

"I'faith! I neither know nor care. What I do care for now, is to make my way into the Jesuits' convent; so to horse and let us knock at their door. Happen what will, the devil take them, they can't eat us."

And he mounted his horse. Planchet had just done the same when an unexpected weight fell upon the back of the horse, which sank down.

"Hey! your honor!" cried Planchet, "I've a man behind me."

D'Artagnan turned around and plainly saw two human forms on Planchet's horse.

"'Tis then the devil that pursues!" he cried; drawing his sword and preparing to attack the new foe.

"No, no, dear D'Artagnan," said the figure, "'tis not the devil, 'tis Aramis; gallop fast, Planchet, and when you come to the end of the village turn swiftly to the left."

And Planchet, with Aramis behind him, set off at full gallop, followed by D'Artagnan, who began to think he was in the merry maze of some fantastic dream.

9. The Abbe D'Herblay.

At the extremity of the village Planchet turned to the left in obedience to the orders of Aramis, and stopped underneath the window which had light in it. Aramis alighted and clapped his hands three times. Immediately the window was opened and a ladder of rope was let down from it.

"My friend," said Aramis, "if you like to ascend I shall be delighted to receive you."

"Ah," said D'Artagnan, "is that the way you return to your apartment?"

"After nine at night, pardieu!" said Aramis, "the rule of the convent is very severe."

"Pardon me, my dear friend," said D'Artagnan, "I think you said 'pardieu!'"

"Do you think so?" said Aramis, smiling; "it is possible. You have no idea, my dear fellow, how one acquires bad habits in these cursed convents, or what evil ways all these men of the church have, with whom I am obliged to live. But will you not go up?"

"Pass on before me, I beg of you."

"As the late cardinal used to say to the late king, 'only to show you the way, sire.'" And Aramis ascended the ladder quickly and reached the window in an instant.

D'Artagnan followed, but less nimbly, showing plainly that this mode of ascent was not one to which he was accustomed.

"I beg your pardon," said Aramis, noticing his awkwardness; "if I had known that I was to have the honor of your visit I should have procured the gardener's ladder; but for me alone this is good enough."

"Sir," said Planchet when he saw D'Artagnan on the summit of the ladder, "this way is easy for Monsieur Aramis and even for you; in case of necessity I might also climb up, but my two horses cannot mount the ladder."

"Take them to yonder shed, my friend," said Aramis, pointing to a low building on the plain; "there you will find hay and straw for them; then come back here and clap your hands three times, and we will give you wine and food. Marry, forsooth, people don't die of hunger here."

And Aramis, drawing in the ladder, closed the window. D'Artagnan then looked around attentively.

Never was there an apartment at the same time more warlike and more elegant. At each corner were arranged trophies, presenting to view swords of all sorts, and on the walls hung four great pictures representing in their ordinary military costume the Cardinal de Lorraine, the Cardinal de Richelieu, the Cardinal de la Valette, and the Archbishop of Bordeaux. Exteriorly, nothing in the room showed that it was the habitation of an abbe. The hangings were of damask, the carpets from Alencon, and the bed, especially, had more the look of a fine lady's couch, with its trimmings of fine lace and its embroidered counterpane, than that of a man who had made a vow that he would endeavor to gain Heaven by fasting and mortification.

"You are examining my den," said Aramis. "Ah, my dear fellow, excuse me; I am lodged like a Chartreux. But what are you looking for?"

"I am looking for the person who let down the ladder. I see no one and yet the ladder didn't come down of itself."

"No, it is Bazin."

"Ah! ah!" said D'Artagnan.

"But," continued Aramis, "Bazin is a well trained servant, and seeing that I was not alone he discreetly retired. Sit down, my dear friend, and let us talk." And Aramis pushed forward a large easy-chair, in which D'Artagnan stretched himself out.

"In the first place, you will sup with me, will you not?" asked Aramis.

"Yes, if you really wish it," said D'Artagnan, "and even with great pleasure, I confess; the journey has given me a devil of an appetite."

"Ah, my poor friend!" said Aramis, "you will find meagre fare; you were not expected."

"Am I then threatened with the omelet of Crevecoeur?"

"Oh, let us hope," said Aramis, "that with the help of God and of Bazin we shall find something better than that in the larder of the worthy Jesuit fathers. Bazin, my friend, come here."

The door opened and Bazin entered; on perceiving the musketeer he uttered an exclamation that was almost a cry of despair.

"My dear Bazin," said D'Artagnan, "I am delighted to see with what wonderful composure you can tell a lie even in church!"

"Sir," replied Bazin, "I have been taught by the good Jesuit fathers that it is permitted to tell a falsehood when it is told in a good cause."

"So far well," said Aramis; "we are dying of hunger. Serve us up the best supper you can, and especially give us some good wine."

Bazin bowed low, sighed, and left the room.

"Now we are alone, dear Aramis," said D'Artagnan, "tell me how the devil you managed to alight upon the back of Planchet's horse."

"I'faith!" answered Aramis, "as you see, from Heaven."

"From Heaven," replied D'Artagnan, shaking his head; "you have no more the appearance of coming from thence than you have of going there."

"My friend," said Aramis, with a look of imbecility on his face which D'Artagnan had never observed whilst he was in the musketeers, "if I did not come from Heaven, at least I was leaving Paradise, which is almost the same."

"Here, then, is a puzzle for the learned," observed D'Artagnan, "until now they have never been able to agree as to the situation of Paradise; some place it on Mount Ararat, others between the rivers Tigris and Euphrates; it seems that they have been looking very far away for it, while it was actually very near. Paradise is at Noisy le Sec, upon the site of the archbishop's chateau. People do not go out from it by the door, but by the window; one doesn't descend here by the marble steps of a peristyle, but by the branches of a lime-tree; and the angel with a flaming sword who guards this elysium seems to have changed his celestial name of Gabriel into that of the more terrestrial one of the Prince de Marsillac."

Aramis burst into a fit of laughter.

"You were always a merry companion, my dear D'Artagnan," he said, "and your witty Gascon fancy has not deserted you. Yes, there is something in what you say; nevertheless, do not believe that it is Madame de Longueville with whom I am in love."

"A plague on't! I shall not do so. After having been so long in love with Madame de Chevreuse, you would hardly lay your heart at the feet of her mortal enemy!"

"Yes," replied Aramis, with an absent air; "yes, that poor duchess! I once loved her much, and to do her justice, she was very useful to us. Eventually she was obliged to leave France. He was a relentless enemy, that damned cardinal," continued Aramis, glancing at the portrait of the old minister. "He had even given orders to arrest her and would have cut off her head had she not escaped with her waiting-maid--poor Kitty! I have heard that she met with a strange adventure in I don't know what village, with I don't know what cure, of whom she asked hospitality and who, having but one chamber, and taking her for a cavalier, offered to share it with her. For she had a wonderful way of dressing as a man, that dear Marie; I know only one other woman who can do it as well. So they made this song about her: 'Laboissiere, dis moi.' You know it, don't you?"

"No, sing it, please."

Aramis immediately complied, and sang the song in a very lively manner.

"Bravo!" cried D'Artagnan, "you sing charmingly, dear Aramis. I do not perceive that singing masses has spoiled your voice."

"My dear D'Artagnan," replied Aramis, "you understand, when I was a musketeer I mounted guard as seldom as I could; now when I am an abbe I say as few masses as I can. But to return to our duchess."

"Which--the Duchess de Chevreuse or the Duchess de Longueville?"

"Have I not already told you that there is nothing between me and the Duchess de Longueville? Little flirtations, perhaps, and that's all. No, I spoke of the Duchess de Chevreuse; did you see her after her return from Brussels, after the king's death?"

"Yes, she is still beautiful."

"Yes," said Aramis, "I saw her also at that time. I gave her good advice, by which she did not profit. I ventured to tell her that Mazarin was the lover of Anne of Austria. She wouldn't believe me, saying that she knew Anne of Austria, who was too proud to love such a worthless coxcomb. After that she plunged into the cabal headed by the Duke of Beaufort; and the 'coxcomb' arrested De Beaufort and banished Madame de Chevreuse."

"You know," resumed D'Artagnan, "that she has had leave to return to France?"

"Yes she is come back and is going to commit some fresh folly or another."

"Oh, but this time perhaps she will follow your advice."

"Oh, this time," returned Aramis, "I haven't seen her; she is much changed."

"In that respect unlike you, my dear Aramis, for you are still the same; you have still your beautiful dark hair, still your elegant figure, still your feminine hands, which are admirably suited to a prelate."

"Yes," replied Aramis, "I am extremely careful of my appearance. Do you know that I am growing old? I am nearly thirty-seven."

"Mind, Aramis"--D'Artagnan smiled as he spoke--"since we are together again, let us agree on one point: what age shall we be in future?"

"How?"

"Formerly I was your junior by two or three years, and if I am not mistaken I am turned forty years old."

"Indeed! Then 'tis I who am mistaken, for you have always been a good chronologist. By your reckoning I must be forty-three at least. The devil I am! Don't let it out at the Hotel Rambouillet; it would ruin me," replied the abbe.

"Don't be afraid," said D'Artagnan. "I never go there."

"Why, what in the world," cried Aramis, "is that animal Bazin doing? Bazin! Hurry up there, you rascal; we are mad with hunger and thirst!"

Bazin entered at that moment carrying a bottle in each hand.

"At last," said Aramis, "we are ready, are we?"

"Yes, monsieur, quite ready," said Bazin; "but it took me some time to bring up all the----"

"Because you always think you have on your shoulders your beadle's robe, and spend all your time reading your breviary. But I give you warning that if in polishing your chapel utensils you forget how to brighten up my sword, I will make a great fire of your blessed images and will see that you are roasted on it."

Bazin, scandalized, made a sign of the cross with the bottle in his hand. D'Artagnan, more surprised than ever at the tone and manners of the Abbe d'Herblay, which contrasted so strongly with those of the Musketeer Aramis, remained staring with wide-open eyes at the face of his friend.

Bazin quickly covered the table with a damask cloth and arranged upon it so many things, gilded, perfumed, appetizing, that D'Artagnan was quite overcome.

"But you expected some one then?" asked the officer.

"Oh," said Aramis, "I always try to be prepared; and then I knew you were seeking me."

"From whom?"

"From Master Bazin, to be sure; he took you for the devil, my dear fellow, and hastened to warn me of the danger that threatened my soul if I should meet again a companion so wicked as an officer of musketeers."

"Oh, monsieur!" said Bazin, clasping his hands supplicatingly.

"Come, no hypocrisy! you know that I don't like it. You will do much better to open the window and let down some bread, a chicken and a bottle of wine to your friend Planchet, who has been this last hour killing himself clapping his hands."

Planchet, in fact, had bedded and fed his horses, and then coming back under the window had repeated two or three times the signal agreed upon.

Bazin obeyed, fastened to the end of a cord the three articles designated and let them down to Planchet, who then went satisfied to his shed.

"Now to supper," said Aramis.

The two friends sat down and Aramis began to cut up fowls, partridges and hams with admirable skill.

"The deuce!" cried D'Artagnan; "do you live in this way always?"

"Yes, pretty well. The coadjutor has given me dispensations from fasting on the jours maigres, on account of my health; then I have engaged as my cook the cook who lived with Lafollone--you know the man I mean?--the friend of the cardinal, and the famous epicure whose grace after dinner used to be, 'Good Lord, do me the favor to cause me to digest what I have eaten.'"

"Nevertheless he died of indigestion, in spite of his grace," said D'Artagnan.

"What can you expect?" replied Aramis, in a tone of resignation. "Every man that's born must fulfil his destiny."

"If it be not an indelicate question," resumed D'Artagnan, "have you grown rich?"

"Oh, Heaven! no. I make about twelve thousand francs a year, without counting a little benefice of a thousand crowns the prince gave me."

"And how do you make your twelve thousand francs? By your poems?"

"No, I have given up poetry, except now and then to write a drinking song, some gay sonnet or some innocent epigram; I compose sermons, my friend."

"What! sermons? Do you preach them?"

"No; I sell them to those of my cloth who wish to become great orators."

"Ah, indeed! and you have not been tempted by the hopes of reputation yourself?"

"I should, my dear D'Artagnan, have been so, but nature said 'No.' When I am in the pulpit, if by chance a pretty woman looks at me, I look at her again: if she smiles, I smile too. Then I speak at random; instead of preaching about the torments of hell I talk of the joys of Paradise. An event took place in the Church of St. Louis au Marais. A gentleman laughed in my face. I stopped short to tell him that he was a fool; the congregation went out to get stones to stone me with, but whilst they were away I found means to conciliate the priests who were present, so that my foe was pelted instead of me. 'Tis true that he came the next morning to my house, thinking that he had to do with an abbe--like all other abbes."

"And what was the end of the affair?"

"We met in the Place Royale--Egad! you know about it."

"Was I not your second?" cried D'Artagnan.

"You were; you know how I settled the matter."

"Did he die?"

"I don't know. But, at all events, I gave him absolution in articulo mortis. 'Tis enough to kill the body, without killing the soul."

Bazin made a despairing sign which meant that while perhaps he approved the moral he altogether disapproved the tone in which it was uttered.

"Bazin, my friend," said Aramis, "you don't seem to be aware that I can see you in that mirror, and you forget that once for all I have forbidden all signs of approbation or disapprobation. You will do me the favor to bring us some Spanish wine and then to withdraw. Besides, my friend D'Artagnan has something to say to me privately, have you not, D'Artagnan?"

D'Artagnan nodded his head and Bazin retired, after placing on the table the Spanish wine.

The two friends, left alone, remained silent, face to face. Aramis seemed to await a comfortable digestion; D'Artagnan, to be preparing his exordium. Each of them, when the other was not looking, hazarded a sly glance. It was Aramis who broke the silence.

"What are you thinking of, D'Artagnan?" he began.

"I was thinking, my dear old friend, that when you were a musketeer you turned your thoughts incessantly to the church, and now that you are an abbe you are perpetually longing to be once more a musketeer."

"'Tis true; man, as you know," said Aramis, "is a strange animal, made up of contradictions. Since I became an abbe I dream of nothing but battles."

"That is apparent in your surroundings; you have rapiers here of every form and to suit the most exacting taste. Do you still fence well?"

"I--I fence as well as you did in the old time--better still, perhaps; I do nothing else all day."

"And with whom?"

"With an excellent master-at-arms that we have here."

"What! here?"

"Yes, here, in this convent, my dear fellow. There is everything in a Jesuit convent."

"Then you would have killed Monsieur de Marsillac if he had come alone to attack you, instead of at the head of twenty men?"

"Undoubtedly," said Aramis, "and even at the head of his twenty men, if I could have drawn without being recognized."

"God pardon me!" said D'Artagnan to himself, "I believe he has become more Gascon than I am!" Then aloud: "Well, my dear Aramis, do you ask me why I came to seek you?"

"No, I have not asked you that," said Aramis, with his subtle manner; "but I have expected you to tell me."

"Well, I sought you for the single purpose of offering you a chance to kill Monsieur de Marsillac whenever you please, prince though he is."

"Hold on! wait!" said Aramis; "that is an idea!"

"Of which I invite you to take advantage, my friend. Let us see; with your thousand crowns from the abbey and the twelve thousand francs you make by selling sermons, are you rich? Answer frankly."

"I? I am as poor as Job, and were you to search my pockets and my boxes I don't believe you would find a hundred pistoles."

"Peste! a hundred pistoles!" said D'Artagnan to himself; "he calls that being as poor as Job! If I had them I should think myself as rich as Croesus." Then aloud: "Are you ambitious?"

"As Enceladus."

"Well, my friend, I bring you the means of becoming rich, powerful, and free to do whatever you wish."

The shadow of a cloud passed over Aramis's face as quickly as that which in August passes over the field of grain; but quick as it was, it did not escape D'Artagnan's observation.

"Speak on," said Aramis.

"One question first. Do you take any interest in politics?"

A gleam of light shone in Aramis's eyes, as brief as the shadow that had passed over his face, but not so brief but that it was seen by D'Artagnan.

"No," Aramis replied.

"Then proposals from any quarter will be agreeable to you, since for the moment you have no master but God?"

"It is possible."

"Have you, my dear Aramis, thought sometimes of those happy, happy, happy days of youth we passed laughing, drinking, and fighting each other for play?"

"Certainly, and more than once regretted them; it was indeed a glorious time."

"Well, those splendidly wild days may chance to come again; I am commissioned to find out my companions and I began by you, who were the very soul of our society."

Aramis bowed, rather with respect than pleasure at the compliment.

"To meddle in politics," he exclaimed, in a languid voice, leaning back in his easy-chair. "Ah! dear D'Artagnan! see how regularly I live and how easy I am here. We have experienced the ingratitude of 'the great,' as you well know."

"'Tis true," replied D'Artagnan. "Yet the great sometimes repent of their ingratitude."

"In that case it would be quite another thing. Come! let's be merciful to every sinner! Besides, you are right in another respect, which is in thinking that if we were to meddle in politics there could not be a better time than the present."

"How can you know that? You who never interest yourself in politics?"

"Ah! without caring about them myself, I live among those who are much occupied in them. Poet as I am, I am intimate with Sarazin, who is devoted to the Prince de Conti, and with Monsieur de Bois-Robert, who, since the death of Cardinal Richelieu, is of all parties or any party; so that political discussions have not altogether been uninteresting to me."

"I have no doubt of it," said D'Artagnan.

"Now, my dear friend, look upon all I tell you as merely the statement of a monk--of a man who resembles an echo--repeating simply what he hears. I understand that Mazarin is at this very moment extremely uneasy as to the state of affairs; that his orders are not respected like those of our former bugbear, the deceased cardinal, whose portrait as you see hangs yonder--for whatever may be thought of him, it must be allowed that Richelieu was great."

"I will not contradict you there," said D'Artagnan.

"My first impressions were favorable to the minister; I said to myself that a minister is never loved, but that with the genius this one was said to have he would eventually triumph over his enemies and would make himself feared, which in my opinion is much more to be desired than to be loved----"

D'Artagnan made a sign with his head which indicated that he entirely approved that doubtful maxim.

"This, then," continued Aramis, "was my first opinion; but as I am very ignorant in matters of this kind and as the humility which I profess obliges me not to rest on my own judgment, but to ask the opinion of others, I have inquired--Eh!--my friend----"

Aramis paused.

"Well? what?" asked his friend.

"Well, I must mortify myself. I must confess that I was mistaken. Monsieur de Mazarin is not a man of genius, as I thought, he is a man of no origin--once a servant of Cardinal Bentivoglio, and he got on by intrigue. He is an upstart, a man of no name, who will only be the tool of a party in France. He will amass wealth, he will injure the king's revenue and pay to himself the pensions which Richelieu paid to others. He is neither a gentleman in manner nor in feeling, but a sort of buffoon, a punchinello, a pantaloon. Do you know him? I do not."

"Hem!" said D'Artagnan, "there is some truth in what you say."

"Ah! it fills me with pride to find that, thanks to a common sort of penetration with which I am endowed, I am approved by a man like you, fresh from the court."

"But you speak of him, not of his party, his resources."

"It is true--the queen is for him."

"Something in his favor."

"But he will never have the king."

"A mere child."

"A child who will be of age in four years. Then he has neither the parliament nor the people with him--they represent the wealth of the country; nor the nobles nor the princes, who are the military power of France."

D'Artagnan scratched his ear. He was forced to confess to himself that this reasoning was not only comprehensive, but just.

"You see, my poor friend, that I am sometimes bereft of my ordinary thoughtfulness; perhaps I am wrong in speaking thus to you, who have evidently a leaning to Mazarin."

"I!" cried D'Artagnan, "not in the least."

"You spoke of a mission."

"Did I? I was wrong then, no, I said what you say--there is a crisis at hand. Well! let's fly the feather before the wind; let us join with that side to which the wind will carry it and resume our adventurous life. We were once four valiant knights--four hearts fondly united; let us unite again, not our hearts, which have never been severed, but our courage and our fortunes. Here's a good opportunity for getting something better than a diamond."

"You are right, D'Artagnan; I held a similar project, but as I had not nor ever shall have your fruitful, vigorous imagination, the idea was suggested to me. Every one nowadays wants auxiliaries; propositions have been made to me and I confess to you frankly that the coadjutor has made me speak out."

"Monsieur de Gondy! the cardinal's enemy?"

"No; the king's friend," said Aramis; "the king's friend, you understand. Well, it is a question of serving the king, the gentleman's duty."

"But the king is with Mazarin."

"He is, but not willingly; in appearance, not heart; and that is exactly the snare the king's enemies are preparing for the poor child."

"Ah! but this is, indeed, civil war which you propose to me, dear Aramis."

"War for the king."

"Yet the king will be at the head of the army on Mazarin's side."

"But his heart will be in the army commanded by the Duc de Beaufort."

"Monsieur de Beaufort? He is at Vincennes."

"Did I say Monsieur de Beaufort? Monsieur de Beaufort or another. Monsieur de Beaufort or Monsieur le Prince."

"But Monsieur le Prince is to set out for the army; he is entirely devoted to the cardinal."

"Oh oh!" said Aramis, "there are questions between them at this very moment. And besides, if it is not the prince, then Monsieur de Gondy----"

"But Monsieur de Gondy is to be made a cardinal; they are soliciting the hat for him."

"And are there no cardinals that can fight? Come now, recall the four cardinals that at the head of armies have equalled Monsieur de Guebriant and Monsieur de Gassion."

"But a humpbacked general!

"Under the cuirass the hump will not be seen. Besides, remember that Alexander was lame and Hannibal had but one eye."

"Do you see any great advantage in adhering to this party?" asked D'Artagnan.

"I foresee in it the aid of powerful princes."

"With the enmity of the government."

"Counteracted by parliament and insurrections."

"That may be done if they can separate the king from his mother."

"That may be done," said Aramis.

"Never!" cried D'Artagnan. "You, Aramis, know Anne of Austria better than I do. Do you think she will ever forget that her son is her safeguard, her shield, the pledge for her dignity, for her fortune and her life? Should she forsake Mazarin she must join her son and go over to the princes' side; but you know better than I do that there are certain reasons why she can never abandon Mazarin."

"Perhaps you are right," said Aramis, thoughtfully; "therefore I shall not pledge myself."

"To them or to us, do you mean, Aramis?"

"To no one. I am a priest," resumed Aramis. "What have I to do with politics? I am not obliged to read any breviary. I have a jolly little circle of witty abbes and pretty women; everything goes on smoothly, so certainly, dear friend, I shall not meddle in politics."

"Well, listen, my dear Aramis," said D'Artagnan; "your philosophy convinces me, on my honor. I don't know what devil of an insect stung me and made me ambitious. I have a post by which I live; at the death of Monsieur de Treville, who is old, I may be a captain, which is a very snug berth for a once penniless Gascon. Instead of running after adventures I shall accept an invitation from Porthos; I shall go and shoot on his estate. You know he has estates--Porthos?"

"I should think so, indeed. Ten leagues of wood, of marsh land and valleys; he is lord of the hill and the plain and is now carrying on a suit for his feudal rights against the Bishop of Noyon!"

"Good," said D'Artagnan to himself. "That's what I wanted to know. Porthos is in Picardy."

Then aloud:

"And he has taken his ancient name of Vallon?"

"To which he adds that of Bracieux, an estate which has been a barony, by my troth."

"So that Porthos will be a baron."

"I don't doubt it. The 'Baroness Porthos' will sound particularly charming."

And the two friends began to laugh.

"So," D'Artagnan resumed, "you will not become a partisan of Mazarin's?"

"Nor you of the Prince de Conde?"

"No, let us belong to no party, but remain friends; let us be neither Cardinalists nor Frondists."

"Adieu, then." And D'Artagnan poured out a glass of wine.

"To old times," he said.

"Yes," returned Aramis. "Unhappily, those times are past."

"Nonsense! They will return," said D'Artagnan. "At all events, if you want me, remember the Rue Tiquetonne, Hotel de la Chevrette."

"And I shall be at the convent of Jesuits; from six in the morning to eight at night come by the door. From eight in the evening until six in the morning come in by the window."

"Adieu, dear friend."

"Oh, I can't let you go so! I will go with you." And he took his sword and cloak.

"He wants to be sure that I go away," said D'Artagnan to himself.

Aramis whistled for Bazin, but Bazin was asleep in the ante-chamber, and Aramis was obliged to shake him by the ear to awake him.

Bazin stretched his arms, rubbed his eyes, and tried to go to sleep again.

"Come, come, sleepy head; quick, the ladder!"

"But," said Bazin, yawning portentously, "the ladder is still at the window."

"The other one, the gardener's. Didn't you see that Monsieur d'Artagnan mounted with difficulty? It will be even more difficult to descend."

D'Artagnan was about to assure Aramis that he could descend easily, when an idea came into his head which silenced him.

Bazin uttered a profound sigh and went out to look for the ladder. Presently a good, solid, wooden ladder was placed against the window.

"Now then," said D'Artagnan, "this is something like; this is a means of communication. A woman could go up a ladder like that."

Aramis's searching look seemed to seek his friend's thought even at the bottom of his heart, but D'Artagnan sustained the inquisition with an air of admirable simplicity. Besides, at that moment he put his foot on the first step of the ladder and began his descent. In a moment he was on the ground. Bazin remained at the window.

"Stay there," said Aramis; "I shall return immediately."

The two friends went toward the shed. At their approach Planchet came out leading the two horses.

"That is good to see," said Aramis. "There is a servant active and vigilant, not like that lazy fellow Bazin, who is no longer good for anything since he became connected with the church. Follow us, Planchet; we shall continue our conversation to the end of the village."

They traversed the width of the village, talking of indifferent things, then as they reached the last houses:

"Go, then, dear friend," said Aramis, "follow your own career. Fortune lavishes her smiles upon you; do not let her flee from your embrace. As for me, I remain in my humility and indolence. Adieu!"

"Thus 'tis quite decided," said D'Artagnan, "that what I have to offer to you does not tempt you?"

"On the contrary, it would tempt me were I any other man," rejoined Aramis; "but I repeat, I am made up of contradictions. What I hate to-day I adore to-morrow, and vice versa. You see that I cannot, like you, for instance, settle on any fixed plan."

"Thou liest, subtile one," said D'Artagnan to himself. "Thou alone, on the contrary, knowest how to choose thy object and to gain it stealthily."

The friends embraced. They descended into the plain by the ladder. Planchet met them hard by the shed. D'Artagnan jumped into the saddle, then the old companions in arms again shook hands. D'Artagnan and Planchet spurred their steeds and took the road to Paris.

But after he had gone about two hundred steps D'Artagnan stopped short, alighted, threw the bridle of his horse over the arm of Planchet and took the pistols from his saddle-bow to fasten them to his girdle.

"What's the matter?" asked Planchet.

"This is the matter: be he ever so cunning he shall never say I was his dupe. Stand here, don't stir, turn your back to the road and wait for me."

Having thus spoken, D'Artagnan cleared the ditch by the roadside and crossed the plain so as to wind around the village. He had observed between the house that Madame de Longueville inhabited and the convent of the Jesuits, an open space surrounded by a hedge.

The moon had now risen and he could see well enough to retrace his road.

He reached the hedge and hid himself behind it; in passing by the house where the scene which we have related took place, he remarked that the window was again lighted up and he was convinced that Aramis had not yet returned to his own apartment and that when he did it would not be alone.

In truth, in a few minutes he heard steps approaching and low whispers.

Close to the hedge the steps stopped.

D'Artagnan knelt down near the thickest part of the hedge.

Two men, to the astonishment of D'Artagnan, appeared shortly; soon, however, his surprise vanished, for he heard the murmurs of a soft, harmonious voice; one of these two men was a woman disguised as a cavalier.

"Calm yourself, dear Rene," said the soft voice, "the same thing will never happen again. I have discovered a sort of subterranean passage which runs beneath the street and we shall only have to raise one of the marble slabs before the door to open you an entrance and an outlet."

"Oh!" answered another voice, which D'Artagnan instantly recognized as that of Aramis. "I swear to you, princess, that if your reputation did not depend on precautions and if my life alone were jeopardized----"

"Yes, yes! I know you are as brave and venturesome as any man in the world, but you do not belong to me alone; you belong to all our party. Be prudent! sensible!"

"I always obey, madame, when I am commanded by so gentle a voice."

He kissed her hand tenderly.

"Ah!" exclaimed the cavalier with a soft voice.

"What's the matter?" asked Aramis.

"Do you not see that the wind has blown off my hat?"

Aramis rushed after the fugitive hat. D'Artagnan took advantage of the circumstance to find a place in the hedge not so thick, where his glance could penetrate to the supposed cavalier. At that instant, the moon, inquisitive, perhaps, like D'Artagnan, came from behind a cloud and by her light D'Artagnan recognized the large blue eyes, the golden hair and the classic head of the Duchess de Longueville.

Aramis returned, laughing, one hat on his head and the other in his hand; and he and his companion resumed their walk toward the convent.

"Good!" said D'Artagnan, rising and brushing his knees; "now I have thee--thou art a Frondeur and the lover of Madame de Longueville."

10. Monsieur Porthos du Vallon de Bracieux de Pierrefonds.

Thanks to what Aramis had told him, D'Artagnan, who knew already that Porthos called himself Du Vallon, was now aware that he styled himself, from his estate, De Bracieux; and that he was, on account of this estate, engaged in a lawsuit with the Bishop of Noyon. It was, then, in the neighborhood of Noyon that he must seek that estate. His itinerary was promptly determined: he would go to Dammartin, from which place two roads diverge, one toward Soissons, the other toward Compiegne; there he would inquire concerning the Bracieux estate and go to the right or to the left according to the information obtained.

Planchet, who was still a little concerned for his safety after his recent escapade, declared that he would follow D'Artagnan even to the end of the world, either by the road to the right or by that to the left; only he begged his former master to set out in the evening, for greater security to himself. D'Artagnan suggested that he should send word to his wife, so that she might not be anxious about him, but Planchet replied with much sagacity that he was very sure his wife would not die of anxiety through not knowing where he was, while he, Planchet, remembering her incontinence of tongue, would die of anxiety if she did know.

This reasoning seemed to D'Artagnan so satisfactory that he no further insisted; and about eight o'clock in the evening, the time when the vapors of night begin to thicken in the streets, he left the Hotel de la Chevrette, and followed by Planchet set forth from the capital by way of the Saint Denis gate.

At midnight the two travelers were at Dammartin, but it was then too late to make inquiries--the host of the Cygne de la Croix had gone to bed.

The next morning D'Artagnan summoned the host, one of those sly Normans who say neither yes nor no and fear to commit themselves by giving a direct answer. D'Artagnan, however, gathered from his equivocal replies that the road to the right was the one he ought to take, and on that uncertain information he resumed his journey. At nine in the morning he reached Nanteuil and stopped for breakfast. His host here was a good fellow from Picardy, who gave him all the information he needed. The Bracieux estate was a few leagues from Villars-Cotterets.

D'Artagnan was acquainted with Villars-Cotterets, having gone thither with the court on several occasions; for at that time Villars-Cotterets was a royal residence. He therefore shaped his course toward that place and dismounted at the Dauphin d'Or. There he ascertained that the Bracieux estate was four leagues distant, but that Porthos was not at Bracieux. Porthos had, in fact, been involved in a dispute with the Bishop of Noyon in regard to the Pierrefonds property, which adjoined his own, and weary at length of a legal controversy which was beyond his comprehension, he put an end to it by purchasing Pierrefonds and added that name to his others. He now called himself Du Vallon de Bracieux de Pierrefonds, and resided on his new estate.

The travelers were therefore obliged to stay at the hotel until the next day; the horses had done ten leagues that day and needed rest. It is true they might have taken others, but there was a great forest to pass through and Planchet, as we have seen, had no liking for forests after dark.

There was another thing that Planchet had no liking for and that was starting on a journey with a hungry stomach. Accordingly, D'Artagnan, on awaking, found his breakfast waiting for him. It need not be said that Planchet in resuming his former functions resumed also his former humility and was not ashamed to make his breakfast on what was left by D'Artagnan.

It was nearly eight o'clock when they set out again. Their course was clearly defined: they were to follow the road toward Compiegne and on emerging from the forest turn to the right.

The morning was beautiful, and in this early springtime the birds sang on the trees and the sunbeams shone through the misty glades, like curtains of golden gauze.

In other parts of the forest the light could scarcely penetrate through the foliage, and the stems of two old oak trees, the refuge of the squirrel, startled by the travelers, were in deep shadow.

There came up from all nature in the dawn of day a perfume of herbs, flowers and leaves, which delighted the heart. D'Artagnan, sick of the closeness of Paris, thought that when a man had three names of his different estates joined one to another, he ought to be very happy in such a paradise; then he shook his head, saying, "If I were Porthos and D'Artagnan came to make me such a proposition as I am going to make to him, I know what I should say to it."

As to Planchet, he thought of little or nothing, but was happy as a hunting-hound in his old master's company.

At the extremity of the wood D'Artagnan perceived the road that had been described to him, and at the end of the road he saw the towers of an immense feudal castle.

"Oh! oh!" he said, "I fancied this castle belonged to the ancient branch of Orleans. Can Porthos have negotiated for it with the Duc de Longueville?"

"Faith!" exclaimed Planchet, "here's land in good condition; if it belongs to Monsieur Porthos I wish him joy."

"Zounds!" cried D'Artagnan, "don't call him Porthos, nor even Vallon; call him De Bracieux or De Pierrefonds; thou wilt knell out damnation to my mission otherwise."

As he approached the castle which had first attracted his eye, D'Artagnan was convinced that it could not be there that his friend dwelt; the towers, though solid and as if built yesterday, were open and broken. One might have fancied that some giant had cleaved them with blows from a hatchet.

On arriving at the extremity of the castle D'Artagnan found himself overlooking a beautiful valley, in which, at the foot of a charming little lake, stood several scattered houses, which, humble in their aspect, and covered, some with tiles, others with thatch, seemed to acknowledge as their sovereign lord a pretty chateau, built about the beginning of the reign of Henry IV., and surmounted by four stately, gilded weather-cocks. D'Artagnan no longer doubted that this was Porthos's pleasant dwelling place.

The road led straight up to the chateau which, compared to its ancestor on the hill, was exactly what a fop of the coterie of the Duc d'Enghein would have been beside a knight in steel armor in the time of Charles VII. D'Artagnan spurred his horse on and pursued his road, followed by Planchet at the same pace.

In ten minutes D'Artagnan reached the end of an alley regularly planted with fine poplars and terminating in an iron gate, the points and crossed bars of which were gilt. In the midst of this avenue was a nobleman, dressed in green and with as much gilding about him as the iron gate, riding on a tall horse. On his right hand and his left were two footmen, with the seams of their dresses laced. A considerable number of clowns were assembled and rendered homage to their lord.

"Ah!" said D'Artagnan to himself, "can this be the Seigneur du Vallon de Bracieux de Pierrefonds? Well-a-day! how he has shrunk since he gave up the name of Porthos!"

"This cannot be Monsieur Porthos," observed Planchet replying, as it were, to his master's thoughts. "Monsieur Porthos was six feet high; this man is scarcely five."

"Nevertheless," said D'Artagnan, "the people are bowing very low to this person."

As he spoke, he rode toward the tall horse--to the man of importance and his valets. As he approached he seemed to recognize the features of this individual.

"Jesu!" cried Planchet, "can it be?"

At this exclamation the man on horseback turned slowly and with a lofty air, and the two travelers could see, displayed in all their brilliancy, the large eyes, the vermilion visage, and the eloquent smile of--Mousqueton.

It was indeed Mousqueton--Mousqueton, as fat as a pig, rolling about with rude health, puffed out with good living, who, recognizing D'Artagnan and acting very differently from the hypocrite Bazin, slipped off his horse and approached the officer with his hat off, so that the homage of the assembled crowd was turned toward this new sun, which eclipsed the former luminary.

"Monsieur d'Artagnan! Monsieur d'Artagnan!" cried Mousqueton, his fat cheeks swelling out and his whole frame perspiring with joy; "Monsieur d'Artagnan! oh! what joy for my lord and master, Du Vallon de Bracieux de Pierrefonds!"

"Thou good Mousqueton! where is thy master?"

"You stand upon his property!"

"But how handsome thou art--how fat! thou hast prospered and grown stout!" and D'Artagnan could not restrain his astonishment at the change good fortune had produced on the once famished one.

"Hey, yes, thank God, I am pretty well," said Mousqueton.

"But hast thou nothing to say to thy friend Planchet?"

"How, my friend Planchet? Planchet--art thou there?" cried Mousqueton, with open arms and eyes full of tears.

"My very self," replied Planchet; "but I wanted first to see if thou wert grown proud."

"Proud toward an old friend? never, Planchet! thou wouldst not have thought so hadst thou known Mousqueton well."

"So far so well," answered Planchet, alighting, and extending his arms to Mousqueton, the two servants embraced with an emotion which touched those who were present and made them suppose that Planchet was a great lord in disguise, so highly did they estimate the position of Mousqueton.

"And now, sir," resumed Mousqueton, when he had rid himself of Planchet, who had in vain tried to clasp his hands behind his friend's fat back, "now, sir, allow me to leave you, for I could not permit my master to hear of your arrival from any but myself; he would never forgive me for not having preceded you."

"This dear friend," said D'Artagnan, carefully avoiding to utter either the former name borne by Porthos or his new one, "then he has not forgotten me?"

"Forgotten--he!" cried Mousqueton; "there's not a day, sir, that we don't expect to hear that you were made marshal either instead of Monsieur de Gassion, or of Monsieur de Bassompierre."

On D'Artagnan's lips there played one of those rare and melancholy smiles which seemed to emanate from the depth of his soul--the last trace of youth and happiness that had survived life's disillusions.

"And you--fellows," resumed Mousqueton, "stay near Monsieur le Comte d'Artagnan and pay him every attention in your power whilst I go to prepare my lord for his visit."

And mounting his horse Mousqueton rode off down the avenue on the grass at a hand gallop.

"Ah, there! there's something promising," said D'Artagnan. "No mysteries, no cloak to hide one's self in, no cunning policy here; people laugh outright, they weep for joy here. I see nothing but faces a yard broad; in short, it seems to me that nature herself wears a holiday garb, and that the trees, instead of leaves and flowers, are covered with red and green ribbons as on gala days."

"As for me," said Planchet, "I seem to smell, from this place, even, a most delectable perfume of fine roast meat, and to see the scullions in a row by the hedge, hailing our approach. Ah! sir, what a cook must Monsieur Pierrefonds have, when he was so fond of eating and drinking, even whilst he was only called Monsieur Porthos!"

"Say no more!" cried D'Artagnan. "If the reality corresponds with appearances I am lost; for a man so well off will never change his happy condition, and I shall fail with him, as I have already done with Aramis."

11. Wealth does not necessarily produce Happiness.

D'Artagnan passed through the iron gate and arrived in front of the chateau. He alighted as he saw a species of giant on the steps. Let us do justice to D'Artagnan. Independently of every selfish wish, his heart palpitated with joy when he saw that tall form and martial demeanor, which recalled to him a good and brave man.

He ran to Porthos and threw himself into his arms; the whole body of servants, arranged in a semi-circle at a respectful distance, looked on with humble curiosity. Mousqueton, at the head of them, wiped his eyes. Porthos linked his arm in that of his friend.

"Ah! how delightful to see you again, dear friend!" he cried, in a voice which was now changed from a baritone into a bass, "you've not then forgotten me?"

"Forget you! oh! dear Du Vallon, does one forget the happiest days of flowery youth, one's dearest friends, the dangers we have dared together? On the contrary, there is not an hour we have passed together that is not present to my memory."

"Yes, yes," said Porthos, trying to give to his mustache a curl which it had lost whilst he had been alone. "Yes, we did some fine things in our time and we gave that poor cardinal a few threads to unravel."

And he heaved a sigh.

"Under any circumstances," he resumed, "you are welcome, my dear friend; you will help me to recover my spirits; to-morrow we will hunt the hare on my plain, which is a superb tract of land, or pursue the deer in my woods, which are magnificent. I have four harriers which are considered the swiftest in the county, and a pack of hounds which are unequalled for twenty leagues around."

And Porthos heaved another sigh.

"But, first," interposed D'Artagnan, "you must present me to Madame du Vallon."

A third sigh from Porthos.

"I lost Madame du Vallon two years ago," he said, "and you find me still in affliction on that account. That was the reason why I left my Chateau du Vallon near Corbeil, and came to my estate, Bracieux. Poor Madame du Vallon! her temper was uncertain, but she came at last to accustom herself to my little ways and understand my little wishes."

"So you are free now, and rich?"

"Alas!" groaned Porthos, "I am a widower and have forty thousand francs a year. Let us go to breakfast."

"I shall be happy to do so; the morning air has made me hungry."

"Yes," said Porthos; "my air is excellent."

They went into the chateau; there was nothing but gilding, high and low; the cornices were gilt, the mouldings were gilt, the legs and arms of the chairs were gilt. A table, ready set out, awaited them.

"You see," said Porthos, "this is my usual style."

"Devil take me!" answered D'Artagnan, "I wish you joy of it. The king has nothing like it."

"No," answered Porthos, "I hear it said that he is very badly fed by the cardinal, Monsieur de Mazarin. Taste this cutlet, my dear D'Artagnan; 'tis off one of my sheep."

"You have very tender mutton and I wish you joy of it." said D'Artagnan.

"Yes, the sheep are fed in my meadows, which are excellent pasture."

"Give me another cutlet."

"No, try this hare, which I had killed yesterday in one of my warrens."

"Zounds! what a flavor!" cried D'Artagnan; "ah! they are fed on thyme only, your hares."

"And how do you like my wine?" asked Porthos; "it is pleasant, isn't it?"

"Capital!"

"It is nothing, however, but a wine of the country."

"Really?"

"Yes, a small declivity to the south, yonder on my hill, gives me twenty hogsheads."

"Quite a vineyard, hey?"

Porthos sighed for the fifth time--D'Artagnan had counted his sighs. He became curious to solve the problem.

"Well now," he said, "it seems, my dear friend, that something vexes you; you are ill, perhaps? That health, which----"

"Excellent, my dear friend; better than ever. I could kill an ox with a blow of my fist."

"Well, then, family affairs, perhaps?"

"Family! I have, happily, only myself in the world to care for."

"But what makes you sigh?"

"My dear fellow," replied Porthos, "to be candid with you, I am not happy."

"You are not happy, Porthos? You who have chateau, meadows, mountains, woods--you who have forty thousand francs a year--you--are--not--happy?"

"My dear friend, all those things I have, but I am a hermit in the midst of superfluity."

"Surrounded, I suppose, only by clodhoppers, with whom you could not associate."

Porthos turned rather pale and drank off a large glass of wine.

"No; but just think, there are paltry country squires who have all some title or another and pretend to go back as far as Charlemagne, or at least to Hugh Capet. When I first came here; being the last comer, it was for me to make the first advances. I made them, but you know, my dear friend, Madame du Vallon----"

Porthos, in pronouncing these words, seemed to gulp down something.

"Madame du Vallon was of doubtful gentility. She had, in her first marriage--I don't think, D'Artagnan, I am telling you anything new--married a lawyer; they thought that 'nauseous;' you can understand that's a word bad enough to make one kill thirty thousand men. I have killed two, which has made people hold their tongues, but has not made me their friend. So that I have no society; I live alone; I am sick of it--my mind preys on itself."

D'Artagnan smiled. He now saw where the breastplate was weak, and prepared the blow.

"But now," he said, "that you are a widower, your wife's connection cannot injure you."

"Yes, but understand me; not being of a race of historic fame, like the De Courcys, who were content to be plain sirs, or the Rohans, who didn't wish to be dukes, all these people, who are all either vicomtes or comtes go before me at church in all the ceremonies, and I can say nothing to them. Ah! If I only were a----"

"A baron, don't you mean?" cried D'Artagnan, finishing his friend's sentence.

"Ah!" cried Porthos; "would I were but a baron!"

"Well, my friend, I am come to give you this very title which you wish for so much."

Porthos gave a start that shook the room; two or three bottles fell and were broken. Mousqueton ran thither, hearing the noise.

Porthos waved his hand to Mousqueton to pick up the bottles.

"I am glad to see," said D'Artagnan, "that you have still that honest lad with you."

"He is my steward," replied Porthos; "he will never leave me. Go away now, Mouston."

"So he's called Mouston," thought D'Artagnan; "'tis too long a word to pronounce 'Mousqueton.'"

"Well," he said aloud, "let us resume our conversation later, your people may suspect something; there may be spies about. You can suppose, Porthos, that what I have to say relates to most important matters."

"Devil take them; let us walk in the park," answered Porthos, "for the sake of digestion."

"Egad," said D'Artagnan, "the park is like everything else and there are as many fish in your pond as rabbits in your warren; you are a happy man, my friend since you have not only retained your love of the chase, but acquired that of fishing."

"My friend," replied Porthos, "I leave fishing to Mousqueton,--it is a vulgar pleasure,--but I shoot sometimes; that is to say, when I am dull, and I sit on one of those marble seats, have my gun brought to me, my favorite dog, and I shoot rabbits."

"Really, how very amusing!"

"Yes," replied Porthos, with a sigh, "it is amusing."

D'Artagnan now no longer counted the sighs. They were innumerable.

"However, what had you to say to me?" he resumed; "let us return to that subject."

"With pleasure," replied D'Artagnan; "I must, however, first frankly tell you that you must change your mode of life."

"How?"

"Go into harness again, gird on your sword, run after adventures, and leave as in old times a little of your fat on the roadside."

"Ah! hang it!" said Porthos.

"I see you are spoiled, dear friend; you are corpulent, your arm has no longer that movement of which the late cardinal's guards have so many proofs."

"Ah! my fist is strong enough I swear," cried Porthos, extending a hand like a shoulder of mutton.

"So much the better."

"Are we then to go to war?"

"By my troth, yes."

"Against whom?"

"Are you a politician, friend?"

"Not in the least."

"Are you for Mazarin or for the princes?"

"I am for no one."

"That is to say, you are for us. Well, I tell you that I come to you from the cardinal."

This speech was heard by Porthos in the same sense as if it had still been in the year 1640 and related to the true cardinal.

"Ho! ho! What are the wishes of his eminence?"

"He wishes to have you in his service."

"And who spoke to him of me?"

"Rochefort--you remember him?"

"Yes, pardieu! It was he who gave us so much trouble and kept us on the road so much; you gave him three sword-wounds in three separate engagements."

"But you know he is now our friend?"

"No, I didn't know that. So he cherishes no resentment?"

"You are mistaken, Porthos," said D'Artagnan. "It is I who cherish no resentment."

Porthos didn't understand any too clearly; but then we know that understanding was not his strong point. "You say, then," he continued, "that the Count de Rochefort spoke of me to the cardinal?"

"Yes, and the queen, too."

"The queen, do you say?"

"To inspire us with confidence she has even placed in Mazarin's hands that famous diamond--you remember all about it--that I once sold to Monsieur des Essarts and of which, I don't know how, she has regained possession."

"But it seems to me," said Porthos, "that she would have done much better if she had given it back to you."

"So I think," replied D'Artagnan; "but kings and queens are strange beings and have odd fancies; nevertheless, since they are the ones who have riches and honors, we are devoted to them."

"Yes, we are devoted to them," repeated Porthos; "and you--to whom are you devoted now?"

"To the king, the queen, and to the cardinal; moreover, I have answered for your devotion also."

"And you say that you have made certain conditions on my behalf?"

"Magnificent, my dear fellow, magnificent! In the first place you have plenty of money, haven't you? forty thousand francs income, I think you said."

Porthos began to be suspicious. "Eh! my friend," said he, "one never has too much money. Madame du Vallon left things in much disorder; I am not much of a hand at figures, so that I live almost from hand to mouth."

"He is afraid I have come to borrow money," thought D'Artagnan. "Ah, my friend," said he, "it is all the better if you are in difficulties."

"How is it all the better?"

"Yes, for his eminence will give you all that you want--land, money, and titles."

"Ah! ah! ah!" said Porthos, opening his eyes at that last word.

"Under the other cardinal," continued D'Artagnan, "we didn't know enough to make our profits; this, however, doesn't concern you, with your forty thousand francs income, the happiest man in the world, it seems to me."

Porthos sighed.

"At the same time," continued D'Artagnan, "notwithstanding your forty thousand francs a year, and perhaps even for the very reason that you have forty thousand francs a year, it seems to me that a little coronet would do well on your carriage, hey?"

"Yes indeed," said Porthos.

"Well, my dear friend, win it--it is at the point of your sword. We shall not interfere with each other--your object is a title; mine, money. If I can get enough to rebuild Artagnan, which my ancestors, impoverished by the Crusades, allowed to fall into ruins, and to buy thirty acres of land about it, that is all I wish. I shall retire and die tranquilly--at home."

"For my part," said Porthos, "I desire to be made a baron."

"You shall be one."

"And have you not seen any of our other friends?"

"Yes, I have seen Aramis."

"And what does he wish? To be a bishop?"

"Aramis," answered D'Artagnan, who did not wish to undeceive Porthos, "Aramis, fancy, has become a monk and a Jesuit, and lives like a bear. My offers did not arouse him,--did not even tempt him."

"So much the worse! He was a clever man. And Athos?"

"I have not yet seen him. Do you know where I shall find him?"

"Near Blois. He is called Bragelonne. Only imagine, my dear friend. Athos, who was of as high birth as the emperor and who inherits one estate which gives him the title of comte, what is he to do with all those dignities--the Comte de la Fere, Comte de Bragelonne?"

"And he has no children with all these titles?"

"Ah!" said Porthos, "I have heard that he had adopted a young man who resembles him greatly."

"What, Athos? Our Athos, who was as virtuous as Scipio? Have you seen him?

"No."

"Well, I shall see him to-morrow and tell him about you; but I'm afraid, entre nous, that his liking for wine has aged and degraded him."

"Yes, he used to drink a great deal," replied Porthos.

"And then he was older than any of us," added D'Artagnan.

"Some years only. His gravity made him look older than he was."

"Well then, if we can get Athos, all will be well. If we cannot, we will do without him. We two are worth a dozen."

"Yes," said Porthos, smiling at the remembrance of his former exploits; "but we four, altogether, would be equal to thirty-six, more especially as you say the work will not be child's play. Will it last long?"

"By'r Lady! two or three years perhaps."

"So much the better," cried Porthos. "You have no idea, my friend, how my bones ache since I came here. Sometimes on a Sunday, I take a ride in the fields and on the property of my neighbours, in order to pick up a nice little quarrel, which I am really in want of, but nothing happens. Either they respect or they fear me, which is more likely, but they let me trample down the clover with my dogs, insult and obstruct every one, and I come back still more weary and low-spirited, that's all. At any rate, tell me: there's more chance of fighting in Paris, is there not?"

"In that respect, my dear friend, it's delightful. No more edicts, no more of the cardinal's guards, no more De Jussacs, nor other bloodhounds. I'Gad! underneath a lamp in an inn, anywhere, they ask 'Are you one of the Fronde?' They unsheathe, and that's all that is said. The Duke de Guise killed Monsieur de Coligny in the Place Royale and nothing was said of it."

"Ah, things go on gaily, then," said Porthos.

"Besides which, in a short time," resumed D'Artagnan, "We shall have set battles, cannonades, conflagrations and there will be great variety."

"Well, then, I decide."

"I have your word, then?"

"Yes, 'tis given. I shall fight heart and soul for Mazarin; but----"

"But?"

"But he must make me a baron."

"Zounds!" said D'Artagnan, "that's settled already; I will be responsible for the barony."

On this promise being given, Porthos, who had never doubted his friend's assurance, turned back with him toward the castle.

12. Porthos was Discontented with his Condition.

As they returned toward the castle, D'Artagnan thought of the miseries of poor human nature, always dissatisfied with what it has, ever desirous of what it has not.

In the position of Porthos, D'Artagnan would have been perfectly happy; and to make Porthos contented there was wanting--what? five letters to put before his three names, a tiny coronet to paint upon the panels of his carriage!

"I shall pass all my life," thought D'Artagnan, "in seeking for a man who is really contented with his lot."

Whilst making this reflection, chance seemed, as it were, to give him the lie direct. When Porthos had left him to give some orders he saw Mousqueton approaching. The face of the steward, despite one slight shade of care, light as a summer cloud, seemed a physiognomy of absolute felicity.

"Here is what I am looking for," thought D'Artagnan; "but alas! the poor fellow does not know the purpose for which I am here."

He then made a sign for Mousqueton to come to him.

"Sir," said the servant, "I have a favour to ask you."

"Speak out, my friend."

"I am afraid to do so. Perhaps you will think, sir, that prosperity has spoiled me?"

"Art thou happy, friend?" asked D'Artagnan.

"As happy as possible; and yet, sir, you may make me even happier than I am."

"Well, speak, if it depends on me."

"Oh, sir! it depends on you only."

"I listen--I am waiting to hear."

"Sir, the favor I have to ask of you is, not to call me 'Mousqueton' but 'Mouston.' Since I have had the honor of being my lord's steward I have taken the last name as more dignified and calculated to make my inferiors respect me. You, sir, know how necessary subordination is in any large establishment of servants."

D'Artagnan smiled; Porthos wanted to lengthen out his names, Mousqueton to cut his short.

"Well, my dear Mouston," he said, "rest satisfied. I will call thee Mouston; and if it makes thee happy I will not 'tutoyer' you any longer."

"Oh!" cried Mousqueton, reddening with joy; "if you do me, sir, such honor, I shall be grateful all my life; it is too much to ask."

"Alas!" thought D'Artagnan, "it is very little to offset the unexpected tribulations I am bringing to this poor devil who has so warmly welcomed me."

"Will monsieur remain long with us?" asked Mousqueton, with a serene and glowing countenance.

"I go to-morrow, my friend," replied D'Artagnan.

"Ah, monsieur," said Mousqueton, "then you have come here only to awaken our regrets."

"I fear that is true," said D'Artagnan, in a low tone.

D'Artagnan was secretly touched with remorse, not at inducing Porthos to enter into schemes in which his life and fortune would be in jeopardy, for Porthos, in the title of baron, had his object and reward; but poor Mousqueton, whose only wish was to be called Mouston--was it not cruel to snatch him from the delightful state of peace and plenty in which he was?

He was thinking of these matters when Porthos summoned him to dinner.

"What! to dinner?" said D'Artagnan. "What time is it, then?"

"Eh! why, it is after one o'clock."

"Your home is a paradise, Porthos; one takes no note of time. I follow you, though I am not hungry."

"Come, if one can't always eat, one can always drink--a maxim of poor Athos, the truth of which I have discovered since I began to be lonely."

D'Artagnan, who as a Gascon, was inclined to sobriety, seemed not so sure as his friend of the truth of Athos's maxim, but he did his best to keep up with his host. Meanwhile his misgivings in regard to

Mousqueton recurred to his mind and with greater force because Mousqueton, though he did not himself wait on the table, which would have been beneath him in his new position, appeared at the door from time to time and evinced his gratitude to D'Artagnan by the quality of the wine he directed to be served. Therefore, when, at dessert, upon a sign from D'Artagnan, Porthos had sent away his servants and the two friends were alone:

"Porthos," said D'Artagnan, "who will attend you in your campaigns?"

"Why," replied Porthos, "Mouston, of course."

This was a blow to D'Artagnan. He could already see the intendant's beaming smile change to a contortion of grief. "But," he said, "Mouston is not so young as he was, my dear fellow; besides, he has grown fat and perhaps has lost his fitness for active service."

"That may be true," replied Porthos; "but I am used to him, and besides, he wouldn't be willing to let me go without him, he loves me so much."

"Oh, blind self-love!" thought D'Artagnan.

"And you," asked Porthos, "haven't you still in your service your old lackey, that good, that brave, that intelligent---what, then, is his name?"

"Planchet--yes, I have found him again, but he is lackey no longer."

"What is he, then?"

"With his sixteen hundred francs--you remember, the sixteen hundred francs he earned at the siege of La Rochelle by carrying a letter to Lord de Winter--he has set up a little shop in the Rue des Lombards and is now a confectioner."

"Ah, he is a confectioner in the Rue des Lombards! How does it happen, then, that he is in your service?"

"He has been guilty of certain escapades and fears he may be disturbed." And the musketeer narrated to his friend Planchet's adventure.

"Well," said Porthos, "if any one had told you in the old times that the day would come when Planchet would rescue Rochefort and that you would protect him in it----"

"I should not have believed him; but men are changed by events."

"There is nothing truer than that," said Porthos; "but what does not change, or changes for the better, is wine. Taste of this; it is a Spanish wine which our friend Athos thought much of."

At that moment the steward came in to consult his master upon the proceedings of the next day and also with regard to the shooting party which had been proposed.

"Tell me, Mouston," said Porthos, "are my arms in good condition?"

"Your arms, my lord--what arms?"

"Zounds! my weapons."

"What weapons?"

"My military weapons."

"Yes, my lord; at any rate, I think so."

"Make sure of it, and if they want it, have them burnished up. Which is my best cavalry horse?"

"Vulcan."

"And the best hack?"

"Bayard."

"What horse dost thou choose for thyself?"

"I like Rustaud, my lord; a good animal, whose paces suit me."

"Strong, thinkest thou?"

"Half Norman, half Mecklenburger; will go night and day."

"That will do for us. See to these horses. Polish up or make some one else polish my arms. Then take pistols with thee and a hunting-knife."

"Are we then going to travel, my lord?" asked Mousqueton, rather uneasy.

"Something better still, Mouston."

"An expedition, sir?" asked the steward, whose roses began to change into lilies.

"We are going to return to the service, Mouston," replied Porthos, still trying to restore his mustache to the military curl it had long lost.

"Into the service--the king's service?" Mousqueton trembled; even his fat, smooth cheeks shook as he spoke, and he looked at D'Artagnan with an air of reproach; he staggered, and his voice was almost choked.

"Yes and no. We shall serve in a campaign, seek out all sorts of adventures--return, in short, to our former life."

These last words fell on Mousqueton like a thunderbolt. It was those very terrible old days that made the present so excessively delightful, and the blow was so great he rushed out, overcome, and forgot to shut the door.

The two friends remained alone to speak of the future and to build castles in the air. The good wine which Mousqueton had placed before them traced out in glowing drops to D'Artagnan a fine perspective, shining with quadruples and pistoles, and showed to Porthos a blue ribbon and a ducal mantle; they were, in fact, asleep on the table when the servants came to light them to their bed.

Mousqueton was, however, somewhat consoled by D'Artagnan, who the next day told him that in all probability war would always be carried on in the heart of Paris and within reach of the Chateau du Vallon, which was near Corbeil, or Bracieux, which was near Melun, and of Pierrefonds, which was between Compiegne and Villars-Cotterets.

"But--formerly--it appears," began Mousqueton timidly.

"Oh!" said D'Artagnan, "we don't now make war as we did formerly. To-day it's a sort of diplomatic arrangement; ask Planchet."

Mousqueton inquired, therefore, the state of the case of his old friend, who confirmed the statement of D'Artagnan. "But," he added, "in this war prisoners stand a chance of being hung."

"The deuce they do!" said Mousqueton; "I think I should like the siege of Rochelle better than this war, then!"

Porthos, meantime, asked D'Artagnan to give him his instructions how to proceed on his journey.

"Four days," replied his friend, "are necessary to reach Blois; one day to rest there; three or four days to return to Paris. Set out, therefore, in a week, with your suite, and go to the Hotel de la Chevrette, Rue Tiquetonne, and there await me."

"That's agreed," said Porthos.

"As to myself, I shall go around to see Athos; for though I don't think his aid worth much, one must with one's friends observe all due politeness," said D'Artagnan.

The friends then took leave of each other on the very border of the estate of Pierrefonds, to which Porthos escorted his friend.

"At least," D'Artagnan said to himself, as he took the road to Villars-Cotterets, "at least I shall not be alone in my undertaking. That devil, Porthos, is a man of prodigious strength; still, if Athos joins us, well, we shall be three of us to laugh at Aramis, that little coxcomb with his too good luck."

At Villars-Cotterets he wrote to the cardinal:

"My Lord,--I have already one man to offer to your eminence, and he is well worth twenty men. I am just setting out for Blois. The Comte de la Fere inhabits the Castle of Bragelonne, in the environs of that city."

13. Two Angelic Faces.

The road was long, but the horses upon which D'Artagnan and Planchet rode had been refreshed in the well supplied stables of the Lord of Bracieux; the master and servant rode side by side, conversing as they went, for D'Artagnan had by degrees thrown off the master and Planchet had entirely ceased to assume the manners of a servant. He had been raised by circumstances to the rank of a confidant to his master. It was many years since D'Artagnan had opened his heart to any one; it happened, however, that these two men, on meeting again, assimilated perfectly. Planchet was in truth no vulgar companion in these new adventures; he was a man of uncommonly sound sense. Without courting danger he never shrank from an encounter; in short, he had been a soldier and arms ennoble a man; it was, therefore, on the footing of friends that D'Artagnan and Planchet arrived in the neighborhood of Blois.

Going along, D'Artagnan, shaking his head, said:

"I know that my going to Athos is useless and absurd; but still I owe this courtesy to my old friend, a man who had in him material for the most noble and generous of characters."

"Oh, Monsieur Athos was a noble gentleman," said Planchet, "was he not? Scattering money round about him as Heaven sprinkles rain. Do you remember, sir, that duel with the Englishman in the inclosure des Carmes? Ah! how lofty, how magnificent Monsieur Athos was that day, when he said to his adversary: 'You have insisted on knowing my name, sir; so much the worse for you, since I shall be obliged to kill you.' I was near him, those were his exact words, when he stabbed his foe as he said he would, and his adversary fell without saying, 'Oh!' 'Tis a noble gentleman--Monsieur Athos."

"Yes, true as Gospel," said D'Artagnan; "but one single fault has swallowed up all these fine qualities."

"I remember well," said Planchet, "he was fond of drinking--in truth, he drank, but not as other men drink. One seemed, as he raised the wine to his lips, to hear him say, 'Come, juice of the grape, and chase away my sorrows.' And how he used to break the stem of a glass or the neck of a bottle! There was no one like him for that."

"And now," replied D'Artagnan, "behold the sad spectacle that awaits us. This noble gentleman with his lofty glance, this handsome cavalier, so brilliant in feats of arms that every one was surprised that he held in his hand a sword only instead of a baton of command! Alas! we shall find him changed into a broken down old man, with garnet nose and eyes that slobber; we shall find him extended on some lawn, whence he will look at us with a languid eye and peradventure will not recognize us. God knows, Planchet, that I should fly from a sight so sad if I did not wish to show my respect for the illustrious shadow of what was once the Comte de la Fere, whom we loved so much."

Planchet shook his head and said nothing. It was evident that he shared his master's apprehensions.

"And then," resumed D'Artagnan, "to this decrepitude is probably added poverty, for he must have neglected the little that he had, and the dirty scoundrel, Grimaud, more taciturn than ever and still more drunken than his master--stay, Planchet, it breaks my heart to merely think of it."

"I fancy myself there and that I see him staggering and hear him stammering," said Planchet, in a piteous tone, "but at all events we shall soon know the real state of things, for I imagine that those lofty walls, now turning ruby in the setting sun, are the walls of Blois."

"Probably; and those steeples, pointed and sculptured, that we catch a glimpse of yonder, are similar to those that I have heard described at Chambord."

At this moment one of those heavy wagons, drawn by bullocks, which carry the wood cut in the fine forests of the country to the ports of the Loire, came out of a byroad full of ruts and turned on that which the two horsemen were following. A man carrying a long switch with a nail at the end of it, with which he urged on his slow team, was walking with the cart.

"Ho! friend," cried Planchet.

"What's your pleasure, gentlemen?" replied the peasant, with a purity of accent peculiar to the people of that district and which might have put to shame the cultured denizens of the Sorbonne and the Rue de l'Universite.

"We are looking for the house of Monsieur de la Fere," said D'Artagnan.

The peasant took off his hat on hearing this revered name.

"Gentlemen," he said, "the wood that I am carting is his; I cut it in his copse and I am taking it to the chateau."

D'Artagnan determined not to question this man; he did not wish to hear from another what he had himself said to Planchet.

"The chateau!" he said to himself, "what chateau? Ah, I understand! Athos is not a man to be thwarted; he, like Porthos, has obliged his peasantry to call him 'my lord,' and to dignify his pettifogging place by the name of chateau. He had a heavy hand--dear old Athos--after drinking."

D'Artagnan, after asking the man the right way, continued his route, agitated in spite of himself at the idea of seeing once more that singular man whom he had so truly loved and who had contributed so much by advice and example to his education as a gentleman. He checked by degrees the speed of his horse and went on, his head drooping as if in deep thought.

Soon, as the road turned, the Chateau de la Valliere appeared in view; then, a quarter of a mile beyond, a white house, encircled in sycamores, was visible at the farther end of a group of trees, which spring had powdered with a snow of flowers.

On beholding this house, D'Artagnan, calm as he was in general, felt an unusual disturbance within his heart--so powerful during the whole course of life are the recollections of youth. He proceeded, nevertheless, and came opposite to an iron gate, ornamented in the taste of the period.

Through the gate was seen kitchen-gardens, carefully attended to, a spacious courtyard, in which neighed several horses held by valets in various liveries, and a carriage, drawn by two horses of the country.

"We are mistaken," said D'Artagnan. "This cannot be the establishment of Athos. Good heavens! suppose he is dead and that this property now belongs to some one who bears his name. Alight, Planchet, and inquire, for I confess that I have scarcely courage so to do."

Planchet alighted.

"Thou must add," said D'Artagnan, "that a gentleman who is passing by wishes to have the honor of paying his respects to the Comte de la Fere, and if thou art satisfied with what thou hearest, then mention my name!"

Planchet, leading his horse by the bridle, drew near to the gate and rang the bell, and immediately a servant-man with white hair and of erect stature, notwithstanding his age, presented himself.

"Does Monsieur le Comte de la Fere live here?" asked Planchet.

"Yes, monsieur, it is here he lives," the servant replied to Planchet, who was not in livery.

"A nobleman retired from service, is he not?"

"Yes."

"And who had a lackey named Grimaud?" persisted Planchet, who had prudently considered that he couldn't have too much information.

"Monsieur Grimaud is absent from the chateau for the time being," said the servitor, who, little used as he was to such inquiries, began to examine Planchet from head to foot.

"Then," cried Planchet joyously, "I see well that it is the same Comte de la Fere whom we seek. Be good enough to open to me, for I wish to announce to monsieur le comte that my master, one of his friends, is here, and wishes to greet him."

"Why didn't you say so?" said the servitor, opening the gate. "But where is your master?"

"He is following me."

The servitor opened the gate and walked before Planchet, who made a sign to D'Artagnan. The latter, his heart palpitating more than ever, entered the courtyard without dismounting.

Whilst Planchet was standing on the steps before the house he heard a voice say:

"Well, where is this gentleman and why do they not bring him here?"

This voice, the sound of which reached D'Artagnan, reawakened in his heart a thousand sentiments, a thousand recollections that he had forgotten. He vaulted hastily from his horse, whilst Planchet, with a smile on his lips, advanced toward the master of the house.

"But I know you, my lad," said Athos, appearing on the threshold.

"Oh, yes, monsieur le comte, you know me and I know you. I am Planchet--Planchet, whom you know well." But the honest servant could say no more, so much was he overcome by this unexpected interview.

"What, Planchet, is Monsieur d'Artagnan here?"

"Here I am, my friend, dear Athos!" cried D'Artagnan, in a faltering voice and almost staggering from agitation.

At these words a visible emotion was expressed on the beautiful countenance and calm features of Athos. He rushed toward D'Artagnan with eyes fixed upon him and clasped him in his arms. D'Artagnan, equally moved, pressed him also closely to him, whilst tears stood in his eyes. Athos then took him by the hand and led him into the drawing-room, where there were several people. Every one arose.

"I present to you," he said, "Monsieur le Chevalier D'Artagnan, lieutenant of his majesty's musketeers, a devoted friend and one of the most excellent, brave gentlemen that I have ever known."

D'Artagnan received the compliments of those who were present in his own way, and whilst the conversation became general he looked earnestly at Athos.

Strange! Athos was scarcely aged at all! His fine eyes, no longer surrounded by that dark line which nights of dissipation pencil too infallibly, seemed larger, more liquid than ever. His face, a little elongated, had gained in calm dignity what it had lost in feverish excitement. His hand, always wonderfully beautiful and strong, was set off by a ruffle of lace, like certain hands by Titian and Vandyck. He was less stiff than formerly. His long, dark hair, softly powdered here and there with silver tendrils, fell elegantly over his shoulders in wavy curls; his voice was still youthful, as if belonging to a Hercules of twenty-five, and his magnificent teeth, which he had preserved white and sound, gave an indescribable charm to his smile.

Meanwhile the guests, seeing that the two friends were longing to be alone, prepared to depart, when a noise of dogs barking resounded through the courtyard and many persons said at the same moment:

"Ah! 'tis Raoul, who is come home."

Athos, as the name of Raoul was pronounced, looked inquisitively at D'Artagnan, in order to see if any curiosity was painted on his face. But D'Artagnan was still in confusion and turned around almost mechanically when a fine young man of fifteen years of age, dressed simply, but in perfect taste, entered the room, raising, as he came, his hat, adorned with a long plume of scarlet feathers.

Nevertheless, D'Artagnan was struck by the appearance of this new personage. It seemed to explain to him the change in Athos; a resemblance between the boy and the man explained the mystery of this regenerated existence. He remained listening and gazing.

"Here you are, home again, Raoul," said the comte.

"Yes, sir," replied the youth, with deep respect, "and I have performed the commission that you gave me."

"But what's the matter, Raoul?" said Athos, very anxiously. "You are pale and agitated."

"Sir," replied the young man, "it is on account of an accident which has happened to our little neighbor."

"To Mademoiselle de la Valliere?" asked Athos, quickly.

"What is it?" cried many persons present.

"She was walking with her nurse Marceline, in the place where the woodmen cut the wood, when, passing on horseback, I stopped. She saw me also and in trying to jump from the end of a pile of wood on which she had mounted, the poor child fell and was not able to rise again. I fear that she has badly sprained her ankle."

"Oh, heavens!" cried Athos. "And her mother, Madame de Saint-Remy, have they yet told her of it?"

"No, sir, Madame de Saint-Remy is at Blois with the Duchess of Orleans. I am afraid that what was first done was unskillful, if not worse than useless. I am come, sir, to ask your advice."

"Send directly to Blois, Raoul; or, rather, take horse and ride immediately yourself."

Raoul bowed.

"But where is Louise?" asked the comte.

"I have brought her here, sir, and I have deposited her in charge of Charlotte, who, till better advice comes, has bathed the foot in cold well-water."

The guests now all took leave of Athos, excepting the old Duc de Barbe, who, as an old friend of the family of La Valliere, went to see little Louise and offered to take her to Blois in his carriage.

"You are right, sir," said Athos. "She will be the sooner with her mother. As for you, Raoul, I am sure it is your fault, some giddiness or folly."

"No, sir, I assure you," muttered Raoul, "it is not."

"Oh, no, no, I declare it is not!" cried the young girl, while Raoul turned pale at the idea of his being perhaps the cause of her disaster.

"Nevertheless, Raoul, you must go to Blois and you must make your excuses and mine to Madame de Saint-Remy."

The youth looked pleased. He again took in his strong arms the little girl, whose pretty golden head and smiling face rested on his shoulder, and placed her gently in the carriage; then jumping on his horse with the elegance of a first-rate esquire, after bowing to Athos and D'Artagnan, he went off close by the door of the carriage, on somebody inside of which his eyes were riveted.

14. The Castle of Bragelonne.

Whilst this scene was going on, D'Artagnan remained with open mouth and a confused gaze. Everything had turned out so differently from what he expected that he was stupefied with wonder.

Athos, who had been observing him and guessing his thoughts, took his arm and led him into the garden.

"Whilst supper is being prepared," he said, smiling, "you will not, my friend, be sorry to have the mystery which so puzzles you cleared up."

"True, monsieur le comte," replied D'Artagnan, who felt that by degrees Athos was resuming that great influence which aristocracy had over him.

Athos smiled.

"First and foremost, dear D'Artagnan, we have no title such as count here. When I call you 'chevalier,' it is in presenting you to my guests, that they may know who you are. But to you, D'Artagnan, I am, I hope, still dear Athos, your comrade, your friend. Do you intend to stand on ceremony because you are less attached to me than you were?"

"Oh! God forbid!"

"Then let us be as we used to be; let us be open with each other. You are surprised at what you see here?"

"Extremely."

"But above all things, I am a marvel to you?"

"I confess it."

"I am still young, am I not? Should you not have known me again, in spite of my eight-and-forty years of age?"

"On the contrary, I do not find you the same person at all."

"I understand," cried Athos, with a gentle blush. "Everything, D'Artagnan, even folly, has its limit."

"Then your means, it appears, are improved; you have a capital house--your own, I presume? You have a park, and horses, servants."

Athos smiled.

"Yes, I inherited this little property when I quitted the army, as I told you. The park is twenty acres--twenty, comprising kitchen-gardens and a common. I have two horses,--I do not count my servant's bobtailed nag. My sporting dogs consist of two pointers, two harriers and two setters. But then all this extravagance is not for myself," added Athos, laughing.

"Yes, I see, for the young man Raoul," said D'Artagnan.

"You guess aright, my friend; this youth is an orphan, deserted by his mother, who left him in the house of a poor country priest. I have brought him up. It is Raoul who has worked in me the change you see; I was dried up like a miserable tree, isolated, attached to nothing on earth; it was only a deep affection that could make me take root again and drag me back to life. This child has caused me to recover what I had lost. I had no longer any wish to live for myself, I have lived for him. I have corrected the vices that I had; I have assumed the virtues that I had not. Precept something, but example more. I may be mistaken, but I believe that Raoul will be as accomplished a gentleman as our degenerate age could display."

The remembrance of Milady recurred to D'Artagnan.

"And you are happy?" he said to his friend.

"As happy as it is allowed to one of God's creatures to be on this earth; but say out all you think, D'Artagnan, for you have not yet done so."

"You are too bad, Athos; one can hide nothing from you," answered D'Artagnan. "I wished to ask you if you ever feel any emotions of terror resembling----"

"Remorse! I finish your phrase. Yes and no. I do not feel remorse, because that woman, I profoundly hold, deserved her punishment. Had she one redeeming trait? I doubt it. I do not feel remorse, because had we allowed her to live she would have persisted in her work of destruction. But I do not mean, my friend that we were right in what we did. Perhaps all blood demands some expiation. Hers had been accomplished; it remains, possibly, for us to accomplish ours."

"I have sometimes thought as you do, Athos."

"She had a son, that unhappy woman?"

"Yes."

"Have you ever heard of him?"

"Never."

"He must be about twenty-three years of age," said Athos, in a low tone. "I often think of that young man, D'Artagnan."

"Strange! for I had forgotten him," said the lieutenant.

Athos smiled; the smile was melancholy.

"And Lord de Winter--do you know anything about him?"

"I know that he is in high favor with Charles I."

"The fortunes of that monarch now are at low water. He shed the blood of Strafford; that confirms what I said just now--blood will have blood. And the queen?"

"What queen?"

"Madame Henrietta of England, daughter of Henry IV."

"She is at the Louvre, as you know."

"Yes, and I hear in bitter poverty. Her daughter, during the severest cold, was obliged for want of fire to remain in bed. Do you grasp that?" said Athos, shrugging his shoulders; "the daughter of Henry IV. shivering for want of a fagot! Why did she not ask from any one of us a home instead of from Mazarin? She should have wanted nothing."

"Have you ever seen the queen of England?" inquired D'Artagnan.

"No; but my mother, as a child, saw her. Did I ever tell you that my mother was lady of honor to Marie de Medici?"

"Never. You know, Athos, you never spoke much of such matters."

"Ah, mon Dieu, yes, you are right," Athos replied; "but then there must be some occasion for speaking."

"Porthos wouldn't have waited for it so patiently," said D'Artagnan, with a smile.

"Every one according to his nature, my dear D'Artagnan. Porthos, in spite of a touch of vanity, has many excellent qualities. Have you seen him?"

"I left him five days ago," said D'Artagnan, and he portrayed with Gascon wit and sprightliness the magnificence of Porthos in his Chateau of Pierrefonds; nor did he neglect to launch a few arrows of wit at the excellent Monsieur Mouston.

"I sometimes wonder," replied Athos, smiling at that gayety which recalled the good old days, "that we could form an association of men who would be, after twenty years of separation, still so closely bound together. Friendship throws out deep roots in honest hearts, D'Artagnan. Believe me, it is only the evil-minded who deny friendship; they cannot understand it. And Aramis?"

"I have seen him also," said D'Artagnan; "but he seemed to me cold."

"Ah, you have seen Aramis?" said Athos, turning on D'Artagnan a searching look. "Why, it is a veritable pilgrimage, my dear friend, that you are making to the Temple of Friendship, as the poets would say."

"Why, yes," replied D'Artagnan, with embarrassment.

"Aramis, you know," continued Athos, "is naturally cold, and then he is always involved in intrigues with women."

"I believe he is at this moment in a very complicated one," said D'Artagnan.

Athos made no reply.

"He is not curious," thought D'Artagnan.

Athos not only failed to reply, he even changed the subject of conversation.

"You see," said he, calling D'Artagnan's attention to the fact that they had come back to the chateau after an hour's walk, "we have made a tour of my domains."

"All is charming and everything savors of nobility," replied D'Artagnan.

At this instant they heard the sound of horses' feet.

"'Tis Raoul who has come back," said Athos; "and we can now hear how the poor child is."

In fact, the young man appeared at the gate, covered with dust, entered the courtyard, leaped from his horse, which he consigned to the charge of a groom, and then went to greet the count and D'Artagnan.

"Monsieur," said Athos, placing his hand on D'Artagnan's shoulder, "monsieur is the Chevalier D'Artagnan of whom you have often heard me speak, Raoul."

"Monsieur," said the young man, saluting again and more profoundly, "monsieur le comte has pronounced your name before me as an example whenever he wished to speak of an intrepid and generous gentleman."

That little compliment could not fail to move D'Artagnan. He extended a hand to Raoul and said:

"My young friend, all the praises that are given me should be passed on to the count here; for he has educated me in everything and it is not his fault that his pupil profited so little from his instructions. But he will make it up in you I am sure. I like your manner, Raoul, and your politeness has touched me."

Athos was more delighted than can be told. He looked at D'Artagnan with an expression of gratitude and then bestowed on Raoul one of those strange smiles, of which children are so proud when they receive them.

"Now," said D'Artagnan to himself, noticing that silent play of countenance, "I am sure of it."

"I hope the accident has been of no consequence?"

"They don't yet know, sir, on account of the swelling; but the doctor is afraid some tendon has been injured."

At this moment a little boy, half peasant, half foot-boy, came to announce supper.

Athos led his guest into a dining-room of moderate size, the windows of which opened on one side on a garden, on the other on a hot-house full of magnificent flowers.

D'Artagnan glanced at the dinner service. The plate was magnificent, old, and appertaining to the family. D'Artagnan stopped to look at a sideboard on which was a superb ewer of silver.

"That workmanship is divine!" he exclaimed.

"Yes, a chef d'oeuvre of the great Florentine sculptor, Benvenuto Cellini," replied Athos.

"What battle does it represent?"

"That of Marignan, just at the point where one of my forefathers is offering his sword to Francis I., who has broken his. It was on that occasion that my ancestor, Enguerrand de la Fere, was made a knight of the Order of St. Michael; besides which, the king, fifteen years afterward, gave him also this ewer and a sword which you may have seen formerly in my house, also a lovely specimen of workmanship. Men were giants in those times," said Athos; "now we are pigmies in comparison. Let us sit down to supper. Call Charles," he added, addressing the boy who waited.

"My good Charles, I particularly recommend to your care Planchet, the laquais of Monsieur D'Artagnan. He likes good wine; now you have the key of the cellar. He has slept a long time on a hard bed, so he won't object to a soft one; take every care of him, I beg of you." Charles bowed and retired.

"You think of everything," said D'Artagnan; "and I thank you for Planchet, my dear Athos."

Raoul stared on hearing this name and looked at the count to be quite sure that it was he whom the lieutenant thus addressed.

"That name sounds strange to you," said Athos, smiling; "it was my nom de guerre when Monsieur D'Artagnan, two other gallant friends and myself performed some feats of arms at the siege of La Rochelle, under the deceased cardinal and Monsieur de Bassompierre. My friend is still so kind as to address me by that old and well beloved appellation, which makes my heart glad when I hear it."

"'Tis an illustrious name," said the lieutenant, "and had one day triumphal honors paid to it."

"What do you mean, sir?" inquired Raoul.

"You have not forgotten St. Gervais, Athos, and the napkin which was converted into a banner?" and he then related to Raoul the story of the bastion, and Raoul fancied he was listening to one of those deeds of arms belonging to days of chivalry, so gloriously recounted by Tasso and Ariosto.

"D'Artagnan does not tell you, Raoul," said Athos, in his turn, "that he was reckoned one of the finest swordsmen of his time--a knuckle of iron, a wrist of steel, a sure eye and a glance of fire; that's what his adversary met with. He was eighteen, only three years older than you are, Raoul, when I saw him set to work, pitted against tried men."

"And did Monsieur D'Artagnan come off the conqueror?" asked the young man, with glistening eye.

"I killed one man, if I recollect rightly," replied D'Artagnan, with a look of inquiry directed to Athos; "another I disarmed or wounded, I don't remember which."

"Wounded!" said Athos; "it was a phenomenon of skill."

The young man would willingly have prolonged this conversation far into the night, but Athos pointed out to him that his guest must need repose. D'Artagnan would fain have declared that he was not fatigued, but Athos insisted on his retiring to his chamber, conducted thither by Raoul.

15. Athos as a Diplomatist.

D'Artagnan retired to bed--not to sleep, but to think over all he had heard that evening. Being naturally goodhearted, and having had once a liking for Athos, which had grown into a sincere friendship, he was delighted at thus meeting a man full of intelligence and moral strength, instead of a drunkard. He admitted without annoyance the continued superiority of Athos over himself, devoid as he was of that jealousy which might have saddened a less generous disposition; he was delighted also that the high qualities of Athos appeared to promise favorably for his mission. Nevertheless, it seemed to him that Athos was not in all respects sincere and frank. Who was the youth he had adopted and who bore so striking a resemblance to him? What could explain Athos's having re-entered the world and the extreme sobriety he had observed at table? The absence of Grimaud, whose name had never once been uttered by Athos, gave D'Artagnan uneasiness. It was evident either that he no longer possessed the confidence of his friend, or that Athos was bound by some invisible chain, or that he had been forewarned of the lieutenant's visit.

He could not help thinking of M. Rochefort, whom he had seen in Notre Dame; could De Rochefort have forestalled him with Athos? Again, the moderate fortune which Athos possessed, concealed as it was, so skillfully, seemed to show a regard for appearances and to betray a latent ambition which might be easily aroused. The clear and vigorous intellect of Athos would render him more open to conviction than a less able man would be. He would enter into the minister's schemes with the more ardor, because his natural activity would be doubled by necessity.

Resolved to seek an explanation on all these points on the following day, D'Artagnan, in spite of his fatigue, prepared for an attack and determined that it should take place after breakfast. He determined to cultivate the good-will of the youth Raoul and, either whilst fencing with him or when out shooting, to extract from his simplicity some information which would connect the Athos of old times with the Athos of the present. But D'Artagnan at the same time, being a man of extreme caution, was quite aware what injury he should do himself, if by any indiscretion or awkwardness he should betray has manoeuvering to the experienced eye of Athos. Besides, to tell truth, whilst D'Artagnan was quite disposed to adopt a subtle course against the cunning of Aramis or the vanity of Porthos, he was ashamed to equivocate with Athos, true-hearted, open Athos. It seemed to him that if Porthos and Aramis deemed him superior to them in the arts of diplomacy, they would like him all the better for it; but that Athos, on the contrary, would despise him.

"Ah! why is not Grimaud, the taciturn Grimaud, here?" thought D'Artagnan, "there are so many things his silence would have told me; with Grimaud silence was another form of eloquence!"

There reigned a perfect stillness in the house. D'Artagnan had heard the door shut and the shutters barred; the dogs became in their turn silent. At last a nightingale, lost in a thicket of shrubs, in the midst of its most melodious cadences had fluted low and lower into stillness and fallen asleep. Not a sound was heard in the castle, except of a footstep up and down, in the chamber above--as he supposed, the bedroom of Athos.

"He is walking about and thinking," thought D'Artagnan; "but of what? It is impossible to know; everything else might be guessed, but not that."

At length Athos went to bed, apparently, for the noise ceased.

Silence and fatigue together overcame D'Artagnan and sleep overtook him also. He was not, however, a good sleeper. Scarcely had dawn gilded his window curtains when he sprang out of bed and opened the windows. Somebody, he perceived, was in the courtyard, moving stealthily. True to his custom of never passing anything over that it was within his power to know, D'Artagnan looked out of the window and perceived the close red coat and brown hair of Raoul.

The young man was opening the door of the stable. He then, with noiseless haste, took out the horse that he had ridden on the previous evening, saddled and bridled it himself and led the animal into the alley to the right of the kitchen-garden, opened a side door which conducted him to a bridle road, shut it after him, and D'Artagnan saw him pass by like a dart, bending, as he went, beneath the pendent flowery branches of maple and acacia. The road, as D'Artagnan had observed, was the way to Blois.

"So!" thought the Gascon "here's a young blade who has already his love affair, who doesn't at all agree with Athos in his hatred to the fair sex. He's not going to hunt, for he has neither dogs nor arms; he's not going on a message, for he goes secretly. Why does he go in secret? Is he afraid of me or of his father? for I am sure the count is his father. By Jove! I shall know about that soon, for I shall soon speak out to Athos."

Day was now advanced; all the noises that had ceased the night before reawakened, one after the other. The bird on the branch, the dog in his kennel, the sheep in the field, the boats moored in the Loire, even, became alive and vocal. The latter, leaving the shore, abandoned themselves gaily to the current. The Gascon gave a last twirl to his mustache, a last turn to his hair, brushed, from habit, the brim of his hat with the sleeve of his doublet, and went downstairs. Scarcely had he descended the last step of the threshold when he saw Athos bent down toward the ground, as if he were looking for a crown-piece in the dust.

"Good-morning, my dear host," cried D'Artagnan.

"Good-day to you; have you slept well?"

"Excellently, Athos, but what are you looking for? You are perhaps a tulip fancier?"

"My dear friend, if I am, you must not laugh at me for being so. In the country people alter; one gets to like, without knowing it, all those beautiful objects that God causes to spring from the earth, which are despised in cities. I was looking anxiously for some iris roots I planted here, close to this reservoir, and which some one has trampled upon this morning. These gardeners are the most careless people in the world; in bringing the horse out to the water they've allowed him to walk over the border."

D'Artagnan began to smile.

"Ah! you think so, do you?"

And he took his friend along the alley, where a number of tracks like those which had trampled down the flowerbeds, were visible.

"Here are the horse's hoofs again, it seems, Athos," he said carelessly.

"Yes, indeed, the marks are recent."

"Quite so," replied the lieutenant.

"Who went out this morning?" Athos asked, uneasily. "Has any horse got loose?"

"Not likely," answered the Gascon; "these marks are regular."

"Where is Raoul?" asked Athos; "how is it that I have not seen him?"

"Hush!" exclaimed D'Artagnan, putting his finger on his lips; and he related what he had seen, watching Athos all the while.

"Ah, he's gone to Blois; the poor boy----"

"Wherefore?"

"Ah, to inquire after the little La Valliere; she has sprained her foot, you know."

"You think he has?"

"I am sure of it," said Athos; "don't you see that Raoul is in love?"

"Indeed! with whom--with a child seven years old?"

"Dear friend, at Raoul's age the heart is so expansive that it must encircle one object or another, fancied or real. Well, his love is half real, half fanciful. She is the prettiest little creature in the world, with flaxen hair, blue eyes,--at once saucy and languishing."

"But what say you to Raoul's fancy?"

"Nothing--I laugh at Raoul; but this first desire of the heart is imperious. I remember, just at his age, how deep in love I was with a Grecian statue which our good king, then Henry IV., gave my father, insomuch that I was mad with grief when they told me that the story of Pygmalion was nothing but a fable."

"It is mere want of occupation. You do not make Raoul work, so he takes his own way of employing himself."

"Exactly; therefore I think of sending him away from here."

"You will be wise to do so."

"No doubt of it; but it will break his heart. So long as three or four years ago he used to adorn and adore his little idol, whom he will some day fall in love with in right earnest if he remains here. The parents of little La Valliere have for a long time perceived and been amused at it; now they begin to look concerned."

"Nonsense! However, Raoul must be diverted from this fancy. Send him away or you will never make a man of him."

"I think I shall send him to Paris."

"So!" thought D'Artagnan, and it seemed to him that the moment for attack had arrived.

"Suppose," he said, "we roughly chalk out a career for this young man. I wish to consult you about some thing."

"Do so."

"Do you think it is time for us to enter the service?"

"But are you not still in the service--you, D'Artagnan?"

"I mean active service. Our former life, has it still no attractions for you? would you not be happy to begin anew in my society and in that of Porthos, the exploits of our youth?"

"Do you propose to me to do so, D'Artagnan?"

"Decidedly and honestly."

"On whose side?" asked Athos, fixing his clear, benevolent glance on the countenance of the Gascon.

"Ah, devil take it, you speak in earnest----"

"And must have a definite answer. Listen, D'Artagnan. There is but one person, or rather, one cause, to whom a man like me can be useful--that of the king."

"Exactly," answered the musketeer.

"Yes, but let us understand each other," returned Athos, seriously. "If by the cause of the king you mean that of Monsieur de Mazarin, we do not understand each other."

"I don't say exactly," answered the Gascon, confused.

"Come, D'Artagnan, don't let us play a sidelong game; your hesitation, your evasion, tells me at once on whose side you are; for that party no one dares openly to recruit, and when people recruit for it, it is with averted eyes and humble voice."

"Ah! my dear Athos!"

"You know that I am not alluding to you; you are the pearl of brave, bold men. I speak of that spiteful and intriguing Italian--of the pedant who has tried to put on his own head a crown which he stole from under a pillow--of the scoundrel who calls his party the party of the king--who wants to send the princes of the blood to prison, not daring to kill them, as our great cardinal--our cardinal did--of the miser, who weighs his gold pieces and keeps the clipped ones for fear, though he is rich, of losing them at play next morning--of the impudent fellow who insults the queen, as they say--so much the worse for her--and who is going in three months to make war upon us, in order that he may retain his pensions; is that the master whom you propose to me? I thank you, D'Artagnan."

"You are more impetuous than you were," returned D'Artagnan. "Age has warmed, not chilled your blood. Who informed you this was the master I propose to you? Devil take it," he muttered to himself, "don't let me betray my secrets to a man not inclined to entertain them."

"Well, then," said Athos, "what are your schemes? what do you propose?"

"Zounds! nothing more than natural. You live on your estate, happy in golden mediocrity. Porthos has, perhaps, sixty thousand francs income. Aramis has always fifty duchesses quarreling over the priest, as they quarreled formerly over the musketeer; but I--what have I in the world? I have worn my cuirass these twenty years, kept down in this inferior rank, without going forward or backward, hardly half living. In fact, I am dead. Well! when there is some idea of being resuscitated, you say he's a scoundrel, an impudent fellow, a miser, a bad master! By Jove! I am of your opinion, but find me a better one or give me the means of living."

Athos was for a few moments thoughtful.

"Good! D'Artagnan is for Mazarin," he said to himself.

From that moment he grew very guarded.

On his side D'Artagnan became more cautious also.

"You spoke to me," Athos resumed, "of Porthos; have you persuaded him to seek his fortune? But he has wealth, I believe, already."

"Doubtless he has. But such is man, we always want something more than we already have."

"What does Porthos wish for?"

"To be a baron."

"Ah, true! I forgot," said Athos, laughing.

"'Tis true!" thought the Gascon, "where has he heard it? Does he correspond with Aramis? Ah! if I knew that he did I should know all."

The conversation was interrupted by the entrance of Raoul.

"Is our little neighbor worse?" asked D'Artagnan, seeing a look of vexation on the face of the youth.

"Ah, sir!" replied Raoul, "her fall is a very serious one, and without any ostensible injury, the physician fears she will be lame for life."

"This is terrible," said Athos.

"And what makes me all the more wretched, sir, is, that I was the cause of this misfortune."

"How so?" asked Athos.

"It was to run to meet me that she leaped from that pile of wood."

"There's only one remedy, dear Raoul--that is, to marry her as a compensation." remarked D'Artagnan.

"Ah, sir!" answered Raoul, "you joke about a real misfortune; that is cruel, indeed."

The good understanding between the two friends was not in the least altered by the morning's skirmish. They breakfasted with a good appetite, looking now and then at poor Raoul, who with moist eyes and a full heart, scarcely ate at all.

After breakfast two letters arrived for Athos, who read them with profound attention, whilst D'Artagnan could not restrain himself from jumping up several times on seeing him read these epistles, in one of which, there being at the time a very strong light, he perceived the fine writing of Aramis. The other was in a feminine hand, long, and crossed.

"Come," said D'Artagnan to Raoul, seeing that Athos wished to be alone, "come, let us take a turn in the fencing gallery; that will amuse you."

And they both went into a low room where there were foils, gloves, masks, breastplates, and all the accessories for a fencing match.

In a quarter of an hour Athos joined them and at the same moment Charles brought in a letter for D'Artagnan, which a messenger had just desired might be instantly delivered.

It was now Athos's turn to take a sly look.

D'Artagnan read the letter with apparent calmness and said, shaking his head:

"See, dear friend, what it is to belong to the army. Faith, you are indeed right not to return to it. Monsieur de Treville is ill, so my company can't do without me; there! my leave is at an end!"

"Do you return to Paris?" asked Athos, quickly.

"Egad! yes; but why don't you come there also?"

Athos colored a little and answered:

"Should I go, I shall be delighted to see you there."

"Halloo, Planchet!" cried the Gascon from the door, "we must set out in ten minutes; give the horses some hay."

Then turning to Athos he added:

"I seem to miss something here. I am really sorry to go away without having seen Grimaud."

"Grimaud!" replied Athos. "I'm surprised you have never so much as asked after him. I have lent him to a friend----"

"Who will understand the signs he makes?" returned D'Artagnan.

"I hope so."

The friends embraced cordially; D'Artagnan pressed Raoul's hand.

"Will you not come with me?" he said; "I shall pass by Blois."

Raoul turned toward Athos, who showed him by a secret sign that he did not wish him to go.

"No, monsieur," replied the young man; "I will remain with monsieur le comte."

"Adieu, then, to both, my good friends," said D'Artagnan; "may God preserve you! as we used to say when we said good-bye to each other in the late cardinal's time."

Athos waved his hand, Raoul bowed, and D'Artagnan and Planchet set out.

The count followed them with his eyes, his hands resting on the shoulders of the youth, whose height was almost equal to his own; but as soon as they were out of sight he said:

"Raoul, we set out to-night for Paris."

"Eh?" cried the young man, turning pale.

"You may go and offer your adieux and mine to Madame de Saint-Remy. I shall wait for you here till seven."

The young man bent low, with an expression of sorrow and gratitude mingled, and retired in order to saddle his horse.

As to D'Artagnan, scarcely, on his side, was he out of sight when he drew from his pocket a letter, which he read over again:

"Return immediately to Paris.--J. M----."

"The epistle is laconic," said D'Artagnan; "and if there had not been a postscript, probably I should not have understood it; but happily there is a postscript."

And he read that welcome postscript, which made him forget the abruptness of the letter.

"P. S.--Go to the king's treasurer, at Blois; tell him your name and show him this letter; you will receive two hundred pistoles."

"Assuredly," said D'Artagnan, "I admire this piece of prose. The cardinal writes better than I thought. Come, Planchet, let us pay a visit to the king's treasurer and then set off."

"Toward Paris, sir?"

"Toward Paris."

And they set out at as hard a canter as their horses could maintain.

16. The Duc de Beaufort.

The circumstances that had hastened the return of D'Artagnan to Paris were as follows:

One evening, when Mazarin, according to custom, went to visit the queen, in passing the guard-chamber he heard loud voices; wishing to know on what topic the soldiers were conversing, he approached with his wonted wolf-like step, pushed open the door and put his head close to the chink.

There was a dispute among the guards.

"I tell you," one of them was saying, "that if Coysel predicted that, 'tis as good as true; I know nothing about it, but I have heard say that he's not only an astrologer, but a magician."

"Deuce take it, friend, if he's one of thy friends thou wilt ruin him in saying so."

"Why?"

"Because he may be tried for it."

"Ah! absurd! they don't burn sorcerers nowadays."

"No? 'Tis not a long time since the late cardinal burnt Urban Grandier, though."

"My friend, Urban Grandier wasn't a sorcerer, he was a learned man. He didn't predict the future, he knew the past--often a more dangerous thing."

Mazarin nodded an assent, but wishing to know what this prediction was, about which they disputed, he remained in the same place.

"I don't say," resumed the guard, "that Coysel is not a sorcerer, but I say that if his prophecy gets wind, it's a sure way to prevent it's coming true."

"How so?"

"Why, in this way: if Coysel says loud enough for the cardinal to hear him, on such or such a day such a prisoner will escape, 'tis plain that the cardinal will take measures of precaution and that the prisoner will not escape."

"Good Lord!" said another guard, who might have been thought asleep on a bench, but who had lost not a syllable of the conversation, "do you suppose that men can escape their destiny? If it is written yonder, in Heaven, that the Duc de Beaufort is to escape, he will escape; and all the precautions of the cardinal will not prevent it."

Mazarin started. He was an Italian and therefore superstitious. He walked straight into the midst of the guards, who on seeing him were silent.

"What were you saying?" he asked with his flattering manner; "that Monsieur de Beaufort had escaped, were you not?"

"Oh, no, my lord!" said the incredulous soldier. "He's well guarded now; we only said he would escape."

"Who said so?"

"Repeat your story, Saint Laurent," replied the man, turning to the originator of the tale.

"My lord," said the guard, "I have simply mentioned the prophecy I heard from a man named Coysel, who believes that, be he ever so closely watched and guarded, the Duke of Beaufort will escape before Whitsuntide."

"Coysel is a madman!" returned the cardinal.

"No," replied the soldier, tenacious in his credulity; "he has foretold many things which have come to pass; for instance, that the queen would have a son; that Monsieur Coligny would be killed in a duel with the Duc de Guise; and finally, that the coadjutor would be made cardinal. Well! the queen has not only one son, but two; then, Monsieur de Coligny was killed, and----"

"Yes," said Mazarin, "but the coadjutor is not yet made cardinal!"

"No, my lord, but he will be," answered the guard.

Mazarin made a grimace, as if he meant to say, "But he does not wear the cardinal's cap;" then he added:

"So, my friend, it's your opinion that Monsieur de Beaufort will escape?"

"That's my idea, my lord; and if your eminence were to offer to make me at this moment governor of the castle of Vincennes, I should refuse it. After Whitsuntide it would be another thing."

There is nothing so convincing as a firm conviction. It has its own effect upon the most incredulous; and far from being incredulous, Mazarin was superstitious. He went away thoughtful and anxious and returned to his own room, where he summoned Bernouin and desired him to fetch thither in the morning the special guard he had placed over Monsieur de Beaufort and to awaken him whenever he should arrive.

The guard had, in fact, touched the cardinal in the tenderest point. During the whole five years in which the Duc de Beaufort had been in prison not a day had passed in which the cardinal had not felt a secret dread of his escape. It was not possible, as he knew well, to confine for the whole of his life the grandson of Henry IV., especially when this young prince was scarcely thirty years of age. But however and whensoever he did escape, what hatred he must cherish against him to whom he owed his long imprisonment; who had taken him, rich, brave, glorious, beloved by women, feared by men, to cut off his life's best, happiest years; for it is not life, it is merely existence, in prison! Meantime, Mazarin redoubled his surveillance over the duke. But like the miser in the fable, he could not sleep for thinking of his treasure. Often he awoke in the night, suddenly, dreaming that he had been robbed of Monsieur de Beaufort. Then he inquired about him and had the vexation of hearing that the prisoner played, drank, sang, but that whilst playing, drinking, singing, he often stopped short to vow that Mazarin should pay dear for all the amusements he had forced him to enter into at Vincennes.

So much did this one idea haunt the cardinal even in his sleep, that when at seven in the morning Bernouin came to arouse him, his first words were: "Well, what's the matter? Has Monsieur de Beaufort escaped from Vincennes?"

"I do not think so, my lord," said Bernouin; "but you will hear about him, for La Ramee is here and awaits the commands of your eminence."

"Tell him to come in," said Mazarin, arranging his pillows, so that he might receive the visitor sitting up in bed.

The officer entered, a large fat man, with an open physiognomy. His air of perfect serenity made Mazarin uneasy.

"Approach, sir," said the cardinal.

The officer obeyed.

"Do you know what they are saying here?"

"No, your eminence."

"Well, they say that Monsieur de Beaufort is going to escape from Vincennes, if he has not done so already."

The officer's face expressed complete stupefaction. He opened at once his little eyes and his great mouth, to inhale better the joke his eminence deigned to address to him, and ended by a burst of laughter, so violent that his great limbs shook in hilarity as they would have done in an ague.

"Escape! my lord--escape! Your eminence does not then know where Monsieur de Beaufort is?"

"Yes, I do, sir; in the donjon of Vincennes."

"Yes, sir; in a room, the walls of which are seven feet thick, with grated windows, each bar as thick as my arm."

"Sir," replied Mazarin, "with perseverance one may penetrate through a wall; with a watch-spring one may saw through an iron bar."

"Then my lord does not know that there are eight guards about him, four in his chamber, four in the antechamber, and that they never leave him."

"But he leaves his room, he plays at tennis at the Mall?"

"Sir, those amusements are allowed; but if your eminence wishes it, we will discontinue the permission."

"No, no!" cried Mazarin, fearing that should his prisoner ever leave his prison he would be the more exasperated against him if he thus retrenched his amusement. He then asked with whom he played.

"My lord, either with the officers of the guard, with the other prisoners, or with me."

"But does he not approach the walls while playing?"

"Your eminence doesn't know those walls; they are sixty feet high and I doubt if Monsieur de Beaufort is sufficiently weary of life to risk his neck by jumping off."

"Hum!" said the cardinal, beginning to feel more comfortable. "You mean to say, then, my dear Monsieur la Ramee----"

"That unless Monsieur de Beaufort can contrive to metamorphose himself into a little bird, I will continue answerable for him."

"Take care! you assert a great deal," said Mazarin. "Monsieur de Beaufort told the guards who took him to Vincennes that he had often thought what he should do in case he were put into prison, and that he had found out forty ways of escaping."

"My lord, if among these forty there had been one good way he would have been out long ago."

"Come, come; not such a fool as I fancied!" thought Mazarin.

"Besides, my lord must remember that Monsieur de Chavigny is governor of Vincennes," continued La Ramee, "and that Monsieur de Chavigny is not friendly to Monsieur de Beaufort."

"Yes, but Monsieur de Chavigny is sometimes absent."

"When he is absent I am there."

"But when you leave him, for instance?"

"Oh! when I leave him, I place in my stead a bold fellow who aspires to be his majesty's special guard. I promise you he keeps a good watch over the prisoner. During the three weeks that he has been with me, I have only had to reproach him with one thing--being too severe with the prisoners."

"And who is this Cerberus?"

"A certain Monsieur Grimaud, my lord."

"And what was he before he went to Vincennes?"

"He was in the country, as I was told by the person who recommended him to me."

"And who recommended this man to you?"

"The steward of the Duc de Grammont."

"He is not a gossip, I hope?"

"Lord a mercy, my lord! I thought for a long time that he was dumb; he answers only by signs. It seems his former master accustomed him to that."

"Well, dear Monsieur la Ramee," replied the cardinal "let him prove a true and thankful keeper and we will shut our eyes upon his rural misdeeds and put on his back a uniform to make him respectable, and in the pockets of that uniform some pistoles to drink to the king's health."

Mazarin was large in promises,--quite unlike the virtuous Monsieur Grimaud so bepraised by La Ramee; for he said nothing and did much.

It was now nine o'clock. The cardinal, therefore, got up, perfumed himself, dressed, and went to the queen to tell her what had detained him. The queen, who was scarcely less afraid of Monsieur de Beaufort than the cardinal himself, and who was almost as superstitious as he was, made him repeat word for word all La Ramee's praises of his deputy. Then, when the cardinal had ended:

"Alas, sir! why have we not a Grimaud near every prince?"

"Patience!" replied Mazarin, with his Italian smile; "that may happen one day; but in the meantime----"

"Well, in the meantime?"

"I shall still take precautions."

And he wrote to D'Artagnan to hasten his return.

17. Duc de Beaufort amused his Leisure Hours in the Donjon of Vincennes.

The captive who was the source of so much alarm to the cardinal and whose means of escape disturbed the repose of the whole court, was wholly unconscious of the terror he caused at the Palais Royal.

He had found himself so strictly guarded that he soon perceived the fruitlessness of any attempt at escape. His vengeance, therefore, consisted in coining curses on the head of Mazarin; he even tried to make some verses on him, but soon gave up the attempt, for Monsieur de Beaufort had not only not received from Heaven the gift of versifying, he had the greatest difficulty in expressing himself in prose.

The duke was the grandson of Henry VI. and Gabrielle d'Estrees--as good-natured, as brave, as proud, and above all, as Gascon as his ancestor, but less elaborately educated. After having been for some time after the death of Louis XIII. the favorite, the confidant, the first man, in short, at the court, he had been obliged to yield his place to Mazarin and so became the second in influence and favor; and eventually, as he was stupid enough to be vexed at this change of position, the queen had had him arrested and sent to Vincennes in charge of Guitant, who made his appearance in these pages in the beginning of this history and whom we shall see again. It is understood, of course, that when we say "the queen," Mazarin is meant.

During the five years of this seclusion, which would have improved and matured the intellect of any other man, M. de Beaufort, had he not affected to brave the cardinal, despise princes, and walk alone without adherents or disciples, would either have regained his liberty or made partisans. But these considerations never occurred to the duke and every day the cardinal received fresh accounts of him which were as unpleasant as possible to the minister.

After having failed in poetry, Monsieur de Beaufort tried drawing. He drew portraits, with a piece of coal, of the cardinal; and as his talents did not enable him to produce a very good likeness, he wrote under the picture that there might be little doubt regarding the original: "Portrait of the Illustrious Coxcomb, Mazarin." Monsieur de Chavigny, the governor of Vincennes, waited upon the duke to request that he would amuse himself in some other way, or that at all events, if he drew likenesses, he would not put mottoes underneath them. The next day the prisoner's room was full of pictures and mottoes. Monsieur de Beaufort, in common with many other prisoners, was bent upon doing things that were prohibited; and the only resource the governor had was, one day when the duke was playing at tennis, to efface all these drawings, consisting chiefly of profiles. M. de Beaufort did not venture to draw the cardinal's fat face.

The duke thanked Monsieur de Chavigny for having, as he said, cleaned his drawing-paper for him; he then divided the walls of his room into compartments and dedicated each of these compartments to some incident in Mazarin's life. In one was depicted the "Illustrious Coxcomb" receiving a shower of blows from Cardinal Bentivoglio, whose servant he had been; another, the "Illustrious Mazarin" acting the part of Ignatius Loyola in a tragedy of that name; a third, the "Illustrious Mazarin" stealing the portfolio of prime minister from Monsieur de Chavigny, who had expected to have it; a fourth, the "Illustrious Coxcomb Mazarin" refusing to give Laporte, the young king's valet, clean sheets, and saying that "it was quite enough for the king of France to have clean sheets every three months."

The governor, of course, thought proper to threaten his prisoner that if he did not give up drawing such pictures he should be obliged to deprive him of all the means of amusing himself in that manner. To this Monsieur de Beaufort replied that since every opportunity of distinguishing himself in arms was taken from him, he wished to make himself celebrated in the arts; since he could not be a Bayard, he would become a Raphael or a Michael Angelo. Nevertheless, one day when Monsieur de Beaufort was walking in the meadow his fire was put out, his charcoal all removed, taken away; and thus his means of drawing utterly destroyed.

The poor duke swore, fell into a rage, yelled, and declared that they wished to starve him to death as they had starved the Marechal Ornano and the Grand Prior of Vendome; but he refused to promise that he would not make any more drawings and remained without any fire in the room all the winter.

His next act was to purchase a dog from one of his keepers. With this animal, which he called Pistache, he was often shut up for hours alone, superintending, as every one supposed, its education. At last, when Pistache was sufficiently well trained, Monsieur de Beaufort invited the governor and officers of Vincennes to attend a representation which he was going to have in his apartment.

The party assembled, the room was lighted with waxlights, and the prisoner, with a bit of plaster he had taken out of the wall of his room, had traced a long white line, representing a cord, on the floor. Pistache, on a signal from his master, placed himself on this line, raised himself on his hind paws, and holding in his front paws a wand with which clothes used to be beaten, he began to dance upon the line with as many contortions as a rope-dancer. Having been several times up and down it, he gave the wand back to his master and began without hesitation to perform the same evolutions over again.

The intelligent creature was received with loud applause.

The first part of the entertainment being concluded Pistache was desired to say what o'clock it was; he was shown Monsieur de Chavigny's watch; it was then half-past six; the dog raised and dropped his paw six times; the seventh he let it remain upraised. Nothing could be better done; a sun-dial could not have shown the hour with greater precision.

Then the question was put to him who was the best jailer in all the prisons in France.

The dog performed three evolutions around the circle and laid himself, with the deepest respect, at the feet of Monsieur de Chavigny, who at first seemed inclined to like the joke and laughed long and loud, but a frown succeeded, and he bit his lips with vexation.

Then the duke put to Pistache this difficult question, who was the greatest thief in the world?

Pistache went again around the circle, but stopped at no one, and at last went to the door and began to scratch and bark.

"See, gentlemen," said M. de Beaufort, "this wonderful animal, not finding here what I ask for, seeks it out of doors; you shall, however, have his answer. Pistache, my friend, come here. Is not the greatest thief in the world, Monsieur (the king's secretary) Le Camus, who came to Paris with twenty francs in his pocket and who now possesses ten millions?"

The dog shook his head.

"Then is it not," resumed the duke, "the Superintendent Emery, who gave his son, when he was married, three hundred thousand francs and a house, compared to which the Tuileries are a heap of ruins and the Louvre a paltry building?"

The dog again shook his head as if to say "no."

"Then," said the prisoner, "let's think who it can be. Can it be, can it possibly be, the 'Illustrious Coxcomb, Mazarin de Piscina,' hey?"

Pistache made violent signs that it was, by raising and lowering his head eight or ten times successively.

"Gentlemen, you see," said the duke to those present, who dared not even smile, "that it is the 'Illustrious Coxcomb' who is the greatest thief in the world; at least, according to Pistache."

"Let us go on to another of his exercises."

"Gentlemen!"--there was a profound silence in the room when the duke again addressed them--"do you not remember that the Duc de Guise taught all the dogs in Paris to jump for Mademoiselle de Pons, whom he styled 'the fairest of the fair?' Pistache is going to show you how superior he is to all other dogs. Monsieur de Chavigny, be so good as to lend me your cane."

Monsieur de Chavigny handed his cane to Monsieur de Beaufort. Monsieur de Beaufort placed it horizontally at the height of one foot.

"Now, Pistache, my good dog, jump the height of this cane for Madame de Montbazon."

"But," interposed Monsieur de Chavigny, "it seems to me that Pistache is only doing what other dogs have done when they jumped for Mademoiselle de Pons."

"Stop," said the duke, "Pistache, jump for the queen." And he raised his cane six inches higher.

The dog sprang, and in spite of the height jumped lightly over it.

"And now," said the duke, raising it still six inches higher, "jump for the king."

The dog obeyed and jumped quickly over the cane.

"Now, then," said the duke, and as he spoke, lowered the cane almost level with the ground; "Pistache, my friend, jump for the 'Illustrious Coxcomb, Mazarin de Piscina.'"

The dog turned his back to the cane.

"What," asked the duke, "what do you mean?" and he gave him the cane again, first making a semicircle from the head to the tail of Pistache. "Jump then, Monsieur Pistache."

But Pistache, as at first, turned round on his legs and stood with his back to the cane.

Monsieur de Beaufort made the experiment a third time, but by this time Pistache's patience was exhausted; he threw himself furiously upon the cane, wrested it from the hands of the prince and broke it with his teeth.

Monsieur de Beaufort took the pieces out of his mouth and presented them with great formality to Monsieur de Chavigny, saying that for that evening the entertainment was ended, but in three months it should be repeated, when Pistache would have learned a few new tricks.

Three days afterward Pistache was found dead--poisoned.

Then the duke said openly that his dog had been killed by a drug with which they meant to poison him; and one day after dinner he went to bed, calling out that he had pains in his stomach and that Mazarin had poisoned him.

This fresh impertinence reached the ears of the cardinal and alarmed him greatly. The donjon of Vincennes was considered very unhealthy and Madame de Rambouillet had said that the room in which the Marechal Ornano and the Grand Prior de Vendome had died was worth its weight in arsenic--a bon mot which had great success. So it was ordered the prisoner was henceforth to eat nothing that had not previously been tasted, and La Ramee was in consequence placed near him as taster.

Every kind of revenge was practiced upon the duke by the governor in return for the insults of the innocent Pistache. De Chavigny, who, according to report, was a son of Richelieu's, and had been a creature of the late cardinal's, understood tyranny. He took from the duke all the steel knives and silver forks and replaced them with silver knives and wooden forks, pretending that as he had been informed that the duke was to pass all his life at Vincennes, he was afraid of his prisoner attempting suicide. A fortnight afterward the duke, going to the tennis court, found two rows of trees about the size of his little finger planted by the roadside; he asked what they were for and was told that they were to shade him from the sun on some future day. One morning the gardener went to him and told him, as if to please him, that he was going to plant a bed of asparagus for his especial use. Now, since, as every one knows, asparagus takes four years in coming to perfection, this civility infuriated Monsieur de Beaufort.

At last his patience was exhausted. He assembled his keepers, and notwithstanding his well-known difficulty of utterance, addressed them as follows:

"Gentlemen! will you permit a grandson of Henry IV. to be overwhelmed with insults and ignominy?

"Odds fish! as my grandfather used to say, I once reigned in Paris! do you know that? I had the king and Monsieur the whole of one day in my care. The queen at that time liked me and called me the most honest man in the kingdom. Gentlemen and citizens, set me free; I shall go to the Louvre and strangle Mazarin. You shall be my body-guard. I will make you all captains, with good pensions! Odds fish! On! march forward!"

But eloquent as he might be, the eloquence of the grandson of Henry IV. did not touch those hearts of stone; not one man stirred, so Monsieur de Beaufort was obliged to be satisfied with calling them all kinds of rascals underneath the sun.

Sometimes, when Monsieur de Chavigny paid him a visit, the duke used to ask him what he should think if he saw an army of Parisians, all fully armed, appear at Vincennes to deliver him from prison.

"My lord," answered De Chavigny, with a low bow, "I have on the ramparts twenty pieces of artillery and in my casemates thirty thousand guns. I should bombard the troops till not one grain of gunpowder was unexploded."

"Yes, but after you had fired off your thirty thousand guns they would take the donjon; the donjon being taken, I should be obliged to let them hang you--at which I should be most unhappy, certainly."

And in his turn the duke bowed low to Monsieur de Chavigny.

"For myself, on the other hand, my lord," returned the governor, "when the first rebel should pass the threshold of my postern doors I should be obliged to kill you with my own hand, since you were confided peculiarly to my care and as I am obliged to give you up, dead or alive."

And once more he bowed low before his highness.

These bitter-sweet pleasantries lasted ten minutes, sometimes longer, but always finished thus:

Monsieur de Chavigny, turning toward the door, used to call out: "Halloo! La Ramee!"

La Ramee came into the room.

"La Ramee, I recommend Monsieur le Duc to you, particularly; treat him as a man of his rank and family ought to be treated; that is, never leave him alone an instant."

La Ramee became, therefore, the duke's dinner guest by compulsion--an eternal keeper, the shadow of his person; but La Ramee--gay, frank, convivial, fond of play, a great hand at tennis, had one defect in the duke's eyes--his incorruptibility.

Now, although La Ramee appreciated, as of a certain value, the honor of being shut up with a prisoner of so great importance, still the pleasure of living in intimacy with the grandson of Henry IV. hardly compensated for the loss of that which he had experienced in going from time to time to visit his family.

One may be a jailer or a keeper and at the same time a good father and husband. La Ramee adored his wife and children, whom now he could only catch a glimpse of from the top of the wall, when in order to please him they used to walk on the opposite side of the moat. 'Twas too brief an enjoyment, and La Ramee felt that the gayety of heart he had regarded as the cause of health (of which it was perhaps rather the result) would not long survive such a mode of life.

He accepted, therefore, with delight, an offer made to him by his friend the steward of the Duc de Grammont, to give him a substitute; he also spoke of it to Monsieur de Chavigny, who promised that he would not oppose it in any way--that is, if he approved of the person proposed.

We consider it useless to draw a physical or moral portrait of Grimaud; if, as we hope, our readers have not wholly forgotten the first part of this work, they must have preserved a clear idea of that estimable individual, who is wholly unchanged, except that he is twenty years older, an advance in life that has made him only more silent; although, since the change that had been working in himself, Athos had given Grimaud permission to speak.

But Grimaud had for twelve or fifteen years preserved habitual silence, and a habit of fifteen or twenty years' duration becomes second nature.

18. Grimaud begins his Functions.

Grimaud thereupon presented himself with his smooth exterior at the donjon of Vincennes. Now Monsieur de Chavigny piqued himself on his infallible penetration; for that which almost proved that he was the son of Richelieu was his everlasting pretension; he examined attentively the countenance of the applicant for place and fancied that the contracted eyebrows, thin lips, hooked nose, and prominent cheek-bones of Grimaud were favorable signs. He addressed about twelve words to him; Grimaud answered in four.

"Here's a promising fellow and it is I who have found out his merits," said Monsieur de Chavigny. "Go," he added, "and make yourself agreeable to Monsieur la Ramee, and tell him that you suit me in all respects."

Grimaud had every quality that could attract a man on duty who wishes to have a deputy. So, after a thousand questions which met with only a word in reply, La Ramee, fascinated by this sobriety in speech, rubbed his hands and engaged Grimaud.

"My orders?" asked Grimaud.

"They are these; never to leave the prisoner alone; to keep away from him every pointed or cutting instrument, and to prevent his conversing any length of time with the keepers."

"Those are all?" asked Grimaud.

"All now," replied La Ramee.

"Good," answered Grimaud; and he went right to the prisoner.

The duke was in the act of combing his beard, which he had allowed to grow, as well as his hair, in order to reproach Mazarin with his wretched appearance and condition. But having some days previously seen from the top of the donjon Madame de Montbazon pass in her carriage, and still cherishing an affection for that beautiful woman, he did not wish to be to her what he wished to be to Mazarin, and in the hope of seeing her again, had asked for a leaden comb, which was allowed him. The comb was to be a leaden one, because his beard, like that of most fair people, was rather red; he therefore dyed it thus whilst combing it.

As Grimaud entered he saw this comb on the tea-table; he took it up, and as he took it he made a low bow.

The duke looked at this strange figure with surprise. The figure put the comb in its pocket.

"Ho! hey! what's that?" cried the duke. "Who is this creature?"

Grimaud did not answer, but bowed a second time.

"Art thou dumb?" cried the duke.

Grimaud made a sign that he was not.

"What art thou, then? Answer! I command thee!" said the duke.

"A keeper," replied Grimaud.

"A keeper!" reiterated the duke; "there was nothing wanting in my collection, except this gallows-bird. Halloo! La Ramee! some one!"

La Ramee ran in haste to obey the call.

"Who is this wretch who takes my comb and puts it in his pocket?" asked the duke.

"One of your guards, my prince; a man of talent and merit, whom you will like, as I and Monsieur de Chavigny do, I am sure."

"Why does he take my comb?"

"Why do you take my lord's comb?" asked La Ramee.

Grimaud drew the comb from his pocket and passing his fingers over the largest teeth, pronounced this one word, "Pointed."

"True," said La Ramee.

"What does the animal say?" asked the duke.

"That the king has forbidden your lordship to have any pointed instrument."

"Are you mad, La Ramee? You yourself gave me this comb."

"I was very wrong, my lord, for in giving it to you I acted in opposition to my orders."

The duke looked furiously at Grimaud.

"I perceive that this creature will be my particular aversion," he muttered.

Grimaud, nevertheless, was resolved for certain reasons not at once to come to a full rupture with the prisoner; he wanted to inspire, not a sudden repugnance, but a good, sound, steady hatred; he retired, therefore, and gave place to four guards, who, having breakfasted, could attend on the prisoner.

A fresh practical joke now occurred to the duke. He had asked for crawfish for his breakfast on the following morning; he intended to pass the day in making a small gallows and hang one of the finest of these fish in the middle of his room--the red color evidently conveying an allusion to the cardinal--so that he might have the pleasure of hanging Mazarin in effigy without being accused of having hung anything more significant than a crawfish.

The day was employed in preparations for the execution. Every one grows childish in prison, but the character of Monsieur de Beaufort was particularly disposed to become so. In the course of his morning's walk he collected two or three small branches from a tree and found a small piece of broken glass, a discovery that quite delighted him. When he came home he formed his handkerchief into a loop.

Nothing of all this escaped Grimaud, but La Ramee looked on with the curiosity of a father who thinks that he may perhaps get a cheap idea concerning a new toy for his children. The guards looked on it with indifference. When everything was ready, the gallows hung in the middle of the room, the loop made, and when the duke had cast a glance upon the plate of crawfish, in order to select the finest specimen among them, he looked around for his piece of glass; it had disappeared.

"Who has taken my piece of glass?" asked the duke, frowning. Grimaud made a sign to denote that he had done so.

"What! thou again! Why didst thou take it?"

"Yes--why?" asked La Ramee.

Grimaud, who held the piece of glass in his hand, said: "Sharp."

"True, my lord!" exclaimed La Ramee. "Ah! deuce take it! we have a precious fellow here!"

"Monsieur Grimaud!" said the duke, "for your sake I beg of you, never come within the reach of my fist!"

"Hush! hush!" cried La Ramee, "give me your gibbet, my lord. I will shape it out for you with my knife."

And he took the gibbet and shaped it out as neatly as possible.

"That's it," said the duke, "now make me a little hole in the floor whilst I go and fetch the culprit."

La Ramee knelt down and made a hole in the floor; meanwhile the duke hung the crawfish up by a thread. Then he placed the gibbet in the middle of the room, bursting with laughter.

La Ramee laughed also and the guards laughed in chorus; Grimaud, however, did not even smile. He approached La Ramee and showing him the crawfish hung up by the thread:

"Cardinal," he said.

"Hung by order of his Highness the Duc de Beaufort!" cried the prisoner, laughing violently, "and by Master Jacques Chrysostom La Ramee, the king's commissioner."

La Ramee uttered a cry of horror and rushed toward the gibbet, which he broke at once and threw the pieces out of the window. He was going to throw the crawfish out also, when Grimaud snatched it from his hands.

"Good to eat!" he said, and put it in his pocket.

This scene so enchanted the duke that at the moment he forgave Grimaud for his part in it; but on reflection he hated him more and more, being convinced he had some evil motive for his conduct.

But the story of the crab made a great noise through the interior of the donjon and even outside. Monsieur de Chavigny, who at heart detested the cardinal, took pains to tell the story to two or three friends, who put it into immediate circulation.

The prisoner happened to remark among the guards one man with a very good countenance; and he favored this man the more as Grimaud became the more and more odious to him. One morning he took this man on one side and had succeeded in speaking to him, when Grimaud entered and seeing what was going on approached the duke respectfully, but took the guard by the arm.

"Go away," he said.

The guard obeyed.

"You are insupportable!" cried the duke; "I shall beat you."

Grimaud bowed.

"I will break every bone in your body!" cried the duke.

Grimaud bowed, but stepped back.

"Mr. Spy," cried the duke, more and more enraged, "I will strangle you with my own hands."

And he extended his hands toward Grimaud, who merely thrust the guard out and shut the door behind him. At the same time he felt the duke's arms on his shoulders like two iron claws; but instead either of calling out or defending himself, he placed his forefinger on his lips and said in a low tone:

"Hush!" smiling as he uttered the word.

A gesture, a smile and a word from Grimaud, all at once, were so unusual that his highness stopped short, astounded.

Grimaud took advantage of that instant to draw from his vest a charming little note with an aristocratic seal, and presented it to the duke without a word.

The duke, more and more bewildered, let Grimaud loose and took the note.

"From Madame de Montbazon?" he cried.

Grimaud nodded assent.

The duke tore open the note, passed his hands over his eyes, for he was dazzled and confused, and read:

"My Dear Duke,--You may entirely confide in the brave lad who will give you this note; he has consented to enter the service of your keeper and to shut himself up at Vincennes with you, in order to prepare and assist your escape, which we are contriving. The moment of your deliverance is at hand; have patience and courage and remember that in spite of time and absence all your friends continue to cherish for you the sentiments they have so long professed and truly entertained.

"Yours wholly and most affectionately

"Marie de Montbazon.

"P.S.--I sign my full name, for I should be vain if I could suppose that after five years of absence you would remember my initials."

The poor duke became perfectly giddy. What for five years he had been wanting--a faithful servant, a friend, a helping hand--seemed to have fallen from Heaven just when he expected it the least.

"Oh, dearest Marie! she thinks of me, then, after five years of separation! Heavens! there is constancy!" Then turning to Grimaud, he said:

"And thou, my brave fellow, thou consentest thus to aid me?"

Grimaud signified his assent.

"And you have come here with that purpose?"

Grimaud repeated the sign.

"And I was ready to strangle you!" cried the duke.

Grimaud smiled.

"Wait, then," said the duke, fumbling in his pocket. "Wait," he continued, renewing his fruitless search; "it shall not be said that such devotion to a grandson of Henry IV. went without recompense."

The duke's endeavors evinced the best intention in the world, but one of the precautions taken at Vincennes was that of allowing prisoners to keep no money. Whereupon Grimaud, observing the duke's disappointment, drew from his pocket a purse filled with gold and handed it to him.

"Here is what you are looking for," he said.

The duke opened the purse and wanted to empty it into Grimaud's hands, but Grimaud shook his head.

"Thank you, monseigneur," he said, drawing back; "I am paid."

The duke went from one surprise to another. He held out his hand. Grimaud drew near and kissed it respectfully. The grand manner of Athos had left its mark on Grimaud.

"What shall we do? and when? and how proceed?"

"It is now eleven," answered Grimaud. "Let my lord at two o'clock ask leave to make up a game at tennis with La Ramee and let him send two or three balls over the ramparts."

"And then?"

"Your highness will approach the walls and call out to a man who works in the moat to send them back again."

"I understand," said the duke.

Grimaud made a sign that he was going away.

"Ah!" cried the duke, "will you not accept any money from me?"

"I wish my lord would make me one promise."

"What! speak!"

"'Tis this: when we escape together, that I shall go everywhere and be always first; for if my lord should be overtaken and caught, there's every chance of his being brought back to prison, whereas if I am caught the least that can befall me is to be--hung."

"True, on my honor as a gentleman it shall be as thou dost suggest."

"Now," resumed Grimaud, "I've only one thing more to ask--that your highness will continue to detest me."

"I'll try," said the duke.

At this moment La Ramee, after the interview we have described with the cardinal, entered the room. The duke had thrown himself, as he was wont to do in moments of dullness and vexation, on his bed. La Ramee cast an inquiring look around him and observing the same signs of antipathy between the prisoner and his guardian he smiled in token of his inward satisfaction. Then turning to Grimaud:

"Very good, my friend, very good. You have been spoken of in a promising quarter and you will soon, I hope, have news that will be agreeable to you."

Grimaud saluted in his politest manner and withdrew, as was his custom on the entrance of his superior.

"Well, my lord," said La Ramee, with his rude laugh, "you still set yourself against this poor fellow?"

"So! 'tis you, La Ramee; in faith, 'tis time you came back again. I threw myself on the bed and turned my nose to the wall, that I mightn't break my promise and strangle Grimaud."

"I doubt, however," said La Ramee, in sprightly allusion to the silence of his subordinate, "if he has said anything disagreeable to your highness."

"Pardieu! you are right--a mute from the East! I swear it was time for you to come back, La Ramee, and I was eager to see you again."

"Monseigneur is too good," said La Ramee, flattered by the compliment.

"Yes," continued the duke, "really, I feel bored today beyond the power of description."

"Then let us have a match in the tennis court," exclaimed La Ramee.

"If you wish it."

"I am at your service, my lord."

"I protest, my dear La Ramee," said the duke, "that you are a charming fellow and that I would stay forever at Vincennes to have the pleasure of your society."

"My lord," replied La Ramee, "I think if it depended on the cardinal your wishes would be fulfilled."

"What do you mean? Have you seen him lately?"

"He sent for me to-day."

"Really! to speak to you about me?"

"Of what else do you imagine he would speak to me? Really, my lord, you are his nightmare."

The duke smiled with bitterness.

"Ah, La Ramee! if you would but accept my offers! I would make your fortune."

"How? you would no sooner have left prison than your goods would be confiscated."

"I shall no sooner be out of prison than I shall be master of Paris."

"Pshaw! pshaw! I cannot hear such things said as that; this is a fine conversation with an officer of the king! I see, my lord, I shall be obliged to fetch a second Grimaud!"

"Very well, let us say no more about it. So you and the cardinal have been talking about me? La Ramee, some day when he sends for you, you must let me put on your clothes; I will go in your stead; I will strangle him, and upon my honor, if that is made a condition I will return to prison."

"Monseigneur, I see well that I must call Grimaud."

"Well, I am wrong. And what did the cuistre [pettifogger] say about me?"

"I admit the word, monseigneur, because it rhymes with ministre [minister]. What did he say to me? He told me to watch you."

"And why so? why watch me?" asked the duke uneasily.

"Because an astrologer had predicted that you would escape."

"Ah! an astrologer predicted that?" said the duke, starting in spite of himself.

"Oh, mon Dieu! yes! those imbeciles of magicians can only imagine things to torment honest people."

"And what did you reply to his most illustrious eminence?"

"That if the astrologer in question made almanacs I would advise him not to buy one."

"Why not?"

"Because before you could escape you would have to be turned into a bird."

"Unfortunately, that is true. Let us go and have a game at tennis, La Ramee."

"My lord--I beg your highness's pardon--but I must beg for half an hour's leave of absence."

"Why?"

"Because Monseigneur Mazarin is a prouder man than his highness, though not of such high birth: he forgot to ask me to breakfast."

"Well, shall I send for some breakfast here?"

"No, my lord; I must tell you that the confectioner who lived opposite the castle--Daddy Marteau, as they called him----"

"Well?"

"Well, he sold his business a week ago to a confectioner from Paris, an invalid, ordered country air for his health."

"Well, what have I to do with that?"

"Why, good Lord! this man, your highness, when he saw me stop before his shop, where he has a display of things which would make your mouth water, my lord, asked me to get him the custom of the prisoners in the donjon. 'I bought,' said he, 'the business of my predecessor on the strength of his assurance that he supplied the castle; whereas, on my honor, Monsieur de Chavigny, though I've been here a week, has not ordered so much as a tartlet.' 'But,' I then replied, 'probably Monsieur de Chavigny is afraid your pastry is not good.' 'My pastry not good! Well, Monsieur La Ramee, you shall judge of it yourself and at once.' 'I cannot,' I replied; 'it is absolutely necessary for me to return to the chateau.' 'Very well,' said he, 'go and attend to your affairs, since you seem to be in a hurry, but come back in half an hour.' 'In half an hour?' 'Yes, have you breakfasted?' 'Faith, no.' 'Well, here is a pate that will be ready for you, with a bottle of old Burgundy.' So, you see, my lord, since I am hungry, I would, with your highness's leave----" And La Ramee bent low.

"Go, then, animal," said the duke; "but remember, I only allow you half an hour."

"May I promise your custom to the successor of Father Marteau, my lord?"

"Yes, if he does not put mushrooms in his pies; thou knowest that mushrooms from the wood of Vincennes are fatal to my family."

La Ramee went out, but in five minutes one of the officers of the guard entered in compliance with the strict orders of the cardinal that the prisoner should never be left alone a moment.

But during these five minutes the duke had had time to read again the note from Madame de Montbazon, which proved to the prisoner that his friends were concerting plans for his deliverance, but in what way he knew not.

But his confidence in Grimaud, whose petty persecutions he now perceived were only a blind, increased, and he conceived the highest opinion of his intellect and resolved to trust entirely to his guidance.

19. Pates made by the Successor of Father Marteau are described.

In half an hour La Ramee returned, full of glee, like most men who have eaten, and more especially drank to their heart's content. The pates were excellent, the wine delicious.

The weather was fine and the game at tennis took place in the open air.

At two o'clock the tennis balls began, according to Grimaud's directions, to take the direction of the moat, much to the joy of La Ramee, who marked fifteen whenever the duke sent a ball into the moat; and very soon balls were wanting, so many had gone over. La Ramee then proposed to send some one to pick them up, but the duke remarked that it would be losing time; and going near the rampart himself and looking over, he saw a man working in one of the numerous little gardens cleared out by the peasants on the opposite side of the moat.

"Hey, friend!" cried the duke.

The man raised his head and the duke was about to utter a cry of surprise. The peasant, the gardener, was Rochefort, whom he believed to be in the Bastile.

"Well? Who's up there?" said the man.

"Be so good as to collect and throw us back our balls," said the duke.

The gardener nodded and began to fling up the balls, which were picked up by La Ramee and the guard. One, however, fell at the duke's feet, and seeing that it was intended for him, he put it into his pocket.

La Ramee was in ecstasies at having beaten a prince of the blood.

The duke went indoors and retired to bed, where he spent, indeed, the greater part of every day, as they had taken his books away. La Ramee carried off all his clothes, in order to be certain that the duke would not stir. However, the duke contrived to hide the ball under his bolster and as soon as the door was closed he tore off the cover of the ball with his teeth and found underneath the following letter:

My Lord,--Your friends are watching over you and the hour of your deliverance is at hand. Ask day after to-morrow to have a pie supplied you by the new confectioner opposite the castle, and who is no other than Noirmont, your former maitre d'hotel. Do not open the pie till you are alone. I hope you will be satisfied with its contents.

"Your highness's most devoted servant,

"In the Bastile, as elsewhere,

"Comte de Rochefort."

The duke, who had latterly been allowed a fire, burned the letter, but kept the ball, and went to bed, hiding the ball under his bolster. La Ramee entered; he smiled kindly on the prisoner, for he was an excellent man and had taken a great liking for the captive prince. He endeavored to cheer him up in his solitude.

"Ah, my friend!" cried the duke, "you are so good; if I could but do as you do, and eat pates and drink Burgundy at the house of Father Marteau's successor."

"'Tis true, my lord," answered La Ramee, "that his pates are famous and his wine magnificent."

"In any case," said the duke, "his cellar and kitchen might easily excel those of Monsieur de Chavigny."

"Well, my lord," said La Ramee, falling into the trap, "what is there to prevent your trying them? Besides, I have promised him your patronage."

"You are right," said the duke. "If I am to remain here permanently, as Monsieur Mazarin has kindly given me to understand, I must provide myself with a diversion for my old age, I must turn gourmand."

"My lord," said La Ramee, "if you will take a bit of good advice, don't put that off till you are old."

"Good!" said the Duc de Beaufort to himself, "every man in order that he may lose his heart and soul, must receive from celestial bounty one of the seven capital sins, perhaps two; it seems that Master La Ramee's is gluttony. Let us then take advantage of it." Then, aloud:

"Well, my dear La Ramee! the day after to-morrow is a holiday."

"Yes, my lord--Pentecost."

"Will you give me a lesson the day after to-morrow?"

"In what?"

"In gastronomy?"

"Willingly, my lord."

"But tete-a-tete. Send the guards to take their meal in the canteen of Monsieur de Chavigny; we'll have a supper here under your direction."

"Hum!" said La Ramee.

The proposal was seductive, but La Ramee was an old stager, acquainted with all the traps a prisoner was likely to set. Monsieur de Beaufort had said that he had forty ways of getting out of prison. Did this proposed breakfast cover some stratagem? He reflected, but he remembered that he himself would have charge of the food and the wine and therefore that no powder could be mixed with the food, no drug with the wine. As to getting him drunk, the duke couldn't hope to do that, and he laughed at the mere thought of it. Then an idea came to him which harmonized everything.

The duke had followed with anxiety La Ramee's unspoken soliloquy, reading it from point to point upon his face. But presently the exempt's face suddenly brightened.

"Well," he asked, "that will do, will it not?"

"Yes, my lord, on one condition."

"What?"

"That Grimaud shall wait on us at table."

Nothing could be more agreeable to the duke, however, he had presence of mind enough to exclaim:

"To the devil with your Grimaud! He will spoil the feast."

"I will direct him to stand behind your chair, and since he doesn't speak, your highness will neither see nor hear him and with a little effort can imagine him a hundred miles away."

"Do you know, my friend, I find one thing very evident in all this, you distrust me."

"My lord, the day after to-morrow is Pentecost."

"Well, what is Pentecost to me? Are you afraid that the Holy Spirit will come as a tongue of fire to open the doors of my prison?"

"No, my lord; but I have already told you what that damned magician predicted."

"And what was it?"

"That the day of Pentecost would not pass without your highness being out of Vincennes."

"You believe in sorcerers, then, you fool?"

"I---I mind them no more than that----" and he snapped his fingers; "but it is my Lord Giulio who cares about them; as an Italian he is superstitious."

The duke shrugged his shoulders.

"Well, then," with well acted good-humor, "I allow Grimaud, but no one else; you must manage it all. Order whatever you like for supper--the only thing I specify is one of those pies; and tell the confectioner that I will promise him my custom if he excels this time in his pies--not only now, but when I leave my prison."

"Then you think you will some day leave it?" said La Ramee.

"The devil!" replied the prince; "surely, at the death of Mazarin. I am fifteen years younger than he is. At Vincennes, 'tis true, one lives faster----"

"My lord," replied La Ramee, "my lord----"

"Or dies sooner, for it comes to the same thing."

La Ramee was going out. He stopped, however, at the door for an instant.

"Whom does your highness wish me to send to you?"

"Any one, except Grimaud."

"The officer of the guard, then, with his chess-board?"

"Yes."

Five minutes afterward the officer entered and the duke seemed to be immersed in the sublime combinations of chess.

A strange thing is the mind, and it is wonderful what revolutions may be wrought in it by a sign, a word, a hope. The duke had been five years in prison, and now to him, looking back upon them, those five years, which had passed so slowly, seemed not so long a time as were the two days, the forty-eight hours, which still parted him from the time fixed for his escape. Besides, there was one thing that engaged his most anxious thought--in what way was the escape to be effected? They had told him to hope for it, but had not told him what was to be hidden in the mysterious pate. And what friends awaited him without? He had friends, then, after five years in prison? If that were so he was indeed a highly favored prince. He forgot that besides his friends of his own sex, a woman, strange to say, had remembered him. It is true that she had not, perhaps, been scrupulously faithful to him, but she had remembered him; that was something.

So the duke had more than enough to think about; accordingly he fared at chess as he had fared at tennis; he made blunder upon blunder and the officer with whom he played found him easy game.

But his successive defeats did service to the duke in one way--they killed time for him till eight o'clock in the evening; then would come night, and with night, sleep. So, at least, the duke believed; but sleep is a capricious fairy, and it is precisely when one invokes her presence that she is most likely to keep him waiting. The duke waited until midnight, turning on his mattress like St. Laurence on his gridiron. Finally he slept.

But at daybreak he awoke. Wild dreams had disturbed his repose. He dreamed that he was endowed with wings--he wished to fly away. For a time these wings supported him, but when he reached a certain height this new aid failed him. His wings were broken and he seemed to sink into a bottomless abyss, whence he awoke, bathed in perspiration and nearly as much overcome as if he had really fallen. He fell asleep again and another vision appeared. He was in a subterranean passage by which he was to leave Vincennes. Grimaud was walking before him with a lantern. By degrees the passage narrowed, yet the duke continued his course. At last it became so narrow that the fugitive tried in vain to proceed. The sides of the walls seem to close in, even to press against him. He made fruitless efforts to go on; it was impossible. Nevertheless, he still saw Grimaud with his lantern in front, advancing. He wished to call out to him but could not utter a word. Then at the other extremity he heard the footsteps of those who were pursuing him. These steps came on, came fast. He was discovered; all hope of flight was gone. Still the walls seemed to be closing on him; they appeared to be in concert with his enemies. At last he heard the voice of La Ramee. La Ramee took his hand and laughed aloud. He was captured again, and conducted to the low and vaulted chamber, in which Ornano, Puylaurens, and his uncle had died. Their three graves were there, rising above the ground, and a fourth was also there, yawning for its ghastly tenant.

The duke was obliged to make as many efforts to awake as he had done to go to sleep; and La Ramee found him so pale and fatigued that he inquired whether he was ill.

"In fact," said one of the guards who had remained in the chamber and had been kept awake by a toothache, brought on by the dampness of the atmosphere, "my lord has had a very restless night and two or three times, while dreaming, he called for help."

"What is the matter with your highness?" asked La Ramee.

"'Tis your fault, you simpleton," answered the duke. "With your idle nonsense yesterday about escaping, you worried me so that I dreamed that I was trying to escape and broke my neck in doing so."

La Ramee laughed.

"Come," he said, "'tis a warning from Heaven. Never commit such an imprudence as to try to escape, except in your dreams."

"And you are right, my dear La Ramee," said the duke, wiping away the sweat that stood on his brow, wide awake though he was; "after this I will think of nothing but eating and drinking."

"Hush!" said La Ramee; and one by one he sent away the guards, on various pretexts.

"Well?" asked the duke when they were alone.

"Well!" replied La Ramee, "your supper is ordered."

"Ah! and what is it to be? Monsieur, my majordomo, will there be a pie?"

"I should think so, indeed--almost as high as a tower."

"You told him it was for me?"

"Yes, and he said he would do his best to please your highness."

"Good!" exclaimed the duke, rubbing his hands.

"Devil take it, my lord! what a gourmand you are growing; I haven't seen you with so cheerful a face these five years."

The duke saw that he had not controlled himself as he ought, but at that moment, as if he had listened at the door and comprehended the urgent need of diverting La Ramee's ideas, Grimaud entered and made a sign to La Ramee that he had something to say to him.

La Ramee drew near to Grimaud, who spoke to him in a low voice.

The duke meanwhile recovered his self-control.

"I have already forbidden that man," he said, "to come in here without my permission."

"You must pardon him, my lord," said La Ramee, "for I directed him to come."

"And why did you so direct when you know that he displeases me?"

"My lord will remember that it was agreed between us that he should wait upon us at that famous supper. My lord has forgotten the supper."

"No, but I have forgotten Monsieur Grimaud."

"My lord understands that there can be no supper unless he is allowed to be present."

"Go on, then; have it your own way."

"Come here, my lad," said La Ramee, "and hear what I have to say."

Grimaud approached, with a very sullen expression on his face.

La Ramee continued: "My lord has done me the honor to invite me to a supper to-morrow en tete-a-tete."

Grimaud made a sign which meant that he didn't see what that had to do with him.

"Yes, yes," said La Ramee, "the matter concerns you, for you will have the honor to serve us; and besides, however good an appetite we may have and however great our thirst, there will be something left on the plates and in the bottles, and that something will be yours."

Grimaud bowed in thanks.

"And now," said La Ramee, "I must ask your highness's pardon, but it seems that Monsieur de Chavigny is to be away for a few days and he has sent me word that he has certain directions to give me before his departure."

The duke tried to exchange a glance with Grimaud, but there was no glance in Grimaud's eyes.

"Go, then," said the duke, "and return as soon as possible."

"Does your highness wish to take revenge for the game of tennis yesterday?"

Grimaud intimated by a scarcely perceptible nod that he should consent.

"Yes," said the duke, "but take care, my dear La Ramee, for I propose to beat you badly."

La Ramee went out. Grimaud looked after him, and when the door was closed he drew out of his pocket a pencil and a sheet of paper.

"Write, my lord," he said.

"And what?"

Grimaud dictated.

"All is ready for to-morrow evening. Keep watch from seven to nine. Have two riding horses ready. We shall descend by the first window in the gallery."

"What next?"

"Sign your name, my lord."

The duke signed.

"Now, my lord, give me, if you have not lost it, the ball--that which contained the letter."

The duke took it from under his pillow and gave it to Grimaud. Grimaud gave a grim smile.

"Well?" asked the duke.

"Well, my lord, I sew up the paper in the ball and you, in your game of tennis, will send the ball into the ditch."

"But will it not be lost?"

"Oh no; there will be some one at hand to pick it up."

"A gardener?"

Grimaud nodded.

"The same as yesterday?"

Another nod on the part of Grimaud.

"The Count de Rochefort?"

Grimaud nodded the third time.

"Come, now," said the duke, "give some particulars of the plan for our escape."

"That is forbidden me," said Grimaud, "until the last moment."

"Who will be waiting for me beyond the ditch?"

"I know nothing about it, my lord."

"But at least, if you don't want to see me turn crazy, tell what that famous pate will contain."

"Two poniards, a knotted rope and a poire d'angoisse[1]."

"Yes, I understand."

"My lord observes that there will be enough to go around."

"We shall take to ourselves the poniards and the rope," replied the duke.

"And make La Ramee eat the pear," answered Grimaud.

"My dear Grimaud, thou speakest seldom, but when thou dost, one must do thee justice--thy words are words of gold."

---

[1] This poire d'angoisse was a famous gag, in the form of a pear, which, being thrust into the mouth, by the aid of a spring, dilated, so as to distend the jaws to their greatest width.

20. One of Marie Michon's Adventures.

Whilst these projects were being formed by the Duc de Beaufort and Grimaud, the Comte de la Fere and the Vicomte de Bragelonne were entering Paris by the Rue du Faubourg Saint Marcel.

They stopped at the sign of the Fox, in the Rue du Vieux Colombier, a tavern known for many years by Athos, and asked for two bedrooms.

"You must dress yourself, Raoul," said Athos, "I am going to present you to some one."

"To-day, monsieur?" asked the young man.

"In half an hour."

The young man bowed. Perhaps, not being endowed with the endurance of Athos, who seemed to be made of iron, he would have preferred a bath in the river Seine of which he had heard so much, and afterward his bed; but the Comte de la Fere had spoken and he had no thought but to obey.

"By the way," said Athos, "take some pains with your toilet, Raoul; I want you to be approved."

"I hope, sir," replied the youth, smiling, "that there's no idea of a marriage for me; you know of my engagement to Louise?"

Athos, in his turn, smiled also.

"No, don't be alarmed, although it is to a lady that I am going to present you, and I am anxious that you should love her----"

The young man looked at the count with a certain uneasiness, but at a smile from Athos he was quickly reassured.

"How old is she?" inquired the Vicomte de Bragelonne.

"My dear Raoul, learn, once for all, that that is a question which is never asked. When you can find out a woman's age by her face, it is useless to ask it; when you cannot do so, it is indiscreet."

"Is she beautiful?"

"Sixteen years ago she was deemed not only the prettiest, but the most graceful woman in France."

This reply reassured the vicomte. A woman who had been a reigning beauty a year before he was born could not be the subject of any scheme for him. He retired to his toilet. When he reappeared, Athos received him with the same paternal smile as that which he had often bestowed on D'Artagnan, but a more profound tenderness for Raoul was now visibly impressed upon his face.

Athos cast a glance at his feet, hands and hair--those three marks of race. The youth's dark hair was neatly parted and hung in curls, forming a sort of dark frame around his face; such was the fashion of the day. Gloves of gray kid, matching the hat, well displayed the form of a slender and elegant hand; whilst his boots, similar in color to the hat and gloves, confined feet small as those of a boy twelve years old.

"Come," murmured Athos, "if she is not proud of him, she must be hard to please."

It was three o'clock in the afternoon. The two travelers proceeded to the Rue Saint Dominique and stopped at the door of a magnificent hotel, surmounted with the arms of De Luynes.

"'Tis here," said Athos.

He entered the hotel and ascended the front steps, and addressing a footman who waited there in a grand livery, asked if the Duchess de Chevreuse was visible and if she could receive the Comte de la Fere?

The servant returned with a message to say, that, though the duchess had not the honor of knowing Monsieur de la Fere, she would receive him.

Athos followed the footman, who led him through a long succession of apartments and paused at length before a closed door. Athos made a sign to the Vicomte de Bragelonne to remain where he was.

The footman opened the door and announced Monsieur le Comte de la Fere.

Madame de Chevreuse, whose name appears so often in our story "The Three Musketeers," without her actually having appeared in any scene, was still a beautiful woman. Although about forty-four or forty-five years old, she might have passed for thirty-five.

She still had her rich fair hair; her large, animated, intelligent eyes, so often opened by intrigue, so often closed by the blindness of love. She had still her nymph-like form, so that when her back was turned she still was not unlike the girl who had jumped, with Anne of Austria, over the moat of the Tuileries in 1563. In all other respects she was the same mad creature who threw over her amours such an air of originality as to make them proverbial for eccentricity in her family.

She was in a little boudoir, hung with blue damask, adorned by red flowers, with a foliage of gold, looking upon a garden; and reclined upon a sofa, her head supported on the rich tapestry which covered it. She held a book in her hand and her arm was supported by a cushion.

At the footman's announcement she raised herself a little and peeped out, with some curiosity.

Athos appeared.

He was dressed in violet-tinted velvet, trimmed with silk of the same color. His shoulder-knots were of burnished silver, his mantle had no gold nor embroidery on it; a simple plume of violet feathers adorned his hat; his boots were of black leather, and at his girdle hung that sword with a magnificent hilt that Porthos had so often admired in the Rue Feron. Splendid lace adorned the falling collar of his shirt, and lace fell also over the top of his boots.

In his whole person he bore such an impress of high degree, that Madame de Chevreuse half rose from her seat when she saw him and made him a sign to sit down near her.

Athos bowed and obeyed. The footman was withdrawing, but Athos stopped him by a sign.

"Madame," he said to the duchess, "I have had the boldness to present myself at your hotel without being known to you; it has succeeded, since you deign to receive me. I have now the boldness to ask you for an interview of half an hour."

"I grant it, monsieur," replied Madame de Chevreuse with her most gracious smile.

"But that is not all, madame. Oh, I am very presuming, I am aware. The interview for which I ask is of us two alone, and I very earnestly wish that it may not be interrupted."

"I am not at home to any one," said the Duchess de Chevreuse to the footman. "You may go."

The footman went out

There ensued a brief silence, during which these two persons, who at first sight recognized each other so clearly as of noble race, examined each other without embarrassment on either side.

The duchess was the first to speak.

"Well, sir, I am waiting with impatience to hear what you wish to say to me."

"And I, madame," replied Athos, "am looking with admiration."

"Sir," said Madame de Chevreuse, "you must excuse me, but I long to know to whom I am talking. You belong to the court, doubtless, yet I have never seen you at court. Have you, by any chance, been in the Bastile?"

"No, madame, I have not; but very likely I am on the road to it."

"Ah! then tell me who you are, and get along with you upon your journey," replied the duchess, with the gayety which made her so charming, "for I am sufficiently in bad odor already, without compromising myself still more."

"Who I am, madame? My name has been mentioned to you--the Comte de la Fere; you do not know that name. I once bore another, which you knew, but you have certainly forgotten it."

"Tell it me, sir."

"Formerly," said the count, "I was Athos."

Madame de Chevreuse looked astonished. The name was not wholly forgotten, but mixed up and confused with ancient recollections.

"Athos?" said she; "wait a moment."

And she placed her hands on her brow, as if to force the fugitive ideas it contained to concentration in a moment.

"Shall I help you, madame?" asked Athos.

"Yes, do," said the duchess.

"This Athos was connected with three young musketeers, named Porthos, D'Artagnan, and----"

He stopped short.

"And Aramis," said the duchess, quickly.

"And Aramis; I see you have not forgotten the name."

"No," she said; "poor Aramis; a charming man, elegant, discreet, and a writer of poetical verses. I am afraid he has turned out ill," she added.

"He has; he is an abbe."

"Ah, what a misfortune!" exclaimed the duchess, playing carelessly with her fan. "Indeed, sir, I thank you; you have recalled one of the most agreeable recollections of my youth."

"Will you permit me, then, to recall another to you?"

"Relating to him?"

"Yes and no."

"Faith!" said Madame de Chevreuse, "say on. With a man like you I fear nothing."

Athos bowed. "Aramis," he continued, "was intimate with a young needlewoman from Tours, a cousin of his, named Marie Michon."

"Ah, I knew her!" cried the duchess. "It was to her he wrote from the siege of Rochelle, to warn her of a plot against the Duke of Buckingham."

"Exactly so; will you allow me to speak to you of her?"

"If," replied the duchess, with a meaning look, "you do not say too much against her."

"I should be ungrateful," said Athos, "and I regard ingratitude, not as a fault or a crime, but as a vice, which is much worse."

"You ungrateful to Marie Michon, monsieur?" said Madame de Chevreuse, trying to read in Athos's eyes. "But how can that be? You never knew her."

"Eh, madame, who knows?" said Athos. "There is a popular proverb to the effect that it is only mountains that never meet; and popular proverbs contain sometimes a wonderful amount of truth."

"Oh, go on, monsieur, go on!" said Madame de Chevreuse eagerly; "you can't imagine how much this conversation interests me."

"You encourage me," said Athos, "I will continue, then. That cousin of Aramis, that Marie Michon, that needlewoman, notwithstanding her low condition, had acquaintances in the highest rank; she called the grandest ladies of the court her friend, and the queen--proud as she is, in her double character as Austrian and as Spaniard--called her her sister."

"Alas!" said Madame de Chevreuse, with a slight sigh and a little movement of her eyebrows that was peculiarly her own, "since that time everything has changed."

"And the queen had reason for her affection, for Marie was devoted to her--devoted to that degree that she served her as medium of intercourse with her brother, the king of Spain."

"Which," interrupted the duchess, "is now brought up against her as a great crime."

"And therefore," continued Athos, "the cardinal--the true cardinal, the other one--determined one fine morning to arrest poor Marie Michon and send her to the Chateau de Loches. Fortunately the affair was not managed so secretly but that it became known to the queen. The case had been provided for: if Marie Michon should be threatened with any danger the queen was to send her a prayer-book bound in green velvet."

"That is true, monsieur, you are well informed."

"One morning the green book was brought to her by the Prince de Marsillac. There was no time to lose. Happily Marie and a follower of hers named Kitty could disguise themselves admirably in men's clothes. The prince procured for Marie Michon the dress of a cavalier and for Kitty that of a lackey; he sent them two excellent horses, and the fugitives went out hastily from Tours, shaping their course toward Spain, trembling at the least noise, following unfrequented roads, and asking for hospitality when they found themselves where there was no inn."

"Why, really, it was all exactly as you say!" cried Madame de Chevreuse, clapping her hands. "It would indeed be strange if----" she checked herself.

"If I should follow the two fugitives to the end of their journey?" said Athos. "No, madame, I will not thus waste your time. We will accompany them only to a little village in Limousin, lying between Tulle and Angouleme--a little village called Roche-l'Abeille."

Madame de Chevreuse uttered a cry of surprise, and looked at Athos with an expression of astonishment that made the old musketeer smile.

"Wait, madame," continued Athos, "what remains for me to tell you is even more strange than what I have narrated."

"Monsieur," said Madame de Chevreuse, "I believe you are a sorcerer; I am prepared for anything. But really--No matter, go on."

"The journey of that day had been long and wearing; it was a cold day, the eleventh of October, there was no inn or chateau in the village and the homes of the peasants were poor and unattractive. Marie Michon was a very aristocratic person; like her sister the queen, she had been accustomed to pleasing perfumes and fine linen; she resolved, therefore, to seek hospitality of the priest."

Athos paused.

"Oh, continue!" said the duchess. "I have told you that I am prepared for anything."

"The two travelers knocked at the door. It was late; the priest, who had gone to bed, cried out to them to come in. They entered, for the door was not locked--there is much confidence among villagers. A lamp burned in the chamber occupied by the priest. Marie Michon, who made the most charming cavalier in the world, pushed open the door, put her head in and asked for hospitality. 'Willingly, my young cavalier,' said the priest, 'if you will be content with the remains of my supper and with half my chamber.'

"The two travelers consulted for a moment. The priest heard a burst of laughter and then the master, or rather, the mistress, replied: 'Thank you, monsieur le cure, I accept.' 'Sup, then, and make as little noise as possible,' said the priest, 'for I, too, have been on the go all day and shall not be sorry to sleep to-night.'"

Madame de Chevreuse evidently went from surprise to astonishment, and from astonishment to stupefaction. Her face, as she looked at Athos, had taken on an expression that cannot be described. It could be seen that she had wished to speak, but she had remained silent through fear of losing one of her companion's words.

"What happened then?" she asked.

"Then?" said Athos. "Ah, I have come now to what is most difficult."

"Speak, speak! One can say anything to me. Besides, it doesn't concern me; it relates to Mademoiselle Marie Michon."

"Ah, that is true," said Athos. "Well, then, Marie Michon had supper with her follower, and then, in accordance with the permission given her, she entered the chamber of her host, Kitty meanwhile taking possession of an armchair in the room first entered, where they had taken their supper."

"Really, monsieur," said Madame de Chevreuse, "unless you are the devil in person I don't know how you could become acquainted with all these details."

"A charming woman was that Marie Michon," resumed Athos, "one of those wild creatures who are constantly conceiving the strangest ideas. Now, thinking that her host was a priest, that coquette took it into her head that it would be a happy souvenir for her old age, among the many happy souvenirs she already possessed, if she could win that of having damned an abbe."

"Count," said the duchess, "upon my word, you frighten me."

"Alas!" continued Athos, "the poor abbe was not a St. Ambroise, and I repeat, Marie Michon was an adorable creature."

"Monsieur!" cried the duchess, seizing Athos's hands, "tell me this moment how you know all these details, or I will send to the convent of the Vieux Augustins for a monk to come and exorcise you."

Athos laughed. "Nothing is easier, madame. A cavalier, charged with an important mission, had come an hour before your arrival, seeking hospitality, at the very moment that the cure, summoned to the bedside of a dying person, left not only his house but the village, for the entire night. The priest having all confidence in his guest, who, besides, was a nobleman, had left to him his house, his supper and his chamber. And therefore Marie came seeking hospitality from the guest of the good abbe and not from the good abbe himself."

"And that cavalier, that guest, that nobleman who arrived before she came?"

"It was I, the Comte de la Fere," said Athos, rising and bowing respectfully to the Duchess de Chevreuse.

The duchess remained a moment stupefied; then, suddenly bursting into laughter:

"Ah! upon my word," said she, "it is very droll, and that mad Marie Michon fared better than she expected. Sit down, dear count, and go on with your story."

"At this point I have to accuse myself of a fault, madame. I have told you that I was traveling on an important mission. At daybreak I left the chamber without noise, leaving my charming companion asleep. In the front room the follower was also still asleep, her head leaning back on the chair, in all respects worthy of her mistress. Her pretty face arrested my attention; I approached and recognized that little Kitty whom our friend Aramis had placed with her. In that way I discovered that the charming traveler was----"

"Marie Michon!" said Madame de Chevreuse, hastily.

"Marie Michon," continued Athos. "Then I went out of the house; I proceeded to the stable and found my horse saddled and my lackey ready. We set forth on our journey."

"And have you never revisited that village?" eagerly asked Madame de Chevreuse.

"A year after, madame."

"Well?"

"I wanted to see the good cure again. I found him much preoccupied with an event that he could not at all comprehend. A week before he had received, in a cradle, a beautiful little boy three months old, with a purse filled with gold and a note containing these simple words: '11 October, 1633.'"

"It was the date of that strange adventure," interrupted Madame de Chevreuse.

"Yes, but he couldn't understand what it meant, for he had spent that night with a dying person and Marie Michon had left his house before his return."

"You must know, monsieur, that Marie Michon, when she returned to France in 1643, immediately sought for information about that child; as a fugitive she could not take care of it, but on her return she wished to have it near her."

"And what said the abbe?" asked Athos.

"That a nobleman whom he did not know had wished to take charge of it, had answered for its future, and had taken it away."

"That was true."

"Ah! I see! That nobleman was you; it was his father!"

"Hush! do not speak so loud, madame; he is there."

"He is there! my son! the son of Marie Michon! But I must see him instantly."

"Take care, madame," said Athos, "for he knows neither his father nor his mother."

"You have kept the secret! you have brought him to see me, thinking to make me happy. Oh, thanks! sir, thanks!" cried Madame de Chevreuse, seizing his hand and trying to put it to her lips; "you have a noble heart."

"I bring him to you, madame," said Athos, withdrawing his hand, "hoping that in your turn you will do something for him; till now I have watched over his education and I have made him, I hope, an accomplished gentleman; but I am now obliged to return to the dangerous and wandering life of party faction. To-morrow I plunge into an adventurous affair in which I may be killed. Then it will devolve on you to push him on in that world where he is called on to occupy a place."

"Rest assured," cried the duchess, "I shall do what I can. I have but little influence now, but all that I have shall most assuredly be his. As to his title and fortune----"

"As to that, madame, I have made over to him the estate of Bragelonne, my inheritance, which will give him ten thousand francs a year and the title of vicomte."

"Upon my soul, monsieur," said the duchess, "you are a true nobleman! But I am eager to see our young vicomte. Where is he?"

"There, in the salon. I will have him come in, if you really wish it."

Athos moved toward the door; the duchess held him back.

"Is he handsome?" she asked.

Athos smiled.

"He resembles his mother."

So he opened the door and beckoned the young man in.

The duchess could not restrain a cry of joy on seeing so handsome a young cavalier, so far surpassing all that her maternal pride had been able to conceive.

"Vicomte, come here," said Athos; "the duchess permits you to kiss her hand."

The youth approached with his charming smile and his head bare, and kneeling down, kissed the hand of the Duchess de Chevreuse.

"Sir," he said, turning to Athos, "was it not in compassion to my timidity that you told me that this lady was the Duchess de Chevreuse, and is she not the queen?"

"No, vicomte," said Madame de Chevreuse, taking his hand and making him sit near her, while she looked at him with eyes sparkling with pleasure; "no, unhappily, I am not the queen. If I were I should do for you at once the most that you deserve. But let us see; whatever I may be," she added, hardly restraining herself from kissing that pure brow, "let us see what profession you wish to follow."

Athos, standing, looked at them both with indescribable pleasure.

"Madame," answered the youth in his sweet voice, "it seems to me that there is only one career for a gentleman--that of the army. I have been brought up by monsieur le comte with the intention, I believe, of making me a soldier; and he gave me reason to hope that at Paris he would present me to some one who would recommend me to the favor of the prince."

"Yes, I understand it well. Personally, I am on bad terms with him, on account of the quarrels between Madame de Montbazon, my mother-in-law, and Madame de Longueville. But the Prince de Marsillac! Yes, indeed, that's the right thing. The Prince de Marsillac--my old friend--will recommend our young friend to Madame de Longueville, who will give him a letter to her brother, the prince, who loves her too tenderly not to do what she wishes immediately."

"Well, that will do charmingly," said the count; "but may I beg that the greatest haste may be made, for I have reasons for wishing the vicomte not to sleep longer than to-morrow night in Paris!"

"Do you wish it known that you are interested about him, monsieur le comte?"

"Better for him in future that he should be supposed never to have seen me."

"Oh, sir!" cried Raoul.

"You know, Bragelonne," said Athos, "I never speak without reflection."

"Well, comte, I am going instantly," interrupted the duchess, "to send for the Prince de Marsillac, who is happily, in Paris just now. What are you going to do this evening?"

"We intend to visit the Abbe Scarron, for whom I have a letter of introduction and at whose house I expect to meet some of my friends."

"'Tis well; I will go there also, for a few minutes," said the duchess; "do not quit his salon until you have seen me."

Athos bowed and prepared to leave.

"Well, monsieur le comte," said the duchess, smiling, "does one leave so solemnly his old friends?"

"Ah," murmured Athos, kissing her hand, "had I only sooner known that Marie Michon was so charming a creature!" And he withdrew, sighing.

21. The Abbe Scarron.

There was once in the Rue des Tournelles a house known by all the sedan chairmen and footmen of Paris, and yet, nevertheless, this house was neither that of a great lord nor of a rich man. There was neither dining, nor playing at cards, nor dancing in that house. Nevertheless, it was the rendezvous of the great world and all Paris went there. It was the abode of the little Abbe Scarron.

In the home of the witty abbe dwelt incessant laughter; there all the items of the day had their source and were so quickly transformed, misrepresented, metamorphosed, some into epigrams, some into falsehoods, that every one was anxious to pass an hour with little Scarron, listening to what he said, reporting it to others.

The diminutive Abbe Scarron, who, however, was an abbe only because he owned an abbey, and not because he was in orders, had formerly been one of the gayest prebendaries in the town of Mans, which he inhabited. On a day of the carnival he had taken a notion to provide an unusual entertainment for that good town, of which he was the life and soul. He had made his valet cover him with honey; then, opening a feather bed, he had rolled in it and had thus become the most grotesque fowl it is possible to imagine. He then began to visit his friends of both sexes, in that strange costume. At first he had been followed through astonishment, then with derisive shouts, then the porters had insulted him, then children had thrown stones at him, and finally he was obliged to run, to escape the missiles. As soon as he took to flight every one pursued him, until, pressed on all sides, Scarron found no way of escaping his escort, except by throwing himself into the river; but the water was icy cold. Scarron was heated, the cold seized on him, and when he reached the farther bank he found himself crippled.

Every means had been employed in vain to restore the use of his limbs. He had been subjected to a severe disciplinary course of medicine, at length he sent away all his doctors, declaring that he preferred the disease to the treatment, and came to Paris, where the fame of his wit had preceded him. There he had a chair made on his own plan, and one day, visiting Anne of Austria in this chair, she asked him, charmed as she was with his wit, if he did not wish for a title.

"Yes, your majesty, there is a title which I covet much," replied Scarron.

"And what is that?"

"That of being your invalid," answered Scarron.

So he was called the queen's invalid, with a pension of fifteen hundred francs.

From that lucky moment Scarron led a happy life, spending both income and principal. One day, however, an emissary of the cardinal's gave him to understand that he was wrong in receiving the coadjutor so often.

"And why?" asked Scarron; "is he not a man of good birth?"

"Certainly."

"Agreeable?"

"Undeniably."

"Witty?"

"He has, unfortunately, too much wit."

"Well, then, why do you wish me to give up seeing such a man?"

"Because he is an enemy."

"Of whom?"

"Of the cardinal."

"What?" answered Scarron, "I continue to receive Monsieur Gilles Despreaux, who thinks ill of me, and you wish me to give up seeing the coadjutor, because he thinks ill of another man. Impossible!"

The conversation had rested there and Scarron, through sheer obstinacy, had seen Monsieur de Gondy only the more frequently.

Now, the very morning of which we speak was that of his quarter-day payment, and Scarron, as usual, had sent his servant to get his money at the pension-office, but the man had returned and said that the government had no more money to give Monsieur Scarron.

It was on Thursday, the abbe's reception day; people went there in crowds. The cardinal's refusal to pay the pension was known about the town in half an hour and he was abused with wit and vehemence.

In the Rue Saint Honore Athos fell in with two gentlemen whom he did not know, on horseback like himself, followed by a lackey like himself, and going in the same direction that he was. One of them, hat in hand, said to him:

"Would you believe it, monsieur? that contemptible Mazarin has stopped poor Scarron's pension."

"That is unreasonable," said Athos, saluting in his turn the two cavaliers. And they separated with courteous gestures.

"It happens well that we are going there this evening," said Athos to the vicomte; "we will pay our compliments to that poor man."

"What, then, is this Monsieur Scarron, who thus puts all Paris in commotion? Is he some minister out of office?"

"Oh, no, not at all, vicomte," Athos replied; "he is simply a gentleman of great genius who has fallen into disgrace with the cardinal through having written certain verses against him."

"Do gentlemen, then, make verses?" asked Raoul, naively, "I thought it was derogatory."

"So it is, my dear vicomte," said Athos, laughing, "to make bad ones; but to make good ones increases fame--witness Monsieur de Rotrou. Nevertheless," he continued, in the tone of one who gives wholesome advice, "I think it is better not to make them."

"Then," said Raoul, "this Monsieur Scarron is a poet?"

"Yes; you are warned, vicomte. Consider well what you do in that house. Talk only by gestures, or rather always listen."

"Yes, monsieur," replied Raoul.

"You will see me talking with one of my friends, the Abbe d'Herblay, of whom you have often heard me speak."

"I remember him, monsieur."

"Come near to us from time to time, as if to speak; but do not speak, and do not listen. That little stratagem may serve to keep off interlopers."

"Very well, monsieur; I will obey you at all points."

Athos made two visits in Paris; at seven o'clock he and Raoul directed their steps to the Rue des Tournelles; it was stopped by porters, horses and footmen. Athos forced his way through and entered, followed by the young man. The first person that struck him on his entrance was Aramis, planted near a great chair on castors, very large, covered with a canopy of tapestry, under which there moved, enveloped in a quilt of brocade, a little face, youngish, very merry, somewhat pallid, whilst its eyes never ceased to express a sentiment at once lively, intellectual, and amiable. This was the Abbe Scarron, always laughing, joking, complimenting--yet suffering--and toying nervously with a small switch.

Around this kind of rolling tent pressed a crowd of gentlemen and ladies. The room was neatly, comfortably furnished. Large valances of silk, embroidered with flowers of gay colors, which were rather faded, fell from the wide windows; the fittings of the room were simple, but in excellent taste. Two well trained servingmen were in attendance on the company. On perceiving Athos, Aramis advanced toward him, took him by the hand and presented him to Scarron. Raoul remained silent, for he was not prepared for the dignity of the bel esprit.

After some minutes the door opened and a footman announced Mademoiselle Paulet.

Athos touched the shoulder of the vicomte.

"Look at this lady, Raoul, she is an historic personage; it was to visit her King Henry IV. was going when he was assassinated."

Every one thronged around Mademoiselle Paulet, for she was always very much the fashion. She was a tall woman, with a slender figure and a forest of golden curls, such as Raphael was fond of and Titian has painted all his Magdalens with. This fawn-colored hair, or, perhaps the sort of ascendancy which she had over other women, gave her the name of "La Lionne." Mademoiselle Paulet took her accustomed seat, but before sitting down, she cast, in all her queen-like grandeur, a look around the room, and her eyes rested on Raoul.

Athos smiled.

"Mademoiselle Paulet has observed you, vicomte; go and bow to her; don't try to appear anything but what you are, a true country youth; on no account speak to her of Henry IV."

"When shall we two walk together?" Athos then said to Aramis.

"Presently--there are not a sufficient number of people here yet; we shall be remarked."

At this moment the door opened and in walked the coadjutor.

At this name every one looked around, for his was already a very celebrated name. Athos did the same. He knew the Abbe de Gondy only by report.

He saw a little dark man, ill made and awkward with his hands in everything--except drawing a sword and firing a pistol--with something haughty and contemptuous in his face.

Scarron turned around toward him and came to meet him in his chair.

"Well," said the coadjutor, on seeing him, "you are in disgrace, then, abbe?"

This was the orthodox phrase. It had been said that evening a hundred times--and Scarron was at his hundredth bon mot on the subject; he was very nearly at the end of his humoristic tether, but one despairing effort saved him.

"Monsieur, the Cardinal Mazarin has been so kind as to think of me," he said.

"But how can you continue to receive us?" asked the coadjutor; "if your income is lessened I shall be obliged to make you a canon of Notre Dame."

"Oh, no!" cried Scarron, "I should compromise you too much."

"Perhaps you have resources of which we are ignorant?"

"I shall borrow from the queen."

"But her majesty has no property," interposed Aramis.

At this moment the door opened and Madame de Chevreuse was announced. Every one arose. Scarron turned his chair toward the door, Raoul blushed, Athos made a sign to Aramis, who went and hid himself in the enclosure of a window.

In the midst of all the compliments that awaited her on her entrance, the duchess seemed to be looking for some one; at last she found out Raoul and her eyes sparkled; she perceived Athos and became thoughtful; she saw Aramis in the seclusion of the window and gave a start of surprise behind her fan.

"Apropos," she said, as if to drive away thoughts that pursued her in spite of herself, "how is poor Voiture, do you know, Scarron?"

"What, is Monsieur Voiture ill?" inquired a gentleman who had spoken to Athos in the Rue Saint Honore; "what is the matter with him?"

"He was acting, but forgot to take the precaution to have a change of linen ready after the performance," said the coadjutor, "so he took cold and is about to die."

"Is he then so ill, dear Voiture?" asked Aramis, half hidden by the window curtain.

"Die!" cried Mademoiselle Paulet, bitterly, "he! Why, he is surrounded by sultanas, like a Turk. Madame de Saintot has hastened to him with broth; La Renaudot warms his sheets; the Marquise de Rambouillet sends him his tisanes."

"You don't like him, my dear Parthenie," said Scarron.

"What an injustice, my dear invalid! I hate him so little that I should be delighted to order masses for the repose of his soul."

"You are not called 'Lionne' for nothing," observed Madame de Chevreuse, "your teeth are terrible."

"You are unjust to a great poet, it seems to me," Raoul ventured to say.

"A great poet! come, one may easily see, vicomte, that you are lately from the provinces and have never so much as seen him. A great poet! he is scarcely five feet high."

"Bravo bravo!" cried a tall man with an enormous mustache and a long rapier, "bravo, fair Paulet, it is high time to put little Voiture in his right place. For my part, I always thought his poetry detestable, and I think I know something about poetry."

"Who is this officer," inquired Raoul of Athos, "who is speaking?"

"Monsieur de Scudery, the author of 'Clelie,' and of 'Le Grand Cyrus,' which were composed partly by him and partly by his sister, who is now talking to that pretty person yonder, near Monsieur Scarron."

Raoul turned and saw two faces just arrived. One was perfectly charming, delicate, pensive, shaded by beautiful dark hair, and eyes soft as velvet, like those lovely flowers, the heartsease, in which shine out the golden petals. The other, of mature age, seemed to have the former one under her charge, and was cold, dry and yellow--the true type of a duenna or a devotee.

Raoul resolved not to quit the room without having spoken to the beautiful girl with the soft eyes, who by a strange fancy, although she bore no resemblance, reminded him of his poor little Louise, whom he had left in the Chateau de la Valliere and whom, in the midst of all the party, he had never for one moment quite forgotten. Meantime Aramis had drawn near to the coadjutor, who, smiling all the while, contrived to drop some words into his ear. Aramis, notwithstanding his self-control, could not refrain from a slight movement of surprise.

"Laugh, then," said Monsieur de Retz; "they are looking at us." And leaving Aramis he went to talk with Madame de Chevreuse, who was in the midst of a large group.

Aramis affected a laugh, to divert the attention of certain curious listeners, and perceiving that Athos had betaken himself to the embrasure of a window and remained there, he proceeded to join him, throwing out a few words carelessly as he moved through the room.

As soon as the two friends met they began a conversation which was emphasized by frequent gesticulation.

Raoul then approached them as Athos had directed him to do.

"'Tis a rondeau by Monsieur Voiture that monsieur l'abbe is repeating to me." said Athos in a loud voice, "and I confess I think it incomparable."

Raoul stayed only a few minutes near them and then mingled with the group round Madame de Chevreuse.

"Well, then?" asked Athos, in a low tone.

"It is to be to-morrow," said Aramis hastily.

"At what time?"

"Six o'clock."

"Where?"

"At Saint Mande."

"Who told you?"

"The Count de Rochefort."

Some one drew near.

"And then philosophic ideas are wholly wanting in Voiture's works, but I am of the same opinion as the coadjutor--he is a poet, a true poet." Aramis spoke so as to be heard by everybody.

"And I, too," murmured the young lady with the velvet eyes. "I have the misfortune also to admire his poetry exceedingly."

"Monsieur Scarron, do me the honor," said Raoul, blushing, "to tell me the name of that young lady whose opinion seems so different from that of others of the company."

"Ah! my young vicomte," replied Scarron, "I suppose you wish to propose to her an alliance offensive and defensive."

Raoul blushed again.

"You asked the name of that young lady. She is called the fair Indian."

"Excuse me, sir," returned Raoul, blushing still more deeply, "I know no more than I did before. Alas! I am from the country."

"Which means that you know very little about the nonsense which here flows down our streets. So much the better, young man! so much the better! Don't try to understand it--you will only lose your time."

"You forgive me, then, sir," said Raoul, "and you will deign to tell me who is the person that you call the young Indian?"

"Certainly; one of the most charming persons that lives--Mademoiselle Frances d'Aubigne."

"Does she belong to the family of the celebrated Agrippa, the friend of Henry IV.?"

"His granddaughter. She comes from Martinique, so I call her the beautiful Indian."

Raoul looked surprised and his eyes met those of the young lady, who smiled.

The company went on speaking of the poet Voiture.

"Monsieur," said Mademoiselle d'Aubigne to Scarron, as if she wished to join in the conversation he was engaged in with Raoul, "do you not admire Monsieur Voiture's friends? Listen how they pull him to pieces even whilst they praise him; one takes away from him all claim to good sense, another robs him of his poetry, a third of his originality, another of his humor, another of his independence of character, a sixth--but, good heavens! what will they leave him? as Mademoiselle de Scudery remarks."

Scarron and Raoul laughed. The fair Indian, astonished at the sensation her observation produced, looked down and resumed her air of naivete.

Athos, still within the inclosure of the window, watched this scene with a smile of disdain on his lips.

"Tell the Comte de la Fere to come to me," said Madame de Chevreuse, "I want to speak to him."

"And I," said the coadjutor, "want it to be thought that I do not speak to him. I admire, I love him--for I know his former adventures--but I shall not speak to him until the day after to-morrow."

"And why day after to-morrow?" asked Madame de Chevreuse.

"You will know that to-morrow evening," said the coadjutor, smiling.

"Really, my dear Gondy," said the duchess, "you remind one of the Apocalypse. Monsieur d'Herblay," she added, turning toward Aramis, "will you be my servant once more this evening?"

"How can you doubt it?" replied Aramis; "this evening, to-morrow, always; command me."

"I will, then. Go and look for the Comte de la Fere; I wish to speak with him."

Aramis found Athos and brought him.

"Monsieur le comte," said the duchess, giving him a letter, "here is what I promised you; our young friend will be extremely well received."

"Madame, he is very happy in owing any obligation to you."

"You have no reason to envy him on that score, for I owe to you the pleasure of knowing him," replied the witty woman, with a smile which recalled Marie Michon to Aramis and to Athos.

As she uttered that bon mot, she arose and asked for her carriage. Mademoiselle Paulet had already gone; Mademoiselle de Scudery was going.

"Vicomte," said Athos to Raoul, "follow the duchess; beg her to do you the favor to take your arm in going downstairs, and thank her as you descend."

The fair Indian approached Scarron.

"You are going already?" he said.

"One of the last, as you see; if you hear anything of Monsieur Voiture, be so kind as to send me word to-morrow."

"Oh!" said Scarron, "he may die now."

"Why?" asked the young girl with the velvet eyes.

"Certainly; his panegyric has been uttered."

They parted, laughing, she turning back to gaze at the poor paralytic man with interest, he looking after her with eyes of love.

One by one the several groups broke up. Scarron seemed not to observe that certain of his guests had talked mysteriously, that letters had passed from hand to hand and that the assembly had seemed to have a secret purpose quite apart from the literary discussion carried on with so much ostentation. What was all that to Scarron? At his house rebellion could be planned with impunity, for, as we have said, since that morning he had ceased to be "the queen's invalid."

As to Raoul, he had attended the duchess to her carriage, where, as she took her seat, she gave him her hand to kiss; then, by one of those wild caprices which made her so adorable and at the same time so dangerous, she had suddenly put her arm around his neck and kissed his forehead, saying:

"Vicomte, may my good wishes and this kiss bring you good fortune!"

Then she had pushed him away and directed the coachman to stop at the Hotel de Luynes. The carriage had started, Madame de Chevreuse had made a parting gesture to the young man, and Raoul had returned in a state of stupefaction.

Athos surmised what had taken place and smiled. "Come, vicomte," he said, "it is time for you to go to bed; you will start in the morning for the army of monsieur le prince. Sleep well your last night as citizen."

"I am to be a soldier then?" said the young man. "Oh, monsieur, I thank you with all my heart."

"Adieu, count," said the Abbe d'Herblay; "I return to my convent."

"Adieu, abbe," said the coadjutor, "I am to preach to-morrow and have twenty texts to examine this evening."

"Adieu, gentlemen," said the count; "I am going to sleep twenty-four hours; I am just falling down with fatigue."

The three men saluted one another, whilst exchanging a last look.

Scarron followed their movements with a glance from the corner of his eye.

"Not one of them will do as he says," he murmured, with his little monkey smile; "but they may do as they please, the brave gentlemen! Who knows if they will not manage to restore to me my pension? They can move their arms, they can, and that is much. Alas, I have only my tongue, but I will try to show that it is good for something. Ho, there, Champenois! here, it is eleven o'clock. Come and roll me to bed. Really, that Demoiselle d'Aubigne is very charming!"

So the invalid disappeared soon afterward and went into his sleeping-room; and one by one the lights in the salon of the Rue des Tournelles were extinguished.

22. Saint Denis.

The day had begun to break when Athos arose and dressed himself. It was plain, by a paleness still greater than usual, and by those traces which loss of sleep leaves on the face, that he must have passed almost the whole of the night without sleeping. Contrary to the custom of a man so firm and decided, there was this morning in his personal appearance something tardy and irresolute.

He was occupied with the preparations for Raoul's departure and was seeking to gain time. In the first place he himself furbished a sword, which he drew from its perfumed leather sheath; he examined it to see if its hilt was well guarded and if the blade was firmly attached to the hilt. Then he placed at the bottom of the valise belonging to the young man a small bag of louis, called Olivain, the lackey who had followed him from Blois, and made him pack the valise under his own eyes, watchful to see that everything should be put in which might be useful to a young man entering on his first campaign.

At length, after occupying about an hour in these preparations, he opened the door of the room in which the vicomte slept, and entered.

The sun, already high, penetrated into the room through the window, the curtains of which Raoul had neglected to close on the previous evening. He was still sleeping, his head gracefully reposing on his arm.

Athos approached and hung over the youth in an attitude full of tender melancholy; he looked long on this young man, whose smiling mouth and half closed eyes bespoke soft dreams and lightest slumber, as if his guardian angel watched over him with solicitude and affection. By degrees Athos gave himself up to the charms of his reverie in the proximity of youth, so pure, so fresh. His own youth seemed to reappear, bringing with it all those savoury remembrances, which are like perfumes more than thoughts. Between the past and the present was an ineffable abyss. But imagination has the wings of an angel of light and travels safely through or over the seas where we have been almost shipwrecked, the darkness in which our illusions are lost, the precipice whence our happiness has been hurled and swallowed up. He remembered that all the first part of his life had been embittered by a woman and he thought with alarm of the influence love might assume over so fine, and at the same time so vigorous an organization as that of Raoul.

In recalling all he had been through, he foresaw all that Raoul might suffer; and the expression of the deep and tender compassion which throbbed in his heart was pictured in the moist eye with which he gazed on the young man.

At this moment Raoul awoke, without a cloud on his face without weariness or lassitude; his eyes were fixed on those of Athos and perhaps he comprehended all that passed in the heart of the man who was awaiting his awakening as a lover awaits the awakening of his mistress, for his glance, in return, had all the tenderness of love.

"You are there, sir?" he said, respectfully.

"Yes, Raoul," replied the count.

"And you did not awaken me?"

"I wished to leave you still to enjoy some moments of sleep, my child; you must be fatigued from yesterday."

"Oh, sir, how good you are!"

Athos smiled.

"How do you feel this morning?" he inquired.

"Perfectly well; quite rested, sir."

"You are still growing," Athos continued, with that charming and paternal interest felt by a grown man for a youth.

"Oh, sir, I beg your pardon!" exclaimed Raoul, ashamed of so much attention; "in an instant I shall be dressed."

Athos then called Olivain.

"Everything," said Olivain to Athos, "has been done according to your directions; the horses are waiting."

"And I was asleep," cried Raoul, "whilst you, sir, you had the kindness to attend to all these details. Truly, sir, you overwhelm me with benefits!"

"Therefore you love me a little, I hope," replied Athos, in a tone of emotion.

"Oh, sir! God knows how much I love, revere you."

"See that you forget nothing," said Athos, appearing to look about him, that he might hide his emotion.

"No, indeed, sir," answered Raoul.

The servant then approached Athos and said, hesitatingly:

"Monsieur le vicomte has no sword."

"'Tis well," said Athos, "I will take care of that."

They went downstairs, Raoul looking every now and then at the count to see if the moment of farewell was at hand, but Athos was silent. When they reached the steps Raoul saw three horses.

"Oh, sir! then you are going with me?"

"I will accompany you a portion of the way," said Athos.

Joy shone in Raoul's eyes and he leaped lightly to his saddle.

Athos mounted more slowly, after speaking in a low voice to the lackey, who, instead of following them immediately, returned to their rooms. Raoul, delighted at the count's companionship, perceived, or affected to perceive nothing of this byplay.

They set out, passing over the Pont Neuf; they pursued their way along the quay then called L'Abreuvoir Pepin, and went along by the walls of the Grand Chatelet. They proceeded to the Rue Saint Denis.

After passing through the Porte Saint Denis, Athos looked at Raoul's way of riding and observed:

"Take care, Raoul! I have already often told you of this; you must not forget it, for it is a great defect in a rider. See! your horse is tired already, he froths at the mouth, whilst mine looks as if he had only just left the stable. You hold the bit too tight and so make his mouth hard, so that you will not be able to make him manoeuvre quickly. The safety of a cavalier often depends on the prompt obedience of his horse. In a week, remember, you will no longer be performing your manoeuvres for practice, but on a field of battle."

Then suddenly, in order not to give too uncomfortable an importance to this observation:

"See, Raoul!" he resumed; "what a fine plain for partridge shooting."

The young man stored in his mind the admonition whilst he admired the delicate tenderness with which it was bestowed.

"I have remarked also another thing," said Athos, "which is, that in firing off your pistol you hold your arm too far outstretched. This tension lessens the accuracy of the aim. So in twelve times you thrice missed the mark."

"Which you, sir, struck twelve times," answered Raoul, smiling.

"Because I bent my arm and rested my hand on my elbow--so; do you understand what I mean?"

"Yes, sir. I have fired since in that manner and have been quite successful."

"What a cold wind!" resumed Athos; "a wintry blast. Apropos, if you fire--and you will do so, for you are recommended to a young general who is very fond of powder--remember that in single combat, which often takes place in the cavalry, never to fire the first shot. He who fires the first shot rarely hits his man, for he fires with the apprehension of being disarmed, before an armed foe; then, whilst he fires, make your horse rear; that manoeuvre has saved my life several times."

"I shall do so, if only in gratitude----"

"Eh!" cried Athos, "are not those fellows poachers they have arrested yonder? They are. Then another important thing, Raoul: should you be wounded in a battle, and fall from your horse, if you have any strength left, disentangle yourself from the line that your regiment has formed; otherwise, it may be driven back and you will be trampled to death by the horses. At all events, should you be wounded, write to me that very instant, or get some one at once to write to me. We are judges of wounds, we old soldiers," Athos added, smiling.

"Thank you, sir," answered the young man, much moved.

They arrived that very moment at the gate of the town, guarded by two sentinels.

"Here comes a young gentleman," said one of them, "who seems as if he were going to join the army."

"How do you make that out?" inquired Athos.

"By his manner, sir, and his age; he's the second to-day."

"Has a young man, such as I am, gone through this morning, then?" asked Raoul.

"Faith, yes, with a haughty presence, a fine equipage; such as the son of a noble house would have."

"He will be my companion on the journey, sir," cried Raoul. "Alas! he cannot make me forget what I shall have lost!"

Thus talking, they traversed the streets, full of people on account of the fete, and arrived opposite the old cathedral, where first mass was going on.

"Let us alight; Raoul," said Athos. "Olivain, take care of our horses and give me my sword."

The two gentlemen then went into the church. Athos gave Raoul some of the holy water. A love as tender as that of a lover for his mistress dwells, undoubtedly, in some paternal hearts toward a son.

Athos said a word to one of the vergers, who bowed and proceeded toward the basement.

"Come, Raoul," he said, "let us follow this man."

The verger opened the iron grating that guarded the royal tombs and stood on the topmost step, whilst Athos and Raoul descended. The sepulchral depths of the descent were dimly lighted by a silver lamp on the lowest step; and just below this lamp there was laid, wrapped in a flowing mantle of violet velvet, worked with fleurs-de-lis of gold, a catafalque resting on trestles of oak. The young man, prepared for this scene by the state of his own feelings, which were mournful, and by the majesty of the cathedral which he had passed through, descended in a slow and solemn manner and stood with head uncovered before these mortal spoils of the last king, who was not to be placed by the side of his forefathers until his successor should take his place there; and who appeared to abide on that spot, that he might thus address human pride, so sure to be exalted by the glories of a throne: "Dust of the earth! Here I await thee!"

There was profound silence.

Then Athos raised his hand and pointing to the coffin:

"This temporary sepulture is," he said, "that of a man who was of feeble mind, yet one whose reign was full of great events; because over this king watched the spirit of another man, even as this lamp keeps vigil over this coffin and illumines it. He whose intellect was thus supreme, Raoul, was the actual sovereign; the other, nothing but a phantom to whom he lent a soul; and yet, so powerful is majesty amongst us, this man has not even the honor of a tomb at the feet of him in whose service his life was worn away. Remember, Raoul, this! If Richelieu made the king, by comparison, seem small, he made royalty great. The Palace of the Louvre contains two things--the king, who must die, and royalty, which never dies. The minister, so feared, so hated by his master, has descended into the tomb, drawing after him the king, whom he would not leave alone on earth, lest his work should be destroyed. So blind were his contemporaries that they regarded the cardinal's death as a deliverance; and I, even I, opposed the designs of the great man who held the destinies of France within the hollow of his hand. Raoul, learn how to distinguish the king from royalty; the king is but a man; royalty is the gift of God. Whenever you hesitate as to whom you ought to serve, abandon the exterior, the material appearance for the invisible principle, for the invisible principle is everything. Raoul, I seem to read your future destiny as through a cloud. It will be happier, I think, than ours has been. Different in your fate from us, you will have a king without a minister, whom you may serve, love, respect. Should the king prove a tyrant, for power begets tyranny, serve, love, respect royalty, that Divine right, that celestial spark which makes this dust still powerful and holy, so that we--gentlemen, nevertheless, of rank and condition--are as nothing in comparison with the cold corpse there extended."

"I shall adore God, sir," said Raoul, "respect royalty and ever serve the king. And if death be my lot, I hope to die for the king, for royalty and for God. Have I, sir, comprehended your instructions?"

Athos smiled.

"Yours is a noble nature." he said; "here is your sword."

Raoul bent his knee to the ground.

"It was worn by my father, a loyal gentleman. I have worn it in my turn and it has sometimes not been disgraced when the hilt was in my hand and the sheath at my side. Should your hand still be too weak to use this sword, Raoul, so much the better. You will have the more time to learn to draw it only when it ought to be used."

"Sir," replied Raoul, putting the sword to his lips as he received it from the count, "I owe you everything and yet this sword is the most precious gift you have yet made me. I will wear it, I swear to you, as a grateful man should do."

"'Tis well; arise, vicomte, embrace me."

Raoul arose and threw himself with emotion into the count's arms.

"Adieu," faltered the count, who felt his heart die away within him; "adieu, and think of me."

"Oh! for ever and ever!" cried the youth; "oh! I swear to you, sir, should any harm befall me, your name will be the last name that I shall utter, the remembrance of you my last thought."

Athos hastened upstairs to conceal his emotion, and regained with hurried steps the porch where Olivain was waiting with the horses.

"Olivain," said Athos, showing the servant Raoul's shoulder-belt, "tighten the buckle of the sword, it falls too low. You will accompany monsieur le vicomte till Grimaud rejoins you. You know, Raoul, Grimaud is an old and zealous servant; he will follow you."

"Yes, sir," answered Raoul.

"Now to horse, that I may see you depart!"

Raoul obeyed.

"Adieu, Raoul," said the count; "adieu, my dearest boy!"

"Adieu, sir, adieu, my beloved protector."

Athos waved his hand--he dared not trust himself to speak: and Raoul went away, his head uncovered. Athos remained motionless, looking after him until he turned the corner of the street.

Then the count threw the bridle of his horse into the hands of a peasant, remounted the steps, went into the cathedral, there to kneel down in the darkest corner and pray.

23. One of the Forty Methods of Escape of the Duc de Beaufort.

Meanwhile time was passing on for the prisoner, as well as for those who were preparing his escape; only for him it passed more slowly. Unlike other men, who enter with ardor upon a perilous resolution and grow cold as the moment of execution approaches, the Duc de Beaufort, whose buoyant courage had become a proverb, seemed to push time before him and sought most eagerly to hasten the hour of action. In his escape alone, apart from his plans for the future, which, it must be admitted, were for the present sufficiently vague and uncertain, there was a beginning of vengeance which filled his heart. In the first place his escape would be a serious misfortune to Monsieur de Chavigny, whom he hated for the petty persecutions he owed to him. It would be a still worse affair for Mazarin, whom he execrated for the greater offences he had committed. It may be observed that there was a proper proportion in his sentiments toward the governor of the prison and the minister--toward the subordinate and the master.

Then Monsieur de Beaufort, who was so familiar with the interior of the Palais Royal, though he did not know the relations existing between the queen and the cardinal, pictured to himself, in his prison, all that dramatic excitement which would ensue when the rumor should run from the minister's cabinet to the chamber of Anne of Austria: "Monsieur de Beaufort has escaped!" Whilst saying that to himself, Monsieur de Beaufort smiled pleasantly and imagined himself already outside, breathing the air of the plains and the forests, pressing a strong horse between his knees and crying out in a loud voice, "I am free!"

It is true that on coming to himself he found that he was still within four walls; he saw La Ramee twirling his thumbs ten feet from him, and his guards laughing and drinking in the ante-chamber. The only thing that was pleasant to him in that odious tableau--such is the instability of the human mind--was the sullen face of Grimaud, for whom he had at first conceived such a hatred and who now was all his hope. Grimaud seemed to him an Antinous. It is needless to say that this transformation was visible only to the prisoner's feverish imagination. Grimaud was still the same, and therefore he retained the entire confidence of his superior, La Ramee, who now relied upon him more than he did upon himself, for, as we have said, La Ramee felt at the bottom of his heart a certain weakness for Monsieur de Beaufort.

And so the good La Ramee made a festivity of the little supper with his prisoner. He had but one fault--he was a gourmand; he had found the pates good, the wine excellent. Now the successor of Pere Marteau had promised him a pate of pheasant instead of a pate of fowl, and Chambertin wine instead of Macon. All this, set off by the presence of that excellent prince, who was so good-natured, who invented so droll tricks against Monsieur de Chavigny and so fine jokes against Mazarin, made for La Ramee the approaching Pentecost one of the four great feasts of the year. He therefore looked forward to six o'clock with as much impatience as the duke himself.

Since daybreak La Ramee had been occupied with the preparations, and trusting no one but himself, he had visited personally the successor of Pere Marteau. The latter had surpassed himself; he showed La Ramee a monstrous pate, ornamented with Monsieur de Beaufort's coat-of-arms. It was empty as yet, but a pheasant and two partridges were lying near it. La Ramee's mouth watered and he returned to the duke's chamber rubbing his hands. To crown his happiness, Monsieur de Chavigny had started on a journey that morning and in his absence La Ramee was deputy-governor of the chateau.

As for Grimaud, he seemed more sullen than ever.

In the course of the forenoon Monsieur de Beaufort had a game of tennis with La Ramee; a sign from Grimaud put him on the alert. Grimaud, going in advance, followed the course which they were to take in the evening. The game was played in an inclosure called the little court of the chateau, a place quite deserted except when Monsieur de Beaufort was playing; and even then the precaution seemed superfluous, the wall was so high.

There were three gates to open before reaching the inclosure, each by a different key. When they arrived Grimaud went carelessly and sat down by a loophole in the wall, letting his legs dangle outside. It was evident that there the rope ladder was to be attached.

This manoeuvre, transparent to the Duc de Beaufort, was quite unintelligible to La Ramee.

The game at tennis, which, upon a sign from Grimaud, Monsieur de Beaufort had consented to play, began in the afternoon. The duke was in full strength and beat La Ramee completely.

Four of the guards, who were constantly near the prisoner, assisted in picking up the tennis balls. When the game was over, the duke, laughing at La Ramee for his bad play, offered these men two louis d'or to go and drink his health, with their four other comrades.

The guards asked permission of La Ramee, who gave it to them, but not till the evening, however; until then he had business and the prisoner was not to be left alone.

Six o'clock came and, although they were not to sit down to table until seven o'clock, dinner was ready and served up. Upon a sideboard appeared the colossal pie with the duke's arms on it, and seemingly cooked to a turn, as far as one could judge by the golden color which illuminated the crust.

The rest of the dinner was to come.

Every one was impatient, La Ramee to sit down to table, the guards to go and drink, the duke to escape.

Grimaud alone was calm as ever. One might have fancied that Athos had educated him with the express forethought of such a great event.

There were moments when, looking at Grimaud, the duke asked himself if he was not dreaming and if that marble figure was really at his service and would grow animated when the moment came for action.

La Ramee sent away the guards, desiring them to drink to the duke's health, and as soon as they were gone shut all the doors, put the keys in his pocket and showed the table to the prince with an air that signified:

"Whenever my lord pleases."

The prince looked at Grimaud, Grimaud looked at the clock; it was hardly a quarter-past six. The escape was fixed to take place at seven o'clock; there was therefore three-quarters of an hour to wait.

The duke, in order to pass away another quarter of an hour, pretended to be reading something that interested him and muttered that he wished they would allow him to finish his chapter. La Ramee went up to him and looked over his shoulder to see what sort of a book it was that had so singular an influence over the prisoner as to make him put off taking his dinner.

It was "Caesar's Commentaries," which La Ramee had lent him, contrary to the orders of the governor; and La Ramee resolved never again to disobey these injunctions.

Meantime he uncorked the bottles and went to smell if the pie was good.

At half-past six the duke arose and said very gravely:

"Certainly, Caesar was the greatest man of ancient times."

"You think so, my lord?" answered La Ramee.

"Yes."

"Well, as for me, I prefer Hannibal."

"And why, pray, Master La Ramee?" asked the duke.

"Because he left no Commentaries," replied La Ramee, with his coarse laugh.

The duke vouchsafed no reply, but sitting down at the table made a sign that La Ramee should seat himself opposite. There is nothing so expressive as the face of an epicure who finds himself before a well spread table, so La Ramee, when receiving his plate of soup from Grimaud, presented a type of perfect bliss.

The duke smiled.

"Zounds!" he said; "I don't suppose there is a more contented man at this moment in all the kingdom than yourself!"

"You are right, my lord duke," answered the officer; "I don't know any pleasanter sight on earth than a well covered table; and when, added to that, he who does the honors is the grandson of Henry IV., you will, my lord duke, easily comprehend that the honor fairly doubles the pleasure one enjoys."

The duke, in his turn, bowed, and an imperceptible smile appeared on the face of Grimaud, who kept behind La Ramee.

"My dear La Ramee," said the duke, "you are the only man to turn such faultless compliments."

"No, my lord duke," replied La Ramee, in the fullness of his heart; "I say what I think; there is no compliment in what I say to you----"

"Then you are attached to me?" asked the duke.

"To own the truth, I should be inconsolable if you were to leave Vincennes."

"A droll way of showing your affliction." The duke meant to say "affection."

"But, my lord," returned La Ramee, "what would you do if you got out? Every folly you committed would embroil you with the court and they would put you into the Bastile, instead of Vincennes. Now, Monsieur de Chavigny is not amiable, I allow, but Monsieur du Tremblay is considerably worse."

"Indeed!" exclaimed the duke, who from time to time looked at the clock, the fingers of which seemed to move with sickening slowness.

"But what can you expect from the brother of a capuchin monk, brought up in the school of Cardinal Richelieu? Ah, my lord, it is a great happiness that the queen, who always wished you well, had a fancy to send you here, where there's a promenade and a tennis court, good air, and a good table."

"In short," answered the duke, "if I comprehend you aright, La Ramee, I am ungrateful for having ever thought of leaving this place?"

"Oh! my lord duke, 'tis the height of ingratitude; but your highness has never seriously thought of it?"

"Yes," returned the duke, "I must confess I sometimes think of it."

"Still by one of your forty methods, your highness?"

"Yes, yes, indeed."

"My lord," said La Ramee, "now we are quite at our ease and enjoying ourselves, pray tell me one of those forty ways invented by your highness."

"Willingly," answered the duke, "give me the pie!"

"I am listening," said La Ramee, leaning back in his armchair and raising his glass of Madeira to his lips, and winking his eye that he might see the sun through the rich liquid that he was about to taste.

The duke glanced at the clock. In ten minutes it would strike seven.

Grimaud placed the pie before the duke, who took a knife with a silver blade to raise the upper crust; but La Ramee, who was afraid of any harm happening to this fine work of art, passed his knife, which had an iron blade, to the duke.

"Thank you, La Ramee," said the prisoner.

"Well, my lord! this famous invention of yours?"

"Must I tell you," replied the duke, "on what I most reckon and what I determine to try first?"

"Yes, that's the thing, my lord!" cried his custodian, gaily.

"Well, I should hope, in the first instance, to have for keeper an honest fellow like you."

"And you have me, my lord. Well?"

"Having, then, a keeper like La Ramee, I should try also to have introduced to him by some friend or other a man who would be devoted to me, who would assist me in my flight."

"Come, come," said La Ramee, "that's not a bad idea."

"Capital, isn't it? for instance, the former servingman of some brave gentleman, an enemy himself to Mazarin, as every gentleman ought to be."

"Hush! don't let us talk politics, my lord."

"Then my keeper would begin to trust this man and to depend upon him, and I should have news from those without the prison walls."

"Ah, yes! but how can the news be brought to you?"

"Nothing easier; in a game of tennis, for example."

"In a game of tennis?" asked La Ramee, giving more serious attention to the duke's words.

"Yes; see, I send a ball into the moat; a man is there who picks it up; the ball contains a letter. Instead of returning the ball to me when I call for it from the top of the wall, he throws me another; that other ball contains a letter. Thus we have exchanged ideas and no one has seen us do it."

"The devil it does! The devil it does!" said La Ramee, scratching his head; "you are in the wrong to tell me that, my lord. I shall have to watch the men who pick up balls."

The duke smiled.

"But," resumed La Ramee, "that is only a way of corresponding."

"And that is a great deal, it seems to me."

"But not enough."

"Pardon me; for instance, I say to my friends, Be on a certain day, on a certain hour, at the other side of the moat with two horses."

"Well, what then?" La Ramee began to be uneasy; "unless the horses have wings to mount the ramparts and come and fetch you."

"That's not needed. I have," replied the duke, "a way of descending from the ramparts."

"What?"

"A rope ladder."

"Yes, but," answered La Ramee, trying to laugh, "a ladder of ropes can't be sent around a ball, like a letter."

"No, but it may be sent in something else."

"In something else--in something else? In what?"

"In a pate, for example."

"In a pate?" said La Ramee.

"Yes. Let us suppose one thing," replied the duke "let us suppose, for instance, that my maitre d'hotel, Noirmont, has purchased the shop of Pere Marteau----"

"Well?" said La Ramee, shuddering.

"Well, La Ramee, who is a gourmand, sees his pates, thinks them more attractive than those of Pere Marteau and proposes to me that I shall try them. I consent on condition that La Ramee tries them with me. That we may be more at our ease, La Ramee removes the guards, keeping only Grimaud to wait on us. Grimaud is the man whom a friend has sent to second me in everything. The moment for my escape is fixed--seven o'clock. Well, at a few minutes to seven----"

"At a few minutes to seven?" cried La Ramee, cold sweat upon his brow.

"At a few minutes to seven," returned the duke (suiting the action to the words), "I raise the crust of the pie; I find in it two poniards, a ladder of rope, and a gag. I point one of the poniards at La Ramee's breast and I say to him, 'My friend, I am sorry for it, but if thou stirrest, if thou utterest one cry, thou art a dead man!'"

The duke, in pronouncing these words, suited, as we have said, the action to the words. He was standing near the officer and he directed the point of the poniard in such a manner, close to La Ramee's heart, that there could be no doubt in the mind of that individual as to his determination. Meanwhile, Grimaud, still mute as ever, drew from the pie the other poniard, the rope ladder and the gag.

La Ramee followed all these objects with his eyes, his alarm every moment increasing.

"Oh, my lord," he cried, with an expression of stupefaction in his face; "you haven't the heart to kill me!"

"No; not if thou dost not oppose my flight."

"But, my lord, if I allow you to escape I am a ruined man."

"I will compensate thee for the loss of thy place."

"You are determined to leave the chateau?"

"By Heaven and earth! This night I am determined to be free."

"And if I defend myself, or call, or cry out?"

"I will kill thee, on the honor of a gentleman."

At this moment the clock struck.

"Seven o'clock!" said Grimaud, who had not spoken a word.

La Ramee made one movement, in order to satisfy his conscience. The duke frowned, the officer felt the point of the poniard, which, having penetrated through his clothes, was close to his heart.

"Let us dispatch," said the duke.

"My lord, one last favor."

"What? speak, make haste."

"Bind my arms, my lord, fast."

"Why bind thee?"

"That I may not be considered as your accomplice."

"Your hands?" asked Grimaud.

"Not before me, behind me."

"But with what?" asked the duke.

"With your belt, my lord!" replied La Ramee.

The duke undid his belt and gave it to Grimaud, who tied La Ramee in such a way as to satisfy him.

"Your feet, too," said Grimaud.

La Ramee stretched out his legs, Grimaud took a table-cloth, tore it into strips and tied La Ramee's feet together.

"Now, my lord," said the poor man, "let me have the poire d'angoisse. I ask for it; without it I should be tried in a court of justice because I did not raise the alarm. Thrust it into my mouth, my lord, thrust it in."

Grimaud prepared to comply with this request, when the officer made a sign as if he had something to say.

"Speak," said the duke.

"Now, my lord, do not forget, if any harm happens to me on your account, that I have a wife and four children."

"Rest assured; put the gag in, Grimaud."

In a second La Ramee was gagged and laid prostrate. Two or three chairs were thrown down as if there had been a struggle. Grimaud then took from the pocket of the officer all the keys it contained and first opened the door of the room in which they were, then shut it and double-locked it, and both he and the duke proceeded rapidly down the gallery which led to the little inclosure. At last they reached the tennis court. It was completely deserted. No sentinels, no one at any of the windows. The duke ran to the rampart and perceived on the other side of the ditch, three cavaliers with two riding horses. The duke exchanged a signal with them. It was indeed for him that they were there.

Grimaud, meantime, undid the means of escape.

This was not, however, a rope ladder, but a ball of silk cord, with a narrow board which was to pass between the legs, the ball to unwind itself by the weight of the person who sat astride upon the board.

"Go!" said the duke.

"First, my lord?" inquired Grimaud.

"Certainly. If I am caught, I risk nothing but being taken back again to prison. If they catch thee, thou wilt be hung."

"True," replied Grimaud.

And instantly, Grimaud, sitting upon the board as if on horseback, commenced his perilous descent.

The duke followed him with his eyes, with involuntary terror. He had gone down about three-quarters of the length of the wall when the cord broke. Grimaud fell--precipitated into the moat.

The duke uttered a cry, but Grimaud did not give a single moan. He must have been dreadfully hurt, for he did not stir from the place where he fell.

Immediately one of the men who were waiting slipped down into the moat, tied under Grimaud's shoulders the end of a cord, and the remaining two, who held the other end, drew Grimaud to them.

"Descend, my lord," said the man in the moat. "There are only fifteen feet more from the top down here, and the grass is soft."

The duke had already begun to descend. His task was the more difficult, as there was no board to support him. He was obliged to let himself down by his hands and from a height of fifty feet. But as we have said he was active, strong, and full of presence of mind. In less than five minutes he arrived at the end of the cord. He was then only fifteen feet from the ground, as the gentlemen below had told him. He let go the rope and fell upon his feet, without receiving any injury.

He instantly began to climb up the slope of the moat, on the top of which he met De Rochefort. The other two gentlemen were unknown to him. Grimaud, in a swoon, was tied securely to a horse.

"Gentlemen," said the duke, "I will thank you later; now we have not a moment to lose. On, then! on! those who love me, follow me!"

And he jumped on his horse and set off at full gallop, snuffing the fresh air in his triumph and shouting out, with an expression of face which it would be impossible to describe:

"Free! free! free!"

24. The timely Arrival of D'Artagnan in Paris.

At Blois, D'Artagnan received the money paid to him by Mazarin for any future service he might render the cardinal.

From Blois to Paris was a journey of four days for ordinary travelers, but D'Artagnan arrived on the third day at the Barriere Saint Denis. In turning the corner of the Rue Montmartre, in order to reach the Rue Tiquetonne and the Hotel de la Chevrette, where he had appointed Porthos to meet him, he saw at one of the windows of the hotel, that friend himself dressed in a sky-blue waistcoat, embroidered with silver, and gaping, till he showed every one of his white teeth; whilst the people passing by admiringly gazed at this gentleman, so handsome and so rich, who seemed to weary of his riches and his greatness.

D'Artagnan and Planchet had hardly turned the corner when Porthos recognized them.

"Eh! D'Artagnan!" he cried. "Thank God you have come!"

"Eh! good-day, dear friend!" replied D'Artagnan.

Porthos came down at once to the threshold of the hotel.

"Ah, my dear friend!" he cried, "what bad stabling for my horses here."

"Indeed!" said D'Artagnan; "I am most unhappy to hear it, on account of those fine animals."

"And I, also--I was also wretchedly off," he answered, moving backward and forward as he spoke; "and had it not been for the hostess," he added, with his air of vulgar self-complacency, "who is very agreeable and understands a joke, I should have got a lodging elsewhere."

The pretty Madeleine, who had approached during this colloquy, stepped back and turned pale as death on hearing Porthos's words, for she thought the scene with the Swiss was about to be repeated. But to her great surprise D'Artagnan remained perfectly calm, and instead of being angry he laughed, and said to Porthos:

"Yes, I understand, the air of La Rue Tiquetonne is not like that of Pierrefonds; but console yourself, I will soon conduct you to one much better."

"When will you do that?"

"Immediately, I hope."

"Ah! so much the better!"

To that exclamation of Porthos's succeeded a groaning, low and profound, which seemed to come from behind a door. D'Artagnan, who had just dismounted, then saw, outlined against the wall, the enormous stomach of Mousqueton, whose down-drawn mouth emitted sounds of distress.

"And you, too, my poor Monsieur Mouston, are out of place in this poor hotel, are you not?" asked D'Artagnan, in that rallying tone which may indicate either compassion or mockery.

"He finds the cooking detestable," replied Porthos.

"Why, then, doesn't he attend to it himself, as at Chantilly?"

"Ah, monsieur, I have not here, as I had there, the ponds of monsieur le prince, where I could catch those beautiful carp, nor the forests of his highness to provide me with partridges. As for the cellar, I have searched every part and poor stuff I found."

"Monsieur Mouston," said D'Artagnan, "I should indeed condole with you had I not at this moment something very pressing to attend to."

Then taking Porthos aside:

"My dear Du Vallon," he said, "here you are in full dress most fortunately, for I am going to take you to the cardinal's."

"Gracious me! really!" exclaimed Porthos, opening his great wondering eyes.

"Yes, my friend."

"A presentation? indeed!"

"Does that alarm you?"

"No, but it agitates me."

"Oh! don't be distressed; you have to deal with a cardinal of another kind. This one will not oppress you by his dignity."

"'Tis the same thing--you understand me, D'Artagnan--a court."

"There's no court now. Alas!"

"The queen!"

"I was going to say, there's no longer a queen. The queen! Rest assured, we shall not see her."

"And you say that we are going from here to the Palais Royal?"

"Immediately. Only, that there may be no delay, I shall borrow one of your horses."

"Certainly; all the four are at your service."

"Oh, I need only one of them for the time being."

"Shall we take our valets?"

"Yes, you may as well take Mousqueton. As to Planchet, he has certain reasons for not going to court."

"And what are they?"

"Oh, he doesn't stand well with his eminence."

"Mouston," said Porthos, "saddle Vulcan and Bayard."

"And for myself, monsieur, shall I saddle Rustaud?"

"No, take a more stylish horse, Phoebus or Superbe; we are going with some ceremony."

"Ah," said Mousqueton, breathing more freely, "you are only going, then, to make a visit?"

"Oh! yes, of course, Mouston; nothing else. But to avoid risk, put the pistols in the holsters. You will find mine on my saddle, already loaded."

Mouston breathed a sigh; he couldn't understand visits of ceremony made under arms.

"Indeed," said Porthos, looking complacently at his old lackey as he went away, "you are right, D'Artagnan; Mouston will do; Mouston has a very fine appearance."

D'Artagnan smiled.

"But you, my friend--are you not going to change your dress?"

"No, I shall go as I am. This traveling dress will serve to show the cardinal my haste to obey his commands."

They set out on Vulcan and Bayard, followed by Mousqueton on Phoebus, and arrived at the Palais Royal at about a quarter to seven. The streets were crowded, for it was the day of Pentecost, and the crowd looked in wonder at these two cavaliers; one as fresh as if he had come out of a bandbox, the other so covered with dust that he looked as if he had but just come off a field of battle.

Mousqueton also attracted attention; and as the romance of Don Quixote was then the fashion, they said that he was Sancho, who, after having lost one master, had found two.

On reaching the palace, D'Artagnan sent to his eminence the letter in which he had been ordered to return without delay. He was soon ordered to the presence of the cardinal.

"Courage!" he whispered to Porthos, as they proceeded. "Do not be intimidated. Believe me, the eye of the eagle is closed forever. We have only the vulture to deal with. Hold yourself as bolt upright as on the day of the bastion of St. Gervais, and do not bow too low to this Italian; that might give him a poor idea of you."

"Good!" answered Porthos. "Good!"

Mazarin was in his study, working at a list of pensions and benefices, of which he was trying to reduce the number. He saw D'Artagnan and Porthos enter with internal pleasure, yet showed no joy in his countenance.

"Ah! you, is it? Monsieur le lieutenant, you have been very prompt. 'Tis well. Welcome to ye."

"Thanks, my lord. Here I am at your eminence's service, as well as Monsieur du Vallon, one of my old friends, who used to conceal his nobility under the name of Porthos."

Porthos bowed to the cardinal.

"A magnificent cavalier," remarked Mazarin.

Porthos turned his head to the right and to the left, and drew himself up with a movement full of dignity.

"The best swordsman in the kingdom, my lord," said D'Artagnan.

Porthos bowed to his friend.

Mazarin was as fond of fine soldiers as, in later times, Frederick of Prussia used to be. He admired the strong hands, the broad shoulders and the steady eye of Porthos. He seemed to see before him the salvation of his administration and of the kingdom, sculptured in flesh and bone. He remembered that the old association of musketeers was composed of four persons.

"And your two other friends?" he asked.

Porthos opened his mouth, thinking it a good opportunity to put in a word in his turn; D'Artagnan checked him by a glance from the corner of his eye.

"They are prevented at this moment, but will join us later."

Mazarin coughed a little.

"And this gentleman, being disengaged, takes to the service willingly?" he asked.

"Yes, my lord, and from pure devotion to the cause, for Monsieur de Bracieux is rich."

"Rich!" said Mazarin, whom that single word always inspired with a great respect.

"Fifty thousand francs a year," said Porthos.

These were the first words he had spoken.

"From pure zeal?" resumed Mazarin, with his artful smile; "from pure zeal and devotion then?"

"My lord has, perhaps, no faith in those words?" said D'Artagnan.

"Have you, Monsieur le Gascon?" asked Mazarin, supporting his elbows on his desk and his chin on his hands.

"I," replied the Gascon, "I believe in devotion as a word at one's baptism, for instance, which naturally comes before one's proper name; every one is naturally more or less devout, certainly; but there should be at the end of one's devotion something to gain."

"And your friend, for instance; what does he expect to have at the end of his devotion?"

"Well, my lord, my friend has three magnificent estates: that of Vallon, at Corbeil; that of Bracieux, in the Soissonais; and that of Pierrefonds, in the Valois. Now, my lord, he would like to have one of his three estates erected into a barony."

"Only that?" said Mazarin, his eyes twinkling with joy on seeing that he could pay for Porthos's devotion without opening his purse; "only that? That can be managed."

"I shall be baron!" explained Porthos, stepping forward.

"I told you so," said D'Artagnan, checking him with his hand; "and now his eminence confirms it."

"And you, Monsieur D'Artagnan, what do you want?"

"My lord," said D'Artagnan, "it is twenty years since Cardinal de Richelieu made me lieutenant."

"Yes, and you would be gratified if Cardinal Mazarin should make you captain."

D'Artagnan bowed.

"Well, that is not impossible. We will see, gentlemen, we will see. Now, Monsieur de Vallon," said Mazarin, "what service do you prefer, in the town or in the country?"

Porthos opened his mouth to reply.

"My lord," said D'Artagnan, "Monsieur de Vallon is like me, he prefers service extraordinary--that is to say, enterprises that are considered mad and impossible."

That boastfulness was not displeasing to Mazarin; he fell into meditation.

"And yet," he said, "I must admit that I sent for you to appoint you to quiet service; I have certain apprehensions--well, what is the meaning of that?"

In fact, a great noise was heard in the antechamber; at the same time the door of the study was burst open and a man, covered with dust, rushed into it, exclaiming:

"My lord the cardinal! my lord the cardinal!"

Mazarin thought that some one was going to assassinate him and he drew back, pushing his chair on the castors. D'Artagnan and Porthos moved so as to plant themselves between the person entering and the cardinal.

"Well, sir," exclaimed Mazarin, "what's the matter? and why do you rush in here, as if you were about to penetrate a crowded market-place?"

"My lord," replied the messenger, "I wish to speak to your eminence in secret. I am Monsieur du Poins, an officer in the guards, on duty at the donjon of Vincennes."

Mazarin, perceiving by the paleness and agitation of the messenger that he had something of importance to say, made a sign that D'Artagnan and Porthos should give place.

D'Artagnan and Porthos withdrew to a corner of the cabinet.

"Speak, monsieur, speak at once!" said Mazarin "What is the matter?"

"The matter is, my lord, that the Duc de Beaufort has contrived to escape from the Chateau of Vincennes."

Mazarin uttered a cry and became paler than the man who had brought the news. He fell back, almost fainting, in his chair.

"Escaped? Monsieur de Beaufort escaped?"

"My lord, I saw him run off from the top of the terrace."

"And you did not fire on him?"

"He was out of range."

"Monsieur de Chavigny--where was he?"

"Absent."

"And La Ramee?"

"Was found locked up in the prisoner's room, a gag in his mouth and a poniard near him."

"But the man who was under him?"

"Was an accomplice of the duke's and escaped along with him."

Mazarin groaned.

"My lord," said D'Artagnan, advancing toward the cardinal, "it seems to me that your eminence is losing precious time. It may still be possible to overtake the prisoner. France is large; the nearest frontier is sixty leagues distant."

"And who is to pursue him?" cried Mazarin.

"I, pardieu!"

"And you would arrest him?"

"Why not?"

"You would arrest the Duc de Beaufort, armed, in the field?"

"If your eminence should order me to arrest the devil, I would seize him by the horns and would bring him in."

"So would I," said Porthos.

"So would you!" said Mazarin, looking with astonishment at those two men. "But the duke will not yield himself without a furious battle."

"Very well," said D'Artagnan, his eyes aflame, "battle! It is a long time since we have had a battle, eh, Porthos?"

"Battle!" cried Porthos.

"And you think you can catch him?"

"Yes, if we are better mounted than he."

"Go then, take what guards you find here, and pursue him."

"You command us, my lord, to do so?"

"And I sign my orders," said Mazarin, taking a piece of paper and writing some lines; "Monsieur du Vallon, your barony is on the back of the Duc de Beaufort's horse; you have nothing to do but to overtake it. As for you, my dear lieutenant, I promise you nothing; but if you bring him back to me, dead or alive, you may ask all you wish."

"To horse, Porthos!" said D'Artagnan, taking his friend by the hand.

"Here I am," smiled Porthos, with his sublime composure.

They descended the great staircase, taking with them all the guards they found on their road, and crying out, "To arms! To arms!" and immediately put spur to horse, which set off along the Rue Saint Honore with the speed of the whirlwind.

"Well, baron, I promise you some good exercise!" said the Gascon.

"Yes, my captain."

As they went, the citizens, awakened, left their doors and the street dogs followed the cavaliers, barking. At the corner of the Cimetiere Saint Jean, D'Artagnan upset a man; it was too insignificant an occurrence to delay people so eager to get on. The troop continued its course as though their steeds had wings.

Alas! there are no unimportant events in this world and we shall see that this apparently slight incident came near endangering the monarchy.

25. An Adventure on the High Road.

The musketeers rode the whole length of the Faubourg Saint Antoine and of the road to Vincennes, and soon found themselves out of the town, then in a forest and then within sight of a village.

The horses seemed to become more lively with each successive step; their nostrils reddened like glowing furnaces. D'Artagnan, freely applying his spurs, was in advance of Porthos two feet at the most; Mousqueton followed two lengths behind; the guards were scattered according to the varying excellence of their respective mounts.

From the top of an eminence D'Artagnan perceived a group of people collected on the other side of the moat, in front of that part of the donjon which looks toward Saint Maur. He rode on, convinced that in this direction he would gain intelligence of the fugitive. In five minutes he had arrived at the place, where the guards joined him, coming up one by one.

The several members of that group were much excited. They looked at the cord, still hanging from the loophole and broken at about twenty feet from the ground. Their eyes measured the height and they exchanged conjectures. On the top of the wall sentinels went and came with a frightened air.

A few soldiers, commanded by a sergeant, drove away idlers from the place where the duke had mounted his horse. D'Artagnan went straight to the sergeant.

"My officer," said the sergeant, "it is not permitted to stop here."

"That prohibition is not for me," said D'Artagnan. "Have the fugitives been pursued?"

"Yes, my officer; unfortunately, they are well mounted."

"How many are there?"

"Four, and a fifth whom they carried away wounded."

"Four!" said D'Artagnan, looking at Porthos. "Do you hear, baron? They are only four!"

A joyous smile lighted Porthos's face.

"How long a start have they?"

"Two hours and a quarter, my officer."

"Two hours and a quarter--that is nothing; we are well mounted, are we not, Porthos?"

Porthos breathed a sigh; he thought of what was in store for his poor horses.

"Very good," said D'Artagnan; "and now in what direction did they set out?"

"That I am forbidden to tell."

D'Artagnan drew from his pocket a paper. "Order of the king," he said.

"Speak to the governor, then."

"And where is the governor?"

"In the country."

Anger mounted to D'Artagnan's face; he frowned and his cheeks were colored.

"Ah, you scoundrel!" he said to the sergeant, "I believe you are impudent to me! Wait!"

He unfolded the paper, presented it to the sergeant with one hand and with the other took a pistol from his holsters and cocked it.

"Order of the king, I tell you. Read and answer, or I will blow out your brains!"

The sergeant saw that D'Artagnan was in earnest. "The Vendomois road," he replied.

"And by what gate did they go out?"

"By the Saint Maur gate."

"If you are deceiving me, rascal, you will be hanged to-morrow."

"And if you catch up with them you won't come back to hang me," murmured the sergeant.

D'Artagnan shrugged his shoulders, made a sign to his escort and started.

"This way, gentlemen, this way!" he cried, directing his course toward the gate that had been pointed out.

But, now that the duke had escaped, the concierge had seen fit to fasten the gate with a double lock. It was necessary to compel him to open it, as the sergeant had been compelled to speak, and this took another ten minutes. This last obstacle having been overcome, the troop pursued their course with their accustomed ardor; but some of the horses could no longer sustain this pace; three of them stopped after an hour's gallop, and one fell down.

D'Artagnan, who never turned his head, did not perceive it. Porthos told him of it in his calm manner.

"If only we two arrive," said D'Artagnan, "it will be enough, since the duke's troop are only four in number."

"That is true," said Porthos

And he spurred his courser on.

At the end of another two hours the horses had gone twelve leagues without stopping; their legs began to tremble, and the foam they shed whitened the doublets of their masters.

"Let us rest here an instant to give these poor creatures breathing time," said Porthos.

"Let us rather kill them! yes, kill them!" cried D'Artagnan; "I see fresh tracks; 'tis not a quarter of an hour since they passed this place."

In fact, the road was trodden by horses' feet, visible even in the approaching gloom of evening.

They set out; after a run of two leagues, Mousqueton's horse sank.

"Gracious me!" said Porthos, "there's Phoebus ruined."

"The cardinal will pay you a hundred pistoles."

"I'm above that."

"Let us set out again, at full gallop."

"Yes, if we can."

But at last the lieutenant's horse refused to go on; he could not breathe; one last spur, instead of making him advance, made him fall.

"The devil!" exclaimed Porthos; "there's Vulcan foundered."

"Zounds!" cried D'Artagnan, "then we must stop! Give me your horse, Porthos. What the devil are you doing?"

"By Jove, I am falling, or rather, Bayard is falling," answered Porthos.

All three then cried: "All's over."

"Hush!" said D'Artagnan.

"What is it?"

"I hear a horse."

"It belongs to one of our companions, who is overtaking us."

"No," said D'Artagnan, "it is in advance."

"That is another thing," said Porthos; and he listened toward the quarter indicated by D'Artagnan.

"Monsieur," said Mousqueton, who, abandoning his horse on the high road, had come on foot to rejoin his master, "Phoebus could no longer hold out and----"

"Silence!" said Porthos.

In fact, at that moment a second neighing was borne to them on the night wind.

"It is five hundred feet from here, in advance," said D'Artagnan.

"True, monsieur," said Mousqueton; "and five hundred feet from here is a small hunting-house."

"Mousqueton, thy pistols," said D'Artagnan.

"I have them at hand, monsieur."

"Porthos, take yours from your holsters."

"I have them."

"Good!" said D'Artagnan, seizing his own; "now you understand, Porthos?"

"Not too well."

"We are out on the king's service."

"Well?"

"For the king's service we need horses."

"That is true," said Porthos.

"Then not a word, but set to work!"

They went on through the darkness, silent as phantoms; they saw a light glimmering in the midst of some trees.

"Yonder is the house, Porthos," said the Gascon; "let me do what I please and do you what I do."

They glided from tree to tree till they arrived at twenty steps from the house unperceived and saw by means of a lantern suspended under a hut, four fine horses. A groom was rubbing them down; near them were saddles and bridles.

D'Artagnan approached quickly, making a sign to his two companions to remain a few steps behind.

"I buy those horses," he said to the groom.

The groom turned toward him with a look of surprise, but made no reply.

"Didn't you hear, fellow?"

"Yes, I heard."

"Why, then, didn't you reply?"

"Because these horses are not to be sold," was the reply.

"I take them, then," said the lieutenant.

And he took hold of one within his reach; his two companions did the same thing.

"Sir," cried the groom, "they have traversed six leagues and have only been unsaddled half an hour."

"Half an hour's rest is enough," replied the Gascon.

The groom cried aloud for help. A kind of steward appeared, just as D'Artagnan and his companions were prepared to mount. The steward attempted to expostulate.

"My dear friend," cried the lieutenant, "if you say a word I will blow out your brains."

"But, sir," answered the steward, "do you know that these horses belong to Monsieur de Montbazon?"

"So much the better; they must be good animals, then."

"Sir, I shall call my people."

"And I, mine; I've ten guards behind me, don't you hear them gallop? and I'm one of the king's musketeers. Come, Porthos; come, Mousqueton."

They all mounted the horses as quickly as possible.

"Halloo! hi! hi!" cried the steward; "the house servants, with the carbines!"

"On! on!" cried D'Artagnan; "there'll be firing! on!"

They all set off, swift as the wind.

"Here!" cried the steward, "here!" whilst the groom ran to a neighboring building.

"Take care of your horses!" cried D'Artagnan to him.

"Fire!" replied the steward.

A gleam, like a flash of lightning, illumined the road, and with the flash was heard the whistling of balls, which were fired wildly in the air.

"They fire like grooms," said Porthos. "In the time of the cardinal people fired better than that, do you remember the road to Crevecoeur, Mousqueton?"

"Ah, sir! my left side still pains me!"

"Are you sure we are on the right track, lieutenant?"

"Egad, didn't you hear? these horses belong to Monsieur de Montbazon; well, Monsieur de Montbazon is the husband of Madame de Montbazon----"

"And----"

"And Madame de Montbazon is the mistress of the Duc de Beaufort."

"Ah! I understand," replied Porthos; "she has ordered relays of horses."

"Exactly so."

"And we are pursuing the duke with the very horses he has just left?"

"My dear Porthos, you are really a man of most superior understanding," said D'Artagnan, with a look as if he spoke against his conviction.

"Pooh!" replied Porthos, "I am what I am."

They rode on for an hour, till the horses were covered with foam and dust.

"Zounds! what is yonder?" cried D'Artagnan.

"You are very lucky if you see anything such a night as this," said Porthos.

"Something bright."

"I, too," cried Mousqueton, "saw them also."

"Ah! ah! have we overtaken them?"

"Good! a dead horse!" said D'Artagnan, pulling up his horse, which shied; "it seems their horses, too, are breaking down, as well as ours."

"I seem to hear the noise of a troop of horsemen," exclaimed Porthos, leaning over his horse's mane.

"Impossible."

"They appear to be numerous."

"Then 'tis something else."

"Another horse!" said Porthos.

"Dead?"

"No, dying."

"Saddled?"

"Yes, saddled and bridled."

"Then we are upon the fugitives."

"Courage, we have them!"

"But if they are numerous," observed Mousqueton, "'tis not we who have them, but they who have us."

"Nonsense!" cried D'Artagnan, "they'll suppose us to be stronger than themselves, as we're in pursuit; they'll be afraid and will disperse."

"Certainly," remarked Porthos.

"Ah! do you see?" cried the lieutenant.

"The lights again! this time I, too, saw them," said Porthos.

"On! on! forward! forward!" cried D'Artagnan, in his stentorian voice; "we shall laugh over all this in five minutes."

And they darted on anew. The horses, excited by pain and emulation, raced over the dark road, in the midst of which was now seen a moving mass, denser and more obscure than the rest of the horizon.

26. The Rencontre.

They rode on in this way for ten minutes. Suddenly two dark forms seemed to separate from the mass, advanced, grew in size, and as they loomed up larger and larger, assumed the appearance of two horsemen.

"Aha!" cried D'Artagnan, "they're coming toward us."

"So much the worse for them," said Porthos.

"Who goes there?" cried a hoarse voice.

The three horsemen made no reply, stopped not, and all that was heard was the noise of swords drawn from the scabbards and the cocking of the pistols with which the two phantoms were armed.

"Bridle in mouth!" said D'Artagnan.

Porthos understood him and he and the lieutenant each drew with the left hand a pistol from their bolsters and cocked it in their turn.

"Who goes there?" was asked a second time. "Not a step forward, or you're dead men."

"Stuff!" cried Porthos, almost choked with dust and chewing his bridle as a horse chews his bit. "Stuff and nonsense; we have seen plenty of dead men in our time."

Hearing these words, the two shadows blockaded the road and by the light of the stars might be seen the shining of their arms.

"Back!" shouted D'Artagnan, "or you are dead!"

Two shots were the reply to this threat; but the assailants attacked their foes with such velocity that in a moment they were upon them; a third pistol-shot was heard, aimed by D'Artagnan, and one of his adversaries fell. As for Porthos, he assaulted the foe with such violence that, although his sword was thrust aside, the enemy was thrown off his horse and fell about ten steps from it.

"Finish, Mouston, finish the work!" cried Porthos. And he darted on beside his friend, who had already begun a fresh pursuit.

"Well?" said Porthos.

"I've broken my man's skull," cried D'Artagnan. "And you----"

"I've only thrown the fellow down, but hark!"

Another shot of a carbine was heard. It was Mousqueton, who was obeying his master's command.

"On! on!" cried D'Artagnan; "all goes well! we have the first throw."

"Ha! ha!" answered Porthos, "behold, other players appear."

And in fact, two other cavaliers made their appearance, detached, as it seemed, from the principal group; they again disputed the road.

This time the lieutenant did not wait for the opposite party to speak.

"Stand aside!" he cried; "stand off the road!"

"What do you want?" asked a voice.

"The duke!" Porthos and D'Artagnan roared out both at once.

A burst of laughter was the answer, but finished with a groan. D'Artagnan had, with his sword, cut in two the poor wretch who had laughed.

At the same time Porthos and his adversary fired on each other and D'Artagnan turned to him.

"Bravo! you've killed him, I think."

"No, wounded his horse only."

"What would you have, my dear fellow? One doesn't hit the bull's-eye every time; it is something to hit inside the ring. Ho! parbleau! what is the matter with my horse?"

"Your horse is falling," said Porthos, reining in his own.

In truth, the lieutenant's horse stumbled and fell on his knees; then a rattling in his throat was heard and he lay down to die. He had received in the chest the bullet of D'Artagnan's first adversary. D'Artagnan swore loud enough to be heard in the skies.

"Does your honor want a horse?" asked Mousqueton.

"Zounds! want one!" cried the Gascon.

"Here's one, your honor----"

"How the devil hast thou two horses?" asked D'Artagnan, jumping on one of them.

"Their masters are dead! I thought they might be useful, so I took them."

Meantime Porthos had reloaded his pistols.

"Be on the qui vive!" cried D'Artagnan. "Here are two other cavaliers."

As he spoke, two horsemen advanced at full speed.

"Ho! your honor!" cried Mousqueton, "the man you upset is getting up."

"Why didn't thou do as thou didst to the first man?" said Porthos.

"I held the horses, my hands were full, your honor."

A shot was fired that moment; Mousqueton shrieked with pain.

"Ah, sir! I'm hit in the other side! exactly opposite the other! This hurt is just the fellow of the one I had on the road to Amiens."

Porthos turned around like a lion, plunged on the dismounted cavalier, who tried to draw his sword; but before it was out of the scabbard, Porthos, with the hilt of his had struck him such a terrible blow on the head that he fell like an ox beneath the butcher's knife.

Mousqueton, groaning, slipped from his horse, his wound not allowing him to keep the saddle.

On perceiving the cavaliers, D'Artagnan had stopped and charged his pistol afresh; besides, his horse, he found, had a carbine on the bow of the saddle.

"Here I am!" exclaimed Porthos. "Shall we wait, or shall we charge?"

"Let us charge them," answered the Gascon.

"Charge!" cried Porthos.

They spurred on their horses; the other cavaliers were only twenty steps from them.

"For the king!" cried D'Artagnan.

"The king has no authority here!" answered a deep voice, which seemed to proceed from a cloud, so enveloped was the cavalier in a whirlwind of dust.

"'Tis well, we will see if the king's name is not a passport everywhere," replied the Gascon.

"See!" answered the voice.

Two shots were fired at once, one by D'Artagnan, the other by the adversary of Porthos. D'Artagnan's ball took off his enemy's hat. The ball fired by Porthos's foe went through the throat of his horse, which fell, groaning.

"For the last time, where are you going?"

"To the devil!" answered D'Artagnan.

"Good! you may be easy, then--you'll get there."

D'Artagnan then saw a musket-barrel leveled at him; he had no time to draw from his holsters. He recalled a bit of advice which Athos had once given him, and made his horse rear.

The ball struck the animal full in front. D'Artagnan felt his horse giving way under him and with his wonderful agility threw himself to one side.

"Ah! this," cried the voice, the tone of which was at once polished and jeering, "this is nothing but a butchery of horses and not a combat between men. To the sword, sir! the sword!"

And he jumped off his horse.

"To the swords! be it so!" replied D'Artagnan; "that is exactly what I want."

D'Artagnan, in two steps, was engaged with the foe, whom, according to custom, he attacked impetuously, but he met this time with a skill and a strength of arm that gave him pause. Twice he was obliged to step back; his opponent stirred not one inch. D'Artagnan returned and again attacked him.

Twice or thrice thrusts were attempted on both sides, without effect; sparks were emitted from the swords like water spouting forth.

At last D'Artagnan thought it was time to try one of his favorite feints in fencing. He brought it to bear, skillfully executed it with the rapidity of lightning, and struck the blow with a force which he fancied would prove irresistible.

The blow was parried.

"'Sdeath!" he cried, with his Gascon accent.

At this exclamation his adversary bounded back and, bending his bare head, tried to distinguish in the gloom the features of the lieutenant.

As to D'Artagnan, afraid of some feint, he still stood on the defensive.

"Have a care," cried Porthos to his opponent; "I've still two pistols charged."

"The more reason you should fire the first!" cried his foe.

Porthos fired; the flash threw a gleam of light over the field of battle.

As the light shone on them a cry was heard from the other two combatants.

"Athos!" exclaimed D'Artagnan.

"D'Artagnan!" ejaculated Athos.

Athos raised his sword; D'Artagnan lowered his.

"Aramis!" cried Athos, "don't fire!"

"Ah! ha! is it you, Aramis?" said Porthos.

And he threw away his pistol.

Aramis pushed his back into his saddle-bags and sheathed his sword.

"My son!" exclaimed Athos, extending his hand to D'Artagnan.

This was the name which he gave him in former days, in their moments of tender intimacy.

"Athos!" cried D'Artagnan, wringing his hands. "So you defend him! And I, who have sworn to take him dead or alive, I am dishonored--and by you!"

"Kill me!" replied Athos, uncovering his breast, "if your honor requires my death."

"Oh! woe is me! woe is me!" cried the lieutenant; "there's only one man in the world who could stay my hand; by a fatality that very man bars my way. What shall I say to the cardinal?"

"You can tell him, sir," answered a voice which was the voice of high command in the battle-field, "that he sent against me the only two men capable of getting the better of four men; of fighting man to man, without discomfiture, against the Comte de la Fere and the Chevalier d'Herblay, and of surrendering only to fifty men!

"The prince!" exclaimed at the same moment Athos and Aramis, unmasking as they addressed the Duc de Beaufort, whilst D'Artagnan and Porthos stepped backward.

"Fifty cavaliers!" cried the Gascon and Porthos.

"Look around you, gentlemen, if you doubt the fact," said the duke.

The two friends looked to the right, to the left; they were encompassed by a troop of horsemen.

"Hearing the noise of the fight," resumed the duke, "I fancied you had about twenty men with you, so I came back with those around me, tired of always running away, and wishing to draw my sword in my own cause; but you are only two."

"Yes, my lord; but, as you have said, two that are a match for twenty," said Athos.

"Come, gentlemen, your swords," said the duke.

"Our swords!" cried D'Artagnan, raising his head and regaining his self-possession. "Never!"

"Never!" added Porthos.

Some of the men moved toward them.

"One moment, my lord," whispered Athos, and he said something in a low voice.

"As you will," replied the duke. "I am too much indebted to you to refuse your first request. Gentlemen," he said to his escort, "withdraw. Monsieur d'Artagnan, Monsieur du Vallon, you are free."

The order was obeyed; D'Artagnan and Porthos then found themselves in the centre of a large circle.

"Now, D'Herblay," said Athos, "dismount and come here."

Aramis dismounted and went to Porthos, whilst Athos approached D'Artagnan.

All four once more together.

"Friends!" said Athos, "do you regret you have not shed our blood?"

"No," replied D'Artagnan; "I regret to see that we, hitherto united, are opposed to each other. Ah! nothing will ever go well with us hereafter!"

"Oh, Heaven! No, all is over!" said Porthos.

"Well, be on our side now," resumed Aramis.

"Silence, D'Herblay!" cried Athos; "such proposals are not to be made to gentlemen such as these. 'Tis a matter of conscience with them, as with us."

"Meantime, here we are, enemies!" said Porthos. "Gramercy! who would ever have thought it?"

D'Artagnan only sighed.

Athos looked at them both and took their hands in his.

"Gentlemen," he said, "this is a serious business and my heart bleeds as if you had pierced it through and through. Yes, we are severed; there is the great, the distressing truth! But we have not as yet declared war; perhaps we shall have to make certain conditions, therefore a solemn conference is indispensable."

"For my own part, I demand it," said Aramis.

"I accept it," interposed D'Artagnan, proudly.

Porthos bowed, as if in assent.

"Let us choose a place of rendezvous," continued Athos, "and in a last interview arrange our mutual position and the conduct we are to maintain toward each other."

"Good!" the other three exclaimed.

"Well, then, the place?"

"Will the Place Royale suit you?" asked D'Artagnan.

"In Paris?"

"Yes."

Athos and Aramis looked at each other.

"The Place Royale--be it so!" replied Athos.

"When?"

"To-morrow evening, if you like!"

"At what hour?"

"At ten in the evening, if that suits you; by that time we shall have returned."

"Good."

"There," continued Athos, "either peace or war will be decided; honor, at all events, will be maintained!"

"Alas!" murmured D'Artagnan, "our honor as soldiers is lost to us forever!"

"D'Artagnan," said Athos, gravely, "I assure you that you do me wrong in dwelling so upon that. What I think of is, that we have crossed swords as enemies. Yes," he continued, sadly shaking his head, "Yes, it is as you said, misfortune, indeed, has overtaken us. Come, Aramis."

"And we, Porthos," said D'Artagnan, "will return, carrying our shame to the cardinal."

"And tell him," cried a voice, "that I am not too old yet for a man of action."

D'Artagnan recognized the voice of De Rochefort.

"Can I do anything for you, gentlemen?" asked the duke.

"Bear witness that we have done all that we could."

"That shall be testified to, rest assured. Adieu! we shall meet soon, I trust, in Paris, where you shall have your revenge." The duke, as he spoke, kissed his hand, spurred his horse into a gallop and disappeared, followed by his troop, who were soon lost in distance and darkness.

D'Artagnan and Porthos were now alone with a man who held by the bridles two horses; they thought it was Mousqueton and went up to him.

"What do I see?" cried the lieutenant. "Grimaud, is it thou?"

Grimaud signified that he was not mistaken.

"And whose horses are these?" cried D'Artagnan.

"Who has given them to us?" said Porthos.

"The Comte de la Fere."

"Athos! Athos!" muttered D'Artagnan; "you think of every one; you are indeed a nobleman! Whither art thou going, Grimaud?"

"To join the Vicomte de Bragelonne in Flanders, your honor."

They were taking the road toward Paris, when groans, which seemed to proceed from a ditch, attracted their attention.

"What is that?" asked D'Artagnan.

"It is I--Mousqueton," said a mournful voice, whilst a sort of shadow arose out of the side of the road.

Porthos ran to him. "Art thou dangerously wounded, my dear Mousqueton?" he said.

"No, sir, but I am severely."

"What can we do?" said D'Artagnan; "we must return to Paris."

"I will take care of Mousqueton," said Grimaud; and he gave his arm to his old comrade, whose eyes were full of tears, nor could Grimaud tell whether the tears were caused by wounds or by the pleasure of seeing him again.

D'Artagnan and Porthos went on, meantime, to Paris. They were passed by a sort of courier, covered with dust, the bearer of a letter from the duke to the cardinal, giving testimony to the valor of D'Artagnan and Porthos.

Mazarin had passed a very bad night when this letter was brought to him, announcing that the duke was free and that he would henceforth raise up mortal strife against him.

"What consoles me," said the cardinal after reading the letter, "is that, at least, in this chase, D'Artagnan has done me one good turn--he has destroyed Broussel. This Gascon is a precious fellow; even his misadventures are of use."

The cardinal referred to that man whom D'Artagnan upset at the corner of the Cimetiere Saint Jean in Paris, and who was no other than the Councillor Broussel.

27. The four old Friends prepare to meet again.

Well," said Porthos, seated in the courtyard of the Hotel de la Chevrette, to D'Artagnan, who, with a long and melancholy face, had returned from the Palais Royal; "did he receive you ungraciously, my dear friend?"

"I'faith, yes! a brute, that cardinal. What are you eating there, Porthos?"

"I am dipping a biscuit in a glass of Spanish wine; do the same."

"You are right. Gimblou, a glass of wine."

"Well, how has all gone off?"

"Zounds! you know there's only one way of saying things, so I went in and said, 'My lord, we were not the strongest party.'

"'Yes, I know that,' he said, 'but give me the particulars.'

"You know, Porthos, I could not give him the particulars without naming our friends; to name them would be to commit them to ruin, so I merely said they were fifty and we were two.

"'There was firing, nevertheless, I heard,' he said; 'and your swords--they saw the light of day, I presume?'

"'That is, the night, my lord,' I answered.

"'Ah!' cried the cardinal, 'I thought you were a Gascon, my friend?'

"'I am a Gascon,' said I, 'only when I succeed.' The answer pleased him and he laughed.

"'That will teach me,' he said, 'to have my guards provided with better horses; for if they had been able to keep up with you and if each one of them had done as much as you and your friend, you would have kept your word and would have brought him back to me dead or alive.'"

"Well, there's nothing bad in that, it seems to me," said Porthos.

"Oh, mon Dieu! no, nothing at all. It was the way in which he spoke. It is incredible how these biscuit soak up wine! They are veritable sponges! Gimblou, another bottle."

The bottle was brought with a promptness which showed the degree of consideration D'Artagnan enjoyed in the establishment. He continued:

"So I was going away, but he called me back.

"'You have had three horses foundered or killed?' he asked me.

"'Yes, my lord.'

"'How much were they worth?'"

"Why," said Porthos, "that was very good of him, it seems to me."

"'A thousand pistoles,' I said."

"A thousand pistoles!" Porthos exclaimed. "Oh! oh! that is a large sum. If he knew anything about horses he would dispute the price."

"Faith! he was very much inclined to do so, the contemptible fellow. He made a great start and looked at me. I also looked at him; then he understood, and putting his hand into a drawer, he took from it a quantity of notes on a bank in Lyons."

"For a thousand pistoles?"

"For a thousand pistoles--just that amount, the beggar; not one too many."

"And you have them?"

"They are here."

"Upon my word, I think he acted very generously."

"Generously! to men who had risked their lives for him, and besides had done him a great service?"

"A great service--what was that?"

"Why, it seems that I crushed for him a parliament councillor."

"What! that little man in black that you upset at the corner of Saint Jean Cemetery?"

"That's the man, my dear fellow; he was an annoyance to the cardinal. Unfortunately, I didn't crush him flat. It seems that he came to himself and that he will continue to be an annoyance."

"See that, now!" said Porthos; "and I turned my horse aside from going plump on to him! That will be for another time."

"He owed me for the councillor, the pettifogger!"

"But," said Porthos, "if he was not crushed completely----"

"Ah! Monsieur de Richelieu would have said, 'Five hundred crowns for the councillor.' Well, let's say no more about it. How much were your animals worth, Porthos?"

"Ah, if poor Mousqueton were here he could tell you to a fraction."

"No matter; you can tell within ten crowns."

"Why, Vulcan and Bayard cost me each about two hundred pistoles, and putting Phoebus at a hundred and fifty, we should be pretty near the amount."

"There will remain, then, four hundred and fifty pistoles," said D'Artagnan, contentedly.

"Yes," said Porthos, "but there are the equipments."

"That is very true. Well, how much for the equipments?"

"If we say one hundred pistoles for the three----"

"Good for the hundred pistoles; there remains, then, three hundred and fifty."

Porthos made a sign of assent.

"We will give the fifty pistoles to the hostess for our expenses," said D'Artagnan, "and share the three hundred."

"We will share," said Porthos.

"A paltry piece of business!" murmured D'Artagnan crumpling his note.

"Pooh!" said Porthos, "it is always that. But tell me----"

"What?"

"Didn't he speak of me in any way?"

"Ah! yes, indeed!" cried D'Artagnan, who was afraid of disheartening his friend by telling him that the cardinal had not breathed a word about him; "yes, surely, he said----"

"He said?" resumed Porthos.

"Stop, I want to remember his exact words. He said, 'As to your friend, tell him he may sleep in peace.'"

"Good, very good," said Porthos; "that signified as clear as daylight that he still intends to make me a baron."

At this moment nine o'clock struck. D'Artagnan started.

"Ah, yes," said Porthos, "there is nine o'clock. We have a rendezvous, you remember, at the Place Royale."

"Ah! stop! hold your peace, Porthos, don't remind me of it; 'tis that which has made me so cross since yesterday. I shall not go."

"Why?" asked Porthos.

"Because it is a grievous thing for me to meet again those two men who caused the failure of our enterprise."

"And yet," said Porthos, "neither of them had any advantage over us. I still had a loaded pistol and you were in full fight, sword in hand."

"Yes," said D'Artagnan; "but what if this rendezvous had some hidden purpose?"

"Oh!" said Porthos, "you can't think that, D'Artagnan!"

D'Artagnan did not believe Athos to be capable of a deception, but he sought an excuse for not going to the rendezvous.

"We must go," said the superb lord of Bracieux, "lest they should say we were afraid. We who have faced fifty foes on the high road can well meet two in the Place Royale."

"Yes, yes, but they took part with the princes without apprising us of it. Athos and Aramis have played a game with me which alarms me. We discovered yesterday the truth; what is the use of going to-day to learn something else?"

"You really have some distrust, then?" said Porthos.

"Of Aramis, yes, since he has become an abbe. You can't imagine, my dear fellow, the sort of man he is. He sees us on the road which leads him to a bishopric, and perhaps will not be sorry to get us out of his way."

"Ah, as regards Aramis, that is another thing," said Porthos, "and it wouldn't surprise me at all."

"Perhaps Monsieur de Beaufort will try, in his turn, to lay hands on us."

"Nonsense! He had us in his power and he let us go. Besides we can be on our guard; let us take arms, let Planchet post himself behind us with his carbine."

"Planchet is a Frondeur," answered D'Artagnan.

"Devil take these civil wars! one can no more now reckon on one's friends than on one's footmen," said Porthos. "Ah! if Mousqueton were here! there's a fellow who will never desert me!"

"So long as you are rich! Ah! my friend! 'tis not civil war that disunites us. It is that we are each of us twenty years older; it is that the honest emotions of youth have given place to suggestions of interest, whispers of ambition, counsels of selfishness. Yes, you are right; let us go, Porthos, but let us go well armed; were we not to keep the rendezvous, they would declare we were afraid. Halloo! Planchet! here! saddle our horses, take your carbine."

"Whom are we going to attack, sir?"

"No one; a mere matter of precaution," answered the Gascon.

"You know, sir, that they wished to murder that good councillor, Broussel, the father of the people?"

"Really, did they?" said D'Artagnan.

"Yes, but he has been avenged. He was carried home in the arms of the people. His house has been full ever since. He has received visits from the coadjutor, from Madame de Longueville, and the Prince de Conti; Madame de Chevreuse and Madame de Vendome have left their names at his door. And now, whenever he wishes----"

"Well, whenever he wishes?"

Planchet began to sing:

"Un vent de fronde S'est leve ce matin; Je crois qu'il gronde Contre le Mazarin. Un vent de fronde S'est leve ce matin."

"It doesn't surprise me," said D'Artagnan, in a low tone to Porthos, "that Mazarin would have been much better satisfied had I crushed the life out of his councillor."

"You understand, then, monsieur," resumed Planchet, "that if it were for some enterprise like that undertaken against Monsieur Broussel that you should ask me to take my carbine----"

"No, don't be alarmed; but where did you get all these details?"

"From a good source, sir; I heard it from Friquet."

"From Friquet? I know that name----"

"A son of Monsieur de Broussel's servant, and a lad that, I promise you, in a revolt will not give away his share to the dogs."

"Is he not a singing boy at Notre Dame?" asked D'Artagnan.

"Yes, that is the very boy; he's patronized by Bazin."

"Ah, yes, I know."

"Of what importance is this little reptile to you?" asked Porthos.

"Gad!" replied D'Artagnan; "he has already given me good information and he may do the same again."

Whilst all this was going on, Athos and Aramis were entering Paris by the Faubourg St. Antoine. They had taken some refreshment on the road and hastened on, that they might not fail at the appointed place. Bazin was their only attendant, for Grimaud had stayed behind to take care of Mousqueton. As they were passing onward, Athos proposed that they should lay aside their arms and military costume, and assume a dress more suited to the city.

"Oh, no, dear count!" cried Aramis, "is it not a warlike encounter that we are going to?"

"What do you mean, Aramis?"

"That the Place Royale is the termination to the main road to Vendomois, and nothing else."

"What! our friends?"

"Are become our most dangerous enemies, Athos. Let us be on our guard."

"Oh! my dear D'Herblay!"

"Who can say whether D'Artagnan may not have betrayed us to the cardinal? who can tell whether Mazarin may not take advantage of this rendezvous to seize us?"

"What! Aramis, you think that D'Artagnan, that Porthos, would lend their hands to such an infamy?"

"Among friends, my dear Athos, no, you are right; but among enemies it would be only a stratagem."

Athos crossed his arms and bowed his noble head.

"What can you expect, Athos? Men are so made; and we are not always twenty years old. We have cruelly wounded, as you know, that personal pride by which D'Artagnan is blindly governed. He has been beaten. Did you not observe his despair on the journey? As to Porthos, his barony was perhaps dependent on that affair. Well, he found us on his road and will not be baron this time. Perhaps that famous barony will have something to do with our interview this evening. Let us take our precautions, Athos."

"But suppose they come unarmed? What a disgrace to us."

"Oh, never fear! besides, if they do, we can easily make an excuse; we came straight off a journey and are insurgents, too."

"An excuse for us! to meet D'Artagnan with a false excuse! to have to make a false excuse to Porthos! Oh, Aramis!" continued Athos, shaking his head mournfully, "upon my soul, you make me the most miserable of men; you disenchant a heart not wholly dead to friendship. Go in whatever guise you choose; for my part, I shall go unarmed."

"No, for I will not allow you to do so. 'Tis not one man, not Athos only, not the Comte de la Fere whom you will ruin by this amiable weakness, but a whole party to whom you belong and who depend upon you."

"Be it so then," replied Athos, sorrowfully.

And they pursued their road in mournful silence.

Scarcely had they reached by the Rue de la Mule the iron gate of the Place Royale, when they perceived three cavaliers, D'Artagnan, Porthos, and Planchet, the two former wrapped up in their military cloaks under which their swords were hidden, and Planchet, his musket by his side. They were waiting at the entrance of the Rue Sainte Catharine, and their horses were fastened to the rings of the arcade. Athos, therefore, commanded Bazin to fasten up his horse and that of Aramis in the same manner.

They then advanced two and two, and saluted each other politely.

"Now where will it be agreeable to you that we hold our conference?" inquired Aramis, perceiving that people were stopping to look at them, supposing that they were going to engage in one of those far-famed duels still extant in the memory of the Parisians, and especially the inhabitants of the Place Royale.

"The gate is shut," said Aramis, "but if these gentlemen like a cool retreat under the trees, and perfect seclusion, I will get the key from the Hotel de Rohan and we shall be well suited."

D'Artagnan darted a look into the obscurity of the Place. Porthos ventured to put his head between the railings, to try if his glance could penetrate the gloom.

"If you prefer any other place," said Athos, in his persuasive voice, "choose for yourselves."

"This place, if Monsieur d'Herblay can procure the key, is the best that we can have," was the answer.

Aramis went off at once, begging Athos not to remain alone within reach of D'Artagnan and Porthos; a piece of advice which was received with a contemptuous smile.

Aramis returned soon with a man from the Hotel de Rohan, who was saying to him:

"You swear, sir, that it is not so?"

"Stop," and Aramis gave him a louis d'or.

"Ah! you will not swear, my master," said the concierge, shaking his head.

"Well, one can never say what may happen; at present we and these gentlemen are excellent friends."

"Yes, certainly," added Athos and the other two.

D'Artagnan had heard the conversation and had understood it.

"You see?" he said to Porthos.

"What do I see?"

"That he wouldn't swear."

"Swear what?"

"That man wanted Aramis to swear that we are not going to the Place Royale to fight."

"And Aramis wouldn't swear?"

"No."

"Attention, then!"

Athos did not lose sight of the two speakers. Aramis opened the gate and faced around in order that D'Artagnan and Porthos might enter. In passing through the gate, the hilt of the lieutenant's sword was caught in the grating and he was obliged to pull off his cloak; in doing so he showed the butt end of his pistols and a ray of the moon was reflected on the shining metal.

"Do you see?" whispered Aramis to Athos, touching his shoulder with one hand and pointing with the other to the arms which the Gascon wore under his belt.

"Alas! I do!" replied Athos, with a deep sigh.

He entered third, and Aramis, who shut the gate after him, last. The two serving-men waited without; but as if they likewise mistrusted each other, they kept their respective distances.

28. The Place Royale.

They proceeded silently to the centre of the Place, but as at this very moment the moon had just emerged from behind a cloud, they thought they might be observed if they remained on that spot and therefore regained the shade of the lime-trees.

There were benches here and there; the four gentlemen stopped near them; at a sign from Athos, Porthos and D'Artagnan sat down, the two others stood in front of them.

After a few minutes of silent embarrassment, Athos spoke.

"Gentlemen," he said, "our presence here is the best proof of former friendship; not one of us has failed the others at this rendezvous; not one has, therefore, to reproach himself."

"Hear me, count," replied D'Artagnan; "instead of making compliments to each other, let us explain our conduct to each other, like men of right and honest hearts."

"I wish for nothing more; have you any cause of complaint against me or Monsieur d'Herblay? If so, speak out," answered Athos.

"I have," replied D'Artagnan. "When I saw you at your chateau at Bragelonne, I made certain proposals to you which you perfectly understood; instead of answering me as a friend, you played with me as a child; the friendship, therefore, that you boast of was not broken yesterday by the shock of swords, but by your dissimulation at your castle."

"D'Artagnan!" said Athos, reproachfully.

"You asked for candor and you have it. You ask what I have against you; I tell you. And I have the same sincerity to show you, if you wish, Monsieur d'Herblay; I acted in a similar way to you and you also deceived me."

"Really, monsieur, you say strange things," said Aramis. "You came seeking me to make to me certain proposals, but did you make them? No, you sounded me, nothing more. Very well what did I say to you? that Mazarin was contemptible and that I wouldn't serve Mazarin. But that is all. Did I tell you that I wouldn't serve any other? On the contrary, I gave you to understand, I think, that I adhered to the princes. We even joked very pleasantly, if I remember rightly, on the very probable contingency of your being charged by the cardinal with my arrest. Were you a party man? There is no doubt of that. Well, why should not we, too, belong to a party? You had your secret and we had ours; we didn't exchange them. So much the better; it proves that we know how to keep our secrets."

"I do not reproach you, monsieur," said D'Artagnan; "'tis only because Monsieur de la Fere has spoken of friendship that I question your conduct."

"And what do you find in it that is worthy of blame?" asked Aramis, haughtily.

The blood mounted instantly to the temples of D'Artagnan, who arose, and replied:

"I consider it worthy conduct of a pupil of Jesuits."

On seeing D'Artagnan rise, Porthos rose also; these four men were therefore all standing at the same time, with a menacing aspect, opposite to each other.

Upon hearing D'Artagnan's reply, Aramis seemed about to draw his sword, when Athos prevented him.

"D'Artagnan," he said, "you are here to-night, still infuriated by yesterday's adventure. I believed your heart noble enough to enable a friendship of twenty years to overcome an affront of a quarter of an hour. Come, do you really think you have anything to say against me? Say it then; if I am in fault I will avow the error."

The grave and harmonious tones of that beloved voice seemed to have still its ancient influence, whilst that of Aramis, which had become harsh and tuneless in his moments of ill-humor, irritated him. He answered therefore:

"I think, monsieur le comte, that you had something to communicate to me at your chateau of

Bragelonne, and that gentleman"--he pointed to Aramis--"had also something to tell me when I was in his convent. At that time I was not concerned in the adventure, in the course of which you have so successfully estopped me! However, because I was prudent you must not take me for a fool. If I had wished to widen the breach between those whom Monsieur d'Herblay chooses to receive with a rope ladder and those whom he receives with a wooden ladder, I could have spoken out."

"What are you meddling with?" cried Aramis, pale with anger, suspecting that D'Artagnan had acted as a spy on him and had seen him with Madame de Longueville.

"I never meddle save with what concerns me, and I know how to make believe that I haven't seen what does not concern me; but I hate hypocrites, and among that number I place musketeers who are abbes and abbes who are musketeers; and," he added, turning to Porthos "here's a gentleman who's of the same opinion as myself."

Porthos, who had not spoken one word, answered merely by a word and a gesture.

He said "yes" and he put his hand on his sword.

Aramis started back and drew his. D'Artagnan bent forward, ready either to attack or to stand on his defense.

Athos at that moment extended his hand with the air of supreme command which characterized him alone, drew out his sword and the scabbard at the same time, broke the blade in the sheath on his knee and threw the pieces to his right. Then turning to Aramis:

"Aramis," he said, "break your sword."

Aramis hesitated.

"It must be done," said Athos; then in a lower and more gentle voice, he added. "I wish it."

Then Aramis, paler than before, but subdued by these words, snapped the serpent blade between his hands, and then folding his arms, stood trembling with rage.

These proceedings made D'Artagnan and Porthos draw back. D'Artagnan did not draw his sword; Porthos put his back into the sheath.

"Never!" exclaimed Athos, raising his right hand to Heaven, "never! I swear before God, who seeth us, and who, in the darkness of this night heareth us, never shall my sword cross yours, never my eye express a glance of anger, nor my heart a throb of hatred, at you. We lived together, we loved, we hated together; we shed, we mingled our blood together, and too probably, I may still add, that there may be yet a bond between us closer even than that of friendship; perhaps there may be the bond of crime; for we four, we once did condemn, judge and slay a human being whom we had not any right to cut off from this world, although apparently fitter for hell than for this life. D'Artagnan, I have always loved you as my son; Porthos, we slept six years side by side; Aramis is your brother as well as mine, and Aramis has once loved you, as I love you now and as I have ever loved you. What can Cardinal Mazarin be to us, to four men who compelled such a man as Richelieu to act as we pleased? What is such or such a prince to us, who fixed the diadem upon a great queen's head? D'Artagnan, I ask your pardon for having yesterday crossed swords with you; Aramis does the same to Porthos; now hate me if you can; but for my own part, I shall ever, even if you do hate me, retain esteem and friendship for you. I repeat my words, Aramis, and then, if you desire it, and if they desire it, let us separate forever from our old friends."

There was a solemn, though momentary silence, which was broken by Aramis.

"I swear," he said, with a calm brow and kindly glance, but in a voice still trembling with recent emotion, "I swear that I no longer bear animosity to those who were once my friends. I regret that I ever crossed swords with you, Porthos; I swear not only that it shall never again be pointed at your breast, but that in the bottom of my heart there will never in future be the slightest hostile sentiment; now, Athos, come."

Athos was about to retire.

"Oh! no! no! do not go away!" exclaimed D'Artagnan, impelled by one of those irresistible impulses which showed the nobility of his nature, the native brightness of his character; "I swear that I would give the last drop of my blood and the last fragment of my limbs to preserve the friendship of such a friend as you, Athos--of such a man as you, Aramis." And he threw himself into the arms of Athos.

"My son!" exclaimed Athos, pressing him in his arms.

"And as for me," said Porthos, "I swear nothing, but I'm choked. Forsooth! If I were obliged to fight against you, I think I should allow myself to be pierced through and through, for I never loved any one but you in the wide world;" and honest Porthos burst into tears as he embraced Athos.

"My friends," said Athos, "this is what I expected from such hearts as yours. Yes, I have said it and I now repeat it: our destinies are irrevocably united, although we now pursue divergent roads. I respect your convictions, and whilst we fight for opposite sides, let us remain friends. Ministers, princes, kings, will pass away like mountain torrents; civil war, like a forest flame; but we--we shall remain; I have a presentiment that we shall."

"Yes," replied D'Artagnan, "let us still be musketeers, and let us retain as our battle-standard that famous napkin of the bastion St. Gervais, on which the great cardinal had three fleurs-de-lis embroidered."

"Be it so," cried Aramis. "Cardinalists or Frondeurs, what matters it? Let us meet again as capital seconds in a duel, devoted friends in business, merry companions in our ancient pleasures."

"And whenever," added Athos, "we meet in battle, at this word, 'Place Royale!' let us put our swords into our left hands and shake hands with the right, even in the very lust and music of the hottest carnage."

"You speak charmingly," said Porthos.

"And are the first of men!" added D'Artagnan. "You excel us all."

Athos smiled with ineffable pleasure.

"'Tis then all settled. Gentlemen, your hands; are we not pretty good Christians?"

"Egad!" said D'Artagnan, "by Heaven! yes."

"We should be so on this occasion, if only to be faithful to our oath," said Aramis.

"Ah, I'm ready to do what you will," cried Porthos; "even to swear by Mahomet. Devil take me if I've ever been so happy as at this moment."

And he wiped his eyes, still moist.

"Has not one of you a cross?" asked Athos.

Aramis smiled and drew from his vest a cross of diamonds, which was hung around his neck by a chain of pearls. "Here is one," he said.

"Well," resumed Athos, "swear on this cross, which, in spite of its magnificent material, is still a cross; swear to be united in spite of everything, and forever, and may this oath bind us to each other, and even, also, our descendants! Does this oath satisfy you?"

"Yes," said they all, with one accord.

"Ah, traitor!" muttered D'Artagnan, leaning toward Aramis and whispering in his ear, "you have made us swear on the crucifix of a Frondeuse."

29. The Ferry across the Oise.

We hope that the reader has not quite forgotten the young traveler whom we left on the road to Flanders.

In losing sight of his guardian, whom he had quitted, gazing after him in front of the royal basilican, Raoul spurred on his horse, in order not only to escape from his own melancholy reflections, but also to hide from Olivain the emotion his face might betray.

One hour's rapid progress, however, sufficed to disperse the gloomy fancies that had clouded the young man's bright anticipations; and the hitherto unfelt pleasure of freedom--a pleasure which is sweet even to those who have never known dependence--seemed to Raoul to gild not only Heaven and earth, but especially that blue but dim horizon of life we call the future.

Nevertheless, after several attempts at conversation with Olivain he foresaw that many days passed thus would prove exceedingly dull; and the count's agreeable voice, his gentle and persuasive eloquence, recurred to his mind at the various towns through which they journeyed and about which he had no longer any one to give him those interesting details which he would have drawn from Athos, the most amusing and the best informed of guides. Another recollection contributed also to sadden Raoul: on their arrival at Sonores he had perceived, hidden behind a screen of poplars, a little chateau which so vividly recalled that of La Valliere to his mind that he halted for nearly ten minutes to gaze at it, and resumed his journey with a sigh too abstracted even to reply to Olivain's respectful inquiry about the cause of so much fixed attention. The aspect of external objects is often a mysterious guide communicating with the fibres of memory, which in spite of us will arouse them at times; this thread, like that of Ariadne, when once unraveled will conduct one through a labyrinth of thought, in which one loses one's self in endeavoring to follow that phantom of the past which is called recollection.

Now the sight of this chateau had taken Raoul back fifty leagues westward and had caused him to review his life from the moment when he had taken leave of little Louise to that in which he had seen her for the first time; and every branch of oak, every gilded weathercock on roof of slates, reminded him that, instead of returning to the friends of his childhood, every instant estranged him further and that perhaps he had even left them forever.

With a full heart and burning head he desired Olivain to lead on the horses to a wayside inn, which he observed within gunshot range, a little in advance of the place they had reached.

As for himself, he dismounted and remained under a beautiful group of chestnuts in flower, amidst which were murmuring a multitude of happy bees, and bade Olivain send the host to him with writing paper and ink, to be placed on a table which he found there, conveniently ready. Olivain obeyed and continued on his way, whilst Raoul remained sitting, with his elbow leaning on the table, from time to time gently shaking the flowers from his head, which fell upon him like snow, and gazing vaguely on the charming landscape spread out before him, dotted over with green fields and groups of trees. Raoul had been there about ten minutes, during five of which he was lost in reverie, when there appeared within the circle comprised in his rolling gaze a man with a rubicund face, who, with a napkin around his body, another under his arm, and a white cap upon his head, approached him, holding paper, pen and ink in hand.

"Ha! ha!" laughed the apparition, "every gentleman seems to have the same fancy, for not a quarter of an hour ago a young lad, well mounted like you, as tall as you and of about your age, halted before this clump of trees and had this table and this chair brought here, and dined here, with an old gentleman who seemed to be his tutor, upon a pie, of which they haven't left a mouthful, and two bottles of Macon wine, of which they haven't left a drop, but fortunately we have still some of the same wine and some of the same pies left, and if your worship will but give your orders----"

"No, friend," replied Raoul, smiling, "I am obliged to you, but at this moment I want nothing but the things for which I have asked--only I shall be very glad if the ink prove black and the pen good; upon these conditions I will pay for the pen the price of the bottle, and for the ink the price of the pie."

"Very well, sir," said the host, "I'll give the pie and the bottle of wine to your servant, and in this way you will have the pen and ink into the bargain."

"Do as you like," said Raoul, who was beginning his apprenticeship with that particular class of society, who, when there were robbers on the highroads, were connected with them, and who, since highwaymen no longer exist, have advantageously and aptly filled their vacant place.

The host, his mind at ease about his bill, placed pen, ink and paper upon the table. By a lucky chance the pen was tolerably good and Raoul began to write. The host remained standing in front of him, looking with a kind of involuntary admiration at his handsome face, combining both gravity and sweetness of expression. Beauty has always been and always will be all-powerful.

"He's not a guest like the other one here just now," observed mine host to Olivain, who had rejoined his master to see if he wanted anything, "and your young master has no appetite."

"My master had appetite enough three days ago, but what can one do? he lost it the day before yesterday."

And Olivain and the host took their way together toward the inn, Olivain, according to the custom of serving-men well pleased with their place, relating to the tavern-keeper all that he could say in favor of the young gentleman; whilst Raoul wrote on thus:

"Sir,--After a four hours' march I stop to write to you, for I miss you every moment, and I am always on the point of turning my head as if to reply when you speak to me. I was so bewildered by your departure and so overcome with grief at our separation, that I am sure I was able to but very feebly express all the affection and gratitude I feel toward you. You will forgive me, sir, for your heart is of such a generous nature that you can well understand all that has passed in mine. I entreat you to write to me, for you form a part of my existence, and, if I may venture to tell you so, I also feel anxious. It seemed to me as if you were yourself preparing for some dangerous undertaking, about which I did not dare to question you, since you told me nothing. I have, therefore, as you see, great need of hearing from you. Now that you are no longer beside me I am afraid every moment of erring. You sustained me powerfully, sir, and I protest to you that to-day I feel very lonely. Will you have the goodness, sir, should you receive news from Blois, to send me a few lines about my little friend Mademoiselle de la Valliere, about whose health, when we left, so much anxiety was felt? You can understand, honored and dear guardian, how precious and indispensable to me is the remembrance of the years that I have passed with you. I hope that you will sometimes, too, think of me, and if at certain hours you should miss me, if you should feel any slight regret at my absence, I shall be overwhelmed with joy at the thought that you appreciate my affection for and my devotion to yourself, and that I have been able to prove them to you whilst I had the happiness of living with you."

After finishing this letter Raoul felt more composed; he looked well around him to see if Olivain and the host might not be watching him, whilst he impressed a kiss upon the paper, a mute and touching caress, which the heart of Athos might well divine on opening the letter.

During this time Olivain had finished his bottle and eaten his pie; the horses were also refreshed. Raoul motioned to the host to approach, threw a crown upon the table, mounted his horse, and posted his letter at Senlis. The rest that had been thus afforded to men and horses enabled them to continue their journey at a good round pace. At Verberie, Raoul desired Olivain to make some inquiry about the young man who was preceding them; he had been observed to pass only three-quarters of an hour previously, but he was well mounted, as the tavern-keeper had already said, and rode at a rapid pace.

"Let us try and overtake this gentleman," said Raoul to Olivain; "like ourselves he is on his way to join the army and may prove agreeable company."

It was about four o'clock in the afternoon when Raoul arrived at Compiegne; there he dined heartily and again inquired about the young gentleman who was in advance of them. He had stopped, like Raoul, at the Hotel of the Bell and Bottle, the best at Compiegne; and had started again on his journey, saying that he should sleep at Noyon.

"Well, let us sleep at Noyon," said Raoul.

"Sir," replied Olivain, respectfully, "allow me to remark that we have already much fatigued the horses this morning. I think it would be well to sleep here and to start again very early to-morrow. Eighteen leagues is enough for the first stage."

"The Comte de la Fere wished me to hasten on," replied Raoul, "that I might rejoin the prince on the morning of the fourth day; let us push on, then, to Noyon; it will be a stage similar to those we traveled from Blois to Paris. We shall arrive at eight o'clock. The horses will have a long night's rest, and at five o'clock to-morrow morning we can be again on the road."

Olivain dared offer no opposition to this determination but he followed his master, grumbling.

"Go on, go on," said he, between his teeth, "expend your ardor the first day; to-morrow, instead of journeying twenty leagues, you will travel ten, the day after to-morrow, five, and in three days you will be in bed. There you must rest; young people are such braggarts."

It was easy to see that Olivain had not been taught in the school of the Planchets and the Grimauds. Raoul really felt tired, but he was desirous of testing his strength, and, brought up in the principles of Athos and certain of having heard him speak a thousand times of stages of twenty-five leagues, he did not wish to fall far short of his model. D'Artagnan, that man of iron, who seemed to be made of nerve and muscle only, had struck him with admiration. Therefore, in spite of Olivain's remarks, he continued to urge his steed more and more, and following a pleasant little path, leading to a ferry, and which he had been assured shortened the journey by the distance of one league, he arrived at the summit of a hill and perceived the river flowing before him. A little troop of men on horseback were waiting on the edge of the stream, ready to embark. Raoul did not doubt this was the gentleman and his escort; he called out to him, but they were too distant to be heard; then, in spite of the weariness of his beast, he made it gallop but the rising ground soon deprived him of all sight of the travelers, and when he had again attained a new height, the ferryboat had left the shore and was making for the opposite bank. Raoul, seeing that he could not arrive in time to cross the ferry with the travelers, halted to wait for Olivain. At this moment a shriek was heard that seemed to come from the river. Raoul turned toward the side whence the cry had sounded, and shaded his eyes from the glare of the setting sun with his hand.

"Olivain!" he exclaimed, "what do I see below there?"

A second scream, more piercing than the first, now sounded.

"Oh, sir!" cried Olivain, "the rope which holds the ferryboat has broken and the boat is drifting. But what do I see in the water--something struggling?"

"Oh, yes," exclaimed Raoul, fixing his glance on one point in the stream, splendidly illumined by the setting sun, "a horse, a rider!"

"They are sinking!" cried Olivain in his turn.

It was true, and Raoul was convinced that some accident had happened and that a man was drowning; he gave his horse its head, struck his spurs into its sides, and the animal, urged by pain and feeling that he had space open before him, bounded over a kind of paling which inclosed the landing place, and fell into the river, scattering to a distance waves of white froth.

"Ah, sir!" cried Olivain, "what are you doing? Good God!"

Raoul was directing his horse toward the unhappy man in danger. This was, in fact, a custom familiar to him. Having been brought up on the banks of the Loire, he might have been said to have been cradled on its waves; a hundred times he had crossed it on horseback, a thousand times had swum across. Athos, foreseeing the period when he should make a soldier of the viscount, had inured him to all kinds of arduous undertakings.

"Oh, heavens!" continued Olivain, in despair, "what would the count say if he only saw you now!"

"The count would do as I do," replied Raoul, urging his horse vigorously forward.

"But I--but I," cried Olivain, pale and disconsolate rushing about on the shore, "how shall I cross?"

"Leap, coward!" cried Raoul, swimming on; then addressing the traveler, who was struggling twenty yards in front of him: "Courage, sir!" said he, "courage! we are coming to your aid."

Olivain advanced, retired, then made his horse rear--turned it and then, struck to the core by shame, leaped, as Raoul had done, only repeating:

"I am a dead man! we are lost!"

In the meantime, the ferryboat had floated away, carried down by the stream, and the shrieks of those whom it contained resounded more and more. A man with gray hair had thrown himself from the boat into the river and was swimming vigorously toward the person who was drowning; but being obliged to go against the current he advanced but slowly. Raoul continued his way and was visibly gaining ground; but the horse and its rider, of whom he did not lose sight, were evidently sinking. The nostrils of the horse were no longer above water, and the rider, who had lost the reins in struggling, fell with his head back and his arms extended. One moment longer and all would disappear.

"Courage!" cried Raoul, "courage!"

"Too late!" murmured the young man, "too late!"

The water closed above his head and stifled his voice.

Raoul sprang from his horse, to which he left the charge of its own preservation, and in three or four strokes was at the gentleman's side; he seized the horse at once by the curb and raised its head above water; the animal began to breathe again and, as if he comprehended that they had come to his aid, redoubled his efforts. Raoul at the same time seized one of the young man's hands and placed it on the mane, which it grasped with the tenacity of a drowning man. Thus, sure that the rider would not release his hold, Raoul now only directed his attention to the horse, which he guided to the opposite bank, helping it to cut through the water and encouraging it with words.

All at once the horse stumbled against a ridge and then placed its foot on the sand.

"Saved!" exclaimed the man with gray hair, who also touched bottom.

"Saved!" mechanically repeated the young gentleman, releasing the mane and sliding from the saddle into Raoul's arms; Raoul was but ten yards from the shore; there he bore the fainting man, and laying him down upon the grass, unfastened the buttons of his collar and unhooked his doublet. A moment later the gray-headed man was beside him. Olivain managed in his turn to land, after crossing himself repeatedly; and the people in the ferryboat guided themselves as well as they were able toward the bank, with the aid of a pole which chanced to be in the boat.

Thanks to the attentions of Raoul and the man who accompanied the young gentleman, the color gradually returned to the pale cheeks of the dying man, who opened his eyes, at first entirely bewildered, but who soon fixed his gaze upon the person who had saved him.

"Ah, sir," he exclaimed, "it was you! Without you I was a dead man--thrice dead."

"But one recovers, sir, as you perceive," replied Raoul, "and we have but had a little bath."

"Oh! sir, what gratitude I feel!" exclaimed the man with gray hair.

"Ah, there you are, my good D'Arminges; I have given you a great fright, have I not? but it is your own fault. You were my tutor, why did you not teach me to swim?"

"Oh, monsieur le comte," replied the old man, "had any misfortune happened to you, I should never have dared to show myself to the marshal again."

"But how did the accident happen?" asked Raoul.

"Oh, sir, in the most natural way possible," replied he to whom they had given the title of count. "We were about a third of the way across the river when the cord of the ferryboat broke. Alarmed by the cries and gestures of the boatmen, my horse sprang into the water. I cannot swim, and dared not throw myself into the river. Instead of aiding the movements of my horse, I paralyzed them; and I was just going to drown myself with the best grace in the world, when you arrived just in time to pull me out of the water; therefore, sir, if you will agree, henceforward we are friends until death."

"Sir," replied Raoul, bowing, "I am entirely at your service, I assure you."

"I am called the Count de Guiche," continued the young man; "my father is the Marechal de Grammont; and now that you know who I am, do me the honor to inform me who you are."

"I am the Viscount de Bragelonne," answered Raoul, blushing at being unable to name his father, as the Count de Guiche had done.

"Viscount, your countenance, your goodness and your courage incline me toward you; my gratitude is already due. Shake hands--I crave your friendship."

"Sir," said Raoul, returning the count's pressure of the hand, "I like you already, from my heart; pray regard me as a devoted friend, I beseech you."

"And now, where are you going, viscount?" inquired De Guiche.

"To join the army, under the prince, count."

"And I, too!" exclaimed the young man, in a transport of joy. "Oh, so much the better, we will fire the first shot together."

"It is well; be friends," said the tutor; "young as you both are, you were perhaps born under the same star and were destined to meet. And now," continued he, "you must change your clothes; your servants, to whom I gave directions the moment they had left the ferryboat, ought to be already at the inn. Linen and wine are both being warmed; come."

The young men had no objection to this proposition; on the contrary, they thought it very timely.

They mounted again at once, whilst looks of admiration passed between them. They were indeed two elegant horsemen, with figures slight and upright, noble faces, bright and proud looks, loyal and intelligent smiles.

29. The Ferry across the Oise.

De Guiche might have been about eighteen years of age, but he was scarcely taller than Raoul, who was only fifteen.

30. Skirmishing.

The halt at Noyon was but brief, every one there being wrapped in profound sleep. Raoul had desired to be awakened should Grimaud arrive, but Grimaud did not arrive. Doubtless, too, the horses on their part appreciated the eight hours of repose and the abundant stabling which was granted them. The Count de Guiche was awakened at five o'clock in the morning by Raoul, who came to wish him good-day. They breakfasted in haste, and at six o'clock had already gone ten miles.

The young count's conversation was most interesting to Raoul, therefore he listened much, whilst the count talked well and long. Brought up in Paris, where Raoul had been but once; at the court, which Raoul had never seen; his follies as page; two duels, which he had already found the means of fighting, in spite of the edicts against them and, more especially, in spite of his tutor's vigilance--these things excited the greatest curiosity in Raoul. Raoul had only been at M. Scarron's house; he named to Guiche the people whom he had seen there. Guiche knew everybody--Madame de Neuillan, Mademoiselle d'Aubigne, Mademoiselle de Scudery, Mademoiselle Paulet, Madame de Chevreuse. He criticised everybody humorously. Raoul trembled, lest he should laugh among the rest at Madame de Chevreuse, for whom he entertained deep and genuine sympathy, but either instinctively, or from affection for the duchess, he said everything in her favor. His praises increased Raoul's friendship twofold. Then came the question of gallantry and love affairs. Under this head, also, Bragelonne had much more to hear than to tell. He listened attentively and fancied that he discovered through three or four rather frivolous adventures, that the count, like himself, had a secret to hide in the depths of his heart.

De Guiche, as we have said before, had been educated at the court, and the intrigues of this court were not unknown to him. It was the same court of which Raoul had so often heard the Comte de la Fere speak, except that its aspect had much changed since the period when Athos had himself been part of it; therefore everything which the Count de Guiche related was new to his traveling companion. The young count, witty and caustic, passed all the world in review; the queen herself was not spared, and Cardinal Mazarin came in for his share of ridicule.

The day passed away as rapidly as an hour. The count's tutor, a man of the world and a bon vivant, up to his eyes in learning, as his pupil described him, often recalled the profound erudition, the witty and caustic satire of Athos to Raoul; but as regarded grace, delicacy, and nobility of external appearance, no one in these points was to be compared to the Comte de la Fere.

The horses, which were more kindly used than on the previous day, stopped at Arras at four o'clock in the evening. They were approaching the scene of war; and as bands of Spaniards sometimes took advantage of the night to make expeditions even as far as the neighborhood of Arras, they determined to remain in the town until the morrow. The French army held all between Pont-a-Marc as far as Valenciennes, falling back upon Douai. The prince was said to be in person at Bethune.

The enemy's army extended from Cassel to Courtray; and as there was no species of violence or pillage it did not commit, the poor people on the frontier quitted their isolated dwellings and fled for refuge into the strong cities which held out a shelter to them. Arras was encumbered with fugitives. An approaching battle was much spoken of, the prince having manoeuvred, until that movement, only in order to await a reinforcement that had just reached him.

The young men congratulated themselves on having arrived so opportunely. The evening was employed in discussing the war; the grooms polished their arms; the young men loaded the pistols in case of a skirmish, and they awoke in despair, having both dreamed that they had arrived too late to participate in the battle. In the morning it was rumored that

Prince de Conde had evacuated Bethune and fallen back on Carvin, leaving, however, a strong garrison in the former city.

But as there was nothing positively certain in this report, the young warriors decided to continue their way toward Bethune, free on the road to diverge to the right and march to Carvin if necessary.

The count's tutor was well acquainted with the country; he consequently proposed to take a cross-road, which lay between that of Lens and that of Bethune. They obtained information at Ablain, and a statement of their route was left for Grimaud. About seven o'clock in the morning they set out. De Guiche, who was young and impulsive, said to Raoul, "Here we are, three masters and three servants. Our valets are well armed and yours seems to be tough enough."

"I have never seen him put to the test," replied Raoul, "but he is a Breton, which promises something."

"Yes, yes," resumed De Guiche; "I am sure he can fire a musket when required. On my side I have two sure men, who have been in action with my father. We therefore represent six fighting men; if we should meet a little troop of enemies, equal or even superior in number to our own, shall we charge them, Raoul?"

"Certainly, sir," replied the viscount.

"Holloa! young people--stop there!" said the tutor, joining in the conversation. "Zounds! how you manoeuvre my instructions, count! You seem to forget the orders I received to conduct you safe and sound to his highness the prince! Once with the army you may be killed at your good pleasure; but until that time, I warn you that in my capacity of general of the army I shall order a retreat and turn my back on the first red coat we come across." De Guiche and Raoul glanced at each other, smiling.

They arrived at Ablain without accident. There they inquired and learned that the prince had in reality quitted Bethune and stationed himself between Cambria and La Venthie. Therefore, leaving directions at every place for Grimaud, they took a crossroad which conducted the little troop by the bank of a small stream flowing into the Lys. The country was beautiful, intersected by valleys as green as the emerald. Here and there they passed little copses crossing the path which they were following. In anticipation of some ambuscade in each of these little woods the tutor placed his two servants at the head of the band, thus forming the advance guard. Himself and the two young men represented the body of the army, whilst Olivain, with his rifle upon his knee and his eyes upon the watch, protected the rear.

They had observed for some time before them, on the horizon, a rather thick wood; and when they had arrived at a distance of a hundred steps from it, Monsieur d'Arminges took his usual precautions and sent on in advance the count's two grooms. The servants had just disappeared under the trees, followed by the tutor, and the young men were laughing and talking about a hundred yards off. Olivain was at the same distance in the rear, when suddenly there resounded five or six musket-shots. The tutor cried halt; the young men obeyed, pulling up their steeds, and at the same moment the two valets were seen returning at a gallop.

The young men, impatient to learn the cause of the firing, spurred on toward the servants. The tutor followed them.

"Were you stopped?" eagerly inquired the two youths.

"No," replied the servants, "it is even probable that we have not been seen; the shots were fired about a hundred paces in advance of us, in the thickest part of the wood, and we returned to ask your advice."

"My advice is this," said Monsieur d'Arminges, "and if needs be, my will, that we beat a retreat. There may be an ambuscade concealed in this wood."

"Did you see nothing there?" asked the count.

"I thought I saw," said one of the servants, "horsemen dressed in yellow, creeping along the bed of the stream.

"That's it," said the tutor. "We have fallen in with a party of Spaniards. Come back, sirs, back."

The two youths looked at each other, and at this moment a pistol-shot and cries for help were heard. Another glance between the young men convinced them both that neither had any wish to go back, and as the tutor had already turned his horse's head, they both spurred forward, Raoul crying: "Follow me, Olivain!" and the Count de Guiche: "Follow, Urban and Planchet!" And before the tutor could recover from his surprise they had both disappeared into the forest. Whilst they spurred their steeds they held their pistols ready also. In five minutes they arrived at the spot whence the noise had proceeded, and then restraining their horses, they advanced cautiously.

"Hush," whispered De Guiche, "these are cavaliers."

"Yes, three on horseback and three who have dismounted."

"Can you see what they are doing?"

"Yes, they appear to be searching a wounded or dead man."

"It is some cowardly assassination," said De Guiche.

"They are soldiers, though," resumed De Bragelonne.

"Yes, skirmishers; that is to say, highway robbers."

"At them!" cried Raoul. "At them!" echoed De Guiche.

"Oh! gentlemen! gentlemen! in the name of Heaven!" cried the poor tutor.

But he was not listened to, and his cries only served to arouse the attention of the Spaniards.

The men on horseback at once rushed at the two youths, leaving the three others to complete the plunder of the dead or wounded travelers; for on approaching nearer, instead of one extended figure, the young men discovered two. De Guiche fired the first shot at ten paces and missed his man; and the Spaniard, who had advanced to meet Raoul, aimed in his turn, and Raoul felt a pain in the left arm, similar to that of a blow from a whip. He let off his fire at but four paces. Struck in the breast and extending his arms, the Spaniard fell back on the crupper, and the terrified horse, turning around, carried him off.

Raoul at this moment perceived the muzzle of a gun pointed at him, and remembering the recommendation of Athos, he, with the rapidity of lightning, made his horse rear as the shot was fired. His horse bounded to one side, losing its footing, and fell, entangling Raoul's leg under its body. The Spaniard sprang forward and seized the gun by its muzzle, in order to strike Raoul on the head with the butt. In the position in which Raoul lay, unfortunately, he could neither draw his sword from the scabbard, nor his pistols from their holsters. The butt end of the musket hovered over his head, and he could scarcely restrain himself from closing his eyes, when with one bound Guiche reached the Spaniard and placed a pistol at his throat. "Yield!" he cried, "or you are a dead man!" The musket fell from the soldier's hands, who yielded on the instant. Guiche summoned one of his grooms, and delivering the prisoner into his charge, with orders to shoot him through the head if he attempted to escape, he leaped from his horse and approached Raoul.

"Faith, sir," said Raoul, smiling, although his pallor betrayed the excitement consequent on a first affair, "you are in a great hurry to pay your debts and have not been long under any obligation to me. Without your aid," continued he, repeating the count's words "I should have been a dead man--thrice dead."

"My antagonist took flight," replied De Guiche "and left me at liberty to come to your assistance. But are you seriously wounded? I see you are covered with blood!"

"I believe," said Raoul, "that I have got something like a scratch on the arm. If you will help me to drag myself from under my horse I hope nothing need prevent us continuing our journey."

Monsieur d'Arminges and Olivain had already dismounted and were attempting to raise the struggling horse. At last Raoul succeeded in drawing his foot from the stirrup and his leg from under the animal, and in a second he was on his feet again.

"Nothing broken?" asked De Guiche.

"Faith, no, thank Heaven!" replied Raoul; "but what has become of the poor wretches whom these scoundrels were murdering?"

"I fear we arrived too late. They have killed them, I think, and taken flight, carrying off their booty. My servants are examining the bodies."

"Let us go and see whether they are quite dead, or if they can still be helped," suggested Raoul. "Olivain, we have come into possession of two horses, but I have lost my own. Take for yourself the better of the two and give me yours."

They approached the spot where the unfortunate victims lay.

31. The Monk.

Two men lay prone upon the ground, one bathed in blood and motionless, with his face toward the earth; this one was dead. The other leaned against a tree, supported there by the two valets, and was praying fervently, with clasped hands and eyes raised to Heaven. He had received a ball in his thigh, which had broken the bone. The young men first approached the dead man.

"He is a priest," said Bragelonne, "he has worn the tonsure. Oh, the scoundrels! to lift their hands against a minister of God."

"Come here, sir," said Urban, an old soldier who had served under the cardinal duke in all his campaigns; "come here, there is nothing to be done with him, whilst we may perhaps be able to save the other."

The wounded man smiled sadly. "Save me! Oh, no!" said he, "but help me to die, if you can."

"Are you a priest?" asked Raoul.

"No sir."

"I ask, as your unfortunate companion appeared to me to belong to the church."

"He is the curate of Bethune, sir, and was carrying the holy vessels belonging to his church, and the treasure of the chapter, to a safe place, the prince having abandoned our town yesterday; and as it was known that bands of the enemy were prowling about the country, no one dared to accompany the good man, so I offered to do so.

"And, sir," continued the wounded man, "I suffer much and would like, if possible, to be carried to some house."

"Where you can be relieved?" asked De Guiche.

"No, where I can confess."

"But perhaps you are not so dangerously wounded as you think," said Raoul.

"Sir," replied the wounded man, "believe me, there is no time to lose; the ball has broken the thigh bone and entered the intestines."

"Are you a surgeon?" asked De Guiche.

"No, but I know a little about wounds, and mine, I know, is mortal. Try, therefore, either to carry me to some place where I may see a priest or take the trouble to send one to me here. It is my soul that must be saved; as for my body, it is lost."

"To die whilst doing a good deed! It is impossible. God will help you."

"Gentlemen, in the name of Heaven!" said the wounded man, collecting all his forces, as if to get up, "let us not lose time in useless words. Either help me to gain the nearest village or swear to me on your salvation that you will send me the first monk, the first cure, the first priest you may meet. But," he added in a despairing tone, "perhaps no one will dare to come for it is known that the Spaniards are ranging through the country, and I shall die without absolution. My God! my God! Good God! good God!" added the wounded man, in an accent of terror which made the young men shudder; "you will not allow that? that would be too terrible!"

"Calm yourself, sir," replied De Guiche. "I swear to you, you shall receive the consolation that you ask. Only tell us where we shall find a house at which we can demand aid and a village from which we can fetch a priest."

"Thank you, and God reward you! About half a mile from this, on the same road, there is an inn, and about a mile further on, after leaving the inn, you will reach the village of Greney. There you must find the curate, or if he is not at home, go to the convent of the Augustines, which is the last house on the right, and bring me one of the brothers. Monk or priest, it matters not, provided only that he has received from holy church the power of absolving in articulo mortis."

"Monsieur d'Arminges," said De Guiche, "remain beside this unfortunate man and see that he is removed as gently as possible. The vicomte and myself will go and find a priest."

"Go, sir," replied the tutor; "but in Heaven's name do not expose yourself to danger!"

"Do not fear. Besides, we are safe for to-day; you know the axiom, 'Non bis in idem.'"

"Courage, sir," said Raoul to the wounded man. "We are going to execute your wishes."

"May Heaven prosper you!" replied the dying man, with an accent of gratitude impossible to describe.

The two young men galloped off in the direction mentioned and in ten minutes reached the inn. Raoul, without dismounting, called to the host and announced that a wounded man was about to be brought to his house and begged him in the meantime to prepare everything needful. He desired him also, should he know in the neighborhood any doctor or chirurgeon, to fetch him, taking on himself the payment of the messenger.

The host, who saw two young noblemen, richly clad, promised everything they required, and our two cavaliers, after seeing that preparations for the reception were actually begun, started off again and proceeded rapidly toward Greney.

They had gone rather more than a league and had begun to descry the first houses of the village, the red-tiled roofs of which stood out from the green trees which surrounded them, when, coming toward them mounted on a mule, they perceived a poor monk, whose large hat and gray worsted dress made them take him for an Augustine brother. Chance for once seemed to favor them in sending what they were so assiduously seeking. He was a man about twenty-two or twenty-three years old, but who appeared much older from ascetic exercises. His complexion was pale, not of that deadly pallor which is a kind of neutral beauty, but of a bilious, yellow hue; his colorless hair was short and scarcely extended beyond the circle formed by the hat around his head, and his light blue eyes seemed destitute of any expression.

"Sir," began Raoul, with his usual politeness, "are you an ecclesiastic?"

"Why do you ask me that?" replied the stranger, with a coolness which was barely civil.

"Because we want to know," said De Guiche, haughtily.

The stranger touched his mule with his heel and continued his way.

In a second De Guiche had sprung before him and barred his passage. "Answer, sir," exclaimed he; "you have been asked politely, and every question is worth an answer."

"I suppose I am free to say or not to say who I am to two strangers who take a fancy to ask me."

It was with difficulty that De Guiche restrained the intense desire he had of breaking the monk's bones.

"In the first place," he said, making an effort to control himself, "we are not people who may be treated anyhow; my friend there is the Viscount of Bragelonne and I am the Count de Guiche. Nor was it from caprice we asked the question, for there is a wounded and dying man who demands the succor of the church. If you be a priest, I conjure you in the name of humanity to follow me to aid this man; if you be not, it is a different matter, and I warn you in the name of courtesy, of which you appear profoundly ignorant, that I shall chastise you for your insolence."

The pale face of the monk became so livid and his smile so strange, that Raoul, whose eyes were still fixed upon him, felt as if this smile had struck to his heart like an insult.

"He is some Spanish or Flemish spy," said he, putting his hand to his pistol. A glance, threatening and transient as lightning, replied to Raoul.

"Well, sir," said De Guiche, "are you going to reply?"

"I am a priest," said the young man.

"Then, father," said Raoul, forcing himself to convey a respect by speech that did not come from his heart, "if you are a priest you have an opportunity, as my friend has told you, of exercising your vocation. At the next inn you will find a wounded man, now being attended by our servants, who has asked the assistance of a minister of God."

"I will go," said the monk.

And he touched his mule.

"If you do not go, sir," said De Guiche, "remember that we have two steeds able to catch your mule and the power of having you seized wherever you may be; and then I swear your trial will be summary; one can always find a tree and a cord."

The monk's eye again flashed, but that was all; he merely repeated his phrase, "I will go,"--and he went.

"Let us follow him," said De Guiche; "it will be the surest plan."

"I was about to propose so doing," answered De Bragelonne.

In the space of five minutes the monk turned around to ascertain whether he was followed or not.

"You see," said Raoul, "we have done wisely."

"What a horrible face that monk has," said De Guiche.

"Horrible!" replied Raoul, "especially in expression."

"Yes, yes," said De Guiche, "a strange face; but these monks are subject to such degrading practices; their fasts make them pale, the blows of the discipline make them hypocrites, and their eyes become inflamed through weeping for the good things of this life we common folk enjoy, but they have lost."

"Well," said Raoul, "the poor man will get his priest, but, by Heaven, the penitent appears to me to have a better conscience than the confessor. I confess I am accustomed to priests of a very different appearance."

"Ah!" exclaimed De Guiche, "you must understand that this is one of those wandering brothers, who go begging on the high road until some day a benefice falls down from Heaven on them; they are mostly foreigners--Scotch, Irish or Danish. I have seen them before."

"As ugly?"

"No, but reasonably hideous."

"What a misfortune for the wounded man to die under the hands of such a friar!"

"Pshaw!" said De Guiche. "Absolution comes not from him who administers it, but from God. However, for my part, I would rather die unshriven than have anything to say to such a confessor. You are of my opinion, are you not, viscount? and I see you playing with the pommel of your sword, as if you had a great inclination to break the holy father's head."

"Yes, count, it is a strange thing and one which might astonish you, but I feel an indescribable horror at the sight of yonder man. Have you ever seen a snake rise up on your path?"

"Never," answered De Guiche.

"Well, it has happened to me to do so in our Blaisois forests, and I remember that the first time I encountered one with its eyes fixed upon me, curled up, swinging its head and pointing its tongue, I remained fixed, pale and as though fascinated, until the moment when the Comte de la Fere----"

"Your father?" asked De Guiche.

"No, my guardian," replied Raoul, blushing.

"Very well----"

"Until the moment when the Comte de la Fere," resumed Raoul, "said, 'Come, Bragelonne, draw your sword;' then only I rushed upon the reptile and cut it in two, just at the moment when it was rising on its tail and hissing, ere it sprang upon me. Well, I vow I felt exactly the same sensation at sight of that man when he said, 'Why do you ask me that?' and looked so strangely at me."

"Then you regret that you did not cut your serpent in two morsels?"

"Faith, yes, almost," said Raoul.

They had now arrived within sight of the little inn and could see on the opposite side the procession bearing the wounded man and guided by Monsieur d'Arminges. The youths spurred on.

"There is the wounded man," said De Guiche, passing close to the Augustine brother. "Be good enough to hurry yourself a little, monsieur monk."

As for Raoul, he avoided the monk by the whole width of the road and passed him, turning his head away in repulsion.

The young men rode up to the wounded man to announce that they were followed by the priest. He raised himself to glance in the direction which they pointed out, saw the monk, and fell back upon the litter, his face illumined by joy.

"And now," said the youths, "we have done all we can for you; and as we are in haste to rejoin the prince's army we must continue our journey. You will excuse us, sir, but we are told that a battle is expected and we do not wish to arrive the day after it."

"Go, my young sirs," said the sick man, "and may you both be blessed for your piety. You have done for me, as you promised, all that you could do. As for me I can only repeat, may God protect you and all dear to you!"

"Sir," said De Guiche to his tutor, "we will precede you, and you can rejoin us on the road to Cambrin."

The host was at his door and everything was prepared--bed, bandages, and lint; and a groom had gone to Lens, the nearest village, for a doctor.

"Everything," said he to Raoul, "shall be done as you desire; but you will not stop to have your wound dressed?"

"Oh, my wound--mine--'tis nothing," replied the viscount; "it will be time to think about it when we next halt; only have the goodness, should you see a cavalier who makes inquiries about a young man on a chestnut horse followed by a servant, to tell him, in fact, that you have seen me, but that I have continued my journey and intend to dine at Mazingarbe and to stop at Cambrin. This cavalier is my attendant."

"Would it not be safer and more certain if I should ask him his name and tell him yours?" demanded the host.

"There is no harm in over-precaution. I am the Viscount de Bragelonne and he is called Grimaud."

At this moment the wounded man arrived from one direction and the monk from the other, the latter dismounting from his mule and desiring that it should be taken to the stables without being unharnessed.

"Sir monk," said De Guiche, "confess well that brave man; and be not concerned for your expenses or for those of your mule; all is paid."

"Thanks, monsieur," said the monk, with one of those smiles that made Bragelonne shudder.

"Come, count," said Raoul, who seemed instinctively to dislike the vicinity of the Augustine; "come, I feel ill here," and the two young men spurred on.

The litter, borne by two servants, now entered the house. The host and his wife were standing on the steps, whilst the unhappy man seemed to suffer dreadful pain and yet to be concerned only to know if he was followed by the monk. At sight of this pale, bleeding man, the wife grasped her husband's arm.

"Well, what's the matter?" asked the latter, "are you going to be ill just now?"

"No, but look," replied the hostess, pointing to the wounded man; "I ask you if you recognize him?"

"That man--wait a bit."

"Ah! I see you know him," exclaimed the wife; "for you have become pale in your turn."

"Truly," cried the host, "misfortune is coming on our house; it is the former executioner of Bethune."

"The former executioner of Bethune!" murmured the young monk, shrinking back and showing on his countenance the feeling of repugnance which his penitent inspired.

Monsieur d'Arminges, who was at the door, perceived his hesitation.

"Sir monk," said he, "whether he is now or has been an executioner, this unfortunate being is none the less a man. Render to him, then, the last service he can by any possibility ask of you, and your work will be all the more meritorious."

The monk made no reply, but silently wended his way to the room where the two valets had deposited the dying man on a bed. D'Arminges and Olivain and the two grooms then mounted their horses, and all four started off at a quick trot to rejoin Raoul and his companion. Just as the tutor and his escort disappeared in their turn, a new traveler stopped on the threshold of the inn.

"What does your worship want?" demanded the host, pale and trembling from the discovery he had just made.

The traveler made a sign as if he wished to drink, and then pointed to his horse and gesticulated like a man who is brushing something.

"Ah, diable!" said the host to himself; "this man seems dumb. And where will your worship drink?"

"There," answered the traveler, pointing to the table.

"I was mistaken," said the host, "he's not quite dumb. And what else does your worship wish for?"

"To know if you have seen a young man pass, fifteen years of age, mounted on a chestnut horse and followed by a groom?"

"The Viscount de Bragelonne?

"Just so."

"Then you are called Monsieur Grimaud?"

The traveler made a sign of assent.

"Well, then," said the host, "your young master was here a quarter of an hour ago; he will dine at Mazingarbe and sleep at Cambrin."

"How far is Mazingarbe?"

"Two miles and a half."

"Thank you."

Grimaud was drinking his wine silently and had just placed his glass on the table to be filled a second time, when a terrific scream resounded from the room occupied by the monk and the dying man. Grimaud sprang up.

"What is that?" said he; "whence comes that cry?"

"From the wounded man's room," replied the host.

"What wounded man?"

"The former executioner of Bethune, who has just been brought in here, assassinated by Spaniards, and who is now being confessed by an Augustine friar."

"The old executioner of Bethune," muttered Grimaud; "a man between fifty-five and sixty, tall, strong, swarthy, black hair and beard?"

"That is he, except that his beard has turned gray and his hair is white; do you know him?" asked the host.

"I have seen him once," replied Grimaud, a cloud darkening his countenance at the picture so suddenly summoned to the bar of recollection.

At this instant a second cry, less piercing than the first, but followed by prolonged groaning, was heard.

The three listeners looked at one another in alarm.

"We must see what it is," said Grimaud.

"It sounds like the cry of one who is being murdered," murmured the host.

"Mon Dieu!" said the woman, crossing herself.

If Grimaud was slow in speaking, we know that he was quick to act; he sprang to the door and shook it violently, but it was bolted on the other side.

"Open the door!" cried the host; "open it instantly, sir monk!"

No reply.

"Unfasten it, or I will break it in!" said Grimaud.

The same silence, and then, ere the host could oppose his design, Grimaud seized a pair of pincers he perceived in a corner and forced the bolt. The room was inundated with blood, dripping from the mattresses upon which lay the wounded man, speechless; the monk had disappeared.

"The monk!" cried the host; "where is the monk?"

Grimaud sprang toward an open window which looked into the courtyard.

"He has escaped by this means," exclaimed he.

"Do you think so?" said the host, bewildered; "boy, see if the mule belonging to the monk is still in the stable."

"There is no mule," cried he to whom this question was addressed.

The host clasped his hands and looked around him suspiciously, whilst Grimaud knit his brows and approached the wounded man, whose worn, hard features awoke in his mind such awful recollections of the past.

"There can be no longer any doubt but that it is himself," said he.

"Does he still live?" inquired the innkeeper.

Making no reply, Grimaud opened the poor man's jacket to feel if the heart beat, whilst the host approached in his turn; but in a moment they both fell back, the host uttering a cry of horror and Grimaud becoming pallid. The blade of a dagger was buried up to the hilt in the left side of the executioner.

"Run! run for help!" cried Grimaud, "and I will remain beside him here."

The host quitted the room in agitation, and as for his wife, she had fled at the sound of her husband's cries.

32. The Absolution.

This is what had taken place: We have seen that it was not of his own free will, but, on the contrary, very reluctantly, that the monk attended the wounded man who had been recommended to him in so strange a manner. Perhaps he would have sought to escape by flight had he seen any possibility of doing so. He was restrained by the threats of the two gentlemen and by the presence of their attendants, who doubtless had received their instructions. And besides, he considered it most expedient, without exhibiting too much ill-will, to follow to the end his role as confessor.

The monk entered the chamber and approached the bed of the wounded man. The executioner searched his face with the quick glance peculiar to those who are about to die and have no time to lose. He made a movement of surprise and said:

"Father, you are very young."

"Men who bear my robe have no age," replied the monk, dryly.

"Alas, speak to me more gently, father; in my last moments I need a friend."

"Do you suffer much?" asked the monk.

"Yes, but in my soul much more than in my body."

"We will save your soul," said the young man; "but are you really the executioner of Bethune, as these people say?"

"That is to say," eagerly replied the wounded man, who doubtless feared that the name of executioner would take from him the last help that he could claim--"that is to say, I was, but am no longer; it is fifteen years since I gave up the office. I still assist at executions, but no longer strike the blow myself--no, indeed."

"You have, then, a repugnance to your profession?"

"So long as I struck in the name of the law and of justice my profession allowed me to sleep quietly, sheltered as I was by justice and law; but since that terrible night when I became an instrument of private vengeance and when with personal hatred I raised the sword over one of God's creatures--since that day----"

The executioner paused and shook his head with an expression of despair.

"Tell me about it," said the monk, who, sitting on the foot of the bed, began to be interested in a story so strangely introduced.

"Ah!" cried the dying man, with all the effusiveness of a grief declared after long suppression, "ah! I have sought to stifle remorse by twenty years of good deeds; I have assuaged the natural ferocity of those who shed blood; on every occasion I have exposed my life to save those who were in danger, and I have preserved lives in exchange for that I took away. That is not all; the money gained in the exercise of my profession I have distributed to the poor; I have been assiduous in attending church and those who formerly fled from me have become accustomed to seeing me. All have forgiven me, some have even loved me; but I think that God has not pardoned me, for the memory of that execution pursues me constantly and every night I see that woman's ghost rising before me."

"A woman! You have assassinated a woman, then?" cried the monk.

"You also!" exclaimed the executioner, "you use that word which sounds ever in my ears--'assassinated!' I have assassinated, then, and not executed! I am an assassin, then, and not an officer of justice!" and he closed his eyes with a groan.

The monk doubtless feared that he would die without saying more, for he exclaimed eagerly:

"Go on, I know nothing, as yet; when you have finished your story, God and I will judge."

"Oh, father," continued the executioner, without opening his eyes, as if he feared on opening them to see some frightful object, "it is especially when night comes on and when I have to cross a river, that this terror which I have been unable to conquer comes upon me; it then seems as if my hand grew heavy, as if the cutlass was still in its grasp, as if the water had the color of blood, and all the voices of nature--the whispering of the trees, the murmur of the wind, the lapping of the wave--united in a voice tearful, despairing, terrible, crying to me, 'Place for the justice of God!'"

"Delirium!" murmured the monk, shaking his head.

The executioner opened his eyes, turned toward the young man and grasped his arm.

"'Delirium,'" he repeated; "'delirium,' do you say? Oh, no! I remember too well. It was evening; I had thrown the body into the river and those words which my remorse repeats to me are those which I in my pride pronounced. After being the instrument of human justice I aspired to be that of the justice of God."

"But let me see, how was it done? Speak," said the monk.

"It was at night. A man came to me and showed me an order and I followed him. Four other noblemen awaited me. They led me away masked. I reserved the right of refusing if the office they required of me should seem unjust. We traveled five or six leagues, serious, silent, and almost without speaking. At length, through the window of a little hut, they showed me a woman sitting, leaning on a table, and said, 'there is the person to be executed.'"

"Horrible!" said the monk. "And you obeyed?"

"Father, that woman was a monster. It was said that she had poisoned her second husband; she had tried to assassinate her brother-in-law; she had just poisoned a young woman who was her rival, and before leaving England she had, it was believed, caused the favorite of the king to be murdered."

"Buckingham?" cried the monk.

"Yes, Buckingham."

"The woman was English, then?"

"No, she was French, but she had married in England."

The monk turned pale, wiped his brow and went and bolted the door. The executioner thought that he had abandoned him and fell back, groaning, upon his bed.

"No, no; I am here," said the monk, quickly coming back to him. "Go on; who were those men?"

"One of them was a foreigner, English, I think. The four others were French and wore the uniform of musketeers."

"Their names?" asked the monk.

"I don't know them, but the four other noblemen called the Englishman 'my lord.'"

"Was the woman handsome?"

"Young and beautiful. Oh, yes, especially beautiful. I see her now, as on her knees at my feet, with her head thrown back, she begged for life. I have never understood how I could have laid low a head so beautiful, with a face so pale."

The monk seemed agitated by a strange emotion; he trembled all over; he seemed eager to put a question which yet he dared not ask. At length, with a violent effort at self-control:

"The name of that woman?" he said.

"I don't know what it was. As I have said, she was twice married, once in France, the second time in England."

"She was young, you say?"

"Twenty-five years old."

"Beautiful?"

"Ravishingly."

"Blond?"

"Yes."

"Abundance of hair--falling over her shoulders?"

"Yes."

"Eyes of an admirable expression?"

"When she chose. Oh, yes, it is she!"

"A voice of strange sweetness?"

"How do you know it?"

The executioner raised himself on his elbow and gazed with a frightened air at the monk, who became livid.

"And you killed her?" the monk exclaimed. "You were the tool of those cowards who dared not kill her themselves? You had no pity for that youthfulness, that beauty, that weakness? you killed that woman?"

"Alas! I have already told you, father, that woman, under that angelic appearance, had an infernal soul, and when I saw her, when I recalled all the evil she had done to me----"

"To you? What could she have done to you? Come, tell me!"

"She had seduced and ruined my brother, a priest. She had fled with him from her convent."

"With your brother?"

"Yes, my brother was her first lover, and she caused his death. Oh, father, do not look in that way at me! Oh, I am guilty, then; you will not pardon me?"

The monk recovered his usual expression.

"Yes, yes," he said, "I will pardon you if you tell me all."

"Oh!" cried the executioner, "all! all! all!"

"Answer, then. If she seduced your brother--you said she seduced him, did you not?"

"Yes."

"If she caused his death--you said that she caused his death?"

"Yes," repeated the executioner.

"Then you must know what her name was as a young girl."

"Oh, mon Dieu!" cried the executioner, "I think I am dying. Absolution, father! absolution."

"Tell me her name and I will give it."

"Her name was----My God, have pity on me!" murmured the executioner; and he fell back on the bed, pale, trembling, and apparently about to die.

"Her name!" repeated the monk, bending over him as if to tear from him the name if he would not utter it; "her name! Speak, or no absolution!"

The dying man collected all his forces.

The monk's eyes glittered.

"Anne de Bueil," murmured the wounded man.

"Anne de Bueil!" cried the monk, standing up and lifting his hands to Heaven. "Anne de Bueil! You said Anne de Bueil, did you not?"

"Yes, yes, that was her name; and now absolve me, for I am dying."

"I, absolve you!" cried the priest, with a laugh which made the dying man's hair stand on end; "I, absolve you? I am not a priest."

"You are not a priest!" cried the executioner. "What, then, are you?"

"I am about to tell you, wretched man."

"Oh, mon Dieu!"

"I am John Francis de Winter."

"I do not know you," said the executioner.

"Wait, wait; you are going to know me. I am John Francis de Winter," he repeated, "and that woman----"

"Well, that woman?"

"Was my mother!"

The executioner uttered the first cry, that terrible cry which had been first heard.

"Oh, pardon me, pardon me!" he murmured; "if not in the name of God, at least in your own name; if not as priest, then as son."

"Pardon you!" cried the pretended monk, "pardon you! Perhaps God will pardon you, but I, never!"

"For pity's sake," said the executioner, extending his arms.

"No pity for him who had no pity! Die, impenitent, die in despair, die and be damned!" And drawing a poniard from beneath his robe he thrust it into the breast of the wounded man, saying, "Here is my absolution!"

Then was heard that second cry, not so loud as the first and followed by a long groan.

The executioner, who had lifted himself up, fell back upon his bed. As to the monk, without withdrawing the poniard from the wound, he ran to the window, opened it, leaped out into the flowers of a small garden, glided onward to the stable, took out his mule, went out by a back gate, ran to a neighbouring thicket, threw off his monkish garb, took from his valise the complete habiliment of a cavalier, clothed himself in it, went on foot to the first post, secured there a horse and continued with a loose rein his journey to Paris.

33. Grimaud Speaks.

Grimaud was left alone with the executioner, who in a few moments opened his eyes.

"Help, help," he murmured; "oh, God! have I not a single friend in the world who will aid me either to live or to die?"

"Take courage," said Grimaud; "they are gone to find assistance."

"Who are you?" asked the wounded man, fixing his half opened eyes on Grimaud.

"An old acquaintance," replied Grimaud.

"You?" and the wounded man sought to recall the features of the person now before him.

"Under what circumstances did we meet?" he asked again.

"One night, twenty years ago, my master fetched you from Bethune and conducted you to Armentieres."

"I know you well now," said the executioner; "you were one of the four grooms."

"Just so."

"Where do you come from now?"

"I was passing by and drew up at this inn to rest my horse. They told me the executioner of Bethune was here and wounded, when you uttered two piercing cries. At the first we ran to the door and at the second forced it open."

"And the monk?" exclaimed the executioner, "did you see the monk?"

"What monk?"

"The monk that was shut in with me."

"No, he was no longer here; he appears to have fled by the window. Was he the man that stabbed you?"

"Yes," said the executioner.

Grimaud moved as if to leave the room.

"What are you going to do?" asked the wounded man.

"He must be apprehended."

"Do not attempt it; he has revenged himself and has done well. Now I may hope that God will forgive me, since my crime is expiated."

"Explain yourself." said Grimaud.

"The woman whom you and your masters commanded me to kill----"

"Milady?"

"Yes, Milady; it is true you called her thus."

"What has the monk to do with this Milady?"

"She was his mother."

Grimaud trembled and stared at the dying man in a dull and leaden manner.

"His mother!" he repeated.

"Yes, his mother."

"But does he know this secret, then?"

"I mistook him for a monk and revealed it to him in confession."

"Unhappy man!" cried Grimaud, whose face was covered with sweat at the bare idea of the evil results such a revelation might cause; "unhappy man, you named no one, I hope?"

"I pronounced no name, for I knew none, except his mother's, as a young girl, and it was by this name that he recognized her, but he knows that his uncle was among her judges."

Thus speaking, he fell back exhausted. Grimaud, wishing to relieve him, advanced his hand toward the hilt of the dagger.

"Touch me not!" said the executioner; "if this dagger is withdrawn I shall die."

Grimaud remained with his hand extended; then, striking his forehead, he exclaimed:

"Oh! if this man should ever discover the names of the others, my master is lost."

"Haste! haste to him and warn him," cried the wounded man, "if he still lives; warn his friends, too. My death, believe me, will not be the end of this atrocious misadventure."

"Where was the monk going?" asked Grimaud.

"Toward Paris."

"Who stopped him?"

"Two young gentlemen, who were on their way to join the army and the name of one of whom I heard his companion mention--the Viscount de Bragelonne."

"And it was this young man who brought the monk to you? Then it was the will of God that it should be so and this it is which makes it all so awful," continued Grimaud. "And yet that woman deserved her fate; do you not think so?"

"On one's death-bed the crimes of others appear very small in comparison with one's own," said the executioner; and falling back exhausted he closed his eyes.

Grimaud was reluctant to leave the man alone and yet he perceived the necessity of starting at once to bear these tidings to the Comte de la Fere. Whilst he thus hesitated the host re-entered the room, followed not only by a surgeon, but by many other persons, whom curiosity had attracted to the spot. The surgeon approached the dying man, who seemed to have fainted.

"We must first extract the steel from the side," said he, shaking his head in a significant manner.

The prophecy which the wounded man had just uttered recurred to Grimaud, who turned away his head. The weapon, as we have already stated, was plunged into the body to the hilt, and as the surgeon, taking it by the end, drew it forth, the wounded man opened his eyes and fixed them on him in a manner truly frightful. When at last the blade had been entirely withdrawn, a red froth issued from the mouth of the wounded man and a stream of blood spouted afresh from the wound when he at length drew breath; then, fixing his eyes upon Grimaud with a singular expression, the dying man uttered the last death-rattle and expired.

Then Grimaud, lifting the dagger from the pool of blood which was gliding along the room, to the horror of all present, made a sign to the host to follow him, paid him with a generosity worthy of his master and again mounted his horse. Grimaud's first intention had been to return to Paris, but he remembered the anxiety which his prolonged absence might occasion Raoul, and reflecting that there were now only two miles between the vicomte and himself and a quarter of an hour's riding would unite them, and that the going, returning and explanation would not occupy an hour, he put spurs to his horse and a few minutes after had reached the only inn of Mazingarbe.

Raoul was seated at table with the Count de Guiche and his tutor, when all at once the door opened and Grimaud presented himself, travel-stained, dirty, and sprinkled with the blood of the unhappy executioner.

"Grimaud, my good Grimaud!" exclaimed Raoul "here you are at last! Excuse me, sirs, this is not a servant, but a friend. How did you leave the count?" continued he. "Does he regret me a little? Have you seen him since I left him? Answer, for I have many things to tell you, too; indeed, the last three days some odd adventures have happened--but what is the matter? how pale you are! and blood, too! What is this?"

"It is the blood of the unfortunate man whom you left at the inn and who died in my arms."

"In your arms?--that man! but know you who he was?"

"He used to be the headsman of Bethune."

"You knew him? and he is dead?"

"Yes."

"Well, sir," said D'Arminges, "it is the common lot; even an executioner is not exempted. I had a bad opinion of him the moment I saw his wound, and since he asked for a monk you know that it was his opinion, too, that death would follow."

At the mention of the monk, Grimaud became pale.

"Come, come," continued D'Arminges, "to dinner;" for like most men of his age and generation he did not allow sentiment or sensibility to interfere with a repast.

"You are right, sir," said Raoul. "Come, Grimaud, order dinner for yourself and when you have rested a little we can talk."

"No, sir, no," said Grimaud. "I cannot stop a moment; I must start for Paris again immediately."

"What? You start for Paris? You are mistaken; it is Olivain who leaves me; you are to remain."

"On the contrary, Olivain is to stay and I am to go. I have come for nothing else but to tell you so."

"But what is the meaning of this change?"

"I cannot tell you."

"Explain yourself."

"I cannot explain myself."

"Come, tell me, what is the joke?"

"Monsieur le vicomte knows that I never joke."

"Yes, but I know also that Monsieur le Comte de la Fere arranged that you were to remain with me and that Olivain should return to Paris. I shall follow the count's directions."

"Not under present circumstances, monsieur."

"Perhaps you mean to disobey me?"

"Yes, monsieur, I must."

"You persist, then?"

"Yes, I am going; may you be happy, monsieur," and Grimaud saluted and turned toward the door to go out.

Raoul, angry and at the same time uneasy, ran after him and seized him by the arm. "Grimaud!" he cried; "remain; I wish it."

"Then," replied Grimaud, "you wish me to allow monsieur le comte to be killed." He saluted and made a movement to depart.

"Grimaud, my friend," said the viscount, "will you leave me thus, in such anxiety? Speak, speak, in Heaven's name!" And Raoul fell back trembling upon his chair.

"I can tell you but one thing, sir, for the secret you wish to know is not my own. You met a monk, did you not?"

"Yes."

The young men looked at each other with an expression of fear.

"You conducted him to the wounded man and you had time to observe him, and perhaps you would know him again were you to meet him."

"Yes, yes!" cried both young men.

"Very well; if ever you meet him again, wherever it may be, whether on the high road or in the street or in a church, anywhere that he or you may be, put your foot on his neck and crush him without pity, without mercy, as you would crush a viper or a scorpion! destroy him utterly and quit him not until he is dead; the lives of five men are not safe, in my opinion, as long as he is on the earth."

And without adding another word, Grimaud, profiting by the astonishment and terror into which he had thrown his auditors, rushed from the room. Two minutes later the thunder of a horse's hoofs was heard upon the road; it was Grimaud, on his way to Paris. When once in the saddle Grimaud reflected on two things; first, that at the pace he was going his horse would not carry him ten miles, and secondly, that he had no money. But Grimaud's ingenuity was more prolific than his speech, and therefore at the first halt he sold his steed and with the money obtained from the purchase took post horses.

34. On the Eve of Battle.

Raoul was aroused from his sombre reflections by his host, who rushed into the apartment crying out, "The Spaniards! the Spaniards!"

That cry was of such importance as to overcome all preoccupation. The young men made inquiries and ascertained that the enemy was advancing by way of Houdin and Bethune.

While Monsieur d'Arminges gave orders for the horses to be made ready for departure, the two young men ascended to the upper windows of the house and saw in the direction of Marsin and of Lens a large body of infantry and cavalry. This time it was not a wandering troop of partisans; it was an entire army. There was therefore nothing for them to do but to follow the prudent advice of Monsieur d'Arminges and beat a retreat. They quickly went downstairs. Monsieur d'Arminges was already mounted. Olivain had ready the horses of the young men, and the lackeys of the Count de Guiche guarded carefully between them the Spanish prisoner, mounted on a pony which had been bought for his use. As a further precaution they had bound his hands.

The little company started off at a trot on the road to Cambrin, where they expected to find the prince. But he was no longer there, having withdrawn on the previous evening to La Bassee, misled by false intelligence of the enemy's movements. Deceived by this intelligence he had concentrated his forces between Vieille-Chapelle and La Venthie; and after a reconnoissance along the entire line, in company with Marshal de Grammont, he had returned and seated himself before a table, with his officers around him. He questioned them as to the news they had each been charged to obtain, but nothing positive had been learned. The hostile army had disappeared two days before and seemed to have gone out of existence.

Now an enemy is never so near and consequently so threatening, as when he has completely disappeared. The prince was, therefore, contrary to his custom, gloomy and anxious, when an officer entered and announced to Marshal de Grammont that some one wished to see him.

The Duc de Grammont received permission from the prince by a glance and went out. The prince followed him with his eyes and continued looking at the door; no one ventured to speak, for fear of disturbing him.

Suddenly a dull and heavy noise was heard. The prince leaped to his feet, extending his hand in the direction whence came the sound, there was no mistaking it--it was the noise of cannon. Every one stood up.

At that moment the door opened.

"Monseigneur," said Marshal de Grammont, with a radiant face, "will your highness permit my son, Count de Guiche, and his traveling companion, Viscount de Bragelonne, to come in and give news of the enemy, whom they have found while we were looking for him?"

"What!" eagerly replied the prince, "will I permit? I not only permit, I desire; let them come in."

The marshal introduced the two young men and placed them face to face with the prince.

"Speak, gentlemen," said the prince, saluting them; "first speak; we shall have time afterward for the usual compliments. The most urgent thing now is to learn where the enemy is and what he is doing."

It fell naturally to the Count de Guiche to make reply; not only was he the elder, but he had been presented to the prince by his father. Besides, he had long known the prince, whilst Raoul now saw him for the first time. He therefore narrated to the prince what they had seen from the inn at Mazingarbe.

Meanwhile Raoul closely observed the young general, already made so famous by the battles of Rocroy, Fribourg, and Nordlingen.

Louis de Bourbon, Prince de Conde, who, since the death of his father, Henri de Bourbon, was called, in accordance with the custom of that period, Monsieur le Prince, was a young man, not more than twenty-six or twenty-seven years old, with the eye of an eagle--agl' occhi grifani, as Dante says--aquiline nose, long, waving hair, of medium height, well formed, possessed of all the qualities essential to the successful soldier--that is to say, the rapid glance, quick decision, fabulous courage. At the same time he was a man of elegant manners and strong mind, so that in addition to the revolution he had made in war, by his new contributions to its methods, he had also made a revolution at Paris, among the young noblemen of the court, whose natural chief he was and who, in distinction from the social leaders of the ancient court, modeled after Bassompierre, Bellegarde and the Duke d'Angouleme, were called the petits-maitres.

At the first words of the Count de Guiche, the prince, having in mind the direction whence came the sound of cannon, had understood everything. The enemy was marching upon Lens, with the intention, doubtless, of securing possession of that town and separating from France the army of France. But in what force was the enemy? Was it a corps sent out to make a diversion? Was it an entire army? To this question De Guiche could not respond.

Now, as these questions involved matters of gravest consequence, it was these to which the prince had especially desired an answer, exact, precise, positive.

Raoul conquered the very natural feeling of timidity he experienced and approaching the prince:

"My lord," he said, "will you permit me to hazard a few words on that subject, which will perhaps relieve you of your uncertainty?"

The prince turned and seemed to cover the young man with a single glance; he smiled on perceiving that he was a child hardly fifteen years old.

"Certainly, monsieur, speak," he said, softening his stern, accented tones, as if he were speaking to a woman.

"My lord," said Raoul, blushing, "might examine the Spanish prisoner."

"Have you a Spanish prisoner?" cried the prince.

"Yes, my lord."

"Ah, that is true," said De Guiche; "I had forgotten it."

"That is easily understood; it was you who took him, count," said Raoul, smiling.

The old marshal turned toward the viscount, grateful for that praise of his son, whilst the prince exclaimed:

"The young man is right; let the prisoner be brought in."

Meanwhile the prince took De Guiche aside and asked him how the prisoner had been taken and who this young man was.

"Monsieur," said the prince, turning toward Raoul, "I know that you have a letter from my sister, Madame de Longueville; but I see that you have preferred commending yourself to me by giving me good counsel."

"My lord," said Raoul, coloring up, "I did not wish to interrupt your highness in a conversation so important as that in which you were engaged with the count. But here is the letter."

"Very well," said the prince; "give it to me later. Here is the prisoner; let us attend to what is most pressing."

The prisoner was one of those military adventurers who sold their blood to whoever would buy, and grew old in stratagems and spoils. Since he had been taken he had not uttered a word, so that it was not known to what country he belonged. The prince looked at him with unspeakable distrust.

"Of what country are you?" asked the prince.

The prisoner muttered a few words in a foreign tongue.

"Ah! ah! it seems that he is a Spaniard. Do you speak Spanish, Grammont?"

"Faith, my lord, but indifferently."

"And I not at all," said the prince, laughing. "Gentlemen," he said, turning to those who were near him "can any one of you speak Spanish and serve me as interpreter?"

"I can, my lord," said Raoul.

"Ah, you speak Spanish?"

"Enough, I think, to fulfill your highness's wishes on this occasion."

Meanwhile the prisoner had remained impassive and as if he had no understanding of what was taking place.

"My lord asks of what country you are," said the young man, in the purest Castilian.

"Ich bin ein Deutscher," replied the prisoner.

"What in the devil does he say?" asked the prince. "What new gibberish is that?"

"He says he is German, my lord," replied Raoul; "but I doubt it, for his accent is bad and his pronunciation defective."

"Then you speak German, also?" asked the prince.

"Yes, my lord."

"Well enough to question him in that language?"

"Yes, my lord."

"Question him, then."

Raoul began the examination, but the result justified his opinion. The prisoner did not understand, or seemed not to understand, what Raoul said to him; and Raoul could hardly understand his replies, containing a mixture of Flemish and Alsatian. However, amidst all the prisoner's efforts to elude a systematic examination, Raoul had recognized his natural accent.

"Non siete Spagnuolo," he said; "non siete Tedesco; siete Italiano."

The prisoner started and bit his lips.

"Ah, that," said the prince, "I understand that language thoroughly; and since he is Italian I will myself continue the examination. Thank you, viscount," continued the prince, laughing, "and I appoint you from this moment my interpreter."

But the prisoner was not less unwilling to respond in Italian than in the other languages; his aim was to elude the examination. Therefore, he knew nothing either of the enemy's numbers, or of those in command, or of the purpose of the army.

"Very good," said the prince, understanding the reason of that ignorance; "the man was caught in the act of assassination and robbery; he might have purchased his life by speaking; he doesn't wish to speak. Take him out and shoot him."

The prisoner turned pale. The two soldiers who had brought him in took him, each by one arm, and led him toward the door, whilst the prince, turning to Marshal de Grammont, seemed to have already forgotten the order he had given.

When he reached the threshold of the door the prisoner stopped. The soldiers, who knew only their orders, attempted to force him along.

"One moment," said the prisoner, in French. "I am ready to speak, my lord."

"Ah! ah!" said the prince, laughing, "I thought we should come to that. I have a sure method of limbering tongues. Young men, take advantage of it against the time when you may be in command."

"But on condition," continued the prisoner, "that your highness will swear that my life shall be safe."

"Upon my honor," said the prince.

"Question, then, my lord."

"Where did the army cross the Lys?"

"Between Saint-Venant and Aire."

"By whom is it commanded?"

"By Count de Fuonsaldagna, General Beck and the archduke."

"Of how many does it consist?"

"Eighteen thousand men and thirty-six cannon."

"And its aim is?"

"Lens."

"You see; gentlemen!" said the prince, turning with a triumphant air toward Marshal de Grammont and the other officers.

"Yes, my lord," said the marshal, "you have divined all that was possible to human genius."

"Recall Le Plessis, Bellievre, Villequier and D'Erlac," said the prince, "recall all the troops that are on this side of the Lys. Let them hold themselves in readiness to march to-night. To-morrow, according to all probability, we shall attack the enemy."

"But, my lord," said Marshal de Grammont, "consider that when we have collected all our forces we shall have hardly thirteen thousand men."

"Monsieur le marechal," said the prince, with that wonderful glance that was peculiar to him, "it is with small armies that great battles are won."

Then turning toward the prisoner, "Take away that man," he said, "and keep him carefully in sight. His life is dependent on the information he has given us; if it is true, he shall be free; if false, let him be shot."

The prisoner was led away.

"Count de Guiche," said the prince, "it is a long time since you saw your father, remain here with him. Monsieur," he continued, addressing Raoul, "if you are not too tired, follow me."

"To the end of the world, my lord!" cried Raoul, feeling an unknown enthusiasm for that young general, who seemed to him so worthy of his renown.

The prince smiled; he despised flatterers, but he appreciated enthusiasts.

"Come, monsieur," he said, "you are good in council, as we have already discovered; to-morrow we shall know if you are good in action."

"And I," said the marshal, "what am I to do?"

"Wait here to receive the troops. I shall either return for them myself or shall send a courier directing you to bring them to me. Twenty guards, well mounted, are all that I shall need for my escort."

"That is very few," said the marshal.

"It is enough," replied the prince. "Have you a good horse, Monsieur de Bragelonne?"

"My horse was killed this morning, my lord, and I am mounted provisionally on my lackey's."

"Choose for yourself in my stables the horse you like best. No false modesty; take the best horse you can find. You will need it this evening, perhaps; you will certainly need it to-morrow."

Raoul didn't wait to be told twice; he knew that with superiors, especially when those superiors are princes, the highest politeness is to obey without delay or argument; he went down to the stables, picked out a pie-bald Andalusian horse, saddled and bridled it himself, for Athos had advised him to trust no one with those important offices at a time of danger, and went to rejoin the prince, who at that moment mounted his horse.

"Now, monsieur," he said to Raoul, "will you give me the letter you have brought?"

Raoul handed the letter to the prince.

"Keep near me," said the latter.

The prince threw his bridle over the pommel of the saddle, as he was wont to do when he wished to have both hands free, unsealed the letter of Madame de Longueville and started at a gallop on the road to Lens, attended by Raoul and his small escort, whilst messengers sent to recall the troops set out with a loose rein in other directions. The prince read as he hastened on.

"Monsieur," he said, after a moment, "they tell me great things of you. I have only to say, after the little that I have seen and heard, that I think even better of you than I have been told."

Raoul bowed.

Meanwhile, as the little troop drew nearer to Lens, the noise of the cannon sounded louder. The prince kept his gaze fixed in the direction of the sound with the steadfastness of a bird of prey. One would have said that his gaze could pierce the branches of trees which limited his horizon. From time to time his nostrils dilated as if eager for the smell of powder, and he panted like a horse.

At length they heard the cannon so near that it was evident they were within a league of the field of battle, and at a turn of the road they perceived the little village of Aunay.

The peasants were in great commotion. The report of Spanish cruelty had gone out and every one was frightened. The women had already fled, taking refuge in Vitry; only a few men remained. On seeing the prince they hastened to meet him. One of them recognized him.

"Ah, my lord," he said, "have you come to drive away those rascal Spaniards and those Lorraine robbers?"

"Yes," said the prince, "if you will serve me as guide."

"Willingly, my lord. Where does your highness wish to go?"

"To some elevated spot whence I can look down on Lens and the surrounding country----"

"In that case, I'm your man."

"I can trust you--you are a true Frenchman?"

"I am an old soldier of Rocroy, my lord."

"Here," said the prince, handing him a purse, "here is for Rocroy. Now, do you want a horse, or will you go afoot?"

"Afoot, my lord; I have served always in the infantry. Besides, I expect to lead your highness into places where you will have to walk."

"Come, then," said the prince; "let us lose no time."

The peasant started off, running before the prince's horse; then, a hundred steps from the village, he took a narrow road hidden at the bottom of the valley. For a half league they proceeded thus, the cannon-shot sounding so near that they expected at each discharge to hear the hum of the balls. At length they entered a path which, going out from the road, skirted the mountainside. The prince dismounted, ordered one of his aids and Raoul to follow his example, and directed the others to await his orders, keeping themselves meanwhile on the alert. He then began to ascend the path.

In about ten minutes they reached the ruins of an old chateau; those ruins crowned the summit of a hill which overlooked the surrounding country. At a distance of hardly a quarter of a league they looked down on Lens, at bay, and before Lens the enemy's entire army.

With a single glance the prince took in the extent of country that lay before him, from Lens as far as Vimy. In a moment the plan of the battle which on the following day was to save France the second time from invasion was unrolled in his mind. He took a pencil, tore a page from his tablets and wrote:

"My Dear Marshal,--In an hour Lens will be in the enemy's possession. Come and rejoin me; bring with you the whole army. I shall be at Vendin to place it in position. To-morrow we shall retake Lens and beat the enemy."

Then, turning toward Raoul: "Go, monsieur," he said; "ride fast and give this letter to Monsieur de Grammont."

Raoul bowed, took the letter, went hastily down the mountain, leaped on his horse and set out at a gallop. A quarter of an hour later he was with the marshal.

A portion of the troops had already arrived and the remainder was expected from moment to moment. Marshal de Grammont put himself at the head of all the available cavalry and infantry and took the road to Vendin, leaving the Duc de Chatillon to await and bring on the rest. All the artillery was ready to move, and started off at a moment's notice.

It was seven o'clock in the evening when the marshal arrived at the appointed place. The prince awaited him there. As he had foreseen, Lens had fallen into the hands of the enemy immediately after Raoul's departure. The event was announced by the cessation of the firing.

As the shadows of night deepened the troops summoned by the prince arrived in successive detachments. Orders were given that no drum should be beaten, no trumpet sounded.

At nine o'clock the night had fully come. Still a last ray of twilight lighted the plain. The army marched silently, the prince at the head of the column. Presently the army came in sight of Lens; two or three houses were in flames and a dull noise was heard which indicated what suffering was endured by a town taken by assault.

The prince assigned to every one his post. Marshal de Grammont was to hold the extreme left, resting on Mericourt. The Duc de Chatillon commanded the centre. Finally, the prince led the right wing, resting on Aunay. The order of battle on the morrow was to be that of the positions taken in the evening. Each one, on awaking, would find himself on the field of battle.

The movement was executed in silence and with precision. At ten o'clock every one was in his appointed position; at half-past ten the prince visited the posts and gave his final orders for the following day.

Three things were especially urged upon the officers, who were to see that the soldiers observed them scrupulously: the first, that the different corps should so march that cavalry and infantry should be on the same line and that each body should protect its gaps; the second, to go to the charge no faster than a walk; the third, to let the enemy fire first.

The prince assigned the Count de Guiche to his father and kept Bragelonne near his own person; but the two young men sought the privilege of passing the night together and it was accorded them. A tent was erected for them near that of the marshal.

Although the day had been fatiguing, neither of them was inclined to sleep. And besides, even for old soldiers the evening before a battle is a serious time; it was so with greater reason to two young men who were about to witness for the first time that terrible spectacle. On the evening before a battle one thinks of a thousand things forgotten till then; those who are indifferent to one another become friends and those who are friends become brothers. It need not be said that if in the depths of the heart there is a sentiment more tender, it reaches then, quite naturally, the highest exaltation of which it is capable. Some sentiment of this kind must have been cherished by each one of these two friends, for each of them almost immediately sat down by himself at an end of the tent and began to write.

The letters were long--the four pages were covered with closely written words. The writers sometimes looked up at each other and smiled; they understood without speaking, their organizations were so delicate and sympathetic. The letters being finished, each put his own into two envelopes, so that no one, without tearing the first envelope, could discover to whom the second was addressed; then they drew near to each other and smilingly exchanged their letters.

"In case any evil should happen to me," said Bragelonne.

"In case I should be killed," said De Guiche.

They then embraced each other like two brothers, and each wrapping himself in his cloak they soon passed into that kindly sleep of youth which is the prerogative of birds, flowers and infants.

35. A Dinner in the Old Style.

The second interview between the former musketeers was not so formal and threatening as the first. Athos, with his superior understanding, wisely deemed that the supper table would be the most complete and satisfactory point of reunion, and at the moment when his friends, in deference to his deportment and sobriety, dared scarcely speak of some of their former good dinners, he was the first to propose that they should all assemble around some well spread table and abandon themselves unreservedly to their own natural character and manners--a freedom which had formerly contributed so much to that good understanding between them which gave them the name of the inseparables. For different reasons this was an agreeable proposition to them all, and it was therefore agreed that each should leave a very exact address and that upon the request of any of the associates a meeting should be convoked at a famous eating house in the Rue de la Monnaie, of the sign of the Hermitage. The first rendezvous was fixed for the following Wednesday, at eight o'clock in the evening precisely.

On that day, in fact, the four friends arrived punctually at the hour, each from his own abode or occupation. Porthos had been trying a new horse; D'Artagnan was on guard at the Louvre; Aramis had been to visit one of his penitents in the neighborhood; and Athos, whose domicile was established in the Rue Guenegaud, found himself close at hand. They were, therefore, somewhat surprised to meet altogether at the door of the Hermitage, Athos starting out from the Pont Neuf, Porthos by the Rue de la Roule, D'Artagnan by the Rue des Fosse Saint Germain l'Auxerrois, and Aramis by the Rue de Bethisy.

The first words exchanged between the four friends, on account of the ceremony which each of them mingled with their demonstration, were somewhat forced and even the repast began with a kind of stiffness. Athos perceived this embarrassment, and by way of supplying an effectual remedy, called for four bottles of champagne.

At this order, given in Athos's habitually calm manner, the face of the Gascon relaxed and Porthos's brow grew smooth. Aramis was astonished. He knew that Athos not only never drank, but more, that he had a kind of repugnance to wine. This astonishment was doubled when Aramis saw Athos fill a bumper and toss it off with all his former enthusiasm. His companions followed his example. In a very few minutes the four bottles were empty and this excellent specific succeeded in dissipating even the slightest cloud that might have rested on their spirits. Now the four friends began to speak loud, scarcely waiting till one had finished before another began, and each assumed his favorite attitude on or at the table. Soon--strange fact--Aramis undid two buttons of his doublet, seeing which, Porthos unfastened his entirely.

Battles, long journeys, blows given and received, sufficed for the first themes of conversation, which turned upon the silent struggles sustained against him who was now called the great cardinal.

"Faith," said Aramis, laughing, "we have praised the dead enough, let us revile the living a little; I should like to say something evil of Mazarin; is it permissible?"

"Go on, go on," replied D'Artagnan, laughing heartily; "relate your story and I will applaud it if it is a good one."

"A great prince," said Aramis, "with whom Mazarin sought an alliance, was invited by him to send him a list of the conditions on which he would do him the honor to negotiate with him. The prince, who had a great repugnance to treat with such an illbred fellow, made out a list, against the grain, and sent it. In this list there were three conditions which displeased Mazarin and he offered the prince ten thousand crowns to renounce them."

"Ah, ha, ha!" laughed the three friends, "not a bad bargain; and there was no fear of being taken at his word; what did the prince do then?"

"The prince immediately sent fifty thousand francs to Mazarin, begging him never to write to him again, and offered twenty thousand francs more, on condition that he would never speak to him. What did Mazarin do?"

"Stormed!" suggested Athos.

"Beat the messenger!" cried Porthos.

"Accepted the money!" said D'Artagnan.

"You have guessed it," answered Aramis; and they all laughed so heartily that the host appeared in order to inquire whether the gentlemen wanted anything; he thought they were fighting.

At last their hilarity calmed down and:

"Faith!" exclaimed D'Artagnan to the two friends, "you may well wish ill to Mazarin; for I assure you, on his side he wishes you no good."

"Pooh! really?" asked Athos. "If I thought the fellow knew me by my name I would be rebaptized, for fear it might be thought I knew him."

"He knows you better by your actions than your name; he is quite aware that there are two gentlemen who greatly aided the escape of Monsieur de Beaufort, and he has instigated an active search for them, I can answer for it."

"By whom?"

"By me; and this morning he sent for me to ask me if I had obtained any information."

"And what did you reply?"

"That I had none as yet; but that I was to dine today with two gentlemen, who would be able to give me some."

"You told him that?" said Porthos, a broad smile spreading over his honest face. "Bravo! and you are not afraid of that, Athos?"

"No," replied Athos, "it is not the search of Mazarin that I fear."

"Now," said Aramis, "tell me a little what you do fear."

"Nothing for the present; at least, nothing in good earnest."

"And with regard to the past?" asked Porthos.

"Oh! the past is another thing," said Athos, sighing; "the past and the future."

"Are you afraid for your young Raoul?" asked Aramis.

"Well," said D'Artagnan, "one is never killed in a first engagement."

"Nor in the second," said Aramis

"Nor in the third," returned Porthos; "and even when one is killed, one rises again, the proof of which is, that here we are!"

"No," said Athos, "it is not Raoul about whom I am anxious, for I trust he will conduct himself like a gentleman; and if he is killed--well, he will die bravely; but hold--should such a misfortune happen--well--" Athos passed his hand across his pale brow.

"Well?" asked Aramis.

"Well, I shall look upon it as an expiation."

"Ah!" said D'Artagnan; "I know what you mean."

"And I, too," added Aramis; "but you must not think of that, Athos; what is past, is past."

"I don't understand," said Porthos.

"The affair at Armentieres," whispered D'Artagnan.

"The affair at Armentieres?" asked he again.

"Milady."

"Oh, yes!" said Porthos; "true, I had forgotten it!"

Athos looked at him intently.

"You have forgotten it, Porthos?" said he.

"Faith! yes, it is so long ago," answered Porthos.

"This affair does not, then, weigh upon your conscience?"

"Faith, no."

"And you, D'Artagnan?"

"I--I own that when my mind returns to that terrible period I have no recollection of anything but the rigid corpse of poor Madame Bonancieux. Yes, yes," murmured he, "I have often felt regret for the victim, but never the very slightest remorse for the assassin."

Athos shook his dead doubtfully.

"Consider," said Aramis, "if you admit divine justice and its participation in the things of this world, that woman was punished by the will of heaven. We were but the instruments, that is all."

"But as to free will, Aramis?"

"How acts the judge? He has a free will, yet he fearlessly condemns. What does the executioner? He is master of his arm, yet he strikes without remorse."

"The executioner!" muttered Athos, as if arrested by some recollection.

"I know that it is terrible," said D'Artagnan; "but when I reflect that we have killed English, Rochellais, Spaniards, nay, even French, who never did us any other harm but to aim at and to miss us, whose only fault was to cross swords with us and to be unable to ward off our blows--I can, on my honor, find an excuse for my share in the murder of that woman."

"As for me," said Porthos, "now that you have reminded me of it, Athos, I have the scene again before me, as if I now were there. Milady was there, as it were, where you sit." (Athos changed color.) "I--I was where D'Artagnan stands. I wore a long sword which cut like a Damascus--you remember it, Aramis for you always called it Balizarde. Well, I swear to you, all three, that had the executioner of Bethune--was he not of Bethune?--yes, egad! of Bethune!--not been there, I would have cut off the head of that infamous being without thinking of it, or even after thinking of it. She was a most atrocious woman."

"And then," said Aramis, with the tone of philosophical indifference which he had assumed since he had belonged to the church and in which there was more atheism than confidence in God, "what is the use of thinking of it all? At the last hour we must confess this action and God knows better than we can whether it is a crime, a fault, or a meritorious deed. I repent of it? Egad! no. Upon my honor and by the holy cross; I only regret it because she was a woman."

"The most satisfactory part of the matter," said D'Artagnan, "is that there remains no trace of it."

"She had a son," observed Athos.

"Oh! yes, I know that," said D'Artagnan, "and you mentioned it to me; but who knows what has become of him? If the serpent be dead, why not its brood? Do you think his uncle De Winter would have brought up that young viper? De Winter probably condemned the son as he had done the mother."

"Then," said Athos, "woe to De Winter, for the child had done no harm."

"May the devil take me, if the child be not dead," said Porthos. "There is so much fog in that detestable country, at least so D'Artagnan declares."

Just as the quaint conclusion reached by Porthos was about to bring back hilarity to faces now more or less clouded, hasty footsteps were heard upon the stair and some one knocked at the door.

"Come in," cried Athos.

"Please your honors," said the host, "a person in a great hurry wishes to speak to one of you."

"To which of us?" asked all the four friends.

"To him who is called the Comte de la Fere."

"It is I," said Athos, "and what is the name of the person?"

"Grimaud."

"Ah!" exclaimed Athos, turning pale. "Back already! What can have happened, then, to Bragelonne?"

"Let him enter," cried D'Artagnan; "let him come up."

But Grimaud had already mounted the staircase and was waiting on the last step; so springing into the room he motioned the host to leave it. The door being closed, the four friends waited in expectation. Grimaud's agitation, his pallor, the sweat which covered his face, the dust which soiled his clothes, all indicated that he was the messenger of some important and terrible news.

"Your honors," said he, "that woman had a child; that child has become a man; the tigress had a little one, the tiger has roused himself; he is ready to spring upon you--beware!"

Athos glanced around at his friends with a melancholy smile. Porthos turned to look at his sword, which was hanging on the wall; Aramis seized his knife; D'Artagnan arose.

"What do you mean, Grimaud?" he exclaimed.

"That Milady's son has left England, that he is in France, on his road to Paris, if he be not here already."

"The devil he is!" said Porthos. "Are you sure of it?"

"Certain," replied Grimaud.

This announcement was received in silence. Grimaud was so breathless, so exhausted, that he had fallen back upon a chair. Athos filled a beaker with champagne and gave it to him.

"Well, after all," said D'Artagnan, "supposing that he lives, that he comes to Paris; we have seen many other such. Let him come."

"Yes," echoed Porthos, glancing affectionately at his sword, still hanging on the wall; "we can wait for him; let him come."

"Moreover, he is but a child," said Aramis.

Grimaud rose.

"A child!" he exclaimed. "Do you know what he has done, this child? Disguised as a monk he discovered the whole history in confession from the executioner of Bethune, and having confessed him, after having learned everything from him, he gave him absolution by planting this dagger into his heart. See, it is on fire yet with his hot blood, for it is not thirty hours since it was drawn from the wound."

And Grimaud threw the dagger on the table.

D'Artagnan, Porthos and Aramis rose and in one spontaneous motion rushed to their swords. Athos alone remained seated, calm and thoughtful.

"And you say he is dressed as a monk, Grimaud?"

"Yes, as an Augustine monk."

"What sized man is he?"

"About my height; thin, pale, with light blue eyes and tawny flaxen hair."

"And he did not see Raoul?" asked Athos.

"Yes, on the contrary, they met, and it was the viscount himself who conducted him to the bed of the dying man."

Athos, in his turn, rising without speaking, went and unhooked his sword.

"Heigh, sir," said D'Artagnan, trying to laugh, "do you know we look very much like a flock of silly, mouse-evading women! How is it that we, four men who have faced armies without blinking, begin to tremble at the mention of a child?"

"It is true," said Athos, "but this child comes in the name of Heaven."

And very soon they left the inn.

36. A Letter from Charles the First.

The reader must now cross the Seine with us and follow us to the door of the Carmelite Convent in the Rue Saint Jacques. It is eleven o'clock in the morning and the pious sisters have just finished saying mass for the success of the armies of King Charles I. Leaving the church, a woman and a young girl dressed in black, the one as a widow and the other as an orphan, have re-entered their cell.

The woman kneels on a prie-dieu of painted wood and at a short distance from her stands the young girl, leaning against a chair, weeping.

The woman must have once been handsome, but traces of sorrow have aged her. The young girl is lovely and her tears only embellish her; the lady appears to be about forty years of age, the girl about fourteen.

"Oh, God!" prayed the kneeling suppliant, "protect my husband, guard my son, and take my wretched life instead!"

"Oh, God!" murmured the girl, "leave me my mother!"

"Your mother can be of no use to you in this world, Henrietta," said the lady, turning around. "Your mother has no longer either throne or husband; she has neither son, money nor friends; the whole world, my poor child, has abandoned your mother!" And she fell back, weeping, into her daughter's arms.

"Courage, take courage, my dear mother!" said the girl.

"Ah! 'tis an unfortunate year for kings," said the mother. "And no one thinks of us in this country, for each must think about his own affairs. As long as your brother was with me he kept me up; but he is gone and can no longer send us news of himself, either to me or to your father. I have pledged my last jewels, sold your clothes and my own to pay his servants, who refused to accompany him unless I made this sacrifice. We are now reduced to live at the expense of these daughters of Heaven; we are the poor, succored by God."

"But why not address yourself to your sister, the queen?" asked the girl.

"Alas! the queen, my sister, is no longer queen, my child. Another reigns in her name. One day you will be able to understand how all this is."

"Well, then, to the king, your nephew. Shall I speak to him? You know how much he loves me, my mother.

"Alas! my nephew is not yet king, and you know Laporte has told us twenty times that he himself is in need of almost everything."

"Then let us pray to Heaven," said the girl.

The two women who thus knelt in united prayer were the daughter and grand-daughter of Henry IV., the wife and daughter of Charles I.

They had just finished their double prayer, when a nun softly tapped at the door of the cell.

"Enter, my sister," said the queen.

"I trust your majesty will pardon this intrusion on her meditations, but a foreign lord has arrived from England and waits in the parlor, demanding the honor of presenting a letter to your majesty."

"Oh, a letter! a letter from the king, perhaps. News from your father, do you hear, Henrietta? And the name of this lord?"

"Lord de Winter."

"Lord de Winter!" exclaimed the queen, "the friend of my husband. Oh, bid him enter!"

And the queen advanced to meet the messenger, whose hand she seized affectionately, whilst he knelt down and presented a letter to her, contained in a case of gold.

"Ah! my lord!" said the queen, "you bring us three things which we have not seen for a long time. Gold, a devoted friend, and a letter from the king, our husband and master."

De Winter bowed again, unable to reply from excess of emotion.

On their side the mother and daughter retired into the embrasure of a window to read eagerly the following letter:

"Dear Wife,--We have now reached the moment of decision. I have concentrated here at Naseby camp all the resources Heaven has left me, and I write to you in haste from thence. Here I await the army of my rebellious subjects. I am about to struggle for the last time with them. If victorious, I shall continue the struggle; if beaten, I am lost. I shall try, in the latter case (alas! in our position, one must provide for everything), I shall try to gain the coast of France. But can they, will they receive an unhappy king, who will bring such a sad story into a country already agitated by civil discord? Your wisdom and your affection must serve me as guides. The bearer of this letter will tell you, madame, what I dare not trust to pen and paper and the risks of transit. He will explain to you the steps that I expect you to pursue. I charge him also with my blessing for my children and with the sentiments of my soul for yourself, my dearest sweetheart."

The letter bore the signature, not of "Charles, King," but of "Charles--still king."

"And let him be no longer king," cried the queen. "Let him be conquered, exiled, proscribed, provided he still lives. Alas! in these days the throne is too dangerous a place for me to wish him to retain it. But my lord, tell me," she continued, "hide nothing from me--what is, in truth, the king's position? Is it as hopeless as he thinks?"

"Alas! madame, more hopeless than he thinks. His majesty has so good a heart that he cannot understand hatred; is so loyal that he does not suspect treason! England is torn in twain by a spirit of disturbance which, I greatly fear, blood alone can exorcise."

"But Lord Montrose," replied the queen, "I have heard of his great and rapid successes of battles gained. I heard it said that he was marching to the frontier to join the king."

"Yes, madame; but on the frontier he was met by Lesly; he had tried victory by means of superhuman undertakings. Now victory has abandoned him. Montrose, beaten at Philiphaugh, was obliged to disperse the remains of his army and to fly, disguised as a servant. He is at Bergen, in Norway."

"Heaven preserve him!" said the queen. "It is at least a consolation to know that some who have so often risked their lives for us are safe. And now, my lord, that I see how hopeless the position of the king is, tell me with what you are charged on the part of my royal husband."

"Well, then, madame," said De Winter, "the king wishes you to try and discover the dispositions of the king and queen toward him."

"Alas! you know that even now the king is but a child and the queen a woman weak enough. Here, Monsieur Mazarin is everything."

"Does he desire to play the part in France that Cromwell plays in England?"

"Oh, no! He is a subtle, conscienceless Italian, who though he very likely dreams of crime, dares not commit it; and unlike Cromwell, who disposes of both Houses, Mazarin has had the queen to support him in his struggle with the parliament."

"More reason, then, he should protect a king pursued by parliament."

The queen shook her head despairingly.

"If I judge for myself, my lord," she said, "the cardinal will do nothing, and will even, perhaps, act against us. The presence of my daughter and myself in France is already irksome to him; much more so would be that of the king. My lord," added Henrietta, with a melancholy smile, "it is sad and almost shameful to be obliged to say that we have passed the winter in the Louvre without money, without linen, almost without bread, and often not rising from bed because we wanted fire."

"Horrible!" cried De Winter; "the daughter of Henry IV., and the wife of King Charles! Wherefore did you not apply, then, madame, to the first person you saw from us?"

"Such is the hospitality shown to a queen by the minister from whom a king demands it."

"But I heard that a marriage between the Prince of Wales and Mademoiselle d'Orleans was spoken of," said De Winter.

"Yes, for an instant I hoped it was so. The young people felt a mutual esteem; but the queen, who at first sanctioned their affection, changed her mind, and Monsieur, the Duc d'Orleans, who had encouraged the familiarity between them, has forbidden his daughter to think any more about the union. Oh, my lord!" continued the queen, without restraining her tears, "it is better to fight as the king has done, and to die, as perhaps he will, than live in beggary like me."

"Courage, madame! courage! Do not despair! The interests of the French crown, endangered at this moment, are to discountenance rebellion in a neighboring nation. Mazarin, as a statesman, will understand the politic necessity."

"Are you sure," said the queen doubtfully, "that you have not been forestalled?"

"By whom?"

"By the Joices, the Prinns, the Cromwells?"

"By a tailor, a coachmaker, a brewer! Ah! I hope, madame, that the cardinal will not enter into negotiations with such men!"

"Ah! what is he himself?" asked Madame Henrietta.

"But for the honor of the king--of the queen."

"Well, let us hope he will do something for the sake of their honor," said the queen. "A true friend's eloquence is so powerful, my lord, that you have reassured me. Give me your hand and let us go to the minister; and yet," she added, "suppose he should refuse and that the king loses the battle?"

"His majesty will then take refuge in Holland, where I hear his highness the Prince of Wales now is."

"And can his majesty count upon many such subjects as yourself for his flight?"

"Alas! no, madame," answered De Winter; "but the case is provided for and I am come to France to seek allies."

"Allies!" said the queen, shaking her head.

"Madame," replied De Winter, "provided I can find some of my good old friends of former times I will answer for anything."

"Come then, my lord," said the queen, with the painful doubt that is felt by those who have suffered much; "come, and may Heaven hear you."

37. Cromwell's Letter.

At the very moment when the queen quitted the convent to go to the Palais Royal, a young man dismounted at the gate of this royal abode and announced to the guards that he had something of importance to communicate to Cardinal Mazarin. Although the cardinal was often tormented by fear, he was more often in need of counsel and information, and he was therefore sufficiently accessible. The true difficulty of being admitted was not to be found at the first door, and even the second was passed easily enough; but at the third watched, besides the guard and the doorkeepers, the faithful Bernouin, a Cerberus whom no speech could soften, no wand, even of gold, could charm.

It was therefore at the third door that those who solicited or were bidden to an audience underwent their formal interrogatory.

The young man having left his horse tied to the gate in the court, mounted the great staircase and addressed the guard in the first chamber.

"Cardinal Mazarin?" said he.

"Pass on," replied the guard.

The cavalier entered the second hall, which was guarded by the musketeers and doorkeepers.

"Have you a letter of audience?" asked a porter, advancing to the new arrival.

"I have one, but not one from Cardinal Mazarin."

"Enter, and ask for Monsieur Bernouin," said the porter, opening the door of the third room. Whether he only held his usual post or whether it was by accident, Monsieur Bernouin was found standing behind the door and must have heard all that had passed.

"You seek me, sir," said he. "From whom may the letter be you bear to his eminence?"

"From General Oliver Cromwell," said the new comer. "Be so good as to mention this name to his eminence and to bring me word whether he will receive me--yes or no."

Saying which, he resumed the proud and sombre bearing peculiar at that time to Puritans. Bernouin cast an inquisitorial glance at the person of the young man and entered the cabinet of the cardinal, to whom he transmitted the messenger's words.

"A man bringing a letter from Oliver Cromwell?" said Mazarin. "And what kind of a man?"

"A genuine Englishman, your eminence. Hair sandy-red--more red than sandy; gray-blue eyes--more gray than blue; and for the rest, stiff and proud."

"Let him give in his letter."

"His eminence asks for the letter," said Bernouin, passing back into the ante-chamber.

"His eminence cannot see the letter without the bearer of it," replied the young man; "but to convince you that I am really the bearer of a letter, see, here it is; and kindly add," continued he, "that I am not a simple messenger, but an envoy extraordinary."

Bernouin re-entered the cabinet, returning in a few seconds. "Enter, sir," said he.

The young man appeared on the threshold of the minister's closet, in one hand holding his hat, in the other the letter. Mazarin rose. "Have you, sir," asked he, "a letter accrediting you to me?"

"There it is, my lord," said the young man.

Mazarin took the letter and read it thus:

"Mr. Mordaunt, one of my secretaries, will remit this letter of introduction to His Eminence, the Cardinal Mazarin, in Paris. He is also the bearer of a second confidential epistle for his eminence.

"Oliver Cromwell."

"Very well, Monsieur Mordaunt," said Mazarin, "give me this second letter and sit down."

The young man drew from his pocket a second letter, presented it to the cardinal, and took his seat. The cardinal, however, did not unseal the letter at once, but continued to turn it again and again in his hand; then, in accordance with his usual custom and judging from experience that few people could hide anything from him when he began to question them, fixing his eyes upon them at the same time, he thus addressed the messenger:

"You are very young, Monsieur Mordaunt, for this difficult task of ambassador, in which the oldest diplomatists often fail."

"My lord, I am twenty-three years of age; but your eminence is mistaken in saying that I am young. I am older than your eminence, although I possess not your wisdom. Years of suffering, in my opinion, count double, and I have suffered for twenty years."

"Ah, yes, I understand," said Mazarin; "want of fortune, perhaps. You are poor, are you not?" Then he added to himself: "These English Revolutionists are all beggars and ill-bred."

"My lord, I ought to have a fortune of six millions, but it has been taken from me."

"You are not, then, a man of the people?" said Mazarin, astonished.

"If I bore my proper title I should be a lord. If I bore my name you would have heard one of the most illustrious names of England."

"What is your name, then?" asked Mazarin.

"My name is Mordaunt," replied the young man, bowing.

Mazarin now understood that Cromwell's envoy desired to retain his incognito. He was silent for an instant, and during that time he scanned the young man even more attentively than he had done at first. The messenger was unmoved.

"Devil take these Puritans," said Mazarin aside; "they are carved from granite." Then he added aloud, "But you have relations left you?"

"I have one remaining. Three times I presented myself to ask his support and three times he ordered his servants to turn me away."

"Oh, mon Dieu! my dear Mr. Mordaunt," said Mazarin, hoping by a display of affected pity to catch the young man in a snare, "how extremely your history interests me! You know not, then, anything of your birth--you have never seen your mother?"

"Yes, my lord; she came three times, whilst I was a child, to my nurse's house; I remember the last time she came as well as if it were to-day."

"You have a good memory," said Mazarin.

"Oh! yes, my lord," said the young man, with such peculiar emphasis that the cardinal felt a shudder run through every vein.

"And who brought you up?" he asked again.

"A French nurse, who sent me away when I was five years old because no one paid her for me, telling me the name of a relation of whom she had heard my mother often speak."

"What became of you?"

"As I was weeping and begging on the high road, a minister from Kingston took me in, instructed me in the Calvinistic faith, taught me all he knew himself and aided me in my researches after my family."

"And these researches?"

"Were fruitless; chance did everything."

"You discovered what had become of your mother?"

"I learned that she had been assassinated by my relation, aided by four friends, but I was already aware that I had been robbed of my wealth and degraded from my nobility by King Charles I."

"Oh! I now understand why you are in the service of Cromwell; you hate the king."

"Yes, my lord, I hate him!" said the young man.

Mazarin marked with surprise the diabolical expression with which the young man uttered these words. Just as, ordinarily, faces are colored by blood, his face seemed dyed by hatred and became livid.

"Your history is a terrible one, Mr. Mordaunt, and touches me keenly; but happily for you, you serve an all-powerful master; he ought to aid you in your search; we have so many means of gaining information."

"My lord, to a well-bred dog it is only necessary to show one end of a track; he is certain to reach the other."

"But this relation you mentioned--do you wish me to speak to him?" said Mazarin, who was anxious to make a friend about Cromwell's person.

"Thanks, my lord, I will speak to him myself. He will treat me better the next time I see him."

"You have the means, then, of touching him?"

"I have the means of making myself feared."

Mazarin looked at the young man, but at the fire which shot from his glance he bent his head; then, embarrassed how to continue such a conversation, he opened Cromwell's letter.

The young man's eyes gradually resumed their dull and glassy appearance and he fell into a profound reverie. After reading the first lines of the letter Mazarin gave a side glance at him to see if he was watching the expression of his face as he read. Observing his indifference, he shrugged his shoulders, saying:

"Send on your business those who do theirs at the same time! Let us see what this letter contains."

We here present the letter verbatim:

"To his Eminence, Monseigneur le Cardinal Mazarini:

"I have wished, monseigneur, to learn your intentions relating to the existing state of affairs in

England. The two kingdoms are so near that France must be interested in our situation, as we are interested in that of France. The English are almost of one mind in contending against the tyranny of Charles and his adherents. Placed by popular confidence at the head of that movement, I can appreciate better than any other its significance and its probable results. I am at present in the midst of war, and am about to deliver a decisive battle against King Charles. I shall gain it, for the hope of the nation and the Spirit of the Lord are with me. This battle won by me, the king will have no further resources in England or in Scotland; and if he is not captured or killed, he will endeavor to pass over into France to recruit soldiers and to refurnish himself with arms and money. France has already received Queen Henrietta, and, unintentionally, doubtless, has maintained a centre of inextinguishable civil war in my country. But Madame Henrietta is a daughter of France and was entitled to the hospitality of France. As to King Charles, the question must be viewed differently; in receiving and aiding him, France will censure the acts of the English nation, and thus so essentially harm England, and especially the well-being of the government, that such a proceeding will be equivalent to pronounced hostilities."

At this moment Mazarin became very uneasy at the turn which the letter was taking and paused to glance under his eyes at the young man. The latter continued in thought. Mazarin resumed his reading:

"It is important, therefore, monseigneur, that I should be informed as to the intentions of France. The interests of that kingdom and those of England, though taking now diverse directions, are very nearly the same. England needs tranquillity at home, in order to consummate the expulsion of her king; France needs tranquillity to establish on solid foundations the throne of her young monarch. You need, as much as we do, that interior condition of repose which, thanks to the energy of our government, we are about to attain.

"Your quarrels with the parliament, your noisy dissensions with the princes, who fight for you today and to-morrow will fight against you, the popular following directed by the coadjutor, President Blancmesnil, and Councillor Broussel--all that disorder, in short, which pervades the several departments of the state, must lead you to view with uneasiness the possibility of a foreign war; for in that event England, exalted by the enthusiasm of new ideas, will ally herself with Spain, already seeking that alliance. I have therefore believed, monseigneur, knowing your prudence and your personal relation to the events of the present time, that you will choose to hold your forces concentrated in the interior of the French kingdom and leave to her own the new government of England. That neutrality consists simply in excluding King Charles from the territory of France and in refraining from helping him--a stranger to your country--with arms, with money or with troops.

"My letter is private and confidential, and for that reason I send it to you by a man who shares my most intimate counsels. It anticipates, through a sentiment which your eminence will appreciate, measures to be taken after the events. Oliver Cromwell considered it more expedient to declare himself to a mind as intelligent as Mazarin's than to a queen admirable for firmness, without doubt, but too much guided by vain prejudices of birth and of divine right.

"Farewell, monseigneur; should I not receive a reply in the space of fifteen days, I shall presume my letter will have miscarried.

"Oliver Cromwell."

"Mr. Mordaunt," said the cardinal, raising his voice, as if to arouse the dreamer, "my reply to this letter will be more satisfactory to General Cromwell if I am convinced that all are ignorant of my having given one; go, therefore, and await it at Boulogne-sur-Mer, and promise me to set out to-morrow morning."

"I promise, my lord," replied Mordaunt; "but how many days does your eminence expect me to await your reply?"

"If you do not receive it in ten days you can leave."

Mordaunt bowed.

"That is not all, sir," continued Mazarin; "your private adventures have touched me to the quick; besides, the letter from Mr. Cromwell makes you an important person as ambassador; come, tell me, what can I do for you?"

Mordaunt reflected a moment and, after some hesitation, was about to speak, when Bernouin entered hastily and bending down to the ear of the cardinal, whispered:

"My lord, the Queen Henrietta Maria, accompanied by an English noble, is entering the Palais Royal at this moment."

Mazarin made a bound from his chair, which did not escape the attention of the young man and suppressed the confidence he was about to make.

"Sir," said the cardinal, "you have heard me? I fix on Boulogne because I presume that every town in

France is indifferent to you; if you prefer another, name it; but you can easily conceive that, surrounded as I am by influences I can only muzzle by discretion, I desire your presence in Paris to be unknown."

"I go, sir," said Mordaunt, advancing a few steps to the door by which he had entered.

"No, not that way, I beg, sir," quickly exclaimed the cardinal, "be so good as to pass by yonder gallery, by which you can regain the hall. I do not wish you to be seen leaving; our interview must be kept secret."

Mordaunt followed Bernouin, who led him through the adjacent chamber and left him with a doorkeeper, showing him the way out.

38. Henrietta Maria and Mazarin.

The cardinal rose, and advanced in haste to receive the queen of England. He showed the more respect to this queen, deprived of every mark of pomp and stripped of followers, as he felt some self-reproach for his own want of heart and his avarice. But supplicants for favor know how to accommodate the expression of their features, and the daughter of Henry IV. smiled as she advanced to meet a man she hated and despised.

"Ah!" said Mazarin to himself, "what a sweet face; does she come to borrow money of me?"

And he threw an uneasy glance at his strong box; he even turned inside the bevel of the magnificent diamond ring, the brilliancy of which drew every eye upon his hand, which indeed was white and handsome.

"Your eminence," said the august visitor, "it was my first intention to speak of the matters that have brought me here to the queen, my sister, but I have reflected that political affairs are more especially the concern of men."

"Madame," said Mazarin, "your majesty overwhelms me with flattering distinction."

"He is very gracious," thought the queen; "can he have guessed my errand?"

"Give," continued the cardinal, "your commands to the most respectful of your servants."

"Alas, sir," replied the queen, "I have lost the habit of commanding and have adopted instead that of making petitions. I am here to petition you, too happy should my prayer be favorably heard."

"I am listening, madame, with the greatest interest," said Mazarin.

"Your eminence, it concerns the war which the king, my husband, is now sustaining against his rebellious subjects. You are perhaps ignorant that they are fighting in England," added she, with a melancholy smile, "and that in a short time they will fight in a much more decided fashion than they have done hitherto."

"I am completely ignorant of it, madame," said the cardinal, accompanying his words with a slight shrug of the shoulders; "alas, our own wars quite absorb the time and the mind of a poor, incapable, infirm old minister like me."

"Well, then, your eminence," said the queen, "I must inform you that Charles I., my husband, is on the eve of a decisive engagement. In case of a check" (Mazarin made a slight movement), "one must foresee everything; in the case of a check, he desires to retire into France and to live here as a private individual. What do you say to this project?"

The cardinal had listened without permitting a single fibre of his face to betray what he felt, and his smile remained as it ever was--false and flattering; and when the queen finished speaking, he said:

"Do you think, madame, that France, agitated and disturbed as it is, would be a safe retreat for a dethroned king? How will the crown, which is scarce firmly set on the head of Louis XIV., support a double weight?"

"The weight was not so heavy when I was in peril," interrupted the queen, with a sad smile, "and I ask no more for my husband than has been done for me; you see that we are very humble monarchs, sir."

"Oh, you, madame," the cardinal hastened to say, in order to cut short the explanation he foresaw was coming, "with regard to you, that is another thing. A daughter of Henry IV., of that great, that sublime sovereign----"

"All which does not prevent you refusing hospitality to his son-in-law, sir! Nevertheless, you ought to remember that that great, that sublime monarch, when proscribed at one time, as my husband may be, demanded aid from England and England accorded it to him; and it is but just to say that Queen Elizabeth was not his niece."

"Peccato!" said Mazarin, writhing beneath this simple eloquence, "your majesty does not understand me; you judge my intentions wrongly, and that is partly because, doubtless, I explain myself in French."

"Speak Italian, sir. Ere the cardinal, your predecessor, sent our mother, Marie de Medicis, to die in exile, she taught us that language. If anything yet remains of that great, that sublime king, Henry, of whom you have just spoken, he would be much surprised at so little pity for his family being united to such a profound admiration of himself."

The perspiration stood in large drops on Mazarin's brow.

"That admiration is, on the contrary, so great, so real, madame," returned Mazarin, without noticing the change of language offered to him by the queen, "that if the king, Charles I.--whom Heaven protect from evil!--came into France, I would offer him my house--my own house; but, alas! it would be but an unsafe retreat. Some day the people will burn that house, as they burned that of the Marechal d'Ancre. Poor Concino Concini! And yet he but desired the good of the people."

"Yes, my lord, like yourself!" said the queen, ironically.

Mazarin pretended not to understand the double meaning of his own sentence, but continued to compassionate the fate of Concino Concini.

"Well then, your eminence," said the queen, becoming impatient, "what is your answer?"

"Madame," cried Mazarin, more and more moved, "will your majesty permit me to give you counsel?"

"Speak, sir," replied the queen; "the counsels of so prudent a man as yourself ought certainly to be available."

"Madame, believe me, the king ought to defend himself to the last."

"He has done so, sir, and this last battle, which he encounters with resources much inferior to those of the enemy, proves that he will not yield without a struggle; but in case he is beaten?"

"Well, madame, in that case, my advice--I know that I am very bold to offer advice to your majesty--my advice is that the king should not leave his kingdom. Absent kings are very soon forgotten; if he passes over into France his cause is lost."

"But," persisted the queen, "if such be your advice and you have his interest at heart, send him help of men and money, for I can do nothing for him; I have sold even to my last diamond to aid him. If I had had a single ornament left, I should have bought wood this winter to make a fire for my daughter and myself."

"Oh, madame," said Mazarin, "your majesty knows not what you ask. On the day when foreign succor follows in the train of a king to replace him on his throne, it is an avowal that he no longer possesses the help and love of his own subjects."

"To the point, sir," said the queen, "to the point, and answer me, yes or no; if the king persists in remaining in England will you send him succor? If he comes to France will you accord him hospitality? What do you intend to do? Speak."

"Madame," said the cardinal, affecting an effusive frankness of speech, "I shall convince your majesty, I trust, of my devotion to you and my desire to terminate an affair which you have so much at heart. After which your majesty will, I think, no longer doubt my zeal in your behalf."

The queen bit her lips and moved impatiently on her chair.

"Well, what do you propose to do?" she, said at length; "come, speak."

"I will go this instant and consult the queen, and we will refer the affair at once to parliament."

"With which you are at war--is it not so? You will charge Broussel to report it. Enough, sir, enough. I understand you or rather, I am wrong. Go to the parliament, for it was from this parliament, the enemy of monarchs, that the daughter of the great, the sublime Henry IV., whom you so much admire, received the only relief this winter which prevented her from dying of hunger and cold!"

And with these words Henrietta rose in majestic indignation, whilst the cardinal, raising his hands clasped toward her, exclaimed, "Ah, madame, madame, how little you know me, mon Dieu!"

But Queen Henrietta, without even turning toward him who made these hypocritical pretensions, crossed the cabinet, opened the door for herself and passing through the midst of the cardinal's numerous guards, courtiers eager to pay homage, the luxurious show of a competing royalty, she went and took the hand of De Winter, who stood apart in isolation. Poor queen, already fallen! Though all bowed before her, as etiquette required, she had now but a single arm on which she could lean.

"It signifies little," said Mazarin, when he was alone. "It gave me pain and it was an ungracious part to play, but I have said nothing either to the one or to the other. Bernouin!"

Bernouin entered.

"See if the young man with the black doublet and the short hair, who was with me just now, is still in the palace."

Bernouin went out and soon returned with Comminges, who was on guard.

"Your eminence," said Comminges, "as I was reconducting the young man for whom you have asked, he approached the glass door of the gallery, and gazed intently upon some object, doubtless the picture by Raphael, which is opposite the door. He reflected for a second and then descended the stairs. I believe I saw him mount a gray horse and leave the palace court. But is not your eminence going to the queen?"

"For what purpose?"

"Monsieur de Guitant, my uncle, has just told me that her majesty had received news of the army."

"It is well; I will go."

Comminges had seen rightly, and Mordaunt had really acted as he had related. In crossing the gallery parallel to the large glass gallery, he perceived De Winter, who was waiting until the queen had finished her negotiation.

At this sight the young man stopped short, not in admiration of Raphael's picture, but as if fascinated at the sight of some terrible object. His eyes dilated and a shudder ran through his body. One would have said that he longed to break through the wall of glass which separated him from his enemy; for if Comminges had seen with what an expression of hatred the eyes of this young man were fixed upon De Winter, he would not have doubted for an instant that the Englishman was his eternal foe.

But he stopped, doubtless to reflect; for instead of allowing his first impulse, which had been to go straight to Lord de Winter, to carry him away, he leisurely descended the staircase, left the palace with his head down, mounted his horse, which he reined in at the corner of the Rue Richelieu, and with his eyes fixed on the gate, waited until the queen's carriage had left the court.

He had not long to wait, for the queen scarcely remained a quarter of an hour with Mazarin, but this quarter of an hour of expectation appeared a century to him. At last the heavy machine, which was called a chariot in those days, came out, rumbling against the gates, and De Winter, still on horseback, bent again to the door to converse with her majesty.

The horses started on a trot and took the road to the Louvre, which they entered. Before leaving the convent of the Carmelites, Henrietta had desired her daughter to attend her at the palace, which she had inhabited for a long time and which she had only left because their poverty seemed to them more difficult to bear in gilded chambers.

Mordaunt followed the carriage, and when he had watched it drive beneath the sombre arches he went and stationed himself under a wall over which the shadow was extended, and remained motionless, amidst the moldings of Jean Goujon, like a bas-relievo, representing an equestrian statue.

39. How, sometimes, the Unhappy mistake Chance for Providence.

"Well, madame," said De Winter, when the queen had dismissed her attendants.

"Well, my lord, what I foresaw has come to pass."

"What? does the cardinal refuse to receive the king? France refuse hospitality to an unfortunate prince? Ay, but it is for the first time, madame!"

"I did not say France, my lord; I said the cardinal, and the cardinal is not even a Frenchman."

"But did you see the queen?"

"It is useless," replied Henrietta, "the queen will not say yes when the cardinal says no. Are you not aware that this Italian directs everything, both indoors and out? And moreover, I should not be surprised had we been forestalled by Cromwell. He was embarrassed whilst speaking to me and yet quite firm in his determination to refuse. Then did you not observe the agitation in the Palais Royal, the passing to and fro of busy people? Can they have received any news, my lord?"

"Not from England, madame. I made such haste that I am certain of not having been forestalled. I set out three days ago, passing miraculously through the Puritan army, and I took post horses with my servant Tony; the horses upon which we were mounted were bought in Paris. Besides, the king, I am certain, awaits your majesty's reply before risking anything."

"You will tell him, my lord," resumed the queen, despairingly, "that I can do nothing; that I have suffered as much as himself--more than he has--obliged as I am to eat the bread of exile and to ask hospitality from false friends who smile at my tears; and as regards his royal person, he must sacrifice it generously and die like a king. I shall go and die by his side."

"Madame, madame," exclaimed De Winter, "your majesty abandons yourself to despair; and yet, perhaps, there still remains some hope."

"No friends left, my lord; no other friends left in the wide world but yourself! Oh, God!" exclaimed the poor queen, raising her eyes to Heaven, "have You indeed taken back all the generous hearts that once existed in the world?"

"I hope not, madame," replied De Winter, thoughtfully; "I once spoke to you of four men."

"What can be done with four?"

"Four devoted, resolute men can do much, assure yourself, madame; and those of whom I speak performed great things at one time."

"And where are these four men?"

"Ah, that is what I do not know. It is twenty years since I saw them, and yet whenever I have seen the king in danger I have thought of them."

"And these men were your friends?"

"One of them held my life in his hands and gave it to me. I know not whether he is still my friend, but since that time I have remained his."

"And these men are in France, my lord?"

"I believe so."

"Tell me their names; perhaps I may have heard them mentioned and might be able to aid you in finding them."

"One of them was called the Chevalier d'Artagnan."

"Ah, my lord, if I mistake not, the Chevalier d'Artagnan is lieutenant of royal guards; but take care, for I fear that this man is entirely devoted to the cardinal."

"That would be a misfortune," said De Winter, "and I shall begin to think that we are really doomed."

"But the others," said the queen, who clung to this last hope as a shipwrecked man clings to the hull of his vessel. "The others, my lord!"

"The second--I heard his name by chance; for before fighting us, these four gentlemen told us their names; the second was called the Comte de la Fere. As for the two others, I had so much the habit of calling them by nicknames that I have forgotten their real ones."

"Oh, mon Dieu, it is a matter of the greatest urgency to find them out," said the queen, "since you think these worthy gentlemen might be so useful to the king."

"Oh, yes," said De Winter, "for they are the same men. Listen, madame, and recall your remembrances. Have you never heard that Queen Anne of Austria was once saved from the greatest danger ever incurred by a queen?"

"Yes, at the time of her relations with Monsieur de Buckingham; it had to do in some way with certain studs and diamonds."

"Well, it was that affair, madame; these men are the ones who saved her; and I smile with pity when I reflect that if the names of those gentlemen are unknown to you it is because the queen has forgotten them, who ought to have made them the first noblemen of the realm."

"Well, then, my lord, they must be found; but what can four men, or rather three men do--for I tell you, you must not count on Monsieur d'Artagnan."

"It will be one valiant sword the less, but there will remain still three, without reckoning my own; now four devoted men around the king to protect him from his enemies, to be at his side in battle, to aid him with counsel, to escort him in flight, are sufficient, not to make the king a conqueror, but to save him if conquered; and whatever Mazarin may say, once on the shores of France your royal husband may find as many retreats and asylums as the seabird finds in a storm."

"Seek, then, my lord, seek these gentlemen; and if they will consent to go with you to England, I will give to each a duchy the day that we reascend the throne, besides as much gold as would pave Whitehall. Seek them, my lord, and find them, I conjure you."

"I will search for them, madame," said De Winter "and doubtless I shall find them; but time fails me. Has your majesty forgotten that the king expects your reply and awaits it in agony?"

"Then indeed we are lost!" cried the queen, in the fullness of a broken heart.

At this moment the door opened and the young Henrietta appeared; then the queen, with that wonderful strength which is the privilege of parents, repressed her tears and motioned to De Winter to change the subject.

But that act of self-control, effective as it was, did not escape the eyes of the young princess. She stopped on the threshold, breathed a sigh, and addressing the queen:

"Why, then, do you always weep, mother, when I am away from you?" she said.

The queen smiled, but instead of answering:

"See, De Winter," she said, "I have at least gained one thing in being only half a queen; and that is that my children call me 'mother' instead of 'madame.'"

Then turning toward her daughter:

"What do you want, Henrietta?" she demanded.

"My mother," replied the young princess, "a cavalier has just entered the Louvre and wishes to present his respects to your majesty; he arrives from the army and has, he says, a letter to remit to you, on the part of the Marechal de Grammont, I think."

"Ah!" said the queen to De Winter, "he is one of my faithful adherents; but do you not observe, my dear lord, that we are so poorly served that it is left to my daughter to fill the office of doorkeeper?"

"Madame, have pity on me," exclaimed De Winter; "you wring my heart!"

"And who is this cavalier, Henrietta?" asked the queen.

"I saw him from the window, madame; he is a young man that appears scarce sixteen years of age, and is called the Viscount de Bragelonne."

The queen, smiling, made a sign with her head; the young princess opened the door and Raoul appeared on the threshold.

Advancing a few steps toward the queen, he knelt down.

"Madame," said he, "I bear to your majesty a letter from my friend the Count de Guiche, who told me he had the honor of being your servant; this letter contains important news and the expression of his respect."

At the name of the Count de Guiche a blush spread over the cheeks of the young princess and the queen glanced at her with some degree of severity.

"You told me that the letter was from the Marechal de Grammont, Henrietta!" said the queen.

"I thought so, madame," stammered the young girl.

"It is my fault, madame," said Raoul. "I did announce myself, in truth, as coming on the part of the Marechal de Grammont; but being wounded in the right arm he was unable to write and therefore the Count de Guiche acted as his secretary."

"There has been fighting, then?" asked the queen, motioning to Raoul to rise.

"Yes, madame," said the young man.

At this announcement of a battle having taken place, the princess opened her mouth as though to ask a question of interest; but her lips closed again without articulating a word, while the color gradually faded from her cheeks.

The queen saw this, and doubtless her maternal heart translated the emotion, for addressing Raoul again:

"And no evil has happened to the young Count de Guiche?" she asked; "for not only is he our servant, as you say, sir, but more--he is one of our friends."

"No, madame," replied Raoul; "on the contrary, he gained great glory and had the honor of being embraced by his highness, the prince, on the field of battle."

The young princess clapped her hands; and then, ashamed of having been betrayed into such a demonstration of joy, she half turned away and bent over a vase of roses, as if to inhale their odor.

"Let us see," said the queen, "what the count says." And she opened the letter and read:

"Madame,--Being unable to have the honor of writing to you myself, by reason of a wound I have received in my right hand, I have commanded my son, the Count de Guiche, who, with his father, is equally your humble servant, to write to tell you that we have just gained the battle of Lens, and that this victory cannot fail to give great power to Cardinal Mazarin and to the queen over the affairs of Europe. If her majesty will have faith in my counsels she ought to profit by this event to address at this moment, in favor of her august husband, the court of France. The Vicomte de Bragelonne, who will have the honor of remitting this letter to your majesty, is the friend of my son, who owes to him his life; he is a gentleman in whom your majesty may confide entirely, in case your majesty may have some verbal or written order to remit to me.

"I have the honor to be, with respect, etc.,

"Marechal de Grammont."

At the moment mention occurred of his having rendered a service to the count, Raoul could not help turning his glance toward the young princess, and then he saw in her eyes an expression of infinite gratitude to the young man; he no longer doubted that the daughter of King Charles I. loved his friend.

"The battle of Lens gained!" said the queen; "they are lucky here indeed; they can gain battles! Yes, the Marechal de Grammont is right; this will change the aspect of French affairs, but I much fear it will do nothing for English, even if it does not harm them. This is recent news, sir," continued she, "and I thank you for having made such haste to bring it to me; without this letter I should not have heard till to-morrow, perhaps after to-morrow--the last of all Paris."

"Madame," said Raoul, "the Louvre is but the second palace this news has reached; it is as yet unknown to all, and I had sworn to the Count de Guiche to remit this letter to your majesty before even I should embrace my guardian."

"Your guardian! is he, too, a Bragelonne?" asked Lord de Winter. "I once knew a Bragelonne--is he still alive?"

"No, sir, he is dead; and I believe it is from him my guardian, whose near relation he was, inherited the estate from which I take my name."

"And your guardian, sir," asked the queen, who could not help feeling some interest in the handsome young man before her, "what is his name?"

"The Comte de la Fere, madame," replied the young man, bowing.

De Winter made a gesture of surprise and the queen turned to him with a start of joy.

"The Comte de la Fere!" she cried. "Have you not mentioned that name to me?"

As for De Winter he could scarcely believe that he had heard aright. "The Comte de la Fere!" he cried in his turn. "Oh, sir, reply, I entreat you--is not the Comte de la Fere a noble whom I remember, handsome and brave, a musketeer under Louis XIII., who must be now about forty-seven or forty-eight years of age?"

"Yes, sir, you are right in every particular!"

"And who served under an assumed name?"

"Under the name of Athos. Latterly I heard his friend, Monsieur d'Artagnan, give him that name."

"That is it, madame, that is the same. God be praised! And he is in Paris?" continued he, addressing Raoul; then turning to the queen: "We may still hope. Providence has declared for us, since I have found this brave man again in so miraculous a manner. And, sir, where does he reside, pray?"

"The Comte de la Fere lodges in the Rue Guenegaud, Hotel du Grand Roi Charlemagne."

"Thanks, sir. Inform this dear friend that he may remain within, that I shall go and see him immediately."

"Sir, I obey with pleasure, if her majesty will permit me to depart."

"Go, Monsieur de Bragelonne," said the queen, "and rest assured of our affection."

Raoul bent respectfully before the two princesses, and bowing to De Winter, departed.

The queen and De Winter continued to converse for some time in low voices, in order that the young princess should not overhear them; but the precaution was needless: she was in deep converse with her own thoughts.

Then, when De Winter rose to take leave:

"Listen, my lord," said the queen; "I have preserved this diamond cross which came from my mother, and this order of St. Michael which came from my husband. They are worth about fifty thousand pounds. I had sworn to die of hunger rather than part with these precious pledges; but now that this ornament may be useful to him or his defenders, everything must be sacrificed. Take them, and if you need money for your expedition, sell them fearlessly, my lord. But should you find the means of retaining them, remember, my lord, that I shall esteem you as having rendered the greatest service that a gentleman can render to a queen; and in the day of my prosperity he who brings me this order and this cross shall be blessed by me and my children."

"Madame," replied De Winter, "your majesty will be served by a man devoted to you. I hasten to deposit these two objects in a safe place, nor should I accept them if the resources of our ancient fortune were left to us, but our estates are confiscated, our ready money is exhausted, and we are reduced to turn to service everything we possess. In an hour hence I shall be with the Comte de la Fere, and tomorrow your majesty shall have a definite reply."

The queen tendered her hand to Lord de Winter, who, kissing it respectfully, went out and traversed alone and unconducted those large, dark and deserted apartments, brushing away tears which, blase as he was by fifty years spent as a courtier, he could not withhold at the spectacle of royal distress so dignified, yet so intense.

40. Uncle and Nephew.

The horse and servant belonging to De Winter were waiting for him at the door; he proceeded toward his abode very thoughtfully, looking behind him from time to him to contemplate the dark and silent frontage of the Louvre. It was then that he saw a horseman, as it were, detach himself from the wall and follow him at a little distance. In leaving the Palais Royal he remembered to have observed a similar shadow.

"Tony," he said, motioning to his groom to approach.

"Here I am, my lord."

"Did you remark that man who is following us?"

"Yes, my lord."

"Who is he?"

"I do not know, only he has followed your grace from the Palais Royal, stopped at the Louvre to wait for you, and now leaves the Louvre with you."

"Some spy of the cardinal," said De Winter to him, aside. "Let us pretend not to notice that he is watching us."

And spurring on he plunged into the labyrinth of streets which led to his hotel, situated near the Marais, for having for so long a time lived near the Place Royale, Lord de Winter naturally returned to lodge near his ancient dwelling.

The unknown spurred his horse to a gallop.

De Winter dismounted at his hotel and went up into his apartment, intending to watch the spy; but as he was about to place his gloves and hat on a table, he saw reflected in a glass opposite to him a figure which stood on the threshold of the room. He turned around and Mordaunt stood before him.

There was a moment of frozen silence between these two.

"Sir," said De Winter, "I thought I had already made you aware that I am weary of this persecution; withdraw, then, or I shall call and have you turned out as you were in London. I am not your uncle, I know you not."

"My uncle," replied Mordaunt, with his harsh and bantering tone, "you are mistaken; you will not have me turned out this time as you did in London--you dare not. As for denying that I am your nephew, you will think twice about it, now that I have learned some things of which I was ignorant a year ago."

"And how does it concern me what you have learned?" said De Winter.

"Oh, it concerns you very closely, my uncle, I am sure, and you will soon be of my opinion," added he, with a smile which sent a shudder through the veins of him he thus addressed. "When I presented myself before you for the first time in London, it was to ask you what had become of my fortune; the second time it was to demand who had sullied my name; and this time I come before you to ask a question far more terrible than any other, to say to you as God said to the first murderer: 'Cain, what hast thou done to thy brother Abel?' My lord, what have you done with your sister--your sister, who was my mother?"

De Winter shrank back from the fire of those scorching eyes.

"Your mother?" he said.

"Yes, my lord, my mother," replied the young man, advancing into the room until he was face to face with Lord de Winter, and crossing his arms. "I have asked the headsman of Bethune," he said, his voice hoarse and his face livid with passion and grief. "And the headsman of Bethune gave me a reply."

De Winter fell back in a chair as though struck by a thunderbolt and in vain attempted a reply.

"Yes," continued the young man; "all is now explained; with this key I open the abyss. My mother inherited an estate from her husband, you have assassinated her; my name would have secured me the paternal estate, you have deprived me of it; you have despoiled me of my fortune. I am no longer astonished that you knew me not. I am not surprised that you refused to recognize me. When a man is a robber it is hard to call him nephew whom he has impoverished; when one is a murderer, to recognize the man whom one has made an orphan."

These words produced a contrary effect to that which Mordaunt had anticipated. De Winter remembered the monster that Milady had been; he rose, dignified and calm, restraining by the severity of his look the wild glance of the young man.

"You desire to fathom this horrible secret?" said De Winter; "well, then, so be it. Know, then, what manner of woman it was for whom to-day you call me to account. That woman had, in all probability, poisoned my brother, and in order to inherit from me she was about to assassinate me in my turn. I have proof of it. What say you to that?"

"I say that she was my mother."

"She caused the unfortunate Duke of Buckingham to be stabbed by a man who was, ere that, honest, good and pure. What say you to that crime, of which I have the proof?"

"She was my mother."

"On our return to France she had a young woman who was attached to one of her opponents poisoned in the convent of the Augustines at Bethune. Will this crime persuade you of the justice of her punishment--for of all this I have the proofs?"

"She was my mother!" cried the young man, who uttered these three successive exclamations with constantly increasing force.

"At last, charged with murders, with debauchery, hated by every one and yet threatening still, like a panther thirsting for blood, she fell under the blows of men whom she had rendered desperate, though they had never done her the least injury; she met with judges whom her hideous crimes had evoked; and that executioner you saw--that executioner who you say told you everything--that executioner, if he told you everything, told you that he leaped with joy in avenging on her his brother's shame and suicide. Depraved as a girl, adulterous as a wife, an unnatural sister, homicide, poisoner, execrated by all who knew her, by every nation that had been visited by her, she died accursed by Heaven and earth."

A sob which Mordaunt could not repress burst from his throat and his livid face became suffused with blood; he clenched his fists, sweat covered his face, his hair, like Hamlet's, stood on end, and racked with fury he cried out:

"Silence, sir! she was my mother! Her crimes, I know them not; her disorders, I know them not; her vices, I know them not. But this I know, that I had a mother, that five men leagued against one woman, murdered her clandestinely by night--silently--like cowards. I know that you were one of them, my uncle, and that you cried louder than the others: 'She must die.' Therefore I warn you, and listen well to my words, that they may be engraved upon your memory, never to be forgotten: this murder, which has robbed me of everything--this murder, which has deprived me of my name--this murder, which has impoverished me--this murder, which has made me corrupt, wicked, implacable--I shall summon you to account for it first and then those who were your accomplices, when I discover them!"

With hatred in his eyes, foaming at his mouth, and his fist extended, Mordaunt had advanced one more step, a threatening, terrible step, toward De Winter. The latter put his hand to his sword, and said, with the smile of a man who for thirty years has jested with death:

"Would you assassinate me, sir? Then I shall recognize you as my nephew, for you would be a worthy son of such a mother."

"No," replied Mordaunt, forcing his features and the muscles of his body to resume their usual places and be calm; "no, I shall not kill you; at least not at this moment, for without you I could not discover the others. But when I have found them, then tremble, sir. I stabbed to the heart the headsman of Bethune, without mercy or pity, and he was the least guilty of you all."

With these words the young man went out and descended the stairs with sufficient calmness to pass unobserved; then upon the lowest landing place he passed Tony, leaning over the balustrade, waiting only for a call from his master to mount to his room.

But De Winter did not call; crushed, enfeebled, he remained standing and with listening ear; then only when he had heard the step of the horse going away he fell back on a chair, saying:

"My God, I thank Thee that he knows me only."

41. Paternal Affection.

Whilst this terrible scene was passing at Lord de Winter's, Athos, seated near his window, his elbow on the table and his head supported on his hand, was listening intently to Raoul's account of the adventures he met with on his journey and the details of the battle.

Listening to the relation of those emotions so fresh and pure, the fine, noble face of Athos betrayed indescribable pleasure; he inhaled the tones of that young voice, as harmonious music. He forgot all that was dark in the past and that was cloudy in the future. It almost seemed as if the return of this much loved boy had changed his fears to hopes. Athos was happy--happy as he had never been before.

"And you assisted and took part in this great battle, Bragelonne!" cried the former musketeer.

"Yes, sir."

"And it was a fierce one?"

"His highness the prince charged eleven times in person."

"He is a great commander, Bragelonne."

"He is a hero, sir. I did not lose sight of him for an instant. Oh! how fine it is to be called Conde and to be so worthy of such a name!"

"He was calm and radiant, was he not?"

"As calm as at parade, radiant as at a fete. When we went up to the enemy it was slowly; we were forbidden to draw first and we were marching toward the Spaniards, who were on a height with lowered muskets. When we arrived about thirty paces from them the prince turned around to the soldiers: 'Comrades,' he said, 'you are about to suffer a furious discharge; but after that you will make short work with those fellows.' There was such dead silence that friends and enemies could have heard these words; then raising his sword, 'Sound trumpets!' he cried."

"Well, very good; you will do as much when the opportunity occurs, will you, Raoul?"

"I know not, sir, but I thought it really very fine and grand!"

"Were you afraid, Raoul?" asked the count.

"Yes, sir," replied the young man naively; "I felt a great chill at my heart, and at the word 'fire,' which resounded in Spanish from the enemy's ranks, I closed my eyes and thought of you."

"In honest truth, Raoul?" said Athos, pressing his hand.

"Yes, sir; at that instant there was such a rataplan of musketry that one might have imagined the infernal regions had opened. Those who were not killed felt the heat of the flames. I opened my eyes, astonished to find myself alive and even unhurt; a third of the squadron were lying on the ground, wounded, dead or dying. At that moment I encountered the eye of the prince. I had but one thought and that was that he was observing me. I spurred on and found myself in the enemy's ranks."

"And the prince was pleased with you?"

"He told me so, at least, sir, when he desired me to return to Paris with Monsieur de Chatillon, who was charged to carry the news to the queen and to bring the colors we had taken. 'Go,' said he; 'the enemy will not rally for fifteen days and until that time I have no need of your service. Go and see those whom you love and who love you, and tell my sister De Longueville that I thank her for the present that she made me of you.' And I came, sir," added Raoul, gazing at the count with a smile of real affection, "for I thought you would be glad to see me again."

Athos drew the young man toward him and pressed his lips to his brow, as he would have done to a young daughter.

"And now, Raoul," said he, "you are launched; you have dukes for friends, a marshal of France for godfather, a prince of the blood as commander, and on the day of your return you have been received by two queens; it is not so bad for a novice."

"Oh sir," said Raoul, suddenly, "you recall something, which, in my haste to relate my exploits, I had forgotten; it is that there was with Her Majesty the Queen of England, a gentleman who, when I pronounced your name, uttered a cry of surprise and joy;

he said he was a friend of yours, asked your address, and is coming to see you."

"What is his name?"

"I did not venture to ask, sir; he spoke elegantly, although I thought from his accent he was an Englishman."

"Ah!" said Athos, leaning down his head as if to remember who it could be. Then, when he raised it again, he was struck by the presence of a man who was standing at the open door and was gazing at him with a compassionate air.

"Lord de Winter!" exclaimed the count.

"Athos, my friend!"

And the two gentlemen were for an instant locked in each other's arms; then Athos, looking into his friend's face and taking him by both hands, said:

"What ails you, my lord? you appear as unhappy as I am the reverse."

"Yes, truly, dear friend; and I may even say the sight of you increases my dismay."

And De Winter glancing around him, Raoul quickly understood that the two friends wished to be alone and he therefore left the room unaffectedly.

"Come, now that we are alone," said Athos, "let us talk of yourself."

"Whilst we are alone let us speak of ourselves," replied De Winter. "He is here."

"Who?"

"Milady's son."

Athos, again struck by this name, which seemed to pursue him like an echo, hesitated for a moment, then slightly knitting his brows, he calmly said:

"I know it, Grimaud met him between Bethune and Arras and then came here to warn me of his presence."

"Does Grimaud know him, then?"

"No; but he was present at the deathbed of a man who knew him."

"The headsman of Bethune?" exclaimed De Winter.

"You know about that?" cried Athos, astonished.

"He has just left me," replied De Winter, "after telling me all. Ah! my friend! what a horrible scene! Why did we not destroy the child with the mother?"

"What need you fear?" said Athos, recovering from the instinctive fear he had at first experienced, by the aid of reason; "are we not men accustomed to defend ourselves? Is this young man an assassin by profession--a murderer in cold blood? He has killed the executioner of Bethune in an access of passion, but now his fury is assuaged."

De Winter smiled sorrowfully and shook his head.

"Do you not know the race?" said he.

"Pooh!" said Athos, trying to smile in his turn. "It must have lost its ferocity in the second generation. Besides, my friend, Providence has warned us, that we may be on our guard. All we can now do is to wait. Let us wait; and, as I said before, let us speak of yourself. What brings you to Paris?"

"Affairs of importance which you shall know later. But what is this that I hear from Her Majesty the Queen of England? Monsieur d'Artagnan sides with Mazarin! Pardon my frankness, dear friend. I neither hate nor blame the cardinal, and your opinions will be held ever sacred by me. But do you happen to belong to him?"

"Monsieur d'Artagnan," replied Athos, "is in the service; he is a soldier and obeys all constitutional authority. Monsieur d'Artagnan is not rich and has need of his position as lieutenant to enable him to live. Millionaires like yourself, my lord, are rare in France."

"Alas!" said De Winter, "I am at this moment as poor as he is, if not poorer. But to return to our subject."

"Well, then, you wish to know if I am of Mazarin's party? No. Pardon my frankness, too, my lord."

"I am obliged to you, count, for this pleasing intelligence! You make me young and happy again by it. Ah! so you are not a Mazarinist? Delightful! Indeed, you could not belong to him. But pardon me, are you free? I mean to ask if you are married?"

"Ah! as to that, no," replied Athos, laughing.

"Because that young man, so handsome, so elegant, so polished----"

"Is a child I have adopted and who does not even know who was his father."

"Very well; you are always the same, Athos, great and generous. Are you still friends with Monsieur Porthos and Monsieur Aramis?"

"Add Monsieur d'Artagnan, my lord. We still remain four friends devoted to each other; but when it becomes a question of serving the cardinal or of fighting him, of being Mazarinists or Frondists, then we are only two."

"Is Monsieur Aramis with D'Artagnan?" asked Lord de Winter.

"No," said Athos; "Monsieur Aramis does me the honor to share my opinions."

"Could you put me in communication with your witty and agreeable friend? Is he much changed?"

"He has become an abbe, that is all."

"You alarm me; his profession must have made him renounce any great undertakings."

"On the contrary," said Athos, smiling, "he has never been so much a musketeer as since he became an abbe, and you will find him a veritable soldier."

"Could you engage to bring him to me to-morrow morning at ten o'clock, on the Pont du Louvre?"

"Oh, oh!" exclaimed Athos, smiling, "you have a duel in prospect."

"Yes, count, and a splendid duel, too; a duel in which I hope you will take your part."

"Where are we to go, my lord?"

"To Her Majesty the Queen of England, who has desired me to present you to her."

"This is an enigma," said Athos, "but it matters not; since you know the solution of it I ask no further. Will your lordship do me the honor to sup with me?"

"Thanks, count, no," replied De Winter. "I own to you that that young man's visit has subdued my appetite and probably will rob me of my sleep. What undertaking can have brought him to Paris? It was not to meet me that he came, for he was ignorant of my journey. This young man terrifies me, my lord; there lies in him a sanguinary predisposition."

"What occupies him in England?"

"He is one of Cromwell's most enthusiastic disciples."

"But what attached him to the cause? His father and mother were Catholics, I believe?"

"His hatred of the king, who deprived him of his estates and forbade him to bear the name of De Winter."

"And what name does he now bear?"

"Mordaunt."

"A Puritan, yet disguised as a monk he travels alone in France."

"Do you say as a monk?"

"It was thus, and by mere accident--may God pardon me if I blaspheme--that he heard the confession of the executioner of Bethune."

"Then I understand it all! he has been sent by Cromwell to Mazarin, and the queen guessed rightly; we have been forestalled. Everything is clear to me now. Adieu, count, till to-morrow."

"But the night is dark," said Athos, perceiving that Lord de Winter seemed more uneasy than he wished to appear; "and you have no servant."

"I have Tony, a safe if simple youth."

"Halloo, there, Grimaud, Olivain, and Blaisois! call the viscount and take the musket with you."

Blaisois was the tall youth, half groom, half peasant, whom we saw at the Chateau de Bragelonne, whom Athos had christened by the name of his province.

"Viscount," said Athos to Raoul, as he entered, "you will conduct my lord as far as his hotel and permit no one to approach him."

"Oh! count," said De Winter, "for whom do you take me?"

"For a stranger who does not know Paris," said Athos, "and to whom the viscount will show the way."

De Winter shook him by the hand.

"Grimaud," said Athos, "put yourself at the head of the troop and beware of the monk."

Grimaud shuddered, and nodding, awaited the departure, regarding the butt of his musket with silent eloquence. Then obeying the orders given him by Athos, he headed the small procession, bearing the torch in one hand and the musket in the other, until it reached De Winter's inn, when pounding on the portal with his fist, he bowed to my lord and faced about without a word.

The same order was followed in returning, nor did Grimaud's searching glance discover anything of a suspicious appearance, save a dark shadow, as it were, in ambuscade, at the corner of the Rue Guenegaud and of the Quai. He fancied, also, that in going he had already observed the street watcher who had attracted his attention. He pushed on toward him, but before he could reach it the shadow had disappeared into an alley, into which Grimaud deemed it scarcely prudent to pursue it.

The next day, on awaking, the count perceived Raoul by his bedside. The young man was already dressed and was reading a new book by M. Chapelain.

"Already up, Raoul?" exclaimed the count.

"Yes, sir," replied Raoul, with slight hesitation; "I did not sleep well."

"You, Raoul, not sleep well! then you must have something on your mind!" said Athos.

"Sir, you will perhaps think that I am in a great hurry to leave you when I have only just arrived, but---"

"Have you only two days of leave, Raoul?"

"On the contrary, sir, I have ten; nor is it to the camp I wish to go."

"Where, then?" said Athos, smiling, "if it be not a secret. You are now almost a man, since you have made your first passage of arms, and have acquired the right to go where you will without consulting me."

"Never, sir," said Raoul, "as long as I possess the happiness of having you for a protector, shall I deem I have the right of freeing myself from a guardianship so valuable to me. I have, however, a wish to go and pass a day at Blois. You look at me and you are going to laugh at me."

"No, on the contrary, I am not inclined to laugh," said Athos, suppressing a sigh. "You wish to see Blois again; it is but natural."

"Then you permit me to go, you are not angry in your heart?" exclaimed Raoul, joyously.

"Certainly; and why should I regret what gives you pleasure?"

"Oh! how kind you are," exclaimed the young man, pressing his guardian's hand; "and I can set out immediately?"

"When you like, Raoul."

"Sir," said Raoul, as he turned to leave the room, "I have thought of one thing, and that is about the Duchess of Chevreuse, who was so kind to me and to whom I owe my introduction to the prince."

"And you ought to thank her, Raoul. Well, try the Hotel de Luynes, Raoul, and ask if the duchess can receive you. I am glad to see you pay attention to the usages of the world. You must take Grimaud and Olivain."

"Both, sir?" asked Raoul, astonished.

"Both."

Raoul went out, and when Athos heard his young, joyous voice calling to Grimaud and Olivain, he sighed.

"It is very soon to leave me," he thought, "but he follows the common custom. Nature has made us thus; she makes the young look ever forward, not behind. He certainly likes the child, but will he love me less as his affection grows for her?"

And Athos confessed to himself that, he was unprepared for so prompt a departure; but Raoul was so happy that this reflection effaced everything else from the consideration of his guardian.

Everything was ready at ten o'clock for the departure, and as Athos was watching Raoul mount, a groom rode up from the Duchess de Chevreuse. He was charged to tell the Comte de la Fere, that she had learned of the return of her youthful protege, and also the manner he had conducted himself on the field, and she added that she should be very glad to offer him her congratulations.

"Tell her grace," replied Athos, "that the viscount has just mounted his horse to proceed to the Hotel de Luynes."

Then, with renewed instructions to Grimaud, Athos signified to Raoul that he could set out, and ended by reflecting that it was perhaps better that Raoul should be away from Paris at that moment.

42. Another Queen in Want of Help.

Athos had not failed to send early to Aramis and had given his letter to Blaisois, the only serving-man whom he had left. Blaisois found Bazin donning his beadle's gown, his services being required that day at Notre Dame.

Athos had desired Blaisois to try to speak to Aramis himself. Blaisois, a tall, simple youth, who understood nothing but what he was expressly told, asked, therefore for the Abbe d'Herblay, and in spite of Bazin's assurances that his master was not at home, he persisted in such a manner as to put Bazin into a passion. Blaisois seeing Bazin in clerical guise, was a little discomposed at his denials and wanted to pass at all risks, believing too, that the man with whom he had to do was endowed with the virtues of his cloth, namely, patience and Christian charity.

But Bazin, still the servant of a musketeer, when once the blood mounted to his fat cheeks, seized a broomstick and began belaboring Blaisois, saying:

"You have insulted the church, my friend, you have insulted the church!"

At this moment Aramis, aroused by this unusual disturbance, cautiously opened the door of his room; and Blaisois, looking reproachfully at the Cerberus, drew the letter from his pocket and presented it to Aramis.

"From the Comte de la Fere," said Aramis. "All right." And he retired into his room without even asking the cause of so much noise.

Blaisois returned disconsolate to the Hotel of the Grand Roi Charlemagne and when Athos inquired if his commission was executed, he related his adventure.

"You foolish fellow!" said Athos, laughing. "And you did not tell him that you came from me?"

"No, sir."

At ten o'clock Athos, with his habitual exactitude, was waiting on the Pont du Louvre and was almost immediately joined by Lord de Winter.

They waited ten minutes and then his lordship began to fear Aramis was not coming to join them.

"Patience," said Athos, whose eyes were fixed in the direction of the Rue du Bac, "patience; I see an abbe cuffing a man, then bowing to a woman; it must be Aramis."

It was indeed Aramis. Having run against a young shopkeeper who was gaping at the crows and who had splashed him, Aramis with one blow of his fist had distanced him ten paces.

At this moment one of his penitents passed, and as she was young and pretty Aramis took off his cap to her with his most gracious smile.

A most affectionate greeting, as one can well believe took place between him and Lord de Winter.

"Where are we going?" inquired Aramis; "are we going to fight, perchance? I carry no sword this morning and cannot return home to procure one."

"No," said Lord de Winter, "we are going to pay a visit to Her Majesty the Queen of England."

"Oh, very well," replied Aramis; then bending his face down to Athos's ear, "what is the object of this visit?" continued he.

"Nay, I know not; some evidence required from us, perhaps."

"May it not be about that cursed affair?" asked Aramis, "in which case I do not greatly care to go, for it will be to pocket a lecture; and since it is my function to give them to others I am rather averse to receiving them myself."

"If it were so," answered Athos, "we should not be taken there by Lord de Winter, for he would come in for his share; he was one of us."

"You're right; yes, let us go."

On arriving at the Louvre Lord de Winter entered first; indeed, there was but one porter there to receive them at the gate.

It was impossible in daylight for the impoverished state of the habitation grudging charity had conceded to an unfortunate queen to pass unnoticed by Athos, Aramis, and even the Englishman. Large rooms, completely stripped of furniture, bare walls upon which, here and there, shone the old gold moldings which had resisted time and neglect, windows with broken panes (impossible to close), no carpets, neither guards nor servants: this is what first met the eyes of Athos, to which he, touching his companion's elbow, directed his attention by his glances.

"Mazarin is better lodged," said Aramis.

"Mazarin is almost king," answered Athos; "Madame Henrietta is almost no longer queen."

"If you would condescend to be clever, Athos," observed Aramis, "I really do think you would be wittier than poor Monsieur de Voiture."

Athos smiled.

The queen appeared to be impatiently expecting them, for at the first slight noise she heard in the hall leading to her room she came herself to the door to receive these courtiers in the corridors of Misfortune.

"Enter. You are welcome, gentlemen," she said.

The gentlemen entered and remained standing, but at a motion from the queen they seated themselves. Athos was calm and grave, but Aramis was furious; the sight of such royal misery exasperated him and his eyes examined every new trace of poverty that presented itself.

"You are examining the luxury I enjoy," said the queen, glancing sadly around her.

"Madame," replied Aramis, "I must ask your pardon, but I know not how to hide my indignation at seeing how a daughter of Henry IV. is treated at the court of France."

"Monsieur Aramis is not an officer?" asked the queen of Lord de Winter.

"That gentleman is the Abbe d'Herblay," replied he.

Aramis blushed. "Madame," he said, "I am an abbe, it is true, but I am so against my will. I never had a vocation for the bands; my cassock is fastened by one button only, and I am always ready to become a musketeer once more. This morning, being ignorant that I should have the honor of seeing your majesty, I encumbered myself with this dress, but you will find me none the less a man devoted to your majesty's service, in whatever way you may see fit to use me."

"The Abbe d'Herblay," resumed De Winter, "is one of those gallant musketeers formerly belonging to His Majesty King Louis XIII., of whom I have spoken to you, madame." Then turning to Athos, he continued, "And this gentleman is that noble Comte de la Fere, whose high reputation is so well known to your majesty."

"Gentlemen," said the queen, "a few years ago I had around me ushers, treasures, armies; and by the lifting of a finger all these were busied in my service. To-day, look around you, and it may astonish you, that in order to accomplish a plan which is dearer to me than life I have only Lord de Winter, the friend of twenty years, and you, gentlemen, whom I see for the first time and whom I know but as my countrymen."

"It is enough," said Athos, bowing low, "if the lives of three men can purchase yours, madame."

"I thank you, gentlemen. But hear me," continued she. "I am not only the most miserable of queens, but the most unhappy of mothers, the most wretched of wives. My children, two of them, at least, the Duke of York and the Princess Elizabeth, are far away from me, exposed to the blows of the ambitious and our foes; my husband, the king, is leading in England so wretched an existence that it is no exaggeration to aver that he seeks death as a thing to be desired. Hold! gentlemen, here is the letter conveyed to me by Lord de Winter. Read it."

Obeying the queen, Athos read aloud the letter which we have already seen, in which King Charles demanded to know whether the hospitality of France would be accorded him.

"Well?" asked Athos, when he had closed the letter.

"Well," said the queen, "it has been refused."

The two friends exchanged a smile of contempt.

"And now," said Athos, "what is to be done? I have the honor to inquire from your majesty what you desire Monsieur d'Herblay and myself to do in your service. We are ready."

"Ah, sir, you have a noble heart!" exclaimed the queen, with a burst of gratitude; whilst Lord de Winter turned to her with a glance which said, "Did I not answer for them?"

"But you, sir?" said the queen to Aramis.

"I, madame," replied he, "follow Monsieur de la Fere wherever he leads, even were it on to death, without demanding wherefore; but when it concerns your majesty's service, then," added he, looking at the queen with all the grace of former days, "I precede the count."

"Well, then, gentlemen," said the queen, "since it is thus, and since you are willing to devote yourselves to the service of a poor princess whom the whole world has abandoned, this is what is required to be done for me. The king is alone with a few gentlemen, whom he fears to lose every day; surrounded by the Scotch, whom he distrusts, although he be himself a Scotchman. Since Lord de Winter left him I am distracted, sirs. I ask much, too much, perhaps, for I have no title to request it. Go to England, join the king, be his friends, protectors, march to battle at his side, and be near him in his house, where conspiracies, more dangerous than the perils of war, are hatching every day. And in exchange for the sacrifice that you make, gentlemen, I promise--not to reward you, I believe that word would offend you--but to love you as a sister, to prefer you, next to my husband and my children, to every one. I swear it before Heaven."

And the queen raised her eyes solemnly upward.

"Madame," said Athos, "when must we set out?"

"You consent then?" exclaimed the queen, joyfully.

"Yes, madame; only it seems to me that your majesty goes too far in engaging to load us with a friendship so far above our merit. We render service to God, madame, in serving a prince so unfortunate, a queen so virtuous. Madame, we are yours, body and soul."

"Oh, sirs," said the queen, moved even to tears, "this is the first time for five years I have felt the least approach to joy or hope. God, who can read my heart, all the gratitude I feel, will reward you! Save my husband! Save the king, and although you care not for the price that is placed upon a good action in this world, leave me the hope that we shall meet again, when I may be able to thank you myself. In the meantime, I remain here. Have you anything to ask of me? From this moment I become your friend, and since you are engaged in my affairs I ought to occupy myself in yours."

"Madame," replied Athos, "I have only to ask your majesty's prayers."

"And I," said Aramis, "I am alone in the world and have only your majesty to serve."

The queen held out her hand, which they kissed, and she said in a low tone to De Winter:

"If you need money, my lord, separate the jewels I have given you; detach the diamonds and sell them to some Jew. You will receive for them fifty or sixty thousand francs; spend them if necessary, but let these gentlemen be treated as they deserve, that is to say, like kings."

The queen had two letters ready, one written by herself, the other by her daughter, the Princess Henrietta. Both were addressed to King Charles. She gave the first to Athos and the other to Aramis, so that should they be separated by chance they might make themselves known to the king; after which they withdrew.

At the foot of the staircase De Winter stopped.

"Not to arouse suspicions, gentlemen," said he, "go your way and I will go mine, and this evening at nine o'clock we will assemble again at the Gate Saint Denis. We will travel on horseback as far as our horses can go and afterward we can take the post. Once more, let me thank you, my good friends, both in my own name and the queen's."

The three gentlemen then shook hands, Lord de Winter taking the Rue Saint Honore, and Athos and Aramis remaining together.

"Well," said Aramis, when they were alone, "what do you think of this business, my dear count?"

"Bad," replied Athos, "very bad."

"But you received it with enthusiasm."

"As I shall ever receive the defense of a great principle, my dear D'Herblay. Monarchs are only strong by the assistance of the aristocracy, but aristocracy cannot survive without the countenance of monarchs. Let us, then, support monarchy, in order to support ourselves.

"We shall be murdered there," said Aramis. "I hate the English--they are coarse, like every nation that swills beer."

"Would it be better to remain here," said Athos, "and take a turn in the Bastile or the dungeon of Vincennes for having favored the escape of Monsieur de Beaufort? I'faith, Aramis, believe me, there is little left to regret. We avoid imprisonment and we play the part of heroes; the choice is easy."

"It is true; but in everything, friend, one must always return to the same question--a stupid one, I admit, but very necessary--have you any money?"

"Something like a hundred pistoles, that my farmer sent to me the day before I left Bragelonne; but out of that sum I ought to leave fifty for Raoul--a young man must live respectably. I have then about fifty pistoles. And you?"

"As for me, I am quite sure that after turning out all my pockets and emptying my drawers I shall not find ten louis at home. Fortunately Lord de Winter is rich."

"Lord de Winter is ruined for the moment; Oliver Cromwell has annexed his income resources."

"Now is the time when Baron Porthos would be useful."

"Now it is that I regret D'Artagnan."

"Let us entice them away."

"This secret, Aramis, does not belong to us; take my advice, then, and let no one into our confidence.

And moreover, in taking such a step we should appear to be doubtful of ourselves. Let us regret their absence to ourselves for our own sakes, but not speak of it."

"You are right; but what are you going to do until this evening? I have two things to postpone."

"And what are they?"

"First, a thrust with the coadjutor, whom I met last night at Madame de Rambouillet's and whom I found particular in his remarks respecting me."

"Oh, fie--a quarrel between priests, a duel between allies!"

"What can I do, friend? he is a bully and so am I; his cassock is a burden to him and I imagine I have had enough of mine; in fact, there is so much resemblance between us that I sometimes believe he is Aramis and I am the coadjutor. This kind of life fatigues and oppresses me; besides, he is a turbulent fellow, who will ruin our party. I am convinced that if I gave him a box on the ear, such as I gave this morning to the little citizen who splashed me, it would change the appearance of things."

"And I, my dear Aramis," quietly replied Athos, "I think it would only change Monsieur de Retz's appearance. Take my advice, leave things just as they are; besides, you are neither of you now your own masters; he belongs to the Fronde and you to the queen of England. So, if the second matter which you regret being unable to attend to is not more important than the first----"

"Oh! that is of the first importance."

"Attend to it, then, at once."

"Unfortunately, it is a thing that I can't perform at any time I choose. It was arranged for the evening and no other time will serve."

"I understand," said Athos smiling, "midnight."

"About that time."

"But, my dear fellow, those are things that bear postponement and you must put it off, especially with so good an excuse to give on your return----"

"Yes, if I return."

"If you do not return, how does it concern you? Be reasonable. Come, you are no longer twenty years old."

"To my great regret, mordieu! Ah, if I were but twenty years old!"

"Yes," said Athos, "doubtless you would commit great follies! But now we must part. I have one or two visits to make and a letter yet to write. Call for me at eight o'clock or shall I wait supper for you at seven?"

"That will do very well," said Aramis. "I have twenty visits to make and as many letters to write."

They then separated. Athos went to pay a visit to Madame de Vendome, left his name at Madame de Chevreuse's and wrote the following letter to D'Artagnan:

"Dear Friend,--I am about to set off with Aramis on important business. I wished to make my adieux to you, but time does not permit. Remember that I write to you now to repeat how much affection for you I still cherish.

"Raoul is gone to Blois and is ignorant of my departure; watch over him in my absence as much as you possibly can; and if by chance you receive no news of me three months hence, tell him to open a packet which he will find addressed to him in my bronze casket at Blois, of which I send you now the key.

"Embrace Porthos from Aramis and myself. Adieu, perhaps farewell."

At the hour agreed upon Aramis arrived; he was dressed as an officer and had the old sword at his side which he had drawn so often and which he was more than ever ready to draw.

"By-the-bye," he said, "I think that we are decidedly wrong to depart thus, without leaving a line for Porthos and D'Artagnan."

"The thing is done, dear friend," said Athos; "I foresaw that and have embraced them both from you and myself."

"You are a wonderful man, my dear count," said Aramis; "you think of everything."

"Well, have you made up your mind to this journey?"

"Quite; and now that I reflect about it, I am glad to leave Paris at this moment."

"And so am I," replied Athos; "my only regret is not having seen D'Artagnan; but the rascal is so cunning, he might have guessed our project."

When supper was over Blaisois entered. "Sir," said he, "here is Monsieur d'Artagnan's answer."

"But I did not tell you there would be an answer, stupid!" said Athos.

"And I set off without waiting for one, but he called me back and gave me this;" and he presented a little leather bag, plump and giving out a golden jingle.

Athos opened it and began by drawing forth a little note, written in these terms:

"My dear Count,--When one travels, and especially for three months, one never has a superfluity of money. Now, recalling former times of mutual distress, I send you half my purse; it is money to obtain which I made Mazarin sweat. Don't make a bad use of it, I entreat you.

"As to what you say about not seeing you again, I believe not a word of it; with such a heart as yours--and such a sword--one passes through the valley of the shadow of death a dozen times, unscathed and unalarmed. Au revoir, not farewell.

"It is unnecessary to say that from the day I saw Raoul I loved him; nevertheless, believe that I heartily pray that I may not become to him a father, however much I might be proud of such a son.

"Your

"D'Artagnan.

"P.S.--Be it well understood that the fifty louis which I send are equally for Aramis as for you--for you as Aramis."

Athos smiled, and his fine eye was dimmed by a tear. D'Artagnan, who had loved him so tenderly, loved him still, although a Mazarinist.

"There are the fifty louis, i'faith," said Aramis, emptying the purse on the table, all bearing the effigy of Louis XIII. "Well, what shall you do with this money, count? Shall you keep it or send it back?"

"I shall keep it, Aramis, and even though I had no need of it I still should keep it. What is offered from a generous heart should be accepted generously. Take twenty-five of them, Aramis, and give me the remaining twenty-five."

"All right; I am glad to see you are of my opinion. There now, shall we start?"

"When you like; but have you no groom?"

"No; that idiot Bazin had the folly to make himself verger, as you know, and therefore cannot leave Notre Dame.

"Very well, take Blaisois, with whom I know not what to do, since I already have Grimaud."

"Willingly," said Aramis.

At this moment Grimaud appeared at the door. "Ready," said he, with his usual curtness.

"Let us go, then," said Athos.

The two friends mounted, as did their servants. At the corner of the Quai they encountered Bazin, who was running breathlessly.

"Oh, sir!" exclaimed he, "thank Heaven I have arrived in time. Monsieur Porthos has just been to your house and has left this for you, saying that the letter was important and must be given to you before you left."

"Good," said Aramis, taking a purse which Bazin presented to him. "What is this?"

"Wait, your reverence, there is a letter."

"You know I have already told you that if you ever call me anything but chevalier I will break every bone in your body. Give me the letter."

"How can you read?" asked Athos, "it is as dark as a cold oven."

"Wait," said Bazin, striking a flint, and setting afire a twisted wax-light, with which he started the church candles. Thus illumined, Aramis read the following epistle:

"My dear D'Herblay,--I learned from D'Artagnan who has embraced me on the part of the Comte de la Fere and yourself, that you are setting out on a journey which may perhaps last two or three months; as I know that you do not like to ask money of your friends I offer you some of my own accord. Here are two hundred pistoles, which you can dispose of as you wish and return to me when opportunity occurs. Do not fear that you put me to inconvenience; if I want money I can send for some to any of my chateaux; at Bracieux alone, I have twenty thousand francs in gold. So, if I do not send you more it is because I fear you would not accept a larger sum.

"I address you, because you know, that although I esteem him from my heart I am a little awed by the Comte de la Fere; but it is understood that what I offer you I offer him at the same time.

"I am, as I trust you do not doubt, your devoted

"Du Vallon de Bracieux de Pierrefonds."

"Well," said Aramis, "what do you say to that?"

"I say, my dear D'Herblay, that it is almost sacrilege to distrust Providence when one has such friends, and therefore we will divide the pistoles from Porthos, as we divided the louis sent by D'Artagnan."

The division being made by the light of Bazin's taper, the two friends continued their road and a quarter of an hour later they had joined De Winter at the Porte Saint Denis.

43. In which it is proved that first Impulses are oftentimes the best.

The three gentlemen took the road to Picardy, a road so well known to them and which recalled to Athos and Aramis some of the most picturesque adventures of their youth.

"If Mousqueton were with us," observed Athos, on reaching the spot where they had had a dispute with the paviers, "how he would tremble at passing this! Do you remember, Aramis, that it was here he received that famous bullet wound?"

"By my faith, 'twould be excusable in him to tremble," replied Aramis, "for even I feel a shudder at the recollection; hold, just above that tree is the little spot where I thought I was killed."

It was soon time for Grimaud to recall the past. Arriving before the inn at which his master and himself had made such an enormous repast, he approached Athos and said, showing him the airhole of the cellar:

"Sausages!"

Athos began to laugh, for this juvenile escapade of his appeared to be as amusing as if some one had related it of another person.

At last, after traveling two days and a night, they arrived at Boulogne toward the evening, favored by magnificent weather. Boulogne was a strong position, then almost a deserted town, built entirely on the heights; what is now called the lower town did not then exist.

"Gentlemen," said De Winter, on reaching the gate of the town, "let us do here as at Paris--let us separate to avoid suspicion. I know an inn, little frequented, but of which the host is entirely devoted to me. I will go there, where I expect to find letters, and you go to the first tavern in the town, to L'Epee du Grand Henri for instance, refresh yourselves, and in two hours be upon the jetty; our boat is waiting for us there."

The matter being thus decided, the two friends found, about two hundred paces further, the tavern indicated. Their horses were fed, but not unsaddled; the grooms supped, for it was already late, and their two masters, impatient to return, appointed a place of meeting with them on the jetty and desired them on no account to exchange a word with any one. It is needless to say that this caution concerned Blaisois alone--long enough since it had been a useless one to Grimaud.

Athos and Aramis walked down toward the port. From their dress, covered with dust, and from a certain easy manner by means of which a man accustomed to travel is always recognizable, the two friends excited the attention of a few promenaders. There was more especially one upon whom their arrival had produced a decided impression. This man, whom they had noticed from the first for the same reason they had themselves been remarked by others, was walking in a listless way up and down the jetty. From the moment he perceived them he did not cease to look at them and seemed to burn with the wish to speak to them.

On reaching the jetty Athos and Aramis stopped to look at a little boat made fast to a pile and ready rigged as if waiting to start.

"That is doubtless our boat," said Athos.

"Yes," replied Aramis, "and the sloop out there making ready to sail must be that which is to take us to our destination; now," continued he, "if only De Winter does not keep us waiting. It is not at all amusing here; there is not a single woman passing."

"Hush!" said Athos, "we are overheard."

In truth, the walker, who, during the observations of the two friends, had passed and repassed behind them several times, stopped at the name of De Winter; but as his face betrayed no emotion at mention of this name, it might have been by chance he stood so still.

"Gentlemen," said the man, who was young and pale, bowing with ease and courtesy, "pardon my curiosity, but I see you come from Paris, or at least that you are strangers at Boulogne."

"We come from Paris, yes," replied Athos, with the same courtesy; "what is there we can do for you?"

"Sir," said the young man, "will you be so good as to tell me if it be true that Cardinal Mazarin is no longer minister?"

"That is a strange question," said Aramis.

"He is and he is not," replied Athos; "that is to say, he is dismissed by one-half of France, but by intrigues and promises he makes the other half sustain him; you will perceive that this may last a long time."

"However, sir," said the stranger, "he has neither fled nor is in prison?"

"No, sir, not at this moment at least."

"Sirs, accept my thanks for your politeness," said the young man, retreating.

"What do you think of that interrogator?" asked Aramis.

"I think he is either a dull provincial person or a spy in search of information."

"And you replied to him with that notion?"

"Nothing warranted me to answer him otherwise; he was polite to me and I was so to him."

"But if he be a spy----"

"What do you think a spy would be about here? We are not living in the time of Cardinal Richelieu, who would have closed the ports on bare suspicion."

"It matters not; you were wrong to reply to him as you did," continued Aramis, following with his eyes the young man, now vanishing behind the cliffs.

"And you," said Athos, "you forget that you committed a very different kind of imprudence in pronouncing Lord de Winter's name. Did you not see that at that name the young man stopped?"

"More reason, then, when he spoke to you, for sending him about his business."

"A quarrel?" asked Athos.

"And since when have you become afraid of a quarrel?"

"I am always afraid of a quarrel when I am expected at any place and when such a quarrel might possibly prevent my reaching it. Besides, let me own something to you. I am anxious to see that young man nearer."

"And wherefore?"

"Aramis, you will certainly laugh at me, you will say that I am always repeating the same thing, you will call me the most timorous of visionaries; but to whom do you see a resemblance in that young man?"

"In beauty or on the contrary?" asked Aramis, laughing.

"In ugliness, in so far as a man can resemble a woman."

"Ah! Egad!" cried Aramis, "you set me thinking. No, in truth you are no visionary, my dear friend, and now I think of it--you--yes, i'faith, you're right--those delicate, yet firm-set lips, those eyes which seem always at the command of the intellect and never of the heart! Yes, it is one of Milady's bastards!"

"You laugh Aramis."

"From habit, that is all. I swear to you, I like no better than yourself to meet that viper in my path."

"Ah! here is De Winter coming," said Athos.

"Good! one thing now is only awanting and that is, that our grooms should not keep us waiting."

"No," said Athos. "I see them about twenty paces behind my lord. I recognize Grimaud by his long legs and his determined slouch. Tony carries our muskets."

"Then we set sail to-night?" asked Aramis, glancing toward the west, where the sun had left a single golden cloud, which, dipping into the ocean, appeared by degrees to be extinguished.

"Probably," said Athos.

"Diable!" resumed Aramis, "I have little fancy for the sea by day, still less at night; the sounds of wind and wave, the frightful movements of the vessel; I confess I prefer the convent of Noisy."

Athos smiled sadly, for it was evident that he was thinking of other things as he listened to his friend and moved toward De Winter.

"What ails our friend?" said Aramis, "he resembles one of Dante's damned, whose neck Apollyon has dislocated and who are ever looking at their heels. What the devil makes him glower thus behind him?"

When De Winter perceived them, in his turn he advanced toward them with surprising rapidity.

"What is the matter, my lord?" said Athos, "and what puts you out of breath thus?"

"Nothing," replied De Winter; "nothing; and yet in passing the heights it seemed to me----" and he again turned round.

Athos glanced at Aramis.

"But let us go," continued De Winter; "let us be off; the boat must be waiting for us and there is our sloop at anchor--do you see it there? I wish I were on board already," and he looked back again.

"He has seen him," said Athos, in a low tone, to Aramis.

They had reached the ladder which led to the boat. De Winter made the grooms who carried the arms and the porters with the luggage descend first and was about to follow them.

At this moment Athos perceived a man walking on the seashore parallel to the jetty, and hastening his steps, as if to reach the other side of the port, scarcely twenty steps from the place of embarking. He fancied in the darkness that he recognized the young man who had questioned him. Athos now descended the ladder in his turn, without losing sight of the young man. The latter, to make a short cut, had appeared on a sluice.

"He certainly bodes us no good," said Athos; "but let us embark; once out at sea, let him come."

And Athos sprang into the boat, which was immediately pushed off and which soon sped seawards under the efforts of four stalwart rowers.

But the young man had begun to follow, or rather to advance before the boat. She was obliged to pass between the point of the jetty, surmounted by a beacon just lighted, and a rock which jutted out. They saw him in the distance climbing the rock in order to look down upon the boat as it passed.

"Ay, but," said Aramis, "that young fellow is decidedly a spy."

"Which is the young man?" asked De Winter, turning around.

"He who followed us and spoke to us awaits us there; behold!"

De Winter turned and followed the direction of Aramis's finger. The beacon bathed with light the little strait through which they were about to pass and the rock where the young man stood with bare head and crossed arms.

"It is he!" exclaimed De Winter, seizing the arm of Athos; "it is he! I thought I recognized him and I was not mistaken."

"Whom do you mean?" asked Aramis.

"Milady's son," replied Athos.

"The monk!" exclaimed Grimaud.

The young man heard these words and bent so forward over the rock that one might have supposed he was about to precipitate himself from it.

"Yes, it is I, my uncle--I, the son of Milady--I, the monk--I, the secretary and friend of Cromwell--I know you now, both you and your companions."

In that boat sat three men, unquestionably brave, whose courage no man would have dared dispute; nevertheless, at that voice, that accent and those gestures, they felt a chill access of terror cramp their veins. As for Grimaud, his hair stood on end and drops of sweat ran down his brow.

"Ah!" exclaimed Aramis, "that is the nephew, the monk, and the son of Milady, as he says himself."

"Alas, yes," murmured De Winter.

"Then wait," said Aramis; and with the terrible coolness which on important occasions he showed, he took one of the muskets from Tony, shouldered and aimed it at the young man, who stood, like the accusing angel, upon the rock.

"Fire!" cried Grimaud, unconsciously.

Athos threw himself on the muzzle of the gun and arrested the shot which was about to be fired.

"The devil take you," said Aramis. "I had him so well at the point of my gun I should have sent a ball into his breast."

"It is enough to have killed the mother," said Athos, hoarsely.

"The mother was a wretch, who struck at us all and at those dear to us."

"Yes, but the son has done us no harm."

Grimaud, who had risen to watch the effect of the shot, fell back hopeless, wringing his hands.

The young man burst into a laugh.

"Ah, it is certainly you!" he cried. "I know you even better now."

His mocking laugh and threatening words passed over their heads, carried by the breeze, until lost in the depths of the horizon. Aramis shuddered.

"Be calm," exclaimed Athos, "for Heaven's sake! have we ceased to be men?"

"No," said Aramis, "but that fellow is a fiend; and ask the uncle whether I was wrong to rid him of his dear nephew."

De Winter only replied by a groan.

"It was all up with him," continued Aramis; "ah I much fear that with all your wisdom such mercy yet will prove supernal folly."

Athos took Lord de Winter's hand and tried to turn the conversation.

"When shall we land in England?" he asked; but De Winter seemed not to hear his words and made no reply.

"Hold, Athos," said Aramis, "perhaps there is yet time. See if he is still in the same place."

Athos turned around with an effort; the sight of the young man was evidently painful to him, and there he still was, in fact, on the rock, the beacon shedding around him, as it were, a doubtful aureole.

"Decidedly, Aramis," said Athos, "I think I was wrong not to let you fire."

"Hold your tongue," replied Aramis; "you would make me weep, if such a thing were possible."

43. In which it is proved that first Impulses are oftentimes the best.

At this moment they were hailed by a voice from the sloop and a few seconds later men, servants and baggage were aboard. The captain was only waiting for his passengers; hardly had they put foot on deck ere her head was turned towards Hastings, where they were to disembark. At this instant the three friends turned, in spite of themselves, a last look on the rock, upon the menacing figure which pursued them and now stood out with a distinctness still. Then a voice reached them once more, sending this threat: "To our next meeting, sirs, in England."

44. Te Deum for the Victory of Lens.

The bustle which had been observed by Henrietta Maria and for which she had vainly sought to discover a reason, was occasioned by the battle of Lens, announced by the prince's messenger, the Duc de Chatillon, who had taken such a noble part in the engagement; he was, besides, charged to hang five and twenty flags, taken from the Lorraine party, as well as from the Spaniards, upon the arches of Notre Dame.

Such news was decisive; it destroyed, in favor of the court, the struggle commenced with parliament. The motive given for all the taxes summarily imposed and to which the parliament had made opposition, was the necessity of sustaining the honor of France and the uncertain hope of beating the enemy. Now, since the affair of Nordlingen, they had experienced nothing but reverses; the parliament had a plea for calling Mazarin to account for imaginary victories, always promised, ever deferred; but this time there really had been fighting, a triumph and a complete one. And this all knew so well that it was a double victory for the court, a victory at home and abroad; so that even when the young king learned the news he exclaimed, "Ah, gentlemen of the parliament, we shall see what you will say now!" Upon which the queen had pressed the royal child to her heart, whose haughty and unruly sentiments were in such harmony with her own. A council was called on the same evening, but nothing transpired of what had been decided on. It was only known that on the following Sunday a Te Deum would be sung at Notre Dame in honor of the victory of Lens.

The following Sunday, then, the Parisians arose with joy; at that period a Te Deum was a grand affair; this kind of ceremony had not then been abused and it produced a great effect. The shops were deserted, houses closed; every one wished to see the young king with his mother, and the famous Cardinal Mazarin whom they hated so much that no one wished to be deprived of his presence. Moreover, great liberty prevailed throughout the immense crowd; every opinion was openly expressed and chorused, so to speak, of coming insurrection, as the thousand bells of all the Paris churches rang out the Te Deum. The police belonging to the city being formed by the city itself, nothing threatening presented itself to disturb this concert of universal hatred or freeze the frequent scoffs of slanderous lips.

Nevertheless, at eight o'clock in the morning the regiment of the queen's guards, commanded by Guitant, under whom was his nephew Comminges, marched publicly, preceded by drums and trumpets, filing off from the Palais Royal as far as Notre Dame, a manoeuvre which the Parisians witnessed tranquilly, delighted as they were with military music and brilliant uniforms.

Friquet had put on his Sunday clothes, under the pretext of having a swollen face which he had managed to simulate by introducing a handful of cherry kernels into one side of his mouth, and had procured a whole holiday from Bazin. On leaving Bazin, Friquet started off to the Palais Royal, where he arrived at the moment of the turning out of the regiment of guards; and as he had only gone there for the enjoyment of seeing it and hearing the music, he took his place at their head, beating the drum on two pieces of slate and passing from that exercise to that of the trumpet, which he counterfeited quite naturally with his mouth in a manner which had more than once called forth the praises of amateurs of imitative harmony.

This amusement lasted from the Barriere des Sergens to the place of Notre Dame, and Friquet found in it very real enjoyment; but when at last the regiment separated, penetrated the heart of the city and placed itself at the extremity of the Rue Saint Christophe, near the Rue Cocatrix, in which Broussel lived, then Friquet remembered that he had not had breakfast; and after thinking in which direction he had better turn his steps in order to accomplish this important act of the day, he reflected deeply and decided that Councillor Broussel should bear the cost of this repast.

In consequence he took to his heels, arrived breathlessly at the councillor's door, and knocked violently.

His mother, the councillor's old servant, opened it.

"What doest thou here, good-for-nothing?" she said, "and why art thou not at Notre Dame?"

"I have been there, mother," said Friquet, "but I saw things happen of which Master Broussel ought to be warned, and so with Monsieur Bazin's permission--you know, mother, Monsieur Bazin, the verger--I came to speak to Monsieur Broussel."

"And what hast thou to say, boy, to Monsieur Broussel?"

"I wish to tell him," replied Friquet, screaming with all his might, "that there is a whole regiment of guards coming this way. And as I hear everywhere that at the court they are ill-disposed to him, I wish to warn him, that he may be on his guard."

Broussel heard the scream of the young oddity, and, enchanted with this excess of zeal, came down to the first floor, for he was, in truth, working in his room on the second.

"Well," said he, "friend, what matters the regiment of guards to us, and art thou not mad to make such a disturbance? Knowest thou not that it is the custom of these soldiers to act thus and that it is usual for the regiment to form themselves into two solid walls when the king goes by?"

Friquet counterfeited surprise, and twisting his new cap around in his fingers, said:

"It is not astonishing for you to know it, Monsieur Broussel, who knows everything; but as for me, by holy truth, I did not know it and I thought I would give you good advice; you must not be angry with me for that, Monsieur Broussel."

"On the contrary, my boy, on the contrary, I am pleased with your zeal. Dame Nanette, look for those apricots which Madame de Longueville sent to us yesterday from Noisy and give half a dozen of them to your son, with a crust of new bread."

"Oh, thank you, sir, thank you, Monsieur Broussel," said Friquet; "I am so fond of apricots!"

Broussel then proceeded to his wife's room and asked for breakfast; it was nine o'clock. The councillor placed himself at the window; the street was completely deserted, but in the distance was heard, like the noise of the tide rushing in, the deep hum of the populous waves increasing now around Notre Dame.

This noise redoubled when D'Artagnan, with a company of musketeers, placed himself at the gates of Notre Dame to secure the service of the church. He had instructed Porthos to profit by this opportunity to see the ceremony; and Porthos, in full dress, mounted his finest horse, taking the part of supernumerary musketeer, as D'Artagnan had so often done formerly. The sergeant of this company, a veteran of the Spanish wars, had recognized Porthos, his old companion, and very soon all those who served under him were placed in possession of startling facts concerning the honor of the ancient musketeers of Treville. Porthos had not only been well received by the company, but he was moreover looked on with great admiration.

At ten o'clock the guns of the Louvre announced the departure of the king, and then a movement, similar to that of trees in a stormy wind that bend and writhe with agitated tops, ran though the multitude, which was compressed behind the immovable muskets of the guard. At last the king appeared with the queen in a gilded chariot. Ten other carriages followed, containing the ladies of honor, the officers of the royal household, and the court.

"God save the king!" was the cry in every direction; the young monarch gravely put his head out of the window, looked sufficiently grateful and even bowed; at which the cries of the multitude were renewed.

Just as the court was settling down in the cathedral, a carriage, bearing the arms of Comminges, quitted the line of the court carriages and proceeded slowly to the end of the Rue Saint Christophe, now entirely deserted. When it arrived there, four guards and a police officer, who accompanied it, mounted into the heavy machine and closed the shutters; then through an opening cautiously made, the policeman began to watch the length of the Rue Cocatrix, as if he was waiting for some one.

All the world was occupied with the ceremony, so that neither the chariot nor the precautions taken by those who were within it had been observed. Friquet, whose eye, ever on the alert, could alone have discovered them, had gone to devour his apricots upon the entablature of a house in the square of Notre Dame. Thence he saw the king, the queen and Monsieur Mazarin, and heard the mass as well as if he had been on duty.

Toward the end of the service, the queen, seeing Comminges standing near her, waiting for a confirmation of the order she had given him before quitting the Louvre, said in a whisper:

"Go, Comminges, and may God aid you!"

Comminges immediately left the church and entered the Rue Saint Christophe. Friquet, seeing this fine officer thus walk away, followed by two guards, amused himself by pursuing them and did this so much the more gladly as the ceremony ended at that instant and the king remounted his carriage.

Hardly had the police officer observed Comminges at the end of the Rue Cocatrix when he said one word to the coachman, who at once put his vehicle into motion and drove up before Broussel's door. Comminges knocked at the door at the same moment, and Friquet was waiting behind Comminges until the door should be opened.

"What dost thou there, rascal?" asked Comminges.

"I want to go into Master Broussel's house, captain," replied Friquet, in that wheedling way the "gamins" of Paris know so well how to assume when necessary.

"And on what floor does he live?" asked Comminges.

"In the whole house," said Friquet; "the house belongs to him; he occupies the second floor when he works and descends to the first to take his meals; he must be at dinner now; it is noon."

"Good," said Comminges.

At this moment the door was opened, and having questioned the servant the officer learned that Master Broussel was at home and at dinner.

Broussel was seated at the table with his family, having his wife opposite to him, his two daughters by his side, and his son, Louvieres, whom we have already seen when the accident happened to the councillor--an accident from which he had quite recovered--at the bottom of the table. The worthy man, restored to perfect health, was tasting the fine fruit which Madame de Longueville had sent to him.

At sight of the officer Broussel was somewhat moved, but seeing him bow politely he rose and bowed also. Still, in spite of this reciprocal politeness, the countenances of the women betrayed a certain amount of uneasiness; Louvieres became very pale and waited impatiently for the officer to explain himself.

"Sir," said Comminges, "I am the bearer of an order from the king."

"Very well, sir," replied Broussel, "what is this order?" And he held out his hand.

"I am commissioned to seize your person, sir," said Comminges, in the same tone and with the same politeness; "and if you will believe me you had better spare yourself the trouble of reading that long letter and follow me."

A thunderbolt falling in the midst of these good people, so peacefully assembled there, would not have produced a more appalling effect. It was a horrible thing at that period to be imprisoned by the enmity of the king. Louvieres sprang forward to snatch his sword, which stood against a chair in a corner of the room; but a glance from the worthy Broussel, who in the midst of it all did not lose his presence of mind, checked this foolhardy action of despair. Madame Broussel, separated by the width of the table from her husband, burst into tears, and the young girls clung to their father's arms.

"Come, sir," said Comminges, "make haste; you must obey the king."

"Sir," said Broussel, "I am in bad health and cannot give myself up a prisoner in this state; I must have time."

"It is impossible," said Comminges; "the order is strict and must be put into execution this instant."

"Impossible!" said Louvieres; "sir, beware of driving us to despair."

"Impossible!" cried a shrill voice from the end of the room.

Comminges turned and saw Dame Nanette, her eyes flashing with anger and a broom in her hand.

"My good Nanette, be quiet, I beseech you," said Broussel.

"Me! keep quiet while my master is being arrested! he, the support, the liberator, the father of the people! Ah! well, yes; you have to know me yet. Are you going?" added she to Comminges.

The latter smiled.

"Come, sir," said he, addressing Broussel, "silence that woman and follow me."

"Silence me! me! me!" said Nanette. "Ah! yet one wants some one besides you for that, my fine king's cockatoo! You shall see." And Dame Nanette sprang to the window, threw it open, and in such a piercing voice that it might have been heard in the square of Notre Dame:

"Help!" she screamed, "my master is being arrested; the Councillor Broussel is being arrested! Help!"

"Sir," said Comminges, "declare yourself at once; will you obey or do you intend to rebel against the king?"

"I obey, I obey, sir!" cried Broussel, trying to disengage himself from the grasp of his two daughters and by a look restrain his son, who seemed determined to dispute authority.

"In that case," commanded Comminges, "silence that old woman."

"Ah! old woman!" screamed Nanette.

And she began to shriek more loudly, clinging to the bars of the window:

"Help! help! for Master Broussel, who is arrested because he has defended the people! Help!"

Comminges seized the servant around the waist and would have dragged her from her post; but at that instant a treble voice, proceeding from a kind of entresol, was heard screeching:

"Murder! fire! assassins! Master Broussel is being killed! Master Broussel is being strangled."

It was Friquet's voice; and Dame Nanette, feeling herself supported, recommenced with all her strength to sound her shrilly squawk.

Many curious faces had already appeared at the windows and the people attracted to the end of the street began to run, first men, then groups, and then a crowd of people; hearing cries and seeing a chariot they could not understand it; but Friquet sprang from the entresol on to the top of the carriage.

"They want to arrest Master Broussel!" he cried; "the guards are in the carriage and the officer is upstairs!"

The crowd began to murmur and approached the house. The two guards who had remained in the lane mounted to the aid of Comminges; those who were in the chariot opened the doors and presented arms.

"Don't you see them?" cried Friquet, "don't you see? there they are!"

The coachman turning around, gave Friquet a slash with his whip which made him scream with pain.

"Ah! devil's coachman!" cried Friquet, "you're meddling too! Wait!"

And regaining his entresol he overwhelmed the coachman with every projectile he could lay hands on.

The tumult now began to increase; the street was not able to contain the spectators who assembled from every direction; the crowd invaded the space which the dreaded pikes of the guards had till then kept clear between them and the carriage. The soldiers, pushed back by these living walls, were in danger of being crushed against the spokes of the wheels and the panels of the carriages. The cries which the police officer repeated twenty times: "In the king's name," were powerless against this formidable multitude--seemed, on the contrary, to exasperate it still more; when, at the shout, "In the name of the king," an officer ran up, and seeing the uniforms ill-treated, he sprang into the scuffle sword in hand, and brought unexpected help to the guards. This gentleman was a young man, scarcely sixteen years of age, now white with anger. He leaped from his charger, placed his back against the shaft of the carriage, making a rampart of his horse, drew his pistols from their holsters and fastened them to his belt, and began to fight with the back sword, like a man accustomed to the handling of his weapon.

During ten minutes he alone kept the crowd at bay; at last Comminges appeared, pushing Broussel before him.

"Let us break the carriage!" cried the people.

"In the king's name!" cried Comminges.

"The first who advances is a dead man!" cried Raoul, for it was in fact he, who, feeling himself pressed and almost crushed by a gigantic citizen, pricked him with the point of his sword and sent him howling back.

Comminges, so to speak, threw Broussel into the carriage and sprang in after him. At this moment a shot was fired and a ball passed through the hat of Comminges and broke the arm of one of the guards. Comminges looked up and saw amidst the smoke the threatening face of Louvieres appearing at the window of the second floor.

"Very well, sir," said Comminges, "you shall hear of this anon."

"And you of me, sir," said Louvieres; "and we shall see then who can speak the loudest."

Friquet and Nanette continued to shout; the cries, the noise of the shot and the intoxicating smell of powder produced their usual maddening effects.

"Down with the officer! down with him!" was the cry.

"One step nearer," said Comminges, putting down the sashes, that the interior of the carriage might be well seen, and placing his sword on his prisoner's breast, "one step nearer, and I kill the prisoner; my orders were to carry him off alive or dead. I will take him dead, that's all."

A terrible cry was heard, and the wife and daughters of Broussel held up their hands in supplication to the people; the latter knew that this officer, who was so pale, but who appeared so determined, would keep his word; they continued to threaten, but they began to disperse.

"Drive to the palace," said Comminges to the coachman, who was by then more dead than alive.

The man whipped his animals, which cleared a way through the crowd; but on arriving on the Quai they were obliged to stop; the carriage was upset, the horses carried off, stifled, mangled by the crowd. Raoul, on foot, for he had not time to mount his horse again, tired, like the guards, of distributing blows with the flat of his sword, had recourse to its point. But this last and dreaded resource served only to exasperate the multitude. From time to time a shot from a musket or the blade of a rapier flashed among the crowd; projectiles continued to hail down from the windows and some shots were heard, the echo of which, though they were probably fired in the air, made all hearts vibrate. Voices, unheard except on days of revolution, were distinguished; faces were seen that only appeared on days of bloodshed. Cries of "Death! death to the guards! to the Seine with the officer!" were heard above all the noise, deafening as it was. Raoul, his hat in ribbons, his face bleeding, felt not only his strength but also his reason going; a red mist covered his sight, and through this mist he saw a hundred threatening arms stretched over him, ready to seize upon him when he fell. The guards were unable to help any one--each one was occupied with his self-preservation. All was over; carriages, horses, guards, and perhaps even the prisoner were about to be torn to shreds, when all at once a voice well known to Raoul was heard, and suddenly a great sword glittered in the air; at the same time the crowd opened, upset, trodden down, and an officer of the musketeers, striking and cutting right and left, rushed up to Raoul and took him in his arms just as he was about to fall.

"God's blood!" cried the officer, "have they killed him? Woe to them if it be so!"

And he turned around, so stern with anger, strength and threat, that the most excited rebels hustled back on one another, in order to escape, and some of them even rolled into the Seine.

"Monsieur d'Artagnan!" murmured Raoul.

"Yes, 'sdeath! in person, and fortunately it seems for you, my young friend. Come on, here, you others," he continued, rising in his stirrups, raising his sword, and addressing those musketeers who had not been able to follow his rapid onslaught. "Come, sweep away all that for me! Shoulder muskets! Present arms! Aim----"

At this command the mountain of populace thinned so suddenly that D'Artagnan could not repress a burst of Homeric laughter.

"Thank you, D'Artagnan," said Comminges, showing half of his body through the window of the broken vehicle, "thanks, my young friend; your name--that I may mention it to the queen."

Raoul was about to reply when D'Artagnan bent down to his ear.

"Hold your tongue," said he, "and let me answer. Do not lose time, Comminges," he continued; "get out of the carriage if you can and make another draw up; be quick, or in five minutes the mob will be on us again with swords and muskets and you will be killed. Hold! there's a carriage coming over yonder."

Then bending again to Raoul, he whispered: "Above all things do not divulge your name."

"That's right. I will go," said Comminges; "and if they come back, fire!"

"Not at all--not at all," replied D'Artagnan; "let no one move. On the contrary, one shot at this moment would be paid for dearly to-morrow."

Comminges took his four guards and as many musketeers and ran to the carriage, from which he made the people inside dismount, and brought them to the vehicle which had upset. But when it was necessary to convey the prisoner from one carriage to the other, the people, catching sight of him whom they called their liberator, uttered every imaginable cry and knotted themselves once more around the vehicle.

"Start, start!" said D'Artagnan. "There are ten men to accompany you. I will keep twenty to hold in check the mob; go, and lose not a moment. Ten men for Monsieur de Comminges."

As the carriage started off the cries were redoubled and more than ten thousand people thronged the Quai and overflowed the Pont Neuf and adjacent streets. A few shots were fired and one musketeer was wounded.

"Forward!" cried D'Artagnan, driven to extremities, biting his moustache; and then he charged with his twenty men and dispersed them in fear. One man alone remained in his place, gun in hand.

"Ah!" he exclaimed, "it is thou who wouldst have him assassinated? Wait an instant." And he pointed his gun at D'Artagnan, who was riding toward him at full speed. D'Artagnan bent down to his horse's neck, the young man fired, and the ball severed the feathers from the hat. The horse started, brushed against the imprudent man, who thought by his strength alone to stay the tempest, and he fell against the wall. D'Artagnan pulled up his horse, and whilst his musketeers continued to charge, he returned and bent with drawn sword over the man he had knocked down.

"Oh, sir!" exclaimed Raoul, recognizing the young man as having seen him in the Rue Cocatrix, "spare him! it is his son!"

D'Artagnan's arm dropped to his side. "Ah, you are his son!" he said; "that is a different thing."

"Sir, I surrender," said Louvieres, presenting his unloaded musket to the officer.

"Eh, no! do not surrender, egad! On the contrary, be off, and quickly. If I take you, you will be hung!"

The young man did not wait to be told twice, but passing under the horse's head disappeared at the corner of the Rue Guenegaud.

"I'faith!" said D'Artagnan to Raoul, "you were just in time to stay my hand. He was a dead man; and on my honor, if I had discovered that it was his son, I should have regretted having killed him."

"Ah! sir!" said Raoul, "allow me, after thanking you for that poor fellow's life, to thank you on my own account. I too, sir, was almost dead when you arrived."

"Wait, wait, young man; do not fatigue yourself with speaking. We can talk of it afterward."

Then seeing that the musketeers had cleared the Quai from the Pont Neuf to the Quai Saint Michael, he raised his sword for them to double their speed. The musketeers trotted up, and at the same time the ten men whom D'Artagnan had given to Comminges appeared.

"Halloo!" cried D'Artagnan; "has something fresh happened?"

"Eh, sir!" replied the sergeant, "their vehicle has broken down a second time; it really must be doomed."

"They are bad managers," said D'Artagnan, shrugging his shoulders. "When a carriage is chosen, it ought to be strong. The carriage in which a Broussel is to be arrested ought to be able to bear ten thousand men."

"What are your commands, lieutenant?"

"Take the detachment and conduct him to his place."

"But you will be left alone?"

"Certainly. So you suppose I have need of an escort? Go."

The musketeers set off and D'Artagnan was left alone with Raoul.

"Now," he said, "are you in pain?"

"Yes; my head is not only swimming but burning."

"What's the matter with this head?" said D'Artagnan, raising the battered hat. "Ah! ah! a bruise."

"Yes, I think I received a flower-pot upon my head."

"Brutes!" said D'Artagnan. "But were you not on horseback? you have spurs."

"Yes, but I got down to defend Monsieur de Comminges and my horse was taken away. Here it is, I see."

At this very moment Friquet passed, mounted on Raoul's horse, waving his parti-colored cap and crying, "Broussel! Broussel!"

"Halloo! stop, rascal!" cried D'Artagnan. "Bring hither that horse."

Friquet heard perfectly, but he pretended not to do so and tried to continue his road. D'Artagnan felt inclined for an instant to pursue Master Friquet, but not wishing to leave Raoul alone he contented himself with taking a pistol from the holster and cocking it.

Friquet had a quick eye and a fine ear. He saw D'Artagnan's movement, heard the sound of the click, and stopped at once.

"Ah! it is you, your honor," he said, advancing toward D'Artagnan; "and I am truly pleased to meet you."

D'Artagnan looked attentively at Friquet and recognized the little chorister of the Rue de la Calandre.

"Ah! 'tis thou, rascal!" said he, "come here: so thou hast changed thy trade; thou art no longer a choir boy nor a tavern boy; thou hast become a horse stealer?"

"Ah, your honor, how can you say so?" exclaimed Friquet. "I was seeking the gentleman to whom this horse belongs--an officer, brave and handsome as a youthful Caesar;" then, pretending to see Raoul for the first time:

"Ah! but if I mistake not," continued he, "here he is; you won't forget the boy, sir."

Raoul put his hand in his pocket.

"What are you about?" asked D'Artagnan.

"To give ten francs to this honest fellow," replied Raoul, taking a pistole from his pocket.

"Ten kicks on his back!" said D'Artagnan; "be off, you little villain, and forget not that I have your address."

Friquet, who did not expect to be let off so cheaply, bounded off like a gazelle up the Quai a la Rue Dauphine, and disappeared. Raoul mounted his horse, and both leisurely took their way to the Rue Tiquetonne.

D'Artagnan watched over the youth as if he had been his own son.

They arrived without accident at the Hotel de la Chevrette.

The handsome Madeleine announced to D'Artagnan that Planchet had returned, bringing

Mousqueton with him, who had heroically borne the extraction of the ball and was as well as his state would permit.

D'Artagnan desired Planchet to be summoned, but he had disappeared.

"Then bring some wine," said D'Artagnan. "You are much pleased with yourself," said he to Raoul when they were alone, "are you not?"

"Well, yes," replied Raoul. "It seems to me I did my duty. I defended the king."

"And who told you to defend the king?"

"The Comte de la Fere himself."

"Yes, the king; but to-day you have not fought for the king, you have fought for Mazarin; which is not quite the same thing."

"But you yourself?"

"Oh, for me; that is another matter. I obey my captain's orders. As for you, your captain is the prince, understand that rightly; you have no other. But has one ever seen such a wild fellow," continued he, "making himself a Mazarinist and helping to arrest Broussel! Breathe not a word of that, or the Comte de la Fere will be furious."

"You think the count will be angry with me?"

"Think it? I'm certain of it; were it not for that, I should thank you, for you have worked for us. However, I scold you instead of him, and in his place; the storm will blow over more easily, believe me. And moreover, my dear child," continued D'Artagnan, "I am making use of the privilege conceded to me by your guardian."

"I do not understand you, sir," said Raoul.

D'Artagnan rose, and taking a letter from his writing-desk, presented it to Raoul. The face of the latter became serious when he had cast his eyes upon the paper.

"Oh, mon Dieu!" he said, raising his fine eyes to D'Artagnan, moist with tears, "the count has left Paris without seeing me?"

"He left four days ago," said D'Artagnan.

"But this letter seems to intimate that he is about to incur danger, perhaps death."

"He--he--incur danger of death! No, be not anxious; he is traveling on business and will return ere long. I hope you have no repugnance to accept me as your guardian in the interim."

"Oh, no, Monsieur d'Artagnan," said Raoul, "you are such a brave gentleman and the Comte de la Fere has so much affection for you!"

"Eh! Egad! love me too; I will not torment you much, but only on condition that you become a Frondist, my young friend, and a hearty Frondist, too."

"But can I continue to visit Madame de Chevreuse?"

"I should say you could! and the coadjutor and Madame de Longueville; and if the worthy Broussel were there, whom you so stupidly helped arrest, I should tell you to excuse yourself to him at once and kiss him on both cheeks."

"Well, sir, I will obey you, although I do not understand you."

"It is unnecessary for you to understand. Hold," continued D'Artagnan, turning toward the door, which had just opened, "here is Monsieur du Vallon, who comes with his coat torn."

"Yes, but in exchange," said Porthos, covered with perspiration and soiled by dust, "in exchange, I have torn many skins. Those wretches wanted to take away my sword! Deuce take 'em, what a popular commotion!" continued the giant, in his quiet manner; "but I knocked down more than twenty with the hilt of Balizarde. A draught of wine, D'Artagnan."

"Oh, I'll answer for you," said the Gascon, filling Porthos's glass to the brim; "but when you have drunk, give me your opinion."

"Upon what?" asked Porthos.

"Look here," resumed D'Artagnan; "here is Monsieur de Bragelonne, who determined at all risks to aid the arrest of Broussel and whom I had great difficulty to prevent defending Monsieur de Comminges."

"The devil!" said Porthos; "and his guardian, what would he have said to that?"

"Do you hear?" interrupted D'Artagnan; "become a Frondist, my friend, belong to the Fronde, and remember that I fill the count's place in everything;" and he jingled his money.

"Will you come?" said he to Porthos.

"Where?" asked Porthos, filling a second glass of wine.

"To present our respects to the cardinal."

Porthos swallowed the second glass with the same grace with which he had imbibed the first, took his beaver and followed D'Artagnan. As for Raoul, he remained bewildered with what he had seen, having been forbidden by D'Artagnan to leave the room until the tumult was over.

45. The Beggar of St. Eustache.

D'Artagnan had calculated that in not going at once to the Palais Royal he would give Comminges time to arrive before him, and consequently to make the cardinal acquainted with the eminent services which he, D'Artagnan, and his friend had rendered to the queen's party in the morning.

They were indeed admirably received by Mazarin, who paid them numerous compliments, and announced that they were more than half on their way to obtain what they desired, namely, D'Artagnan his captaincy, Porthos his barony.

D'Artagnan would have preferred money in hand to all that fine talk, for he knew well that to Mazarin it was easy to promise and hard to perform. But, though he held the cardinal's promises as of little worth, he affected to be completely satisfied, for he was unwilling to discourage Porthos.

Whilst the two friends were with the cardinal, the queen sent for him. Mazarin, thinking that it would be the means of increasing the zeal of his two defenders if he procured them personal thanks from the queen, motioned them to follow him. D'Artagnan and Porthos pointed to their dusty and torn dresses, but the cardinal shook his head.

"Those costumes," he said, "are of more worth than most of those which you will see on the backs of the queen's courtiers; they are costumes of battle."

D'Artagnan and Porthos obeyed. The court of Anne of Austria was full of gayety and animation; for, after having gained a victory over the Spaniard, it had just gained another over the people. Broussel had been conducted out of Paris without further resistance, and was at this time in the prison of Saint Germain; while Blancmesnil, who was arrested at the same time, but whose arrest had been made without difficulty or noise, was safe in the Castle of Vincennes.

Comminges was near the queen, who was questioning him upon the details of his expedition, and every one was listening to his account, when D'Artagnan and Porthos were perceived at the door, behind the cardinal.

"Ah, madame," said Comminges, hastening to D'Artagnan, "here is one who can tell you better than myself, for he was my protector. Without him I should probably at this moment be a dead fish in the nets at Saint Cloud, for it was a question of nothing less than throwing me into the river. Speak, D'Artagnan, speak."

D'Artagnan had been a hundred times in the same room with the queen since he had become lieutenant of the musketeers, but her majesty had never once spoken to him.

"Well, sir," at last said Anne of Austria, "you are silent, after rendering such a service?"

"Madame," replied D'Artagnan, "I have nought to say, save that my life is ever at your majesty's service, and that I shall only be happy the day I lose it for you."

"I know that, sir; I have known that," said the queen, "a long time; therefore I am delighted to be able thus publicly to mark my gratitude and my esteem."

"Permit me, madame," said D'Artagnan, "to reserve a portion for my friend; like myself" (he laid an emphasis on these words) "an ancient musketeer of the company of Treville; he has done wonders."

"His name?" asked the queen.

"In the regiment," said D'Artagnan, "he is called Porthos" (the queen started), "but his true name is the Chevalier du Vallon."

"De Bracieux de Pierrefonds," added Porthos.

"These names are too numerous for me to remember them all, and I will content myself with the first," said the queen, graciously. Porthos bowed. At this moment the coadjutor was announced; a cry of surprise ran through the royal assemblage. Although the coadjutor had preached that same morning it was well known that he leaned much to the side of the Fronde; and Mazarin, in requesting the archbishop of Paris to make his nephew preach, had evidently had the intention of administering to Monsieur de Retz one of those Italian kicks he so much enjoyed giving.

The fact was, in leaving Notre Dame the coadjutor had learned the event of the day. Although almost engaged to the leaders of the Fronde he had not gone so far but that retreat was possible should the court offer him the advantages for which he was ambitious and to which the coadjutorship was but a stepping-stone. Monsieur de Retz wished to become archbishop in his uncle's place, and cardinal, like Mazarin; and the popular party could with difficulty accord him favors so entirely royal. He therefore hastened to the palace to congratulate the queen on the battle of Lens, determined beforehand to act with or against the court, as his congratulations were well or ill received.

The coadjutor possessed, perhaps, as much wit as all those put together who were assembled at the court to laugh at him. His speech, therefore, was so well turned, that in spite of the great wish felt by the courtiers to laugh, they could find no point on which to vent their ridicule. He concluded by saying that he placed his feeble influence at her majesty's command.

During the whole time he was speaking, the queen appeared to be well pleased with the coadjutor's harangue; but terminating as it did with such a phrase, the only one which could be caught at by the jokers, Anne turned around and directed a glance toward her favorites, which announced that she delivered up the coadjutor to their tender mercies. Immediately the wits of the court plunged into satire. Nogent-Beautin, the fool of the court, exclaimed that "the queen was very happy to have the succor of religion at such a moment." This caused a universal burst of laughter. The Count de Villeroy said that "he did not know how any fear could be entertained for a moment, when the court had, to defend itself against the parliament and the citizens of Paris, his holiness the coadjutor, who by a signal could raise an army of curates, church porters and vergers."

The Marechal de la Meilleraie added that in case the coadjutor should appear on the field of battle it would be a pity that he should not be distinguished in the melee by wearing a red hat, as Henry IV. had been distinguished by his white plume at the battle of Ivry.

During this storm, Gondy, who had it in his power to make it most unpleasant for the jesters, remained calm and stern. The queen at last asked him if he had anything to add to the fine discourse he had just made to her.

"Yes, madame," replied the coadjutor; "I have to beg you to reflect twice ere you cause a civil war in the kingdom."

The queen turned her back and the laughing recommenced.

The coadjutor bowed and left the palace, casting upon the cardinal such a glance as is best understood by mortal foes. That glance was so sharp that it penetrated the heart of Mazarin, who, reading in it a declaration of war, seized D'Artagnan by the arm and said:

"If occasion requires, monsieur, you will remember that man who has just gone out, will you not?"

"Yes, my lord," he replied. Then, turning toward Porthos, "The devil!" said he, "this has a bad look. I dislike these quarrels among men of the church."

Gondy withdrew, distributing benedictions on his way, and finding a malicious satisfaction in causing the adherents of his foes to prostrate themselves at his feet.

"Oh!" he murmured, as he left the threshold of the palace: "ungrateful court! faithless court! cowardly court! I will teach you how to laugh to-morrow--but in another manner."

But whilst they were indulging in extravagant joy at the Palais Royal, to increase the hilarity of the queen, Mazarin, a man of sense, and whose fear, moreover, gave him foresight, lost no time in making idle and dangerous jokes; he went out after the coadjutor, settled his account, locked up his gold, and had confidential workmen to contrive hiding places in his walls.

On his return home the coadjutor was informed that a young man had come in after his departure and was waiting for him; he started with delight when, on demanding the name of this young man, he learned that it was Louvieres. He hastened to his cabinet. Broussel's son was there, still furious, and still bearing bloody marks of his struggle with the king's officers. The only precaution he had taken in coming to the archbishopric was to leave his arquebuse in the hands of a friend.

The coadjutor went to him and held out his hand. The young man gazed at him as if he would have read the secret of his heart.

"My dear Monsieur Louvieres," said the coadjutor, "believe me, I am truly concerned for the misfortune which has happened to you."

"Is that true, and do you speak seriously?" asked Louvieres.

"From the depth of my heart," said Gondy.

"In that case, my lord, the time for words has passed and the hour for action is at hand; my lord, in three days, if you wish it, my father will be out of prison and in six months you may be cardinal."

The coadjutor started.

"Oh! let us speak frankly," continued Louvieres, "and act in a straightforward manner. Thirty thousand crowns in alms is not given, as you have done for the last six months, out of pure Christian charity; that would be too grand. You are ambitious--it is natural; you are a man of genius and you know your worth. As for me, I hate the court and have but one desire at this moment--vengeance. Give us the clergy and the people, of whom you can dispose, and I will bring you the citizens and the parliament; with these four elements Paris is ours in a week; and believe me, monsieur coadjutor, the court will give from fear what it will not give from good-will."

It was now the coadjutor's turn to fix his piercing eyes on Louvieres.

"But, Monsieur Louvieres, are you aware that it is simply civil war you are proposing to me?"

"You have been preparing long enough, my lord, for it to be welcome to you now."

"Never mind," said the coadjutor; "you must be well aware that this requires reflection."

"And how many hours of reflection do you ask?"

"Twelve hours, sir; is it too long?"

"It is now noon; at midnight I will be at your house."

"If I should not be in, wait for me."

"Good! at midnight, my lord."

"At midnight, my dear Monsieur Louvieres."

When once more alone Gondy sent to summon all the curates with whom he had any connection to his house. Two hours later, thirty officiating ministers from the most populous, and consequently the most disturbed parishes of Paris had assembled there. Gondy related to them the insults he had received at the Palais Royal and retailed the jests of Beautin, the Count de Villeroy and Marechal de la Meilleraie. The curates asked him what was to be done.

"Simply this," said the coadjutor. "You are the directors of all consciences. Well, undermine in them the miserable prejudice of respect and fear of kings; teach your flocks that the queen is a tyrant; and repeat often and loudly, so that all may know it, that the misfortunes of France are caused by Mazarin, her lover and her destroyer; begin this work to-day, this instant even, and in three days I shall expect the result. For the rest, if any one of you have further or better counsel to expound, I will listen to him with the greatest pleasure."

Three curates remained--those of St. Merri, St. Sulpice and St. Eustache. The others withdrew.

"You think, then, that you can help me more efficaciously than your brothers?" said Gondy.

"We hope so," answered the curates.

"Let us hear. Monsieur de St. Merri, you begin."

"My lord, I have in my parish a man who might be of the greatest use to you."

"Who and what is this man?"

"A shopkeeper in the Rue des Lombards, who has great influence upon the commerce of his quarter."

"What is his name?"

"He is named Planchet, who himself also caused a rising about six weeks ago; but as he was searched for after this emeute he disappeared."

"And can you find him?"

"I hope so. I think he has not been arrested, and as I am his wife's confessor, if she knows where he is I shall know it too."

"Very well, sir, find this man, and when you have found him bring him to me."

"We will be with you at six o'clock, my lord."

"Go, my dear curate, and may God assist you!"

"And you, sir?" continued Gondy, turning to the curate of St. Sulpice.

"I, my lord," said the latter, "I know a man who has rendered great services to a very popular prince and who would make an excellent leader of revolt. Him I can place at your disposal; it is Count de Rochefort."

"I know him also, but unfortunately he is not in Paris."

"My lord, he has been for three days at the Rue Cassette."

"And wherefore has he not been to see me?"

"He was told--my lord will pardon me----"

"Certainly, speak."

"That your lordship was about to treat with the court."

Gondy bit his lips.

"They are mistaken; bring him here at eight o'clock, sir, and may Heaven bless you as I bless you!"

"And now 'tis your turn," said the coadjutor, turning to the last that remained; "have you anything as good to offer me as the two gentlemen who have left us?"

"Better, my lord."

"Diable! think what a solemn engagement you are making; one has offered a wealthy shopkeeper, the other a count; you are going, then, to offer a prince, are you?"

"I offer you a beggar, my lord."

"Ah! ah!" said Gondy, reflecting, "you are right, sir; some one who could raise the legion of paupers who choke up the crossings of Paris; some one who would know how to cry aloud to them, that all France might hear it, that it is Mazarin who has reduced them to poverty."

"Exactly your man."

"Bravo! and the man?"

"A plain and simple beggar, as I have said, my lord, who asks for alms, as he gives holy water; a practice he has carried on for six years on the steps of St. Eustache."

"And you say that he has a great influence over his compeers?"

"Are you aware, my lord, that mendacity is an organized body, a kind of association of those who have nothing against those who have everything; an association in which every one takes his share; one that elects a leader?"

"Yes, I have heard it said," replied the coadjutor.

"Well, the man whom I offer you is a general syndic."

"And what do you know of him?"

"Nothing, my lord, except that he is tormented with remorse."

"What makes you think so?"

"On the twenty-eighth of every month he makes me say a mass for the repose of the soul of one who died a violent death; yesterday I said this mass again."

"And his name?"

"Maillard; but I do not think it is his right one."

"And think you that we should find him at this hour at his post?"

"Certainly."

"Let us go and see your beggar, sir, and if he is such as you describe him, you are right--it will be you who have discovered the true treasure."

Gondy dressed himself as an officer, put on a felt cap with a red feather, hung on a long sword, buckled spurs to his boots, wrapped himself in an ample cloak and followed the curate.

The coadjutor and his companion passed through all the streets lying between the archbishopric and the St. Eustache Church, watching carefully to ascertain the popular feeling. The people were in an excited mood, but, like a swarm of frightened bees, seemed not to know at what point to concentrate; and it was very evident that if leaders of the people were not provided all this agitation would pass off in idle buzzing.

On arriving at the Rue des Prouvaires, the curate pointed toward the square before the church.

"Stop!" he said, "there he is at his post."

Gondy looked at the spot indicated and perceived a beggar seated in a chair and leaning against one of the moldings; a little basin was near him and he held a holy water brush in his hand.

"Is it by permission that he remains there?" asked Gondy.

"No, my lord; these places are bought. I believe this man paid his predecessor a hundred pistoles for his."

"The rascal is rich, then?"

"Some of those men sometimes die worth twenty thousand and twenty-five and thirty thousand francs and sometimes more."

"Hum!" said Gondy, laughing; "I was not aware my alms were so well invested."

In the meantime they were advancing toward the square, and the moment the coadjutor and the curate put their feet on the first church step the mendicant arose and proffered his brush.

He was a man between sixty-six and sixty-eight years of age, little, rather stout, with gray hair and light eyes. His countenance denoted the struggle between two opposite principles--a wicked nature, subdued by determination, perhaps by repentance.

He started on seeing the cavalier with the curate. The latter and the coadjutor touched the brush with the tips of their fingers and made the sign of the cross; the coadjutor threw a piece of money into the hat, which was on the ground.

"Maillard," began the curate, "this gentleman and I have come to talk with you a little."

"With me!" said the mendicant; "it is a great honor for a poor distributor of holy water."

There was an ironical tone in his voice which he could not quite disguise and which astonished the coadjutor.

"Yes," continued the curate, apparently accustomed to this tone, "yes, we wish to know your opinion of the events of to-day and what you have heard said by people going in and out of the church."

The mendicant shook his head.

"These are melancholy doings, your reverence, which always fall again upon the poor. As to what is said, everybody is discontented, everybody complains, but 'everybody' means 'nobody.'"

"Explain yourself, my good friend," said the coadjutor.

"I mean that all these cries, all these complaints, these curses, produce nothing but storms and flashes and that is all; but the lightning will not strike until there is a hand to guide it."

"My friend," said Gondy, "you seem to be a clever and a thoughtful man; are you disposed to take a part in a little civil war, should we have one, and put at the command of the leader, should we find one, your personal influence and the influence you have acquired over your comrades?"

"Yes, sir, provided this war were approved of by the church and would advance the end I wish to attain--I mean, the remission of my sins."

"The war will not only be approved of, but directed by the church. As for the remission of your sins, we have the archbishop of Paris, who has the very greatest power at the court of Rome, and even the coadjutor, who possesses some plenary indulgences; we will recommend you to him."

"Consider, Maillard," said the curate, "that I have recommended you to this gentleman, who is a powerful lord, and that I have made myself responsible for you."

"I know, monsieur le cure," said the beggar, "that you have always been very kind to me, and therefore I, in my turn, will be serviceable to you."

"And do you think your power as great with the fraternity as monsieur le cure told me it was just now?"

"I think they have some esteem for me," said the mendicant with pride, "and that not only will they obey me, but wherever I go they will follow me."

"And could you count on fifty resolute men, good, unemployed, but active souls, brawlers, capable of bringing down the walls of the Palais Royal by crying, 'Down with Mazarin,' as fell those at Jericho?"

"I think," said the beggar, "I can undertake things more difficult and more important than that."

"Ah, ah," said Gondy, "you will undertake, then, some night, to throw up some ten barricades?"

"I will undertake to throw up fifty, and when the day comes, to defend them."

"I'faith!" exclaimed Gondy, "you speak with a certainty that gives me pleasure; and since monsieur le cure can answer for you----"

"I answer for him," said the curate.

"Here is a bag containing five hundred pistoles in gold; make all your arrangements, and tell me where I shall be able to find you this evening at ten o'clock."

"It must be on some elevated place, whence a given signal may be seen in every part of Paris."

"Shall I give you a line for the vicar of St. Jacques de la Boucherie? he will let you into the rooms in his tower," said the curate.

"Capital," answered the mendicant.

"Then," said the coadjutor, "this evening, at ten o'clock, and if I am pleased with you another bag of five hundred pistoles will be at your disposal."

The eyes of the mendicant dashed with cupidity, but he quickly suppressed his emotion.

"This evening, sir," he replied, "all will be ready."

46. The Tower of St. Jacques de la Boucherie.

At a quarter to six o'clock, Monsieur de Gondy, having finished his business, returned to the archiepiscopal palace.

At six o'clock the curate of St. Merri was announced.

The coadjutor glanced rapidly behind and saw that he was followed by another man. The curate then entered, followed by Planchet.

"Your holiness," said the curate, "here is the person of whom I had the honor to speak to you."

Planchet saluted in the manner of one accustomed to fine houses.

"And you are disposed to serve the cause of the people?" asked Gondy.

"Most undoubtedly," said Planchet. "I am a Frondist from my heart. You see in me, such as I am, a person sentenced to be hung."

"And on what account?"

"I rescued from the hands of Mazarin's police a noble lord whom they were conducting back to the Bastile, where he had been for five years."

"Will you name him?"

"Oh, you know him well, my lord--it is Count de Rochefort."

"Ah! really, yes," said the coadjutor, "I have heard this affair mentioned. You raised the whole district, so they told me!"

"Very nearly," replied Planchet, with a self-satisfied air.

"And your business is----"

"That of a confectioner, in the Rue des Lombards."

"Explain to me how it happens that, following so peaceful a business, you had such warlike inclinations."

"Why does my lord, belonging to the church, now receive me in the dress of an officer, with a sword at his side and spurs to his boots?"

"Not badly answered, i'faith," said Gondy, laughing; "but I have, you must know, always had, in spite of my bands, warlike inclinations."

"Well, my lord, before I became a confectioner I myself was three years sergeant in the Piedmontese regiment, and before I became sergeant I was for eighteen months the servant of Monsieur d'Artagnan."

"The lieutenant of musketeers?" asked Gondy.

"Himself, my lord."

"But he is said to be a furious Mazarinist."

"Phew!" whistled Planchet.

"What do you mean by that?"

"Nothing, my lord; Monsieur d'Artagnan belongs to the service; Monsieur d'Artagnan makes it his business to defend the cardinal, who pays him, as much as we make it ours, we citizens, to attack him, whom he robs."

"You are an intelligent fellow, my friend; can we count upon you?"

"You may count upon me, my lord, provided you want to make a complete upheaval of the city."

"'Tis that exactly. How many men, think you, you could collect together to-night?"

"Two hundred muskets and five hundred halberds."

"Let there be only one man in every district who can do as much and by to-morrow we shall have quite a powerful army. Are you disposed to obey Count de Rochefort?"

"I would follow him to hell, and that is saying not a little, as I believe him entirely capable of the descent."

"Bravo!"

"By what sign to-morrow shall we be able to distinguish friends from foes?"

"Every Frondist must put a knot of straw in his hat."

"Good! Give the watchword."

"Do you want money?"

"Money never comes amiss at any time, my lord; if one has it not, one must do without it; with it, matters go on much better and more rapidly."

Gondy went to a box and drew forth a bag.

"Here are five hundred pistoles," he said; "and if the action goes off well you may reckon upon a similar sum to-morrow."

"I will give a faithful account of the sum to your lordship," said Planchet, putting the bag under his arm.

"That is right; I recommend the cardinal to your attention."

"Make your mind easy, he is in good hands."

Planchet went out, the curate remaining for a moment.

"Are you satisfied, my lord?" he asked.

"Yes; he appears to be a resolute fellow."

"Well, he will do more than he has promised."

"He will do wonders then."

The curate rejoined Planchet, who was waiting for him on the stairs. Ten minutes later the curate of St. Sulpice was announced. As soon as the door of Gondy's study was opened a man rushed in. It was the Count de Rochefort.

"'Tis you, then, my dear count," cried Gondy, offering his hand.

"You have made up your mind at last, my lord?" said Rochefort.

"It has been made up a long time," said Gondy.

"Let us say no more on the subject; you tell me so, I believe you. Well, we are going to give a ball to Mazarin."

"I hope so."

"And when will the dance begin?"

"The invitations are given for this evening," said the coadjutor, "but the violins will not begin to play until to-morrow morning."

"You may reckon upon me and upon fifty soldiers which the Chevalier d'Humieres has promised me whenever I need them."

"Upon fifty soldiers?"

"Yes, he is making recruits and he will lend them to me; if any are missing when the fete is over, I shall replace them."

"Good, my dear Rochefort; but that is not all. What have you done with Monsieur de Beaufort?"

"He is in Vendome, where he will wait until I write to him to return to Paris."

"Write to him; now's the time."

"You are sure of your enterprise?"

"Yes, but he must make haste; for hardly will the people of Paris have revolted before we shall have a score of princes begging to lead them. If he defers he will find the place of honor taken."

"Shall I send word to him as coming from you?"

"Yes certainly."

"Shall I tell him that he can count on you?"

"To the end."

"And you will leave the command to him?"

"Of the war, yes, but in politics----"

"You must know it is not his element."

"He must leave me to negotiate for my cardinal's hat in my own fashion."

"You care about it, then, so much?"

"Since they force me to wear a hat of a form which does not become me," said Gondy, "I wish at least that the hat should be red."

"One must not dispute matters of taste and colors," said Rochefort, laughing. "I answer for his consent."

"How soon can he be here?"

"In five days."

"Let him come and he will find a change, I will answer for it."

"Therefore, go and collect your fifty men and hold yourself in readiness."

"For what?"

"For everything."

"Is there any signal for the general rally?"

"A knot of straw in the hat."

"Very good. Adieu, my lord."

"Adieu, my dear Rochefort."

"Ah, Monsieur Mazarin, Monsieur Mazarin," said Rochefort, leading off his curate, who had not found an opportunity of uttering a single word during the foregoing dialogue, "you will see whether I am too old to be a man of action."

It was half-past nine o'clock and the coadjutor required half an hour to go from the archbishop's palace to the tower of St. Jacques de la Boucherie. He remarked that a light was burning in one of the highest windows of the tower. "Good," said he, "our syndic is at his post."

He knocked and the door was opened. The vicar himself awaited him, conducted him to the top of the tower, and when there pointed to a little door, placed the light which he had brought with him in a corner of the wall, that the coadjutor might be able to find it on his return, and went down again. Although the key was in the door the coadjutor knocked.

"Come in," said a voice which he recognized as that of the mendicant, whom he found lying on a kind of truckle bed. He rose on the entrance of the coadjutor, and at that moment ten o'clock struck.

"Well," said Gondy, "have you kept your word with me?"

"Not exactly," replied the mendicant.

"How is that?"

"You asked me for five hundred men, did you not? Well, I have ten thousand for you."

"You are not boasting?"

"Do you wish for a proof?"

"Yes."

There were three candles alight, each of which burnt before a window, one looking upon the city, the other upon the Palais Royal, and a third upon the Rue Saint Denis.

The man went silently to each of the candles and blew them out one after the other.

"What are you doing?" asked the coadjutor.

"I have given the signal."

"For what?"

"For the barricades. When you leave this you will behold my men at work. Only take care you do not break your legs in stumbling over some chain or your neck by falling in a hole."

"Good! there is your money, the same sum as that you have received already. Now remember that you are a general and do not go and drink."

"For twenty years I have tasted nothing but water."

The man took the bag from the hands of the coadjutor, who heard the sound of his fingers counting and handling the gold pieces.

"Ah! ah!" said the coadjutor, "you are avaricious, my good fellow."

The mendicant sighed and threw down the bag.

"Must I always be the same?" said he, "and shall I never succeed in overcoming the old leaven? Oh, misery, oh, vanity!"

"You take it, however."

"Yes, but I make hereby a vow in your presence, to employ all that remains to me in pious works."

His face was pale and drawn, like that of a man who had just undergone some inward struggle.

"Singular man!" muttered Gondy, taking his hat to go away; but on turning around he saw the beggar between him and the door. His first idea was that this man intended to do him some harm, but on the contrary he saw him fall on his knees before him with his hands clasped.

"Your blessing, your holiness, before you go, I beseech you!" he cried.

"Your holiness!" said Gondy; "my friend, you take me for some one else."

"No, your holiness, I take you for what you are, that is to say, the coadjutor; I recognized you at the first glance."

Gondy smiled. "And you want my blessing?" he said.

"Yes, I have need of it."

The mendicant uttered these words in a tone of such humility, such earnest repentance, that Gondy placed his hand upon him and gave him his benediction with all the unction of which he was capable.

"Now," said Gondy, "there is a communion between us. I have blessed you and you are sacred to me. Come, have you committed some crime, pursued by human justice, from which I can protect you?"

The beggar shook his head. "The crime which I have committed, my lord, has no call upon human justice, and you can only deliver me from it by blessing me frequently, as you have just done."

"Come, be candid," said the coadjutor, "you have not all your life followed the trade which you do now?"

"No, my lord. I have pursued it for six years only."

"And previously, where were you?"

"In the Bastile."

"And before you went to the Bastile?"

"I will tell you, my lord, on the day when you are willing to hear my confession."

"Good! At whatsoever hour of the day or night you may present yourself, remember that I shall be ready to give you absolution."

"Thank you, my lord," said the mendicant in a hoarse voice. "But I am not yet ready to receive it."

"Very well. Adieu."

"Adieu, your holiness," said the mendicant, opening the door and bending low before the prelate.

47. The Riot.

It was about eleven o'clock at night. Gondy had not walked a hundred steps ere he perceived the strange change which had been made in the streets of Paris.

The whole city seemed peopled with fantastic beings; silent shadows were seen unpaving the streets and others dragging and upsetting great wagons, whilst others again dug ditches large enough to ingulf whole regiments of horsemen. These active beings flitted here and there like so many demons completing some unknown labor; these were the beggars of the Court of Miracles--the agents of the giver of holy water in the Square of Saint Eustache, preparing barricades for the morrow.

Gondy gazed on these deeds of darkness, on these nocturnal laborers, with a kind of fear; he asked himself, if, after having called forth these foul creatures from their dens, he should have the power of making them retire again. He felt almost inclined to cross himself when one of these beings happened to approach him. He reached the Rue Saint Honore and went up it toward the Rue de la Ferronnerie; there the aspect changed; here it was the tradesmen who were running from shop to shop; their doors seemed closed like their shutters, but they were only pushed to in such a manner as to open and allow the men, who seemed fearful of showing what they carried, to enter, closing immediately. These men were shopkeepers, who had arms to lend to those who had none.

One individual went from door to door, bending under the weight of swords, guns, muskets and every kind of weapon, which he deposited as fast as he could. By the light of a lantern the coadjutor recognized Planchet.

The coadjutor proceeded onward to the quay by way of the Rue de la Monnaie; there he found groups of bourgeois clad in black cloaks or gray, according as they belonged to the upper or lower bourgeoisie. They were standing motionless, while single men passed from one group to another. All these cloaks, gray or black, were raised behind by the point of a sword, or before by the barrel of an arquebuse or a musket.

On reaching the Pont Neuf the coadjutor found it strictly guarded and a man approached him.

"Who are you?" asked the man. "I do not know you for one of us."

"Then it is because you do not know your friends, my dear Monsieur Louvieres," said the coadjutor, raising his hat.

Louvieres recognized him and bowed.

Gondy continued his way and went as far as the Tour de Nesle. There he saw a lengthy chain of people gliding under the walls. They might be said to be a procession of ghosts, for they were all wrapped in white cloaks. When they reached a certain spot these men appeared to be annihilated, one after the other, as if the earth had opened under their feet. Gondy, edged into a corner, saw them vanish from the first until the last but one. The last raised his eyes, to ascertain, doubtless, that neither his companions nor himself had been watched, and, in spite of the darkness, he perceived Gondy. He walked straight up to him and placed a pistol to his throat.

"Halloo! Monsieur de Rochefort," said Gondy, laughing, "are you a boy to play with firearms?"

Rochefort recognized the voice.

"Ah, it is you, my lord!" said he.

"The very same. What people are you leading thus into the bowels of the earth?"

"My fifty recruits from the Chevalier d'Humieres, who are destined to enter the light cavalry and who have only received as yet for their equipment their white cloaks."

"And where are you going?"

"To the house of one of my friends, a sculptor, only we enter by the trap through which he lets down his marble."

"Very good," said Gondy, shaking Rochefort by the hand, who descended in his turn and closed the trap after him.

It was now one o'clock in the morning and the coadjutor returned home. He opened a window and leaned out to listen. A strange, incomprehensible, unearthly sound seemed to pervade the whole city; one felt that something unusual and terrible was happening in all the streets, now dark as ocean's most unfathomable caves. From time to time a dull sound was heard, like that of a rising tempest or a billow of the sea; but nothing clear, nothing distinct, nothing intelligible; it was like those mysterious subterraneous noises that precede an earthquake.

The work of revolt continued the whole night thus. The next morning, on awaking, Paris seemed to be startled at her own appearance. It was like a besieged town. Armed men, shouldering muskets, watched over the barricades with menacing looks; words of command, patrols, arrests, executions, even, were encountered at every step. Those bearing plumed hats and gold swords were stopped and made to cry, "Long live Broussel!" "Down with Mazarin!" and whoever refused to comply with this ceremony was hooted at, spat upon and even beaten. They had not yet begun to slay, but it was well felt that the inclination to do so was not wanting.

The barricades had been pushed as far as the Palais Royal. From the Rue de Bons Enfants to that of the Ferronnerie, from the Rue Saint Thomas-du-Louvre to the Pont Neuf, from the Rue Richelieu to the Porte Saint Honore, there were more than ten thousand armed men; those who were at the front hurled defiance at the impassive sentinels of the regiment of guards posted around the Palais Royal, the gates of which were closed behind them, a precaution which made their situation precarious. Among these thousands moved, in bands numbering from one hundred to two hundred, pale and haggard men, clothed in rags, who bore a sort of standard on which was inscribed these words: "Behold the misery of the people!" Wherever these men passed, frenzied cries were heard; and there were so many of these bands that the cries were to be heard in all directions.

The astonishment of Mazarin and of Anne of Austria was great when it was announced to them that the city, which the previous evening they had left entirely tranquil, had awakened to such feverish commotion; nor would either the one or the other believe the reports that were brought to them, declaring they would rather rely on the evidence of their own eyes and ears. Then a window was opened and when they saw and heard they were convinced.

Mazarin shrugged his shoulders and pretended to despise the populace; but he turned visibly pale and ran to his closet, trembling all over, locked up his gold and jewels in his caskets and put his finest diamonds on his fingers. As for the queen, furious, and left to her own guidance, she went for the Marechal de la Meilleraie and desired him to take as many men as he pleased and to go and see what was the meaning of this pleasantry.

The marshal was ordinarily very adventurous and was wont to hesitate at nothing; and he had that lofty contempt for the populace which army officers usually profess. He took a hundred and fifty men and attempted to go out by the Pont du Louvre, but there he met Rochefort and his fifty horsemen, attended by more than five hundred men. The marshal made no attempt to force that barrier and returned up the quay. But at Pont Neuf he found Louvieres and his bourgeois. This time the marshal charged, but he was welcomed by musket shots, while stones fell like hail from all the windows. He left there three men.

He beat a retreat toward the market, but there he met Planchet with his halberdiers; their halberds were leveled at him threateningly. He attempted to ride over those gray cloaks, but the gray cloaks held their ground and the marshal retired toward the Rue Saint Honore, leaving four of his guards dead on the field of battle.

The marshal then entered the Rue Saint Honore, but there he was opposed by the barricades of the mendicant of Saint Eustache. They were guarded, not only by armed men, but even by women and children. Master Friquet, the owner of a pistol and of a sword which Louvieres had given him, had organized a company of rogues like himself and was making a tremendous racket.

The marshal thought this barrier not so well fortified as the others and determined to break through it. He dismounted twenty men to make a breach in the barricade, whilst he and others, remaining on their horses, were to protect the assailants. The twenty men marched straight toward the barrier, but from behind the beams, from among the wagon-wheels and from the heights of the rocks a terrible fusillade burst forth and at the same time Planchet's halberdiers appeared at the corner of the Cemetery of the Innocents, and Louvieres's bourgeois at the corner of the Rue de la Monnaie.

The Marechal de la Meilleraie was caught between two fires, but he was brave and made up his mind to die where he was. He returned blow for blow and cries of pain began to be heard in the crowd. The guards, more skillful, did greater execution; but the bourgeois, more numerous, overwhelmed them with a veritable hurricane of iron. Men fell around him as they had fallen at Rocroy or at Lerida. Fontrailles, his aide-de-camp, had an arm broken; his horse had received a bullet in his neck and he had difficulty in controlling him, maddened by pain. In short, he had reached that supreme moment when the bravest feel a shudder in their veins, when suddenly, in the direction of the Rue de l'Arbre-Sec, the crowd opened, crying: "Long live the coadjutor!" and Gondy, in surplice and cloak, appeared, moving tranquilly in the midst of the fusillade and bestowing his benedictions to the right and left, as undisturbed as if he were leading a procession of the Fete Dieu.

All fell to their knees. The marshal recognized him and hastened to meet him.

"Get me out of this, in Heaven's name!" he said, "or I shall leave my carcass here and those of all my men."

A great tumult arose, in the midst of which even the noise of thunder could not have been heard. Gondy raised his hand and demanded silence. All were still.

"My children," he said, "this is the Marechal de la Meilleraie, as to whose intentions you have been deceived and who pledges himself, on returning to the Louvre, to demand of the queen, in your name, our Broussel's release. You pledge yourself to that, marshal?" added Gondy, turning to La Meilleraie.

"Morbleu!" cried the latter, "I should say that I do pledge myself to it! I had no hope of getting off so easily."

"He gives you his word of honor," said Gondy.

The marshal raised his hand in token of assent.

"Long live the coadjutor!" cried the crowd. Some voices even added: "Long live the marshal!" But all took up the cry in chorus: "Down with Mazarin!"

The crowd gave place, the barricade was opened, and the marshal, with the remnant of his company, retreated, preceded by Friquet and his bandits, some of them making a presence of beating drums and others imitating the sound of the trumpet. It was almost a triumphal procession; only, behind the guards the barricades were closed again. The marshal bit his fingers.

In the meantime, as we have said, Mazarin was in his closet, putting his affairs in order. He called for D'Artagnan, but in the midst of such tumult he little expected to see him, D'Artagnan not being on service. In about ten minutes D'Artagnan appeared at the door, followed by the inseparable Porthos.

"Ah, come in, come in, Monsieur d'Artagnan!" cried the cardinal, "and welcome your friend too. But what is going on in this accursed Paris?"

"What is going on, my lord? nothing good," replied D'Artagnan, shaking his head. "The town is in open revolt, and just now, as I was crossing the Rue Montorgueil with Monsieur du Vallon, who is here, and is your humble servant, they wanted in spite of my uniform, or perhaps because of my uniform, to make us cry 'Long live Broussel!' and must I tell you, my lord what they wished us to cry as well?"

"Speak, speak."

"'Down with Mazarin!' I'faith, the treasonable word is out."

Mazarin smiled, but became very pale.

"And you did cry?" he asked.

"I'faith, no," said D'Artagnan; "I was not in voice; Monsieur du Vallon has a cold and did not cry either. Then, my lord----"

"Then what?" asked Mazarin.

"Look at my hat and cloak."

And D'Artagnan displayed four gunshot holes in his cloak and two in his beaver. As for Porthos's coat, a blow from a halberd had cut it open on the flank and a pistol shot had cut his feather in two.

"Diavolo!" said the cardinal, pensively gazing at the two friends with lively admiration; "I should have cried, I should."

At this moment the tumult was heard nearer.

Mazarin wiped his forehead and looked around him. He had a great desire to go to the window, but he dared not.

"See what is going on, Monsieur D'Artagnan," said he.

D'Artagnan went to the window with his habitual composure. "Oho!" said he, "what is this? Marechal de la Meilleraie returning without a hat--Fontrailles with his arm in a sling--wounded guards--horses bleeding; eh, then, what are the sentinels about? They are aiming--they are going to fire!"

"They have received orders to fire on the people if the people approach the Palais Royal!" exclaimed Mazarin.

"But if they fire, all is lost!" cried D'Artagnan.

"We have the gates."

"The gates! to hold for five minutes--the gates, they will be torn down, twisted into iron wire, ground to powder! God's death, don't fire!" screamed D'Artagnan, throwing open the window.

In spite of this recommendation, which, owing to the noise, could scarcely have been heard, two or three musket shots resounded, succeeded by a terrible discharge. The balls might be heard peppering the facade of the Palais Royal, and one of them, passing under D'Artagnan's arm, entered and broke a mirror, in which Porthos was complacently admiring himself.

"Alack! alack!" cried the cardinal, "a Venetian glass!"

"Oh, my lord," said D'Artagnan, quietly shutting the window, "it is not worth while weeping yet, for probably an hour hence there will not be one of your mirrors remaining in the Palais Royal, whether they be Venetian or Parisian."

"But what do you advise, then?" asked Mazarin, trembling.

"Eh, egad, to give up Broussel as they demand! What the devil do you want with a member of the parliament? He is of no earthly use to anybody."

"And you, Monsieur du Vallon, is that your advice? What would you do?"

"I should give up Broussel," said Porthos.

"Come, come with me, gentlemen!" exclaimed Mazarin. "I will go and discuss the matter with the queen."

He stopped at the end of the corridor and said:

"I can count upon you, gentlemen, can I not?"

"We do not give ourselves twice over," said D'Artagnan; "we have given ourselves to you; command, we shall obey."

"Very well, then," said Mazarin; "enter this cabinet and wait till I come back."

And turning off he entered the drawing-room by another door.

48. The Riot becomes a Revolution.

The closet into which D'Artagnan and Porthos had been ushered was separated from the drawing-room where the queen was by tapestried curtains only, and this thin partition enabled them to hear all that passed in the adjoining room, whilst the aperture between the two hangings, small as it was, permitted them to see.

The queen was standing in the room, pale with anger; her self-control, however, was so great that it might have been imagined that she was calm. Comminges, Villequier and Guitant were behind her and the women again were behind the men. The Chancellor Sequier, who twenty years previously had persecuted her so ruthlessly, stood before her, relating how his carriage had been smashed, how he had been pursued and had rushed into the Hotel d'O----, that the hotel was immediately invaded, pillaged and devastated; happily he had time to reach a closet hidden behind tapestry, in which he was secreted by an old woman, together with his brother, the Bishop of Meaux. Then the danger was so imminent, the rioters came so near, uttering such threats, that the chancellor thought his last hour had come and confessed himself to his brother priest, so as to be all ready to die in case he was discovered. Fortunately, however, he had not been taken; the people, believing that he had escaped by some back entrance, retired and left him at liberty to retreat. Then, disguised in he clothes of the Marquis d'O----, he had left the hotel, stumbling over the bodies of an officer and two guards who had been killed whilst defending the street door.

During the recital Mazarin entered and glided noiselessly up to the queen to listen.

"Well," said the queen, when the chancellor had finished speaking; "what do you think of it all?"

"I think that matters look very gloomy, madame."

"But what step would you propose to me?"

"I could propose one to your majesty, but I dare not."

"You may, you may, sir," said the queen with a bitter smile; "you were not so timid once."

The chancellor reddened and stammered some words.

"It is not a question of the past, but of the present," said the queen; "you said you could give me advice--what is it?"

"Madame," said the chancellor, hesitating, "it would be to release Broussel."

The queen, although already pale, became visibly paler and her face was contracted.

"Release Broussel!" she cried, "never!"

At this moment steps were heard in the ante-room and without any announcement the Marechal de la Meilleraie appeared at the door.

"Ah, there you are, marechal," cried Anne of Austria joyfully. "I trust you have brought this rabble to reason."

"Madame," replied the marechal, "I have left three men on the Pont Neuf, four at the Halle, six at the corner of the Rue de l'Arbre-Sec and two at the door of your palace--fifteen in all. I have brought away ten or twelve wounded. I know not where I have left my hat, and in all probability I should have been left with my hat, had the coadjutor not arrived in time to rescue me."

"Ah, indeed," said the queen, "it would have much astonished me if that low cur, with his distorted legs, had not been mixed up with all this."

"Madame," said La Meilleraie, "do not say too much against him before me, for the service he rendered me is still fresh."

"Very good," said the queen, "be as grateful as you like, it does not implicate me; you are here safe and sound, that is all I wished for; you are not only welcome, but welcome back."

"Yes, madame; but I only came back on one condition--that I would transmit to your majesty the will of the people."

"The will!" exclaimed the queen, frowning. "Oh! oh! monsieur marechal, you must indeed have found yourself in wondrous peril to have undertaken so strange a commission!"

The irony with which these words were uttered did not escape the marechal.

"Pardon, madame," he said, "I am not a lawyer, I am a mere soldier, and probably, therefore, I do not quite comprehend the value of certain words; I ought to have said the wishes, and not the will, of the people. As for what you do me the honor to say, I presume you mean I was afraid?"

The queen smiled.

"Well, then, madame, yes, I did feel fear; and though I have been through twelve pitched battles and I cannot count how many charges and skirmishes, I own for the third time in my life I was afraid. Yes, and I would rather face your majesty, however threatening your smile, than face those demons who accompanied me hither and who sprung from I know not whence, unless from deepest hell."

("Bravo," said D'Artagnan in a whisper to Porthos; "well answered.")

"Well," said the queen, biting her lips, whilst her courtiers looked at each other with surprise, "what is the desire of my people?"

"That Broussel shall be given up to them, madame."

"Never!" said the queen, "never!"

"Your majesty is mistress," said La Meilleraie, retreating a few steps.

"Where are you going, marechal?" asked the queen.

"To give your majesty's reply to those who await it."

"Stay, marechal; I will not appear to parley with rebels."

"Madame, I have pledged my word, and unless you order me to be arrested I shall be forced to return."

Anne of Austria's eyes shot glances of fire.

"Oh! that is no impediment, sir," said she; "I have had greater men than you arrested--Guitant!"

Mazarin sprang forward.

"Madame," said he, "if I dared in my turn advise----"

"Would it be to give up Broussel, sir? If so, you can spare yourself the trouble."

"No," said Mazarin; "although, perhaps, that counsel is as good as any other."

"Then what may it be?"

"To call for monsieur le coadjuteur."

"The coadjutor!" cried the queen, "that dreadful mischief maker! It is he who has raised all this revolt."

"The more reason," said Mazarin; "if he has raised it he can put it down."

"And hold, madame," suggested Comminges, who was near a window, out of which he could see; "hold, the moment is a happy one, for there he is now, giving his blessing in the square of the Palais Royal."

The queen sprang to the window.

"It is true," she said, "the arch hypocrite--see!"

"I see," said Mazarin, "that everybody kneels before him, although he be but coadjutor, whilst I, were I in his place, though I am cardinal, should be torn to pieces. I persist, then, madame, in my wish" (he laid an emphasis on the word), "that your majesty should receive the coadjutor."

"And wherefore do you not say, like the rest, your will?" replied the queen, in a low voice.

Mazarin bowed.

"Monsieur le marechal," said the queen, after a moment's reflection, "go and find the coadjutor and bring him to me."

"And what shall I say to the people?"

"That they must have patience," said Anne, "as I have."

The fiery Spanish woman spoke in a tone so imperative that the marechal made no reply; he bowed and went out.

(D'Artagnan turned to Porthos. "How will this end?" he said.

"We shall soon see," said Porthos, in his tranquil way.)

In the meantime Anne of Austria approached Comminges and conversed with him in a subdued tone, whilst Mazarin glanced uneasily at the corner occupied by D'Artagnan and Porthos. Ere long the door opened and the marechal entered, followed by the coadjutor.

"There, madame," he said, "is Monsieur Gondy, who hastens to obey your majesty's summons."

The queen advanced a few steps to meet him, and then stopped, cold, severe, unmoved, with her lower lip scornfully protruded.

Gondy bowed respectfully.

"Well, sir," said the queen, "what is your opinion of this riot?"

"That it is no longer a riot, madame," he replied, "but a revolt."

"The revolt is at the door of those who think my people can rebel," cried Anne, unable to dissimulate before the coadjutor, whom she looked upon, and probably with reason, as the promoter of the tumult. "Revolt! thus it is called by those who have wished for this demonstration and who are, perhaps, the cause of it; but, wait, wait! the king's authority will put all this to rights."

"Was it to tell me that, madame," coldly replied Gondy, "that your majesty admitted me to the honor of entering your presence?"

"No, my dear coadjutor," said Mazarin; "it was to ask your advice in the unhappy dilemma in which we find ourselves."

"Is it true," asked Gondy, feigning astonishment, "that her majesty summoned me to ask for my opinion?"

"Yes," said the queen, "it is requested."

The coadjutor bowed.

"Your majesty wishes, then----"

"You to say what you would do in her place," Mazarin hastened to reply.

The coadjutor looked at the queen, who replied by a sign in the affirmative.

"Were I in her majesty's place," said Gondy, coldly, "I should not hesitate; I should release Broussel."

"And if I do not give him up, what think you will be the result?" exclaimed the queen.

"I believe that not a stone in Paris will remain unturned," put in the marechal.

"It was not your opinion that I asked," said the queen, sharply, without even turning around.

"If it is I whom your majesty interrogates," replied the coadjutor in the same calm manner, "I reply that I hold monsieur le marechal's opinion in every respect."

The color mounted to the queen's face; her fine blue eyes seemed to start out of her head and her carmine lips, compared by all the poets of the day to a pomegranate in flower, were trembling with anger. Mazarin himself, who was well accustomed to the domestic outbreaks of this disturbed household, was alarmed.

"Give up Broussel!" she cried; "fine counsel, indeed. Upon my word! one can easily see it comes from a priest."

Gondy remained firm, and the abuse of the day seemed to glide over his head as the sarcasms of the evening before had done; but hatred and revenge were accumulating in his heart silently and drop by drop. He looked coldly at the queen, who nudged Mazarin to make him say something in his turn.

Mazarin, according to his custom, was thinking much and saying little.

"Ho! ho!" said he, "good advice, advice of a friend. I, too, would give up that good Monsieur Broussel, dead or alive, and all would be at an end."

"If you yield him dead, all will indeed be at an end, my lord, but quite otherwise than you mean."

"Did I say 'dead or alive?'" replied Mazarin. "It was only a way of speaking. You know I am not familiar with the French language, which you, monsieur le coadjuteur, both speak and write so well."

("This is a council of state," D'Artagnan remarked to Porthos; "but we held better ones at La Rochelle, with Athos and Aramis."

"At the Saint Gervais bastion," said Porthos.

"There and elsewhere.")

The coadjutor let the storm pass over his head and resumed, still with the same tranquillity:

"Madame, if the opinion I have submitted to you does not please you it is doubtless because you have better counsels to follow. I know too well the wisdom of the queen and that of her advisers to suppose that they will leave the capital long in trouble that may lead to a revolution."

"Thus, then, it is your opinion," said Anne of Austria, with a sneer and biting her lips with rage, "that yesterday's riot, which to-day is already a rebellion, to-morrow may become a revolution?"

"Yes, madame," replied the coadjutor, gravely.

"But if I am to believe you, sir, the people seem to have thrown off all restraint."

"It is a bad year for kings," said Gondy, shaking his head; "look at England, madame."

"Yes; but fortunately we have no Oliver Cromwell in France," replied the queen.

"Who knows?" said Gondy; "such men are like thunderbolts--one recognizes them only when they have struck."

Every one shuddered and there was a moment of silence, during which the queen pressed her hand to her side, evidently to still the beatings of her heart.

("Porthos," murmured D'Artagnan, "look well at that priest."

"Yes," said Porthos, "I see him. What then?"

"Well, he is a man."

Porthos looked at D'Artagnan in astonishment. Evidently he did not understand his meaning.)

"Your majesty," continued the coadjutor, pitilessly, "is about to take such measures as seem good to you, but I foresee that they will be violent and such as will still further exasperate the rioters."

"In that case, you, monsieur le coadjuteur, who have such power over them and are at the same time friendly to us," said the queen, ironically, "will quiet them by bestowing your blessing upon them."

"Perhaps it will be too late," said Gondy, still unmoved; "perhaps I shall have lost all influence; while by giving up Broussel your majesty will strike at the root of the sedition and will gain the right to punish severely any revival of the revolt."

"Have I not, then, that right?" cried the queen.

"If you have it, use it," replied Gondy.

("Peste!" said D'Artagnan to Porthos. "There is a man after my own heart. Oh! if he were minister and I were his D'Artagnan, instead of belonging to that beast of a Mazarin, mordieu! what fine things we would do together!"

"Yes," said Porthos.)

The queen made a sign for every one, except Mazarin, to quit the room; and Gondy bowed, as if to leave with the rest.

"Stay, sir," said Anne to him.

"Good," thought Gondy, "she is going to yield."

("She is going to have him killed," said D'Artagnan to Porthos, "but at all events it shall not be by me. I swear to Heaven, on the contrary, that if they fall upon him I will fall upon them."

"And I, too," said Porthos.)

"Good," muttered Mazarin, sitting down, "we shall soon see something startling."

The queen's eyes followed the retreating figures and when the last had closed the door she turned away. It was evident that she was making unnatural efforts to subdue her anger; she fanned herself, smelled at her vinaigrette and walked up and down. Gondy, who began to feel uneasy, examined the tapestry with his eyes, touched the coat of mail which he wore under his long gown and felt from time to time to see if the handle of a good Spanish dagger, which was hidden under his cloak, was well within reach.

"And now," at last said the queen, "now that we are alone, repeat your counsel, monsieur le coadjuteur."

"It is this, madame: that you should appear to have reflected, and publicly acknowledge an error, which constitutes the extra strength of a strong government; release Broussel from prison and give him back to the people."

"Oh!" cried Anne, "to humble myself thus! Am I, or am I not, the queen? This screaming mob, are they, or are they not, my subjects? Have I friends? Have I guards? Ah! by Notre Dame! as Queen Catherine used to say," continued she, excited by her own words, "rather than give up this infamous Broussel to them I will strangle him with my own hands!"

And she sprang toward Gondy, whom assuredly at that moment she hated more than Broussel, with outstretched arms. The coadjutor remained immovable and not a muscle of his face was discomposed; only his glance flashed like a sword in returning the furious looks of the queen.

("He were a dead man" said the Gascon, "if there were still a Vitry at the court and if Vitry entered at this moment; but for my part, before he could reach the good prelate I would kill Vitry at once; the cardinal would be infinitely pleased with me."

"Hush!" said Porthos; "listen.")

"Madame," cried the cardinal, seizing hold of Anne and drawing her back, "Madame, what are you about?"

Then he added in Spanish, "Anne, are you mad? You, a queen to quarrel like a washerwoman! And do you not perceive that in the person of this priest is represented the whole people of Paris and that it is dangerous to insult him at this moment, and if this priest wished it, in an hour you would be without a crown? Come, then, on another occasion you can be firm and strong; but to-day is not the proper time; to-day, flatter and caress, or you are only a common woman."

(At the first words of this address D'Artagnan had seized Porthos's arm, which he pressed with gradually increasing force. When Mazarin ceased speaking he said to Porthos in a low tone:

"Never tell Mazarin that I understand Spanish, or I am a lost man and you are also."

"All right," said Porthos.)

This rough appeal, marked by the eloquence which characterized Mazarin when he spoke in Italian or Spanish and which he lost entirely in speaking French, was uttered with such impenetrable expression that Gondy, clever physiognomist as he was, had no suspicion of its being more than a simple warning to be more subdued.

The queen, on her part, thus chided, softened immediately and sat down, and in an almost weeping voice, letting her arms fall by her side, said:

"Pardon me, sir, and attribute this violence to what I suffer. A woman, and consequently subject to the weaknesses of my sex, I am alarmed at the idea of civil war; a queen, accustomed to be obeyed, I am excited at the first opposition."

"Madame," replied Gondy, bowing, "your majesty is mistaken in qualifying my sincere advice as opposition. Your majesty has none but submissive and respectful subjects. It is not the queen with whom the people are displeased; they ask for Broussel and are only too happy, if you release him to them, to live under your government."

Mazarin, who at the words, "It is not the queen with whom the people are displeased," had pricked up his ears, thinking that the coadjutor was about to speak of the cries, "Down with Mazarin," and pleased with Gondy's suppression of this fact, he said with his sweetest voice and his most gracious expression:

"Madame, credit the coadjutor, who is one of the most able politicians we have; the first available cardinal's hat seems to belong already to his noble brow."

"Ah! how much you have need of me, cunning rogue!" thought Gondy.

("And what will he promise us?" said D'Artagnan. "Peste, if he is giving away hats like that, Porthos, let us look out and both demand a regiment to-morrow. Corbleu! let the civil war last but one year and I will have a constable's sword gilt for me."

"And for me?" put in Porthos.

"For you? I will give you the baton of the Marechal de la Meilleraie, who does not seem to be much in favor just now.")

"And so, sir," said the queen, "you are seriously afraid of a public tumult."

"Seriously," said Gondy, astonished at not having further advanced; "I fear that when the torrent has broken its embankment it will cause fearful destruction."

"And I," said the queen, "think that in such a case other embankments should be raised to oppose it. Go; I will reflect."

Gondy looked at Mazarin, astonished, and Mazarin approached the queen to speak to her, but at this moment a frightful tumult arose from the square of the Palais Royal.

Gondy smiled, the queen's color rose and Mazarin grew even paler.

"What is that again?" he asked.

At this moment Comminges rushed into the room.

"Pardon, your majesty," he cried, "but the people have dashed the sentinels against the gates and they are now forcing the doors; what are your commands?"

"Listen, madame," said Gondy.

The moaning of waves, the noise of thunder, the roaring of a volcano, cannot be compared with the tempest of cries heard at that moment.

"What are my commands?" said the queen.

"Yes, for time presses."

"How many men have you about the Palais Royal?"

"Six hundred."

"Place a hundred around the king and with the remainder sweep away this mob for me."

"Madame," cried Mazarin, "what are you about?"

"Go!" said the queen.

Comminges went out with a soldier's passive obedience.

At this moment a monstrous battering was heard. One of the gates began to yield.

"Oh! madame," cried Mazarin, "you have ruined us all--the king, yourself and me."

At this cry from the soul of the frightened cardinal, Anne became alarmed in her turn and would have recalled Comminges.

"It is too late," said Mazarin, tearing his hair, "too late!"

The gale had given way. Hoarse shouts were heard from the excited mob. D'Artagnan put his hand to his sword, motioning to Porthos to follow his example.

"Save the queen!" cried Mazarin to the coadjutor.

Gondy sprang to the window and threw it open; he recognized Louvieres at the head of a troop of about three or four thousand men.

"Not a step further," he shouted, "the queen is signing!"

"What are you saying?" asked the queen.

"The truth, madame," said Mazarin, placing a pen and a paper before her, "you must;" then he added: "Sign, Anne, I implore you--I command you."

The queen fell into a chair, took the pen and signed.

The people, kept back by Louvieres, had not made another step forward; but the awful murmuring, which indicates an angry people, continued.

The queen had written, "The keeper of the prison at Saint Germain will set Councillor Broussel at liberty;" and she had signed it.

The coadjutor, whose eyes devoured her slightest movements, seized the paper immediately the signature had been affixed to it, returned to the window and waved it in his hand.

"This is the order," he said.

All Paris seemed to shout with joy, and then the air resounded with the cries of "Long live Broussel!" "Long live the coadjutor!"

"Long live the queen!" cried De Gondy; but the cries which replied to his were poor and few, and perhaps he had but uttered it to make Anne of Austria sensible of her weakness.

"And now that you have obtained what you want, go," said she, "Monsieur de Gondy."

"Whenever her majesty has need of me," replied the coadjutor, bowing, "her majesty knows I am at her command."

"Ah, cursed priest!" cried Anne, when he had retired, stretching out her arm to the scarcely closed door, "one day I will make you drink the dregs of the atrocious gall you have poured out on me to-day."

Mazarin wished to approach her. "Leave me!" she exclaimed; "you are not a man!" and she went out of the room.

"It is you who are not a woman," muttered Mazarin.

Then, after a moment of reverie, he remembered where he had left D'Artagnan and Porthos and that they must have overheard everything. He knit his brows and went direct to the tapestry, which he pushed aside. The closet was empty.

At the queen's last word, D'Artagnan had dragged Porthos into the gallery. Thither Mazarin went in his turn and found the two friends walking up and down.

"Why did you leave the closet, Monsieur d'Artagnan?" asked the cardinal.

"Because," replied D'Artagnan, "the queen desired every one to leave and I thought that this command was intended for us as well as for the rest."

"And you have been here since----"

"About a quarter of an hour," said D'Artagnan, motioning to Porthos not to contradict him.

Mazarin saw the sign and remained convinced that D'Artagnan had seen and heard everything; but he was pleased with his falsehood.

"Decidedly, Monsieur d'Artagnan, you are the man I have been seeking. You may reckon upon me and so may your friend." Then bowing to the two musketeers with his most gracious smile, he re-entered his closet more calmly, for on the departure of De Gondy the uproar had ceased as though by enchantment.

49. Misfortune refreshes the Memory.

Anne of Austria returned to her oratory, furious.

"What!" she cried, wringing her beautiful hands, "What! the people have seen Monsieur de Conde, a prince of the blood royal, arrested by my mother-in-law, Maria de Medicis; they saw my mother-in-law, their former regent, expelled by the cardinal; they saw Monsieur de Vendome, that is to say, the son of Henry IV., a prisoner at Vincennes; and whilst these great personages were imprisoned, insulted and threatened, they said nothing; and now for a Broussel--good God! what, then, is to become of royalty?"

The queen unconsciously touched here upon the exciting question. The people had made no demonstration for the princes, but they had risen for Broussel; they were taking the part of a plebeian and in defending Broussel they instinctively felt they were defending themselves.

During this time Mazarin walked up and down the study, glancing from time to time at his beautiful Venetian mirror, starred in every direction. "Ah!" he said, "it is sad, I know well, to be forced to yield thus; but, pshaw! we shall have our revenge. What matters it about Broussel--it is a name, not a thing."

Mazarin, clever politician as he was, was for once mistaken; Broussel was a thing, not a name.

The next morning, therefore, when Broussel made his entrance into Paris in a large carriage, having his son Louvieres at his side and Friquet behind the vehicle, the people threw themselves in his way and cries of "Long live Broussel!" "Long live our father!" resounded from all parts and was death to Mazarin's ears; and the cardinal's spies brought bad news from every direction, which greatly agitated the minister, but was calmly received by the queen. The latter seemed to be maturing in her mind some great stroke, a fact which increased the uneasiness of the cardinal, who knew the proud princess and dreaded much the determination of Anne of Austria.

The coadjutor returned to parliament more a monarch than king, queen, and cardinal, all three together. By his advice a decree from parliament summoned the citizens to lay down their arms and demolish the barricades. They now knew that it required but one hour to take up arms again and one night to reconstruct the barricades.

Rochefort had returned to the Chevalier d'Humieres his fifty horsemen, less two, missing at roll call. But the chevalier was himself at heart a Frondist and would hear nothing said of compensation.

The mendicant had gone to his old place on the steps of Saint Eustache and was again distributing holy water with one hand and asking alms with the other. No one could suspect that those two hands had been engaged with others in drawing out from the social edifice the keystone of royalty.

Louvieres was proud and satisfied; he had taken revenge on Mazarin and had aided in his father's deliverance from prison. His name had been mentioned as a name of terror at the Palais Royal. Laughingly he said to the councillor, restored to his family:

"Do you think, father, that if now I should ask for a company the queen would give it to me?"

D'Artagnan profited by this interval of calm to send away Raoul, whom he had great difficulty in keeping shut up during the riot, and who wished positively to strike a blow for one party or the other. Raoul had offered some opposition at first; but D'Artagnan made use of the Comte de la Fere's name, and after paying a visit to Madame de Chevreuse, Raoul started to rejoin the army.

Rochefort alone was dissatisfied with the termination of affairs. He had written to the Duc de Beaufort to come and the duke was about to arrive, and he world find Paris tranquil. He went to the coadjutor to consult with him whether it would not be better to send word to the duke to stop on the road, but Gondy reflected for a moment, and then said:

"Let him continue his journey."

"All is not then over?" asked Rochefort.

"My dear count, we have only just begun."

"What induces you to think so?"

"The knowledge that I have of the queen's heart; she will not rest contented beaten."

"Is she, then, preparing for a stroke?"

"I hope so."

"Come, let us see what you know."

"I know that she has written to the prince to return in haste from the army."

"Ah! ha!" said Rochefort, "you are right. We must let Monsieur de Beaufort come."

In fact, the evening after this conversation the report was circulated that the Prince de Conde had arrived. It was a very simple, natural circumstance and yet it created a profound sensation. It was said that Madame de Longueville, for whom the prince had more than a brother's affection and in whom he had confided, had been indiscreet. His confidence had unveiled the sinister project of the queen.

Even on the night of the prince's return, some citizens, bolder than the rest, such as the sheriffs, captains and the quartermaster, went from house to house among their friends, saying:

"Why do we not take the king and place him in the Hotel de Ville? It is a shame to leave him to be educated by our enemies, who will give him evil counsel; whereas, brought up by the coadjutor, for instance, he would imbibe national principles and love his people."

That night the question was secretly agitated and on the morrow the gray and black cloaks, the patrols of armed shop-people, and the bands of mendicants reappeared.

The queen had passed the night in lonely conference with the prince, who had entered the oratory at midnight and did not leave till five o'clock in the morning.

At five o'clock Anne went to the cardinal's room. If she had not yet taken any repose, he at least was already up. Six days had already passed out of the ten he had asked from Mordaunt; he was therefore occupied in revising his reply to Cromwell, when some one knocked gently at the door of communication with the queen's apartments. Anne of Austria alone was permitted to enter by that door. The cardinal therefore rose to open it.

The queen was in a morning gown, but it became her still; for, like Diana of Poictiers and Ninon, Anne of Austria enjoyed the privilege of remaining ever beautiful; nevertheless, this morning she looked handsomer than usual, for her eyes had all the sparkle inward satisfaction adds to expression.

"What is the matter, madame?" said Mazarin, uneasily. "You seem secretly elated."

"Yes, Giulio," she said, "proud and happy; for I have found the means of strangling this hydra."

"You are a great politician, my queen," said Mazarin; "let us hear the means." And he hid what he had written by sliding the letter under a folio of blank paper.

"You know," said the queen, "that they want to take the king away from me?"

"Alas! yes, and to hang me."

"They shall not have the king."

"Nor hang me."

"Listen. I want to carry off my son from them, with yourself. I wish that this event, which on the day it is known will completely change the aspect of affairs, should be accomplished without the knowledge of any others but yourself, myself, and a third person."

"And who is this third person?"

"Monsieur le Prince."

"He has come, then, as they told me?"

"Last evening."

"And you have seen him?"

"He has just left me."

"And will he aid this project?"

"The plan is his own."

"And Paris?"

"He will starve it out and force it to surrender at discretion."

"The plan is not wanting in grandeur; I see but one impediment."

"What is it?"

"Impossibility."

"A senseless word. Nothing is impossible."

"On paper."

"In execution. We have money?"

"A little," said Mazarin, trembling, lest Anne should ask to draw upon his purse.

"Troops?"

"Five or six thousand men."

"Courage?"

"Plenty."

"Then the thing is easy. Oh! do think of it, Giulio! Paris, this odious Paris, waking up one morning without queen or king, surrounded, besieged, famished--having for its sole resource its stupid parliament and their coadjutor with crooked limbs!"

"Charming! charming!" said Mazarin. "I can imagine the effect, I do not see the means."

"I will find the means myself."

"You are aware it will be war, civil war, furious, devouring, implacable?"

"Oh! yes, yes, war," said Anne of Austria. "Yes, I will reduce this rebellious city to ashes. I will extinguish the fire with blood! I will perpetuate the crime and punishment by making a frightful example. Paris!; I--I detest, I loathe it!"

"Very fine, Anne. You are now sanguinary; but take care. We are not in the time of Malatesta and Castruccio Castracani. You will get yourself decapitated, my beautiful queen, and that would be a pity."

"You laugh."

"Faintly. It is dangerous to go to war with a nation. Look at your brother monarch, Charles I. He is badly off, very badly."

"We are in France, and I am Spanish."

"So much the worse; I had much rather you were French and myself also; they would hate us both less."

"Nevertheless, you consent?"

"Yes, if the thing be possible."

"It is; it is I who tell you so; make preparations for departure."

"I! I am always prepared to go, only, as you know, I never do go, and perhaps shall go this time as little as before."

"In short, if I go, will you go too?"

"I will try."

"You torment me, Giulio, with your fears; and what are you afraid of, then?"

"Of many things."

"What are they?"

Mazarin's face, smiling as it was, became clouded.

"Anne," said he, "you are but a woman and as a woman you may insult men at your ease, knowing that you can do it with impunity. You accuse me of fear; I have not so much as you have, since I do not fly as you do. Against whom do they cry out? is it against you or against myself? Whom would they hang, yourself or me? Well, I can weather the storm--I, whom, notwithstanding, you tax with fear--not with bravado, that is not my way; but I am firm. Imitate me. Make less hubbub and think more deeply. You cry very loud, you end by doing nothing; you talk of flying----"

Mazarin shrugged his shoulders and taking the queen's hand led her to the window.

"Look!" he said.

"Well?" said the queen, blinded by her obstinacy.

"Well, what do you see from this window? If I am not mistaken those are citizens, helmeted and mailed, armed with good muskets, as in the time of the League, and whose eyes are so intently fixed on this window that they will see you if you raise that curtain much; and now come to the other side--what do you see? Creatures of the people, armed with halberds, guarding your doors. You will see the same at every opening from this palace to which I should lead you. Your doors are guarded, the airholes of your cellars are guarded, and I could say to you, as that good La Ramee said to me of the Duc de Beaufort, you must be either bird or mouse to get out."

"He did get out, nevertheless."

"Do you think of escaping in the same way?"

"I am a prisoner, then?"

"Parbleu!" said Mazarin, "I have been proving it to you this last hour."

And he quietly resumed his dispatch at the place where he had been interrupted.

Anne, trembling with anger and scarlet with humiliation, left the room, shutting the door violently after her. Mazarin did not even turn around. When once more in her own apartment Anne fell into a chair and wept; then suddenly struck with an idea:

"I am saved!" she exclaimed, rising; "oh, yes! yes! I know a man who will find the means of taking me from Paris, a man I have too long forgotten." Then falling into a reverie, she added, however, with an expression of joy, "Ungrateful woman that I am, for twenty years I have forgotten this man, whom I ought to have made a marechal of France. My mother-in-law expended gold, caresses, dignities on Concini, who ruined her; the king made Vitry marechal of France for an assassination: while I have left in obscurity, in poverty, the noble D'Artagnan, who saved me!"

And running to a table, on which were paper, pens and ink, she hastily began to write.

50. The Interview.

It had been D'Artagnan's practice, ever since the riots, to sleep in the same room as Porthos, and on this eventful morning he was still there, sleeping, and dreaming that a yellow cloud had overspread the sky and was raining gold pieces into his hat, which he held out till it was overflowing with pistoles. As for Porthos, he dreamed that the panels of his carriage were not capacious enough to contain the armorial bearings he had ordered to be painted on them. They were both aroused at seven o'clock by the entrance of an unliveried servant, who brought a letter for D'Artagnan.

"From whom?" asked the Gascon.

"From the queen," replied the servant.

"Ho!" said Porthos, raising himself in his bed; "what does she say?"

D'Artagnan requested the servant to wait in the next room and when the door was closed he sprang up from his bed and read rapidly, whilst Porthos looked at him with starting eyes, not daring to ask a single question.

"Friend Porthos," said D'Artagnan, handing the letter to him, "this time, at least, you are sure of your title of baron, and I of my captaincy. Read for yourself and judge."

Porthos took the letter and with a trembling voice read the following words:

"The queen wishes to speak to Monsieur d'Artagnan, who must follow the bearer."

"Well!" exclaimed Porthos; "I see nothing in that very extraordinary."

"But I see much that is very extraordinary in it," replied D'Artagnan. "It is evident, by their sending for me, that matters are becoming complicated. Just reflect a little what an agitation the queen's mind must be in for her to have remembered me after twenty years."

"It is true," said Porthos.

"Sharpen your sword, baron, load your pistols, and give some corn to the horses, for I will answer for it, something lightning-like will happen ere tomorrow."

"But, stop; do you think it can be a trap that they are laying for us?" suggested Porthos, incessantly thinking how his greatness must be irksome to inferior people.

"If it is a snare," replied D'Artagnan, "I shall scent it out, be assured. If Mazarin is an Italian, I am a Gascon."

And D'Artagnan dressed himself in an instant.

Whilst Porthos, still in bed, was hooking on his cloak for him, a second knock at the door was heard.

"Come in," exclaimed D'Artagnan; and another servant entered.

"From His Eminence, Cardinal Mazarin," presenting a letter.

D'Artagnan looked at Porthos.

"A complicated affair," said Porthos; "where will you begin?"

"It is arranged capitally; his eminence expects me in half an hour."

"Good."

"My friend," said D'Artagnan, turning to the servant, "tell his eminence that in half an hour I shall be at his command."

"It is very fortunate," resumed the Gascon, when the valet had retired, "that he did not meet the other one."

"Do you not think that they have sent for you, both for the same thing?"

"I do not think it, I am certain of it."

"Quick, quick, D'Artagnan. Remember that the queen awaits you, and after the queen, the cardinal, and after the cardinal, myself."

D'Artagnan summoned Anne of Austria's servant and signified that he was ready to follow him into the queen's presence.

The servant conducted him by the Rue des Petits Champs and turning to the left entered the little garden gate leading into the Rue Richelieu; then they gained the private staircase and D'Artagnan was ushered into the oratory. A certain emotion, for which he could not account, made the lieutenant's heart beat: he had no longer the assurance of youth; experience had taught him the importance of past events. Formerly he would have approached the queen as a young man who bends before a woman; but now it was a different thing; he answered her summons as an humble soldier obeys an illustrious general.

The silence of the oratory was at last disturbed by the slight rustling of silk, and D'Artagnan started when he perceived the tapestry raised by a white hand, which, by its form, its color and its beauty he recognized as that royal hand which had one day been presented to him to kiss. The queen entered.

"It is you, Monsieur d'Artagnan," she said, fixing a gaze full of melancholy interest on the countenance of the officer, "and I know you well. Look at me well in your turn. I am the queen; do you recognize me?"

"No, madame," replied D'Artagnan.

"But are you no longer aware," continued Anne, giving that sweet expression to her voice which she could do at will, "that in former days the queen had once need of a young, brave and devoted cavalier--that she found this cavalier--and that, although he might have thought that she had forgotten him, she had kept a place for him in the depths of her heart?"

"No, madame, I was ignorant of that," said the musketeer.

"So much the worse, sir," said Anne of Austria; "so much the worse, at least for the queen, for to-day she has need of the same courage and the same devotion."

"What!" exclaimed D'Artagnan, "does the queen, surrounded as she is by such devoted servants, such wise counselors, men, in short, so great by merit or position--does she deign to cast her eyes on an obscure soldier?"

Anne understood this covert reproach and was more moved than irritated by it. She had many a time felt humiliated by the self-sacrifice and disinterestedness shown by the Gascon gentleman. She had allowed herself to be exceeded in generosity.

"All that you tell me of those by whom I am surrounded, Monsieur d'Artagnan, is doubtless true," said the queen, "but I have confidence in you alone. I know that you belong to the cardinal, but belong to me as well, and I will take upon myself the making of your fortune. Come, will you do to-day what formerly the gentleman you do not know did for the queen?"

"I will do everything your majesty commands," replied D'Artagnan.

The queen reflected for a moment and then, seeing the cautious demeanor of the musketeer:

"Perhaps you like repose?" she said.

"I do not know, for I have never had it, madame."

"Have you any friends?"

"I had three, two of whom have left Paris, to go I know not where. One alone is left to me, but he is one of those known, I believe, to the cavalier of whom your majesty did me the honor to speak."

"Very good," said the queen; "you and your friend are worth an army."

"What am I to do, madame?"

"Return at five o'clock and I will tell you; but do not breathe to a living soul, sir, the rendezvous which I give you."

"No, madame."

"Swear it upon the cross."

"Madame, I have never been false to my word; when I say I will not do a thing, I mean it."

The queen, although astonished at this language, to which she was not accustomed from her courtiers, argued from it a happy omen of the zeal with which D'Artagnan would serve her in the accomplishment of her project. It was one of the Gascon's artifices to hide his deep cunning occasionally under an appearance of rough loyalty.

"Has the queen any further commands for me now?" asked D'Artagnan.

"No, sir," replied Anne of Austria, "and you may retire until the time that I mentioned to you."

D'Artagnan bowed and went out.

"Diable!" he exclaimed when the door was shut, "they seem to have the greatest need of me just now."

Then, as the half hour had already glided by, he crossed the gallery and knocked at the cardinal's door.

Bernouin introduced him.

"I come for your commands, my lord," he said.

And according to his custom D'Artagnan glanced rapidly around and remarked that Mazarin had a sealed letter before him. But it was so placed on the desk that he could not see to whom it was addressed.

"You come from the queen?" said Mazarin, looking fixedly at D'Artagnan.

"I! my lord--who told you that?"

"Nobody, but I know it."

"I regret infinitely to tell you, my lord, that you are mistaken," replied the Gascon, impudently, firm to the promise he had just made to Anne of Austria.

"I opened the door of the ante-room myself and I saw you enter at the end of the corridor."

"Because I was shown up the private stairs."

"How so?"

"I know not; it must have been a mistake."

Mazarin was aware that it was not easy to make D'Artagnan reveal anything he was desirous of hiding, so he gave up, for the time, the discovery of the mystery the Gascon was concealing.

"Let us speak of my affairs," said Mazarin, "since you will tell me naught of yours. Are you fond of traveling?"

"My life has been passed on the high road."

"Would anything retain you particularly in Paris?"

"Nothing but an order from a superior would retain me in Paris."

"Very well. Here is a letter, which must be taken to its address."

"To its address, my lord? But it has none."

In fact, the side of the letter opposite the seal was blank.

"I must tell you," resumed Mazarin, "that it is in a double envelope."

"I understand; and I am to take off the first one when I have reached a certain place?"

"Just so, take it and go. You have a friend, Monsieur du Vallon, whom I like much; let him accompany you."

"The devil!" said D'Artagnan to himself. "He knows that we overheard his conversation yesterday and he wants to get us away from Paris."

"Do you hesitate?" asked Mazarin.

"No, my lord, and I will set out at once. There is one thing only which I must request."

"What is it? Speak."

"That your eminence will go at once to the queen."

"What for?"

"Merely to say these words: 'I am going to send Monsieur d'Artagnan away and I wish him to set out directly.'"

"I told you," said Mazarin, "that you had seen the queen."

"I had the honor of saying to your eminence that there had been some mistake."

"What is the meaning of that?"

"May I venture to repeat my prayer to your eminence?"

"Very well; I will go. Wait here for me." And looking attentively around him, to see if he had left any of his keys in his closets, Mazarin went out. Ten minutes elapsed, during which D'Artagnan made every effort to read through the first envelope what was written on the second. But he did not succeed.

Mazarin returned, pale, and evidently thoughtful. He seated himself at his desk and D'Artagnan proceeded to examine his face, as he had just examined the letter he held, but the envelope which covered his countenance appeared as impenetrable as that which covered the letter.

"Ah!" thought the Gascon; "he looks displeased. Can it be with me? He meditates. Is it about sending me to the Bastile? All very fine, my lord, but at the very first hint you give of such a thing I will strangle you and become Frondist. I should be carried home in triumph like Monsieur Broussel and Athos would proclaim me the French Brutus. It would be exceedingly droll."

The Gascon, with his vivid imagination, had already seen the advantage to be derived from his situation. Mazarin gave, however, no order of the kind, but on the contrary began to be insinuating.

"You were right," he said, "my dear Monsieur d'Artagnan, and you cannot set out yet. I beg you to return me that dispatch."

D'Artagnan obeyed, and Mazarin ascertained that the seal was intact.

"I shall want you this evening," he said "Return in two hours."

"My lord," said D'Artagnan, "I have an appointment in two hours which I cannot miss."

"Do not be uneasy," said Mazarin; "it is the same."

"Good!" thought D'Artagnan; "I fancied it was so."

"Return, then, at five o'clock and bring that worthy Monsieur du Vallon with you. Only, leave him in the ante-room, as I wish to speak to you alone."

D'Artagnan bowed, and thought: "Both at the same hour; both commands alike; both at the Palais Royal. Monsieur de Gondy would pay a hundred thousand francs for such a secret!"

"You are thoughtful," said Mazarin, uneasily.

"Yes, I was thinking whether we ought to come armed or not."

"Armed to the teeth!" replied Mazarin.

"Very well, my lord; it shall be so."

D'Artagnan saluted, went out and hastened to repeat to his friend Mazarin's flattering promises, which gave Porthos an indescribable happiness.

51. The Flight.

When D'Artagnan returned to the Palais Royal at five o'clock, it presented, in spite of the excitement which reigned in the town, a spectacle of the greatest rejoicing. Nor was that surprising. The queen had restored Broussel and Blancmesnil to the people and had therefore nothing to fear, since the people had nothing more just then to ask for. The return, also, of the conqueror of Lens was the pretext for giving a grand banquet. The princes and princesses were invited and their carriages had crowded the court since noon; then after dinner the queen was to have a play in her apartment. Anne of Austria had never appeared more brilliant than on that day--radiant with grace and wit. Mazarin disappeared as they rose from table. He found D'Artagnan waiting for him already at his post in the ante-room.

The cardinal advanced to him with a smile and taking him by the hand led him into his study.

"My dear M. d'Artagnan," said the minister, sitting down, "I am about to give you the greatest proof of confidence that a minister can give an officer."

"I hope," said D'Artagnan, bowing, "that you give it, my lord, without hesitation and with the conviction that I am worthy of it."

"More worthy than any one in Paris my dear friend; therefore I apply to you. We are about to leave this evening," continued Mazarin. "My dear M. d'Artagnan, the welfare of the state is deposited in your hands." He paused.

"Explain yourself, my lord, I am listening."

"The queen has resolved to make a little excursion with the king to Saint Germain."

"Aha!" said D'Artagnan, "that is to say, the queen wishes to leave Paris."

"A woman's caprice--you understand."

"Yes, I understand perfectly," said D'Artagnan.

"It was for this she summoned you this morning and that she told you to return at five o'clock."

"Was it worth while to wish me to swear this morning that I would mention the appointment to no one?" muttered D'Artagnan. "Oh, women! women! whether queens or not, they are always the same."

"Do you disapprove of this journey, my dear M. d'Artagnan?" asked Mazarin, anxiously.

"I, my lord?" said D'Artagnan; "why should I?"

"Because you shrug your shoulders."

"It is a way I have of speaking to myself. I neither approve nor disapprove, my lord; I merely await your commands."

"Good; it is you, accordingly, that I have pitched upon to conduct the king and the queen to Saint Germain."

"Liar!" thought D'Artagnan.

"You see, therefore," continued the cardinal, perceiving D'Artagnan's composure, "that, as I have told you, the welfare of the state is placed in your hands."

"Yes, my lord, and I feel the whole responsibility of such a charge."

"You accept, however?"

"I always accept."

"Do you think the thing possible?"

"Everything is possible."

"Shall you be attacked on the road?"

"Probably."

"And what will you do in that case?"

"I shall pass through those who attack me."

"And suppose you cannot pass through them?"

"So much the worse for them; I shall pass over them."

"And you will place the king and queen in safety also, at Saint Germain?"

"Yes."

"On your life?"

"On my life."

"You are a hero, my friend," said Mazarin, gazing at the musketeer with admiration.

D'Artagnan smiled.

"And I?" asked Mazarin, after a moment's silence.

"How? and you, my lord?"

"If I wish to leave?"

"That would be much more difficult."

"Why so?"

"Your eminence might be recognized."

"Even under this disguise?" asked Mazarin, raising a cloak which covered an arm-chair, upon which lay a complete dress for an officer, of pearl-gray and red, entirely embroidered with silver.

"If your eminence is disguised it will be almost easy."

"Ah!" said Mazarin, breathing more freely.

"But it will be necessary for your eminence to do what the other day you declared you should have done in our place--cry, 'Down with Mazarin!'"

"I will: 'Down with Mazarin'"

"In French, in good French, my lord, take care of your accent; they killed six thousand Angevins in Sicily because they pronounced Italian badly. Take care that the French do not take their revenge on you for the Sicilian vespers."

"I will do my best."

"The streets are full of armed men," continued D'Artagnan. "Are you sure that no one is aware of the queen's project?"

Mazarin reflected.

"This affair would give a fine opportunity for a traitor, my lord; the chance of being attacked would be an excuse for everything."

Mazarin shuddered, but he reflected that a man who had the least intention to betray would not warn first.

"And therefore," added he, quietly, "I have not confidence in every one; the proof of which is, that I have fixed upon you to escort me."

"Shall you not go with the queen?"

"No," replied Mazarin.

"Then you will start after the queen?"

"No," said Mazarin again.

"Ah!" said D'Artagnan, who began to understand.

"Yes," continued the cardinal. "I have my plan. With the queen I double her risk; after the queen her departure would double mine; then, the court once safe, I might be forgotten. The great are often ungrateful."

"Very true," said D'Artagnan, fixing his eyes, in spite of himself, on the queen's diamond, which Mazarin wore on his finger. Mazarin followed the direction of his eyes and gently turned the hoop of the ring inside.

"I wish," he said, with his cunning smile, "to prevent them from being ungrateful to me."

"It is but Christian charity," replied D'Artagnan, "not to lead one's neighbors into temptation."

"It is exactly for that reason," said Mazarin, "that I wish to start before them."

D'Artagnan smiled--he was just the man to understand the astute Italian. Mazarin saw the smile and profited by the moment.

"You will begin, therefore, by taking me first out of Paris, will you not, my dear M. d'Artagnan?"

"A difficult commission, my lord," replied D'Artagnan, resuming his serious manner.

"But," said Mazarin, "you did not make so many difficulties with regard to the king and queen."

"The king and the queen are my king and queen," replied the musketeer, "my life is theirs and I must give it for them. If they ask it what have I to say?"

"That is true," murmured Mazarin, in a low tone, "but as thy life is not mine I suppose I must buy it, must I not?" and sighing deeply he began to turn the hoop of his ring outside again. D'Artagnan smiled. These two men met at one point and that was, cunning; had they been actuated equally by courage, the one would have done great things for the other.

"But, also," said Mazarin, "you must understand that if I ask this service from you it is with the intention of being grateful."

"Is it still only an intention, your eminence?" asked D'Artagnan.

"Stay," said Mazarin, drawing the ring from his finger, "my dear D'Artagnan, there is a diamond which belonged to you formerly, it is but just it should return to you; take it, I pray."

D'Artagnan spared Mazarin the trouble of insisting, and after looking to see if the stone was the same and assuring himself of the purity of its water, he took it and passed it on his finger with indescribable pleasure.

"I valued it much," said Mazarin, giving a last look at it; "nevertheless, I give it to you with great pleasure."

"And I, my lord," said D'Artagnan, "accept it as it is given. Come, let us speak of your little affairs. You wish to leave before everybody and at what hour?"

"At ten o'clock."

"And the queen, at what time is it her wish to start?"

"At midnight."

"Then it is possible. I can get you out of Paris and leave you beyond the barriere, and can return for her."

"Capital; but how will you get me out of Paris?"

"Oh! as to that, you must leave it to me."

"I give you absolute power, therefore; take as large an escort as you like."

D'Artagnan shook his head.

"It seems to me, however," said Mazarin, "the safest method."

"Yes, for you, my lord, but not for the queen; you must leave it to me and give me the entire direction of the undertaking."

"Nevertheless----"

"Or find some one else," continued D'Artagnan, turning his back.

"Oh!" muttered Mazarin, "I do believe he is going off with the diamond! M. d'Artagnan, my dear M. d'Artagnan," he called out in a coaxing voice, "will you answer for everything?"

"I will answer for nothing. I will do my best."

"Well, then, let us go--I must trust to you."

"It is very fortunate," said D'Artagnan to himself.

"You will be here at half-past nine."

"And I shall find your eminence ready?"

"Certainly, quite ready."

"Well, then, it is a settled thing; and now, my lord, will you obtain for me an audience with the queen?"

"For what purpose?"

"I wish to receive her majesty's commands from her own lips."

"She desired me to give them to you."

"She may have forgotten something."

"You really wish to see her?"

"It is indispensable, my lord."

Mazarin hesitated for one instant, but D'Artagnan was firm.

"Come, then," said the minister; "I will conduct you to her, but remember, not one word of our conversation."

"What has passed between us concerns ourselves alone, my lord," replied D'Artagnan.

"Swear to be mute."

"I never swear, my lord, I say yes or no; and, as I am a gentleman, I keep my word."

"Come, then, I see that I must trust unreservedly to you."

"Believe me, my lord, it will be your best plan."

"Come," said Mazarin, conducting D'Artagnan into the queen's oratory and desiring him to wait there. He did not wait long, for in five minutes the queen entered in full gala costume. Thus dressed she scarcely appeared thirty-five years of age. She was still exceedingly handsome.

"It is you, Monsieur D'Artagnan," she said, smiling graciously; "I thank you for having insisted on seeing me."

"I ought to ask your majesty's pardon, but I wished to receive your commands from your own mouth."

"Do you accept the commission which I have intrusted to you?"

"With gratitude."

"Very well, be here at midnight."

"I will not fail."

"Monsieur d'Artagnan," continued the queen, "I know your disinterestedness too well to speak of my own gratitude at such a moment, but I swear to you that I shall not forget this second service as I forgot the first."

"Your majesty is free to forget or to remember, as it pleases you; and I know not what you mean," said D'Artagnan, bowing.

"Go, sir," said the queen, with her most bewitching smile, "go and return at midnight."

And D'Artagnan retired, but as he passed out he glanced at the curtain through which the queen had entered and at the bottom of the tapestry he remarked the tip of a velvet slipper.

"Good," thought he; "Mazarin has been listening to discover whether I betrayed him. In truth, that Italian puppet does not deserve the services of an honest man."

D'Artagnan was not less exact to his appointment and at half-past nine o'clock he entered the anteroom.

He found the cardinal dressed as an officer, and he looked very well in that costume, which, as we have already said, he wore elegantly; only he was very pale and trembled slightly.

"Quite alone?" he asked.

"Yes, my lord."

"And that worthy Monsieur du Vallon, are we not to enjoy his society?"

"Certainly, my lord; he is waiting in his carriage at the gate of the garden of the Palais Royal."

"And we start in his carriage, then?"

"Yes, my lord."

"And with us no other escort but you two?"

"Is it not enough? One of us would suffice."

"Really, my dear Monsieur d'Artagnan," said the cardinal, "your coolness startles me."

"I should have thought, on the contrary, that it ought to have inspired you with confidence."

"And Bernouin--do I not take him with me?"

"There is no room for him, he will rejoin your eminence."

"Let us go," said Mazarin, "since everything must be done as you wish."

"My lord, there is time to draw back," said D'Artagnan, "and your eminence is perfectly free."

"Not at all, not at all," said Mazarin; "let us be off."

And so they descended the private stair, Mazarin leaning on the arm of D'Artagnan a hand the musketeer felt trembling. At last, after crossing the courts of the Palais Royal, where there still remained some of the conveyances of late guests, they entered the garden and reached the little gate. Mazarin attempted to open it by a key which he took from his pocket, but with such shaking fingers that he could not find the keyhole.

"Give it to me," said D'Artagnan, who when the gate was open deposited the key in his pocket, reckoning upon returning by that gate.

The steps were already down and the door open. Mousqueton stood at the door and Porthos was inside the carriage.

"Mount, my lord," said D'Artagnan to Mazarin, who sprang into the carriage without waiting for a second bidding. D'Artagnan followed him, and Mousqueton, having closed the door, mounted behind the carriage with many groans. He had made some difficulties about going, under pretext that he still suffered from his wound, but D'Artagnan had said to him:

"Remain if you like, my dear Monsieur Mouston, but I warn you that Paris will be burnt down tonight;" upon which Mousqueton had declared, without asking anything further, that he was ready to follow his master and Monsieur d'Artagnan to the end of the world.

The carriage started at a measured pace, without betraying by the slightest sign that it contained people in a hurry. The cardinal wiped his forehead with his handkerchief and looked around him. On his left was Porthos, whilst D'Artagnan was on his right; each guarded a door and served as a rampart to him on either side. Before him, on the front seat, lay two pairs of pistols--one in front of Porthos and the other of D'Artagnan. About a hundred paces from the Palais Royal a patrol stopped the carriage.

"Who goes?" asked the captain.

"Mazarin!" replied D'Artagnan, bursting into a laugh. The cardinal's hair stood on end. But the joke appeared an excellent one to the citizens, who, seeing the conveyance without escort and unarmed, would never have believed in the possibility of so great an imprudence.

"A good journey to ye," they cried, allowing it to pass.

"Hem!" said D'Artagnan, "what does my lord think of that reply?"

"Man of talent!" cried Mazarin.

"In truth," said Porthos, "I understand; but now----"

About the middle of the Rue des Petits Champs they were stopped by a second patrol.

"Who goes there?" inquired the captain of the patrol.

"Keep back, my lord," said D'Artagnan. And Mazarin buried himself so far behind the two friends that he disappeared, completely hidden between them.

"Who goes there?" cried the same voice, impatiently whilst D'Artagnan perceived that they had rushed to the horses' heads. But putting his head out of the carriage:

"Eh! Planchet," said he.

The chief approached, and it was indeed Planchet; D'Artagnan had recognized the voice of his old servant.

"How, sir!" said Planchet, "is it you?"

"Eh! mon Dieu! yes, my good friend, this worthy Porthos has just received a sword wound and I am taking him to his country house at Saint Cloud."

"Oh! really," said Planchet.

"Porthos," said D'Artagnan, "if you can still speak, say a word, my dear Porthos, to this good Planchet."

"Planchet, my friend," said Porthos, in a melancholy voice, "I am very ill; should you meet a doctor you will do me a favor by sending him to me."

"Oh! good Heaven," said Planchet, "what a misfortune! and how did it happen?"

"I will tell you all about it," replied Mousqueton.

Porthos uttered a deep groan.

"Make way for us, Planchet," said D'Artagnan in a whisper to him, "or he will not arrive alive; the lungs are attacked, my friend."

Planchet shook his head with the air of a man who says, "In that case things look ill." Then he exclaimed, turning to his men:

"Let them pass; they are friends."

The carriage resumed its course, and Mazarin, who had held his breath, ventured to breathe again.

"Bricconi!" muttered he.

A few steps in advance of the gate of Saint Honore they met a third troop; this latter party was composed of ill-looking fellows, who resembled bandits more than anything else; they were the men of the beggar of Saint Eustache.

"Attention, Porthos!" cried D'Artagnan.

Porthos placed his hand on the pistols.

"What is it?" asked Mazarin.

"My lord, I think we are in bad company."

A man advanced to the door with a kind of scythe in his hand. "Qui vive?" he asked.

"Eh, rascal!" said D'Artagnan, "do you not recognize his highness the prince's carriage?"

"Prince or not," said the man, "open. We are here to guard the gate, and no one whom we do not know shall pass."

"What is to be done?" said Porthos.

"Pardieu! pass," replied D'Artagnan.

"But how?" asked Mazarin.

"Through or over; coachman, gallop on."

The coachman raised his whip.

"Not a step further," said the man, who appeared to be the captain, "or I will hamstring your horses."

"Peste!" said Porthos, "it would be a pity; animals which cost me a hundred pistoles each."

"I will pay you two hundred for them," said Mazarin.

"Yes, but when once they are hamstrung, our necks will be strung next."

"If one of them comes to my side," asked Porthos, "must I kill him?"

"Yes, by a blow of your fist, if you can; we will not fire but at the last extremity."

"I can do it," said Porthos.

"Come and open, then!" cried D'Artagnan to the man with the scythe, taking one of the pistols up by the muzzle and preparing to strike with the handle. And as the man approached, D'Artagnan, in order to have more freedom for his actions, leaned half out of the door; his eyes were fixed upon those of the mendicant, which were lighted up by a lantern. Without doubt he recognized D'Artagnan, for he became deadly pale; doubtless the musketeer knew him, for his hair stood up on his head.

"Monsieur d'Artagnan!" he cried, falling back a step; "it is Monsieur d'Artagnan! let him pass."

D'Artagnan was perhaps about to reply, when a blow, similar to that of a mallet falling on the head of an ox, was heard. The noise was caused by Porthos, who had just knocked down his man.

D'Artagnan turned around and saw the unfortunate man upon his back about four paces off.

"'Sdeath!" cried he to the coachman. "Spur your horses! whip! get on!"

The coachman bestowed a heavy blow of the whip upon his horses; the noble animals bounded forward; then cries of men who were knocked down were heard; then a double concussion was felt, and two of the wheels seemed to pass over a round and flexible body. There was a moment's silence, then the carriage cleared the gate.

"To Cours la Reine!" cried D'Artagnan to the coachman; then turning to Mazarin he said, "Now, my lord, you can say five paters and five aves, in thanks to Heaven for your deliverance. You are safe--you are free."

Mazarin replied only by a groan; he could not believe in such a miracle. Five minutes later the carriage stopped, having reached Cours la Reine.

"Is my lord pleased with his escort?" asked D'Artagnan.

"Enchanted, monsieur," said Mazarin, venturing his head out of one of the windows; "and now do as much for the queen."

"It will not be so difficult," replied D'Artagnan, springing to the ground. "Monsieur du Vallon, I commend his eminence to your care."

"Be quite at ease," said Porthos, holding out his hand, which D'Artagnan took and shook in his.

"Oh!" cried Porthos, as if in pain.

D'Artagnan looked with surprise at his friend.

"What is the matter, then?" he asked.

"I think I have sprained my wrist,' said Porthos.

"The devil! why, you strike like a blind or a deaf man."

"It was necessary; my man was going to fire a pistol at me; but you--how did you get rid of yours?"

"Oh, mine," replied D'Artagnan, "was not a man."

"What was it then?"

"It was an apparition."

"And----"

"I charmed it away."

Without further explanation D'Artagnan took the pistols which were upon the front seat, placed them in his belt, wrapped himself in his cloak, and not wishing to enter by the same gate as that through which they had left, he took his way toward the Richelieu gate.

52. The Carriage of Monsieur le Coadjuteur.

Instead of returning, then, by the Saint Honore gate, D'Artagnan, who had time before him, walked around and re-entered by the Porte Richelieu. He was approached to be examined, and when it was discovered by his plumed hat and his laced coat, that he was an officer of the musketeers, he was surrounded, with the intention of making him cry, "Down with Mazarin!" The demonstration did not fail to make him uneasy at first; but when he discovered what it meant, he shouted it in such a voice that even the most exacting were satisfied. He walked down the Rue Richelieu, meditating how he should carry off the queen in her turn, for to take her in a carriage bearing the arms of France was not to be thought of, when he perceived an equipage standing at the door of the hotel belonging to Madame de Guemenee.

He was struck by a sudden idea.

"Ah, pardieu!" he exclaimed; "that would be fair play."

And approaching the carriage, he examined the arms on the panels and the livery of the coachman on his box. This scrutiny was so much the more easy, the coachman being sound asleep.

"It is, in truth, monsieur le coadjuteur's carriage," said D'Artagnan; "upon my honor I begin to think that Heaven favors us."

He mounted noiselessly into the chariot and pulled the silk cord which was attached to the coachman's little finger.

"To the Palais Royal," he called out.

The coachman awoke with a start and drove off in the direction he was desired, never doubting but that the order had come from his master. The porter at the palace was about to close the gates, but seeing such a handsome equipage he fancied that it was some visit of importance and the carriage was allowed to pass and to stop beneath the porch. It was then only the coachman perceived the grooms were not behind the vehicle; he fancied monsieur le coadjuteur had sent them back, and without dropping the reins he sprang from his box to open the door. D'Artagnan, in his turn, sprang to the ground, and just at the moment when the coachman, alarmed at not seeing his master, fell back a step, he seized him by his collar with the left, whilst with the right hand he placed the muzzle of a pistol at his breast.

"Pronounce one single word," muttered D'Artagnan, "and you are a dead man."

The coachman perceived at once, by the expression of the man who thus addressed him, that he had fallen into a trap, and he remained with his mouth wide open and his eyes portentously staring.

Two musketeers were pacing the court, to whom D'Artagnan called by their names.

"Monsieur de Belliere," said he to one of them, "do me the favor to take the reins from the hands of this worthy man, mount upon the box and drive to the door of the private stair, and wait for me there; it is an affair of importance on the service of the king."

The musketeer, who knew that his lieutenant was incapable of jesting with regard to the service, obeyed without a word, although he thought the order strange. Then turning toward the second musketeer, D'Artagnan said:

"Monsieur du Verger, help me to place this man in a place of safety."

The musketeer, thinking that his lieutenant had just arrested some prince in disguise, bowed, and drawing his sword, signified that he was ready. D'Artagnan mounted the staircase, followed by his prisoner, who in his turn was followed by the soldier, and entered Mazarin's ante-room. Bernouin was waiting there, impatient for news of his master.

"Well, sir?" he said.

"Everything goes on capitally, my dear Monsieur Bernouin, but here is a man whom I must beg you to put in a safe place."

"Where, then, sir?"

"Where you like, provided that the place which you shall choose has iron shutters secured by padlocks and a door that can be locked."

"We have that, sir," replied Bernouin; and the poor coachman was conducted to a closet, the windows of which were barred and which looked very much like a prison.

"And now, my good friend," said D'Artagnan to him, "I must invite you to deprive yourself, for my sake, of your hat and cloak."

The coachman, as we can well understand, made no resistance; in fact, he was so astonished at what had happened to him that he stammered and reeled like a drunken man; D'Artagnan deposited his clothes under the arm of one of the valets.

"And now, Monsieur du Verger," he said, "shut yourself up with this man until Monsieur Bernouin returns to open the door. The duty will be tolerably long and not very amusing, I know; but," added he, seriously, "you understand, it is on the king's service."

"At your command, lieutenant," replied the musketeer, who saw the business was a serious one.

"By-the-bye," continued D'Artagnan, "should this man attempt to fly or to call out, pass your sword through his body."

The musketeer signified by a nod that these commands should be obeyed to the letter, and D'Artagnan went out, followed by Bernouin. Midnight struck.

"Lead me into the queen's oratory," said D'Artagnan, "announce to her I am here, and put this parcel, with a well-loaded musket, under the seat of the carriage which is waiting at the foot of the private stair."

Bernouin conducted D'Artagnan to the oratory, where he sat down pensively. Everything had gone on as usual at the Palais Royal. As we said before, by ten o'clock almost all the guests had dispersed; those who were to fly with the court had the word of command and they were each severally desired to be from twelve o'clock to one at Cours la Reine.

At ten o'clock Anne of Austria had entered the king's room. Monsieur had just retired, and the youthful Louis, remaining the last, was amusing himself by placing some lead soldiers in a line of battle, a game which delighted him much. Two royal pages were playing with him.

"Laporte," said the queen, "it is time for his majesty to go to bed."

The king asked to remain up, having, he said, no wish to sleep; but the queen was firm.

"Are you not going to-morrow morning at six o'clock, Louis, to bathe at Conflans? I think you wished to do so of your own accord?"

"You are right, madame," said the king, "and I am ready to retire to my room when you have kissed me. Laporte, give the light to Monsieur the Chevalier de Coislin."

The queen touched with her lips the white, smooth brow the royal child presented to her with a gravity which already partook of etiquette.

"Go to sleep soon, Louis," said the queen, "for you must be awakened very early."

"I will do my best to obey you, madame," said the youthful king, "but I have no inclination to sleep."

"Laporte," said Anne of Austria, in an undertone, "find some very dull book to read to his majesty, but do not undress yourself."

The king went out, accompanied by the Chevalier de Coislin, bearing the candlestick, and then the queen returned to her own apartment. Her ladies--that is to say Madame de Bregy, Mademoiselle de Beaumont, Madame de Motteville, and Socratine, her sister, so called on account of her sense--had just brought into her dressing-room the remains of the dinner, on which, according to her usual custom, she supped. The queen then gave her orders, spoke of a banquet which the Marquis de Villequier was to give to her on the day after the morrow, indicated the persons she would admit to the honor of partaking of it, announced another visit on the following day to Val-de-Grace, where she intended to pay her devotions, and gave her commands to her senior valet to accompany her. When the ladies had finished their supper the queen feigned extreme fatigue and passed into her bedroom. Madame de Motteville, who was on especial duty that evening, followed to aid and undress her. The queen then began to read, and after conversing with her affectionately for a few minutes, dismissed her.

It was at this moment D'Artagnan entered the courtyard of the palace, in the coadjutor's carriage, and a few seconds later the carriages of the ladies-in-waiting drove out and the gates were shut after them.

A few minutes after twelve o'clock Bernouin knocked at the queen's bedroom door, having come by the cardinal's secret corridor. Anne of Austria opened the door to him herself. She was dressed, that is to say, in dishabille, wrapped in a long, warm dressing-gown.

"It is you, Bernouin," she said. "Is Monsieur d'Artagnan there?"

"Yes, madame, in your oratory. He is waiting till your majesty is ready."

"I am. Go and tell Laporte to wake and dress the king, and then pass on to the Marechal de Villeroy and summon him to me."

Bernouin bowed and retired.

The queen entered her oratory, which was lighted by a single lamp of Venetian crystal, She saw D'Artagnan, who stood expecting her.

"Is it you?" she said.

"Yes, madame."

"Are you ready?"

"I am."

"And his eminence, the cardinal?"

"Has got off without any accident. He is awaiting your majesty at Cours la Reine."

"But in what carriage do we start?"

"I have provided for everything; a carriage below is waiting for your majesty."

"Let us go to the king."

D'Artagnan bowed and followed the queen. The young Louis was already dressed, with the exception of his shoes and doublet; he had allowed himself to be dressed, in great astonishment, overwhelming Laporte with questions, who replied only in these words, "Sire, it is by the queen's commands."

The bedclothes were thrown back, exposing the king's bed linen, which was so worn that here and there holes could be seen. It was one of the results of Mazarin's niggardliness.

The queen entered and D'Artagnan remained at the door. As soon as the child perceived the queen he escaped from Laporte and ran to meet her. Anne then motioned to D'Artagnan to approach, and he obeyed.

"My son," said Anne of Austria, pointing to the musketeer, calm, standing uncovered, "here is Monsieur d'Artagnan, who is as brave as one of those ancient heroes of whom you like so much to hear from my women. Remember his name well and look at him well, that his face may not be forgotten, for this evening he is going to render us a great service."

The young king looked at the officer with his large-formed eye, and repeated:

"Monsieur d'Artagnan."

"That is it, my son."

The young king slowly raised his little hand and held it out to the musketeer; the latter bent on his knee and kissed it.

"Monsieur d'Artagnan," repeated Louis; "very well, madame."

At this moment they were startled by a noise as if a tumult were approaching.

"What is that?" exclaimed the queen.

"Oh, oh!" replied D'Artagnan, straining both at the same time his quick ear and his intelligent glance, "it is the murmur of the populace in revolution."

"We must fly," said the queen.

"Your majesty has given me the control of this business; we had better wait and see what they want."

"Monsieur d'Artagnan!"

"I will answer for everything."

Nothing is so catching as confidence. The queen, full of energy and courage, was quickly alive to these two virtues in others.

"Do as you like," she said, "I rely upon you."

"Will your majesty permit me to give orders in your name throughout this business?"

"Command, sir."

"What do the people want this time?" demanded the king.

"We are about to ascertain, sire," replied D'Artagnan, as he rapidly left the room.

The tumult continued to increase and seemed to surround the Palais Royal entirely. Cries were heard from the interior, of which they could not comprehend the sense. It was evident that there was clamor and sedition.

The king, half dressed, the queen and Laporte remained each in the same state and almost in the same place, where they were listening and waiting. Comminges, who was on guard that night at the Palais Royal, ran in. He had about two hundred men in the courtyards and stables, and he placed them at the queen's disposal.

"Well," asked Anne of Austria, when D'Artagnan reappeared, "what does it mean?"

"It means, madame, that the report has spread that the queen has left the Palais Royal, carrying off the king, and the people ask to have proof to the contrary, or threaten to demolish the Palais Royal."

"Oh, this time it is too much!" exclaimed the queen, "and I will prove to them I have not left."

D'Artagnan saw from the expression of the queen's face that she was about to issue some violent command. He approached her and said in a low voice:

"Has your majesty still confidence in me?"

This voice startled her. "Yes, sir," she replied, "every confidence; speak."

"Will the queen deign to follow my advice?"

"Speak."

"Let your majesty dismiss M. de Comminges and desire him to shut himself up with his men in the guardhouse and in the stables."

Comminges glanced at D'Artagnan with the envious look with which every courtier sees a new favorite spring up.

"You hear, Comminges?" said the queen.

D'Artagnan went up to him; with his usual quickness he caught the anxious glance.

"Monsieur de Comminges," he said, "pardon me; we both are servants of the queen, are we not? It is my turn to be of use to her; do not envy me this happiness."

Comminges bowed and left.

"Come," said D'Artagnan to himself, "I have got one more enemy."

"And now," said the queen, addressing D'Artagnan, "what is to be done? for you hear that, instead of becoming calmer, the noise increases."

"Madame," said D'Artagnan, "the people want to see the king and they must see him."

"What! must see him! Where--on the balcony?"

"Not at all, madame, but here, sleeping in his bed."

"Oh, your majesty," exclaimed Laporte, "Monsieur d'Artagnan is right."

The queen became thoughtful and smiled, like a woman to whom duplicity is no stranger.

"Without doubt," she murmured.

"Monsieur Laporte," said D'Artagnan, "go and announce to the people through the grating that they are going to be satisfied and that in five minutes they shall not only see the king, but they shall see him in bed; add that the king sleeps and that the queen begs that they will keep silence, so as not to awaken him."

"But not every one; a deputation of two or four people."

"Every one, madame."

"But reflect, they will keep us here till daybreak."

"It shall take but a quarter of an hour, I answer for everything, madame; believe me, I know the people; they are like a great child, who only wants humoring. Before the sleeping king they will be mute, gentle and timid as lambs."

"Go, Laporte," said the queen.

The young king approached his mother and said, "Why do as these people ask?"

"It must be so, my son," said Anne of Austria.

"But if they say, 'it must be' to me, am I no longer king?"

The queen remained silent.

"Sire," said D'Artagnan, "will your majesty permit me to ask you a question?"

Louis XIV. turned around, astonished that any one should dare to address him. But the queen pressed the child's hand.

"Yes, sir." he said.

"Does your majesty remember, when playing in the park of Fontainebleau, or in the palace courts at Versailles, ever to have seen the sky grow suddenly dark and heard the sound of thunder?"

"Yes, certainly."

"Well, then, this noise of thunder, however much your majesty may have wished to continue playing, has said, 'go in, sire. You must do so.'"

"Certainly, sir; but they tell me that the noise of thunder is the voice of God."

"Well then, sire," continued D'Artagnan, "listen to the noise of the people; you will perceive that it resembles that of thunder."

In truth at that moment a terrible murmur was wafted to them by the night breeze; then all at once it ceased.

"Hold, sire," said D'Artagnan, "they have just told the people that you are asleep; you see, you still are king."

The queen looked with surprise at this strange man, whose brilliant courage made him the equal of the bravest, and who was, by his fine and quick intelligence, the equal of the most astute.

Laporte entered.

"Well, Laporte?" asked the queen.

"Madame," he replied, "Monsieur d'Artagnan's prediction has been accomplished; they are calm, as if by enchantment. The doors are about to be opened and in five minutes they will be here."

"Laporte," said the queen, "suppose you put one of your sons in the king's place; we might be off during the time."

"If your majesty desires it," said Laporte, "my sons, like myself, are at the queen's service."

"Not at all," said D'Artagnan; "should one of them know his majesty and discover but a substitute, all would be lost."

"You are right, sir, always right," said Anne of Austria. "Laporte, place the king in bed."

Laporte placed the king, dressed as he was, in the bed and then covered him as far as the shoulders with the sheet. The queen bent over him and kissed his brow.

"Pretend to sleep, Louis," said she.

"Yes," said the king, "but I do not wish to be touched by any of those men."

"Sire, I am here," said D'Artagnan, "and I give you my word, that if a single man has the audacity, his life shall pay for it."

"And now what is to be done?" asked the queen, "for I hear them."

"Monsieur Laporte, go to them and again recommend silence. Madame, wait at the door, whilst I shall be at the head of the king's bed, ready to die for him."

Laporte went out; the queen remained standing near the hangings, whilst D'Artagnan glided behind the curtains.

Then the heavy and collected steps of a multitude of men were heard, and the queen herself raised the tapestry hangings and put her finger on her lips.

On seeing the queen, the men stopped short, respectfully.

"Enter, gentlemen, enter," said the queen.

There was then amongst that crowd a moment's hesitation, which looked like shame. They had expected resistance, they had expected to be thwarted, to have to force the gates, to overturn the guards. The gates had opened of themselves, and the king, ostensibly at least, had no other guard at his bed-head but his mother. The foremost of them stammered and attempted to fall back.

"Enter, gentlemen," said Laporte, "since the queen desires you so to do."

Then one more bold than the rest ventured to pass the door and to advance on tiptoe. This example was imitated by the rest, until the room filled silently, as if these men had been the humblest, most devoted courtiers. Far beyond the door the heads of those who were not able to enter could be seen, all craning to their utmost height to try and see.

D'Artagnan saw it all through an opening he had made in the curtain, and in the very first man who entered he recognized Planchet.

"Sir," said the queen to him, thinking he was the leader of the band, "you wished to see the king and therefore I determined to show him to you myself. Approach and look at him and say if we have the appearance of people who wish to run away."

"No, certainly," replied Planchet, rather astonished at the unexpected honor conferred upon him.

"You will say, then, to my good and faithful Parisians," continued Anne, with a smile, the expression of which did not deceive D'Artagnan, "that you have seen the king in bed, asleep, and the queen also ready to retire."

"I shall tell them, madame, and those who accompany me will say the same thing; but----"

"But what?" asked Anne of Austria.

"Will your majesty pardon me," said Planchet, "but is it really the king who is lying there?"

Anne of Austria started. "If," she said, "there is one among you who knows the king, let him approach and say whether it is really his majesty lying there."

A man wrapped in a cloak, in the folds of which his face was hidden, approached and leaned over the bed and looked.

For one second, D'Artagnan thought the man had some evil design and he put his hand to his sword; but in the movement made by the man in stooping a portion of his face was uncovered and D'Artagnan recognized the coadjutor.

"It is certainly the king," said the man, rising again. "God bless his majesty!"

"Yes," repeated the leader in a whisper, "God bless his majesty!" and all these men, who had entered enraged, passed from anger to pity and blessed the royal infant in their turn.

"Now," said Planchet, "let us thank the queen. My friends, retire."

They all bowed, and retired by degrees as noiselessly as they had entered. Planchet, who had been the first to enter, was the last to leave. The queen stopped him.

"What is your name, my friend?" she said.

Planchet, much surprised at the inquiry, turned back.

"Yes," continued the queen, "I think myself as much honored to have received you this evening as if you had been a prince, and I wish to know your name."

"Yes," thought Planchet, "to treat me as a prince. No, thank you."

D'Artagnan trembled lest Planchet, seduced, like the crow in the fable, should tell his name, and that the queen, knowing his name, would discover that Planchet had belonged to him.

"Madame," replied Planchet, respectfully, "I am called Dulaurier, at your service."

"Thank you, Monsieur Dulaurier," said the queen; "and what is your business?"

"Madame, I am a clothier in the Rue Bourdonnais."

"That is all I wished to know," said the queen. "Much obliged to you, Monsieur Dulaurier. You will hear again from me."

"Come, come," thought D'Artagnan, emerging from behind the curtain, "decidedly Monsieur

Planchet is no fool; it is evident he has been brought up in a good school."

The different actors in this strange scene remained facing one another, without uttering a single word; the queen standing near the door, D'Artagnan half out of his hiding place, the king raised on his elbow, ready to fall down on his bed again at the slightest sound that would indicate the return of the multitude, but instead of approaching, the noise became more and more distant and very soon it died entirely away.

The queen breathed more freely. D'Artagnan wiped his damp forehead and the king slid off his bed, saying, "Let us go."

At this moment Laporte reappeared.

"Well?" asked the queen

"Well, madame," replied the valet, "I followed them as far as the gates. They announced to all their comrades that they had seen the king and that the queen had spoken to them; and, in fact, they went away quite proud and happy."

"Oh, the miserable wretches!" murmured the queen, "they shall pay dearly for their boldness, and it is I who promise this."

Then turning to D'Artagnan, she said:

"Sir, you have given me this evening the best advice I have ever received. Continue, and say what we must do now."

"Monsieur Laporte," said D'Artagnan, "finish dressing his majesty."

"We may go, then?" asked the queen.

"Whenever your majesty pleases. You have only to descend by the private stairs and you will find me at the door."

"Go, sir," said the queen; "I will follow you."

D'Artagnan went down and found the carriage at its post and the musketeer on the box. D'Artagnan took out the parcel which he had desired Bernouin to place under the seat. It may be remembered that it was the hat and cloak belonging to Monsieur de Gondy's coachman.

He placed the cloak on his shoulders and the hat on his head, whilst the musketeer got off the box.

"Sir," said D'Artagnan, "you will go and release your companion, who is guarding the coachman. You must mount your horse and proceed to the Rue Tiquetonne, Hotel de la Chevrette, whence you will take my horse and that of Monsieur du Vallon, which you must saddle and equip as if for war, and then you will leave Paris, bringing them with you to Cours la Reine. If, when you arrive at Cours la Reine, you find no one, you must go on to Saint Germain. On the king's service."

The musketeer touched his cap and went away to execute the orders thus received.

D'Artagnan mounted the box, having a pair of pistols in his belt, a musket under his feet and a naked sword behind him.

The queen appeared, and was followed by the king and the Duke d'Anjou, his brother.

"Monsieur the coadjutor's carriage!" she exclaimed, falling back.

"Yes, madame," said D'Artagnan; "but get in fearlessly, for I myself will drive you."

The queen uttered a cry of surprise and entered the carriage, and the king and monsieur took their places at her side.

"Come, Laporte," said the queen.

"How, madame!" said the valet, "in the same carriage as your majesties?"

"It is not a matter of royal etiquette this evening, but of the king's safety. Get in, Laporte."

Laporte obeyed.

"Pull down the blinds," said D'Artagnan.

"But will that not excite suspicion, sir?" asked the queen.

"Your majesty's mind may be quite at ease," replied the officer; "I have my answer ready."

The blinds were pulled down and they started at a gallop by the Rue Richelieu. On reaching the gate the captain of the post advanced at the head of a dozen men, holding a lantern in his hand.

D'Artagnan signed to them to draw near.

"Do you recognize the carriage?" he asked the sergeant.

"No," replied the latter.

"Look at the arms."

The sergeant put the lantern near the panel.

"They are those of monsieur le coadjuteur," he said.

"Hush; he is enjoying a ride with Madame de Guemenee."

The sergeant began to laugh.

"Open the gate," he cried. "I know who it is!" Then putting his face to the lowered blinds, he said:

"I wish you joy, my lord!"

"Impudent fellow!" cried D'Artagnan, "you will get me turned off."

The gate groaned on its hinges, and D'Artagnan, seeing the way clear, whipped his horses, who started at a canter, and five minutes later they had rejoined the cardinal.

"Mousqueton!" exclaimed D'Artagnan, "draw up the blinds of his majesty's carriage."

"It is he!" cried Porthos.

"Disguised as a coachman!" exclaimed Mazarin.

"And driving the coadjutor's carriage!" said the queen.

"Corpo di Dio! Monsieur d'Artagnan!" said Mazarin, "you are worth your weight in gold."

53. How D'Artagnan and Porthos earned by selling Straw.

Mazarin was desirous of setting out instantly for Saint Germain, but the queen declared that she should wait for the people whom she had appointed to meet her. However, she offered the cardinal Laporte's place, which he accepted and went from one carriage to the other.

It was not without foundation that a report of the king's intention to leave Paris by night had been circulated. Ten or twelve persons had been in the secret since six o'clock, and howsoever great their prudence might be, they could not issue the necessary orders for the departure without suspicion being generated. Besides, each individual had one or two others for whom he was interested; and as there could be no doubt but that the queen was leaving Paris full of terrible projects of vengeance, every one had warned parents and friends of what was about to transpire; so that the news of the approaching exit ran like a train of lighted gunpowder along the streets.

The first carriage which arrived after that of the queen was that of the Prince de Conde, with the princess and dowager princess. Both these ladies had been awakened in the middle of the night and did not know what it all was about. The second contained the Duke and Duchess of Orleans, the tall young Mademoiselle and the Abbe de la Riviere; and the third, the Duke de Longueville and the Prince de Conti, brother and brother-in-law of Conde. They all alighted and hastened to pay their respects to the king and queen in their coach. The queen fixed her eyes upon the carriage they had left, and seeing that it was empty, she said:

"But where is Madame de Longueville?"

"Ah, yes, where is my sister?" asked the prince.

"Madame de Longueville is ill," said the duke, "and she desired me to excuse her to your majesty."

Anne gave a quick glance to Mazarin, who answered by an almost imperceptible shake of his head.

"What do you say of this?" asked the queen.

"I say that she is a hostage for the Parisians," answered the cardinal.

"Why is she not come?" asked the prince in a low voice, addressing his brother.

"Silence," whispered the duke, "she has her reasons."

"She will ruin us!" returned the prince.

"She will save us," said Conti.

Carriages now arrived in crowds; those of the Marechal de Villeroy, Guitant, Villequier and Comminges came into the line. The two musketeers arrived in their turn, holding the horses of D'Artagnan and Porthos in their hands. These two instantly mounted, the coachman of the latter replacing D'Artagnan on the coach-box of the royal coach. Mousqueton took the place of the coachman, and drove standing, for reasons known to himself, like Automedon of antiquity.

The queen, though occupied by a thousand details, tried to catch the Gascon's eye; but he, with his wonted prudence, had mingled with the crowd.

"Let us be the avant guard," said he to Porthos, "and find good quarters at Saint Germain; nobody will think of us, and for my part I am greatly fatigued."

"As for me," replied Porthos, "I am falling asleep, which is strange, considering we have not had any fighting; truly the Parisians are idiots."

"Or rather, we are very clever," said D'Artagnan.

"Perhaps."

"And how is your wrist?"

"Better; but do you think that we've got them this time?"

"Got what?"

"You your command, and I my title?"

"I'faith! yes--I should expect so; besides, if they forget, I shall take the liberty of reminding them."

"The queen's voice! she is speaking," said Porthos; "I think she wants to ride on horseback."

"Oh, she would like it, but----"

"But what?"

"The cardinal won't allow it. Gentlemen," he said, addressing the two musketeers, "accompany the royal carriage, we are going forward to look for lodgings."

D'Artagnan started off for Saint Germain, followed by Porthos.

"We will go on, gentlemen," said the queen.

And the royal carriage drove on, followed by the other coaches and about fifty horsemen.

They reached Saint German without any accident; on descending, the queen found the prince awaiting her, bare-headed, to offer her his hand.

"What an awakening for the Parisians!" said the queen, radiant.

"It is war," said the prince.

"Well, then, let it be war! Have we not on our side the conqueror of Rocroy, of Nordlingen, of Lens?"

The prince bowed low.

It was then three o'clock in the morning. The queen walked first, every one followed her. About two hundred persons had accompanied her in her flight.

"Gentlemen," said the queen, laughing, "pray take up your abode in the chateau; it is large, and there will be no want of room for you all; but, as we never thought of coming here, I am informed that there are, in all, only three beds in the whole establishment, one for the king, one for me----"

"And one for the cardinal," muttered the prince.

"Am I--am I, then, to sleep on the floor?" asked Gaston d'Orleans, with a forced smile.

"No, my prince," replied Mazarin, "the third bed is intended for your highness."

"But your eminence?" replied the prince.

"I," answered Mazarin, "I shall not sleep at all; I have work to do."

Gaston desired that he should be shown into the room wherein he was to sleep, without in the least concerning himself as to where his wife and daughter were to repose.

"Well, for my part, I shall go to bed," said D'Artagnan; "come, Porthos."

Porthos followed the lieutenant with that profound confidence he ever had in the wisdom of his friend. They walked from one end of the chateau to the other, Porthos looking with wondering eyes at D'Artagnan, who was counting on his fingers.

"Four hundred, at a pistole each, four hundred pistoles."

"Yes," interposed Porthos, "four hundred pistoles; but who is to make four hundred pistoles?"

"A pistole is not enough," said D'Artagnan, "'tis worth a louis."

"What is worth a louis?"

"Four hundred, at a louis each, make four hundred louis."

"Four hundred?" said Porthos.

"Yes, there are two hundred of them, and each of them will need two, which will make four hundred."

"But four hundred what?"

"Listen!" cried D'Artagnan.

But as there were all kinds of people about, who were in a state of stupefaction at the unexpected arrival of the court, he whispered in his friend's ear.

"I understand," answered Porthos, "I understand you perfectly, on my honor; two hundred louis, each of us, would be making a pretty thing of it; but what will people say?"

"Let them say what they will; besides, how will they know that we are doing it?"

"But who will distribute these things?" asked Porthos.

"Isn't Mousqueton there?"

"But he wears my livery; my livery will be known," replied Porthos.

"He can turn his coat inside out."

"You are always in the right, my dear friend," cried Porthos; "but where the devil do you discover all the notions you put into practice?"

D'Artagnan smiled. The two friends turned down the first street they came to. Porthos knocked at the door of a house to the right, whilst D'Artagnan knocked at the door of a house to the left.

"Some straw," they said.

"Sir, we don't keep any," was the reply of the people who opened the doors; "but please ask at the hay dealer's."

"Where is the hay dealer's?"

"At the last large door in the street."

"Are there any other people in Saint Germain who sell straw?"

"Yes; there's the landlord of the Lamb, and Gros-Louis the farmer; they both live in the Rue des Ursulines."

"Very well."

D'Artagnan went instantly to the hay dealer and bargained with him for a hundred and fifty trusses of straw, which he obtained, at the rate of three pistoles each. He went afterward to the innkeeper and bought from him two hundred trusses at the same price. Finally, Farmer Louis sold them eighty trusses, making in all four hundred and thirty.

There was no more to be had in Saint Germain. This foraging did not occupy more than half an hour. Mousqueton, duly instructed, was put at the head of this sudden and new business. He was cautioned not to let a bit of straw out of his hands under a louis the truss, and they intrusted to him straw to the amount of four hundred and thirty louis. D'Artagnan, taking with him three trusses of straw, returned to the chateau, where everybody, freezing with cold and more than half asleep, envied the king, the queen, and the Duke of Orleans, on their camp beds. The lieutenant's entrance produced a burst of laughter in the great drawing-room; but he did not appear to notice that he was the object of general attention, but began to arrange, with so much cleverness, nicety and gayety, his straw bed, that the mouths of all these poor creatures, who could not go to sleep, began to water.

"Straw!" they all cried out, "straw! where is there any to be found?"

"I can show you," answered the Gascon.

And he conducted them to Mousqueton, who freely distributed the trusses at the rate of a louis apiece. It was thought rather dear, but people wanted to sleep, and who would not give even two or three louis for a few hours of sound sleep?

D'Artagnan gave up his bed to any one who wanted it, making it over about a dozen times; and since he was supposed to have paid, like the others, a louis for his truss of straw, he pocketed in that way thirty louis in less than half an hour. At five o'clock in the morning the straw was worth eighty francs a truss and there was no more to be had.

D'Artagnan had taken the precaution to set apart four trusses for his own use. He put in his pocket the key of the room where he had hidden them, and accompanied by Porthos returned to settle with Mousqueton, who, naively, and like the worthy steward that he was, handed them four hundred and thirty louis and kept one hundred for himself.

Mousqueton, who knew nothing of what was going on in the chateau, wondered that the idea had not occurred to him sooner. D'Artagnan put the gold in his hat, and in going back to the chateau settled the reckoning with Porthos, each of them had cleared two hundred and fifteen louis.

Porthos, however, found that he had no straw left for himself. He returned to Mousqueton, but the steward had sold the last wisp. He then repaired to D'Artagnan, who, thanks to his four trusses of straw, was in the act of making up and tasting, by anticipation, the luxury of a bed so soft, so well stuffed at the head, so well covered at the foot, that it would have excited the envy of the king himself, if his majesty had not been fast asleep in his own. D'Artagnan could on no account consent to pull his bed to pieces again for Porthos, but for a consideration of four louis that the latter paid him for it, he consented that Porthos should share his couch with him. He laid his sword at the head, his pistols by his side, stretched his cloak over his feet, placed his felt hat on the top of his cloak and extended himself luxuriously on the straw, which rustled under him. He was already enjoying the sweet dream engendered by the possession of two hundred and nineteen louis, made in a quarter of an hour, when a voice was heard at the door of the hall, which made him stir.

"Monsieur d'Artagnan!" it cried.

"Here!" cried Porthos, "here!"

Porthos foresaw that if D'Artagnan was called away he should remain the sole possessor of the bed. An officer approached.

"I am come to fetch you, Monsieur d'Artagnan."

"From whom?"

"His eminence sent me."

"Tell my lord that I'm going to sleep, and I advise him, as a friend, to do the same."

"His eminence is not gone to bed and will not go to bed, and wants you instantly."

"The devil take Mazarin, who does not know when to sleep at the proper time. What does he want with me? Is it to make me a captain? In that case I will forgive him."

And the musketeer rose, grumbling, took his sword, hat, pistols, and cloak, and followed the officer, whilst Porthos, alone and sole possessor of the bed, endeavored to follow the good example of falling asleep, which his predecessor had set him.

"Monsieur d'Artagnan," said the cardinal, on perceiving him, "I have not forgotten with what zeal you have served me. I am going to prove to you that I have not."

"Good," thought the Gascon, "this is a promising beginning."

"Monsieur d'Artagnan," he resumed, "do you wish to become a captain?"

"Yes, my lord."

"And your friend still longs to be made a baron?"

"At this very moment, my lord, he no doubt dreams that he is one already."

"Then," said Mazarin, taking from his portfolio the letter which he had already shown D'Artagnan, "take this dispatch and carry it to England."

D'Artagnan looked at the envelope; there was no address on it.

"Am I not to know to whom to present it?"

"You will know when you reach London; at London you may tear off the outer envelope."

"And what are my instructions?"

"To obey in every particular the man to whom this letter is addressed. You must set out for Boulogne. At the Royal Arms of England you will find a young gentleman named Mordaunt."

"Yes, my lord; and what am I to do with this young gentleman?"

"Follow wherever he leads you."

D'Artagnan looked at the cardinal with a stupefied air.

"There are your instructions," said Mazarin; "go!"

"Go! 'tis easy to say so, but that requires money, and I haven't any."

"Ah!" replied Mazarin, "so you have no money?"

"None, my lord."

"But the diamond I gave you yesterday?"

"I wish to keep it in remembrance of your eminence."

Mazarin sighed.

"'Tis very dear living in England, my lord, especially as envoy extraordinary."

"Zounds!" replied Mazarin, "the people there are very sedate, and their habits, since the revolution, simple; but no matter."

He opened a drawer and took out a purse.

"What do you say to a thousand crowns?"

D'Artagnan pouted out his lower lip in a most extraordinary manner.

"I reply, my lord, 'tis but little, as certainly I shall not go alone."

"I suppose not. Monsieur du Vallon, that worthy gentleman, for, with the exception of yourself, Monsieur d'Artagnan, there's not a man in France that I esteem and love so much as him----"

"Then, my lord," replied D'Artagnan, pointing to the purse which Mazarin still held, "if you love and esteem him so much, you--understand me?"

"Be it so! on his account I add two hundred crowns."

"Scoundrel!" muttered D'Artagnan. "But on our return," he said aloud, "may we, that is, my friend and I, depend on having, he his barony, and I my promotion?"

"On the honor of Mazarin."

"I should like another sort of oath better," said D'Artagnan to himself; then aloud, "May I not offer my duty to her majesty the queen?"

"Her majesty is asleep and you must set off directly," replied Mazarin; "go, pray, sir----"

"One word more, my lord; if there's any fighting where I'm going, must I fight?"

"You are to obey the commands of the personage to whom I have addressed the inclosed letter."

"'Tis well," said D'Artagnan, holding out his hand to receive the money. "I offer my best respects and services to you, my lord."

D'Artagnan then, returning to the officer, said:

"Sir, have the kindness also to awaken Monsieur du Vallon and to say 'tis by his eminence's order, and that I shall await him at the stables."

The officer went off with an eagerness that showed the Gascon that he had some personal interest in the matter.

Porthos was snoring most musically when some one touched him on the shoulder.

"I come from the cardinal," said the officer.

"Heigho!" said Porthos, opening his large eyes; "what have you got to say?"

"That his eminence has ordered you to England and that Monsieur d'Artagnan is waiting for you in the stables."

Porthos sighed heavily, arose, took his hat, his pistols, and his cloak, and departed, casting a look of regret upon the couch where he had hoped to sleep so well.

No sooner had he turned his back than the officer laid himself down in it, and he had scarcely crossed the threshold before his successor, in his turn, was snoring immoderately. It was very natural, he being the only person in the whole assemblage, except the king, the queen, and the Duke of Orleans, who slept gratuitously.

54. In which we hear Tidings of Aramis.

D'Artagnan went straight to the stables; day was just dawning. He found his horse and that of Porthos fastened to the manger, but to an empty manger. He took pity on these poor animals and went to a corner of the stable, where he saw a little straw, but in doing so he struck his foot against a human body, which uttered a cry and arose on its knees, rubbing its eyes. It was Mousqueton, who, having no straw to lie upon, had helped himself to that of the horses.

"Mousqueton," cried D'Artagnan, "let us be off! Let us set off."

Mousqueton, recognizing the voice of his master's friend, got up suddenly, and in doing so let fall some louis which he had appropriated to himself illegally during the night.

"Ho! ho!" exclaimed D'Artagnan, picking up a louis and displaying it; "here's a louis that smells confoundedly of straw."

Mousqueton blushed so confusedly that the Gascon began to laugh at him and said:

"Porthos would be angry, my dear Monsieur Mousqueton, but I pardon you, only let us remember that this gold must serve us as a joke, so be gay--come along."

Mousqueton instantly assumed a jovial countenance, saddled the horses quickly and mounted his own without making faces over it.

Whilst this went on, Porthos arrived with a very cross look on his face, and was astonished to find the lieutenant resigned and Mousqueton almost merry.

"Ah, that's it!" he cried, "you have your promotion and I my barony."

"We are going to fetch our brevets," said D'Artagnan, "and when we come back, Master Mazarin will sign them."

"And where are we going?" asked Porthos.

"To Paris first; I have affairs to settle."

And they both set out for Paris.

On arriving at its gates they were astounded to see the threatening aspect of the capital. Around a broken-down carriage the people were uttering imprecations, whilst the persons who had attempted to escape were made prisoners--that is to say, an old man and two women. On the other hand, as the two friends approached to enter, they showed them every kind of civility, thinking them deserters from the royal party and wishing to bind them to their own.

"What is the king doing?" they asked.

"He is asleep."

"And the Spanish woman?"

"Dreaming."

"And the cursed Italian?"

"He is awake, so keep on the watch, as they are gone away; it's for some purpose, rely on it. But as you are the strongest, after all," continued D'Artagnan, "don't be furious with old men and women, and keep your wrath for more appropriate occasions."

The people listened to these words and let go the ladies, who thanked D'Artagnan with an eloquent look.

"Now! onward!" cried the Gascon.

And they continued their way, crossing the barricades, getting the chains about their legs, pushed about, questioning and questioned.

In the place of the Palais Royal D'Artagnan saw a sergeant, who was drilling six or seven hundred citizens. It was Planchet, who brought into play profitably the recollections of the regiment of Piedmont.

In passing before D'Artagnan he recognized his former master.

"Good-day, Monsieur d'Artagnan," said Planchet proudly.

"Good-day, Monsieur Dulaurier," replied D'Artagnan.

Planchet stopped short, staring at D'Artagnan. The first row, seeing their sergeant stop, stopped in their turn, and so on to the very last.

"These citizens are dreadfully ridiculous," observed D'Artagnan to Porthos and went on his way.

Five minutes afterward he entered the hotel of La Chevrette, where pretty Madeleine, the hostess, came to him.

"My dear Mistress Turquaine," said the Gascon, "if you happen to have any money, lock it up quickly; if you happen to have any jewels, hide them directly; if you happen to have any debtors, make them pay you, or any creditors, don't pay them."

"Why, prithee?" asked Madeleine.

"Because Paris is going to be reduced to dust and ashes like Babylon, of which you have no doubt heard tell."

"And are you going to leave me at such a time?"

"This very instant."

"And where are you going?"

"Ah, if you could tell me that, you would be doing me a service."

"Ah, me! ah, me!

"Have you any letters for me?" inquired D'Artagnan, wishing to signify to the hostess that her lamentations were superfluous and that therefore she had better spare him demonstrations of her grief.

"There's one just arrived," and she handed the letter to D'Artagnan.

"From Athos!" cried D'Artagnan, recognizing the handwriting.

"Ah!" said Porthos, "let us hear what he says."

D'Artagnan opened the letter and read as follows:

"Dear D'Artagnan, dear Du Vallon, my good friends, perhaps this may be the last time that you will ever hear from me. Aramis and I are very unhappy; but God, our courage, and the remembrance of our friendship sustain us. Think often of Raoul. I intrust to you certain papers which are at Blois; and in two months and a half, if you do not hear of us, take possession of them.

"Embrace, with all your heart, the vicomte, for your devoted, friend,

"ATHOS." "I believe, by Heaven," said D'Artagnan, "that I shall embrace him, since he's upon our road; and if he is so unfortunate as to lose our dear Athos, from that very day he becomes my son."

"And I," said Porthos, "shall make him my sole heir."

"Let us see, what more does Athos say?"

"Should you meet on your journey a certain Monsieur Mordaunt, distrust him, in a letter I cannot say more."

"Monsieur Mordaunt!" exclaimed the Gascon, surprised.

"Monsieur Mordaunt! 'tis well," said Porthos, "we shall remember that; but see, there is a postscript from Aramis."

"So there is," said D'Artagnan, and he read:

"We conceal the place where we are, dear friends, knowing your brotherly affection and that you would come and die with us were we to reveal it."

"Confound it," interrupted Porthos, with an explosion of passion which sent Mousqueton to the other end of the room; "are they in danger of dying?"

D'Artagnan continued:

"Athos bequeaths to you Raoul, and I bequeath to you my revenge. If by any good luck you lay your hand on a certain man named Mordaunt, tell Porthos to take him into a corner and to wring his neck. I dare not say more in a letter.

"ARAMIS." "If that is all, it is easily done," said Porthos.

"On the contrary," observed D'Artagnan, with a vexed look; "it would be impossible."

"How so?"

"It is precisely this Monsieur Mordaunt whom we are going to join at Boulogne and with whom we cross to England."

"Well, suppose instead of joining this Monsieur Mordaunt we were to go and join our friends?" said Porthos, with a gesture fierce enough to have frightened an army.

"I did think of it, but this letter has neither date nor postmark."

"True," said Porthos. And he began to wander about the room like a man beside himself, gesticulating and half drawing his sword out of the scabbard.

As to D'Artagnan, he remained standing like a man in consternation, with the deepest affliction depicted on his face.

"Ah, this is not right; Athos insults us; he wishes to die alone; it is bad, bad, bad."

Mousqueton, witnessing this despair, melted into tears in a corner of the room.

"Come," said D'Artagnan, "all this leads to nothing. Let us go on. We will embrace Raoul, and perhaps he will have news of Athos."

"Stop--an idea!" cried Porthos; "indeed, my dear D'Artagnan, I don't know how you manage, but you are always full of ideas; let us go and embrace Raoul."

"Woe to that man who should happen to contradict my master at this moment," said Mousqueton to himself; "I wouldn't give a farthing for his life."

They set out. On arriving at the Rue Saint Denis, the friends found a vast concourse of people. It was the Duc de Beaufort, who was coming from the Vendomois and whom the coadjutor was showing to the Parisians, intoxicated with joy. With the duke's aid they already considered themselves invincible.

The two friends turned off into a side street to avoid meeting the prince, and so reached the Saint Denis gate.

"Is it true," said the guard to the two cavaliers, "that the Duc de Beaufort has arrived in Paris?"

"Nothing more certain; and the best proof of it is," said D'Artagnan, "that he has dispatched us to meet the Duc de Vendome, his father, who is coming in his turn."

"Long live De Beaufort!" cried the guards, and they drew back respectfully to let the two friends pass. Once across the barriers these two knew neither fatigue nor fear. Their horses flew, and they never ceased speaking of Athos and Aramis.

The camp had entered Saint Omer; the friends made a little detour and went to the camp, and gave the army an exact account of the flight of the king and queen. They found Raoul near his tent, reclining on a truss of hay, of which his horse stole some mouthfuls; the young man's eyes were red and he seemed dejected. The Marechal de Grammont and the Comte de Guiche had returned to Paris and he was quite lonely. And as soon as he saw the two cavaliers he ran to them with open arms.

"Oh, is it you, dear friends? Did you come here to fetch me? Will you take me away with you? Do you bring me tidings of my guardian?"

"Have you not received any?" said D'Artagnan to the youth.

"Alas! sir, no, and I do not know what has become of him; so that I am really so unhappy that I weep."

In fact, tears rolled down his cheeks.

Porthos turned aside, in order not to show by his honest round face what was passing in his mind.

"Deuce take it!" cried D'Artagnan, more moved than he had been for a long time, "don't despair, my friend, if you have not received any letters from the count, we have received one."

"Oh, really!" cried Raoul.

"And a comforting one, too," added D'Artagnan, seeing the delight that his intelligence gave the young man.

"Have you it?" asked Raoul

"Yes--that is, I had it," repined the Gascon, making believe to find it. "Wait, it ought to be there in my pocket; it speaks of his return, does it not, Porthos?"

All Gascon as he was, D'Artagnan could not bear alone the weight of that falsehood.

"Yes," replied Porthos, coughing.

"Eh, give it to me!" said the young man.

"Eh! I read it a little while since. Can I have lost it? Ah! confound it! yes, my pocket has a hole in it."

"Oh, yes, Monsieur Raoul!" said Mousqueton, "the letter was very consoling. These gentlemen read it to me and I wept for joy."

"But at any rate, you know where he is, Monsieur d'Artagnan?" asked Raoul, somewhat comforted.

"Ah! that's the thing!" replied the Gascon. "Undoubtedly I know it, but it is a mystery."

"Not to me, I hope?"

"No, not to you, so I am going to tell you where he is."

Porthos devoured D'Artagnan with wondering eyes.

"Where the devil shall I say that he is, so that he cannot try to rejoin him?" thought D'Artagnan.

"Well, where is he, sir?" asked Raoul, in a soft and coaxing voice.

"He is at Constantinople."

"Among the Turks!" exclaimed Raoul, alarmed. "Good heavens! how can you tell me that?"

"Does that alarm you?" cried D'Artagnan. "Pooh! what are the Turks to such men as the Comte de la Fere and the Abbe d'Herblay?"

"Ah, his friend is with him?" said Raoul. "That comforts me a little."

"Has he wit or not--this demon D'Artagnan?" said Porthos, astonished at his friend's deception.

"Now, sir," said D'Artagnan, wishing to change the conversation, "here are fifty pistoles that the count has sent you by the same courier. I suppose you have no more money and that they will be welcome."

"I have still twenty pistoles, sir."

"Well, take them; that makes seventy."

"And if you wish for more," said Porthos, putting his hand to his pocket----

"Thank you, sir," replied Raoul, blushing; "thank you a thousand times."

At this moment Olivain appeared. "Apropos," said D'Artagnan, loud enough for the servant to hear him, "are you satisfied with Olivain?"

"Yes, in some respects, tolerably well."

Olivain pretended to have heard nothing and entered the tent.

"What fault do you find with the fellow?"

"He is a glutton."

"Oh, sir!" cried Olivain, reappearing at this accusation.

"And a little bit of a thief."

"Oh, sir! oh!"

"And, more especially, a notorious coward."

"Oh, oh! sir! you really vilify me!" cried Olivain.

"The deuce!" cried D'Artagnan. "Pray learn, Monsieur Olivain, that people like us are not to be served by cowards. Rob your master, eat his sweetmeats, and drink his wine; but, by Jove! don't be a coward, or I shall cut off your ears. Look at Monsieur Mouston, see the honorable wounds he has received, observe how his habitual valor has given dignity to his countenance."

Mousqueton was in the third heaven and would have embraced D'Artagnan had he dared; meanwhile he resolved to sacrifice his life for him on the next occasion that presented itself.

"Send away that fellow, Raoul," said the Gascon; "for if he's a coward he will disgrace thee some day."

"Monsieur says I am coward," cried Olivain, "because he wanted the other day to fight a cornet in Grammont's regiment and I refused to accompany him."

"Monsieur Olivain, a lackey ought never to disobey," said D'Artagnan, sternly; then taking him aside, he whispered to him: "Thou hast done right; thy master was in the wrong; here's a crown for thee, but should he ever be insulted and thou dost not let thyself be cut in quarters for him, I will cut out thy tongue. Remember that."

Olivain bowed and slipped the crown into his pocket.

"And now, Raoul," said the Gascon, "Monsieur du Vallon and I are going away as ambassadors, where, I know not; but should you want anything, write to Madame Turquaine, at La Chevrette, Rue Tiquetonne and draw upon her purse as on a banker--with economy; for it is not so well filled as that of Monsieur d'Emery."

And having, meantime, embraced his ward, he passed him into the robust arms of Porthos, who lifted him up from the ground and held him a moment suspended near the noble heart of the formidable giant.

"Come," said D'Artagnan, "let us go."

And they set out for Boulogne, where toward evening they arrived, their horses flecked with foam and dark with perspiration.

At ten steps from the place where they halted was a young man in black, who seemed waiting for some one, and who, from the moment he saw them enter the town, never took his eyes off them.

D'Artagnan approached him, and seeing him stare so fixedly, said:

"Well, friend! I don't like people to quiz me!"

"Sir," said the young man, "do you not come from Paris, if you please?"

D'Artagnan thought it was some gossip who wanted news from the capital.

"Yes, sir," he said, in a softened tone.

"Are you not going to put up at the 'Arms of England'?"

"Yes, sir."

"Are you not charged with a mission from his eminence, Cardinal Mazarin?"

"Yes, sir."

"In that case, I am the man you have to do with. I am M. Mordaunt."

"Ah!" thought D'Artagnan, "the man I am warned against by Athos."

"Ah!" thought Porthos, "the man Aramis wants me to strangle."

They both looked searchingly at the young man, who misunderstood the meaning of that inquisition.

"Do you doubt my word?" he said. "In that case I can give you proofs."

"No, sir," said D'Artagnan; "and we place ourselves at your orders."

"Well, gentlemen," resumed Mordaunt, "we must set out without delay, to-day is the last day granted me by the cardinal. My ship is ready, and had you not come I must have set off without you, for General Cromwell expects my return impatiently."

"So!" thought the lieutenant, "'tis to General Cromwell that our dispatches are addressed."

"Have you no letter for him?" asked the young man.

"I have one, the seal of which I am not to break till I reach London; but since you tell me to whom it is addressed, 'tis useless to wait till then."

D'Artagnan tore open the envelope of the letter. It was directed to "Monsieur Oliver Cromwell, General of the Army of the English Nation."

"Ah!" said D'Artagnan; "a singular commission."

"Who is this Monsieur Oliver Cromwell?" inquired Porthos.

"Formerly a brewer," replied the Gascon.

"Perhaps Mazarin wishes to make a speculation in beer, as we did in straw," said Porthos.

"Come, come, gentlemen," said Mordaunt, impatiently, "let us depart."

"What!" exclaimed Porthos "without supper? Cannot Monsieur Cromwell wait a little?"

"Yes, but I?" said Mordaunt.

"Well, you," said Porthos, "what then?"

"I cannot wait."

"Oh! as to you, that is not my concern, and I shall sup either with or without your permission."

The young man's eyes kindled in secret, but he restrained himself.

"Monsieur," said D'Artagnan, "you must excuse famished travelers. Besides, our supper can't delay you much. We will hasten on to the inn; you will meanwhile proceed on foot to the harbor. We will take a bite and shall be there as soon as you are."

"Just as you please, gentlemen, provided we set sail," he said.

"The name of your ship?" inquired D'Artagnan.

"The Standard."

"Very well; in half an hour we shall be on board."

And the friends, spurring on their horses, rode to the hotel, the "Arms of England."

"What do you say of that young man?" asked D'Artagnan, as they hurried along.

"I say that he doesn't suit me at all," said Porthos, "and that I feel a strong itching to follow Aramis's advice."

"By no means, my dear Porthos; that man is a messenger of General Cromwell; it would insure for us a poor reception, I imagine, should it be announced to him that we had twisted the neck of his confidant."

"Nevertheless," said Porthos, "I have always noticed that Aramis gives good advice."

"Listen," returned D'Artagnan, "when our embassy is finished----"

"Well?"

"If it brings us back to France----"

"Well?"

"Well, we shall see."

At that moment the two friends reached the hotel, "Arms of England," where they supped with hearty appetite and then at once proceeded to the port.

There they found a brig ready to set sail, upon the deck of which they recognized Mordaunt walking up and down impatiently.

"It is singular," said D'Artagnan, whilst the boat was taking them to the Standard, "it is astonishing how that young man resembles some one I must have known, but who it was I cannot yet remember."

A few minutes later they were on board, but the embarkation of the horses was a longer matter than that of the men, and it was eight o'clock before they raised anchor.

The young man stamped impatiently and ordered all sail to be spread.

Porthos, completely used up by three nights without sleep and a journey of seventy leagues on horseback, retired to his cabin and went to sleep.

D'Artagnan, overcoming his repugnance to Mordaunt, walked with him upon the deck and invented a hundred stories to make him talk.

Mousqueton was seasick.

55. The Scotchman.

And now our readers must leave the Standard to sail peaceably, not toward London, where D'Artagnan and Porthos believed they were going, but to Durham, whither Mordaunt had been ordered to repair by the letter he had received during his sojourn at Boulogne, and accompany us to the royalist camp, on this side of the Tyne, near Newcastle.

There, placed between two rivers on the borders of Scotland, but still on English soil, the tents of a little army extended. It was midnight. Some Highlanders were listlessly keeping watch. The moon, which was partially obscured by heavy clouds, now and then lit up the muskets of the sentinels, or silvered the walls, the roofs, and the spires of the town that Charles I. had just surrendered to the parliamentary troops, whilst Oxford and Newark still held out for him in the hopes of coming to some arrangement.

At one of the extremities of the camp, near an immense tent, in which the Scottish officers were holding a kind of council, presided over by Lord Leven, their commander, a man attired as a cavalier lay sleeping on the turf, his right hand extended over his sword.

About fifty paces off, another man, also appareled as a cavalier, was talking to a Scotch sentinel, and, though a foreigner, he seemed to understand without much difficulty the answers given in the broad Perthshire dialect.

As the town clock of Newcastle struck one the sleeper awoke, and with all the gestures of a man rousing himself out of deep sleep he looked attentively about him; perceiving that he was alone he rose and making a little circuit passed close to the cavalier who was speaking to the sentinel. The former had no doubt finished his questions, for a moment later he said good-night and carelessly followed the same path taken by the first cavalier.

In the shadow of a tent the former was awaiting him.

"Well, my dear friend?" said he, in as pure French as has ever been uttered between Rouen and Tours.

"Well, my friend, there is not a moment to lose; we must let the king know immediately."

"Why, what is the matter?"

"It would take too long to tell you, besides, you will hear it all directly and the least word dropped here might ruin all. We must go and find Lord Winter."

They both set off to the other end of the camp, but as it did not cover more than a surface of five hundred feet they quickly arrived at the tent they were looking for.

"Tony, is your master sleeping?" said one of the two cavaliers to a servant who was lying in the outer compartment, which served as a kind of ante-room.

"No, monsieur le comte," answered the servant, "I think not; or at least he has not long been so, for he was pacing up and down for more than two hours after he left the king, and the sound of his footsteps has only ceased during the last ten minutes. However, you may look and see," added the lackey, raising the curtained entrance of the tent.

Lord Winter was seated near an aperture, arranged as a window to let in the night air, his eyes mechanically following the course of the moon, intermittently veiled, as we before observed, by heavy clouds. The two friends approached Winter, who, with his head on his hands, was gazing at the heavens; he did not hear them enter and remained in the same attitude till he felt a hand upon his shoulder.

He turned around, recognized Athos and Aramis and held out his hand to them.

"Have you observed," said he to them, "what a blood-red color the moon has to-night?"

"No," replied Athos; "I thought it looked much the same as usual."

"Look, again, chevalier," returned Lord Winter.

"I must own," said Aramis, "I am like the Comte de la Fere--I can see nothing remarkable about it."

"My lord," said Athos, "in a position so precarious as ours we must examine the earth and not the heavens. Have you studied our Scotch troops and have you confidence in them?"

"The Scotch?" inquired Winter. "What Scotch?"

"Ours, egad!" exclaimed Athos. "Those in whom the king has confided--Lord Leven's Highlanders."

"No," said Winter, then he paused; "but tell me, can you not perceive the russet tint which marks the heavens?"

"Not the least in the world," said Aramis and Athos at once.

"Tell me," continued Winter, always possessed by the same idea, "is there not a tradition in France that Henry IV., the evening before the day he was assassinated, when he was playing at chess with M. de Bassompiere, saw clots of blood upon the chessboard?"

"Yes," said Athos, "and the marechal has often told me so himself."

"Then it was so," murmured Winter, "and the next day Henry IV. was killed."

"But what has this vision of Henry IV. to do with you, my lord?" inquired Aramis.

"Nothing; and indeed I am mad to trouble you with such things, when your coming to my tent at such an hour announces that you are the bearers of important news."

"Yes, my lord," said Athos, "I wish to speak to the king."

"To the king! but the king is asleep."

"I have something important to reveal to him."

"Can it not be put off till to-morrow?"

"He must know it this moment, and perhaps it is already too late."

"Come, then," said Lord Winter.

Lord Winter's tent was pitched by the side of the royal marquee, a kind of corridor communicating between the two. This corridor was guarded, not by a sentinel, but by a confidential servant, through whom, in case of urgency, Charles could communicate instantly with his faithful subject.

"These gentlemen are with me," said Winter.

The lackey bowed and let them pass. As he had said, on a camp bed, dressed in his black doublet, booted, unbelted, with his felt hat beside him, lay the king, overcome by sleep and fatigue. They advanced, and Athos, who was the first to enter, gazed a moment in silence on that pale and noble face, framed in its long and now untidy, matted hair, the blue veins showing through the transparent temples, his eyes seemingly swollen by tears.

Athos sighed deeply; the sigh woke the king, so lightly did he sleep.

He opened his eyes.

"Ah!" said he, raising himself on his elbow, "is it you, Comte de la Fere?"

"Yes, sire," replied Athos.

"You watch while I sleep and you have come to bring me some news?"

"Alas, sire," answered Athos, "your majesty has guessed aright."

"It is bad news?"

"Yes, sire."

"Never mind; the messenger is welcome. You never come to me without conferring pleasure. You whose devotion recognizes neither country nor misfortune, you who are sent to me by Henrietta; whatever news you bring, speak out."

"Sire, Cromwell has arrived this night at Newcastle."

"Ah!" exclaimed the king, "to fight?"

"No, sire, but to buy your majesty."

"What did you say?"

"I said, sire, that four hundred thousand pounds are owing to the Scottish army."

"For unpaid wages; yes, I know it. For the last year my faithful Highlanders have fought for honor alone."

Athos smiled.

"Well, sir, though honor is a fine thing, they are tired of fighting for it, and to-night they have sold you for two hundred thousand pounds--that is to say, for half what is owing them."

"Impossible!" cried the king, "the Scotch sell their king for two hundred thousand pounds! And who is the Judas who has concluded this infamous bargain?"

"Lord Leven."

"Are you certain of it, sir?"

"I heard it with my own ears."

The king sighed deeply, as if his heart would break, and then buried his face in his hands.

"Oh! the Scotch," he exclaimed, "the Scotch I called 'my faithful,' to whom I trusted myself when I could have fled to Oxford! the Scotch, my brothers! But are you well assured, sir?"

"Lying behind the tent of Lord Leven, I raised it and saw all, heard all!"

"And when is this to be consummated?"

"To-day--this morning; so your majesty must perceive there is no time to lose!"

"To do what? since you say I am sold."

"To cross the Tyne, reach Scotland and rejoin Lord Montrose, who will not sell you."

"And what shall I do in Scotland? A war of partisans, unworthy of a king."

"The example of Robert Bruce will absolve you, sire."

"No, no! I have fought too long; they have sold me, they shall give me up, and the eternal shame of treble treason shall fall on their heads."

"Sire," said Athos, "perhaps a king should act thus, but not a husband and a father. I have come in the name of your wife and daughter and of the children you have still in London, and I say to you, 'Live, sire,'--it is the will of Heaven."

The king raised himself, buckled on his belt, and passing his handkerchief over his moist forehead, said:

"Well, what is to be done?"

"Sire, have you in the army one regiment on which you can implicitly rely?"

"Winter," said the king, "do you believe in the fidelity of yours?"

"Sire, they are but men, and men are become both weak and wicked. I will not answer for them. I would confide my life to them, but I should hesitate ere I trusted them with your majesty's."

"Well!" said Athos, "since you have not a regiment, we are three devoted men. It is enough. Let your majesty mount on horseback and place yourself in the midst of us; we will cross the Tyne, reach Scotland, and you will be saved."

"Is this your counsel also, Winter?" inquired the king.

"Yes, sire."

"And yours, Monsieur d'Herblay?"

"Yes, sire."

"As you wish, then. Winter, give the necessary orders."

Winter then left the tent; in the meantime the king finished his toilet. The first rays of daybreak penetrated the aperture of the tent as Winter re-entered it.

"All is ready, sire," said he.

"For us, also?" inquired Athos.

"Grimaud and Blaisois are holding your horses, ready saddled."

"In that case," exclaimed Athos, "let us not lose an instant, but set off."

"Come," added the king.

"Sire," said Aramis, "will not your majesty acquaint some of your friends of this?"

"Friends!" answered Charles, sadly, "I have but three--one of twenty years, who has never forgotten me, and two of a week's standing, whom I shall never forget. Come, gentlemen, come!"

The king quitted his tent and found his horse ready waiting for him. It was a chestnut that the king had ridden for three years and of which he was very fond.

The horse neighed with pleasure at seeing him.

"Ah!" said the king, "I was unjust; here is a creature that loves me. You at least will be faithful to me, Arthur."

The horse, as if it understood these words, bent its red nostrils toward the king's face, and parting his lips displayed all its teeth, as if with pleasure.

"Yes, yes," said the king, caressing it with his hand, "yes, my Arthur, thou art a fond and faithful creature."

After this little scene Charles threw himself into the saddle, and turning to Athos, Aramis and Winter, said:

"Now, gentlemen, I am at your service."

But Athos was standing with his eyes fixed on a black line which bordered the banks of the Tyne and seemed to extend double the length of the camp.

"What is that line?" cried Athos, whose vision was still rather obscured by the uncertain shades and demi-tints of daybreak. "What is that line? I did not observe it yesterday."

"It must be the fog rising from the river," said the king.

"Sire, it is something more opaque than the fog."

"Indeed!" said Winter, "it appears to me like a bar of red color."

"It is the enemy, who have made a sortie from Newcastle and are surrounding us!" exclaimed Athos.

"The enemy!" cried the king.

"Yes, the enemy. It is too late. Stop a moment; does not that sunbeam yonder, just by the side of the town, glitter on the Ironsides?"

This was the name given the cuirassiers, whom Cromwell had made his body-guard.

"Ah!" said the king, "we shall soon see whether my Highlanders have betrayed me or not."

"What are you going to do?" exclaimed Athos.

"To give them the order to charge, and run down these miserable rebels."

And the king, putting spurs to his horse, set off to the tent of Lord Leven.

"Follow him," said Athos.

"Come!" exclaimed Aramis.

"Is the king wounded?" cried Lord Winter. "I see spots of blood on the ground." And he set off to follow the two friends.

He was stopped by Athos.

"Go and call out your regiment," said he; "I can foresee that we shall have need of it directly."

Winter turned his horse and the two friends rode on. It had taken but two minutes for the king to reach the tent of the Scottish commander; he dismounted and entered.

The general was there, surrounded by the more prominent chiefs.

"The king!" they exclaimed, as all rose in bewilderment.

Charles was indeed in the midst of them, his hat on his head, his brows bent, striking his boot with his riding whip.

"Yes, gentlemen, the king in person, the king who has come to ask for some account of what has happened."

"What is the matter, sire?" exclaimed Lord Leven.

"It is this, sir," said the king, angrily, "that General Cromwell has reached Newcastle; that you knew it and I was not informed of it; that the enemy have left the town and are now closing the passages of the Tyne against us; that our sentinels have seen this movement and I have been left unacquainted with it; that, by an infamous treaty you have sold me for two hundred thousand pounds to Parliament. Of this treaty, at least, I have been warned. This is the matter, gentlemen; answer and exculpate yourselves, for I stand here to accuse you."

"Sire," said Lord Leven, with hesitation, "sire, your majesty has been deceived by false reports."

"My own eyes have seen the enemy extend itself between myself and Scotland; and I can almost say that with my own ears I have heard the clauses of the treaty debated."

The Scotch chieftains looked at each other in their turn with frowning brows.

"Sire," murmured Lord Leven, crushed by shame, "sire, we are ready to give you every proof of our fidelity."

"I ask but one," said the king; "put the army in battle array and face the enemy."

"That cannot be, sire," said the earl.

"How, cannot be? What hinders it?" exclaimed the king.

"Your majesty is well aware that there is a truce between us and the English army."

"And if there is a truce the English army has broken it by quitting the town, contrary to the agreement which kept it there. Now, I tell you, you must pass with me through this army across to Scotland, and if you refuse you may choose betwixt two names, which the contempt of all honest men will brand you with--you are either cowards or traitors!"

The eyes of the Scotch flashed fire; and, as often happens on such occasions, from shame they passed to effrontery and two heads of clans advanced upon the king.

"Yes," said they, "we have promised to deliver Scotland and England from him who for the last five-and-twenty years has sucked the blood and gold of Scotland and England. We have promised and we will keep our promise. Charles Stuart, you are our prisoner."

And both extended their hands as if to seize the king, but before they could touch him with the tips of their fingers, both had fallen, one dead, the other stunned.

Aramis had passed his sword through the body of the first and Athos had knocked down the other with the butt end of his pistol.

Then, as Lord Leven and the other chieftains recoiled before this unexpected rescue, which seemed to come from Heaven for the prince they already thought was their prisoner, Athos and Aramis dragged the king from the perjured assembly into which he had so imprudently ventured, and throwing themselves on horseback all three returned at full gallop to the royal tent.

On their road they perceived Lord Winter marching at the head of his regiment. The king motioned him to accompany them.

56. The Avenger.

They all four entered the tent; they had no plan ready--they must think of one.

The king threw himself into an arm-chair. "I am lost," said he.

"No, sire," replied Athos. "You are only betrayed."

The king sighed deeply.

"Betrayed! yes betrayed by the Scotch, amongst whom I was born, whom I have always loved better than the English. Oh, traitors that ye are!"

"Sire," said Athos, "this is not a moment for recrimination, but a time to show yourself a king and a gentleman. Up, sire! up! for you have here at least three men who will not betray you. Ah! if we had been five!" murmured Athos, thinking of D'Artagnan and Porthos.

"What do you say?" inquired Charles, rising.

"I say, sire, that there is now but one way open. Lord Winter answers for his regiment, or at least very nearly so--we will not split straws about words--let him place himself at the head of his men, we will place ourselves at the side of your majesty, and we will mow a swath through Cromwell's army and reach Scotland."

"There is another method," said Aramis. "Let one of us put on the dress and mount the king's horse. Whilst they pursue him the king might escape."

"It is good advice," said Athos, "and if the king will do one of us the honor we shall be truly grateful to him."

"What do you think of this counsel, Winter?" asked the king, looking with admiration at these two men, whose chief idea seemed to be how they could take on their shoulders all the dangers that assailed him.

"I think the only chance of saving your majesty has just been proposed by Monsieur d'Herblay. I humbly entreat your majesty to choose quickly, for we have not an instant to lose."

"But if I accept, it is death, or at least imprisonment, for him who takes my place."

"He will have had the glory of having saved his king," cried Winter.

The king looked at his old friend with tears in his eyes; undid the Order of the Saint Esprit which he wore, to honor the two Frenchmen who were with him, and passed it around Winter's neck, who received on his knees this striking proof of his sovereign's confidence and friendship.

"It is right," said Athos; "he has served your majesty longer than we have."

The king overheard these words and turned around with tears in his eyes.

"Wait a moment, sir," said he; "I have an order for each of you also."

He turned to a closet where his own orders were locked up, and took out two ribbons of the Order of the Garter.

"These cannot be for us," said Athos.

"Why not, sir?" asked Charles.

"Such are for royalty, and we are simple commoners."

"Speak not of crowns. I shall not find amongst them such great hearts as yours. No, no, you do yourselves injustice; but I am here to do you justice. On your knees, count."

Athos knelt down and the king passed the ribbon down from left to right as usual, raised his sword, and instead of pronouncing the customary formula, "I make you a knight. Be brave, faithful and loyal," he said, "You are brave, faithful and loyal. I knight you, monsieur le comte."

Then turning to Aramis, he said:

"It is now your turn, monsieur le chevalier."

The same ceremony recommenced, with the same words, whilst Winter unlaced his leather cuirass, that he might disguise himself like the king. Charles, having proceeded with Aramis as with Athos, embraced them both.

"Sire," said Winter, who in this trying emergency felt all his strength and energy fire up, "we are ready."

The king looked at the three gentlemen. "Then we must fly!" said he.

"Flying through an army, sire," said Athos, "in all countries in the world is called charging."

"Then I shall die, sword in hand," said Charles. "Monsieur le comte, monsieur le chevalier, if ever I am king----"

"Sire, you have already done us more honor than simple gentlemen could ever aspire to, therefore gratitude is on our side. But we must not lose time. We have already wasted too much."

The king again shook hands with all three, exchanged hats with Winter and went out.

Winter's regiment was ranged on some high ground above the camp. The king, followed by the three friends, turned his steps that way. The Scotch camp seemed as if at last awakened; the soldiers had come out of their tents and taken up their station in battle array.

"Do you see that?" said the king. "Perhaps they are penitent and preparing to march."

"If they are penitent," said Athos, "let them follow us."

"Well!" said the king, "what shall we do?"

"Let us examine the enemy's army."

At the same instant the eyes of the little group were fixed on the same line which at daybreak they had mistaken for fog and which the morning sun now plainly showed was an army in order of battle. The air was soft and clear, as it generally is at that early hour of the morning. The regiments, the standards, and even the colors of the horses and uniforms were now clearly distinct.

On the summit of a rising ground, a little in advance of the enemy, appeared a short and heavy looking man; this man was surrounded by officers. He turned a spyglass toward the little group amongst which the king stood.

"Does this man know your majesty personally?" inquired Aramis.

Charles smiled.

"That man is Cromwell," said he.

"Then draw down your hat, sire, that he may not discover the substitution."

"Ah!" said Athos, "how much time we have lost."

"Now," said the king, "give the word and let us start."

"Will you not give it, sire?" asked Athos.

"No; I make you my lieutenant-general," said the king.

"Listen, then, Lord Winter. Proceed, sire, I beg. What we are going to say does not concern your majesty."

The king, smiling, turned a few steps back.

"This is what I propose to do," said Athos. "We will divide our regiments into two squadrons. You will put yourself at the head of the first. We and his majesty will lead the second. If no obstacle occurs we will both charge together, force the enemy's line and throw ourselves into the Tyne, which we must cross, either by fording or swimming; if, on the contrary, any repulse should take place, you and your men must fight to the last man, whilst we and the king proceed on our road. Once arrived at the brink of the river, should we even find them three ranks deep, as long as you and your regiment do your duty, we will look to the rest."

"To horse!" said Lord Winter.

"To horse!" re-echoed Athos; "everything is arranged and decided."

"Now, gentlemen," cried the king, "forward! and rally to the old cry of France, 'Montjoy and St. Denis!' The war cry of England is too often in the mouths of traitors."

They mounted--the king on Winter's horse and Winter on that of the king; then Winter took his place at the head of the first squadron, and the king, with Athos on his right and Aramis on his left, at the head of the second.

The Scotch army stood motionless and silent, seized with shame at sight of these preparations.

Some of the chieftains left the ranks and broke their swords in two.

"There," said the king, "that consoles me; they are not all traitors."

At this moment Winter's voice was raised with the cry of "Forward!"

The first squadron moved off; the second followed, and descended from the plateau. A regiment of cuirassiers, nearly equal as to numbers, issued from behind the hill and came full gallop toward it.

The king pointed this out.

"Sire," said Athos, "we foresaw this; and if Lord Winter's men but do their duty, we are saved, instead of lost."

At this moment they heard above all the galloping and neighing of the horses Winter's voice crying out:

"Sword in hand!"

At these words every sword was drawn, and glittered in the air like lightning.

"Now, gentlemen," said the king in his turn, excited by this sight, "come, gentlemen, sword in hand!"

But Aramis and Athos were the only ones to obey this command and the king's example.

"We are betrayed," said the king in a low voice.

"Wait a moment," said Athos, "perhaps they do not recognize your majesty's voice, and await the order of their captain."

"Have they not heard that of their colonel? But look! look!" cried the king, drawing up his horse with a sudden jerk, which threw it on its haunches, and seizing the bridle of Athos's horse.

"Ah, cowards! traitors!" screamed Lord Winter, whose voice they heard, whilst his men, quitting their ranks, dispersed all over the plain.

About fifteen men were ranged around him and awaited the charge of Cromwell's cuirassiers.

"Let us go and die with them!" said the king.

"Let us go," said Athos and Aramis.

"All faithful hearts with me!" cried out Winter.

This voice was heard by the two friends, who set off, full gallop.

"No quarter!" cried a voice in French, answering to that of Winter, which made them tremble.

As for Winter, at the sound of that voice he turned pale, and was, as it were, petrified.

It was the voice of a cavalier mounted on a magnificent black horse, who was charging at the head of the English regiment, of which, in his ardor, he was ten steps in advance.

"'Tis he!" murmured Winter, his eyes glazed and he allowed his sword to fall to his side.

"The king! the king!" cried out several voices, deceived by the blue ribbon and chestnut horse of Winter; "take him alive."

"No! it is not the king!" exclaimed the cavalier. "Lord Winter, you are not the king; you are my uncle."

At the same moment Mordaunt, for it was he, leveled his pistol at Winter; it went off and the ball entered the heart of the old cavalier, who with one bound on his saddle fell back into the arms of Athos, murmuring: "He is avenged!"

"Think of my mother!" shouted Mordaunt, as his horse plunged and darted off at full gallop.

"Wretch!" exclaimed Aramis, raising his pistol as he passed by him; but the powder flashed in the pan and it did not go off.

At this moment the whole regiment came up and they fell upon the few men who had held out, surrounding the two Frenchmen. Athos, after making sure that Lord Winter was really dead, let fall the corpse and said:

"Come, Aramis, now for the honor of France!" and the two Englishmen who were nearest to them fell, mortally wounded.

At the same moment a fearful "hurrah!" rent the air and thirty blades glittered about their heads.

Suddenly a man sprang out of the English ranks, fell upon Athos, twined arms of steel around him, and tearing his sword from him, said in his ear:

"Silence! yield--you yield to me, do you not?"

A giant had seized also Aramis's two wrists, who struggled in vain to release himself from this formidable grasp.

"D'Art----" exclaimed Athos, whilst the Gascon covered his mouth with his hand.

"I am your prisoner," said Aramis, giving up his sword to Porthos.

"Fire, fire!" cried Mordaunt, returning to the group surrounding the two friends.

"And wherefore fire?" said the colonel; "every one has yielded."

"It is the son of Milady," said Athos to D'Artagnan.

"I recognize him."

"It is the monk," whispered Porthos to Aramis.

"I know it."

And now the ranks began to open. D'Artagnan held the bridle of Athos's horse and Porthos that of Aramis. Both of them attempted to lead his prisoner off the battle-field.

This movement revealed the spot where Winter's body had fallen. Mordaunt had found it out and was gazing on his dead relative with an expression of malignant hatred.

Athos, though now cool and collected, put his hand to his belt, where his loaded pistols yet remained.

"What are you about?" said D'Artagnan.

"Let me kill him."

"We are all four lost, if by the least gesture you discover that you recognize him."

Then turning to the young man he exclaimed:

"A fine prize! a fine prize, friend Mordaunt; we have both myself and Monsieur du Vallon, taken two Knights of the Garter, nothing less."

"But," said Mordaunt, looking at Athos and Aramis with bloodshot eyes, "these are Frenchmen, I imagine."

"I'faith, I don't know. Are you French, sir?" said he to Athos.

"I am," replied the latter, gravely.

"Very well, my dear sir, you are the prisoner of a fellow countryman."

"But the king--where is the king?" exclaimed Athos, anxiously.

D'Artagnan vigorously seized his prisoner's hand, saying:

"Eh! the king? We have secured him."

"Yes," said Aramis, "through an infamous act of treason."

Porthos pressed his friend's hand and said to him:

"Yes, sir, all is fair in war, stratagem as well as force; look yonder!"

At this instant the squadron, that ought to have protected Charles's retreat, was advancing to meet the English regiments. The king, who was entirely surrounded, walked alone in a great empty space. He appeared calm, but it was evidently not without a mighty effort. Drops of perspiration trickled down his face, and from time to time he put a handkerchief to his mouth to wipe away the blood that rilled from it.

"Behold Nebuchadnezzar!" exclaimed an old Puritan soldier, whose eyes flashed at the sight of the man they called the tyrant.

"Do you call him Nebuchadnezzar?" said Mordaunt, with a terrible smile; "no, it is Charles the First, the king, the good King Charles, who despoils his subjects to enrich himself."

Charles glanced a moment at the insolent creature who uttered this, but did not recognize him. Nevertheless, the calm religious dignity of his countenance abashed Mordaunt.

"Bon jour, messieurs!" said the king to the two gentlemen who were held by D'Artagnan and Porthos. "The day has been unfortunate, but it is not your fault, thank God! But where is my old friend Winter?"

The two gentlemen turned away their heads in silence.

"In Strafford's company," said Mordaunt, tauntingly.

Charles shuddered. The demon had known how to wound him. The remembrance of Strafford was a source of lasting remorse to him, the shadow that haunted him by day and night. The king looked around him. He saw a corpse at his feet. It was Winter's. He uttered not a word, nor shed a tear, but a deadly pallor spread over his face; he knelt down on the ground, raised Winter's head, and unfastening the Order of the Saint Esprit, placed it on his own breast.

"Lord Winter is killed, then?" inquired D'Artagnan, fixing his eyes on the corpse.

"Yes," said Athos, "by his own nephew."

"Come, he was the first of us to go; peace be to him! he was an honest man," said D'Artagnan.

"Charles Stuart," said the colonel of the English regiment, approaching the king, who had just put on the insignia of royalty, "do you yield yourself a prisoner?"

"Colonel Tomlison," said Charles, "kings cannot yield; the man alone submits to force."

"Your sword."

The king drew his sword and broke it on his knee.

At this moment a horse without a rider, covered with foam, his nostrils extended and eyes all fire, galloped up, and recognizing his master, stopped and neighed with pleasure; it was Arthur.

The king smiled, patted it with his hand and jumped lightly into the saddle.

"Now, gentlemen," said he, "conduct me where you will."

Turning back again, he said, "I thought I saw Winter move; if he still lives, by all you hold most sacred, do not abandon him."

"Never fear, King Charles," said Mordaunt, "the bullet pierced his heart."

"Do not breathe a word nor make the least sign to me or Porthos," said D'Artagnan to Athos and Aramis, "that you recognize this man, for Milady is not dead; her soul lives in the body of this demon."

The detachment now moved toward the town with the royal captive; but on the road an aide-de-camp, from Cromwell, sent orders that Colonel Tomlison should conduct him to Holdenby Castle.

At the same time couriers started in every direction over England and Europe to announce that Charles Stuart was the prisoner of Oliver Cromwell.

57. Oliver Cromwell.

"Have you been to the general?" said Mordaunt to D'Artagnan and Porthos; "you know he sent for you after the action."

"We want first to put our prisoners in a place of safety," replied D'Artagnan. "Do you know, sir, these gentlemen are each of them worth fifteen hundred pounds?"

"Oh, be assured," said Mordaunt, looking at them with an expression he vainly endeavoured to soften, "my soldiers will guard them, and guard them well, I promise you."

"I shall take better care of them myself," answered D'Artagnan; "besides, all they require is a good room, with sentinels, or their simple parole that they will not attempt escape. I will go and see about that, and then we shall have the honor of presenting ourselves to the general and receiving his commands for his eminence."

"You think of starting at once, then?" inquired Mordaunt.

"Our mission is ended, and there is nothing more to detain us now but the good pleasure of the great man to whom we were sent."

The young man bit his lips and whispered to his sergeant:

"You will follow these men and not lose sight of them; when you have discovered where they lodge, come and await me at the town gate."

The sergeant made a sign of comprehension.

Instead of following the knot of prisoners that were being taken into the town, Mordaunt turned his steps toward the rising ground from whence Cromwell had witnessed the battle and on which he had just had his tent pitched.

Cromwell had given orders that no one was to be allowed admission; but the sentinel, who knew that Mordaunt was one of the most confidential friends of the general, thought the order did not extend to the young man. Mordaunt, therefore, raised the canvas, and saw Cromwell seated before a table, his head buried in his hands, his back being turned.

Whether he heard Mordaunt or not as he entered, Cromwell did not move. Mordaunt remained standing near the door. At last, after a few moments, Cromwell raised his head, and, as if he divined that some one was there, turned slowly around.

"I said I wished to be alone," he exclaimed, on seeing the young man.

"They thought this order did not concern me, sir; nevertheless, if you wish it, I am ready to go."

"Ah! is it you, Mordaunt?" said Cromwell, the cloud passing away from his face; "since you are here, it is well; you may remain."

"I come to congratulate you."

"To congratulate me--what for?"

"On the capture of Charles Stuart. You are now master of England."

"I was much more really so two hours ago."

"How so, general?"

"Because England had need of me to take the tyrant, and now the tyrant is taken. Have you seen him?"

"Yes, sir." said Mordaunt.

"What is his bearing?"

Mordaunt hesitated; but it seemed as though he was constrained to tell the truth.

"Calm and dignified," said he.

"What did he say?"

"Some parting words to his friends."

"His friends!" murmured Cromwell. "Has he any friends?" Then he added aloud, "Did he make any resistance?"

"No, sir, with the exception of two or three friends every one deserted him; he had no means of resistance."

"To whom did he give up his sword?"

"He did not give it up; he broke it."

"He did well; but instead of breaking it, he might have used it to still more advantage."

There was a momentary pause.

"I heard that the colonel of the regiment that escorted Charles was killed," said Cromwell, staring very fixedly at Mordaunt.

"Yes, sir."

"By whom?" inquired Cromwell.

"By me."

"What was his name?"

"Lord Winter."

"Your uncle?" exclaimed Cromwell.

"My uncle," answered Mordaunt; "but traitors to England are no longer members of my family."

Cromwell observed the young man a moment in silence, then, with that profound melancholy Shakespeare describes so well:

"Mordaunt," he said, "you are a terrible servant."

"When the Lord commands," said Mordaunt, "His commands are not to be disputed. Abraham raised the knife against Isaac, and Isaac was his son."

"Yes," said Cromwell, "but the Lord did not suffer that sacrifice to be accomplished."

"I have looked around me," said Mordaunt, "and I have seen neither goat nor kid caught among the bushes of the plain."

Cromwell bowed. "You are strong among the strong, Mordaunt," he said; "and the Frenchmen, how did they behave?"

"Most fearlessly."

"Yes, yes," murmured Cromwell; "the French fight well; and if my glass was good and I mistake not, they were foremost in the fight."

"They were," replied Mordaunt.

"After you, however," said Cromwell.

"It was the fault of their horses, not theirs."

Another pause.

"And the Scotch?"

"They kept their word and never stirred," said Mordaunt.

"Wretched men!"

"Their officers wish to see you, sir."

"I have no time to see them. Are they paid?"

"Yes, to-night."

"Let them be off and return to their own country, there to hide their shame, if its hills are high enough; I have nothing more to do with them nor they with me. And now go, Mordaunt."

"Before I go," said Mordaunt, "I have some questions and a favor to ask you, sir."

"A favor from me?"

Mordaunt bowed.

"I come to you, my leader, my head, my father, and I ask you, master, are you contented with me?"

Cromwell looked at him with astonishment. The young man remained immovable.

"Yes," said Cromwell; "you have done, since I knew you, not only your duty, but more than your duty; you have been a faithful friend, a cautious negotiator, a brave soldier."

"Do you remember, sir it was my idea, the Scotch treaty, for giving up the king?"

"Yes, the idea was yours. I had no such contempt for men before."

"Was I not a good ambassador in France?"

"Yes, for Mazarin has granted what I desire."

"Have I not always fought for your glory and interests?"

"Too ardently, perhaps; it is what I have just reproached you for. But what is the meaning of all these questions?"

"To tell you, my lord, that the moment has now arrived when, with a single word, you may recompense all these services."

"Oh!" said Oliver, with a slight curl of his lip, "I forgot that every service merits some reward and that up to this moment you have not been paid."

"Sir, I can take my pay at this moment, to the full extent of my wishes."

"How is that?"

"I have the payment under my hand; I almost possess it."

"What is it? Have they offered you money? Do you wish a step, or some place in the government?"

"Sir, will you grant me my request?"

"Let us hear what it is, first."

"Sir, when you have told me to obey an order did I ever answer, 'Let me see that order '?"

"If, however, your wish should be one impossible to fulfill?"

"When you have cherished a wish and have charged me with its fulfillment, have I ever replied, 'It is impossible'?"

"But a request preferred with so much preparation----"

"Ah, do not fear, sir," said Mordaunt, with apparent simplicity: "it will not ruin you."

"Well, then," said Cromwell, "I promise, as far as lies in my power, to grant your request; proceed."

"Sir, two prisoners were taken this morning, will you let me have them?"

"For their ransom? have they then offered a large one?" inquired Cromwell.

"On the contrary, I think they are poor, sir."

"They are friends of yours, then?"

"Yes, sir," exclaimed Mordaunt, "they are friends, dear friends of mine, and I would lay down my life for them."

"Very well, Mordaunt," exclaimed Cromwell, pleased at having his opinion of the young man raised once more; "I will give them to you; I will not even ask who they are; do as you like with them."

"Thank you, sir!" exclaimed Mordaunt, "thank you; my life is always at your service, and should I lose it I should still owe you something; thank you; you have indeed repaid me munificently for my services."

He threw himself at the feet of Cromwell, and in spite of the efforts of the Puritan general, who did not like this almost kingly homage, he took his hand and kissed it.

"What!" said Cromwell, arresting him for a moment as he arose; "is there nothing more you wish? neither gold nor rank?"

"You have given me all you can give me, and from to-day your debt is paid."

And Mordaunt darted out of the general's tent, his heart beating and his eyes sparkling with joy.

Cromwell gazed a moment after him.

"He has slain his uncle!" he murmured. "Alas! what are my servants? Possibly this one, who asks nothing or seems to ask nothing, has asked more in the eyes of Heaven than those who tax the country and steal the bread of the poor. Nobody serves me for nothing. Charles, who is my prisoner, may still have friends, but I have none!"

And with a deep sigh he again sank into the reverie that had been interrupted by Mordaunt.

58. Jesus Seigneur.

Whilst Mordaunt was making his way to Cromwell's tent, D'Artagnan and Porthos had brought their prisoners to the house which had been assigned to them as their dwelling at Newcastle.

The order given by Mordaunt to the sergeant had been heard by D'Artagnan, who accordingly, by an expressive glance, warned Athos and Aramis to exercise extreme caution. The prisoners, therefore, had remained silent as they marched along in company with their conquerors--which they could do with the less difficulty since each of them had occupation enough in answering his own thoughts.

It would be impossible to describe Mousqueton's astonishment when from the threshold of the door he saw the four friends approaching, followed by a sergeant with a dozen men. He rubbed his eyes, doubting if he really saw before him Athos and Aramis; and forced at last to yield to evidence, he was on the point of breaking forth in exclamations when he encountered a glance from the eyes of Porthos, the repressive force of which he was not inclined to dispute.

Mousqueton remained glued to the door, awaiting the explanation of this strange occurrence. What upset him completely was that the four friends seemed to have no acquaintance with one another.

The house to which D'Artagnan and Porthos conducted Athos and Aramis was the one assigned to them by General Cromwell and of which they had taken possession on the previous evening. It was at the corner of two streets and had in the rear, bordering on the side street, stables and a sort of garden. The windows on the ground floor, according to a custom in provincial villages, were barred, so that they strongly resembled the windows of a prison.

The two friends made the prisoners enter the house first, whilst they stood at the door, desiring Mousqueton to take the four horses to the stable.

"Why don't we go in with them?" asked Porthos.

"We must first see what the sergeant wishes us to do," replied D'Artagnan.

The sergeant and his men took possession of the little garden.

D'Artagnan asked them what they wished and why they had taken that position.

"We have had orders," answered the man, "to help you in taking care of your prisoners."

There could be no fault to find with this arrangement; on the contrary, it seemed to be a delicate attention, to be gratefully received; D'Artagnan, therefore, thanked the man and gave him a crown piece to drink to General Cromwell's health.

The sergeant answered that Puritans never drank, and put the crown piece in his pocket.

"Ah!" said Porthos, "what a fearful day, my dear D'Artagnan!"

"What! a fearful day, when to-day we find our friends?"

"Yes; but under what circumstances?"

"'Tis true that our position is an awkward one; but let us go in and see more clearly what is to be done."

"Things look black enough," replied Porthos; "I understand now why Aramis advised me to strangle that horrible Mordaunt."

"Silence!" cried the Gascon; "do not utter that name."

"But," argued Porthos, "I speak French and they are all English."

D'Artagnan looked at Porthos with that air of wonder which a cunning man cannot help feeling at displays of crass stupidity.

But as Porthos on his side could not comprehend his astonishment, he merely pushed him indoors, saying, "Let us go in."

They found Athos in profound despondency; Aramis looked first at Porthos and then at D'Artagnan, without speaking, but the latter understood his meaningful look.

"You want to know how we came here? 'Tis easily guessed. Mazarin sent us with a letter to General Cromwell."

"But how came you to fall into company with Mordaunt, whom I bade you distrust?" asked Athos.

"And whom I advised you to strangle, Porthos," said Aramis.

"Mazarin again. Cromwell had sent him to Mazarin. Mazarin sent us to Cromwell. There is a certain fatality in it."

"Yes, you are right, D'Artagnan, a fatality that will separate and ruin us! So, my dear Aramis, say no more about it and let us prepare to submit to destiny."

"Zounds! on the contrary, let us speak about it; for it was agreed among us, once for all, that we should always hold together, though engaged on opposing sides."

"Yes," added Athos, "I now ask you, D'Artagnan, what side you are on? Ah! behold for what end the wretched Mazarin has made use of you. Do you know in what crime you are to-day engaged? In the capture of a king, his degradation and his murder."

"Oh! oh!" cried Porthos, "do you think so?"

"You are exaggerating, Athos; we are not so far gone as that," replied the lieutenant.

"Good heavens! we are on the very eve of it. I say, why is the king taken prisoner? Those who wish to respect him as a master would not buy him as a slave. Do you think it is to replace him on the throne that Cromwell has paid for him two hundred thousand pounds sterling? They will kill him, you may be sure of it."

"I don't maintain the contrary," said D'Artagnan. "But what's that to us? I am here because I am a soldier and have to obey orders--I have taken an oath to obey, and I do obey; but you who have taken no such oath, why are you here and what cause do you represent?"

"That most sacred in the world," said Athos; "the cause of misfortune, of religion, royalty. A friend, a wife, a daughter, have done us the honor to call us to their aid. We have served them to the best of our poor means, and God will recompense the will, forgive the want of power. You may see matters differently, D'Artagnan, and think otherwise. I will not attempt to argue with you, but I blame you."

"Heyday!" cried D'Artagnan, "what matters it to me, after all, if Cromwell, who's an Englishman, revolts against his king, who is a Scotchman? I am myself a Frenchman. I have nothing to do with these things--why hold me responsible?"

"Yes," said Porthos.

"Because all gentlemen are brothers, because you are a gentleman, because the kings of all countries are the first among gentlemen, because the blind populace, ungrateful and brutal, always takes pleasure in pulling down what is above them. And you, you, D'Artagnan, a man sprung from the ancient nobility of France, bearing an honorable name, carrying a good sword, have helped to give up a king to beersellers, shopkeepers, and wagoners. Ah! D'Artagnan! perhaps you have done your duty as a soldier, but as a gentleman, I say that you are very culpable."

D'Artagnan was chewing the stalk of a flower, unable to reply and thoroughly uncomfortable; for when turned from the eyes of Athos he encountered those of Aramis.

"And you, Porthos," continued the count, as if in consideration for D'Artagnan's embarrassment, "you, the best heart, the best friend, the best soldier that I know--you, with a soul that makes you worthy of a birth on the steps of a throne, and who, sooner or later, must receive your reward from an intelligent king--you, my dear Porthos, you, a gentleman in manners, in tastes and in courage, you are as culpable as D'Artagnan."

Porthos blushed, but with pleasure rather than with confusion; and yet, bowing his head, as if humiliated, he said:

"Yes, yes, my dear count, I feel that you are right."

Athos arose.

"Come," he said, stretching out his hand to D'Artagnan, "come, don't be sullen, my dear son, for I have said all this to you, if not in the tone, at least with the feelings of a father. It would have been easier to me merely to have thanked you for preserving my life and not to have uttered a word of all this."

"Doubtless, doubtless, Athos. But here it is: you have sentiments, the devil knows what, such as every one can't entertain. Who could suppose that a sensible man could leave his house, France, his ward--a charming youth, for we saw him in the camp--to fly to the aid of a rotten, worm-eaten royalty, which is going to crumble one of these days like an old hovel. The sentiments you air are certainly fine, so fine that they are superhuman."

"However that may be, D'Artagnan," replied Athos, without falling into the snare which his Gascon friend had prepared for him by an appeal to his parental love, "however that may be, you know in the bottom of your heart that it is true; but I am wrong to dispute with my master. D'Artagnan, I am your prisoner--treat me as such."

"Ah! pardieu!" said D'Artagnan, "you know you will not be my prisoner very long."

"No," said Aramis, "they will doubtless treat us like the prisoners of the Philipghauts."

"And how were they treated?" asked D'Artagnan.

"Why," said Aramis, "one-half were hanged and the other half were shot."

"Well, I," said D'Artagnan "I answer that while there remains a drop of blood in my veins you will be neither hanged nor shot. Sang Diou! let them come on! Besides--do you see that door, Athos?"

"Yes; what then?"

"Well, you can go out by that door whenever you please; for from this moment you are free as the air."

"I recognize you there, my brave D'Artagnan," replied Athos; "but you are no longer our masters. That door is guarded, D'Artagnan; you know that."

"Very well, you will force it," said Porthos. "There are only a dozen men at the most."

"That would be nothing for us four; it is too much for us two. No, divided as we now are, we must perish. See the fatal example: on the Vendomois road, D'Artagnan, you so brave, and you, Porthos, so valiant and so strong--you were beaten; to-day Aramis and I are beaten in our turn. Now that never happened to us when we were four together. Let us die, then, as De Winter has died; as for me, I will fly only on condition that we all fly together."

"Impossible," said D'Artagnan; "we are under Mazarin's orders."

"I know it and I have nothing more to say; my arguments lead to nothing; doubtless they are bad, since they have not determined minds so just as yours."

"Besides," said Aramis, "had they taken effect it would be still better not to compromise two excellent friends like D'Artagnan and Porthos. Be assured, gentlemen, we shall do you honor in our dying. As for myself, I shall be proud to face the bullets, or even the rope, in company with you, Athos; for you have never seemed to me so grand as you are to-day."

D'Artagnan said nothing, but, after having gnawed the flower stalk, he began to bite his nails. At last:

"Do you imagine," he resumed, "that they mean to kill you? And wherefore should they do so? What interest have they in your death? Moreover, you are our prisoners."

"Fool!" cried Aramis; "knowest thou not, then, Mordaunt? I have but exchanged with him one look, yet that look convinced me that we were doomed."

"The truth is, I'm very sorry that I did not strangle him as you advised me," said Porthos.

"Eh! I make no account of the harm Mordaunt can do!" cried D'Artagnan. "Cap de Diou! if he troubles me too much I will crush him, the insect! Do not fly, then. It is useless; for I swear to you that you are as safe here as you were twenty years, ago--you, Athos, in the Rue Ferou, and you, Aramis, in the Rue de Vaugirard."

"Stop," cried Athos, extending his hand to one of the grated windows by which the room was lighted; "you will soon know what to expect, for here he is."

"Who?"

"Mordaunt."

In fact, looking at the place to which Athos pointed, D'Artagnan saw a cavalier coming toward the house at full gallop.

It was Mordaunt.

D'Artagnan rushed out of the room.

Porthos wanted to follow him.

"Stay," said D'Artagnan, "and do not come till you hear me drum my fingers on the door."

When Mordaunt arrived opposite the house he saw D'Artagnan on the threshold and the soldiers lying on the grass here and there, with their arms.

"Halloo!" he cried, "are the prisoners still there?"

"Yes, sir," answered the sergeant, uncovering.

"'Tis well; order four men to conduct them to my lodging."

Four men prepared to do so.

"What is it?" said D'Artagnan, with that jeering manner which our readers have so often observed in him since they made his acquaintance. "What is the matter, if you please?"

"Sir," replied Mordaunt, "I have ordered the two prisoners we made this morning to be conducted to my lodging."

"Wherefore, sir? Excuse curiosity, but I wish to be enlightened on the subject."

"Because these prisoners, sir, are at my disposal and I choose to dispose of them as I like."

"Allow me--allow me, sir," said D'Artagnan, "to observe you are in error. The prisoners belong to those who take them and not to those who only saw them taken. You might have taken Lord Winter--who, 'tis said, was your uncle--prisoner, but you preferred killing him; 'tis well; we, that is, Monsieur du Vallon and I, could have killed our prisoners--we preferred taking them."

Mordaunt's very lips grew white with rage.

D'Artagnan now saw that affairs were growing worse and he beat the guard's march upon the door. At the first beat Porthos rushed out and stood on the other side of the door.

This movement was observed by Mordaunt.

"Sir!" he thus addressed D'Artagnan, "your resistance is useless; these prisoners have just been given me by my illustrious patron, Oliver Cromwell."

These words struck D'Artagnan like a thunderbolt. The blood mounted to his temples, his eyes became dim; he saw from what fountainhead the ferocious hopes of the young man arose, and he put his hand to the hilt of his sword.

As for Porthos, he looked inquiringly at D'Artagnan.

This look of Porthos's made the Gascon regret that he had summoned the brute force of his friend to aid him in an affair which seemed to require chiefly cunning.

"Violence," he said to himself, "would spoil all; D'Artagnan, my friend, prove to this young serpent that thou art not only stronger, but more subtle than he is."

"Ah!" he said, making a low bow, "why did you not begin by saying that, Monsieur Mordaunt? What! are you sent by General Oliver Cromwell, the most illustrious captain of the age?"

"I have this instant left him," replied Mordaunt, alighting, in order to give his horse to a soldier to hold.

"Why did you not say so at once, my dear sir! all England is with Cromwell; and since you ask for my prisoners, I bend, sir, to your wishes. They are yours; take them."

Mordaunt, delighted, advanced, Porthos looking at D'Artagnan with open-mouthed astonishment. Then D'Artagnan trod on his foot and Porthos began to understand that this was merely acting.

Mordaunt put his foot on the first step of the door and, with his hat in hand, prepared to pass by the two friends, motioning to the four men to follow him.

"But, pardon," said D'Artagnan, with the most charming smile and putting his hand on the young man's shoulder, "if the illustrious General Oliver Cromwell has disposed of our prisoners in your favour, he has, of course, made that act of donation in writing."

Mordaunt stopped short.

"He has given you some little writing for me--the least bit of paper which may show that you come in his name. Be pleased to give me that scrap of paper so that I may justify, by a pretext at least, my abandoning my countrymen. Otherwise, you see, although I am sure that General Oliver Cromwell can intend them no harm, it would have a bad appearance."

Mordaunt recoiled; he felt the blow and discharged a terrible look at D'Artagnan, who responded by the most amiable expression that ever graced a human countenance.

"When I tell you a thing, sir," said Mordaunt, "you insult me by doubting it."

"I!" cried D'Artagnan, "I doubt what you say! God keep me from it, my dear Monsieur Mordaunt! On the contrary, I take you to be a worthy and accomplished gentleman. And then, sir, do you wish me to speak freely to you?" continued D'Artagnan, with his frank expression.

"Speak out, sir," said Mordaunt.

"Monsieur du Vallon, yonder, is rich and has forty thousand francs yearly, so he does not care about money. I do not speak for him, but for myself."

"Well, sir? What more?"

"Well--I--I'm not rich. In Gascony 'tis no dishonor, sir, nobody is rich; and Henry IV., of glorious memory, who was the king of the Gascons, as His Majesty Philip IV. is the king of the Spaniards, never had a penny in his pocket."

"Go on, sir, I see what you wish to get at; and if it is simply what I think that stops you, I can obviate the difficulty."

"Ah, I knew well," said the Gascon, "that you were a man of talent. Well, here's the case, here's where the saddle hurts me, as we French say. I am an officer of fortune, nothing else; I have nothing but what my sword brings me in--that is to say, more blows than banknotes. Now, on taking prisoners, this morning, two Frenchmen, who seemed to me of high birth--in short, two knights of the Garter--I said to myself, my fortune is made. I say two, because in such circumstances, Monsieur du Vallon, who is rich, always gives me his prisoners."

Mordaunt, completely deceived by the wordy civility of D'Artagnan, smiled like a man who understands perfectly the reasons given him, and said:

"I shall have the order signed directly, sir, and with it two thousand pistoles; meanwhile, let me take these men away."

"No," replied D'Artagnan; "what signifies a delay of half an hour? I am a man of order, sir; let us do things in order."

"Nevertheless," replied Mordaunt, "I could compel you; I command here."

"Ah, sir!" said D'Artagnan, "I see that although we have had the honor of traveling in your company you do not know us. We are gentlemen; we are, both of us, able to kill you and your eight men--we two only. For Heaven's sake don't be obstinate, for when others are obstinate I am obstinate likewise, and then I become ferocious and headstrong, and there's my friend, who is even more headstrong and ferocious than myself. Besides, we are sent here by Cardinal Mazarin, and at this moment represent both the king and the cardinal, and are, therefore, as ambassadors, able to act with impunity, a thing that General Oliver Cromwell, who is assuredly as great a politician as he is a general, is quite the man to understand. Ask him then, for the written order. What will that cost you my dear Monsieur Mordaunt?"

"Yes, the written order," said Porthos, who now began to comprehend what D'Artagnan was aiming at, "we ask only for that."

However inclined Mordaunt was to have recourse to violence, he understood the reasons D'Artagnan had given him; besides, completely ignorant of the friendship which existed between the four Frenchmen, all his uneasiness disappeared when he heard of the plausible motive of the ransom. He decided, therefore, not only to fetch the order, but the two thousand pistoles, at which he estimated the prisoners. He therefore mounted his horse and disappeared.

"Good!" thought D'Artagnan; "a quarter of an hour to go to the tent, a quarter of an hour to return; it is more than we need." Then turning, without the least change of countenance, to Porthos, he said, looking him full in the face: "Friend Porthos, listen to this; first, not a syllable to either of our friends of what you have heard; it is unnecessary for them to know the service we are going to render them."

"Very well; I understand."

"Go to the stable; you will find Mousqueton there; saddle your horses, put your pistols in your saddle-bags, take out the horses and lead them to the street below this, so that there will be nothing to do but mount them; all the rest is my business."

Porthos made no remark, but obeyed, with the sublime confidence he had in his friend.

"I go," he said, "only, shall I enter the chamber where those gentlemen are?"

"No, it is not worth while."

"Well, do me the kindness to take my purse, which I left on the mantelpiece."

"All right."

He then proceeded, with his usual calm gait, to the stable and went into the very midst of the soldiery, who, foreigner as he was, could not help admiring his height and the enormous strength of his great limbs.

At the corner of the street he met Mousqueton and took him with him.

D'Artagnan, meantime, went into the house, whistling a tune which he had begun before Porthos went away.

"My dear Athos, I have reflected on your arguments and I am convinced. I am sorry to have had anything to do with this matter. As you say, Mazarin is a knave. I have resolved to fly with you, not a word--be ready. Your swords are in the corner; do not forget them, they are in many circumstances very useful; there is Porthos's purse, too."

He put it into his pocket. The two friends were perfectly stupefied.

"Well, pray, is there anything to be so surprised at?" he said. "I was blind; Athos has made me see, that's all; come here."

The two friends went near him.

"Do you see that street? There are the horses. Go out by the door, turn to the right, jump into your saddles, all will be right; don't be uneasy at anything except mistaking the signal. That will be the signal when I call out--Jesus Seigneur!"

"But give us your word that you will come too, D'Artagnan," said Athos.

"I swear I will, by Heaven."

"'Tis settled," said Aramis; "at the cry 'Jesus Seigneur' we go out, upset all that stands in our way, run to our horses, jump into our saddles, spur them; is that all?"

"Exactly."

"See, Aramis, as I have told you, D'Artagnan is first amongst us all," said Athos.

"Very true," replied the Gascon, "but I always run away from compliments. Don't forget the signal: 'Jesus Seigneur!'" and he went out as he came in, whistling the self-same air.

The soldiers were playing or sleeping; two of them were singing in a corner, out of tune, the psalm: "On the rivers of Babylon."

D'Artagnan called the sergeant. "My dear friend, General Cromwell has sent Monsieur Mordaunt to fetch me. Guard the prisoners well, I beg of you."

The sergeant made a sign, as much as to say he did not understand French, and D'Artagnan tried to make him comprehend by signs and gestures. Then he went into the stable; he found the five horses saddled, his own amongst the rest.

"Each of you take a horse by the bridle," he said to Porthos and Mousqueton; "turn to the left, so that Athos and Aramis may see you clearly from the window."

"They are coming, then?" said Porthos.

"In a moment."

"You didn't forget my purse?"

"No; be easy."

"Good."

Porthos and Mousqueton each took a horse by the bridle and proceeded to their post.

Then D'Artagnan, being alone, struck a light and lighted a small bit of tinder, mounted his horse and stopped at the door in the midst of the soldiers. There, caressing as he pretended, the animal with his hand, he put this bit of burning tinder in his ear. It was necessary to be as good a horseman as he was to risk such a scheme, for no sooner had the animal felt the burning tinder than he uttered a cry of pain and reared and jumped as if he had been mad.

The soldiers, whom he was nearly trampling, ran away.

"Help! help!" cried D'Artagnan; "stop--my horse has the staggers."

In an instant the horse's eyes grew bloodshot and he was white with foam.

"Help!" cried D'Artagnan. "What! will you let me be killed? Jesus Seigneur!"

No sooner had he uttered this cry than the door opened and Athos and Aramis rushed out. The coast, owing to the Gascon's stratagem, was clear.

"The prisoners are escaping! the prisoners are escaping!" cried the sergeant.

"Stop! stop!" cried D'Artagnan, giving rein to his famous steed, who, darting forth, overturned several men.

"Stop! stop!" cried the soldiers, and ran for their arms.

But the prisoners were in their saddles and lost no time hastening to the nearest gate.

In the middle of the street they saw Grimaud and Blaisois, who were coming to find their masters. With one wave of his hand Athos made Grimaud, who followed the little troop, understand everything, and they passed on like a whirlwind, D'Artagnan still directing them from behind with his voice.

They passed through the gate like apparitions, without the guards thinking of detaining them, and reached the open country.

All this time the soldiers were calling out, "Stop! stop!" and the sergeant, who began to see that he was the victim of an artifice, was almost in a frenzy of despair. Whilst all this was going on, a cavalier in full gallop was seen approaching. It was Mordaunt with the order in his hand.

"The prisoners!" he exclaimed, jumping off his horse.

The sergeant had not the courage to reply; he showed him the open door, the empty room. Mordaunt darted to the steps, understood all, uttered a cry, as if his very heart was pierced, and fell fainting on the stone steps.

59. Noble Natures never lose Courage, nor good Stomachs their Appetites.

The little troop, without looking behind them or exchanging a word, fled at a rapid gallop, fording a little stream, of which none of them knew the name, and leaving on their left a town which Athos declared to be Durham. At last they came in sight of a small wood, and spurring their horses afresh, rode in its direction.

As soon as they had disappeared behind a green curtain sufficiently thick to conceal them from the sight of any one who might be in pursuit they drew up to hold a council together. The two grooms held the horses, that they might take a little rest without being unsaddled, and Grimaud was posted as sentinel.

"Come, first of all," said Athos to D'Artagnan, "my friend, that I may shake hands with you--you, our rescuer--you, the true hero of us all."

"Athos is right--you have my adoration," said Aramis, in his turn pressing his hand. "To what are you not equal, with your superior intelligence, infallible eye, your arm of iron and your enterprising mind!"

"Now," said the Gascon, "that is all well, I accept for Porthos and myself everything--thanks and compliments; we have plenty of time to spare."

The two friends, recalled by D'Artagnan to what was also due to Porthos, pressed his hand in their turn.

"And now," said Athos, "it is not our plan to run anywhere and like madmen, but we must map up our campaign. What shall we do?"

"What are we going to do, i'faith? It is not very difficult to say."

"Tell us, then, D'Artagnan."

"We are going to reach the nearest seaport, unite our little resources, hire a vessel and return to France. As for me I will give my last sou for it. Life is the greatest treasure, and speaking candidly, ours hangs by a thread."

"What do you say to this, Du Vallon?"

"I," said Porthos, "I am entirely of D'Artagnan's opinion; this is a 'beastly' country, this England."

"You are quite decided, then, to leave it?" asked Athos of D'Artagnan.

"Egad! I don't see what is to keep me here."

A glance was exchanged between Athos and Aramis.

"Go, then, my friends," said the former, sighing.

"How, go then?" exclaimed D'Artagnan. "Let us go, you mean?"

"No, my friend," said Athos, "you must leave us."

"Leave you!" cried D'Artagnan, quite bewildered at this unexpected announcement.

"Bah!" said Porthos, "why separate, since we are all together?"

"Because you can and ought to return to France; your mission is accomplished, but ours is not."

"Your mission is not accomplished?" exclaimed D'Artagnan, looking in astonishment at Athos.

"No, my friend," replied Athos, in his gentle but decided voice, "we came here to defend King Charles; we have but ill defended him--it remains for us to save him!"

"To save the king?" said D'Artagnan, looking at Aramis as he had looked at Athos.

Aramis contented himself by making a sign with his head.

D'Artagnan's countenance took an expression of the deepest compassion; he began to think he had to do with madmen.

"You cannot be speaking seriously, Athos!" said he; "the king is surrounded by an army, which is conducting him to London. This army is commanded by a butcher, or the son of a butcher--it matters little--Colonel Harrison. His majesty, I can assure you, will be tried on his arrival in London; I have heard enough from the lips of Oliver Cromwell to know what to expect."

A second look was exchanged between Athos and Aramis.

"And when the trial is ended there will be no delay in putting the sentence into execution," continued D'Artagnan.

"And to what penalty do you think the king will be condemned?" asked Athos.

"The penalty of death, I greatly fear; they have gone too far for him to pardon them, and there is nothing left to them but one thing, and that is to kill him. Have you never heard what Oliver Cromwell said when he came to Paris and was shown the dungeon at Vincennes where Monsieur de Vendome was imprisoned?"

"What did he say?" asked Porthos.

"'Princes must be knocked on the head.'"

"I remember it," said Athos.

"And you fancy he will not put his maxim into execution, now that he has got hold of the king?"

"On the contrary, I am certain he will do so. But then that is all the more reason why we should not abandon the august head so threatened."

"Athos, you are becoming mad."

"No, my friend," Athos gently replied, "but De Winter sought us out in France and introduced us, Monsieur d'Herblay and myself, to Madame Henrietta. Her majesty did us the honor to ask our aid for her husband. We engaged our word; our word included everything. It was our strength, our intelligence, our life, in short, that we promised. It remains now for us to keep our word. Is that your opinion, D'Herblay?"

"Yes," said Aramis, "we have promised."

"Then," continued Athos, "we have another reason; it is this--listen: In France at this moment everything is poor and paltry. We have a king ten years old, who doesn't yet know what he wants; we have a queen blinded by a belated passion; we have a minister who governs France as he would govern a great farm--that is to say, intent only on turning out all the gold he can by the exercise of Italian cunning and invention; we have princes who set up a personal and egotistic opposition, who will draw from Mazarin's hands only a few ingots of gold or some shreds of power granted as bribes. I have served them without enthusiasm--God knows that I estimated them at their real value, and that they are not high in my esteem--but on principle. To-day I am engaged in a different affair. I have encountered misfortune in a high place, a royal misfortune, a European misfortune; I attach myself to it. If we can succeed in saving the king it will be good; if we die for him it will be grand."

"So you know beforehand you must perish!" said D'Artagnan.

"We fear so, and our only regret is to die so far from both of you."

"What will you do in a foreign land, an enemy's country?"

"I traveled in England when I was young, I speak English like an Englishman, and Aramis, too, knows something of the language. Ah! if we had you, my friends! With you, D'Artagnan, with you, Porthos--all four reunited for the first time for twenty years--we would dare not only England, but the three kingdoms put together!"

"And did you promise the queen," resumed D'Artagnan, petulantly, "to storm the Tower of London, to kill a hundred thousand soldiers, to fight victoriously against the wishes of the nation and the ambition of a man, and when that man is Cromwell? Do not exaggerate your duty. In Heaven's name, my dear Athos, do not make a useless sacrifice. When I see you merely, you look like a reasonable being; when you speak, I seem to have to do with a madman. Come, Porthos, join me; say frankly, what do you think of this business?"

"Nothing good," replied Porthos.

"Come," continued D'Artagnan, who, irritated that instead of listening to him Athos seemed to be attending to his own thoughts, "you have never found yourself the worse for my advice. Well, then, believe me, Athos, your mission is ended, and ended nobly; return to France with us."

"Friend," said Athos, "our resolution is irrevocable."

"Then you have some other motive unknown to us?"

Athos smiled and D'Artagnan struck his hand together in anger and muttered the most convincing reasons that he could discover; but to all these reasons Athos contented himself by replying with a calm, sweet smile and Aramis by nodding his head.

"Very well," cried D'Artagnan, at last, furious, "very well, since you wish it, let us leave our bones in this beggarly land, where it is always cold, where fine weather is a fog, fog is rain, and rain a deluge; where the sun represents the moon and the moon a cream cheese; in truth, whether we die here or elsewhere matters little, since we must die."

"Only reflect, my good fellow," said Athos, "it is but dying rather sooner."

"Pooh! a little sooner or a little later, it isn't worth quarreling over."

"If I am astonished at anything," remarked Porthos, sententiously, "it is that it has not already happened."

"Oh, it will happen, you may be sure," said D'Artagnan. "So it is agreed, and if Porthos makes no objection----"

"I," said Porthos, "I will do whatever you please; and besides, I think what the Comte de la Fere said just now is very good."

"But your future career, D'Artagnan--your ambition, Porthos?"

"Our future, our ambition!" replied D'Artagnan, with feverish volubility. "Need we think of that since we are to save the king? The king saved--we shall assemble our friends together--we will head the Puritans--reconquer England; we shall re-enter London--place him securely on his throne----"

"And he will make us dukes and peers," said Porthos, whose eyes sparkled with joy at this imaginary prospect.

"Or he will forget us," added D'Artagnan.

"Oh!" said Porthos.

"Well, that has happened, friend Porthos. It seems to me that we once rendered Anne of Austria a service not much less than that which to-day we are trying to perform for Charles I.; but, none the less, Anne of Austria has forgotten us for twenty years."

"Well, in spite of that, D'Artagnan," said Athos, "you are not sorry that you were useful to her?"

"No, indeed," said D'Artagnan; "I admit even that in my darkest moments I find consolation in that remembrance."

"You see, then, D'Artagnan, though princes often are ungrateful, God never is."

"Athos," said D'Artagnan, "I believe that were you to fall in with the devil, you would conduct yourself so well that you would take him with you to Heaven."

"So, then?" said Athos, offering his hand to D'Artagnan.

"'Tis settled," replied D'Artagnan. "I find England a charming country, and I stay--but on one condition only."

"What is it?"

"That I am not forced to learn English."

"Well, now," said Athos, triumphantly, "I swear to you, my friend, by the God who hears us--I believe that there is a power watching over us, and that we shall all four see France again."

"So be it!" said D'Artagnan, "but I--I confess I have a contrary conviction."

"Our good D'Artagnan," said Aramis, "represents among us the opposition in parliament, which always says no, and always does aye."

"But in the meantime saves the country," added Athos.

"Well, now that everything is decided," cried Porthos, rubbing his hands, "suppose we think of dinner! It seems to me that in the most critical positions of our lives we have always dined."

"Oh! yes, speak of dinner in a country where for a feast they eat boiled mutton, and as a treat drink beer. What the devil did you come to such a country for, Athos? But I forgot," added the Gascon, smiling, "pardon, I forgot you are no longer Athos; but never mind, let us hear your plan for dinner, Porthos."

"My plan!"

"Yes, have you a plan?"

"No! I am hungry, that is all."

"Pardieu, if that is all, I am hungry, too; but it is not everything to be hungry, one must find something to eat, unless we browse on the grass, like our horses----"

"Ah!" exclaimed Aramis, who was not quite so indifferent to the good things of the earth as Athos, "do you remember, when we were at Parpaillot, the beautiful oysters that we ate?"

"And the legs of mutton of the salt marshes," said Porthos, smacking his lips.

"But," suggested D'Artagnan, "have we not our friend Mousqueton, who managed for us so well at Chantilly, Porthos?"

"Yes," said Porthos, "we have Mousqueton, but since he has been steward, he has become very heavy; never mind, let us call him, and to make sure that he will reply agreeably----

"Here! Mouston," cried Porthos.

Mouston appeared, with a most piteous face.

"What is the matter, my dear M. Mouston?" asked D'Artagnan. "Are you ill?"

"Sir, I am very hungry," replied Mouston.

"Well, it is just for that reason that we have called you, my good M. Mouston. Could you not procure us a few of those nice little rabbits, and some of those delicious partridges, of which you used to make fricassees at the hotel----? 'Faith, I do not remember the name of the hotel."

"At the hotel of----," said Porthos; "by my faith--nor do I remember it either."

"It does not matter; and a few of those bottles of old Burgundy wine, which cured your master so quickly of his sprain!"

"Alas! sir," said Mousqueton, "I much fear that what you ask for are very rare things in this detestable and barren country, and I think we should do better to go and seek hospitality from the owner of a little house we see on the fringe of the forest."

"How! is there a house in the neighborhood?" asked D'Artagnan.

"Yes, sir," replied Mousqueton.

"Well, let us, as you say, go and ask a dinner from the master of that house. What is your opinion, gentlemen, and does not M. Mouston's suggestion appear to you full of sense?"

"Oh!" said Aramis, "suppose the master is a Puritan?"

"So much the better, mordioux!" replied D'Artagnan; "if he is a Puritan we will inform him of the capture of the king, and in honor of the news he will kill for us his fatted hens."

"But if he should be a cavalier?" said Porthos.

"In that case we will put on an air of mourning and he will pluck for us his black fowls."

"You are very happy," exclaimed Athos, laughing, in spite of himself, at the sally of the irresistible Gascon; "for you see the bright side of everything."

"What would you have?" said D'Artagnan. "I come from a land where there is not a cloud in the sky."

"It is not like this, then," said Porthos stretching out his hand to assure himself whether a chill sensation he felt on his cheek was not really caused by a drop of rain.

"Come, come," said D'Artagnan, "more reason why we should start on our journey. Halloo, Grimaud!"

Grimaud appeared.

"Well, Grimaud, my friend, have you seen anything?" asked the Gascon.

"Nothing!" replied Grimaud.

"Those idiots!" cried Porthos, "they have not even pursued us. Oh! if we had been in their place!"

"Yes, they are wrong," said D'Artagnan. "I would willingly have said two words to Mordaunt in this little desert. It is an excellent spot for bringing down a man in proper style."

"I think, decidedly," observed Aramis, "gentlemen, that the son hasn't his mother's energy."

"What, my good fellow!" replied Athos, "wait awhile; we have scarcely left him two hours ago--he does not know yet in what direction we came nor where we are. We may say that he is not equal to his mother when we put foot in France, if we are not poisoned or killed before then."

"Meanwhile, let us dine," suggested Porthos.

"I'faith, yes," said Athos, "for I am hungry."

"Look out for the black fowls!" cried Aramis.

And the four friends, guided by Mousqueton, took up the way toward the house, already almost restored to their former gayety; for they were now, as Athos had said, all four once more united and of single mind.

60. Respect to Fallen Majesty.

As our fugitives approached the house, they found the ground cut up, as if a considerable body of horsemen had preceded them. Before the door the traces were yet more apparent; these horsemen, whoever they might be, had halted there.

"Egad!" cried D'Artagnan, "it's quite clear that the king and his escort have been by here."

"The devil!" said Porthos; "in that case they have eaten everything."

"Bah!" said D'Artagnan, "they will have left a chicken, at least." He dismounted and knocked on the door. There was no response.

He pushed open the door and found the first room empty and deserted.

"Well?" cried Porthos.

"I can see nobody," said D'Artagnan. "Aha!"

"What?"

"Blood!"

At this word the three friends leaped from their horses and entered. D'Artagnan had already opened the door of the second room, and from the expression of his face it was clear that he there beheld some extraordinary object.

The three friends drew near and discovered a young man stretched on the ground, bathed in a pool of blood. It was evident that he had attempted to regain his bed, but had not had sufficient strength to do so.

Athos, who imagined that he saw him move, was the first to go up to him.

"Well?" inquired D'Artagnan.

"Well, if he is dead," said Athos, "he has not been so long, for he is still warm. But no, his heart is beating. Ho, there, my friend!"

The wounded man heaved a sigh. D'Artagnan took some water in the hollow of his hand and threw it upon his face. The man opened his eyes, made an effort to raise his head, and fell back again. The wound was in the top of his skull and blood was flawing copiously.

Aramis dipped a cloth into some water and applied it to the gash. Again the wounded man opened his eyes and looked in astonishment at these strangers, who appeared to pity him.

"You are among friends," said Athos, in English; "so cheer up, and tell us, if you have the strength to do so, what has happened?"

"The king," muttered the wounded man, "the king is a prisoner."

"You have seen him?" asked Aramis, in the same language.

The man made no reply.

"Make your mind easy," resumed Athos, "we are all faithful servants of his majesty."

"Is what you tell me true?" asked the wounded man.

"On our honor as gentlemen."

"Then I may tell you all. I am brother to Parry, his majesty's lackey."

Athos and Aramis remembered that this was the name by which De Winter had called the man they had found in the passage of the king's tent.

"We know him," said Athos, "he never left the king."

"Yes, that is he. Well, he thought of me, when he saw the king was taken, and as they were passing before the house he begged in the king's name that they would stop, as the king was hungry. They brought him into this room and placed sentinels at the doors and windows. Parry knew this room, as he had often been to see me when the king was at Newcastle. He knew that there was a trap-door communicating with a cellar, from which one could get into the orchard. He made a sign, which I understood, but the king's guards must have noticed it and held themselves on guard. I went out as if to fetch wood, passed through the subterranean passage into the cellar, and whilst Parry was gently bolting the door, pushed up the board and beckoned to the king to follow me. Alas! he would not. But Parry clasped his hands and implored him, and at last he agreed. I went on first, fortunately. The king was a few steps behind me, when suddenly I saw something rise up in front of me like a huge shadow. I wanted to cry out to warn the king, but that very moment I felt a blow as if the house was falling on my head, and fell insensible. When I came to myself again, I was stretched in the same place. I dragged myself as far as the yard. The king and his escort were no longer there. I spent perhaps an hour in coming from the yard to this place; then my strength gave out and I fainted again."

"And now how are you feeling?"

"Very ill," replied the wounded man.

"Can we do anything for you?" asked Athos.

"Help to put me on the bed; I think I shall feel better there."

"Have you any one to depend on for assistance?"

"My wife is at Durham and may return at any moment. But you--is there nothing that you want?"

"We came here with the intention of asking for something to eat."

"Alas, they have taken everything; there isn't a morsel of bread in the house."

"You hear, D'Artagnan?" said Athos; "we shall have to look elsewhere for our dinner."

"It is all one to me now," said D'Artagnan; "I am no longer hungry."

"Faith! neither am I," said Porthos.

They carried the man to his bed and called Grimaud to dress the wound. In the service of the four friends Grimaud had had so frequent occasion to make lint and bandages that he had become something of a surgeon.

In the meantime the fugitives had returned to the first room, where they took counsel together.

"Now," said Aramis, "we know how the matter stands. The king and his escort have gone this way; we had better take the opposite direction, eh?"

Athos did not reply; he reflected.

"Yes," said Porthos, "let us take the opposite direction; if we follow the escort we shall find everything devoured and die of hunger. What a confounded country this England is! This is the first time I have gone without my dinner for ten years, and it is generally my best meal."

"What do you think, D'Artagnan?" asked Athos. "Do you agree with Aramis?"

"Not at all," said D'Artagnan; "I am precisely of the contrary opinion."

"What! you would follow the escort?" exclaimed Porthos, in dismay.

"No, I would join the escort."

Athos's eyes shone with joy.

"Join the escort!" cried Aramis.

"Let D'Artagnan speak," said Athos; "you know he always has wise advice to give."

"Clearly," said D'Artagnan, "we must go where they will not look for us. Now, they will be far from looking for us among the Puritans; therefore, with the Puritans we must go."

"Good, my friend, good!" said Athos. "It is excellent advice. I was about to give it when you anticipated me."

"That, then, is your opinion?" asked Aramis.

"Yes. They will think we are trying to leave England and will search for us at the ports; meanwhile we shall reach London with the king. Once in London we shall be hard to find--without considering," continued Athos, throwing a glance at Aramis, "the chances that may come to us on the way."

"Yes," said Aramis, "I understand."

"I, however, do not understand," said Porthos. "But no matter; since it is at the same time the opinion of D'Artagnan and of Athos, it must be the best."

"But," said Aramis, "shall we not be suspected by Colonel Harrison?"

"Egad!" cried D'Artagnan, "he's just the man I count upon. Colonel Harrison is one of our friends. We have met him twice at General Cromwell's. He knows that we were sent from France by Monsieur Mazarin; he will consider us as brothers. Besides, is he not a butcher's son? Well, then, Porthos shall show him how to knock down an ox with a blow of the fist, and I how to trip up a bull by taking him by the horns. That will insure his confidence."

Athos smiled. "You are the best companion that I know, D'Artagnan," he said, offering his hand to the Gascon; "and I am very happy in having found you again, my dear son."

This was, as we have seen, the term which Athos applied to D'Artagnan in his more expansive moods.

At this moment Grimaud came in. He had stanched the wound and the man was better.

The four friends took leave of him and asked if they could deliver any message for him to his brother.

"Tell him," answered the brave man, "to let the king know that they have not killed me outright. However insignificant I am, I am sure that his majesty is concerned for me and blames himself for my death."

"Be easy," said D'Artagnan, "he will know all before night."

The little troop recommenced their march, and at the end of two hours perceived a considerable body of horsemen about half a league ahead.

"My dear friends," said D'Artagnan, "give your swords to Monsieur Mouston, who will return them to you at the proper time and place, and do not forget you are our prisoners."

It was not long before they joined the escort. The king was riding in front, surrounded by troopers, and when he saw Athos and Aramis a glow of pleasure lighted his pale cheeks.

D'Artagnan passed to the head of the column, and leaving his friends under the guard of Porthos, went straight to Harrison, who recognized him as having met him at Cromwell's and received him as politely as a man of his breeding and disposition could. It turned out as D'Artagnan had foreseen. The colonel neither had nor could have any suspicion.

They halted for the king to dine. This time, however, due precautions were taken to prevent any attempt at escape. In the large room of the hotel a small table was placed for him and a large one for the officers.

"Will you dine with me?" asked Harrison of D'Artagnan.

"Gad, I should be very happy, but I have my companion, Monsieur du Vallon, and the two prisoners, whom I cannot leave. Let us manage it better. Have a table set for us in a corner and send us whatever you like from yours."

"Good," answered Harrison.

The matter was arranged as D'Artagnan had suggested, and when he returned he found the king already seated at his little table, where Parry waited on him, Harrison and his officers sitting together at another table, and, in a corner, places reserved for himself and his companions.

The table at which the Puritan officers were seated was round, and whether by chance or coarse intention, Harrison sat with his back to the king.

The king saw the four gentlemen come in, but appeared to take no notice of them.

They sat down in such a manner as to turn their backs on nobody. The officers, table and that of the king were opposite to them.

"I'faith, colonel," said D'Artagnan, "we are very grateful for your gracious invitation; for without you we ran the risk of going without dinner, as we have without breakfast. My friend here, Monsieur du Vallon, shares my gratitude, for he was particularly hungry."

"And I am so still," said Porthos bowing to Harrison.

"And how," said Harrison, laughing, "did this serious calamity of going without breakfast happen to you?"

"In a very simple manner, colonel," said D'Artagnan. "I was in a hurry to join you and took the road you had already gone by. You can understand our disappointment when, arriving at a pretty little house on the skirts of a wood, which at a distance had quite a gay appearance, with its red roof and green shutters, we found nothing but a poor wretch bathed--Ah! colonel, pay my respects to the officer of yours who struck that blow."

"Yes," said Harrison, laughing, and looking over at one of the officers seated at his table. "When Groslow undertakes this kind of thing there's no need to go over the ground a second time."

"Ah! it was this gentleman?" said D'Artagnan, bowing to the officer. "I am sorry he does not speak French, that I might tender him my compliments."

"I am ready to receive and return them, sir," said the officer, in pretty good French, "for I resided three years in Paris."

"Then, sir, allow me to assure you that your blow was so well directed that you have nearly killed your man."

"Nearly? I thought I had quite," said Groslow.

"No. It was a very near thing, but he is not dead."

As he said this, D'Artagnan gave a glance at Parry, who was standing in front of the king, to show him that the news was meant for him.

The king, too, who had listened in the greatest agony, now breathed again.

"Hang it," said Groslow, "I thought I had succeeded better. If it were not so far from here to the house I would return and finish him."

"And you would do well, if you are afraid of his recovering; for you know, if a wound in the head does not kill at once, it is cured in a week."

And D'Artagnan threw a second glance toward Parry, on whose face such an expression of joy was manifested that Charles stretched out his hand to him, smiling.

Parry bent over his master's hand and kissed it respectfully.

"I've a great desire to drink the king's health," said Athos.

"Let me propose it, then," said D'Artagnan.

"Do," said Aramis.

Porthos looked at D'Artagnan, quite amazed at the resources with which his companion's Gascon sharpness continually supplied him. D'Artagnan took up his camp tin cup, filled it with wine and arose.

"Gentlemen," said he, "let us drink to him who presides at the repast. Here's to our colonel, and let him know that we are always at his commands as far as London and farther."

And as D'Artagnan, as he spoke, looked at Harrison, the colonel imagined the toast was for himself. He arose and bowed to the four friends, whose eyes were fixed on Charles, while Harrison emptied his glass without the slightest misgiving.

The king, in return, looked at the four gentlemen and drank with a smile full of nobility and gratitude.

"Come, gentlemen," cried Harrison, regardless of his illustrious captive, "let us be off."

"Where do we sleep, colonel?"

"At Thirsk," replied Harrison.

"Parry," said the king, rising too, "my horse; I desire to go to Thirsk."

"Egad!" said D'Artagnan to Athos, "your king has thoroughly taken me, and I am quite at his service."

"If what you say is sincere," replied Athos, "he will never reach London."

"How so?"

"Because before then we shall have carried him off."

"Well, this time, Athos," said D'Artagnan, "upon my word, you are mad."

"Have you some plan in your head then?" asked Aramis.

"Ay!" said Porthos, "the thing would not be impossible with a good plan."

"I have none," said Athos; "but D'Artagnan will discover one."

D'Artagnan shrugged his shoulders and they proceeded.

61. D'Artagnan hits on a Plan.

As night closed in they arrived at Thirsk. The four friends appeared to be entire strangers to one another and indifferent to the precautions taken for guarding the king. They withdrew to a private house, and as they had reason every moment to fear for their safety, they occupied but one room and provided an exit, which might be useful in case of an attack. The lackeys were sent to their several posts, except that Grimaud lay on a truss of straw across the doorway.

D'Artagnan was thoughtful and seemed for the moment to have lost his usual loquacity. Porthos, who could never see anything that was not self-evident, talked to him as usual. He replied in monosyllables and Athos and Aramis looked significantly at one another.

Next morning D'Artagnan was the first to rise. He had been down to the stables, already taken a look at the horses and given the necessary orders for the day, whilst Athos and Aramis were still in bed and Porthos snoring.

At eight o'clock the march was resumed in the same order as the night before, except that D'Artagnan left his friends and began to renew the acquaintance which he had already struck up with Monsieur Groslow.

Groslow, whom D'Artagnan's praises had greatly pleased, welcomed him with a gracious smile.

"Really, sir," D'Artagnan said to him, "I am pleased to find one with whom to talk in my own poor tongue. My friend, Monsieur du Vallon, is of a very melancholy disposition, so much so, that one can scarcely get three words out of him all day. As for our two prisoners, you can imagine that they are but little in the vein for conversation."

"They are hot royalists," said Groslow.

"The more reason they should be sulky with us for having captured the Stuart, for whom, I hope, you're preparing a pretty trial."

"Why," said Groslow, "that is just what we are taking him to London for."

"And you never by any chance lose sight of him, I presume?"

"I should think not, indeed. You see he has a truly royal escort."

"Ay, there's no fear in the daytime; but at night?"

"We redouble our precautions."

"And what method of surveillance do you employ?"

"Eight men remain constantly in his room."

"The deuce, he is well guarded, then. But besides these eight men, you doubtless place some guard outside?"

"Oh, no! Just think. What would you have two men without arms do against eight armed men?"

"Two men--how do you mean?"

"Yes, the king and his lackey."

"Oh! then they allow the lackey to remain with him?"

"Yes; Stuart begged this favor and Harrison consented. Under pretense that he's a king it appears he cannot dress or undress without assistance."

"Really, captain," said D'Artagnan, determined to continue on the laudatory tack on which he had commenced, "the more I listen to you the more surprised I am at the easy and elegant manner in which you speak French. You have lived three years in Paris? May I ask what you were doing there?"

"My father, who is a merchant, placed me with his correspondent, who in turn sent his son to join our house in London."

"Were you pleased with Paris, sir?"

"Yes, but you are much in want of a revolution like our own--not against your king, who is a mere child, but against that lazar of an Italian, the queen's favorite."

"Ah! I am quite of your opinion, sir, and we should soon make an end of Mazarin if we had only a dozen officers like yourself, without prejudices, vigilant and incorruptible."

"But," said the officer, "I thought you were in his service and that it was he who sent you to General Cromwell."

"That is to say I am in the king's service, and that knowing he wanted to send some one to England, I solicited the appointment, so great was my desire to know the man of genius who now governs the three kingdoms. So that when he proposed to us to draw our swords in honor of old England you see how we snapped up the proposition."

"Yes, I know that you charged by the side of Mordaunt."

"On his right and left, sir. Ah! there's another brave and excellent young man."

"Do you know him?" asked the officer.

"Yes, very well. Monsieur du Vallon and myself came from France with him."

"It appears, too, you kept him waiting a long time at Boulogne."

"What would you have? I was like you, and had a king in keeping."

"Aha!" said Groslow; "what king?"

"Our own, to be sure, the little one--Louis XIV."

"And how long had you to take care of him?"

"Three nights; and, by my troth, I shall always remember those three nights with a certain pleasure."

"How do you mean?"

"I mean that my friends, officers in the guards and mousquetaires, came to keep me company and we passed the night in feasting, drinking, dicing."

"Ah true," said the Englishman, with a sigh; "you Frenchmen are born boon companions."

"And don't you play, too, when you are on guard?"

"Never," said the Englishman.

"In that case you must be horribly bored, and have my sympathy."

"The fact is, I look to my turn for keeping guard with horror. It's tiresome work to keep awake a whole night."

"Yes, but with a jovial partner and dice, and guineas clinking on the cloth, the night passes like a dream. You don't like playing, then?"

"On the contrary, I do."

"Lansquenet, for instance?"

"Devoted to it. I used to play almost every night in France."

"And since your return to England?"

"I have not handled a card or dice-box."

"I sincerely pity you," said D'Artagnan, with an air of profound compassion.

"Look here," said the Englishman.

"Well?"

"To-morrow I am on guard."

"In Stuart's room?"

"Yes; come and pass the night with me."

"Impossible!"

"Impossible! why so?"

"I play with Monsieur du Vallon every night. Sometimes we don't go to bed at all!"

"Well, what of that?"

"Why, he would be annoyed if I did not play with him."

"Does he play well?"

"I have seen him lose as much as two thousand pistoles, laughing all the while till the tears rolled down."

"Bring him with you, then."

"But how about our prisoners?"

"Let your servants guard them."

"Yes, and give them a chance of escaping," said D'Artagnan. "Why, one of them is a rich lord from Touraine and the other a knight of Malta, of noble family. We have arranged the ransom of each of them--2,000 on arriving in France. We are reluctant to leave for a single moment men whom our lackeys know to be millionaires. It is true we plundered them a little when we took them, and I will even confess that it is their purse that Monsieur du Vallon and I draw on in our nightly play. Still, they may have concealed some precious stone, some valuable diamond; so that we are like those misers who are unable to absent themselves from their treasures. We have made ourselves the constant guardians of our men, and while I sleep Monsieur du Vallon watches."

"Ah! ah!" said Groslow.

"You see, then, why I must decline your polite invitation, which is especially attractive to me, because nothing is so wearisome as to play night after night with the same person; the chances always balance and at the month's end nothing is gained or lost."

"Ah!" said Groslow, sighing; "there is something still more wearisome, and that is not to play at all."

"I can understand that," said D'Artagnan.

"But, come," resumed the Englishman, "are these men of yours dangerous?"

"In what respect?"

"Are they capable of attempting violence?"

D'Artagnan burst out laughing at the idea.

"Jesus Dieu!" he cried; "one of them is trembling with fever, having failed to adapt himself to this charming country of yours, and the other is a knight of Malta, as timid as a young girl; and for greater security we have taken from them even their penknives and pocket scissors."

"Well, then," said Groslow, "bring them with you."

"But really----" said D'Artagnan.

"I have eight men on guard, you know. Four of them can guard the king and the other four your prisoners. I'll manage it somehow, you will see."

"But," said D'Artagnan, "now I think of it--what is to prevent our beginning to-night?"

"Nothing at all," said Groslow.

"Just so. Come to us this evening and to-morrow we'll return your visit."

"Capital! This evening with you, to-morrow at Stuart's, the next day with me."

"You see, that with a little forethought one can lead a merry life anywhere and everywhere," said D'Artagnan.

"Yes, with Frenchmen, and Frenchmen like you."

"And Monsieur du Vallon," added the other. "You will see what a fellow he is; a man who nearly killed Mazarin between two doors. They employ him because they are afraid of him. Ah, there he is calling me now. You'll excuse me, I know."

They exchanged bows and D'Artagnan returned to his companions.

"What on earth can you have been saying to that bulldog?" exclaimed Porthos.

"My dear fellow, don't speak like that of Monsieur Groslow. He's one of my most intimate friends."

"One of your friends!" cried Porthos, "this butcher of unarmed farmers!"

"Hush! my dear Porthos. Monsieur Groslow is perhaps rather hasty, it's true, but at bottom I have discovered two good qualities in him--he is conceited and stupid."

Porthos opened his eyes in amazement; Athos and Aramis looked at one another and smiled; they knew D'Artagnan, and knew that he did nothing without a purpose.

"But," continued D'Artagnan, "you shall judge of him for yourself. He is coming to play with us this evening."

"Oho!" said Porthos, his eyes glistening at the news. "Is he rich?"

"He's the son of one of the wealthiest merchants in London."

"And knows lansquenet?"

"Adores it."

"Basset?"

"His mania."

"Biribi?"

"Revels in it."

"Good," said Porthos; "we shall pass an agreeable evening."

"The more so, as it will be the prelude to a better."

"How so?"

"We invite him to play to-night; he has invited us in return to-morrow. But wait. To-night we stop at Derby; and if there is a bottle of wine in the town let Mousqueton buy it. It will be well to prepare a light supper, of which you, Athos and Aramis, are not to partake--Athos, because I told him you had a fever; Aramis, because you are a knight of Malta and won't mix with fellows like us. Do you understand?"

"That's no doubt very fine," said Porthos; "but deuce take me if I understand at all."

"Porthos, my friend, you know I am descended on the father's side from the Prophets and on the mother's from the Sybils, and that I only speak in parables and riddles. Let those who have ears hear and those who have eyes see; I can tell you nothing more at present."

"Go ahead, my friend," said Athos; "I am sure that whatever you do is well done."

"And you, Aramis, are you of that opinion?"

"Entirely so, my dear D'Artagnan."

"Very good," said D'Artagnan; "here indeed are true believers; it is a pleasure to work miracles before them; they are not like that unbelieving Porthos, who must see and touch before he will believe."

"The fact is," said Porthos, with an air of finesse, "I am rather incredulous."

D'Artagnan gave him playful buffet on the shoulder, and as they had reached the station where they were to breakfast, the conversation ended there.

At five in the evening they sent Mousqueton on before as agreed upon. Blaisois went with him.

In crossing the principal street in Derby the four friends perceived Blaisois standing in the doorway of a handsome house. It was there a lodging was prepared for them.

At the hour agreed upon Groslow came. D'Artagnan received him as he would have done a friend of twenty years' standing. Porthos scanned him from head to foot and smiled when he discovered that in spite of the blow he had administered to Parry's brother, he was not nearly so strong as himself. Athos and Aramis suppressed as well as they could the disgust they felt in the presence of such coarseness and brutality.

In short, Groslow seemed to be pleased with his reception.

Athos and Aramis kept themselves to their role. At midnight they withdrew to their chamber, the door of which was left open on the pretext of kindly consideration. Furthermore, D'Artagnan went with them, leaving Porthos at play with Groslow.

Porthos gained fifty pistoles from Groslow, and found him a more agreeable companion than he had at first believed him to be.

As to Groslow, he promised himself that on the following evening he would recover from D'Artagnan what he had lost to Porthos, and on leaving reminded the Gascon of his appointment.

The next day was spent as usual. D'Artagnan went from Captain Groslow to Colonel Harrison and from Colonel Harrison to his friends. To any one not acquainted with him he seemed to be in his normal condition; but to his friends--to Athos and Aramis--was apparent a certain feverishness in his gayety.

"What is he contriving?" asked Aramis.

"Wait," said Athos.

Porthos said nothing, but he handled in his pocket the fifty pistoles he had gained from Groslow with a degree of satisfaction which betrayed itself in his whole bearing.

Arrived at Ryston, D'Artagnan assembled his friends. His face had lost the expression of careless gayety it had worn like a mask the whole day. Athos pinched Aramis's hand.

"The moment is at hand," he said.

"Yes," returned D'Artagnan, who had overheard him, "to-night, gentlemen, we rescue the king."

"D'Artagnan," said Athos, "this is no joke, I trust? It would quite cut me up."

"You are a very odd man, Athos," he replied, "to doubt me thus. Where and when have you seen me trifle with a friend's heart and a king's life? I have told you, and I repeat it, that to-night we rescue Charles I. You left it to me to discover the means and I have done so."

Porthos looked at D'Artagnan with an expression of profound admiration. Aramis smiled as one who hopes. Athos was pale, and trembled in every limb.

"Speak," said Athos.

"We are invited," replied D'Artagnan, "to pass the night with M. Groslow. But do you know where?"

"No."

"In the king's room."

"The king's room?" cried Athos.

"Yes, gentlemen, in the king's room. Groslow is on guard there this evening, and to pass the time away he has invited us to keep him company."

"All four of us?" asked Athos.

"Pardieu! certainly, all four; we couldn't leave our prisoners, could we?"

"Ah! ah!" said Aramis.

"Tell us about it," said Athos, palpitating.

"We are going, then, we two with our swords, you with daggers. We four have got to master these eight fools and their stupid captain. Monsieur Porthos, what do you say to that?"

"I say it is easy enough," answered Porthos.

"We dress the king in Groslow's clothes. Mousqueton, Grimaud and Blaisois have our horses saddled at the end of the first street. We mount them and before daylight are twenty leagues distant."

Athos placed his two hands on D'Artagnan's shoulders, and gazed at him with his calm, sad smile.

"I declare, my friend," said he, "that there is not a creature under the sky who equals you in prowess and in courage. Whilst we thought you indifferent to our sorrows, which you couldn't share without crime, you alone among us have discovered what we were searching for in vain. I repeat it, D'Artagnan, you are the best one among us; I bless and love you, my dear son."

"And to think that I couldn't find that out," said Porthos, scratching his head; "it is so simple."

"But," said Aramis, "if I understand rightly we are to kill them all, eh?"

Athos shuddered and turned pale.

"Mordioux!" answered D'Artagnan, "I believe we must. I confess I can discover no other safe and satisfactory way."

"Let us see," said Aramis, "how are we to act?"

"I have arranged two plans. Firstly, at a given signal, which shall be the words 'At last,' you each plunge a dagger into the heart of the soldier nearest to you. We, on our side, do the same. That will be four killed. We shall then be matched, four against the remaining five. If these five men give themselves up we gag them; if they resist, we kill them. If by chance our Amphitryon changes his mind and receives only Porthos and myself, why, then, we must resort to heroic measures and each give two strokes instead of one. It will take a little longer time and may make a greater disturbance, but you will be outside with swords and will rush in at the proper time."

"But if you yourselves should be struck?" said Athos.

"Impossible!" said D'Artagnan; "those beer drinkers are too clumsy and awkward. Besides, you will strike at the throat, Porthos; it kills as quickly and prevents all outcry."

"Very good," said Porthos; "it will be a nice little throat cutting."

"Horrible, horrible," exclaimed Athos.

"Nonsense," said D'Artagnan; "you would do as much, Mr. Humanity, in a battle. But if you think the king's life is not worth what it must cost there's an end of the matter and I send to Groslow to say I am ill."

"No, you are right," said Athos.

At this moment a soldier entered to inform them that Groslow was waiting for them.

"Where?" asked D'Artagnan.

"In the room of the English Nebuchadnezzar," replied the staunch Puritan.

"Good," replied Athos, whose blood mounted to his face at the insult offered to royalty; "tell the captain we are coming."

The Puritan then went out. The lackeys had been ordered to saddle eight horses and to wait, keeping together and without dismounting, at the corner of a street about twenty steps from the house where the king was lodged.

It was nine o'clock in the evening; the sentinels had been relieved at eight and Captain Groslow had been on guard for an hour. D'Artagnan and Porthos, armed with their swords, and Athos and Aramis, each carrying a concealed poniard, approached the house which for the time being was Charles Stuart's prison. The two latter followed their captors in the humble guise of captives, without arms.

"Od's bodikins," said Groslow, as the four friends entered, "I had almost given you up."

D'Artagnan went up to him and whispered in his ear:

"The fact is, we, that is, Monsieur du Vallon and I, hesitated a little."

"And why?"

D'Artagnan looked significantly toward Athos and Aramis.

"Aha," said Groslow; "on account of political opinions? No matter. On the contrary," he added, laughing, "if they want to see their Stuart they shall see him.

"Are we to pass the night in the king's room?" asked D'Artagnan.

"No, but in the one next to it, and as the door will remain open it comes to the same thing. Have you provided yourself with money? I assure you I intend to play the devil's game to-night."

D'Artagnan rattled the gold in his pockets.

"Very good," said Groslow, and opened the door of the room. "I will show you the way," and he went in first.

D'Artagnan turned to look at his friends. Porthos was perfectly indifferent; Athos, pale, but resolute; Aramis was wiping a slight moisture from his brow.

The eight guards were at their posts. Four in the king's room, two at the door between the rooms and two at that by which the friends had entered. Athos smiled when he saw their bare swords; he felt it was no longer to be a butchery, but a fight, and he resumed his usual good humor.

Charles was perceived through the door, lying dressed upon his bed, at the head of which Parry was seated, reading in a low voice a chapter from the Bible.

A candle of coarse tallow on a black table lighted up the handsome and resigned face of the king and that of his faithful retainer, far less calm.

From time to time Parry stopped, thinking the king, whose eyes were closed, was really asleep, but Charles would open his eyes and say with a smile:

"Go on, my good Parry, I am listening."

Groslow advanced to the door of the king's room, replaced on his head the hat he had taken off to receive his guests, looked for a moment contemptuously at this simple, yet touching scene, then turning to D'Artagnan, assumed an air of triumph at what he had achieved.

"Capital!" cried the Gascon, "you would make a distinguished general."

"And do you think," asked Groslow, "that Stuart will ever escape while I am on guard?"

"No, to be sure," replied D'Artagnan; "unless, forsooth, the sky rains friends upon him."

Groslow's face brightened.

It is impossible to say whether Charles, who kept his eyes constantly closed, had noticed the insolence of the Puritan captain, but the moment he heard the clear tone of D'Artagnan's voice his eyelids rose, in spite of himself.

Parry, too, started and stopped reading.

"What are you thinking about?" said the king; "go on, my good Parry, unless you are tired."

Parry resumed his reading.

On a table in the next room were lighted candles, cards, two dice-boxes, and dice.

"Gentlemen," said Groslow, "I beg you will take your places. I will sit facing Stuart, whom I like so much to see, especially where he now is, and you, Monsieur d'Artagnan, opposite to me."

Athos turned red with rage. D'Artagnan frowned at him.

"That's it," said D'Artagnan; "you, Monsieur le Comte de la Fere, to the right of Monsieur Groslow. You, Chevalier d'Herblay, to his left. Du Vallon next me. You'll bet for me and those gentlemen for Monsieur Groslow."

By this arrangement D'Artagnan could nudge Porthos with his knee and make signs with his eyes to Athos and Aramis.

At the names Comte de la Fere and Chevalier d'Herblay, Charles opened his eyes, and raising his noble head, in spite of himself, threw a glance at all the actors in the scene.

At that moment Parry turned over several leaves of his Bible and read with a loud voice this verse in Jeremiah:

"God said, 'Hear ye the words of the prophets my servants, whom I have sent unto you.'"

The four friends exchanged glances. The words that Parry had read assured them that their presence was understood by the king and was assigned to its real motive. D'Artagnan's eyes sparkled with joy.

"You asked me just now if I was in funds," said D'Artagnan, placing some twenty pistoles upon the table. "Well, in my turn I advise you to keep a sharp lookout on your treasure, my dear Monsieur Groslow, for I can tell you we shall not leave this without robbing you of it."

"Not without my defending it," said Groslow.

"So much the better," said D'Artagnan. "Fight, my dear captain, fight. You know or you don't know, that that is what we ask of you."

"Oh! yes," said Groslow, bursting with his usual coarse laugh, "I know you Frenchmen want nothing but cuts and bruises."

Charles had heard and understood it all. A slight color mounted to his cheeks. The soldiers then saw him stretch his limbs, little by little, and under the pretense of much heat throw off the Scotch plaid which covered him.

Athos and Aramis started with delight to find that the king was lying with his clothes on.

The game began. The luck had turned, and Groslow, having won some hundred pistoles, was in the merriest possible humor.

Porthos, who had lost the fifty pistoles he had won the night before and thirty more besides, was very cross and questioned D'Artagnan with a nudge of the knee as to whether it would not soon be time to change the game. Athos and Aramis looked at him inquiringly. But D'Artagnan remained impassible.

It struck ten. They heard the guard going its rounds.

"How many rounds do they make a night?" asked D'Artagnan, drawing more pistoles from his pocket.

"Five," answered Groslow, "one every two hours."

D'Artagnan glanced at Athos and Aramis and for the first time replied to Porthos's nudge of the knee by a nudge responsive. Meanwhile, the soldiers whose duty it was to remain in the king's room, attracted by that love of play so powerful in all men, had stolen little by little toward the table, and standing on tiptoe, lounged, watching the game, over the shoulders of D'Artagnan and Porthos. Those on the other side had followed their example, thus favoring the views of the four friends, who preferred having them close at hand to chasing them about the chamber. The two sentinels at the door still had their swords unsheathed, but they were leaning on them while they watched the game.

Athos seemed to grow calm as the critical moment approached. With his white, aristocratic hands he played with the louis, bending and straightening them again, as if they were made of pewter. Aramis, less self-controlled, fumbled continually with his hidden poniard. Porthos, impatient at his continued losses, kept up a vigorous play with his knee.

D'Artagnan turned, mechanically looking behind him, and between the figures of two soldiers he could see Parry standing up and Charles leaning on his elbow with his hands clasped and apparently offering a fervent prayer to God.

D'Artagnan saw that the moment was come. He darted a preparatory glance at Athos and Aramis, who slyly pushed their chairs a little back so as to leave themselves more space for action. He gave Porthos a second nudge of the knee and Porthos got up as if to stretch his legs and took care at the same time to ascertain that his sword could be drawn smoothly from the scabbard.

"Hang it!" cried D'Artagnan, "another twenty pistoles lost. Really, Captain Groslow, you are too much in fortune's way. This can't last," and he drew another twenty from his pocket. "One more turn, captain; twenty pistoles on one throw--only one, the last."

"Done for twenty," replied Groslow.

And he turned up two cards as usual, a king for D'Artagnan and an ace for himself.

"A king," said D'Artagnan; "it's a good omen, Master Groslow--look out for the king."

And in spite of his extraordinary self-control there was a strange vibration in the Gascon's voice which made his partner start.

Groslow began turning the cards one after another. If he turned up an ace first he won; if a king he lost.

He turned up a king.

"At last!" cried D'Artagnan.

At this word Athos and Aramis jumped up. Porthos drew back a step. Daggers and swords were just about to shine, when suddenly the door was thrown open and Harrison appeared in the doorway, accompanied by a man enveloped in a large cloak. Behind this man could be seen the glistening muskets of half a dozen soldiers.

Groslow jumped up, ashamed at being surprised in the midst of wine, cards, and dice. But Harrison paid not the least attention to him, and entering the king's room, followed by his companion:

"Charles Stuart," said he, "an order has come to conduct you to London without stopping day or night. Prepare yourself, then, to start at once."

"And by whom is this order given?" asked the king.

"By General Oliver Cromwell. And here is Mr. Mordaunt, who has brought it and is charged with its execution."

"Mordaunt!" muttered the four friends, exchanging glances.

D'Artagnan swept up the money that he and Porthos had lost and buried it in his huge pocket. Athos and Aramis placed themselves behind him. At this movement Mordaunt turned around, recognized them, and uttered an exclamation of savage delight.

"I'm afraid we are prisoners," whispered D'Artagnan to his friend.

"Not yet," replied Porthos.

"Colonel, colonel," cried Mordaunt, "you are betrayed. These four Frenchmen have escaped from Newcastle, and no doubt want to carry off the king. Arrest them."

"Ah! my young man," said D'Artagnan, drawing his sword, "that is an order sooner given than executed. Fly, friends, fly!" he added, whirling his sword around him.

The next moment he darted to the door and knocked down two of the soldiers who guarded it, before they had time to cock their muskets. Athos and Aramis followed him. Porthos brought up the rear, and before soldiers, officers, or colonel had time to recover their surprise all four were in the street.

"Fire!" cried Mordaunt; "fire upon them!"

Three or four shots were fired, but with no other result than to show the four fugitives turning the corner of the street safe and sound.

The horses were at the place fixed upon, and they leaped lightly into their saddles.

"Forward!" cried D'Artagnan, "and spur for your dear lives!"

They galloped away and took the road they had come by in the morning, namely, in the direction toward Scotland. A few hundred yards beyond the town D'Artagnan drew rein.

"Halt!" he cried, "this time we shall be pursued. We must let them leave the village and ride after us on the northern road, and when they have passed we will take the opposite direction."

There was a stream close by and a bridge across it.

D'Artagnan led his horse under the arch of the bridge. The others followed. Ten minutes later they heard the rapid gallop of a troop of horsemen. A few minutes more and the troop passed over their heads.

62. London.

As soon as the noise of the hoofs was lost in the distance D'Artagnan remounted the bank of the stream and scoured the plain, followed by his three friends, directing their course, as well as they could guess, toward London.

"This time," said D'Artagnan, when they were sufficiently distant to proceed at a trot, "I think all is lost and we have nothing better to do than to reach France. What do you say, Athos, to that proposition? Isn't it reasonable?"

"Yes, dear friend," Athos replied, "but you said a word the other day that was more than reasonable--it was noble and generous. You said, 'Let us die here!' I recall to you that word."

"Oh," said Porthos, "death is nothing: it isn't death that can disquiet us, since we don't know what it is. What troubles me is the idea of defeat. As things are turning out, I foresee that we must give battle to London, to the provinces, to all England, and certainly in the end we can't fail to be beaten."

"We ought to witness this great tragedy even to its last scene," said Athos. "Whatever happens, let us not leave England before the crisis. Don't you agree with me, Aramis?"

"Entirely, my dear count. Then, too, I confess I should not be sorry to come across Mordaunt again. It appears to me that we have an account to settle with him, and that it is not our custom to leave a place without paying our debts, of this kind, at least."

"Ah! that's another thing," said D'Artagnan, "and I should not mind waiting in London a whole year for a chance of meeting this Mordaunt in question. Only let us lodge with some one on whom we can count; for I imagine, just now, that Noll Cromwell would not be inclined to trifle with us. Athos, do you know any inn in the whole town where one can find white sheets, roast beef reasonably cooked, and wine which is not made of hops and gin?"

"I think I know what you want," replied Athos. "De Winter took us to the house of a Spaniard, who, he said, had become naturalized as an Englishman by the guineas of his new compatriots. What do you say to it, Aramis?"

"Why, the idea of taking quarters with Senor Perez seems to me very reasonable, and for my part I agree to it. We will invoke the remembrance of that poor De Winter, for whom he seemed to have a great regard; we will tell him that we have come as amateurs to see what is going on; we will spend with him a guinea each per day; and I think that by taking all these precautions we can be quite undisturbed."

"You forget, Aramis, one precaution of considerable importance."

"What is that?"

"The precaution of changing our clothes."

"Changing our clothes!" exclaimed Porthos. "I don't see why; we are very comfortable in those we wear."

"To prevent recognition," said D'Artagnan. "Our clothes have a cut which would proclaim the Frenchman at first sight. Now, I don't set sufficient store on the cut of my jerkin to risk being hung at Tyburn or sent for change of scene to the Indies. I shall buy a chestnut-colored suit. I've remarked that your Puritans revel in that color."

"But can you find your man?" said Aramis to Athos.

"Oh! to be sure, yes. He lives at the Bedford Tavern, Greenhall Street. Besides, I can find my way about the city with my eyes shut."

"I wish we were already there," said D'Artagnan; "and my advice is that we reach London before daybreak, even if we kill our horses."

"Come on, then," said Athos, "for unless I am mistaken in my calculations we have only eight or ten leagues to go."

The friends urged on their horses and arrived, in fact, at about five o'clock in the morning. They were stopped and questioned at the gate by which they sought to enter the city, but Athos replied, in excellent English, that they had been sent forward by Colonel Harrison to announce to his colleague, Monsieur Bridge, the approach of the king. That reply led to several questions about the king's capture, and Athos gave details so precise and positive that if the gatekeepers had any suspicions they vanished completely. The way was therefore opened to the four friends with all sorts of Puritan congratulations.

Athos was right. He went direct to the Bedford Tavern, and the host, who recognized him, was delighted to see him again with such a numerous and promising company.

Though it was scarcely daylight our four travelers found the town in a great bustle, owing to the reported approach of Harrison and the king.

The plan of changing their clothes was unanimously adopted. The landlord sent out for every description of garment, as if he wanted to fit up his wardrobe. Athos chose a black coat, which gave him the appearance of a respectable citizen. Aramis, not wishing to part with his sword, selected a dark-blue cloak of a military cut. Porthos was seduced by a wine-colored doublet and sea-green breeches. D'Artagnan, who had fixed on his color beforehand, had only to select the shade, and looked in his chestnut suit exactly like a retired sugar dealer.

"Now," said D'Artagnan, "for the actual man. We must cut off our hair, that the populace may not insult us. As we no longer wear the sword of the gentleman we may as well have the head of the Puritan. This, as you know, is the important point of distinction between the Covenanter and the Cavalier."

After some discussion this was agreed to and Mousqueton played the role of barber.

"We look hideous," said Athos.

"And smack of the Puritan to a frightful extent," said Aramis.

"My head feels actually cold," said Porthos.

"As for me, I feel anxious to preach a sermon," said D'Artagnan.

"Now," said Athos, "that we cannot even recognize one another and have therefore no fear of others recognizing us, let us go and see the king's entrance."

They had not been long in the crowd before loud cries announced the king's arrival. A carriage had been sent to meet him, and the gigantic Porthos, who stood a head above the entire rabble, soon announced that he saw the royal equipage approaching. D'Artagnan raised himself on tiptoe, and as the carriage passed, saw Harrison at one window and Mordaunt at the other.

The next day, Athos, leaning out of his window, which looked upon the most populous part of the city, heard the Act of Parliament, which summoned the ex-king, Charles I., to the bar, publicly cried.

"Parliament indeed!" cried Athos. "Parliament can never have passed such an act as that."

At this moment the landlord came in.

"Did parliament pass this act?" Athos asked of him in English.

"Yes, my lord, the pure parliament."

"What do you mean by 'the pure parliament'? Are there, then, two parliaments?"

"My friend," D'Artagnan interrupted, "as I don't understand English and we all understand Spanish, have the kindness to speak to us in that language, which, since it is your own, you must find pleasure in using when you have the chance."

"Ah! excellent!" said Aramis.

As to Porthos, all his attention was concentrated on the allurements of the breakfast table.

"You were asking, then?" said the host in Spanish.

"I asked," said Athos, in the same language, "if there are two parliaments, a pure and an impure?"

"Why, how extraordinary!" said Porthos, slowly raising his head and looking at his friends with an air of astonishment, "I understand English, then! I understand what you say!"

"That is because we are talking Spanish, my dear friend," said Athos.

"Oh, the devil!" said Porthos, "I am sorry for that; it would have been one language more."

"When I speak of the pure parliament," resumed the host, "I mean the one which Colonel Bridge has weeded."

"Ah! really," said D'Artagnan, "these people are very ingenious. When I go back to France I must suggest some such convenient course to Cardinal Mazarin and the coadjutor. One of them will weed the parliament in the name of the court, and the other in the name of the people; and then there won't be any parliament at all."

"And who is this Colonel Bridge?" asked Aramis, "and how does he go to work to weed the parliament?"

"Colonel Bridge," replied the Spaniard, "is a retired wagoner, a man of much sense, who made one valuable observation whilst driving his team, namely, that where there happened to be a stone on the road, it was much easier to remove the stone than try and make the wheel pass over it. Now, of two hundred and fifty-one members who composed the parliament, there were one hundred and ninety-one who were in the way and might have upset his political wagon. He took them up, just as he formerly used to take up the stones from the road, and threw them out of the house."

"Neat," remarked D'Artagnan. "Very!"

"And all these one hundred and ninety-one were Royalists?" asked Athos.

"Without doubt, senor; and you understand that they would have saved the king."

"To be sure," said Porthos, with majestic common sense; "they were in the majority."

"And you think," said Aramis, "he will consent to appear before such a tribunal?"

"He will be forced to do so," smiled the Spaniard.

"Now, Athos!" said D'Artagnan, "do you begin to believe that it's a ruined cause, and that what with your Harrisons, Joyces, Bridges and Cromwells, we shall never get the upper hand?"

"The king will be delivered at the tribunal," said Athos; "the very silence of his supporters indicates that they are at work."

D'Artagnan shrugged his shoulders.

"But," said Aramis, "if they dare to condemn their king, it can only be to exile or imprisonment."

D'Artagnan whistled a little air of incredulity.

"We shall see," said Athos, "for we shall go to the sittings, I presume."

"You will not have long to wait," said the landlord; "they begin to-morrow."

"So, then, they drew up the indictments before the king was taken?"

"Of course," said D'Artagnan; "they began the day he was sold."

"And you know," said Aramis, "that it was our friend Mordaunt who made, if not the bargain, at least the overtures."

"And you know," added D'Artagnan, "that whenever I catch him I will kill him, this Mordaunt."

"And I, too," exclaimed Porthos.

"And I, too," added Aramis.

"Touching unanimity!" cried D'Artagnan, "which well becomes good citizens like us. Let us take a turn around the town and imbibe a little fog."

"Yes," said Porthos, "'twill be at least a little change from beer."

63. The Trial.

The next morning King Charles I. was haled by a strong guard before the high court which was to judge him. All London was crowding to the doors of the house. The throng was terrific, and it was not till after much pushing and some fighting that our friends reached their destination. When they did so they found the three lower rows of benches already occupied; but being anxious not to be too conspicuous, all, with the exception of Porthos, who had a fancy to display his red doublet, were quite satisfied with their places, the more so as chance had brought them to the centre of their row, so that they were exactly opposite the arm-chair prepared for the royal prisoner.

Toward eleven o'clock the king entered the hall, surrounded by guards, but wearing his head covered, and with a calm expression turned to every side with a look of complete assurance, as if he were there to preside at an assembly of submissive subjects, rather than to meet the accusations of a rebel court.

The judges, proud of having a monarch to humiliate, evidently prepared to enjoy the right they had arrogated to themselves, and sent an officer to inform the king that it was customary for the accused to uncover his head.

Charles, without replying a single word, turned his head in another direction and pulled his felt hat over it. Then when the officer was gone he sat down in the arm-chair opposite the president and struck his boots with a little cane which he carried in his hand. Parry, who accompanied him, stood behind him.

D'Artagnan was looking at Athos, whose face betrayed all those emotions which the king, possessing more self-control, had banished from his own. This agitation in one so cold and calm as Athos, frightened him.

"I hope," he whispered to him, "that you will follow his majesty's example and not get killed for your folly in this den."

"Set your mind at rest," replied Athos.

"Aha!" continued D'Artagnan, "it is clear that they are afraid of something or other; for look, the sentinels are being reinforced. They had only halberds before, now they have muskets. The halberds were for the audience in the rear; the muskets are for us."

"Thirty, forty, fifty, sixty-five men," said Porthos, counting the reinforcements.

"Ah!" said Aramis, "but you forget the officer."

D'Artagnan grew pale with rage. He recognized Mordaunt, who with bare sword was marshalling the musketeers behind the king and opposite the benches.

"Do you think they have recognized us?" said D'Artagnan. "In that case I should beat a retreat. I don't care to be shot in a box."

"No," said Aramis, "he has not seen us. He sees no one but the king. Mon Dieu! how he stares at him, the insolent dog! Does he hate his majesty as much as he does us?"

"Pardi," answered Athos "we only carried off his mother; the king has spoiled him of his name and property."

"True," said Aramis; "but silence! the president is speaking to the king."

"Stuart," Bradshaw was saying, "listen to the roll call of your judges and address to the court any observations you may have to make."

The king turned his head away, as if these words had not been intended for him. Bradshaw waited, and as there was no reply there was a moment of silence.

Out of the hundred and sixty-three members designated there were only seventy-three present, for the rest, fearful of taking part in such an act, had remained away.

When the name of Colonel Fairfax was called, one of those brief but solemn silences ensued, which announced the absence of the members who had no wish to take a personal part in the trial.

"Colonel Fairfax," repeated Bradshaw.

"Fairfax," answered a laughing voice, the silvery tone of which betrayed it as that of a woman, "is not such a fool as to be here."

A loud laugh followed these words, pronounced with that boldness which women draw from their own weakness--a weakness which removes them beyond the power of vengeance.

"It is a woman's voice," cried Aramis; "faith, I would give a good deal if she is young and pretty." And he mounted on the bench to try and get a sight of her.

"By my soul," said Aramis, "she is charming. Look D'Artagnan; everybody is looking at her; and in spite of Bradshaw's gaze she has not turned pale."

"It is Lady Fairfax herself," said D'Artagnan. "Don't you remember, Porthos, we saw her at General Cromwell's?"

The roll call continued.

"These rascals will adjourn when they find that they are not in sufficient force," said the Comte de la Fere.

"You don't know them. Athos, look at Mordaunt's smile. Is that the look of a man whose victim is likely to escape him? Ah, cursed basilisk, it will be a happy day for me when I can cross something more than a look with you."

"The king is really very handsome," said Porthos; "and look, too, though he is a prisoner, how carefully he is dressed. The feather in his hat is worth at least five-and-twenty pistoles. Look at it, Aramis."

The roll call finished, the president ordered them to read the act of accusation. Athos turned pale. A second time he was disappointed in his expectation. Notwithstanding the judges were so few the trial was to continue; the king then, was condemned in advance.

"I told you so, Athos," said D'Artagnan, shrugging his shoulders. "Now take your courage in both hands and hear what this gentleman in black is going to say about his sovereign, with full license and privilege."

Never till then had a more brutal accusation or meaner insults tarnished kingly majesty.

Charles listened with marked attention, passing over the insults, noting the grievances, and, when hatred overflowed all bounds and the accuser turned executioner beforehand, replying with a smile of lofty scorn.

"The fact is," said D'Artagnan, "if men are punished for imprudence and triviality, this poor king deserves punishment. But it seems to me that that which he is just now undergoing is hard enough."

"In any case," Aramis replied, "the punishment should fall not on the king, but on his ministers; for the first article of the constitution is, 'The king can do no wrong.'"

"As for me," thought Porthos, giving Mordaunt his whole attention, "were it not for breaking in on the majesty of the situation I would leap down from the bench, reach Mordaunt in three bounds and strangle him; I would then take him by the feet and knock the life out of these wretched musketeers who parody the musketeers of France. Meantime, D'Artagnan, who is full of invention, would find some way to save the king. I must speak to him about it."

As to Athos, his face aflame, his fists clinched, his lips bitten till they bled, he sat there foaming with rage at that endless parliamentary insult and that long enduring royal patience; the inflexible arm and steadfast heart had given place to a trembling hand and a body shaken by excitement.

At this moment the accuser concluded with these words: "The present accusation is preferred by us in the name of the English people."

At these words there was a murmur along the benches, and a second voice, not that of a woman, but a man's, stout and furious, thundered behind D'Artagnan.

"You lie!" it cried. "Nine-tenths of the English people are horrified at what you say."

This voice was that of Athos, who, standing up with outstretched hand and quite out of his mind, thus assailed the public accuser.

King, judges, spectators, all turned their eyes to the bench where the four friends were seated. Mordaunt did the same and recognized the gentleman, around whom the three other Frenchmen were standing, pale and menacing. His eyes glittered with delight. He had discovered those to whose death he had devoted his life. A movement of fury called to his side some twenty of his musketeers, and pointing to the bench where his enemies were: "Fire on that bench!" he cried.

But with the rapidity of thought D'Artagnan seized Athos by the waist, and followed by Porthos with Aramis, leaped down from the benches, rushed into the passages, and flying down the staircase were lost in the crowd without, while the muskets within were pointed on some three thousand spectators, whose piteous cries and noisy alarm stopped the impulse already given to bloodshed.

Charles also had recognized the four Frenchmen. He put one hand on his heart to still its beating and the other over his eyes, that he might not witness the slaying of his faithful friends.

Mordaunt, pale and trembling with anger, rushed from the hall sword in hand, followed by six pikemen, pushing, inquiring and panting in the crowd; and then, having found nothing, returned.

The tumult was indescribable. More than half an hour passed before any one could make himself heard. The judges were looking for a new outbreak from the benches. The spectators saw the muskets leveled at them, and divided between fear and curiosity, remained noisy and excited.

Quiet was at length restored.

"What have you to say in your defense?" asked Bradshaw of the king.

Then rising, with his head still covered, in the tone of a judge rather than a prisoner, Charles began.

"Before questioning me," he said, "reply to my question. I was free at Newcastle and had there concluded a treaty with both houses. Instead of performing your part of this contract, as I performed mine, you bought me from the Scotch, cheaply, I know, and that does honor to the economic talent of your government. But because you have paid the price of a slave, do you imagine that I have ceased to be your king? No. To answer you would be to forget it. I shall only reply to you when you have satisfied me of your right to question me. To answer you would be to acknowledge you as my judges, and I only acknowledge you as my executioners." And in the middle of a deathlike silence, Charles, calm, lofty, and with his head still covered, sat down again in his arm-chair.

"Why are not my Frenchmen here?" he murmured proudly and turning his eyes to the benches where they had appeared for a moment; "they would have seen that their friend was worthy of their defense while alive, and of their tears when dead."

"Well," said the president, seeing that Charles was determined to remain silent, "so be it. We will judge you in spite of your silence. You are accused of treason, of abuse of power, and murder. The evidence will support it. Go, and another sitting will accomplish what you have postponed in this."

Charles rose and turned toward Parry, whom he saw pale and with his temples dewed with moisture.

"Well, my dear Parry," said he, "what is the matter, and what can affect you in this manner?"

"Oh, my king," said Parry, with tears in his eyes and in a tone of supplication, "do not look to the left as we leave the hall."

"And why, Parry?"

"Do not look, I implore you, my king."

"But what is the matter? Speak," said Charles, attempting to look across the hedge of guards which surrounded him.

"It is--but you will not look, will you?--it is because they have had the axe, with which criminals are executed, brought and placed there on the table. The sight is hideous."

"Fools," said Charles, "do they take me for a coward, like themselves? You have done well to warn me. Thank you, Parry."

When the moment arrived the king followed his guards out of the hall. As he passed the table on which the axe was laid, he stopped, and turning with a smile, said:

"Ah! the axe, an ingenious device, and well worthy of those who know not what a gentleman is; you frighten me not, executioner's axe," added he, touching it with the cane which he held in his hand, "and I strike you now, waiting patiently and Christianly for you to return the blow."

And shrugging his shoulders with unaffected contempt he passed on. When he reached the door a stream of people, who had been disappointed in not being able to get into the house and to make amends had collected to see him come out, stood on each side, as he passed, many among them glaring on him with threatening looks.

"How many people," thought he, "and not one true friend."

And as he uttered these words of doubt and depression within his mind, a voice beside him said:

"Respect to fallen majesty."

The king turned quickly around, with tears in his eyes and heart. It was an old soldier of the guards who could not see his king pass captive before him without rendering him this final homage. But the next moment the unfortunate man was nearly killed with heavy blows of sword-hilts, and among those who set upon him the king recognized Captain Groslow.

"Alas!" said Charles, "that is a severe chastisement for a very trifling fault."

He continued his walk, but he had scarcely gone a hundred paces, when a furious fellow, leaning between two soldiers, spat in the king's face, as once an infamous and accursed Jew spit in the face of Jesus of Nazareth. Loud roars of laughter and sullen murmurs arose together. The crowd opened and closed again, undulating like a stormy sea, and the king imagined that he saw shining in the midst of this living wave the bright eyes of Athos.

Charles wiped his face and said with a sad smile: "Poor wretch, for half a crown he would do as much to his own father."

The king was not mistaken. Athos and his friends, again mingling with the throng, were taking a last look at the martyr king.

When the soldier saluted Charles, Athos's heart bounded for joy; and that unfortunate, on coming to himself, found ten guineas that the French gentleman had slipped into his pocket. But when the cowardly insulter spat in the face of the captive monarch Athos grasped his dagger. But D'Artagnan stopped his hand and in a hoarse voice cried, "Wait!"

Athos stopped. D'Artagnan, leaning on Athos, made a sign to Porthos and Aramis to keep near them and then placed himself behind the man with the bare arms, who was still laughing at his own vile pleasantry and receiving the congratulations of several others.

The man took his way toward the city. The four friends followed him. The man, who had the appearance of being a butcher, descended a little steep and isolated street, looking on to the river, with two of his friends. Arrived at the bank of the river the three men perceived that they were followed, turned around, and looking insolently at the Frenchmen, passed some jests from one to another.

"I don't know English, Athos," said D'Artagnan; "but you know it and will interpret for me."

Then quickening their steps they passed the three men, but turned back immediately, and D'Artagnan walked straight up to the butcher and touching him on the chest with the tip of his finger, said to Athos:

"Say this to him in English: 'You are a coward. You have insulted a defenseless man. You have befouled the face of your king. You must die.'"

Athos, pale as a ghost, repeated these words to the man, who, seeing the bodeful preparations that were making, put himself in an attitude of defense. Aramis, at this movement, drew his sword.

"No," cried D'Artagnan, "no steel. Steel is for gentlemen."

And seizing the butcher by the throat:

"Porthos," said he, "kill this fellow for me with a single blow."

Porthos raised his terrible fist, which whistled through the air like a sling, and the portentous mass fell with a smothered crash on the insulter's skull and crushed it. The man fell like an ox beneath the pole-axe. His companions, horror-struck, could neither move nor cry out.

"Tell them this, Athos," resumed D'Artagnan; "thus shall all die who forget that a captive man is sacred and that a captive king doubly represents the Lord."

Athos repeated D'Artagnan's words.

The fellows looked at the body of their companion, swimming in blood, and then recovering voice and legs together, ran screaming off.

"Justice is done," said Porthos, wiping his forehead.

"And now," said D'Artagnan to Athos, "entertain no further doubts about me; I undertake all that concerns the king."

64. Whitehall.

The parliament condemned Charles to death, as might have been foreseen. Political judgments are generally vain formalities, for the same passions which give rise to the accusation ordain to the condemnation. Such is the atrocious logic of revolutions.

Although our friends were expecting that condemnation, it filled them with grief. D'Artagnan, whose mind was never more fertile in resources than in critical emergencies, swore again that he would try all conceivable means to prevent the denouement of the bloody tragedy. But by what means? As yet he could form no definite plan; all must depend on circumstances. Meanwhile, it was necessary at all hazards, in order to gain time, to put some obstacle in the way of the execution on the following day--the day appointed by the judges. The only way of doing that was to cause the disappearance of the London executioner. The headsman out of the way, the sentence could not be executed. True, they could send for the headsman of the nearest town, but at least a day would be gained, and a day might be sufficient for the rescue. D'Artagnan took upon himself that more than difficult task.

Another thing, not less essential, was to warn Charles Stuart of the attempt to be made, so that he might assist his rescuers as much as possible, or at least do nothing to thwart their efforts. Aramis assumed that perilous charge. Charles Stuart had asked that Bishop Juxon might be permitted to visit him. Mordaunt had called on the bishop that very evening to apprise him of the religious desire expressed by the king and also of Cromwell's permission. Aramis determined to obtain from the bishop, through fear or by persuasion, consent that he should enter in the bishop's place, and clad in his sacerdotal robes, the prison at Whitehall.

Finally, Athos undertook to provide, in any event, the means of leaving England--in case either of failure or of success.

The night having come they made an appointment to meet at eleven o'clock at the hotel, and each started out to fulfill his dangerous mission.

The palace of Whitehall was guarded by three regiments of cavalry and by the fierce anxiety of Cromwell, who came and went or sent his generals or his agents continually. Alone in his usual room, lighted by two candles, the condemned monarch gazed sadly on the luxury of his past greatness, just as at the last hour one sees the images of life more mildly brilliant than of yore.

Parry had not quitted his master, and since his condemnation had not ceased to weep. Charles, leaning on a table, was gazing at a medallion of his wife and daughter; he was waiting first for Juxon, then for martyrdom.

At times he thought of those brave French gentlemen who had appeared to him from a distance of a hundred leagues fabulous and unreal, like the forms that appear in dreams. In fact, he sometimes asked himself if all that was happening to him was not a dream, or at least the delirium of a fever. He rose and took a few steps as if to rouse himself from his torpor and went as far as the window; he saw glittering below him the muskets of the guards. He was thereupon constrained to admit that he was indeed awake and that his bloody dream was real.

Charles returned in silence to his chair, rested his elbow on the table, bowed his head upon his hand and reflected.

"Alas!" he said to himself, "if I only had for a confessor one of those lights of the church, whose soul has sounded all the mysteries of life, all the littlenesses of greatness, perhaps his utterance would overawe the voice that wails within my soul. But I shall have a priest of vulgar mind, whose career and fortune I have ruined by my misfortune. He will speak to me of God and death, as he has spoken to many another dying man, not understanding that this one leaves his throne to an usurper, his children to the cold contempt of public charity."

And he raised the medallion to his lips.

It was a dull, foggy night. A neighboring church clock slowly struck the hour. The flickering light of the two candles showed fitful phantom shadows in the lofty room. These were the ancestors of Charles, standing back dimly in their tarnished frames.

An awful sadness enveloped the heart of Charles. He buried his brow in his hands and thought of the world, so beautiful when one is about to leave it; of the caresses of children, so pleasing and so sweet, especially when one is parting from his children never to see them again; then of his wife, the noble and courageous woman who had sustained him to the last moment. He drew from his breast the diamond cross and the star of the Garter which she had sent him by those generous Frenchmen; he kissed it, and then, as he reflected, that she would never again see those things till he lay cold and mutilated in the tomb, there passed over him one of those icy shivers which may be called forerunners of death.

Then, in that chamber which recalled to him so many royal souvenirs, whither had come so many courtiers, the scene of so much flattering homage, alone with a despairing servant, whose feeble soul could afford no support to his own, the king at last yielded to sorrow, and his courage sank to a level with that feebleness, those shadows, and that wintry cold. That king, who was so grand, so sublime in the hour of death, meeting his fate with a smile of resignation on his lips, now in that gloomy hour wiped away a tear which had fallen on the table and quivered on the gold embroidered cloth.

Suddenly the door opened, an ecclesiastic in episcopal robes entered, followed by two guards, to whom the king waved an imperious gesture. The guards retired; the room resumed its obscurity.

"Juxon!" cried Charles, "Juxon, thank you, my last friend; you come at a fitting moment."

The bishop looked anxiously at the man sobbing in the ingle-nook.

"Come, Parry," said the king, "cease your tears."

"If it's Parry," said the bishop, "I have nothing to fear; so allow me to salute your majesty and to tell you who I am and for what I am come."

At this sight and this voice Charles was about to cry out, when Aramis placed his finger on his lips and bowed low to the king of England.

"The chevalier!" murmured Charles.

"Yes, sire," interrupted Aramis, raising his voice, "Bishop Juxon, the faithful knight of Christ, obedient to your majesty's wishes."

Charles clasped his hands, amazed and stupefied to find that these foreigners, without other motive than that which their conscience imposed on them, thus combated the will of a people and the destiny of a king.

"You!" he said, "you! how did you penetrate hither? If they recognize you, you are lost."

"Care not for me, sire; think only of yourself. You see, your friends are wakeful. I know not what we shall do yet, but four determined men can do much. Meanwhile, do not be surprised at anything that happens; prepare yourself for every emergency."

Charles shook his head.

"Do you know that I die to-morrow at ten o'clock?"

"Something, your majesty, will happen between now and then to make the execution impossible."

The king looked at Aramis with astonishment.

At this moment a strange noise, like the unloading of a cart, and followed by a cry of pain, was heard beneath the window.

"Do you hear?" said the king.

"I hear," said Aramis, "but I understand neither the noise nor the cry of pain."

"I know not who can have uttered the cry," said the king, "but the noise is easily understood. Do you know that I am to be beheaded outside this window? Well, these boards you hear unloaded are the posts and planks to build my scaffold. Some workmen must have fallen underneath them and been hurt."

Aramis shuddered in spite of himself.

"You see," said the king, "that it is useless for you to resist. I am condemned; leave me to my death."

"My king," said Aramis, "they well may raise a scaffold, but they cannot make an executioner."

"What do you mean?" asked the king.

"I mean that at this hour the headsman has been got out of the way by force or persuasion. The scaffold will be ready by to-morrow, but the headsman will be wanting and they will put it off till the day after to-morrow."

"What then?" said the king.

"To-morrow night we shall rescue you."

"How can that be?" cried the king, whose face was lighted up, in spite of himself, by a flash of joy.

"Oh! sir," cried Parry, "may you and yours be blessed!"

"How can it be?" repeated the king. "I must know, so that I may assist you if there is any chance."

"I know nothing about it," continued Aramis, "but the cleverest, the bravest, the most devoted of us four said to me when I left him, 'Tell the king that to-morrow at ten o'clock at night, we shall carry him off.' He has said it and will do it."

"Tell me the name of that generous friend," said the king, "that I may cherish for him an eternal gratitude, whether he succeeds or not."

"D'Artagnan, sire, the same who had so nearly rescued you when Colonel Harrison made his untimely entrance."

"You are, indeed, wonderful men," said the king; "if such things had been related to me I should not have believed them."

"Now, sire," resumed Aramis, "listen to me. Do not forget for a single instant that we are watching over your safety; observe the smallest gesture, the least bit of song, the least sign from any one near you; watch everything, hear everything, interpret everything."

"Oh, chevalier!" cried the king, "what can I say to you? There is no word, though it should come from the profoundest depth of my heart, that can express my gratitude. If you succeed I do not say that you will save a king; no, in presence of the scaffold as I am, royalty, I assure you, is a very small affair; but you will save a husband to his wife, a father to his children. Chevalier, take my hand; it is that of a friend who will love you to his last sigh."

Aramis stooped to kiss the king's hand, but Charles clasped his and pressed it to his heart.

At this moment a man entered, without even knocking at the door. Aramis tried to withdraw his hand, but the king still held it. The man was one of those Puritans, half preacher and half soldier, who swarmed around Cromwell.

"What do you want, sir?" said the king.

"I desire to know if the confession of Charles Stuart is at an end?" said the stranger.

"And what is it to you?" replied the king; "we are not of the same religion."

"All men are brothers," said the Puritan. "One of my brothers is about to die and I come to prepare him."

"Bear with him," whispered Aramis; "it is doubtless some spy."

"After my reverend lord bishop," said the king to the man, "I shall hear you with pleasure, sir."

The man retired, but not before examining the supposed Juxon with an attention which did not escape the king.

"Chevalier," said the king, when the door was closed, "I believe you are right and that this man only came here with evil intentions. Take care that no misfortune befalls you when you leave."

"I thank your majesty," said Aramis, "but under these robes I have a coat of mail, a pistol and a dagger."

"Go, then, sir, and God keep you!"

The king accompanied him to the door, where Aramis pronounced his benediction upon him, and passing through the ante-rooms, filled with soldiers, jumped into his carriage and drove to the bishop's palace. Juxon was waiting for him impatiently.

"Well?" said he, on perceiving Aramis.

"Everything has succeeded as I expected; spies, guards, satellites, all took me for you, and the king blesses you while waiting for you to bless him."

"May God protect you, my son; for your example has given me at the same time hope and courage."

Aramis resumed his own attire and left Juxon with the assurance that he might again have recourse to him.

He had scarcely gone ten yards in the street when he perceived that he was followed by a man, wrapped in a large cloak. He placed his hand on his dagger and stopped. The man came straight toward him. It was Porthos.

"My dear friend," cried Aramis.

"You see, we had each our mission," said Porthos; "mine was to guard you and I am doing so. Have you seen the king?"

"Yes, and all goes well."

"We are to meet our friends at the hotel at eleven."

It was then striking half-past ten by St. Paul's.

Arrived at the hotel it was not long before Athos entered.

"All's well," he cried, as he entered; "I have hired a cedar wherry, as light as a canoe, as easy on the wing as any swallow. It is waiting for us at Greenwich, opposite the Isle of Dogs, manned by a captain and four men, who for the sum of fifty pounds sterling will keep themselves at our disposition three successive nights. Once on board we drop down the Thames and in two hours are on the open sea. In case I am killed, the captain's name is Roger and the skiff is called the Lightning. A handkerchief, tied at the four corners, is to be the signal."

Next moment D'Artagnan entered.

"Empty your pockets," said he; "I want a hundred pounds, and as for my own----" and he emptied them inside out.

The sum was collected in a minute. D'Artagnan ran out and returned directly after.

"There," said he, "it's done. Ough! and not without a deal of trouble, too."

"Has the executioner left London?" asked Athos.

"Ah, you see that plan was not sure enough; he might go out by one gate and return by another."

"Where is he, then?"

"In the cellar."

"The cellar--what cellar?"

"Our landlord's, to be sure. Mousqueton is propped against the door and here's the key."

"Bravo!" said Aramis, "how did you manage it?"

"Like everything else, with money; but it cost me dear."

"How much?" asked Athos.

"Five hundred pounds."

"And where did you get so much money?" said Athos. "Had you, then, that sum?"

"The queen's famous diamond," answered D'Artagnan, with a sigh.

"Ah, true," said Aramis. "I recognized it on your finger."

"You bought it back, then, from Monsieur des Essarts?" asked Porthos.

"Yes, but it was fated that I should not keep it."

"So, then, we are all right as regards the executioner," said Athos; "but unfortunately every executioner has his assistant, his man, or whatever you call him."

"And this one had his," said D'Artagnan; "but, as good luck would have it, just as I thought I should have two affairs to manage, our friend was brought home with a broken leg. In the excess of his zeal he had accompanied the cart containing the scaffolding as far as the king's window, and one of the crossbeams fell on his leg and broke it."

"Ah!" cried Aramis, "that accounts for the cry I heard."

"Probably," said D'Artagnan, "but as he is a thoughtful young man he promised to send four expert workmen in his place to help those already at the scaffold, and wrote the moment he was brought home to Master Tom Lowe, an assistant carpenter and friend of his, to go down to Whitehall, with three of his friends. Here's the letter he sent by a messenger, for sixpence, who sold it to me for a guinea."

"And what on earth are you going to do with it?" asked Athos.

"Can't you guess, my dear Athos? You, who speak English like John Bull himself, are Master Tom Lowe, we, your three companions. Do you understand it now?"

Athos uttered a cry of joy and admiration, ran to a closet and drew forth workmen's clothes, which the four friends immediately put on; they then left the hotel, Athos carrying a saw, Porthos a vise, Aramis an axe and D'Artagnan a hammer and some nails.

The letter from the executioner's assistant satisfied the master carpenter that those were the men he expected.

65. The Workmen.

Toward midnight Charles heard a great noise beneath his window. It arose from blows of hammer and hatchet, clinking of pincers and cranching of saws.

Lying dressed upon his bed, the noise awoke him with a start and found a gloomy echo in his heart. He could not endure it, and sent Parry to ask the sentinel to beg the workmen to strike more gently and not disturb the last slumber of one who had been their king. The sentinel was unwilling to leave his post, but allowed Parry to pass.

Arriving at the window Parry found an unfinished scaffold, over which they were nailing a covering of black serge. Raised to the height of twenty feet, so as to be on a level with the window, it had two lower stories. Parry, odious as was this sight to him, sought for those among some eight or ten workmen who were making the most noise; and fixed on two men, who were loosening the last hooks of the iron balcony.

"My friends," said Parry, mounting the scaffold and standing beside them, "would you work a little more quietly? The king wishes to get a sleep."

One of the two, who was standing up, was of gigantic size and was driving a pick with all his might into the wall, whilst the other, kneeling beside him, was collecting the pieces of stone. The face of the first was lost to Parry in the darkness; but as the second turned around and placed his finger on his lips Parry started back in amazement.

"Very well, very well," said the workman aloud, in excellent English. "Tell the king that if he sleeps badly to-night he will sleep better to-morrow night."

These blunt words, so terrible if taken literally, were received by the other workmen with a roar of laughter. But Parry withdrew, thinking he was dreaming.

Charles was impatiently awaiting his return. At the moment he re-entered, the sentinel who guarded the door put his head through the opening, curious as to what the king was doing. The king was lying on his bed, resting on his elbow. Parry closed the door and approaching the king, his face radiant with joy:

"Sire," he said, in a low voice, "do you know who these workmen are who are making so much noise?"

"I? No; how would you have me know?"

Parry bent his head and whispered to the king: "It is the Comte de la Fere and his friends."

"Raising my scaffold!" cried the king, astounded.

"Yes, and at the same time making a hole in the wall."

The king clasped his hands and raised his eyes to Heaven; then leaping down from his bed he went to the window, and pulling aside the curtain tried to distinguish the figures outside, but in vain.

Parry was not wrong. It was Athos he had recognized, and Porthos who was boring a hole through the wall.

This hole communicated with a kind of loft--the space between the floor of the king's room and the ceiling of the one below it. Their plan was to pass through the hole they were making into this loft and cut out from below a piece of the flooring of the king's room, so as to form a kind of trap-door.

Through this the king was to escape the next night, and, hidden by the black covering of the scaffold, was to change his dress for that of a workman, slip out with his deliverers, pass the sentinels, who would suspect nothing, and so reach the skiff that was waiting for him at Greenwich.

Day gilded the tops of the houses. The aperture was finished and Athos passed through it, carrying the clothes destined for the king wrapped in black cloth, and the tools with which he was to open a communication with the king's room. He had only two hours' work to do to open communication with the king and, according to the calculations of the four friends, they had the entire day before them, since, the executioner being absent, another must be sent for to Bristol.

D'Artagnan returned to change his workman's clothes for his chestnut-colored suit, and Porthos to put on his red doublet. As for Aramis, he went off to the bishop's palace to see if he could possibly pass in with Juxon to the king's presence. All three agreed to meet at noon in Whitehall Place to see how things went on.

Before leaving the scaffold Aramis had approached the opening where Athos was concealed to tell him that he was about to make an attempt to gain another interview with the king.

"Adieu, then, and be of good courage," said Athos. "Report to the king the condition of affairs. Say to him that when he is alone it will help us if he will knock on the floor, for then I can continue my work in safety. Try, Aramis, to keep near the king. Speak loud, very loud, for they will be listening at the door. If there is a sentinel within the apartment, kill him without hesitation. If there are two, let Parry kill one and you the other. If there are three, let yourself be slain, but save the king."

"Be easy," said Aramis; "I will take two poniards and give one to Parry. Is that all?"

"Yes, go; but urge the king strongly not to stand on false generosity. While you are fighting if there is a fight, he must flee. The trap once replaced over his head, you being on the trap, dead or alive, they will need at least ten minutes to find the hole by which he has escaped. In those ten minutes we shall have gained the road and the king will be saved."

"Everything shall be done as you say, Athos. Your hand, for perhaps we shall not see each other again."

Athos put his arm around Aramis's neck and embraced him.

"For you," he said. "Now if I die, say to D'Artagnan that I love him as a son, and embrace him for me. Embrace also our good and brave Porthos. Adieu."

"Adieu," said Aramis. "I am as sure now that the king will be saved as I am sure that I clasp the most loyal hand in the world."

Aramis parted from Athos, went down from the scaffold in his turn and took his way to the hotel, whistling the air of a song in praise of Cromwell. He found the other two friends sitting at table before a good fire, drinking a bottle of port and devouring a cold chicken. Porthos was cursing the infamous parliamentarians; D'Artagnan ate in silence, revolving in his mind the most audacious plans.

Aramis related what had been agreed upon. D'Artagnan approved with a movement of the head and Porthos with his voice.

"Bravo!" he said; "besides, we shall be there at the time of the flight. What with D'Artagnan, Grimaud and Mousqueton, we can manage to dispatch eight of them. I say nothing about Blaisois, for he is only fit to hold the horses. Two minutes a man makes four minutes. Mousqueton will lose another, that's five; and in five minutes we shall have galloped a quarter of a league."

Aramis swallowed a hasty mouthful, gulped a glass of wine and changed his clothes.

"Now," said he, "I'm off to the bishop's. Take care of the executioner, D'Artagnan."

"All right. Grimaud has relieved Mousqueton and has his foot on the cellar door."

"Well, don't be inactive."

"Inactive, my dear fellow! Ask Porthos. I pass my life upon my legs."

Aramis again presented himself at the bishop's. Juxon consented the more readily to take him with him, as he would require an assistant priest in case the king should wish to communicate. Dressed as Aramis had been the night before, the bishop got into his carriage, and the former, more disguised by his pallor and sad countenance than his deacon's dress, got in by his side. The carriage stopped at the door of the palace.

It was about nine o'clock in the morning.

Nothing was changed. The ante-rooms were still full of soldiers, the passages still lined by guards. The king was already sanguine, but when he perceived Aramis his hope turned to joy. He embraced Juxon and pressed the hand of Aramis. The bishop affected to speak in a loud voice, before every one, of their previous interview. The king replied that the words spoken in that interview had borne their fruit, and that he desired another under the same conditions. Juxon turned to those present and begged them to leave him and his assistant alone with the king. Every one withdrew. As soon as the door was closed:

"Sire," said Aramis, speaking rapidly, "you are saved; the London executioner has vanished. His assistant broke his leg last night beneath your majesty's window--the cry we heard was his--and there is no executioner nearer at hand than Bristol."

"But the Comte de la Fere?" asked the king.

"Two feet below you; take the poker from the fireplace and strike three times on the floor. He will answer you."

The king did so, and the moment after, three muffled knocks, answering the given signal, sounded beneath the floor.

"So," said Charles, "he who knocks down there----"

"Is the Comte de la Fere, sire," said Aramis. "He is preparing a way for your majesty to escape. Parry, for his part, will raise this slab of marble and a passage will be opened."

"Oh, Juxon," said the king, seizing the bishop's two hands in his own, "promise that you will pray all your life for this gentleman and for the other that you hear beneath your feet, and for two others also, who, wherever they may be, are on the watch for my safety."

"Sire," replied Juxon, "you shall be obeyed."

Meanwhile, the miner underneath was heard working away incessantly, when suddenly an unexpected noise resounded in the passage. Aramis seized the poker and gave the signal to stop; the noise came nearer and nearer. It was that of a number of men steadily approaching. The four men stood motionless. All eyes were fixed on the door, which opened slowly and with a kind of solemnity.

A parliamentary officer, clothed in black and with a gravity that augured ill, entered, bowed to the king, and unfolding a parchment, read the sentence, as is usually done to criminals before their execution.

"What is this?" said Aramis to Juxon.

Juxon replied with a sign which meant that he knew no more than Aramis about it.

"Then it is for to-day?" asked the king.

"Was not your majesty warned that it was to take place this morning?"

"Then I must die like a common criminal by the hand of the London executioner?"

"The London executioner has disappeared, your majesty, but a man has offered his services instead. The execution will therefore only be delayed long enough for you to arrange your spiritual and temporal affairs."

A slight moisture on his brow was the only trace of emotion that Charles evinced, as he learned these tidings. But Aramis was livid. His heart ceased beating, he closed his eyes and leaned upon the table. Charles perceived it and took his hand.

"Come, my friend," said he, "courage." Then he turned to the officer. "Sir, I am ready. There is but little reason why I should delay you. Firstly, I wish to communicate; secondly, to embrace my children and bid them farewell for the last time. Will this be permitted me?"

"Certainly," replied the officer, and left the room.

Aramis dug his nails into his flesh and groaned aloud.

"Oh! my lord bishop," he cried, seizing Juxon's hands, "where is Providence? where is Providence?"

"My son," replied the bishop, with firmness, "you see Him not, because the passions of the world conceal Him."

"My son," said the king to Aramis, "do not take it so to heart. You ask what God is doing. God beholds your devotion and my martyrdom, and believe me, both will have their reward. Ascribe to men, then, what is happening, and not to God. It is men who drive me to death; it is men who make you weep."

"Yes, sire," said Aramis, "yes, you are right. It is men whom I should hold responsible, and I will hold them responsible."

"Be seated, Juxon," said the king, falling upon his knees. "I have now to confess to you. Remain, sir," he added to Aramis, who had moved to leave the room. "Remain, Parry. I have nothing to say that cannot be said before all."

Juxon sat down, and the king, kneeling humbly before him, began his confession.

66. Remember!

The mob had already assembled when the confession terminated. The king's children next arrived--the Princess Charlotte, a beautiful, fair-haired child, with tears in her eyes, and the Duke of Gloucester, a boy eight or nine years old, whose tearless eyes and curling lip revealed a growing pride. He had wept all night long, but would not show his grief before the people.

Charles's heart melted within him at the sight of those two children, whom he had not seen for two years and whom he now met at the moment of death. He turned to brush away a tear, and then, summoning up all his firmness, drew his daughter toward him, recommending her to be pious and resigned. Then he took the boy upon his knee.

"My son," he said to him, "you saw a great number of people in the streets as you came here. These men are going to behead your father. Do not forget that. Perhaps some day they will want to make you king, instead of the Prince of Wales, or the Duke of York, your elder brothers. But you are not the king, my son, and can never be so while they are alive. Swear to me, then, never to let them put a crown upon your head unless you have a legal right to the crown. For one day--listen, my son--one day, if you do so, they will doom you to destruction, head and crown, too, and then you will not be able to die with a calm conscience, as I die. Swear, my son."

The child stretched out his little hand toward that of his father and said, "I swear to your majesty."

"Henry," said Charles, "call me your father."

"Father," replied the child, "I swear to you that they shall kill me sooner than make me king."

"Good, my child. Now kiss me; and you, too, Charlotte. Never forget me."

"Oh! never, never!" cried both the children, throwing their arms around their father's neck.

"Farewell," said Charles, "farewell, my children. Take them away, Juxon; their tears will deprive me of the courage to die."

Juxon led them away, and this time the doors were left open.

Meanwhile, Athos, in his concealment, waited in vain the signal to recommence his work. Two long hours he waited in terrible inaction. A deathlike silence reigned in the room above. At last he determined to discover the cause of this stillness. He crept from his hole and stood, hidden by the black drapery, beneath the scaffold. Peeping out from the drapery, he could see the rows of halberdiers and musketeers around the scaffold and the first ranks of the populace swaying and groaning like the sea.

"What is the matter, then?" he asked himself, trembling more than the wind-swayed cloth he was holding back. "The people are hurrying on, the soldiers under arms, and among the spectators I see D'Artagnan. What is he waiting for? What is he looking at? Good God! have they allowed the headsman to escape?"

Suddenly the dull beating of muffled drums filled the square. The sound of heavy steps was heard above his head. The next moment the very planks of the scaffold creaked with the weight of an advancing procession, and the eager faces of the spectators confirmed what a last hope at the bottom of his heart had prevented him till then believing. At the same moment a well-known voice above him pronounced these words:

"Colonel, I want to speak to the people."

Athos shuddered from head to foot. It was the king speaking on the scaffold.

In fact, after taking a few drops of wine and a piece of bread, Charles, weary of waiting for death, had suddenly decided to go to meet it and had given the signal for movement. Then the two wings of the window facing the square had been thrown open, and the people had seen silently advancing from the interior of the vast chamber, first, a masked man, who, carrying an axe in his hand, was recognized as the executioner. He approached the block and laid his axe upon it. Behind him, pale indeed, but marching with a firm step, was Charles Stuart, who advanced between two priests, followed by a few superior officers appointed to preside at the execution and attended by two files of partisans who took their places on opposite sides of the scaffold.

The sight of the masked man gave rise to a prolonged sensation. Every one was full of curiosity as to who that unknown executioner could be who presented himself so opportunely to assure to the people the promised spectacle, when the people believed it had been postponed until the following day. All gazed at him searchingly.

But they could discern nothing but a man of middle height, dressed in black, apparently of a certain age, for the end of a gray beard peeped out from the bottom of the mask that hid his features.

The king's request had undoubtedly been acceded to by an affirmative sign, for in firm, sonorous accents, which vibrated in the depths of Athos's heart, the king began his speech, explaining his conduct and counseling the welfare of the kingdom.

"Oh!" said Athos to himself, "is it indeed possible that I hear what I hear and that I see what I see? Is it possible that God has abandoned His representative on earth and left him to die thus miserably? And I have not seen him! I have not said adieu to him!"

A noise was heard like that the instrument of death would make if moved upon the block.

"Do not touch the axe," said the king, and resumed his speech.

At the end of his speech the king looked tenderly around upon the people. Then unfastening the diamond ornament which the queen had sent him, he placed it in the hands of the priest who accompanied Juxon. Then he drew from his breast a little cross set in diamonds, which, like the order, had been the gift of Henrietta Maria.

"Sir," said he to the priest, "I shall keep this cross in my hand till the last moment. Take it from me when I am--dead."

"Yes, sire," said a voice, which Athos recognized as that of Aramis.

He then took his hat from his head and threw it on the ground. One by one he undid the buttons of his doublet, took it off and deposited it by the side of his hat. Then, as it was cold, he asked for his gown, which was brought to him.

All the preparations were made with a frightful calmness. One would have thought the king was going to bed and not to his coffin.

"Will these be in your way?" he said to the executioner, raising his long locks; "if so, they can be tied up."

Charles accompanied these words with a look designed to penetrate the mask of the unknown headsman. His calm, noble gaze forced the man to turn away his head. But after the searching look of the king he encountered the burning eyes of Aramis.

The king, seeing that he did not reply, repeated his question.

"It will do," replied the man, in a tremulous voice, "if you separate them across the neck."

The king parted his hair with his hands, and looking at the block he said:

"This block is very low, is there no other to be had?"

"It is the usual block," answered the man in the mask.

"Do you think you can behead me with a single blow?" asked the king.

"I hope so," was the reply. There was something so strange in these three words that everybody, except the king, shuddered.

"I do not wish to be taken by surprise," added the king. "I shall kneel down to pray; do not strike then."

"When shall I strike?"

"When I shall lay my head on the block and say 'Remember!' then strike boldly."

"Gentlemen," said the king to those around him, "I leave you to brave the tempest; I go before you to a kingdom which knows no storms. Farewell."

He looked at Aramis and made a special sign to him with his head.

"Now," he continued, "withdraw a little and let me say my prayer, I beseech you. You, also, stand aside," he said to the masked man. "It is only for a moment and I know that I belong to you; but remember that you are not to strike till I give the signal."

Then he knelt down, made the sign of the cross, and lowering his face to the planks, as if he would have kissed them, said in a low tone, in French, "Comte de la Fere, are you there?"

"Yes, your majesty," he answered, trembling.

"Faithful friend, noble heart!" said the king, "I should not have been rescued. I have addressed my people and I have spoken to God; last of all I speak to you. To maintain a cause which I believed sacred I have lost the throne and my children their inheritance. A million in gold remains; it is buried in the cellars of Newcastle Keep. You only know that this money exists. Make use of it, then, whenever you think it will be most useful, for my eldest son's welfare. And now, farewell."

"Farewell, saintly, martyred majesty," lisped Athos, chilled with terror.

A moment's silence ensued and then, in a full, sonorous voice, the king exclaimed: "Remember!"

He had scarcely uttered the word when a heavy blow shook the scaffold and where Athos stood immovable a warm drop fell upon his brow. He reeled back with a shudder and the same moment the drops became a crimson cataract.

Athos fell on his knees and remained some minutes as if bewildered or stunned. At last he rose and taking his handkerchief steeped it in the blood of the martyred king. Then as the crowd gradually dispersed he leaped down, crept from behind the drapery, glided between two horses, mingled with the crowd and was the first to arrive at the inn.

Having gained his room he raised his hand to his face, and observing that his fingers were covered with the monarch's blood, fell down insensible.

67. The Man in the Mask.

The snow was falling thick and icy. Aramis was the next to come in and to discover Athos almost insensible. But at the first words he uttered the comte roused himself from the kind of lethargy in which he had sunk.

"Well," said Aramis, "beaten by fate!"

"Beaten!" said Athos. "Noble and unhappy king!"

"Are you wounded?" cried Aramis.

"No, this is his blood."

"Where were you, then?"

"Where you left me--under the scaffold."

"Did you see it all?"

"No, but I heard all. God preserve me from another such hour as I have just passed."

"Then you know that I did not leave him?"

"I heard your voice up to the last moment."

"Here is the order he gave me and the cross I took from his hand; he desired they should be returned to the queen."

"Then here is a handkerchief to wrap them in," replied Athos, drawing from his pocket the one he had steeped in the king's blood.

"And what," he continued, "has been done with the poor body?"

"By order of Cromwell royal honors will be accorded to it. The doctors are embalming the corpse, and when it is ready it will be placed in a lighted chapel."

"Mockery," muttered Athos, savagely; "royal honors to one whom they have murdered!"

"Well, cheer up!" said a loud voice from the staircase, which Porthos had just mounted. "We are all mortal, my poor friends."

"You are late, my dear Porthos."

"Yes, there were some people on the way who delayed me. The wretches were dancing. I took one of them by the throat and three-quarters throttled him. Just then a patrol rode up. Luckily the man I had had most to do with was some minutes before he could speak, so I took advantage of his silence to walk off."

"Have you seen D'Artagnan?"

"We got separated in the crowd and I could not find him again."

"Oh!" said Athos, satirically, "I saw him. He was in the front row of the crowd, admirably placed for seeing; and as on the whole the sight was curious, he probably wished to stay to the end."

"Ah Comte de la Fere," said a calm voice, though hoarse with running, "is it your habit to calumniate the absent?"

This reproof stung Athos to the heart, but as the impression produced by seeing D'Artagnan foremost in a coarse, ferocious crowd had been very strong, he contented himself with replying:

"I am not calumniating you, my friend. They were anxious about you here; I simply told them where you were. You didn't know King Charles; to you he was only a foreigner and you were not obliged to love him."

So saying, he stretched out his hand, but the other pretended not to see it and he let it drop again slowly by his side.

"Ugh! I am tired," cried D'Artagnan, sitting down.

"Drink a glass of port," said Aramis; "it will refresh you."

"Yes, let us drink," said Athos, anxious to make it up by hobnobbing with D'Artagnan, "let us drink and get away from this hateful country. The felucca is waiting for us, you know; let us leave to-night, we have nothing more to do here."

"You are in a hurry, sir count," said D'Artagnan.

"But what would you have us to do here, now that the king is dead?"

"Go, sir count," replied D'Artagnan, carelessly; "you see nothing to keep you a little longer in England? Well, for my part, I, a bloodthirsty ruffian, who can go and stand close to a scaffold, in order to have a better view of the king's execution--I remain."

Athos turned pale. Every reproach his friend uttered struck deeply in his heart.

"Ah! you remain in London?" said Porthos.

"Yes. And you?"

"Hang it!" said Porthos, a little perplexed between the two, "I suppose, as I came with you, I must go away with you. I can't leave you alone in this abominable country."

"Thanks, my worthy friend. So I have a little adventure to propose to you when the count is gone. I want to find out who was the man in the mask, who so obligingly offered to cut the king's throat."

"A man in a mask?" cried Athos. "You did not let the executioner escape, then?"

"The executioner is still in the cellar, where, I presume, he has had an interview with mine host's bottles. But you remind me. Mousqueton!"

"Sir," answered a voice from the depths of the earth.

"Let out your prisoner. All is over."

"But," said Athos, "who is the wretch that has dared to raise his hand against his king?"

"An amateur headsman," replied Aramis, "who however, does not handle the axe amiss."

"Did you not see his face?" asked Athos.

"He wore a mask."

"But you, Aramis, who were close to him?"

"I could see nothing but a gray beard under the fringe of the mask."

"Then it must be a man of a certain age."

"Oh!" said D'Artagnan, "that matters little. When one puts on a mask, it is not difficult to wear a beard under it."

"I am sorry I did not follow him," said Porthos.

"Well, my dear Porthos," said D'Artagnan, "that's the very thing it came into my head to do."

Athos understood all now.

"Pardon me, D'Artagnan," he said. "I have distrusted God; I could the more easily distrust you. Pardon me, my friend."

"We will see about that presently," said D'Artagnan, with a slight smile.

"Well, then?" said Aramis.

"Well, while I was watching--not the king, as monsieur le comte thinks, for I know what it is to see a man led to death, and though I ought to be accustomed to the sight it always makes me ill--while I was watching the masked executioner, the idea came to me, as I said, to find out who he was. Now, as we are wont to complete ourselves each by all the rest and to depend on one another for assistance, as one calls his other hand to aid the first, I looked around instinctively to see if Porthos was there; for I had seen you, Aramis, with the king, and you, count, I knew would be under the scaffold, and for that reason I forgive you," he added, offering Athos his hand, "for you must have suffered much. I was looking around for Porthos when I saw near me a head which had been broken, but which, for better or worse, had been patched with plaster and with black silk. 'Humph!' thought I, 'that looks like my handiwork; I fancy I must have mended that skull somewhere or other.' And, in fact, it was that unfortunate Scotchman, Parry's brother, you know, on whom Groslow amused himself by trying his strength. Well, this man was making signs to another at my left, and turning around I recognized the honest Grimaud. 'Oh!' said I to him. Grimaud turned round with a jerk, recognized me, and pointed to the man in the mask. 'Eh!' said he, which meant, 'Do you see him?' 'Parbleu!' I answered, and we perfectly understood one another. Well, everything was finished as you know. The mob dispersed. I made a sign to Grimaud and the Scotchman, and we all three retired into a corner of the square. I saw the executioner return into the king's room, change his clothes, put on a black hat and a large cloak and disappear. Five minutes later he came down the grand staircase."

"You followed him?" cried Athos.

"I should think so, but not without difficulty. Every few minutes he turned around, and thus obliged us to conceal ourselves. I might have gone up to him and killed him. But I am not selfish, and I thought it might console you all a little to have a share in the matter. So we followed him through the lowest streets in the city, and in half an hour's time he stopped before a little isolated house. Grimaud drew out a pistol. 'Eh?' said he, showing it. I held back his arm. The man in the mask stopped before a low door and drew out a key; but before he placed it in the lock he turned around to see if he was being followed. Grimaud and I got behind a tree, and the Scotchman having nowhere to hide himself, threw himself on his face in the road. Next moment the door opened and the man disappeared."

"The scoundrel!" said Aramis. "While you have been returning hither he will have escaped and we shall never find him."

"Come, now, Aramis," said D'Artagnan, "you must be taking me for some one else."

"Nevertheless," said Athos, "in your absence----"

"Well, in my absence haven't I put in my place Grimaud and the Scotchman? Before he had taken ten steps beyond the door I had examined the house on all sides. At one of the doors, that by which he had entered, I placed our Scotchman, making a sign to him to follow the man wherever he might go, if he came out again. Then going around the house I placed Grimaud at the other exit, and here I am. Our game is beaten up. Now for the tally-ho."

Athos threw himself into D'Artagnan's arms.

"Friend," he said, "you have been too good in pardoning me; I was wrong, a hundred times wrong. I ought to have known you better by this time; but we are all possessed of a malignant spirit, which bids us doubt."

"Humph!" said Porthos. "Don't you think the executioner might be Master Cromwell, who, to make sure of this affair, undertook it himself?"

"Ah! just so. Cromwell is stout and short, and this man thin and lanky, rather tall than otherwise."

"Some condemned soldier, perhaps," suggested Athos, "whom they have pardoned at the price of regicide."

"No, no," continued D'Artagnan, "it was not the measured step of a foot soldier, nor was it the gait of a horseman. If I am not mistaken we have to do with a gentleman."

"A gentleman!" exclaimed Athos. "Impossible! It would be a dishonor to all the nobility."

"Fine sport, by Jove!" cried Porthos, with a laugh that shook the windows. "Fine sport!"

"Are you still bent on departure, Athos?" asked D'Artagnan.

"No, I remain," replied Athos, with a threatening gesture that promised no good to whomsoever it was addressed.

"Swords, then!" cried Aramis, "swords! let us not lose a moment."

The four friends resumed their own clothes, girded on their swords, ordered Mousqueton and Blaisois to pay the bill and to arrange everything for immediate departure, and wrapped in their large cloaks left in search of their game.

The night was dark, snow was falling, the streets were silent and deserted. D'Artagnan led the way through the intricate windings and narrow alleys of the city and ere long they had reached the house in question. For a moment D'Artagnan thought that Parry's brother had disappeared; but he was mistaken. The robust Scotchman, accustomed to the snows of his native hills, had stretched himself against a post, and like a fallen statue, insensible to the inclemency of the weather, had allowed the snow to cover him. He rose, however, as they approached.

"Come," said Athos, "here's another good servant. Really, honest men are not so scarce as I thought."

"Don't be in a hurry to weave crowns for our Scotchman. I believe the fellow is here on his own account, for I have heard that these gentlemen born beyond the Tweed are very vindictive. I should not like to be Groslow, if he meets him."

"Well?" said Athos, to the man, in English.

"No one has come out," he replied.

"Then, Porthos and Aramis, will you remain with this man while we go around to Grimaud?"

Grimaud had made himself a kind of sentry box out of a hollow willow, and as they drew near he put his head out and gave a low whistle.

"Soho!" cried Athos.

"Yes," said Grimaud.

"Well, has anybody come out?"

"No, but somebody has gone in."

"A man or a woman?"

"A man."

"Ah! ah!" said D'Artagnan, "there are two of them, then!"

"I wish there were four," said Athos; "the two parties would then be equal."

"Perhaps there are four," said D'Artagnan.

"What do you mean?"

"Other men may have entered before them and waited for them."

"We can find out," said Grimaud. At the same time he pointed to a window, through the shutters of which a faint light streamed.

"That is true," said D'Artagnan, "let us call the others."

They returned around the house to fetch Porthos and Aramis.

"Have you seen anything?" they asked.

"No, but we are going to," replied D'Artagnan, pointing to Grimaud, who had already climbed some five or six feet from the ground.

All four came up together. Grimaud continued to climb like a cat and succeeded at last in catching hold of a hook, which served to keep one of the shutters back when opened. Then resting his foot on a small ledge he made a sign to show all was right.

"Well?" asked D'Artagnan.

Grimaud showed his closed hand, with two fingers spread out.

"Speak," said Athos; "we cannot see your signs. How many are there?"

"Two. One opposite to me, the other with his back to me."

"Good. And the man opposite to you is----

"The man I saw go in."

"Do you know him?"

"I thought I recognized him, and was not mistaken. Short and stout."

"Who is it?" they all asked together in a low tone.

"General Oliver Cromwell."

The four friends looked at one another.

"And the other?" asked Athos.

"Thin and lanky."

"The executioner," said D'Artagnan and Aramis at the same time.

"I can see nothing but his back," resumed Grimaud. "But wait. He is moving; and if he has taken off his mask I shall be able to see. Ah----"

And as if struck in the heart he let go the hook and dropped with a groan.

"Did you see him?" they all asked.

"Yes," said Grimaud, with his hair standing on end.

"The thin, spare man?"

"Yes."

"The executioner, in short?" asked Aramis.

"Yes."

"And who is it?" said Porthos.

"He--he--is----" murmured Grimaud, pale as a ghost and seizing his master's hand.

"Who? He?" asked Athos.

"Mordaunt," replied Grimaud.

D'Artagnan, Porthos and Aramis uttered a cry of joy.

Athos stepped back and passed his hand across his brow.

"Fatality!" he muttered.

68. Cromwell's House.

It was, in fact, Mordaunt whom D'Artagnan had followed, without knowing it. On entering the house he had taken off his mask and imitation beard, then, mounting a staircase, had opened a door, and in a room lighted by a single lamp found himself face to face with a man seated behind a desk.

This man was Cromwell.

Cromwell had two or three of these retreats in London, unknown except to the most intimate of his friends. Mordaunt was among these.

"It is you, Mordaunt," he said. "You are late."

"General, I wished to see the ceremony to the end, which delayed me."

"Ah! I scarcely thought you were so curious as that."

"I am always curious to see the downfall of your honor's enemies, and he was not among the least of them. But you, general, were you not at Whitehall?"

"No," said Cromwell.

There was a moment's silence.

"Have you had any account of it?"

"None. I have been here since the morning. I only know that there was a conspiracy to rescue the king."

"Ah, you knew that?" said Mordaunt.

"It matters little. Four men, disguised as workmen, were to get the king out of prison and take him to Greenwich, where a vessel was waiting."

"And knowing all that, your honor remained here, far from the city, tranquil and inactive."

"Tranquil, yes," replied Cromwell. "But who told you I was inactive?"

"But--if the plot had succeeded?"

"I wished it to do so."

"I thought your excellence considered the death of Charles I. as a misfortune necessary to the welfare of England."

"Yes, his death; but it would have been more seemly not upon the scaffold."

"Why so?" asked Mordaunt.

Cromwell smiled. "Because it could have been said that I had had him condemned for the sake of justice and had let him escape out of pity."

"But if he had escaped?"

"Impossible; my precautions were taken."

"And does your honor know the four men who undertook to rescue him?"

"The four Frenchmen, of whom two were sent by the queen to her husband and two by Mazarin to me."

"And do you think Mazarin commissioned them to act as they have done?"

"It is possible. But he will not avow it."

"How so?"

"Because they failed."

"Your honor gave me two of these Frenchmen when they were only guilty of fighting for Charles I. Now that they are guilty of a conspiracy against England will your honor give me all four of them?"

"Take them," said Cromwell.

Mordaunt bowed with a smile of triumphant ferocity.

"Did the people shout at all?" Cromwell asked.

"Very little, except 'Long live Cromwell!'"

"Where were you placed?"

Mordaunt tried for a moment to read in the general's face if this was simply a useless question, or whether he knew everything. But his piercing eyes could by no means penetrate the sombre depths of Cromwell's.

"I was so situated as to hear and see everything," he answered.

It was now Cromwell's turn to look fixedly at Mordaunt, and Mordaunt to make himself impenetrable.

"It appears," said Cromwell, "that this improvised executioner did his duty remarkably well. The blow, so they tell me at least, was struck with a master's hand."

Mordaunt remembered that Cromwell had told him he had had no detailed account, and he was now quite convinced that the general had been present at the execution, hidden behind some screen or curtain.

"In fact," said Mordaunt, with a calm voice and immovable countenance, "a single blow sufficed."

"Perhaps it was some one in that occupation," said Cromwell.

"Do you think so, sir? He did not look like an executioner."

"And who else save an executioner would have wished to fill that horrible office?"

"But," said Mordaunt, "it might have been some personal enemy of the king, who had made a vow of vengeance and accomplished it in this way. Perhaps it was some man of rank who had grave reasons for hating the fallen king, and who, learning that the king was about to flee and escape him, threw himself in the way, with a mask on his face and an axe in his hand, not as substitute for the executioner, but as an ambassador of Fate."

"Possibly."

"And if that were the case would your honor condemn his action?"

"It is not for me to judge. It rests between his conscience and his God."

"But if your honor knew this man?"

"I neither know nor wish to know him. Provided Charles is dead, it is the axe, not the man, we must thank."

"And yet, without the man, the king would have been rescued."

Cromwell smiled.

"They would have carried him to Greenwich," he said, "and put him on board a felucca with five barrels of powder in the hold. Once out to sea, you are too good a politician not to understand the rest, Mordaunt."

"Yes, they would have all been blown up."

"Just so. The explosion would have done what the axe had failed to do. Men would have said that the king had escaped human justice and been overtaken by God's. You see now why I did not care to know your gentleman in the mask; for really, in spite of his excellent intentions, I could not thank him for what he has done."

Mordaunt bowed humbly. "Sir," he said, "you are a profound thinker and your plan was sublime."

"Say absurd, since it has become useless. The only sublime ideas in politics are those which bear fruit. So to-night, Mordaunt, go to Greenwich and ask for the captain of the felucca Lightning. Show him a white handkerchief knotted at the four corners and tell the crew to disembark and carry the powder back to the arsenal, unless, indeed----"

"Unless?" said Mordaunt, whose face was lighted by a savage joy as Cromwell spoke:

"This skiff might be of use to you for personal projects."

"Oh, my lord, my lord!"

"That title," said Cromwell, laughing, "is all very well here, but take care a word like that does not escape your lips in public."

"But your honor will soon be called so generally."

"I hope so, at least," said Cromwell, rising and putting on his cloak.

"You are going, sir?"

"Yes," said Cromwell. "I slept here last night and the night before, and you know it is not my custom to sleep three times in the same bed."

"Then," said Mordaunt, "your honor gives me my liberty for to-night?"

"And even for all day to-morrow, if you want it. Since last evening," he added, smiling, "you have done enough in my service, and if you have any personal matters to settle it is just that I should give you time."

"Thank you, sir; it will be well employed, I hope."

Cromwell turned as he was going.

"Are you armed?" he asked.

"I have my sword."

"And no one waiting for you outside?"

"No."

"Then you had better come with me."

"Thank you, sir, but the way by the subterranean passage would take too much time and I have none to lose."

Cromwell placed his hand on a hidden handle and opened a door so well concealed by the tapestry that the most practiced eye could not have discovered it. It closed after him with a spring. This door communicated with a subterranean passage, leading under the street to a grotto in the garden of a house about a hundred yards from that of the future Protector.

It was just before this that Grimaud had perceived the two men seated together.

D'Artagnan was the first to recover from his surprise.

"Mordaunt," he cried. "Ah! by Heaven! it is God Himself who sent us here."

"Yes," said Porthos, "let us break the door in and fall upon him."

"No," replied D'Artagnan, "no noise. Now, Grimaud, you come here, climb up to the window again and tell us if Mordaunt is alone and whether he is preparing to go out or go to bed. If he comes out we shall catch him. If he stays in we will break in the window. It is easier and less noisy than the door."

Grimaud began to scale the wall again.

"Keep guard at the other door, Athos and Aramis. Porthos and I will stay here."

The friends obeyed.

"He is alone," said Grimaud.

"We did not see his companion come out."

"He may have gone by the other door."

"What is he doing?"

"Putting on his cloak and gloves."

"He's ours," muttered D'Artagnan.

Porthos mechanically drew his dagger from the scabbard.

"Put it up again, my friend," said D'Artagnan. "We must proceed in an orderly manner."

"Hush!" said Grimaud, "he is coming out. He has put out the lamp, I can see nothing now."

"Get down then and quickly."

Grimaud leaped down. The snow deadened the noise of his fall.

"Now go and tell Athos and Aramis to stand on each side of the door and clap their hands if they catch him. We will do the same."

The next moment the door opened and Mordaunt appeared on the threshold, face to face with D'Artagnan. Porthos clapped his hands and the other two came running around. Mordaunt was livid, but he uttered no cry nor called for assistance. D'Artagnan quietly pushed him in again, and by the light of a lamp on the staircase made him ascend the steps backward one by one, keeping his eyes all the time on Mordaunt's hands, who, however, knowing that it was useless, attempted no resistance. At last they stood face to face in the very room where ten minutes before Mordaunt had been talking to Cromwell.

Porthos came up behind, and unhooking the lamp on the staircase relit that in the room. Athos and Aramis entered last and locked the door behind them.

"Oblige me by taking a seat," said D'Artagnan, pushing a chair toward Mordaunt, who sat down, pale but calm. Aramis, Porthos and D'Artagnan drew their chairs near him. Athos alone kept away and sat in the furthest corner of the room, as if determined to be merely a spectator of the proceedings. He seemed to be quite overcome. Porthos rubbed his hands in feverish impatience. Aramis bit his lips till the blood came.

D'Artagnan alone was calm, at least in appearance.

"Monsieur Mordaunt," he said, "since, after running after one another so long, chance has at last brought us together, let us have a little conversation, if you please."

69. Conversational.

Though Mordaunt had been so completely taken by surprise and had mounted the stairs in such utter confusion, when once seated he recovered himself, as it were, and prepared to seize any possible opportunity of escape. His eye wandered to a long stout sword on his flank and he instinctively slipped it around within reach of his right hand.

D'Artagnan was waiting for a reply to his remark and said nothing. Aramis muttered to himself, "We shall hear nothing but the usual commonplace things."

Porthos sucked his mustache, muttering, "A good deal of ceremony to-night about crushing an adder." Athos shrunk into his corner, pale and motionless as a bas-relief.

The silence, however, could not last forever. So D'Artagnan began:

"Sir," he said, with desperate politeness, "it seems to me that you change your costume almost as rapidly as I have seen the Italian mummers do, whom the Cardinal Mazarin brought over from Bergamo and whom he doubtless took you to see during your travels in France."

Mordaunt did not reply.

"Just now," D'Artagnan continued, "you were disguised--I mean to say, attired--as a murderer, and now----"

"And now I look very much like a man who is going to be murdered."

"Oh! sir," said D'Artagnan, "how can you talk like that when you are in the company of gentlemen and have such an excellent sword at your side?"

"No sword is excellent enough to be of use against four swords and daggers."

"Well, that is scarcely the question. I had the honor of asking you why you altered your costume. The mask and beard became you very well, and as to the axe, I do not think it would be out of keeping even at this moment. Why, then, have you laid it aside?"

"Because, remembering the scene at Armentieres, I thought I should find four axes for one, as I was to meet four executioners."

"Sir," replied D'Artagnan, in the calmest manner possible, "you are very young; I shall therefore overlook your frivolous remarks. What took place at Armentieres has no connection whatever with the present occasion. We could scarcely have requested your mother to take a sword and fight us."

"Aha! It is a duel, then?" cried Mordaunt, as if disposed to reply at once to the provocation.

Porthos rose, always ready for this kind of adventure.

"Pardon me," said D'Artagnan. "Do not let us do things in a hurry. We will arrange the matter rather better. Confess, Monsieur Mordaunt, that you are anxious to kill some of us."

"All," replied Mordaunt.

"Then, my dear sir; I am convinced that these gentlemen return your kind wishes and will be delighted to kill you also. Of course they will do so as honorable gentlemen, and the best proof I can furnish is this----"

So saying, he threw his hat on the ground, pushed back his chair to the wall and bowed to Mordaunt with true French grace.

"At your service, sir," he continued. "My sword is shorter than yours, it's true, but, bah! I think the arm will make up for the sword."

"Halt!" cried Porthos coming forward. "I begin, and without any rhetoric."

"Allow me, Porthos," said Aramis.

Athos did not move. He might have been taken for a statue. Even his breathing seemed to be arrested.

"Gentlemen," said D'Artagnan, "you shall have your turn. Monsieur Mordaunt dislikes you sufficiently not to refuse you afterward. You can see it in his eye. So pray keep your places, like Athos, whose calmness is entirely laudable. Besides, we will have no words about it. I have particular business to settle with this gentleman and I shall and will begin."

Porthos and Aramis drew back, disappointed, and drawing his sword D'Artagnan turned to his adversary:

"Sir, I am waiting for you."

"And for my part, gentlemen, I admire you. You are disputing which shall fight me first, but you do not consult me who am most concerned in the matter. I hate you all, but not equally. I hope to kill all four of you, but I am more likely to kill the first than the second, the second than the third, and the third than the last. I claim, then, the right to choose my opponent. If you refuse this right you may kill me, but I shall not fight."

"It is but fair," said Porthos and Aramis, hoping he would choose one of them.

Athos and D'Artagnan said nothing, but their silence seemed to imply consent.

"Well, then," said Mordaunt, "I choose for my adversary the man who, not thinking himself worthy to be called Comte de la Fere, calls himself Athos."

Athos sprang up, but after an instant of motionless silence he said, to the astonishment of his friends, "Monsieur Mordaunt, a duel between us is impossible. Submit this honour to somebody else." And he sat down.

"Ah!" said Mordaunt, with a sneer, "there's one who is afraid."

"Zounds!" exclaimed D'Artagnan, bounding toward him, "who says that Athos is afraid?"

"Let him have his say, D'Artagnan," said Athos, with a smile of sadness and contempt.

"Is it your decision, Athos?" resumed the Gascon.

"Irrevocably."

"You hear, sir," said D'Artagnan, turning to Mordaunt. "The Comte de la Fere will not do you the honor of fighting with you. Choose one of us to replace the Comte de la Fere."

"As long as I don't fight with him it is the same to me with whom I fight. Put your names into a hat and draw lots."

"A good idea," said D'Artagnan.

"At least that will conciliate us all," said Aramis.

"I should never have thought of that," said Porthos, "and yet it is very simple."

"Come, Aramis," said D'Artagnan, "write this for us in those neat little characters in which you wrote to Marie Michon that the mother of this gentleman intended to assassinate the Duke of Buckingham."

Mordaunt sustained this new attack without wincing. He stood with his arms folded, apparently as calm as any man could be in such circumstances. If he had not courage he had what is very like it, namely, pride.

Aramis went to Cromwell's desk, tore off three bits of paper of equal size, wrote on the first his own name and on the others those of his two companions, and presented them open to Mordaunt, who by a movement of his head indicated that he left the matter entirely to Aramis. He then rolled them separately and put them in a hat, which he handed to Mordaunt.

Mordaunt put his hand into the hat, took out one of the three papers and disdainfully dropped it on the table without reading it.

"Ah! serpent," muttered D'Artagnan, "I would give my chance of a captaincy in the mousquetaires for that to be my name."

Aramis opened the paper, and in a voice trembling with hate and vengeance read "D'Artagnan."

The Gascon uttered a cry of joy and turning to Mordaunt:

"I hope, sir," said he, "you have no objection to make."

"None, whatever," replied the other, drawing his sword and resting the point on his boot.

The moment that D'Artagnan saw that his wish was accomplished and his man would not escape him, he recovered his usual tranquillity. He turned up his cuffs neatly and rubbed the sole of his right boot on the floor, but did not fail, however, to remark that Mordaunt was looking about him in a singular manner.

"Are you ready, sir?" he said at last.

"I was waiting for you, sir," said Mordaunt, raising his head and casting at his opponent a look it would be impossible to describe.

"Well, then," said the Gascon, "take care of yourself, for I am not a bad hand at the rapier."

"Nor I either."

"So much the better; that sets my mind at rest. Defend yourself."

"One minute," said the young man. "Give me your word, gentlemen, that you will not attack me otherwise than one after the other."

"Is it to have the pleasure of insulting us that you say that, my little viper?"

"No, but to set my mind at rest, as you observed just now."

"It is for something else than that, I imagine," muttered D'Artagnan, shaking his head doubtfully.

"On the honor of gentlemen," said Aramis and Porthos.

"In that case, gentlemen, have the kindness to retire into the corners, so as to give us ample room. We shall require it."

"Yes, gentlemen," said D'Artagnan, "we must not leave this person the slightest pretext for behaving badly, which, with all due respect, I fancy he is anxious still to do."

This new attack made no impression on Mordaunt. The space was cleared, the two lamps placed on Cromwell's desk, in order that the combatants might have as much light as possible; and the swords crossed.

D'Artagnan was too good a swordsman to trifle with his opponent. He made a rapid and brilliant feint which Mordaunt parried.

"Aha!" he cried with a smile of satisfaction.

And without losing a minute, thinking he saw an opening, he thrust his right in and forced Mordaunt to parry a counter en quarte so fine that the point of the weapon might have turned within a wedding ring.

This time it was Mordaunt who smiled.

"Ah, sir," said D'Artagnan, "you have a wicked smile. It must have been the devil who taught it you, was it not?"

Mordaunt replied by trying his opponent's weapon with an amount of strength which the Gascon was astonished to find in a form apparently so feeble; but thanks to a parry no less clever than that which Mordaunt had just achieved, he succeeded in meeting his sword, which slid along his own without touching his chest.

Mordaunt rapidly sprang back a step.

"Ah! you lose ground, you are turning? Well, as you please, I even gain something by it, for I no longer see that wicked smile of yours. You have no idea what a false look you have, particularly when you are afraid. Look at my eyes and you will see what no looking-glass has ever shown you--a frank and honorable countenance."

To this flow of words, not perhaps in the best taste, but characteristic of D'Artagnan, whose principal object was to divert his opponent's attention, Mordaunt did not reply, but continuing to turn around he succeeded in changing places with D'Artagnan.

He smiled more and more sarcastically and his smile began to make the Gascon anxious.

"Come, come," cried D'Artagnan, "we must finish with this," and in his turn he pressed Mordaunt hard, who continued to lose ground, but evidently on purpose and without letting his sword leave the line for a moment. However, as they were fighting in a room and had not space to go on like that forever, Mordaunt's foot at last touched the wall, against which he rested his left hand.

"Ah, this time you cannot lose ground, my fine friend!" exclaimed D'Artagnan. "Gentlemen, did you ever see a scorpion pinned to a wall? No. Well, then, you shall see it now."

In a second D'Artagnan had made three terrible thrusts at Mordaunt, all of which touched, but only pricked him. The three friends looked on, panting and astonished. At last D'Artagnan, having got up too close, stepped back to prepare a fourth thrust, but the moment when, after a fine, quick feint, he was attacking as sharply as lightning, the wall seemed to give way, Mordaunt disappeared through the opening, and D'Artagnan's blade, caught between the panels, shivered like a sword of glass. D'Artagnan sprang back; the wall had closed again.

Mordaunt, in fact, while defending himself, had manoeuvred so as to reach the secret door by which Cromwell had left, had felt for the knob with his left hand, pressed it and disappeared.

The Gascon uttered a furious imprecation, which was answered by a wild laugh on the other side of the iron panel.

"Help me, gentlemen," cried D'Artagnan, "we must break in this door."

"It is the devil in person!" said Aramis, hastening forward.

"He escapes us," growled Porthos, pushing his huge shoulder against the hinges, but in vain. "'Sblood! he escapes us."

"So much the better," muttered Athos.

"I thought as much," said D'Artagnan, wasting his strength in useless efforts. "Zounds, I thought as much when the wretch kept moving around the room. I thought he was up to something."

"It's a misfortune, to which his friend, the devil, treats us," said Aramis.

"It's a piece of good fortune sent from Heaven," said Athos, evidently much relieved.

"Really!" said D'Artagnan, abandoning the attempt to burst open the panel after several ineffectual attempts, "Athos, I cannot imagine how you can talk to us in that way. You cannot understand the position we are in. In this kind of game, not to kill is to let one's self be killed. This fox of a fellow will be sending us a hundred iron-sided beasts who will pick us off like sparrows in this place. Come, come, we must be off. If we stay here five minutes more there's an end of us."

"Yes, you are right."

"But where shall we go?" asked Porthos.

"To the hotel, to be sure, to get our baggage and horses; and from there, if it please God, to France, where, at least, I understand the architecture of the houses."

So, suiting the action to the word, D'Artagnan thrust the remnant of his sword into its scabbard, picked up his hat and ran down the stairs, followed by the others.

70. The Skiff "Lightning."

D'Artagnan had judged correctly; Mordaunt felt that he had no time to lose, and he lost none. He knew the rapidity of decision and action that characterized his enemies and resolved to act with reference to that. This time the musketeers had an adversary who was worthy of them.

After closing the door carefully behind him Mordaunt glided into the subterranean passage, sheathing on the way his now useless sword, and thus reached the neighboring house, where he paused to examine himself and to take breath.

"Good!" he said, "nothing, almost nothing--scratches, nothing more; two in the arm and one in the breast. The wounds that I make are better than that--witness the executioner of Bethune, my uncle and King Charles. Now, not a second to lose, for a second lost will perhaps save them. They must die--die all together--killed at one stroke by the thunder of men in default of God's. They must disappear, broken, scattered, annihilated. I will run, then, till my legs no longer serve, till my heart bursts in my bosom but I will arrive before they do."

Mordaunt proceeded at a rapid pace to the nearest cavalry barracks, about a quarter of a league distant. He made that quarter of a league in four or five minutes. Arrived at the barracks he made himself known, took the best horse in the stables, mounted and gained the high road. A quarter of an hour later he was at Greenwich.

"There is the port," he murmured. "That dark point yonder is the Isle of Dogs. Good! I am half an hour in advance of them, an hour, perhaps. Fool that I was! I have almost killed myself by my needless haste. Now," he added, rising in the stirrups and looking about him, "which, I wonder, is the Lightning?"

At this moment, as if in reply to his words, a man lying on a coil of cables rose and advanced a few steps toward him. Mordaunt drew a handkerchief from his pocket, and tying a knot at each corner--the signal agreed upon--waved it in the air and the man came up to him. He was wrapped in a large rough cape, which concealed his form and partly his face.

"Do you wish to go on the water, sir?" said the sailor.

"Yes, just so. Along the Isle of Dogs."

"And perhaps you have a preference for one boat more than another. You would like one that sails as rapidly as----"

"Lightning," interrupted Mordaunt.

"Then mine is the boat you want, sir. I'm your man."

"I begin to think so, particularly if you have not forgotten a certain signal."

"Here it is, sir," and the sailor took from his coat a handkerchief, tied at each corner.

"Good, quite right!" cried Mordaunt, springing off his horse. "There's not a moment to lose; now take my horse to the nearest inn and conduct me to your vessel."

"But," asked the sailor, "where are your companions? I thought there were four of you."

"Listen to me, sir. I'm not the man you take me for; you are in Captain Rogers's post, are you not? under orders from General Cromwell. Mine, also, are from him!"

"Indeed, sir, I recognize you; you are Captain Mordaunt."

Mordaunt was startled.

"Oh, fear nothing," said the skipper, showing his face. "I am a friend."

"Captain Groslow!" cried Mordaunt.

"Himself. The general remembered that I had formerly been a naval officer and he gave me the command of this expedition. Is there anything new in the wind?"

"Nothing."

"I thought, perhaps, that the king's death----"

"Has only hastened their flight; in ten minutes they will perhaps be here."

"What have you come for, then?"

"To embark with you."

"Ah! ah! the general doubted my fidelity?"

"No, but I wish to have a share in my revenge. Haven't you some one who will relieve me of my horse?"

Groslow whistled and a sailor appeared.

"Patrick," said Groslow, "take this horse to the stables of the nearest inn. If any one asks you whose it is you can say that it belongs to an Irish gentleman."

The sailor departed without reply.

"Now," said Mordaunt, "are you not afraid that they will recognize you?"

"There is no danger, dressed as I am in this pilot coat, on a night as dark as this. Besides even you didn't recognize me; they will be much less likely to."

"That is true," said Mordaunt, "and they will be far from thinking of you. Everything is ready, is it not?"

"Yes."

"The cargo on board?"

"Yes."

"Five full casks?"

"And fifty empty ones."

"Good."

"We are carrying port wine to Anvers."

"Excellent. Now take me aboard and return to your post, for they will soon be here."

"I am ready."

"It is important that none of your crew should see me."

"I have but one man on board, and I am as sure of him as I am of myself. Besides, he doesn't know you; like his mates he is ready to obey our orders knowing nothing of our plan."

"Very well; let us go."

They then went down to the Thames. A boat was fastened to the shore by a chain fixed to a stake. Groslow jumped in, followed by Mordaunt, and in five minutes they were quite away from that world of houses which then crowded the outskirts of London; and Mordaunt could discern the little vessel riding at anchor near the Isle of Dogs. When they reached the side of this felucca, Mordaunt, dexterous in his eagerness for vengeance, seized a rope and climbed up the side of the vessel with a coolness and agility very rare among landsmen. He went with Groslow to the captain's berth, a sort of temporary cabin of planks, for the chief apartment had been given up by Captain Rogers to the passengers, who were to be accommodated at the other end of the boat.

"They will have nothing to do, then at this end?" said Mordaunt.

"Nothing at all."

"That's a capital arrangement. Return to Greenwich and bring them here. I shall hide myself in your cabin. You have a longboat?"

"That in which we came."

"It appeared light and well constructed."

"Quite a canoe."

"Fasten it to the poop with a rope; put the oars into it, so that it may follow in the track and there will be nothing to do except to cut the cord. Put a good supply of rum and biscuit in it for the seamen; should the night happen to be stormy they will not be sorry to find something to console themselves with."

"Consider all this done. Do you wish to see the powder-room?"

"No. When you return I will set the fuse myself, but be careful to conceal your face, so that you cannot be recognized by them."

"Never fear."

"There's ten o'clock striking at Greenwich."

Groslow, then, having given the sailor on duty an order to be on the watch with more than usual vigilance, went down into the longboat and soon reached Greenwich. The wind was chilly and the jetty was deserted, as he approached it; but he had no sooner landed than he heard a noise of horses galloping upon the paved road.

These horsemen were our friends, or rather, an avant garde, composed of D'Artagnan and Athos. As soon as they arrived at the spot where Groslow stood they stopped, as if guessing that he was the man they wanted. Athos alighted and calmly opened the handkerchief tied at each corner, whilst D'Artagnan, ever cautious, remained on horseback, one hand upon his pistol, leaning forward watchfully.

On seeing the appointed signal, Groslow, who had at first crept behind one of the cannon planted on that spot, walked straight up to the gentlemen. He was so well wrapped up in his cloak that it would have been impossible to see his face even if the night had not been so dark as to render precaution superfluous; nevertheless, the keen glance of Athos perceived at once it was not Rogers who stood before them.

"What do you want with us?" he asked of Groslow.

"I wish to inform you, my lord," replied Groslow, with an Irish accent, feigned of course, "that if you are looking for Captain Rogers you will not find him. He fell down this morning and broke his leg. But I'm his cousin; he told me everything and desired me to watch instead of him, and in his place to conduct, wherever they wished to go, the gentlemen who should bring me a handkerchief tied at each corner, like that one which you hold and one which I have in my pocket."

And he drew out the handkerchief.

"Was that all he said?" inquired Athos.

"No, my lord; he said you had engaged to pay seventy pounds if I landed you safe and sound at Boulogne or any other port you choose in France."

"What do you think of all this?" said Athos, in a low tone to D'Artagnan, after explaining to him in French what the sailor had said in English.

"It seems a likely story to me."

"And to me, too."

"Besides, we can but blow out his brains if he proves false," said the Gascon; "and you, Athos, you know something of everything and can be our captain. I dare say you know how to navigate, should he fail us."

"My dear friend, you guess well. My father meant me for the navy and I have some vague notions about navigation."

"You see!" cried D'Artagnan.

They then summoned their friends, who, with Blaisois, Mousqueton and Grimaud, promptly joined them, leaving Parry behind them, who was to take back to London the horses of the gentlemen and of their lackeys, which had been sold to the host in settlement of their account with him. Thanks to this stroke of business the four friends were able to take away with them a sum of money which, if not large, was sufficient as a provision against delays and accidents.

Parry parted from his friends regretfully; they had proposed his going with them to France, but he had straightway declined.

"It is very simple," Mousqueton had said; "he is thinking of Groslow."

It was Captain Groslow, the reader will remember, who had broken Parry's head.

D'Artagnan resumed immediately the attitude of distrust that was habitual with him. He found the wharf too completely deserted, the night too dark, the captain too accommodating. He had reported to Aramis what had taken place, and Aramis, not less distrustful than he, had increased his suspicions. A slight click of the tongue against his teeth informed Athos of the Gascon's uneasiness.

"We have no time now for suspicions," said Athos. "The boat is waiting for us; come."

"Besides," said Aramis, "what prevents our being distrustful and going aboard at the same time? We can watch the skipper."

"And if he doesn't go straight I will crush him, that's all."

"Well said, Porthos," replied D'Artagnan. "Let us go, then. You first, Mousqueton," and he stopped his friends, directing the valets to go first, in order to test the plank leading from the pier to the boat.

The three valets passed without accident. Athos followed them, then Porthos, then Aramis. D'Artagnan went last, still shaking his head.

"What in the devil is the matter with you, my friend?" said Porthos. "Upon my word you would make Caesar afraid."

"The matter is," replied D'Artagnan, "that I can see upon this pier neither inspector nor sentinel nor exciseman."

"And you complain of that!" said Porthos. "Everything goes as if in flowery paths."

"Everything goes too well, Porthos. But no matter; we must trust in God."

As soon as the plank was withdrawn the captain took his place at the tiller and made a sign to one of the sailors, who, boat-hook in hand, began to push out from the labyrinth of boats in which they were involved. The other sailor had already seated himself on the port side and was ready to row. As soon as there was room for rowing, his companion rejoined him and the boat began to move more rapidly.

"At last we are off!" exclaimed Porthos.

"Alas," said Athos, "we depart alone."

"Yes; but all four together and without a scratch; which is a consolation."

"We are not yet at our destination," observed the prudent D'Artagnan; "beware of misadventure."

"Ah, my friend!" cried Porthos, "like the crows, you always bring bad omens. Who could intercept us on such a night as this, pitch dark, when one does not see more than twenty yards before one?"

"Yes, but to-morrow morning----"

"To-morrow we shall be at Boulogne."

"I hope so, with all my heart," said the Gascon, "and I confess my weakness. Yes, Athos, you may laugh, but as long as we were within gunshot of the pier or of the vessels lying by it I was looking for a frightful discharge of musketry which would crush us."

"But," said Porthos, with great wisdom, "that was impossible, for they would have killed the captain and the sailors."

"Bah! much Monsieur Mordaunt would care. You don't imagine he would consider a little thing like that?"

"At any rate," said Porthos, "I am glad to hear D'Artagnan admit that he is afraid."

"I not only confess it, but am proud of it," returned the Gascon; "I'm not such a rhinoceros as you are. Oho! what's that?"

"The Lightning," answered the captain, "our felucca."

"So far, so good," laughed Athos.

They went on board and the captain instantly conducted them to the berth prepared for them--a cabin which was to serve for all purposes and for the whole party; he then tried to slip away under pretext of giving orders to some one.

"Stop a moment," cried D'Artagnan; "pray how many men have you on board, captain?"

"I don't understand," was the reply.

"Explain it, Athos."

Groslow, on the question being interpreted, answered, "Three, without counting myself."

D'Artagnan understood, for while replying the captain had raised three fingers. "Oh!" he exclaimed, "I begin to be more at my ease, however, whilst you settle yourselves, I shall make the round of the boat."

"As for me," said Porthos, "I will see to the supper."

"A very good idea, Porthos," said the Gascon. "Athos lend me Grimaud, who in the society of his friend Parry has perhaps picked up a little English, and can act as my interpreter."

"Go, Grimaud," said Athos.

D'Artagnan, finding a lantern on the deck, took it up and with a pistol in his hand he said to the captain, in English, "Come," (being, with the classic English oath, the only English words he knew), and so saying he descended to the lower deck.

This was divided into three compartments--one which was covered by the floor of that room in which Athos, Porthos and Aramis were to pass the night; the second was to serve as the sleeping-room for the servants, the third, under the prow of the ship, was under the temporary cabin in which Mordaunt was concealed.

"Oho!" cried D'Artagnan, as he went down the steps of the hatchway, preceded by the lantern, "what a number of barrels! one would think one was in the cave of Ali Baba. What is there in them?" he added, putting his lantern on one of the casks.

The captain seemed inclined to go upon deck again, but controlling himself he answered:

"Port wine."

"Ah! port wine! 'tis a comfort," said the Gascon, "since we shall not die of thirst. Are they all full?"

Grimaud translated the question, and Groslow, who was wiping the perspiration from off his forehead, answered:

"Some full, others empty."

D'Artagnan struck the barrels with his hand, and having ascertained that he spoke the truth, pushed his lantern, greatly to the captain's alarm, into the interstices between the barrels, and finding that there was nothing concealed in them:

"Come along," he said; and he went toward the door of the second compartment.

"Stop!" said the Englishman, "I have the key of that door;" and he opened the door, with a trembling hand, into the second compartment, where Mousqueton and Blaisois were preparing supper.

Here there was evidently nothing to seek or to apprehend and they passed rapidly to examine the third compartment.

This was the room appropriated to the sailors. Two or three hammocks hung upon the ceiling, a table and two benches composed the entire furniture. D'Artagnan picked up two or three old sails hung on the walls, and meeting nothing to suspect, regained by the hatchway the deck of the vessel.

"And this room?" he asked, pointing to the captain's cabin.

"That's my room," replied Groslow.

"Open the door."

The captain obeyed. D'Artagnan stretched out his arm in which he held the lantern, put his head in at the half opened door, and seeing that the cabin was nothing better than a shed:

"Good," he said. "If there is an army on board it is not here that it is hidden. Let us see what Porthos has found for supper." And thanking the captain, he regained the state cabin, where his friends were.

Porthos had found nothing, and with him fatigue had prevailed over hunger. He had fallen asleep and was in a profound slumber when D'Artagnan returned. Athos and Aramis were beginning to close their eyes, which they half opened when their companion came in again.

"Well!" said Aramis.

"All is well; we may sleep tranquilly."

On this assurance the two friends fell asleep; and D'Artagnan, who was very weary, bade good-night to Grimaud and laid himself down in his cloak, with naked sword at his side, in such a manner that his body barricaded the passage, and it should be impossible to enter the room without upsetting him.

71. Port Wine.

In ten minutes the masters slept; not so the servants---hungry, and more thirsty than hungry.

Blaisois and Mousqueton set themselves to preparing their bed which consisted of a plank and a valise. On a hanging table, which swung to and fro with the rolling of the vessel, were a pot of beer and three glasses.

"This cursed rolling!" said Blaisois. "I know it will serve me as it did when we came over."

"And to think," said Mousqueton, "that we have nothing to fight seasickness with but barley bread and hop beer. Pah!"

"But where is your wicker flask, Monsieur Mousqueton? Have you lost it?" asked Blaisois.

"No," replied Mousqueton, "Parry kept it. Those devilish Scotchmen are always thirsty. And you, Grimaud," he said to his companion, who had just come in after his round with D'Artagnan, "are you thirsty?"

"As thirsty as a Scotchman!" was Grimaud's laconic reply.

And he sat down and began to cast up the accounts of his party, whose money he managed.

"Oh, lackadaisy! I'm beginning to feel queer!" cried Blaisois.

"If that's the case," said Mousqueton, with a learned air, "take some nourishment."

"Do you call that nourishment?" said Blaisois, pointing to the barley bread and pot of beer upon the table.

"Blaisois," replied Mousqueton, "remember that bread is the true nourishment of a Frenchman, who is not always able to get bread, ask Grimaud."

"Yes, but beer?" asked Blaisois sharply, "is that their true drink?"

"As to that," answered Mousqueton, puzzled how to get out of the difficulty, "I must confess that to me beer is as disagreeable as wine is to the English."

"What! Monsieur Mousqueton! The English--do they dislike wine?"

"They hate it."

"But I have seen them drink it."

"As a punishment. For example, an English prince died one day because they had put him into a butt of Malmsey. I heard the Chevalier d'Herblay say so."

"The fool!" cried Blaisois, "I wish I had been in his place."

"Thou canst be," said Grimaud, writing down his figures.

"How?" asked Blaisois, "I can? Explain yourself."

Grimaud went on with his sum and cast up the whole.

"Port," he said, extending his hand in the direction of the first compartment examined by D'Artagnan and himself.

"Eh? eh? ah? Those barrels I saw through the door?"

"Port!" replied Grimaud, beginning a fresh sum.

"I have heard," said Blaisois, "that port is a very good wine."

"Excellent!" exclaimed Mousqueton, smacking his lips. "Excellent; there is port wine in the cellar of Monsieur le Baron de Bracieux."

"Suppose we ask these Englishmen to sell us a bottle," said the honest Blaisois.

"Sell!" cried Mousqueton, about whom there was a remnant of his ancient marauding character left. "One may well perceive, young man, that you are inexperienced. Why buy what one can take?"

"Take!" said Blaisois; "covet the goods of your neighbor? That is forbidden, it seems to me."

"Where forbidden?" asked Mousqueton.

"In the commandments of God, or of the church, I don't know which. I only know it says, 'Thou shalt not covet thy neighbor's goods, nor yet his wife.'"

"That is a child's reason, Monsieur Blaisois," said Mousqueton in his most patronizing manner. "Yes, you talk like a child--I repeat the word. Where have you read in the Scriptures, I ask you, that the English are your neighbors?"

"Where, that is true," said Blaisois; "at least, I can't now recall it."

"A child's reason--I repeat it," continued Mousqueton. "If you had been ten years engaged in war, as Grimaud and I have been, my dear Blaisois, you would know the difference there is between the goods of others and the goods of enemies. Now an Englishman is an enemy; this port wine belongs to the English, therefore it belongs to us."

"And our masters?" asked Blaisois, stupefied by this harangue, delivered with an air of profound sagacity, "will they be of your opinion?"

Mousqueton smiled disdainfully.

"I suppose that you think it necessary that I should disturb the repose of these illustrious lords to say, 'Gentlemen, your servant, Mousqueton, is thirsty.' What does Monsieur Bracieux care, think you, whether I am thirsty or not?"

"'Tis a very expensive wine," said Blaisois, shaking his head.

"Were it liquid gold, Monsieur Blaisois, our masters would not deny themselves this wine. Know that Monsieur de Bracieux is rich enough to drink a tun of port wine, even if obliged to pay a pistole for every drop." His manner became more and more lofty every instant; then he arose and after finishing off the beer at one draught he advanced majestically to the door of the compartment where the wine was. "Ah! locked!" he exclaimed; "these devils of English, how suspicious they are!"

"Locked!" said Blaisois; "ah! the deuce it is; unlucky, for my stomach is getting more and more upset."

"Locked!" repeated Mousqueton.

"But," Blaisois ventured to say, "I have heard you relate, Monsieur Mousqueton, that once on a time, at Chantilly, you fed your master and yourself by taking partridges in a snare, carp with a line, and bottles with a slipnoose."

"Perfectly true; but there was an airhole in the cellar and the wine was in bottles. I cannot throw the loop through this partition nor move with a packthread a cask of wine which may perhaps weigh two hundred pounds."

"No, but you can take out two or three boards of the partition," answered Blaisois, "and make a hole in the cask with a gimlet."

Mousqueton opened his great round eyes to the utmost, astonished to find in Blaisois qualities for which he did not give him credit.

"'Tis true," he said; "but where can I get a chisel to take the planks out, a gimlet to pierce the cask?"

"Trousers," said Grimaud, still squaring his accounts.

"Ah, yes!" said Mousqueton.

Grimaud, in fact, was not only the accountant, but the armorer of the party; and as he was a man full of forethought, these trousers, carefully rolled up in his valise, contained every sort of tool for immediate use.

Mousqueton, therefore, was soon provided with tools and he began his task. In a few minutes he had extracted three boards. He tried to pass his body through the aperture, but not being like the frog in the fable, who thought he was larger than he really was, he found he must take out three or four more before he could get through.

He sighed and set to work again.

Grimaud had now finished his accounts. He arose and stood near Mousqueton.

"I," he said.

"What?" said Mousqueton.

"I can pass."

"That is true," said Mousqueton, glancing at his friend's long and thin body, "you will pass easily."

"And he knows the full casks," said Blaisois, "for he has already been in the hold with Monsieur le Chevalier d'Artagnan. Let Monsieur Grimaud go in, Monsieur Mouston."

"I could go in as well as Grimaud," said Mousqueton, a little piqued.

"Yes, but that would take too much time and I am thirsty. I am getting more and more seasick."

"Go in, then, Grimaud," said Mousqueton, handing him the beer pot and gimlet.

"Rinse the glasses," said Grimaud. Then with a friendly gesture toward Mousqueton, that he might forgive him for finishing an enterprise so brilliantly begun by another, he glided like a serpent through the opening and disappeared.

Blaisois was in a state of great excitement; he was in ecstasies. Of all the exploits performed since their arrival in England by the extraordinary men with whom he had the honor to be associated, this seemed without question to be the most wonderful.

"You are about to see," said Mousqueton, looking at Blaisois with an expression of superiority which the latter did not even think of questioning, "you are about to see, Blaisois, how we old soldiers drink when we are thirsty."

"My cloak," said Grimaud, from the bottom of the hold.

"What do you want?" asked Blaisois.

"My cloak--stop up the aperture with it."

"Why?" asked Blaisois.

"Simpleton!" exclaimed Mousqueton; "suppose any one came into the room."

"Ah, true," cried Blaisois, with evident admiration; "but it will be dark in the cellar."

"Grimaud always sees, dark or light, night as well as day," answered Mousqueton.

"That is lucky," said Blaisois. "As for me, when I have no candle I can't take two steps without knocking against something."

"That's because you haven't served," said Mousqueton. "Had you been in the army you would have been able to pick up a needle on the floor of a closed oven. But hark! I think some one is coming."

Mousqueton made, with a low whistling sound, the sign of alarm well known to the lackeys in the days of their youth, resumed his place at the table and made a sign to Blaisois to follow his example.

Blaisois obeyed.

The door of their cabin was opened. Two men, wrapped in their cloaks, appeared.

"Oho!" said they, "not in bed at a quarter past eleven. That's against all rules. In a quarter of an hour let every one be in bed and snoring."

These two men then went toward the compartment in which Grimaud was secreted; opened the door, entered and shut it after them.

"Ah!" cried Blaisois, "he is lost!"

"Grimaud's a cunning fellow," murmured Mousqueton.

They waited for ten minutes, during which time no noise was heard that might indicate that Grimaud was discovered, and at the expiration of that anxious interval the two men returned, closed the door after them, and repeating their orders that the servants should go to bed and extinguish their lights, disappeared.

"Shall we obey?" asked Blaisois. "All this looks suspicious."

"They said a quarter of an hour. We still have five minutes," replied Mousqueton.

"Suppose we warn the masters."

"Let's wait for Grimaud."

"But perhaps they have killed him."

"Grimaud would have cried out."

"You know he is almost dumb."

"We should have heard the blow, then."

"But if he doesn't return?"

"Here he is."

At that very moment Grimaud drew back the cloak which hid the aperture and came in with his face livid, his eyes staring wide open with terror, so that the pupils were contracted almost to nothing, with a large circle of white around them. He held in his hand a tankard full of a dark substance, and approaching the gleam of light shed by the lamp he uttered this single monosyllable: "Oh!" with such an expression of extreme terror that Mousqueton started, alarmed, and Blaisois was near fainting from fright.

Both, however, cast an inquisitive glance into the tankard--it was full of gunpowder.

Convinced that the ship was full of powder instead of having a cargo of wine, Grimaud hastened to awake D'Artagnan, who had no sooner beheld him than he perceived that something extraordinary had taken place. Imposing silence, Grimaud put out the little night lamp, then knelt down and poured into the lieutenant's ear a recital melodramatic enough not to require play of feature to give it pith.

This was the gist of his strange story:

The first barrel that Grimaud had found on passing into the compartment he struck--it was empty. He passed on to another--it, also, was empty, but the third which he tried was, from the dull sound it gave out, evidently full. At this point Grimaud stopped and was preparing to make a hole with his gimlet, when he found a spigot; he therefore placed his tankard under it and turned the spout; something, whatever it was the cask contained, fell silently into the tankard.

Whilst he was thinking that he should first taste the liquor which the tankard contained before taking it to his companions, the door of the cellar opened and a man with a lantern in his hands and enveloped in a cloak, came and stood just before the hogshead, behind which Grimaud, on hearing him come in, instantly crept. This was Groslow. He was accompanied by another man, who carried in his hand something long and flexible rolled up, resembling a washing line. His face was hidden under the wide brim of his hat. Grimaud, thinking that they had come, as he had, to try the port wine, effaced himself behind his cask and consoled himself with the reflection that if he were discovered the crime was not a great one.

"Have you the wick?" asked the one who carried the lantern.

"Here it is," answered the other.

At the voice of this last speaker, Grimaud started and felt a shudder creeping through his very marrow. He rose gently, so that his head was just above the round of the barrel, and under the large hat he recognized the pale face of Mordaunt.

"How long will this fuse burn?" asked this person.

"About five minutes," replied the captain.

That voice also was known to Grimaud. He looked from one to the other and after Mordaunt he recognized Groslow.

"Then tell the men to be in readiness--don't tell them why now. When the clock strikes a quarter after midnight collect your men. Get down into the longboat."

"That is, when I have lighted the match?"

"I will undertake that. I wish to be sure of my revenge. Are the oars in the boat?"

"Everything is ready."

"'Tis well."

Mordaunt knelt down and fastened one end of the train to the spigot, in order that he might have nothing to do but to set it on fire at the opposite end with the match.

He then arose.

"You hear me--at a quarter past midnight--in fact, in twenty minutes."

"I understand all perfectly, sir," replied Groslow; "but allow me to say there is great danger in what you undertake; would it not be better to intrust one of the men to set fire to the train?"

"My dear Groslow," answered Mordaunt, "you know the French proverb, 'Nothing one does not do one's self is ever well done.' I shall abide by that rule."

Grimaud had heard all this, if he had not understood it. But what he saw made good what he lacked in perfect comprehension of the language. He had seen the two mortal enemies of the musketeers, had seen Mordaunt adjust the fuse; he had heard the proverb, which Mordaunt had given in French. Then he felt and felt again the contents of the tankard he held in his hand; and, instead of the lively liquor expected by Blaisois and Mousqueton, he found beneath his fingers the grains of some coarse powder.

Mordaunt went away with the captain. At the door he stopped to listen.

"Do you hear how they sleep?" he asked.

In fact, Porthos could be heard snoring through the partition.

"'Tis God who gives them into our hands," answered Groslow.

"This time the devil himself shall not save them," rejoined Mordaunt.

And they went out together.

72. End of the Port Wine Mystery.

Grimaud waited till he heard the bolt grind in the lock and when he was satisfied that he was alone he slowly rose from his recumbent posture.

"Ah!" he said, wiping with his sleeve large drops of sweat from his forehead, "how lucky it was that Mousqueton was thirsty!"

He made haste to pass out by the opening, still thinking himself in a dream; but the sight of the gunpowder in the tankard proved to him that his dream was a fatal nightmare.

It may be imagined that D'Artagnan listened to these details with increasing interest; before Grimaud had finished he rose without noise and putting his mouth to Aramis's ear, and at the same time touching him on the shoulder to prevent a sudden movement:

"Chevalier," he said, "get up and don't make the least noise."

Aramis awoke. D'Artagnan, pressing his hand, repeated his call. Aramis obeyed.

"Athos is near you," said D'Artagnan; "warn him as I have warned you."

Aramis easily aroused Athos, whose sleep was light, like that of all persons of a finely organized constitution. But there was more difficulty in arousing Porthos. He was beginning to ask full explanation of that breaking in on his sleep, which was very annoying to him, when D'Artagnan, instead of explaining, closed his mouth with his hand.

Then our Gascon, extending his arms, drew to him the heads of his three friends till they almost touched one another.

"Friends," he said, "we must leave this craft at once or we are dead men."

"Bah!" said Athos, "are you still afraid?"

"Do you know who is captain of this vessel?"

"No."

"Captain Groslow."

The shudder of the three musketeers showed to D'Artagnan that his words began to make some impression on them.

"Groslow!" said Aramis; "the devil!

"Who is this Groslow?" asked Porthos. "I don't remember him."

"Groslow is the man who broke Parry's head and is now getting ready to break ours."

"Oh! oh!"

"And do you know who is his lieutenant?"

"His lieutenant? There is none," said Athos. "They don't have lieutenants in a felucca manned by a crew of four."

"Yes, but Monsieur Groslow is not a captain of the ordinary kind; he has a lieutenant, and that lieutenant is Monsieur Mordaunt."

This time the musketeers did more than shudder--they almost cried out. Those invincible men were subject to a mysterious and fatal influence which that name had over them; the mere sound of it filled them with terror.

"What shall we do?" said Athos.

"We must seize the felucca," said Aramis.

"And kill him," said Porthos.

"The felucca is mined," said D'Artagnan. "Those casks which I took for casks of port wine are filled with powder. When Mordaunt finds himself discovered he will destroy all, friends and foes; and on my word he would be bad company in going either to Heaven or to hell."

"You have some plan, then?" asked Athos.

"Yes."

"What is it?"

"Have you confidence in me?"

"Give your orders," said the three musketeers.

"Very well; come this way."

D'Artagnan went toward a very small, low window, just large enough to let a man through. He turned it gently on its hinges.

"There," he said, "is our road."

"The deuce! it is a very cold one, my dear friend," said Aramis.

"Stay here, if you like, but I warn you 'twill be rather too warm presently."

"But we cannot swim to the shore."

"The longboat is yonder, lashed to the felucca. We will take possession of it and cut the cable. Come, my friends."

"A moment's delay," said Athos; "our servants?"

"Here we are!" they cried.

Meantime the three friends were standing motionless before the awful sight which D'Artagnan, in raising the shutters, had disclosed to them through the narrow opening of the window.

Those who have once beheld such a spectacle know that there is nothing more solemn, more striking, than the raging sea, rolling, with its deafening roar, its dark billows beneath the pale light of a wintry moon.

"Gracious Heaven, we are hesitating!" cried D'Artagnan; "if we hesitate what will the servants do?"

"I do not hesitate, you know," said Grimaud.

"Sir," interposed Blaisois, "I warn you that I can only swim in rivers."

"And I not at all," said Mousqueton.

But D'Artagnan had now slipped through the window.

"You have decided, friend?" said Athos.

"Yes," the Gascon answered; "Athos! you, who are a perfect being, bid spirit triumph over body. Do you, Aramis, order the servants. Porthos, kill every one who stands in your way."

And after pressing the hand of Athos, D'Artagnan chose a moment when the ship rolled backward, so that he had only to plunge into the water, which was already up to his waist.

Athos followed him before the felucca rose again on the waves; the cable which tied the boat to the vessel was then seen plainly rising out of the sea.

D'Artagnan swam to it and held it, suspending himself by this rope, his head alone out of water.

In one second Athos joined him.

Then they saw, as the felucca turned, two other heads peeping, those of Aramis and Grimaud.

"I am uneasy about Blaisois," said Athos; "he can, he says, only swim in rivers."

"When people can swim at all they can swim anywhere. To the boat! to the boat!"

"But Porthos, I do not see him."

"Porthos is coming--he swims like Leviathan."

In fact, Porthos did not appear; for a scene, half tragedy and half comedy, had been performed by him with Mousqueton and Blaisois, who, frightened by the noise of the sea, by the whistling of the wind, by the sight of that dark water yawning like a gulf beneath them, shrank back instead of going forward.

"Come, come!" said Porthos; "jump in."

"But, monsieur," said Mousqueton, "I can't swim; let me stay here."

"And me, too, monsieur," said Blaisois.

"I assure you, I shall be very much in the way in that little boat," said Mousqueton.

"And I know I shall drown before reaching it," continued Blaisois.

"Come along! I shall strangle you both if you don't get out," said Porthos at last, seizing Mousqueton by the throat. "Forward, Blaisois!"

A groan, stifled by the grasp of Porthos, was all the reply of poor Blaisois, for the giant, taking him neck and heels, plunged him into the water headforemost, pushing him out of the window as if he had been a plank.

"Now, Mousqueton," he said, "I hope you don't mean to desert your master?"

"Ah, sir," replied Mousqueton, his eyes filling with tears, "why did you re-enter the army? We were all so happy in the Chateau de Pierrefonds!"

And without any other complaint, passive and obedient, either from true devotion to his master or from the example set by Blaisois, Mousqueton leaped into the sea headforemost. A sublime action, at all events, for Mousqueton looked upon himself as dead. But Porthos was not a man to abandon an old servant, and when Mousqueton rose above the water, blind as a new-born puppy, he found he was supported by the large hand of Porthos and that he was thus enabled, without having occasion even to move, to advance toward the cable with the dignity of a very triton.

In a few minutes Porthos had rejoined his companions, who were already in the boat; but when, after they had all got in, it came to his turn, there was great danger that in putting his huge leg over the edge of the boat he would upset the little vessel. Athos was the last to enter.

"Are you all here?" he asked.

"Ah! have you your sword, Athos?" cried D'Artagnan.

"Yes."

"Cut the cable, then."

Athos drew a sharp poniard from his belt and cut the cord. The felucca went on, the boat continued stationary, rocked only by the swashing waves.

"Come, Athos!" said D'Artagnan, giving his hand to the count; "you are going to see something curious," added the Gascon.

73. Fatality.

Scarcely had D'Artagnan uttered these words when a ringing and sudden noise was heard resounding through the felucca, which had now become dim in the obscurity of the night.

"That, you may be sure," said the Gascon, "means something."

They then at the same instant perceived a large lantern carried on a pole appear on the deck, defining the forms of shadows behind it.

Suddenly a terrible cry, a cry of despair, was wafted through space; and as if the shrieks of anguish had driven away the clouds, the veil which hid the moon was cleated away and the gray sails and dark shrouds of the felucca were plainly visible beneath the silvery light.

Shadows ran, as if bewildered, to and fro on the vessel, and mournful cries accompanied these delirious walkers. In the midst of these screams they saw Mordaunt upon the poop with a torch in hand.

The agitated figures, apparently wild with terror, consisted of Groslow, who at the hour fixed by Mordaunt had collected his men and the sailors. Mordaunt, after having listened at the door of the cabin to hear if the musketeers were still asleep, had gone down into the cellar, convinced by their silence that they were all in a deep slumber. Then he had run to the train, impetuous as a man who is excited by revenge, and full of confidence, as are those whom God blinds, he had set fire to the wick of nitre.

All this while Groslow and his men were assembled on deck.

"Haul up the cable and draw the boat to us," said Groslow.

One of the sailors got down the side of the ship, seized the cable, and drew it; it came without the least resistance.

"The cable is cut!" he cried, "no boat!"

"How! no boat!" exclaimed Groslow; "it is impossible."

"'Tis true, however," answered the sailor; "there's nothing in the wake of the ship; besides, here's the end of the cable."

"What's the matter?" cried Mordaunt, who, coming up out of the hatchway, rushed to the stern, waving his torch.

"Only that our enemies have escaped; they have cut the cord and gone off with the boat."

Mordaunt bounded with one step to the cabin and kicked open the door.

"Empty!" he exclaimed; "the infernal demons!"

"We must pursue them," said Groslow, "they can't be gone far, and we will sink them, passing over them."

"Yes, but the fire," ejaculated Mordaunt; "I have lighted it."

"Ten thousand devils!" cried Groslow, rushing to the hatchway; "perhaps there is still time to save us."

Mordaunt answered only by a terrible laugh, threw his torch into the sea and plunged in after it. The instant Groslow put his foot upon the hatchway steps the ship opened like the crater of a volcano. A burst of flame rose toward the skies with an explosion like that of a hundred cannon; the air burned, ignited by flaming embers, then the frightful lightning disappeared, the brands sank, one after another, into the abyss, where they were extinguished, and save for a slight vibration in the air, after a few minutes had elapsed one would have thought that nothing had happened.

Only--the felucca had disappeared from the surface of the sea and Groslow and his three sailors were consumed.

The four friends saw all this--not a single detail of this fearful scene escaped them. At one moment, bathed as they were in a flood of brilliant light, which illumined the sea for the space of a league, they might each be seen, each by his own peculiar attitude and manner expressing the awe which, even in their hearts of bronze, they could not help experiencing. Soon a torrent of vivid sparks fell around them--then, at last, the volcano was extinguished--then all was dark and still--the floating bark and heaving ocean.

They sat silent and dejected.

"By Heaven!" at last said Athos, the first to speak, "by this time, I think, all must be over."

"Here, my lords! save me! help!" cried a voice, whose mournful accents, reaching the four friends, seemed to proceed from some phantom of the ocean.

All looked around; Athos himself stared.

"'Tis he! it is his voice!"

All still remained silent, the eyes of all were turned in the direction where the vessel had disappeared, endeavoring in vain to penetrate the darkness. After a minute or two they were able to distinguish a man, who approached them, swimming vigorously.

Athos extended his arm toward him, pointing him out to his companions.

"Yes, yes, I see him well enough," said D'Artagnan.

"He--again!" cried Porthos, who was breathing like a blacksmith's bellows; "why, he is made of iron."

"Oh, my God!" muttered Athos.

Aramis and D'Artagnan whispered to each other.

Mordaunt made several strokes more, and raising his arm in sign of distress above the waves: "Pity, pity on me, gentlemen, in Heaven's name! my strength is failing me; I am dying."

The voice that implored aid was so piteous that it awakened pity in the heart of Athos.

"Poor fellow!" he exclaimed.

"Indeed!" said D'Artagnan, "monsters have only to complain to gain your sympathy. I believe he's swimming toward us. Does he think we are going to take him in? Row, Porthos, row." And setting the example he plowed his oar into the sea; two strokes took the bark on twenty fathoms further.

"Oh! you will not abandon me! You will not leave me to perish! You will not be pitiless!" cried Mordaunt.

"Ah! ah!" said Porthos to Mordaunt, "I think we have you now, my hero! and there are no doors by which you can escape this time but those of hell."

"Oh! Porthos!" murmured the Comte de la Fere.

"Oh, pray, for mercy's sake, don't fly from me. For pity's sake!" cried the young man, whose agony-drawn breath at times, when his head went under water, under the wave, exhaled and made the icy waters bubble.

D'Artagnan, however, who had consulted with Aramis, spoke to the poor wretch. "Go away," he said; "your repentance is too recent to inspire confidence. See! the vessel in which you wished to fry us is still smoking; and the situation in which you are is a bed of roses compared to that in which you wished to place us and in which you have placed Monsieur Groslow and his companions."

"Sir!" replied Mordaunt, in a tone of deep despair, "my penitence is sincere. Gentlemen, I am young, scarcely twenty-three years old. I was drawn on by a very natural resentment to avenge my mother. You would have done what I did."

Mordaunt wanted now only two or three fathoms to reach the boat, for the approach of death seemed to give him supernatural strength.

"Alas!" he said, "I am then to die? You are going to kill the son, as you killed the mother! Surely, if I am culpable and if I ask for pardon, I ought to be forgiven."

Then, as if his strength failed him, he seemed unable to sustain himself above the water and a wave passed over his head, which drowned his voice.

"Oh! this is torture to me," cried Athos.

Mordaunt reappeared.

"For my part," said D'Artagnan, "I say this must come to an end; murderer, as you were, of your uncle! executioner, as you were, of King Charles! incendiary! I recommend you to sink forthwith to the bottom of the sea; and if you come another fathom nearer, I'll stave your wicked head in with this oar."

"D'Artagnan! D'Artagnan!" cried Athos, "my son, I entreat you; the wretch is dying, and it is horrible to let a man die without extending a hand to save him. I cannot resist doing so; he must live."

"Zounds!" replied D'Artagnan, "why don't you give yourself up directly, feet and hands bound, to that wretch? Ah! Comte de la Fere, you wish to perish by his hands! I, your son, as you call me--I will not let you!"

'Twas the first time D'Artagnan had ever refused a request from Athos.

Aramis calmly drew his sword, which he had carried between his teeth as he swam.

"If he lays his hand on the boat's edge I will cut it off, regicide that he is."

"And I," said Porthos. "Wait."

"What are you going to do?" asked Aramis.

"Throw myself in the water and strangle him."

"Oh, gentlemen!" cried Athos, "be men! be Christians! See! death is depicted on his face! Ah! do not bring on me the horrors of remorse! Grant me this poor wretch's life. I will bless you--I----"

"I am dying!" cried Mordaunt, "come to me! come to me!"

D'Artagnan began to be touched. The boat at this moment turned around, and the dying man was by that turn brought nearer Athos.

"Monsieur the Comte de la Fere," he cried, "I supplicate you! pity me! I call on you--where are you? I see you no longer--I am dying--help me! help me!"

"Here I am, sir!" said Athos, leaning and stretching out his arm to Mordaunt with that air of dignity and nobility of soul habitual to him; "here I am, take my hand and jump into our boat."

Mordaunt made a last effort--rose--seized the hand thus extended to him and grasped it with the vehemence of despair.

"That's right," said Athos; "put your other hand here." And he offered him his shoulder as another stay and support, so that his head almost touched that of Mordaunt; and these two mortal enemies were in as close an embrace as if they had been brothers.

"Now, sir," said the count, "you are safe--calm yourself."

"Ah! my mother," cried Mordaunt, with eyes on fire with a look of hate impossible to paint, "I can only offer thee one victim, but it shall at any rate be the one thou wouldst thyself have chosen!"

And whilst D'Artagnan uttered a cry, Porthos raised the oar, and Aramis sought a place to strike, a frightful shake given to the boat precipitated Athos into the sea; whilst Mordaunt, with a shout of triumph, grasped the neck of his victim, and in order to paralyze his movements, twined arms and legs around the musketeer. For an instant, without an exclamation, without a cry for help, Athos tried to sustain himself on the surface of the waters, but the weight dragged him down; he disappeared by degrees; soon nothing was to be seen except his long, floating hair; then both men disappeared and the bubbling of the water, which, in its turn, was soon effaced, alone indicated the spot where these two had sunk.

Mute with horror, the three friends had remained open-mouthed, their eyes dilated, their arms extended like statues, and, motionless as they were, the beating of their hearts was audible. Porthos was the first who came to himself. He tore his hair.

"Oh!" he cried, "Athos! Athos! thou man of noble heart; woe is me! I have let thee perish!"

At this instant, in the midst of the silver circle illumined by the light of the moon the same whirlpool which had been made by the sinking men was again obvious, and first were seen, rising above the waves, a wisp of hair, then a pale face with open eyes, yet, nevertheless, the eyes of death; then a body, which, after rising of itself even to the waist above the sea, turned gently on its back, according to the caprice of the waves, and floated.

In the bosom of this corpse was plunged a poniard, the gold hilt of which shone in the moonbeams.

"Mordaunt! Mordaunt!" cried the three friends; "'tis Mordaunt!"

"But Athos!" exclaimed D'Artagnan.

Suddenly the boat leaned on one side beneath a new and unexpected weight and Grimaud uttered a shout of joy; every one turned around and beheld Athos, livid, his eyes dim and his hands trembling, supporting himself on the edge of the boat. Eight vigorous arms lifted him up immediately and laid him in the boat, where directly Athos was warmed and reanimated, reviving with the caresses and cares of his friends, who were intoxicated with joy.

"You are not hurt?" asked D'Artagnan.

"No," replied Athos; "and he----"

"Oh, he! now we may say at last, thank Heaven! he is really dead. Look!" and D'Artagnan, obliging Athos to look in the direction he pointed, showed him the body of Mordaunt floating on its back, which, sometimes submerged, sometimes rising, seemed still to pursue the four friends with looks of insult and mortal hatred.

At last he sank. Athos had followed him with a glance in which the deepest melancholy and pity were expressed.

"Bravo! Athos!" cried Aramis, with an emotion very rare in him.

"A capital blow you gave!" cried Porthos.

"I have a son. I wished to live," said Athos.

"In short," said D'Artagnan, "this has been the will of God."

"It was not I who killed him," said Athos in a soft, low tone, "'twas destiny."

74. How Mousqueton had a Narrow Escape of being eaten.

A deep silence reigned for a long time in the boat after the fearful scene described.

The moon, which had shone for a short time, disappeared behind the clouds; every object was again plunged in the obscurity that is so awful in the deserts and still more so in that liquid desert, the ocean, and nothing was heard save the whistling of the west wind driving along the tops of the crested billows.

Porthos was the first to speak.

"I have seen," he said, "many dreadful things, but nothing that ever agitated me so much as what I have just witnessed. Nevertheless, even in my present state of perturbation, I protest that I feel happy. I have a hundred pounds' weight less upon my chest. I breathe more freely." In fact, Porthos breathed so loud as to do credit to the free play of his powerful lungs.

"For my part," observed Aramis, "I cannot say the same as you do, Porthos. I am still terrified to such a degree that I scarcely believe my eyes. I look around the boat, expecting every moment to see that poor wretch holding between his hands the poniard plunged into his heart."

"Oh! I feel easy," replied Porthos. "The poniard was pointed at the sixth rib and buried up to the hilt in his body. I do not reproach you, Athos, for what you have done. On the contrary, when one aims a blow that is the regulation way to strike. So now, I breathe again--I am happy!"

"Don't be in haste to celebrate a victory, Porthos," interposed D'Artagnan; "never have we incurred a greater danger than we are now encountering. Men may subdue men--they cannot overcome the elements. We are now on the sea, at night, without any pilot, in a frail bark; should a blast of wind upset the boat we are lost."

Mousqueton heaved a deep sigh.

"You are ungrateful, D'Artagnan," said Athos; "yes, ungrateful to Providence, to whom we owe our safety in the most miraculous manner. Let us sail before the wind, and unless it changes we shall be drifted either to Calais or Boulogne. Should our bark be upset we are five of us good swimmers, able enough to turn it over again, or if not, to hold on by it. Now we are on the very road which all the vessels between Dover and Calais take, 'tis impossible but that we should meet with a fisherman who will pick us up."

"But should we not find any fisherman and should the wind shift to the north?"

"That," said Athos, "would be quite another thing; and we should nevermore see land until we were upon the other side of the Atlantic."

"Which implies that we may die of hunger," said Aramis.

"'Tis more than possible," answered the Comte de la Fere.

Mousqueton sighed again, more deeply than before.

"What is the matter? what ails you?" asked Porthos.

"I am cold, sir," said Mousqueton.

"Impossible! your body is covered with a coating of fat which preserves it from the cold air."

"Ah! sir, 'tis this very coating of fat that makes me shiver."

"How is that, Mousqueton?

"Alas! your honor, in the library of the Chateau of Bracieux there are a lot of books of travels."

"What then?"

"Amongst them the voyages of Jean Mocquet in the time of Henry IV."

"Well?"

"In these books, your honor, 'tis told how hungry voyagers, drifting out to sea, have a bad habit of eating each other and beginning with----"

"The fattest among them!" cried D'Artagnan, unable in spite of the gravity of the occasion to help laughing.

"Yes, sir," answered Mousqueton; "but permit me to say I see nothing laughable in it. However," he added, turning to Porthos, "I should not regret dying, sir, were I sure that by doing so I might still be useful to you."

"Mouston," replied Porthos, much affected, "should we ever see my castle of Pierrefonds again you shall have as your own and for your descendants the vineyard that surrounds the farm."

"And you should call it 'Devotion,'" added Aramis; "the vineyard of self-sacrifice, to transmit to latest ages the recollection of your devotion to your master."

"Chevalier," said D'Artagnan, laughing, "you could eat a piece of Mouston, couldn't you, especially after two or three days of fasting?"

"Oh, no," replied Aramis, "I should much prefer Blaisois; we haven't known him so long."

One may readily conceive that during these jokes which were intended chiefly to divert Athos from the scene which had just taken place, the servants, with the exception of Grimaud, were not silent. Suddenly Mousqueton uttered a cry of delight, taking from beneath one of the benches a bottle of wine; and on looking more closely in the same place he discovered a dozen similar bottles, bread, and a monster junk of salted beef.

"Oh, sir!" he cried, passing the bottle to Porthos, "we are saved--the bark is supplied with provisions."

This intelligence restored every one save Athos to gayety.

"Zounds!" exclaimed Porthos, "'tis astonishing how empty violent agitation makes the stomach."

And he drank off half a bottle at a draught and bit great mouthfuls of the bread and meat.

"Now," said Athos, "sleep, or try to sleep, my friends, and I will watch."

In a few moments, notwithstanding their wet clothes, the icy blast that blew and the previous scene of terror, these hardy adventurers, with their iron frames, inured to every hardship, threw themselves down, intending to profit by the advice of Athos, who sat at the helm, pensively wakeful, guiding the little bark the way it was to go, his eyes fixed on the heavens, as if he sought to verify not only the road to France, but the benign aspect of protecting Providence. After some hours of repose the sleepers were aroused by Athos.

Dawn was shedding its pallid, placid glimmer on the purple ocean, when at the distance of a musket shot from them was seen a dark gray mass, above which gleamed a triangular sail; then masters and servants joined in a fervent cry to the crew of that vessel to hear them and to save.

"A bark!" all cried together.

It was, in fact, a small craft from Dunkirk bound for Boulogne.

A quarter of an hour afterward the rowboat of this craft took them all aboard. Grimaud tendered twenty guineas to the captain, and at nine o'clock in the morning, having a fair wind, our Frenchmen set foot on their native land.

"Egad! how strong one feels here!" said Porthos, almost burying his large feet in the sands. "Zounds! I could defy a nation!"

"Be quiet, Porthos," said D'Artagnan, "we are observed."

"We are admired, i'faith," answered Porthos.

"These people who are looking at us are only merchants," said Athos, "and are looking more at the cargo than at us."

"I shall not trust to that," said the lieutenant, "and I shall make for the Dunes[1] as soon as possible."

The party followed him and soon disappeared with him behind the hillocks of sand unobserved. Here, after a short conference, they proposed to separate.

"And why separate?" asked Athos.

"Because," answered the Gascon, "we were sent, Porthos and I, by Cardinal Mazarin to fight for Cromwell; instead of fighting for Cromwell we have served Charles I.--not the same thing by any means. In returning with the Comte de la Fere and Monsieur d'Herblay our crime would be confirmed. We have circumvented Cromwell, Mordaunt, and the sea, but we shall find a certain difficulty in circumventing Mazarin."

"You forget," replied Athos, "that we consider ourselves your prisoners and not free from the engagement we entered into."

"Truly, Athos," interrupted D'Artagnan, "I am vexed that such a man as you are should talk nonsense which schoolboys would be ashamed of. Chevalier," he continued, addressing Aramis, who, leaning proudly on his sword, seemed to agree with his companion, "Chevalier, Porthos and I run no risk; besides, should any ill-luck happen to two of us, will it not be much better that the other two should be spared to assist those who may be apprehended? Besides, who knows whether, divided, we may not obtain a pardon--you from the queen, we from Mazarin--which, were we all four together, would never be granted. Come, Athos and Aramis, go to the

[1] Sandy hills about Dunkirk, from which it derives its name.

right; Porthos, come with me to the left; these gentlemen should file off into Normandy, whilst we, by the nearest road, reach Paris."

He then gave his friends minute directions as to their route.

"Ah! my dear friend," exclaimed Athos, "how I should admire the resources of your mind did I not stop to adore those of your heart."

And he gave him his hand.

"Isn't this fox a genius, Athos?" asked the Gascon. "No! he knows how to crunch fowls, to dodge the huntsman and to find his way home by day or by night, that's all. Well, is all said?"

"All."

"Then let's count our money and divide it. Ah! hurrah! there's the sun! A merry morning to you, Sunshine. 'Tis a long time since I saw thee!"

"Come, come, D'Artagnan," said Athos, "do not affect to be strong-minded; there are tears in your eyes. Let us be open with each other and sincere."

"What!" cried the Gascon, "do you think, Athos, we can take leave, calmly, of two friends at a time not free from danger to you and Aramis?"

"No," answered Athos; "embrace me, my son."

"Zounds!" said Porthos, sobbing, "I believe I'm crying; but how foolish all this is!"

Then they embraced. At that moment their fraternal bond of union was closer than ever, and when they parted, each to take the route agreed on, they turned back to utter affectionate expressions, which the echoes of the Dunes repeated. At last they lost sight of each other.

"Sacrebleu! D'Artagnan," said Porthos, "I must out with it at once, for I can't keep to myself anything I have against you; I haven't been able to recognize you in this matter."

"Why not?" said D'Artagnan, with his wise smile.

"Because if, as you say, Athos and Aramis are in real danger, this is not the time to abandon them. For my part, I confess to you that I was all ready to follow them and am still ready to rejoin them, in spite of all the Mazarins in the world."

"You would be right, Porthos, but for one thing, which may change the current of your ideas; and that is, that it is not those gentlemen who are in the greatest danger, it is ourselves; it is not to abandon them that we have separated, but to avoid compromising them."

"Really?" said Porthos, opening his eyes in astonishment.

"Yes, no doubt. If they are arrested they will only be put in the Bastile; if we are arrested it is a matter of the Place de Greve."

"Oh! oh!" said Porthos, "there is quite a gap between that fate and the baronial coronet you promised me, D'Artagnan."

"Bah! perhaps not so great as you think, Porthos; you know the proverb, 'All roads lead to Rome.'"

"But how is it that we are incurring greater risks than Athos and Aramis?" asked Porthos.

"Because they have but fulfilled the mission confided to them by Queen Henrietta and we have betrayed that confided to us by Mazarin; because, going hence as emissaries to Cromwell, we became partisans of King Charles; because, instead of helping cut off the royal head condemned by those fellows called Mazarin, Cromwell, Joyce, Bridge, Fairfax, etc., we very nearly succeeded in saving it."

"Upon my word that is true," said Porthos; "but how can you suppose, my dear friend, that in the midst of his great preoccupations General Cromwell has had time to think----"

"Cromwell thinks of everything; Cromwell has time for everything; and believe me, dear friend, we ought not to lose our time--it is precious. We shall not be safe till we have seen Mazarin, and then----"

"The devil!" said Porthos; "what can we say to Mazarin?"

"Leave that to me--I have my plan. He laughs best who laughs last. Cromwell is mighty, Mazarin is tricky, but I would rather have to do with them than with the late Monsieur Mordaunt."

"Ah!" said Porthos, "it is very pleasant to be able to say 'the late Monsieur Mordaunt.'"

"My faith, yes," said D'Artagnan. "But we must be going."

The two immediately started across country toward the road to Paris, followed by Mousqueton, who, after being too cold all night, at the end of a quarter of an hour found himself too warm.

75. The Return.

During the six weeks that Athos and Aramis had been absent from France, the Parisians, finding themselves one morning without either queen or king, were greatly annoyed at being thus deserted, and the absence of Mazarin, a thing so long desired, did not compensate for that of the two august fugitives.

The first feeling that pervaded Paris on hearing of the flight to Saint Germain, was that sort of affright which seizes children when they awake in the night and find themselves alone. A deputation was therefore sent to the queen to entreat her to return to Paris; but she not only declined to receive the deputies, but sent an intimation by Chancellor Seguier, implying that if the parliament did not humble itself before her majesty by negativing all the questions that had been the cause of the quarrel, Paris would be besieged the very next day.

This threatening answer, unluckily for the court, produced quite a different effect to that which was intended. It wounded the pride of the parliament, which, supported by the citizens, replied by declaring that Cardinal Mazarin was the cause of all the discontent; denounced him as the enemy both of the king and the state, and ordered him to retire from the court that same day and from France within a week afterward; enjoining, in case of disobedience on his part, all the subjects of the king to pursue and take him.

Mazarin being thus placed beyond the pale of the protection of the law, preparations on both sides were commenced--by the queen, to attack Paris, by the citizens, to defend it. The latter were occupied in breaking up the pavement and stretching chains across the streets, when, headed by the coadjutor, appeared the Prince de Conti (the brother of the Prince de Conde) and the Duc de Longueville, his brother-in-law. This unexpected band of auxiliaries arrived in Paris on the tenth of January and the Prince of Conti was named, but not until after a stormy discussion, generalissimo of the army of the king, out of Paris.

As for the Duc de Beaufort, he arrived from Vendome, according to the annals of the day, bringing with him his high bearing and his long and beautiful hair, qualifications which gained him the sovereignty of the marketplaces.

The Parisian army had organized with the promptness characteristic of the bourgeois whenever they are moved by any sentiment whatever to disguise themselves as soldiers. On the nineteenth the impromptu army had attempted a sortie, more to assure itself and others of its actual existence than with any more serious intention. They carried a banner, on which could be read this strange device: "We are seeking our king."

The next following days were occupied in trivial movements which resulted only in the carrying off of a few herds of cattle and the burning of two or three houses.

That was still the situation of affairs up to the early days of February. On the first day of that month our four companions had landed at Boulogne, and, in two parties, had set out for Paris. Toward the end of the fourth day of the journey Athos and Aramis reached Nanterre, which place they cautiously passed by on the outskirts, fearing that they might encounter some troop from the queen's army.

It was against his will that Athos took these precautions, but Aramis had very judiciously reminded him that they had no right to be imprudent, that they had been charged by King Charles with a supreme and sacred mission, which, received at the foot of the scaffold, could be accomplished only at the feet of Queen Henrietta. Upon that, Athos yielded.

On reaching the capital Athos and Aramis found it in arms. The sentinel at the gate refused even to let them pass, and called his sergeant.

The sergeant, with the air of importance which such people assume when they are clad with military dignity, said:

"Who are you, gentlemen?"

"Two gentlemen."

"And where do you come from?"

"From London."

"And what are you going to do in Paris?"

"We are going with a mission to Her Majesty, the Queen of England."

"Ah, every one seems to be going to see the queen of England. We have already at the station three gentlemen whose passports are under examination, who are on their way to her majesty. Where are your passports?"

"We have none; we left England, ignorant of the state of politics here, having left Paris before the departure of the king."

"Ah!" said the sergeant, with a cunning smile, "you are Mazarinists, who are sent as spies."

"My dear friend," here Athos spoke, "rest assured, if we were Mazarinists we should come well prepared with every sort of passport. In your situation distrust those who are well provided with every formality."

"Enter the guardroom," said the sergeant; "we will lay your case before the commandant of the post."

The guardroom was filled with citizens and common people, some playing, some drinking, some talking. In a corner, almost hidden from view, were three gentlemen, who had preceded Athos and Aramis, and an officer was examining their passports. The first impulse of these three, and of those who last entered, was to cast an inquiring glance at each other. The first arrivals wore long cloaks, in whose drapery they were carefully enveloped; one of them, shorter than the rest, remained pertinaciously in the background.

When the sergeant on entering the room announced that in all probability he was bringing in two Mazarinists, it appeared to be the unanimous opinion of the officers on guard that they ought not to pass.

"Be it so," said Athos; "yet it is probable, on the contrary, that we shall enter, because we seem to have to do with sensible people. There seems to be only one thing to do, which is, to send our names to Her Majesty the Queen of England, and if she engages to answer for us I presume we shall be allowed to enter."

On hearing these words the shortest of the other three men seemed more attentive than ever to what was going on, wrapping his cloak around him more carefully than before.

"Merciful goodness!" whispered Aramis to Athos, "did you see?"

"What?" asked Athos.

"The face of the shortest of those three gentlemen?"

"No."

"He looked to me--but 'tis impossible."

At this instant the sergeant, who had been for his orders, returned, and pointing to the three gentlemen in cloaks, said:

"The passports are in order; let these three gentlemen pass."

The three gentlemen bowed and hastened to take advantage of this permission.

Aramis looked after them, and as the last of them passed close to him he pressed the hand of Athos.

"What is the matter with you, my friend?" asked the latter.

"I have--doubtless I am dreaming; tell me, sir," he said to the sergeant, "do you know those three gentlemen who are just gone out?"

"Only by their passports; they are three Frondists, who are gone to rejoin the Duc de Longueville."

"'Tis strange," said Aramis, almost involuntarily; "I fancied that I recognized Mazarin himself."

The sergeant burst into a fit of laughter.

"He!" he cried; "he venture himself amongst us, to be hung! Not so foolish as all that."

"Ah!" muttered Athos, "I may be mistaken, I haven't the unerring eye of D'Artagnan."

"Who is speaking of Monsieur D'Artagnan?" asked an officer who appeared at that moment upon the threshold of the room.

"What!" cried Aramis and Athos, "what! Planchet!"

"Planchet," added Grimaud; "Planchet, with a gorget, indeed!"

"Ah, gentlemen!" cried Planchet, "so you are back again in Paris. Oh, how happy you make us! no doubt you come to join the princes!"

"As thou seest, Planchet," said Aramis, whilst Athos smiled on seeing what important rank was held in the city militia by the former comrade of Mousqueton, Bazin and Grimaud.

"And Monsieur d'Artagnan, of whom you spoke just now, Monsieur d'Herblay; may I ask if you have any news of him?"

"We parted from him four days ago and we have reason to believe that he has reached Paris before us."

"No, sir; I am sure he hasn't yet arrived. But then he may have stopped at Saint Germain."

"I don't think so; we appointed to meet at La Chevrette."

"I was there this very day."

"And had the pretty Madeleine no news?" asked Aramis, smiling.

"No, sir, and it must be admitted that she seemed very anxious."

"In fact," said Aramis, "there is no time lost and we made our journey quickly. Permit me, then, my dear Athos, without inquiring further about our friend, to pay my respects to M. Planchet."

"Ah, monsieur le chevalier," said Planchet, bowing.

"Lieutenant?" asked Aramis.

"Lieutenant, with a promise of becoming captain."

"'Tis capital; and pray, how did you acquire all these honors?"

"In the first place, gentlemen, you know that I was the means of Monsieur de Rochefort's escape; well, I was very near being hung by Mazarin and that made me more popular than ever."

"So, owing to your popularity----"

"No; thanks to something better. You know, gentlemen, that I served the Piedmont regiment and had the honor of being a sergeant?"

"Yes."

"Well, one day when no one could drill a mob of citizens, who began to march, some with the right foot, others with the left, I succeeded, I did, in making them all begin with the same foot, and I was made lieutenant on the spot."

"So I presume," said Athos, "that you have a large number of the nobles with you?"

"Certainly. There are the Prince de Conti, the Duc de Longueville, the Duc de Beaufort, the Duc de Bouillon, the Marechal de la Mothe, the Marquis de Sevigne, and I don't know who, for my part."

"And the Vicomte Raoul de Bragelonne?" inquired Athos, in a tremulous voice. "D'Artagnan told me that he had recommended him to your care, in parting."

"Yes, count; nor have I lost sight of him for a single instant since."

"Then," said Athos in a tone of delight, "he is well? no accident has happened to him?"

"None, sir."

"And he lives?"

"Still at the Hotel of the Great Charlemagne."

"And passes his time?"

"Sometimes with the queen of England, sometimes with Madame de Chevreuse. He and the Count de Guiche are like each other's shadows."

"Thanks, Planchet, thanks!" cried Athos, extending his hand to the lieutenant.

"Oh, sir!" Planchet only touched the tips of the count's fingers.

"Well, what are you doing, count--to a former lackey?

"My friend," said Athos, "he has given me news of Raoul."

"And now, gentlemen," said Planchet, who had not heard what they were saying, "what do you intend to do?"

"Re-enter Paris, if you will let us, my good Planchet."

"Let you, sir? Now, as ever, I am nothing but your servant." Then turning to his men:

"Allow these gentlemen to pass," he said; "they are friends of the Duc de Beaufort."

"Long live the Duc de Beaufort!" cried the sentinels.

The sergeant drew near to Planchet.

"What! without passports?" he murmured.

"Without passports," said Planchet.

"Take notice, captain," he continued, giving Planchet his expected title, "take notice that one of the three men who just now went out from here told me privately to distrust these gentlemen."

"And I," said Planchet, with dignity, "I know them and I answer for them."

As he said this, he pressed Grimaud's hand, who seemed honored by the distinction.

"Farewell till we meet again," said Aramis, as they took leave of Planchet; "if anything happens to us we shall blame you for it."

"Sir," said Planchet, "I am in all things at your service."

"That fellow is no fool," said Aramis, as he got on his horse.

"How should he be?" replied Athos, whilst mounting also, "seeing he was used so long to brush your hats."

76. The Ambassadors.

The two friends rode rapidly down the declivity of the Faubourg, but on arriving at the bottom were surprised to find that the streets of Paris had become rivers, and the open places lakes; after the great rains which fell in January the Seine had overflowed its banks and the river inundated half the capital. The two gentlemen were obliged, therefore, to get off their horses and take a boat; and in that strange manner they approached the Louvre.

Night had closed in, and Paris, seen thus, by the light of lanterns flickering on the pools of water, crowded with ferry-boats of every kind, including those that glittered with the armed patrols, with the watchword, passing from post to post--Paris presented such an aspect as to strongly seize the senses of Aramis, a man most susceptible to warlike impressions.

They reached the queen's apartments, but were compelled to stop in the ante-chamber, since her majesty was at that moment giving audience to gentlemen bringing her news from England.

"We, too," said Athos, to the footman who had given him that answer, "not only bring news from England, but have just come from there."

"What? then, are your names, gentlemen?"

"The Comte de la Fere and the Chevalier d'Herblay," said Aramis.

"Ah! in that case, gentlemen," said the footman, on hearing the names which the queen had so often pronounced with hope, "in that case it is another thing, and I think her majesty will pardon me for not keeping you here a moment. Please follow me," and he went on before, followed by Athos and Aramis.

On arriving at the door of the room where the queen was receiving he made a sign for them to wait and opening the door:

"Madame," he said, "I hope your majesty will forgive me for disobeying your orders, when you learn that the gentlemen I have come to announce are the Comte de la Fere and the Chevalier d'Herblay."

On hearing those two names the queen uttered a cry of joy, which the two gentlemen heard.

"Poor queen!" murmured Athos.

"Oh, let them come in! let them come in," cried the young princess, bounding to the door.

The poor child was constant in her attendance on her mother and sought by her filial attentions to make her forget the absence of her two sons and her other daughter.

"Come in, gentlemen," repeated the princess, opening the door herself.

The queen was seated on a fauteuil and before her were standing two or three gentlemen, and among them the Duc de Chatillon, the brother of the nobleman killed eight or nine years previously in a duel on account of Madame de Longueville, on the Place Royale. All these gentlemen had been noticed by Athos and Aramis in the guardhouse, and when the two friends were announced they started and exchanged some words in a low tone. "Well, sirs!" cried the queen, on perceiving the two friends, "you have come, faithful friends! But the royal couriers have been more expeditious than you, and here are Monsieur de Flamarens and Monsieur de Chatillon, who bring me from Her Majesty the Queen Anne of Austria, the very latest intelligence."

Aramis and Athos were astounded by the calmness, even the gayety of the queen's manner.

"Go on with your recital, sirs," said the queen, turning to the Duc de Chatillon. "You said that His Majesty, King Charles, my august consort, had been condemned to death by a majority of his subjects!"

"Yes, madame," Chatillon stammered out.

Athos and Aramis were more and more astonished.

"And that being conducted to the scaffold," resumed the queen--"oh, my lord! oh, my king!--and that being led to the scaffold he had been saved by an indignant people."

"Just so madame," replied Chatillon, in so low a voice that though the two friends were listening eagerly they could hardly hear this affirmation.

The queen clasped her hands in enthusiastic gratitude, whilst her daughter threw her arms around her mother's neck and kissed her--her own eyes streaming with tears.

"Now, madame, nothing remains to me except to proffer my respectful homage," said Chatillon, who felt confused and ashamed beneath the stern gaze of Athos.

"One moment, yes," answered the queen. "One moment--I beg--for here are the Chevalier d'Herblay and the Comte de la Fere, just arrived from London, and they can give you, as eye-witnesses, such details as you can convey to the queen, my royal sister. Speak, gentlemen, speak--I am listening; conceal nothing, gloss over nothing. Since his majesty still lives, since the honor of the throne is safe, everything else is a matter of indifference to me."

Athos turned pale and laid his hand on his heart.

"Well!" exclaimed the queen, who remarked this movement and his paleness. "Speak, sir! I beg you to do so."

"I beg you to excuse me, madame; I wish to add nothing to the recital of these gentlemen until they perceive themselves that they have perhaps been mistaken."

"Mistaken!" cried the queen, almost suffocated by emotion; "mistaken! what has happened, then?"

"Sir," interposed Monsieur de Flamarens to Athos, "if we are mistaken the error has originated with the queen. I do not suppose you will have the presumption to set it to rights--that would be to accuse Her Majesty, Queen Anne, of falsehood."

"With the queen, sir?" replied Athos, in his calm, vibrating voice.

"Yes," murmured Flamarens, lowering his eyes.

Athos sighed deeply.

"Or rather, sir," said Aramis, with his peculiar irritating politeness, "the error of the person who was with you when we met you in the guardroom; for if the Comte de la Fere and I are not mistaken, we saw you in the company of a third gentleman."

Chatillon and Flamarens started.

"Explain yourself, count!" cried the queen, whose anxiety grew greater every moment. "On your brow I read despair--your lips falter ere you announce some terrible tidings--your hands tremble. Oh, my God! my God! what has happened?"

"Lord!" ejaculated the young princess, falling on her knees, "have mercy on us!"

"Sir," said Chatillon, "if you bring bad tidings it will be cruel in you to announce them to the queen."

Aramis went so close to Chatillon as almost to touch him.

"Sir," said he, with compressed lips and flashing eyes, "you have not the presumption to instruct the Comte de la Fere and myself what we ought to say here?"

During this brief altercation Athos, with his hands on his heart, his head bent low, approached the queen and in a voice of deepest sorrow said:

"Madame, princes--who by nature are above other men--receive from Heaven courage to support greater misfortunes than those of lower rank, for their hearts are elevated as their fortunes. We ought not, therefore, I think, to act toward a queen so illustrious as your majesty as we should act toward a woman of our lowlier condition. Queen, destined as you are to endure every sorrow on this earth, hear the result of our unhappy mission."

Athos, kneeling down before the queen, trembling and very cold, drew from his bosom, inclosed in the same case, the order set in diamonds which the queen had given to Lord de Winter and the wedding ring which Charles I. before his death had placed in the hands of Aramis. Since the moment he had first received these two mementoes Athos had never parted with them.

He opened the case and offered them to the queen with deep and silent anguish.

The queen stretched out her hand, seized the ring, pressed it convulsively to her lips--and without being able to breathe a sigh, to give vent to a sob, she extended her arms, became deadly pale, and fell senseless in the arms of her attendants and her daughter.

Athos kissed the hem of the robe of the widowed queen and rising, with a dignity that made a deep impression on those around:

"I, the Comte de la Fere, a gentleman who has never deceived any human being, swear before God and before this unhappy queen, that all that was possible to save the king of England was done whilst we were on English ground. Now, chevalier," he added, turning to Aramis, "let us go. Our duty is fulfilled."

"Not yet." said Aramis; "we have still a word to say to these gentlemen."

And turning to Chatillon: "Sir, be so good as not to go away without giving me an opportunity to tell you something I cannot say before the queen."

Chatillon bowed in token of assent and they all went out, stopping at the window of a gallery on the ground floor.

"Sir," said Aramis, "you allowed yourself just now to treat us in a most extraordinary manner. That would not be endurable in any case, and is still less so on the part of those who came to bring the queen the message of a liar."

"Sir!" cried De Chatillon.

"What have you done with Monsieur de Bruy? Has he by any possibility gone to change his face which was too like that of Monsieur de Mazarin? There is an abundance of Italian masks at the Palais Royal, from harlequin even to pantaloon."

"Chevalier! chevalier!" said Athos.

"Leave me alone," said Aramis impatiently. "You know well that I don't like to leave things half finished."

"Conclude, then, sir," answered De Chatillon, with as much hauteur as Aramis.

"Gentlemen," resumed Aramis, "any one but the Comte de la Fere and myself would have had you arrested--for we have friends in Paris--but we are contented with another course. Come and converse with us for just five minutes, sword in hand, upon this deserted terrace."

"One moment, gentlemen," cried Flamarens. "I know well that the proposition is tempting, but at present it is impossible to accept it."

"And why not?" said Aramis, in his tone of raillery. "Is it Mazarin's proximity that makes you so prudent?"

"Oh, you hear that, Flamarens!" said Chatillon. "Not to reply would be a blot on my name and my honor."

"That is my opinion," said Aramis.

"You will not reply, however, and these gentlemen, I am sure, will presently be of my opinion."

Aramis shook his head with a motion of indescribable insolence.

Chatillon saw the motion and put his hand to his sword.

"Willingly," replied De Chatillon.

"Duke," said Flamarens, "you forget that to-morrow you are to command an expedition of the greatest importance, projected by the prince, assented to by the queen. Until to-morrow evening you are not at your own disposal."

"Let it be then the day after to-morrow," said Aramis.

"To-morrow, rather," said De Chatillon, "if you will take the trouble of coming so far as the gates of Charenton."

"How can you doubt it, sir? For the pleasure of a meeting with you I would go to the end of the world."

"Very well, to-morrow, sir."

"I shall rely on it. Are you going to rejoin your cardinal? Swear first, on your honor, not to inform him of our return."

"Conditions?"

"Why not?"

"Because it is for victors to make conditions, and you are not yet victors, gentlemen."

"Then let us draw on the spot. It is all one to us--to us who do not command to-morrow's expedition."

Chatillon and Flamarens looked at each other. There was such irony in the words and in the bearing of Aramis that the duke had great difficulty in bridling his anger, but at a word from Flamarens he restrained himself and contented himself with saying:

"You promise, sir--that's agreed--that I shall find you to-morrow at Charenton?"

"Oh, don't be afraid, sir," replied Aramis; and the two gentlemen shortly afterward left the Louvre.

"For what reason is all this fume and fury?" asked Athos. "What have they done to you?"

"They--did you not see what they did?"

"No."

"They laughed when we swore that we had done our duty in England. Now, if they believed us, they laughed in order to insult us; if they did not believe it they insulted us all the more. However, I'm glad not to fight them until to-morrow. I hope we shall have something better to do to-night than to draw the sword."

"What have we to do?"

"Egad! to take Mazarin."

Athos curled his lip with disdain.

"These undertakings do not suit me, as you know, Aramis."

"Why?"

"Because it is taking people unawares."

"Really, Athos, you would make a singular general. You would fight only by broad daylight, warn your foe before an attack, and never attempt anything by night lest you should be accused of taking advantage of the darkness."

Athos smiled.

"You know one cannot change his nature," he said. "Besides, do you know what is our situation, and whether Mazarin's arrest wouldn't be rather an encumbrance than an advantage?"

"Say at once you disapprove of my proposal."

"I think you ought to do nothing, since you exacted a promise from these gentlemen not to let Mazarin know that we were in France."

"I have entered into no engagement and consider myself quite free. Come, come."

"Where?"

"Either to seek the Duc de Beaufort or the Duc de Bouillon, and to tell them about this."

"Yes, but on one condition--that we begin by the coadjutor. He is a priest, learned in cases of conscience, and we will tell him ours."

It was then agreed that they were to go first to Monsieur de Bouillon, as his house came first; but first of all Athos begged that he might go to the Hotel du Grand Charlemagne, to see Raoul.

They re-entered the boat which had brought them to the Louvre and thence proceeded to the Halles; and taking up Grimaud and Blaisois, they went on foot to the Rue Guenegaud.

But Raoul was not at the Hotel du Grand Charlemagne. He had received a message from the prince, to whom he had hastened with Olivain the instant he had received it.

77. The three Lieutenants of the Generalissimo.

The night was dark, but still the town resounded with those noises that disclose a city in a state of siege. Athos and Aramis did not proceed a hundred steps without being stopped by sentinels placed before the barricades, who demanded the watchword; and on their saying that they were going to Monsieur de Bouillon on a mission of importance a guide was given them under pretext of conducting them, but in fact as a spy over their movements.

On arriving at the Hotel de Bouillon they came across a little troop of three cavaliers, who seemed to know every possible password; for they walked without either guide or escort, and on arriving at the barricades had nothing to do but to speak to those who guarded them, who instantly let them pass with evident deference, due probably to their high birth.

On seeing them Athos and Aramis stood still.

"Oh!" cried Aramis, "do you see, count?"

"Yes," said Athos.

"Who do these three cavaliers appear to you to be?"

"What do you think, Aramis?"

"Why, they are our men."

"You are not mistaken; I recognize Monsieur de Flamarens."

"And I, Monsieur de Chatillon."

"As to the cavalier in the brown cloak----"

"It is the cardinal."

"In person."

"How the devil do they venture so near the Hotel de Bouillon?"

Athos smiled, but did not reply. Five minutes afterward they knocked at the prince's door.

This door was guarded by a sentinel and there was also a guard placed in the courtyard, ready to obey the orders of the Prince de Conti's lieutenant.

Monsieur de Bouillon had the gout, but notwithstanding his illness, which had prevented his mounting on horseback for the last month---that is, since Paris had been besieged--he was ready to receive the Comte de la Fere and the Chevalier d'Herblay.

He was in bed, but surrounded with all the paraphernalia of war. Everywhere were swords, pistols, cuirasses, and arquebuses, and it was plain that as soon as his gout was better Monsieur de Bouillon would give a pretty tangle to the enemies of the parliament to unravel. Meanwhile, to his great regret, as he said, he was obliged to keep his bed.

"Ah, gentlemen," he cried, as the two friends entered, "you are very happy! you can ride, you can go and come and fight for the cause of the people. But I, as you see, am nailed to my bed--ah! this demon, gout--this demon, gout!"

"My lord," said Athos, "we are just arrived from England and our first concern is to inquire after your health."

"Thanks, gentlemen, thanks! As you see, my health is but indifferent. But you come from England. And King Charles is well, as I have just heard?"

"He is dead, my lord!" said Aramis.

"Pooh!" said the duke, too much astonished to believe it true.

"Dead on the scaffold; condemned by parliament."

"Impossible!"

"And executed in our presence."

"What, then, has Monsieur de Flamarens been telling me?"

"Monsieur de Flamarens?"

"Yes, he has just gone out."

Athos smiled. "With two companions?" he said.

"With two companions, yes," replied the duke. Then he added with a certain uneasiness, "Did you meet them?"

"Why, yes, I think so--in the street," said Athos; and he looked smilingly at Aramis, who looked at him with an expression of surprise.

"The devil take this gout!" cried Monsieur de Bouillon, evidently ill at ease.

"My lord," said Athos, "we admire your devotion to the cause you have espoused, in remaining at the head of the army whilst so ill, in so much pain."

"One must," replied Monsieur de Bouillon, "sacrifice one's comfort to the public good; but I confess to you I am now almost exhausted. My spirit is willing, my head is clear, but this demon, the gout, o'ercrows me. I confess, if the court would do justice to my claims and give the head of my house the title of prince, and if my brother De Turenne were reinstated in his command I would return to my estates and leave the court and parliament to settle things between themselves as they might."

"You are perfectly right, my lord."

"You think so? At this very moment the court is making overtures to me; hitherto I have repulsed them; but since such men as you assure me that I am wrong in doing so, I've a good mind to follow your advice and to accept a proposition made to me by the Duc de Chatillon just now."

"Accept it, my lord, accept it," said Aramis.

"Faith! yes. I am even sorry that this evening I almost repulsed--but there will be a conference to-morrow and we shall see."

The two friends saluted the duke.

"Go, gentlemen," he said; "you must be much fatigued after your voyage. Poor King Charles! But, after all, he was somewhat to blame in all that business and we may console ourselves with the reflection that France has no cause of reproach in the matter and did all she could to serve him."

"Oh! as to that," said Aramis, "we are witnesses. Mazarin especially----"

"Yes, do you know, I am very glad to hear you give that testimony; the cardinal has some good in him, and if he were not a foreigner--well, he would be more justly estimated. Oh! the devil take this gout!"

Athos and Aramis took their leave, but even in the ante-chamber they could still hear the duke's cries; he was evidently suffering the tortures of the damned.

When they reached the street, Aramis said:

"Well, Athos, what do you think?"

"Of whom?"

"Pardieu! of Monsieur de Bouillon."

"My friend, I think that he is much troubled with gout."

"You noticed that I didn't breathe a word as to the purpose of our visit?"

"You did well; you would have caused him an access of his disease. Let us go to Monsieur de Beaufort."

The two friends went to the Hotel de Vendome. It was ten o'clock when they arrived. The Hotel de Vendome was not less guarded than the Hotel de Bouillon, and presented as warlike an appearance. There were sentinels, a guard in the court, stacks of arms, and horses saddled. Two horsemen going out as Athos and Aramis entered were obliged to give place to them.

"Ah! ah! gentlemen," said Aramis, "decidedly it is a night for meetings. We shall be very unfortunate if, after meeting so often this evening, we should not succeed in meeting to-morrow."

"Oh, as to that, sir," replied Chatillon (for it was he who, with Flamarens, was leaving the Duc de Beaufort), "you may be assured; for if we meet by night without seeking each other, much more shall we meet by day when wishing it."

"I hope that is true," said Aramis.

"As for me, I am sure of it," said the duke.

De Flamarens and De Chatillon continued on their way and Athos and Aramis dismounted.

Hardly had they given the bridles of their horses to their lackeys and rid themselves of their cloaks when a man approached them, and after looking at them for an instant by the doubtful light of the lantern hung in the centre of the courtyard he uttered an exclamation of joy and ran to embrace them.

"Comte de la Fere!" the man cried out; "Chevalier d'Herblay! How does it happen that you are in Paris?"

"Rochefort!" cried the two friends.

"Yes! we arrived four or five days ago from the Vendomois, as you know, and we are going to give Mazarin something to do. You are still with us, I presume?"

"More than ever. And the duke?"

"Furious against the cardinal. You know his success--our dear duke? He is really king of Paris; he can't go out without being mobbed by his admirers."

"Ah! so much the better! Can we have the honor of seeing his highness?"

"I shall be proud to present you," and Rochefort walked on. Every door was opened to him. Monsieur de Beaufort was at supper, but he rose quickly on hearing the two friends announced.

"Ah!" he cried, "by Jove! you're welcome, sirs. You are coming to sup with me, are you not? Boisgoli, tell Noirmont that I have two guests. You know Noirmont, do you not? The successor of Father Marteau who makes the excellent pies you know of. Boisgoli, let him send one of his best, but not such a one as he made for La Ramee. Thank God! we don't want either rope ladders or gag-pears now."

"My lord," said Athos, "do not let us disturb you. We came merely to inquire after your health and to take your orders."

"As to my health, since it has stood five years of prison, with Monsieur de Chavigny to boot, 'tis excellent! As to my orders, since every one gives his own commands in our party, I shall end, if this goes on, by giving none at all."

"In short, my lord," said Athos, glancing at Aramis, "your highness is discontented with your party?"

"Discontented, sir! say my highness is furious! To such a degree, I assure you, though I would not say so to others, that if the queen, acknowledging the injuries she has done me, would recall my mother and give me the reversion of the admiralty, which belonged to my father and was promised me at his death, well! it would not be long before I should be training dogs to say that there were greater traitors in France than the Cardinal Mazarin!"

At this Athos and Aramis could not help exchanging not only a look but a smile; and had they not known it for a fact, this would have told them that De Chatillon and De Flamarens had been there.

"My lord," said Athos, "we are satisfied; we came here only to express our loyalty and to say that we are at your lordship's service and his most faithful servants."

"My most faithful friends, gentlemen, my most faithful friends; you have proved it. And if ever I am reconciled with the court I shall prove to you, I hope, that I remain your friend, as well as that of--what the devil are their names--D'Artagnan and Porthos?"

"D'Artagnan and Porthos."

"Ah, yes. You understand, then, Comte de la Fere, you understand, Chevalier d'Herblay, that I am altogether and always at your service."

Athos and Aramis bowed and went out.

"My dear Athos," cried Aramis, "I think you consented to accompany me only to give me a lesson--God forgive me!"

"Wait a little, Aramis; it will be time for you to perceive my motive when we have paid our visit to the coadjutor."

"Let us then go to the archiepiscopal palace," said Aramis.

They directed their horses to the city. On arriving at the cradle from which Paris sprang they found it inundated with water, and it was again necessary to take a boat. The palace rose from the bosom of the water, and to see the number of boats around it one would have fancied one's self not in Paris, but in Venice. Some of these boats were dark and mysterious, others noisy and lighted up with torches. The friends slid in through this congestion of embarkation and landed in their turn. The palace was surrounded with water, but a kind of staircase had been fixed to the lower walls; and the only difference was, that instead of entering by the doors, people entered by the windows.

Thus did Athos and Aramis make their appearance in the ante-chamber, where about a dozen noblemen were collected in waiting.

"Good heavens!" said Aramis to Athos, "does the coadjutor intend to indulge himself in the pleasure of making us cool our hearts off in his ante-chamber?"

"My dear friend, we must take people as we find them. The coadjutor is at this moment one of the seven kings of Paris, and has a court. Let us send in our names, and if he does not send us a suitable message we will leave him to his own affairs or those of France. Let us call one of these lackeys, with a demi-pistole in the left hand."

"Exactly so," cried Aramis. "Ah! if I'm not mistaken here's Bazin. Come here, fellow."

Bazin, who was crossing the ante-chamber majestically in his clerical dress, turned around to see who the impertinent gentleman was who thus addressed him; but seeing his friends he went up to them quickly and expressed delight at seeing them.

"A truce to compliments," said Aramis; "we want to see the coadjutor, and instantly, as we are in haste."

"Certainly, sir--it is not such lords as you are who are allowed to wait in the ante-chamber, only just now he has a secret conference with Monsieur de Bruy."

"De Bruy!" cried the friends, "'tis then useless our seeing monsieur the coadjutor this evening," said Aramis, "so we give it up."

And they hastened to quit the palace, followed by Bazin, who was lavish of bows and compliments.

"Well," said Athos, when Aramis and he were in the boat again, "are you beginning to be convinced that we should have done a bad turn to all these people in arresting Mazarin?"

"You are wisdom incarnate, Athos," Aramis replied.

What had especially been observed by the two friends was the little interest taken by the court of France in the terrible events which had occurred in

England, which they thought should have arrested the attention of all Europe.

In fact, aside from a poor widow and a royal orphan who wept in the corner of the Louvre, no one appeared to be aware that Charles I. had ever lived and that he had perished on the scaffold.

The two friends made an appointment for ten o'clock on the following day; for though the night was well advanced when they reached the door of the hotel, Aramis said that he had certain important visits to make and left Athos to enter alone.

At ten o'clock the next day they met again. Athos had been out since six o'clock.

"Well, have you any news?" Athos asked.

"Nothing. No one has seen D'Artagnan and Porthos has not appeared. Have you anything?"

"Nothing."

"The devil!" said Aramis.

"In fact," said Athos, "this delay is not natural; they took the shortest route and should have arrived before we did."

"Add to that D'Artagnan's rapidity in action and that he is not the man to lose an hour, knowing that we were expecting him."

"He expected, you will remember, to be here on the fifth."

"And here we are at the ninth. This evening the margin of possible delay expires."

"What do you think should be done," asked Athos, "if we have no news of them to-night?"

"Pardieu! we must go and look for them."

"All right," said Athos.

"But Raoul?" said Aramis.

A light cloud passed over the count's face.

"Raoul gives me much uneasiness," he said. "He received yesterday a message from the Prince de Conde; he went to meet him at Saint Cloud and has not returned."

"Have you seen Madame de Chevreuse?"

"She was not at home. And you, Aramis, you were going, I think, to visit Madame de Longueville."

"I did go there."

"Well?"

"She was no longer there, but she had left her new address."

"Where was she?"

"Guess; I give you a thousand chances."

"How should I know where the most beautiful and active of the Frondists was at midnight? for I presume it was when you left me that you went to visit her."

"At the Hotel de Ville, my dear fellow."

"What! at the Hotel de Ville? Has she, then, been appointed provost of merchants?"

"No; but she has become queen of Paris, ad interim, and since she could not venture at once to establish herself in the Palais Royal or the Tuileries, she is installed at the Hotel de Ville, where she is on the point of giving an heir or an heiress to that dear duke."

"You didn't tell me of that, Aramis."

"Really? It was my forgetfulness then; pardon me."

"Now," asked Athos, "what are we to do with ourselves till evening? Here we are without occupation, it seems to me."

"You forget, my friend, that we have work cut out for us in the direction of Charenton; I hope to see Monsieur de Chatillon, whom I've hated for a long time, there."

"Why have you hated him?"

"Because he is the brother of Coligny."

"Ah, true! he who presumed to be a rival of yours, for which he was severely punished; that ought to satisfy you."

"'Yes, but it does not; I am rancorous--the only stigma that proves me to be a churchman. Do you understand? You understand that you are in no way obliged to go with me."

"Come, now," said Athos, "you are joking."

"In that case, my dear friend, if you are resolved to accompany me there is no time to lose; the drum beats; I observed cannon on the road; I saw the citizens in order of battle on the Place of the Hotel de Ville; certainly the fight will be in the direction of Charenton, as the Duc de Chatillon said."

"I supposed," said Athos, "that last night's conferences would modify those warlike arrangements."

"No doubt; but they will fight, none the less, if only to mask the conferences."

"Poor creatures!" said Athos, "who are going to be killed, in order that Monsieur de Bouillon may have his estate at Sedan restored to him, that the reversion of the admiralty may be given to the Duc de Beaufort, and that the coadjutor may be made a cardinal."

"Come, come, dear Athos, confess that you would not be so philosophical if your Raoul were to be involved in this affair."

"Perhaps you speak the truth, Aramis."

"Well, let us go, then, where the fighting is, for that is the most likely place to meet with D'Artagnan, Porthos, and possibly even Raoul. Stop, there are a fine body of citizens passing; quite attractive, by Jupiter! and their captain--see! he has the true military style."

"What, ho!" said Grimaud.

"What?" asked Athos.

"Planchet, sir."

"Lieutenant yesterday," said Aramis, "captain to-day, colonel, doubtless, to-morrow; in a fortnight the fellow will be marshal of France."

"Question him about the fight," said Athos.

Planchet, prouder than ever of his new duties, deigned to explain to the two gentlemen that he was ordered to take up his position on the Place Royale with two hundred men, forming the rear of the army of Paris, and to march on Charenton when necessary.

"This day will be a warm one," said Planchet, in a warlike tone.

"No doubt," said Aramis, "but it is far from here to the enemy."

"Sir, the distance will be diminished," said a subordinate.

Aramis saluted, then turning toward Athos:

"I don't care to camp on the Place Royale with all these people," he said. "Shall we go forward? We shall see better what is going on."

"And then Monsieur de Chatillon will not come to the Place Royale to look for you. Come, then, my friend, we will go forward."

"Haven't you something to say to Monsieur de Flamarens on your own account?"

"My friend," said Athos, "I have made a resolution never to draw my sword save when it is absolutely necessary."

"And how long ago was that?"

"When I last drew my poniard."

"Ah! Good! another souvenir of Monsieur Mordaunt. Well, my friend, nothing now is lacking except that you should feel remorse for having killed that fellow."

"Hush!" said Athos, putting a finger on his lips, with the sad smile peculiar to him; "let us talk no more of Mordaunt--it will bring bad luck." And Athos set forward toward Charenton, followed closely by Aramis.

78. The Battle of Charenton.

As Athos and Aramis proceeded, and passed different companies on the road, they became aware that they were arriving near the field of battle.

"Ah! my friend!" cried Athos, suddenly, "where have you brought us? I fancy I perceive around us faces of different officers in the royal army; is not that the Duc de Chatillon himself coming toward us with his brigadiers?"

"Good-day, sirs," said the duke, advancing; "you are puzzled by what you see here, but one word will explain everything. There is now a truce and a conference. The prince, Monsieur de Retz, the Duc de Beaufort, the Duc de Bouillon, are talking over public affairs. Now one of two things must happen: either matters will not be arranged, or they will be arranged, in which last case I shall be relieved of my command and we shall still meet again."

"Sir," said Aramis, "you speak to the point. Allow me to ask you a question: Where are the plenipotentiaries?"

"At Charenton, in the second house on the right on entering from the direction of Paris."

"And was this conference arranged beforehand?"

"No, gentlemen, it seems to be the result of certain propositions which Mazarin made last night to the Parisians."

Athos and Aramis exchanged smiles; for they well knew what those propositions were, to whom they had been made and who had made them.

"And that house in which the plenipotentiaries are," asked Athos, "belongs to----"

"To Monsieur de Chanleu, who commands your troops at Charenton. I say your troops, for I presume that you gentlemen are Frondeurs?"

"Yes, almost," said Aramis.

"We are for the king and the princes," added Athos.

"We must understand each other," said the duke. "The king is with us and his generals are the Duke of Orleans and the Prince de Conde, although I must add 'tis almost impossible now to know to which party any one belongs."

"Yes," answered Athos, "but his right place is in our ranks, with the Prince de Conti, De Beaufort, D'Elbeuf, and De Bouillon; but, sir, supposing that the conference is broken off--are you going to try to take Charenton?"

"Such are my orders."

"Sir, since you command the cavalry----"

"Pardon me, I am commander-in-chief."

"So much the better. You must know all your officers--I mean those more distinguished."

"Why, yes, very nearly."

"Will you then kindly tell me if you have in your command the Chevalier d'Artagnan, lieutenant in the musketeers?"

"No, sir, he is not with us; he left Paris more than six weeks ago and is believed to have gone on a mission to England."

"I knew that, but I supposed he had returned."

"No, sir; no one has seen him. I can answer positively on that point, for the musketeers belong to our forces and Monsieur de Cambon, the substitute for Monsieur d'Artagnan, still holds his place."

The two friends looked at each other.

"You see," said Athos.

"It is strange," said Aramis.

"It is absolutely certain that some misfortune has happened to them on the way."

"If we have no news of them this evening, tomorrow we must start."

Athos nodded affirmatively, then turning:

"And Monsieur de Bragelonne, a young man fifteen years of age, attached to the Prince de Conde--has he the honor of being known to you?" diffident in allowing the sarcastic Aramis to perceive how strong were his paternal feelings.

"Yes, surely, he came with the prince; a charming young man; he is one of your friends then, monsieur le comte?"

"Yes, sir," answered Athos, agitated; "so much so that I wish to see him if possible."

"Quite possible, sir; do me the favor to accompany me and I will conduct you to headquarters."

"Halloo, there!" cried Aramis, turning around; "what a noise behind us!"

"A body of cavaliers is coming toward us," said Chatillon.

"I recognize the coadjutor by his Frondist hat."

"And I the Duc de Beaufort by his white plume of ostrich feathers."

"They are coming, full gallop; the prince is with them--ah! he is leaving them!"

"They are beating the rappel!" cried Chatillon; "we must discover what is going on."

In fact, they saw the soldiers running to their arms; the trumpets sounded; the drums beat; the Duc de Beaufort drew his sword. On his side the prince sounded a rappel and all the officers of the royalist army, mingling momentarily with the Parisian troops, ran to him.

"Gentlemen," cried Chatillon, "the truce is broken, that is evident; they are going to fight; go, then, into Charenton, for I shall begin in a short time--there's a signal from the prince!"

The cornet of a troop had in fact just raised the standard of the prince.

"Farewell, till the next time we meet," cried Chatillon, and he set off, full gallop.

Athos and Aramis turned also and went to salute the coadjutor and the Duc de Beaufort. As to the Duc de Bouillon, he had such a fit of gout as obliged him to return to Paris in a litter; but his place was well filled by the Duc d'Elbeuf and his four sons, ranged around him like a staff. Meantime, between Charenton and the royal army was left a space which looked ready to serve as a last resting place for the dead.

"Gentlemen," cried the coadjutor, tightening his sash, which he wore, after the fashion of the ancient military prelates, over his archiepiscopal simar, "there's the enemy approaching. Let us save them half of their journey."

And without caring whether he were followed or not he set off; his regiment, which bore the name of the regiment of Corinth, from the name of his archbishopric, darted after him and began the fight. Monsieur de Beaufort sent his cavalry, toward Etampes and Monsieur de Chanleu, who defended the place, was ready to resist an assault, or if the enemy were repulsed, to attempt a sortie.

The battle soon became general and the coadjutor performed miracles of valor. His proper vocation had always been the sword and he was delighted whenever he could draw it from the scabbard, no matter for whom or against whom.

Chanleu, whose fire at one time repulsed the royal regiment, thought that the moment was come to pursue it; but it was reformed and led again to the charge by the Duc de Chatillon in person. This charge was so fierce, so skillfully conducted, that Chanleu was almost surrounded. He commanded a retreat, which began, step by step, foot by foot; unhappily, in an instant he fell, mortally wounded. De Chatillon saw him fall and announced it in a loud voice to his men, which raised their spirits and completely disheartened their enemies, so that every man thought only of his own safety and tried to gain the trenches, where the coadjutor was trying to reform his disorganized regiment.

Suddenly a squadron of cavalry galloped up to encounter the royal troops, who were entering, pelemele, the intrenchments with the fugitives. Athos and Aramis charged at the head of their squadrons; Aramis with sword and pistol in his hands, Athos with his sword in his scabbard, his pistol in his saddlebags; calm and cool as if on the parade, except that his noble and beautiful countenance became sad as he saw slaughtered so many men who were sacrificed on the one side to the obstinacy of royalty and on the other to the personal rancor of the princes. Aramis, on the contrary, struck right and left and was almost delirious with excitement. His bright eyes kindled, and his mouth, so finely formed, assumed a wicked smile; every blow he aimed was sure, and his pistol finished the deed--annihilated the wounded wretch who tried to rise again.

On the opposite side two cavaliers, one covered with a gilt cuirass, the other wearing simply a buff doublet, from which fell the sleeves of a vest of blue velvet, charged in front. The cavalier in the gilt cuirass fell upon Aramis and struck a blow that Aramis parried with his wonted skill.

"Ah! 'tis you, Monsieur de Chatillon," cried the chevalier; "welcome to you--I expected you."

"I hope I have not made you wait too long, sir," said the duke; "at all events, here I am."

"Monsieur de Chatillon," cried Aramis, taking from his saddle-bags a second pistol, "I think if your pistols have been discharged you are a dead man."

"Thank God, sir, they are not!"

And the duke, pointing his pistol at Aramis, fired. But Aramis bent his head the instant he saw the duke's finger press the trigger and the ball passed without touching him.

"Oh! you've missed me," cried Aramis, "but I swear to Heaven! I will not miss you."

"If I give you time!" cried the duke, spurring on his horse and rushing upon him with his drawn sword.

Aramis awaited him with that terrible smile which was peculiar to him on such occasions, and Athos, who saw the duke advancing toward Aramis with the rapidity of lightning, was just going to cry out, "Fire! fire, then!" when the shot was fired. De Chatillon opened his arms and fell back on the crupper of his horse.

The ball had entered his breast through a notch in the cuirass.

"I am a dead man," he said, and fell from his horse to the ground.

"I told you this, I am now grieved I have kept my word. Can I be of any use to you?"

Chatillon made a sign with his hand and Aramis was about to dismount when he received a violent shock; 'twas a thrust from a sword, but his cuirass turned aside the blow.

He turned around and seized his new antagonist by the wrist, when he started back, exclaiming, "Raoul!"

"Raoul?" cried Athos.

The young man recognized at the same instant the voices of his father and the Chevalier d'Herblay; two officers in the Parisian forces rushed at that instant on Raoul, but Aramis protected him with his sword.

"My prisoner!" he cried.

Athos took his son's horse by the bridle and led him forth out of the melee.

At this crisis of the battle, the prince, who had been seconding De Chatillon in the second line, appeared in the midst of the fight; his eagle eye made him known and his blows proclaimed the hero.

On seeing him, the regiment of Corinth, which the coadjutor had not been able to reorganize in spite of all his efforts, threw itself into the midst of the Parisian forces, put them into confusion and reentered Charenton flying. The coadjutor, dragged along with his fugitive forces, passed near the group formed by Athos, Raoul and Aramis. Aramis could not in his jealousy avoid being pleased at the coadjutor's misfortune, and was about to utter some bon mot more witty than correct, when Athos stopped him.

"On, on!" he cried, "this is no moment for compliments; or rather, back, for the battle seems to be lost by the Frondeurs."

"It is a matter of indifference to me," said Aramis; "I came here only to meet De Chatillon; I have met him, I am contented; 'tis something to have met De Chatillon in a duel!"

"And besides, we have a prisoner," said Athos, pointing to Raoul.

The three cavaliers continued their road on full gallop.

"What were you doing in the battle, my friend?" inquired Athos of the youth; "'twas not your right place, I think, as you were not equipped for an engagement!"

"I had no intention of fighting to-day, sir; I was charged, indeed, with a mission to the cardinal and had set out for Rueil, when, seeing Monsieur de Chatillon charge, an invincible desire possessed me to charge at his side. It was then that he told me two cavaliers of the Parisian army were seeking me and named the Comte de la Fere."

"What! you knew we were there and yet wished to kill your friend the chevalier?"

"I did not recognize the chevalier in armor, sir!" said Raoul, blushing; "though I might have known him by his skill and coolness in danger."

"Thank you for the compliment, my young friend," replied Aramis, "we can see from whom you learned courtesy. Then you were going to Rueil?"

"Yes! I have a despatch from the prince to his eminence."

"You must still deliver it," said Athos.

"No false generosity, count! the fate of our friends, to say nothing of our own, is perhaps in that very despatch."

"This young man must not, however, fail in his duty," said Athos.

"In the first place, count, this youth is our prisoner; you seem to forget that. What I propose to do is fair in war; the vanquished must not be dainty in the choice of means. Give me the despatch, Raoul."

The young man hesitated and looked at Athos as if seeking to read in his eyes a rule of conduct.

"Give him the despatch, Raoul! you are the chevalier's prisoner."

Raoul gave it up reluctantly; Aramis instantly seized and read it.

"You," he said, "you, who are so trusting, read and reflect that there is something in this letter important for us to see."

Athos took the letter, frowning, but an idea that he should find something in this letter about D'Artagnan conquered his unwillingness to read it.

"My lord, I shall send this evening to your eminence in order to reinforce the troop of Monsieur de Comminges, the ten men you demand. They are good soldiers, fit to confront the two violent adversaries whose address and resolution your eminence is fearful of."

"Oh!" cried Athos.

"Well," said Aramis, "what think you about these two enemies whom it requires, besides Comminges's troop, ten good soldiers to confront; are they not as like as two drops of water to D'Artagnan and Porthos?"

"We'll search Paris all day long," said Athos, "and if we have no news this evening we will return to the road to Picardy; and I feel no doubt that, thanks to D'Artagnan's ready invention, we shall then find some clew which will solve our doubts."

"Yes, let us search Paris and especially inquire of Planchet if he has yet heard from his former master."

"That poor Planchet! You speak of him very much at your ease, Aramis; he has probably been killed. All those fighting citizens went out to battle and they have been massacred."

It was, then, with a sentiment of uneasiness whether Planchet, who alone could give them information, was alive or dead, that the friends returned to the Place Royale; to their great surprise they found the citizens still encamped there, drinking and bantering each other, although, doubtless, mourned by their families, who thought they were at Charenton in the thickest of the fighting.

Athos and Aramis again questioned Planchet, but he had seen nothing of D'Artagnan; they wished to take Planchet with them, but he could not leave his troop, who at five o'clock returned home, saying that they were returning from the battle, whereas they had never lost sight of the bronze equestrian statue of Louis XIII.

79. The Road to Picardy.

On leaving Paris, Athos and Aramis well knew that they would be encountering great danger; but we know that for men like these there could be no question of danger. Besides, they felt that the denouement of this second Odyssey was at hand and that there remained but a single effort to make.

Besides, there was no tranquillity in Paris itself. Provisions began to fail, and whenever one of the Prince de Conti's generals wished to gain more influence he got up a little popular tumult, which he put down again, and thus for the moment gained a superiority over his colleagues.

In one of these risings, the Duc de Beaufort pillaged the house and library of Mazarin, in order to give the populace, as he put it, something to gnaw at. Athos and Aramis left Paris after this coup-d'etat, which took place on the very evening of the day in which the Parisians had been beaten at Charenton.

They quitted Paris, beholding it abandoned to extreme want, bordering on famine; agitated by fear, torn by faction. Parisians and Frondeurs as they were, the two friends expected to find the same misery, the same fears, the same intrigue in the enemy's camp; but what was their surprise, after passing Saint Denis, to hear that at Saint Germain people were singing and laughing, and leading generally cheerful lives. The two gentlemen traveled by byways in order not to encounter the Mazarinists scattered about the Isle of France, and also to escape the Frondeurs, who were in possession of Normandy and who never failed to conduct captives to the Duc de Longueville, in order that he might ascertain whether they were friends or foes. Having escaped these dangers, they returned by the main road to Boulogne, at Abbeville, and followed it step by step, examining every track.

Nevertheless, they were still in a state of uncertainty. Several inns were visited by them, several innkeepers questioned, without a single clew being given to guide their inquiries, when at Montreuil Athos felt upon the table that something rough was touching his delicate fingers. He turned up the cloth and found these hieroglyphics carved upon the wood with a knife:

"Port.... D'Art.... 2d February."

"This is capital!" said Athos to Aramis, "we were to have slept here, but we cannot--we must push on." They rode forward and reached Abbeville. There the great number of inns puzzled them; they could not go to all; how could they guess in which those whom they were seeking had stayed?

"Trust me," said Aramis, "do not expect to find anything in Abbeville. If we had only been looking for Porthos, Porthos would have stationed himself in one of the finest hotels and we could easily have traced him. But D'Artagnan is devoid of such weaknesses. Porthos would have found it very difficult even to make him see that he was dying of hunger; he has gone on his road as inexorable as fate and we must seek him somewhere else."

They continued their route. It had now become a weary and almost hopeless task, and had it not been for the threefold motives of honor, friendship and gratitude, implanted in their hearts, our two travelers would have given up many a time their rides over the sand, their interrogatories of the peasantry and their close inspection of faces.

They proceeded thus to Peronne.

Athos began to despair. His noble nature felt that their ignorance was a sort of reflection upon them. They had not looked carefully enough for their lost friends. They had not shown sufficient pertinacity in their inquiries. They were willing and ready to retrace their steps, when, in crossing the suburb which leads to the gates of the town, upon a white wall which was at the corner of a street turning around the rampart, Athos cast his eyes upon a drawing in black chalk, which represented, with the awkwardness of a first attempt, two cavaliers riding furiously; one of them carried a roll of paper on which were written these words: "They are following us."

"Oh!" exclaimed Athos, "here it is, as clear as day; pursued as he was, D'Artagnan would not have tarried here five minutes had he been pressed very closely, which gives us hopes that he may have succeeded in escaping."

Aramis shook his head.

"Had he escaped we should either have seen him or have heard him spoken of."

"You are right, Aramis, let us travel on."

To describe the impatience and anxiety of these two friends would be impossible. Uneasiness took possession of the tender, constant heart of Athos, and fearful forecasts were the torment of the impulsive Aramis. They galloped on for two or three hours as furiously as the cavaliers on the wall. All at once, in a narrow pass, they perceived that the road was partially barricaded by an enormous stone. It had evidently been rolled across the pass by some arm of giant strength.

Aramis stopped.

"Oh!" he said, looking at the stone, "this is the work of either Hercules or Porthos. Let us get down, count, and examine this rock."

They both alighted. The stone had been brought with the evident intention of barricading the road, but some one having perceived the obstacle had partially turned it aside.

With the assistance of Blaisois and Grimaud the friends succeeded in turning the stone over. Upon the side next the ground were scratched the following words:

"Eight of the light dragoons are pursuing us. If we reach Compiegne we shall stop at the Peacock. It is kept by a friend of ours."

"At last we have something definite," said Athos; "let us go to the Peacock."

"Yes," answered Aramis, "but if we are to get there we must rest our horses, for they are almost broken-winded."

Aramis was right; they stopped at the first tavern and made each horse swallow a double quantity of corn steeped in wine; they gave them three hours' rest and then set off again. The men themselves were almost dead with fatigue, but hope supported them.

In six hours they reached Compiegne and alighted at the Peacock. The host proved to be a worthy man, as bald as a Chinaman. They asked him if some time ago he had not received in his house two gentlemen who were pursued by dragoons; without answering he went out and brought in the blade of a rapier.

"Do you know that?" he asked.

Athos merely glanced at it.

"'Tis D'Artagnan's sword," he said.

"Does it belong to the smaller or to the larger of the two?" asked the host.

"To the smaller."

"I see that you are the friends of these gentlemen."

"Well, what has happened to them?"

"They were pursued by eight of the light dragoons, who rode into the courtyard before they had time to close the gate."

"Eight!" said Aramis; "it surprises me that two such heroes as Porthos and D'Artagnan should have allowed themselves to be arrested by eight men."

"The eight men would doubtless have failed had they not been assisted by twenty soldiers of the regiment of Italians in the king's service, who are in garrison in this town so that your friends were overpowered by numbers."

"Arrested, were they?" inquired Athos; "is it known why?"

"No, sir, they were carried off instantly, and had not even time to tell me why; but as soon as they were gone I found this broken sword-blade, as I was helping to raise two dead men and five or six wounded ones."

"'Tis still a consolation that they were not wounded," said Aramis.

"Where were they taken?" asked Athos.

"Toward the town of Louvres," was the reply.

The two friends having agreed to leave Blaisois and Grimaud at Compiegne with the horses, resolved to take post horses; and having snatched a hasty dinner they continued their journey to Louvres. Here they found only one inn, in which was consumed a liqueur which preserves its reputation to our time and which is still made in that town.

"Let us alight here," said Athos. "D'Artagnan will not have let slip an opportunity of drinking a glass of this liqueur, and at the same time leaving some trace of himself."

They went into the town and asked for two glasses of liqueur, at the counter--as their friends must have done before them. The counter was covered with a plate of pewter; upon this plate was written with the point of a large pin: "Rueil... D.."

"They went to Rueil," cried Aramis.

"Let us go to Rueil," said Athos.

"It is to throw ourselves into the wolf's jaws," said Aramis.

"Had I been as great a friend of Jonah as I am of D'Artagnan I should have followed him even into the inside of the whale itself; and you would have done the same, Aramis."

"Certainly--but you make me out better than I am, dear count. Had I been alone I should scarcely have gone to Rueil without great caution. But where you go, I go."

They then set off for Rueil. Here the deputies of the parliament had just arrived, in order to enter upon those famous conferences which were to last three weeks, and produced eventually that shameful peace, at the conclusion of which the prince was arrested. Rueil was crowded with advocates, presidents and councillors, who came from the Parisians, and, on the side of the court, with officers and guards; it was therefore easy, in the midst of this confusion, to remain as unobserved as any one might wish; besides, the conferences implied a truce, and to arrest two gentlemen, even Frondeurs, at this time, would have been an attack on the rights of the people.

The two friends mingled with the crowd and fancied that every one was occupied with the same thought that tormented them. They expected to hear some mention made of D'Artagnan or of Porthos, but every one was engrossed by articles and reforms. It was the advice of Athos to go straight to the minister.

"My friend," said Aramis, "take care; our safety lies in our obscurity. If we were to make ourselves known we should be sent to rejoin our friends in some deep ditch, from which the devil himself could not take us out. Let us try not to find them out by accident, but from our notions. Arrested at Compiegne, they have been carried to Rueil; at Rueil they have been questioned by the cardinal, who has either kept them near him or sent them to Saint Germain. As to the Bastile, they are not there, though the Bastile is especially for the Frondeurs. They are not dead, for the death of D'Artagnan would make a sensation. As for Porthos, I believe him to be eternal, like God, although less patient. Do not let us despond, but wait at Rueil, for my conviction is that they are at Rueil. But what ails you? You are pale."

"It is this," answered Athos, with a trembling voice.

"I remember that at the Castle of Rueil the Cardinal Richelieu had some horrible 'oubliettes' constructed."

"Oh! never fear," said Aramis. "Richelieu was a gentleman, our equal in birth, our superior in position. He could, like the king, touch the greatest of us on the head, and touching them make such heads shake on their shoulders. But Mazarin is a low-born rogue, who can at the most take us by the collar, like an archer. Be calm--for I am sure that D'Artagnan and Porthos are at Rueil, alive and well."

"But," resumed Athos, "I recur to my first proposal. I know no better means than to act with candor. I shall seek, not Mazarin, but the queen, and say to her, 'Madame, restore to us your two servants and our two friends.'"

Aramis shook his head.

"'Tis a last resource, but let us not employ it till it is imperatively called for; let us rather persevere in our researches."

They continued their inquiries and at last met with a light dragoon who had formed one of the guard which had escorted D'Artagnan to Rueil.

Athos, however, perpetually recurred to his proposed interview with the queen.

"In order to see the queen," said Aramis, "we must first see the cardinal; and when we have seen the cardinal--remember what I tell you, Athos--we shall be reunited to our friends, but not in the way you wish. Now, that way of joining them is not very attractive to me, I confess. Let us act in freedom, that we may act well and quickly."

"I shall go," he said, "to the queen."

"Well, then," answered Aramis, "pray tell me a day or two beforehand, that I may take that opportunity of going to Paris."

"To whom?"

"Zounds! how do I know? perhaps to Madame de Longueville. She is all-powerful yonder; she will help me. But send me word should you be arrested, for then I will return directly."

"Why do you not take your chance and be arrested with me?"

"No, I thank you."

"Should we, by being arrested, be all four together again, we should not, I am not sure, be twenty-four hours in prison without getting free."

"My friend, since I killed Chatillon, adored of the ladies of Saint Germain, I am too great a celebrity not to fear a prison doubly. The queen is likely to follow Mazarin's counsels and to have me tried."

"Do you think she loves this Italian so much as they say she does?"

"Did she not love an Englishman?"

"My friend, she is a woman."

"No, no, you are deceived--she is a queen."

"Dear friend, I shall sacrifice myself and go and see Anne of Austria."

"Adieu, Athos, I am going to raise an army."

"For what purpose?"

"To come back and besiege Rueil."

"Where shall we meet again?"

"At the foot of the cardinal's gallows."

The two friends departed--Aramis to return to Paris, Athos to take measures preparatory to an interview with the queen.

80. The Gratitude of Anne of Austria.

Athos found much less difficulty than he had expected in obtaining an audience of Anne of Austria. It was granted, and was to take place after her morning's "levee," at which, in accordance with his rights of birth, he was entitled to be present. A vast crowd filled the apartments of Saint Germain. Anne had never at the Louvre had so large a court; but this crowd represented chiefly the second class of nobility, while the Prince de Conti, the Duc de Beaufort and the coadjutor assembled around them the first nobility of France.

The greatest possible gayety prevailed at court. The particular characteristic of this was that more songs were made than cannons fired during its continuance. The court made songs on the Parisians and the Parisians on the court; and the casualties, though not mortal, were painful, as are all wounds inflicted by the weapon of ridicule.

In the midst of this seeming hilarity, nevertheless, people's minds were uneasy. Was Mazarin to remain the favorite and minister of the queen? Was he to be carried back by the wind which had blown him there? Every one hoped so, so that the minister felt that all around him, beneath the homage of the courtiers, lay a fund of hatred, ill disguised by fear and interest. He felt ill at ease and at a loss what to do.

Conde himself, whilst fighting for him, lost no opportunity of ridiculing, of humbling him. The queen, on whom he threw himself as sole support, seemed to him now not much to be relied upon.

When the hour appointed for the audience arrived Athos was obliged to stay until the queen, who was waited upon by a new deputation from Paris, had consulted with her minister as to the propriety and manner of receiving them. All were fully engrossed with the affairs of the day; Athos could not therefore have chosen a more inauspicious moment to speak of his friends--poor atoms, lost in that raging whirlwind.

But Athos was a man of inflexible determination; he firmly adhered to a purpose once formed, when it seemed to him to spring from conscience and to be prompted by a sense of duty. He insisted on being introduced, saying that although he was not a deputy from Monsieur de Conti, or Monsieur de Beaufort, or Monsieur de Bouillon, or Monsieur d'Elbeuf, or the coadjutor, or Madame de Longueville, or Broussel, or the Parliament, and although he had come on his own private account, he nevertheless had things to say to her majesty of the utmost importance.

The conference being finished, the queen summoned him to her cabinet.

Athos was introduced and announced by name. It was a name that too often resounded in her majesty's ears and too often vibrated in her heart for Anne of Austria not to recognize it; yet she remained impassive, looking at him with that fixed stare which is tolerated only in women who are queens, either by the power of beauty or by the right of birth.

"It is then a service which you propose to render us, count?" asked Anne of Austria, after a moment's silence.

"Yes, madame, another service," said Athos, shocked that the queen did not seem to recognize him.

Athos had a noble heart, and made, therefore, but a poor courtier.

Anne frowned. Mazarin, who was sitting at a table folding up papers, as if he had only been a secretary of state, looked up.

"Speak," said the queen.

Mazarin turned again to his papers.

"Madame," resumed Athos, "two of my friends, named D'Artagnan and Monsieur du Vallon, sent to England by the cardinal, suddenly disappeared when they set foot on the shores of France; no one knows what has become of them."

"Well?" said the queen.

"I address myself, therefore, first to the benevolence of your majesty, that I may know what has become of my friends, reserving to myself, if necessary, the right of appealing hereafter to your justice."

"Sir," replied Anne, with a degree of haughtiness which to certain persons became impertinence, "this is the reason that you trouble me in the midst of so many absorbing concerns! an affair for the police! Well, sir, you ought to know that we no longer have a police, since we are no longer at Paris."

"I think your majesty will have no need to apply to the police to know where my friends are, but that if you will deign to interrogate the cardinal he can reply without any further inquiry than into his own recollections."

"But, God forgive me!" cried Anne, with that disdainful curl of the lips peculiar to her, "I believe that you are yourself interrogating."

"Yes, madame, here I have a right to do so, for it concerns Monsieur d'Artagnan---d'Artagnan," he repeated, in such a manner as to bow the regal brow with recollections of the weak and erring woman.

The cardinal saw that it was now high time to come to the assistance of Anne.

"Sir," he said, "I can tell you what is at present unknown to her majesty. These individuals are under arrest. They disobeyed orders."

"I beg of your majesty, then," said Athos, calmly and not replying to Mazarin, "to quash these arrests of Messieurs d'Artagnan and du Vallon."

"What you ask is merely an affair of discipline and does not concern me," said the queen.

"Monsieur d'Artagnan never made such an answer as that when the service of your majesty was concerned," said Athos, bowing with great dignity. He was going toward the door when Mazarin stopped him.

"You, too, have been in England, sir?" he said, making a sign to the queen, who was evidently going to issue a severe order.

"I was a witness of the last hours of Charles I. Poor king! culpable, at the most, of weakness, how cruelly punished by his subjects! Thrones are at this time shaken and it is to little purpose for devoted hearts to serve the interests of princes. This is the second time that Monsieur d'Artagnan has been in England. He went the first time to save the honor of a great queen; the second, to avert the death of a great king."

"Sir," said Anne to Mazarin, with an accent from which daily habits of dissimulation could not entirely chase the real expression, "see if we can do something for these gentlemen."

"I wish to do, madame, all that your majesty pleases."

"Do what Monsieur de la Fere requests; that is your name, is it not, sir?"

"I have another name, madame--I am called Athos."

"Madame," said Mazarin, with a smile, "you may rest easy; your wishes shall be fulfilled."

"You hear, sir?" said the queen.

"Yes, madame, I expected nothing less from the justice of your majesty. May I not go and see my friends?"

"Yes, sir, you shall see them. But, apropos, you belong to the Fronde, do you not?"

"Madame, I serve the king."

"Yes, in your own way."

"My way is the way of all gentlemen, and I know only one way," answered Athos, haughtily.

"Go, sir, then," said the queen; "you have obtained what you wish and we know all we desire to know."

Scarcely, however, had the tapestry closed behind Athos when she said to Mazarin:

"Cardinal, desire them to arrest that insolent fellow before he leaves the court."

"Your majesty," answered Mazarin, "desires me to do only what I was going to ask you to let me do. These bravoes who resuscitate in our epoch the traditions of another reign are troublesome; since there are two of them already there, let us add a third."

Athos was not altogether the queen's dupe, but he was not a man to run away on suspicion--above all, when distinctly told that he should see his friends again. He waited, then, in the ante-chamber with impatience, till he should be conducted to them.

He walked to the window and looked into the court. He saw the deputation from the Parisians enter it; they were coming to assign the definitive place for the conference and to make their bow to the queen. A very imposing escort awaited them without the gates.

Athos was looking on attentively, when some one touched him softly on the shoulder.

"Ah! Monsieur de Comminges," he said.

"Yes, count, and charged with a commission for which I beg of you to accept my excuses."

"What is it?"

"Be so good as to give me up your sword, count."

Athos smiled and opened the window.

"Aramis!" he cried.

A gentleman turned around. Athos fancied he had seen him among the crowd. It was Aramis. He bowed with great friendship to the count.

"Aramis," cried Athos, "I am arrested."

"Good," replied Aramis, calmly.

"Sir," said Athos, turning to Comminges and giving him politely his sword by the hilt, "here is my sword; have the kindness to keep it safely for me until I quit my prison. I prize it--it was given to my ancestor by King Francis I. In his time they armed gentlemen, not disarmed them. Now, whither do you conduct me?"

"Into my room first," replied Comminges; "the queen will ultimately decide your place of domicile."

Athos followed Comminges without saying a single word.

81. Cardinal Mazarin as King.

The arrest produced no sensation, indeed was almost unknown, and scarcely interrupted the course of events. To the deputation it was formally announced that the queen would receive it.

Accordingly, it was admitted to the presence of Anne, who, silent and lofty as ever, listened to the speeches and complaints of the deputies; but when they had finished their harangues not one of them could say, so calm remained her face, whether or no she had heard them.

On the other hand, Mazarin, present at that audience, heard very well what those deputies demanded. It was purely and simply his removal, in terms clear and precise.

The discourse being finished, the queen remained silent.

"Gentlemen," said Mazarin, "I join with you in supplicating the queen to put an end to the miseries of her subjects. I have done all in my power to ameliorate them and yet the belief of the public, you say, is that they proceed from me, an unhappy foreigner, who has been unable to please the French. Alas! I have never been understood, and no wonder. I succeeded a man of the most sublime genius that ever upheld the sceptre of France. The memory of Richelieu annihilates me. In vain--were I an ambitious man--should I struggle against such remembrances as he has left; but that I am not ambitious I am going to prove to you. I own myself conquered. I shall obey the wishes of the people. If Paris has injuries to complain of, who has not some wrongs to be redressed? Paris has been sufficiently punished; enough blood has flowed, enough misery has humbled a town deprived of its king and of justice. 'Tis not for me, a private individual, to disunite a queen from her kingdom. Since you demand my resignation, I retire."

"Then," said Aramis, in his neighbor's ear, "the conferences are over. There is nothing to do but to send Monsieur Mazarin to the most distant frontier and to take care that he does not return even by that, nor any other entrance into France."

"One instant, sir," said the man in a gown, whom he addressed; "a plague on't! how fast you go! one may soon see that you're a soldier. There's the article of remunerations and indemnifications to be discussed and set to rights."

"Chancellor," said the queen, turning to Seguier, our old acquaintance, "you will open the conferences. They can take place at Rueil. The cardinal has said several things which have agitated me, therefore I will not speak more fully now. As to his going or staying, I feel too much gratitude to the cardinal not to leave him free in all his actions; he shall do what he wishes to do."

A transient pallor overspread the speaking countenance of the prime minister; he looked at the queen with anxiety. Her face was so passionless, that he, as every one else present, was incapable of reading her thoughts.

"But," added the queen, "in awaiting the cardinal's decision let there be, if you please, a reference to the king only."

The deputies bowed and left the room.

"What!" exclaimed the queen, when the last of them had quitted the apartment, "you would yield to these limbs of the law--these advocates?"

"To promote your majesty's welfare, madame," replied Mazarin, fixing his penetrating eyes on the queen, "there is no sacrifice that I would not make."

Anne dropped her head and fell into one of those reveries so habitual with her. A recollection of Athos came into her mind. His fearless deportment, his words, so firm, yet dignified, the shades which by one word he had evoked, recalled to her the past in all its intoxication of poetry and romance, youth, beauty, the eclat of love at twenty years of age, the bloody death of Buckingham, the only man whom she had ever really loved, and the heroism of those obscure champions who had saved her from the double hatred of Richelieu and the king.

Mazarin looked at her, and whilst she deemed herself alone and freed from the world of enemies who sought to spy into her secret thoughts, he read her thoughts in her countenance, as one sees in a transparent lake clouds pass--reflections, like thoughts, of the heavens.

"Must we, then," asked Anne of Austria, "yield to the storm, buy peace, and patiently and piously await better times?"

Mazarin smiled sarcastically at this speech, which showed that she had taken the minister's proposal seriously.

Anne's head was bent down--she had not seen the Italian's smile; but finding that her question elicited no reply she looked up.

"Well, you do not answer, cardinal, what do you think about it?"

"I am thinking, madame, of the allusion made by that insolent gentleman, whom you have caused to be arrested, to the Duke of Buckingham--to him whom you allowed to be assassinated--to the Duchess de Chevreuse, whom you suffered to be exiled--to the Duc de Beaufort, whom you imprisoned; but if he made allusion to me it was because he is ignorant of the relation in which I stand to you."

Anne drew up, as she always did, when anything touched her pride. She blushed, and that she might not answer, clasped her beautiful hands till her sharp nails almost pierced them.

"That man has sagacity, honor and wit, not to mention likewise that he is a man of undoubted resolution. You know something about him, do you not, madame? I shall tell him, therefore, and in doing so I shall confer a personal favor on him, how he is mistaken in regard to me. What is proposed to me would be, in fact, almost an abdication, and an abdication requires reflection."

"An abdication?" repeated Anne; "I thought, sir, that it was kings alone who abdicated!"

"Well," replied Mazarin, "and am I not almost a king--king, indeed, of France? Thrown over the foot of the royal bed, my simar, madame, looks not unlike the mantle worn by kings."

This was one of the humiliations which Mazarin made Anne undergo more frequently than any other, and one that bowed her head with shame. Queen Elizabeth and Catherine II. of Russia are the only two monarchs of their set on record who were at once sovereigns and lovers. Anne of Austria looked with a sort of terror at the threatening aspect of the cardinal--his physiognomy in such moments was not destitute of a certain grandeur.

"Sir," she replied, "did I not say, and did you not hear me say to those people, that you should do as you pleased?"

"In that case," said Mazarin, "I think it must please me best to remain; not only on account of my own interest, but for your safety."

"Remain, then, sir; nothing can be more agreeable to me; only do not allow me to be insulted."

"You are referring to the demands of the rebels and to the tone in which they stated them? Patience! They have selected a field of battle on which I am an abler general than they--that of a conference. No, we shall beat them by merely temporizing. They want food already. They will be ten times worse off in a week."

"Ah, yes! Good heavens! I know it will end in that way; but it is not they who taunt me with the most wounding reproaches, but----"

"I understand; you mean to allude to the recollections perpetually revived by these three gentlemen. However, we have them safe in prison, and they are just sufficiently culpable for us to keep them in prison as long as we find it convenient. One only is still not in our power and braves us. But, devil take him! we shall soon succeed in sending him to join his boon companions. We have accomplished more difficult things than that. In the first place I have as a precaution shut up at Rueil, near me, under my own eyes, within reach of my hand, the two most intractable ones. To-day the third will be there also."

"As long as they are in prison all will be well," said Anne, "but one of these days they will get out."

"Yes, if your majesty releases them."

"Ah!" exclaimed Anne, following the train of her own thoughts on such occasions, "one regrets Paris!"

"Why so?"

"On account of the Bastile, sir, which is so strong and so secure."

"Madame, these conferences will bring us peace; when we have peace we shall regain Paris; with Paris, the Bastile, and our four bullies shall rot therein."

Anne frowned slightly when Mazarin, in taking leave, kissed her hand.

Mazarin, after this half humble, half gallant attention, went away. Anne followed him with her eyes, and as he withdrew, at every step he took, a disdainful smile was seen playing, then gradually burst upon her lips.

"I once," she said, "despised the love of a cardinal who never said 'I shall do,' but, 'I have done so and so.' That man knew of retreats more secure than

Rueil, darker and more silent even than the Bastile. Degenerate world!"

82. Precautions.

After quitting Anne, Mazarin took the road to Rueil, where he usually resided; in those times of disturbance he went about with numerous followers and often disguised himself. In military dress he was, indeed, as we have stated, a very handsome man.

In the court of the old Chateau of Saint Germain he entered his coach, and reached the Seine at Chatou. The prince had supplied him with fifty light horse, not so much by way of guard as to show the deputies how readily the queen's generals dispersed their troops and to prove that they might be safely scattered at pleasure. Athos, on horseback, without his sword and kept in sight by Comminges, followed the cardinal in silence. Grimaud, finding that his master had been arrested, fell back into the ranks near Aramis, without saying a word and as if nothing had happened.

Grimaud had, indeed, during twenty-two years of service, seen his master extricate himself from so many difficulties that nothing less than Athos's imminent death was likely to make him uneasy.

At the branching off of the road toward Paris, Aramis, who had followed in the cardinal's suite, turned back. Mazarin went to the right hand and Aramis could see the prisoner disappear at the turning of the avenue. Athos, at the same moment, moved by a similar impulse, looked back also. The two friends exchanged a simple inclination of the head and Aramis put his finger to his hat, as if to bow, Athos alone comprehending by that signal that he had some project in his head.

Ten minutes afterward Mazarin entered the court of that chateau which his predecessor had built for him at Rueil; as he alighted, Comminges approached him.

"My lord," he asked, "where does your eminence wish Monsieur Comte de la Fere to be lodged?"

"In the pavilion of the orangery, of course, in front of the pavilion where the guard is. I wish every respect to be shown the count, although he is the prisoner of her majesty the queen."

"My lord," answered Comminges, "he begs to be taken to the place where Monsieur d'Artagnan is confined--that is, in the hunting lodge, opposite the orangery."

Mazarin thought for an instant.

Comminges saw that he was undecided.

"'Tis a very strong post," he resumed, "and we have forty good men, tried soldiers, having no connection with Frondeurs nor any interest in the Fronde."

"If we put these three men together, Monsieur Comminges," said Mazarin, "we must double the guard, and we are not rich enough in fighting men to commit such acts of prodigality."

Comminges smiled; Mazarin read and construed that smile.

"You do not know these men, Monsieur Comminges, but I know them, first personally, also by hearsay. I sent them to carry aid to King Charles and they performed prodigies to save him; had it not been for an adverse destiny, that beloved monarch would this day have been among us."

"But since they served your eminence so well, why are they, my lord cardinal, in prison?"

"In prison?" said Mazarin, "and when has Rueil been a prison?"

"Ever since there were prisoners in it," answered Comminges.

"These gentlemen, Comminges, are not prisoners," returned Mazarin, with his ironical smile, "only guests; but guests so precious that I have put a grating before each of their windows and bolts to their doors, that they may not refuse to continue my visitors. So much do I esteem them that I am going to make the Comte de la Fere a visit, that I may converse with him tete-a-tete, and that we may not be disturbed at our interview you must conduct him, as I said before, to the pavilion of the orangery; that, you know, is my daily promenade. Well, while taking my walk I will call on him and we will talk. Although he professes to be my enemy I have sympathy for him, and if he is reasonable perhaps we shall arrange matters."

Comminges bowed, and returned to Athos, who was awaiting with apparent calmness, but with real anxiety, the result of the interview.

"Well?" he said to the lieutenant.

"Sir," replied Comminges, "it seems that it is impossible."

"Monsieur de Comminges," said Athos, "I have been a soldier all my life and I know the force of orders; but outside your orders there is a service you can render me."

"I will do it with all my heart," said Comminges; "for I know who you are and what service you once performed for her majesty; I know, too, how dear to you is the young man who came so valiantly to my aid when that old rogue of a Broussel was arrested. I am entirely at your service, except only for my orders."

"Thank you, sir; what I am about to ask will not compromise you in any degree."

"If it should even compromise me a little," said Monsieur de Comminges, with a smile, "still make your demand. I don't like Mazarin any better than you do. I serve the queen and that draws me naturally into the service of the cardinal; but I serve the one with joy and the other against my will. Speak, then, I beg of you; I wait and listen."

"Since there is no harm," said Athos, "in my knowing that D'Artagnan is here, I presume there will be none in his knowing that I am here."

"I have received no orders on that point."

"Well, then, do me the kindness to give him my regards and tell him that I am his neighbor. Tell him also what you have just told me--that Mazarin has placed me in the pavilion of the orangery in order to make me a visit, and assure him that I shall take advantage of this honor he proposes to accord to me to obtain from him some amelioration of our captivity."

"Which cannot last," interrupted Comminges; "the cardinal said so; there is no prison here."

"But there are oubliettes!" replied Athos, smiling.

"Oh! that's a different thing; yes, I know there are traditions of that sort," said Comminges. "It was in the time of the other cardinal, who was a great nobleman; but our Mazarin--impossible! an Italian adventurer would not dare to go such lengths with such men as ourselves. Oubliettes are employed as a means of kingly vengeance, and a low-born fellow such as he is would not have recourse to them. Your arrest is known, that of your friends will soon be known; and all the nobility of France would demand an explanation of your disappearance. No, no, be easy on that score. I will, however, inform Monsieur d'Artagnan of your arrival here."

Comminges then led the count to a room on the ground floor of a pavilion, at the end of the orangery. They passed through a courtyard as they went, full of soldiers and courtiers. In the centre of this court, in the form of a horseshoe, were the buildings occupied by Mazarin, and at each wing the pavilion (or smaller building), where D'Artagnan was confined, and that, level with the orangery, where Athos was to be. From the ends of these two wings extended the park.

Athos, when he reached his appointed room, observed through the gratings of his window, walls and roofs; and was told, on inquiry, by Comminges, that he was looking on the back of the pavilion where D'Artagnan was confined.

"Yes, 'tis too true," said Comminges, "'tis almost a prison; but what a singular fancy this is of yours, count--you, who are the very flower of our nobility--to squander your valor and loyalty amongst these upstarts, the Frondists! Really, count, if ever I thought that I had a friend in the ranks of the royal army, it was you. A Frondeur! you, the Comte de la Fere, on the side of Broussel, Blancmesnil and Viole! For shame! you, a Frondeur!"

"On my word of honor," said Athos, "one must be either a Mazarinist or a Frondeur. For a long time I had these words whispered in my ears, and I chose the latter; at any rate, it is a French word. And now, I am a Frondeur--not of Broussel's party, nor of Blancmesnil's, nor am I with Viole; but with the Duc de Beaufort, the Ducs de Bouillon and d'Elbeuf; with princes, not with presidents, councillors and low-born lawyers. Besides, what a charming outlook it would have been to serve the cardinal! Look at that wall--without a single window--which tells you fine things about Mazarin's gratitude!"

"Yes," replied De Comminges, "more especially if it could reveal how Monsieur d'Artagnan for this last week has been anathematizing him."

"Poor D'Artagnan'" said Athos, with the charming melancholy that was one of the traits of his character, "so brave, so good, so terrible to the enemies of those he loves. You have two unruly prisoners there, sir."

"Unruly," Comminges smiled; "you wish to terrify me, I suppose. When he came here, Monsieur D'Artagnan provoked and braved the soldiers and inferior officers, in order, I suppose, to have his sword back. That mood lasted some time; but now he's as gentle as a lamb and sings Gascon songs, which make one die of laughing."

"And Du Vallon?" asked Athos.

"Ah, he's quite another sort of person--a formidable gentleman, indeed. The first day he broke all the doors in with a single push of his shoulder; and I expected to see him leave Rueil in the same way as Samson left Gaza. But his temper cooled down, like his friend's; he not only gets used to his captivity, but jokes about it."

"So much the better," said Athos.

"Do you think anything else was to be expected of them?" asked Comminges, who, putting together what Mazarin had said of his prisoners and what the Comte de la Fere had said, began to feel a degree of uneasiness.

Athos, on the other hand, reflected that this recent gentleness of his friends most certainly arose from some plan formed by D'Artagnan. Unwilling to injure them by praising them too highly, he replied: "They? They are two hotheads--the one a Gascon, the other from Picardy; both are easily excited, but they quiet down immediately. You have had a proof of that in what you have just related to me."

This, too, was the opinion of Comminges, who withdrew somewhat reassured. Athos remained alone in the vast chamber, where, according to the cardinal's directions, he was treated with all the courtesy due to a nobleman. He awaited Mazarin's promised visit to get some light on his present situation.

83. Strength and Sagacity.

Now let us pass the orangery to the hunting lodge. At the extremity of the courtyard, where, close to a portico formed of Ionic columns, were the dog kennels, rose an oblong building, the pavilion of the orangery, a half circle, inclosing the court of honor. It was in this pavilion, on the ground floor, that D'Artagnan and Porthos were confined, suffering interminable hours of imprisonment in a manner suitable to each different temperament.

D'Artagnan was pacing to and fro like a caged tiger; with dilated eyes, growling as he paced along by the bars of a window looking upon the yard of servant's offices.

Porthos was ruminating over an excellent dinner he had just demolished.

The one seemed to be deprived of reason, yet he was meditating. The other seemed to meditate, yet he was more than half asleep. But his sleep was a nightmare, which might be guessed by the incoherent manner in which he sometimes snored and sometimes snorted.

"Look," said D'Artagnan, "day is declining. It must be nearly four o'clock. We have been in this place nearly eighty-three hours."

"Hem!" muttered Porthos, with a kind of pretense of answering.

"Did you hear, eternal sleeper?" cried D'Artagnan, irritated that any one could doze during the day, when he had the greatest difficulty in sleeping during the night.

"What?" said Porthos.

"I say we have been here eighty-three hours."

"'Tis your fault," answered Porthos.

"How, my fault?"

"Yes, I offered you escape."

"By pulling out a bar and pushing down a door?"

"Certainly."

"Porthos, men like us can't go out from here purely and simply."

"Faith!" said Porthos, "as for me, I could go out with that purity and that simplicity which it seems to me you despise too much."

D'Artagnan shrugged his shoulders.

"And besides," he said, "going out of this chamber isn't all."

"Dear friend," said Porthos, "you appear to be in a somewhat better humor to-day than you were yesterday. Explain to me why going out of this chamber isn't everything."

"Because, having neither arms nor password, we shouldn't take fifty steps in the court without knocking against a sentinel."

"Very well," said Porthos, "we will kill the sentinel and we shall have his arms."

"Yes, but before we can kill him--and he will be hard to kill, that Swiss--he will shriek out and the whole picket will come, and we shall be taken like foxes, we, who are lions, and thrown into some dungeon, where we shall not even have the consolation of seeing this frightful gray sky of Rueil, which no more resembles the sky of Tarbes than the moon is like the sun. Lack-a-day! if we only had some one to instruct us about the physical and moral topography of this castle. Ah! when one thinks that for twenty years, during which time I did not know what to do with myself, it never occurred to me to come to study Rueil."

"What difference does that make?" said Porthos. "We shall go out all the same."

"Do you know, my dear fellow, why master pastrycooks never work with their hands?"

"No," said Porthos, "but I should be glad to be informed."

"It is because in the presence of their pupils they fear that some of their tarts or creams may turn out badly cooked."

"What then?"

"Why, then they would be laughed at, and a master pastrycook must never be laughed at."

"And what have master pastrycooks to do with us?"

"We ought, in our adventures, never to be defeated or give any one a chance to laugh at us. In England, lately, we failed, we were beaten, and that is a blemish on our reputation."

"By whom, then, were we beaten?" asked Porthos.

"By Mordaunt."

"Yes, but we have drowned Monsieur Mordaunt."

"That is true, and that will redeem us a little in the eyes of posterity, if posterity ever looks at us. But listen, Porthos: though Monsieur Mordaunt was a man not to be despised, Mazarin is not less strong than he, and we shall not easily succeed in drowning him. We must, therefore, watch and play a close game; for," he added with a sigh, "we two are equal, perhaps, to eight others; but we are not equal to the four that you know of."

"That is true," said Porthos, echoing D'Artagnan's sigh.

"Well, Porthos, follow my examples; walk back and forth till some news of our friends reaches us or till we are visited by a good idea. But don't sleep as you do all the time; nothing dulls the intellect like sleep. As to what may lie before us, it is perhaps less serious than we at first thought. I don't believe that Monsieur de Mazarin thinks of cutting off our heads, for heads are not taken off without previous trial; a trial would make a noise, and a noise would get the attention of our friends, who would check the operations of Monsieur de Mazarin."

"How well you reason!" said Porthos, admiringly.

"Well, yes, pretty well," replied D'Artagnan; "and besides, you see, if they put us on trial, if they cut off our heads, they must meanwhile either keep us here or transfer us elsewhere."

"Yes, that is inevitable," said Porthos.

"Well, it is impossible but that Master Aramis, that keen-scented bloodhound, and Athos, that wise and prudent nobleman, will discover our retreat. Then, believe me, it will be time to act."

"Yes, we will wait. We can wait the more contentedly, that it is not absolutely bad here, but for one thing, at least."

"What is that?"

"Did you observe, D'Artagnan, that three days running they have brought us braised mutton?"

"No; but if it occurs a fourth time I shall complain of it, so never mind."

"And then I feel the loss of my house, 'tis a long time since I visited my castles."

"Forget them for a time; we shall return to them, unless Mazarin razes them to the ground."

"Do you think that likely?"

"No, the other cardinal would have done so, but this one is too mean a fellow to risk it."

"You reconcile me, D'Artagnan."

"Well, then, assume a cheerful manner, as I do; we must joke with the guards, we must gain the good-will of the soldiers, since we can't corrupt them. Try, Porthos, to please them more than you are wont to do when they are under our windows. Thus far you have done nothing but show them your fist; and the more respectable your fist is, Porthos, the less attractive it is. Ah, I would give much to have five hundred louis, only."

"So would I," said Porthos, unwilling to be behind D'Artagnan in generosity; "I would give as much as a hundred pistoles."

The two prisoners were at this point of their conversation when Comminges entered, preceded by a sergeant and two men, who brought supper in a basket with two handles, filled with basins and plates.

"What!" exclaimed Porthos, "mutton again?"

"My dear Monsieur de Comminges," said D'Artagnan, "you will find that my friend, Monsieur du Vallon, will go to the most fatal lengths if Cardinal Mazarin continues to provide us with this sort of meat; mutton every day."

"I declare," said Porthos, "I shall eat nothing if they do not take it away."

"Remove the mutton," cried Comminges; "I wish Monsieur du Vallon to sup well, more especially as I have news to give him that will improve his appetite."

"Is Mazarin dead?" asked Porthos.

"No; I am sorry to tell you he is perfectly well."

"So much the worse," said Porthos.

"What is that news?" asked D'Artagnan. "News in prison is a fruit so rare that I trust, Monsieur de Comminges, you will excuse my impatience--the more eager since you have given us to understand that the news is good."

"Should you be glad to hear that the Comte de la Fere is well?" asked De Comminges.

D'Artagnan's penetrating gray eyes were opened to the utmost.

"Glad!" he cried; "I should be more than glad! Happy--beyond measure!"

"Well, I am desired by him to give you his compliments and to say that he is in good health."

D'Artagnan almost leaped with joy. A quick glance conveyed his thought to Porthos: "If Athos knows where we are, if he opens communication with us, before long Athos will act."

Porthos was not very quick to understand the language of glances, but now since the name of Athos had suggested to him the same idea, he understood.

"Do you say," asked the Gascon, timidly, "that the Comte de la Fere has commissioned you to give his compliments to Monsieur du Vallon and myself?"

"Yes, sir."

"Then you have seen him?"

"Certainly I have."

"Where? if I may ask without indiscretion."

"Near here," replied De Comminges, smiling; "so near that if the windows which look on the orangery were not stopped up you could see him from where you are."

"He is wandering about the environs of the castle," thought D'Artagnan. Then he said aloud:

"You met him, I dare say, in the park--hunting, perhaps?"

"No; nearer, nearer still. Look, behind this wall," said De Comminges, knocking against the wall.

"Behind this wall? What is there, then, behind this wall? I was brought here by night, so devil take me if I know where I am."

"Well," said Comminges, "suppose one thing."

"I will suppose anything you please."

"Suppose there were a window in this wall."

"Well?"

"From that window you would see Monsieur de la Fere at his."

"The count, then, is in the chateau?"

"Yes."

"For what reason?"

"The same as yourself."

"Athos--a prisoner?"

"You know well," replied De Comminges, "that there are no prisoners at Rueil, because there is no prison."

"Don't let us play upon words, sir. Athos has been arrested."

"Yesterday, at Saint Germain, as he came out from the presence of the queen."

The arms of D'Artagnan fell powerless by his side. One might have supposed him thunderstruck; a paleness ran like a cloud over his dark skin, but disappeared immediately.

"A prisoner?" he reiterated.

"A prisoner," repeated Porthos, quite dejected.

Suddenly D'Artagnan looked up and in his eyes there was a gleam which scarcely even Porthos observed; but it died away and he appeared more sorrowful than before.

"Come, come," said Comminges, who, since D'Artagnan, on the day of Broussel's arrest, had saved him from the hands of the Parisians, had entertained a real affection for him, "don't be unhappy; I never thought of bringing you bad news. Laugh at the chance which has brought your friend near to you and Monsieur du Vallon, instead of being in the depths of despair about it."

But D'Artagnan was still in a desponding mood.

"And how did he look?" asked Porthos, who, perceiving that D'Artagnan had allowed the conversation to drop, profited by it to put in a word or two.

"Very well, indeed, sir," replied Comminges; "at first, like you, he seemed distressed; but when he heard that the cardinal was going to pay him a visit this very evening----"

"Ah!" cried D'Artagnan, "the cardinal is about to visit the Comte de la Fere?"

"Yes; and the count desired me to tell you that he should take advantage of this visit to plead for you and for himself."

"Ah! our dear count!" said D'Artagnan.

"A fine thing, indeed!" grunted Porthos. "A great favor! Zounds! Monsieur the Comte de la Fere, whose family is allied to the Montmorency and the Rohan, is easily the equal of Monsieur de Mazarin."

"No matter," said D'Artagnan, in his most wheedling tone. "On reflection, my dear Du Vallon, it is a great honor for the Comte de la Fere, and gives good reason to hope. In fact, it seems to me so great an honor for a prisoner that I think Monsieur de Comminges must be mistaken."

"What? I am mistaken?"

"Monsieur de Mazarin will not come to visit the Comte de la Fere, but the Comte de la Fere will be sent for to visit him."

"No, no, no," said Comminges, who made a point of having the facts appear exactly as they were, "I clearly understood what the cardinal said to me. He will come and visit the Comte de la Fere."

D'Artagnan tried to gather from the expression of his eyes whether Porthos understood the importance of that visit, but Porthos did not even look toward him.

"It is, then, the cardinal's custom to walk in his orangery?" asked D'Artagnan.

"Every evening he shuts himself in there. That, it seems, is where he meditates on state affairs."

"In that case," said D'Artagnan, "I begin to believe that Monsieur de la Fere will receive the visit of his eminence; he will, of course, have an escort."

"Yes--two soldiers."

"And will he talk thus of affairs in presence of two strangers?"

"The soldiers are Swiss, who understand only German. Besides, according to all probability they will wait at the door."

D'Artagnan made a violent effort over himself to keep his face from being too expressive.

"Let the cardinal take care of going alone to visit the Comte de la Fere," said D'Artagnan; "for the count must be furious."

Comminges began to laugh. "Oh, oh! why, really, one would say that you four were anthropaphagi! The count is an affable man; besides, he is unarmed; at the first word from his eminence the two soldiers about him would run to his assistance."

"Two soldiers," said D'Artagnan, seeming to remember something, "two soldiers, yes; that, then, is why I hear two men called every evening and see them walking sometimes for half an hour, under my window."

"That is it; they are waiting for the cardinal, or rather for Bernouin, who comes to call them when the cardinal goes out."

"Fine-looking men, upon my word!" said D'Artagnan.

"They belong to the regiment that was at Lens, which the prince assigned to the cardinal."

"Ah, monsieur," said D'Artagnan, as if to sum up in a word all that conversation, "if only his eminence would relent and grant to Monsieur de la Fere our liberty."

"I wish it with all my heart," said Comminges.

"Then, if he should forget that visit, you would find no inconvenience in reminding him of it?"

"Not at all."

"Ah, that gives me more confidence."

This skillful turn of the conversation would have seemed a sublime manoeuvre to any one who could have read the Gascon's soul.

"Now," said D'Artagnan, "I've one last favor to ask of you, Monsieur de Comminges."

"At your service, sir."

"You will see the count again?"

"To-morrow morning."

"Will you remember us to him and ask him to solicit for me the same favor that he will have obtained?"

"You want the cardinal to come here?"

"No; I know my place and am not so presumptuous. Let his eminence do me the honor to give me a hearing; that is all I want."

"Oh!" muttered Porthos, shaking his head, "never should I have thought this of him! How misfortune humbles a man!"

"I promise you it shall be done," answered De Comminges.

"Tell the count that I am well; that you found me sad, but resigned."

"I am pleased, sir, to hear that."

"And the same, also, for Monsieur du Vallon----"

"Not for me," cried Porthos; "I am not by any means resigned."

"But you will be resigned, my friend."

"Never!"

"He will become so, monsieur; I know him better than he knows himself. Be silent, dear Du Vallon, and resign yourself."

"Adieu, gentlemen," said De Comminges; "sleep well!"

"We will try."

De Comminges went away, D'Artagnan remaining apparently in the same attitude of humble resignation; but scarcely had he departed when he turned and clasped Porthos in his arms with an expression not to be doubted.

"Oh!" cried Porthos; "what's the matter now? Have you gone mad, my dear friend?"

"What is the matter?" returned D'Artagnan; "we are saved!"

"I don't see that at all," answered Porthos. "I think we are all taken prisoners, except Aramis, and that our chances of getting out are lessened since one more of us is caught in Mazarin's mousetrap."

"Which is far too strong for two of us, but not strong enough for three of us," returned D'Artagnan.

"I don't understand," said Porthos.

"Never mind; let's sit down to table and take something to strengthen us for the night."

"What are we to do, then, to-night?"

"To travel--perhaps."

"But----"

"Sit down, dear friend, to table. When one is eating, ideas flow easily. After supper, when they are perfected, I will communicate my plans to you."

So Porthos sat down to table without another word and ate with an appetite that did honor to the confidence that was ever inspired in him by D'Artagnan's inventive imagination.

84. Strength and Sagacity--Continued.

Supper was eaten in silence, but not in sadness; for from time to time one of those sweet smiles which were habitual to him in moments of good-humor illumined the face of D'Artagnan. Not a scintilla of these was lost on Porthos; and at every one he uttered an exclamation which betrayed to his friend that he had not lost sight of the idea which possessed his brain.

At dessert D'Artagnan reposed in his chair, crossed one leg over the other and lounged about like a man perfectly at his ease.

Porthos rested his chin on his hands, placed his elbows on the table and looked at D'Artagnan with an expression of confidence which imparted to that colossus an admirable appearance of good-fellowship.

"Well?" said D'Artagnan, at last.

"Well!" repeated Porthos.

"You were saying, my dear friend----"

"No; I said nothing."

"Yes; you were saying you wished to leave this place."

"Ah, indeed! the will was never wanting."

"To get away you would not mind, you added, knocking down a door or a wall."

"'Tis true--I said so, and I say it again."

"And I answered you, Porthos, that it was not a good plan; that we couldn't go a hundred steps without being recaptured, because we were without clothes to disguise ourselves and arms to defend ourselves."

"That is true; we should need clothes and arms."

"Well," said D'Artagnan, rising, "we have them, friend Porthos, and even something better."

"Bah!" said Porthos, looking around.

"Useless to look; everything will come to us when wanted. At about what time did we see the two Swiss guards walking yesterday?"

"An hour after sunset."

"If they go out to-day as they did yesterday we shall have the honor, then, of seeing them in half an hour?"

"In a quarter of an hour at most."

"Your arm is still strong enough, is it not, Porthos?"

Porthos unbuttoned his sleeve, raised his shirt and looked complacently on his strong arm, as large as the leg of any ordinary man.

"Yes, indeed," said he, "I believe so."

"So that you could without trouble convert these tongs into a hoop and yonder shovel into a corkscrew?"

"Certainly." And the giant took up these two articles, and without any apparent effort produced in them the metamorphoses suggested by his companion.

"There!" he cried.

"Capital!" exclaimed the Gascon. "Really, Porthos, you are a gifted individual!"

"I have heard speak," said Porthos, "of a certain Milo of Crotona, who performed wonderful feats, such as binding his forehead with a cord and bursting it--of killing an ox with a blow of his fist and carrying it home on his shoulders, et cetera. I used to learn all these feat by heart yonder, down at Pierrefonds, and I have done all that he did except breaking a cord by the corrugation of my temples."

"Because your strength is not in your head, Porthos," said his friend.

"No; it is in my arms and shoulders," answered Porthos with gratified naivete.

"Well, my dear friend, let us approach the window and there you can match your strength against that of an iron bar."

Porthos went to the window, took a bar in his hands, clung to it and bent it like a bow; so that the two ends came out of the sockets of stone in which for thirty years they had been fixed.

"Well! friend, the cardinal, although such a genius, could never have done that."

"Shall I take out any more of them?" asked Porthos.

"No; that is sufficient; a man can pass through that."

Porthos tried, and passed the upper portion of his body through.

"Yes," he said.

"Now pass your arm through this opening."

"Why?"

"You will know presently--pass it."

Porthos obeyed with military promptness and passed his arm through the opening.

"Admirable!" said D'Artagnan.

"The scheme goes forward, it seems."

"On wheels, dear friend."

"Good! What shall I do now?"

"Nothing."

"It is finished, then?"

"No, not yet."

"I should like to understand," said Porthos.

"Listen, my dear friend; in two words you will know all. The door of the guardhouse opens, as you see."

"Yes, I see."

"They are about to send into our court, which Monsieur de Mazarin crosses on his way to the orangery, the two guards who attend him."

"There they are, coming out."

"If only they close the guardhouse door! Good! They close it."

"What, then?"

"Silence! They may hear us."

"I don't understand it at all."

"As you execute you will understand."

"And yet I should have preferred----"

"You will have the pleasure of the surprise."

"Ah, that is true."

"Hush!"

Porthos remained silent and motionless.

In fact, the two soldiers advanced on the side where the window was, rubbing their hands, for it was cold, it being the month of February.

At this moment the door of the guardhouse was opened and one of the soldiers was summoned away.

"Now," said D'Artagnan, "I am going to call this soldier and talk to him. Don't lose a word of what I'm going to say to you, Porthos. Everything lies in the execution."

"Good, the execution of plots is my forte."

"I know it well. I depend on you. Look, I shall turn to the left, so that the soldier will be at your right, as soon as he mounts on the bench to talk to us."

"But supposing he doesn't mount?"

"He will; rely upon it. As soon as you see him get up, stretch out your arm and seize him by the neck. Then, raising him up as Tobit raised the fish by the gills, you must pull him into the room, taking care to squeeze him so tight that he can't cry out."

"Oh!" said Porthos. "Suppose I happen to strangle him?"

"To be sure there would only be a Swiss the less in the world; but you will not do so, I hope. Lay him down here; we'll gag him and tie him--no matter where--somewhere. So we shall get from him one uniform and a sword."

"Marvelous!" exclaimed Porthos, looking at the Gascon with the most profound admiration.

"Pooh!" replied D'Artagnan.

"Yes," said Porthos, recollecting himself, "but one uniform and one sword will not suffice for two."

"Well; but there's his comrade."

"True," said Porthos.

"Therefore, when I cough, stretch out your arm."

"Good!"

The two friends then placed themselves as they had agreed, Porthos being completely hidden in an angle of the window.

"Good-evening, comrade," said D'Artagnan in his most fascinating voice and manner.

"Good-evening, sir," answered the soldier, in a strong provincial accent.

"'Tis not too warm to walk," resumed D'Artagnan.

"No, sir."

"And I think a glass of wine will not be disagreeable to you?"

"A glass of wine will be extremely welcome."

"The fish bites--the fish bites!" whispered the Gascon to Porthos.

"I understand," said Porthos.

"A bottle, perhaps?"

"A whole bottle? Yes, sir."

"A whole bottle, if you will drink my health."

"Willingly," answered the soldier.

"Come, then, and take it, friend," said the Gascon.

"With all my heart. How convenient that there's a bench here. Egad! one would think it had been placed here on purpose."

"Get on it; that's it, friend."

And D'Artagnan coughed.

That instant the arm of Porthos fell. His hand of iron grasped, quick as lightning, firm as a pair of blacksmith's pincers, the soldier's throat. He raised him, almost stifling him as he drew him through the aperture, at the risk of flaying him in the passage. He then laid him down on the floor, where D'Artagnan, after giving him just time enough to draw his breath, gagged him with his long scarf; and the moment he had done so began to undress him with the promptitude and dexterity of a man who had learned his business on the field of battle. Then the soldier, gagged and bound, was placed upon the hearth, the fire of which had been previously extinguished by the two friends.

"Here's a sword and a dress," said Porthos.

"I take them," said D'Artagnan, "for myself. If you want another uniform and sword you must play the same trick over again. Stop! I see the other soldier issue from the guardroom and come toward us."

"I think," replied Porthos, "it would be imprudent to attempt the same manoeuvre again; it is said that no man can succeed twice in the same way, and a failure would be ruinous. No; I will go down, seize the man unawares and bring him to you ready gagged."

"That is better," said the Gascon.

"Be ready," said Porthos, as he slipped through the opening.

He did as he said. Porthos seized his opportunity, caught the next soldier by his neck, gagged him and pushed him like a mummy through the bars into the room, and entered after him. Then they undressed him as they had done the first, laid him on their bed and bound him with the straps which composed the bed--the bedstead being of oak. This operation proved as great a success as the first.

"There," said D'Artagnan, "this is capital! Now let me try on the dress of yonder chap. Porthos, I doubt if you can wear it; but should it be too tight, never mind, you can wear the breastplate and the hat with the red feathers."

It happened, however, that the second soldier was a Swiss of gigantic proportions, so, save that some few of the seams split, his uniform fitted Porthos perfectly.

They then dressed themselves.

"'Tis done!" they both exclaimed at once. "As to you, comrades," they said to the men, "nothing will happen to you if you are discreet; but if you stir you are dead men."

The soldiers were complaisant; they had found the grasp of Porthos pretty powerful and that it was no joke to fight against it.

"Now," said D'Artagnan, "you wouldn't be sorry to understand the plot, would you, Porthos?"

"Well, no, not very."

"Well, then, we shall go down into the court."

"Yes."

"We shall take the place of those two fellows."

"Well?"

"We will walk back and forth."

"That's a good idea, for it isn't warm."

"In a moment the valet-de-chambre will call the guard, as he did yesterday and the day before."

"And we shall answer?"

"No, on the contrary, we shall not answer."

"As you please; I don't insist on answering."

"We will not answer, then; we will simply settle our hats on our heads and we will escort his eminence."

"Where shall we escort him?"

"Where he is going--to visit Athos. Do you think Athos will be sorry to see us?"

"Oh!" cried Porthos, "oh! I understand."

"Wait a little, Porthos, before crying out; for, on my word, you haven't reached the end," said the Gascon, in a jesting tone.

"What is to happen?" said Porthos.

"Follow me," replied D'Artagnan. "The man who lives to see shall see."

And slipping through the aperture, he alighted in the court. Porthos followed him by the same road, but with more difficulty and less diligence. They could hear the two soldiers shivering with fear, as they lay bound in the chamber.

Scarcely had the two Frenchmen touched the ground when a door opened and the voice of the valet-de-chambre called out:

"Make ready!"

At the same moment the guardhouse was opened and a voice called out:

"La Bruyere and Du Barthois! March!"

"It seems that I am named La Bruyere," remarked D'Artagnan.

"And I, Du Barthois," added Porthos.

"Where are you?" asked the valet-de-chambre, whose eyes, dazzled by the light, could not clearly distinguish our heroes in the gloom.

"Here we are," said the Gascon.

"What say you to that, Monsieur du Vallon?" he added in a low tone to Porthos.

"If it but lasts, most capital," responded Porthos.

These two newly enlisted soldiers marched gravely after the valet-de-chambre, who opened the door of the vestibule, then another which seemed to be that of a waiting-room, and showing them two stools:

"Your orders are very simple," he said; "don't allow anybody, except one person, to enter here. Do you hear--not a single creature! Obey that person implicitly. On your return you cannot make a mistake. You have only to wait here till I release you."

D'Artagnan was known to this valet-de-chambre, who was no other than Bernouin, and he had during the last six or eight months introduced the Gascon a dozen times to the cardinal. The Gascon, therefore, instead of answering, growled out "Ja! Ja!" in the most German and the least Gascon accent possible.

As for Porthos, on whom D'Artagnan had impressed the necessity of absolute silence and who did not even now begin to comprehend the scheme of his friend, which was to follow Mazarin in his visit to Athos, he was simply mute. All that he was allowed to say, in case of emergencies, was the proverbial Der Teufel!

Bernouin shut the door and went away. When Porthos heard the key turn in the lock he began to be alarmed, lest they should only have exchanged one prison for another.

"Porthos, my friend," said D'Artagnan, "don't distrust Providence! Let me meditate and consider."

"Meditate and consider as much as you like," replied Porthos, who was now quite out of humor at seeing things take this turn.

"We have walked eight paces," whispered D'Artagnan, "and gone up six steps, so hereabouts is the pavilion called the pavilion of the orangery. The Comte de la Fere cannot be far off, only the doors are locked."

"That is a slight difficulty," said Porthos, "and a good push with the shoulders----"

"For God's sake, Porthos my friend, reserve your feats of strength, or they will not have, when needed, the honor they deserve. Have you not heard that some one is coming here?"

"Yes."

"Well, that some one will open the doors."

"But, my dear fellow, if that some one recognizes us, if that some one cries out, we are lost; for you don't propose, I imagine, that I shall kill that man of the church. That might do if we were dealing with Englishmen or Germans."

"Oh, may God keep me from it, and you, too!" said D'Artagnan. "The young king would, perhaps, show us some gratitude; but the queen would never forgive us, and it is she whom we have to consider. And then, besides, the useless blood! never! no, never! I have my plan; let me carry it out and we shall laugh."

"So much the better," said Porthos; "I feel some need of it."

"Hush!" said D'Artagnan; "the some one is coming."

The sound of a light step was heard in the vestibule. The hinges of the door creaked and a man appeared in the dress of a cavalier, wrapped in a brown cloak, with a lantern in one hand and a large beaver hat pulled down over his eyes.

Porthos effaced himself against the wall, but he could not render himself invisible; and the man in the cloak said to him, giving him his lantern:

"Light the lamp which hangs from the ceiling."

Then addressing D'Artagnan:

"You know the watchword?" he said.

"Ja!" replied the Gascon, determined to confine himself to this specimen of the German tongue.

"Tedesco!" answered the cavalier; "va bene."

And advancing toward the door opposite to that by which he came in, he opened it and disappeared behind it, shutting it as he went.

"Now," asked Porthos, "what are we to do?"

"Now we shall make use of your shoulder, friend Porthos, if this door proves to be locked. Everything in its proper time, and all comes right to those who know how to wait patiently. But first barricade the first door well; then we will follow yonder cavalier."

The two friends set to work and crowded the space before the door with all the furniture in the room, as not only to make the passage impassable, but so to block the door that by no means could it open inward.

"There!" said D'Artagnan, "we can't be overtaken. Come! forward!"

85. The Oubliettes of Cardinal Mazarin.

At first, on arriving at the door through which Mazarin had passed, D'Artagnan tried in vain to open it, but on the powerful shoulder of Porthos being applied to one of the panels, which gave way, D'Artagnan introduced the point of his sword between the bolt and the staple of the lock. The bolt gave way and the door opened.

"As I told you, everything can be attained, Porthos, women and doors, by proceeding with gentleness."

"You're a great moralist, and that's the fact," said Porthos.

They entered; behind a glass window, by the light of the cardinal's lantern, which had been placed on the floor in the midst of the gallery, they saw the orange and pomegranate trees of the Castle of Rueil, in long lines, forming one great alley and two smaller side alleys.

"No cardinal!" said D'Artagnan, "but only his lantern; where the devil, then, is he?"

Exploring, however, one of the side wings of the gallery, after making a sign to Porthos to explore the other, he saw, all at once, at his left, a tub containing an orange tree, which had been pushed out of its place and in its place an open aperture.

Ten men would have found difficulty in moving that tub, but by some mechanical contrivance it had turned with the flagstone on which it rested.

D'Artagnan, as we have said, perceived a hole in that place and in this hole the steps of a winding staircase.

He called Porthos to look at it.

"Were our object money only," he said, "we should be rich directly."

"How's that?"

"Don't you understand, Porthos? At the bottom of that staircase lies, probably, the cardinal's treasury of which folk tell such wonders, and we should only have to descend, empty a chest, shut the cardinal up in it, double lock it, go away, carrying off as much gold as we could, put back this orange-tree over the place, and no one in the world would ever ask us where our fortune came from--not even the cardinal."

"It would be a happy hit for clowns to make, but as it seems to be unworthy of two gentlemen----" said Porthos.

"So I think; and therefore I said, 'Were our object money only;' but we want something else," replied the Gascon.

At the same moment, whilst D'Artagnan was leaning over the aperture to listen, a metallic sound, as if some one was moving a bag of gold, struck on his ear; he started; instantly afterward a door opened and a light played upon the staircase.

Mazarin had left his lamp in the gallery to make people believe that he was walking about, but he had with him a waxlight, to help him to explore his mysterious strong box.

"Faith," he said, in Italian, as he was reascending the steps and looking at a bag of reals, "faith, there's enough to pay five councillors of parliament, and two generals in Paris. I am a great captain--that I am! but I make war in my own way."

The two friends were crouching down, meantime, behind a tub in the side alley.

Mazarin came within three steps of D'Artagnan and pushed a spring in the wall; the slab turned and the orange tree resumed its place.

Then the cardinal put out the waxlight, slipped it into his pocket, and taking up the lantern: "Now," he said, "for Monsieur de la Fere."

"Very good," thought D'Artagnan, "'tis our road likewise; we will go together."

All three set off on their walk, Mazarin taking the middle alley and the friends the side ones.

The cardinal reached a second door without perceiving he was being followed; the sand with which the alleys were covered deadened the sound of footsteps.

He then turned to the left, down a corridor which had escaped the attention of the two friends, but as he opened the door he paused, as if in thought.

"Ah! Diavolo!" he exclaimed, "I forgot the recommendation of De Comminges, who advised me to take a guard and place it at this door, in order not to put myself at the mercy of that four-headed combination of devils." And with a movement of impatience he turned to retrace his steps.

"Do not give yourself the trouble, my lord," said D'Artagnan, with his right foot forward, his beaver in his hand, a smile on his face, "we have followed your eminence step by step and here we are."

"Yes--here we are," said Porthos.

And he made the same friendly salute as D'Artagnan.

Mazarin gazed at each of them with an affrighted stare, recognized them, and let drop his lantern, uttering a cry of terror.

D'Artagnan picked it up; by good luck it had not been extinguished.

"Oh, what imprudence, my lord," said D'Artagnan; "'tis not good to be about just here without a light. Your eminence might knock against something, or fall into a hole."

"Monsieur d'Artagnan!" muttered Mazarin, unable to recover from his astonishment.

"Yes, my lord, it is I. I have the honor to present to you Monsieur du Vallon, that excellent friend of mine, in whom your eminence had the kindness to interest yourself formerly."

And D'Artagnan held the lamp before the merry face of Porthos, who now began to comprehend the affair and be very proud of the whole undertaking.

"You were going to visit Monsieur de la Fere?" said D'Artagnan. "Don't let us disarrange your eminence. Be so good as to show us the way and we will follow you."

Mazarin was by degrees recovering his senses.

"Have you been long in the orangery?" he asked in a trembling voice, remembering the visits he had been paying to his treasury.

Porthos opened his mouth to reply; D'Artagnan made him a sign, and his mouth, remaining silent, gradually closed.

"This moment come, my lord," said D'Artagnan.

Mazarin breathed again. His fears were now no longer for his hoard, but for himself. A sort of smile played on his lips.

"Come," he said, "you have me in a snare, gentlemen. I confess myself conquered. You wish to ask for liberty, and--I give it you."

"Oh, my lord!" answered D'Artagnan, "you are too good; as to our liberty, we have that; we want to ask something else of you."

"You have your liberty?" repeated Mazarin, in terror.

"Certainly; and on the other hand, my lord, you have lost it, and now, in accordance with the law of war, sir, you must buy it back again."

Mazarin felt a shiver run through him--a chill even to his heart's core. His piercing look was fixed in vain on the satirical face of the Gascon and the unchanging countenance of Porthos. Both were in shadow and the Sybil of Cuma herself could not have read them.

"To purchase back my liberty?" said the cardinal.

"Yes, my lord."

"And how much will that cost me, Monsieur d'Artagnan?"

"Zounds, my lord, I don't know yet. We must ask the Comte de la Fere the question. Will your eminence deign to open the door which leads to the count's room, and in ten minutes all will be settled."

Mazarin started.

"My lord," said D'Artagnan, "your eminence sees that we wish to act with all formality and due respect; but I must warn you that we have no time to lose; open the door then, my lord, and be so good as to remember, once for all, that on the slightest attempt to escape or the faintest cry for help, our position being very critical indeed, you must not be angry with us if we go to extremities."

"Be assured," answered Mazarin, "that I shall attempt nothing; I give you my word of honor."

D'Artagnan made a sign to Porthos to redouble his watchfulness; then turning to Mazarin:

"Now, my lord, let us enter, if you please."

86. Conferences.

Mazarin turned the lock of a double door, on the threshold of which they found Athos ready to receive his illustrious guests according to the notice Comminges had given him.

On perceiving Mazarin he bowed.

"Your eminence," he said, "might have dispensed with your attendants; the honor bestowed on me is too great for me to be unmindful of it."

"And so, my dear count," said D'Artagnan, "his eminence didn't actually insist on our attending him; it is Du Vallon and I who have insisted, and even in a manner somewhat impolite, perhaps, so great was our longing to see you."

At that voice, that mocking tone, and that familiar gesture, accenting voice and tone, Athos made a bound of surprise.

"D'Artagnan! Porthos!" he exclaimed.

"My very self, dear friend."

"Me, also!" repeated Porthos.

"What means this?" asked the count.

"It means," replied Mazarin, trying to smile and biting his lips in the attempt, "that our parts are changed, and that instead of these gentlemen being my prisoners I am theirs; but, gentlemen, I warn you, unless you kill me, your victory will be of very short duration; people will come to the rescue."

"Ah! my lord!" cried the Gascon, "don't threaten! 'tis a bad example. We are so good and gentle to your eminence. Come, let us put aside all rancor and talk pleasantly."

"There's nothing I wish more," replied Mazarin. "But don't think yourselves in a better position than you are. In ensnaring me you have fallen into the trap yourselves. How are you to get away from here? remember the soldiers and sentinels who guard these doors. Now, I am going to show you how sincere I am."

"Good," thought D'Artagnan; "we must look about us; he's going to play us a trick."

"I offered you your liberty," continued the minister; "will you take it? Before an hour has passed you will be discovered, arrested, obliged to kill me, which would be a crime unworthy of loyal gentlemen like you."

"He is right," thought Athos.

And, like every other reflection passing in a mind that entertained none but noble thoughts, this feeling was expressed in his eyes.

"And therefore," said D'Artagnan, to clip the hope which Athos's tacit adhesion had imparted to Mazarin, "we shall not proceed to that violence save in the last extremity."

"If on the contrary," resumed Mazarin, "you accept your liberty----"

"Why you, my lord, might take it away from us in less than five minutes afterward; and from my knowledge of you I believe you will so take it away from us."

"No--on the faith of a cardinal. You do not believe me?"

"My lord, I never believe cardinals who are not priests."

"Well, on the faith of a minister."

"You are no longer a minister, my lord; you are a prisoner."

"Then, on the honor of a Mazarin, as I am and ever shall be, I hope," said the cardinal.

"Hem," replied D'Artagnan. "I have heard speak of a Mazarin who had not much religion when his oaths were in question. I fear he may have been an ancestor of your eminence."

"Monsieur d'Artagnan, you are a great wit and I am really sorry to be on bad terms with you."

"My lord, let us come to terms; I ask nothing better."

"Very well," said Mazarin, "if I place you in security, in a manner evident, palpable----"

"Ah! that is another thing," said Porthos.

"Let us see," said Athos.

"Let us see," said D'Artagnan.

"In the first place, do you accept?" asked the cardinal.

"Unfold your plan, my lord, and we will see."

"Take notice that you are shut up--captured."

"You well know, my lord, that there always remains to us a last resource."

"What?"

"That of dying together."

Mazarin shuddered.

"Listen," he said; "at the end of yonder corridor is a door, of which I have the key, it leads into the park. Go, and take this key with you; you are active, vigorous, and you have arms. At a hundred steps, on turning to the left, you will find the wall of the park; get over it, and in three leaps you will be on the road and free."

"Ah! by Jove, my lord," said D'Artagnan, "you have well said, but these are only words. Where is the key you speak of?"

"Here it is."

"Ah, my lord! You will conduct us yourself, then, to that door?"

"Very willingly, if it be necessary to reassure you," answered the minister, and Mazarin, who was delighted to get off so cheaply, led the way, in high spirits, to the corridor and opened the door.

It led into the park, as the three fugitives perceived by the night breeze which rushed into the corridor and blew the wind into their faces.

"The devil!" exclaimed the Gascon, "'tis a dreadful night, my lord. We don't know the locality, and shall never find the wall. Since your eminence has come so far, come a few steps further; conduct us, my lord, to the wall."

"Be it so," replied the cardinal; and walking in a straight line he went to the wall, at the foot of which they all four arrived at the same instant.

"Are you satisfied, gentlemen?" asked Mazarin.

"I think so, indeed; we should be hard to please if we were not. Deuce take it! three poor gentlemen escorted by a prince of the church! Ah! apropos, my lord! you remarked that we were all active, vigorous and armed."

"Yes."

"You are mistaken. Monsieur du Vallon and I are the only two who are armed. The count is not; and should we meet with one of your patrol we must defend ourselves."

"'Tis true."

"Where can we find another sword?" asked Porthos.

"My lord," said D'Artagnan, "will lend his, which is of no use to him, to the Comte de la Fere."

"Willingly," said the cardinal; "I will even ask the count to keep it for my sake."

"I promise you, my lord, never to part with it," replied Athos.

"Well, well," cried D'Artagnan, "this reconciliation is truly touching; have you not tears in your eyes, Porthos?"

"Yes," said Porthos; "but I do not know if it is feeling or the wind that makes me weep; I think it is the wind."

"Now climb up, Athos, quickly," said D'Artagnan. Athos, assisted by Porthos, who lifted him up like a feather, arrived at the top.

"Now, jump down, Athos."

Athos jumped and disappeared on the other side of the wall.

"Are you on the ground?" asked D'Artagnan.

"Yes."

"Without accident?"

"Perfectly safe and sound."

"Porthos, whilst I get up, watch the cardinal. No, I don't want your help, watch the cardinal."

"I am watching," said Porthos. "Well?"

"You are right; it is more difficult than I thought. Lend me your back--but don't let the cardinal go."

Porthos lent him his back and D'Artagnan was soon on the summit of the wall, where he seated himself.

Mazarin pretended to laugh.

"Are you there?" asked Porthos.

"Yes, my friend; and now----"

"Now, what?" asked Porthos.

"Now give me the cardinal up here; if he makes any noise stifle him."

Mazarin wished to call out, but Porthos held him tight and passed him to D'Artagnan, who seized him by the neck and made him sit down by him; then in a menacing tone, he said:

"Sir! jump directly down, close to Monsieur de la Fere, or, on the honor of a gentleman, I'll kill you!"

"Monsieur, monsieur," cried Mazarin, "you are breaking your word to me!"

"I--did I promise you anything, my lord?"

Mazarin groaned.

"You are free," he said, "through me; your liberty was my ransom."

"Agreed; but the ransom of that immense treasure buried under the gallery, to which one descends on pushing a spring hidden in the wall, which causes a tub to turn, revealing a staircase--must not one speak of that a little, my lord?"

"Diavolo!" cried Mazarin, almost choked, and clasping his hands; "I am a lost and ruined man!"

But without listening to his protestations of alarm, D'Artagnan slipped him gently down into the arms of Athos, who stood immovable at the bottom of the wall.

Porthos next made an effort which shook the solid wall, and by the aid of his friend's hand gained the summit.

"I didn't understand it all," he said, "but I understand now; how droll it is!"

"You think so? so much the better; but that it may prove laughter-worthy even to the end, let us not lose time." And he jumped off the wall.

Porthos did the same.

"Attend to monsieur le cardinal, gentlemen," said D'Artagnan; "for myself, I will reconnoitre."

The Gascon then drew his sword and marched as avant guard.

"My lord," he said, "which way do we go? Think well of your reply, for should your eminence be mistaken, there might ensue most grave results for all of us."

"Along the wall, sir," said Mazarin, "there will be no danger of losing yourselves."

The three friends hastened on, but in a short time were obliged to slacken the pace. The cardinal could not keep up with them, though with every wish to do so.

Suddenly D'Artagnan touched something warm, which moved.

"Stop! a horse!" he cried; "I have found a horse!"

"And I, likewise," said Athos.

"I, too," said Porthos, who, faithful to the instructions, still held the cardinal's arm.

"There's luck, my lord! just as you were complaining of being tired and obliged to walk."

But as he spoke the barrel of a pistol was presented at his breast and these words were pronounced:

"Touch it not!"

"Grimaud!" he cried; "Grimaud! what art thou about? Why, thou art posted here by Heaven!"

"No, sir," said the honest servant, "it was Monsieur Aramis who posted me here to take care of the horses."

"Is Aramis here?"

"Yes, sir; he has been here since yesterday."

"What are you doing?"

"On the watch----"

"What! Aramis here?" cried Athos.

"At the lesser gate of the castle; he's posted there."

"Are you a large party?"

"Sixty."

"Let him know."

"This moment, sir."

And believing that no one could execute the commission better than himself, Grimaud set off at full speed; whilst, enchanted at being all together again, the friends awaited his return.

There was no one in the whole group in a bad humor except Cardinal Mazarin.

87. Thinking that Porthos will be at last a Baron, and D'Artagnan a Captain.

At the expiration of ten minutes Aramis arrived, accompanied by Grimaud and eight or ten followers. He was excessively delighted and threw himself into his friends' arms.

"You are free, my brothers! free without my aid! and I shall have succeeded in doing nothing for you in spite of all my efforts."

"Do not be unhappy, dear friend, on that account; if you have done nothing as yet, you will do something soon," replied Athos.

"I had well concerted my plans," pursued Aramis; "the coadjutor gave me sixty men; twenty guard the walls of the park, twenty the road from Rueil to Saint Germain, twenty are dispersed in the woods. Thus I was able, thanks to the strategic disposition of my forces, to intercept two couriers from Mazarin to the queen."

Mazarin listened intently.

"But," said D'Artagnan, "I trust that you honorably sent them back to monsieur le cardinal!"

"Ah, yes!" said Aramis, "toward him I should be very likely to practice such delicacy of sentiment! In one of the despatches the cardinal declares to the queen that the treasury is empty and that her majesty has no more money. In the other he announces that he is about to transport his prisoners to Melun, since Rueil seemed to him not sufficiently secure. You can understand, dear friend, with what hope I was inspired by that last letter. I placed myself in ambuscade with my sixty men; I encircled the castle; the riding horses I entrusted to Grimaud and I awaited your coming out, which I did not expect till tomorrow, and I didn't hope to free you without a skirmish. You are free to-night, without fighting; so much the better! How did you manage to escape that scoundrel Mazarin? You must have much reason to complain of him."

"Not very much," said D'Artagnan.

"Really!"

"I might even say that we have some reason to praise him."

"Impossible!"

"Yes, really; it is owing to him that we are free."

"Owing to him?"

"Yes, he had us conducted into the orangery by Monsieur Bernouin, his valet-de-chambre, and from there we followed him to visit the Comte de la Fere. Then he offered us our liberty and we accepted it. He even went so far as to show us the way out; he led us to the park wall, which we climbed over without accident, and then we fell in with Grimaud."

"Well!" exclaimed Aramis, "this will reconcile me to him; but I wish he were here that I might tell him that I did not believe him capable of so noble an act."

"My lord," said D'Artagnan, no longer able to contain himself, "allow me to introduce to you the Chevalier d'Herblay, who wishes--as you may have heard--to offer his congratulations to your eminence."

And he retired, discovering Mazarin, who was in great confusion, to the astonished gaze of Aramis.

"Ho! ho!" exclaimed the latter, "the cardinal! a glorious prize! Halloo! halloo! friends! to horse! to horse!"

Several horsemen ran quickly to him.

"Zounds!" cried Aramis, "I may have done some good; so, my lord, deign to receive my most respectful homage! I will lay a wager that 'twas that Saint Christopher, Porthos, who performed this feat! Apropos! I forgot----" and he gave some orders in a low voice to one of the horsemen.

"I think it will be wise to set off," said D'Artagnan.

"Yes; but I am expecting some one, a friend of Athos."

"A friend!" exclaimed the count.

"And here he comes, by Jupiter! galloping through the bushes."

"The count! the count!" cried a young voice that made Athos start.

"Raoul! Raoul!" he ejaculated.

For one moment the young man forgot his habitual respect--he threw himself on his father's neck.

"Look, my lord cardinal," said Aramis, "would it not have been a pity to have separated men who love each other as we love? Gentlemen," he continued, addressing the cavaliers, who became more and more numerous every instant; "gentlemen, encircle his eminence, that you may show him the greater honor. He will, indeed give us the favor of his company; you will, I hope, be grateful for it; Porthos, do not lose sight of his eminence."

Aramis then joined Athos and D'Artagnan, who were consulting together.

"Come," said D'Artagnan, after a conference of five minutes' duration, "let us begin our journey."

"Where are we to go?" asked Porthos.

"To your house, dear Porthos, at Pierrefonds; your fine chateau is worthy of affording its princely hospitality to his eminence; it is, likewise, well situated--neither too near Paris, nor too far from it; we can establish a communication between it and the capital with great facility. Come, my lord, you shall be treated like a prince, as you are."

"A fallen prince!" exclaimed Mazarin, piteously.

"The chances of war," said Athos, "are many, but be assured we shall take no improper advantage of them."

"No, but we shall make use of them," said D'Artagnan.

The rest of the night was employed by these cavaliers in traveling with the wonderful rapidity of former days. Mazarin, still sombre and pensive, permitted himself to be dragged along in this way; it looked a race of phantoms. At dawn twelve leagues had been passed without drawing rein; half the escort were exhausted and several horses fell down.

"Horses, nowadays, are not what they were formerly," observed Porthos; "everything degenerates."

"I have sent Grimaud to Dammartin," said Aramis. "He is to bring us five fresh horses--one for his eminence, four for us. We, at least, must keep close to monseigneur; the rest of the start will rejoin us later. Once beyond Saint Denis we shall have nothing to fear."

Grimaud, in fact, brought back five horses. The nobleman to whom he applied, being a friend of Porthos, was very ready, not to sell them, as was proposed, but to lend them. Ten minutes later the escort stopped at Ermenonville, but the four friends went on with well sustained ardor, guarding Mazarin carefully. At noon they rode into the avenue of Pierrefonds.

"Ah!" said Mousqueton, who had ridden by the side of D'Artagnan without speaking a word on the journey, "you may think what you will, sir, but I can breathe now for the first time since my departure from Pierrefonds;" and he put his horse to a gallop to announce to the other servants the arrival of Monsieur du Vallon and his friends.

"We are four of us," said D'Artagnan; "we must relieve each other in mounting guard over my lord and each of us must watch three hours at a time. Athos is going to examine the castle, which it will be necessary to render impregnable in case of siege; Porthos will see to the provisions and Aramis to the troops of the garrison. That is to say, Athos will be chief engineer, Porthos purveyor-in-general, and Aramis governor of the fortress."

Meanwhile, they gave up to Mazarin the handsomest room in the chateau.

"Gentlemen," he said, when he was in his room, "you do not expect, I presume, to keep me here a long time incognito?"

"No, my lord," replied the Gascon; "on the contrary, we think of announcing very soon that we have you here."

"Then you will be besieged."

"We expect it."

"And what shall you do?"

"Defend ourselves. Were the late Cardinal Richelieu alive he would tell you a certain story of the Bastion Saint Gervais, which we four, with our four lackeys and twelve dead men, held out against a whole army."

"Such feats, sir, are done once--and never repeated."

"However, nowadays there's no need of so much heroism. To-morrow the army of Paris will be summoned, the day after it will be here! The field of battle, instead, therefore, of being at Saint Denis or at Charenton, will be near Compiegne or Villars-Cotterets."

"The prince will vanquish you, as he has always done."

"'Tis possible; my lord; but before an engagement ensues we shall move your eminence to another castle belonging to our friend Du Vallon, who has three. We will not expose your eminence to the chances of war."

"Come," answered Mazarin, "I see it will be necessary for me to capitulate."

"Before a siege?"

"Yes; the conditions will be better than afterward."

"Ah, my lord! as to conditions, you would soon see how moderate and reasonable we are!"

"Come, now, what are your conditions?"

"Rest yourself first, my lord, and we--we will reflect."

"I do not need rest, gentlemen; I need to know whether I am among enemies or friends."

"Friends, my lord! friends!"

"Well, then, tell me at once what you want, that I may see if any arrangement be possible. Speak, Comte de la Fere!"

"My lord," replied Athos, "for myself I have nothing to demand. For France, were I to specify my wishes, I should have too much. I beg you to excuse me and propose to the chevalier."

And Athos, bowing, retired and remained leaning against the mantelpiece, a spectator of the scene.

"Speak, then, chevalier!" said the cardinal. "What do you want? Nothing ambiguous, if you please. Be clear, short and precise."

"As for me," replied Aramis, "I have in my pocket the very programme of the conditions which the deputation--of which I formed one--went yesterday to Saint Germain to impose on you. Let us consider first the ancient rights. The demands in that programme must be granted."

"We were almost agreed on those," replied Mazarin; "let us pass on to private and personal stipulations."

"You suppose, then, that there are some?" said Aramis, smiling.

"I do not suppose that you will all be quite so disinterested as Monsieur de la Fere," replied the cardinal, bowing to Athos.

"My lord, you are right, and I am glad to see that you do justice to the count at last. The count has a mind above vulgar desires and earthly passions. He is a proud soul--he is a man by himself! You are right--he is worth us all, and we avow it to you!"

"Aramis," said Athos, "are you jesting?"

"No, no, dear friend; I state only what we all know. You are right; it is not you alone this matter concerns, but my lord and his unworthy servant, myself."

"Well, then, what do you require besides the general conditions before recited?"

"I require, my lord, that Normandy should be given to Madame de Longueville, with five hundred thousand francs and full absolution. I require that his majesty should deign to be godfather to the child she has just borne; and that my lord, after having been present at the christening, should go to proffer his homage to our Holy Father the Pope."

"That is, you wish me to lay aside my ministerial functions, to quit France and be an exile."

"I wish his eminence to become pope on the first opportunity, allowing me then the right of demanding full indulgences for myself and my friends."

Mazarin made a grimace which was quite indescribable, and then turned to D'Artagnan.

"And you, sir?" he said.

"I, my lord," answered the Gascon, "I differ from Monsieur d'Herblay entirely as to the last point, though I agree with him on the first. Far from wishing my lord to quit Paris, I hope he will stay there and continue to be prime minister, as he is a great statesman. I shall try also to help him to down the Fronde, but on one condition--that he sometimes remembers the king's faithful servants and gives the first vacant company of musketeers to a man that I could name. And you, Monsieur du Vallon----"

"Yes, you, sir! Speak, if you please," said Mazarin.

"As for me," answered Porthos, "I wish my lord cardinal, in order to do honor to my house, which gives him an asylum, would in remembrance of this adventure erect my estate into a barony, with a promise to confer that order on one of my particular friends, whenever his majesty next creates peers."

"You know, sir, that before receiving the order one must submit proofs."

"My friends will submit them. Besides, should it be necessary, monseigneur will show him how that formality may be avoided."

Mazarin bit his lips; the blow was direct and he replied rather dryly:

"All this appears to me to be ill conceived, disjointed, gentlemen; for if I satisfy some I shall displease others. If I stay in Paris I cannot go to Rome; if I became pope I could not continue to be prime minister; and it is only by continuing prime minister that I can make Monsieur d'Artagnan a captain and Monsieur du Vallon a baron."

"True," said Aramis, "so, as I am in a minority, I withdraw my proposition, so far as it relates to the voyage to Rome and monseigneur's resignation."

"I am to remain minister, then?" said Mazarin.

"You remain minister; that is understood," said D'Artagnan; "France needs you."

"And I desist from my pretensions," said Aramis. "His eminence will continue to be prime minister and her majesty's favorite, if he will grant to me and my friends what we demand for France and for ourselves."

"Occupy yourselves with your own affairs, gentlemen, and let France settle matters as she will with me," resumed Mazarin.

"Ho! ho!" replied Aramis. "The Frondeurs will have a treaty and your eminence must sign it before us, promising at the same time to obtain the queen's consent to it."

"I can answer only for myself," said Mazarin. "I cannot answer for the queen. Suppose her majesty refuses?"

"Oh!" said D'Artagnan, "monseigneur knows very well that her majesty refuses him nothing."

"Here, monseigneur," said Aramis, "is the treaty proposed by the deputation of Frondeurs. Will your eminence please read and examine?"

"I am acquainted with it."

"Sign it, then."

"Reflect, gentlemen, that a signature given under circumstances like the present might be regarded as extorted by violence."

"Monseigneur will be at hand to testify that it was freely given."

"Suppose I refuse?"

"Then," said D'Artagnan, "your eminence must expect the consequences of a refusal."

"Would you dare to touch a cardinal?"

"You have dared, my lord, to imprison her majesty's musketeers."

"The queen will revenge me, gentlemen."

"I do not think so, although inclination might lead her to do so, but we shall take your eminence to Paris, and the Parisians will defend us."

"How uneasy they must be at this moment at Rueil and Saint Germain," said Aramis. "How they must be asking, 'Where is the cardinal?' 'What has become of the minister?' 'Where has the favorite gone?' How they must be looking for monseigneur in all corners! What comments must be made; and if the Fronde knows that monseigneur has disappeared, how the Fronde must triumph!"

"It is frightful," murmured Mazarin.

"Sign the treaty, then, monseigneur," said Aramis.

"Suppose the queen should refuse to ratify it?"

"Ah! nonsense!" cried D'Artagnan, "I can manage so that her majesty will receive me well; I know an excellent method."

"What?"

"I shall take her majesty the letter in which you tell her that the finances are exhausted."

"And then?" asked Mazarin, turning pale.

"When I see her majesty embarrassed, I shall conduct her to Rueil, make her enter the orangery and show her a certain spring which turns a box."

"Enough, sir," muttered the cardinal, "you have said enough; where is the treaty?"

"Here it is," replied Aramis. "Sign, my lord," and he gave him a pen.

Mazarin arose, walked some moments, thoughtful, but not dejected.

"And when I have signed," he said, "what is to be my guarantee?"

"My word of honor, sir," said Athos.

Mazarin started, turned toward the Comte de la Fere, and looking for an instant at that grand and honest countenance, took the pen.

"It is sufficient, count," he said, and signed the treaty.

"And now, Monsieur d'Artagnan," he said, "prepare to set off for Saint Germain and take a letter from me to the queen."

88. Shows how with Threat and Pen more is effected than by the Sword.

D'Artagnan knew his part well; he was aware that opportunity has a forelock only for him who will take it and he was not a man to let it go by him without seizing it. He soon arranged a prompt and certain manner of traveling, by sending relays of horses to Chantilly, so that he might be in Paris in five or six hours. But before setting out he reflected that for a lad of intelligence and experience he was in a singular predicament, since he was proceeding toward uncertainty and leaving certainty behind him.

"In fact," he said, as he was about to mount and start on his dangerous mission, "Athos, for generosity, is a hero of romance; Porthos has an excellent disposition, but is easily influenced; Aramis has a hieroglyphic countenance, always illegible. What will come out of those three elements when I am no longer present to combine them? The deliverance of the cardinal, perhaps. Now, the deliverance of the cardinal would be the ruin of our hopes; and our hopes are thus far the only recompense we have for labors in comparison with which those of Hercules were pygmean."

He went to find Aramis.

"You, my dear Chevalier d'Herblay," he said, "are the Fronde incarnate. Mistrust Athos, therefore, who will not prosecute the affairs of any one, even his own. Mistrust Porthos, especially, who, to please the count whom he regards as God on earth, will assist him in contriving Mazarin's escape, if Mazarin has the wit to weep or play the chivalric."

Aramis smiled; his smile was at once cunning and resolute.

"Fear nothing," he said; "I have my conditions to impose. My private ambition tends only to the profit of him who has justice on his side."

"Good!" thought D'Artagnan: "in this direction I am satisfied." He pressed Aramis's hand and went in search of Porthos.

"Friend," he said, "you have worked so hard with me toward building up our fortune, that, at the moment when we are about to reap the fruits of our labours, it would be a ridiculous piece of silliness in you to allow yourself to be controlled by Aramis, whose cunning you know--a cunning which, we may say between ourselves, is not always without egotism; or by Athos, a noble and disinterested man, but blase, who, desiring nothing further for himself, doesn't sympathize with the desires of others. What should you say if either of these two friends proposed to you to let Mazarin go?"

"Why, I should say that we had too much trouble in taking him to let him off so easily."

"Bravo, Porthos! and you would be right, my friend; for in losing him you would lose your barony, which you have in your grasp, to say nothing of the fact that, were he once out of this, Mazarin would have you hanged."

"Do you think so?"

"I am sure of it."

"Then I would kill him rather than let him go."

"And you would act rightly. There is no question, you understand, provided we secure our own interests, of securing those of the Frondeurs; who, besides, don't understand political matters as we old soldiers do."

"Never fear, dear friend," said Porthos. "I shall see you through the window as you mount your horse; I shall follow you with my eyes as long as you are in sight; then I shall place myself at the cardinal's door--a door with glass windows. I shall see everything, and at the least suspicious sign I shall begin to exterminate."

"Bravo!" thought D'Artagnan; "on this side I think the cardinal will be well guarded." He pressed the hand of the lord of Pierrefonds and went in search of Athos.

"My dear Athos," he said, "I am going away. I have only one thing to say to you. You know Anne of Austria; the captivity of Mazarin alone guarantees my life; if you let him go I am a dead man."

"I needed nothing less than that consideration, my dear D'Artagnan, to persuade myself to adopt the role of jailer. I give you my word that you will find the cardinal where you leave him."

"This reassures me more than all the royal signatures," thought D'Artagnan. "Now that I have the word of Athos I can set out."

D'Artagnan started alone on his journey, without other escort than his sword, and with a simple passport from Mazarin to secure his admission to the queen's presence. Six hours after he left Pierrefonds he was at Saint Germain.

The disappearance of Mazarin was not as yet generally known. Anne of Austria was informed of it and concealed her uneasiness from every one. In the chamber of D'Artagnan and Porthos the two soldiers had been found bound and gagged. On recovering the use of their limbs and tongues they could, of course, tell nothing but what they knew--that they had been seized, stripped and bound. But as to what had been done by Porthos and D'Artagnan afterward they were as ignorant as all the inhabitants of the chateau.

Bernouin alone knew a little more than the others. Bernouin, seeing that his master did not return and hearing the stroke of midnight, had made an examination of the orangery. The first door, barricaded with furniture, had aroused in him certain suspicions, but without communicating his suspicions to any one he had patiently worked his way into the midst of all that confusion. Then he came to the corridor, all the doors of which he found open; so, too, was the door of Athos's chamber and that of the park. From the latter point it was easy to follow tracks on the snow. He saw that these tracks tended toward the wall; on the other side he found similar tracks, then footprints of horses and then signs of a troop of cavalry which had moved away in the direction of Enghien. He could no longer cherish any doubt that the cardinal had been carried off by the three prisoners, since the prisoners had disappeared at the same time; and he had hastened to Saint Germain to warn the queen of that disappearance.

Anne had enforced the utmost secrecy and had disclosed the event to no one except the Prince de Conde, who had sent five or six hundred horsemen into the environs of Saint Germain with orders to bring in any suspicious person who was going away from Rueil, in whatsoever direction it might be.

Now, since D'Artagnan did not constitute a body of horsemen, since he was alone, since he was not going away from Rueil and was going to Saint Germain, no one paid any attention to him and his journey was not obstructed in any way.

On entering the courtyard of the old chateau the first person seen by our ambassador was Maitre Bernouin in person, who, standing on the threshold, awaited news of his vanished master.

At the sight of D'Artagnan, who entered the courtyard on horseback, Bernouin rubbed his eyes and thought he must be mistaken. But D'Artagnan made a friendly sign to him with his head, dismounted, and throwing his bridle to a lackey who was passing, he approached the valet-de-chambre with a smile on his lips.

"Monsieur d'Artagnan!" cried the latter, like a man who has the nightmare and talks in his sleep, "Monsieur d'Artagnan!"

"Himself, Monsieur Bernouin."

"And why have you come here?"

"To bring news of Monsieur de Mazarin--the freshest news there is."

"What has become of him, then?"

"He is as well as you and I."

"Nothing bad has happened to him, then?"

"Absolutely nothing. He felt the need of making a trip in the Ile de France, and begged us--the Comte de la Fere and Monsieur du Vallon--to accompany him. We were too devoted servants to refuse him a request of that sort. We set out last evening and here we are."

"Here you are."

"His eminence had something to communicate to her majesty, something secret and private--a mission that could be confided only to a sure man--and so has sent me to Saint Germain. And therefore, my dear Monsieur Bernouin, if you wish to do what will be pleasing to your master, announce to her majesty that I have come, and tell her with what purpose."

Whether he spoke seriously or in jest, since it was evident that under existing circumstances D'Artagnan was the only man who could relieve the queen's uneasiness, Bernouin went without hesitation to announce to her this strange embassy; and as he had foreseen, the queen gave orders to introduce Monsieur d'Artagnan at once.

D'Artagnan approached the sovereign with every mark of profound respect, and having fallen on his knees presented to her the cardinal's letter

It was, however, merely a letter of introduction. The queen read it, recognized the writing, and, since there were no details in it of what had occurred, asked for particulars. D'Artagnan related everything with that simple and ingenuous air which he knew how to assume on occasions. The queen, as he went on, looked at him with increasing astonishment. She could not comprehend how a man could conceive such an enterprise and still less how he could have the audacity to disclose it to her whose interest and almost duty it was to punish him.

"How, sir!" she cried, as D'Artagnan finished, "you dare to tell me the details of your crime--to give me an account of your treason!"

"Pardon, madame, but I think that either I have expressed myself badly or your majesty has imperfectly understood me. There is here no question of crime or treason. Monsieur de Mazarin held us in prison, Monsieur du Vallon and myself, because we could not believe that he had sent us to England to quietly look on while they cut off the head of Charles I., brother-in-law of the late king, your husband, the consort of Madame Henrietta, your sister and your guest, and because we did all that we could do to save the life of the royal martyr. We were then convinced, my friend and I, that there was some error of which we were the victims, and that an explanation was called for between his eminence and ourselves. Now, that an explanation may bear fruit, it is necessary that it should be quietly conducted, far from noise and interruption. We have therefore taken away monsieur le cardinal to my friend's chateau and there we have come to an understanding. Well, madame, it proved to be as we had supposed; there was a mistake. Monsieur de Mazarin had thought that we had rendered service to General Cromwell, instead of King Charles, which would have been a disgrace, rebounding from us to him, and from him to your majesty--a dishonor which would have tainted the royalty of your illustrious son. We were able to prove the contrary, and that proof we are ready to give to your majesty, calling in support of it the august widow weeping in the Louvre, where your royal munificence has provided for her a home. That proof satisfied him so completely that, as a sign of satisfaction, he has sent me, as your majesty may see, to consider with you what reparation should be made to gentlemen unjustly treated and wrongfully persecuted."

"I listen to you, and I wonder at you, sir," said the queen. "In fact, I have rarely seen such excess of impudence."

"Your majesty, on your side," said D'Artagnan, "is as much mistaken as to our intentions as the Cardinal Mazarin has always been."

"You are in error, sir," answered the queen. "I am so little mistaken that in ten minutes you shall be arrested, and in an hour I shall set off at the head of my army to release my minister."

"I am sure your majesty will not commit such an act of imprudence, first, because it would be useless and would produce the most disastrous results. Before he could be possibly set free the cardinal would be dead; and indeed, so convinced is he of this, that he entreated me, should I find your majesty disposed to act in this way, to do all I could to induce you to change your resolution."

"Well, then, I will content myself with arresting you!"

"Madame, the possibility of my arrest has been foreseen, and should I not have returned by tomorrow, at a certain hour the next day the cardinal will be brought to Paris and delivered to the parliament."

"It is evident, sir, that your position has kept you out of relation to men and affairs; otherwise you would know that since we left Paris monsieur le cardinal has returned thither five or six times; that he has there met De Beaufort, De Bouillon, the coadjutor and D'Elbeuf and that not one of them had any desire to arrest him."

"Your pardon, madame, I know all that. And therefore my friends will conduct monsieur le cardinal neither to De Beaufort, nor to De Bouillon, nor to the coadjutor, nor to D'Elbeuf. These gentlemen wage war on private account, and in buying them up, by granting them what they wished, monsieur le cardinal has made a good bargain. He will be delivered to the parliament, members of which can, of course, be bought, but even Monsieur de Mazarin is not rich enough to buy the whole body."

"I think," returned Anne of Austria, fixing upon him a glance, which in any woman's face would have expressed disdain, but in a queen's, spread terror to those she looked upon, "nay, I perceive you dare to threaten the mother of your sovereign."

"Madame," replied D'Artagnan, "I threaten simply and solely because I am obliged to do so. Believe me, madame, as true a thing as it is that a heart beats in this bosom--a heart devoted to you--believe that you have been the idol of our lives; that we have, as you well know--good Heaven!--risked our lives twenty times for your majesty. Have you, then, madame, no compassion for your servants who for twenty years have vegetated in obscurity, without betraying in a single sigh the solemn and sacred secrets they have had the honor to share with you? Look at me, madame--at me, whom you accuse of speaking loud and threateningly. What am I? A poor officer, without fortune, without protection, without a future, unless the eye of my queen, which I have sought so long, rests on me for a moment. Look at the Comte de la Fere, a type of nobility, a flower of chivalry. He has taken part against his queen, or rather, against her minister. He has not been unreasonably exacting, it seems to me. Look at Monsieur du Vallon, that faithful soul, that arm of steel, who for twenty years has awaited the word from your lips which will make him in rank what he is in sentiment and in courage. Consider, in short, your people who love you and who yet are famished, who have no other wish than to bless you, and who, nevertheless--no, I am wrong, your subjects, madame, will never curse you; say one word to them and all will be ended--peace succeed war, joy tears, and happiness to misfortune!"

Anne of Austria looked with wonderment on the warlike countenance of D'Artagnan, which betrayed a singular expression of deep feeling.

"Why did you not say all this before you took action, sir?" she said.

"Because, madame, it was necessary to prove to your majesty one thing of which you doubted---that is, that we still possess amongst us some valor and are worthy of some consideration at your hands."

"And that valor would shrink from no undertaking, according to what I see."

"It has hesitated at nothing in the past; why, then, should it be less daring in the future?"

"Then, in case of my refusal, this valor, should a struggle occur, will even go the length of carrying me off in the midst of my court, to deliver me into the hands of the Fronde, as you propose to deliver my minister?"

"We have not thought about it yet, madame," answered D'Artagnan, with that Gascon effrontery which had in him the appearance of naivete; "but if we four had resolved upon it we should do it most certainly."

"I ought," muttered Anne to herself, "by this time to remember that these men are giants."

"Alas, madame!" exclaimed D'Artagnan, "this proves to me that not till to-day has your majesty had a just idea of us."

"Perhaps," said Anne; "but that idea, if at last I have it----"

"Your majesty will do us justice. In doing us justice you will no longer treat us as men of vulgar stamp. You will see in me an ambassador worthy of the high interests he is authorized to discuss with his sovereign."

"Where is the treaty?"

"Here it is."

Anne of Austria cast her eyes upon the treaty that D'Artagnan presented to her.

"I do not see here," she said, "anything but general conditions; the interests of the Prince de Conti or of the Ducs de Beaufort, de Bouillon and d'Elbeuf and of the coadjutor, are herein consulted; but with regard to yours?"

"We do ourselves justice, madame, even in assuming the high position that we have. We do not think ourselves worthy to stand near such great names."

"But you, I presume, have decided to assert your pretensions viva voce?"

"I believe you, madame, to be a great and powerful queen, and that it will be unworthy of your power and greatness if you do not recompense the arms which will bring back his eminence to Saint Germain."

"It is my intention so to do; come, let us hear you. Speak."

"He who has negotiated these matters (forgive me if I begin by speaking of myself, but I must claim that importance which has been given to me, not assumed by me) he who has arranged matters for the return of the cardinal, ought, it appears to me, in order that his reward may not be unworthy of your majesty, to be made commandant of the guards--an appointment something like that of captain of the musketeers."

"'Tis the appointment Monsieur de Treville held, you ask of me."

"The place, madame, is vacant, and although 'tis a year since Monsieur de Treville has left it, it has not been filled."

"But it is one of the principal military appointments in the king's household."

"Monsieur de Treville was but a younger son of a simple Gascon family, like me, madame; he occupied that post for twenty years."

"You have an answer ready for everything," replied the queen, and she took from her bureau a document, which she filled up and signed.

"Undoubtedly, madame," said D'Artagnan, taking the document and bowing, "this is a noble reward; but everything in the world is unstable, and the man who happened to fall into disgrace with your majesty might lose this office to-morrow."

"What more do you want?" asked the queen, coloring, as she found that she had to deal with a mind as subtle as her own.

"A hundred thousand francs for this poor captain of musketeers, to be paid whenever his services shall no longer be acceptable to your majesty."

Anne hesitated.

"To think of the Parisians," soliloquized D'Artagnan, "offering only the other day, by an edict of the parliament, six hundred thousand francs to any man soever who would deliver up the cardinal to them, dead or alive--if alive, in order to hang him; if dead, to deny him the rites of Christian burial!"

"Come," said Anne, "'tis reasonable, since you only ask from a queen the sixth of what the parliament has proposed;" and she signed an order for a hundred thousand francs.

"Now, then," she said, "what next?"

"Madame, my friend Du Vallon is rich and has therefore nothing in the way of fortune to desire; but I think I remember that there was a question between him and Monsieur Mazarin as to making his estate a barony. Nay, it must have been a promise."

"A country clown," said Anne of Austria, "people will laugh."

"Let them," answered D'Artagnan. "But I am sure of one thing--that those who laugh at him in his presence will never laugh a second time."

"Here goes the barony." said the queen; she signed a patent.

"Now there remains the chevalier, or the Abbe d'Herblay, as your majesty pleases."

"Does he wish to be a bishop?"

"No, madame, something easier to grant."

"What?"

"It is that the king should deign to stand godfather to the son of Madame de Longueville."

The queen smiled.

"Monsieur de Longueville is of royal blood, madame," said D'Artagnan.

"Yes," said the queen; "but his son?"

"His son, madame, must be, since the husband of the son's mother is."

"And your friend has nothing more to ask for Madame de Longueville?"

"No, madame, for I presume that the king, standing godfather to him, could do no less than present him with five hundred thousand francs, giving his father, also, the government of Normandy."

"As to the government of Normandy," replied the queen, "I think I can promise; but with regard to the present, the cardinal is always telling me there is no more money in the royal coffers."

"We shall search for some, madame, and I think we can find a little, and if your majesty approves, we will seek for some together."

"What next?"

"What next, madame?"

"Yes."

"That is all."

"Haven't you, then, a fourth companion?"

"Yes, madame, the Comte de la Fere."

"What does he ask?"

"Nothing."

"There is in the world, then, one man who, having the power to ask, asks--nothing!"

"There is the Comte de la Fere, madame. The Comte de la Fere is not a man."

"What is he, then?"

"The Comte de la Fere is a demi-god."

"Has he not a son, a young man, a relative, a nephew, of whom Comminges spoke to me as being a brave boy, and who, with Monsieur de Chatillon, brought the standards from Lens?"

"He has, as your majesty has said, a ward, who is called the Vicomte de Bragelonne."

"If that young man should be appointed to a regiment what would his guardian say?"

"Perhaps he would accept."

"Perhaps?"

"Yes, if your majesty herself should beg him to accept."

"He must be indeed a strange man. Well, we will reflect and perhaps we will beg him. Are you satisfied, sir?"

"There is one thing the queen has not signed--her assent to the treaty."

"Of what use to-day? I will sign it to-morrow."

"I can assure her majesty that if she does not sign to-day she will not have time to sign to-morrow. Consent, then, I beg you, madame, to write at the bottom of this schedule, which has been drawn up by Mazarin, as you see:

"'I consent to ratify the treaty proposed by the Parisians.'"

Anne was caught, she could not draw back--she signed; but scarcely had she done so when pride burst forth and she began to weep.

D'Artagnan started on seeing these tears. Since that period of history queens have shed tears, like other women.

The Gascon shook his head, these tears from royalty melted his heart.

"Madame," he said, kneeling, "look upon the unhappy man at your feet. He begs you to believe that at a gesture of your majesty everything will be possible to him. He has faith in himself; he has faith in his friends; he wishes also to have faith in his queen. And in proof that he fears nothing, that he counts on nothing, he will restore Monsieur de Mazarin to your majesty without conditions. Behold, madame! here are the august signatures of your majesty's hand; if you think you are right in giving them to me, you shall do so, but from this very moment you are free from any obligation to keep them."

And D'Artagnan, full of splendid pride and manly intrepidity, placed in Anne's hands, in a bundle, the papers that he had one by one won from her with so much difficulty.

There are moments--for if everything is not good, everything in this world is not bad--in which the most rigid and the coldest soul is softened by the tears of strong emotion, heart-arraigning sentiment: one of these momentary impulses actuated Anne. D'Artagnan, when he gave way to his own feelings--which were in accordance with those of the queen--had accomplished more than the most astute diplomacy could have attempted. He was therefore instantly recompensed, either for his address or for his sensibility, whichever it might be termed.

"You were right, sir," said Anne. "I misunderstood you. There are the acts signed; I deliver them to you without compulsion. Go and bring me back the cardinal as soon as possible."

"Madame," faltered D'Artagnan, "'tis twenty years ago--I have a good memory--since I had the honor behind a piece of tapestry in the Hotel de Ville, of kissing one of those lovely hands."

"There is the other," replied the queen; "and that the left hand should not be less liberal than the right," she drew from her finger a diamond similar to the one formerly given to him, "take and keep this ring in remembrance of me.

"Madame," said D'Artagnan, rising, "I have only one thing more to wish, which is, that the next thing you ask from me, shall be--my life."

And with this conclusion--a way peculiar to himself--he rose and left the room.

"I never rightly understood those men," said the queen, as she watched him retiring from her presence; "and it is now too late, for in a year the king will be of age."

In twenty-four hours D'Artagnan and Porthos conducted Mazarin to the queen; and the one received his commission, the other his patent of nobility.

On the same day the Treaty of Paris was signed, and it was everywhere announced that the cardinal had shut himself up for three days in order to draw it up with the greatest care.

Here is what each of the parties concerned gained by that treaty:

Monsieur de Conti received Damvilliers, and having made his proofs as general, he succeeded in remaining a soldier, instead of being made cardinal. Moreover, something had been said of a marriage with Mazarin's niece. The idea was welcomed by the prince, to whom it was of little importance whom he married, so long as he married some one.

The Duc de Beaufort made his entrance at court, receiving ample reparation for the wrongs he had suffered, and all the honor due to his rank. Full pardon was accorded to those who had aided in his escape. He received also the office of admiral, which had been held by his father, the Duc de Vendome and an indemnity for his houses and castles, demolished by the Parliament of Bretagne.

The Duc de Bouillon received domains of a value equal to that of his principality of Sedan, and the title of prince, granted to him and to those belonging to his house.

The Duc de Longueville gained the government of Pont-de-l'Arche, five hundred thousand francs for his wife and the honor of seeing her son held at the baptismal font by the young king and Henrietta of England.

Aramis stipulated that Bazin should officiate at that ceremony and that Planchet should furnish the christening sugar plums.

The Duc d'Elbeuf obtained payment of certain sums due to his wife, one hundred thousand francs for his eldest son and twenty-five thousand for each of the three others.

The coadjutor alone obtained nothing. They promised, indeed, to negotiate with the pope for a cardinal's hat for him; but he knew how little reliance should be placed on such promises, made by the queen and Mazarin. Quite contrary to the lot of Monsieur de Conti, unable to be cardinal, he was obliged to remain a soldier.

And therefore, when all Paris was rejoicing in the expected return of the king, appointed for the next day, Gondy alone, in the midst of the general happiness, was dissatisfied; he sent for the two men whom he was wont to summon when in especially bad humor. Those two men were the Count de Rochefort and the mendicant of Saint Eustache. They came with their usual promptness, and the coadjutor spent with them a part of the night.

89. Difficult for Kings to return to the Capitals of their Kingdoms.

Whilst D'Artagnan and Porthos were engaged in conducting the cardinal to Saint Germain, Athos and Aramis returned to Paris.

Each had his own particular visit to make.

Aramis rushed to the Hotel de Ville, where Madame de Longueville was sojourning. The duchess loudly lamented the announcement of peace. War had made her a queen; peace brought her abdication. She declared that she would never assent to the treaty and that she wished eternal war.

But when Aramis had presented that peace to her in a true light--that is to say, with all its advantages; when he had pointed out to her, in exchange for the precarious and contested royalty of Paris, the vice-royalty of Font-de-l'Arche, in other words, of all Normandy; when he had rung in her ears the five hundred thousand francs promised by the cardinal; when he had dazzled her eyes with the honor bestowed on her by the king in holding her child at the baptismal font, Madame de Longueville contended no longer, except as is the custom with pretty women to contend, and defended herself only to surrender at last.

Aramis made a presence of believing in the reality of her opposition and was unwilling to deprive himself in his own view of the credit of her conversion.

"Madame," he said, "you have wished to conquer the prince your brother--that is to say, the greatest captain of the age; and when women of genius wish anything they always succeed in attaining it. You have succeeded; the prince is beaten, since he can no longer fight. Now attach him to our party. Withdraw him gently from the queen, whom he does not like, from Mazarin, whom he despises. The Fronde is a comedy, of which the first act only is played. Let us wait for a denouement--for the day when the prince, thanks to you, shall have turned against the court."

Madame de Longueville was persuaded. This Frondist duchess trusted so confidently to the power of her fine eyes, that she could not doubt their influence even over Monsieur de Conde; and the chronicles of the time aver that her confidence was justified.

Athos, on quitting Aramis, went to Madame de Chevreuse. Here was another frondeuse to persuade, and she was even less open to conviction than her younger rival. There had been no stipulation in her favor. Monsieur de Chevreuse had not been appointed governor of a province, and if the queen should consent to be godmother it could be only of her grandson or granddaughter. At the first announcement of peace Madame de Chevreuse frowned, and in spite of all the logic of Athos to show her that a prolonged war would have been impracticable, contended in favor of hostilities.

"My fair friend," said Athos, "allow me to tell you that everybody is tired of war. You will get yourself exiled, as you did in the time of Louis XIII. Believe me, we have passed the time of success in intrigue, and your fine eyes are not destined to be eclipsed by regretting Paris, where there will always be two queens as long as you are there."

"Oh," cried the duchess, "I cannot make war alone, but I can avenge myself on that ungrateful queen and most ambitious favorite-on the honor of a duchess, I will avenge myself."

"Madame," replied Athos, "do not injure the Vicomte de Bragelonne--do not ruin his prospects. Alas! excuse my weakness! There are moments when a man grows young again in his children."

The duchess smiled, half tenderly, half ironically.

"Count," she said, "you are, I fear, gained over to the court. I suppose you have a blue ribbon in your pocket?"

"Yes, madame; I have that of the Garter, which King Charles I. gave me some days before he died."

"Come, I am growing an old woman!" said the duchess, pensively.

Athos took her hand and kissed it. She sighed, as she looked at him.

"Count," she said, "Bragelonne must be a charming place. You are a man of taste. You have water--woods--flowers there?"

She sighed again and leaned her charming head, gracefully reclined, on her hand, still beautiful in form and color.

"Madame!" exclaimed Athos, "what were you saying just now about growing old? Never have I seen you look so young, so beautiful!"

The duchess shook her head.

"Does Monsieur de Bragelonne remain in Paris?" she inquired.

"What think you of it?" inquired Athos.

"Leave him with me," replied the duchess.

"No, madame; if you have forgotten the history of Oedipus, I, at least, remember it."

"Really, sir, you are delightful, and I should like to spend a month at Bragelonne."

"Are you not afraid of making people envious of me, duchess?" replied Athos.

"No, I shall go incognito, count, under the name of Marie Michon."

"You are adorable, madame."

"But do not keep Raoul with you."

"Why not?"

"Because he is in love."

"He! he is quite a child!"

"And 'tis a child he loves."

Athos became thoughtful.

"You are right, duchess. This singular passion for a child of seven may some day make him very unhappy. There is to be war in Flanders. He shall go thither."

"And at his return you will send him to me. I will arm him against love."

"Alas, madame!" exclaimed Athos, "to-day love is like war--the breastplate is becoming useless."

Raoul entered at this moment; he came to announce that the solemn entrance of the king, queen, and her ministers was to take place on the ensuing day.

The next day, in fact, at daybreak, the court made preparations to quit Saint Germain.

Meanwhile, the queen every hour had been sending for D'Artagnan.

"I hear," she said, "that Paris is not quiet. I am afraid for the king's safety; place yourself close to the coach door on the right."

"Reassure yourself, madame, I will answer for the king's safety."

As he left the queen's presence Bernouin summoned him to the cardinal.

"Sir," said Mazarin to him "an emeute is spoken of in Paris. I shall be on the king's left and as I am the chief person threatened, remain at the coach door to the left."

"Your eminence may be perfectly easy," replied D'Artagnan; "they will not touch a hair of your head."

"Deuce take it!" he thought to himself, "how can I take care of both? Ah! plague on't, I will guard the king and Porthos shall guard the cardinal."

This arrangement pleased every one. The queen had confidence in the courage of D'Artagnan, which she knew, and the cardinal in the strength of Porthos, which he had experienced.

The royal procession set out for Paris. Guitant and Comminges, at the head of the guards, marched first; then came the royal carriage, with D'Artagnan on one side, Porthos on the other; then the musketeers, for two and twenty years staunch friends of D'Artagnan. During twenty he had been lieutenant, their captain since the night before.

The cortege proceeded to Notre Dame, where a Te Deum was chanted. All Paris were in the streets. The Swiss were drawn up along the road, but as the road was long, they were placed at six or eight feet distant from each other and one deep only. This force was therefore wholly insufficient, and from time to time the line was broken through by the people and was formed again with difficulty. Whenever this occurred, although it proceeded only from goodwill and a desire to see the king and queen, Anne looked at D'Artagnan anxiously.

Mazarin, who had dispensed a thousand louis to make the people cry "Long live Mazarin," and who had accordingly no confidence in acclamations bought at twenty pistoles each, kept one eye on Porthos; but that gigantic body-guard replied to the look with his great bass voice, "Be tranquil, my lord," and Mazarin became more and more composed.

At the Palais Royal, the crowd, which had flowed in from the adjacent street was still greater; like an impetuous mob, a wave of human beings came to meet the carriage and rolled tumultuously into the Rue Saint Honore.

When the procession reached the palace, loud cries of "Long live their majesties!" resounded. Mazarin leaned out of the window. One or two shouts of "Long live the cardinal" saluted his shadow; but instantly hisses and yells stifled them remorselessly. Mazarin turned pale and shrank back in the coach.

"Low-born fellows!" ejaculated Porthos.

D'Artagnan said nothing, but twirled his mustache with a peculiar gesture which showed that his fine Gascon humor was awake.

Anne of Austria bent down and whispered in the young king's ear:

"Say something gracious to Monsieur d'Artagnan, my son."

The young king leaned toward the door.

"I have not said good-morning to you, Monsieur d'Artagnan," he said; "nevertheless, I have remarked you. It was you who were behind my bed-curtains that night the Parisians wished to see me asleep."

"And if the king permits me," returned the Gascon, "I shall be near him always when there is danger to be encountered."

"Sir," said Mazarin to Porthos, "what would you do if the crowd fell upon us?"

"Kill as many as I could, my lord."

"Hem! brave as you are and strong as you are, you could not kill them all."

"'Tis true," answered Porthos, rising on his saddle, in order that he might appraise the immense crowd, "there are a lot of them."

"I think I should like the other fellow better than this one," said Mazarin to himself, and he threw himself back in his carriage.

The queen and her minister, more especially the latter, had reason to feel anxious. The crowd, whilst preserving an appearance of respect and even of affection for the king and queen regent, began to be tumultuous. Reports were whispered about, like certain sounds which announce, as they whistle from wave to wave, the coming storm--and when they pass athwart a multitude, presage an emeute.

D'Artagnan turned toward the musketeers and made a sign imperceptible to the crowd, but very easily understood by that chosen regiment, the flower of the army.

The ranks closed firmly in and a kind of majestic tremor ran from man to man.

At the Barriere des Sergents the procession was obliged to stop. Comminges left the head of the escort and went to the queen's carriage. Anne questioned D'Artagnan by a look. He answered in the same language.

"Proceed," she said.

Comminges returned to his post. An effort was made and the living barrier was violently broken through.

Some complaints arose from the crowd and were addressed this time to the king as well as the minister.

"Onward!" cried D'Artagnan, in a loud voice.

"Onward!" cried Porthos.

But as if the multitude had waited only for this demonstration to burst out, all the sentiments of hostility that possessed it exploded simultaneously. Cries of "Down with Mazarin!" "Death to the cardinal!" resounded on all sides.

At the same time through the streets of Grenelle, Saint Honore, and Du Coq, a double stream of people broke the feeble hedge of Swiss guards and came like a whirlwind even to the very legs of Porthos's horse and that of D'Artagnan.

This new eruption was more dangerous than the others, being composed of armed men. It was plain that it was not the chance combination of those who had collected a number of the malcontents at the same spot, but a concerted organized attack.

Each of these mobs was led by a chief, one of whom appeared to belong, not to the people, but to the honorable corporation of mendicants, and the other, notwithstanding his affected imitation of the people, might easily be discerned to be a gentleman. Both were evidently stimulated by the same impulse.

There was a shock which was perceived even in the royal carriage. Myriads of hoarse cries, forming one vast uproar, were heard, mingled with guns firing.

"Ho! Musketeers!" cried D'Artagnan.

The escort divided into two files. One of them passed around to the right of the carriage, the other to the left. One went to support D'Artagnan, the other Porthos. Then came a skirmish, the more terrible because it had no definite object; the more melancholy, because those engaged in it knew not for whom they were fighting. Like all popular movements, the shock given by the rush of this mob was formidable. The musketeers, few in number, not being able, in the midst of this crowd, to make their horses wheel around, began to give way. D'Artagnan offered to lower the blinds of the royal carriage, but the young king stretched out his arm, saying:

"No, sir! I wish to see everything."

"If your majesty wishes to look out--well, then, look!" replied D'Artagnan. And turning with that fury which made him so formidable, he rushed toward the chief of the insurgents, a man who, with a huge sword in his hand, was trying to hew a passage to the coach door through the musketeers.

"Make room!" cried D'Artagnan. "Zounds! give way!"

At these words the man with a pistol and sword raised his head, but it was too late. The blow was sped by D'Artagnan; the rapier had pierced his bosom.

"Ah! confound it!" cried the Gascon, trying in vain, too late, to retract the thrust. "What the devil are you doing here, count?"

"Accomplishing my destiny," replied Rochefort, falling on one knee. "I have already got up again after three stabs from you, I shall never rise after this fourth."

"Count!" said D'Artagnan, with some degree of emotion, "I struck without knowing that it was you. I am sorry, if you die, that you should die with sentiments of hatred toward me."

Rochefort extended his hand to D'Artagnan, who took it. The count wished to speak, but a gush of blood stifled him. He stiffened in the last convulsions of death and expired.

"Back, people!" cried D'Artagnan, "your leader is dead; you have no longer any business here."

Indeed, as if De Rochefort had been the very soul of the attack, the crowd who had followed and obeyed him took to flight on seeing him fall. D'Artagnan charged, with a party of musketeers, up the Rue du Coq, and the portion of the mob he assailed disappeared like smoke, dispersing near the Place Saint Germain-l'Auxerrois and taking the direction of the quays.

D'Artagnan returned to help Porthos, if Porthos needed help; but Porthos, for his part, had done his work as conscientiously as D'Artagnan. The left of the carriage was as well cleared as the right, and they drew up the blind of the window which Mazarin, less heroic than the king, had taken the precaution to lower.

Porthos looked very melancholy.

"What a devil of a face you have, Porthos! and what a strange air for a victor!"

"But you," answered Porthos, "seem to me agitated."

"There's a reason! Zounds! I have just killed an old friend."

"Indeed!" replied Porthos, "who?"

"That poor Count de Rochefort."

"Well! exactly like me! I have just killed a man whose face is not unknown to me. Unluckily, I hit him on the head and immediately his face was covered with blood."

"And he said nothing as he died?"

"Yes; he exclaimed, 'Oh!'"

"I suppose," answered D'Artagnan, laughing, "if he only said that, it did not enlighten you much."

"Well, sir!" cried the queen.

"Madame, the passage is quite clear and your majesty can continue your road."

In fact, the procession arrived, in safety at Notre Dame, at the front gate of which all the clergy, with the coadjutor at their head, awaited the king, the queen and the minister, for whose happy return they chanted a Te Deum.

As the service was drawing to a close a boy entered the church in great excitement, ran to the sacristy, dressed himself quickly in the choir robes, and cleaving, thanks to that uniform, the crowd that filled the temple, approached Bazin, who, clad in his blue robe, was standing gravely in his place at the entrance to the choir.

Bazin felt some one pulling his sleeve. He lowered to earth his eyes, beatifically raised to Heaven, and recognized Friquet.

"Well, you rascal, what is it? How do you dare to disturb me in the exercise of my functions?" asked the beadle.

"Monsieur Bazin," said Friquet, "Monsieur Maillard--you know who he is, he gives holy water at Saint Eustache----"

"Well, go on."

"Well, he received in the scrimmage a sword stroke on the head. That great giant who was there gave it to him."

"In that case," said Bazin, "he must be pretty sick."

"So sick that he is dying, and he wants to confess to the coadjutor, who, they say, has power to remit great sins."

"And does he imagine that the coadjutor will put himself out for him?"

"To be sure; the coadjutor has promised."

"Who told you that?"

"Monsieur Maillard himself."

"You have seen him, then?"

"Certainly; I was there when he fell."

"What were you doing there?"

"I was shouting, 'Down with Mazarin!' 'Death to the cardinal!' 'The Italian to the gallows!' Isn't that what you would have me shout?"

"Be quiet, you rascal!" said Bazin, looking uneasily around.

"So that he told me, that poor Monsieur Maillard, 'Go find the coadjutor, Friquet, and if you bring him to me you shall be my heir.' Say, then, Father Bazin--

the heir of Monsieur Maillard, the giver of holy water at Saint Eustache! Hey! I shall have nothing to do but to fold my arms! All the same, I should like to do him that service--what do you say to it?"

"I will tell the coadjutor," said Bazin.

In fact, he slowly and respectfully approached the prelate and spoke to him privately a few words, to which the latter responded by an affirmative sign. He then returned with the same slow step and said:

"Go and tell the dying man that he must be patient. Monseigneur will be with him in an hour."

"Good!" said Friquet, "my fortune is made."

"By the way," said Bazin, "where was he carried?"

"To the tower Saint Jacques la Boucherie;" and delighted with the success of his embassy, Friquet started off at the top of his speed.

When the Te Deum was over, the coadjutor, without stopping to change his priestly dress, took his way toward that old tower which he knew so well. He arrived in time. Though sinking from moment to moment, the wounded man was not yet dead. The door was opened to the coadjutor of the room in which the mendicant was suffering.

A moment later Friquet went out, carrying in his hand a large leather bag; he opened it as soon as he was outside the chamber and to his great astonishment found it full of gold. The mendicant had kept his word and made Friquet his heir.

"Ah! Mother Nanette!" cried Friquet, suffocating; "ah! Mother Nanette!"

He could say no more; but though he hadn't strength to speak he had enough for action. He rushed headlong to the street, and like the Greek from Marathon who fell in the square at Athens, with his laurel in his hand, Friquet reached Councillor Broussel's threshold, and then fell exhausted, scattering on the floor the louis disgorged by his leather bag.

Mother Nanette began by picking up the louis; then she picked up Friquet.

In the meantime the cortege returned to the Palais Royal.

"That Monsieur d'Artagnan is a very brave man, mother," said the young king.

"Yes, my son; and he rendered very important services to your father. Treat him kindly, therefore, in the future."

"Captain," said the young king to D'Artagnan, on descending from the carriage, "the queen has charged me to invite you to dinner to-day--you and your friend the Baron du Vallon."

That was a great honor for D'Artagnan and for Porthos. Porthos was delighted; and yet during the entire repast he seemed to be preoccupied.

"What was the matter with you, baron?" D'Artagnan said to him as they descended the staircase of the Palais Royal. "You seemed at dinner to be anxious about something."

"I was trying," said Porthos, "to recall where I had seen that mendicant whom I must have killed."

"And you couldn't remember?"

"No."

"Well, search, my friend, search; and when you have found, you will tell me, will you not?"

"Pardieu!" said Porthos.

90. Conclusion.

On going home, the two friends found a letter from Athos, who desired them to meet him at the Grand Charlemagne on the following day.

The friends went to bed early, but neither of them slept. When we arrive at the summit of our wishes, success has usually the power to drive away sleep on the first night after the fulfilment of long cherished hopes.

The next day at the appointed hour they went to see Athos and found him and Aramis in traveling costume.

"What!" cried Porthos, "are we all going away, then? I, so, have made my preparations this morning."

"Oh, heavens! yes," said Aramis. "There's nothing to do in Paris now there's no Fronde. The Duchess de Longueville has invited me to pass a few days in Normandy, and has deputed me, while her son is being baptized, to go and prepare her residence at Rouen; after which, if nothing new occurs, I shall go and bury myself in my convent at Noisy-le-Sec."

"And I," said Athos, "am returning to Bragelonne. You know, dear D'Artagnan, I am nothing more than a good honest country gentleman. Raoul has no fortune other than I possess, poor child! and I must take care of it for him, since I only lend him my name."

"And Raoul--what shall you do with him?"

"I leave him with you, my friend. War has broken out in Flanders. You shall take him with you there. I am afraid that remaining at Blois would be dangerous to his youthful mind. Take him and teach him to be as brave and loyal as you are yourself."

"Then," replied D'Artagnan, "though I shall not have you, Athos, at all events I shall have that dear fair-haired head by me; and though he's but a boy, yet, since your soul lives again in him, dear Athos, I shall always fancy that you are near me, sustaining and encouraging me."

The four friends embraced with tears in their eyes.

Then they departed, without knowing whether they would ever see each other again.

D'Artagnan returned to the Rue Tiquetonne with Porthos, still possessed by the wish to find out who the man was that he had killed. On arriving at the Hotel de la Chevrette they found the baron's equipage all really and Mousqueton on his saddle.

"Come, D'Artagnan," said Porthos, "bid adieu to your sword and go with me to Pierrefonds, to Bracieux, or to Du Vallon. We will grow old together and talk of our companions."

"No!" replied D'Artagnan, "deuce take it, the campaign is going to begin; I wish to be there, I expect to get something by it."

"What do you expect to get?"

"Why, I expect to be made Marechal of France!"

"Ha! ha!" cried Porthos, who was not completely taken in by D'Artagnan's Gasconades.

"Come my brother, go with me," added D'Artagnan, "and I will see that you are made a duke!"

"No," answered Porthos, "Mouston has no desire to fight; besides, they have erected a triumphal arch for me to enter my barony, which will kill my neighbors with envy."

"To that I can say nothing," returned D'Artagnan, who knew the vanity of the new baron. "Then, here's to our next merry meeting!"

"Adieu, dear captain," said Porthos, "I shall always be happy to welcome you to my barony."

"Yes, yes, when the campaign is over," replied the Gascon.

"His honor's equipage is waiting," said Mousqueton.

The two friends, after a cordial pressure of the hands, separated. D'Artagnan was standing at the door looking after Porthos with a mournful gaze, when the baron, after walking scarcely more than twenty paces, returned--stood still--struck his forehead with his finger and exclaimed:

"I recollect!"

"What?" inquired D'Artagnan.

"Who the beggar was that I killed."

"Ah! indeed! and who was he?"

"'Twas that low fellow, Bonacieux."

And Porthos, enchanted at having relieved his mind, rejoined Mousqueton and they disappeared around an angle of the street. D'Artagnan stood for an instant, mute, pensive and motionless; then, as he went in, he saw the fair Madeleine, his hostess, standing on the threshold.

"Madeleine," said the Gascon, "give me your apartment on the first floor; now that I am a captain in the royal musketeers I must make an appearance; nevertheless, reserve my old room on the fifth story for me; one never knows what may happen."

The Scarlet Pimpernel Omnibus - Unabridged - The Scarlet Pimpernel, I Will Repay, Eldorado, Sir Percy Hits Back
Baroness Orczy
Oxford City Press, 2012
824 pages
ISBN: 978-1-78139-228-7

Available from www.amazon.com, www.amazon.co.uk

The Scarlet Pimpernel appears in a play and a series of novels and short stories by Baroness Emmuska Orczy. They are set at the start of the French Revolution, Pimpernel being a master of disguise and a precursor to other heroes such as Zorro and Batman. The play and the tales brought Orczy international acclaim, being translated into sixteen languages. This omnibus edition includes the following unabridged stories: The Scarlet Pimpernel, I Will Repay, Eldorado, and Sir Percy Hits Back

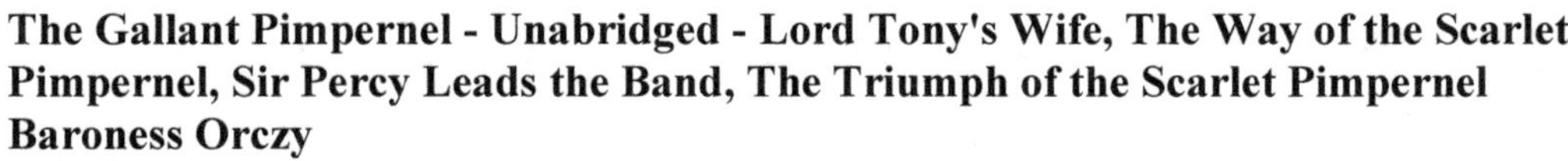

The Gallant Pimpernel - Unabridged - Lord Tony's Wife, The Way of the Scarlet Pimpernel, Sir Percy Leads the Band, The Triumph of the Scarlet Pimpernel
Baroness Orczy

Oxford City Press, 2012
804 pages
ISBN: 978-1-78139-227-0

Available from www.amazon.com, www.amazon.co.uk

The Scarlet Pimpernel appears in a play and a series of novels and short stories by Baroness Emmuska Orczy. They are set at the start of the French Revolution, Pimpernel being a master of disguise and a precursor to other heroes such as Zorro and Batman. The play and the tales brought Orczy international acclaim, being translated into sixteen languages. This omnibus edition includes the following unabridged stories: Lord Tony's Wife, The Way of the Scarlet Pimpernel, Sir Percy Leads the Band, and The Triumph of the Scarlet Pimpernel.

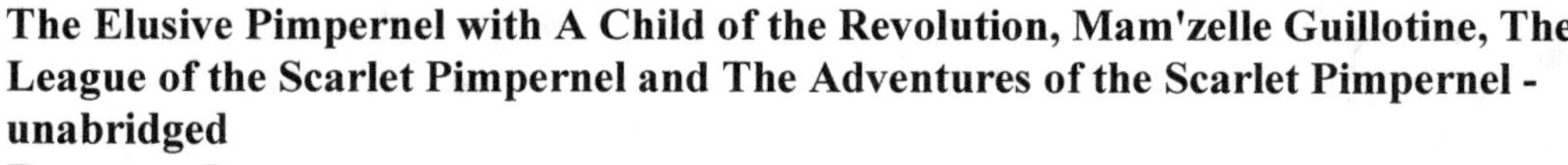

The Elusive Pimpernel with A Child of the Revolution, Mam'zelle Guillotine, The League of the Scarlet Pimpernel and The Adventures of the Scarlet Pimpernel - unabridged
Baroness Orczy
Oxford City Press, 2012
882 pages
ISBN: 978-1-78139-284-3

Available from www.amazon.com, www.amazon.co.uk

The Scarlet Pimpernel appears in a play and a series of novels and short stories by Baroness Emmuska Orczy. They are set at the start of the French Revolution, Pimpernel being a master of disguise and a precursor to other heroes such as Zorro and Batman. The play and the tales brought Orczy international acclaim, being translated into sixteen languages. This omnibus edition includes the following unabridged novels: The Elusive Pimpernel, A child of the Revolution, Mam'zelle Guillotine and the following collections of short stories: The League of the Scarlet Pimpernel and The Adventures of the Scarlet Pimpernel.

Pimpernel and Rosemary
Baroness Orczy
Oxford City Press, 2012
280 pages
ISBN: 978-1-78139-245-4

Available from www.amazon.com, www.amazon.co.uk

This story takes place three generations after Sir Percy, and is similar in many ways to "The Scarlet Pimpernel" with its intrigue, romance and twists and turns in the plot. However, it is different enough to surprise and delight the reader. It is a must-read for fans of Baroness Orczy and her beloved 'Pimpernel'.

The Complete Captain Blood and other Famous Sabatini Novels (unabridged) - Captain Blood, Captain Blood Returns (or The Chronicles of Captain Blood), The Fortunes of Captain Blood, Scaramouche and The Sea-Hawk
Rafael Sabatini
Oxford City Press, 2012
1064 pages
ISBN: 978-1-78139-251-5

Available from www.amazon.com, www.amazon.co.uk

This volume contains the Captain Blood novel, plus the series of short stories - Captain Blood Returns (or the Chronicles of Captain Blood) and The Fortunes of Captain Blood, plus the novels Scaramouche and The Sea-Hawk. Rafael Sabatini is a master storyteller, his stories full of action and intrigue. The Daily Telegraph described him thus: 'One wonders if there is another storyteller so adroit at filling his pages with intrigue and counter-intrigue, with danger threaded with romance, with a background of lavish colour, of silks and velvets, of swords and jewels'. This book is a must-have for fans of action-packed swashbuckling stories.

Anthony Hope Omnibus, containing Dolly Dialogues,The Prisoner of Zenda, Rupert of Hentzau, Simon Dale, The King's Mirror and Quisanté (all unabridged)
Anthony Hope
Benediction Classics, 2012
1032 pages
ISBN: 978-1-78139-255-3

Available from www.amazon.com, www.amazon.co.uk

This Omnibus edition contains: Dolly Dialogues, The Prisoner of Zenda, Rupert of Hentzau, Simon Dale, The King's Mirror, Quisanté. Anthony Hope (1863 - 1933), more fully Sir Anthony Hope Hawkins was an English novelist and playwright. He was a prolific writer of adventure novels and his stories "The Prisoner of Zenda" and "Rupert of Hentzau" are minor classics of English Literature, inspiring many adaptations. These books offer the greatest swashbuckling of all time with cliffhanging chapters, romance, swordfights and foreign intrigue. In addition, Hope's other works - "Dolly Dialogues" which gave him his first major literary success - A.E.W. Mason deemed these conversations "so truly set in the London of their day that the social historian would be unwise to neglect them" and said they were written with "delicate wit [and] a shade of sadness." Then "Simon Dale" is an historical novel involving the actress and courtesan Nell Gwyn. Hope considered "The King's Mirror" to be one of his best works and he was elected chairman of the committee of the Society of Authors after he published Quisanté.

Also from Benediction Books …
Wandering Between Two Worlds: Essays on Faith and Art
Anita Mathias
Benediction Books, 2007
152 pages
ISBN: 0955373700

Available from www.amazon.com, www.amazon.co.uk

In these wide-ranging lyrical essays, Anita Mathias writes, in lush, lovely prose, of her naughty Catholic childhood in Jamshedpur, India; her large, eccentric family in Mangalore, a sea-coast town converted by the Portuguese in the sixteenth century; her rebellion and atheism as a teenager in her Himalayan boarding school, run by German missionary nuns, St. Mary's Convent, Nainital; and her abrupt religious conversion after which she entered Mother Teresa's convent in Calcutta as a novice. Later rich, elegant essays explore the dualities of her life as a writer, mother, and Christian in the United States-- Domesticity and Art, Writing and Prayer, and the experience of being "an alien and stranger" as an immigrant in America, sensing the need for roots.

About the Author

Anita Mathias is the author of *Wandering Between Two Worlds: Essays on Faith and Art*. She has a B.A. and M.A. in English from Somerville College, Oxford University, and an M.A. in Creative Writing from the Ohio State University, USA. Anita won a National Endowment of the Arts fellowship in Creative Nonfiction in 1997. She lives in Oxford, England with her husband, Roy, and her daughters, Zoe and Irene.

Anita's website:
    http://www.anitamathias.com, and
Anita's blog Dreaming Beneath the Spires:
    http://dreamingbeneaththespires.blogspot.com

The Church That Had Too Much
Anita Mathias
Benediction Books, 2010
52 pages
ISBN: 9781849026567

Available from www.amazon.com, www.amazon.co.uk

The Church That Had Too Much was very well-intentioned. She wanted to love God, she wanted to love people, but she was both hampered by her muchness and the abundance of her possessions, and beset by ambition, power struggles and snobbery. Read about the surprising way The Church That Had Too Much began to resolve her problems in this deceptively simple and enchanting fable.

About the Author

Anita Mathias is the author of *Wandering Between Two Worlds: Essays on Faith and Art*. She has a B.A. and M.A. in English from Somerville College, Oxford University, and an M.A. in Creative Writing from the Ohio State University, USA. Anita won a National Endowment of the Arts fellowship in Creative Nonfiction in 1997. She lives in Oxford, England with her husband, Roy, and her daughters, Zoe and Irene.

Anita's website:
http://www.anitamathias.com, and
Anita's blog Dreaming Beneath the Spires:
http://dreamingbeneaththespires.blogspot.com

www.ingramcontent.com/pod-product-compliance
Lightning Source LLC
Chambersburg PA
CBHW081133300726
48982CB00005B/951

* 9 7 8 1 7 8 1 3 9 3 5 2 9 *